THE PENGUIN BOOK OF

Irish Fiction

Edited with an Introduction
by Colm Tóibín

VIKING

VIKING

Published by the Penguin Group
Penguin Books Ltd, 27 Wrights Lane, London w 8 5 tz, England
Penguin Putnam Inc., 375 Hudson Street, New York, New York 10014, USA
Penguin Books Australia Ltd, Ringwood, Victoria, Australia
Penguin Books Canada Ltd, 10 Alcorn Avenue, Toronto, Ontario, Canada m 4 v 3 b 2
Penguin Books (NZ) Ltd, Private Bag 102902, NSMC, Auckland, New Zealand

Penguin Books Ltd, Registered Offices: Harmondsworth, Middlesex, England

First published 1999
10 9 8 7 6 5 4 3 2 1

Set in 10/12pt Monotype Garamond
Typeset by Rowland Phototypesetting Ltd, Bury St Edmunds, Suffolk
Printed in Great Britain by Clays Ltd, St Ives plc

A CIP catalogue record for this book is available from the British Library

UK ISBN 0–670–85497–2
USA ISBN 0–670–89108–8

CONTENTS

Contents

INTRODUCTION

The weakness of Goethe, according to J. M. Synge, was that he had 'no national and intellectual mood to interpret. The individual mood is often trivial, perverse, fleeting, [but the] national mood [is] broad, serious, provisionally permanent.'[1] In all the surveys we have of the canon of Irish fiction, there is no such complaint. Ireland, from the time of Jonathan Swift to the present, has been, it seems, awash with 'national and intellectual mood', especially national mood, so that those writers who have sought to evade the opportunities to interpret this, who have sought to deal with the individual mood, however trivial, perverse and fleeting, seem now oddly heroic and hard to place. The purpose of much Irish fiction, it seems, is to become involved in the Irish argument, and the purpose of much Irish criticism has been to relate the fiction to the argument.

Thus if you want to read about the vagaries of the human heart, or the fleeting nature of love or time, read Goethe's lyrics; but if you want to know about the unreliable nature of narrative in a time of landlords, read Maria Edgeworth. If you want to know how love can lead to marriage, read Jane Austen; but if you want to delve into the secret and dark unconscious of an embattled ruling class, read Bram Stoker, Charles Maturin and Joseph Sheridan Le Fanu. If you want to read prose in which language is presented as neutral, barely noticeable, then read English fiction, because, as Terry Eagleton points out, 'language is strategic for the oppressed and representational for their rulers', and Ireland is, of course, oppressed and language in Ireland 'is weapon, dissemblance, seduction, apologia – anything, in fact, but representational'.[2]

'Reality' in Ireland, as well as language, has been a problem from the beginning. Maria Edgeworth wrote to her brother about it in 1834: 'It is impossible to draw Ireland as she now is in the book of fiction – realities are too strong, party passions too violent, to bear to see, or care to look at their faces in a looking-glass. The people would only break the glass and curse the fool who held the mirror up to nature – distorted nature in a fever.'[3] Lady Morgan, in the previous year, wrote, 'we are living in an era of transition. Changes moral and political are in progress. The frame of the constitution, the frame of society itself, are sustaining a shock, which occupies all minds, to avert or modify.' Under such conditions, she wrote, 'There is no legitimate literature, as there is no legitimate drama.'[4]

If you wanted to write a history of love in Ireland in the nineteenth century, or a history of adultery, you could more fruitfully look to politics rather than to literature: the love which Robert Emmet had for Sarah Curran; the life and times of Daniel O'Connell; Parnell's relationship with Katharine O'Shea. If you want accounts of the male hero facing destiny, equipped with will and talent and sex appeal, or accounts of the doomed protagonist, and you want these to be story-shaped, in Ireland you look to the lives of the nineteenth-century leaders, whereas in England you look to Daniel Deronda or in France to Emma Bovary.

Irish history reads like a form of fiction, full of love stories with ill-fated lovers dying with a smile, so daring and sweet their thought. Those central moments in French history are communal and urban, but the crucial moments in Irish history seem more like a nineteenth-century novel in which the individual, tragic hero is broken by the society he lives in. We have no communards, no rabble in the streets. Instead, we have personal sacrifice as a metaphor for general sacrifice.

It is striking how much this activity self-consciously resembles literature. Just as a poem may move and influence the reader, so too a song or a story or a novel, and so too Irish political action from Wolfe Tone to Bobby Sands. This is perhaps why historical revisionism since the 1970s in Ireland has so been so powerful and persuasive: many of the events themselves in their first telling had the shape and tone of fiction. Many of the revisionists, for very good reasons, took considerable offence at this idea.

And then, if you want to observe what it is like to inherit a tradition in which it is readily accepted that the novel cannot compete with the world, which is something that Tolstoy never accepted, nor Dickens, nor Melville, then follow the strange literary careers of those who sought a way out: Gerald Griffin attempting a love story and a murder story in *The Collegians*, using the rise of a new Catholic class as his background; or Oscar Wilde or Robert Tressell moving over to taunt the English; or George Moore desperately, and at times successfully, trying to become a French novelist in Ireland.

In his *The Irish Novelists* Thomas Flanagan wrote that

the nineteenth-century Irish novel established no tradition. Between Carleton's death [in 1869] and the beginning of the new century Ireland produced no prose writer of real stature . . . When a novelist of commanding talent did appear – the greatest perhaps of his age – he owed little to the work of his predecessors. Ireland was Joyce's theme, as it had been theirs, and he shared their involvement in issues of race, culture and nationality. But in his work the theme finds its expression in irony, in a passion which mocks both itself and its object . . . It matters not at all that there were Irish novelists before Joyce, for their work was entirely useless to him. They had established no conventions by which the actualities of Irish life could be represented.[5]

It seems to me, however, that it matters a great deal that there were Irish novelists before Joyce. The absence of conventions left him free to understand that the English and French novel, the novel which played with the conflict between restriction and freedom, depended for its even tone, its sense of stable character, even its use of linear time, on certain connections between the writer and the reader which were uncertain in Ireland, and indeed between the individual and the society which were equally uncertain. Anyone, with the exception of George Moore, who had tried, failed. This failure, this great peculiar gap between Edgeworth (1767–1849) and Moore (1852–1933), filled by the Gothic novelists, or by half-geniuses like Carleton who would have flourished in any other society, or by Anthony Trollope adapting himself so happily to local conditions, made that much clear. Ireland, in the years around the Famine, could produce songs and stories, but had trouble with a deeply layered structure like a novel, in which the individual choice and the individual destiny are central.

Both Moore and Joyce understood this. 'Moore,' Seamus Deane has written, 'amalgamated so much of Irish literary and social experience in his life and writings that he is a perfectly appropriate stepfather to the dishevelled brood of novelists who were to succeed and, in some instances, outshine him.'[6]

It is not an accident that Moore's best novel, and one of the best Irish novels of all time, *Esther Waters*, is set in England. It is interesting to look at the difference between *Esther Waters* (1894) and Moore's earlier novel, *A Drama in Muslin* (1886), set in Ireland. *A Drama in Muslin* deals with a number of daughters of landed holdings on the social scene in Dublin in search of husbands. The portraits of a number of the young women, led by clever, sensitive and plain Alice Barton, are delicately drawn; they could belong in any novel from Zola to Edith Wharton, and any talented novelist would know what to do with their destinies, and would be able to dramatize their season in the capital in the most personal way. But Moore is not entirely free to do this: he has to examine the system of land-holding, which he knew well since he owned twelve thousand acres in County Mayo, and to deal with its decline. He has to include a malevolent peasantry watching over the revelry of his young heroines. And, perhaps most significantly, he has to deal – and he researched this scene in some detail – with Dublin Castle and its mores, the shabby manners of the Viceregal Court in the time of Parnell. His version of Dublin as a centre of paralysis is more direct and stark, and more heavy-handed, than Joyce's, but he also offers a consolation which is not available to Joyce's characters in *Dubliners*: this landed society cannot last, it will self-destruct, *A Drama in Muslin* tells us, and that story is more vivid and passionate than the story of Alice Barton and her friends. The tragedy of the novel is that, in the 1880s, the conditions which Maria Edgeworth and Lady Morgan described at the beginning of the century are still in place. The drama of a sensitive consciousness entering into conflict with the wider world cannot compete with the assassination of Cavendish and Burke by the Invincibles in the Phoenix Park, which is also dramatized in the novel. It is not a coincidence that Alice Barton eventually finds happiness and fulfilment in England at the end of the novel, it being clear that there is no future for people like her, nor indeed for novelists in the half-formed chaos of Ireland.

In *Esther Waters* the social and political background – which takes in religion, class politics, women's rights, horse-racing and betting – adds to the novel's power and authority rather than taking away from it, or competing with it, as in *A Drama in Muslin*. Esther is a servant girl who comes to a big house, most of whose denizens are dedicated to horse-racing, as were the denizens of Moore Hall, during George Moore's childhood, his father having owned a number of famous race-horses. If this were Ireland, and there are moments when it sounds very like Ireland, the issues of big house versus peasantry, Catholic versus Protestant, Fenian versus Parnellite, Irish versus Anglo-Irish, would have to be portrayed. But because this is England, and the large questions in the society are, at least for the moment, settled, Moore can create his illiterate servant girl Esther Waters with an extraordinary delicacy and sympathy, render her consciousness with great sensitivity, so that when she becomes pregnant and then tries to bring up the child, the reader is concerned not about the issue of single mothers, or about the uncaring nature of the society, but rather about Esther herself, her plight, her future.

Moore remained concerned about what could be done, and not done, in Ireland. He wrote the first version of his series of short stories, *The Untilled Field* (1903), to be translated into Irish, to furnish 'the young Irish of the future with models'.[7] They were then translated back into English, being, Moore said, 'much improved after their bath in Irish'.[8] Terence Brown has written that 'the manner suggests the book has been translated from some more culturally innocent language',[9] but it also reads like Moore was wandering in an unknown country, in which the possibility of sophisticated psychological portraits, such as that of Esther Waters, did not exist. These are half-formed narratives, full of raw desires and a quaintness which Moore would have mercilessly mocked in any other writer. They are of interest for two reasons. They are the first concerted efforts to explore this hidden Ireland since William Carleton. Also, they stand in relation to the stories in Joyce's *Dubliners*, written in the same decade, as shadow does to light. In fact, the last scene of 'The Dead', a story for which George Moore expressed great admiration ('I regretted that I was not the author of it'), owes much to the ending of Moore's *Vain Fortune*. 'In that book,' Richard Ellmann writes,

a bridal couple receive, on their wedding night, a message that a young woman whom the husband jilted has just committed suicide. The news holds them apart, she asks him not to kiss her, and both are tormented by remorse. The wife, her marriage unconsummated, falls off at last to sleep, and her husband goes to the window and looks out at 'the melancholy greyness of the dawn'. For the first time he recognizes, with the force of a revelation, that his life is a failure, and that his wife lacks the passion of the girl who has killed herself.[10]

Also, Joyce was scathing about Moore's *The Lake*, but, Ellmann writes, 'this rejection did not keep him from making use of the book later. He remembered the ending when he came to write the visionary scene at the end of the fourth chapter of *A Portrait of the Artist as a Young Man* . . . Joyce winnowed Moore of the preposterous; he found him a good man to improve on.'[11] (In 1904, in Pola, Joyce gave Nora Barnacle a copy of 'Mildred Lawson', the first story in Moore's *Celibates*, to read. The story ends with a woman ruminating in bed. Nora thought that Moore didn't know how to finish a story; for Joyce, it helped to inspire Molly Bloom's soliloquy.)

George Moore, of course, could make no sense of *Ulysses*. He was locked into a system of novel-writing which had cost him dear to learn. 'It is absurd to imagine that any good end can be served by trying to record every single thought and sensation of any human being,' he said.[12] Moore, who specialized in seeing no reason, could see no reason why the minor acts of Leopold Bloom should be associated with the acts of Ulysses. He was out of his depth.

James Stephens, who may or may not have been born on the same day as Joyce, was more sympathetic to the later work, having called *Dubliners* 'a rather disconnected, unpleasant prose work'.[13] In 1927 Joyce decided that Stephens should finish *Finnegans Wake*, if he should prove unable to. Stephens had attempted a grim, spare poetic realism in the short novel *The Charwoman's Daughter*, but was also interested in myth and story and legend, which he explored, fluently and confidently, in his masterpiece *The Crock of Gold*. The problem which faced Stephens as an artist, a dealer in both disillusion and pure illusion, has been clearly identified by Seamus Deane:

The repeated attempts . . . to conjoin these worlds of Gaelic myth and Irish reality is, of course, a symptom of the increasing strain to which the heroicizing impulse of the Revival was subjected, especially in the aftermath of the political settlement of 1922. The society itself made the discrepancy between mythological grandeurs and quotidian pettiness so severe that it became impossible to incorporate them satisfactorily in fiction.[14]

Stephens's work and, indeed, his silence as a writer of fiction for the last quarter-century of his life (he was, like George Moore, a great talker) are instructive. He was interested in language, tone and form as much as Moore was interested in psychology and society. And both Moore and Stephens remain fascinating figures in the same way as Catalan painters like Santiago Rusinol or Isidre Nonell remain fascinating for their connection with Picasso. The story of how they were prepared to go a certain length with him (including to Paris, like Moore and Stephens) but no further is like the story of Moore and Stephens, crippled by the very problems which were the making of Joyce: how to find a formal structure and a tone in language which would not only reflect the Irish heritage – the mixture of poor realities and grand dreams – but become the Irish heritage.

During the years when Joyce was writing *Ulysses* the Catalan painter Joan Miró, who viewed Barcelona as a centre of paralysis and moved to Paris as soon as the First World War ended, was becoming increasingly uneasy about inherited ideas of perspective. Just as Joyce attempted what T. S. Eliot called 'an anti-style' in *Ulysses*, Miró viewed perspective as a great lie and sought to find a system for his art which would deal with the true shape of things. 'With the exception of the primitives and the Japanese,' he wrote, 'everyone has painted only the great masses of trees and mountains . . . that which interests me above all else is the calligraphy of a tree or the tiles of a roof, and I mean leaf by leaf, branch by branch, blade by blade of grass.'[15]

Joyce realized that if he did not find a language, a form and a style which were new and inventive, he would be lost as Moore, to some extent, and certainly Stephens were lost. He was against plot-lines and character development and closure, as Miró was against perspective. He tried, then, to find a system which would capture the strange beauty of consciousness, just as Miró developed a dream iconography for his paintings.

We grow to love Leopold Bloom not because of the story in which he plays a part, nor for his adventures in the plot, but because of the rich way he notices things, because of the way he remembers, and then becomes distracted, then is reminded of something, and then watches, notices again, wishes and makes calculations. Some of his observations are desperately funny, as when he agrees with himself that wine is a suitable drink for the chalice, rather than Guinness, say, or ginger ale. But he is always burdened with other matters, such as his father's death, his son's death and his marriage, and then once more he is distracted.

Leopold Bloom in *Ulysses* is, however, more than anything else a verbal construct; he is made with language, and this making is on display, much as Miró's flat colours or Picasso's theatricality are on display. Joyce is not answerable to any earlier tradition in fiction or conditions in Ireland, yet he feels free to play with both, at times as though history were the fit of laughing from which he was trying to recover.

Joyce's sense of Irish society, as we know from *Dubliners*, was more acute and vivid than that of contemporaries like Moore or Stephens. (Indeed, as a young man, he taunted Stephens with this.) And in the years between the rise of Parnell and the rise of de Valera there was a peculiar and intense aura around politics and religion in Ireland. Ireland was to be, after the fall of Parnell, in Yeats's phrase, 'like soft wax'.[16] Ireland was about to become a vacuum which various competing forces sought to fill – the Irish Parliamentary Party, Sinn Féin, the Gaelic League, the Gaelic Athletic Association, the Catholic Church, the rabble, the Abbey Theatre and the Unionists. The possibilities surrounding this aura gave Joyce his great subject, which was language.

The language of *Ulysses* moves from the plain, clipped, almost throwaway style for solitary moments – shitting, masturbating, thinking – to the cross-talk of friends, associates and colleagues in which speaking is half-claptrap or small talk, full of witticisms, quotations and half-baked opinions, laced like all of the book with snatches of song. The style is always fluid. Bloom's stream-of-consciousness can be broken by clear description of what is going on around him. The pub talk can be broken, as in Barney Kiernan's, by Bloom's efforts to be serious and almost solemn. Other scenes and situations are described in a language which is playfully baroque. Molly Bloom's soliloquy is direct and passionate.

Throughout the book there is a game being played between public and private discourse. The language of provincial (or indeed cosmopolitan) journalism, the language of nationalism and religion, and public rhetoric of all sorts are parodied, thrown up in the air and let float back down, all the more to tease them and humiliate them. Ireland was slowly becoming 'Ireland' with its Gaelic League, its Sinn Féin, its Abbey Theatre, its urgent need to de-Anglicize, its feeling, as John O'Leary said to Yeats, that 'a man must have upon his side the Church or the Fenians'.[17] The supposed ancientness of Ireland is the source of much laughter and many jokes in *Ulysses*, so too Ireland's natural resources, which both the Citizen and Skin-the-Goat (assuming it was he) extol in different sections of the book. 'And our wool that was sold in Rome in the time of Juvenal and our flax and our damask from the looms of Antrim and our Limerick lace, our tanneries and our white flint glass down there by Ballybough.'[18]

Joyce loved lists, the longer and more incongruous the better, as Miró loved painting squiggles and Picasso loved painting eyes. Joyce loved the aura around proper names. There is a sense in *Ulysses* that anything which is held sacred in Ireland, especially respectability, history, nationalism and Catholicism, will be ridiculed – Joyce did not need the Church or the Fenians. Instead, sanctity will be offered to ordinary experience – something which had not figured much in previous Irish writing – and also to memory, love and sex, to companionship, to long, shapeless days and city life, to men half down on their luck, to song.

To that extent *Ulysses* is a deeply political book in which Joyce too joins those who sought to mould the soft wax of Ireland. He set his masterpiece against any narrow idea of a nation; his nation of 1904 was made up of different people in the same place. Yet *Ulysses* is also, in an odd and admirable way, a deeply patriotic and liberating book. Most of the Irish fiction written before Joyce was written for an English audience; much of it sought to describe Ireland's history and landscape and people as peculiar and alarmingly dramatic. Some of the most talented writers, from Oliver Goldsmith to Joseph Sheridan

Le Fanu to George Moore, had set their novels in England. But Joyce's work is almost hermetically sealed in Ireland.

Ulysses is full of local references – names of people, streets, places; it is full of figures of speech and lines of songs. Nothing is ever explained in the book, but Irish readers get most of the references. The book depends on the idea that the city being described is not the centre of paralysis, but rather the centre of the world. Local references and proper names are not there to add colour to the book; most of the time the effect is entirely natural and often poetic. When names appear which have also appeared in *Dubliners* (and this happens throughout) there is a double pleasure in knowing what a name like Gretta Conroy means and then in meeting her briefly once more.

To understand the idea that this book was written first for an Irish audience, all one has to do is imagine Virginia Woolf reading the book and coming across the many proper names and missing the resonance which each one has in Ireland. Take the list of clergy, for example, who appear in the 'Cyclops' section at an imagined meeting to discuss the revival of Irish sport: 'the rev. T. Brangan, O. S. A.; the rev. J. Flavin, C. C.; the rev. M. A. Hackett, C. C.; the rev. W. Hurley, C. C.; the rt rev. Mgr M'Manus, V. G.; the rev. B. R. Slattery, O. M. I.; the very rev. M. D. Scally, P. P.; the rev. F. T. Purcell, O. P.; the very rev. Timothy canon Gorman, P. P.; the rev. J. Flanagan, C. C. . . .'[19] This list is, first of all, funny because it is based on the lists you still read in Irish provincial and indeed daily newspapers, and because it plays with titles and hierarchy but it is also graphic – it is easy to imagine these priests in a group photo, strong farmers' sons. None of this is explained anywhere, and most of it could not be felt by a non-Irish reader. This is merely one example of the ways in which Joyce handed Ireland back to Irish readers in his book, how he made Ireland the centre of the known world. The Citizen would have been proud of him.

Joan Miró, throughout his long career, tried to return painting to two dimensions, to the making of marks on a surface. He wanted to erase the pretense of depth. He loved the flatness of the Romanesque tradition, it was like the blood in his veins, he said. Joyce too found in the *Odyssey* a map that he could follow so that his use of detail and his creation of structure in *Ulysses* was not simply a matter of establishing verisimilitude but of unleashing irony. He made it clear that words and sentences are marks on a page, sounds we make, rhetorical systems and ways for us to perform. The idea offered Joyce a new beginning in the creation of fiction.

Between Carleton and Joyce there remains one extraordinary phenomenon in Irish literary history, and that is what Roy Foster calls 'Protestant Magic', the tradition of Gothic fiction which includes Maturin, Le Fanu, Stoker and leads on to Yeats and certain elements in the work of Elizabeth Bowen. 'The fact that Anglo-Irish writers . . . should have exhibited such fascination with madness and the occult, terror and the supernatural, is in one sense surprising,' Terry Eagleton writes.

They belonged, after all, to a notoriously hard-headed social class which habitually chided the Catholic masses for their infantile superstition. But Protestant Gothic might be dubbed the political unconscious of Anglo-Irish society, the place where its fears and fantasies most definitively emerge . . . And if Irish Gothic is a specifically Protestant phenomenon, it is because nothing lent itself more to the genre than the decaying gentry in their crumbling houses, isolated and sinisterly eccentric, haunted by the sins of the past. Gothic carries with it a freight of guilt and self-torment, and these are arguably more Protestant than Catholic obsessions . . . For Gothic is the nightmare of the besieged and reviled . . . in this case a minority marooned within a largely hostile people to whom they are socially, religiously alien.[20]

The Catholic natives, in other words, put the fear of God into Protestants of all sorts, even though it didn't seem like that to either party at the time. The Catholics also, through their religion and superstition and their abiding sense of community (not to speak of the open nature of their suffering), got all their fears out of their system. The other crowd became anal-retentive, neurotic and paranoid. Thus we got *Melmoth* and *Dracula* and *Uncle Silas*.

'*Uncle Silas*,' Elizabeth Bowen wrote,

has always struck me as an Irish story transposed to an English setting. The hermetic solitude and the autocracy of the great country house, the demonic power of the family myth, fatalism, feudalism and the 'ascendancy' outlook are accepted facts of life for the race of hybrids from which Le Fanu sprang. For the psychological background of *Uncle Silas* it was necessary for him to invent nothing.[21]

'The line of Irish Protestant supernatural fiction,' Roy Foster writes,

is an obvious one . . . marginalized Irish Protestants . . . often living in England but regretting Ireland, stemming from families with strong clerical and professional colorations, whose occult preoccupations surely mirror a sense of displacement, a loss of social and psychological integration, and an escapism motivated by the threat of a takeover by the Catholic middle classes – a threat all the more inexorable because it is being accomplished by peaceful means and with the free legal aid of British governments. The supernatural theme of a corrupt bargain recurs again.

Indeed, a strong theme in Protestant gothic is a mingled repulsion and envy where Catholic magic is concerned. The Jesuit order in *Melmoth* manipulated darker forces than the eponymous hero. In *Dracula*, Van Helsing is a Dutch Catholic who brings the Host, with a papal dispensation, to combat the undead at Whitby.[22]

This shape of Irish history in one of its manifestations gave life to the Gothic imagination – that is, the idea of history as unfinished business, the idea of the dispossessed locals lying in wait, impelled by the wrongs done to their ancestors, the idea that the crimes committed by the settlers still hang in the air. Joep Leerssen in his *Remembrance and Imagination* describes this

recurrence of the dead past, bursting into the living present; the awareness of buried, unfinished business yet awaiting definitive settlement . . . is present in much of the tradition of the Irish Gothic . . . It is no surprise that the figure of the aristocratic vampire, undead remnant of a feudal past battening on the vitality of the living, is an appealing one for Irish authors. The frisson of Irish Gothic (from *Melmoth* to *Dracula*) and the appeal of the Big House theme . . . lay partly in the fact that 'the lively expectation of the young' tended to be 'devoured by the guilt and errors of their elders'. The theme reverberates with worried reservations as to the straightforwardness of time, with an uncanny sense that Irish history, the sheer weight and bloodiness and persistence of it, will trouble the present's course to the future.[23]

In his essay 'The Argentine Writer and Tradition', Jorge Luis Borges wrote that the South American writer, by virtue of being distant and close at the same time, had more 'rights' to Western culture than anyone in any Western nation. He went on to explore the extraordinary contribution of the Jewish artist to Western culture and the Irish writer to English literature. Jewish artists, he wrote, 'work within the culture and at the same time do not feel tied to it through any special devotion'. For Irish writers, he argued, it was 'enough, the fact of feeling Irish, different, to become innovators within English culture'.[24]

He wanted to emphasize that there was nothing 'racial' about this, because

many of these illustrious Irish writers (Shaw, Berkeley, Swift) were of English descent, they had no Celtic blood; nevertheless, it was enough, the fact of feeling Irish, different, to become innovators within English culture. I believe that Argentine writers, and South American writers in general, are in an analogous situation; we can handle all the European themes, handle them without superstition, but with an irreverence which can have, and does have, fortunate consequences.[25]

Borges's essay was published in 1932, the year after Daniel Corkery's *Synge and Anglo-Irish Literature*. 'Anglo-Irish literature,' Corkery wrote in the first essay, 'as the phrase is understood, is mostly the product of Irishmen who neither live at home nor write primarily for their own people.' Exile, or, in Corkery's term, 'expatriation', has been 'a chronic disease from Goldsmith's time, Steele's time, Sheridan's time, Burke's time, [Thomas] Moore's time, Prout's time, Wilde's time, to our own time of Shaw, Joyce and [George] Moore'.[26]

Writers not in exile from Ireland are in exile within Ireland. These Corkery deems 'colonial' and they include Maria Edgeworth: 'No other book [*Castle Rackrent*] did as much in the creation of what was to prove the most favoured of the moulds which subsequent writers were to use. This Colonial literature was written to explain the quaintness of the humankind of this land, especially the native humankind, to another humankind that was not quaint, that was standard, normal.' The work of Edgeworth and others, including Somerville and Ross, according to Corkery, 'is all written for their motherland, England, by spiritual exiles'.[27]

Borges versus Corkery, then. Ireland as a state of mind, when it is 'enough to feel Irish, different', or Ireland as a matter of class and race. In *Writers and Politics*, Conor Cruise O'Brien tried to define Irishness: 'Irishness,' he wrote, 'is not primarily a question of birth or blood or language: it is the condition of being involved with the Irish situation, and usually of being mauled by it.'[28] This is surely too grim. Perhaps it would be closer to the truth if it read: Irishness is not primarily a question of birth or blood or language: it is the condition of being involved with the Irish situation, and, if the candidate is a writer, often being crowned by it.

'Anthony Trollope's connection with Ireland is unique among the British major creative writers of the nineteenth century,' Owen Dudley Edwards has written.

For all the many differences of their response to Ireland, Trollope has one quality lacking in the rest of them. Britain made them. Everyone of them saw Ireland as outsiders. Trollope did not. His view of Ireland from first to last was that of a participant: Ireland made him . . . Trollope, almost alone of all British-born writers on Ireland in the nineteenth century, reminds us of the twentieth-century error which assumes Irish and British separation to have been inevitable . . . In the nineteenth century Ireland was part of the United Kingdom, and it was possible for an Anthony Trollope, going from Britain to Ireland, or for a Phineas Finn going from Ireland to Britain, to have a single as well as a dual identity . . . They could and did experience both an Irish and a British identity.[29]

This dual identity existed among many Irish writers including Swift, Frances Sheridan, Sterne, Goldsmith, George Moore, Elizabeth Bowen (who felt most at home, according to Roy Foster, 'in mid-Irish Sea'), right down to Iris Murdoch and William Trevor. When Anthony Trollope came to Ireland in 1841, at the age of twenty-six, he had not succeeded in writing fiction. He was, in many respects, including his career in the Post Office, a failure. He took to Ireland immediately, while being at the same time shocked by much of it. He hunted with relish, and, when he was finished hunting, he danced; he also reorganized the postal system with skill; since no one knew he was a failure, he could reinvent himself. He immersed himself in Irish writing, including Maria Edgeworth, Charles Robert Maturin, Lady Morgan, William Carleton, John Banim, Gerald Griffin and Charles Lever. Being English, he could become friends with people in Ireland who could never become friends with each other. Thus he saw a great deal of Charles Bianconi, who was a close friend of Daniel O'Connell (his daughter was to marry O'Connell's nephew, his son O'Connell's granddaughter). Bianconi was, in Victoria Glendinning's phrase, 'loud for Catholic rights'.[30]

Trollope had been in school in England with Sir William Gregory (later husband of Augusta Gregory), who was now a landlord in Galway, being groomed for political stardom by Peel, with some outward similarities to Phineas Finn. Trollope met Charles Lever in Gregory's house as well as many Irish landlords unsympathetic to O'Connell, to say the least. Victoria Glendinning writes:

As Gregory's guest at Coole [Trollope] listened to the social and political gossip and did not forget it. He heard stories about the doings and the personalities of famous men and of people in public life long before he ever met such people himself. It was the best possible fodder for a novelist. He was also buying and keeping political pamphlets of all kinds. It was the politics and the sexual scandals of the 1840s, when he knew almost no one, which were to be the starting points for his fiction long after he left Ireland.[31]

It was this sense of ferment and conflict that gave him his start as a novelist. His first two novels, *The Macdermots of Ballycloran* (1847) and *The Kellys and the O'Kellys* (1848), are set entirely in Ireland. He managed to create credible characters and use the sharp and subtle conflicts within the society for both colour and drama. He was the missing novelist between Carleton and George Moore; and because he went back to England in 1859, after eighteen years in Ireland, and became a famous English novelist, his involvement with the Irish situation and his being crowned by it are harder to establish as central for him and central for the Irish situation.

'His Irish experience,' Roy Foster writes, 'gave him one consistent theme in all his political fiction: a fascination with the outsider who enters a closed society.' On the idea that Phineas Finn can be viewed as Trollope's alter ego, Foster writes, 'it is significant that this alter ego comes from Ireland, the adopted country where Trollope discovered happiness, in order to conquer England, the mother country which broke his youthful heart'.[32] Both Foster and Dudley Edwards make clear that Irish themes and echoes continued right through Trollope's career, even in novels not ostensibly about Ireland. 'He went to the frontier, for in a linguistic, religious, political, social and economic sense Ireland was one,' Dudley Edwards writes.

He learned his literary trade on the frontier. He discovered that frontier-made goods were not good selling material in the metropolis. Hence he began to build his literary achievements in forms acceptable to England and apparently English. But the tools and perceptions were Irish in the initial instance, and much of the workmanship after his return to England was still based on the rough designs he had initially executed on Irish soil, with Irish themes, about Irish characters and with Irish insights.[33]

For Borges and his generation in Buenos Aires, the real world was elsewhere: they spoke and read French and English, and in their imagination they belonged to Europe, but when they lifted their heads from books, or came back from abroad, they were in a cultural backwater, and they had no intention of becoming chroniclers of their half-formed time or their badly formed country. They realized that they had no choice but to invent their own time and their own country. They believed, as many Irish writers came to believe (and later writers García Márquez in Colombia and Amos Tutuola in Nigeria came to believe), that you cannot write social realism in an underdeveloped country.

There are certain odd similarities between Borges and the Jonathan Swift of *Gulliver's Travels*. Both lived far from what they believed was the centre of things. Both mimicked the language of reportage, using a tone which was po-faced, dry, factual and elaborate to describe invented worlds and systems. There is a central urge in both their imaginations to make things strange, to refuse to deal with the familiar world. Although Borges suffered from a savage lack of indignation, neither had much regard for mankind. (Borges wrote: 'Mirrors and copulation are abominable, for they multiply the number of mankind.'[34]) They both spent their formative years in cities – Dublin and Buenos Aires – which were being substantially rebuilt and re-created.

Gulliver's Travels is a suitable beginning for this anthology. It stands alone in its playful use of narrative. It is hard to categorize, belonging to no tradition, or to no tradition which can be easily identified. It is the beginning, perhaps, of the Great Tradition of Irish masterpieces, which includes *Castle Rackrent*, *Tristram Shandy*, *The Vicar of Wakefield*, *Ulysses*, *At Swim-Two-Birds* and Beckett's trilogy, books which delight in the shifting, uneven tone, the unreliable structure, the comic turn, which read as though the writer believed that no one had ever written a book before.

'In English writing we seldom speak of tradition, though we occasionally apply its name in deploring its absence,' T. S. Eliot wrote at the beginning of his essay 'Tradition and the Individual Talent'.[35] How would such an essay begin if we were to ask: 'In Irish fiction . . .'?

In Irish fiction we speak of tradition all the time, because of its strangeness. Because of our proximity to England and France, we are constantly alert to what is missing here. 'I recall being in Thurles at a hurling match for the championship of Ireland,' Daniel Corkery wrote in *Synge and Anglo-Irish Literature*.

There were 30,000 onlookers. They were as typical of this nation as any of the great crowds that assemble of Saturday afternoons in England to witness Association football matches are typical of the English nation. It was while I looked around on that great crowd I first became acutely conscious that as a nation we were without self-expression in literary form. The life of this people I looked upon – there were all sorts of individuals present, from bishops to tramps off the road – was not being explored in a natural way by any except one or two writers of any standing . . . On the other hand, there seems to be no difficulty in posing Galsworthy, Masefield, Bennett, Wells, against corresponding assemblies in England.[36]

In Ireland there seemed to be no middle ground between work of pure genius and ballads. Corkery identified 'the three great forces which, working for long in the Irish national being, have made it so different from the English national being . . . (1) The Religious Consciousness of the People; (2) Irish Nationalism; and (3) The Land.' And he went on: 'Now the mentality of that crowd of 30,000 I looked upon in Thurles was chiefly the result of the interplay of these forces. To let one's mind, filled with this thought, rest on that crowd, scanning the faces for confirmation of it, and then suddenly to shift one's thought on to the mass of Anglo-Irish Literature, is to turn from solid reality to a pale ghost.'[37]

Corkery (1878–1964), as we can see, was not short of attitude, and as a writer of fiction himself – he wrote one novel and several volumes of short stories – he was not a genius. But there was, as in Joyce's *Dubliners*, a subdued and melancholy tone in the prose as hidden moments in small lives were being described, with a sense of mystery about time passing and a sadness about the unaccountable nature of love. This sense of quiet desolation was to emerge – and perhaps was already there in earlier writers – as an important element in the Irish tradition. Corkery's story in this anthology is one of five stories included here about returned exiles. Each story – Corkery's 'Nightfall', George Moore's 'Homesickness', Bryan MacMahon's 'Exile's Return', Máirtín Ó Cadhain's 'Floodtide' and Benedict Kiely's 'Homes on the Mountain' – is rich in drama and irony. These stories also belong to Corkery's famous 30,000 faces at the hurling match in Thurles; they have, as their basis, ideas of community and land among a class with a deep fear of dispossession. The people in these stories have a nightmare that the millions who have left will return and the returning emigrants will forget they are no longer young (Corkery), will be unstable, unsettled and unreliable (Moore), will arrive without warning and discover what has been happening (MacMahon), will build a house in an unsuitable spot (Kiely). Or, in the case of Ó Cadhain's heroine, will be put to work as though she has never been away.

A similar intensity emerges when writers describe a dance. From Katherine Cecil

Thurston, born in 1875, to Mary Dorcey, born in 1951, this offers a way of showing the society at its most formal and threatening, but it also offers an occasion, perhaps the only occasion, for an individual to escape and thus an opportunity for the writers to show the relationship between restriction and freedom. Those hours in the dance-hall, or the formal party, become then a cauldron which many Irish writers have chosen to stir. There are four accounts of dances in this anthology – and there could have been many more. 'The Dead' is, of course, included, as well as a section from Maurice Leitch's *Stamping Ground*, which is a dramatic and chilling use of public space and private fears. In all these stories, with the possible exception of Thurston's, the dance results in a degree of misery for the individual, offers us a microscope so we can see all the more clearly how harsh and vicious the society is (Leitch and Dorcey) or how oddly isolated the individual is (Joyce). In the Irish tradition, no one writes well or easily about happiness. (Mary Lavin's story 'Happiness' is about death.)

There are three other subjects which seem to engage Irish writers deeply. The first one is fire. The burning down of houses has a distinguished career in Irish writing, from the extraordinary, incandescent prose of William Carleton's 'Wildgoose Lodge' to some marvellous conflagrations in Frances Sheridan's *Memoirs of Miss Sidney Bidulph* and *The Vicar of Wakefield* to the burning of big houses as the final act in novels (the locals arriving, the odd intimacy between the locals and the quality, the sense of the fire as the end of history) like Elizabeth's Bowen's *The Last September* and Molly Keane's *Two Days in Aragon*. Prose is attracted to fire, like Maeve Brennan's heroine in 'The Morning after the Big Fire' it loves the drama of fire, its sweeping destruction.

The second subject which makes prose become vivid is the killing of women by men. In novels like *The Collegians* or John Banville's *The Book of Evidence* or Carlo Gébler's *The Cure*, the murders are loosely based on real murders which were amply documented. The murders themselves are the hinges on which the novels turn. In the other accounts included here, James Stephens's 'A Glass of Beer', Leland Bardwell's 'The Hairdresser' and Patrick McCabe's *The Butcher Boy*, the murders are fictional, but no less chilling and shocking for that.

The third subject is fathers and sons. In several stories a battle between love and fear, hatred and duty, takes place. The urge to kill or destroy or learn to hate is the central drama in Bernard Mac Laverty's 'Life Drawing' and Neil Jordan's 'Night in Tunisia'.

The murdering of women, the fascination with fire, the use of the dance-hall as an arena for terror and fear, the dread of the familiar figure turned stranger back from exile, the urge to kill the father – these are some of the tropes which followers of the Irish tradition will recognize. The preponderance of vast, ambitious and ironic masterpieces, matched by an astonishing flowering of Gothic fiction. And the absence of images of domestic harmony, the dead fathers and mothers and dead children. Leopold Bloom's father committed suicide, his son is dead, his wife is being unfaithful to him, Stephen's mother is dead. The dying of parents gives Kate O'Brien her most powerful moments. John McGahern's novels are haunted by the dead and the dying, and in many other pieces from this century in this anthology (Brian Moore, Val Mulkerns, John Broderick, Eugene McCabe, Tom Mac Intyre, David Park, Mary Morrissy, Frank Ronan, Colum McCann) death and illness provide the governing theme.

Is it possible, then, to talk about a national style, a way of approaching language, form and character, which is specifically Irish? Most commentators, in this context, will cite the famous encounter between the English Jesuit and young Stephen in James Joyce's *A Portrait of the Artist as a Young Man*. Stephen uses the word 'tundish' to describe what the Jesuit calls a funnel, and then begins to contemplate his own relationship to the English language: 'The language in which we are speaking is his before it is mine. How different are the words *home, Christ, ale, master*, on his lips and on mine! I cannot speak or write these words without unrest of spirit. His language, so familiar and so foreign, will always be for me an acquired speech . . . My soul frets in the shadow of his language.'[38]

In this context too it is worth quoting from Seamus Heaney's essay on Derek Walcott in *The Government of the Tongue*: 'Walcott possesses English more deeply and sonorously than most of the English themselves.'[39] English in Ireland, like English in Walcott's Caribbean, is both a plague inflicted on us, brought here by armies and imperial designs, and a language we have come to feel free with. Capitalism had no heroic phase in Ireland, and Ireland does not have many natural resources, but there is language, which, like software skills in the 1990s, we have come to possess and repossess deeply and sonorously. Language in Ireland, it seems, is both culture and nature.

In Irish writing, we have survived to inherit the tension between the Latin of *non serviam*, Satan's and Stephen Dedalus's insistence on remaining apart from the fold, and the Anglo-Saxon of the groans and moans which fill the work of Samuel Beckett. One language has faded to a large extent, which means that the other one, English, the one we use now, could fade too, slip and fail. In Beckett's play *All That Fall* Mr Rooney says 'sometimes one would think you were struggling with a dead language', and Mrs Rooney replies: 'Well, you know, it will be dead in time, just like our own poor dear Gaelic, there is that to be said.'[40] And, in this version of things, the Irish tradition in English, from Jonathan Swift to the new generation, begins from that point: the language must be worked for all it is worth until, as John Banville's narrator in his early novel *Nightspawn* says, 'we are all up to our balls in paper, and this same testimony would remain: I love words and I hate death. Beyond this, nothing.'[41]

English, in this argument, both belongs to the Irish writer and does not. And the idea of this dual and ambiguous inheritance sounds true – just as does Stephen's unrest of spirit. But it may not be true; it may even be pure nonsense. The terms seem plausible when used to describe an entire culture, but, when used to describe an individual's relationship with language, the gestures are too broad. Every writer's soul, including writers in Wolverhampton and London, frets in the shadow of his or her language. George Eliot, Virginia Woolf, Graham Swift possessed and possess the language more sonorously than most of the English themselves. That is what writers, whether in England or in her former colonies, try to do. Not a word out of place and yet every word somehow under suspicion, and the play between the two. In this way, all of us who use language are Irish; all of us fret in its shadow.

When you write, whether in England or in Ireland, it feels like an act of will. You decide each sentence, you cut and reshape, you reimagine; you change the ending; you make an infinite number of choices and decisions. The process of imagining and writing seems like an entirely autonomous process. What I do comes from me, the writer feels. It is entirely mine. I am free.

How is it then that we can find a shape for Irish writing which goes beyond the personal into the communal? How is it then that we can make the following statements about Irish writing: there is almost no version of domestic harmony at the end of an Irish novel; there is almost no version of domestic harmony at the beginning of an Irish novel; there is no Irish novel which ends in a wedding, or a match being made. Irish fiction is not like that; Irish fiction is full of dislocation and displacement.

There are, however, two Irish novels (and perhaps there are only two) which have happy families. These are Oliver Goldsmith's *The Vicar of Wakefield* (1766) and Roddy Doyle's *The Snapper* (1990). Both these novels also have good, if somewhat foolish, fathers; it is hard to think of any other good fathers in the canon of Irish fiction and drama. Fathers in Irish writing are absent, or angry, or mad, or strangely silent. In Goldsmith and Doyle the families – the Primroses and the Rabbittes – undergo a number of catastrophes, in Goldsmith imprisonment, ruination, fire, in Doyle the pregnancy of Sharon. It is as though in both books the images of family stability and domestic order are set up only to be destroyed, and in both books the reader is allowed to enjoy the comedy, to relish the reversal of fortune the gods are inflicting on these people for daring to be happy.

In 1891 W. B. Yeats published his *Representative Irish Tales*. 'I notice very distinctly in all Irish literature,' he wrote in the introduction,

two different accents – the accent of the gentry, and the less polished accent of the peasantry and those near them; a division roughly into the voice of those who lived lightly and gaily, and those who took man and his fortunes with much seriousness and even at times mournfully . . . There is perhaps no other country in the world the style and nature of whose writers have been so completely governed by their birth and social standing.[42]

Yeats then took us through the names of the Irish prose writers, praising especially the work of Maria Edgeworth and William Carleton, and then he wrote,

In Gerald Griffin, the most finished storyteller among Irish novelists . . . I think I notice a new accent – not quite clear enough to be wholly distinct; the accent of people who have not the recklessness of the landowning classes, nor the violent passions of the peasantry, nor the good frankness of either. The accent of those middle-class people who find Carleton rough and John Banim coarse, who when they write stories cloak all unpleasant matters and moralise with ease and have yet a sense of order and comeliness that may yet give Ireland a new literature.[43]

Yeats was unsure about this new accent which lacked recklessness and frankness, more at ease with Protestant Gothic and tales of simple folk. That new accent was for a voice which set out to dramatize the life of the Irish middle classes, emerging between the peasantry and the hard-riding country gentlemen. A number of writers sought to become chroniclers of this class, notably in the twentieth century: Kate O'Brien, the later Sean O'Faolain, Mary Lavin, Val Mulkerns, John Broderick, Clare Boylan.

The tradition which Kate O'Brien (1897–1974) inherited was, for the novelist she intended to be, disabling and unhelpful. There was fear and decay around the big house (and this would be an abiding theme in the twentieth century in the work of Bowen and Keane, Jennifer Johnston, William Trevor, Aidan Higgins and John Banville), and there was wildness and drunkenness in the village as well, and there was the story of Ireland, omnipresent like the bad weather. The real world was not part of this narrative. There is something so wild and disturbed in the world of Lady Morgan or the Banim brothers or the fiction of Charles Lever or William Carleton that even when historical events such as the rise of the United Irishmen or the Rising of 1798 are being described, the notion of character gets lost in the detail of battle and background. And when the plight of the tenant is described, it reads as though the tenant is barely human.

The rise of the Catholic middle classes in Ireland, the Irish men who would benefit from O'Connell's battle for Catholics to take silk, say, or the building of the great Catholic cathedrals, the rise of a new sort of manners and morals in Ireland, is barely described in the fiction of the nineteenth century. Thomas Flanagan describes Gerald Griffin (1803–40) as 'the most alert eye which had yet looked upon the Irish scene'.[44] In *The Collegians*, Flanagan wrote, 'Griffin had not written a novel about Ireland; he had written an Irish novel. The Ireland of *The Collegians* is not presented to the reader as an object of sympathy or commiseration or indulgent humour. It simply exists. It exists in rich and exact detail. It is given to us as a work of art, not as a disguised tract.'[45]

The Collegians (1829) bears an odd and interesting resemblance to Kate O'Brien's novel *The Last of Summer* (1943). *The Collegians* is the story of the murder of the Colleen Bawn, but it is also the story of our hero Hardress Cregan and his mother's ambition for him as Catholics begin to repossess Ireland, her interest in his marrying Anne Chute of Castle Chute. It shows Catholic society in Ireland as graded and complex, it hardly mentions England, and thus it allows the enemy to be within. But it needs to play, in a way which often seems laboured and exaggerated, with a phenomenon which has not loomed large in Irish fiction: the interior of houses.

The Dalys, friends of the Cregans, live in a 'cottage' overlooking the Shannon:

The interior of the cottage was not less interesting to contemplate than the landscape which lay before it. The principal breakfast table (for there were two spread in the room) was placed before the window, the neat and snow white damask cloth covered with fare that spoke satisfactorily for the circumstances of the proprietor, and for the housewifery of his helpmate . . . The furniture of the apartment was in accordance with the appearance and manners of its inhabitants. The floor was handsomely carpetted, a lofty green fender fortified the fire-place . . . A small book case, with the edges of the shelves handsomely gilded, was suspended in one corner of the room . . .[46]

The Collegians has its faults and is perhaps of more interest to literary historians than to the general reader. It is overwritten and melodramatic, but what remains with the reader afterwards is the extraordinary intensity – I can think of nothing like it – of Hardress's mother's concern for him. It burns through the book, neurotic and obsessive. It is as though, if Mrs Cregan loses concentration for one moment, she and her son will stare into the abyss. *The Collegians* offers us a picture of a rising class in a changing social and political scene. There is a desperation in the intensity of Mrs Cregan's ambition, and the fear that if this opportunity be lost, no more will come. The power of the book comes from the moral vacuum at Hardress's core, the feeling that he and his mother will do anything to survive. The reader is asked to become them both in their nihilism and in their extraordinary need to rise in the world.

Kate O'Brien's *The Last of Summer* is also set in a house close to a river, the seat of the Kernehan family. (O'Brien, like Griffin, was born in Limerick.) As in *The Collegians*, the world of Catholic ease and privilege is surrounded by another world which offers colour and variety in the book: peculiar servants and scatterings of children at the entrance to the big house and local characters up and down on their luck. The novel is set in 1939 on the eve of war. Hannah Kernehan walks in her garden with an 'open parasol, lined with dark green silk'; the family later will drink some 1933 Moselle wine; the following Sunday for the picnic there will be lobster mayonnaise and a luncheon basket; the son of the house, Kate O'Brien's version of Hardress Cregan, will have spent time after his father's death 'in conclave with lawyers and bankers'; three local families will drive home in a Ford, a Buick and a Fraser-Nash; there is lump sugar and the plum harvest is very fine this year.

There are constant references to paintings, furniture, nice food and fine manners. This is a new Ireland we have not read about previously, where people in Limerick use French phrases and collect Sèvres china and speak at times like characters from Henry James. It is not that this world did not exist, it existed in abundance, but it had not been included in Irish narrative in this way before. Kate O'Brien was starting from scratch, just like Gerald Griffin more than a hundred years before her. There was no Irish fiction to help her, and there was something heroic about her insistence on dealing with this world, sticking to it, rather than describing a rising Catholic class which she could satirize and laugh at. She took these people seriously; she gave them enough money so that they could have choices. They remain, however, oddly brittle under pressure.

As in *The Collegians*, the mother's ferocious attachment to her son begins to burn the pages as you turn them. While *The Last of Summer* is not Kate O'Brien at her best, the mother's fear and longing is perfect, and the idea too that her son is an empty vessel is superb. In these two novels, the mothers watch their sons' weakness and sublime moral emptiness knowing what it will lead to if it is not checked and controlled. Griffin and O'Brien deal with this so intensely that it moves beyond the merely personal into some dark vision of the society: an illustration of the idea that survival is fragile in this ostensibly settled Catholic Ireland, the prospect of ruin is still haunting them all and governing their actions and their relations.

Kate O'Brien and Brian Moore are among the very few Irish writers after Joyce to take a serious interest in Catholicism. In much of the fiction, it appears in the background, or is taken for granted. (Borges insisted that there were no camels mentioned in the Koran.) In Patrick Kavanagh's *Tarry Flynn*, it is a further aspect of the tragi-comic nature of things.

So much, then, for one of Daniel Corkery's three qualities of the Irish people. The other two, land and nationalism, fare rather better in Irish fiction. Haunting, fragmented images of the Famine appear in Carleton's *The Black Prophet* or Rosa Mulholland's 'The Hungry Death' or Seosamh Mac Grianna's 'On the Empty Shore'. And in other writing about rural life, there are no comforting images either, but an insistence on harshness, cruelty and loneliness, as in the work of Kavanagh or John McGahern or Edna O'Brien or Eugene McCabe or Tom Mac Intyre. It is hard to think of a version of rural life as dark as that of Eugene McCabe's masterpiece 'Music at Annahullion'.

The treatment of nationalism in Irish fiction is not celebratory either, from the fierce argument about Parnell in *A Portrait of the Artist as a Young Man* to the account of political violence and its legacy in Liam O'Flaherty, Francis Stuart, Michael McLaverty, Frank O'Connor, Mary Leland, Seamus Deane and Sebastian Barry. In works like O'Connor's 'Guests of the Nation' and Deane's *Reading in the Dark* and Barry's *The Whereabouts of Eneas McNulty*, violence is presented as haunting and disabling, just as the Kenyan struggle for independence is presented in Ngugi wa Thong's *Petals of Blood*: the violence may have led to what seemed for one illusory moment like political liberation, but the legacy of what happened in the struggle has maimed those who took part and those around them.

In her essay on *Uncle Silas* Elizabeth Bowen found two qualities besides those listed above which made it an Irish novel: 'it is sexless,' she wrote, 'and it shows a sublimated infantalism'.[47] In much Irish fiction there is a reticence on sexual matters. Molly Bloom lies down alone in Irish fiction. In the work of other writers sex is furtive and dangerous or never mentioned. In the years after the foundation of the state, one common wisdom was that the Irish imagination and conditions in Ireland made it easier to write short stories than novels (and short stories of course never dealt with sex). Frank O'Connor, Denis Donoghue writes,

regarded the difference between the novel and the short story as only incidentally a matter of length, scale and capacity: the real difference, he thought, was in implication, and the rhythm of implication. The novel refers to a world in which it is possible, however difficult, to live: it implies continuity, latitude of possibility, space to breathe. The short story may offer the same implication, but it rarely does; in common practice, it presents life mainly in the form of constraint and through the feelings of tramps, widows, spoiled priests, monks and only children. O'Connor's affection for the short story speaks of his affection for marginal people, men withering, caught in the duress of circumstance and passion.[48]

Ireland, it is clear, in the years between independence and the First Programme for Economic Expansion (1958), offered 'constraint' rather than 'space to breathe'. A number of short-story writers – Frank O'Connor, Sean O'Faolain, Liam O'Flaherty, Bryan MacMahon, Michael McLaverty and Mary Lavin – flourished in this period. Their work was formally conservative, with the Joyce of *Dubliners* and nineteenth-century short fiction as its governing influences, and dealt with states of loneliness and isolation, or used the anecdote, the story told around the fire, as the model. The men wrote a great deal about childhood. 'There is a sense in which,' Donoghue says,

Frank O'Connor stayed, imaginatively, in the towns of his boyhood, and let the new Ireland mind its own grubby business. Liam O'Flaherty, too, wrote as if his first experiences were definitive and could only be lost if pestered by later matters. Michael McLaverty . . . stayed where he started: perhaps the experience of childhood and boyhood was too cherished to admit a rival or the fear of a lapse.[49]

Sean O'Faolain got away, however. He too wrote about childhood and told anecdotes about peasant life, but, as Donogue has pointed out, the stories he wrote after 1945 'cast an ironic but not a cold eye upon Dublin, its upper-middle-class life, its lawyers and doctors, the remnants of Ascendancy Ireland, their marriages, their mistresses'.[50] Like the pictures of upper-middle-class Irish Catholic life in Gerald Griffin and Kate O'Brien, there are moments when you feel that O'Faolain is forcing things – images of new wealth and new liberalism – in his later work, just as he forces things in creating images of purity and simplicity in his early work.

Many of the short stories written by this generation of Irish writers now seem dated. This has not happened, however, to the work of Mary Lavin. She set much of her work among the prosperous Catholic business classes, but she took this and the wider society for granted; she concentrated, instead, on her characters and her sentences and the creation of a subdued and flawless tone. Love, memory, family, age, death, hope and hopelessness became her themes, and there is a sense of ease in her work which is absent in most Irish writing of the century. She is prepared to dramatize the small details, the moments of pure truth. Her stories tell you very little about 'Irish society' and a great deal about the human heart.

'A happy ending was imperative,' E. M. Forster wrote about his novel *Maurice*. 'I shouldn't have bothered to write otherwise. I was determined that in fiction anyway two men should fall in love and remain in it for the ever and ever that fiction allows . . . Happiness is the keynote.'[51] Forster was aware that writing about gay relationships tended towards the tragic. Indeed, there was a movement among gay literary activists in the 1970s to stop this trend. 'Gay critics made gay writers self-conscious about their sense of appropriate endings,' Gregory Woods wrote in *A History of Gay Literature*. 'No central gay character could be murdered or commit suicide, even if for reasons clearly represented as being other than homosexuality itself, for fear of enforcing the myth of the tragic queer.'[52]

Irish writing and gay writing have the myth of a tragic destiny in common. It is easy to see why homosexuality as a theme has attracted so many Irish writers. Oscar Wilde's *The Picture of Dorian Gray* still remains the greatest gay novel ever written, even if Joyce thought that it was too cloaked and tame. Joyce himself dealt with the theme in 'An Encounter', one of the stories in *Dubliners* which caused the greatest alarm among publishers. Some of the most powerful scenes in the work of Kate O'Brien centre on homosexuality and its discontents, and this is also true in the work of John Broderick. It is remarkable how many times in Irish fiction of the past twenty years the theme has emerged: in the work of John Banville, Val Mulkerns, Ita Daly, Desmond Hogan, Mary Dorcey, Patrick McCabe, Dermot Bolger, Frank Ronan, Joseph O'Connor, Colum McCann, Emma Donoghue.

There is a moment in Samuel Beckett's story 'The Expelled' in which our hero watches a funeral pass:

Personally if I were reduced to making the sign of the cross I would set my heart on doing it right, nose, navel, left nipple, right nipple. But the way they did it slovenly and wild, he seemed crucified all of a heap, no dignity, his knees under his chin and his hands anyhow . . . As for the policeman he stiffened to attention, closed his eyes and saluted . . . The horses were farting and shitting as though they were going to the fair.[53]

This is one of Beckett's common modes. Our rueful narrator, a Leopold Bloom who has read Descartes and Kant, muses to himself, intrigued and obsessed by the rigours of things, loving lists, locked into the mind's peculiar capacity to gather information, analyse it, store some of it and then forget most of it, lacking all respect for what Yeats called 'custom and ceremony', having it in for tradition and authority, and delighted by the body's ability to undo whatever grandeur society or the mind had constructed.

Beckett's work is at its best when the author seems to forget himself, forget his great mission to undo the power of words, which he explained in a letter, written in German, to the translator Axel Kaun in 1937:

It is indeed becoming more and more difficult, even senseless, for me to write an official English. And more and more my own language appears to me like a veil that must be torn apart in order to get at the things (or the Nothingness) behind it. Grammar and Style. To me they seem to have become as irrelevant as a Victorian bathing suit or the imperturbability of a true gentleman. A mask. Let us hope the time will come, thank God that in certain circles it has already come, when language is most efficiently used when it is most efficiently misused. As we cannot eliminate language all at once, we should at least leave nothing undone that might contribute to its falling into disrepute. To bore one hole after another in it, until what lurks behind it – be it something or nothing – begins to seep through; I cannot imagine a higher goal for a writer today.[54]

And yet we look back to that last sentence quoted from 'The Expelled': 'The horses were farting and shitting as though they were going to the fair' or the celebrated first sentence of *Murphy*, published in 1938, a year after the letter was written ('The sun shone, having no alternative, on the nothing new') or sentences chosen at random from Beckett's trilogy of novels *Molloy*, *Malone Dies* and *The Unnameable*, and we find that he is half in love with Grammar and Style, and that he is somehow prevented from putting his own agenda into operation, that the 'higher goal' constantly eludes him. And it is this tension – Beckett with his agenda and Beckett failing, becoming too distracted by the world, to put his agenda into operation – that fills his work between *Murphy* and the later prose.

There were, of course, other tensions too, not least a philosophical tension between the notion of *cogito* and the idea of *sum*. Beckett characters take a dim view of the connection, the *ergo* part of the equation. Cogitating is the nightmare from which they are trying to awake, and Being is a sour trick played on them by some force with whom they are desperately trying not to reckon. Beckett produces infinite amounts of comedy about the business of thinking as boring, invalid, quite unnecessary. His characters know they exist because of the discomforts and odd habits of their bodies. In some cases they are left in no doubt: 'The smell of corpses, distinctly perceptible under those of grass and humus mingled, I do not find unpleasant, a trifle on the sweet side perhaps, a trifle heady, but how infinitely preferable to what the living emit, their feet, teeth, armpits, arses, sticky foreskins and frustrated ovules.'[55]

There are times when you feel that Beckett genuinely means this: not alone are many of his narrators half dead, but he would be happier too if his readers were also dead, but no wiser for that. In 1929 the Censorship of Publications Act was passed in Ireland, and work by most Irish writers and many foreign writers was banned; this did not encourage Irish writers to feel that there was an audience out there hungry for their work. The sense that there was no reader fed into a tradition which was already strong in Irish writing, a tradition which insisted that a book could read itself, hermetically sealed in a deep self-consciousness. From *Tristram Shandy* to *Ulysses* to *At Swim-Two-Birds* to Beckett's fiction to John Banville's *Birchwood* to John McGahern's *The Pornographer*, pastiche and parody combine with the idea of the built-in reader.

There was little space between history and destiny for these novelists to pitch their tents. In John Banville's world everything has to be imagined and contructed; nothing was there before the novel. In John McGahern's work the fate of the Irishman becomes the fate of all mankind: alone, lost, in search of some whole, unbroken place which may have existed in the past, which may be possible in the future in a personal and intimate way, but which will probably not be possible at all. But in Beckett's austere universe, nothing is there after the novel, nor within the novel either, and there is no search, except for time to pass, and nothing is possible, but certain things are probable, and those probabilities, in all their infinite absurdity, haunt the books and plays from the very beginning.

Beckett's short prose works from the 1980s represent an astonishing end to his career. They have not been helped by his later works for the theatre, which often seem like flat parodies of Beckett's supposed views on the human condition. Since both the prose and the drama insist on brevity and lessness, it is easy to feel that they come from the same impulse and should be taken as part of the same process. But the late fictions are written with a sympathy for the human voice which is not in the later plays. This is a broken voice, full of memory, or what seems like memory, gasps of fresh thought and insight, only too willing to stop as though for good, but suddenly starting again, stirring still in a closed room, suddenly more words, further statements, the rhythm repetitious and mesmerizing.

This prose is modulated with beauty and care; there is no time for jokes or casual ironies. This is the language of the body, found at last after a lifetime's search; 'Company', *Ill Seen Ill Said*, *Worstword Ho* and *Stirrings Still* are grave works of art which deserve our attention and our gratitude.

Francis Stuart remembered meeting Beckett in the back room of Davy Byrne's pub in Dublin in the 1920s. There was a bond between them, Stuart believed, as both felt awkward and did not fit in. By the 1930s they fitted in even less 'when the so-called Cork school of writers [Frank O'Connor, Sean O'Faolain] dominated the Irish (and Irish-American) literary scene', as Stuart wrote in his obituary of Beckett.[56] They lived and wrote in a world light years away from their Irish contemporaries.

Like Beckett, Stuart had no time for current pieties. He disowned his early work, saw it as a preparation for his post-war novels, but again in the 1930s, before he set out for Berlin where he lived in the war years, he wrote of the redemption of outcasts and strangers, a world of possibility outside society, the healing power of catastrophe and suffering, the lone and isolated figure against materialism and the filthy, modern tide.

The notion of writing to explore a deep personal wound arises over and over in Stuart's fiction. After the war, he wrote two novels, *The Pillar of Cloud* (1948) and *Redemption* (1949). Later, in the early 1960s, he set to work on his masterpiece, *Black List, Section H*. He surrounded H, his central figure (whose life resembles Stuart's), with a mass of rich detail. Horse-racing, poultry, farming, houses, hotels, social gatherings, journeys were made interesting, exciting, even funny. But the novel never lost its main focus, its awkwardness, never ceased to insist on H's alienation from the fixed moral world and his inability to feel part of what was happening either in Ireland or Germany. The detail, relayed with a sense of truth and accuracy, forced the reader to see the world through H's eyes and slowly to join him in his status as renegade, man without qualities and outsider.

Brian Moore is as elusive as Stuart in any contemplation of Irish fiction. He too was interested in renegades, men without qualities and outsiders. But while Stuart's imagination was fired by the re-creation of the self, Moore remained invisible. Much of his work, especially his later work, would have satisfied the man on the golf course in E. M. Forster's *Aspects of the Novel*: 'You can take your art, you can take your literature, you can take your music, but give me a good story.'[57] (The man on the golf course, it should be said, would have made Francis Stuart puke.) Moore's first novel, *The Lonely Passion of Judith Hearne* (1955), remains his most intense and complete; he never again managed to create such a powerful single consciousness, concentrating instead on the portrayal of moral dilemmas. Once or twice, he struck gold in these. It is possible to read *Black Robe* (1985) as a subtle allegory for the Irish experience. Here, the terse style, which is too terse in later books, is perfect. Moore's eye, which was capable of a deep sympathy, managed to catch both sides in this conflict between two civilizations in seventeenth-century Canada. He remains a fascinating figure for the way in which he flits in and out of an Irish tradition.

William Trevor, as has already been pointed out, comes as the last in a long line of writers who have been able to write about both England and Ireland with equal authority and ease. In her essay in memory of Marianne Moore, Elizabeth Bishop wrote, 'She said her poem "Spenser's Ireland" was not about *loving* Ireland, as people seemed to think, but about *disapproving* of it.'[58] In much of his fiction set in Ireland, William Trevor also seems to disapprove of Ireland, often finding it hopeless, feckless and chaotic, as opposed to the England of his stories, which is dry, structured and severe, or 'dear, safe, uncomplicated' as Mrs Pulvertaft would have it in Trevor's story 'The News from Ireland'. The first Irishman appears early on in Trevor's work in a story called 'Memories of Youghal'. Miss Grimshaw and Miss Titcher are on holiday in the Mediterranean. They represent England: they are settled and sober. Quillan, the Irishman, is drunk, however, and obsessed with the past, and not very coherent. And yet one of the women is drawn to him, to his wounded self. He remains enigmatic, while the two ladies are only too real. It is a slight story, it lacks the skill and feeling which Trevor can bring to other work. The people are caricatures of Ireland and England. Yet, in other, better stories about Ireland, drink and drunkenness come up over and over. And in stories about England we read again and again of a comic austerity. Early on in his career, William Trevor found a theme. And then he began to soften his attitudes and become more sympathetic and open, and in doing so he created a number of wonderful stories. Unlike writers such as John McGahern and Eugene McCabe, whose work takes place in an exact and contoured landscape, Trevor has no fiefdom in Ireland, no landscape which he knows in detail. He is more at home in boarding houses, shops, public houses, or in the minds of his characters. In his best Irish stories – 'An Evening with John Joe Dempsey', 'A Choice of Butchers', 'Teresa's Wedding', 'Death in Jerusalem', 'Honeymoon in Tramore' and 'Kathleen's Field' – he abandons most of the brittleness and wryness of his earlier work. In the last two he tells the story of someone poor and innocent coming up against a harsher world, and he places himself in that long Irish tradition of melancholy.

John McGahern is the Irish writer who has worked best within that tradition and produced the most impressive body of work of any Irish writer in the second half of the century. The very narrowness and modesty of his scope has served to heighten his powers of expression, and the clarity of his prose can be matched by a poetic impulse. The same names and the same resonant landscape appear again and again in his fiction. The name Luke Moran first appears in *Korea* (1970) and surfaces again in *Amongst Women* (1990), just as the names Mona and Sheila had appeared in earlier fiction. The same gruff father appears in the novels and many stories. The same beech trees and yew trees, the same shadows, the same battle between desolation and communion. McGahern's fictional universe is fired not by memory, or by autobiography, because the crafting is too self-conscious, the artistry too complete. McGahern writes with the simplicity, sense of inevitability and poetic turn of phrase of a nineteenth-century ballad. He is able to move effortlessly – and this perhaps is the real genius in his work – from minute dramatization to sweeping statements about character and motive. He is especially good at rendering ordinary moments luminous and daily routine a powerful ritual. The opening passage of *The Barracks*, which he wrote in his twenties, is among the finest and most expressive prose by any Irish writer, showing, as Denis Sampson has pointed out, in a slow and searing sequence the battle between darkness and light.[59] No relationship in his work is easy; love is hard-won, but love too can include moments of pure savagery or sourness. McGahern has remained true to his art, irrespective of fashion or taste. He is an exemplary presence in contemporary Irish writing.

Two books appeared in the 1970s which changed the face of Irish fiction. John Banville's *Birchwood* appeared in 1973; Neil Jordan's *Night in Tunisia* appeared in 1976. The first offered closure, tried to put an end once and for all to certain tropes and themes in Irish fiction; the other, being cinematic, half American in its rhythms and full of post-1960s angst, offered a beginning which had an impact on many younger writers. Banville's novel appeared just as Ireland was getting ready to join what became the European Union. It suited its moment because it made fun of rebellion and land wars and famine, Irish myths of origin, which had been dear to the heart of the founding fathers. Full of dark laughter, *Birchwood* was, more than any historian's work, the most radical text in Irish revisionism. It also parodied its literary precedents in prose both ironic and purple: big houses and Gothic moments and the plight of the decayed landed class. Nabokov meets Maria Edgeworth meets Walter Pater.

The tone of *Birchwood* was knowing and slyly comic. It was exactly what Ireland needed then: to rid itself stylishly of the burden of history. Banville followed this with two novels set at the heart of the European achievement, and these too, oddly enough, since Banville has shown little interest in 'society' or the *Zeitgeist*, suited the ambitions of post-nationalist Ireland. But to match his work with changes in the society is to belittle it and miss its point. Banville is interested in the age-old and essential questions – order and chaos, language and silence, art and invention. His language manages to be luxuriant and comic at the same time, his narrators and protagonists are both puzzled and dazzled by the world. Banville's tone is often Olympian; the lives of mere mortals are both beyond him and beneath his contempt, and yet he writes with a pure wonder about the world and its central mysteries.

In music and cinema, as the 1970s progressed, Ireland became open to America. Among Irish intellectuals, there was almost no gut anti-American feeling as there was among English or Continental intellectuals. Ireland lay down and let America wash over it. Thus in the 1980s and 1990s it was possible to detect the spare poetic realism of Raymond Carver and Richard Ford, or the eccentric voices of Flannery O'Connor and Grace Paley, in many of the younger writers, but more than that the influence of American cinema and American music.

While there has been stylistic innovation in the work of, say, Anne Enright and Roddy Doyle and Patrick McCabe and Aidan Mathews, a playing with tone, an ability to write sentences like no one had ever written them before, most of the work being produced in Ireland now is formally conservative. This may be because, for the first time, there is an audience for books in Ireland. You can have readers outside the book as well as within it. This new conservatism among fiction writers both north and south of the border is most clear when you compare the calmness of contemporary Irish writing with the wildness of contemporary Scottish writing. It is as though the legacy of Sterne and Swift, Joyce, Beckett and Flann O'Brien had taken the Larne–Stranraer ferry; in the writing of James Kelman, Alasdair Gray, Irvine Welsh, Janice Galloway and Alan Warner there is political anger, stylistic experiment and formal trickery. Books are written, as in Ireland in the old days, to replace a country.

In Ireland now, for the first time, the exiles tell their own stories to the whole country. Writers like Edna O'Brien, Julia O'Faolain, Desmond Hogan, Patrick McCabe, Joseph O'Connor, Frank Ronan, Colum McCann and Emma Donoghue can explore Irish identity in England or the United States or Europe. In the nineteenth century, and for much of the twentieth, the emigrants were too busy finding work to write stories. They melted into England and America, and when their children or grandchildren came to write stories – Henry James, Eugene O'Neill, T. Coraghessan Boyle, Alice McDermot – the stories had changed.

The violence of the past thirty years has also come back to haunt Irish fiction in the work of Dermot Healy, Deirdre Madden, David Park, Eoin McNamee, Glenn Patterson and Robert McLiam Wilson. But now that the violence is fading and the society moves slowly towards Anglo-Irish Agreement and European Union, will we see a waning of the national themes in Irish writing? Some clues about what might replace this can be seen in the work of several women writers, most notably K. Arnold Price, whose account of a marriage in *The New Perspective* could equally be set in contemporary Scandinavia, or Deirdre Madden, whose novel *Remembering Light and Stone* concentrates on the experiences of an Irishwoman in Italy, or Emma Donoghue, whose dramatizations of sexual politics have set a new tone in Irish fiction, or Anne Enright, who has taken up and refined the legacy of Sterne and Flann O'Brien and placed it in a Dublin which, for the first time in its long life in fiction, has become post-Freudian and post-feminist and, of course (three cheers!), post-nationalist.

Notes

1. Quoted in Fintan O'Toole, 'Irish Theatre: The State of the Art in Ireland' in *Towards New Identities?*, edited by Karl-Heinz Westarp and Michael Boss (Aarhaus University Press, 1998).
2. Terry Eagleton, *Heathcliff and the Great Hunger: Studies in Irish Culture* (Verso, 1995), pp. 171–2.
3. Quoted in David Lloyd Duke, *Anomalous States* (Lilliput, 1993), p. 134.
4. ibid., p. 135.
5. Thomas Flanagan, *The Irish Novelists 1800–1850* (Columbia University Press, 1958), pp. 333–5.
6. Seamus Deane, *A Short History of Irish Literature* (Hutchinson, 1986), p. 169.
7. Quoted in the introduction by Terence Brown to *The Untilled Field* (Gill & Macmillan, 1990), p. xii.
8. ibid., p. xiii.
9. ibid., p. xvi.
10. Richard Ellmann, *James Joyce* (1959; revised edn 1982), p. 250.
11. ibid., p. 234.
12. Quoted in ibid., p. 529.
13. Quoted in ibid., p. 334.
14. Seamus Deane, *A Short History of Irish Literature*, p. 202.
15. Carolyn Lanchner, *Joan Miró* (Museum of Modern Art, New York, 1993), p. 34.
16. W. B. Yeats, *Autobiographies* (Macmillan, 1955), p. 199.
17. ibid., p. 209.
18. James Joyce, *Ulysses* (Penguin edn, 1982), p. 923.
19. ibid., p. 411.
20. Terry Eagleton, *Heathcliff and the Great Hunger*, p. 187.
21. Elizabeth Bowen, *The Mulberry Tree: The Writings of Elizabeth Bowen* (Virago, 1986), p. 101.
22. R. F. Foster, *Paddy and Mr Punch: Connections in Irish and English History* (Allen Lane, 1993), p. 220.
23. Joep Leerssen, *Remembrance and Imagination: Patterns in the Historical and Literary Representation of Ireland in the Nineteenth Century* (Cork University Press, 1996), pp. 222–3.
24. Jorge Luis Borges, *Obras completas*, vol. 1 (Emecé, Buenos Aires, 1974), p. 272.
25. ibid., p. 273.
26. Daniel Corkery, *Synge and Anglo-Irish Literature* (Longman, 1931), pp. 6–7.
27. ibid., pp. 7–10.
28. Conor Cruise O'Brien, *Writers and Politics* (Chatto & Windus, 1965), p. 134.
29. Owen Dudley Edwards, 'Trollope as an Irish Writer', *Nineteenth Century Fiction*, vol. 38, no. 1 (1983–4), p. 1.
30. Victoria Glendinning, *Trollope* (Hutchinson, 1992), p. 155.
31. ibid., p. 152.

32. R. F. Foster, *Paddy and Mr Punch*, p. 145.
33. Owen Dudley Edwards, 'Trollope as an Irish Writer', p. 41.
34. Jorge Luis Borges, *Collected Stories* (Penguin, 1998), p. 68.
35. T. S. Eliot, *Selected Essays 1917–1932* (Faber, 1932), p. 13.
36. Daniel Corkery, *Synge and Anglo-Irish Literature*, p. 12.
37. ibid., p. 19.
38. James Joyce, *A Portrait of the Artist as a Young Man* (Cape, 1917), p. 215.
39. Seamus Heaney, *The Government of the Tongue* (Faber, 1988), p. 26.
40. Samuel Beckett, *The Collected Shorter Plays of Samuel Beckett* (Faber, 1984), p. 34.
41. John Banville, *Nightspawn* (Secker & Warburg, 1971), p. 224.
42. W. B. Yeats, *Representative Irish Tales* (Colin Smythe edn, 1979), p. 25.
43. ibid., p. 31.
44. Thomas Flanagan, *The Irish Novelists 1800–1850*, p. 30.
45. ibid., p. 230.
46. Gerald Griffin, *The Collegians* (Appletree, 1992), pp. 10–11.
47. Elizabeth Bowen, *The Mulberry Tree*.
48. Denis Donoghue, *We Irish* (Harvester, 1986), p. 232.
49. ibid., p. 239.
50. ibid.
51. E. M. Forster, *Maurice* (Edward Arnold, 1971), p. 250.
52. Gregory Woods, *A History of Gay Literature* (Yale University Press, 1998), p. 265.
53. Samuel Beckett, *The Expelled and Other Novellas* (Penguin, 1980), pp. 39–40.
54. Samuel Beckett, quoted in Seamus Deane, ed., *The Field Day Anthology of Irish Writing* (Field Day, 1991), vol. III, p. 258.
55. Samuel Beckett, *The Complete Short Prose* (Grove Press, 1955), pp. 52–3.
56. Francis Stuart, *Sunday Press*, 31 December 1989.
57. E. M. Forster, *Aspects of the Novel* (Edward Arnold, 1927), p. 40.
58. Elizabeth Bishop, *The Collected Prose* (Chatto & Windus, 1984), p. 133.
59. Denis Sampson, *Outstaring Nature's Eye: The Fiction of John McGahern* (Lilliput Press, 1993), p. 38.

THE PENGUIN BOOK OF *Irish Fiction*

JONATHAN SWIFT

from *Gulliver's Travels*

The author giveth some account of himself and family, his first inducements to travel. He is shipwrecked, and swims for his life, gets safe on shore in the country of Lilliput, is made a prisoner, and carried up the country.

My father had a small estate in Nottinghamshire; I was the third of five sons. He sent me to Emanuel College in Cambridge, at fourteen years old, where I resided three years, and applied myself close to my studies: but the charge of maintaining me (although I had a very scanty allowance) being too great for a narrow fortune, I was bound apprentice to Mr James Bates, an eminent surgeon in London, with whom I continued four years; and my father now and then sending me small sums of money, I laid them out in learning navigation, and other parts of the mathematics, useful to those who intend to travel, as I always believed it would be some time or other my fortune to do. When I left Mr Bates, I went down to my father; where, by the assistance of him and my uncle John, and some other relations, I got forty pounds, and a promise of thirty pounds a year to maintain me at Leyden: there I studied physic two years and seven months, knowing it would be useful in long voyages.

Soon after my return from Leyden, I was recommended by my good master Mr Bates, to be surgeon to the *Swallow*, Captain Abraham Pannell commander; with whom I continued three years and a half, making a voyage or two into the Levant, and some other parts. When I came back, I resolved to settle in London, to which Mr Bates, my master, encouraged me, and by him I was recommended to several patients. I took part of a small house in the Old Jury; and being advised to alter my condition, I married Mrs Mary Burton, second daughter to Mr Edmond Burton hosier in Newgate Street, with whom I received four hundred pounds for a portion.

But, my good master Bates dying in two years after, and I having few friends, my business began to fail; for my conscience would not suffer me to imitate the bad practice of too many among my brethren. Having therefore consulted with my wife, and some of my acquaintance, I determined to go again to sea. I was surgeon successively in two ships, and made several voyages, for six years, to the East and West Indies, by which I got some addition to my fortune. My hours of leisure I spent in reading the best authors ancient and modern, being always provided with a good number of books; and when I was ashore, in observing the manners and dispositions of the people, as well as learning their language, wherein I had a great facility by the strength of my memory.

The last of these voyages not proving very fortunate, I grew weary of the sea, and intended to stay at home with my wife and family. I removed from the Old Jury to Fetter Lane, and from thence to Wapping, hoping to get business among the sailors;

but it would not turn to account. After three years' expectation that things would mend, I accepted an advantageous offer from Captain William Prichard, master of the *Antelope*, who was making a voyage to the South Sea. We set sail from Bristol, May 4th, 1699, and our voyage at first was prosperous.

It would not be proper, for some reasons, to trouble the reader with the particulars of our adventures in those seas: let it suffice to inform him, that in our passage from thence to the East Indies, we were driven by a violent storm to the north-west of Van Diemen's Land. By an observation, we found ourselves in the latitude of 30 degrees 2 minutes south. Twelve of our crew were dead by immoderate labour, and ill food, the rest were in a very weak condition. On the fifth of November, which was the beginning of summer in those parts, the weather being very hazy, the seamen spied a rock, within half a cable's length of the ship; but the wind was so strong, that we were driven directly upon it, and immediately split. Six of the crew, of whom I was one, having let down the boat into the sea, made a shift to get clear of the ship, and the rock. We rowed by my computation about three leagues, till we were able to work no longer, being already spent with labour while we were in the ship. We therefore trusted ourselves to the mercy of the waves, and in about half an hour the boat was overset by a sudden flurry from the north. What became of my companions in the boat, as well as of those who escaped on the rock, or were left in the vessel, I cannot tell; but conclude they were all lost. For my own part, I swam as Fortune directed me, and was pushed forward by wind and tide. I often let my legs drop, and could feel no bottom: but when I was almost gone, and able to struggle no longer, I found myself within my depth; and by this time the storm was much abated. The declivity was so small, that I walked near a mile before I got to the shore, which I conjectured was about eight o'clock in the evening. I then advanced forward near half a mile, but could not discover any sign of houses or inhabitants; at least I was in so weak a condition, that I did not observe them. I was extremely tired, and with that, and the heat of the weather, and about half a pint of brandy that I drank as I left the ship, I found myself much inclined to sleep. I lay down on the grass, which was very short and soft, where I slept sounder than ever I remember to have done in my life, and as I reckoned, above nine hours; for when I awaked, it was just daylight. I attempted to rise, but was not able to stir: for as I happened to lie on my back, I found my arms and legs were strongly fastened on each side to the ground; and my hair, which was long and thick, tied down in the same manner. I likewise felt several slender ligatures across my body, from my armpits to my thighs. I could only look upwards, the sun began to grow hot, and the light offended mine eyes. I heard a confused noise about me, but in the posture I lay, could see nothing except the sky. In a little time I felt something alive moving on my left leg, which advancing gently forward over my breast, came almost up to my chin; when bending mine eyes downwards as much as I could, I perceived it to be a human creature not six inches high, with a bow and arrow in his hands, and a quiver at his back. In the meantime, I felt at least forty more of the same kind (as I conjectured) following the first. I was in the utmost astonishment, and roared so loud, that they all ran back in a fright; and some of them, as I was afterwards told, were hurt with the falls they got by leaping from my sides upon the ground. However, they soon returned, and one of them, who ventured so far as to get a full sight of my face, lifting up his hands and eyes by way of admiration, cried out in a shrill, but distinct voice, *Hekinah degul*: the others repeated the same words several times, but I then knew not what they meant. I lay all this while, as the reader may believe, in great uneasiness: at length, struggling to get loose, I had the fortune to break the strings, and wrench out the pegs that fastened my left arm to the ground; for, by lifting it up to my face, I discovered the methods they had taken to bind me; and, at the same time, with a violent pull, which gave me excessive pain, I a little loosened the strings that tied down my hair on the left side, so that I was just able to turn my head about two inches. But the creatures ran off a second time, before I could seize them; whereupon there was a great shout in a very shrill accent, and after it ceased, I heard one of them cry aloud, *Tolgo phonac*; when in an instant I felt above an hundred arrows discharged on my left hand, which pricked me like so many needles; and besides, they shot another flight into the air, as we do bombs in Europe, whereof many, I suppose, fell on my body (though I felt them not), and some on my face, which I immediately covered with my left hand. When this shower of arrows was over, I fell a groaning with grief and pain, and then striving again to get loose, they discharged another volley larger than the first, and some of them attempted with spears to stick me in the sides; but, by good luck, I had on me a buff jerkin, which they could not pierce. I thought it the most prudent method to lie still, and my design was to continue so till night, when, my left hand being already loose, I could easily free myself: and as for the inhabitants, I had reason to believe I might be a match for the greatest armies they could bring against me, if they were all of the same size with him that I saw. But Fortune disposed otherwise of me. When the people observed I was quiet, they discharged no more arrows: but, by the noise increasing, I knew their numbers were greater; and about four yards from me, over-against my right ear, I heard a knocking for above an hour, like people at work; when, turning my head that way, as well as the pegs and strings would permit me, I saw a stage erected about a foot and a half from the ground, capable of holding four of the inhabitants, with two or three ladders to mount it: from whence one of them, who seemed to be a person of quality, made me a long speech, whereof I understood not one syllable. But I should have mentioned, that before the principal person began his oration, he cried out three times *Langro dehul san* (these words and the former were afterwards repeated and explained to me): whereupon immediately about fifty of the inhabitants came, and cut the strings that fastened the left side of my head, which gave me the liberty of turning it to the right, and of observing the person and gesture of him who was to speak. He appeared to be of a middle age, and taller than any of the other three who attended him, whereof one was a page who held up his train, and seemed to be somewhat longer than my middle finger; the other two stood one on each side to support him. He acted every part of an orator, and I could observe many periods of threatenings, and others of promises, pity and kindness. I answered in a few words, but in the most submissive manner, lifting up my left hand and both mine eyes to the sun, as calling him for a witness; and being almost famished with hunger, having not eaten a morsel for some hours before I left the ship, I found the demands of nature so strong upon me, that I could not forbear showing my impatience (perhaps against the strict rules of decency) by putting my finger frequently on my mouth, to signify that I wanted food. The *Hurgo* (for so they call a great lord, as I afterwards learnt) understood me very well. He descended from the stage, and commanded that several ladders should be applied to my sides, on which above an hundred of the inhabitants mounted, and walked towards my mouth, laden with baskets full of meat, which had been provided and sent thither by the King's orders upon the first intelligence he received of me. I observed there was the flesh of several animals, but could not distinguish them by the taste. There were shoulders, legs and loins, shaped like those of mutton, and very well dressed, but smaller than the wings of a lark. I ate them by two or three at a mouthful, and took three loaves at a time, about the bigness of musket bullets. They supplied me as fast as they could, showing a thousand marks of wonder and astonishment at my bulk and appetite. I then made another sign that I wanted drink. They found by my eating that a small quantity would not suffice me; and being a most ingenious people, they slung up with great dexterity one of their largest hogsheads, then rolled it towards my hand, and beat out the top; I drank it off at a draught, which I might well do, for it hardly held half a pint, and tasted like a small wine of Burgundy, but much more delicious. They brought me a second hogshead, which I drank in the same manner, and made signs for more, but they had none to give me. When I had performed these wonders, they shouted for joy, and danced upon my breast, repeating several times as they did at first, *Hekinah degul*. They made me a sign that I should throw down the two hogsheads, but first warned the people below to stand out of the way, crying aloud, *Borach mivola*, and when they saw the vessels in the air, there was an universal shout of *Hekinah degul*. I confess I was often tempted, while they were passing backwards and forwards on my body, to seize forty or fifty of the first that came in my reach, and dash them against the ground. But the remembrance of what I had felt, which probably might not be the worst they could do, and the promise of honour I made them, for so I interpreted my submissive behaviour, soon drove out those imaginations. Besides, I now considered myself as bound by the laws of hospitality to a people who had treated me with so much expense and magnificence. However, in my thoughts I could not sufficiently wonder at the intrepidity of these diminutive mortals, who durst venture to mount and walk on my body, while one of my hands was at liberty, without trembling at the very sight of so prodigious a creature as I must appear to them. After some time, when they observed that I made no more demands for meat, there appeared before me a person of high rank from his Imperial Majesty. His Excellency having mounted on the small of my right leg, advanced forwards up to my face, with about a dozen of his retinue. And producing his credentials under the Signet Royal, which he applied close to mine eyes, spoke about ten minutes, without any signs of anger, but with a kind of determinate resolution; often pointing forwards, which, as I afterwards found, was towards the capital city, about half a mile distant, whither it was agreed by his Majesty in council that I must be conveyed. I answered in few words, but to no purpose, and made a sign with my hand that was loose, putting it to the other (but over his Excellency's head, for fear of hurting him or his train) and then to my own head and body, to signify that I desired my liberty. It appeared that he understood me well enough, for he shook his head by way of disapprobation, and held his hand in a posture to show that I must be carried as a prisoner. However, he made other signs to let me understand that I should have meat and drink enough, and very good treatment. Whereupon I once more thought of attempting to break my bonds, but again, when I felt the smart of their arrows upon my face and hands, which were all in blisters, and many of the darts still sticking in them, and observing likewise that the number of my enemies increased, I gave tokens to let them know that they might do with me what they pleased. Upon this, the *Hurgo* and his train withdrew with much civility and cheerful countenances. Soon after I heard a general shout, with frequent repetitions of the words, *Peplom selan*, and I felt great numbers of the people on my left side relaxing the cords to such a degree, that I was able to turn upon my right, and to ease myself with making water; which I very plentifully did, to the great astonishment of the people, who conjecturing by my motions what I was going to do, immediately opened to the right and left on that side, to avoid the torrent which fell with such noise and violence from me. But before this, they had daubed my face and both my hands with a sort of ointment very pleasant to the smell, which in a few minutes removed all the smart of their arrows. These circumstances, added to the refreshment I had received by their victuals and drink, which were very nourishing, disposed me to sleep. I slept about eight hours, as I was afterwards assured; and it was no wonder, for the physicians, by the Emperor's order, had mingled a sleepy potion in the hogsheads of wine.

It seems that upon the first moment I was discovered sleeping on the ground after my landing, the Emperor had early notice of it by an express, and determined in council that I should be tied in the manner I have related (which was done in the night while I slept), that plenty of meat and drink should be sent me, and a machine prepared to carry me to the capital city.

This resolution perhaps may appear very bold and dangerous, and I am confident would not be imitated by any prince in Europe on the like occasion; however, in my opinion it was extremely prudent as well as generous. For supposing these people had endeavoured to kill me with their spears and arrows while I was asleep, I should certainly have awaked with the first sense of smart, which might so far have roused my rage and strength, as to enable me to break the strings wherewith I was tied; after which, as they were not able to make resistance, so they could expect no mercy.

These people are most excellent mathematicians, and arrived to a great perfection in mechanics by the countenance and encouragement of the Emperor, who is a renowned patron of learning. This prince hath several machines fixed on wheels for the carriage of trees and other great weights. He often buildeth his largest men-of-war, whereof some are nine foot long, in the woods where the timber grows, and has them carried on these engines three or four hundred yards to the sea. Five hundred carpenters and engineers were immediately set at work to prepare the greatest engine they had. It was a frame of wood raised three inches from the ground, about seven foot long and four wide, moving upon twenty-two wheels. The shout I heard was upon the arrival of this engine, which it seems set out in four hours after my landing. It was brought parallel to me as I lay. But the principal difficulty was to raise and place me in this vehicle. Eighty poles, each of one foot high, were erected for this purpose, and very strong cords of the bigness of pack-thread were fastened by hooks to many bandages, which the workmen had girt round my neck, my hands, my body, and my legs. Nine hundred of the strongest men were employed to draw up these cords by many pulleys fastened on the poles, and thus in less than three hours, I was raised and slung into the engine, and there tied fast. All this I was told, for while the whole operation was performing, I lay in a profound sleep, by the force of that soporiferous medicine infused into my liquor. Fifteen hundred of the Emperor's largest horses, each about four inches and a half high, were employed to draw me towards the metropolis, which, as I said, was half a mile distant.

About four hours after we began our journey, I awaked by a very ridiculous accident; for the carriage being stopped a while to adjust something that was out of order, two or three of the young natives had the curiosity to see how I looked when I was asleep; they climbed up into the engine, and advancing very softly to my face, one of them, an officer in the Guards, put the sharp end of his half-pike a good way up into my left nostril, which tickled my nose like a straw, and made me sneeze violently: whereupon they stole off unperceived, and it was three weeks before I knew the cause of my awaking so suddenly. We made a long march the remaining part of that day, and rested at night with five hundred guards on each side of me, half with torches, and half with bows and arrows, ready to shoot me if I should offer to stir. The next morning at sunrise we continued our march, and arrived within two hundred yards of the city gates about noon. The Emperor and all his Court came out to meet us, but his great officers would by no means suffer his Majesty to endanger his person by mounting on my body.

At the place where the carriage stopped, there stood an ancient temple, esteemed to be the largest in the whole kingdom, which having been polluted some years before by an unnatural murder, was, according to the zeal of those people, looked upon as profane, and therefore had been applied to common uses, and all the ornaments and furniture carried away. In this edifice it was determined I should lodge. The great gate fronting to the north was about four foot high, and almost two foot wide, through which I could easily creep. On each side of the gate was a small window not above six inches from the ground: into that on the left side, the King's smiths conveyed fourscore and eleven chains, like those that hang to a lady's watch in Europe, and almost as large, which were locked to my left leg with six and thirty padlocks. Over against this temple, on t'other side of the great highway, at twenty foot distance, there was a turret at least five foot high. Here the Emperor ascended with many principal lords of his Court, to have an opportunity of viewing me, as I was told, for I could not see them. It was reckoned that above an hundred thousand inhabitants came out of the town upon the same errand; and in spite of my guards, I believe there could not be fewer than ten thousand, at several times, who mounted upon my body by the help of ladders. But a proclamation was soon issued to forbid it upon pain of death. When the workmen found it was impossible for me to break loose, they cut all the strings that bound me; whereupon I rose up with as melancholy a disposition as ever I had in my life. But the noise and astonishment of the people at seeing me rise and walk are not to be expressed. The chains that held my left leg were about two yards long, and gave me not only the liberty of walking backwards and forwards in a semicircle; but being fixed within four inches of the gate, allowed me to creep in, and lie at my full length in the temple.

2

The Emperor of Lilliput, attended by several of the nobility, comes to see the author in his confinement. The Emperor's person and habit described. Learned men appointed to teach the author their language. He gains favour by his mild disposition. His pockets are searched, and his sword and pistols taken from him.

When I found myself on my feet, I looked about me, and must confess I never beheld a more entertaining prospect. The country round appeared like a continued garden, and the inclosed fields, which were generally forty foot square, resembled so many beds of flowers. These fields were intermingled with woods of half a stang, and the tallest trees, as I could judge, appeared to be seven foot high. I viewed the town on my left hand, which looked like the painted scene of a city in a theatre.

I had been for some hours extremely pressed by the necessities of nature; which was no wonder, it being almost two days since I had last disburthened myself. I was under great difficulties between urgency and shame. The best expedient I could think on, was to creep into my house, which I accordingly did; and shutting the gate after me, I went as far as the length of my chain would suffer, and discharged my body of that uneasy load. But this was the only time I was ever guilty of so uncleanly an action; for which I cannot but hope the candid reader will give some allowance, after he hath maturely and impartially considered my case, and the distress I was in. From this time my constant practice was, as soon as I rose, to perform that business in open air, at the full extent of my chain, and due care was taken every morning before company came, that the offensive matter should be carried off in wheelbarrows by two servants appointed for that purpose. I would not have dwelt so long upon a circumstance, that perhaps at first sight may appear not very momentous, if I had not thought it necessary to justify my character in point of cleanliness to the world; which I am told some of my maligners have been pleased, upon this and other occasions, to call in question.

When this adventure was at an end, I came back out of my house, having occasion for fresh air. The Emperor was already descended from the tower, and advancing on horseback towards me, which had like to have cost him dear; for the beast, although very well trained, yet wholly unused to such a sight, which appeared as if a mountain moved before him, reared up on his hinder feet: but that prince, who is an excellent horseman, kept his seat, till his attendants ran in, and held the bridle, while his Majesty had time to dismount. When he alighted, he surveyed me round with great admiration, but kept beyond the length of my chain. He ordered his cooks and butlers, who were already prepared, to give me victuals and drink, which they pushed forward in a sort of vehicles upon wheels till I could reach them. I took these vehicles, and soon emptied them all; twenty of them were filled with meat, and ten with liquor; each of the former afforded me two or three good mouthfuls, and I emptied the liquor of ten vessels, which was contained in earthen vials, into one vehicle, drinking it off at a draught, and so I did with the rest. The Empress, and young Princes of the Blood, of both sexes, attended by many ladies, sat at some distance in their chairs; but upon the accident that happened to the Emperor's horse, they alighted, and came near his person, which I am now going to describe. He is taller by almost the breadth of my nail, than any of his Court, which alone is enough to strike an awe into the beholders. His features are strong and masculine, with an Austrian lip and arched nose, his complexion olive, his countenance erect, his body and limbs well proportioned, all his motions graceful, and his deportment majestic. He was then past his prime, being twenty-eight years and three quarters old, of which he had reigned about seven, in great felicity, and generally victorious. For the better convenience of beholding him, I lay on my side, so that my face was parallel to his, and he stood but three yards off: however, I have had him since many times in my hand, and therefore cannot be deceived in the description. His dress was very plain and simple, the fashion of it between the Asiatic and the European; but he had on his head a light helmet of gold, adorned with jewels, and a plume on the crest. He held his sword drawn in his hand, to defend himself, if I should happen to break loose; it was almost three inches long, the hilt and scabbard were gold enriched with diamonds. His voice was shrill, but very clear and articulate, and I could distinctly hear it when I stood up. The ladies and courtiers were all most magnificently clad, so that the spot they stood upon seemed to resemble a petticoat spread on the ground, embroidered with figures of gold and silver. His Imperial Majesty spoke often to me, and I returned answers, but neither of us could understand a syllable. There were several of his priests and lawyers present (as I conjectured by their habits) who were commanded to address themselves to me, and I spoke to them in as many languages as I had the least smattering of, which were High and Low Dutch, Latin, French, Spanish, Italian, and Lingua Franca; but all to no purpose. After about two hours the Court retired, and I was left with a strong guard, to prevent the impertinence, and probably the malice of the rabble, who were very impatient to crowd about me as near as they durst, and some of them had the impudence to shoot their arrows at me as I sat on the ground by the door of my house, whereof one very narrowly missed my left eye. But the colonel ordered six of the ringleaders to be seized, and thought no punishment so proper as to deliver them bound into my hands, which some of his soldiers accordingly did, pushing them forwards with the butt-ends of their pikes into my reach; I took them all in my right hand, put five of them into my coat-pocket, and as to the sixth, I made a countenance as if I would eat him alive. The poor man squalled terribly, and the colonel and his officers were in much pain, especially when they saw me take out my penknife: but I soon put them out of fear; for, looking mildly, and immediately cutting the strings he was bound with, I set him gently on the ground, and away he ran; I treated the rest in the same manner, taking them one by one out of my pocket, and I observed both the soldiers and people were highly obliged at this mark of my clemency, which was represented very much to my advantage at Court.

Towards night I got with some difficulty into my house, where I lay on the ground, and continued to do so about a fortnight; during which time the Emperor gave orders to have a bed prepared for me. Six hundred beds of the common measure were brought in carriages, and worked up in my house; an hundred and fifty of their beds sewn together made up the breadth and length, and these were four double, which however kept me but very indifferently from the hardness of the floor, that was of smooth stone. By the same computation they provided me with sheets, blankets, and coverlets, tolerable enough for one who had been so long inured to hardships as I.

As the news of my arrival spread through the kingdom, it brought prodigious numbers of rich, idle, and curious people to see me; so that the villages were almost emptied, and great neglect of tillage and household affairs must have ensued, if his Imperial Majesty had not provided by several proclamations and orders of state against this inconveniency. He directed that those, who had already beheld me, should return home, and not presume to come within fifty yards of my house without licence from Court; whereby the Secretaries of State got considerable fees.

In the meantime, the Emperor held frequent councils to debate what course should be taken with me; and I was afterwards assured by a particular friend, a person of great quality, who was as much in the *secret* as any, that the Court was under many difficulties concerning me. They apprehended my breaking loose, that my diet would be very expensive, and might cause a famine. Sometimes they determined to starve me, or at least to shoot me in the face and hands with poisoned arrows, which would soon dispatch me: but again they considered, that the stench of so large a carcass might produce a plague in the metropolis, and probably spread through the whole kingdom. In the midst of these consultations, several officers of the army went to the door of the great council-chamber; and two of them being admitted, gave an account of my behaviour to the six criminals above-mentioned, which made so favourable an impression in the breast of his Majesty and the whole Board in my behalf, that an Imperial Commission was issued out, obliging all the villages nine hundred yards round the city, to deliver in every morning six beeves, forty sheep, and other victuals for my sustenance; together with a proportionable quantity of bread, and wine, and other liquors: for the due payment of which, his Majesty gave assignments upon his Treasury. For this Prince lives chiefly upon his own demesnes, seldom except upon great occasions raising any subsidies upon his subjects, who are bound to attend him in his wars at their own expense. An establishment was also made of six hundred persons to be my domestics, who had board-wages allowed for their maintenance, and tents built for them very conveniently on each side of my door. It was likewise ordered, that three hundred tailors should make me a suit of clothes after the fashion of the country: that six of his Majesty's greatest scholars should be employed to instruct me in their language: and, lastly, that the Emperor's horses, and those of the nobility and troops of guards, should be exercised in my sight, to accustom themselves to me. All these orders were duly put in execution, and in about three weeks I made a great progress in learning their language; during which time, the Emperor frequently honoured me with his visits, and was pleased to assist my masters in teaching me. We began already to converse together in some sort; and the first words I learnt were to express my desire that he would please to give me my liberty, which I every day repeated on my knees. His answer, as I could apprehend, was, that this must be a work of time, not to be thought on without the advice of his Council, and that first I must *lumos kelmin pesso desmar lon emposo*; that is, swear a peace with him and his kingdom. However, that I should be used with all kindness, and he advised me to acquire by my patience, and discreet behaviour, the good opinion of himself and his subjects. He desired I would not take it ill, if he gave orders to certain proper officers to search me; for probably I might carry about me several weapons, which must needs be dangerous things, if they answered the bulk of so prodigious a person. I said, his Majesty should be satisfied, for I was ready to strip myself, and turn up my pockets before him. This I delivered part in words, and part in signs. He replied, that by the laws of the kingdom I must be searched by two of his officers; that he knew this could not be done without my consent and assistance; that he had so good an opinion of my generosity and justice, as to trust their persons in my hands: that whatever they took from me should be returned when I left the country, or paid for at the rate which I would set upon them. I took up the two officers in my hands, put them first into my coat-pockets, and then into every other pocket about me, except my two fobs, and another secret pocket which I had no mind should be searched, wherein I had some little necessaries of no consequence to any but myself. In one of my fobs there was a silver watch, and in the other a small quantity of gold in a purse. These gentlemen, having pen, ink and paper about them, made an exact inventory of everything they saw; and when they had done, desired I would set them down, that they might deliver it to the Emperor. This inventory I afterwards translated into English, and is word for word as follows.

IMPRIMIS, In the right coat-pocket of the Great Man-Mountain (for so I interpret the words *Quinbus Flestrin*) after the strictest search, we found only one great piece of coarse cloth, large enough to be a foot-cloth for your Majesty's chief room of state. In the left pocket, we saw a huge silver chest, with a cover of the same metal, which we the searchers were not able to lift. We desired it should be opened, and one of us stepping into it, found himself up to the mid leg in a sort of dust, some part whereof flying up to our faces, set us both a sneezing for several times together. In his right waistcoat-pocket, we found a prodigious bundle of white thin substances, folded one over another, about the bigness of three men, tied with a strong cable, and marked with black figures; which we humbly conceive to be writings, every letter almost half as large as the palm of our hands. In the left, there was a sort of engine, from the back of which were extended twenty long poles, resembling the palisados before your Majesty's Court; wherewith we conjecture the Man-Mountain combs his head, for we did not always trouble him with questions, because we found it a great difficulty to make him understand us. In the large pocket on the right side of his middle cover (so I translate the word *ranfu-lo*, by which they meant my breeches), we saw a hollow pillar of iron, about the length of a man, fastened to a strong piece of timber, larger than the pillar; and upon one side of the pillar were huge pieces of iron sticking out, cut into strange figures, which we know not what to make of. In the left pocket, another engine of the same kind. In the smaller pocket on the right side, were several round flat pieces of white and red metal, of different bulk; some of the white, which seemed to be silver, were so large and heavy, that my comrade and I could hardly lift them. In the left pocket were two black pillars irregularly shaped: we could not, without difficulty, reach the top of them as we stood at the bottom of his pocket. One of them was covered, and seemed all of a piece: but at the upper end of the other, there appeared a white round substance, about twice the bigness of our heads. Within each of these was enclosed a prodigious plate of steel; which, by our orders, we obliged him to show us, because we apprehended they might be dangerous engines. He took them out of their cases, and told us, that in his own country his practice was to shave his beard with one of these, and to cut his meat with the other. There were two pockets which we could not enter: these he called his fobs; they were two large slits cut into the top of his middle cover, but squeezed close by the pressure of his belly. Out of the right fob hung a great silver chain, with a wonderful kind of engine at the bottom. We directed him to draw out whatever was at the end of that chain; which appeared to be a globe, half silver, and half of some transparent metal: for on the transparent side we saw certain strange figures circularly drawn, and thought we could touch them, till we found our fingers stopped with that lucid substance. He put this engine to our ears, which made an incessant noise like that of a watermill. And we conjecture it is either some unknown animal, or the god that he worships: but we are more inclined to the latter opinion, because he assured us (if we understood him right, for he expressed himself very imperfectly), that he seldom did anything without consulting it. He called it his oracle, and said it pointed out the time for every action of his life. From the left fob he took out a net almost large enough for a fisherman, but contrived to open and shut like a purse, and served him for the same use: we found therein several massy pieces of yellow metal, which if they be of real gold, must be of immense value.

Having thus, in obedience to your Majesty's commands, diligently searched all his pockets, we observed a girdle about his waist made of the hide of some prodigious animal; from which, on the left side, hung a sword of the length of five men; and on the right, a bag or pouch divided into two cells, each cell capable of holding three of your Majesty's subjects. In one of these cells were several globes or balls of a most ponderous metal, about the bigness of our heads, and required a strong hand to lift them: the other cell contained a heap of certain black grains, but of no great bulk or weight, for we could hold above fifty of them in the palms of our hands.

This is an exact inventory of what we found about the body of the Man-Mountain, who used us with great civility, and due respect to your Majesty's Commission. Signed and sealed on the fourth day of the eighty-ninth moon of your Majesty's auspicious reign.

Clefven Frelock, Marsi Frelock

When this inventory was read over to the Emperor, he directed me to deliver up the several particulars. He first called for my scimitar, which I took out, scabbard and all. In the meantime he ordered three thousand of his choicest troops (who then attended him) to surround me at a distance, with their bows and arrows just ready to discharge: but I did not observe it, for mine eyes were wholly fixed upon his Majesty. He then desired me to draw my scimitar, which, although it had got some rust by the seawater, was in most parts exceeding bright. I did so, and immediately all the troops gave a shout between terror and surprise; for the sun shone clear, and the reflection dazzled their eyes as I waved the scimitar to and fro in my hand. His Majesty, who is a most magnanimous prince, was less daunted than I could expect; he ordered me to return it into the scabbard, and cast it on the ground as gently as I could, about six foot from the end of my chain. The next thing he demanded was one of the hollow iron pillars, by which he meant my pocket-pistols. I drew it out, and at his desire, as well as I could, expressed to him the use of it; and charging it only with powder, which by the closeness of my pouch happened to scape wetting in the sea (an inconvenience that all prudent mariners take special care to provide against), I first cautioned the Emperor not to be afraid, and then I let it off in the air. The astonishment here was much greater than at the sight of my scimitar. Hundreds fell down as if they had been struck dead; and even the Emperor, although he stood his ground, could not recover himself in some time. I delivered up both my pistols in the same manner as I had done my scimitar, and then my pouch of powder and bullets; begging him that the former might be kept from fire, for it would kindle with the smallest spark, and blow up his imperial palace into the air. I likewise delivered up my watch, which the Emperor was very curious to see, and commanded two of his tallest Yeomen of the Guards to bear it on a pole upon their shoulders, as draymen in England do a barrel of ale. He was amazed at the continual noise it made, and the motion of the minute-hand, which he could easily discern; for their sight is much more acute than ours: he asked the opinions of his learned men about him, which were various and remote, as the reader may well imagine without my repeating; although indeed I could not very perfectly understand them. I then gave up my silver and copper money, my purse with nine large pieces of gold, and some smaller ones; my knife and razor, my comb and silver snuff-box, my handkerchief and journal book. My scimitar, pistols, and pouch, were conveyed in carriages to his Majesty's stores; but the rest of my goods were returned me.

I had, as I before observed, one private pocket which escaped their search, wherein there was a pair of spectacles (which I sometimes use for the weakness of mine eyes), a pocket perspective, and several other little conveniences; which being of no consequence to the Emperor, I did not think myself bound in honour to discover, and I apprehended they might be lost or spoiled if I ventured them out of my possession.

3

The author diverts the Emperor and his nobility of both sexes in a very uncommon manner. The diversions of the Court of Lilliput described. The author hath his liberty granted him upon certain conditions.

My gentleness and good behaviour had gained so far on the Emperor and his Court, and indeed upon the army and people in general, that I began to conceive hopes of getting my liberty in a short time. I took all possible methods to cultivate this favourable disposition. The natives came by degrees to be less apprehensive of any danger from me. I would sometimes lie down, and let five or six of them dance on my hand. And at last the boys and girls would venture to come and play at hide and seek in my hair. I had now made a good progress in understanding and speaking their language. The Emperor had a mind one day to entertain me with several of the country shows, wherein they exceed all nations I have known, both for dexterity and magnificence. I was diverted with none so much as that of the rope-dancers, performed upon a slender white thread, extended about two foot, and twelve inches from the ground. Upon which I shall desire liberty, with the reader's patience, to enlarge a little.

This diversion is only practised by those persons who are candidates for great employments, and high favour, at Court. They are trained in this art from their youth, and are not always of noble birth, or liberal education. When a great office is vacant either by death or disgrace (which often happens) five or six of those candidates petition the Emperor to entertain his Majesty and the Court with a dance on the rope, and whoever jumps the highest without falling, succeeds in the office. Very often the chief Ministers themselves are commanded to show their skill, and to convince the Emperor that they have not lost their faculty. Flimnap, the Treasurer, is allowed to cut a caper on the strait rope, at least an inch higher than any other lord in the whole Empire. I have seen him do the summerset several times together upon a trencher fixed on the rope, which is no thicker than a common pack-thread in England. My friend Reldresal, Principal Secretary for Private Affairs, is, in my opinion, if I am not partial, the second after the Treasurer; the rest of the great officers are much upon a par.

These diversions are often attended with fatal accidents, whereof great numbers are on record. I myself have seen two or three candidates break a limb. But the danger is much greater when the Ministers themselves are commanded to show their dexterity; for by contending to excel themselves and their fellows, they strain so far, that there is hardly one of them who hath not received a fall, and some of them two or three. I was assured that a year or two before my arrival, Flimnap would have infallibly broke his neck, if one of the *King's cushions*, that accidentally lay on the ground, had not weakened the force of his fall.

There is likewise another diversion, which is only shown before the Emperor and Empress, and first Minister, upon particular occasions. The Emperor lays on a table three fine silken threads of six inches long. One is blue, the other red, and the third green. These threads are proposed as prizes for those persons whom the Emperor hath a mind to distinguish by a peculiar mark of his favour. The ceremony is performed in his Majesty's great chamber of state, where the candidates are to undergo a trial of dexterity very different from the former, and such as I have not observed the least resemblance of in any other country of the old or the new world. The Emperor holds a stick in his hands, both ends parallel to the horizon, while the candidates, advancing one by one, sometimes leap over the stick, sometimes creep under it backwards and forwards several times, according as the stick is advanced or depressed. Sometimes the Emperor holds one end of the stick, and his first Minister the other; sometimes the Minister has it entirely to himself. Whoever performs his part with most agility, and holds out the longest in *leaping* and *creeping*, is rewarded with the blue-coloured silk; the red is given to the next, and the green to the third, which they all wear girt twice round about the middle; and you see few great persons about this Court who are not adorned with one of these girdles.

The horses of the army, and those of the royal stables, having been daily led before me, were no longer shy, but would come up to my very feet without starting. The riders would leap them over my hand as I held it on the ground, and one of the Emperor's huntsmen, upon a large courser, took my foot, shoe and all; which was indeed a prodigious leap. I had the good fortune to divert the Emperor one day after a very extraordinary manner. I desired he would order several sticks of two foot high, and the thickness of an ordinary cane, to be brought me; whereupon his Majesty commanded the Master of his Woods to give directions accordingly, and the next morning six woodmen arrived with as many carriages, drawn by eight horses to each. I took nine of these sticks, and fixing them firmly in the ground in a quadrangular figure, two foot and a half square, I took four other sticks, and tied them parallel at each corner, about two foot from the ground; then I fastened my handkerchief to the nine sticks that stood erect, and extended it on all sides till it was as tight as the top of a drum; and the four parallel sticks, rising about five inches higher than the handkerchief, served as ledges on each side. When I had finished my work, I desired the Emperor to let a troop of his best horse, twenty-four in number, come and exercise upon this plain. His Majesty approved of the proposal, and I took them up one by one in my hands, ready mounted and armed, with the proper officers to exercise them. As soon as they got into order, they divided into two parties, performed mock skirmishes, discharged blunt arrows, drew their swords, fled and pursued, attacked and retired, and in short discovered the best military discipline I ever beheld. The parallel sticks secured them and their horses from falling over the stage; and the Emperor was so much delighted, that he ordered this entertainment to be repeated several days, and once was pleased to be lifted up, and give the word of command; and, with great difficulty, persuaded even the Empress herself to let me hold her in her close chair within two yards of the stage, from whence she was able to take a full view of the whole performance. It was my good fortune that no ill accident happened in these entertainments, only once a fiery horse that belonged to one of the captains pawing with his hoof struck a hole in my handkerchief, and his foot slipping, he overthrew his rider and himself; but I immediately relieved them both, and covering the hole with one hand, I set down the troop with the other, in the same manner as I took them up. The horse that fell was strained in the left shoulder, but the rider got no hurt, and I repaired my handkerchief as well as I could; however, I would not trust to the strength of it any more in such dangerous enterprises.

About two or three days before I was set at liberty, as I was entertaining the Court with these kinds of feats, there arrived an express to inform his Majesty, that some of his subjects, riding near the place where I was first taken up, had seen a great black substance lying on the ground, very oddly shaped, extending its edges round as wide as his Majesty's bed-chamber, and rising up in the middle as high as a man; that it was no living creature, as they at first apprehended, for it lay on the grass without motion, and some of them had walked round it several times; that by mounting upon each others' shoulders, they had got to the top, which was flat and even, and stamping upon it they found it was hollow within; that they humbly conceived it might be something belonging to the Man-Mountain, and if his Majesty pleased, they would undertake to bring it with only five horses. I presently knew what they meant, and was glad at heart to receive this intelligence. It seems upon my first reaching the shore after our shipwreck, I was in such confusion, that before I came to the place where I went to sleep, my hat, which I had fastened with a string to my head while I was rowing, and had stuck on all the time I was swimming, fell off after I came to land; the string, as I conjecture, breaking by some accident which I never observed, but thought my hat had been lost at sea. I entreated his Imperial Majesty to give orders it might be brought to me as soon as possible, describing to him the use and the nature of it: and the next day the waggoners arrived with it, but not in a very good condition; they had bored two holes in the brim, within an inch and a half of the edge, and fastened two hooks in the holes; these hooks were tied by a long cord to the harness, and thus my hat was dragged along for above half an English mile: but the ground in that country being extremely smooth and level, it received less damage than I expected.

Two days after this adventure, the Emperor having ordered that part of his army which quarters in and about his metropolis to be in a readiness, took a fancy of diverting himself in a very singular manner. He desired I would stand like a colossus, with my legs as far asunder as I conveniently could. He then commanded his General (who was an old experienced leader, and a great patron of mine) to draw up the troops in close order, and march them under me, the foot by twenty-four in a breast, and the horse by sixteen, with drums beating, colours flying, and pikes advanced. This body consisted of three thousand foot, and a thousand horse. His Majesty gave orders, upon pain of death, that every soldier in his march should observe the strictest decency with regard to my person; which, however, could not prevent some of the younger officers from turning up their eyes as they passed under me. And, to confess the truth, my breeches were at that time in so ill a condition, that they afforded some opportunities for laughter and admiration.

I had sent so many memorials and petitions for my liberty, that his Majesty at length mentioned the matter, first in the Cabinet, and then in a full council; where it was opposed by none, except Skyresh Bolgolam, who was pleased, without any provocation, to be my mortal enemy. But it was carried against him by the whole Board, and confirmed by the Emperor. That Minister was *Galbet*, or Admiral of the Realm, very much in his master's confidence, and a person well versed in affairs, but of a morose and sour complexion. However, he was at length persuaded to comply; but prevailed that the articles and conditions upon which I should be set free, and to which I must swear, should be drawn up by himself. These articles were brought to me by Skyresh Bolgolam in person, attended by two Under-Secretaries, and several persons of distinction. After they were read, I was demanded to swear to the performance of them; first in the manner of my own country, and afterwards in the method prescribed by their laws; which was to hold my right foot in my left hand, to place the middle finger of my right hand on the crown of my head, and my thumb on the tip of my right ear. But, because the reader may perhaps be curious to have some idea of the style and manner of expression peculiar to that people, as well as to know the articles upon which I recovered my liberty, I have made a translation of the whole instrument word for word, as near as I was able, which I here offer to the public.

GOLBASTO MOMAREN EVLAME GURDILO SHEFIN MULLY ULLY GUE, most mighty Emperor of Lilliput, Delight and Terror of the Universe, whose dominions extend five thousand blustrugs (about twelve miles in circumference), to the extremities of the globe; Monarch of all Monarchs, taller than the sons of men; whose feet press down to the centre, and whose head strikes against the sun: at whose nod the princes of the earth shake their knees; pleasant as the spring, comfortable as the summer, fruitful as autumn, dreadful as winter. His most sublime Majesty proposeth to the Man-Mountain, lately arrived to our celestial dominions, the following articles, which by a solemn oath he shall be obliged to perform.

First, The Man-Mountain shall not depart from our dominions, without our licence under our great seal.

2nd, He shall not presume to come into our metropolis, without our express order; at which time the inhabitants shall have two hours warning to keep within their doors.

3rd, The said Man-Mountain shall confine his walks to our principal high roads, and not offer to walk or lie down in a meadow or field of corn.

4th, As he walks the said roads, he shall take the utmost care not to trample upon the bodies of any of our loving subjects, their horses, or carriages, nor take any of our said subjects into his hands, without their own consent.

5th, If an express require extraordinary dispatch, the Man-Mountain shall be obliged to carry in his pocket the messenger and horse a six days' journey once in every moon, and return the said messenger back (if so required) safe to our Imperial Presence.

6th, He shall be our ally against our enemies in the island of Blefuscu, and do his utmost to destroy their fleet, which is now preparing to invade us.

7th, That the said Man-Mountain shall, at his times of leisure, be aiding and assisting to our workmen, in helping to raise certain great stones, towards covering the wall of the principal park, and other our royal buildings.

8th, That the said Man-Mountain shall, in two moons' time, deliver in an exact survey of the circumference of our dominions by a computation of his own paces round the coast.

Lastly, That upon his solemn oath to observe all the above articles, the said Man-Mountain shall have a daily allowance of meat and drink sufficient for the support of 1,728 of our subjects, with free access to our Royal Person, and other marks of our favour. Given at our palace at Belfaborac the twelfth day of the ninety-first moon of our reign.

I swore and subscribed to these articles with great cheerfulness and content, although some of them were not so honourable as I could have wished; which proceeded wholly from the malice of Skyresh Bolgolam the High Admiral: whereupon my chains were immediately unlocked, and I was at full liberty; the Emperor himself in person did me the honour to be by at the whole ceremony. I made my acknowledgements by prostrating myself at his Majesty's feet: but he commanded me to rise; and after many gracious expressions, which, to avoid the censure of vanity, I shall not repeat, he added, that he hoped I should prove a useful servant, and well deserve all the favours he had already conferred upon me, or might do for the future.

The reader may please to observe, that in the last article for the recovery of my liberty, the Emperor stipulates to allow me a quantity of meat and drink sufficient for the support of 1,728 Lilliputians. Some time after, asking a friend at Court how they came to fix on that determinate number, he told me, that his Majesty's mathematicians, having taken the height of my body by the help of a quadrant, and finding it to exceed theirs in the proportion of twelve to one, they concluded from the similarity of their bodies, that mine must contain at least 1,728 of theirs, and consequently would require as much food as was necessary to support that number of Lilliputians. By which, the reader may conceive an idea of the ingenuity of that people, as well as the prudent and exact economy of so great a prince.

4

Mildendo, the metropolis of Lilliput, described, together with the Emperor's palace. A conversation between the author and a principal Secretary, concerning the affairs of that Empire; the author's offers to serve the Emperor in his wars.

The first request I made after I had obtained my liberty, was, that I might have licence to see Mildendo, the metropolis; which the Emperor easily granted me, but with a special charge to do no hurt, either to the inhabitants, or their houses. The people had notice by proclamation of my design to visit the town. The wall which encompassed it is two foot and an half high, and at least eleven inches broad, so that a coach and horses may be driven very safely round it; and it is flanked with strong towers at ten foot distance. I stepped over the great western gate, and passed very gently and sideling through the two principal streets, only in my short waistcoat, for fear of damaging the roofs and eaves of the houses with the skirts of my coat. I walked with the utmost circumspection, to avoid treading on any stragglers, who might remain in the streets, although the orders were very strict, that all people should keep in their houses, at their own peril. The garret windows and tops of houses were so crowded with spectators, that I thought in all my travels I had not seen a more populous place. The city is an exact square, each side of the wall being five hundred foot long. The two great streets, which run cross and divide it into four quarters, are five foot wide. The lanes and alleys, which I could not enter, but only viewed them as I passed, are from twelve to eighteen inches. The town is capable of holding five hundred thousand souls. The houses are from three to five stories. The shops and markets well provided.

The Emperor's palace is in the centre of the city, where the two great streets meet. It is enclosed by a wall of two foot high, and twenty foot distant from the buildings. I had his Majesty's permission to step over this wall; and the space being so wide between that and the palace, I could easily view it on every side. The outward court is a square of forty foot, and includes two other courts: in the inmost are the royal apartments, which I was very desirous to see, but found it extremely difficult; for the great gates, from one square into another, were but eighteen inches high, and seven inches wide. Now the buildings of the outer court were at least five foot high, and it was impossible for me to stride over them, without infinite damage to the pile, though the walls were strongly built of hewn stone, and four inches thick. At the same time the Emperor had a great desire that I should see the magnificence of his palace; but this I was not able to do till three days after, which I spent in cutting down with my knife some of the largest trees in the royal park, about an hundred yards distant from the city. Of these trees I made two stools, each about three foot high, and strong enough to bear my weight. The people having received notice a second time, I went again through the city to the palace, with my two stools in my hands. When I came to the side of the outer court, I stood upon one stool, and took the other in my hand: this I lifted over the roof, and gently set it down on the space between the first and second court, which was eight foot wide. I then stepped over the buildings very conveniently from one stool to the other, and drew up the first after me with a hooked stick. By this contrivance I got into the inmost court; and lying down upon my side, I applied my face to the windows of the middle stories, which were left open on purpose, and discovered the most splendid apartments that can be imagined. There I saw the Empress, and the young Princes in their several lodgings, with their chief attendants about them. Her Imperial Majesty was pleased to smile very graciously upon me, and gave me out of the window her hand to kiss.

But I shall not anticipate the reader with farther descriptions of this kind, because I reserve them for a greater work, which is now almost ready for the press, containing a general description of this Empire, from its first erection, through a long series of princes, with a particular account of their wars and politics, laws, learning, and religion; their plants and animals, their peculiar manners and customs, with other matters very curious and useful; my chief design at present being only to relate such events and transactions as happened to the public, or to myself, during a residence of about nine months in that Empire.

One morning, about a fortnight after I had obtained my liberty, Reldresal, Principal Secretary (as they style him) of Private Affairs, came to my house, attended only by one servant. He ordered his coach to wait at a distance, and desired I would give him an hour's audience; which I readily consented to, on account of his quality, and personal merits, as well as of the many good offices he had done me during my solicitations at Court. I offered to lie down, that he might the more conveniently reach my ear; but he chose rather to let me hold him in my hand during our conversation. He began with compliments on my liberty, said he might pretend to some merit in it; but, however, added, that if it had not been for the present situation of things at Court, perhaps I might not have obtained it so soon. For, *said he*, as flourishing a condition as we appear to be in to foreigners, we labour under two mighty evils; a violent faction at home, and the danger of an invasion by a most potent enemy from abroad. As to the first, you are to understand, that for above seventy moons past, there have been two struggling parties in this Empire, under the names of *Tramecksan* and *Slamecksan*, from the high and low heels on their shoes, by which they distinguish themselves. It is alleged indeed, that the high heels are most agreeable to our ancient constitution: but however this be, his Majesty hath determined to make use of only low heels in the administration of the government, and all offices in the gift of the Crown, as you cannot but observe; and particularly, that his Majesty's imperial heels are lower at least by a *drurr* than any of his Court (*drurr* is a measure about the fourteenth part of an inch). The animosities between these two parties run so high, that they will neither eat nor drink, nor talk with each other. We compute the *Tramecksan*, or High-Heels, to exceed us in number; but the power is wholly on our side. We apprehend his Imperial Highness, the heir to the Crown, to have some tendency towards the High-Heels; at least we can plainly discover one of his heels higher than the other, which gives him a hobble in his gait. Now, in the midst of these intestine disquiets, we are threatened with an invasion from the island of Blefuscu, which is the other great Empire of the universe, almost as large and powerful as this of his Majesty. For as to what we have heard you affirm, that there are other kingdoms and states in the world, inhabited by human creatures as large as yourself, our philosophers are in much doubt, and would rather conjecture that you dropped from the moon, or one of the stars; because it is certain, that an hundred mortals of your bulk would, in a short time, destroy all the fruits and cattle of his Majesty's dominions. Besides, our histories of six thousand moons make no mention of any other regions, than the two great Empires of Lilliput and Blefuscu. Which two mighty powers have, as I was going to tell you, been engaged in a most obstinate war for six and thirty moons past. It began upon the following occasion. It is allowed on all hands, that the primitive way of breaking eggs before we eat them, was upon the larger end: but his present Majesty's grandfather, while he was a boy, going to eat an egg, and breaking it according to the ancient practice, happened to cut one of his fingers. Whereupon the Emperor his father published an edict, commanding all his subjects, upon great penalties, to break the smaller end of their eggs. The people so highly resented this law, that our Histories tell us there have been six rebellions raised on that account; wherein one Emperor lost his life, and another his crown. These civil commotions were constantly formented by the monarchs of Blefuscu; and when they were quelled, the exiles always fled for refuge to that Empire. It is computed, that eleven thousand persons have, at several times, suffered death, rather than submit to break their eggs at the smaller end. Many hundred large volumes have been published upon this controversy: but the books of the Big-Endians have been long forbidden, and the whole patty rendered incapable by law of holding employments. During the course of these troubles, the Emperors of Blefuscu did frequently expostulate by their ambassadors, accusing us of making a schism in religion, by offending against a fundamental doctrine of our great prophet Lustrog, in the fifty-fourth chapter of the *Brundecral* (which is their Alcoran). This, however, is thought to be a mere strain upon the text: for the words are these; *That all true believers shall break their eggs at the convenient end*: and which is the convenient end, seems, in my humble opinion, to be left to every man's conscience, or at least in the power of the chief magistrate to determine. Now the Big-Endian exiles have found so much credit in the Emperor of Blefuscu's Court, and so much private assistance and encouragement from their party here at home, that a bloody war hath been carried on between the two Empires for six and thirty moons with various success; during which time we have lost forty capital ships, and a much greater number of smaller vessels, together with thirty thousand of our best seamen and soldiers; and the damage received by the enemy is reckoned to be somewhat greater than ours. However, they have now equipped a numerous fleet, and are just preparing to make a descent upon us; and his Imperial Majesty, placing great confidence in your valour and strength, hath commanded me to lay this account of his affairs before you.

I desired the Secretary to present my humble duty to the Emperor, and to let him know, that I thought it would not become me, who was a foreigner, to interfere with parties; but I was ready, with the hazard of my life, to defend his person and state against all invaders.

5

The author by an extraordinary stratagem prevents an invasion. A high title of honour is conferred upon him. Ambassadors arrive from the Emperor of Blefuscu, and sue for peace. The Empress's apartment on fire by an accident; the author instrumental in saving the rest of the palace.

The Empire of Blefuscu is an island situated to the north-north-east side of Lilliput, from whence it is parted only by a channel of eight hundred yards wide. I had not yet seen it, and upon this notice of an intended invasion, I avoided appearing on that side of the coast, for fear of being discovered by some of the enemy's ships, who had received no intelligence of me, all intercourse between the two Empires having been strictly forbidden during the war, upon pain of death, and an embargo laid by our Emperor upon all vessels whatsoever. I communicated to his Majesty a project I had formed of seizing the enemy's whole fleet; which, as our scouts assured us, lay at anchor in the harbour ready to sail with the first fair wind. I consulted the most experienced seamen upon the depth of the channel, which they had often plumbed, who told me, that in the middle at high water it was seventy *glumgluffs* deep, which is about six foot of European measure; and the rest of it fifty *glumgluffs* at most. I walked to the north-east coast over against Blefuscu; where, lying down behind a hillock, I took out my small pocket perspective-glass, and viewed the enemy's fleet at anchor, consisting of about fifty men-of-war, and a great number of transports: I then came back to my house, and gave order (for which I had a warrant) for a great quantity of the strongest cable and bars of iron. The cable was about as thick as pack-thread, and the bars of the length and size of a knitting-needle. I trebled the cable to make it stronger, and for the same reason I twisted three of the iron bars together, bending the extremities into a hook. Having thus fixed fifty hooks to as many cables, I went back to the north-east coast, and putting off my coat, shoes, and stockings, walked into the sea in my leathern jerkin, about half an hour before high water. I waded with what haste I could, and swam in the middle about thirty yards till I felt ground; I arrived at the fleet in less than half an hour. The enemy was so frighted when they saw me, that they leaped out of their ships, and swam to shore, where there could not be fewer than thirty thousand souls. I then took my tackling, and fastening a hook to the hole at the prow of each, I tied all the cords together at the end. While I was thus employed, the enemy discharged several thousand arrows, many of which stuck in my hands and face; and besides the excessive smart, gave me much disturbance in my work. My greatest apprehension was for mine eyes, which I should have infallibly lost, if I had not suddenly thought of an expedient. I kept among other little necessaries a pair of spectacles in a private pocket, which, as I observed before, had scaped the Emperor's searchers. These I took out and fastened as strongly as I could upon my nose, and thus armed went on boldly with my work in spite of the enemy's arrows, many of which struck against the glasses of my spectacles, but without any other effect, further than a little to discompose them. I had now fastened all the hooks, and taking the knot in my hand, began to pull; but not a ship would stir, for they were all too fast held by their anchors, so that the boldest part of my enterprise remained. I therefore let go the cord, and leaving the hooks fixed to the ships, I resolutely cut with my knife the cables that fastened the anchors, receiving above two hundred shots in my face and hands; then I took up the knotted end of the cables to which my hooks were tied, and with great ease drew fifty of the enemy's largest men-of-war after me.

The Blefuscudians, who had not the least imagination of what I intended, were at first confounded with astonishment. They had seen me cut the cables, and thought my design was only to let the ships run adrift, or fall foul on each other: but when they perceived the whole fleet moving in order, and saw me pulling at the end, they set up such a scream of grief and despair, that it is almost impossible to describe or conceive. When I had got out of danger, I stopped a while to pick out the arrows that stuck in my hands and face, and rubbed on some of the same ointment that was given me at my first arrival, as I have formerly mentioned. I then took off my spectacles, and waiting about an hour till the tide was a little fallen, I waded through the middle with my cargo, and arrived safe at the royal port of Lilliput.

The Emperor and his whole Court stood on the shore expecting the issue of this great adventure. They saw the ships move forward in a large half-moon, but could not discern me, who was up to my breast in water. When I advanced to the middle of the channel, they were yet more in pain, because I was under water to my neck. The Emperor concluded me to be drowned, and that the enemy's fleet was approaching in a hostile manner: but he was soon eased of his fears, for the channel growing shallower every step I made, I came in a short time within hearing, and holding up the end of the cable by which the fleet was fastened, I cried in a loud voice, *Long live the most puissant Emperor of Lilliput!* This great prince received me at my landing with all possible encomiums, and created me a *Nardac* upon the spot, which is the highest title of honour among them.

His Majesty desired I would take some other opportunity of bringing all the rest of his enemy's ships into his ports. And so unmeasureable is the ambition of princes, that he seemed to think of nothing less than reducing the whole Empire of Blefuscu into a province, and governing it by a Viceroy; of destroying the Big-Endian exiles, and compelling that people to break the smaller end of their eggs, by which he would remain sole monarch of the whole world. But I endeavoured to divert him from this design, by many arguments drawn from the topics of policy as well as justice: and I plainly protested, that I would never be an instrument of bringing a free and brave people into slavery. And when the matter was debated in Council, the wisest part of the Ministry were of my opinion.

This open bold declaration of mine was so opposite to the schemes and politics of his Imperial Majesty, that he could never forgive me; he mentioned it in a very artful manner at Council, where I was told that some of the wisest appeared, at least, by their silence, to be of my opinion; but others, who were my secret enemies, could not forbear some expressions, which by a side-wind reflected on me. And from this time began an intrigue between his Majesty and a junto of Ministers maliciously bent against me, which broke out in less than two months, and had like to have ended in my utter destruction. Of so little weight are the greatest services to princes, when put into the balance with a refusal to gratify their passions.

About three weeks after this exploit, there arrived a solemn embassy from Blefuscu, with humble offers of a peace; which was soon concluded upon conditions very advantageous to our Emperor, wherewith I shall not trouble the reader. There were six ambassadors, with a train of about five hundred persons, and their entry was very magnificent, suitable to the grandeur of their master, and the importance of their business. When their Treaty was finished, wherein I did them several good offices by the credit I now had, or at least appeared to have at Court, their Excellencies, who were privately told how much I had been their friend, made me a visit in form. They began with many compliments upon my valour and generosity, invited me to that kingdom in the Emperor their master's name, and desired me to show them some proofs of my prodigious strength, of which they had heard so many wonders; wherein I readily obliged them, but shall not interrupt the reader with the particulars.

When I had for some time entertained their Excellencies to their infinite satisfaction and surprise, I desired they would do me the honour to present my most humble respects to the Emperor their master, the renown of whose virtues had so justly filled the whole world with admiration, and whose royal person I resolved to attend before I returned to my own country: accordingly, the next time I had the honour to see our Emperor, I desired his general licence to wait on the Blefuscudian monarch, which he was pleased to grant me, as I could plainly perceive, in a very cold manner; but could not guess the reason, till I had a whisper from a certain person, that Flimnap and Bolgolam had represented my intercourse with those ambassadors as a mark of disaffection, from which I am sure my heart was wholly free. And this was the first time I began to conceive some imperfect idea of Courts and Ministers.

It is to be observed, that these ambassadors spoke to me by an interpreter, the languages of both Empires differing as much from each other as any two in Europe, and each nation priding itself upon the antiquity, beauty, and energy of their own tongues, with an avowed contempt for that of their neighbour; yet our Emperor, standing upon the advantage he had got by the seizure of their fleet, obliged them to deliver their credentials, and make their speech, in the Lilliputian tongue. And it must be confessed, that from the great intercourse of trade and commerce between both realms, from the continual reception of exiles, which is mutual among them, and from the custom in each Empire to send their young nobility and richer gentry to the other, in order to polish themselves, by seeing the world, and understanding men and manners, there are few persons of distinction, or merchants, or seamen, who dwell in the maritime parts, but what can hold conversation in both tongues; as I found some weeks after, when I went to pay my respects to the Emperor of Blefuscu, which in the midst of great misfortunes, through the malice of my enemies, proved a very happy adventure to me, as I shall relate in its proper place.

The reader may remember, that when I signed those articles upon which I recovered my liberty, there were some which I disliked upon account of their being too servile, neither could anything but an extreme necessity have forced me to submit. But being now a *Nardac*, of the highest rank in that Empire, such offices were looked upon as below my dignity, and the Emperor (to do him justice) never once mentioned them to me. However, it was not long before I had an opportunity of doing his Majesty, at least, as I then thought, a most signal service. I was alarmed at midnight with the cries of many hundred people at my door; by which being suddenly awaked, I was in some kind of terror. I heard the word *burglum* repeated incessantly: several of the Emperor's Court, making their way through the crowd, entreated me to come immediately to the palace, where her Imperial Majesty's apartment was on fire, by the carelessness of a Maid of Honour, who fell asleep while she was reading a romance. I got up in an instant; and orders being given to clear the way before me, and it being likewise a moonshine night, I made a shift to get to the palace without trampling on any of the people. I found they had already applied ladders to the walls of the apartment, and were well provided with buckets, but the water was at some distance. These buckets were about the size of a large thimble, and the poor people supplied me with them as fast as they could; but the flame was so violent, that they did little good. I might easily have stifled it with my coat, which I unfortunately left behind me for haste, and came away only in my leathern jerkin. The case seemed wholly desperate and deplorable, and this magnificent palace would have infallibly been burnt down to the ground, if, by a presence of mind, unusual to me, I had not suddenly thought of an expedient. I had the evening before drank plentifully of a most delicious wine, called *glimigrim* (the Blefuscudians call it *flunec*, but ours is esteemed the better sort), which is very diuretic. By the luckiest chance in the world, I had not discharged myself of any part of it. The heat I had contracted by coming very near the flames, and by my labouring to quench them, made the wine begin to operate by urine; which I voided in such a quantity, and applied so well to the proper places, that in three minutes the fire was wholly extinguished, and the rest of that noble pile, which had cost so many ages in erecting, preserved from destruction.

It was now daylight, and I returned to my house, without waiting to congratulate with the Emperor; because, although I had done a very eminent piece of service, yet I could not tell how his Majesty might resent the manner by which I had performed it: for, by the fundamental laws of the realm, it is capital in any person, of what quality soever, to make water within the precincts of the palace. But I was a little comforted by a message from his Majesty, that he would give orders to the Grand Justiciary for passing my pardon in form; which, however, I could not obtain. And I was privately assured, that the Empress, conceiving the greatest abhorrence of what I had done, removed to the most distant side of the court, firmly resolved that those buildings should never be repaired for her use; and, in the presence of her chief confidants, could not forbear vowing revenge.

6

Of the inhabitants of Lilliput; their learning, laws, and customs, the manner of educating their children. The author's way of living in that country. His vindication of a great Lady.

Although I intend to leave the description of this Empire to a particular treatise, yet in the meantime I am content to gratify the curious reader with some general ideas. As the common size of the natives is somewhat under six inches, so there is an exact proportion in all other animals, as well as plants and trees: for instance, the tallest horses and oxen are between four and five inches in height, the sheep an inch and a half, more or less; their geese about the bigness of a sparrow, and so the several gradations downwards, till you come to the smallest, which, to my sight, were almost invisible; but Nature hath adapted the eyes of the Lilliputians to all objects proper for their view: they see with great exactness, but at no great distance. And to show the sharpness of their sight towards objects that are near, I have been much pleased with observing a cook pulling a lark, which was not so large as a common fly; and a young girl threading an invisible needle with invisible silk. Their tallest trees are about seven foot high; I mean some of those in the great royal park, the tops whereof I could but just reach with my fist clinched. The other vegetables are in the same proportion; but this I leave to the reader's imagination.

I shall say but little at present of their learning, which for many ages hath flourished in all its branches among them: but their manner of writing is very peculiar, being neither from the left to the right, like the Europeans; nor from the right to the left, like the Arabians; nor from up to down, like the Chinese; nor from down to up, like the Cascagians; but aslant from one corner of the paper to the other, like our ladies in England.

They bury their dead with their heads directly downwards, because they hold an opinion that in eleven thousand moons they are all to rise again, in which period the earth (which they conceive to be flat) will turn upside down, and by this means they shall, at their resurrection, be found ready standing on their feet. The learned among them confess the absurdity of this doctrine, but the practice still continues, in compliance to the vulgar.

There are some laws and customs in this Empire very peculiar, and if they were not so directly contrary to those of my own dear country, I should be tempted to say a little in their justification. It is only to be wished, that they were as well executed. The first I shall mention, relateth to informers. All crimes against the state are punished here with the utmost severity; but if the person accused make his innocence plainly to appear upon his trial, the accuser is immediately put to an ignominious death; and out of his goods or lands, the innocent person is quadruply recompensed for the loss of his time, for the danger he underwent, for the hardship of his imprisonment, and for all the charges he hath been at in making his defence. Or, if that fund be deficient, it is largely supplied by the Crown. The Emperor doth also confer on him some public mark of his favour, and proclamation is made of his innocence through the whole city.

They look upon fraud as a greater crime than theft, and therefore seldom fail to punish it with death; for they allege, that care and vigilance, with a very common understanding, may preserve a man's goods from thieves, but honesty hath no fence against superior cunning: and since it is necessary that there should be a perpetual intercourse of buying and selling, and dealing upon credit, where fraud is permitted or connived at, or hath no law to punish it, the honest dealer is always undone, and the knave gets the advantage. I remember when I was once interceding with the King for a criminal who had wronged his master of a great sum of money, which he had received by order, and ran away with; and happening to tell his Majesty, by way of extenuation, that it was only a breach of trust; the Emperor thought it monstrous in me to offer, as a defence, the greatest aggravation of the crime: and truly, I had little to say in return, farther than the common answer, that different nations had different customs; for, I confess, I was heartily ashamed.

Although we usually call reward and punishment the two hinges upon which all government turns, yet I could never observe this maxim to be put in practice by any nation except that of Lilliput. Whoever can there bring sufficient proof that he hath strictly observed the laws of his country for seventy-three moons, hath a claim to certain privileges, according to his quality and condition of life, with a proportionable sum of money out of a fund appropriated for that use: he likewise acquires the title of *Snilpall*, or *Legal*, which is added to his name, but doth not descend to his posterity. And these people thought it a prodigious defect of policy among us, when I told them that our laws were enforced only by penalties without any mention of reward. It is upon this account that the image of Justice, in their courts of judicature, is formed with six eyes, two before, as many behind, and on each side one, to signify circumspection; with a bag of gold open in her right hand, and a sword sheathed in her left, to show she is more disposed to reward than to punish.

In choosing persons for all employments, they have more regard to good morals than to great abilities; for, since government is necessary to mankind, they believe that the common size of human understandings is fitted to some station or other, and that Providence never intended to make the management of public affairs a mystery, to be comprehended only by a few persons of sublime genius, of which there seldom are three born in an age: but, they suppose truth, justice, temperance, and the like, to be in every man's power; the practice of which virtues, assisted by experience and a good intention, would qualify any man for the service of his country, except where a course of study is required. But they thought the want of moral virtues was so far from being supplied by superior endowments of the mind, that employments could never be put into such dangerous hands as those of persons so qualified; and at least, that the mistakes committed by ignorance in a virtuous disposition, would never be of such fatal consequence to the public weal, as the practices of a man whose inclinations led him to be corrupt, and had great abilities to manage, and multiply, and defend his corruptions.

In like manner, the disbelief of a Divine Providence renders a man uncapable of holding any public station; for since kings avow themselves to be the deputies of Providence, the Lilliputians think nothing can be more absurd than for a prince to employ such men as disown the authority under which he acteth.

In relating these and the following laws, I would only be understood to mean the original institutions, and not the most scandalous corruptions into which these people are fallen by the degenerate nature of man. For as to that infamous practice of acquiring great employments by dancing on the ropes, or badges of favour and distinction by leaping over sticks, and creeping under them, the reader is to observe, that they were first introduced by the grandfather of the Emperor now reigning, and grew to the present height by the gradual increase of party and faction.

Ingratitude is among them a capital crime, as we read it to have been in some other countries; for they reason thus, that whoever makes ill returns to his benefactor, must needs be a common enemy to the rest of mankind, from whom he hath received no obligation, and therefore such a man is not fit to live.

Their notions relating to the duties of parents and children differ extremely from ours. For, since the conjunction of male and female is founded upon the great Law of Nature, in order to propagate and continue the species, the Lilliputians will needs have it, that men and women are joined together like other animals, by the motives of concupiscence; and that their tenderness towards their young, proceedeth from the like natural principle: for which reason they will never allow, that a child is under any obligation to his father for begetting him, or to his mother for bringing him into the world; which, considering the miseries of human life, was neither a benefit in itself, nor intended so by his parents, whose thoughts in their love-encounters were otherwise employed. Upon these, and the like reasonings, their opinion is, that parents are the last of all others to be trusted with the education of their own children: and therefore they have in every town public nurseries, where all parents, except cottagers and labourers, are obliged to send their infants of both sexes to be reared and educated when they come to the age of twenty moons, at which time they are supposed to have some rudiments of docility. These schools are of several kinds, suited to different qualities, and to both sexes. They have certain professors well skilled in preparing children for such a condition of life as befits the rank of their parents, and their own capacities as well as inclinations. I shall first say something of the male nurseries, and then of the female.

The nurseries for males of noble or eminent birth are provided with grave and learned professors, and their several deputies. The clothes and food of the children are plain and simple. They are bred up in the principles of honour, justice, courage, modesty, clemency, religion, and love of their country; they are always employed in some business, except in the times of eating and sleeping, which are very short, and two hours for diversions, consisting of bodily exercises. They are dressed by men till four years of age, and then are obliged to dress themselves, although their quality be ever so great; and the women attendants, who are aged proportionably to ours at fifty, perform only the most menial offices. They are never suffered to converse with servants, but go together in small or greater numbers to take their diversions, and always in the presence of a professor, or one of his deputies; whereby they avoid those early bad impressions of folly and vice to which our children are subject. Their parents are suffered to see them only twice a year; the visit is not to last above an hour. They are allowed to kiss the child at meeting and parting; but a professor, who always standeth by on those occasions, will not suffer them to whisper, or use any fondling expressions, or bring any presents of toys, sweetmeats, and the like.

The pension from each family for the education and entertainment of a child, upon failure of due payment, is levied by the Emperor's officers.

The nurseries for children of ordinary gentlemen, merchants, traders, and handicrafts, are managed proportionably after the same manner; only those designed for trades are put out apprentices at seven years old, whereas those of persons of quality continue in their nurseries till fifteen, which answers to one and twenty with us: but the confinement is gradually lessened for the last three years.

In the female nurseries, the young girls of quality are educated much like the males, only they are dressed by orderly servants of their own sex, but always in the presence of a professor or deputy, till they come to dress themselves, which is at five years old. And if it be found that these nurses ever presume to entertain the girls with frightful or foolish stories, or the common follies practised by chambermaids among us, they are publicly whipped thrice about the city, imprisoned for a year, and banished for life to the most desolate parts of the country. Thus the young ladies there are as much ashamed of being cowards and fools as the men, and despise all personal ornaments beyond decency and cleanliness: neither did I perceive any difference in their education, made by their difference of sex, only that the exercises of the females were not altogether so robust, and that some rules were given them relating to domestic life, and a smaller compass of learning was enjoined them: for their maxim is, that among people of quality, a wife should be always a reasonable and agreeable companion, because she cannot always be young. When the girls are twelve years old, which among them is the marriageable age, their parents or guardians take them home, with great expressions of gratitude to the professors, and seldom without tears of the young lady and her companions.

In the nurseries of females of the meaner sort, the children are instructed in all kinds of works proper for their sex, and their several degrees: those intended for apprentices are dismissed at seven years old, the rest are kept to eleven.

The meaner families who have children at these nurseries are obliged, besides their annual pension, which is as low as possible, to return to the steward of the nursery a small monthly share of their gettings, to be a portion for the child; and therefore all parents are limited in their expenses by the law. For the Lilliputians think nothing can be more unjust, than that people, in subservience to their own appetites, should bring children into the world, and leave the burthen of supporting them on the public. As to persons of quality, they give security to appropriate a certain sum for each child, suitable to their condition; and these funds are always managed with good husbandry, and the most exact justice.

The cottagers and labourers keep their children at home, their business being only to till and cultivate the earth, and therefore their education is of little consequence to the public; but the old and diseased among them are supported by hospitals: for begging is a trade unknown in this Empire.

And here it may perhaps divert the curious reader, to give some account of my domestic, and my manner of living in this country, during a residence of nine months and thirteen days. Having a head mechanically turned, and being likewise forced by necessity, I had made for myself a table and chair convenient enough, out of the largest trees in the royal park. Two hundred sempstresses were employed to make me shirts, and linen for my bed and table, all of the strongest and coarsest kind they could get; which, however, they were forced to quilt together in several folds, for the thickest was some degrees finer than lawn. Their linen is usually three inches wide, and three foot make a piece. The sempstresses took my measure as I lay on the ground, one standing at my neck, and another at my mid leg, with a strong cord extended, that each held by the end, while the third measured the length of the cord with a rule of an inch long. Then they measured my right thumb, and desired no more; for by a mathematical computation, that twice round the thumb is once round the wrist, and so on to the neck and the waist, and by the help of my old shirt, which I displayed on the ground before them for a pattern, they fitted me exactly. Three hundred tailors were employed in the same manner to make me clothes; but they had another contrivance for taking my measure. I kneeled down, and they raised a ladder from the ground to my neck; upon this ladder one of them mounted, and let fall a plumb-line from my collar to the floor, which just answered the length of my coat; but my waist and arms I measured myself. When my clothes were finished, which was done in my house (for the largest of theirs would not have been able to hold them), they looked like the patchwork made by the ladies in England, only that mine were all of a colour.

I had three hundred cooks to dress my victuals, in little convenient huts built about my house, where they and their families lived, and prepared me two dishes apiece. I took up twenty waiters in my hand, and placed them on the table; an hundred more attended below on the ground, some with dishes of meat, and some with barrels of wine, and other liquors, slung on their shoulders; all which the waiters above drew up as I wanted, in a very ingenious manner, by certain cords, as we draw the bucket up a well in Europe. A dish of their meat was a good mouthful, and a barrel of their liquor a reasonable draught. Their mutton yields to ours, but their beef is excellent. I have had a sirloin so large, that I have been forced to make three bits of it; but this is rare. My servants were astonished to see me eat it bones and all, as in our country we do the leg of a lark. Their geese and turkeys I usually ate at a mouthful, and I must confess they far exceed ours. Of their smaller fowl I could take up twenty or thirty at the end of my knife.

One day his Imperial Majesty, being informed of my way of living, desired that himself, and his Royal Consort, with the young Princes of the Blood of both sexes, might have the happiness (as he was pleased to call it) of dining with me. They came accordingly, and I placed 'em upon chairs of state on my table, just over-against me, with their guards about them. Flimnap the Lord High Treasurer attended there likewise, with his white staff; and I observed he often looked on me with a sour countenance, which I would not seem to regard, but ate more than usual, in honour to my dear country, as well as to fill the Court with admiration. I have some private reasons to believe, that this visit from his Majesty gave Flimnap an opportunity of doing me ill offices to his master. That Minister had always been my secret enemy, although he outwardly caressed me more than was usual to the moroseness of his nature. He represented to the Emperor the low condition of his Treasury; that he was forced to take up money at great discount; that Exchequer bills would not circulate under nine per cent below par; that I had cost his Majesty above a million and a half of *sprugs* (their greatest gold coin, about the bigness of a spangle); and upon the whole, that it would be advisable in the Emperor to take the first fair occasion of dismissing me.

I am here obliged to vindicate the reputation of an excellent Lady, who was an innocent sufferer upon my account. The Treasurer took a fancy to be jealous of his wife, from the malice of some evil tongues, who informed him that her Grace had taken a violent affection for my person, and the Court-scandal ran for some time, that she once came privately to my lodging. This I solemnly declare to be a most infamous falsehood, without any grounds, farther than that her Grace was pleased to treat me with all innocent marks of freedom and friendship. I own she came often to my house, but always publicly, nor ever without three more in the coach, who were usually her sister, and young daughter, and some particular acquaintance; but this was common to many other ladies of the Court. And I still appeal to my servants round, whether they at any time saw a coach at my door without knowing what persons were in it. On those occasions, when a servant had given me notice, my custom was to go immediately to the door; and after paying my respects, to take up the coach and two horses very carefully in my hands (for if there were six horses, the postillion always unharnessed four), and place them on a table, where I had fixed a moveable rim quite round, of five inches high, to prevent accidents. And I have often had four coaches and horses at once on my table full of company, while I sat in my chair leaning my face towards them; and when I was engaged with one set, the coachmen would gently drive the others round my table. I have passed many an afternoon very agreeably in these conversations. But I defy the Treasurer, or his two informers (I will name them, and let 'em make their best of it), Clustril and Drunlo, to prove that any person ever came to me *incognito*, except the Secretary Reldresal, who was sent by express command of his Imperial Majesty, as I have before related. I should not have dwelt so long upon this particular, if it had not been a point wherein the reputation of a great Lady is so nearly concerned, to say nothing of my own; though I had the honour to be a *Nardac*, which the Treasurer himself is not, for all the world knows he is only a *Clumglum*, a title inferior by one degree, as that of a marquis is to a duke in England; yet I allow he preceded me in right of his post. These false informations, which I afterwards came to the knowledge of, by an accident not proper to mention, made the Treasurer show his Lady for some time an ill countenance, and me a worse; for although he were at last undeceived and reconciled to her, yet I lost all credit with him, and found my interest decline very fast with the Emperor himself, who was indeed too much governed by that favourite.

7

The author being informed of a design to accuse him of high treason, makes his escape to Blefuscu. His reception there.

Before I proceed to give an account of my leaving this kingdom, it may be proper to inform the reader of a private intrigue which had been for two months forming against me.

I had been hitherto all my life a stranger to Courts, for which I was unqualified by the meanness of my condition. I had indeed heard and read enough of the dispositions of great princes and ministers; but never expected to have found such terrible effects of them in so remote a country, governed, as I thought, by very different maxims from those in Europe.

When I was just preparing to pay my attendance on the Emperor of Blefuscu, a considerable person at Court (to whom I had been very serviceable at a time when he lay under the highest displeasure of his Imperial Majesty) came to my house very privately at night in a close chair, and without sending his name, desired admittance: the chairmen were dismissed; I put the chair, with his Lordship in it, into my coat-pocket; and giving orders to a trusty servant to say I was indisposed and gone to sleep, I fastened the door of my house, placed the chair on the table, according to my usual custom, and sat down by it. After the common salutations were over, observing his Lordship's countenance full of concern, and enquiring into the reason, he desired I would hear him with patience in a matter that highly concerned my honour and my life. His speech was to the following effect, for I took notes of it as soon as he left me.

You are to know, said he, that several Committees of Council have been lately called in the most private manner on your account: and it is but two days since his Majesty came to a full resolution.

You are very sensible that Skyresh Bolgolam (*Galbet*, or High Admiral) hath been your mortal enemy almost ever since your arrival. His original reasons I know not, but his hatred is much increased since your great success against Blefuscu, by which his glory, as Admiral, is obscured. This Lord, in conjunction with Flimnap the High Treasurer, whose enmity against you is notorious on account of his Lady, Limtoc the General, Lalcon the Chamberlain, and Balmuff the Grand Justiciary, have prepared articles of impeachment against you, for treason, and other capital crimes.

This preface made me so impatient, being conscious of my own merits and innocence, that I was going to interrupt; when he entreated me to be silent; and thus proceeded.

Out of gratitude for the favours you have done me, I procured information of the whole proceedings, and a copy of the articles, wherein I venture my head for your service.

Articles of Impeachment against Quinbus Flestrin (*the* Man-Mountain)

ARTICLE I

Whereas, by a statute made in the reign of his Imperial Majesty Calin Deffar Plune, it is enacted, That whoever shall make water within the precincts of the royal palace, shall be liable to the pains and penalties of high treason: notwithstanding, the said Quinbus Flestrin, in open breach of the said law, under colour of extinguishing the fire kindled in the apartment of his Majesty's most dear Imperial Consort, did maliciously, traitorously, and devilishly, by discharge of his urine, put out the said fire kindled in the said apartment, lying and being within the precincts of the said royal palace, against the statute in that case provided, etc., against the duty, etc.

ARTICLE II

That the said Quinbus Flestrin, having brought the imperial fleet of Blefuscu into the royal port, and being afterwards commanded by his Imperial Majesty to seize all the other ships of the said Empire of Blefuscu, and reduce that Empire to a province, to be governed by a Viceroy from hence, and to destroy and put to death not only all the Big-Endian exiles, but likewise all the people of that Empire who would not immediately forsake the Big-Endian heresy: he, the said Flestrin, like a false traitor against his most Auspicious, Serene, Imperial Majesty, did petition to be excused from the said service, upon pretence of unwillingness to force the consciences, or destroy the liberties and lives of an innocent people.

ARTICLE III

That, whereas certain ambassadors arrived from the Court of Blefuscu to sue for peace in his Majesty's Court: he the said Flestrin did, like a false traitor, aid, abet, comfort, and divert the said ambassadors, although he knew them to be servants to a Prince who was lately an open enemy to his Imperial Majesty, and in open war against his said Majesty.

ARTICLE IV

That the said Quinbus Flestrin, contrary to the duty of a faithful subject, is now preparing to make a voyage to the Court and Empire of Blefuscu, for which he hath received only verbal licence from his Imperial Majesty; and under colour of the said licence, doth falsely and traitorously intend to take the said voyage, and thereby to aid, comfort, and abet the Emperor of Blefuscu, so late an enemy, and in open war with his Imperial Majesty aforesaid.

There are some other articles, but these are the most important, of which I have read you an abstract.

In the several debates upon this impeachment, it must be confessed that his Majesty gave many marks of his great *lenity*, often urging the services you had done him, and endeavouring to extenuate your crimes. The Treasurer and Admiral insisted that you should be put to the most painful and ignominious death, by setting fire on your house at night, and the General was to attend with twenty thousand men armed with poisoned arrows to shoot you on the face and hands. Some of your servants were to have private orders to strew a poisonous juice on your shirts and sheets, which would soon make you tear your own flesh, and die in the utmost torture. The General came into the same opinion, so that for a long time there was a majority against you. But his Majesty resolving, if possible, to spare your life, at last brought off the Chamberlain.

Upon this incident, Reldresal, Principal Secretary for Private Affairs, who always approved himself your true friend, was commanded by the Emperor to deliver his opinion, which he accordingly did; and therein justified the good thoughts you have of him. He allowed your crimes to be great, but that still there was room for mercy, the most commendable virtue in a prince, and for which his Majesty was so justly celebrated. He said, the friendship between you and him was so well known to the world, that perhaps the most honourable Board might think him partial: however, in obedience to the command he had received, he would freely offer his sentiments. That if his Majesty, in consideration of your services, and pursuant to his own merciful disposition, would please to spare your life, and only give order to put out both your eyes, he humbly conceived, that by this expedient justice might in some measure be satisfied, and all the world would applaud the *lenity* of the Emperor, as well as the fair and generous proceedings of those who have the honour to be his counsellors. That the loss of your eyes would be no impediment to your bodily strength, by which you might still be useful to his Majesty. That blindness is an addition to courage, by concealing dangers from us; that the fear you had for your eyes, was the greatest difficulty in bringing over the enemy's fleet, and it would be sufficient for you to see by the eyes of the Ministers, since the greatest princes do no more.

This proposal was received with the utmost disapprobation by the whole Board. Bolgolam, the Admiral, could not preserve his temper; but rising up in fury, said, he wondered how the Secretary durst presume to give his opinion for preserving the life of a traitor: that the services you had performed were, by all true reasons of state, the great aggravation of your crimes; that you, who were able to extinguish the fire, by discharge of urine in her Majesty's apartment (which he mentioned with horror), might, at another time, raise an inundation by the same means, to drown the whole palace; and the same strength which enabled you to bring over the enemy's fleet, might serve, upon the first discontent, to carry it back: that he had good reasons to think you were a Big-Endian in your heart; and as treason begins in the heart before it appears in overt acts, so he accused you as a traitor on that account, and therefore insisted you should be put to death.

The Treasurer was of the same opinion; he showed to what straits his Majesty's revenue was reduced by the charge of maintaining you, which would soon grow insupportable: that the Secretary's expedient of putting out your eyes was so far from being a remedy against this evil, that it would probably increase it, as it is manifest from the common practice of blinding some kind of fowl, after which they fed the faster, and grew sooner fat: that his sacred Majesty, and the Council, who are your judges, were in their own consciences fully convinced of your guilt, which was a sufficient argument to condemn you to death, without the *formal proofs required by the strict letter of the law.*

But his Imperial Majesty, fully determined against capital punishment, was graciously pleased to say, that since the Council thought the loss of your eyes too easy a censure, some other may be inflicted hereafter. And your friend the Secretary humbly desiring to be heard again, in answer to what the Treasurer had objected concerning the great charge his Majesty was at in maintaining you, said, that his Excellency, who had the sole disposal of the Emperor's revenue, might easily provide against this evil, by gradually lessening your establishment; by which, for want of sufficient food, you would grow weak and faint, and lose your appetite, and consequently decay and consume in a few months; neither would the stench of your carcass be then so dangerous, when it should become more than half diminished; and immediately upon your death, five or six thousand of his Majesty's subjects might, in two or three days, cut your flesh from your bones, take it away by cart-loads, and bury it in distant parts to prevent infection, leaving the skeleton as a monument of admiration to posterity.

Thus by the great friendship of the Secretary, the whole affair was compromised. It was strictly enjoined, that the project of starving you by degrees should be kept a secret, but the sentence of putting out your eyes was entered on the books; none dissenting except Bolgolam the Admiral, who being a creature of the Empress, was perpetually instigated by her Majesty to insist upon your death, she having borne perpetual malice against you, on account of that infamous and illegal method you took to extinguish the fire in her apartment.

In three days your friend the Secretary will be directed to come to your house, and read before you the articles of impeachment; and then to signify the great *lenity* and favour of his Majesty and Council, whereby you are only condemned to the loss of your eyes, which his Majesty doth not question you will gratefully and humbly submit to; and twenty of his Majesty's surgeons will attend, in order to see the operation well performed, by discharging very sharp-pointed arrows into the balls of your eyes, as you lie on the ground.

I leave to your prudence what measures you will take; and to avoid suspicion, I must immediately return in as private a manner as I came.

His Lordship did so, and I remained alone, under many doubts and perplexities of mind.

It was a custom introduced by this Prince and his Ministry (very different, as I have been assured, from the practices of former times), that after the Court had decreed any cruel execution, either to gratify the monarch's resentment, or the malice of a favourite, the Emperor always made a speech to his whole Council, expressing his *great lenity and tenderness, as qualities known and confessed by all the world.* This speech was immediately published through the kingdom; nor did anything terrify the people so much as those encomiums on his Majesty's mercy; because it was observed, that the more these praises were enlarged and insisted on, the more *inhuman* was the punishment, and the *sufferer more innocent.* Yet, as to myself, I must confess, having never been designed for a courtier either by my birth or education, I was so ill a judge of things, that I could not discover the *lenity* and favour of this sentence, but conceived it (perhaps erroneously) rather to be rigorous than gentle. I sometimes thought of standing my trial, for although I could not deny the facts alleged in the several articles, yet I hoped they would admit of some extenuations. But having in my life perused many state trials, which I ever observed to terminate as the judges thought fit to direct, I durst not rely on so dangerous a decision, in so critical a juncture, and against such powerful enemies. Once I was strongly bent upon resistance, for while I had liberty, the whole strength of that Empire could hardly subdue me, and I might easily with stones pelt the metropolis to pieces; but I soon rejected that project with horror, by remembering the oath I had made to the Emperor, the favours I received from him, and the high title of *Nardac* he conferred upon me. Neither had I so soon learned the gratitude of courtiers, to persuade myself that his Majesty's *present severities acquitted me of all past obligations.*

At last I fixed upon a resolution, for which it is probable I may incur some censure, and not unjustly; for I confess I owe the preserving mine eyes, and consequently my liberty, to my own great rashness and want of experience: because if I had then known the nature of princes and ministers, which I have since observed in many other courts, and their methods of treating criminals less obnoxious than myself, I should with great alacrity and readiness have submitted to so *easy* a punishment. But hurried on by the precipitancy of youth, and having his Imperial Majesty's licence to pay my attendance upon the Emperor of Blefuscu, I took this opportunity, before the three days were elapsed, to send a letter to my friend the Secretary, signifying my resolution of setting out that morning for Blefuscu pursuant to the leave I had got; and without waiting for an answer, I went to that side of the island where our fleet lay. I seized a large man-of-war, tied a cable to the prow, and lifting up the anchors, I stripped myself, put my clothes (together with my coverlet, which I carried under my arm) into the vessel, and drawing it after me between wading and swimming, arrived at the royal port of Blefuscu, where the people had long expected me; they lent me two guides to direct me to the capital city, which is of the same name. I held them in my hands till I came within two hundred yards of the gate, and desired them to signify my arrival to one of the Secretaries, and let him know, I there waited his Majesty's commands. I had an answer in about an hour, that his Majesty, attended by the Royal Family, and great officers of the Court, was coming out to receive me. I advanced a hundred yards. The Emperor, and his train, alighted from their horses, the Empress and ladies from their coaches, and I did not perceive they were in any fright or concern. I lay on the ground to kiss his Majesty's and the Empress's hand. I told his Majesty that I was come according to my promise, and with the licence of the Emperor my master, to have the honour of seeing so mighty a monarch, and to offer him any service in my power, consistent with my duty to my own prince; not mentioning a word of my disgrace, because I had hitherto no regular information of it, and might suppose myself wholly ignorant of any such design; neither could I reasonably conceive that the Emperor would discover the secret while I was out of his power: wherein, however, it soon appeared I was deceived.

I shall not trouble the reader with the particular account of my reception at this Court, which was suitable to the generosity of so great a prince; nor of the difficulties I was in for want of a house and bed, being forced to lie on the ground, wrapped up in my coverlet.

8

The author, by a lucky accident, finds means to leave Blefuscu; and, after some difficulties, returns safe to his native country.

Three days after my arrival, walking out of curiosity to the north-east coast of the island, I observed, about half a league off, in the sea, somewhat that looked like a boat overturned. I pulled off my shoes and stockings, and wading two or three hundred yards, I found the object to approach nearer by force of the tide, and then plainly saw it to be a real boat, which I supposed might, by some tempest, have been driven from a ship; whereupon I returned immediately towards the city, and desired his Imperial Majesty to lend me twenty of the tallest vessels he had left after the loss of his fleet, and three thousand seamen under the command of his Vice-Admiral. This fleet sailed round, while I went back the shortest way to the coast where I first discovered the boat; I found the tide had driven it still nearer. The seamen were all provided with cordage, which I had beforehand twisted to a sufficient strength. When the ships came up, I stripped myself, and waded till I came within an hundred yards of the boat, after which I was forced to swim till I got up to it. The seamen threw me the end of the cord, which I fastened to a hole in the fore-part of the boat, and the other end to a man-of-war: but I found all my labour to little purpose; for being out of my depth, I was not able to work. In this necessity, I was forced to swim behind, and push the boat forwards as often as I could, with one of my hands; and the tide favouring me, I advanced so far, that I could just hold up my chin and feel the ground. I rested two or three minutes, and then gave the boat another shove, and so on till the sea was no higher than my armpits; and now the most laborious part being over, I took out my other cables, which were stowed in one of the ships, and fastening them first to the boat, and then to nine of the vessels which attended me; the wind being favourable, the seamen towed, and I shoved till we arrived within forty yards of the shore, and waiting till the tide was out, I got dry to the boat, and by the assistance of two thousand men, with ropes and engines, I made a shift to turn it on its bottom, and found it was but little damaged.

I shall not trouble the reader with the difficulties I was under by the help of certain paddles, which cost me ten days making, to get my boat to the royal port of Blefuscu, where a mighty concourse of people appeared upon my arrival, full of wonder at the sight of so prodigious a vessel. I told the Emperor, that my good fortune had thrown this boat in my way, to carry me to some place from whence I might return into my native country, and begged his Majesty's orders for getting materials to fit it up, together with his licence to depart; which, after some kind expostulations, he was pleased to grant.

I did very much wonder, in all this time, not to have heard of an express relating to me from our Emperor to the Court of Blefuscu. But I was afterwards given privately to understand, that his Imperial Majesty, never imagining I had the least notice of his designs, believed I was only gone to Blefuscu in performance of my promise, according to the licence he had given me, which was well known at our Court, and would return in a few days when that ceremony was ended. But he was at last in pain at my long absence; and, after consulting with the Treasurer, and the rest of that Cabal, a person of quality was dispatched with the copy of the articles against me. This envoy had instructions to represent to the monarch of Blefuscu the great *lenity* of his master, who was content to punish me no further than with the loss of mine eyes; that I had fled from justice, and if I did not return in two hours, I should be deprived of my title of *Nardac*, and declared a traitor. The envoy further added, that in order to maintain the peace and amity between both Empires, his master expected, that his brother of Blefuscu would give orders to have me sent back to Lilliput, bound hand and foot, to be punished as a traitor.

The Emperor of Blefuscu, having taken three days to consult, returned an answer consisting of many civilities and excuses. He said, that as for sending me bound, his brother knew it was impossible; that although I had deprived him of his fleet, yet he owed great obligations to me for many good offices I had done him in making the peace. That however both their Majesties would soon be made easy; for I had found a prodigious vessel on the shore, able to carry me on the sea, which he had given order to fit up with my own assistance and direction, and he hoped in a few weeks both Empires would be freed from so insupportable an incumbrance.

With this answer the envoy returned to Lilliput, and the Monarch of Blefuscu related to me all that had passed, offering me at the same time (but under the strictest confidence) his gracious protection, if I would continue in his service; wherein although I believed him sincere, yet I resolved never more to put any confidence in princes or ministers, where I could possibly avoid it; and therefore, with all due acknowledgements for his favourable intentions, I humbly begged to be excused. I told him, that since Fortune, whether good or evil, had thrown a vessel in my way, I was resolved to venture myself in the ocean, rather than be an occasion of difference between two such mighty monarchs. Neither did I find the Emperor at all displeased; and I discovered by a certain accident, that he was very glad of my resolution, and so were most of his Ministers.

These considerations moved me to hasten my departure somewhat sooner than I intended; to which the Court, impatient to have me gone, very readily contributed. Five hundred workmen were employed to make two sails to my boat, according to my directions, by quilting thirteen fold of their strongest linen together. I was at the pains of making ropes and cables, by twisting ten, twenty or thirty of the thickest and strongest of theirs. A great stone that I happened to find, after a long search by the seashore, served me for an anchor. I had the tallow of three hundred cows for greasing my boat, and other uses. I was at incredible pains in cutting down some of the largest timber-trees for oars and masts, wherein I was, however, much assisted by his Majesty's ship-carpenters, who helped me in smoothing them, after I had done the rough work.

In about a month, when all was prepared, I sent to receive his Majesty's commands, and to take my leave. The Emperor and Royal Family came out of the palace; I lay down on my face to kiss his hand, which he very graciously gave me; so did the Empress, and young Princes of the Blood. His Majesty presented me with fifty purses of two hundred *sprugs* apiece, together with his picture at full length, which I put immediately into one of my gloves, to keep it from being hurt. The ceremonies at my departure were too many to trouble the reader with at this time.

I stored the boat with the carcasses of an hundred oxen, and three hundred sheep, with bread and drink proportionable, and as much meat ready dressed as four hundred cooks could provide. I took with me six cows and two bulls alive, with as many ewes and rams, intending to carry them into my own country, and propagate the breed. And to feed them on board, I had a good bundle of hay, and a bag of corn. I would gladly have taken a dozen of the natives, but this was a thing the Emperor would by no means permit; and besides a diligent search into my pockets, his Majesty engaged my honour not to carry away any of his subjects, although with their own consent and desire.

Having thus prepared all things as well as I was able, I set sail on the twenty-fourth day of September, 1701, at six in the morning; and when I had gone about four leagues to the northward, the wind being at south-east, at six in the evening, I descried a small island about half a league to the north-west. I advanced forward, and cast anchor on the lee-side of the island, which seemed to be uninhabited. I then took some refreshment, and went to my rest. I slept well, and as I conjecture at least six hours, for I found the day broke in two hours after I awaked. It was a clear night. I ate my breakfast before the sun was up; and heaving anchor, the wind being favourable, I steered the same course that I had done the day before, wherein I was directed by my pocket-compass. My intention was to reach, if possible, one of those islands, which I had reason to believe lay to the north-east of Van Diemen's Land. I discovered nothing all that day; but upon the next, about three in the afternoon, when I had by my computation made twenty-four leagues from Blefuscu, I descried a sail steering to the south-east; my course was due east. I hailed her, but could get no answer; yet I found I gained upon her, for the wind slackened. I made all the sail I could, and in half an hour she spied me, then hung out her ancient, and discharged a gun. It is not easy to express the joy I was in upon the unexpected hope of once more seeing my beloved country, and the dear pledges I had left in it. The ship slackened her sails, and I came up with her between five and six in the evening, September 26; but my heart leapt within me to see her English colours. I put my cows and sheep into my coat-pockets, and got on board with all my little cargo of provisions. The vessel was an English merchantman, returning from Japan by the North and South Seas; the captain, Mr John Biddel of Deptford, a very civil man, and an excellent sailor. We were now in the latitude of 30 degrees south; there were about fifty men in the ship; and here I met an old comrade of mine, one Peter Williams, who gave me a good character to the captain. This gentleman treated me with kindness, and desired I would let him know what place I came from last, and whither I was bound; which I did in few words, but he thought I was raving, and that the dangers I underwent had disturbed my head; whereupon I took my black cattle and sheep out of my pocket, which, after great astonishment, clearly convinced him of my veracity. I then showed him the gold given me by the Emperor of Blefuscu, together with his Majesty's picture at full length, and some other rarities of that country. I gave him two purses of two hundred *sprugs* each, and promised, when we arrived in England, to make him a present of a cow and a sheep big with young.

I shall not trouble the reader with a particular account of this voyage, which was very prosperous for the most part. We arrived in the Downs on the 13th of April, 1702. I had only one misfortune, that the rats on board carried away one of my sheep; I found her bones in a hole, picked clean from the flesh. The rest of my cattle I got safe on shore, and set them a grazing in a bowling-green at Greenwich, where the fineness of the grass made them feed very heartily, though I had always feared the contrary: neither could I possibly have preserved them in so long a voyage, if the captain had not allowed me some of his best biscuit, which, rubbed to powder, and mingled with water, was their constant food. The short time I continued in England, I made a considerable profit by showing my cattle to many persons of quality, and others: and before I began my second voyage, I sold them for six hundred pounds. Since my last return, I find the breed is considerably increased, especially the sheep; which I hope will prove much to the advantage of the woollen manufacture, by the fineness of the fleeces.

I stayed but two months with my wife and family; for my insatiable desire of seeing foreign countries would suffer me to continue no longer. I left fifteen hundred pounds with my wife, and fixed her in a good house at Redriff. My remaining stock I carried with me, part in money, and part in goods, in hopes to improve my fortunes. My eldest uncle John had left me an estate in land, near Epping, of about thirty pounds a year; and I had a long lease of the Black Bull in Fetter Lane, which yielded me as much more: so that I was not in any danger of leaving my family upon the parish. My son Johnny, named so after his uncle, was at the grammar school, and a towardly child. My daughter Betty (who is now well married, and has children) was then at her needlework. I took leave of my wife, and boy and girl, with tears on both sides, and went on board the *Adventure*, a merchant-ship of three hundred tons, bound for Surat, Captain John Nicholas of Liverpool, commander. But my account of this voyage must be referred to the second part of my Travels.

LAURENCE STERNE

from *The Life and Opinions of Tristram Shandy, Gent.*

I

I wish either my father or my mother, or indeed both of them, as they were in duty both equally bound to it, had minded what they were about when they begot me; had they duly considered how much depended upon what they were then doing; – that not only the production of a rational Being was concerned in it, but that possibly the happy formation and temperature of his body, perhaps his genius and the very cast of his mind; – and, for aught they knew to the contrary, even the fortunes of his whole house might take their turn from the humours and dispositions which were then uppermost;— Had they duly weighed and considered all this, and proceeded accordingly,—I am verily persuaded I should have made a quite different figure in the world, from that in which the reader is likely to see me. – Believe me, good folks, this is not so inconsiderable a thing as many of you may think it; – you have all, I dare say, heard of the animal spirits, as how they are transfused from father to son, etc. etc. – and a great deal to that purpose: – Well, you may take my word, that nine parts in ten of a man's sense or his nonsense, his successes and miscarriages in this world depend upon their motions and activity, and the different tracts and trains you put them into, so that when they are once set a-going, whether right or wrong, 'tis not a halfpenny matter, – away they go cluttering like hey-go mad; and by treading the same steps over and over again, they presently make a road of it, as plain and as smooth as a garden-walk, which, when they are once used to, the Devil himself sometimes shall not be able to drive them off it.

'Pray, my Dear,' quoth my mother, 'have you not forgot to wind up the clock?'—— 'Good G—!' cried my father, making an exclamation, but taking care to moderate his voice at the same time,—'Did ever woman, since the creation of the world, interrupt a man with such a silly question?' Pray, what was your father saying?—Nothing.

2

—Then, positively, there is nothing in the question that I can see, either good or bad.— Then, let me tell you, Sir, it was a very unseasonable question at least, – because it scattered and dispersed the animal spirits, whose business it was to have escorted and gone hand in hand with the HOMUNCULUS, and conducted him safe to the place destined for his reception.

The Homunculus, Sir, in however low and ludicrous a light he may appear, in this age of levity, to the eye of folly or prejudice; – to the eye of reason in scientific research, he stands confessed – a Being guarded and circumscribed with rights.—The minutest philosophers, who, by the bye, have the most enlarged understandings, (their souls being inversely as their enquiries) shew us incontestably, that the Homunculus is created by the same hand, – engendered in the same course of nature, – endowed with the same locomotive powers and faculties with us: – That he consists as we do, of skin, hair, fat, flesh, veins, arteries, ligaments, nerves, cartilages, bones, marrow, brains, glands, genitals, humours, and articulations; – is a Being of as much activity, – and, in all senses of the word, as much and as truly our fellow-creature as my Lord Chancellor of England. – He may be benefited, – he may be injured, – he may obtain redress; – in a word, he has all the claims and rights of humanity, which Tully, Puffendorf, or the best ethic writers allow to arise out of that state and relation.

Now, dear Sir, what if any accident had befallen him in his way alone! – or that, through terror of it, natural to so young a traveller, my little Gentleman had got to his journey's end miserably spent; – his muscular strength and virility worn down to a thread; – his own animal spirits ruffled beyond description, – and that in this sad disordered state of nerves, he had lain down a prey to sudden starts, or a series of melancholy dreams and fancies, for nine long, long months together. – I tremble to think what a foundation had been laid for a thousand weaknesses both of body and mind, which no skill of the physician or the philosopher could ever afterwards have set thoroughly to rights.

3

To my uncle Mr Toby Shandy do I stand indebted for the preceding anecdote, to whom my father, who was an excellent natural philosopher, and much given to close reasoning upon the smallest matters, had oft, and heavily complained of the injury; but once more particularly, as my uncle Toby well remembered, upon his observing a most unaccountable obliquity, (as he called it) in my manner of setting up my top, and justifying the principles upon which I had done it, – the old gentleman shook his head, and in a tone more expressive by half of sorrow than reproach, – he said his heart all along foreboded, and he saw it verified in this, and from a thousand other observations he had made upon me, That I should neither think nor act like any other man's child: – 'But alas!' continued he, shaking his head a second time, and wiping away a tear which was trickling down his cheeks, 'My Tristram's misfortunes began nine months before ever he came into the world.'

– My mother, who was sitting by, looked up, – but she knew no more than her backside what my father meant, – but my uncle, Mr Toby Shandy, who had been often informed of the affair, – understood him very well.

4

I know there are readers in the world, as well as many other good people in it, who are no readers at all, – who find themselves ill at ease, unless they are let into the whole secret from first to last, of everything which concerns you.

It is in pure compliance with this humour of theirs, and from a backwardness in my nature to disappoint any one soul living, that I have been so very particular already. As my life and opinions are likely to make some noise in the world, and, if I conjecture right, will take in all ranks, professions, and denominations of men whatever, – be no less read than the *Pilgrim's Progress* itself – and in the end, prove the very thing which Montaigne dreaded his Essays should turn out, that is, a book for a parlour-window; – I find it necessary to consult every one a little in his turn; and therefore must beg pardon for going on a little further in the same way: For which cause, right glad I am, that I have begun the history of myself in the way I have done; and that I am able to go on, tracing every thing in it, as Horace says, *ab Ovo*.

Horace, I know does not recommend this fashion altogether: But that gentleman is speaking only of an epic poem or a tragedy; – (I forget which,) – besides, if it was not so I should beg Mr Horace's pardon; – for in writing what I have set about, I shall confine myself neither to his rules, nor to any man's rules that ever lived.

To such, however, as do not choose to go so far back into these things, I can give no better advice, than that they skip over the remaining part of this chapter; for I declare beforehand, 'tis wrote only for the curious and inquisitive.

———————————————————Shut the door———————————————————

I was begot in the night, betwixt the first Sunday and the first Monday in the month of March, in the year of our Lord one thousand seven hundred and eighteen. I am positive I was, – But how I came to be so very particular in my account of a thing which happened before I was born, is owing to another small anecdote known only in our own family, but now made public for the better clearing up this point.

My father, you must know, who was originally a Turkey merchant, but had left off business for some years, in order to retire to, and die upon, his paternal estate in the county of———, was, I believe, one of the most regular men in everything he did, whether 'twas matter of business, or matter of amusement, that ever lived. As a small specimen of this extreme exactness of his, to which he was in truth a slave, – he had made it a rule for many years of his life – on the first Sunday-night of every month throughout the whole year, – as certain as ever the Sunday-night came,—to wind up a large house-clock, which we had standing on the backstairs head, with his own hands: – And being somewhere between fifty and sixty years of age at the time I have been speaking of, – he had likewise gradually brought some other little family concernments to the same period, in order, as he would often say to my uncle Toby, to get them all out of the way at one time, and be no more plagued and pestered with them the rest of the month.

It was attended with but one misfortune, which, in a great measure, fell upon myself, and the effects of which I fear I shall carry with me to my grave; namely, that from an unhappy association of ideas, which have no connection in nature, it so fell out at length, that my poor mother could never hear the said clock wound up, – but the thoughts of some other things unavoidably popped into her head – and *vice versâ*:— Which strange combination of ideas, the sagacious Locke, who certainly understood the nature of these things better than most men, affirms to have produced more wry actions than all other sources of prejudice whatsoever.

But this by the bye.

Now it appears by a memorandum in my father's pocket-book, which now lies upon the table, 'That on Lady-day, which was on the 25th of the same month in which I date my geniture, – my father set out upon his journey to London, with my eldest brother Bobby, to fix him at Westminster school'; and, as it appears from the same authority, 'That he did not get down to his wife and family till the second week in May following,' – it brings the thing almost to a certainty. However, what follows in the beginning of the next chapter, puts it beyond all possibility of doubt.

—But pray, Sir, What was your father doing all December, – January, and February?—Why, Madam, – he was all that time afflicted with a Sciatica.

5

On the fifth day of November, 1718, which to the era fixed on, was as near nine calendar months as any husband could in reason have expected, – was I Tristram Shandy, Gentleman, brought forth into this scurvy and disastrous world of ours.—I wish I had been born in the Moon, or in any of the planets, (except Jupiter or Saturn, because I never could bear cold weather) for it could not well have fared worse with me in any of them (though I will not answer for Venus) than it has in this vile, dirty planet of ours, – which, o' my conscience, with reverence be it spoken, I take to be made up of the shreds and clippings of the rest;—not but the planet is well enough, provided a man could be born in it to a great title or to a great estate; or could any how contrive to be called up to public charges, and employments of dignity or power;—but that is not my case;—and therefore every man will speak of the fair as his own market has gone in it;—for which cause I affirm it over again to be one of the vilest worlds that ever was made; – for I can truly say, that from the first hour I drew my breath in it, to this, that I can now scarce draw it at all, for an asthma I got in skating against the wind in Flanders; – I have been the continual sport of what the world calls Fortune; and though I will not wrong her by saying, She has ever made me feel the weight of any great or signal evil;—yet with all the good temper in the world, I affirm it of her, that in every stage of my life, and at every turn and corner where she could get fairly at me, the ungracious duchess has pelted me with a set of as pitiful misadventures and cross accidents as ever small Hero sustained.

6

In the beginning of the last chapter, I informed you exactly when I was born; but I did not inform you how, No, that particular was reserved entirely for a chapter by itself; – besides, Sir, as you and I are in a manner perfect strangers to each other, it would not have been proper to have let you into too many circumstances relating to myself all at once. – You must have a little patience. I have undertaken, you see, to write not only my life, but my opinions also; hoping and expecting that your knowledge of my character, and of what kind of a mortal I am, by the one, would give you a better relish for the other: As you proceed farther with me, the slight acquaintance, which is now beginning betwixt us, will grow into familiarity; and that, unless one of us is in fault, will terminate in friendship. – *O diem praeclarum!* – then nothing which has touched me will be thought trifling in its nature, or tedious in its telling. Therefore, my dear friend and companion, if you should think me somewhat sparing of my narrative on my first setting out – bear with me, – and let me go on, and tell my story my own way: – Or, if I should seem now and then to trifle upon the road, – or should sometimes put on a fool's cap with a bell to it, for a moment or two as we pass along, – don't fly off, – but rather courteously give me credit for a little more wisdom than appears upon my outside; – and as we jog on, either laugh with me, or at me, or in short, do any thing, – only keep your temper.

7

In the same village where my father and my mother dwelt, dwelt also a thin, upright, motherly, notable, good old body of a midwife, who with the help of a little plain good sense, and some years' full employment in her business, in which she had all along trusted little to her own efforts, and a great deal to those of dame Nature, – had acquired, in her way, no small degree of reputation in the world:—by which the word *world*, need I in this place inform your worship, that I would be understood to mean no more of it, than a small circle described upon the circle of the great world, of four English miles diameter, or thereabouts, of which the cottage where the good old woman lived, is supposed to be the centre? – She had been left, it seems, a widow in great distress, with three or four small children, in her forty-seventh year; and as she was at that time a person of decent carriage, – grave deportment, – a woman moreover of few words, and withal an object of compassion, whose distress, and silence under it, called out the louder for a friendly lift: the wife of the parson of the parish was touched with pity; and having often lamented an inconvenience, to which her husband's flock had for many years been exposed, inasmuch as there was no such thing as a midwife, of any kind or degree, to be got at, let the case have been never so urgent, within less than six or seven long miles riding; which said seven long miles in dark nights and dismal roads, the country thereabouts being nothing but a deep clay, was almost equal to fourteen; and that in effect was sometimes next to having no midwife at all; it came into her head, that it would be doing as seasonable a kindness to the whole parish, as to the poor creature herself, to get her a little instructed in some of the plain principles of the business, in order to set her up in it. As no woman thereabouts was better qualified to execute the plan she had formed than herself, the gentlewoman very charitably undertook it; and having great influence over the female part of the parish, she found no difficulty in effecting it to the utmost of her wishes. In truth, the parson joined his interest with his wife's in the whole affair; and in order to do things as they should be, and give the poor soul as good a title by law to practice, as his wife had given by institution, – he cheerfully paid the fees for the ordinary's licence himself, amounting in the whole, to the sum of eighteen shillings and four pence; so that betwixt them both, the good woman was fully invested in the real and corporal possession of her office, together with all its rights, members, and appurtenances whatsoever.

These last words, you must know, were not according to the old form in which such licences, faculties, and powers usually ran, which in like cases had heretofore been granted to the sisterhood. But it was according to a neat Formula of Didius his own devising, who having a particular turn for taking to pieces, and new framing over again, all kinds of instruments in that way, not only hit upon this dainty amendment, but coaxed many of the old licensed matrons in the neighbourhood, to open their faculties afresh, in order to have this wham-wham of his inserted.

I own I never could envy Didius in these kinds of fancies of his: – But every man to his own taste. – Did not Dr Kunastrokius, that great man, at his leisure hours, take the greatest delight imaginable in combing of asses tails, and plucking the dead hairs out with his teeth, though he had tweezers always in his pocket? Nay, if you come to that,

Sir, have not the wisest of men in all ages, not excepting Solomon himself, – have they not had their Hobby-Horses; – their running horses, – their coins and their cockle-shells, their drums and their trumpets, their fiddles, their pallets, – their maggots and their butterflies? – and so long as a man rides his Hobby-Horse peaceably and quietly along the King's highway, and neither compels you or me to get up behind him, – pray, Sir, what have either you or I to do with it?

8

– *De gustibus non est disputandum;* – that is, there is no disputing against Hobby-Horses; and for my part, I seldom do; nor could I with any sort of grace, had I been an enemy to them at the bottom; for happening, at certain intervals and changes of the moon, to be both fiddler and painter, according as the fly stings: – Be it known to you, that I keep a couple of pads myself, upon which, in their turns, (nor do I care who knows it) I frequently ride out and take the air; – though sometimes, to my shame be it spoken, I take somewhat longer journeys than what a wise man would think altogether right. – But the truth is, – I am not a wise man; – and besides am a mortal of so little consequence in the world, it is not much matter what I do: so I seldom fret or fume at all about it: Nor does it much disturb my rest, when I see such great Lords and tall Personages as hereafter follow: – such, for instance, as my Lord A, B, C, D, E, F, G, H, I, K, L, M, N, O, P, Q, and so on, all of a row, mounted upon their several horses, some with large stirrups, getting on in a more grave and sober pace;—others on the contrary, tucked up to their very chins, with whips across their mouths, scouring and scampering it away like so many little party-coloured devils astride a mortgage, – and as if some of them were resolved to break their necks.—So much the better – say I to myself; – for in case the worst should happen, the world will make a shift to do excellently well without them; and for the rest,—why—God speed them—e'en let them ride on without opposition from me; for were their lordships unhorsed this very night – 'tis ten to one but that many of them would be worse mounted by one half before to-morrow morning.

Not one of these instances therefore can be said to break in upon my rest.—But there is an instance, which I own puts me off my guard, and that is, when I see one born for great actions, and what is still more for his honour, whose nature ever inclines him to good ones; – when I behold such a one, my Lord, like yourself, whose principles and conduct are as generous and noble as his blood, and whom, for that reason, a corrupt world cannot spare one moment; – when I see such a one, my Lord, mounted, though it is but for a minute beyond the time which my love to my country has prescribed to him, and my zeal for his glory wishes, – then, my Lord, I cease to be a philosopher, and in the first transport of an honest impatience, I wish the Hobby-Horse, with all his fraternity, at the Devil.

'MY LORD,

'I maintain this to be a dedication, notwithstanding its singularity in the three great essentials of matter, form, and place: I beg, therefore, you will accept it as such, and that you will permit me to lay it, with the most respectful humility, at your Lordship's feet, – when you are upon them, – which you can be when you please; – and that is, my Lord, whenever there is occasion for it, and I will add, to the best purposes too. I have the honour to be,

'*My Lord,*
Your Lordship's most obedient,
and most devoted,
and most humble servant,
Tristram Shandy'

9

I solemnly declare to all mankind, that the above dedication was made for no one Prince, Prelate, Pope, or Potentate, – Duke, Marquis, Earl, Viscount, or Baron, of this, or any other Realm in Christendom; – nor has it yet been hawked about, or offered publicly or privately, directly or indirectly, to any one person or personage, great or small; but is honestly a true Virgin-Dedication untried on, upon any soul living.

I labour this point so particularly, merely to remove any offence or objection which might arise against it from the manner in which I propose to make the most of it; – which is the putting it up fairly to public sale; which I now do.

—Every author has a way of his own in bringing his points to bear; – for my own part, as I hate chaffering and higgling for a few guineas in a dark entry; – I resolved within myself, from the very beginning, to deal squarely and openly with your Great Folks in this affair, and try whether I should not come off the better by it.

If therefore there is any one Duke, Marquis, Earl, Viscount, or Baron, in these his Majesty's dominions, who stands in need of a tight, genteel dedication, and whom the above will suit, (for by the bye, unless it suits in some degree I will not part with it)— it is much at his service for fifty guineas;—which I am positive is twenty guineas less than it ought to be afforded for, by any man of genius.

My Lord, if you examine it over again, it is far from being a gross piece of daubing, as some dedications are. The design, your Lordship sees, is good, – the colouring transparent, – the drawing not amiss; – or to speak more like a man of science, – and measure my piece in the painter's scale, divided into 20, – I believe, my Lord, the outlines will turn out as 12, – the composition as 9, – the colouring as 6, – the expression 13 and a half, – and the design, – if I may be allowed, my Lord, to understand my own design, and supposing absolute perfection in designing, to be as 20, – I think it cannot well fall short of 19. Besides all this, – there is keeping in it, and the dark strokes in the Hobby-Horse, (which is a secondary figure, and a kind of back-ground to the whole) give great force to the principal lights in your own figure, and make it come off wonderfully; – and besides, there is an air of originality in the *tout ensemble*.

Be pleased, my good Lord, to order the sum to be paid into the hands of Mr Dodsley, for the benefit of the author, and in the next edition care shall be taken that this chapter be expunged, and your Lordship's titles, distinctions, arms, and good actions, be placed at the front of the preceding chapter: All which, from the words, *De gustibus non est disputandum*, and whatever else in this book relates to Hobby-Horses, but no more, shall stand dedicated to your Lordship. – The rest I dedicate to the Moon, who, by the bye, of all the Patrons or Matrons I can think of, has most power to set my book a-going, and make the world run mad after it.

Bright Goddess,

If thou art not too busy with Candid and Miss Cunegund's affairs, – take Tristram Shandy's under thy protection also.

10

Whatever degree of small merit the act of benignity in favour of the midwife might justly claim, or in whom that claim truly rested, – at first sight seems not very material to this history;—certain however it was, that the gentlewoman, the parson's wife, did run away at that time with the whole of it: And yet, for my life, I cannot help thinking but that the parson himself, though he had not the good fortune to hit upon the design first, – yet, as he heartily concurred in it the moment it was laid before him, and as heartily parted with his money to carry it into execution, had a claim to some share of it, – if not to a full half of whatever honour was due to it.

The world at that time was pleased to determine the matter otherwise.

Lay down the book, and I will allow you half a day to give a probable guess at the grounds of this procedure.

Be it known then, that, for about five years before the date of the midwife's licence, of which you have had so circumstantial an account, – the parson we have to do with had made himself a country-talk by a breach of all decorum, which he had committed against himself, his station, and his office; – and that was in never appearing better, or otherwise mounted, than upon a lean, sorry, jack-ass of a horse, value about one pound fifteen shillings; who, to shorten all description of him, was full brother to Rosinante, as far as similitude congenial could make him; for he answered his description to a hair-breadth in every thing, – except that I do not remember 'tis any where said, that Rosinante was broken-winded; and that, moreover, Rosinante, as is the happiness of most Spanish horses, fat or lean, – was undoubtedly a horse at all points.

I know very well that the Hero's horse was a horse of chaste deportment, which may have given grounds for the contrary opinion: But it is as certain at the same time, that Rosinante's continency (as may be demonstrated from the adventure of the Yanguesian carriers) proceeded from no bodily defect or cause whatsoever, but from the temperance and orderly current of his blood. – And let me tell you, Madam, there is a great deal of very good chastity in the world, in behalf of which you could not say more for your life.

Let that be as it may, as my purpose is to do exact justice to every creature brought upon the stage of this dramatic work, – I could not stifle this distinction in favour of Don Quixote's horse;—in all other points, the parson's horse, I say, was just such another, – for he was as lean, and as lank, and as sorry a jade, as Humility herself could have bestrided.

In the estimation of here and there a man of weak judgment, it was greatly in the parson's power to have helped the figure of this horse of his, – for he was master of a very handsome demi-peaked saddle, quilted on the seat with green plush, garnished with a double row of silver-headed studs, and a noble pair of shining brass stirrups, with a housing altogether suitable, of grey superfine cloth, with an edging of black lace, terminating in a deep, black, silk fringe, *poudré d'or*, – all which he had purchased in the pride and prime of his life, together with a grand embossed bridle, ornamented at all points as it should be.—But not caring to banter his beast, he had hung all these up behind his study door: – and, in lieu of them, had seriously befitted him with just such a bridle and such a saddle, as the figure and value of such a steed might well and truly deserve.

In the several sallies about his parish, and in the neighbouring visits to the gentry who lived around him, – you will easily comprehend, that the parson, so appointed, would both hear and see enough to keep his philosophy from rusting. To speak the truth, he never could enter a village, but he caught the attention of both old and young.— Labour stood still as he passed – the bucket hung suspended in the middle of the well, – the spinning-wheel forgot its round,—even chuck-farthing and shuffle-cap themselves stood gaping till he had got out of sight; and as his movement was not of the quickest, he had generally time enough upon his hands to make his observations, – to hear the groans of the serious, – and the laughter of the light-hearted; – all which he bore with excellent tranquillity. – His character was, – he loved a jest in his heart – and as he saw himself in the true point of ridicule, he would say he could not be angry with others for seeing him in a light, in which he so strongly saw himself: So that to his friends, who knew his foible was not the love of money, and who therefore made the less scruple in bantering the extravagance of his humour – instead of giving the true cause, – he chose rather to join in the laugh against himself; and as he never carried one single ounce of flesh upon his own bones, being altogether as spare a figure as his beast, – he would sometimes insist upon it, that the horse was as good as the rider deserved; – that they were, centaur-like, – both of a piece. At other times, and in other moods, when his spirits were above the temptation of false wit, – he would say, he found himself going off fast in a consumption; and, with great gravity, would pretend, he could not bear the sight of a fat horse, without a dejection of heart, and a sensible alteration in his pulse; and that he had made choice of the lean one he rode upon, not only to keep himself in countenance, but in spirits.

At different times he would give fifty humorous and apposite reasons for riding a meek-spirited jade of a broken-winded horse, preferably to one of mettle; – for on such a one he could sit mechanically, and meditate as delightfully *de vanitate mundi et fugâ saeculi*, as with the advantage of a death's-head before him; – that, in all other exercitations, he could spend his time, as he rode slowly along, – to as much account as in his study; – that he could draw up an argument in his sermon, – or a hole in his breeches, as steadily on the one as in the other; – that brisk trotting and slow argumentation, like wit and judgment, were two incompatible movements. – But that upon his steed – he could unite and reconcile every thing, – he could compose his sermon, – he could compose his cough,—and, in case nature gave a call that way, he could likewise compose himself to sleep. In short, the parson upon such encounters would assign any cause but the true cause, – and he withheld the true one, only out of a nicety of temper, because he thought it did honour to him.

But the truth of the story was as follows: In the first years of this gentleman's life, and about the time when the superb saddle and bridle were purchased by him, it had been his manner, or vanity, or call it what you will, – to run into the opposite extreme. – In the language of the county where he dwelt, he was said to have loved a good horse, and generally had one of the best in the whole parish standing in his stable always ready for saddling; and as the nearest midwife, as I told you, did not live nearer to the village than seven miles, and in a vile country, – it so fell out that the poor gentleman was scarce a whole week together without some piteous application for his beast; and as he was not an unkind-hearted man, and every case was more pressing and more distressful than the last, – as much as he loved his beast, he had never a heart to refuse him; the upshot of which was generally this, that his horse was either clapped, or spavined, or greazed; – or he was twitter-boned, or broken-winded, or something, in short, or other had befallen him, which would let him carry no flesh; – so that he had every nine or ten months a bad horse to get rid of, – and a good horse to purchase in his stead.

What the loss in such a balance might amount to, *communibus annis*, I would leave to a special jury of sufferers in the same traffic, to determine; – but let it be what it would, the honest gentleman bore it for many years without a murmur, till at length, by repeated ill accidents of the kind, he found it necessary to take the thing under consideration; and upon weighing the whole, and summing it up in his mind, he found it not only disproportioned to his other expenses, but withal so heavy an article in itself, as to disable him from any other act of generosity in his parish: Besides this, he considered that with half the sum thus galloped away, he could do ten times as much good; – and what still weighed more with him than all other considerations put together, was this, that it confined all his charity into one particular channel, and where, as he fancied, it was the least wanted, namely to the child-bearing and child-getting part of his parish; reserving nothing for the impotent, – nothing for the aged, – nothing for the many comfortless scenes he was hourly called forth to visit, where poverty, and sickness, and affliction dwelt together.

For these reasons he resolved to discontinue the expense; and there appeared but two possible ways to extricate him clearly out of it; – and these were, either to make it an irrevocable law never more to lend his steed upon any application whatever, – or else be content to ride the last poor devil, such as they had made him, with all his aches and infirmities, to the very end of the chapter.

As he dreaded his own constancy in the first – he very cheerfully betook himself to the second; and though he could very well have explained it, as I said, to his honour, – yet, for that very reason, he had a spirit above it; choosing rather to bear the contempt of his enemies, and the laughter of his friends, than undergo the pain of telling a story, which might seem a panegyric upon himself.

I have the highest idea of the spiritual and refined sentiments of this reverend gentleman, from this single stroke in his character, which I think comes up to any of the honest refinements of the peerless knight of La Mancha, whom, by the bye, with all his follies, I love more, and would actually have gone farther to have paid a visit to, than the greatest hero of antiquity.

But this is not the moral of my story: The thing I had in view was to shew the temper of the world in the whole of this affair. – For you must know, that so long as this explanation would have done the parson credit, – the devil a soul could find it out, – I suppose his enemies would not, and that his friends could not.—But no sooner did he bestir himself in behalf of the midwife, and pay the expenses of the ordinary's licence to set her up, – but the whole secret came out; every horse he had lost, and two horses more than ever he had lost, with all the circumstances of their destruction, were known and distinctly remembered. – The story ran like wildfire – 'The parson had a returning fit of pride which had just seized him; and he was going to be well mounted once again in his life; and if it was so, 'twas plain as the sun at noon-day, he would pocket the expense of the licence, ten times told, the very first year: – So that every body was left to judge what were his views in this act of charity.'

What were his views in this, and in every other action of his life, – or rather what were the opinions which floated in the brains of other people concerning it, was a thought which too much floated in his own, and too often broke in upon his rest, when he should have been sound asleep.

About ten years ago this gentleman had the good fortune to be made entirely easy upon that score, – it being just so long since he left his parish, – and the whole world at the same time behind him, – and stands accountable to a Judge of whom he will have no cause to complain.

But there is a fatality attends the actions of some men. Order them as they will, they pass thro' a certain medium, which so twists and refracts them from their true directions— that, with all the titles to praise which a rectitude of heart can give, the doers of them are nevertheless forced to live and die without it.

Of the truth of which, this gentleman was a painful example.—But to know by what means this came to pass, – and to make that knowledge of use to you, I insist upon it that you read the two following chapters, which contain such a sketch of his life and conversation, as will carry its moral along with it. – When this is done, if nothing stops us in our way, we will go on with the midwife.

II

Yorick was this parson's name, and, what is very remarkable in it, (as appears from a most ancient account of the family, wrote upon strong vellum, and now in perfect preservation) it had been exactly so spelt for near,—I was within an ace of saying nine hundred years;—but I would not shake my credit in telling an improbable truth, however indisputable in itself; – and therefore I shall content myself with only saying – It had been exactly so spelt, without the least variation or transposition of a single letter, for I do not know how long; which is more than I would venture to say of one half of the best surnames in the kingdom; which, in a course of years, have generally undergone as many chops and changes as their owners. – Has this been owing to the pride, or to the shame of the respective proprietors? – In honest truth, I think sometimes to the one, and sometimes to the other, just as the temptation has wrought. But a villainous affair it is, and will one day so blend and confound us altogether, that no one shall be able to stand up and swear, 'That his own great grandfather was the man who did either this or that.'

This evil had been sufficiently fenced against by the prudent care of the Yorick's family, and their religious preservation of these records I quote, which do farther inform us, That the family was originally of Danish extraction, and had been transplanted into England as early as in the reign of Horwendillus, king of Denmark, in whose court, it seems, an ancestor of this Mr Yorick's, and from whom he was lineally descended, held a considerable post to the day of his death. Of what nature this considerable post was, this record saith not; – It only adds, That, for near two centuries, it had been totally abolished, as altogether unnecessary, not only in that court, but in every other court of the Christian world.

It has often come into my head, that this post could be no other than that of the king's chief Jester; – and that Hamlet's Yorick, in our Shakespeare, many of whose plays, you know, are founded upon authenticated facts, was certainly the very man.

I have not the time to look into Saxo-Grammaticus's Danish history to know the certainty of this; – but if you have leisure, and can easily get at the book, you may do it full as well yourself.

I had just time, in my travels through Denmark with Mr Noddy's eldest son, whom, in the year 1741, I accompanied as governor, riding along with him at a prodigious rate thro' most parts of Europe, and of which original journey performed by us two, a most delectable narrative will be given in the progress of this work; I had just time, I say, and that was all, to prove the truth of an observation made by a long sojourner in that country;—namely, 'That nature was neither very lavish, nor was she very stingy in her gifts of genius and capacity to its inhabitants; – but, like a discreet parent, was moderately kind to them all; observing such an equal tenor in the distribution of her favours, as to bring them, in those points, pretty near to a level with each other; so that you will meet with few instances in that kingdom of refined parts; but a great deal of good plain household understanding amongst all ranks of people, of which every body has a share'; which is, I think, very right.

With us, you see, the case is quite different: – we are all ups and downs in this matter; – you are a great genius; or 'tis fifty to one, Sir, you are a great dunce and a blockhead; – not that there is a total want of intermediate steps, – no, – we are not so irregular as that comes to; – but the two extremes are more common, and in a greater degree in this unsettled island, where nature, in her gifts and dispositions of this kind, is most whimsical and capricious; fortune herself not being more so in the bequest of her goods and chattels than she.

This is all that ever staggered my faith in regard to Yorick's extraction, who, by what I can remember of him, and by all the accounts I could ever get of him, seemed not to have had one single drop of Danish blood in his whole crasis; in nine hundred years, it might possibly have all run out:—I will not philosophize one moment with you about it; for happen how it would, the fact was this: – That instead of that cold phlegm and exact regularity of sense and humours, you would have looked for, in one so extracted; – he was, on the contrary, as mercurial and sublimated a composition, – as heteroclite a creature in all his declensions; – with as much life and whim, and *gaité de coeur* about him, as the kindliest climate could have engendered and put together. With all this sail, poor Yorick carried not one ounce of ballast; he was utterly unpractised in the world; and, at the age of twenty-six, knew just about as well how to steer his course in it, as a romping, unsuspicious girl of thirteen: So that upon his first setting out, the brisk gale of his spirits, as you will imagine, ran him foul ten times in a day of somebody's tackling; and as the grave and more slow-paced were oftenest in his way,—you may likewise imagine, 'twas with such he had generally the ill luck to get the most entangled. For aught I know there might be some mixture of unlucky wit at the bottom of such Fracas:—For, to speak the truth, Yorick had an invincible dislike and opposition in his nature to gravity; – not to gravity as such; – for where gravity was wanted, he would be the most grave or serious of mortal men for days and weeks together; – but he was an enemy to the affectation of it, and declared open war against it, only as it appeared a cloak for ignorance, or for folly: and then, whenever it fell in his way, however sheltered and protected, he seldom gave it much quarter.

Sometimes, in his wild way of talking, he would say, that Gravity was an errant scoundrel, and he would add, – of the most dangerous kind too, – because a sly one; and that he verily believed, more honest, well-meaning people were bubbled out of their goods and money by it in one twelve-month, than by pocket-picking and shop-lifting in seven. In the naked temper which a merry heart discovered, he would say there was no danger, – but to itself: – whereas the very essence of gravity was design, and consequently deceit; – 'twas a taught trick to gain credit of the world for more sense and knowledge than a man was worth; and that, with all its pretensions, – it was no better, but often worse, than what a French wit had long ago defined it, – viz. 'A mysterious carriage of the body to cover the defects of the mind'; – which definition of gravity, Yorick, with great imprudence, would say, deserved to be wrote in letters of gold.

But, in plain truth, he was a man unhackneyed and unpractised in the world, and was altogether as indiscreet and foolish on every other subject of discourse where policy is wont to impress restraint. Yorick had no impression but one, and that was what arose from the nature of the deed spoken of; which impression he would usually translate into plain English without any periphrasis; – and too oft without much distinction of either person, time, or place; – so that when mention was made of a pitiful or an ungenerous proceeding—he never gave himself a moment's time to reflect who was the hero of the piece,—what his station,—or how far he had power to hurt him hereafter;—but if it was a dirty action, – without more ado, – The man was a dirty fellow, – and so on. – And as his comments had usually the ill fate to be terminated either in a *bon mot*, or to be enlivened throughout with some drollery or humour of expression, it gave wings to Yorick's indiscretion. In a word, tho' he never sought, yet, at the same time, as he seldom shunned occasions of saying what came uppermost, and without much ceremony:—he had but too many temptations in life, of scattering his wit and his humour, – his gibes and his jests about him.—They were not lost for want of gathering.

What were the consequences, and what was Yorick's catastrophe thereupon, you will read in the next chapter.

12

The Mortgager and Mortgagée differ the one from the other, not more in length of purse, than the Jester and Jestée do, in that of memory. But in this the comparison between them runs, as the scholiasts call it, upon all-four; which, by the bye, is upon one or two legs more than some of the best of Homer's can pretend to; – namely, That the one raises a sum, and the other a laugh at your expense, and thinks no more about it. Interest, however, still runs on in both cases; – the periodical or accidental payments of it, just serving to keep the memory of the affair alive; till, at length, in some evil hour, – pop comes the creditor upon each, and by demanding principal upon the spot, together with full interest to the very day, makes them both feel the full extent of their obligations.

As the reader (for I hate your *ifs*) has a thorough knowledge of human nature, I need not say more to satisfy him, that my Hero could not go on at this rate without some slight experience of these incidental mementos. To speak the truth, he had wantonly involved himself in a multitude of small book-debts of this stamp, which, notwithstanding Eugenius's frequent advice, he too much disregarded; thinking, that as not one of them was contracted thro' any malignancy; – but, on the contrary, from an honesty of mind, and a mere jocundity of humour, they would all of them be crossed out in course.

Eugenius would never admit this; and would often tell him, that one day or other he would certainly be reckoned with; and he would often add, in an accent of sorrowful apprehension, – to the uttermost mite. To which Yorick, with his usual carelessness of heart, would as often answer with a pshaw! – and if the subject was started in the fields, – with a hop, skip, and a jump at the end of it; but if close pent up in the social chimney-corner, where the culprit was barricadoed in, with a table and a couple of arm-chairs, and could not so readily fly off in a tangent, – Eugenius would then go on with his lecture upon discretion in words to this purpose, though somewhat better put together.

Trust me, dear Yorick, this unwary pleasantry of thine will sooner or later bring thee into scrapes and difficulties, which no after-wit can extricate thee out of.—In these sallies, too oft, I see, it happens, that a person laughed at, considers himself in the light of a person injured, with all the rights of such a situation belonging to him; and when thou viewest him in that light too, and reckons up his friends, his family, his kindred and allies,—and musters up with them the many recruits which will list under him from a sense of common danger;—'tis no extravagant arithmetic to say, that for every ten jokes, – thou hast got an hundred enemies; and till thou hast gone on, and raised a swarm of wasps about thine ears, and art half stung to death by them, thou wilt never be convinced it is so.

I cannot suspect it in the man whom I esteem, that there is the least spur from spleen or malevolence of intent in these sallies—I believe and know them to be truly honest and sportive: – But consider, my dear lad, that fools cannot distinguish this, – and that knaves will not: and thou knowest not what it is, either to provoke the one, or to make merry with the other:—whenever they associate for mutual defence, depend upon it, they will carry on the war in such a manner against thee, my dear friend, as to make thee heartily sick of it, and of thy life too.

Revenge from some baneful corner shall level a tale of dishonour at thee, which no innocence of heart or integrity of conduct shall set right.—The fortunes of thy house shall totter, – thy character, which led the way to them, shall bleed on every side of it, – thy faith questioned, – thy works belied, – thy wit forgotten, – thy learning trampled on. To wind up the last scene of thy tragedy, Cruelty and Cowardice, twin ruffians, hired and set on by Malice in the dark, shall strike together at all thy infirmities and mistakes:—

The best of us, my dear lad, lie open there,—and trust me,—trust me, Yorick, when to gratify a private appetite, it is once resolved upon, that an innocent and an helpless creature shall be sacrificed, 'tis an easy matter to pick up sticks enough from any thicket where it has strayed, to make a fire to offer it up with.

Yorick scarce ever heard this sad vatication of his destiny read over to him, but with a tear stealing from his eye, and a promissory look attending it, that he was resolved, for the time to come, to ride his tit with more sobriety. – But, alas, too late! – a grand confederacy, with ***** and ***** at the head of it, was formed before the first prediction of it. – The whole plan of the attack, just as Eugenius had forboded, was put in execution all at once, – with so little mercy on the side of the allies, – and so little suspicion in Yorick, of what was carrying on against him, – that when he thought, good easy man! full surely preferment was o' ripening, – they had smote his root, and then he fell, as many a worthy man had fallen before him.

Yorick, however, fought it out with all imaginable gallantry for some time; till, overpowered by numbers, and worn out at length by the calamities of the war, – but more so, by the ungenerous manner in which it was carried on, – he threw down the sword; and though he kept up his spirits in appearance to the last, he died, nevertheless, as was generally thought, quite broken-hearted.

What inclined Eugenius to the same opinion was as follows:

A few hours before Yorick breathed his last, Eugenius stept in with an intent to take his last sight and last farewell of him. Upon his drawing Yorick's curtain, and asking how he felt himself, Yorick looking up in his face took hold of his hand, – and after thanking him for the many tokens of his friendship to him, for which, he said, if it was their fate to meet hereafter, – he would thank him again and again, – he told him, he was within a few hours of giving his enemies the slip for ever. – I hope not, answered Eugenius, with tears trickling down his cheeks, and with the tenderest tone that ever man spoke. – I hope not, Yorick, said he.—Yorick replied, with a look up, and a gentle squeeze of Eugenius's hand, and that was all, – but it cut Eugenius to his heart. – Come, – come, Yorick, quoth Eugenius, wiping his eyes, and summoning up the man within him, – my dear lad, be comforted, – let not all thy spirits and fortitude forsake thee at this crisis when thou most wants them; – who knows what resources are in store, and what the power of God may yet do for thee?—Yorick laid his hand upon his heart, and gently shook his head; – For my part, continued Eugenius, crying bitterly as he uttered the words, – I declare I know not, Yorick, how to part with thee, and would gladly flatter my hopes, added Eugenius, cheering up his voice, that there is still enough left of thee to make a bishop, and that I may live to see it.—I beseech thee, Eugenius, quoth Yorick, taking off his night-cap as well as he could with his left hand, – his right being still grasped close in that of Eugenius,—I beseech thee to take a view of my head. – I see nothing that ails it, replied Eugenius. Then, alas! my friend, said Yorick, let me tell you, that 'tis so bruised and mis-shapened with the blows which ***** and *****, and some others have so unhandsomely given me in the dark, that I might say with Sancho Pança, that should I recover, and 'Mitres thereupon be suffered to rain down from heaven as thick as hail, not one of them would fit it.'—Yorick's last breath was hanging upon his trembling lips ready to depart as he uttered this: – yet still it was uttered with something of a Cervantick tone; – and as he spoke it, Eugenius could perceive a stream of lambent fire lighted up for a moment in his eyes; – faint picture of those flashes of his spirit, which (as Shakespeare said of his ancestor) were wont to set the table in a roar!

Eugenius was convinced from this, that the heart of his friend was broke: he squeezed his hand,—and then walked softly out of the room, weeping as he walked. Yorick followed Eugenius with his eyes to the door, – he then closed them, – and never opened them more.

He lies buried in the corner of his church-yard, in the parish of——, under a plain marble slab, which his friend Eugenius, by leave of his executors, laid upon his grave, with no more than these three words of inscription, serving both for his epitaph and elegy,

Alas, poor YORICK!

Ten times a day has Yorick's ghost the consolation to hear his monumental inscription read over with such a variety of plaintive tones, as denote a general pity and esteem for him;—a foot-way crossing the church-yard close by the side of his grave, – not a passenger goes by without stopping to cast a look upon it, – and sighing as he walks on,

Alas, poor YORICK!

13

It is so long since the reader of this rhapsodical work has been parted from the midwife, that it is high time to mention her again to him, merely to put him in mind that there is such a body still in the world, and whom, upon the best judgment I can form upon my own plan at present, – I am going to introduce to him for good and all: But as fresh matter may be started, and much unexpected business fall out betwixt the reader and myself, which may require immediate dispatch;—'twas right to take care that the poor woman should not be lost in the meantime; – because when she is wanted we can no way do without her.

I think I told you that this good woman was a person of no small note and consequence throughout our whole village and township; – that her fame had spread itself to the very out-edge and circumference of that circle of importance, of which kind every soul living, whether he has a shirt to his back or no,—has one surrounding him; – which said circle, by the way, whenever 'tis said that such a one is of great weight and importance in the world,—I desire may be enlarged or contracted in your worship's fancy, in a compound ratio of the station, profession, knowledge, abilities, height and depth (measuring both ways) of the personage brought before you.

In the present case, if I remember, I fixed it about four or five miles, which not only comprehended the whole parish, but extended itself to two or three of the adjacent hamlets in the skirts of the next parish; which made a considerable thing of it. I must add, That she was, moreover, very well looked on at one large grange-house, and some other odd houses and farms within two or three miles, as I said, from the smoke of her own chimney:—But I must here, once for all, inform you, that all this will be more exactly delineated and explained in a map, now in the hands of the engraver, which with many other pieces and developements of this work, will be added to the end of the twentieth volume, – not to swell the work, – I detest the thought of such a thing; – but by way of commentary, scholium, illustration, and key to such passages, incidents, or innuendos as shall be thought to be either of private interpretation, or of dark or doubtful meaning, after my life and my opinions shall have been read over (now don't forget the meaning of the word) by all the world; – which, betwixt you and me, and in spite of all the gentlemen-reviewers in Great Britain, and of all that their worships shall undertake to write or say to the contrary, – I am determined shall be the case. – I need not tell your worship, that all this is spoke in confidence.

14

Upon looking into my mother's marriage-settlement, in order to satisfy myself and reader in a point necessary to be cleared up, before we could proceed any farther in this history; – I had the good fortune to pop upon the very thing I wanted before I had read a day and a half straight forwards, – it might have taken me up a month; – which shews plainly that when a man sits down to write a history, – tho' it be but the history of Jack Hickathrift or Tom Thumb, he knows no more than his heels what lets and confounded hindrances he is to meet with in his way, – or what a dance he may be led, by one excursion or another, before all is over. Could a historiographer drive on his history, as a muleteer drives on his mule, – straight forward;—for instance, from Rome all the way to Loretto, without ever once turning his head aside either to the right hand or to the left,—he might venture to foretell you to an hour when he should get to his journey's end:—but the thing is, morally speaking, impossible: For, if he is a man of the least spirit he will have fifty deviations from a straight line to make with this or that party as he goes along, which he can no ways avoid. He will have views and prospects to himself perpetually soliciting his eye, which he can no more help standing still to look at than he can fly; he will moreover have various

Accounts to reconcile:

Anecdotes to pick up:

Inscriptions to make out:

Stories to weave in:

Traditions to sift:

Personages to call upon:

Panegyrics to paste up at this door;

Pasquinades at that:—All which both the man and his mule are quite exempt from. To sum up all; there are archives at every stage to be looked into, and rolls, records, documents, and endless genealogies, which justice ever and anon calls him back to stay the reading of: – In short, there is no end of it; – for my own part, I declare I have been at it these six weeks, making all the speed I possibly could, – and am not yet born: – I have just been able, and that's all, to tell you *when* it happened, but not *how*, – so that you see the thing is yet far from being accomplished.

These unforeseen stoppages, which I own I had no conception of when I first set out; – but which, I am convinced now, will rather increase than diminish as I advance, – have struck out a hint which I am resolved to follow; – and that is, – not to be in a hurry; but to go on leisurely, writing and publishing two volumes of my life every year; – which, if I am suffered to go on quietly, and can make a tolerable bargain with my bookseller, I shall continue to do as long as I live.

15

The article in my mother's marriage-settlement, which I told the reader I was at the pains to search for, and which, now that I have found it, I think proper to lay before him, – is so much more fully expressed in the deed itself, than ever I can pretend to do it, that it would be barbarity to take it out of the lawyer's hand: – It is as follows.

'𝕬𝖓𝖉 𝖙𝖍𝖎𝖘 𝕴𝖓𝖉𝖊𝖓𝖙𝖚𝖗𝖊 𝖋𝖚𝖗𝖙𝖍𝖊𝖗 𝖜𝖎𝖙𝖓𝖊𝖘𝖘𝖊𝖙𝖍, That the said Walter Shandy, merchant, in consideration of the said intended marriage to be had, and, by God's blessing, to be well and truly solemnized and consummated between the said Walter Shandy and Elizabeth Mollineux aforesaid, and divers other good and valuable causes and considerations him thereunto specially moving, – doth grant, covenant, condescend, consent, conclude, bargain, and fully agree to and with John Dixon, and James Turner, Esqrs, the above-named Trustees, &c. &c. – **to wit,** – That in case it should hereafter so fall out, chance, happen, or otherwise come to pass, – That the said Walter Shandy, merchant, shall have left off business before the time or times, that the said Elizabeth Mollineux shall, according to the course of nature or otherwise, have left off bearing and bringing forth children; – and that, in consequence of the said Walter Shandy having so left off business, he shall in despite, and against the free-will, consent, and good-liking of the said Elizabeth Mollineux, – make a departure from the city of London, in order to retire to, and dwell upon, his estate at Shandy Hall, in the county of—, or at any other country-seat, castle, hall, mansion-house, messuage or grange-house, now purchased, or hereafter to be purchased, or upon any part or parcel thereof: – That then, and as often as the said Elizabeth Mollineux shall happen to be enceint with child or children severally and lawfully begot, or to be begotten, upon the body of the said Elizabeth Mollineux, during her said coverture, – he the said Walter Shandy shall, at his own proper cost and charges, and out of his own proper monies, upon good and reasonable notice, which is hereby agreed to be within six weeks of her the said Elizabeth Mollineux's full reckoning, or time of supposed and computed delivery, – pay, or cause to be paid, the sum of one hundred and twenty pounds of good and lawful money, to John Dixon, and James Turner, Esqrs or assigns, – upon TRUST and confidence, and for and unto the use and uses, intent, end, and purpose following: – **That is to say,** – That the said sum of one hundred and twenty pounds shall be paid into the hands of the said Elizabeth Mollineux, or to be otherwise applied by them the said Trustees, for the well and truly hiring of one coach, with able and sufficient horses, to carry and convey the body of the said Elizabeth Mollineux, and the child or children which she shall be then and there enceint and pregnant with, – unto the city of London; and for the further paying and defraying of all other incidental costs, charges, and expenses whatsoever, – in and about, and for, and relating to, her said intended delivery and lying-in, in the said city or suburbs thereof. And that the said Elizabeth Mollineux shall and may, from time to time, and at all such time and times as are here covenanted and agreed upon, – peaceably and quietly hire the said coach and horses, and have free ingress, egress, and regress throughout her journey, in and from the said coach, according to the tenor, true intent, and meaning of these presents, without any let, suit, trouble, disturbance, molestation, discharge, hindrance, forfeiture, eviction, vexation, interruption, or incumbrance whatsoever. – And that it shall moreover be lawful to and for the said Elizabeth Mollineux, from time to time, and as oft or often as she shall well and truly be advanced in her said pregnancy, to the time heretofore stipulated and agreed upon, – to live and reside in such place or places, and in such family or families, and with such relations, friends, and other persons within the said city of London, as she at her own will and pleasure, notwithstanding her present coverture, and as if she was a *femme sole* and unmarried, – shall think fit. – **And this Indenture further witnesseth,** That for the more effectually carrying of the said covenant into execution, the said Walter Shandy, merchant, doth hereby grant, bargain, sell, release, and confirm unto the said John Dixon, and James Turner, Esqrs their heirs, executors, and assigns, in their actual possession now being, by virtue of an indenture of bargain and sale for a year to them the said John Dixon, and James Turner, Esqrs by him the said Walter Shandy, merchant, thereof made; which said bargain and sale for a year, bears date the day next before the date of these presents, and by force and virtue of the statute for transferring of uses into possession, – **All** that the manor and lordship of Shandy, in the county of—, with all the rights, members, and appurtenances thereof; and all and every the messuages, houses, buildings, barns, stables, orchards, gardens, backsides, tofts, crofts, garths, cottages, lands, meadows, feedings, pastures, marshes, commons, woods, underwoods, drains, fisheries, waters, and water-courses; – together with all rents, reversions, services, annuities, fee-farms, knights' fees, views of frankpledge, escheats, reliefs, mines, quarries, goods and chattels of felons and fugitives, felons of themselves, and put in exigent, deodands, free warrens, and all other royalties and seigniories, rights and jurisdictions, privileges and heredita-ments whatsoever.—**And also** the advowson, donation, presentation, and free dispo-sition of the rectory or parsonage of Shandy aforesaid, and all and every the tenths, tithes, glebe-lands.'—In three words,—'My mother was to lay in, (if she chose it) in London.'

But in order to put a stop to the practice of any unfair play on the part of my mother, which a marriage-article of this nature too manifestly opened a door to, and which indeed had never been thought of at all, but for my uncle Toby Shandy; – a clause was added in security of my father, which was this: – 'That in case my mother hereafter should, at any time, put my father to the trouble and expense of a London journey, upon false cries and tokens;—that for every such instance, she should forfeit all the right and title which the covenant gave her to the next turn;—but to no more, – and so on, *toties quoties*, in as effectual a manner, as if such a covenant betwixt them had not been made.' – This, by the way, was no more than what was reasonable; – and yet, as reasonable as it was, I have ever thought it hard that the whole weight of the article should have fallen entirely, as it did, upon myself.

But I was begot and born to misfortunes: – for my poor mother, whether it was wind or water – or a compound of both, – or neither; – or whether it was simply the mere swell of imagination and fancy in her; – or how far a strong wish and desire to have it so, might mislead her judgment: – in short, whether she was deceived or deceiving in this matter, it no way becomes me to decide. The fact was this, That in the latter end of September 1717, which was the year before I was born, my mother having carried my father up to town much against the grain, – he peremptorily insisted upon the clause; – so that I was doomed, by marriage-articles, to have my nose squeezed as flat to my face, as if the destinies had actually spun me without one.

How this event came about, – and what a train of vexatious disappointments, in one stage or other of my life, have pursued me from the mere loss, or rather compression, of this one single member, – shall be laid before the reader all in due time.

16

My father, as any body may naturally imagine, came down with my mother into the country, in but a pettish kind of a humour. The first twenty or five-and-twenty miles he did nothing in the world but fret and teaze himself, and indeed my mother too, about the cursed expense, which he said might every shilling of it have been saved; – then what vexed him more than every thing else was, the provoking time of the year, – which, as I told you, was towards the end of September, when his wall-fruit and green gages especially, in which he was very curious, were just ready for pulling:—'Had he been whistled up to London, upon a Tom Fool's errand, in any other month of the whole year, he should not have said three words about it.'

For the next two whole stages, no subject would go down, but the heavy blow he had sustained from the loss of a son, whom it seems he had fully reckoned upon in his mind, and registered down in his pocket-book, as a second staff for his old age, in case Bobby should fail him. The disappointment of this, he said, was ten times more to a wise man, than all the money which the journey, etc., had cost him, put together, – rot the hundred and twenty pounds,—he did not mind it a rush.

From Stilton, all the way to Grantham, nothing in the whole affair provoked him so much as the condolences of his friends, and the foolish figure they should both make at church, the first Sunday;—of which, in the satirical vehemence of his wit, now sharpened a little by vexation, he would give so many humorous and provoking descriptions, – and place his rib and self in so many tormenting lights and attitudes in the face of the whole congregation; – that my mother declared, these two stages were so truly tragi-comical, that she did nothing but laugh and cry in a breath, from one end to the other of them all the way.

From Grantham, till they had crossed the Trent, my father was out of all kind of patience at the vile trick and imposition which he fancied my mother had put upon him in this affair – 'Certainly,' he would say to himself, over and over again, 'the woman could not be deceived herself—if she could,—what weakness!' – tormenting word! – which led his imagination a thorny dance, and before all was over, played the deuce and all with him; – for sure as ever the word weakness was uttered, and struck full upon his brain – so sure it set him upon running divisions upon how many kinds of weaknesses there were; – that there was such a thing as weakness of the body, – as well as weakness of the mind, – and then he would do nothing but syllogize within himself for a stage or two together, How far the cause of all these vexations might, or might not, have arisen out of himself.

In short, he had so many little subjects of disquietude springing out of this one affair, all fretting successively in his mind as they rose up in it, that my mother, whatever was her journey up, had but an uneasy journey of it down. – In a word, as she complained to my uncle Toby, he would have tired out the patience of any flesh alive.

17

Though my father travelled homewards, as I told you, in none of the best of moods, – pshawing and pishing all the way down, – yet he had the complaisance to keep the worst part of the story still to himself; – which was the resolution he had taken of doing himself the justice, which my uncle Toby's clause in the marriage-settlement empowered him; nor was it till the very night in which I was begot, which was thirteen months after, that she had the least intimation of his design: when my father, happening, as you remember, to be a little chagrined and out of temper, – took occasion as they lay chatting gravely in bed afterwards, talking over what was to come,—to let her know that she must accommodate herself as well as she could to the bargain made between them in their marriage-deeds; which was to lie-in of her next child in the country, to balance the last year's journey.

My father was a gentleman of many virtues, – but he had a strong spice of that in his temper, which might, or might not, add to the number. – 'Tis known by the name of perseverance in a good cause, – and of obstinacy in a bad one: Of this my mother had so much knowledge, that she knew 'twas to no purpose to make any remonstrance, – so she e'en resolved to sit down quietly, and make the most of it.

18

As the point was that night agreed, or rather determined, that my mother should lie-in of me in the country, she took her measures accordingly; for which purpose, when she was three days, or thereabouts, gone with child, she began to cast her eyes upon the midwife, whom you have so often heard me mention; and before the week was well got round, as the famous Dr Manningham was not to be had, she had to come to a final determination in her mind, – notwithstanding there was a scientific operator within so near a call as eight miles of us, and who, moreover, had expressly wrote a five shillings book upon the subject of midwifery, in which he had exposed, not only the blunders of the sisterhood itself, – but had likewise super-added many curious improvements for the quicker extraction of the foetus in cross births, and some other cases of danger, which belay us in getting into the world; notwithstanding all this, my mother, I say, was absolutely determined to trust her life, and mine with it, into no soul's hand but this old woman's only. – Now this I like; – when we cannot get at the very thing we wish – never to take up with the next best in degree to it: – no; that's pitiful beyond description; – it is no more than a week from this very day, in which I am now writing this book for the edification of the world; – which is March 9, 1759,—that my dear, dear Jenny, observing I looked a little grave, as she stood cheapening a silk of five-and-twenty shillings a yard, – told the mercer, she was sorry she had given him so much trouble; – and immediately went and bought herself a yard-wide stuff of ten-pence a yard. – 'Tis the duplication of one and the same greatness of soul; only what lessened the honour of it, somewhat, in my mother's case, was that she could not heroine it into so violent and hazardous an extreme, as one in her situation might have wished, because the old midwife had really some little claim to be depended upon, – as much, at least, as success could give her; having, in the course of her practice of near twenty years in the parish, brought every mother's son of them into the world without any one slip or accident which could fairly be laid to her account.

These facts, tho' they had their weight, yet did not altogether satisfy some few scruples and uneasiness which hung upon my father's spirits in relation to this choice. – To say nothing of the natural workings of humanity and justice – or of the yearnings of parental and connubial love, all which prompted him to leave as little to hazard as possible in a case of this kind; – he felt himself concerned in a particular manner, that all should go right in the present case; – from the accumulated sorrow he lay open to, should any evil betide his wife and child in lying-in at Shandy-Hall. – He knew the world judged by events and would add to his afflictions in such a misfortune, by loading him with the whole blame of it.—'Alas o'day; – had Mrs Shandy, poor gentlewoman! had but her wish in going up to town just to lie-in and come down again; – which, they say, she begged and prayed for upon her bare knees, – and which, in my opinion, considering the fortune which Mr Shandy got with her, – was no such mighty matter to have complied with, the lady and her babe might both of 'em have been alive at this hour.'

This exclamation, my father knew, was unanswerable; – and yet, it was not merely to shelter himself, – nor was it altogether for the care of his offspring and wife that he seemed so extremely anxious about this point; – my father had extensive views of things,—and stood moreover, as he thought, deeply concerned in it for the public good, from the dread he entertained of the bad uses an ill-fated instance might be put to.

He was very sensible that all political writers upon the subject had unanimously agreed and lamented, from the beginning of Queen Elizabeth's reign down to his own time, that the current of men and money towards the metropolis, upon one frivolous errand or another, – set in so strong, – as to become dangerous to our civil rights, – though, by the bye, – a current was not the image he took most delight in, – a distemper was here his favourite metaphor, and he would run it down into a perfect allegory, by maintaining it was identically the same in the body national as in the body natural, where the blood and spirits were driven up into the head faster than they could find their ways down;—a stoppage of circulation must ensue, which was death in both cases.

There was little danger, he would say, of losing our liberties by French politics or French invasions; – nor was he so much in pain of a consumption from the mass of corrupted matter and ulcerated humours in our constitution, which he hoped was not so bad as it was imagined; – but he verily feared, that in some violent push, we should go off, all at once, in a state-apoplexy; – and then he would say, 'The Lord have mercy upon us all.'

My father was never able to give the history of this distemper, – without the remedy along with it.

'Was I an absolute prince,' he would say, pulling up his breeches with both his hands, as he rose from his arm-chair, 'I would appoint able judges, at every avenue of my metropolis, who should take cognizance of every fool's business who came there; – and if, upon a fair and candid hearing, it appeared not of weight sufficient to leave his own home, and come up, bag and baggage, with his wife and children, farmer's sons, etc. etc., at his backside, they should all be sent back, from constable to constable, like vagrants as they were, to the place of their legal settlements. By this means I shall take care, that my metropolis tottered not thro' its own weight; – that the head be no longer too big for the body; – that the extremes, now wasted and pinned in, be restored to their due share of nourishment, and regain with it their natural strength and beauty: – I would effectually provide, That the meadows and corn-fields of my dominions, should laugh and sing; – that good cheer and hospitality flourish once more; – and that such weight and influence be put thereby into the hands of the Squirality of my kingdom, as should counterpoise what I perceive my Nobility are now taking from them.

'Why are there so few palaces and gentlemen's seats,' he would ask, with some emotion, as he walked across the room, 'throughout so many delicious provinces in France? Whence is it that the few remaining Chateaus amongst them are so dismantled, – so unfurnished, and in so ruinous and desolate a condition?—Because, Sir,' (he would say) 'in that kingdom no man has any country-interest to support; – the little interest of any kind which any man has anywhere in it, is concentrated in the court, and the looks of the Grand Monarch: by the sunshine of whose countenance, or the clouds which pass across it, every French man lives or dies.'

Another political reason which prompted my father so strongly to guard against the least evil accident in my mother's lying-in in the country,—was, That any such instance would infallibly throw a balance of power, too great already, into the weaker vessels of the gentry, in his own, or higher stations;—which, with the many other usurped rights which that part of the constitution was hourly establishing, – would, in the end, prove fatal to the monarchical system of domestic government established in the first creation of things by God.

In this point he was entirely of Sir Robert Filmer's opinion, That the plans and institutions of the greatest monarchies in the eastern parts of the world, were, originally, all stolen from that admirable pattern and prototype of this household and paternal power; – which, for a century, he said, and more, had gradually been degenerating away into a mixed government;—the form of which, however desirable in great combinations of the species,—was very troublesome in small ones, – and seldom produced anything, that he saw, but sorrow and confusion.

For all these reasons, private and public, put together, – my father was for having the man-midwife by all means, – my mother by no means. My father begged and intreated, she would for once recede from her prerogative in this matter, and suffer him to choose for her; – my mother, on the contrary, insisted upon her privilege in this matter, to choose for herself, – and have no mortal's help but the old woman's. – What could my father do? He was almost at his wit's end;—talked it over with her in all moods; – placed his arguments in all lights; – argued the matter with her like a christian, – like a heathen, – like a husband, – like a father, – like a patriot, – like a man: – My mother answered every thing only like a woman; which was a little hard upon her; – for as she could not assume and fight it out behind such a variety of characters, – 'twas no fair match: – 'twas seven to one. – What could my mother do?—She had the advantage (otherwise she had been certainly overpowered) of a small reinforcement of chagrin personal at the bottom, which bore her up, and enabled her to dispute the affair with my father with so equal an advantage,—that both sides sung *Te Deum*. In a word, my mother was to have the old woman, – and the operator was to have licence to drink a bottle of wine with my father and my uncle Toby Shandy in the back parlour, – for which he was to be paid five guineas.

I must beg leave, before I finish this chapter, to enter a caveat in the breast of my fair reader; – and it is this,—Not to take it absolutely for granted, from an unguarded word or two which I have dropped in it,—'That I am a married man.' – I own, the tender appellation of my dear, dear Jenny, – with some other strokes of conjugal knowledge, interspersed here and there, might, naturally enough, have misled the most candid judge in the world into such a determination against me. – All I plead for, in this case, Madam, is strict justice, and that you do so much of it, to me as well as to yourself, – as not to prejudge, or receive such an impression of me, till you have better evidence, than, I am positive, at present can be produced against me. – Not that I can be so vain or unreasonable, Madam, as to desire you should therefore think, that my dear, dear Jenny is my kept mistress; – no, – that would be flattering my character in the other extreme, and giving it an air of freedom, which, perhaps, it has no kind of right to. All I contend for, is the utter impossibility, for some volumes, that you, or the most penetrating spirit upon earth, should know how this matter really stands. – It is not impossible, but that my dear, dear Jenny! tender as the appellation is, may be my child.—Consider, – I was born in the year eighteen. – Nor is there anything unnatural or extravagant in the supposition, that my dear Jenny may be my friend. – Friend! – My friend. – Surely, Madam, a friendship between the two sexes may subsist, and be supported without—Fy! Mr Shandy:—Without any thing, Madam, but that tender and delicious sentiment, which ever mixes in friendship, where there is a difference of sex. Let me intreat you to study the pure and sentimental parts of the best French Romances; – it will really, Madam, astonish you to see with what a variety of chaste expressions this delicious sentiment, which I have the honour to speak of, is dressed out.

19

I would sooner undertake to explain the hardest problem in geometry, than pretend to account for it, that a gentleman of my father's great good sense,—knowing, as the reader must have observed him, and curious too in philosophy, – wise also in political reasoning, – and in polemical (as he will find) no way ignorant, – could be capable of entertaining a notion in his head, so out of the common track, – that I fear the reader, when I come to mention it to him, if he is the least of a choleric temper, will immediately throw the book by; if mercurial, he will laugh most heartily at it; – and if he is of a grave and saturnine case, he will, at first sight, absolutely condemn as fanciful and extravagant; and that was in respect to the choice and imposition of christian names, on which he thought a great deal more depended than what superficial minds were capable of conceiving.

His opinion, in this matter, was, That there was a strange kind of magic bias, which good or bad names, as he called them, irresistibly impressed upon our characters and conduct.

The hero of Cervantes argued not the point with more seriousness,—nor had he more faith,—or more to say on the powers of necromancy in dishonouring his deeds, – or on Dulcinea's name, in shedding lustre upon them, than my father had on those of Trismegistus or Archimedes, on the one hand – or of Nyky and Simkin on the other. How many Caesars and Pompeys, he would say, by mere inspiration of the names, have been rendered worthy of them? And how many, he would add, are there, who might have done exceeding well in the world, had not their characters and spirits been totally depressed and Nicodemused into nothing?

I see plainly, Sir, by your looks, (or as the case happened) my father would say – that you do not heartily subscribe to this opinion of mine, – which, to those, he would add, who have not carefully sifted it to the bottom, – I own has an air more of fancy than of solid reasoning in it;—and yet, my dear Sir, if I may presume to know your character, I am morally assured, I should hazard little in stating a case to you, – not as a party in the dispute, – but as a judge, and trusting my appeal upon it to your own good sense and candid disquisition in this matter; – you are a person free from any narrow prejudices of education as most men; – and, if I may presume to penetrate farther into you, – of a liberality of genius above bearing down an opinion, merely because it wants friends. Your son, – your dear son, – from whose sweet and open temper you have so much to expect. – Your Billy, Sir! – would you, for the world, have called him Judas? – Would you, my dear Sir, he would say, laying his hand upon your breast, with the genteelest address, – and in that soft and irresistible piano of voice, which the nature of the *argumentum ad hominem* absolutely requires, – Would you, Sir, if a Jew of a godfather had proposed the name for your child, and offered you his purse along with it, would you have consented to such a desecration of him?—O my God! he would say, looking up, if I know your temper right, Sir – you are incapable of it;—you would have trampled upon the offer; – you would have thrown the temptation at the tempter's head with abhorrence.

Your greatness of mind in this action, which I admire, with that generous contempt of money, which you shew me in the whole transaction, is really noble; – and what renders it more so, is the principle of it; – the working of a parent's love upon the truth and conviction of this very hypothesis, namely, That was your son called Judas, – the sordid and treacherous idea, so inseparable from the name, would have accompanied him through life like his shadow, and, in the end, made a miser and a rascal of him, in spite, Sir, of your example.

I never knew a man able to answer this argument.—But, indeed, to speak of my father as he was; – he was certainly irresistible; – both in his orations and disputations; – he was born an orator; – Θεοδίδακτος. – Persuasion hung upon his lips, and the elements of Logic and Rhetoric were so blended up in him, – and, withal, he had so shrewd a guess at the weaknesses and passions of his respondent,—that Nature might have stood up and said, – 'This man is eloquent.' – In short, whether he was on the weak or the strong side of the question, 'twas hazardous in either case to attack him. – And yet, 'tis strange he had never read Cicero, nor Quintilian *de Oratore*, nor Isocrates, nor Aristotle, nor Longinus amongst the ancients; – nor Vossius, nor Scioppius, nor Ramus, nor Farnaby amongst the moderns; – and what is more astonishing, he had never in his whole life the least light or spark of subtlety struck into his mind, by one single lecture upon Crackenthorp or Burgersdicius, or any Dutch logician or commentator; – he knew not so much as in what the difference of an argument *ad ignorantiam*, and an argument *ad hominem* consisted; so that I well remember, when he went up along with me to enter my name at Jesus College in ****, – it was a matter of just wonder with my worthy tutor, and two or three fellows of that learned society, – that a man who knew not so much as the names of his tools, should be able to work after that fashion with them.

To work with them in the best manner he could, was what my father was, however, perpetually forced upon; – for he had a thousand little sceptical notions of the comic kind to defend – most of which notions, I verily believe, at first entered upon the footing of mere whims, and of a *vive la Bagatelle*; and as such he would make merry with them for half an hour or so, and having sharpened his wit upon them, dismiss them till another day.

I mention this, not only as a matter of hypothesis or conjecture upon the progress and establishment of my father's many odd opinions, – but as a warning to the learned reader against the indiscreet reception of such guests, who, after a free and undisturbed entrance, for some years, into our brains, – at length claim a kind of settlement there,—

65

working sometimes like yeast; – but more generally after the manner of the gentle passion, beginning in jest, – but ending in downright earnest.

Whether this was the case of the singularity of my father's notions – or that his judgment, at length, became the dupe of his wit; – or how far, in many of his notions, he might, though odd, be absolutely right;—the reader, as he comes at them, shall decide. All that I maintain here, is, that in this one, of the influence of christian names, however it gained footing, he was serious; – he was all uniformity; – he was systematical, and, like all systematic reasoners, he would move both heaven and earth, and twist and torture every thing in nature, to support his hypothesis. In a word, I repeat it over again; – he was serious; and, in consequence of it, he would lose all kind of patience whenever he saw people, especially of condition, who should have known better,—as careless and as indifferent about the name they imposed upon their child, – or more so, than in the choice of Ponto or Cupid for their puppy-dog.

This, he would say, looked ill; – and had, moreover, this particular aggravation in it, viz., That when once a vile name was wrongfully or injudiciously given, 'twas not like the case of a man's character, which, when wronged, might hereafter be cleared;—and, possibly, some time or other, if not in the man's life, at least after his death, – be, somehow or other, set to rights with the world: But the injury of this, he would say, could never be undone; – nay, he doubted even whether an act of parliament could reach it:—He knew as well as you, that the legislature assumed a power over surnames; – but for very strong reasons, which he could give, it had never yet adventured, he would say, to go a step farther.

It was observable, that tho' my father, in consequence of this opinion, had, as I have told you, the strongest likings and dislikings towards certain names; – that there were still numbers of names which hung so equally in the balance before him, that they were absolutely indifferent to him. Jack, Dick, and Tom were of this class: These my father called neutral names; – affirming of them, without a satire, That there had been as many knaves and fools, at least, as wise and good men, since the world began, who had indifferently borne them; – so that, like equal forces acting against each other in contrary directions, he thought they mutually destroyed each other's effects; for which reason, he would often declare, He would not give a cherry-stone to choose amongst them. Bob, which was my brother's name, was another of these neutral kinds of christian names, which operated very little either way; and as my father happened to be at Epsom, when it was given him, – he would oft-times thank Heaven it was no worse. Andrew was something like a negative quantity in Algebra with him; – 'twas worse, he said, than nothing. – William stood pretty high: – Numps again was low with him: – and Nick, he said, was the Devil.

But, of all the names in the universe, he had the most unconquerable aversion for Tristram; – he had the lowest and most contemptible opinion of it of any thing in the world, – thinking it could possibly produce nothing in *rerum naturâ*, but what was extremely mean and pitiful: So that in the midst of a dispute on the subject, in which, by the bye, he was frequently involved, – he would sometimes break off in a sudden and spirited Epiphonema, or rather Erotesis, raised a third, and sometimes a full fifth above the key of the discourse, – and demand it categorically of his antagonist, Whether he would take upon him to say, he had ever remembered, – whether he had ever read, – or even whether he had ever heard tell of a man, called Tristram, performing any thing great or worth recording? – No, – he would say, – Tristram! – The thing is impossible.

What could be wanting in my father but to have wrote a book to publish this notion of his to the world? Little boots it to the subtle speculatist to stand single in his opinions, – unless he gives them proper vent: – It was the identical thing which my father did: – for in the year sixteen, which was two years before I was born, he was at the pains of writing an express Dissertation simply upon the word Tristram, – shewing the world, with great candour and modesty, the grounds of his great abhorrence to the name.

When this story is compared with the title-page, – Will not the gentle reader pity my father from his soul? – to see an orderly and well-disposed gentleman, who tho' singular, – yet inoffensive in his notions, – so played upon in them by cross purposes;—to look down upon the stage, and see him baffled and overthrown in all his little systems and wishes; to behold a train of events perpetually falling out against him, and in so critical and cruel a way, as if they had purposely been planned and pointed against him, merely to insult his speculations.—In a word, to behold such a one, in his old age, ill-fitted for troubles, ten times in a day suffering sorrow; – ten times in a day calling the child of his prayers Tristram! – Melancholy dissyllable of sound! which, to his ears, was unison to Nincompoop, and every name vituperative under heaven.—By his ashes! I swear it, – if ever malignant spirit took pleasure, or busied itself in traversing the purposes of mortal man, – it must have been here; – and if it was not necessary I should be born before I was christened, I would this moment give the reader an account of it.

20

——How could you, Madam, be so inattentive in reading the last chapter? I told you in it, That my mother was not a papist.—Papist! You told me no such thing, Sir. – Madam, I beg leave to repeat it over again, that I told you as plain, at least, as words, by direct inference, could tell you such a thing. – Then, Sir, I must have missed a page. – No, Madam, – you have not missed a word.—Then I was asleep, Sir. – My pride, Madam, cannot allow you that refuge.—Then, I declare, I know nothing at all about the matter. – That, Madam, is the very fault I lay to your charge; and as a punishment for it, I do insist upon it, that you immediately turn back, that is, as soon as you get to the next full stop, and read the whole chapter over again. I have imposed this penance upon the lady, neither out of wantonness nor cruelty; but from the best of motives; and therefore shall make her no apology for it when she returns back: – 'Tis to rebuke a vicious taste, which has crept into thousands besides herself, – of reading straight forwards, more in quest of the adventures, than of the deep erudition and knowledge which a book of this cast, if read over as it should be, would infallibly impart with them—The mind should be accustomed to make wise reflections, and draw curious conclusions as it goes along; the habitude of which made Pliny the younger affirm, 'That he never read a book so bad, but he drew some profit from it.' The stories of Greece and Rome, run over without this turn and application, – do less service, I affirm it, than the history of Parismus and Parismenus, or of the Seven Champions of England, read with it.

——But here comes my fair lady. Have you read over again the chapter, Madam, as I desired you? – You have: And did you not observe the passage, upon the second reading, which admits the inference?—Not a word like it! Then, Madam, be pleased to ponder well the last line but one of the chapter, where I take upon me to say, 'It was necessary I should be born before I was christened.' Had my mother, Madam, been a Papist, that consequence did not follow.

It is a terrible misfortune for this same book of mine, but more so to the Republic of letters; – so that my own is quite swallowed up in the consideration of it; – that this self-same vile pruriency for fresh adventures in all things, has got so strongly into our habit and humour, – and so wholly intent are we upon satisfying the impatience of our concupiscence that way, – that nothing but the gross and more carnal parts of a composition will go down: – The subtle hints and sly communications of science fly off, like spirits upwards,—the heavy moral escapes downwards; and both the one and the other are as much lost to the world, as if they were still left in the bottom of the ink-horn.

I wish the male-reader has not passed by many a one, as quaint and curious as this one, in which the female-reader has been detected. I wish it may have its effects; – and that all good people, both male and female, from her example, may be taught to think as well as read.[1]

---

[1] The Romish Rituals direct the baptizing of the child, in cases of danger, before it is born; – but upon this proviso, That some part or other of the child's body be seen by the baptizer:—But the Doctors of the Sorbonne, by a deliberation held amongst them, April 10, 1733, – have enlarged the powers of the midwives, by determining, That though no part of the child's body should appear,—that baptism shall, nevertheless, be administered to it by injection, – *par le moyen d'une petite canule*, – Anglicè *a squirt.*—'Tis very strange that St Thomas Aquinas, who had so good a mechanical head, both for tying and untying the knots of school-divinity, – should, after so much pains bestowed upon this, – give up the point at last, as a second *La chose impossible*, – 'Infantes in maternis uteris existentes (quoth St Thomas!) baptizari possunt *nullo modo*.' – O Thomas! Thomas!

If the reader has the curiosity to see the question upon baptism by injection, as presented to the Doctors of the Sorbonne, with their consultation thereupon, it is as follows.

Memoire presenté à Messieurs les Docteurs de Sorbonne[2]

Un Chirurgien Accoucheur, represente à Messieurs les Docteurs de Sorbonne, qu'il y a des cas, quoique très rares, où une mere ne sçauroit accoucher, & même où l'enfant est tellement renfermé dans le sein de sa mere, qu'il ne fait parôitre aucune partie de son corps, ce qui seroit un cas, suivant les Rituels, de lui conférer, du moins sous condition, le baptême. Le Chirurgien, qui consulte, prétend, par le moyen d'une petite canule, de pouvoir baptiser immediatement l'enfant, sans faire aucun tort à la mere.—Il demand si ce moyen, qu'il vient de proposer, est permis & légitimé, & s'il peut s'en servir dans les cas qu'il vient d'exposer.

---

[2] Vide Deventer, Paris edit., 4to, 1734, p. 366.

Reponse

Le Conseil estime, que la question proposée souffre de grandes difficultés. Les Théologiens posent d'un coté pour principe, que le baptême, qui est une naissance spirituelle, suppose une premiere naissance; il faut être né dans le monde, pour renaître en Jesus Christ, comme ils l'enseignent. S. Thomas, 3 part. quaest. 88, artic. 11, suit cette doctrine comme une verité constante; l'on ne peut, dit ce S. Docteur, baptiser les enfans qui sont renfermés dans le sein de leurs meres, & S. Thomas est fondé sur ce, que les enfans ne sont point nés, & ne peuvent être comptés parmi les autres hommes; d'où il conclud, qu'ils ne peuvent être l'objet d'une action extérieure, pour reçevoir par leur ministére, les sacremens nécessaires au salut: *Pueri in maternis uteris existentes nondum prodierunt in lucem ut cum aliis hominibus vitam ducant; unde non possunt subjici actioni humanae, ut per eorum ministerium sacramenta recipiant ad salutem.* Les rituels ordonnent dans la pratique ce que les théologiens ont établi sur les mêmes matiéres, & ils deffendent tous d'une maniére uniforme, de baptiser les enfans qui sont renfermés dans le sein de leurs meres, s'ils ne font paroître quelque partie de leurs corps. Le concours des théologiens, & des rituels, qui sont les régles des diocéses, paroit former une autorité qui termine la question presente; cependant le conseil de conscience considerant d'un côté, que le raisonnement des théologiens est uniquement fondé sur une raison de convenance, & que la deffense des rituels suppose que l'on ne peut baptiser immediatement les enfans ainsi renfermés dans le sein de leurs meres, ce qui est contre la supposition presente; & d'un autre côté, considerant que les mêmes théologiens enseignent, que l'on peut risquer les sacremens que Jesus Christ a établis comme des moyens faciles, mais nécessaires pour sanctifier les hommes; & d'ailleurs estimant, que les enfans renfermés dans le sein de leurs meres, pourroient être capables de salut, parcequ'ils sont capables de damnation; – pour ces considerations, & en egard à l'exposé, suivant lequel on assure avoir trouvé un moyen certain de baptiser ces enfans ainsi renfermés, sans faire aucun tort à la mere, le Conseil estime que l'on pourroit se servir du moyen proposé, dans la confiance qu'il a, que Dieu n'a point laissé ces sortes d'enfans sans aucuns secours, & supposant, comme il est exposé, que le moyen dont il s'agit est propre à leur procurer le baptême; cependant comme il s'agiroit, en autorisant la pratique propose, de changer une regle universellement établie, le Conseil croit que celui qui consulte doit s'addresser à son evêque, & à qui il appartient de juger de l'utilité, & du danger du moyen proposé, & comme, sous le bon plaisir de l'evêque, le Conseil estime qu'il faudroit recourir au Pape, qui a le droit d'expliquer les régles de l'eglise, & d'y déroger dans le cas, ou la loi ne sçauroit obliger, quelque sage & quelque utile que paroisse la maniére de baptiser dont il s'agit, le Conseil ne pourroit l'approuver sans le concours de ces deux autorités. On conseile au moins à celui qui consulte, de s'addresser à son evêque, & de lui faire part de la presente décision, afin que, si le prelat entre dans les raisons sur lesquelles les docteurs soussignés s'appuyent, il puisse être autorisé dans le cas de nécessité, ou il risqueroit trop d'attendre que la permission fût demandée & accordée d'employer le moyen qu'il propose si avantageux au salut de l'enfant. Au reste, le Conseil, en estimant que l'on pourroit s'en servir, croit cependant, que si les enfans dont il s'agit, venoient au monde, contre l'esperance de ceux qui se seroient servis du même moyen, il seroit nécessaire de les baptiser sous condition; & en cela le Conseil se conforme à tous les rituels, qui en autorisant le baptême d'un enfant qui fait paroître quelque partie de son corps, enjoignent néantmoins, & ordonnent de le baptiser sous condition, s'il vient heureusement au monde.

Déliberé en Sorbonne, le 10 Avril, 1733.

A. LE MOYNE

L. DE ROMIGNY

DE MARCILLY

Mr Tristram Shandy's compliments to Messrs Le Moyne, De Romigny, and De Marcilly; hopes they all rested well the night after so tiresome a consultation. – He begs to know, whether after the ceremony of marriage, and before that of consummation, the baptizing all the Homunculi at once, slapdash, by injection, would not be a shorter and safer cut still; on condition, as above, That if the Homunculi do well, and come safe into the world after this, that each and every of them shall be baptized again (*sous condition*)—And provided, in the second place, That the thing can be done, which Mr Shandy apprehends it may, *par le moyen d'une petite canulle*, and *sans faire aucun tort au pere*.

21

—I wonder what's all that noise, and running backwards and forwards for, above stairs, quoth my father, addressing himself, after an hour and a half's silence, to my uncle Toby—who, you must know, was sitting on the opposite side of the fire, smoking his social pipe all the time, in mute contemplation of a new pair of black plush breeches which he had got on:—What can they be doing, brother?—quoth my father,—we can scarce hear ourselves talk.

I think, replied my uncle Toby, taking his pipe from his mouth, and striking the head of it two or three times upon the nail of his left thumb, as he began his sentence,—I think, says he:—But to enter rightly into my uncle Toby's sentiments upon this matter, you must be made to enter first a little into his character, the outlines of which I shall just give you, and then the dialogue between him and my father will go on as well again.

Pray what was that man's name, – for I write in such a hurry, I have no time to recollect or look for it, – who first made the observation, 'That there was great inconsistency in our air and climate'? Whoever he was, 'twas a just and good observation in him. – But the corollary drawn from it, namely, 'That it is this which has furnished us with such a variety of odd and whimsical characters'; – that was not his; – it was found out by another man, at least a century and a half after him: Then again, – that this copious store-house of original materials, is the true and natural cause that our Comedies are so much better than those of France, or any others that either have, or can be wrote upon the Continent:—that discovery was not fully made till about the middle of King William's reign, – when the great Dryden, in writing one of his long prefaces, (if I mistake not) most fortunately hit upon it. Indeed toward the latter end of Queen Anne, the great Addison began to patronize the notion, and more fully explained it to the world in one or two of his Spectators; – but the discovery was not his. – Then, fourthly and lastly, that this strange irregularity in our climate, producing so strange an irregularity in our characters,—doth thereby, in some sort, make us amends, by giving us somewhat to make us merry with when the weather will not suffer us to go out of doors, – that observation is my own; – and was struck out by me this very rainy day, March 26, 1759, and betwixt the hours of nine and ten in the morning.

Thus – thus, my fellow-labourers and associates in this great harvest of our learning, now ripening before our eyes; thus it is, by slow steps of casual increase, that our knowledge physical, metaphysical, physiological, polemical, nautical, mathematical, enigmatical, technical, biographical, romantical, chemical, and obstetrical, with fifty other branches of it, (most of 'em ending as these do, in *ical*) have for these two centuries and more, gradually been creeping upwards towards that 'Ακμὴ of their perfections, from which, if we may form a conjecture from the advances of these last seven years, we cannot possibly be far off.

When that happens, it is to be hoped, it will put an end to all kind of writings whatsoever; – the want of all kind of writing will put an end to all kind of reading; – and that in time, As war begets poverty; poverty peace,—must, in course, put an end to all kind of knowledge, – and then—we shall have all to begin over again; or, in other words, be exactly where we started.

—Happy! thrice happy times! I only wish that the era of my begetting, as well as the mode and manner of it, had been a little altered, – or that it could have been put off, with any convenience to my father or mother, for some twenty or five-and-twenty years longer, when a man in the literary world might have stood some chance. –

But I forget my uncle Toby, whom all this while we have left knocking the ashes out of his tobacco-pipe.

His humour was of that particular species, which does honour to our atmosphere; and I should have made no scruple of ranking him amongst one of the first-rate productions of it, had not there appeared too many strong lines in it of a family-likeness, which shewed that he derived the singularity of his temper more from blood, than either wind or water, or any modifications or combinations of them whatever: And I have, therefore, oft-times wondered, that my father, tho' I believe he had his reasons for it, upon his observing some tokens of eccentricity, in my course, when I was a boy, – should never once endeavour to account for them in this way: for all the Shandy Family were of an original character throughout:—I mean the males, – the females had no character at all, – except, indeed, my great aunt Dinah, who, about sixty years ago, was married and got with child by the coachman, for which my father, according to his hypothesis of christian names, would often say, She might thank her godfathers and godmothers.

It will seem very strange, – and I would as soon think of dropping a riddle in the reader's way, which is not my interest to do, as set him upon guessing how it could come to pass, that an event of this kind, so many years after it had happened, should be reserved for the interruption of the peace and unity, which otherwise so cordially subsisted, between my father and my uncle Toby. One would have thought, that the whole force of the misfortune should have spent and wasted itself in the family at first, – as is generally the case. – But nothing ever wrought with our family after the ordinary way. Possibly at the very time this happened, it might have something else to afflict it; and as afflictions are sent down for our good, and that as this had never done the Shandy Family any good at all, it might lie waiting till apt times and circumstances should give it an opportunity to discharge its office.—Observe, I determine nothing upon this.—My way is ever to point out to the curious, different tracts of investigation, to come at the first springs of the events I tell; – not with a pedantic Fescue, – or in the decisive manner of Tacitus, who outwits himself and his reader; – but with the officious humility of a heart devoted to the assistance merely of the inquisitive; – to them I write,—and by them I shall be read,—if any such reading as this could be supposed to hold out so long, – to the very end of the world.

Why this cause of sorrow, therefore, was thus reserved for my father and uncle, is undetermined by me. But how and in what direction it exerted itself so as to become the cause of dissatisfaction between them, after it began to operate, is what I am able to explain with great exactness, and is as follows:

My uncle Toby Shandy, Madam, was a gentleman, who, with the virtues which usually constitute the character of a man of honour and rectitude, – possessed one in a very eminent degree, which is seldom or never put into the catalogue; and that was a most extreme and unparalleled modesty of nature; – though I correct the word nature, for this reason, that I may not prejudge a point which must shortly come to a hearing, and that is, Whether this modesty of his was natural or acquired. – Whichever way my uncle Toby came by it, 'twas nevertheless modesty in the truest sense of it; and that is, Madam, not in regard to words, for he was so unhappy as to have very little choice in them – but to things; – and this kind of modesty so possessed him, and it arose to such a height in him, as almost to equal, if such a thing could be, even the modesty of a woman: That female nicety, Madam, and inward cleanliness of mind and fancy, in your sex, which makes you so much the awe of ours.

You will imagine, Madam, that my uncle Toby had contracted all this from this very source; – that he had spent a great part of his time in converse with your sex; and that from a thorough knowledge of you, and the force of imitation which such fair examples render irresistible, he had acquired this amiable turn of mind.

I wish I could say so, – for unless it was with his sister-in-law, my father's wife and my mother – my uncle Toby scarce exchanged three words with the sex in as many years;—no, he got it, Madam, by a blow.—A blow! – Yes, Madam, it was owing to a blow from a stone, broke off by a ball from the parapet of a horn-work at the siege of Namur, which struck full upon my uncle Toby's groin. – Which way could that affect it? The story of that, Madam, is long and interesting; – but it would be running my history all upon heaps to give it you here.—'Tis for an episode hereafter; and every circumstance relating to it, in its proper place, shall be faithfully laid before you: – 'Till then, it is not in my power to give farther light into this matter, or say more than what I have said already,—That my uncle Toby was a gentleman of unparalleled modesty, which happening to be somewhat subtilized and rarified by the constant heat of a little family pride, – they both so wrought together within him, that he could never bear to hear the affair of my aunt Dinah touched upon, but with the greatest emotion. – The least hint of it was enough to make the blood fly into his face; – but when my father enlarged upon the story in mixed companies, which the illustration of his hypothesis frequently obliged him to do, – the unfortunate blight of one of the fairest branches of the family would set my uncle Toby's honour and modesty o'bleeding; and he would often take my father aside, in the greatest concern imaginable, to expostulate and tell him, he would give him any thing in the world, only to let the story rest.

My father, I believe, had the truest love and tenderness for my uncle Toby, that ever one brother bore towards another, and would have done anything in nature, which one brother in reason could have desired of another, to have made my uncle Toby's heart easy in this, or any other point. But this lay out of his power.

—My father, as I told you, was a philosopher in grain, – speculative, – systematical; – and my aunt Dinah's affair was a matter of as much consequence to him, as the retrogradation of the planets to Copernicus: – The backslidings of Venus in her orbit fortified the Copernican system, called so after his name; and the backslidings of my aunt Dinah in her orbit, did the same service in establishing my father's system, which, I trust, will for ever hereafter be called the Shandean System, after his.

In any other family dishonour, my father, I believe, had as nice a sense of shame as any man whatever; – and neither he, nor, I dare say, Copernicus, would have divulged the affair in either case, or have taken the least notice of it to the world, but for the obligations they owed, as they thought, to truth. – *Amicus Plato*, my father would say, construing the words to my uncle Toby, as he went along, *Amicus Plato*; that is, Dinah was my aunt; – *sed magis amica veritas* – but Truth is my sister.

This contrariety of humours betwixt my father and my uncle, was the source of many a fraternal squabble. The one could not bear to hear the tale of family disgrace recorded, – and the other would scarce ever let a day pass to an end without some hint at it.

For God's sake, my uncle Toby would cry, – and for my sake, and for all our sakes, my dear brother Shandy, – do let this story of our aunt's and her ashes sleep in peace;— how can you,—how can you have so little feeling and compassion for the character of our family?—What is the character of a family to an hypothesis? my father would reply.—Nay, if you come to that – what is the life of a family?—The life of a family! – my uncle Toby would say, throwing himself back in his arm-chair, and lifting up his hands, his eyes, and one leg.—Yes, the life, – my father would say, maintaining his point. How many thousands of 'em are there every year that come cast away, (in all civilized countries at least) – and considered as nothing but common air, in competition of an hypothesis. In my plain sense of things, my uncle Toby would answer, – every such instance is downright Murder, let who will commit it. – There lies your mistake, my father would reply;—for, in *Foro Scientiae* there is no such thing as Murder, – 'tis only Death, brother.

My uncle Toby would never offer to answer this by any other kind of argument, than that of whistling half a dozen bars of *Lillabullero*.—You must know it was the usual channel thro' which his passions got vent, when any thing shocked or surprised him:— but especially when any thing, which he deemed very absurd, was offered.

As not one of our logical writers, nor any of the commentators upon them, that I remember, have thought proper to give a name to this particular species of argument, – I here take the liberty to do it myself, for two reasons. First, That, in order to prevent all confusion in disputes, it may stand as much distinguished for ever, from every other species of argument—as the *Argumentum ad Verecundiam, ex Absurdo, ex Fortiori*, or any other argument whatsoever:—And, secondly, That it may be said by my children's children, when my head is laid to rest, – that their learned grandfather's head had been busied to as much purpose once, as other people's; – That he had invented a name, – and generously thrown it into the Treasury of the *Ars Logica*, for one of the most unanswerable arguments in the whole science. And, if the end of disputation is more to silence than convince, – they may add, if they please, to one of the best arguments too.

I do therefore, by these presents, strictly order and command, That it be known and distinguished by the name and title of the *Argumentum Fistulatorium*, and no other; – and that it rank hereafter with the *Argumentum Baculinum* and the *Argumentum ad Crumenam*, and for ever hereafter be treated of in the same chapter.

As for the *Argumentum Tripodium*, which is never used but by the woman against the man; – and the *Argumentum ad Rem*, which, contrarywise, is made use of by the man only against the woman; – As these two are enough in conscience for one lecture;— and, moreover, as the one is the best answer to the other, – let them likewise be kept apart and be treated of in a place by themselves.

22

The learned Bishop Hall, I mean the famous Dr Joseph Hall, who was Bishop of Exeter in King James the First's reign, tells us in one of his *Decads*, at the end of his divine art of meditation, imprinted at London, in the year 1610, by John Beal, dwelling in Aldersgate-street, 'That it is an abominable thing for a man to commend himself';— and I really think it is so.

And yet, on the other hand, when a thing is executed in a masterly kind of a fashion, which thing is not likely to be found out; – I think it is full as abominable, that a man should lose the honour of it, and go out of the world with the conceit of it rotting in his head.

This is precisely my situation.

For in this long digression which I was accidentally led into, as in all my digressions (one only excepted) there is a master-stroke of digressive skill, the merit of which has all along, I fear, been overlooked by my reader, – not for want of penetration in him, – but because 'tis an excellence seldom looked for, or expected indeed, in a digression; – and it is this: That tho' my digressions are all fair, as you observe, – and that I fly off from what I am about, as far, and as often too, as any writer in Great Britain; yet I constantly take care to order affairs so that my main business does not stand still in my absence.

I was just going, for example, to have given you the great outlines of my uncle Toby's most whimsical character; – when my aunt Dinah and the coachman came across us, and led us a vagary some millions of miles into the very heart of the planetary system: Notwithstanding all this, you perceive that the drawing of my uncle Toby's character went on gently all the time; – not the great contours of it – that was impossible, – but some familiar strokes and faint designations of it, were here and there touched on, as we went along, so that you are much better acquainted with my uncle Toby now than you was before.

FRANCES SHERIDAN

from *Memoirs of Miss Sidney Bidulph*

August 26

Oh! my dear! I am mortified to the last degree, lest Mr Arnold should, from some indiscreet tongue, have received a hint of my former engagement; he may think me disingenuous for never having mentioned it, especially since Mr Faulkland has been in the neighbourhood: I think his nature is too open to entertain any suspicions essentially injurious to me; yet may this affair, circumstanced as it is, make an unfavourable impression on him. I wish I had been before-hand with any officious whisperer: he has got so many new acquaintance, and is so much abroad, that the story may have reached his ears. God forbid it should affect his mind with causeless uneasiness! I would Mr Faulkland were a thousand miles from V——hall. I think Mr Arnold is altered since his arrival there – Colder he appears to be – I hope I but *fancy* it – yet there *is* a change – his looks are less kind – his voice has lost that tenderness, that it used to have in speaking to me – yet this may only be his temper – a man cannot *always* be a lover – Oh! I sicken at the very thought of Mr Arnold's entertaining a doubt of my true affection for him. I would not live in this suspence for millions. I would rather he should treat me roughly – if I discovered that to be his humour, though it would frighten me, yet should I patiently conform to it.

August 30

That which was ever the terror of my thoughts is come upon me – Mr Arnold – Ah! my dear Cecilia! Mr Arnold is no longer the same! Coldness and indifference have at length succeeded to love, to complacency, and the fondest attention – What a change! but the *cause*, my dear, that remains a secret locked up in his own breast. It cannot be that a whisper, an idle rumour should affect him thus. What if he *has* heard that Mr Faulkland loved me once? That we were to have been married? Cannot he ask me the question? I long to set his heart at ease – yet cannot mention the affair first, after so long a silence; it would look like a consciousness. A consciousness of what? I have nothing to accuse myself of.

September 1

I am no longer in doubt. The cause, the fatal cause of Mr Arnold's change is discovered. This miserable day has disclosed the secret to me; a black, a complicated scene of mischief.

Mr Arnold rode out this morning. He told me he was to dine with a gentleman at some miles distance, and should not return till late in the evening.

He was but just gone, when a lady of my acquaintance called in upon me, to request I would go with her to a play, that was to be performed at night. You must know we have had a company of players in the neighbourhood for some time past, and it was to one of those poor people's benefits that she desired my company. I promised to attend her, though you know I don't much admire those sort of entertainments in the country, and seldom go to them.

The lady and her husband called upon me at the appointed hour, and I went with them in their coach. The place which the players had fitted up for their purpose, had formerly been a pretty large school-room, and could, with the addition of a gallery (which they had made) with ease contain above three hundred people. The play had been bespoke by some of the principal ladies in the neighbourhood, who had used all their interest for the performer, so that the house was as full as it could hold. The audience consisting chiefly of fashionable people, it was with difficulty that we reached the places which were kept for us in the pit, as they happened to be on the bench next the stage, and the door was at the other end of the house. The first object that I observed on my coming in was Mr Faulkland; he bowed to me at a distance, but made no attempts to approach me. The play was come to the latter end of the fourth act, and the curtain was let down to make some preparation on the stage, when we were alarmed with the cry of fire.

It happened that the carpenters, who had been employed in fitting up this extempore theatre, had left a heap of shavings in a little place behind the stage, which had been converted into a dressing-room; a little boy belonging to the company had found a candle in it, and having piled up the shavings, set them on fire, and left them burning: the flame communicated itself to some dry boards which lay in the room, and in a few minutes the whole was in a blaze. Some persons, who heard the crackling of the wood, opened the door, when the flame burst out with such violence, that the scenes were presently on fire, and the curtain, which as I told you was dropt, soon caught it.

The consternation and terror of the poor people, whose *all* was destroying, is not to be described: the women shrieking, threw themselves off the stage into the pit, as the smoke and flames terrified them from attempting to get out any other way, though there was a door behind the stage.

The audience were in little less confusion than they; for as the house was composed chiefly of wood, every one expected it would soon be consumed to ashes.

The horror and distraction of my mind almost deprived me of the power of motion. My life was in imminent danger; for I was scorched with the fire before I could get at any distance from the stage, though the people were rushing out as fast as they could.

The lady who was with me was exceedingly frightened; but being under her husband's care, had a little more courage than I had. He caught her round the waist, and lifted her over the benches, which were very high, giving me what assistance he could with his other hand. But the terror and hurry I was in occasioned my foot to slip, and I fell between two of the benches, and sprained my ancle.

Some people pushing to get out, rushed between me and my company; the excessive pain I felt, joined to my fright, made me faint away; in this condition Mr Faulkland found me, and carried me out in his arms; for my companion was too anxious for her own safety, to suffer her husband to stay to give me any assistance, so that he had only time to beg of the men about him not to let me perish.

I soon recovered, upon being carried into the open air, and found myself seated on some planks, at a little distance from the booth, Mr Faulkland supporting me, and two or three other people about me, whom he had called to my assistance.

Indebted to him as I was for saving my life, my spirits were at that time too much agitated to thank him as I ought.

He told me, he had stepped behind the scenes to speak to somebody, and was there when the stage took fire; that he then ran to give what assistance he could to the ladies that were in the house (observe he distinguished not *me* in particular), and had just come in when he saw me meet with the accident, which had occasioned my fainting away; and when the gentleman, who was with me, was calling for help, but at the same time getting out as fast as he could.

I now began to recollect myself; I was uneasy at Mr Faulkland's presence; I wished him away. I beseeched him to return once more to the booth, to see if every one had got out safe, for I told him I had seen several of my female acquaintance there, for whom I was alarmed. With the assistance of the people about me, I said I could make a shift to get to the nearest house, which was not above a hundred yards off, from whence I should send home for my chariot, which I had ordered to come to me after the play. He begged I would give him leave to see me safe to that house, but I would not permit him; and he left me in the care of two women and a man, who had come to be spectators of the fire.

With the help of these people, I contrived to hobble (for my ancle pained me exceedingly) to the place I mentioned, which happened to be a public house. All the rooms below were full, and the woman of the house very obligingly helped me up stairs into her own chamber. I called for a glass of water, which was immediately brought me, and I desired the woman to send some one to my house, which was at about a mile's distance, to order my chariot to come to me immediately.

While the woman went to execute my instructions, I had thrown myself into a chair that stood close to the wainscot. I heard a bell ring, and presently a waiter entered, and asked if I wanted any thing; I told him, no. He ran hastily out of the room, and entering the next to that where I was sitting, I heard a voice, which I knew to be Mr Arnold's, ask, Were the servants found? The man replying that they were not, Then, said Mr Arnold, tell your mistress she will oblige me if she will let me have her chaise to carry this lady home. The waiter presently withdrew, and without reflecting on the particularity of Mr Arnold's being there with a lady, about whom I formed no conjectures, I was about to rise off my chair to go in to him; but being almost disabled from walking, I was obliged to creep along, holding by the wainscot; when a tender exclamation of Mr Arnold's stopped me. My dearest creature, said he to his companion, you have not yet recovered your fright. A female voice answered him with some fond expressions, which I could not hear distinctly enough to discover whose it was; but I was soon put out of doubt, when the lady added, in a louder tone, Do you know that your wife was at the play to-night? Mr Arnold answered, No; I hope she did not see me. Mrs Gerrarde, for I perceived it was she who spoke, replied, I hope not, because perhaps she might expect you home after the play. Though Mr Arnold, in his first emotion of surprize at hearing that I was at the play, was only anxious lest I should have observed him, yet he was not so lost to humanity as to be indifferent whether I escaped the flames or not: I am surprized I did not see her, said he; I wish she may have got out of the house safe. You are very sollicitous about her, replied Mrs Gerrarde, peevishly; there was one there perhaps as anxious for her preservation as you are – The conversation I found here was likely to become extremely critical for me; but I was prevented from hearing any more, by the woman of the house, who just then entered the room to ask me how I did, and to know if I wanted any thing.

I had heard enough to convince me that my presence would be very unacceptable both to Mr Arnold and his companion, and I resolved not to interrupt them; nor, if possible, ever let Mr Arnold know that I had made a discovery so fatal to my own peace, and so disadvantageous to him and his friend.

The messenger who had been dispatched for my chariot met it by the way, and was now returned with it; I was told that it was at the door; and it was with difficulty I got down stairs, leaning on the woman of the house.

I found Mr Faulkland at the door; he saw that I wished to disengage myself from him after he had carried me out of the booth; and though probably he did not take the trouble to excuse the sham commission I gave him, which was indeed with no other view than to get him away, yet I believe he had too much respect to intrude on me; and came then with no other design than to enquire if my chariot had come for me, and how I was after the terrible condition he had left me in, sitting at night in the open air, with nobody but two or three ordinary people about me, and those strangers. This was a piece of civility which humanity, had politeness been out of the question, would have obliged him to. He told me the fire was extinguished, and happily nobody had received any hurt; and that he had only called at that house to know if I were safe, and recovered from the fright and pain he had left me in. I thanked him, and was just stepping, assisted by Mr Faulkland, into the chariot, when Mr Arnold appeared at the door: he was alone, and I concluded, that having heard the chariot rattle up the court-yard, he supposed it was the carriage he had ordered for Mrs Gerrarde, and came down to see if it was ready to receive her.

The light which the servant, who attended me out, held in his hand, immediately discovered Mr Arnold and me to each other. I could easily distinguish surprize mixed with displeasure in his countenance. He asked me abruptly, How I came to that place? Which I told him, in few words. The cold civility of a grave bow passed between him and Mr Faulkland, who leaving me in my husband's hands, wished me a good night, and got into my lord V—'s coach, which waited for him.

Though I knew, from the discourse I had overheard, that Mr Arnold did not mean to go home with me, yet as I was now seated in the chariot, I could not avoid asking him. He told me, he was engaged to sup with company at that house, and that probably he should not be at home till late. I knew this beforehand, and, without troubling him with any farther questions, drove home.

I have thrown together the strange occurrences of this evening, as well as the tumult of my spirits would give me leave: I shall now lay down my pen, to consider of them a little more calmly. My heart sinks in me – Oh! that I had remained in ignorance! –

Is it possible, my Cecilia, that Mr Arnold, so good a man, one who married me for love, and who for these two years has been the tenderest, the kindest husband, and to whom I never gave the most distant shadow of offence, should at last be led into – I cannot name it – dare not think of it – yet a thousand circumstances recur to my memory, which now convince me I am unhappy! If I had not been blind, I might have seen it sooner. I recollect some passages, which satisfy me that Mr Arnold's acquaintance with Mrs Gerrarde did not commence at South-park. I remember lady V—once asked me, had she and I been acquainted in London? I said, No. My lord laughed, and in his blunt way said, I will swear your hubsand was, for I have seen him hand her out from the play more than once. I never asked Mr Arnold about this; it made no impression on me at the time it was spoke, and went quick-out of my thoughts.

'Tis one o'clock: I hear Mr Arnold ring at the outer gate; I tremble all over, and feel as if I feared to see him. Yet why should I fear? *I* have not injured *him*.

September 2

Mr Arnold staid long enough in his dressing-room after he came in last night, to give me time to go to-bed before he came up stairs. Not a word passed between us: I slept not the whole night: whether he did or not I cannot tell. He asked me this morning, when he rose, how I did: I told him in great pain. My ancle was prodigiously swelled, and turned quite black, for I had neglected it last night. He said, you had better let a surgeon see it, and went carelessly out of the room. How new is unkindness to me, my friend! you know I have not been used to it. Mr Arnold adds cruelty too – but let it be so; far be reproaches or complaints from my lips; to you only, my second self, shall I utter them; to you I am bound by solemn promise, and reciprocal confidence, to disclose the inmost secrets of my soul, and with you they are as safe as in my own breast. –

I am once more composed, and determined on my behaviour. I have not a doubt remaining of Mr Arnold's infidelity; but let me not aggravate my own griefs, nor to a vicious world justify my husband's conduct, by bringing any reproach on my own. The silent sufferings of the injured, must, to a mind not ungenerous, be a sharper rebuke than it is in the power of language to inflict.

But this is not all: I must endeavour, if possible, to skreen Mr Arnold from censure. I hope his own imprudence may not render these endeavours ineffectual. I am resolved not to drop my acquaintance with Mrs Gerrarde. While we continue upon a footing of seeming intimacy, the frequent visits, which I am sure Mr Arnold makes at her house, will be less taken notice of.

How Sir George would triumph at the knowlege of Mr Arnold's deviating from virtue! How my poor mother would be amazed and afflicted! But I will, as far as lies in my power, disappoint the malice of my stars; my mother shall have no cause to grieve, nor my brother to rejoice; the secret shall die with me in my own bosom, and I will wait patiently, till the hand of time applies a remedy to my grief. Mrs Gerrarde sent a message to enquire how I did. Conscious woman! she would not come herself, though she knew not I had discovered her.

My dear good lady V—hurried to see me the instant she had breakfasted: Mr

Faulkland had told her of my disaster, and her tenderness soothed and comforted me much. She sat by my bed-side two hours, and her discourse alleviated the pain both of my mind and body; but now she has left me, I must again recur to the subject that wrings my heart. Mr Arnold is enslaved to one of the most artful of her sex. I look upon his attachment to be the more dangerous, as I believe it is the first of the kind he ever had; and no woman was ever more formed to please and to deceive, than she who now holds him in her chains. Into what hands am I fallen! Mrs Gerrarde must have heard my story, and by the hint I heard her drop, what cruel misrepresentations may she have made to Mr Arnold! Mr Faulkland, she can have no enmity to; but me she certainly hates, for she has injured me.

'Tis noon: I have not seen Mr Arnold since morning; he has been abroad ever since he rose; Good God! is this the life I am condemned to lead?

A new scene of affliction is opened to me: surely my fate is drawing towards a crisis. Mr Arnold has just left me. What conversation have we had!

After entering my room, he walked about for some minutes without speaking; at last stopping short, and fixing his eyes upon me, How long have you, said he, been acquainted with Mr Faulkland? I told him my acquaintance began with him some months before I was married. He was once your lover I am informed. He was, and a treaty of marriage was concluded on between us. You would have been happier perhaps, madam, if it had taken place. I do not think so Mr Arnold, you have no reason to suppose I do. I had a very great objection to Mr Faulkland, and obeyed my mother willingly, when she forbid me to see him. I ask not what that objection was, said he; but I suppose, madam, you will without reluctance obey *me*, if I make the same request to you. Most chearfully; you cannot make a request with which I should more readily comply. But let me beseech you, Mr Arnold, to tell me, what part of my behaviour has given you cause to think such a prohibition necessary? I do not say, answered Mr Arnold, that I have any suspicion of your virtue; but your acquiescence in this particular is necessary to *my* peace and your *own* honour. A lady's being *married* does not cut off the hopes of a gay man. You give me your promise that you will not see him any more. I *do*, said I; I will give up lady V—, whose acquaintance I so much esteem: I will go no more to her house while Mr Faulkland continues there; and I know of no other family, where I visit, that he is acquainted with.

My pride would not suffer me to enquire where he had got his information: I already knew it too well; and fearing he would rather descend to an untruth than tell me his author, I declined any farther questions. He seemed satisfied with my promise, but quickly left me, as if the whole end of his visit to me was accomplished in having obtained it.

September 8

What painful minutes am I obliged to sustain! Mrs Gerrarde has been to see me, gay and assured as ever. She affected to condole with me on the accident that happened to my foot, with such an overstrained concern, such a tender solicitude, that her insincerity disgusted me, if possible, more than the other part of her behaviour. She told me, she herself had been at the play, but very luckily had got out without receiving any injury.

I said, I was surprized I had not seen her there. O, replied she, I was in a little snug corner, where nobody could see me; for having refused to go with some ladies that asked me, I did not chuse to be visible in the house, and so squeezed myself up into what they called their gallery, for I took nobody with me but my maid. Audacious woman! – Is it not strange, my dear, that Mr Arnold could be so weak as to humour her in the absurd frolick of going with her to such a place? for so it must have been; or perhaps she appointed him only to call for her at the play; and he might have arrived but just in time to assist her in getting out. No matter which it was.

September 9

I was born to sacrifice my own peace to that of other people; my life is become miserable, but I have no remedy for it but patience.

Mr Arnold spends whole days abroad; at night we are separated on account of my indisposition; so that we hardly ever converse together. What a dreadful prospect have I before me! O! Cecilia, may you never experience the bitterness of having your husband's heart alienated from you!

Lady V——, that best of creatures, is with me constantly; she presses me to come to her house, as my ancle is now pretty well, yet I am obliged to excuse myself. I am distressed to the last degree at the conduct I shall be forced to observe towards her, yet dare not explain the motive. Causeless jealousy is always the subject of ridicule, and at all events Mr Arnold must not be exposed to this.

September 12

I am weary of inventing excuses for absenting myself from V—hall. My lady has done sollicting me, yet continues her friendly and affectionate visits; I fear she guesses my situation, though she has not as yet hinted at it; but her forbearing to press me any more on the subject of going to her, and at the same time not requiring a reason for this breach of civility as well as friendship, convinced me, that she suspects the cause of my restraint. I am now perfectly recovered, yet do I still confine myself to my house, to avoid as much as possible giving umbrage to lady V——: but this restraint cannot last much longer; Mrs Gerrarde teazes me to come to her, and I have promised to make her my first visit.

September 27

Said I not that my fate was near its crisis? Where will this impending ruin end? Take, my Cecilia, the occurrences of this frightful day.

Mr Arnold rode out this morning, and told me he should not return till night. He asked me, with that indifference which now accompanies all his words, How I meant to dispose of myself for the day? I told him, I had no design of going abroad, and should spend my time in reading, or at my needle. This was my real intention; but Mr Arnold had but just left the house, when I received a message from Mrs Gerrarde to know how I did, and to tell me she was not well, and much out of spirits, or she would come and pass the day with me; but that she insisted on my dining with her. As I had told Mr Arnold I did not mean to go out, I really had neither intention nor inclination to do so. But shall I confess my weakness to you? I suspected that he purposed spending the day (as he often did) with Mrs Gerrarde, and the more so from the question he had asked me on his going abroad; he thought I might probably pay her a visit; and this intrusion was a circumstance he had a mind to be guarded against, by knowing before-hand my designs. I had not been to see Mrs Gerrarde since my recovery, and it was natural to suppose I would return her visits. Possessed as I was with this opinion, her message gave me a secret satisfaction, as it served to convince me Mr Arnold was not to be with her, for she generally detained me late when I went to her house. From what trivial circumstances will the afflicted draw consolation, or an additional weight of grief? So it was, I felt a sort of pleasure, in thinking, that for all that day at least Mr Arnold would absent himself from my rival – My rival! mean word, she is not worthy to be called so; from his mistress let it be. In short, I resolved to go, especially as she had sent me word she was not well, and I knew my husband would be pleased with my complaisance.

I went accordingly to her house, a little before her hour of dining, which is much later than any body else's in this part of the world. I found her dressed out, and seemingly in perfect health. She looked surprized when she saw me; and I then supposed that she hoped to have received a denial from me, and was disappointed at my coming; though I wondered that the answer she received to her message had not prepared her. This thought rushed into my mind in an instant, and I was sure she expected Mr Arnold. I told her, if I had thought I should have found her so well, that her message should not have brought me to her; for that I had determined not to stir out that day, till her invitation prevailed on me to change my mind. Sure, my dear, said she, there must have been some mistake in delivering the message to you, it was for to-morrow I desired the pleasure of your company to dine with me; for today I am absolutely engaged. However, I am very glad you are come, for I shall not go out till seven o'clock. I was vexed and mortified: either your servant or mine made a mistake, said I, for I was told you desired to see me to-day; besides you sent me word you were not well. She seemed a little abashed at this: I *was* very ill in the morning, she said; and though I was engaged to spend the evening abroad, did intend to have sent an excuse; but finding myself better, I changed my purpose.

Dinner was immediately served, and I sat down, but with a reluctance that prevented me from eating. I would have taken my leave soon after dinner, but Mrs Gerrarde insisted on my staying, and told me, if I refused her, she should think I had taken something amiss of her. She called for cards; I suffered myself to be persuaded, and we fell to piquet.

I played with disgust, and without attention, every minute wishing to break away. Coffee was at length brought in; I begged to be excused from staying, telling Mrs Gerrarde, I was sure I prevented her from going abroad, but she would take no denial. I was constrained to take a dish of coffee, and was hastening to get it down when the parlour door flew open, and lo! Mr Faulkland entered the room. If an object the most horrible to human nature had appeared before me, it could not, at that instant, have shocked me half so much. I let the cup and saucer drop from my hand: to say I turned pale, trembled and was ready to faint, would be too feeble a description of the effect this spectre had on me. I was senseless, I almost died away. Mrs Gerrarde pretended to be greatly alarmed; she ran for drops, and having given me a few in a glass of water, I made a shift to rise off my chair, and telling her, I should be glad of a little air, tottered to the street door. I determined to go home directly, but the universal tremor I was now in, disabled me from walking, and I sat down in the porch to recover myself a little. Mr Faulkland's having been a witness to the agony his presence had thrown me into, did not a little aggravate the horror and confusion of my thoughts. Whatever *his* were, he had not spoke to me, nor was it possible for me to have remarked his behaviour: I staid not more than two minutes in the parlour after he entered. In this situation you will think my distress would hardly admit of any addition; but the final blow was yet to come. Mrs Gerrarde had staid a minute in the parlour to speak to Mr Faulkland after I went out, but presently followed me, and was soothing me with the kindest expressions, when I heard the trampling of horses, and presently beheld Mr Arnold alighting at the door. I now gave myself up for lost. My mind suddenly suggested to me that Mrs Gerrarde had contrived a plot upon my innocence; but how she had been able to bring it about, my thoughts were not then disengaged enough to conceive. My mind was all a chaos; I was not able to answer Mr Arnold when he spoke to me. He soon perceived my disorder, and enquired the cause. Mrs Gerrarde took upon her to answer, that I was just preparing to go home, when I was taken suddenly ill. I was going abroad, said she, and as I ordered the chariot much about this hour, I fancy it is ready, and may as well carry Mrs Arnold home; you had best step into the parlour, my dear, (to me) till it is brought to the door.

I am now able to walk, madam, said I; there is no occasion to give you that trouble. Mr Arnold said, I should not walk by any means; and Mrs Gerrarde immediately calling to a servant to order the chariot to the door, said, as she was going out, she would leave me at home herself. Mr Arnold answered, it would be the best way, and that he should follow soon. The chariot was presently at the door, and I was preparing to get into it, when Mrs Gerrarde cry'd, Bless me, I had forgot, it will not be so civil to leave the gentleman behind, without saying any thing to him. Mr Arnold hastily asked, What Gentleman? Mrs Gerrarde replied, Mr Faulkland, *who took it into his head* to make me a visit this evening. She went quickly into the parlour, and strait returned with Mr Faulkland; who bowing carelessly to Mr Arnold, and civilly to me, walked away.

Mrs Gerrarde stepped into the chariot with me, and ordered it to drive to my house, leaving Mr Arnold standing motionless at her door.

A total silence prevailed on my side during our short journey home, except to answer in monosyllables Mrs Gerrarde's repeated enquiries after my health. She set me down at my own door, and took her leave without alighting. When I found myself alone, I began to consider the consequences of this evening's fatal interview; an interview, which, though unthought of by me, I judged was contrived to ensnare me. I laid all the circumstances together, and endeavoured to unravel the clue. 'Tis plain to me Mr Arnold was expected by Mrs Gerrarde this evening. She sent for me on purpose to betray me; the message, which she pretended was delivered wrong, was only an artifice, in order to impose on Mr Arnold, that he might imagine she did not expect me. Indeed, he could not possibly think she should send for me on the very evening he was to be with her; and she had so well guarded her contrivance, that it was not easily to be detected.

She had sent her message by word of mouth, though she generally wrote them down on paper, but this way would not have been liable to misconstruction: she had told me she was engaged in the evening, yet detained me longer than I meant to stay. From the first of these circumstances, it must appear to Mr Arnold, that as I had come unwished for, she wanted to get rid of me; the latter obviously served her own purpose; for it is as clear as daylight that she laid her plan so as that Mr Arnold should find Mr Faulkland and me together. All this I have deduced from a long train of reasoning on the circumstances. But the inexplicable part of the mystery is how she contrived to get Mr Faulkland, with whom I did not think she was acquainted, to visit her at so fatally critical a juncture. Sure some evil spirit must have assisted her in this wicked scheme: she knew, no doubt, of the promise Mr Arnold had exacted of me, never to see him. The apparent breach of this promise, she may have art enough to persuade Mr Arnold was concerted on my side. But I hope I shall be able to clear myself of this cruel imputation to my husband. Truth *must* force its way into his mind, if he is not resolved on my destruction. Perhaps Mr Faulkland may be secretly Mrs Gerrarde's admirer, and Mr Arnold is the dupe to her perfidy, as I am the sacrifice to her malice and licentiousness. – 'Tis all a strange riddle, but I cannot remain long in this dismal state of suspence; Mr Arnold, perhaps, may discover her treachery, while she is endeavouring to destroy me in his good opinion.

I am waiting here like a poor criminal, in expectation of appearing before my judge. I wish Mr Arnold were come in, yet I dread to see him.

I might have spared myself the anxiety. Mr Arnold is just returned, but he has locked himself into another chamber. I will not molest him tonight; to-morrow, perhaps, he may be in better temper, and I may be able to justify myself to him, and dispel this frightful gloom that hangs over us.

September 13

Hopes and fears are at an end, and the measure of my afflictions is filled up.

I went to bed last night, but slept not; the hours were passed in agonies not to be described. I think all griefs are magnified by silence and darkness. I well knew, prepossessed as Mr Arnold was by my artful enemy, I should find it difficult to excuse myself, or persuade him, that chance, or Mrs Gerrarde's more wicked contrivance, had been the sole cause of what had given him such offence. I was resolved, however, to vindicate my innocence, and was, in my own thoughts, preparing my defence the greatest part of the night. Towards morning, weariness and grief overpowered me, and I fell asleep, but I enjoyed not this repose long. Some noise that was made in the house suddenly awakened me; I saw it was broad day, and looking at my watch, found it was past seven o'clock. I rang my bell, and Patty entering my room, I enquired if her master was yet stirring. The poor girl looked aghast, He is gone away on horseback, madam, said she, almost two hours ago; and he ordered his man to put up some linnen and a few other things in a small portmanteau. I believe he means not to return to-night; for he bid me to deliver this letter to you. I opened the letter with trembling hands, from whence I received my doom in the following words:

'You have broken your faith with me, in seeing the man whom I forbad you to see, and whom you so solemnly promised to avoid. As you have betrayed my confidence in this particular, I can no longer rely on your prudence or your fidelity. Whatever your designs may be, it will be less to my dishonour if you prosecute them from under your husband's roof. I therefore give you till this day se'nnight to consider of a place for your future abode; for one house must no more contain two people, whose hearts are divided. Our children remain with me, and the settlement which was made on you in marriage, shall be appropriated to your separate use.

'I have left home to avoid expostulations, nor shall I return to it till I hear you have removed yourself. Spare the attempt of a justification, which can only aggravate the resentment of your already too-much injured husband.'

I have for a while suppressed the tumult in my soul, to give you this shocking letter.

O my Cecilia! What a wretched lot is thy unhappy friend's! To be neglected, forsaken, despised, by a husband that I love! Yet I could bear that: but to be suspected, accused too! to be at once the miserable object of jealousy and scorn! Surely they know nothing of the human heart, who say that jealousy cannot subsist without affection; I have a fatal proof to the contrary. Mr Arnold loves me not, yet doubts my honour. Cruel, mean, detestable suspicion! Oh that vile woman! 'tis she has done this; like a persecuting daemon she urges on the ruin which she set on foot.

What can I do? Whither can I fly? I cannot remain here any longer; my presence banishes Mr Arnold from his home. If I go to my mother under such circumstances, it will break her heart; yet she must know it. I must not wait to be turned out of my own doors. That thought is not to be borne. I will go this instant, no matter whither.

OLIVER GOLDSMITH

from *The Vicar of Wakefield*

2

Family misfortunes. The loss of fortune only serves to encrease the pride of the worthy

The temporal concerns of our family were chiefly committed to my wife's management, as to the spiritual I took them entirely under my own direction. The profits of my living, which amounted to but thirty-five pounds a year, I made over to the orphans and widows of the clergy of our diocese; for having a sufficient fortune of my own, I was careless of temporalities, and felt a secret pleasure in doing my duty without reward. I also set a resolution of keeping no curate, and of being acquainted with every man in the parish, exhorting the married men to temperance and the bachelors to matrimony; so that in a few years it was a common saying, that there were three strange wants at Wakefield, a parson wanting pride, young men wanting wives, and ale-houses wanting customers.

Matrimony was always one of my favourite topics, and I wrote several sermons to prove its happiness: but there was a peculiar tenet which I made a point of supporting;

for I maintained with Whiston, that it was unlawful for a priest of the church of England, after the death of his first wife, to take a second, or to express it in one word, I valued myself upon being a strict monogamist.

I was early initiated into this important dispute, on which so many laborious volumes have been written. I published some tracts upon the subject myself, which, as they never sold, I have the consolation of thinking are read only by the happy *Few*. Some of my friends called this my weak side; but alas! they had not like me made it the subject of long contemplation. The more I reflected upon it, the more important it appeared. I even went a step beyond Whiston in displaying my principles: as he had engraven upon his wife's tomb that she was the *only* wife of William Whiston; so I wrote a similar epitaph for my wife, though still living, in which I extolled her prudence, œconomy, and obedience till death; and having got it copied fair, with an elegant frame, it was placed over the chimney-piece, where it answered several very useful purposes. It admonished my wife of her duty to me, and my fidelity to her; it inspired her with a passion for fame, and constantly put her in mind of her end.

It was thus, perhaps, from hearing marriage so often recommended, that my eldest son, just upon leaving college, fixed his affections upon the daughter of a neighbouring clergyman, who was a dignitary in the church, and in circumstances to give her a large fortune: but fortune was her smallest accomplishment. Miss Arabella Wilmot was allowed by all, except my two daughters, to be completely pretty. Her youth, health, and innocence, were still heightened by a complexion so transparent, and such an happy sensibility of look, as even age could not gaze on with indifference. As Mr Wilmot knew that I could make a very handsome settlement on my son, he was not averse to the match; so both families lived together in all that harmony which generally precedes an expected alliance. Being convinced by experience that the days of courtship are the most happy of our lives, I was willing enough to lengthen the period; and the various amusements which the young couple every day shared in each other's company, seemed to encrease their passion. We were generally awaked in the morning by music, and on fine days rode a hunting. The hours between breakfast and dinner the ladies devoted to dress and study: they usually read a page, and then gazed at themselves in the glass, which even philosophers might own often presented the page of greatest beauty. At dinner my wife took the lead; for as she always insisted upon carving every thing herself, it being her mother's way, she gave us upon these occasions the history of every dish. When we had dined, to prevent the ladies leaving us, I generally ordered the table to be removed; and sometimes, with the music master's assistance, the girls would give us a very agreeable concert. Walking out, drinking tea, country dances, and forfeits, shortened the rest of the day, without the assistance of cards, as I hated all manner of gaming, except backgammon, at which my old friend and I sometimes took a two-penny hit. Nor can I here pass over an ominous circumstance that happened the last time we played together: I only wanted to fling a quatre, and yet I threw deuce ace five times running.

Some months were elapsed in this manner, till at last it was thought convenient to fix a day for the nuptials of the young couple, who seemed earnestly to desire it. During the preparations for the wedding, I need not describe the busy importance of my wife, nor the sly looks of my daughters: in fact, my attention was fixed on another object, the completing a tract which I intended shortly to publish in defence of my favourite principle. As I looked upon this as a master-piece both for argument and style, I could not in the pride of my heart avoid shewing it to my old friend Mr Wilmot, as I made no doubt of receiving his approbation; but not till too late I discovered that he was most violently attached to the contrary opinion, and with good reason; for he was at that time actually courting a fourth wife. This, as may be expected, produced a dispute attended with some acrimony, which threatened to interrupt our intended alliance: but on the day before that appointed for the ceremony, we agreed to discuss the subject at large.

It was managed with proper spirit on both sides: he asserted that I was heterodox, I retorted the charge: he replied, and I rejoined. In the mean time, while the controversy was hottest, I was called out by one of my relations, who, with a face of concern, advised me to give up the dispute, at least till my son's wedding was over. 'How,' cried I, 'relinquish the cause of truth, and let him be an husband, already driven to the very verge of absurdity. You might as well advise me to give up my fortune as my argument.' 'Your fortune,' returned my friend, 'I am now sorry to inform you, is almost nothing. The merchant in town, in whose hands your money was lodged, has gone off, to avoid a statute of bankruptcy, and is thought not to have left a shilling in the pound. I was unwilling to shock you or the family with the account till after the wedding: but now it may serve to moderate your warmth in the argument; for, I suppose, your own prudence will enforce the necessity of dissembling at least till your son has the young lady's fortune secure.' – 'Well,' returned I, 'if what you tell me be true, and if I am to be a beggar, it shall never make me a rascal, or induce me to disavow my principles. I'll go this moment and inform the company of my circumstances; and as for the argument, I even here retract my former concessions in the old gentleman's favour, nor will I allow him now to be an husband in any sense of the expression.'

It would be endless to describe the different sensations of both families when I divulged the news of our misfortune; but what others felt was slight to what the lovers appeared to endure. Mr Wilmot, who seemed before sufficiently inclined to break off the match, was by this blow soon determined: one virtue he had in perfection, which was prudence, too often the only one that is left us at seventy-two.

*   *   *

12

Fortune seems resolved to humble the family of Wakefield. Mortifications are often more painful than real calamities

When we were returned home, the night was dedicated to schemes of future conquest. Deborah exerted much sagacity in conjecturing which of the two girls was likely to have the best place, and most opportunities of seeing good company. The only obstacle to our preferment was in obtaining the 'Squire's recommendation; but he had already shewn us too many instances of his friendship to doubt of it now. Even in bed my wife kept up the usual theme: 'Well, faith, my dear Charles, between ourselves, I think we have made an excellent day's work of it.' – 'Pretty well,' cried I, not knowing what to say. – 'What only pretty well!' returned she. 'I think it is very well. Suppose the girls should come to make acquaintances of taste in town! This I am assured of, that London is the only place in the world for all manner of husbands. Besides, my dear, stranger things happen every day: and as ladies of quality are so taken with my daughters, what will not men of quality be! Entre nous, I protest I like my Lady Blarney vastly, so very obliging. However, Miss Carolina Wilelmina Amelia Skeggs has my warm heart. But yet, when they came to talk of places in town, you saw at once how I nailed them. Tell me, my dear, don't you think I did for my children there?' – 'Ay,' returned I, not knowing well what to think of the matter, 'heaven grant they may be both the better for it this day three months!' This was one of those observations I usually made to impress my wife with an opinion of my sagacity; for if the girls succeeded, then it was a pious wish fulfilled; but if any thing unfortunate ensued, then it might be looked upon as a prophecy. All this conversation, however, was only preparatory to another scheme, and indeed I dreaded as much. This was nothing less than, that as we were now to hold up our heads a little higher in the world, it would be proper to sell the Colt, which was grown old, at a neighbouring fair, and buy us an horse that would carry single or double upon an occasion, and make a pretty appearance at church or upon a visit. This at first I opposed stoutly; but it was as stoutly defended. However, as I weakened, my antagonist gained strength, till at last it was resolved to part with him.

As the fair happened on the following day, I had intentions of going myself; but my wife persuaded me that I had got a cold, and nothing could prevail upon her to permit me from home. 'No, my dear,' said she, 'our son Moses is a discreet boy, and can buy and sell to very good advantage; you know all our great bargains are of his purchasing. He always stands out and higgles, and actually tires them till he gets a bargain.'

As I had some opinion of my son's prudence, I was willing enough to entrust him with this commission; and the next morning I perceived his sisters mighty busy in fitting out Moses for the fair; trimming his hair, brushing his buckles, and cocking his hat with pins. The business of the toilet being over, we had at last the satisfaction of seeing him mounted upon the Colt, with a deal box before him to bring home groceries in. He had on a coat made of that cloth they call thunder and lightning, which, though grown too short, was much too good to be thrown away. His waistcoat was of gosling green, and his sisters had tied his hair with a broad black ribband. We all followed him several paces from the door, bawling after him good luck, good luck, till we could see him no longer.

He was scarce gone, when Mr Thornhill's butler came to congratulate us upon our good fortune, saying, that he overheard his young master mention our names with great commendation.

Good fortune seemed resolved not to come alone. Another footman from the same family followed, with a card for my daughters, importing, that the two ladies had received such pleasing accounts from Mr Thornhill of us all, that, after a few previous enquiries, they hoped to be perfectly satisfied. 'Ay,' cried my wife, 'I now see it is no easy matter to get into the families of the great; but when one once gets in, then, as Moses says, one may go sleep.' To this piece of humour, for she intended it for wit, my daughters assented with a loud laugh of pleasure. In short, such was her satisfaction at this message, that she actually put her hand in her pocket, and gave the messenger seven-pence halfpenny.

This was to be our visiting-day. The next that came was Mr Burchell, who had been at the fair. He brought my little ones a pennyworth of gingerbread each, which my wife undertook to keep for them, and give them by letters at a time. He brought my daughters also a couple of boxes, in which they might keep wafers, snuff, patches, or even money, when they got it. My wife was usually fond of a weesel skin purse, as being the most lucky; but this by the bye. We had still a regard for Mr Burchell, though his late rude behaviour was in some measure displeasing; nor could we now avoid communicating our happiness to him, and asking his advice: although we seldom followed advice, we were all ready enough to ask it. When he read the note from the two ladies, he shook his head, and observed, that an affair of this sort demanded the utmost circumspection. – This air of diffidence highly displeased my wife. 'I never doubted, Sir,' cried she, 'your readiness to be against my daughters and me. You have more circumspection than is wanted. However, I fancy when we come to ask advice, we will apply to persons who seem to have made use of it themselves.' – 'Whatever my own conduct may have been, madam,' replied he, 'is not the present question; tho' as I have made no use of advice myself, I should in conscience give it to those that will.' – As I was apprehensive this answer might draw on a repartee, making up by abuse what it wanted in wit, I changed the subject, by seeming to wonder what could keep our son so long at the fair, as it was now almost nightfall. – 'Never mind our son,' cried my wife, 'depend upon it he knows what he is about. I'll warrant we'll never see him sell his hen of a rainy day. I have seen him buy such bargains as would amaze one. I'll tell you a good story about that, that will make you split your sides with laughing – But as I live, yonder comes Moses, without an horse, and the box at his back.'

As she spoke, Moses came slowly on foot, and sweating under the deal box, which he had strapt round his shoulders like a pedlar. – 'Welcome, welcome, Moses; well, my boy, what have you brought us from the fair?' – 'I have brought you myself,' cried Moses, with a sly look, and resting the box on the dresser. – 'Ay, Moses,' cried my wife, 'that we know, but where is the horse?' 'I have sold him,' cried Moses, 'for three pounds five shillings and two-pence.' – 'Well done, my good boy,' returned she, 'I knew you would touch them off. Between ourselves, three pounds five shillings and two-pence is no bad day's work. Come, let us have it then.' – 'I have brought back no money,' cried Moses again. 'I have laid it all out in a bargain, and here it is,' pulling out a bundle from his breast: 'here they are; a groce of green spectacles, with silver rims and shagreen cases.' – 'A groce of green spectacles!' repeated my wife in a faint voice. 'And you have parted with the Colt, and brought us back nothing but a groce of green paltry spectacles!' – 'Dear mother,' cried the boy, 'why won't you listen to reason? I had them a dead bargain, or I should not have bought them. The silver rims alone will sell for double money.' – 'A fig for the silver rims,' cried my wife, in a passion: 'I dare swear they won't sell for above half the money at the rate of broken silver, five shillings an ounce.' – 'You need be under no uneasiness,' cried I, 'about selling the rims; for they are not worth six-pence, for I perceive they are only copper varnished over.' – 'What,' cried my wife, 'not silver, the rims not silver!' 'No,' cried I, 'no more silver than your saucepan.' – 'And so,' returned she, 'we have parted with the Colt, and have only got a groce of green spectacles, with copper rims and shagreen cases! A murrain take such trumpery. The blockhead has been imposed upon, and should have known his company better.' – 'There, my dear,' cried I, 'you are wrong, he should not have known them at all.' – 'Marry, hang the ideot,' returned she, 'to bring me such stuff, if I had them, I would throw them in the fire.' 'There again you are wrong, my dear,' cried I; 'for though they be copper, we will keep them by us, as copper spectacles, you know, are better than nothing.'

By this time the unfortunate Moses was undeceived. He now saw that he had indeed been imposed upon by a prowling sharper, who, observing his figure, had marked him for an easy prey. I therefore asked the circumstances of his deception. He sold the horse, it seems, and walked the fair in search of another. A reverend looking man brought him to a tent, under pretence of having one to sell. 'Here,' continued Moses, 'we met another man, very well drest, who desired to borrow twenty pounds upon these, saying, that he wanted money, and would dispose of them for a third of the value. The first gentleman, who pretended to be my friend, whispered me to buy them, and cautioned me not to let so good an offer pass. I sent for Mr Flamborough, and they talked him up as finely as they did me, and so at last we were persuaded to buy the two groce between us.'

13
Mr Burchell is found to be an enemy; for he has the confidence to give disagreeable advice

Our family had now made several attempts to be fine; but some unforeseen disaster demolished each as soon as projected. I endeavoured to take the advantage of every disappointment, to improve their good sense in proportion as they were frustrated in ambition. 'You see, my children,' cried I, 'how little is to be got by attempts to impose upon the world, in coping with our betters. Such as are poor and will associate with none but the rich, are hated by those they avoid, and despised by these they follow. Unequal combinations are always disadvantageous to the weaker side: the rich having the pleasure, and the poor the inconveniencies that result from them. But come, Dick, my boy, and repeat the fable that you were reading to-day, for the good of the company.'

'Once upon a time,' cried the child, 'a Giant and a Dwarf were friends, and kept together. They made a bargain that they would never forsake each other, but go seek adventures. The first battle they fought was with two Saracens, and the Dwarf, who was very courageous, dealt one of the champions a most angry blow. It did the Saracen but very little injury, who lifting up his sword, fairly struck off the poor Dwarf's arm. He was now in a woeful plight; but the Giant coming to his assistance, in a short time left the two Saracens dead on the plain, and the Dwarf cut off the dead man's head out of spite. They then travelled on to another adventure. This was against three bloody-minded Satyrs, who were carrying away a damsel in distress. The Dwarf was not quite so fierce now as before; but for all that, struck the first blow, which was returned by another, that knocked out his eye: but the Giant was soon up with them, and had they not fled, would certainly have killed them every one. They were all very joyful for this victory, and the damsel who was relieved fell in love with the Giant, and married him. They now travelled far, and farther than I can tell, till they met with a company of robbers. The Giant, for the first time, was foremost now; but the Dwarf was not far behind. The battle was stout and long. Wherever the Giant came all fell before him; but the Dwarf had like to have been killed more than once. At last the victory declared for the two adventurers; but the Dwarf lost his leg. The Dwarf was now without an arm, a leg, and an eye, while the Giant was without a single wound. Upon which he cried out to his little companion, My little heroe, this is glorious sport; let us get one victory more, and then we shall have honour for ever. No, cries the Dwarf, who was by this time grown wiser, no, I declare off; I'll fight no more; for I find in every battle that you get all the honour and rewards, but all the blows fall upon me.'

I was going to moralize this fable, when our attention was called off to a warm dispute between my wife and Mr Burchell, upon my daughters' intended expedition to town. My wife very strenuously insisted upon the advantages that would result from it. Mr Burchell, on the contrary, dissuaded her with great ardor, and I stood neuter. His present dissuasions seemed but the second part of those which were received with so ill a grace in the morning. The dispute grew high, while poor Deborah, instead of reasoning stronger, talked louder, and at last was obliged to take shelter from a defeat in clamour. The conclusion of her harangue, however, was highly displeasing to us all: she knew, she said, of some who had their own secret reasons for what they advised; but, for her part, she wished such to stay away from her house for the future. – 'Madam,' cried Burchell, with looks of great composure, which tended to enflame her the more, 'as for secret reasons, you are right: I have secret reasons, which I forbear to mention, because you are not able to answer those of which I make no secret: but I find my visits here are become troublesome; I'll take my leave therefore now, and perhaps come once more to take a final farewell when I am quitting the country.' Thus saying, he took up his hat, nor could the attempts of Sophia, whose looks seemed to upbraid his precipitancy, prevent his going.

When gone, we all regarded each other for some minutes with confusion. My wife, who knew herself to be the cause, strove to hide her concern with a forced smile, and an air of assurance, which I was willing to reprove: 'How, woman,' cried I to her, 'is it thus we treat strangers? Is it thus we return their kindness? Be assured, my dear, that these were the harshest words, and to me the most unpleasing that ever escaped your lips!' – 'Why would he provoke me then,' replied she; 'but I know the motives of his advice perfectly well. He would prevent my girls from going to town, that he may have the pleasure of my youngest daughter's company here at home. But whatever happens, she shall chuse better company than such low-lived fellows as he.' – 'Low-lived, my dear, do you call him,' cried I, 'it is very possible we may mistake this man's character: for he seems upon some occasions the most finished gentleman I ever knew. – Tell me, Sophia, my girl, has he ever given you any secret instances of his attachment?' – 'His conversation with me, sir,' replied my daughter, 'has ever been sensible, modest, and pleasing. As to aught else, no, never. Once, indeed, I remember to have heard him say he never knew a woman who could find merit in a man that seemed poor.' 'Such, my dear,' cried I, 'is the common cant of all the unfortunate or idle. But I hope you have been taught to judge properly of such men, and that it would be even madness to expect happiness from one who has been so very bad an œconomist of his own. Your mother and I have now better prospects for you. The next winter, which you will probably spend in town, will give you opportunities of making a more prudent choice.'

What Sophia's reflections were upon this occasion, I can't pretend to determine; but I was not displeased at the bottom that we were rid of a guest from whom I had much to fear. Our breach of hospitality went to my conscience a little: but I quickly silenced that monitor by two or three specious reasons, which served to satisfy and reconcile me to myself. The pain which conscience gives the man who has already done wrong, is soon got over. Conscience is a coward, and those faults it has not strength enough to prevent, it seldom has justice enough to accuse.

14

Fresh mortifications, or a demonstration that seeming calamities may be real blessings

The journey of my daughters to town was now resolved upon, Mr Thornhill having kindly promised to inspect their conduct himself, and inform us by letter of their behaviour. But it was thought indispensably necessary that their appearance should equal the greatness of their expectations, which could not be done without expence. We debated therefore in full council what were the easiest methods of raising money, or, more properly speaking, what we could most conveniently sell. The deliberation was soon finished, it was found that our remaining horse was utterly useless for the plow, without his companion, and equally unfit for the road, as wanting an eye, it was therefore determined that we should dispose of him for the purposes above-mentioned, at the neighbouring fair, and, to prevent imposition, that I should go with him myself. Though this was one of the first mercantile transactions of my life, yet I had no doubt about acquitting myself with reputation. The opinion a man forms of his own prudence is measured by that of the company he keeps, and as mine was mostly in the family way, I had conceived no unfavourable sentiments of my worldly wisdom. My wife, however, next morning, at parting, after I had got some paces from the door, called me back, to advise me, in a whisper, to have all my eyes about me.

I had, in the usual forms, when I came to the fair, put my horse through all his paces; but for some time had no bidders. At last a chapman approached, and, after he had for a good while examined the horse round, finding him blind of one eye, he would have nothing to say to him: a second came up; but observing he had a spavin, declared he would not take him for the driving home: a third perceived he had a windgall, and would bid no money: a fourth knew by his eye that he had the botts: a fifth, wondered what a plague I could do at the fair with a blind, spavined, galled hack, that was only fit to be cut up for a dog kennel. By this time I began to have a most hearty contempt for the poor animal myself, and was almost ashamed at the approach of every customer; for though I did not entirely believe all the fellows told me; yet I reflected that the number of witnesses was a strong presumption they were right, and St Gregory, upon good works, professes himself to be of the same opinion.

I was in this mortifying situation, when a brother clergyman, an old acquaintance, who had also business to the fair, came up, and shaking me by the hand, proposed adjourning to a public-house and taking a glass of whatever we could get. I readily closed with the offer, and entering an ale-house, we were shewn into a little back room, where there was only a venerable old man, who sat wholly intent over a large book, which he was reading. I never in my life saw a figure that prepossessed me more favourably. His locks of silver grey venerably shaded his temples, and his green old age seemed to be the result of health and benevolence. However, his presence did not interrupt our conversation; my friend and I discoursed on the various turns of fortune we had met: the Whistonean controversy, my last pamphlet, the archdeacon's reply, and the hard measure that was dealt me. But our attention was in a short time taken off by the appearance of a youth, who, entering the room, respectfully said something softly to the old stranger. 'Make no apologies, my child,' said the old man, 'to do good is a duty we owe to all our fellow creatures: take this, I wish it were more; but five pounds will relieve your distress, and you are welcome.' The modest youth shed tears of gratitude, and yet his gratitude was scarce equal to mine. I could have hugged the good old man in my arms, his benevolence pleased me so. He continued to read, and we resumed our conversation, until my companion, after some time, recollecting that he had business to transact in the fair, promised to be soon back; adding, that he always desired to have as much of Dr Primrose's company as possible. The old gentleman, hearing my name mentioned, seemed to look at me with attention, for some time, and when my friend was gone, most respectfully demanded if I was any way related to the great Primrose, that couragious monogamist, who had been the bulwark of the church. Never did my heart feel sincerer rapture than at that moment. 'Sir,' cried I, 'the applause of so good a man, as I am sure you are, adds to that happiness in my breast which your benevolence has already excited. You behold before you, Sir, that Doctor Primrose, the monogamist, whom you have been pleased to call great. You here see that unfortunate Divine, who has so long, and it would ill become me to say, successfully, fought against the deuterogamy of the age.' 'Sir,' cried the stranger, struck with awe, 'I fear I have been too familiar; but you'll forgive my curiosity, Sir: I beg pardon.' 'Sir,' cried I, grasping his hand, 'you are so far from displeasing me by your familiarity, that I must beg you'll accept my friendship, as you already have my esteem.' – 'Then with gratitude I accept the offer,' cried he, squeezing me by the hand, 'thou glorious pillar of unshaken orthodoxy; and do I behold –' I here interrupted what he was going to say; for tho', as an author, I could digest no small share of flattery, yet now my modesty would permit no more. However, no lovers in romance ever cemented a more instantaneous friendship. We talked upon several subjects: at first I thought he seemed rather devout than learned, and began to think he despised all human doctrines as dross. Yet this no way lessened him in my esteem; for I had for some time begun privately to harbour such an opinion myself. I therefore took occasion to observe, that the world in general began to be blameably indifferent as to doctrinal matters, and followed human speculations too much – 'Ay, Sir,' replied he, as if he had reserved all his learning to that moment, 'Ay, Sir, the world is in its dotage, and yet the cosmogony or creation of the world has puzzled philosophers of all ages. What a medly of opinions have they not broached upon the creation of the world? Sanconiathon, Manetho, Berosus, and Ocellus Lucanus, have all attempted it in vain. The latter has these words, *Anarchon ara kai atelutaion to pan*, which imply that all things have neither beginning nor end. Manetho also, who lived about the time of Nebuchadon-Asser, Asser being a Syriac word usually applied as a sirname to the kings of that country, as Teglat Phael-Asser, Nabon-Asser, he, I say, formed a conjecture equally absurd; for as we usually say *ek to biblion kubernetes*, which implies that books will never teach the world; so he attempted to investigate – But, Sir, I ask pardon, I am straying from the question.' – That he actually was; nor could I for my life see how the creation of the world had any thing to do with the business I was talking of; but it was sufficient to shew me that he was a man of letters, and I now reverenced him the more. I was resolved therefore to bring him to the touch-stone; but he was too mild and too gentle to contend for victory. Whenever I made any observation that looked like a challenge to controversy, he would smile, shake his head, and say nothing; by which I understood he could say much, if he thought proper. The subject therefore insensibly changed from the business of antiquity to that which brought us both to the fair; mine I told him was to sell an horse, and very luckily, indeed, his was to buy one for one of his tenants. My horse was soon produced, and in fine we struck a bargain. Nothing now remained but to pay me, and he accordingly pulled out a thirty pound note, and bid me change it. Not being in a capacity of complying with his demand, he ordered his footman to be called up, who made his appearance in a very genteel livery. 'Here, Abraham,' cried he, 'go and get gold for this; you'll do it at neighbour Jackson's, or any where.' While the fellow was gone, he entertained me with a pathetic harangue on the great scarcity of silver, which I undertook to improve, by deploring also the great scarcity of gold; so that by the time Abraham returned, we had both agreed that money was never so hard to be come at as now. Abraham returned to inform us, that he had been over the whole fair and could not get change, tho' he had offered half a crown for doing it. This was a very great disappointment to us all; but the old gentleman having paused a little, asked me if I knew one Solomon Flamborough in my part of the country: upon replying that he was my next door neighbour, 'If that be the case then,' returned he, 'I believe we shall deal. You shall have a draught upon him, payable at sight; and let me tell you he is as warm a man as any within five miles round him. Honest Solomon and I have been acquainted for many years together. I remember I always beat him at three jumps; but he could hop upon one leg farther than I.' A draught upon my neighbour was to me the same as money; for I was sufficiently convinced of his ability: the draught was signed and put into my hands, and Mr Jenkinson, the old gentleman, his man Abraham, and my horse, old Blackberry, trotted off very well pleased with each other.

After a short interval being left to reflection, I began to recollect that I had done wrong in taking a draught from a stranger, and so prudently resolved upon following the purchaser, and having back my horse. But this was now too late: I therefore made directly homewards, resolving to get the draught changed into money at my friend's as fast as possible. I found my honest neighbour smoking his pipe at his own door, and informing him that I had a small bill upon him, he read it twice over. 'You can read the name, I suppose,' cried I, 'Ephraim Jenkinson.' 'Yes,' returned he, 'the name is written plain enough, and I know the gentleman too, the greatest rascal under the canopy of heaven. This is the very same rogue who sold us the spectacles. Was he not a venerable looking man, with grey hair, and no flaps to his pocket-holes? And did he not talk a long string of learning about Greek and cosmogony, and the world?' To this I replied with a groan. 'Aye,' continued he, 'he has but that one piece of learning in the world, and he always talks it away whenever he finds a scholar in company; but I know the rogue, and will catch him yet.'

Though I was already sufficiently mortified, my greatest struggle was to come, in facing my wife and daughters. No truant was ever more afraid of returning to school, there to behold the master's visage, than I was of going home. I was determined, however, to anticipate their fury, by first falling into a passion myself.

But, alas! upon entering, I found the family no way disposed for battle. My wife and girls were all in tears, Mr Thornhill having been there that day to inform them, that their journey to town was entirely over. The two ladies having heard reports of us from some malicious person about us, were that day set out for London. He could neither discover the tendency, nor the author of these, but whatever they might be, or whoever might have broached them, he continued to assure our family of his friendship and protection. I found, therefore, that they bore my disappointment with great resignation, as it was eclipsed in the greatness of their own. But what perplexed us most was to think who could be so base as to asperse the character of a family so harmless as ours, too humble to excite envy, and too inoffensive to create disgust.

MARIA EDGEWORTH

Castle Rackrent

PREFACE

The prevailing taste of the public for anecdote has been censured and ridiculed by critics who aspire to the character of superior wisdom: but if we consider it in a proper point of view, this taste is an incontestible proof of the good sense and profoundly philosophic temper of the present times. Of the numbers who study, or at least who read history, how few derive any advantage from their labours! The heroes of history are so decked out by the fine fancy of the professed historian; they talk in such measured prose, and act from such sublime or such diabolical motives, that few have sufficient taste, wickedness, or heroism, to sympathize in their fate. Besides, there is much uncertainty even in the best authenticated ancient or modern histories; and that love of truth, which in some minds is innate and immutable, necessarily leads to a love of secret memoirs, and private anecdotes. We cannot judge either of the feelings or of the characters of men with perfect accuracy, from their actions or their appearance in public; it is from their careless conversations, their half-finished sentences, that we may hope with the greatest probability of success to discover their real characters. The life of a great or of a little man written by himself, the familiar letters, the diary of any individual published by his friends or by his enemies, after his decease, are esteemed important literary curiosities. We are surely justified, in this eager desire, to collect the most minute facts relative to the domestic lives, not only of the great and good, but even of the worthless and insignificant, since it is only by a comparison of their actual happiness or misery in the privacy of domestic life that we can form a just estimate of the real reward of virtue, or the real punishment of vice. That the great are not as happy as they seem, that the external circumstances of fortune and rank do not constitute felicity, is asserted by every moralist: the historian can seldom, consistently with his dignity, pause to illustrate this truth: it is therefore to the biographer we must have recourse. After we have beheld splendid characters playing their parts on the great theatre of the world, with all the advantages of stage effect and decoration, we anxiously beg to be admitted behind the scenes, that we may take a nearer view of the actors and actresses.

Some may perhaps imagine, that the value of biography depends upon the judgement and taste of the biographer: but on the contrary it may be maintained, that the merits of a biographer are inversely as the extent of his intellectual powers and of his literary talents. A plain unvarnished tale is preferable to the most highly ornamented narrative. Where we see that a man has the power, we may naturally suspect that he has the will to deceive us; and those who are used to literary manufacture know how much is often sacrificed to the rounding of a period, or the pointing of an antithesis.

That the ignorant may have their prejudices as well as the learned cannot be disputed; but we see and despise vulgar errors: we never bow to the authority of him who has no great name to sanction his absurdities. The partiality which blinds a biographer to the defects of his hero, in proportion as it is gross, ceases to be dangerous; but if it be concealed by the appearance of candour, which men of great abilities best know how to assume, it endangers our judgement sometimes, and sometimes our morals. If her grace the Duchess of Newcastle, instead of penning her lord's elaborate eulogium, had undertaken to write the life of Savage, we should not have been in any danger of mistaking an idle, ungrateful libertine for a man of genius and virtue. The talents of a biographer are often fatal to his reader. For these reasons the public often judiciously countenance those, who, without sagacity to discriminate character, without elegance of style to relieve the tediousness of narrative, without enlargement of mind to draw any conclusions from the facts they relate, simply pour forth anecdotes, and retail conversations, with all the minute prolixity of a gossip in a country town.

The author of the following Memoirs has upon these grounds fair claims to the public favour and attention; he was an illiterate old steward, whose partiality to *the family*, in which he was bred and born, must be obvious to the reader. He tells the history of the Rackrent family in his vernacular idiom, and in the full confidence that Sir Patrick, Sir Murtagh, Sir Kit, and Sir Condy Rackrent's affairs will be as interesting to all the world as they were to himself. Those who were acquainted with the manners of a certain class of the gentry of Ireland some years ago will want no evidence of the truth of honest Thady's narrative: to those who are totally unacquainted with Ireland, the following Memoirs will perhaps be scarcely intelligible, or probably they may appear perfectly incredible. For the information of the *ignorant* English reader, a few notes have been subjoined by the editor, and he had it once in contemplation to translate the language of Thady into plain English; but Thady's idiom is incapable of translation, and, besides, the authenticity of his story would have been more exposed to doubt if it were not told in his own characteristic manner. Several years ago he related to the editor the history of the Rackrent family, and it was with some difficulty that he was persuaded to have it committed to writing; however, his feelings for '*the honour of the family*', as he expressed himself, prevailed over his habitual laziness, and he at length completed the narrative which is now laid before the public.

The editor hopes his readers will observe that these are 'tales of other times': that the manners depicted in the following pages are not those of the present age: the race of the Rackrents has long since been extinct in Ireland; and the drunken Sir Patrick, the litigious Sir Murtagh, the fighting Sir Kit, and the slovenly Sir Condy, are characters which could no more be met with at present in Ireland, than Squire Western or Parson Trulliber in England. There is a time, when individuals can bear to be rallied for their past follies and absurdities, after they have acquired new habits, and a new consciousness. Nations as well as individuals gradually lose attachment to their identity, and the present generation is amused rather than offended by the ridicule that is thrown upon its ancestors.

Probably we shall soon have it in our power, in a hundred instances, to verify the truth of these observations.

When Ireland loses her identity by an union with Great Britain, she will look back with a smile of good-humoured complacency on the Sir Kits and Sir Condys of her former existence.

1800

Monday morning

Having, out of friendship for the family, upon whose estate, praised be Heaven! I and mine have lived rent-free, time out of mind, voluntarily undertaken to publish the MEMOIRS of the RACKRENT FAMILY, I think it my duty to say a few words, in the first place, concerning myself. My real name is Thady Quirk, though in the family I have always been known by no other than '*honest Thady*', – afterwards, in the time of Sir Murtagh, deceased, I remember to hear them calling me '*old Thady*', and now I'm come to '*poor Thady*'; for I wear a long great coat* winter and summer, which is very handy,

---

* The cloak, or mantle, as described by Thady, is of high antiquity. Spenser, in his 'View of the State of Ireland', proves that it is not, as some have imagined, peculiarly derived from the Scythians, but that 'most nations of the world anciently used the mantle; for the Jews used it, as you may read of Elias's mantle, &c.; the Chaldees also used it, as you may read in Diodorus; the Egyptians likewise used it, as you may read in Herodotus, and may be gathered by the description of Berenice, in the Greek Commentary upon Callimachus; the Greeks also used it anciently, as appeared by Venus's mantle lined with stars, though afterwards they changed the form thereof into their cloaks, called Pallai, as some of the Irish also use: and the ancient Latins and Romans used it, as you may read in Virgil, who was a very great antiquary, that Evander, when Æneas came to him at his feast, did entertain and feast him sitting on the ground, and lying on mantles: insomuch that he useth the very word mantile for a mantle,

"– Humi mantilia sternunt":

so that it seemeth that the mantle was a general habit to most nations, and not proper to the Scythians only.'

as I never put my arms into the sleeves; they are as good as new, though come Holantide next I've had it these seven years; it holds on by a single button round my neck, cloak fashion. To look at me, you would hardly think 'poor Thady' was the father of attorney Quirk; he is a high gentleman, and never minds what poor Thady says, and having better than fifteen hundred a year, landed estate, looks down upon honest Thady; but I wash my hands of his doings, and as I have lived so will I die, true and loyal to the family. The family of the Rackrents is, I am proud to say, one of the most ancient in the kingdom. Every body knows this is not the old family name, which was O'Shaughlin, related to the kings of Ireland – but that was before my time. My grandfather was driver to the great Sir Patrick O'Shaughlin, and I heard him, when I was a boy, telling how the Castle Rackrent estate came to Sir Patrick; Sir Tallyhoo Rackrent was cousin-german to him, and had a fine estate of his own, only never a gate upon it, it being his maxim that a car was the best gate. Poor gentleman! he lost a fine hunter and his life, at last, by it, all in one day's hunt. But I ought to bless that day, for the estate came straight into *the* family, upon one condition, which Sir Patrick O'Shaughlin at the time took sadly to heart, they say, but thought better of it afterwards, seeing how large a stake depended upon it, that he should by act of parliament, take and bear the surname and arms of Rackrent.

Now it was that the world was to see what was *in* Sir Patrick. On coming into the estate, he gave the finest entertainment ever was heard of in the country: not a man could stand after supper but Sir Patrick himself, who could sit out the best man in Ireland, let alone the three kingdoms itself. He had his house, from one year's end to another, as full of company as ever it could hold, and fuller; for rather than be left out of the parties at Castle Rackrent, many gentlemen, and those men of the first consequence and landed estates in the country, such as the O'Neils of Ballynagrotty, and the Moneygawls of Mount Juliet's Town, and O'Shannons of New Town Tullyhog, made it their choice, often and often, when there was no room to be had for love nor money, in long winter nights, to sleep in the chicken-house, which Sir Patrick had fitted up for the purpose of accommodating his friends and the public in general, who honoured him with their company unexpectedly at Castle Rackrent; and this went on, I can't tell you how long – the whole country rang with his praises! – Long life to him! I'm sure I love to look upon his picture, now opposite to me; though I never saw him, he must have been a portly gentleman – his neck something short, and remarkable for the largest

---

Spenser knew the convenience of the said mantle, as housing, bedding, and clothing.

'*Iren*. Because the commodity doth not countervail the discommodity; for the inconveniences which thereby do arise are much more many; for it is a fit house for an outlaw, a meet bed for a rebel, and an apt cloak for a thief. First, the outlaw being for his many crimes and villanies, banished from the towns and houses of honest men, and wandering in waste places, far from danger of law, maketh his mantle his house, and under it covereth himself from the wrath of Heaven, from the offence of the earth, and from the sight of men. When it raineth, it is his pent-house; when it bloweth, it is his tent; when it freezeth it is his tabernacle. In summer he can wear it loose; in winter he can wrap it close; at all times he can use it; never heavy, never cumbersome. Likewise for a rebel it is as serviceable; for in this war that he maketh (if at least it deserves the name of war), when he still flieth from his foe, and lurketh in the *thick woods* (*this should be black bogs*) and straight passages waiting for advantages, it is his bed, yea, and almost his household stuff.'

pimple on his nose, which, by his particular desire, is still extant in his picture, said to be a striking likeness, though taken when young. He is said also to be the inventor of raspberry whiskey, which is very likely, as nobody has ever appeared to dispute it with him, and as there still exists a broken punch-bowl at Castle Rackrent, in the garret, with an inscription to that effect – a great curiosity. A few days before his death he was very merry; it being his honour's birth-day, he called my grandfather in, God bless him! to drink the company's health, and filled a bumper himself, but could not carry it to his head, on account of the great shake in his hand; on this he cast his joke, saying 'What would my poor father say to me if he was to pop out of the grave, and see me now? I remember when I was a little boy, the first bumper of claret he gave me after dinner, how he praised me for carrying it so steady to my mouth. Here's my thanks to him – a bumper toast.' Then he fell to singing the favourite song he learned from his father – for the last time, poor gentleman – he sung it that night as loud and as hearty as ever with a chorus:

> He that goes to bed, and goes to bed sober,
> Falls as the leaves do, falls as the leaves do, and dies in October;
> But he that goes to bed, and goes to bed mellow,
> Lives as he ought to do, lives as he ought to do, and dies an honest fellow.

Sir Patrick died that night: just as the company rose to drink his health with three cheers, he fell down in a sort of fit, and was carried off; they sat it out, and were surprised, on inquiry, in the morning, to find that it was all over with poor Sir Patrick. Never did any gentleman live and die more beloved in the country by rich and poor. His funeral was such a one as was never known before or since in the county! All the gentlemen in the three counties were at it; far and near, how they flocked: my great grandfather said, that to see all the women even in their red cloaks, you would have taken them for the army drawn out. Then such a fine whillaluh! you might have heard it to the farthest end of the county, and happy the man who could get but a sight of the hearse! But who'd have thought it? just as all was going on right, through his own town they were passing, when the body was seized for debt – a rescue was apprehended from the mob; but the heir who attended the funeral was against that, for fear of consequences, seeing that those villains who came to serve acted under the disguise of the law: so, to be sure, the law must take its course, and little gain had the creditors for their pains. First and foremost, they had the curses of the country: and Sir Murtagh Rackrent, the new heir, in the next place, on account of this affront to the body, refused to pay a shilling of the debts, in which he was countenanced by all the best gentlemen of property, and others of his acquaintance; Sir Murtagh alleging in all companies, that he all along meant to pay his father's debts of honour, but the moment the law was taken of him, there was an end of honour to be sure. It was whispered (but none but the enemies of the family believe it), that this was all a sham seizure to get quit of the debts, which he had bound himself to pay in honour.

It's a long time ago, there's no saying how it was, but this for certain, the new man did not take at all after the old gentleman; the cellars were never filled after his death, and no open house, or any thing as it used to be; the tenants even were sent away without their whiskey. I was ashamed myself, and knew not what to say for the honour of the family; but I made the best of a bad case, and laid it all at my lady's door, for I did not like her any how, nor any body else; she was of the family of the Skinflints, and a widow; it was a strange match for Sir Murtagh; the people in the country thought he demeaned himself greatly, but I said nothing: I knew how it was; Sir Murtagh was a great lawyer, and looked to the great Skinflint estate; there, however, he overshot himself; for though one of the co-heiresses, he was never the better for her, for she outlived him many's the long day – he could not see that to be sure when he married her. I must say for her, she made him the best of wives, being a very notable stirring woman, and looking close to every thing. But I always suspected she had Scotch blood in her veins; any thing else I could have looked over in her from a regard to the family. She was a strict observer for self and servants of Lent, and all fast days, but not holidays. One of the maids having fainted three times the last day of Lent, to keep soul and body together, we put a morsel of roast beef into her mouth, which came from Sir Murtagh's dinner, who never fasted, not he; but somehow or other it unfortunately reached my lady's ears, and the priest of the parish had a complaint made of it the next day, and the poor girl was forced as soon as she could walk to do penance for it, before she could get any peace or absolution, in the house or out of it. However, my lady was very charitable in her own way. She had a charity school for poor children, where they were taught to read and write gratis, and where they were kept well to spinning gratis for my lady in return; for she had always heaps of duty yarn from the tenants, and got all her household linen out of the estate from first to last; for after the spinning, the weavers on the estate took it in hand for nothing, because of the looms my lady's interest could get from the Linen Board to distribute gratis. Then there was a bleach-yard near us, and the tenant dare refuse my lady nothing, for fear of a lawsuit Sir Murtagh kept hanging over him about the water-course. With these ways of managing, 'tis surprising how cheap my lady got things done, and how proud she was of it. Her table the same way, kept for next to nothing; duty fowls, and duty turkies, and duty geese, came as fast as we could eat 'em, for my lady kept a sharp look-out, and knew to a tub of butter every thing the tenants had, all round. They knew her way, and what with fear of driving for rent and Sir Murtagh's lawsuits, they were kept in such good order, they never thought of coming near Castle Rackrent without a present of something or other – nothing too much or too little for my lady – eggs, honey, butter, meal, fish, game, grouse, and herrings, fresh or salt, all went for something. As for their young pigs, we had them, and the best bacon and hams they could make up, with all young chickens in spring; but they were a set of poor wretches, and we had nothing but misfortunes with them, always breaking and running away. This, Sir Murtagh and my lady said, was all their former landlord Sir Patrick's fault, who let 'em get the half year's rent into arrear; there was something in that to be sure. But Sir Murtagh was as much the contrary way; for let alone making English tenants of them, every soul, he was always driving and driving, and pounding and pounding, and canting and canting, and replevying and replevying, and he made a good living of trespassing cattle; there was always some tenant's pig, or horse, or cow, or calf, or goose, trespassing, which was so great a gain to Sir Murtagh, that he did not like to hear me talk of repairing fences. Then his heriots and duty work brought him in something, his turf was cut, his potatoes set and dug, his hay brought home, and, in short, all the work about his house done for nothing; for in all our leases there were strict clauses heavy with penalties, which Sir Murtagh knew well how to enforce; so many days' duty work of man and horse, from every tenant, he was to have, and had, every year; and when a man vexed him, why the finest day he could pitch on, when the cratur was getting in his own harvest, or thatching his cabin, Sir Murtagh made it a principle to call upon him and his horse; so he taught 'em all, as he said, to know the law of landlord and tenant. As for law, I believe no man, dead or alive, ever loved it so well as Sir Murtagh. He had once sixteen suits pending at a time, and I never saw him so much himself; roads, lanes, bogs, wells, ponds, eel-wires, orchards, trees, tithes, vagrants, gravelpits, sandpits, dunghills, and nuisances, every thing upon the face of the earth furnished him good matter for a suit. He used to boast that he had a lawsuit for every letter in the alphabet. How I used to wonder to see Sir Murtagh in the midst of the papers in his office! Why he could hardly turn about for them. I made bold to shrug my shoulders once in his presence, and thanked my stars I was not born a gentleman to so much toil and trouble; but Sir Murtagh took me up short with his old proverb, 'learning is better than house or land'. Out of forty-nine suits which he had, he never lost one but seventeen; the rest he gained with costs, double costs, treble costs sometimes; but even that did not pay. He was a very learned man in the law, and had the character of it; but how it was I can't tell, these suits that he carried cost him a power of money; in the end he sold some hundreds a year of the family estate; but he was a very learned man in the law, and I know nothing of the matter, except having a great regard for the family; and I could not help grieving when he sent me to post up notices of the sale of the fee-simple of the lands and appurtenances of Timoleague. 'I know, honest Thady,' says he, to comfort me, 'what I'm about better than you do; I'm only selling to get the ready money wanting to carry on my suit with spirit with the Nugents of Carrickashaughlin.'

He was very sanguine about that suit with the Nugents of Carrickashaughlin. He could have gained it, they say, for certain, had it pleased Heaven to have spared him to us, and it would have been at the least a plump two thousand a year in his way; but things were ordered otherwise, for the best to be sure. He dug up a fairy-mount* against my advice, and had no luck afterwards. Though a learned man in the law, he was a little too incredulous in other matters. I warned him that I heard the very Banshee† that my grandfather heard under Sir Patrick's window a few days before his death. But Sir Murtagh thought nothing of the Banshee, nor of his cough with a spitting of blood, brought on, I understand, by catching cold in attending the courts, and overstraining

---

* These fairy-mounts are called ant-hills in England. They are held in high reverence by the common people in Ireland. A gentlemen, who in laying out his lawn had occasion to level one of these hillocks, could not prevail upon any of his labourers to begin the ominous work. He was obliged to take a *loy* from one of their reluctant hands, and began the attack himself. The labourers agreed, that the vengeance of the fairies would fall upon the head of the presumptuous mortal, who first disturbed them in their retreat.

† The Banshee is a species of aristocratic fairy, who, in the shape of a little hideous old woman, has been known to appear, and heard to sing in a mournful supernatural voice under the windows of great houses, to warn the family that some of them are soon to die. In the last century every great family in Ireland had a Banshee, who attended regularly; but latterly their visits and songs have been discontinued.

his chest with making himself heard in one of his favourite causes. He was a great speaker with a powerful voice; but his last speech was not in the courts at all. He and my lady, though both of the same way of thinking in some things, and though she was as good a wife and great economist as you could see, and he the best of husbands, as to looking into his affairs, and making money for his family; yet I don't know how it was, they had a great deal of sparring and jarring between them. My lady had her privy purse – and she had her weed ashes, and her sealing money upon the signing of all the leases, with something to buy gloves besides; and besides again often took money from the tenants, if offered properly, to speak for them to Sir Murtagh about abatements and renewals. Now the weed ashes and the glove money he allowed her clear perquisites; though once when he saw her in a new gown saved out of the weed ashes, he told her to my face (for he could say a sharp thing), that she should not put on her weeds before her husband's death. But in a dispute about an abatement, my lady would have the last word, and Sir Murtagh grew mad; I was within hearing of the door, and now I wish I had made bold to step in. He spoke so loud, the whole kitchen was out on the stairs. All of a sudden he stopped and my lady too. Something has surely happened, thought I – and so it was, for Sir Murtagh in his passion broke a blood-vessel, and all the law in the land could do nothing in that case. My lady sent for five physicians, but Sir Murtagh died, and was buried. She had a fine jointure settled upon her, and took herself away to the great joy of the tenantry. I never said any thing one way or the other, whilst she was part of the family, but got up to see her go at three o'clock in the morning. 'It's a fine morning, honest Thady,' said she; 'good bye to ye,' and into the carriage she stept, without a word more, good or bad, or even half a crown; but I made my bow, and stood to see her safe out of sight for the sake of the family.

Then we were all bustle in the house, which made me keep out of the way, for I walk slow and hate a bustle; but the house was all hurry-skurry, preparing for my new master. Sir Murtagh, I forgot to notice, had no childer;* so the Rackrent estate went to his younger brother, a young dashing officer, who came amongst us before I knew for the life of me whereabouts I was, in a gig or some of them things, with another spark along with him, and led horses, and servants, and dogs, and scarce a place to put any Christian of them into; for my late lady had sent all the feather-beds off before her, and blankets and household linen, down to the very knife cloths, on the cars to Dublin, which were all her own, lawfully paid for out of her own money. So the house was quite bare, and my young master, the moment ever he set foot in it out of his gig, thought all those things must come of themselves, I believe, for he never looked after any thing at all, but harum-scarum called for every thing as if we were conjurers, or in a public house. For my part, I could not bestir myself any how; I had been so much used to my late master and mistress, all was upside down with me, and the new servants in the servants' hall were quite out of my way; I had nobody to talk to and if it had not been for my pipe and tobacco, should, I verily believe, have broke my heart for poor Sir Murtagh.

But one morning my new master caught a glimpse of me as I was looking at his

* *Childer:* this is the manner in which many of Thady's rank, and others in Ireland, *formerly* pronounced the word *children.*

horse's heels, in hopes of a word from him. 'And is that old Thady?' says he, as he got into his gig: I loved him from that day to this, his voice was so like the family; and he threw me a guinea out of his waistcoat pocket, as he drew up the reins with the other hand, his horse rearing too; I thought I never set my eyes on a finer figure of a man, quite another sort from Sir Murtagh, though withal, *to me*, a family likeness. A fine life we should have led, had he staid amongst us, God bless him! He valued a guinea as little as any man: money to him was no more than dirt, and his gentleman and groom, and all belonging to him, the same; but the sporting season over, he grew tired of the place, and having got down a great architect for the house, and an improver for the grounds, and seen their plans and elevations, he fixed a day for settling with the tenants, but went off in a whirlwind to town, just as some of them came into the yard in the morning. A circular letter came next post from the new agent, with news that the master was sailed for England, and he must remit £500 to Bath for his use before a fortnight was at an end; bad news still for the poor tenants, no change still for the better with them. Sir Kit Rackrent, my young master, left all to the agent; and though he had the spirit of a prince, and lived away to the honour of his country abroad, which I was proud to hear of, what were we the better for that at home? The agent was one of your middle men,* who grind the face of the poor, and can never bear a man with a hat upon his head: he ferretted the tenants out of their lives; not a week without a call for money, drafts upon drafts from Sir Kit; but I laid it all to the fault of the agent; for, says I, what can Sir Kit do with so much cash, and he a single man? but still it went. Rents must be all paid up to the day, and afore; no allowance for improving tenants, no consideration for those who had built upon their farms: no sooner was a lease out, but the land was advertised to the highest bidder, all the old tenants turned out, when they spent their substance in the hope and trust of a renewal from the landlord. All was now set at the highest penny to a parcel of poor wretches, who meant to run away, and did so, after taking two crops out of the ground. Then fining down the year's rent came into fashion; any thing for the ready penny; and with all this, and presents to the agent and the driver, there was no such thing as standing it. I said nothing, for I had a regard for the family; but I walked about thinking if his honour Sir Kit knew all this, it would go hard with him, but he'd see us righted; not that I had any thing for my own share to complain of, for the agent was always very civil to me, when he came down into the

---

* *Middle men.* – There was a class of men termed middle men in Ireland, who took large farms on long leases from gentlemen of landed property, and set the land again in small portions to the poor, as under-tenants, at exorbitant rents. The *head landlord*, as he was called, seldom saw his *under-tenants*; but if he could not get the *middle man* to pay him his rent punctually, he *went to his land, and drove the land for his rent*, that is to say, he sent his steward or bailiff, or driver, to the land to seize the cattle, hay, corn, flax, oats, or potatoes, belonging to the under-tenants, and proceeded to sell these for his rents: it sometimes happened that these unfortunate tenants paid their rent twice over, once to the *middle man*, and once to the *head landlord*.

The characteristics of a middle man were, servility to his superiors, and tyranny towards his inferiors: the poor detested this race of beings. In speaking to them, however, they always used the most abject language, and the most humble tone and posture. – '*Please your honour*; *and please your honour's honour*,' they knew must be repeated as a charm at the beginning and end of every equivocating, exculpatory, or supplicatory sentence; and they were much more alert in doffing their caps to these new men, than to those of what they call *good old families*. A witty carpenter once termed these middle men *journeymen gentlemen*.

country, and took a great deal of notice of my son Jason. Jason Quirk, though he be my son, I must say, was a good scholar from his birth, and a very 'cute lad: I thought to make him a priest, but he did better for himself: seeing how he was as good a clerk as any in the county, the agent gave him his rent accounts to copy, which he did first of all for the pleasure of obliging the gentleman, and would take nothing at all for his trouble, but was always proud to serve the family. By-and-bye a good farm bounding us to the east fell into his honour's hands, and my son put in a proposal for it: why shouldn't he, as well as another? The proposals all went over to the master at the Bath, who knowing no more of the land than the child unborn, only having once been out a grousing on it before he went to England; and the value of lands, as the agent informed him, falling every year in Ireland, his honour wrote over in all haste a bit of a letter, saying he left it all to the agent, and that he must set it as well as he could to the best bidder, to be sure, and send him over £200 by return of post: with this the agent gave me a hint, and I spoke a good word for my son, and gave out in the country that nobody need bid against us. So his proposal was just the thing, and he a good tenant; and he got a promise of an abatement in the rent, after the first year, for advancing the half year's rent at signing the lease, which was wanting to complete the agent's £200, by the return of the post, with all which my master wrote back he was well satisfied. About this time we learned from the agent as a great secret, how the money went so fast, and the reason of the thick coming of the master's drafts: he was a little too fond of play; and Bath, they say, was no place for a young man of his fortune, where there were so many of his own countrymen too hunting him up and down, day and night, who had nothing to lose. At last, at Christmas, the agent wrote over to stop the drafts, for he could raise no more money on bond or mortgage, or from the tenants, or any how, nor had he any more to lend himself, and desired at the same time to decline the agency for the future, wishing Sir Kit his health and happiness, and the compliments of the season, for I saw the letter before ever it was sealed, when my son copied it. When the answer came, there was a new turn in affairs, and the agent was turned out; and my son Jason, who had corresponded privately with his honour occasionally on business, was forthwith desired by his honour to take the accounts into his own hands, and look them over till further orders. It was a very spirited letter to be sure: Sir Kit sent his service, and the compliments of the season, in return to the agent, and he would fight him with pleasure to-morrow, or any day, for sending him such a letter, if he was born a gentleman, which he was sorry (for both their sakes) to find (too late) he was not. Then, in a private postscript, he condescended to tell us, that all would be speedily settled to his satisfaction, and we should turn over a new leaf, for he was going to be married in a fortnight to the grandest heiress in England and had only immediate occasion at present for £200, as he would not choose to touch his lady's fortune for travelling expences home to Castle Rackrent, where he intended to be, wind and weather permitting, early in the next month; and desired fires, and the house to be painted, and the new building to go on as fast as possible, for the reception of him and his lady before that time; with several words besides in the letter, which we could not make out, because, God bless him! he wrote in such a flurry. My heart warmed to my new lady when I read this; I was almost afraid it was too good news to be true; but the girls fell to scouring, and it was well they did, for we soon saw his marriage in the paper to a lady with I don't know how many tens of thousand pounds to her fortune: then I watched the post-office for his landing; and the news came to my son of his and the bride being in Dublin, and on the way home to Castle Rackrent. We had bonfires all over the country, expecting him down the next day, and we had his coming of age still to celebrate, which he had not time to do properly before he left the country; therefore a great ball was expected, and great doings upon his coming, as it were, fresh to take possession of his ancestors' estate. I never shall forget the day he came home: we had waited and waited all day long till eleven o'clock at night, and I was thinking of sending the boy to lock the gates, and giving them up for that night, when there came the carriages thundering up to the great hall door. I got the first sight of the bride; for when the carriage door opened, just as she had her foot on the steps, I held the flam full in her face to light her, at which she shut her eyes, but I had a full view of the rest of her, and greatly shocked I was, for by that light she was little better than a blackamoor, and seemed crippled, but that was only sitting so long in the chariot. 'You're kindly welcome to Castle Rackrent, my lady,' says I (recollecting who she was); 'did your honour hear of the bonfires?' His honour spoke never a word, nor so much as handed her up the steps – he looked to me no more like himself than nothing at all; I know I took him for the skeleton of his honour: I was not sure what to say next to one or t'other, but seeing she was a stranger in a foreign country, I thought it was right to speak cheerful to her, so I went back again to the bonfires. 'My lady,' says I, as she crossed the hall, 'there would have been fifty times as many, but for fear of the horses and frightening your ladyship: Jason and I forbid them, please your honour.' With that she looked at me a little bewildered. 'Will I have a fire lighted in the state room to-night?' was the next question I put to her, but never a word she answered, so I concluded she could not speak a word of English, and was from foreign parts. The short and the long of it was I couldn't tell what to make of her; so I left her to herself, and went straight down to the servants' hall to learn something for certain about her. Sir Kit's own man was tired, but the groom set him a talking at last, and we had it all out before ever I closed my eyes that night. The bride might well be a great fortune – she was a *Jewish* by all accounts, who are famous for their great riches. I had never seen any of that tribe or nation before, and could only gather, that she spoke a strange kind of English of her own, that she could not abide pork or sausages, and went neither to church or mass. Mercy upon his honour's poor soul, thought I; what will become of him and his, and all of us, with his heretic blackamoor at the head of the Castle Rackrent estate! I never slept a wink all night for thinking of it; but before the servants I put my pipe in my mouth, and kept my mind to myself; for I had a great regard for the family; and after this, when strange gentlemen's servants came to the house, and would begin to talk about the bride, I took care to put the best foot foremost, and passed her for a nabob in the kitchen, which accounted for her dark complexion and every thing.

The very morning after they came home, however, I saw how things were plain enough between Sir Kit and my lady, though they were walking together arm in arm after breakfast, looking at the new building and the improvements. 'Old Thady,' said my master, just as he used to do, 'how do you do?' 'Very well, I thank your honour's honour,' said I; but I saw he was not well pleased, and my heart was in my mouth as I walked along after him. 'Is the large room damp, Thady?' said his honour. 'Oh, damp, your honour! how should it but be as dry as a bone,' says I, 'after all the fires we have kept in it day and night? it's the barrack-room your honour's talking on.' 'And what is a barrack-room, pray, my dear?' were the first words I ever heard out of my lady's lips. 'No matter, my dear!' said he, and went on talking to me, ashamed like I should witness her ignorance. To be sure, to hear her talk one might have taken her for an innocent, for it was, 'what's this, Sir Kit? and what's that, Sir Kit?' all the way we went. To be sure, Sir Kit had enough to do to answer her. 'And what do you call that, Sir Kit?' said she, 'that, that looks like a pile of black bricks, pray, Sir Kit?' 'My turf stack, my dear,' said my master, and bit his lip. Where have you lived, my lady, all your life, not to know a turf stack when you see it, thought I, but I said nothing. Then, by-and-bye, she takes out her glass, and begins spying over the country. 'And what's all that black swamp out yonder, Sir Kit?' says she. 'My bog, my dear,' says he, and went on whistling. 'It's a very ugly prospect, my dear,' says she. 'You don't see it, my dear,' says he, 'for we've planted it out, when the trees grow up in summer time,' says he. 'Where are the trees,' said she, 'my dear?' still looking through her glass. 'You are blind, my dear,' says he; 'what are those under your eyes?' 'These shrubs,' said she. 'Trees,' said he. 'May be they are what you call trees in Ireland, my dear,' said she; 'but they are not a yard high, are they?' 'They were planted out but last year, my lady,' says I, to soften matters between them, for I saw she was going the way to make his honour mad with her – 'they are very well grown for their age, and you'll not see the bog of Allyballycarricko'shaughlin at-all-at-all through the screen, when once the leaves come out. But, my lady, you must not quarrel with any part or parcel of Allyballycarricko'shaughlin, for you don't know how many hundred years that same bit of bog has been in the family; we would not part with the bog of Allyballycarricko'shaughlin upon no account at all; it cost the late Sir Murtagh two hundred good pounds to defend his title to it and boundaries against the O'Leary's who cut a road through it.' Now one would have thought this would have been hint enough for my lady, but she fell to laughing like one out of their right mind, and made me say the name of the bog over for her to get it by heart, a dozen times – then she must ask me how to spell it, and what was the meaning of it in English – Sir Kit standing by whistling all the while; I verily believed she laid the corner stone of all her future misfortunes at that very instant; but I said no more, only looked at Sir Kit.

There was no balls, no dinners, no doings; the country was all disappointed – Sir Kit's gentleman said in a whisper to me, it was all my lady's own fault, because she was so obstinate about the cross. 'What cross?' says I; 'is it about her being a heretic?' 'Oh, no such matter,' says he; 'my master does not mind her heresies, but her diamond cross, it's worth I can't tell you how much; and she has thousands of English pounds concealed in diamonds about her, which she as good as promised to give up to my master before he married, but now she won't part with any of them, and she must take the consequences.'

Her honey-moon, at least her Irish honey-moon, was scarcely well over, when his honour one morning said to me, 'Thady, buy me a pig!' and then the sausages were ordered, and here was the first open breaking-out of my lady's troubles. My lady came down herself into the kitchen, to speak to the cook about the sausages, and desired never to see them more at her table. Now my master had ordered them, and my lady knew that. The cook took my lady's part, because she never came down into the kitchen, and was young and innocent in housekeeping, which raised her pity; besides, said she, at her own table, surely, my lady should order and disorder what she pleases; but the cook soon changed her note, for my master made it a principle to have the sausages, and swore at her for a Jew herself, till he drove her fairly out of the kitchen; then, for fear of her place, and because he threatened that my lady should give her no discharge without the sausages, she gave up, and from that day forward always sausages, or bacon, or pig meat in some shape or other, went up to table; upon which my lady shut herself up in her own room, and my master said she might stay there, with an oath: and to make sure of her, he turned the key in the door, and kept it ever after in his pocket. We none of us ever saw or heard her speak for seven years after that:* he carried her dinner himself. Then his honour had a great deal of company to dine with him, and balls in the house, and was as gay and gallant, and as much himself as before he was married; and at dinner he always drank my lady Rackrent's good health, and so did the company, and he sent out always a servant, with his compliments to my lady Rackrent, and the company was drinking her ladyship's health, and begged to know if there was any thing at table he might send her; and the man came back, after the sham errand, with my lady Rackrent's compliments, and she was very much obliged to Sir Kit – she did not wish for any thing, but drank the company's health. The country, to be sure, talked and wondered at my lady's being shut up, but nobody chose to interfere or ask any impertinent questions, for they knew my master was a man very apt to give a short

* This part of the history of the Rackrent family can scarcely be thought credible; but in justice to honest Thady, it is hoped the reader will recollect the history of the celebrated Lady Cathcart's conjugal imprisonment. – The Editor was acquainted with Colonel M'Guire, Lady Cathcart's husband; he has lately seen and questioned the maid-servant who lived with Colonel M'Guire during the time of Lady Cathcart's imprisonment. Her ladyship was locked up in her own house for many years; during which period her husband was visited by the neighbouring gentry, and it was his regular custom at dinner to send his compliments to Lady Cathcart, informing her that the company had the honour to drink her ladyship's health, and begging to know whether there was any thing at table that she would like to eat? the answer was always, 'Lady Cathcart's compliments, and she has every thing she wants.' An instance of honesty in a poor Irish woman deserves to be recorded: – Lady Cathcart had some remarkably fine diamonds, which she had concealed from her husband, and which she was anxious to get out of the house, lest he should discover them. She had neither servant nor friend to whom she could entrust them; but she had observed a poor beggar woman, who used to come to the house; she spoke to her from the window of the room in which she was confined; the woman promised to do what she desired, and Lady Cathcart threw a parcel, containing the jewels, to her. The poor woman carried them to the person to whom they were directed; and several years afterwards, when Lady Cathcart recovered her liberty, she received her diamonds safely.

At Colonel M'Guire's death her ladyship was released. The editor, within this year, saw the gentleman who accompanied her to England after her husband's death. When she first was told of his death, she imagined that the news was not true, and that it was told only with an intention of deceiving her. At his death she had scarcely clothes sufficient to cover her; she wore a red wig, looked scared and her understanding seemed stupefied; she said that she scarcely knew one human creature from another; her imprisonment lasted above twenty years. These circumstances may appear strange to an English reader, but there is no danger in the present times, that any individual should exercise such tyranny as Colonel M'Guire's with impunity, the power being now all in the hands of government, and there being no possibility of obtaining from parliament an act of indemnity for any cruelties.

answer himself, and likely to call a man out for it afterwards; he was a famous shot; had killed his man before he came of age, and nobody scarce dared look at him whilst at Bath. Sir Kit's character was so well known in the country, that he lived in peace and quietness ever after, and was a great favourite with the ladies, especially when in process of time, in the fifth year of her confinement, my lady Rackrent fell ill, and took entirely to her bed, and he gave out that she was now skin and bone, and could not last through the winter. In this he had two physicians' opinions to back him (for now he called in two physicians for her), and tried all his arts to get the diamond cross from her on her death-bed, and to get her to make a will in his favour of her separate possession; but there she was too tough for him. He used to swear at her behind her back, after kneeling to her to her face, and call her in the presence of his gentleman his stiff-necked Israelite, though before he married her, that same gentleman told me he used to call her (how he could bring it out, I don't know) 'my pretty Jessica!' To be sure it must have been hard for her to guess what sort of a husband he reckoned to make her. When she was lying, to all expectation, on her death-bed of a broken heart, I could not but pity her, though she was a Jewish; and considering too it was no fault of hers to be taken with my master so young as she was at the Bath, and so fine a gentleman as Sir Kit was when he courted her; and considering too, after all they had heard and seen of him as a husband, there were now no less than three ladies in our county talked of for his second wife, all at daggers drawn with each other, as his gentleman swore, at the balls, for Sir Kit for their partner, – I could not but think them bewitched; but they all reasoned with themselves, that Sir Kit would make a good husband to any Christian but a Jewish, I suppose, and especially as he was now a reformed rake; and it was not known how my lady's fortune was settled in her will, nor how the Castle Rackrent estate was all mortgaged, and bonds out against him, for he was never cured of his gaming tricks; but that was the only fault he had, God bless him.

My lady had a sort of fit, and it was given out she was dead, by mistake: this brought things to a sad crisis for my poor master, – one of the three ladies showed his letters to her brother, and claimed his promises, whilst another did the same. I don't mention names. Sir Kit, in his defence, said he would meet any man who dared to question his conduct, and as to the ladies, they must settle it amongst them who was to be his second, and his third, and his fourth, whilst his first was still alive, to his mortification and theirs. Upon this, as upon all former occasions, he had the voice of the country with him, on account of the great spirit and propriety he acted with. He met and shot the first lady's brother; the next day he called out the second, who had a wooden leg; and their place of meeting by appointment being in a new ploughed field, the wooden-leg man stuck fast in it. Sir Kit, seeing his situation, with great candour fired his pistol over his head; upon which the seconds interposed, and convinced the parties there had been a slight misunderstanding between them; thereupon they shook hands cordially, and went home to dinner together. This gentleman, to show the world how they stood together, and by the advice of the friends of both parties, to re-establish his sister's injured reputation, went out with Sir Kit as his second, and carried his message next day to the last of his adversaries: I never saw him in such fine spirits as that day he went out – sure enough he was within ames-ace of getting quit handsomely of all his enemies; but unluckily, after hitting the tooth pick out of his adversary's finger and thumb, he received a ball in a vital part, and was brought home, in little better than an hour after the affair, speechless on a hand-barrow, to my lady. We got the key out of his pocket the first thing we did, and my son Jason ran to unlock the barrack-room, where my lady had been shut up for seven years, to acquaint her with the fatal accident. The surprise bereaved her of her senses at first, nor would she believe but we were putting some new trick upon her, to entrap her out of her jewels, for a great while, till Jason bethought himself of taking her to the window, and showed her the men bringing Sir Kit up the avenue upon the hand-barrow, which had immediately the desired effect; for directly she burst into tears, and pulling her cross from her bosom, she kissed it with as great devotion as ever I witnessed; and lifting up her eyes to heaven, uttered some ejaculation, which none present heard; but I take the sense of it to be, she returned thanks for this unexpected interposition in her favour when she had least reason to expect it. My master was greatly lamented: there was no life in him when we lifted him off the barrow, so he was laid out immediately, and *waked* the same night. The country was all in an uproar about him, and not a soul but cried shame upon his murderer; who would have been hanged surely, if he could have been brought to his trial, whilst the gentlemen in the country were up about it; but he very prudently withdrew himself to the continent before the affair was made public. As for the young lady, who was the immediate cause of the fatal accident, however innocently, she could never show her head after at the balls in the county or any place; and by the advice of her friends and physicians, she was ordered soon after to Bath, where it was expected, if any where on this side of the grave, she would meet with the recovery of her health and lost peace of mind. As a proof of his great popularity, I need only add, that there was a song made upon my master's untimely death in the newspapers, which was in every body's mouth, singing up and down through the country, even down to the mountains, only three days after his unhappy exit. He was also greatly bemoaned at the Curragh, where his cattle were well known; and all who had taken up his bets formerly were particularly inconsolable for his loss to society. His stud sold at the cant at the greatest price ever known in the county; his favourite horses were chiefly disposed of amongst his particular friends, who would give any price for them for his sake; but no ready money was required by the new heir, who wished not to displease any of the gentlemen of the neighbourhood just upon his coming to settle amongst them; so a long credit was given where requisite, and the cash has never been gathered in from that day to this.

But to return to my lady: – She got surprisingly well after my master's decease. No sooner was it known for certain that he was dead, than all the gentlemen within twenty miles of us came in a body, as it were, to set my lady at liberty, and to protest against her confinement, which they now for the first time understood was against her own consent. The ladies too were as attentive as possible, striving who should be foremost with their morning visits; and they that saw the diamonds spoke very handsomely of them, but thought it a pity they were not bestowed, if it had so pleased God, upon a lady who would have become them better. All these civilities wrought little with my lady, for she had taken an unaccountable prejudice against the country, and every thing belonging to it, and was so partial to her native land, that after parting with the cook, which she did immediately upon my master's decease, I never knew her easy one instant, night or day, but when she was packing up to leave us. Had she meant to make any stay in Ireland, I stood a great chance of being a great favourite with her; for when she found I understood the weathercock, she was always finding some pretence to be talking to me, and asking me which way the wind blew, and was it likely, did I think, to continue fair for England. But when I saw she had made up her mind to spend the rest of her days upon her own income and jewels in England, I considered her quite as a foreigner, and not at all any longer as part of the family. She gave no vails to the servants at Castle Rackrent at parting, notwithstanding the old proverb of *'as rich as a Jew'*, which, she being a Jewish, they built upon with reason. But from first to last she brought nothing but misfortunes amongst us; and if it had not been all along with her, his honour, Sir Kit, would have been now alive in all appearance. Her diamond cross was, they say, at the bottom of it all; and it was a shame for her, being his wife, not to show more duty, and to have given it up when he condescended to ask so often for such a bit of a trifle in his distresses, especially when he all along made it no secret he married for money. But we will not bestow another thought upon her. This much I thought it lay upon my conscience to say, in justice to my poor master's memory.

'Tis an ill wind that blows nobody no good – the same wind that took the Jew Lady Rackrent over to England brought over the new heir to Castle Rackrent.

Here let me pause for breath in my story, for though I had a great regard for every member of the family, yet without compare Sir Conolly, commonly called, for short, amongst his friends, Sir Condy Rackrent, was ever my great favourite, and, indeed, the most universally beloved man I had ever seen or heard of, not excepting his great ancestor Sir Patrick, to whose memory he, amongst other instances of generosity, erected a handsome marble stone in the church of Castle Rackrent, setting forth in large letters his age, birth, parentage, and many other virtues, concluding with the compliment so justly due, that 'Sir Patrick Rackrent lived and died a monument of old Irish hospitality.'

CONTINUATION OF THE MEMOIRS OF THE RACKRENT FAMILY

History of Sir Conolly Rackrent

Sir Condy Rackrent, by the grace of God heir at law to the Castle Rackrent estate, was a remote branch of the family: born to little or no fortune of his own, he was bred to the bar; at which, having many friends to push him, and no mean natural abilities of his own, he doubtless would, in process of time, if he could have borne the drudgery of that study, have been rapidly made king's counsel, at the least; but things were disposed otherwise, and he never went the circuit but twice, and then made no figure for want of a fee, and being unable to speak in public. He received his education chiefly in the college of Dublin; but before he came to years of discretion lived in the country, in a small but slated house, within view of the end of the avenue. I remember him bare footed and headed, running through the street of O'Shaughlin's town, and playing at pitch and toss, ball, marbles, and what not, with the boys of the town, amongst whom my son Jason was a great favourite with him. As for me, he was ever my white-headed boy: often's the time when I would call in at his father's, where I was always made welcome; he would slip down to me in the kitchen, and love to sit on my knee, whilst I told him stories of the family, and the blood from which he was sprung, and how he might look forward, if the *then* present man should die without childer, to being at the head of the Castle Rackrent estate. This was then spoke quite and clear at random to please the child, but it pleased Heaven to accomplish my prophecy afterwards, which gave him a great opinion of my judgement in business. He went to a little grammar-school with many others, and my son amongst the rest, who was in his class, and not a little useful to him in his book learning, which he acknowledged with gratitude ever after. These rudiments of his education thus completed, he got a-horseback, to which exercise he was ever addicted, and used to gallop over the country while yet but a slip of a boy, under the care of Sir Kit's huntsman, who was very fond of him, and often lent him his gun, and took him out a-shooting under his own eye. By these means he became well acquainted and popular amongst the poor in the neighbourhood early; for there was not a cabin at which he had not stopped some morning or other, along with the huntsman, to drink a glass of burnt whiskey out of an eggshell, to do him good and warm his heart, and drive the cold out of his stomach. The old people always told him he was a great likeness of Sir Patrick; which made him first have an ambition to take after him, as far as his fortune should allow. He left us when of an age to enter the college, and there completed his education and nineteenth year; for as he was not born to an estate, his friends thought it incumbent on them to give him the best education which could be had for love or money; and a great deal of money consequently was spent upon him at college and Temple. He was a very little altered for the worse by what he saw there of the great world; for when he came down into the country, to pay us a visit, we thought him just the same man as ever, hand and glove with every one, and as far from high, though not without his own proper share of family pride, as any man ever you see. Latterly, seeing how Sir Kit and the Jewish lived together, and that there was no one between him and the Castle Rackrent estate, he neglected to apply to the law as much as was expected of him; and secretly many of the tenants, and others, advanced him cash upon his note of hand value received, promising bargains of leases and lawful interest, should he ever come into the estate. All this was kept a great secret, for fear the present man, hearing of it, should take it into his head to take it ill of poor Condy, and so should cut him off for ever, by levying a fine, and suffering a recovery to dock the entail. Sir Murtagh would have been the man for that; but Sir Kit was too much taken up philandering to consider the law in this case, or any other. These practices I have mentioned, to account for the state of his affairs, I mean Sir Condy's, upon his coming into the Castle Rackrent estate. He could not command a penny of his first year's income; which, and keeping no accounts, and the great sight of company he did, with many other causes too numerous to mention, was the origin of his distresses. My son Jason, who was now established agent, and knew every thing, explained matters out of the face to Sir Conolly, and made him sensible of his embarrassed situation. With a great nominal rent-roll, it was almost all paid away in interest; which being for convenience suffered to run on, soon doubled the principal, and Sir Condy was obliged to pass new bonds for the interest, now grown principal, and so on. Whilst this was going on, my son requiring to be paid for his trouble, and many years' service in the family gratis, and Sir Condy not willing to take his affairs into his own hands, or to look them even in the face, he gave my son a bargain of some acres, which fell out of lease, at a reasonable rent. Jason set the land, as soon as his lease was sealed, to under-tenants, to make the rent, and got two hundred a-year profit rent; which was little enough considering his long agency. He bought the land at twelve years' purchase two years afterwards, when Sir Condy was pushed for money on an execution, and was at the same time allowed for his improvements thereon. There was a sort of hunting-lodge upon the estate, convenient to my son Jason's land, which he had his eye upon about this time; and he was a little jealous of Sir Condy, who talked of setting it to a stranger, who was just come into the country – Captain Moneygawl was the man. He was son and heir to the Moneygawls of Mount Juliet's town, who had a great estate in the next county to ours; and my master was loth to disoblige the young gentleman, whose heart was set upon the lodge; so he wrote him back, that the lodge was at his service, and if he would honour him with his company at Castle Rackrent, they could ride over together some morning, and look at it, before signing the lease. Accordingly the captain came over to us, and he and Sir Condy grew the greatest friends ever you see, and were for ever out a-shooting or hunting together, and were very merry in the evenings; and Sir Condy was invited of course to Mount Juliet's town; and the family intimacy that had been in Sir Patrick's time was now recollected, and nothing would serve Sir Condy but he must be three times a-week at the least with his new friends, which grieved me, who knew, by the captain's groom and gentleman, how they talked of him at Mount Juliet's town, making him quite, as one may say, a laughingstock and a butt for the whole company; but they were soon cured of *that* by an accident that surprised 'em not a little, as it did me. There was a bit of a scrawl found upon the waiting-maid of old Mr Moneygawl's youngest daughter, Miss Isabella, that laid open the whole; and her father, they say, was like one out of his right mind, and swore it was the last thing he ever should have thought of, when he invited my master to his house, that his daughter should think of such a match. But their talk signified not a straw, for, as Miss Isabella's maid reported, her young mistress was fallen over head and ears in love with Sir Condy, from the first time that ever her brother brought him into the house to dinner: the servant who waited that day behind my master's chair was the first who knew it, as he says; though it's hard to believe him, for he did not tell till a great while afterwards; but, however, it's likely enough, as the thing turned out, that he was not far out of the way; for towards the middle of dinner, as he says, they were talking of stage-plays, having a playhouse, and being great play-actors at Mount Juliet's town; and Miss Isabella turns short to my master, and says, 'Have you seen the play-bill, Sir Condy?' 'No, I have not,' said he. 'Then more shame for you,' said the captain her brother, 'not to know that my sister is to play Juliet to-night, who plays it better than any woman on or off the stage in all Ireland.' 'I am very happy to hear it,' said Sir Condy; and there the matter dropped for the present. But Sir Condy all this time, and a great while afterwards, was at a terrible nonplus; for he had no liking, not he, to stage-plays, nor to Miss Isabella either; to his mind, as it came out over a bowl of whiskey punch at home, his little Judy M'Quirk, who was daughter to a sister's son of mine, was worth twenty of Miss Isabella. He had seen her often when he stopped at her father's cabin to drink whiskey out of the eggshell, out hunting, before he came to the estate, and, as she gave out, was under something like a promise of marriage to her. Any how, I could not but pity my poor master, who was so bothered between them, and he an easy-hearted man, that could not disoblige nobody, God bless him! To be sure, it was not his place to behave ungenerous to Miss Isabella, who had disobliged all her relations for his sake, as he remarked; and then she was locked up in her chamber, and forbid to think of him any more, which raised his spirit, because his family was, as he observed, as good as theirs at any rate, and the Rackrents a suitable match for the Moneygawls any day in the year: all which was true enough; but it grieved me to see, that upon the strength of all this, Sir Condy was growing more in the mind to carry off Miss Isabella to Scotland, in spite of her relations, as she desired.

'It's all over with our poor Judy!' said I, with a heavy sigh, making bold to speak to him one night when he was a little cheerful, and standing in the servants' hall all alone with me, as was often his custom. 'Not at all,' said he; 'I never was fonder of Judy than at this present speaking; and to prove it to you,' said he, and he took from my hand a halfpenny, change that I had just got along with my tobacco, 'and to prove it to you, Thady,' says he, 'it's a toss up with me which I should marry this minute, her or Mr Moneygawl of Mount Juliet's town's daughter – so it is.' 'Oh, boo! boo!'* says I, making light of it, to see what he would go on to next; 'your honour's joking, to be sure; there's no compare between our poor Judy and Miss Isabella, who has a great fortune, they say.' 'I'm not a man to mind a fortune, nor never was,' said Sir Condy, proudly, 'whatever her friends may say; and to make short of it,' says he, 'I'm come to a determination upon the spot'; with that he swore such a terrible oath, as made me cross myself; 'and by this book,' said he, snatching up my ballad book, mistaking it for my prayer book, which lay in the window; 'and by this book,' says he, 'and by all the books that ever were shut and opened, it's come to a toss-up with me, and I'll stand or fall by the toss; and so, Thady, hand me over that pin† out of the ink-horn,' and he makes a cross on the smooth side of the halfpenny; 'Judy M'Quirk,' says he, 'her mark.'‡ God bless him! his hand was a little unsteadied by all the whiskey punch he had taken, but it was plain to see his heart was for poor Judy. My heart was all as one as in my mouth when I saw the halfpenny up in the air, but I said nothing at all; and when it came down, I was glad I had kept myself to myself, for to be sure now it was all over with poor Judy. 'Judy's out a luck,' said I, striving to laugh. 'I'm out a luck,' said he; and I never saw a man

---

* Boo! boo! an exclamation equivalent to *pshaw* or *nonsense*.

† *Pin* read *pen*. It formerly was vulgarly pronounced *pin* in Ireland.

‡ *Her mark.* It was the custom in Ireland for those who could not write to make a cross to stand for their signature, as was formerly the practice of our English monarchs. The Editor inserts the fac-simile of an Irish *mark*, which may hereafter be valuable to a judicious antiquary –

Her
Judy × M'Quirk,
Mark.

In bonds or notes, signed in this manner, a witness is requisite, as the name is frequently written by him or her.

look so cast down: he took up the halfpenny off the flag, and walked away quite sober-like by the shock. Now, though as easy a man, you would think, as any in the wide world, there was no such thing as making him unsay one of these sort of vows* which he had learned to reverence when young, as I well remember teaching him to toss up for bog-berries on my knee. So I saw the affair was as good as settled between him and Miss Isabella, and I had no more to say but to wish her joy, which I did the week afterwards, upon her return from Scotland with my poor master.

My new lady was young, as might be supposed of a lady that had been carried off, by her own consent, to Scotland; but I could only see her at first through her veil, which, from bashfulness or fashion, she kept over her face. 'And am I to walk through all this crowd of people, my dearest love?' said she to Sir Condy, meaning us servants and tenants, who had gathered at the back gate. 'My dear,' said Sir Condy, 'there's nothing for it but to walk, or to let me carry you as far as the house, for you see that back road is too narrow for a carriage, and the great piers have tumbled down across the front approach; so there's no driving the right way, by reason of the ruins.' 'Plato, thou reasonest well!' said she, or words to that effect, which I could no ways understand; and again, when her foot stumbled against a broken bit of a car-wheel, she cried out, 'Angels and ministers of grace defend us!' Well, thought I, to be sure if she's no Jewish, like the last, she is a mad woman for certain, which is as bad: it would have been as well for my poor master to have taken up with poor Judy, who is in her right mind, any how.

She was dressed like a mad woman, moreover, more than like any one I ever saw afore or since, and I could not take my eyes off her, but still followed behind her, and her feathers on the top of her hat were broke going in at the low back door, and she pulled out her little bottle out of her pocket to smell to when she found herself in the kitchen, and said, 'I shall faint with the heat of this odious, odious place.' 'My dear, it's only three steps across the kitchen, and there's a fine air if your veil was up,' said Sir Condy, and with that threw back her veil, so that I had then a full sight of her face; she had not at all the colour of one going to faint, but a fine complexion of her own, as I then took it to be, though her maid told me after it was all put on; but even complexion and all taken in, she was no way, in point of good looks, to compare to poor Judy; and with all she had a quality toss with her; but may be it was my over-partiality to Judy, into whose place I may say she stept, that made me notice all this. To do her justice, however, she was, when we came to know her better, very liberal in her housekeeping, nothing at all of the skin-flint in her; she left every thing to the housekeeper; and her own maid, Mrs Jane, who went with her to Scotland, gave her the best of characters for generosity. She seldom or ever wore a thing twice the same way, Mrs Jane told us,

* *Vows* – It has been maliciously and unjustly hinted, that the lower classes of the people in Ireland pay but little regard to oaths; yet it is certain that some oaths have great power over their minds. Sometimes they swear they will be revenged on some of their neighbours; this is an oath that they are never known to break. But, what is infinitely more extraordinary and unaccountable, they sometimes make and keep a vow against whiskey; those vows are usually limited to a short time. A woman who has a drunken husband is most fortunate if she can prevail upon him to go to the priest, and make a vow against whiskey for a year, or a month, or a week, or a day.

and was always pulling her things to pieces, and giving them away, never being used, in her father's house, to think of expence in any thing; and she reckoned, to be sure, to go on the same way at Castle Rackrent; but, when I came to inquire, I learned that her father was so mad with her for running off, after his locking her up, and forbidding her to think any more of Sir Condy, that he would not give her a farthing; and it was lucky for her she had a few thousands of her own, which had been left to her by a good grandmother, and these were very convenient to begin with. My master and my lady set out in great style; they had the finest coach and chariot, and horses and liveries, and cut the greatest dash in the county, returning their wedding visits; and it was immediately reported, that her father had undertaken to pay all my master's debts, and of course all his tradesmen gave him a new credit, and every thing went on smack smooth, and I could not but admire my lady's spirit, and was proud to see Castle Rackrent again in all its glory. My lady had a fine taste for building, and furniture, and playhouses, and she turned every thing topsy-turvy, and made the barrack-room into a theatre, as she called it, and she went on as if she had a mint of money at her elbow; and, to be sure, I thought she knew best, especially as Sir Condy said nothing to it one way or the other. All he asked, God bless him! was to live in peace and quietness, and have his bottle or his whiskey punch at night to himself. Now this was little enough, to be sure, for any gentleman; but my lady couldn't abide the smell of the whiskey punch. 'My dear,' says he, 'you liked it well enough before we were married, and why not now?' 'My dear,' said she, 'I never smelt it, or I assure you I should never have prevailed upon myself to marry you.' 'My dear, I am sorry you did not smell it, but we can't help that now,' returned my master, without putting himself in a passion, or going out of his way, but just fair and easy helped himself to another glass, and drank it off to her good health. All this the butler told me, who was going backwards and forwards unnoticed with the jug, and hot water, and sugar, and all he thought wanting. Upon my master's swallowing the last glass of whiskey punch my lady burst into tears, calling him an ungrateful, base, barbarous wretch! and went off into a fit of hysterics, as I think Mrs Jane called it, and my poor master was greatly frightened, this being the first thing of the kind he had seen; and he fell straight on his knees before her, and, like a good-hearted cratur as he was, ordered the whiskey punch out of the room, and bid 'em throw open all the windows, and cursed himself: and then my lady came to herself again, and when she saw him kneeling there bid him get up, and not forswear himself any more, for that she was sure he did not love her, nor never had; this we learnt from Mrs Jane, who was the only person left present at all this. 'My dear,' returns my master, thinking, to be sure, of Judy, as well he might, 'whoever told you so is an incendiary, and I'll have 'em turned out of the house this minute, if you'll only let me know which of them it was.' 'Told me what?' said my lady, starting upright in her chair. 'Nothing at all, nothing at all,' said my master, seeing he had overshot himself, and that my lady spoke at random; 'but what you said just now, that I did not love you, Bella; who told you that?' 'My own sense,' she said, and she put her handkerchief to her face and leant back upon Mrs Jane, and fell to sobbing as if her heart would break. 'Why now, Bella, this is very strange of you,' said my poor master; 'if nobody has told you nothing, what is it you are taking on for at this rate, and exposing yourself and me for this way?' 'Oh, say no more, say no more; every word you say kills me,' cried my lady; and she ran on like one, as Mrs Jane says, raving, 'Oh, Sir Condy, Sir Condy! I that had hoped to find in you – ' 'Why now, faith, this is a little too much; do Bella, try to recollect yourself, my dear; am not I your husband, and of your own choosing; and is not that enough?' 'Oh, too much! too much!' cried my lady, wringing her hands. 'Why, my dear, come to your right senses, for the love of heaven. See, is not the whiskey punch, jug and bowl, and all, gone out of the room long ago? What is it, in the wide world, you have to complain of?' But still my lady sobbed and sobbed, and called herself the most wretched of women; and among other out-of-the-way provoking things, asked my master, was he fit company for her, and he drinking all night? This nettling him, which it was hard to do, he replied, that as to drinking all night, he was then as sober as she was herself, and that it was no matter how much a man drank, provided it did no ways affect or stagger him: that as to being fit company for her, he thought himself of a family to be fit company for any lord or lady in the land; but that he never prevented her from seeing and keeping what company she pleased, and that he had done his best to make Castle Rackrent pleasing to her since her marriage, having always had the house full of visitors, and if her own relations were not amongst them, he said that was their own fault, and their pride's fault, of which he was sorry to find her ladyship had so unbecoming a share. So concluding, he took his candle and walked off to his room, and my lady was in her tantarums for three days after; and would have been so much longer, no doubt, but some of her friends, young ladies, and cousins, and second cousins, came to Castle Rackrent, by my poor master's express invitation, to see her, and she was in a hurry to get up, as Mrs Jane called it, a play for them, and so got well, and was as finely dressed, and as happy to look at, as ever; and all the young ladies, who used to be in her room dressing of her, said, in Mrs Jane's hearing, that my lady was the happiest bride ever they had seen, and that to be sure a love-match was the only thing for happiness, where the parties could any way afford it.

As to affording it, God knows it was little they knew of the matter; my lady's few thousands could not last for ever, especially the way she went on with them, and letters from tradesfolk came every post thick and threefold with bills as long as my arm, of years' and years' standing; my son Jason had 'em all handed over to him, and the pressing letters were all unread by Sir Condy, who hated trouble, and could never be brought to hear talk of business, but still put it off and put it off, saying, settle it any how, or bid 'em call again to-morrow, or speak to me about it some other time. Now it was hard to find the right time to speak, for in the mornings he was a-bed, and in the evenings over his bottle, where no gentleman chooses to be disturbed. Things in a twelvemonth or so came to such a pass there was no making a shift to go on any longer, though we were all of us well enough used to live from hand to mouth at Castle Rackrent. One day, I remember, when there was a power of company, all sitting after dinner in the dusk, not to say dark, in the drawing-room, my lady having rung five times for candles, and none to go up, the housekeeper sent up the footman, who went to my mistress, and whispered behind her chair how it was. 'My lady,' says he, 'there are no candles in the house'. 'Bless me,' says she, 'then take a horse and gallop off as fast as you can to Carrick O'Fungus, and get some.' 'And in the mean time tell them to step into the playhouse, and try if there are not some bits left,' added Sir Condy, who happened to be within hearing. The man was sent up again to my lady, to let her know there was no horse to go, but one that wanted a shoe. 'Go to Sir Condy, then; I know nothing at all about the horses,' said my lady; 'why do you plague me with these things?' How it was settled I really forget, but to the best of my remembrance, the boy was sent down to my son Jason's to borrow candles for the night. Another time in the winter, and on a desperate cold day, there was no turf in for the parlour and above stairs, and scarce enough for the cook in the kitchen; the little *gossoon** was sent off to the neighbours, to see and beg or borrow some, but none could he bring back with him for love or money; so as needs must, we were forced to trouble Sir Condy – 'Well, and if there's no turf to be had in the town or country, why what signifies talking any more about it; can't ye go and cut down a tree?' 'Which tree, please your honour?' I made bold to say. 'Any tree at all that's good to burn,' said Sir Condy; 'send off smart and get one down, and the fires lighted, before my lady gets up to breakfast, or the house will be too hot to hold us.' He was always very considerate in all things about my lady, and she wanted for nothing whilst he had it to give. Well, when things were tight with them about this time, my son Jason put in a word again about the lodge, and made a genteel offer to lay down the purchase-money, to relieve Sir Condy's distresses. Now Sir Condy had it from the best authority, that there were two writs come down to the sheriff against his person, and the sheriff, as ill luck would have it, was no friend of his, and talked how he must do his duty, and how he would do it, if it was against the first man in the country, or even his own brother; let alone one who had voted against him at the last election, as Sir Condy had done. So Sir Condy was fain to take the purchase-money of the lodge from my son Jason to settle matters; and sure enough it was a good bargain for both parties, for my son bought the fee-simple of a good house for him and his heirs for ever, for little or nothing, and by selling of it for that same, my master saved himself from a gaol. Every way it turned out fortunate for Sir Condy; for before the money was all gone there came a general election, and he being so well beloved in the county, and one of the oldest families, no one had a better right to stand candidate for the vacancy, and he was called upon by all his friends, and the whole county I may say, to declare himself against the old member, who had little thought of a contest. My master did not relish the thought of a troublesome canvass, and all the ill-will he might bring upon himself by disturbing the peace of the county, besides the expence, which was no trifle; but all his friends called upon one another to subscribe, and they formed themselves into a committee, and wrote all his circular letters for him, and engaged all his agents, and did all the business unknown to him; and he was well pleased that it should be so at last, and my lady herself was very sanguine about the election; and there was open house kept night and day at Castle Rackrent, and I thought I never saw my lady look so well in her life as she did at that time; there were grand dinners, and all the gentlemen

---

* *Gossoon*, a little boy – from the French word *garçon*. In most Irish families there used to be a barefooted gossoon, who was slave to the cook and the butler, and who in fact, without wages, did all the hard work of the house. Gossoons were always employed as messengers. The Editor has known a gossoon to go on foot, without shoes or stockings, fifty-one English miles between sunrise and sunset.

drinking success to Sir Condy till they were carried off; and then dances and balls, and the ladies all finishing with a raking pot of tea in the morning. Indeed it was well the company made it their choice to sit up all nights, for there were not half beds enough for the sights of people that were in it, though there were shakedowns in the drawing-room always made up before sunrise for those that liked it. For my part, when I saw the doings that were going on, and the loads of claret that went down the throats of them that had no right to be asking for it, and the sights of meat that went up to table and never came down, besides what was carried off to one or t'other below stairs, I couldn't but pity my poor master, who was to pay for all; but I said nothing, for fear of gaining myself ill-will. The day of election will come some time or other, says I to myself, and all will be over; and so it did, and a glorious day it was as any I ever had the happiness to see. 'Huzza! huzza! Sir Condy Rackrent for ever!' was the first thing I hears in the morning, and the same and nothing else all day, and not a soul sober only just when polling, enough to give their votes as became 'em, and to stand the browbeating of the lawyers, who came tight enough upon us; and many of our freeholders were knocked off, having never a freehold that they could safely swear to, and Sir Condy was not willing to have any man perjure himself for his sake, as was done on the other side, God knows, but no matter for that. Some of our friends were dumb-founded, by the lawyers asking them: Had they ever been upon the ground where their freeholds lay? Now Sir Condy being tender of the consciences of them that had not been on the ground, and so could not swear to a freehold when cross-examined by them lawyers, sent out for a couple of cleaves-full of the sods of his farm of Gulteeshinnagh:* and as soon as the sods came into town he set each man upon his sod, and so then, ever after, you know, they could fairly swear they had been upon the ground.† We gained the day by this piece of honesty. I thought I should have died in the streets for joy when I seed my poor master chaired, and he bareheaded, and it raining as hard as it could pour; but all the crowds following him up and down, and he bowing and shaking hands with the whole town. 'Is that Sir Condy Rackrent in the chair?' says a stranger man in the crowd. 'The same,' says I; 'who else should it be? God bless him!' 'And I take it, then, you belong to him?' says he. 'Not at all,' says I: 'but I live under him, and have done so these two hundred years and upwards, me and mine.' 'It's lucky for you, then,' rejoins he, 'that he is where he is; for was he any where else but in the chair, this minute he'd be in a worse place; for I was sent down on purpose to put him up,‡ and here's my order for so doing in my pocket.' It was a writ that villain the wine merchant had marked against my poor master for some hundreds of an old debt, which it was a shame to be

---

* At St Patrick's meeting, London, March, 1806, the Duke of Sussex said he had the honour of bearing an Irish title, and, with the permission of the company, he should tell them an anecdote of what he had experienced on his travels. When he was at Rome, he went to visit an Irish seminary, and when they heard who he was, and that he had an Irish title, some of them asked him, 'Please your Royal Highness, since you are an Irish peer, will you tell us if you ever trod upon Irish ground?' When he told them he had not, 'O then,' said one of the order, 'you shall soon do so.' Then they spread some earth, which had been brought from Ireland, on a marble slab, and made him stand upon it.

† This was actually done at an election in Ireland.

‡ *To put him up* – to put him in gaol.

talking of at such a time as this. 'Put it in your pocket again, and think no more of it any ways for seven years to come, my honest friend,' says I; 'he's a member of parliament now, praised be God, and such as you can't touch him: and if you'll take a fool's advice, I'd have you keep out of the way this day, or you'll run a good chance of getting your deserts amongst my master's friends, unless you choose to drink his health like every body else.' 'I've no objection to that in life,' said he; so we went into one of the public houses kept open for my master; and we had a great deal of talk about this thing and that. 'And how is it,' says he, 'your master keeps on so well upon his legs? I heard say he was off Holantide twelvemonth past.' 'Never was better or heartier in his life,' said I. 'It's not that I'm after speaking of,' said he; 'but there was a great report of his being ruined.' 'No matter,' says I, 'the sheriffs two years running were his particular friends, and the sub-sheriffs were both of them gentlemen, and were properly spoken to; and so the writs lay snug with them, and they, as I understand by my son Jason the custom in them cases is, returned the writs as they came to them to those that sent 'em; much good may it do them! with a word in Latin, that no such person as Sir Condy Rackrent, bart., was to be found in those parts.' 'Oh, I understand all those ways better, no offence, than you,' says he, laughing, and at the same time filling his glass to my master's good health, which convinced me he was a warm friend in his heart after all, though appearances were a little suspicious or so at first. 'To be sure,' says he, still cutting his joke, 'when a man's over head and shoulders in debt, he may live the faster for it, and the better, if he goes the right way about it; or else how is it so many live on so well, as we see every day, after they are ruined?' 'How is it,' says I, being a little merry at the time; 'how is it but just as you see the ducks in the chicken-yard, just after their heads are cut off by the cook, running round and round faster than when alive?' At which conceit he fell a laughing, and remarked he had never had the happiness yet to see the chicken-yard at Castle Rackrent. 'It won't be long so, I hope,' says I; 'you'll be kindly welcome there, as every body is made by my master; there is not a freer spoken gentleman, or a better beloved, high or low, in all Ireland.' And of what passed after this I'm not sensible, for we drank Sir Condy's good health and the downfall of his enemies till we could stand no longer ourselves. And little did I think at the time, or till long after, how I was harbouring my poor master's greatest of enemies myself. This fellow had the impudence, after coming to see the chicken-yard, to get me to introduce him to my son Jason; little more than the man that never was born did I guess at his meaning by this visit: he gets him a correct list fairly drawn out from my son Jason of all my master's debts, and goes straight round to the creditors and buys them all up, which he did easy enough, seeing the half of them never expected to see their money out of Sir Condy's hands. Then, when this base-minded limb of the law, as I afterward detected him in being, grew to be sole creditor over all, he takes him out a custodiam on all the denominations and sub-denominations, and every carton and half carton upon the estate; and not content with that, must have an execution against the master's goods, and down to the furniture, though little worth, of Castle Rackrent itself. But this is a part of my story I'm not come to yet, and it's bad to be forestalling: ill news flies fast enough all the world over.

To go back to the day of the election, which I never think of but with pleasure and tears of gratitude for those good times; after the election was quite and clean over, there comes shoals of people from all parts, claiming to have obliged my master with their votes, and putting him in mind of promises which he could never remember himself to have made; one was to have a freehold for each of his four sons; another was to have a renewal of a lease; another an abatement; one came to be paid ten guineas for a pair of silver buckles sold my master on the hustings, which turned out to be no better than copper gilt; another had a long bill for oats, the half of which never went into the granary to my certain knowledge, and the other half were not fit for the cattle to touch; but the bargain was made the week before the election, and the coach and saddle horses were got into order for the day, besides a vote fairly got by them oats; so no more reasoning on that head; but then there was no end to them that were telling Sir Condy he had engaged to make their sons excisemen, or high constables, or the like; and as for them that had bills to give in for liquor, and beds, and straw, and ribands, and horses, and postchaises for the gentlemen freeholders that came from all parts and other counties to vote for my master, and were not, to be sure, to be at any charges, there was no standing against all these; and, worse than all, the gentlemen of my master's committee, who managed all for him, and talked how they'd bring him in without costing him a penny, and subscribed by hundreds very genteelly, forgot to pay their subscriptions, and had laid out in agents' and lawyers' fees and secret service money the Lord knows how much; and my master could never ask one of them for their subscription, you are sensible, nor for the price of a fine horse he had sold one of them; so it all was left at his door. He could never, God bless him again! I say, bring himself to ask a gentleman for money, despising such sort of conversation himself; but others, who were not gentlemen born, behaved very uncivil in pressing him at this very time, and all he could do to content 'em all was to take himself out of the way as fast as possible to Dublin, where my lady had taken a house fitting for him as a member of parliament, to attend his duty in there all the winter. I was very lonely when the whole family was gone, and all the things they had ordered to go, and forgot, sent after them by the car. There was then a great silence in Castle Rackrent, and I went moping from room to room, hearing the doors clap for want of right locks, and the wind through the broken windows, that the glazier never would come to mend, and the rain coming through the roof and best ceilings all over the house for want of the slater, whose bill was not paid, besides our having no slates or shingles for that part of the old building which was shingled and burnt when the chimney took fire, and had been open to the weather ever since. I took myself to the servants' hall in the evening to smoke my pipe as usual, but missed the bit of talk we used to have there sadly, and ever after was content to stay in the kitchen and boil my little potatoes,* and put up my bed there; and every post-day I looked in the newspaper, but no news of my master in the house; he never spoke good or bad; but as the butler wrote down word to my son Jason, was very ill used by the government about a place that was promised him and never given, after his supporting them against his conscience very honourably, and being greatly abused for it, which hurt him greatly, he having the name of a great patriot in the

---

* *My little potatoes* – Thady does not mean, by this expression, that his potatoes were less than other people's, or less than the usual size – *little* is here used only as an Italian diminutive, expressive of fondness.

country before. The house and living in Dublin too were not to be had for nothing, and my son Jason said, 'Sir Condy must soon be looking out for a new agent, for I've done my part, and can do no more: – if my lady had the bank of Ireland to spend, it would go all in one winter, and Sir Condy would never gainsay her, though he does not care the rind of a lemon for her all the while.'

Now I could not bear to hear Jason giving out after this manner against the family, and twenty people standing by in the street. Ever since he had lived at the lodge of his own, he looked down, howsomever, upon poor old Thady, and was grown quite a great gentleman, and had none of his relations near him; no wonder he was no kinder to poor Sir Condy than to his own kith or kin.* In the spring it was the villain that got the list of the debts from him brought down the custodiam, Sir Condy still attending his duty in parliament, and I could scarcely believe my own old eyes, or the spectacles with which I read it, when I was shown my son Jason's name joined in the custodiam; but he told me it was only for form's sake, and to make things easier than if all the land was under the power of a total stranger. Well, I did not know what to think; it was hard to be talking ill of my own, and I could not but grieve for my poor master's fine estate, all torn by these vultures of the law; so I said nothing, but just looked on to see how it would all end.

It was not till the month of June that he and my lady came down to the country. My master was pleased to take me aside with him to the brewhouse that same evening, to complain to me of my son and other matters, in which he said he was confident I had neither art nor part; he said a great deal more to me, to whom he had been fond to talk ever since he was my white-headed boy, before he came to the estate; and all that he said about poor Judy I can never forget, but scorn to repeat. He did not say an unkind word of my lady, but wondered, as well he might, her relations would do nothing for him or her, and they in all this great distress. He did not take any thing long to heart, let it be as it would, and had no more malice, or thought of the like in him, than a child that can't speak; this night it was all out of his head before he went to his bed. He took his jug of whiskey punch – my lady was grown quite easy about the whiskey punch by this time, and so I did suppose all was going on right betwixt them, till I learnt the truth through Mrs Jane, who talked over their affairs to the housekeeper, and I within hearing. The night my master came home thinking of nothing at all but just making merry, he drank his bumper toast 'to the deserts of that old curmudgeon my father-in-law, and all enemies at Mount Juliet's town'. Now my lady was no longer in the mind she formerly was, and did no ways relish hearing her own friends abused in her presence, she said. 'Then why don't they show themselves your friends,' said my master, 'and oblige me with the loan of the money I condescended, by your advice, my dear, to ask? It's now three posts since I sent off my letter, desiring in the postscript a speedy answer by the return of the post, and no account at all from them yet.' 'I expect they'll write to *me* next post,' says my lady, and that was all that passed then; but it was easy from this to guess there was a coolness betwixt them, and with good cause.

The next morning, being post-day, I sent off the gossoon early to the post-office, to

* *Kith* and *kin* – family or relations. *Kin* from *kind*; *kith* from we know not what.

see was there any letter likely to set matters to rights, and he brought back one with the proper post-mark upon it, sure enough, and I had no time to examine, or make any conjecture more about it, for into the servants' hall pops Mrs Jane with a blue bandbox in her hand, quite entirely mad. 'Dear ma'am, and what's the matter?' says I. 'Matter enough,' says she; 'don't you see my bandbox is wet through, and my best bonnet here spoiled, besides my lady's, and all by the rain coming in through that gallery window, that you might have got mended, if you'd had any sense, Thady, all the time we were in town in the winter.' 'Sure I could not get the glazier, ma'am,' says I. 'You might have stopped it up any how,' says she. 'So I did, ma'am, to the best of my ability; one of the panes with the old pillow-case, and the other with a piece of the old stage green curtain; sure I was as careful as possible all the time you were away, and not a drop of rain came in at that window of all the windows in the house, all winter, ma'am, when under my care; and now the family's come home, and it's summer time, I never thought no more about it, to be sure; but dear, it's a pity to think of your bonnet, ma'am; but here's what will please you, ma'am, a letter from Mount Juliet's town for my lady.' With that she snatches it from me without a word more, and runs up the back stairs to my mistress; I follows with a slate to make up the window. This window was in the long passage, or gallery, as my lady gave out orders to have it called, in the gallery leading to my master's bedchamber and hers. And when I went up with the slate, the door having no lock, and the bolt spoilt, was a-jar after Mrs Jane, and as I was busy with the window, I heard all that was saying within.

'Well, what's in your letter, Bella, my dear?' says he: 'you're a long time spelling it over.' 'Won't you shave this morning, Sir Condy?' says she, and put the letter into her pocket. 'I shaved the day before yesterday,' says he, 'my dear, and that's not what I'm thinking of now; but any thing to oblige you, and to have peace and quietness, my dear' – and presently I had the glimpse of him at the cracked glass over the chimney-piece, standing up shaving himself to please my lady. But she took no notice, but went on reading her book and Mrs Jane doing her hair behind. 'What is it you're reading there, my dear? – phoo, I've cut myself with this razor; the man's a cheat that sold it me, but I have not paid him for it yet: what is it you're reading there? did you hear me asking you, my dear?' 'The Sorrows of Werter,' replies my lady, as well as I could hear. 'I think more of the sorrows of Sir Condy,' says my master, joking like. 'What news from Mount Juliet's town?' 'No news,' says she, 'but the old story over again, my friends all reproaching me still for what I can't help now.' 'Is it for marrying me?' said my master, still shaving: 'what signifies, as you say, talking of that, when it can't be help'd now?'

With that she heaved a great sigh, that I heard plain enough in the passage. 'And did not you use me basely, Sir Condy,' says she, 'not to tell me you were ruined before I married you?' 'Tell you, my dear,' said he; 'did you ever ask me one word about it? and had not you friends enough of your own, that were telling you nothing else from morning to night, if you'd have listened to them slanders?' 'No slanders, nor are my friends slanderers; and I can't bear to hear them treated with disrespect as I do,' says my lady, and took out her pocket handkerchief; 'they are the best of friends; and if I had taken their advice – But my father was wrong to lock me up, I own; that was the only unkind thing I can charge him with; for if he had not locked me up, I should never have had a serious thought of running away as I did.' 'Well, my dear,' said my master, 'don't cry and make yourself uneasy about it now, when it's all over, and you have the man of your own choice, in spite of 'em all.' 'I was too young, I know, to make a choice at the time you ran away with me, I'm sure,' says my lady, and another sigh, which made my master, half shaved as he was, turn round upon her in surprise. 'Why, Bell,' says he, 'you can't deny what you know as well as I do, that it was at your own particular desire, and that twice under your own hand and seal expressed, that I should carry you off as I did to Scotland, and marry you there.' 'Well, say no more about it, Sir Condy,' said my lady, pettish like – 'I was a child then, you know.' 'And as far as I know, you're little better now, my dear Bella, to be talking in this manner to your husband's *face*; but I won't take it ill of you, for I know it's something in that letter you put into your pocket just now, that has set you against me all on a sudden, and imposed upon your understanding.' 'It is not so very easy as you think it, Sir Condy, to impose upon *my* understanding,' said my lady. 'My dear,' says he, 'I have, and with reason, the best opinion of your understanding of any man now breathing; and you know I have never set my own in competition with it till now, my dear Bella,' says he, taking her hand from her book as kind as could be – 'till now, when I have the great advantage of being quite cool, and you not; so don't believe one word your friends say against your own Sir Condy, and lend me the letter out of your pocket, till I see what it is they can have to say.' 'Take it then,' says she, 'and as you are quite cool, I hope it is a proper time to request you'll allow me to comply with the wishes of all my own friends, and return to live with my father and family, during the remainder of my wretched existence, at Mount Juliet's town.'

At this my poor master fell back a few paces, like one that had been shot. 'You're not serious, Bella,' says he; 'and could you find it in your heart to leave me this way in the very middle of my distresses, all alone?' But recollecting himself after his first surprise, and a moment's time for reflection, he said, with a great deal of consideration for my lady, 'Well, Bella, my dear, I believe you are right; for what could you do at Castle Rackrent, and an execution against the goods coming down, and the furniture to be canted, and an auction in the house all next week? so you have my full consent to go, since that is your desire, only you must not think of my accompanying you, which I could not in honour do upon the terms I always have been, since our marriage, with your friends; besides, I have business to transact at home; so in the mean time, if we are to have any breakfast this morning, let us go down and have it for the last time in peace and comfort, Bella.'

Then as I heard my master coming to the passage door, I finished fastening up my slate against the broken pane; and when he came out, I wiped down the window seat with my wig,* and bade him a good morrow as kindly as I could, seeing he was in

---

* Wigs were formerly used instead of brooms in Ireland, for sweeping or dusting tables, stairs, &c. The Editor doubted the fact, till he saw a labourer of the old school sweep down a flight of stairs with his wig; he afterwards put it on his head again with the utmost composure, and said, 'Oh, please your honour, it's never a bit the worse.'

It must be acknowledged, that these men are not in any danger of catching cold by taking off their wigs occasionally, because they usually have fine crops of hair growing under their wigs. The wigs are often yellow, and the hair which appears from beneath them black; the wigs are usually too small, and are raised up by the hair beneath, or by the ears of the wearers.

trouble, though he strove and thought to hide it from me. 'This window is all racked and tattered,' says I, 'and it's what I'm striving to mend.' 'It *is* all racked and tattered, plain enough,' says he, 'and never mind mending it, honest old Thady,' says he; 'it will do well enough for you and I, and that's all the company we shall have left in the house by-and-bye.' 'I'm sorry to see your honour so low this morning,' says I; 'but you'll be better after taking your breakfast.' 'Step down to the servants' hall,' says he, 'and bring me up the pen and ink into the parlour, and get a sheet of paper from Mrs Jane, for I have business that can't brook to be delayed; and come into the parlour with the pen and ink yourself, Thady, for I must have you to witness my signing a paper I have to execute in a hurry.' Well, while I was getting of the pen and ink-horn, and the sheet of paper, I ransacked my brains to think what could be the papers my poor master could have to execute in such a hurry, he that never thought of such a thing as doing business afore breakfast, in the whole course of his life, for any man living; but this was for my lady, as I afterwards found, and the more genteel of him after all her treatment.

I was just witnessing the paper that he had scrawled over, and was shaking the ink out of my pen upon the carpet, when my lady came into breakfast, and she started as if it had been a ghost! as well she might, when she saw Sir Condy writing at this unseasonable hour. 'That will do very well, Thady,' says he to me, and took the paper I had signed to, without knowing what upon the earth it might be, out of my hands, and walked, folding it up, to my lady.

'You are concerned in this, my lady Rackrent,' says he, putting it into her hands; 'and I beg you'll keep this memorandum safe, and show it to your friends the first thing you do when you get home; but put it in your pocket now, my dear, and let us eat our breakfast, in God's name.' 'What is all this?' said my lady, opening the paper in great curiosity. 'It's only a bit of a memorandum of what I think becomes me to do whenever I am able,' says my master; 'you know my situation, tied hand and foot at the present time being, but that can't last always, and when I'm dead and gone, the land will be to the good, Thady, you know; and take notice, it's my intention your lady should have a clear five hundred a year jointure off the estate afore any of my debts are paid.' 'Oh, please your honour,' says I, 'I can't expect to live to see that time, being now upwards of fourscore years of age, and you a young man, and likely to continue so, by the help of God.' I was vexed to see my lady so insensible too, for all she said was, 'This is very genteel of you, Sir Condy. You need not wait any longer, Thady'; so I just picked up the pen and ink that had tumbled on the floor, and heard my master finish with saying, 'You behaved very genteel to me, my dear, when you threw all the little you had in your own power along with yourself, into my hands; and as I don't deny but what you may have had some things to complain of,' – to be sure he was thinking then of Judy, or of the whiskey punch, one or t'other, or both, – 'and as I don't deny but you may have had something to complain of, my dear, it is but fair you should have something in the form of compensation to look forward to agreeably in future; besides, it's an act of justice to myself, that none of your friends, my dear, may ever have it to say against me, I married for money, and not for love.' 'That is the last thing I should ever have thought of saying of you, Sir Condy,' said my lady, looking very gracious. 'Then, my dear,' said Sir Condy, 'we shall part as good friends as we met; so all's right.'

I was greatly rejoiced to hear this, and went out of the parlour to report it all to the kitchen. The next morning my lady and Mrs Jane set out for Mount Juliet's town in the jaunting car: many wondered at my lady's choosing to go away, considering all things, upon the jaunting car, as if it was only a party of pleasure; but they did not know, till I told them, that the coach was all broke in the journey down, and no other vehicle but the car to be had; besides, my lady's friends were to send their coach to meet her at the cross roads; so it was all done very proper.

My poor master was in great trouble after my lady left us. The execution came down; and every thing at Castle Rackrent was seized by the gripers, and my son Jason, to his shame be it spoken, amongst them. I wondered, for the life of me, how he could harden himself to do it; but then he had been studying the law, and had made himself attorney Quirk; so he brought down at once a heap of accounts upon my master's head. To cash lent, and to ditto, and to ditto, and to ditto, and oats, and bills paid at the milliner's and linen draper's, and many dresses for the fancy balls in Dublin for my lady, and all the bills to the workmen and tradesmen for the scenery of the theatre, and the chandler's and grocer's bills, and tailor's besides butcher's and baker's, and worse than all, the old one at that base wine merchant's, that wanted to arrest my poor master for the amount on the election day, for which amount Sir Condy afterwards passed his note of hand, bearing lawful interest from the date thereof; and the interest and compound interest was now mounted to a terrible deal on many other notes and bonds for money borrowed, and there was besides hush money to the sub-sheriffs, and sheets upon sheets of old and new attorneys' bills, with heavy balances, *as per former account furnished,* brought forward with interest thereon; then there was a powerful deal due to the crown for sixteen years' arrear of quit-rent of the town-lands of Carrickshaughlin, with driver's fees, and a compliment to the receiver every year for letting the quit-rent run on, to oblige Sir Condy, and Sir Kit afore him. Then there were bills for spirits and ribands at the election time, and the gentlemen of the committee's accounts unsettled, and their subscription never gathered; and there were cows to be paid for, with the smith and farrier's bills to be set against the rent of the demesne, with calf and hay money; then there was all the servants' wages, since I don't know when, coming due to them, and sums advanced for them by my son Jason for clothes, and boots, and whips, and odd moneys for sundries expended by them in journeys to town and elsewhere, and pocket-money for the master continually, and messengers and postage before his being a parliament man; I can't myself tell you what besides; but this I know, that when the evening came on the which Sir Condy had appointed to settle all with my son Jason, and when he comes into the parlour, and sees the sight of bills and load of papers all gathered on the great dining-table for him, he puts his hands before both his eyes, and cried out, 'Merciful Jasus! what is it I see before me?' Then I sets an arm-chair at the table for him, and with a deal of difficulty he sits him down, and my son Jason hands him over the pen and ink to sign to this man's bill and t'other man's bill, all which he did without making the least objections. Indeed, to give him his due, I never *seen* a man more fair and honest, and easy in all his dealings, from first to last, as Sir Condy, or more willing to pay every man his own as far as he was able, which is as much as any one can do. 'Well,' says he, joking like with Jason, 'I wish we could settle it all with a stroke of my grey goose quill. What signifies making me wade through all this ocean of papers here; can't you now, who understand drawing out an account, debtor and creditor, just sit down here at the corner of the table, and get it done out for me, that I may have a clear view of the balance, which is all I need be talking about, you know?' 'Very true, Sir Condy; nobody understands business better than yourself,' says Jason. 'So I've a right to do, being born and bred to the bar,' says Sir Condy. 'Thady, do step out and see are they bringing in the things for the punch, for we've just done all we have to do for this evening.' I goes out accordingly, and when I came back, Jason was pointing to the balance, which was a terrible sight to my poor master. 'Pooh! pooh! pooh!' says he, 'here's so many noughts they dazzle my eyes, so they do, and put me in mind of all I suffered, larning of my numeration table, when I was a boy at the day-school along with you, Jason – units, tens, hundreds, tens of hundred. Is the punch ready, Thady?' says he, seeing me. 'Immediately; the boy has the jug in his hand; it's coming up stairs, please your honour, as fast as possible,' says I, for I saw his honour was tired out of his life; but Jason, very short and cruel, cuts me off with – 'Don't be talking of punch yet a while; it's no time for punch yet a bit – units, tens, hundreds,' goes he on, counting over the master's shoulder, units, tens, hundreds, thousands. 'A-a-ah! hold your hand,' cries my master; 'where in this wide world am I to find hundreds, or units itself, let alone thousands?' 'The balance has been running on too long,' says Jason, sticking to him as I could not have done at the time, if you'd have given both the Indies and Cork to boot; 'the balance has been running on too long, and I'm distressed myself on your account, Sir Condy, for money, and the thing must be settled now on the spot, and the balance cleared off,' says Jason. 'I'll thank you if you'll only show me how,' says Sir Condy. 'There's but one way,' says Jason, 'and that's ready enough: when there's no cash, what can a gentleman do, but go to the land?' 'How can you go to the land, and it under custodiam to yourself already,' says Sir Condy, 'and another custodiam hanging over it? and no one at all can touch it, you know, but the custodees.' 'Sure, can't you sell, though at a loss? sure you can sell, and I've a purchaser ready for you,' says Jason. 'Have ye so?' said Sir Condy; 'that's a great point gained; but there's a thing now beyond all, that perhaps you don't know yet, barring Thady has let you into the secret.' 'Sarrah bit of a secret, or any thing at all of the kind, has he learned from me these fifteen weeks come St John's eve,' says I; 'for we have scarce been upon speaking terms of late; but what is it your honour means of a secret?' 'Why, the secret of the little keepsake I gave my lady Rackrent the morning she left us, that she might not go back empty-handed to her friends.' 'My lady Rackrent, I'm sure, has baubles and keepsakes enough, as those bills on the table will show,' says Jason; 'but whatever it is,' says he, taking up his pen, 'we must add it to the balance, for to be sure it can't be paid for.' 'No, nor can't till after my decease,' said Sir Condy; 'that's one good thing.' Then colouring up a good deal, he tells Jason of the memorandum of the five hundred a year jointure he had settled upon my lady; at which Jason was indeed mad, and said a great deal in very high words, that it was using a gentleman, who had the management of his affairs, and was moreover his principal creditor, extremely ill, to do such a thing without consulting him, and against his knowledge and consent. To all which Sir Condy had nothing to reply, but that upon his conscience, it was in a hurry and without a moment's thought on his part, and he was very sorry for it, but if it was to do over again he would do the same; and he appealed to me, and I was ready to give my evidence, if that would do, to the truth of all he said.

So Jason with much ado was brought to agree to a compromise. 'The purchaser that I have ready,' says he, 'will be much displeased, to be sure, at the incumbrance on the land, but I must see and manage him; here's a deed ready drawn up; we have nothing to do but to put in the consideration money and our names to it.' 'And how much am I going to sell? – the lands of O'Shaughlin's town, and the lands of Gruneaghoolaghan, and the lands of Crookaghnawaturgh,' says he, just reading to himself, – 'and – Oh, murder, Jason! sure you won't put this in – the castle, stable, and appurtenances of Castle Rackrent.' 'Oh, murder!' says I, clapping my hands, 'this is too bad, Jason.' 'Why so?' said Jason, 'when it's all, and a great deal more to the back of it, lawfully mine, was I to push for it.' 'Look at him,' says I, pointing to Sir Condy, who was just leaning back in his arm-chair, with his arms falling beside him like one stupified; 'is it you, Jason, that can stand in his presence, and recollect all he has been to us, and all we have been to him, and yet use him so at the last?' 'Who will you find to use him better, I ask you?' said Jason; 'if he can get a better purchaser, I'm content; I only offer to purchase, to make things easy and oblige him: though I don't see what compliment I am under, if you come to that; I have never had, asked, or charged more than sixpence in the pound, receiver's fees; and where would he have got an agent for a penny less?' 'Oh, Jason! Jason! how will you stand to this in the face of the county and all who know you?' says I; 'and what will people think and say, when they see you living here in Castle Rackrent, and the lawful owner turned out of the seat of his ancestors, without a cabin to put his head into, or so much as a potato to eat?' Jason, whilst I was a saying this, and a great deal more, made me signs, and winks, and frowns; but I took no heed; for I was grieved and sick at heart for my poor master, and couldn't but speak.

'Here's the punch,' says Jason, for the door opened; 'here's the punch!' Hearing that, my master starts up in his chair, and recollects himself, and Jason uncorks the whiskey. 'Set down the jug here,' says he, making room for it beside the papers opposite to Sir Condy, but still not stirring the deed that was to make over all. Well, I was in great hopes he had some touch of mercy about him when I saw him making the punch, and my master took a glass; but Jason put it back as he was going to fill again, saying, 'No, Sir Condy, it sha'n't be said of me, I got your signature to this deed when you were half-seas over: you know your name and handwriting in that condition would not, if brought before the courts, benefit me a straw; wherefore let us settle all before we go deeper into the punch-bowl.' 'Settle all as you will,' said Sir Condy, clapping his hands to his ears; 'but let me hear no more; I'm bothered to death this night.' 'You've only to sign,' said Jason, putting the pen to him. 'Take all, and be content,' said my master. So he signed; and the man who brought in the punch witnessed it, for I was not able, but crying like a child; and besides, Jason said, which I was glad of, that I was no fit witness, being so old and doting. It was so bad with me, I could not taste a drop of the punch itself, though my master himself, God bless him! in the midst of his trouble, poured out a glass for me, and brought it up to my lips. 'Not a drop, I thank your honour's honour as much as if I took it though,' and I just set down the glass as it was, and went out, and when I got to the street-door, the neighbour's childer, who were playing at marbles there, seeing me in great trouble, left their play, and gathered about me to know what ailed me; and I told them all, for it was a great relief to me to speak to these poor childer, that seemed to have some natural feeling left in them: and when they were made sensible that Sir Condy was going to leave Castle Rackrent for good and all, they set up a whillalu that could be heard to the farthest end of the street; and one fine boy he was, that my master had given an apple to that morning, cried the loudest, but they all were the same sorry, for Sir Condy was greatly beloved amongst the childer, for letting them go a nutting in the demesne, without saying a word to them, though my lady objected to them. The people in the town, who were the most of them standing at their doors, hearing the childer cry, would know the reason of it; and when the report was made known, the people one and all gathered in great anger against my son Jason, and terror at the notion of his coming to be landlord over them, and they cried, 'No Jason! no Jason! Sir Condy! Sir Condy! Sir Condy Rackrent for ever!' and the mob grew so great and so loud, I was frightened, and made my way back to the house to warn my son to make his escape, or hide himself for fear of the consequences. Jason would not believe me till they came all round the house, and to the windows with great shouts: then he grew quite pale, and asked Sir Condy what had he best do? 'I'll tell you what you'd best do,' said Sir Condy, who was laughing to see his fright; 'finish your glass first, then let's go to the window and show ourselves, and I'll tell 'em, or you shall, if you please, that I'm going to the Lodge for change of air for my health, and by my own desire, for the rest of my days.' 'Do so,' said Jason, who never meant it should have been so, but could not refuse him the Lodge at this unseasonable time. Accordingly Sir Condy threw up the sash, and explained matters, and thanked all his friends, and bid 'em look in at the punch-bowl, and observe that Jason and he had been sitting over it very good friends; so the mob was content, and he sent 'em out some whiskey to drink his health, and that was the last time his honour's health was ever drunk at Castle Rackrent.

The very next day, being too proud, as he said, to me, to stay an hour longer in a house that did not belong to him, he sets off to the Lodge, and I along with him not many hours after. And there was great bemoaning through all O'Shaughlin's town, which I stayed to witness, and gave my poor master a full account of when I got to the Lodge. He was very low and in his bed when I got there, and complained of a great pain about his heart, but I guessed it was only trouble, and all the business, let alone vexation, he had gone through of late; and knowing the nature of him from a boy, I took my pipe, and, whilst smoking it by the chimney, began telling him how he was beloved and regretted in the county, and it did him a deal of good to hear it. 'Your honour has a great many friends yet, that you don't know of, rich and poor, in the county,' says I; 'for as I was coming along the road, I met two gentlemen in their own carriages, who asked after you, knowing me, and wanted to know where you was and all about you, and even how old I was: think of that.' Then he wakened out of his doze, and began questioning me who the gentlemen were. And the next morning it came into my head to go, unknown to any body, with my master's compliments, round to many of the gentlemen's houses, where he and my lady used to visit, and people that I knew were his great friends, and would go to Cork to serve him any day in the year, and I made bold to try to borrow a trifle of cash from them. They all treated me very civil for the most part, and asked a great many questions very kind about my lady, and Sir Condy, and all the family, and were greatly surprised to learn from me Castle Rackrent was sold, and my master at the Lodge for health; and they all pitied him greatly, and he had their good wishes, if that would do, but money was a thing they unfortunately had not any of them at this time to spare. I had my journey for my pains, and I, not used to walking, nor supple as formerly, was greatly tired, and had the satisfaction of telling my master, when I got to the Lodge, all the civil things said by high and low.

'Thady,' says he, 'all you've been telling me brings a strange thought into my head; I've a notion I shall not be long for this world any how, and I've a great fancy to see my own funeral afore I die.' I was greatly shocked, at the first speaking, to hear him speak so light about his funeral, and he, to all appearance, in good health, but recollecting myself, answered, 'To be sure, it would be as fine a sight as one could see, I dared to say, and one I should be proud to witness, and I did not doubt his honour's would be as great a funeral as ever Sir Patrick O'Shaughlin's was, and such a one as that had never been known in the county afore or since.' But I never thought he was in earnest about seeing his own funeral himself, till the next day he returns to it again. 'Thady,' says he, 'as far as the wake* goes, sure I might without any great trouble have the satisfaction of seeing a bit of my own funeral.' 'Well, since your honour's honour's so bent upon it,' says I, not willing to cross him, and he in trouble, 'we must see what we can do.' So he fell into a sort of a sham disorder, which was easy done, as he kept his bed, and no one to see him; and I got my shister, who was an old woman very handy about the sick, and very skilful, to come up to the Lodge, to nurse him; and we gave out, she knowing no better, that he was just at his latter end, and it answered beyond any thing; and there was a great throng of people, men, women, and childer, and there being only two rooms at the Lodge, except what was locked up full of Jason's furniture and things, the house was soon as full and fuller than it could hold, and the heat, and smoke, and noise wonderful great; and standing amongst them that were near the bed, but not thinking at all of the dead, I was started by the sound of my master's voice from under the great coats that had been thrown all at top, and I went close up, no one noticing. 'Thady,' says he, 'I've had enough of this; I'm smothering, and can't hear a word of all they're saying of the deceased.' 'God bless you, and lie still and quiet,' says I, 'a bit longer, for my shister's afraid of ghosts, and would die on the spot with fright, was she to see you come to life all of a sudden this way without the least preparation.' So he lays him still, though well nigh stifled, and I made all haste to tell the secret of the joke, whispering to one and t'other, and there was a great surprise, but not so great as we had laid out it would. 'And aren't we to have the pipes and tobacco, after coming so far to-night?' said some; but they were all well enough pleased when his honour got up to drink with them, and sent for more spirits from a shebean-house,† where they very civilly let him

---

* A wake in England is a meeting avowedly for merriment; in Ireland it is a nocturnal meeting avowedly for the purpose of watching and bewailing the dead; but, in reality, for gossiping and debauchery.

† *Shebean-house*, a hedge-alehouse. Shebean properly means weak small-beer, taplash.

have it upon credit. So the night passed off very merrily, but, to my mind, Sir Condy was rather upon the sad order in the midst of it all, not finding there had been such a great talk about himself after his death as he had always expected to hear.

The next morning, when the house was cleared of them, and none but my shister and myself left in the kitchen with Sir Condy, one opens the door, and walks in, and who should it be but Judy M'Quirk herself! I forgot to notice, that she had been married long since, whilst young Captain Moneygawl lived at the Lodge, to the captain's huntsman, who after a while listed and left her, and was killed in the wars. Poor Judy fell off greatly in her good looks after her being married a year or two; and being smoke-dried in the cabin, and neglecting herself like, it was hard for Sir Condy himself to know her again till she spoke; but when she says, 'It's Judy M'Quirk, please your honour, don't you remember her?' 'Oh, Judy, is it you?' says his honour; 'yes, sure, I remember you very well; but you're greatly altered, Judy.' 'Sure it's time for me,' says she; 'and I think your honour, since I *seen* you last, – but that's a great while ago, – is altered too.' 'And with reason, Judy,' says Sir Condy, fetching a sort of a sigh; 'but how's this, Judy?' he goes on; 'I take it a little amiss of you, that you were not at my wake last night.' 'Ah, don't be being jealous of that,' says she; 'I didn't hear a sentence of your honour's wake till it was all over, or it would have gone hard with me but I would have been at it sure; but I was forced to go ten miles up the country three days ago to a wedding of a relation of my own's, and didn't get home till after the wake was over; but,' says she, 'it won't be so, I hope, the next time,* please your honour.' 'That we shall see, Judy,' says his honour, 'and may be sooner than you think for, for I've been very unwell this while past, and don't reckon any way I'm long for this world.' At this, Judy takes up the corner of her apron, and puts it first to one eye and then to t'other, being to all appearance in great trouble; and my shister put in her word, and bid his honour have a good heart, for she was sure it was only the gout, that Sir Patrick used to have flying about him, and he ought to drink a glass or a bottle extraordinary to keep it out of his stomach; and he promised to take her advice, and sent out for more spirits immediately; and Judy made a sign to me, and I went over to the door to her, and she said, 'I wonder to see Sir Condy so low! has he heard the news?' 'What news?' says I. 'Didn't ye hear it, then?' says she; 'my lady Rackrent that was is kilt and lying for dead, and I don't doubt but it's all over with her by this time.' 'Mercy on us all,' says I; 'how was it?' 'The jaunting car it was that ran away with her,' says Judy. 'I was coming home that same time from Biddy M'Guggin's marriage, and a great crowd of people too upon the road, coming from the fair of Crookaghnawaturgh, and I sees a jaunting car standing in the middle of the road, and with the two wheels off and all tattered. "What's this?" says I. "Didn't ye hear of it?" says they that were looking on; "it's my lady Rackrent's car, that was running away from her husband, and the horse took fright at a carrion that lay across the road, and so ran away with the jaunting car, and my lady Rackrent and her maid screaming, and the horse ran with them against a car that was coming from the fair, with the boy asleep on it, and the lady's petticoat hanging out of the jaunting car caught,

---

* At the coronation of one of our monarchs, the king complained of the confusion which happened in the procession. The great officer who presided told his majesty, 'That it should not be so next time.'

and she was dragged I can't tell you how far upon the road, and it all broken up with the stones just going to be pounded, and one of the road-makers, with his sledge-hammer in his hand, stops the horse at the last; but my lady Rackrent was all kilt* and smashed, and they lifted her into a cabin hard by, and the maid was found after, where she had been thrown, in the gripe of the ditch, her cap and bonnet all full of bog water, and they say my lady can't live any way." Thady, pray now is it true what I'm told for sartain, that Sir Condy has made over all to your son Jason?' 'All,' says I. 'All entirely?' says she again. 'All entirely,' says I. 'Then,' says she, 'that's a great shame, but don't be telling Jason what I say.' 'And what is it you say?' cries Sir Condy, leaning over betwixt us, which made Judy start greatly. 'I know the time when Judy M'Quirk would never have stayed so long talking at the door, and I in the house.' 'Oh!' says Judy, 'for shame, Sir Condy; times are altered since then, and it's my lady Rackrent you ought to be thinking of.' 'And why should I be thinking of her, that's not thinking of me now?' says Sir Condy. 'No matter for that,' says Judy, very properly; 'it's time you should be thinking of her, if ever you mean to do it at all, for don't you know she's lying for death?' 'My lady Rackrent!' says Sir Condy, in a surprise; 'why it's but two days since we parted, as you very well know, Thady, in her full health and spirits, and she and her maid along with her going to Mount Juliet's town on her jaunting car.' 'She'll never ride no more on her jaunting car,' said Judy, 'for it has been the death of her, sure enough.' 'And is she dead, then?' says his honour. 'As good as dead, I hear,' says Judy; 'but there's Thady here has just learnt the whole truth of the story as I had it, and it is fitter he or any body else should be telling it you than I, Sir Condy: I must be going home to the childer.' But he stops her, but rather from civility in him, as I could see very plainly, than any thing else, for Judy was, as his honour remarked at her first coming in, greatly changed, and little likely, as far as I could see – though she did not seem to be clear of it herself – little likely to be my lady Rackrent now, should there be a second toss-up to be made. But I told him the whole story out of the face, just as Judy had told it to me, and he sent off a messenger with his compliments to Mount Juliet's town that evening, to learn the truth of the report, and Judy bid the boy that was going call in at Tim M'Enerney's shop in O'Shaughlin's town and buy her a new shawl. 'Do so,' said Sir Condy, 'and tell Tim to take no money from you, for I must pay him for the shawl myself.' At this my shister throws me over a look, and I says nothing, but turned the tobacco in my mouth, whilst Judy began making a many words about it, and saying how she could not be beholden for shawls to any gentleman. I left her there to consult with my shister, did she think there was any thing in it, and my shister thought I was blind to be asking her the question, and I thought my shister must see more into it than I did; and recollecting all past times and every thing, I changed my mind, and came over to her way of thinking,

---

* *Kilt and smashed.* – Our author is not here guilty of an anti-climax. The mere English reader, from a similarity of sound between the words *kilt* and *killed*, might be induced to suppose that their meanings are similar, yet they are not by any means in Ireland synonymous terms. Thus you may hear a man exclaim, 'I'm kilt and murdered!' but he frequently means only that he has received a black eye, or a slight contusion. – *I'm kilt all over* means that he is in a worse state than being simply *kilt*. Thus, *I'm kilt with the cold* is nothing to *I'm kilt all over with the rheumatism.*

and we settled it that Judy was very like to be my lady Rackrent after all, if a vacancy should have happened.

The next day, before his honour was up, somebody comes with a double knock at the door, and I was greatly surprised to see it was my son Jason. 'Jason, is it you?' said I; 'what brings you to the Lodge?' says I; 'is it my lady Rackrent? we know that already since yesterday.' 'May be so,' says he, 'but I must see Sir Condy about it.' 'You can't see him yet,' says I; 'sure he is not awake.' 'What then,' says he, 'can't he be wakened? and I standing at the door.' 'I'll not be disturbing his honour for you, Jason,' says I; 'many's the hour you've waited in your time, and been proud to do it, till his honour was at leisure to speak to you. His honour,' says I, raising my voice, at which his honour wakens of his own accord, and calls to me from the room to know who it was I was speaking to. Jason made no more ceremony, but follows me into the room. 'How are you, Sir Condy?' says he; 'I'm happy to see you looking so well; I came up to know how you did to-day, and to see did you want for any thing at the Lodge.' 'Nothing at all, Mr Jason, I thank you,' says he; for his honour had his own share of pride, and did not choose, after all that had passed, to be beholden, I suppose, to my son; 'but pray take a chair and be seated, Mr Jason.' Jason sat him down upon the chest, for chair there was none, and after he had sat there some time, and a silence on all sides, 'What news is there stirring in the country, Mr Jason M'Quirk?' says Sir Condy very easy, yet high like. 'None that's news to you, Sir Condy, I hear,' says Jason: 'I am sorry to hear of my lady Rackrent's accident.' 'I'm much obliged to you, and so is her ladyship, I'm sure,' answered Sir Condy, still stiff; and there was another sort of a silence, which seemed to lie the heaviest on my son Jason.

'Sir Condy,' says he at last, seeing Sir Condy disposing himself to go to sleep again, 'Sir Condy, I dare say you recollect mentioning to me the little memorandum you gave to Lady Rackrent about the £500 a-year jointure.' 'Very true,' said Sir Condy; 'it is all in my recollection.' 'But if my lady Rackrent dies, there's an end of all jointure,' says Jason. 'Of course,' says Sir Condy. 'But it's not a matter of certainty that my lady Rackrent won't recover,' says Jason. 'Very true, sir,' says my master. 'It's a fair speculation, then, for you to consider what the chance of the jointure on those lands, when out of custodiam, will be to you.' 'Just five hundred a-year, I take it, without any speculation at all,' said Sir Condy. 'That's supposing the life dropt, and the custodiam off, you know; begging your pardon, Sir Condy, who understands business, that is a wrong calculation.' 'Very likely so,' said Sir Condy; 'but, Mr Jason, if you have any thing to say to me this morning about it, I'd be obliged to you to say it, for I had an indifferent night's rest last night, and wouldn't be sorry to sleep a little this morning.' 'I have only three words to say, and those more of consequence to you, Sir Condy, than me. You are a little cool, I observe; but I hope you will not be offended at what I have brought here in my pocket,' and he pulls out two long rolls, and showers down golden guineas upon the bed. 'What's this?' said Sir Condy; 'it's long since' – but his pride stops him. 'All these are your lawful property this minute, Sir Condy, if you please,' said Jason. 'Not for nothing, I'm sure,' said Sir Condy, and laughs a little – 'nothing for nothing, or I'm under a mistake with you, Jason.' 'Oh, Sir Condy, we'll not be indulging ourselves in any unpleasant retrospects,' says Jason; 'it's my present intention to behave, as I'm sure you will, like a gentleman in this affair. Here's two hundred guineas, and a third I mean to add, if you should think proper to make over to me all your right and title to those lands that you know of.' 'I'll consider of it,' said my master; and a great deal more, that I was tired listening to, was said by Jason, and all that, and the sight of the ready cash upon the bed worked with his honour; and the short and the long of it was, Sir Condy gathered up the golden guineas, and tied them up in a handkerchief, and signed some paper Jason brought with him as usual, and there was an end of the business; Jason took himself away, and my master turned himself round and fell asleep again.

I soon found what had put Jason in such a hurry to conclude this business. The little gossoon we had sent off the day before with my master's compliments to Mount Juliet's town, and to know how my lady did after her accident, was stopped early this morning, coming back with his answer through O'Shaughlin's town, at Castle Rackrent, by my son Jason, and questioned of all he knew of my lady from the servant at Mount Juliet's town; and the gossoon told him my lady Rackrent was not expected to live over night; so Jason thought it high time to be moving to the Lodge, to make his bargain with my master about the jointure afore it should be too late, and afore the little gossoon should reach us with the news. My master was greatly vexed, that is, I may say, as much as ever I *seen* him, when he found how he had been taken in; but it was some comfort to have the ready cash for immediate consumption in the house, any way.

And when Judy came up that evening, and brought the childer to see his honour, he unties the handkerchief, and, God bless him! whether it was little or much he had, 'twas all the same with him, he gives 'em all round guineas a-piece. 'Hold up your head,' says my shister to Judy, as Sir Condy was busy filling out a glass of punch for her eldest boy – 'Hold up your head, Judy; for who knows but we may live to see you yet at the head of the Castle Rackrent estate?' 'May be so,' says she, 'but not the way you are thinking of.' I did not rightly understand which way Judy was looking when she makes this speech, till a-while after. 'Why, Thady, you were telling me yesterday, that Sir Condy had sold all entirely to Jason, and where then does all them guineas in the handkerchief come from?' 'They are the purchase-money of my lady's jointure,' says I. 'A penny for your thoughts, Judy,' says my shister; 'hark, sure Sir Condy is drinking her health.' He was at the table in *the room,** drinking with the exciseman and the gauger, who came up to see his honour, and we were standing over the fire in the kitchen. 'I don't much care is he drinking my health or not,' says Judy; 'and it is not Sir Condy I'm thinking of, with all your jokes, whatever he is of me.' 'Sure you wouldn't refuse to be my lady Rackrent, Judy, if you had the offer?' says I. 'But if I could do better!' says she. 'How better?' says I and my shister both at once. 'How better?' says she; 'why, what signifies it to be my lady Rackrent, and no castle? sure what good is the car, and no horse to draw it?' 'And where will ye get the horse, Judy?' says I. 'Never mind that,' says she; 'may be it is your own son Jason might find that.' 'Jason!' says I; 'don't be trusting to him, Judy. Sir Condy, as I have good reason to know, spoke well of you, when Jason spoke very indifferently of you, Judy.' 'No matter,' says Judy; 'it's often men speak the contrary just to what they think of us.' 'And you the same way of them, no doubt,' answers I. 'Nay, don't be

* *The room* – the principal room in the house.

denying it, Judy, for I think the better of ye for it, and shouldn't be proud to call ye the daughter of a shister's son of mine, if I was to hear ye talk ungrateful, and any way disrespectful of his honour.' 'What disrespect,' says she, 'to say I'd rather, if it was my luck, be the wife of another man?' 'You'll have no luck, mind my words, Judy,' says I; and all I remembered about my poor master's goodness in tossing up for her afore he married at all came across me, and I had a choaking in my throat that hindered me to say more. 'Better luck, any how, Thady,' says she, 'than to be like some folk, following the fortunes of them that have none left.' 'Oh! King of Glory!' says I, 'hear the pride and ungratitude of her, and he giving his last guineas but a minute ago to her childer, and she with the fine shawl on her he made her a present of but yesterday!' 'Oh, troth, Judy, you're wrong now,' says my shister, looking at the shawl. 'And was not he wrong yesterday, then,' says she, 'to be telling me I was greatly altered, to affront me?' 'But, Judy,' says I, 'what is it brings you here then at all in the mind you are in; is it to make Jason think the better of you?' 'I'll tell you no more of my secrets, Thady,' says she, 'nor would have told you this much, had I taken you for such an unnatural fader as I find you are, not to wish your own son preferred to another.' 'Oh, troth, *you* are wrong now, Thady,' says my shister. Well, I was never so put to it in my life: between these womens, and my son and my master, and all I felt and thought just now, I could not, upon my conscience, tell which was the wrong from the right. So I said not a word more, but was only glad his honour had not the luck to hear all Judy had been saying of him, for I reckoned it would have gone nigh to break his heart; not that I was of opinion he cared for her as much as she and my shister fancied, but the ungratitude of the whole from Judy might not plase him; and he could never stand the notion of not being well spoken of or beloved like behind his back. Fortunately for all parties concerned, he was so much elevated at this time, there was no danger of his understanding any thing, even if it had reached his ears. There was a great horn at the Lodge, ever since my master and Captain Moneygawl was in together, that used to belong originally to the celebrated Sir Patrick, his ancestor; and his honour was fond often of telling the story that he learned from me when a child, how Sir Patrick drank the full of this horn without stopping, and this was what no other man afore or since could without drawing breath. Now Sir Condy challenged the gauger, who seemed to think little of the horn, to swallow the contents, and had it filled to the brim with punch; and the gauger said it was what he could not do for nothing, but he'd hold Sir Condy a hundred guineas he'd do it. 'Done,' said my master; 'I'll lay you a hundred golden guineas to a tester* you don't.' 'Done,' says the gauger; and done and done's enough between two gentlemen. The gauger was cast, and my master won the bet, and thought he'd won a hundred guineas, but by the wording it was adjudged to be only a tester that was his due by the exciseman. It was all one to him; he was as well pleased, and I was glad to see him in such spirits again.

The gauger, bad luck to him! was the man that next proposed to my master to try himself could he take at a draught the contents of the great horn. 'Sir Patrick's horn!'

---

* *Tester* – sixpence; from the French word tête, a head: a piece of silver stamped with a head, which in old French was called 'un testion', and which was about the value of an old English sixpence. Tester is used in Shakspeare.

said his honour; 'hand it to me: I'll hold you your own bet over again I'll swallow it.' 'Done,' says the gauger; 'I'll lay ye any thing at all you do no such thing.' 'A hundred guineas to sixpence I do,' says he: 'bring me the handkerchief.' I was loth, knowing he meant the handkerchief with the gold in it, to bring it out in such company, and his honour not very able to reckon it. 'Bring me the handkerchief, then, Thady,' says he, and stamps with his foot; so with that I pulls it out of my great coat pocket, where I had put it for safety. Oh, how it grieved me to see the guineas counting upon the table, and they the last my master had! Says Sir Condy to me, 'Your hand is steadier than mine to-night, old Thady, and that's a wonder; fill you the horn for me.' And so, wishing his honour success, I did; but I filled it, little thinking of what would befall him. He swallows it down, and drops like one shot. We lifts him up, and he was speechless, and quite black in the face. We put him to bed, and in a short time he wakened, raving with a fever on his brain. He was shocking either to see or hear. 'Judy! Judy! have you no touch of feeling? won't you stay to help us nurse him?' says I to her, and she putting on her shawl to go out of the house. 'I'm frightened to see him,' says she, 'and wouldn't nor couldn't stay in it; and what use? he can't last till the morning.' With that she ran off. There was none but my sister and myself left near him of all the many friends he had. The fever came and went, and came and went, and lasted five days, and the sixth he was sensible for a few minutes, and said to me, knowing me very well. 'I'm in burning pain all withinside of me, Thady.' I could not speak, but my shister asked him would he have this thing or t'other to do him good? 'No,' says he, 'nothing will do me good no more,' and he gave a terrible screech with the torture he was in – then again in a minute's ease – 'brought to this by drink,' says he; 'where are all the friends? – where's Judy? – Gone, hey? Ay, Sir Condy has been a fool all his days,' said he; and there was the last word he spoke, and died. He had but a very poor funeral, after all.

If you want to know any more, I'm not very well able to tell you; but my lady Rackrent did not die, as was expected of her, but was only disfigured in the face ever after by the fall and bruises she got; and she and Jason, immediately after my poor master's death, set about going to law about that jointure; the memorandum not being on stamped paper, some say it is worth nothing, others again it may do; others say, Jason won't have the lands at any rate. Many wishes it so: for my part, I'm tired wishing for any thing in this world, after all I've seen in it – but I'll say nothing; it would be a folly to be getting myself ill-will in my old age. Jason did not marry, nor think of marrying Judy, as I prophesied and I am not sorry for it; who is? As for all I have here set down from memory and hearsay of the family, there's nothing but truth in it from beginning to end: that you may depend upon; for where's the use of telling lies about the things which every body knows as well as I do?

The Editor could have readily made the catastrophe of Sir Condy's history more dramatic and more pathetic, if he thought it allowable to varnish the plain round tale of faithful Thady. He lays it before the English reader as a specimen of manners and characters, which are, perhaps, unknown in England. Indeed, the domestic habits of no nation in Europe were less known to the English than those of their sister country, till within these few years.

Mr Young's picture of Ireland, in his tour through that country, was the first faithful portrait of its inhabitants. All the features in the foregoing sketch were taken from the life, and they are characteristic of that mixture of quickness, simplicity, cunning, carelessness, dissipation, disinterestedness, shrewdness, and blunder, which, in different forms, and with various success, has been brought upon the stage, or delineated in novels.

It is a problem of difficult solution to determine, whether an Union will hasten or retard the melioration of this country. The few gentlemen of education, who now reside in this country, will resort to England: they are few, but they are in nothing inferior to men of the same rank in Great Britain. The best that can happen will be the introduction of British manufacturers in their places.

Did the Warwickshire militia, who were chiefly artisans, teach the Irish to drink beer? or did they learn from the Irish to drink whiskey?

1800

ADVERTISEMENT TO THE ENGLISH READER

Some friends who have seen Thady's history since it has been printed have suggested to the Editor, that many of the terms and idiomatic phrases with which it abounds could not be intelligible to the English reader without farther explanation. The Editor has therefore furnished the following Glossary.

GLOSSARY

page 97 Monday morning] Thady begins his Memoirs of the Rackrent Family by dating *Monday morning*, because no great undertaking can be auspiciously commenced in Ireland on any morning but *Monday morning*. – 'Oh, please God we live till Monday morning, we'll set the slater to mend the roof of the house – On Monday morning we'll fall to and cut the turf – On Monday morning we'll see and begin mowing – On Monday morning, please your honour, we'll begin and dig the potatoes,' &c.

All the intermediate days between the making of such speeches and the ensuing Monday are wasted, and when Monday morning comes it is ten to one that the business is deferred to *the next* Monday morning. The Editor knew a gentleman who, to counteract this prejudice, made his workmen and labourers begin all new pieces of work upon a Saturday.

page 98 let alone the three kingdoms itself] *Let alone*, in this sentence, means *put out of the consideration*. This phrase *let alone*, which is now used as the imperative of a verb, may in time become a conjunction, and may exercise the ingenuity of some future etymologist. The celebrated Horne Tooke has proved most satisfactorily, that the conjunction *but* comes from the imperative of the Anglo-Saxon verb (*beonutan*) *to be out*; also that *if* comes from *gif*, the imperative of the Anglo-Saxon verb which signifies *to give*, &c. &c.

page 99 whillaluh] Ullaloo, Gol, or lamentation over the dead –

'Magnoque ululante tumultu.'
VIRGIL

'Ululatibus omne Implevere nemus.'
OVID

A full account of the Irish Gol or Ullaloo, and of the Caoinan or Irish funeral song, with its first semichorus, second semichorus, full chorus of sighs and groans, together with the Irish words and music, may be found in the fourth volume of the Transactions of the Royal Irish Academy. For the advantage of *lazy* readers, who would rather read a page than walk a yard, and from compassion, not to say sympathy with their infirmity, the Editor transcribes the following passages.

'The Irish have been always remarkable for their funeral lamentations, and this peculiarity has been noticed by almost every traveller who visited them. And it seems derived from their Celtic ancestors, the primæval inhabitants of this isle . . .'

'It has been affirmed of the Irish, that to cry was more natural to them than to any other nation, and at length the Irish cry became proverbial . . .'

'Cambrensis in the twelfth century says, the Irish then musically expressed their griefs; that is, they applied the musical art, in which they excelled all others, to the orderly celebration of funeral obsequies, by dividing the mourners into two bodies, each alternately singing their part, and the whole at times joining in full chorus . . . The body of the deceased, dressed in grave clothes and ornamented with flowers, was placed on a bier or some elevated spot. The relations and Keeners (*singing mourners*) ranged themselves in two divisions, one at the head and the other at the feet of the corpse. The bards and croteries had before prepared the funeral Caoinan. The chief bard of the head chorus began by singing the first stanza in a low, doleful tone, which was softly accompanied by the harp: at the conclusion the foot semichorus began the lamentation, or Ullaloo, from the final note of the preceding stanza, in which they were answered by the head semichorus; then both united in one general chorus. The chorus of the first stanza being ended, the chief bard of the foot semichorus began the second Gol or lamentation, in which they were answered by that of the head; and then as before both united in the general full chorus. Thus alternately were the song and choruses performed during the night. The genealogy, rank, possessions, the virtues and vices of the dead were rehearsed, and a number of interrogations were addressed to the deceased: as, Why did he die? If married, whether his wife was faithful to him, his sons dutiful, or good hunters or warriors? If a woman, whether her daughters were fair or chaste? If a young man, whether he had been crossed in love? or if the blue-eyed maids of Erin treated him with scorn?'

We are told that formerly the feet (the metrical feet) of the Caoinan were much attended to, but on the decline of the Irish bards these feet were gradually neglected, the Caoinan fell into a sort of slip-shod metre amongst women. Each province had different Caoinans, or at least different imitations of the original. There was the Munster cry, the Ulster cry, &c. It became an extempore performance, and every set of Keeners varied the melody according to their own fancy.

It is curious to observe how customs and ceremonies degenerate. The present Irish cry or howl cannot boast of much melody, nor is the funeral procession conducted with much dignity. The crowd of people who assemble at these funerals sometimes amounts to a thousand, often to four or five hundred. They gather as the bearers of the hearse proceed on their way, and when they pass through any village, or when they come near any houses, they begin to cry – Oh! Oh! Oh! Oh! Oh! Agh! Agh! raising their notes from the first *Oh!* to the last *Agh!* in a kind of mournful howl. This gives notice to the inhabitants of the village that a *funeral is passing*, and immediately they flock out to follow it. In the province of Munster it is a common thing for the women to follow a funeral, to join in the universal cry with all their might and main for some time, and then to turn and ask – 'Arrah! who is it that's dead? – who is it we're crying for?' – Even the poorest people have their own burying-places, that is, spots of ground in the church-yards, where they say that their ancestors have been buried ever since the wars of Ireland: and if these burial-places are ten miles from the place where a man dies, his friends and neighbours take care to carry his corpse thither. Always one priest, often five or six priests, attend these funerals; each priest repeats a mass, for which he is paid sometimes a shilling, sometimes half a crown, sometimes half a guinea, or a guinea, according to the circumstances, or as they say, according to the *ability* of the deceased. After the burial of any very poor man who has left a widow or children, the priest makes what is called *a collection* for the widow; he goes round to every person present, and each contributes sixpence or a shilling, or what they please. The reader will find in the note upon the word *wake* more particulars respecting the conclusion of the Irish funerals.

Certain old women, who cry particularly loud and well, are in great request, and, as a man said to the Editor, 'Every one would wish and be proud to have such at his funeral, or at that of his friends.' The lower Irish are wonderfully eager to attend the funerals of their friends and relations, and they make their relationships branch out to a great extent. The proof that a poor man has been well beloved during his life, is his having a crowded funeral. To attend a neighbour's funeral is a cheap proof of humanity, but it does not, as some imagine, cost nothing. The time spent in attending funerals may be safely valued at half a million to the Irish nation: the Editor thinks that double that sum would not be too high an estimate. The habits of profligacy and drunkenness which are acquired at *wakes* are here put out of the question. When a labourer, a carpenter, or a smith is not at his work, which frequently happens, ask where he is gone, and ten to one the answer is – 'Oh faith, please your honour, he couldn't do a stroke to-day, for he's gone to *the* funeral.'

Even beggars, when they grow old, go about begging *for their own funerals*; that is, begging for money to buy a coffin, candles, pipes and tobacco. – For the use of the candles, pipes and tobacco, see *wake*.

Those who value customs in proportion to their antiquity, and nations in proportion to their adherence to ancient customs, will doubtless admire the Irish *Ullaloo*, and the Irish nation, for persevering in this usage from time immemorial. The Editor, however, has observed some alarming symptoms, which seem to prognosticate the declining taste for the Ullaloo in Ireland. In a comic theatrical entertainment represented not long since on the Dublin stage, a chorus of old women was introduced, who set up the Irish howl round the relics of a physician, who is supposed to have fallen under the wooden sword of Harlequin. After the old women have continued their Ullaloo for a decent time, with all the necessary accompaniments of wringing their hands, wiping or rubbing their eyes with the corners of their gowns or aprons, &c. one of the mourners suddenly suspends her lamentable cries, and turning to her neighbour, asks – 'Arrh now, honey, who is it we're crying for?'

pages 99–100 the tenants were sent away without their whiskey] It is usual with some landlords to give their inferior tenants a glass of whiskey when they pay their rents. Thady calls it *their* whiskey; not that the whiskey is actually the property of the tenants, but that it becomes their *right*, after it has been often given to them. In this general mode of reasoning respecting *rights*, the lower Irish are not singular, but they are peculiarly quick and tenacious in claiming these rights. 'Last year your honour gave me some straw for the roof of my house, and I *expect* your honour will be after doing the same this year.' – In this manner gifts are frequently turned into tributes. The high and low are not always dissimilar in their habits. It is said that the Sublime Ottoman Porte is very apt to claim gifts as tributes: thus it is dangerous to send the Grand Signior a fine horse on his birth-day one year, lest on his next birth-day he should expect a similar present, and should proceed to demonstrate the reasonableness of his expectations.

page 100 he demeaned himself greatly] Means, he lowered, or disgraced himself much.

page 100 duty fowls – and duty turkies – and duty geese] In many leases in Ireland, tenants were *formerly* bound to supply an inordinate quantity of poultry to their landlords. The Editor knew of sixty turkies being reserved in one lease of a small farm.

page 100 English tenants] An English tenant does not mean a tenant who is an Englishman, but a tenant who pays his rent the day that it is due. It is a common prejudice in Ireland, amongst the poorer classes of people, to believe that all tenants in England pay their rents on the very day when they become due. An Irishman, when he goes to take a farm, if he wants to prove to his landlord that he is a substantial man, offers to become an *English tenant*. If a tenant disobliges his landlord by voting against him, or against his opinion, at an election, the tenant is immediately informed by the agent that he must become *an English tenant*. This threat does not imply that he is to change his language or his country, but that he must pay all the arrear of rent which he owes, and that he must thenceforward pay his rent on the day when it becomes due.

page 100 canting] does not mean talking or writing hypocritical nonsense, but selling substantially by auction.

page 100 duty work] It was formerly common in Ireland to insert clauses in leases, binding tenants to furnish their landlords with labourers and horses for several days in the year. Much petty tyranny and oppression have resulted from this feudal custom. Whenever a poor man disobliged his landlord, the agent sent to him for his duty work, and Thady does not exaggerate when he says, that the tenants were often called from their own work to do that of their landlord. Thus the very means of earning their rent were taken from them: whilst they were getting home their landlord's harvest, their own was often ruined, and yet their rents were expected to be paid as punctually as if their time had been at their own disposal. This appears the height of absurd injustice.

In Esthonia, amongst the poor Sclavonian race of peasant slaves, they pay tributes to their lords, not under the name of duty work, duty geese, duty turkies, &c. but under the name of *righteousnesses*. The following ballad is a curious specimen of Estonian poetry:

This is the cause that the country is ruined,
And the straw of the thatch is eaten away,
The gentry are come to live in the land –
Chimneys between the village,
And the proprietor upon the white floor!
The sheep brings forth a lamb with a white forehead;
This is paid to the lord for a *righteousness sheep.*
The sow farrows pigs,
They go to the spit of the lord.
The hen lays eggs,
They go into the lord's frying-pan.
The cow drops a male calf,
That goes into the lord's herd as a bull.
The mare foals a horse foal,
That must be for my lord's nag.
The boor's wife has sons,
They must go to look after my lord's poultry.

page 101 out of forty-nine suits which he had, he never lost one – but seventeen] Thady's language in this instance is a specimen of a mode of rhetoric common in Ireland. An astonishing assertion is made in the beginning of a sentence, which ceases to be in the least surprising when you hear the qualifying explanation that follows. Thus a man who is in the last stage of staggering drunkenness will, if he can articulate, swear to you – 'Upon his conscience now (and may he never stir from the spot alive if he is telling a lie) upon his conscience he has not tasted a drop of any thing, good or bad, since morning at-all-at-all – but half a pint of whiskey, please your honour.'

page 101 fairy mounts] Barrows. It is said that these high mounts were of great service to the natives of Ireland, when Ireland was invaded by the Danes. Watch was always kept on them, and upon the approach of an enemy a fire was lighted to give notice to the next watch, and thus the intelligence was quickly communicated through the country. *Some years ago,* the common people believed that these barrows were inhabited by fairies, or as they call them, by the *good people.* – 'Oh troth, to the best of my belief, and to the best of my judgment and opinion (said an elderly man to the Editor), it was only the old people that had nothing to do, and got together and were telling stories about them fairies, but to the best of my judgment there's nothing in it. – Only this I heard myself not very many years back, from a decent kind of a man, a grazier, that as he was coming just *fair and easy* (*quietly*) from the fair, with some cattle and sheep that he had not sold, just at the church of—, at an angle of the road like, he was met by a good-looking man, who asked him where was he going? And he answered, 'Oh, far enough, I must be going all night.' – 'No, that you mustn't nor won't (says the man), you'll sleep with me the night, and you'll want for nothing, nor your cattle nor sheep neither, nor your *beast* (*horse*); so come along with me.' – With that the grazier *lit* (alighted) from his horse, and it was dark night; but presently he finds himself, he does not know in the wide world how, in a fine house, and plenty of every thing to eat and drink – nothing at all wanting that he could wish for or think of – And he does not *mind* (*recollect*, or *know*) how at last he falls asleep; and the morning he finds himself lying, not in ever a bed or a house at all, but just in the angle of the road where first he met the strange man: there he finds himself lying on his back on the grass, and all his sheep feeding as quiet as ever all round about him, and his horse the same way, and the bridle of the beast over his wrist. And I asked him what he thought of it, and from first to last he could think of nothing but for certain sure it must have been the fairies that entertained him so well. For there was no house to see any where nigh hand, or any building, or barn, or place at all, but only the church and the *mote* (*barrow*). There's another odd thing enough that they tell about this same church, that if any person's corpse, that had not a right to be buried in that church-yard, went to be burying there in it, no not all the men, women, or childer in all Ireland could get the corpse any way into the church-yard; but as they would be trying to go into the church-yard, their feet would seem to be going backwards instead of forwards; aye, continually backwards the whole funeral would seem to go; and they would never set foot with the corpse in the church-yard. Now they say, that it is the fairies do all this; but it is my opinion it is all idle talk, and people are after being wiser now.'

The country people in Ireland certainly *had* great admiration mixed with reverence, if not dread of fairies. They believed, that beneath these fairy mounts were spacious subterraneous palaces inhabited by *the good people*, who must not on any account be disturbed. When the wind raises a little eddy of dust upon the road, the poor people believe that it is raised by the fairies, that it is a sign that they are journeying from one of the fairy mounts to another, and they say to the fairies, or to the dust as it passes – 'God speed ye, gentlemen, God speed ye.' This averts any evil that *the good people* might be inclined to do them. There are innumerable stories told of the friendly and unfriendly feats of these busy fairies; some of these tales are ludicrous, and some romantic enough for poetry. It is a pity that poets should lose such convenient, though diminutive machinery. – By the by, Parnell, who shewed himself so deeply 'skilled of faerie lore', was an Irishman; and though he has presented his faeries to the world in the ancient English dress of 'Britain's Isle, and Arthur's days', it is probable that his first acquaintance with them began in his native country.

Some remote origin for the most superstitious or romantic popular illusions or vulgar errors may often be discovered. In Ireland, the old churches and church-yards have been usually fixed upon as the scenes of wonders. Now the antiquarians tell us, that near the ancient churches in that kingdom caves of various constructions have from time to time been discovered, which were formerly used as granaries or magazines by the ancient inhabitants, and as places to which they retreated in time of danger. There is (p. 84 of the RIA Transactions for 1789) a particular account of a number of these artificial caves at the west end of the church of Killossy, in the county of Kildare. Under a rising ground, in a dry sandy soil, these subterraneous dwellings were found: they have pediment roofs, and they communicate with each other by small apertures. In the Brehon laws these are mentioned, and there are fines inflicted by those laws upon persons who steal from the subterraneous granaries. All these things shew, that there was a real foundation for the stories which were told of the appearance of lights and the sounds of voices near these places. The persons who had property concealed there very willingly countenanced every wonderful relation that tended to make these places objects of sacred awe or superstitious terror.

page 102 weed-ashes] By antient usage in Ireland, all the weeds on a farm belonged to the farmer's wife, or to the wife of the squire who holds the ground in his own hands. The great demand for alkaline salts in bleaching rendered these ashes no inconsiderable perquisite.

page 102 sealing-money] Formerly it was the custom in Ireland for tenants to give the squire's lady from two to fifty guineas as a perquisite upon the sealing of their leases. The Editor not very long since knew of a baronet's lady accepting fifty guineas as sealing money, upon closing a bargain for a considerable farm.

page 102 Sir Murtagh grew mad] Sir Murtagh grew angry.

page 102 the whole kitchen was out on the stairs] Means that all the inhabitants of the kitchen came out of the kitchen and stood upon the stairs. These, and similar expressions, show how much the Irish are disposed to metaphor and amplification.

page 103 fining down the yearly rent] When an Irish gentleman, like Sir Kit Rackrent, has lived beyond his income, and finds himself distressed for want of ready money, tenants obligingly offer to take his land at a rent far below the value, and to pay him a small sum of money in hand, which they call fining down the yearly rent. The temptation of this ready cash often blinds the landlord to his future interest.

page 103 driver] A man who is employed to drive tenants for rent; that is, to drive the cattle belonging to tenants to pound. The office of driver is by no means a sinecure.

page 104 I thought to make him a priest] It was customary amongst those of Thady's rank, in Ireland, whenever they could get a little money, to send their sons abroad to St Omer's, or to Spain, to be educated as priests. Now they are educated at Maynooth. The Editor has lately known a young lad, who began by being a post-boy, afterwards turn into a carpenter; then quit his plane and work bench to study his *Humanities*, as he said, at the college of Maynooth: but after he had gone through his course of Humanities, he determined to be a soldier instead of a priest.

page 105 flam] Short for flambeau.

page 106 barrack-room] Formerly it was customary, in gentlemen's houses in Ireland, to fit up one large bedchamber with a number of beds for the reception of occasional visitors. These rooms were called barrack-rooms.

page 106 an innocent] In Ireland, means a simpleton, an idiot.

page 109 the Curragh] is the Newmarket of Ireland.

page 109 the cant] The auction.

page 110 and so should cut him off for ever, by levying a fine, and suffering a recovery to dock the entail] The English reader may perhaps be surprised at the extent of Thady's legal knowledge, and at the fluency with which he pours forth law terms; but almost every poor man in Ireland, be he farmer, weaver, shopkeeper, or steward, is, beside his other occupations, occasionally a lawyer. The nature of processes, ejectments, custodians, injunctions, replevins, &c. &c. are perfectly known to them, and the terms are as familiar to them as to any attorney. They all love law. It is a kind of lottery, in which every man, staking his own wit or cunning against his richer neighbour's property, feels that he has little to lose and much to gain.

'I'll have the law of you, so I will!' – is the saying of an Englishman who expects justice. 'I'll have you before his honour' – is the threat of an Irishman who hopes for partiality. Miserable is the life of a justice of the peace in Ireland the day after a fair, especially if he resides near a small town. The multitude of the *kilt* (*kilt* does not mean *killed*, but hurt) and wounded who come before his honour with black eyes or bloody heads is astonishing, but more astonishing is the number of those, who, though they are scarcely able by daily labour to procure daily food, will nevertheless, without the least reluctance, waste six or seven hours of the day lounging in the yard or hall of a justice of the peace, waiting to make some complaint about – nothing. It is impossible to convince them that *time is money*. They do not set any value upon their own time, and they think that others estimate theirs at less than nothing. Hence they make no scruple of telling a justice of the peace a story of an hour long about a *tester* (sixpence): and if he grow impatient, they attribute it to some secret prejudice which he entertains against them.

Their method is to get a story completely by heart, and to tell it, as they call it, *out of the face*, that is, from the beginning to the end, without interruption.

'Well, my good friend, I have seen you lounging about these three hours in the yard; what is your business?'

'Please your honour, it is what I want to speak one word to your honour.'

'Speak then, but be quick – What is the matter?'

'Nothing strange – The matter, please your honour, is nothing at-all-at-all, only just about the grazing of a horse, please your honour, that this man here sold me at the fair of Gurtishannon last Shrove fair, which lay down three times with myself, please your honour, and *kilt* me; not to be telling your honour of how, no later back than yesterday night, he lay down in the house there within, and all the childer standing round, and it was God's mercy he did not fall a'-top of them, or into the fire to burn himself. So please your honour, to-day I took him back to this man, which owned him, and after a great deal to do I got the mare again I *swopped* (*exchanged*) him for, but he won't pay the grazing of the horse for the time I had him, though he promised to pay the grazing in case the horse didn't answer; and he never did a day's work, good or bad, please your honour, all the time he was with me, and I had the doctor to him five times, any how. And so, please your honour, it is what I expect your honour will stand my friend, for I'd sooner come to your honour for justice than to any other in all Ireland. And so I brought him here before your honour, and expect your honour will make him pay me the grazing, or tell me, can I process him for it at the next assizes, please your honour?'

The defendant now, turning a quid of tobacco with his tongue into some secret cavern in his mouth, begins his defence with –

'Please your honour, under favour, and saving your honour's presence, there's not a word of truth in all this man has been saying from beginning to end, upon my conscience, and I wouldn't for the value of the horse itself, grazing and all, be after telling your honour a lie. For please your honour, I have a dependence upon your honour that you'll do me justice, and not be listening to him or the like of him. Please your honour, it's what he has brought me before your honour, because he had a spite against me about some oats I sold your honour, which he was jealous of, and a shawl his wife got at my shister's shop there without, and never paid for; so I offered to set the shawl against the grazing, and give him a receipt in full of all demands, but he wouldn't out of spite, please your honour; so he brought me before your honour, expecting your honour was mad with me for cutting down the tree in the horse park, which was none of my doing, please your honour – ill luck to them that went and belied me to your honour behind my back! - So if your honour is pleasing, I'll tell you the whole truth about the horse that he swopped against my mare, out of the face. – Last Shrove fair I met this man, Jemmy Duffy, please your honour, just at the corner of the road where the bridge is broke down that your honour is to have the presentment for this year – long life to you for it! - And he was at that time coming from the fair of Gurtishannon, and I the same way. "How are you, Jemmy!" says I. – "Very well, I thank ye kindly, Bryan," says he; "shall we turn back to Paddy Salmon's, and take a naggin of whiskey to our better acquaintance?" – "I don't care if I did, Jemmy," says I; "only it is what I can't take the whiskey, because I'm under an oath against it for a month." Ever since, please your honour, the day your honour met me on the road, and observed to me I could hardly stand I had taken so much – though upon my conscience your honour wronged me greatly that same time – ill luck to them that belied me behind my back to your honour! – Well, please your honour, as I was telling you, as he was taking the whiskey, and we talking of one thing or t'other, he makes me an offer to swop his mare that he couldn't sell at the fair of Gurtishannon, because nobody would be troubled with the beast, please your honour, against my horse, and to oblige him I took the mare – sorrow take her! and him along with her! – She kicked me a new car, that was worth three pounds ten, to tatters the first time ever I put her into it, and I expect your honour will make him pay me the price of the car, any how, before I pay the grazing, which I've no right to pay at-all-at-all, only to oblige him. – But I leave it all to your honour – and the whole grazing he ought to be charging for the beast is but two and eightpence half-penny, any how, please your honour. So I'll abide by what your honour says, good or bad. I'll leave it all to your honour.'

I'll leave *it* all to your honour – literally means, I'll leave all the trouble to your honour.

The Editor knew a justice of the peace in Ireland, who had such a dread of *having it all left to his honour*, that he frequently gave the complainants the sum about which they were disputing to make peace between them, and to get rid of the trouble of hearing their stories *out of the face*. But he was soon cured of this method of buying off disputes, by the increasing multitude of those who, out of pure regard to his honour, came 'to get justice from him, because they would sooner come before him than before any man in all Ireland'.

page 118 a raking pot of tea] We should observe, that this custom has long since been banished from the higher orders of Irish gentry. The mysteries of a raking pot of tea, like those of the Bona Dea, are supposed to be sacred to females, but now and then it has happened that some of the male species, who were either more audacious or more highly favoured than the rest of their sex, have been admitted by stealth to these orgies. The time when the festive ceremony begins varies according to circumstances, but it is never earlier than twelve o'clock at night; the joys of a raking pot of tea depending on its being made in secret, and at an unseasonable hour. After a ball, when the more discreet part of the company had departed to rest, a few chosen female spirits, who have footed it till they can foot it no longer, and till the sleepy notes expire under the slurring hand of the musician, retire to a bed-chamber, call the favourite maid, who alone is admitted, bid her *put down the kettle*, lock the door, and amidst as much giggling and scrambling as possible, they get round a tea-table, on which all manner of things are huddled together. Then begin mutual railleries and mutual confidences amongst the young ladies, and the faint scream and the loud laugh is heard, and the romping for letters and pocket-books begins, and gentlemen are called by their surnames, or by the general name of fellows – pleasant fellows! charming fellows! odious fellows! abominable fellows! – and then all prudish decorums are forgotten, and then we might be convinced how much the satyrical poet was mistaken when he said,

'There is no woman where there's no reserve.'

The merit of the original idea of a raking pot of tea evidently belongs to the washerwoman and the laundry-maid. But why should not we have *Low life above stairs*, as well as *High life below stairs*?

page 119 carton and half carton] Thady means cartron or half cartron. 'According to the old record in the black book of Dublin, a *cantred* is said to contain 30 *villatas terras*, which are also called *quarters* of land (quarterons; *cartrons*); every one of which quarters must contain so much ground as will pasture 400 cows and 17 plough-lands. A knight's fee was composed of 8 hydes, which amount to 160 acres, and that is generally deemed about a *ploughland*.'

The Editor was favoured by a learned friend with the above extract, from a MS of Lord Totness's in the Lambeth library.

page 129 wake] A wake, in England, means a festival held upon the anniversary of the saint of the parish. At these wakes rustic games, rustic conviviality, and rustic courtship, are pursued with all the ardour and all the appetite, which accompany such pleasures as occur but seldom. – In Ireland a wake is a midnight meeting, held professedly for the indulgence of holy sorrow, but usually it is converted into orgies of unholy joy. When an Irish man or woman of the lower order dies, the straw which composed his bed, whether it has been contained in a bag to form a mattress, or simply spread upon the earthen floor, is immediately taken out of the house, and burned before the cabin door, the family at the same time setting up the death howl. The ears and eyes of the neighbours being thus alarmed, they flock to the house of the deceased, and by their vociferous sympathy excite and at the same time soothe the sorrows of the family.

It is curious to observe how good and bad are mingled in human institutions. In countries which were thinly inhabited, this custom prevented private attempts against the lives of individuals, and formed a kind of Coroner's inquest upon the body which had recently expired, and burning the straw upon which the sick man lay became a simple preservative against infection. At night the dead body is waked, that is to say, all the friends and neighbours of the deceased collect in a barn or stable, where the corpse is laid upon some boards, or an unhinged door supported upon stools, the face exposed, the rest of the body covered with a white sheet. Round the body are stuck in brass candlesticks, which have been borrowed perhaps at five miles distance, as many candles as the poor person can beg or borrow, observing always to have an odd number. Pipes and tobacco are first distributed, and then according to the *ability* of the deceased, cakes and ale, and sometimes whiskey, are *dealt* to the company.

> 'Deal on, deal on, my merry men all,
> Deal on your cakes and your wine,
> For whatever is dealt at her funeral to-day
> Shall be dealt to-morrow at mine.'

After a fit of universal sorrow, and the comfort of a universal dram, the scandal of the neighbourhood, as in higher circles, occupy the company. The young lads and lasses romp with one another, and when the fathers and mothers are at last overcome with sleep and whiskey (*vino & sommo*), the youth become more enterprising and are frequently successful. It is said that more matches are made at wakes than at weddings.

page 130 kilt] This word frequently occurs in the following pages, where it means not *killed*, but much *hurt*. In Ireland, not only cowards, but the brave 'die many times before their death'. There *Killing is no murder*.

CHARLES ROBERT MATURIN
from *Melmoth the Wanderer*

I

Alive again? Then show me where he is;
I'll give a thousand pounds to look upon him.

SHAKESPEARE

In the autumn of 1816, John Melmoth, a student in Trinity College, Dublin, quitted it to attend a dying uncle on whom his hopes for independence chiefly rested. John was the orphan son of a younger brother, whose small property scarce could pay John's college expences; but the uncle was rich, unmarried, and old; and John, from his infancy, had been brought up to look on him with that mingled sensation of awe, and of the wish, without the means to conciliate, (that sensation at once attractive and repulsive), with which we regard a being who (as nurse, domestic, and parent have tutored us to believe) holds the very threads of our existence in his hands, and may prolong or snap them when he pleases.

On receiving this summons, John set immediately out to attend his uncle.

The beauty of the country through which he travelled (it was the county Wicklow) could not prevent his mind from dwelling on many painful thoughts, some borrowed from the past, and more from the future. His uncle's caprice and moroseness, – the strange reports concerning the cause of the secluded life he had led for many years, – his own dependent state, – fell like blows fast and heavy on his mind. He roused himself to repel them, – sat up in the mail, in which he was a solitary passenger, – looked out on the prospect, – consulted his watch; – then he thought they receded for a moment, – but there was nothing to fill their place, and he was forced to invite them back for company. When the mind is thus active in calling over invaders, no wonder the conquest is soon completed. As the carriage drew near the Lodge, (the name of old Melmoth's seat), John's heart grew heavier every moment.

The recollection of this awful uncle from infancy, – when he was never permitted to approach him without innumerable lectures, – *not to be troublesome*, – not to go too near his uncle, – not to ask him any questions, – on no account to disturb the inviolable arrangement of his snuff-box, hand-bell, and spectacles, nor to suffer the glittering of the gold-headed cane to tempt him to the mortal sin of handling it, – and, finally, to pilot himself aright through his perilous course in and out of the apartment without striking against the piles of books, globes, old newspapers, wig-blocks, tobacco-pipes, and snuff-cannisters, not to mention certain hidden rocks of rat-traps and mouldy books beneath the chairs, – together with the final reverential bow at the door, which was to be closed with cautious gentleness, and the stairs to be descended as if he were 'shod with felt.' – This recollection was carried on to his school-boy years, when at Christmas and Easter, the ragged poney, the jest of the school, was dispatched to bring the reluctant visitor to the Lodge, – where his pastime was to sit vis-à-vis to his uncle, without speaking or moving, till the pair resembled Don Raymond and the ghost of Beatrice in the Monk, – then watching him as he picked the bones of lean mutton out of his mess of weak broth, the latter of which he handed to his nephew with a needless caution not to 'take more than he liked,' – then hurried to bed by daylight, even in winter, to save the expence of an inch of candle, where he lay awake and restless from hunger, till his uncle's retiring at eight o'clock gave signal to the governante of the meagre household to steal up to him with some fragments of her own scanty meal, administering between every mouthful a whispered caution not to tell his uncle. Then his college life, passed in an attic in the second square, uncheered by an invitation to the country; the gloomy summer wasted in walking up and down the deserted streets, as his uncle would not defray the expences of his journey; – the only intimation of his existence, received in quarterly epistles, containing, with the scanty but punctual remittance, complaints of the expences of his education, cautions against extravagance, and lamentations for the failure of tenants and the fall of the value of lands. All these recollections came over him, and along with them the remembrance of that last scene, where his dependence on his uncle was impressed on him by the dying lips of his father.

'John, I must leave you, my poor boy; it has pleased God to take your father from you before he could do for you what would have made this hour less painful to him. You must look up, John, to your uncle for every thing. He has oddities and infirmities, but you must learn to bear with them, and with many other things too, as you will learn too soon. And now, my poor boy, may He who is the father of the fatherless look on your desolate state, and give you favour in the eyes of your uncle.' As this scene rose to John's memory, his eyes filled fast with tears, which he hastened to wipe away as the carriage stopt to let him out at his uncle's gate.

He alighted, and with a change of linen in a handkerchief, (his only travelling equipment), he approached his uncle's gate. The lodge was in ruins, and a barefooted boy from an adjacent cabin ran to lift on its single hinge what had once been a gate, but was now a few planks so villainously put together, that they clattered like a sign in a high wind. The stubborn post of the gate, yielding at last to the united strength of John and his barefooted assistant, grated heavily through the mud and gravel stones, in which it left a deep and sloughy furrow, and the entrance lay open. John, after searching his pocket in vain for a trifle to reward his assistant, pursued his way, while the lad, on his return, cleared the road at a hop step and jump, plunging through the mud with all the dabbling and amphibious delight of a duck, and scarce less proud of his agility than of his 'sarving a gentleman'. As John slowly trod the miry road which had once been the approach, he could discover, by the dim light of an autumnal evening, signs of increasing desolation since he had last visited the spot, – signs that penury had been aggravated and sharpened into downright misery. There was not a fence or a hedge round the domain: an uncemented wall of loose stones, whose numerous gaps were filled with furze or thorns, supplied their place. There was not a tree or shrub on the lawn; the lawn itself was turned into pasture-ground, and a few sheep were picking their scanty food amid the pebblestones, thistles, and hard mould, through which a few blades of grass made their rare and squalid appearance.

The house itself stood strongly defined even amid the darkness of the evening sky; for there were neither wings, or offices, or shrubbery, or tree, to shade or support it, and soften its strong harsh outline. John, after a melancholy gaze at the grass-grown steps and boarded windows, 'addressed himself' to knock at the door; but knocker there was none: loose stones, however, there were in plenty; and John was making vigorous application to the door with one of them, till the furious barking of a mastiff, who threatened at every bound to break his chain, and whose yell and growl, accompanied by 'eyes that glow and fangs that grin,' savoured as much of hunger as of rage, made the assailant raise the siege on the door, and betake himself to a well-known passage that led to the kitchen. A light glimmered in the window as he approached: he raised the latch with a doubtful hand; but, when he saw the party within, he advanced with the step of a man no longer doubtful of his welcome.

Round a turf-fire, whose well-replenished fuel gave testimony to the 'master's' indisposition, who would probably as soon have been placed on the fire himself as seen the whole *kish* emptied on it once, were seated the old housekeeper, two or three *followers*, (*i.e.* people who ate, drank, and lounged about in any kitchen that was open in the neighbourhood, on an occasion of grief or joy, all for his honor's sake, and for the great rispict they bore the family), and an old woman, whom John immediately recognized as the doctress of the neighbourhood, – a withered Sybil, who prolonged her squalid existence by practising on the fears, the ignorance, and the sufferings of beings as miserable as herself. Among the better sort, to whom she sometimes had access by the influence of servants, she tried the effects of some simples, her skill in which was sometimes productive of success. Among the lower orders she talked much of the effects of the 'evil eye', against which she boasted a counter-spell, of unfailing efficacy; and while she spoke, she shook her grizzled locks with such witch-like eagerness, that she never failed to communicate to her half-terrified, half-believing audience, some portion of that enthusiasm which, amid all her consciousness of imposture, she herself probably felt a large share of; still, when the case at last became desperate, when credulity itself lost all patience, and hope and life were departing together, she urged the miserable patient to confess *'there was something about his heart'*; and when this confession was extorted from the weariness of pain and the ignorance of poverty, she nodded and muttered so mysteriously, as to convey to the bystanders, that she had had difficulties to contend with which were invincible by human power. When there was no pretext, from indisposition, for her visiting either 'his honor's' kitchen, or the cottar's hut, – when the stubborn and persevering convalescence of the whole country threatened her with starvation, – she still had a resource: – if there were no lives to be shortened, there were fortunes to be told; – she worked 'by spells, and by such daubry as is beyond our element.' No one twined so well as she the mystic yarn to be dropt into the lime-kiln pit, on the edge of which stood the shivering inquirer into futurity, doubtful whether the answer to her question of 'who holds?' was to be uttered by the voice of demon or lover.

No one knew so well as she to find where the four streams met, in which, on the same portentous season, the chemise was to be immersed, and then displayed before the fire, (in the name of one whom we dare not mention to 'ears polite'), to be turned by the figure of the destined husband before morning. No one but herself (she said) knew the hand in which the comb was to be held, while the other was employed in conveying the apple to the mouth, – while, during the joint operation, the shadow of the phantom-spouse was to pass across the mirror before which it was performed. No one was more skilful or active in removing every iron implement from the kitchen where these ceremonies were usually performed by the credulous and terrified dupes of her wizardry, lest, instead of the form of a comely youth exhibiting a ring on his white finger, an headless figure should stalk to the rack, (*Anglicè*, dresser), take down a long spit, or, in default of that, snatch a poker from the fire-side, and mercilessly take measure with its iron length of the sleeper for a coffin. No one, in short, knew better how to torment or terrify her victims into a belief of that power which may and has reduced the strongest minds to the level of the weakest; and under the influence of which the cultivated sceptic, Lord Lyttleton, yelled and gnashed and writhed in his last hours, like the poor girl who, in the belief of the horrible visitation of the vampire, shrieked aloud, that her grandfather was sucking her vital blood while she slept, and expired under the influence of imaginary horror. Such was the being to whom old Melmoth had committed his life, half from credulity, and (*Hibernicè* speaking) *more than half* from avarice. Among this groupe John advanced, – recognizing some, – disliking more, – distrusting all. The old housekeeper received him with cordiality; – he was always her 'white-headed boy,' she said, – (*imprimis*, his hair was as black as jet), and she tried to lift her withered hand to his head with an action between a benediction and a caress, till the difficulty of the attempt forced on her the conviction that that head was fourteen inches higher than her reach since she had last patted it. The men, with the national deference of the Irish to a person of superior rank, all rose at his approach, (their stools chattering on the broken flags), and wished his honor 'a thousand years, and long life to the back of that; and would not his honor take something to keep the grief out of his heart'; and so saying, five or six red and bony hands tendered him glasses of whiskey all at once. All this time the Sybil sat silent in the ample chimney-corner, sending redoubled whiffs out of her pipe. John gently declined the offer of spirits, received the attentions of the old housekeeper cordially, looked askance at the withered crone who occupied the chimney corner, and then glanced at the table, which displayed other cheer than he had been accustomed to see in his 'honor's time'. There was a wooden dish of potatoes, which old Melmoth would have considered enough for a week's subsistence. There was the salted salmon, (a luxury unknown even in London. *Vide* Miss Edgeworth's Tales, 'The Absentee').

There was the *slink-veal*, flanked with tripe; and, finally, there were lobsters and *fried* turbot enough to justify what the author of the tale asserts, 'suo periculo', that when his great grandfather, the Dean of Killala, hired servants at the deanery, they stipulated that they should not be required to eat turbot or lobster more than twice a-week. There were also bottles of Wicklow ale, long and surreptitiously borrowed from his 'honor's' cellar, and which now made their first appearance on the kitchen hearth, and manifested their impatience of further constraint, by hissing, spitting, and bouncing in the face of the fire that provoked its animosity. But the whiskey (genuine illegitimate potsheen, smelling strongly of weed and smoke, and breathing defiance to excisemen) appeared, the 'veritable Amphitryon' of the feast; every one praised, and drank as deeply as he praised.

John, as he looked round the circle, and thought of his dying uncle was forcibly reminded of the scene at Don Quixote's departure, where, in spite of the grief caused by the dissolution of the worthy knight, we are informed that 'nevertheless the niece eat her victuals, the housekeeper drank to the repose of his soul, and even Sancho cherished his little carcase'. After returning, 'as he might', the courtesies of the party, John asked how his uncle was. 'As bad as he can be'; – 'Much better, and many thanks to your honor,' was uttered in such rapid and discordant unison by the party, that John turned from one to the other, not knowing which or what to believe. 'They say his honour has had a fright,' said a fellow, upwards of six feet high, approaching by way of whispering, and then bellowing the sound six inches above John's head. 'But then his honor has had *a cool* since,' said a man who was quietly swallowing the spirits that John had refused. At these words the Sybil who sat in the chimney-corner slowly drew her pipe from her mouth, and turned towards the party: the oracular movements of a Pythoness on her tripod never excited more awe, or impressed for the moment a deeper silence. 'It's not *here*,' said she, pressing her withered finger on her wrinkled forehead, 'nor *here*, – nor *here*'; and she extended her hand to the foreheads of those who were near her, who all bowed as if they were receiving a benediction, but had immediate recourse to the spirits afterwards, as if to ensure its effects. – 'It's all *here* – it's all *about the heart*'; and as she spoke she spread and pressed her fingers on her hollow bosom with a force of action that thrilled her hearers. – 'It's all *here*,' she added, repeating the action, (probably excited by the effect she had produced), and then sunk on her seat, resumed her pipe, and spoke no more. At this moment of involuntary awe on the part of John, and of terrified silence on that of the rest, an unusual sound was heard in the house, and the whole company started as if a musket had been discharged among them: – it was the unwonted sound of old Melmoth's bell. His domestics were so few, and so constantly near him, that the sound of his bell startled them as much as if he had been ringing the knell for his own interment. 'He used always to *rap down* for me,' said the old housekeeper, hurrying out of the kitchen; 'he said pulling the bells wore out the ropes.'

The sound of the bell produced its full effect. The housekeeper rushed into the room, followed by a number of women, (the Irish præficæ); all ready to prescribe for the dying or weep for the dead, – all clapping their hard hands, or wiping their dry eyes. These hags all surrounded the bed; and to witness their loud, wild, and desperate grief, their cries of 'Oh! he's going, his honor's going, his honor's going,' one would have imagined their lives were bound up in his, like those of the wives in the story of Sinbad the Sailor, who were to be interred alive with their deceased husbands.

Four of them wrung their hands and howled round the bed, while one, with all the adroitness of a Mrs Quickly, felt his honor's feet, and 'upward and upward', and 'all was cold as any stone'.

Old Melmoth withdrew his feet from the grasp of the hag, – counted with his keen eye (keen amid the approaching dimness of death) the number assembled round his bed, – raised himself on his sharp elbow, and pushing away the housekeeper, (who attempted to settle his nightcap, that had been shoved on one side in the struggle, and gave his haggard, dying face, a kind of grotesque fierceness), bellowed out in tones that made the company start, – 'What the devil brought ye all here?' The question scattered the whole party for a moment; but rallying instantly, they communed among themselves in whispers, and frequently using the sign of the cross, muttered 'The devil, – Christ save us, the devil in his mouth the first word he spoke.' 'Aye,' roared the invalid, 'and the devil in my eye the first sight I see.' 'Where, – where?' cried the terrified housekeeper, clinging close to the invalid in her terror, and half-hiding herself in the blanket, which she snatched without mercy from his struggling and exposed limbs. 'There, there,' he repeated, (during the battle of the blanket), pointing to the huddled and terrified women, who stood aghast at hearing themselves arointed as the very demons they came to banish. 'Oh! Lord keep your honor's head,' said the housekeeper in a more soothing tone, when her fright was over; 'and sure your honour knows them all, is'n't *her* name, – and *her* name, – and *her* name,' – and she pointed respectively to each of them, adding their names, which we shall spare the English reader the torture of reciting, (as a proof of our lenity, adding the last only, Cotchleen O'Mulligan), 'Ye lie, ye b——h,' growled old Melmoth; 'their name is Legion, for they are many, – turn them all out of the room, – turn them all out of doors, – if they howl at my death, they shall howl in earnest, – not for my death, for they would see me dead and damned too with dry eyes, but for want of the whiskey that they would have stolen if they could have got at it,' (and here old Melmoth grasped a key which lay under his pillow, and shook it in vain triumph at the old housekeeper, who had long possessed the means of getting at the spirits unknown to his 'honor'), 'and for want of the victuals you have pampered them with.' '*Pampered*, oh Ch—st!' ejaculated the housekeeper. 'Aye, and what are there so many candles for, all *fours*, and the same below I warrant. Ah! you – you – worthless, wasteful old devil.' 'Indeed, your honor, they are all *sixes*.' 'Sixes, – and what the devil are you burning sixes for, d'ye think it's *the wake* already? Ha?' 'Oh! not yet, your honor, not yet,' chorussed the beldams; 'but in God's good time, your honor knows,' in a tone that spoke ill suppressed impatience for the event. 'Oh! that your honor would think of making your soul.' 'That's the first sensible word you have said,' said the dying man, 'fetch me the prayer-book, – you'll find it there under that old boot-jack, – blow off the cobwebs; – it has not been opened this many a year.' It was handed to him by the old governante, on whom he turned a reproaching eye. 'What made you burn sixes in the kitchen, you extravagant jade? How many years have you lived in this house?' 'I don't know, your honor.' 'Did you ever see any extravagance or waste in it?' 'Oh never, never, your honor.' 'Was any thing but a farthing candle ever burned in the kitchen?' 'Never, never, your honor.' 'Were not you kept as tight as hand and head and heart could keep you, were you not? answer me that.' 'Oh yes, sure, your honor; every *sowl* about us knows that, – every one does your honor justice, that you kept the closest house and closest hand in the country, – your honor was always a good warrant for it.' 'And how dare you unlock my hold before death has unlocked it,' said the dying miser, shaking his meagre hand at her. 'I smelt meat in the house, – I heard voices in the house, – I heard the key turn in the door over and over. Oh that I was up,' he added, rolling in impatient agony in his bed, 'Oh that I was up, to see the waste and ruin that is going on. But it would kill me,' he continued, sinking back on the bolster, for he never allowed himself a pillow; 'it would kill me, – the very thought of it is killing me now.' The women, discomfited and defeated, after sundry winks and whispers, were huddling out of the room, till recalled by the sharp eager tones of old Melmoth. – 'Where are ye trooping to now? back to the kitchen to gormandize and guzzle? Won't one of ye stay and listen while there's a prayer read for me? Ye may want it one day for yourselves, ye hags.' Awed by this expostulation and menace, the train silently returned, and placed themselves round the bed, while the housekeeper, though a Catholic, asked if his honor would not have a clergyman to give him *the rights*, (rites) of his church. The eyes of the dying man sparkled with vexation at the proposal. 'What for, – just to have him expect a scarf and hat-band at the funeral. Read the prayers yourself, you old ——; that will save something.' The housekeeper made the attempt, but soon declined it, alleging, as her reason, that her eyes had been watery ever since his honor took ill. 'That's because you had always a drop in them,' said the invalid, with a spiteful sneer, which the contraction of approaching death stiffened into a hideous grin. – 'Here, – is not there one of you that's gnashing and howling there, that can get up a prayer to keep me from it?' So adjured, one of the women offered her services; and of her it might truly be said, as of the 'most desartless man of the watch' in Dogberry's time, that 'her reading and writing came by nature'; for she never had been at school, and had never before seen or opened a Protestant prayer-book in her life; nevertheless, on she went, and with more emphasis than good discretion, read nearly through the service for the 'churching of women'; which in our prayer-books following that of the burial of the dead, she perhaps imagined was someway connected with the state of the invalid.

She read with great solemnity, – it was a pity that two interruptions occurred during the performance, one from old Melmoth who, shortly after the commencement of the prayers, turned towards the old housekeeper, and said, in a tone scandalously audible, 'Go down and draw the niggers of the kitchen fire closer, and lock the door, and let me *hear it locked*. I can't mind any thing till that's done.' The other was from John Melmoth gliding into the room, hearing the inappropriate words uttered by the ignorant woman, taking quietly as he knelt beside her the prayer-book from her hands, and reading in a suppressed voice part of that solemn service which, by the forms of the Church of England, is intended for the consolation of the departing.

'That is John's voice,' said the dying man; and the little kindness he had ever shewed this unfortunate lad rushed on his hard heart at this moment, and touched it. He saw himself, too, surrounded by heartless and rapacious menials; and slight as must have been his dependence on a relative whom he had always treated as a stranger, he felt at this hour he was no stranger, and grasped at his support like a straw amid his wreck. 'John, my good boy, you are there. – I kept you far from me when living, and now you are nearest me when dying. – John, *read on.*' John, affected deeply by the situation in which he beheld this *poor man*, amid all his wealth, as well as by the solemn request to impart consolation to his dying moments, read on; – but in a short time his voice became indistinct, from the horror with which he listened to the increasing hiccup of the patient, which, however, he struggled with from time to time, to ask the housekeeper if *the niggers were closed*. John, who was a lad of feeling, rose from his knees in some degree of agitation. 'What, are you leaving me like the rest?' said old Melmoth, trying to raise himself in the bed. 'No, Sir,' said John; 'but,' observing the altered looks of the dying man, 'I think you want some refreshment, some support, Sir.' 'Aye, I do, I do, but whom can I trust to get it for me. *They*, (and his haggard eye wandered round the groupe), *they* would poison me.' 'Trust me, Sir,' said John; 'I will go to the apothecary's, or whoever you may employ.' The old man grasped his hand, drew him close to his bed, cast a threatening yet fearful eye round the party, and then whispered in a voice of agonized constraint, 'I want a glass of wine, it would keep me alive for some hours, but there is not one I can trust to get it for me, – *they'd steal a bottle, and ruin me.*' John was greatly shocked. 'Sir, for God's sake, let *me* get a glass of wine for you.' 'Do you know where?' said the old man, with an expression in his face John could not understand. 'No, Sir; you know I have been rather a stranger here, Sir.' 'Take this key,' said old Melmoth, after a violent spasm; 'take this key, there is wine in that closet, – *Madeira*. I always told them there was nothing there, but they did not believe me, or I should not have been robbed as I have been. At one time I said it was whiskey, and then I fared worse than ever, for they drank twice as much of it.'

John took the key from his uncle's hand; the dying man pressed it as he did so, and John, interpreting this as a mark of kindness, returned the pressure. He was undeceived by the whisper that followed, – 'John, my lad, don't drink any of that wine while you are there.' 'Good God!' said John, indignantly throwing the key on the bed; then, recollecting that the miserable being before him was no object of resentment, he gave the promise required, and entered the closet, which no foot but that of old Melmoth had entered for nearly sixty years. He had some difficulty in finding out the wine, and indeed staid long enough to justify his uncle's suspicions, – but his mind was agitated, and his hand unsteady. He could not but remark his uncle's extraordinary look, that had the ghastliness of fear superadded to that of death, as he gave him permission to enter his closet. He could not but see the looks of horror which the women exchanged as he approached it. And, finally, when he was in it, his memory was malicious enough to suggest some faint traces of a story, too horrible for imagination, connected with it. He remembered in one moment most distinctly, that no one but his uncle had ever been known to enter it for many years.

Before he quitted it, he held up the dim light, and looked around him with a mixture of terror and curiosity. There was a great deal of decayed and useless lumber, such as might be supposed to be heaped up to rot in a miser's closet; but John's eyes were in a moment, and as if by magic, rivetted on a portrait that hung on the wall, and appeared, even to his untaught eye, far superior to the tribe of family pictures that are left to moulder on the walls of a family mansion. It represented a man of middle age. There was nothing remarkable in the costume, or in the countenance, but *the eyes*, John felt, were such as one feels they wish they had never seen, and feels they can never forget. Had he been acquainted with the poetry of Southey, he might have often exclaimed in his after-life,

> Only the eyes had life,
> They gleamed with demon light.
>
> THALABA

From an impulse equally resistless and painful, he approached the portrait, held the candle towards it, and could distinguish the words on the border of the painting, – Jno. Melmoth, anno 1646. John was neither timid by nature, or nervous by constitution, or superstitious from habit, yet he continued to gaze in stupid horror on this singular picture, till, aroused by his uncle's cough, he hurried into his room. The old man swallowed the wine. He appeared a little revived; it was long since he had tasted such a cordial, – his heart appeared to expand to a momentary confidence. 'John, what did you see in that room?' 'Nothing, Sir.' 'That's a lie; every one wants to cheat or to rob me.' 'Sir, I don't want to do either.' 'Well, what did you see that you – you took notice of?' 'Only a picture, Sir.' 'A picture, Sir! – the original is still alive.' John, though under the impression of his recent feelings, could not but look incredulous. 'John,' whispered his uncle; – 'John, they say I am dying of this and that; and one says it is for want of nourishment, and one says it is for want of medicine, – but, John,' and his face looked hideously ghastly, 'I am dying of a fright. That man,' and he extended his meagre arm toward the closet, as if he was pointing to a living being; 'that man, I have good reason to know, is alive still.' 'How is that possible, Sir?' said John involuntarily, 'the date on the picture is 1646.' 'You have seen it, – you have noticed it,' said his uncle. 'Well,' – he rocked and nodded on his bolster for a moment, then, grasping John's hand with an unutterable look, he exclaimed, 'You will see him again, he is alive.' Then, sinking back on his bolster, he fell into a kind of sleep or stupor, his eyes still open, and fixed on John.

The house was now perfectly silent, and John had time and space for reflection. More thoughts came crowding on him than he wished to welcome, but they would not be repulsed. He thought of his uncle's habits and character, turned the matter over and over again in his mind, and he said to himself, 'The last man on earth to be superstitious. He never thought of any thing but the price of stocks, and the rate of exchange, and my college expences, that hung heavier at his heart than all; and such a man to die of a fright, – a ridiculous fright, that a man living 150 years ago is alive still, and yet – he is dying.' John paused, for facts will confute the most stubborn logician. 'With all his hardness of mind, and of heart, he is dying of a fright. I heard it in the kitchen, I have heard it from himself, – he could not be deceived. If I had ever heard he was nervous, or fanciful, or superstitious, but a character so contrary to all these impressions; – a man that, as poor Butler says, in his Remains, of the Antiquarian, would have "sold Christ over again for the numerical piece of silver which Judas got for him," – such a man to die of fear! Yet he *is* dying,' said John, glancing his fearful eye on the contracted nostril, the glazed eye, the dropping jaw, the whole horrible apparatus of the *facies Hippocratica* displayed, and soon to cease its display.

Old Melmoth at this moment seemed to be in a deep stupor; his eyes lost that little expression they had before, and his hands, that had convulsively been catching at the blankets, let go their short and quivering grasp, and lay extended on the bed like the claws of some bird that had died of hunger, – so meagre, so yellow, so spread. John, unaccustomed to the sight of death, believed this to be only a sign that he was going to sleep; and, urged by an impulse for which he did not attempt to account to himself, caught up the miserable light, and once more ventured into the forbidden room, – the *blue chamber* of the dwelling. The motion roused the dying man; – he sat bolt upright in his bed. This John could not see, for he was now in the closet; but he heard the groan, or rather the choaked and guggling rattle of the throat, that announces the horrible conflict between muscular and mental convulsion. He started, turned away; but, as he turned away, he thought he saw the eyes of the portrait, on which his own was fixed, *move*, and hurried back to his uncle's bedside.

Old Melmoth died in the course of that night, and died as he had lived, in a kind of avaricious delirium. John could not have imagined a scene so horrible as his last hours presented. He cursed and blasphemed about three half-pence, missing, as he said, some weeks before, in an account of change with his groom, about hay to a starving horse that he kept. Then he grasped John's hand, and asked him to give him the sacrament. 'If I send to the clergyman, he will charge me something for it, which I cannot pay, – I cannot. They say I am rich, – look at this blanket; – but I would not mind that, if I could save my soul.' And, raving, he added, 'Indeed, Doctor, I am a very poor man. I never troubled a clergyman before, and all I want is, that you will grant me two trifling requests, very little matters in your way, – save my soul, and (whispering) make interest to get me a parish coffin, – I have not enough left to bury me. I always told every one I was poor, but the more I told them so, the less they believed me.'

John, greatly shocked, retired from the bed-side, and sat down in a distant corner of the room. The women were again in the room, which was very dark. Melmoth was silent from exhaustion, and there was a death-like pause for some time. At this moment John saw the door open, and a figure appear at it, who looked round the room, and then quietly and deliberately retired, but not before John had discovered in his face the living original of the portrait. His first impulse was to utter an exclamation of terror, but his breath felt stopped. He was then rising to pursue the figure, but a moment's reflection checked him. What could be more absurd, than to be alarmed or amazed at a resemblance between a living man and the portrait of a dead one! The likeness was doubtless strong enough to strike him even in that darkened room, but it was doubtless only a likeness; and though it might be imposing enough to terrify an old man of gloomy and retired habits, and with a broken constitution, John resolved it should not produce the same effect on him.

But while he was applauding himself for this resolution, the door opened, and the figure appeared at it, beckoning and nodding to him, with a familiarity somewhat terrifying. John now started up, determined to pursue it; but the pursuit was stopped by the weak but shrill cries of his uncle, who was struggling at once with the agonies of death and his housekeeper. The poor woman, anxious for her master's reputation and her own, was trying to put on him a clean shirt and nightcap, and Melmoth, who had just sensation enough to perceive they were taking something from him, continued exclaiming feebly, 'They are robbing me, – robbing me in my last moments, – robbing a dying man. John, won't you assist me, – I shall die a beggar; they are taking my last shirt, – I shall die a beggar.'—And the miser died.

2

You that wander, scream, and groan,
Round the mansions once your own.

ROWE

A few days after the funeral, the will was opened before proper witnesses, and John was found to be left sole heir to his uncle's property, which, though originally moderate, had, by his grasping habits, and parsimonious life, become very considerable.

As the attorney who read the will concluded, he added, 'There are some words here, at the corner of the parchment, which do not appear to be part of the will, as they are neither in the form of a codicil, nor is the signature of the testator affixed to them; but, to the best of my belief, they are in the hand-writing of the deceased.' As he spoke he shewed the lines to Melmoth, who immediately recognized his uncle's hand, (that perpendicular and penurious hand, that seems determined to make the most of the very paper, thriftily abridging every word, and leaving scarce an atom of margin), and read, not without some emotion, the following words: 'I enjoin my nephew and heir, John Melmoth, to remove, destroy, or cause to be destroyed, the portrait inscribed J. Melmoth, 1646, hanging in my closet. I also enjoin him to search for a manuscript, which I think he will find in the third and lowest left-hand drawer of the mahogany chest standing under that portrait, – it is among some papers of no value, such as manuscript sermons, and pamphlets on the improvement of Ireland, and such stuff; he will distinguish it by its being tied round with a black tape, and the paper being very mouldy and discoloured. He may read it if he will: – I think he had better not. At all events, I adjure him, if there be any power in the adjuration of a dying man, to burn it.'

After reading this singular memorandum, the business of the meeting was again resumed; and as old Melmoth's will was very clear and legally worded, all was soon settled, the party dispersed, and John Melmoth was left alone.

We should have mentioned, that his guardians appointed by the will (for he was not yet of age) advised him to return to College, and complete his education as soon as proper; but John urged the expediency of paying the respect due to his uncle's memory, by remaining a decent time in the house after his decease. This was not his real motive. Curiosity, or something that perhaps deserves a better name, the wild and awful pursuit of an indefinite object, had taken strong hold of his mind. His guardians (who were men of respectability and property in the neighbourhood, and in whose eyes John's consequence had risen rapidly since the reading of the will), pressed him to accept of a temporary residence in their respective houses, till his return to Dublin. This was declined gratefully, but steadily. They called for their horses, shook hands with the heir, and rode off – Melmoth was left alone.

The remainder of the day was passed in gloomy and anxious deliberation, – in traversing his late uncle's room, – approaching the door of the closet, and then retreating from it, – in watching the clouds, and listening to the wind, as if the gloom of the one, or the murmurs of the other, relieved instead of increasing the weight that pressed on his mind. Finally, towards evening, he summoned the old woman, from whom he expected something like an explanation of the extraordinary circumstances he had witnessed since his arrival at his uncle's. The old woman, proud of the summons, readily attended, but she had very little to tell, – her communication was nearly in the following words: (We spare the reader her endless circumlocutions, her Irishcisms, and the frequent interruptions arising from her applications to her snuff-box, and to the glass of whiskey punch with which Melmoth took care to have her supplied). The old woman deposed, 'That his honor (as she always called the deceased) was always intent upon the little room inside his bed-chamber, and reading there, within the last two years; – that people, knowing his honor had money, and thinking it must be there, had broke into that room, (in other words, there was a robbery attempted there), but finding nothing but some papers, they had retired; – that he was so frightened, he had bricked up the window; but *she thought there was more in it than that*, for when his honor missed but a half-penny, he would make the house ring about it, but that, when the closet was bricked up, he never said a word; – that afterwards his honor used to lock himself up in his own room, and though he was never fond of reading, was always found, when his dinner was brought him, hanging over a paper, which he hid the moment any one came into the room, and once there was a great bustle about a picture that he tried to conceal; – that knowing there was an *odd story in the family*, she did her best to come at it, and even went to Biddy Brannigan's, (the medical Sybil before mentioned), to find out the rights of it; but Biddy only shook her head, filled her pipe, uttered some words she did not understand, and smoked on; – that it was but two evenings before his honor *was struck*, (*i.e.* took ill), she was standing at the door of the court, (which had once been surrounded by stables, pigeon-house, and all the usual etceteras of a gentleman's residence, but now presented only a ruinous range of dismantled out-offices, thatched with thistles, and tenanted by pigs), when his honor called to her to lock the door, (his honor was always *keen* about locking the doors early); she was hastening to do so, when he snatched the key from her, swearing at her, (for he was always very keen about locking the doors, though the locks were so bad, and the keys so rusty, that it was always like *the cry of the dead* in the house when the keys were turned); – that she stood aside for a minute, seeing he was angry, and gave him the key, when she heard him utter a scream, and saw him fall across the door-way; – that she hurried to raise him, *hoping* it was a fit; – that she found him stiff and stretched out, and called for help to lift him up; – that then people came from the kitchen to assist; – that she was so bewildered and terrified, she hardly knew what was done or said; but with all her terror remembered, that as they raised him up, the first sign of life he gave was lifting up his arm, and pointing it towards the court, and at that moment she saw the figure of a tall man cross the court, and go out of the court, she knew not where or how, for the outer gate was locked, and had not been opened for years, and they were all gathered round his honor at the other door; – she saw the figure, – she saw the shadow on the wall, – she saw him walk slowly through the court, and in her terror cried, "Stop him," but nobody minded her, all being busy about her master; and when he was brought to his room, nobody thought but of getting him to himself again. And further she could not tell. His honor (young Melmoth) knew as much as she, – he had witnessed his last illness, had heard his last words, he saw him die, – how could she know more than his honor.'

'True,' said Melmoth, 'I certainly saw him die; but – you say *there was an odd story in the family*, do you know any thing about it?' 'Not a word, it was long before my time, as old as I am.' 'Certainly it must have been so; but, was my uncle ever superstitious, fanciful?' – and Melmoth was compelled to use many synonymous expressions, before he could make himself understood. When he did, the answer was plain and decisive, 'No, never, never. When his honor sat in the kitchen in winter, to save a fire in his own room, he could never bear the talk of the old women that came in to light their pipes *betimes*, (from time to time). He used to shew such impatience of their superstitious nonsense, that they were fain to smoke them in silence, without the consolatory accompaniment of one whisper about a child that the evil eye had looked on, or another, that though apparently a mewling, peevish, crippled brat all day, went regularly out at night to dance with the *good people* on the top of a neighbouring mountain, summoned thereto by the sound of a bag-pipe, which was unfailingly heard at the cabin door every night.' Melmoth's thoughts began to take somewhat of a darker hue at this account. If his uncle was not superstitious, might he not have been guilty, and might not his strange and sudden death, and even the terrible visitation that preceded it, have been owing to some wrong that his rapacity had done the widow and the fatherless. He questioned the old woman indirectly and cautiously on the subject, – her answer completely justified the deceased. 'He was a man,' she said, 'of a hard hand, and a hard heart, but he was as jealous of another's right as of his own. He would have starved all the world, but he would not have wronged it of a farthing.'

Melmoth's last resource was to send for Biddy Brannigan, who was still in the house, and from whom he at least hoped to hear the odd story that the old woman confessed was in the family. She came, and, on her introduction to Melmoth, it was curious to observe the mingled look of servility and command, the result of the habits of her life, which was alternately one of abject mendicity, and of arrogant but clever imposture. When she first appeared, she stood at the door, awed and curtseying in the presence, and muttering sounds which, possibly intended for blessings, had, from the harsh tone and witch-like look of the speaker, every appearance of malediction; but when interrogated on the subject of the story, she rose at once into consequence, – her figure seemed frightfully dilated, like that of Virgil's Alecto, who exchanges in a moment the appearance of a feeble old woman for that of a menacing fury. She walked deliberately across the room, seated, or rather squatted herself on the hearth-stone like a hare in her form, spread her bony and withered hands towards the blaze, and rocked for a considerable time in silence before she commenced her tale. When she had finished it, Melmoth remained in astonishment at the state of mind to which the late singular circumstances had reduced him, – at finding himself listening with varying and increasing emotions of interest, curiosity, and terror, to a tale so wild, so improbable, nay, so actually incredible, that he at least blushed for the folly he could not conquer. The result of these impressions was, a resolution to visit the closet, and examine the manuscript that very night.

This resolution he found it impossible to execute immediately, for, on inquiring for lights, the gouvernante confessed the very last had been burnt at *his honor's* wake; and a bare-footed boy was charged to run for life and death to the neighbouring village for candles; and if you could *borry* a couple of candlesticks, added the housekeeper. 'Are there no candlesticks in the house?' said Melmoth. 'There are, honey, plinty, but it's no time to be opening the old chest, for the plated ones, in regard of their being at the bottom of it, and the brass ones that's *in it* (in the house), one of them has no socket, and the other has no bottom.' 'And how did you make shift yourself,' said Melmoth. 'I stuck it in a potatoe,' quoth the housekeeper. So the *gossoon* ran for life and death, and Melmoth, towards the close of the evening, was left alone to meditate.

It was an evening apt for meditation, and Melmoth had his fill of it before the messenger returned. The weather was cold and gloomy; heavy clouds betokened a long and dreary continuance of autumnal rains; cloud after cloud came sweeping on like the dark banners of an approaching host, whose march is for desolation. As Melmoth leaned against the window, whose dismantled frame, and pieced and shattered panes, shook with every gust of wind, his eye encountered nothing but that most cheerless of all prospects, a miser's garden, – walls broken down, grass-grown walks whose grass was not even green, dwarfish, doddered, leafless trees, and a luxuriant crop of nettles and weeds rearing their unlovely heads where there had once been flowers, all waving and bending in capricious and unsightly forms, as the wind sighed over them. It was the verdure of the church-yard, the garden of death. He turned for relief to the room, but no relief was there, – the wainscotting dark with dirt, and in many places cracked and starting from the walls, – the rusty grate, so long unconscious of a fire, that nothing but a sullen smoke could be coaxed to issue from between its dingy bars, – the crazy chairs, their torn bottoms of rush drooping inwards, and the great leathern seat displaying the stuffing round the worn edges, while the nails, though they kept their places, had failed to keep the covering they once fastened, – the chimney-piece, which, tarnished more by time than by smoke, displayed for its garniture half a pair of snuffers, a tattered almanack of 1750, a time-keeper dumb for want of repair, and a rusty fowling-piece without a lock. – No wonder the spectacle of desolation drove Melmoth back to his own thoughts, restless and uncomfortable as they were. He recapitulated the Sybil's story word by word, with the air of a man who is cross-examining an evidence, and trying to make him contradict himself.

'The first of the Melmoths, she says, who settled in Ireland, was an officer in Cromwell's army, who obtained a grant of lands, the confiscated property of an Irish family attached to the royal cause. The elder brother of this man was one who had travelled abroad, and resided so long on the Continent, that his family had lost all recollection of him. Their memory was not stimulated by their affection, for there were strange reports concerning the traveller. He was said to be (like the "damned magician, great Glendower,") "a gentleman profited in strange concealments."

It must be remembered, that at this period, and even to a later, the belief in astrology and witchcraft was very general. Even so late as the reign of Charles II, Dryden calculated the nativity of his son Charles, the ridiculous books of Glanville were in general circulation, and Delrio and Wierus were so popular, that even a dramatic writer (Shadwell) quoted copiously from them, in the notes subjoined to his curious comedy of the Lancashire witches. It was said, that during the life-time of Melmoth, the traveller paid him a visit; and though he must have then been considerably advanced in life, to the astonishment of his family, he did not betray the slightest trace of being a year older than when they last beheld him. His visit was short, he said nothing of the past or the future, nor did his family question him. It was said that they did not feel themselves perfectly at ease in his presence. On his departure he left them his picture, (the same which Melmoth saw in the closet, bearing date 1646), and they saw him no more. Some years after, a person arrived from England, directed to Melmoth's house, in pursuit of the traveller, and exhibiting the most marvellous and unappeasable solicitude to obtain some intelligence of him. The family could give him none, and after some days of restless inquiry and agitation, he departed, leaving behind him, either through negligence or intention, a manuscript, containing an extraordinary account of the circumstances under which he had met John Melmoth the Traveller (as he was called).

The manuscript and portrait were both preserved, and of the original a report spread that he was still alive, and had been frequently seen in Ireland even to the present century, – but that he was never known to appear but on the approaching death of one of the family, nor even then, unless when the evil passions or habits of the individual had cast a shade of gloomy and fearful interest over their dying hour.

It was therefore judged no favourable augury for the spiritual destination of the last Melmoth, that this extraordinary person had visited, or been imagined to visit, the house previous to his decease.'

Such was the account given by Biddy Brannigan, to which she added her own solemnly-attested belief, that John Melmoth the Traveller was still without a hair on his head changed, or a muscle in his frame contracted; – that she had seen those that had seen him, and would confirm their evidence by oath if necessary; – that he was never heard to speak, seen to partake of food, or known to enter any dwelling but that of his family; – and, finally, that she herself believed that his late appearance boded no good either to the living or the dead.

John was still musing on these things when the lights were procured, and, disregarding the pallid countenances and monitory whispers of the attendants, he resolutely entered the closet, shut the door, and proceeded to search for the manuscript. It was soon found, for the directions of old Melmoth were forcibly written, and strongly remembered. The manuscript, old, tattered, and discoloured, was taken from the very drawer in which it was mentioned to be laid. Melmoth's hands felt as cold as those of his dead uncle, when he drew the blotted pages from their nook. He sat down to read, – there was a dead silence through the house. Melmoth looked wistfully at the candles, snuffed them, and still thought they looked dim, (perchance he thought they burned blue, but such thought he kept to himself.) Certain it is, he often changed his posture, and would have changed his chair, had there been more than one in the apartment.

He sunk for a few moments into a fit of gloomy abstraction, till the sound of the clock striking twelve made him start, – it was the only sound he had heard for some hours, and the sounds produced by inanimate things, while all living beings around are as dead, have at such an hour an effect indescribably awful. John looked at his manuscript with some reluctance, opened it, paused over the first lines, and as the wind sighed round the desolate apartment, and the rain pattered with a mournful sound against the dismantled window, wished—what did he wish for?—he wished the sound of the wind less dismal, and the dash of the rain less monotonous.—He may be forgiven, it was past midnight, and there was not a human being awake but himself within ten miles when he began to read.

LADY MORGAN

from *The O'Briens and the O'Flahertys*

4

The Oligarchs

And when we see the figure of the house,
Then must we rate the cost of the erection.

SHAKSPEARE

Proudfort House was one of those magnificent mansions which, before the Union, were the town residences of the Irish aristocracy; and which, since that fatal period, have been converted into public offices. For such have been the anomalies of that country, 'where (Swift says) an honest man ought to be ashamed to live', that its official splendour has increased, in proportion as its resources have dwindled, and its business diminished.

Proudfort House, at all times of the year, the shrine of place-hunters and pension-mongers, – of the needy and of the corrupt, was, – at that particular season, which is the carnival of life, as of society, the *rendezvous* of all the rank and fashion of the country. Ireland, during the last quarter of a century has fallen far behind the rest of Europe; but it was at this period of its active demoralization, more liberal, than it now is in its stultified degradation. Society, though corrupt, was joyous. Party threw no cloud over pleasure. Fashion took no note of faction; and if many of the hereditary guardians of the country and counsellors of the crown – the first in rank as in talents – stood dignified and aloof from the Proudfort cabal and its chiefs; if they boldly entered their protest in the senate* against the scandalous measures originated by these political vampires, they did not suffer their patriotic feelings to interfere with social festivity; nor, in that narrow and illiberal jealousy, which has since broken up society into cliques and côteries, refuse to mingle on public nights in the balls, masquerades, theatricals, and ridottoes of their political opponents. The members of all parties then filled up the ranks of amusement; and by encouraging trade, energizing industry, and stimulating the arts, they enabled the country to make a better stand against its oppressors; and, for a while, to uphold its struggling, but decaying manufactures.†

But if wit and beauty discountenanced the domestic display of party violence, they had not to encounter the resistance of that dark bigotry, which now lies like an incubus on the public pleasures. A feeble race of imbecile fanatics had not yet succeeded to a generation, whose vices, bold as their manners, did not permit them to veil their patricidal enormities under the sanctimonious garb of religious hypocrisy. Even the harpies who devoured the vitals of the land, shewed more sense and more feeling for the people, than their heartless, brainless successors; and if they helped themselves largely and impudently from the public purse, they had not yet exhibited the scandal of purchasing heaven at the expence of their impoverished country, – of congregating to suffocation round the itinerant declaimer, to squander their superfluities upon foreign missions, – nor of overlooking the thousands perishing in their streets and their highways, to administer with profusion to the fanciful wants of proselytes at the furthest extremities of the globe. As yet, the gayest capital of Europe was unclouded by the gloom of controversial theology; and the charities and the graces of life still lingering, where the sterner virtues had disappeared, were neither chilled by ignorant fanaticism, nor reproved by vulgar zeal.

The intimates, the *habitués* of Proudfort House, the daily guests of its lord, were however, exclusively selected from the oligarchy, of which he was the leader. Strenuously occupied in the barter of power and principles, they exercised an unrestrained rule over the less privileged classes, engrossing all the offices of state, owning most of the property in the soil, and supplying from amongst their own cadets, the 'nursing fathers of the

---

* See the protest in the House of Peers, in 1790, signed by such names as Leinster, Charlemont, Moira, Portarlington, &c. &c.

† These remarks apply only to the political and social intercourse between protestant and protestant. At all times catholics rarely and difficultly obtained admission into what is called *bon ton* society. Party feelings were perhaps too rancorous at first to render much intimacy desirable on either side; and eventually, those who were not seen in a particular circle, were deemed unfit for it.

church', (to use a phrase of Archbishop King's) whose fosterage was more fatal to the interests and tranquillity of Ireland, than that of the olden times, against which so many acts were fulminated by early parliaments.

At the head of this caste, in power and in influence, stood the family of the Proudforts; whose numbers, like the '*race d'Agamemnon qui ne finit jamais*', seemed to increase and multiply, with the resources they extorted from the revenues of the country. Arrogating to themselves an exclusive loyalty, as 'King's men', they mistook the subjection of the crown to their will, for *their* devotion to its possessor: and if a minister, offended by their pride, or scandalized at their greediness, hesitated to uphold their political juggling, or questioned their right to a monopoly of place, they were as ready to turn against the sovereign, as against the people. More than once, a concerted *soulèvement* of the whole privy council, a *levée en masse*, against the viceroy, marked their determination to suffer no minister in Ireland, who was not of their own selection: and on one occasion 'seven of the eleven' constituting the Irish ministry, put the King into Coventry, and themselves *hors du combat*. Kings, however, like wits, have sometimes short memories; and his majesty forgetting to call in those who had so foolishly gone out, resigned them to the original obscurity for which nature had intended them.

The foundation of the Proudfort power was the Proudfort property: and this property was based on the church. The founder of the family had been the chaplain of King William's regiment; and a succession of prelates, *de père en fils*, had added to a small original grant of land (made by the military head of the church, to the chaplain of the church militant), a succession of estates, each purchased from the ample dower of the establishment. This vast landed property, spotted as it was with boroughs, (close and rotten,) was the *matériél* of family influence; and amply fulfilled the prophecy, 'that to him who has much, more shall be given'. For the rest, the Proudforts, without one quality which naturally places men above their fellows, were destitute of every means for attaining to eminence, save the pertinacity which usually accompanies the passion for family aggrandizement. They were indeed the happiest illustrations of what dogged dulness may effect, when unencumbered by genius to withdraw it from the beaten track of self-interest, or by sympathy with human suffering to distract it from the steady pursuit of personal ambition. Dull as the Dutchman from whom they were descended, tasteless, as they were talentless, they had yet given princes to the church, and commanders to the army; and stopping short only where distinction was to be exclusively acquired by merit, they had engrossed all places and all patronage, without giving to the Irish senate one orator, or to the Irish bar one advocate of eminence.

The Earl of Knocklofty, the head and representative of this prosperous dynasty, was more distinguished by the family organ of self-appropriation, than by any trait of individual idiosyncracy. Plodding, without an head for business; sensual, without a taste for pleasure; the gravity of his manner passed for wisdom, and the solemnity of his carriage for dignity. Always ready to scoff at public virtue as a phantom, he affected great respect for all the external forms of society; and he talked with plausibility of 'the great bonds which keep men together'. Regular in his attendance at church on Sundays, and at Daly's Club-house, on every other day of the week, he prayed and played with equal devotion. But though religious and loyal in the extreme, a pillar of the state and a corner stone of the church, he was, on certain points and morals, with which going to church has little to do, as relaxed, as the members of his caste then usually were in Ireland. He had long survived the passion, which had led him into a second marriage with Lady Albina O'Blarney, whose portionless rank, and powerful beauty, had suited his ambition, and gratified his vanity. But his liberality of the wealth which she knew so well how to distribute, and which gratified his ostentatious habits, and the pride he took in his handsome children, obtained for him the reputation of an excellent private character; as if the selfishness which leads to public corruption, could be made compatible with private worth. Living with magnificence, his table exhibited all that luxury had then invented, in a department which has since become one of the fine arts; and his wines and his influence brought him a multitude of guests, who learned from his example, to enjoy, without remorse, those public emoluments which were purchased without restraint – by the ruin of the country. He had recently been elevated to the Earldom of Knocklofty; and the higher dignity of a Marquisate was said to be reserved for those future services, which the proprietor of many boroughs can always render to the party of his adoption.

The Countess Knocklofty was, by her social position, the great autocrat of Irish fashion; and she presided over the *bel air* of the Irish capital, as her husband ruled its political junta. Preserving all the beauty which does not exclusively depend on youth, (a passionate expression, a graceful *tournure*), brilliant, though no longer blooming; her rank and influence gave her all the charms she had lost, and heightened all she had retained: for even beauty, in that little world called 'the great', has no intrinsic value. It is the stamp of fashion that gives it currency; and with that stamp the basest metal is received without examination, while the sterling ore of loveliness, that bears not the mark of the mint, is rejected with disdain. Educated by a feeble and bigotted grandmother, with prejudices which passed for principles, and phrases which passed for ideas; and brought up in respect for forms, and in ignorance of realities, she threw off ties, on coming into the world, which, being founded not in influence but in authority, had no hold either on her judgment or her heart. Launched from the romantic solitudes of her father's castle in Connaught, upon the bustle and temptation of the world, she brought into society the unregulated romance of a retired education; with all the headlong propensities to pleasure of a wilful temperament. Vain, credulous, and impetuous, her vivacity was mistaken for passion, and her fancies for feelings. The reigning manners of the day, and the influence of her position, conspired to sanction the boundless indulgence of a disposition, as unregulated as her mind; and even the selfish pursuit of her own gratification passed for devotion to those, who were flattered by being distinguished as its objects. With men of the world, there is a shorter road to the heart than even through their passions – their vanity; and none ever took it with more success than Lady Knocklofty.

It is a maxim of French gallantry (and axioms in love, like dogmas in faith, are always numerous in proportion as the religion is doubtful,) that, '*la femme, quand l'amour est passion, est constante; quand l'amour n'est que goût, elle est légère*'. According to this canon, Lady Knocklofty was the most passionless, as she was the most *engouée* of women. Yet her predilections and her preferences, such as they were, were not the episodes, but the history of her life. Platonic or passionate, the fancy of a day, or the sentiment of a year, her flirtations or attachments were the business of her existence. '*Vertueuse, elle jouit de ses refus; foible, elle jouit de ses remords.*' Hitherto, borne out by that demoralization in the higher circles, which ever goes with despotic governments, and living on those terms of decency with her lord, which the world only requires (for nothing can save an imprudent wife, but the dupery of her husband, – or his depravity), Lady Knocklofty, though blamed by some, suspected by many, and talked of by all, still retained the reins of society in her own possession; and kept opinion in check, by having the whip hand, in the great career of rank, influence, and fortune.

To preserve her Ladyship in this enviable, but critical position, which enabled her to preside over the largest house, and command the highest circles in the Irish capital, was the vigilant, assiduous, and not very disinterested object of her friend, monitor, and constant companion, Lady Honoria Stratton. More gifted, more accomplished, more corrupt, and more experienced, than her noble *protégée*, Lady Honoria, was one of the many illustrations of that golden maxim, 'that gallantry is the least fault of a woman of gallantry'. The '*vertu de moins*' of Lady Honoria was indeed the only point in her character that had the semblance of amiability. But the frailty which, in some, indicates a susceptibility to 'loving too well', was in her the result of a necessitous poverty, which obliged her to love 'too wisely'. In risking her character, she calculated only on the profit and loss of a tender attachment; and with Werter in one hand, and Cocker in the other, she formed her estimates as much by the arithmetical conclusions of the one, as by the high-flown sentimentalities of the other. The world, however, always more apt to pardon the folly of vice, than its wisdom, had nearly thrown her beyond its pale, for the ruin she had brought on a young and popular Irishman of moderate fortune; when, luckily, her well directed coquetry at the cold phlegmatic vanity of Lord Knocklofty, and her knowledge of the world, as cleverly directed at the assumption of his wife, gave her an influence at Proudfort House; which opened the door of every other house in Dublin to her reception, and restored her to the caste which she had nearly lost by that which should have been deemed an additional cause for banishing her for ever from its ranks. Beautiful and witty, bold and adroit, the naturally fine dispositions and brilliant qualities of Lady Honoria had been perverted in her earliest youth by a neglected education at home, and a depraved one abroad. Living on the continent from her fifteenth year to her five-and-twentieth with a libertine father (a poor Irish peer), in the refined but profligate circles of the French court, she married at the epoch (in the expectation of a reversionary title and large fortune), the drivelling brother of an Irish nobleman, whose celibacy was deemed certain, till he wedded his cook; when the birth of an heir blasted the hope for which Lady Honoria had made such sacrifices.

Obliged by circumstances to live in Ireland – niched in a large empty house, in Stephen's Green, belonging to her brother-in-law, who resided habitually on his estate in Munster, – and conscious of her own superiority to those to whom her necessities obliged her to bend, she paid back the obligations her ruined fortunes compelled her to accept, by secret contempt, or by open sallies of wit and bitterness, which frequently purchased civilities that gratitude and complaisance might not have extorted. Admired by the men, and feared by the women, she used both as she wanted them; and called upon to '*désennuyer la sottise*', she repaid the dinners she could not return, and entertainments she could not rival, by a wit which was always amusing, though not always refined; and a humour which was reckoned somewhat too broad even for the Irish court.

A constant and welcome guest at Proudfort House, she gave a life to its festivities, and a style to its entertainments, which the taste and refinement of its owners were insufficient to confer. Flattering the dull vanity of the husband, and engrossing the confidence of the wife, she soon became a necessity to both; and was frequently a mediatrix in disputes, which her cleverness and subtlety prevented from exploding, to the total rupture of the matrimonial tie, that would have involved the overthrow of her own interests.

While Lady Honoria thus acted as *premier* in the diplomacy of the Knocklofty *ménage*, the Honourable Catherine Macguire was not without her utility in the domestic system of those, who by the very fortune which raises them, are disposed to depend so much more upon the resources of others, than on their own. The daughter of an aunt of Lord Knocklofty, who had run away with a landless papist lord, and had been ever afterwards thrown off by the family, the Honourable Catherine was received by her noble kinsman, as poor Irish cousins usually are – partly from pity, and partly from pride: and being destitute of that fine tone of feeling, which makes dependence misery, – and as highly endowed with that stout huckaback fibre, which stands the wear and tear of capricious favour and insolent pretension, she steadily kept the 'even tenor of her way'. False without feigning, insincere without hypocrisy, she frankly shewed up to the world's laughter her present friends and her former creed; and quizzed the Proudforts, and ridiculed the papists, with equally unsparing candour. To the proselyting humour of 'the good Lady Mary' she was indebted for the new creed, which had been the passport to her cousin's protection; and she abandoned the faith of her fathers, with a conviction quite as clear as that with which she had originally received it. Pleasant as she was heartless, she had already passed through the world's hands; and had contracted from its contact, that simple hardihood of manner, which often gives to the hacknied the *naïveté*, that is the charm of the recluse. Sure to please, as long as she amused the solemn mediocrity of her kinsman and host, she was well aware of her tenure at Proudfort House; and, resolved that it should be a lease renewable for ever, she silently inserted a clause of surrender, in case she should attain to the fee-simple of any other more advantageous possession.

'The good Lady Mary', by whose agency Miss Macguire had been induced to accept the thirty-nine articles, and a seat at Lord Knocklofty's luxurious table, – to swallow the precepts of the sister, with the *pâtés* of the brother, – was a happy precursor of all the *good* ladies of the present day, who have come forward in such numbers 'to justify the ways of God to man', to complete what the Redeemer had left undone, and, in the fulness of time, accomplish and expound that revelation, which ordinary Christians imagine to have been perfected some eighteen hundred years ago. She was the first to bring into notice an inspired work, generally thought to have been long well known: and she was the original inventor of the protestant dray for carrying converted papists on their road to salvation. She was likewise the first among the great to send out invitations to tea and tracts; and to open religious shops for go-carts mounted upon protestant principles, toys against tolerance, and bible-only babies. It was in Lady Mary's cheap repository, that employment was given to idle ladies of fashion,* at the slight expence of those humble dependents on their own industry for their daily bread, who are persons of no fashion; and it was in her schools that education was first made subservient to the purposes of an insidious proselytism. Dull and mischievous, arrogant and interfering, she was among the first to contribute and collect for the conversion of Asiatic Jews; while the poor Irish peasant perished at the gates of the Episcopal Palace, unheeded, and the needy artisan fainted under the windows of the metropolitan mansion, unrelieved. In her domestic capacity, too deeply occupied in saving the souls of her neighbour's children, she had no time to attend to the comforts of her own; and, while driving about from school to school, to teach tenets with tent-stitch, and encourage the growth of piety and plain work, she gradually saw the objects of her natural affections disappear beneath her unobserving neglect. One of her children had fallen into a pond, another had fallen out of a window. The eldest, Miss Sullivan, who was thrown from unwholesome confinement into a galloping consumption, *galloped off* with the apothecary; and the youngest, suffered to run wild from apprehension of her sister's fate, had been so much in the habit of trotting behind the coachman, that she trotted away with him one day to Gretna Green. Her three surviving sons, however, following in the Bishop's track, (the 'milky way' of church promotion,) bid fair for the Bishop's fortune. They already engrossed the three best livings in the Bishop's gift.

The Bishop himself, who, as tutor to Lord Knocklofty, had won Lady Mary's heart, and as dean of St Grellan had obtained her hand, was one of those '*personnages de position, qui viennent toujours au secours du vainqueur*'. He had wriggled himself into his proud eminence by siding successively with every party that prospered, and dedicating his various polemical volumes alternately to whig and tory. A Foxite to-day, a Pittite to-morrow – now a catholic advocate, and now the apostle of catholic extermination – his true religion was a mitre, his political principle a peerage; and knowing that the world, like the Baron in *La fausse Agnès*, '*est toujours dans l'admiration de ce qu'il n'entend pas*', he took for the subject of a work, which was designed as the key-stone of his fortune, a theme, which being beyond human comprehension, left no just measure of the intellect which he brought to bear upon its mystery. Having arrived at the object of his ambition, the pliant candidate for church promotion stood erect upon the pediment of church supremacy, with a look that might be translated, '*Sono Papa*'. A little Sixtus Quintus in his way, his air became as papistical, as his infallible pretensions: and whoever saw him mounted upon his ecclesiastical *haquenée*, ambling through the streets of St Grellan, saw the most faithful copy of an Italian Monsignore ever exhibited beyond the Roman corso: – all purple and pertness, pious priggery and foppish formality, with a beetling

---

* She works religious petticoats: for flowers
  She'll make church histories. Her needle doth
  So sanctify my cushionets. – Besides,
  My smock-sleeves have such holy embroidery,
  And are so learned, that I fear in time
  All my apparel will be quoted by
  Some pure instructor.

  Old Play

brow, and the best flapped hat that ever was perched upon three hairs of the erect head of a high, haughty, and overbearing churchman, – the genius of caricature could have added nothing to the picture.

Lord Chesterfield has said, that 'of all men who can read and write, a parson is, perhaps, the most ignorant'. This apothegm described the Archdeacon of St Grellan to a tittle. Ignorant of all but his own interests, his want of *savoir* was well supplied by his *savoir faire*; and the success of his well directed subserviency to the Bishop, to Lady Mary, and to the whole Proudfort dynasty, proved that he had neither mistaken his means nor misunderstood his persons. The nephew of their law agent, Solicitor Hunks, – the son of their chaplain and *protegé*, the late Archdeacon, – he had in his favour the habit of the Proudforts to provide for his family; and he did not suffer that habit to wear out for want of frequent solicitation.

Pertinacious, as men of limited intellects usually are, irascible, as churchmen are accused of being, and envious, as mediocrity ever is, he had viewed the young and hardy 'engrosser of fame' and favour, the hero of the castle frolic, with a deeply founded aversion, sharpened by the sense of hereditary wrongs. O'Brien, as the son of him, who had contrived to embezzle a part of the Archdeacon's family property, by embezzling the daughter of its richest member – of him whose legal knowledge had reduced the Archdeacon's inheritance almost to his hopes in the Proudfort interest, – had claims on his hatred, which he was determined should not lie idle; even at the risk of opposing the impetuous predilections of Lady Knocklofty.

Such was the party, which, with the addition of Lord Kilcolman and Captain O'Mealy, assembled for dinner in the great saloon of Proudfort-house, at the then late hour of six o'clock – a quarter of an hour before the lady of the mansion made her appearance. Miss Macguire, however, received, amused, and talked with the guests; while Lord Knocklofty, always silent and abstracted before dinner, walked up and down, occasionally assenting, by a nod, to the Bishop's emphatic philippics against the bad spirit of the times, as illustrated by the volunteer review of the preceding day, the tumult at the Strugglers, and other signs equally portentous of a state of things, which called on every loyal and religious man to put it down. To this all agreed in their different ways; from Captain O'Mealy's ''tis true for you, my lord, for as the immortal Shakspeare says, "the times themselves are out of sayson"', to the pious ejaculations of Lady Mary, and the never-failing concordance of the Archdeacon with the sentiments of his superior.

'By the by, Albina,' said Lord Knocklofty, turning short upon his wife, as she entered and flung herself in an arm-chair, with a very slight inclination of the head to her guests – 'By the by, how have you disposed of your hero?'

'Disposed of *my* hero?' re-echoed Lady Knocklofty, evasively, and looking for resource to her friend, Lady Honoria.

'What! has she got a hero *de poche*?' asked Lady Honoria, laughing. 'Oh! I suppose you mean the volunteer, who, under heaven, saved our lives yesterday. I hope, Lady Knocklofty, you will assist me in paying the debt, by saying a word in his favour to the Provost; for, of course, he will be brought before the board, with the rest of the college boys concerned in the row last night.'

'I believe,' said the Archdeacon, 'that is past praying for. The Provost can do nothing;

the whole affair being referred to the visitors. The Chancellor, as Vice-chancellor of the University, has been long waiting to make an example of some of those young incendiaries, who are known agents of the jacobinical societies, now so numerous.'

'And this very O'Brien,' observed the Bishop, 'the leader in the riot, to whom your ladyship imagines yourself so much indebted, will, most probably, be rusticated, if not expelled: but as long as the historical society is permitted to exist in the College, and Locke on Government to form part of the College course, you will have a hot-bed of sedition and a code of republicanism, whose influence is obvious.'

'Ay, and of atheism too, as the Archdeacon says,' observed Lady Mary.

'I think,' said the Archdeacon, 'that the denial of innate ideas leads irresistibly to such a conclusion.'

'I am quite of the Archdeacon's opinion,' said O'Mealy, pulling up his stock; 'I am, upon my honour; and so I believe is every loyal man in Dublin, in or out of College. For there is all the difference upon earth between a nate idaya, and an innate idaya.'

A general titter followed the assertion, and Lady Honoria demanded – 'Now, honour bright, O'Mealy, what is the precise difference between a *nate* and an *innate* idea?'

'Why, Lady Honoria?' said O'Mealy, calling fearlessly on a stock of impudence which he knew to be exhaustless, 'an innate idaya may be any man's idaya; but your ladyship's must always be a nate one, intirely, upon my honour.'

'*Pas mal,*' said Lady Honoria, nodding her head approvingly; while Lord Kilcolman cried out, 'Hear him, hear him!'

'You are aware, my Lord,' continued the Archdeacon, returning to the charge, 'that this Mr O'Brien, who affected to stop Lady Knocklofty's horses, when they had stopped of themselves, is –'

'That is not true,' interrupted Lady Knocklofty, vehemently and haughtily; 'it is utterly false: the horses were quite unmanageable, and both Lady Honoria and myself would have been dashed to pieces, but for the interference of *this Mister* O'Brien, who had the humanity to risk his life, and save ours. Is it not true, Lady Honoria?'

'I'll schwear to that,' said Lady Honoria, in the tone and accent of the Jew, in the *School for Scandal.*

'Well, then,' continued the pertinacious Archdeacon, 'this saviour of her ladyship's life is the youth, my lord, who, in the historical society, made a sort of killing-no-murder oration on the death of Cæsar; defending the regicide act of Brutus upon a great principle of popular right, applicable to all times; taking occasion, apropos to nothing at all, to introduce an invective against those whom he called the Dictators of Ireland, and sketching three illustrious characters high in the Irish government, as the triumvirate, who, with the same patricidal views as those of the Roman triumvirs, wanted only the courage and the talents to effect the same ends. The speech got into the opposition journal, which complimented the speaker with the title of the Irish Mirabeau, an imitation of whose eloquence, by the by, he gave us last night at the castle.'

'Indeed!' said Lord Knocklofty, pausing in his measured pace before his wife: 'and is this the person, Lady Knocklofty, whom you brought forward, as I hear you did, in so extraordinary a way, last night; availing yourself of the Duke's complaisance and good nature – is this the hero of your frolic?'

'Pooh, nonsense!' said Lady Knocklofty, carelessly, 'my frolic was every body's frolic; and it was neither as improper as Lady Glenmore's frolic with the sweep; nor as fatal as your lordship's, when you and your friends personated highwaymen, in the Phœnix Park, to frighten the Ladies Butler; when you not only upset their carriage and broke Lady Anne's arm, but shot one of the postilions *by accident*, and scared to death old Lady Castletown, who never recovered the fright. Archdeacon, you are like old Croaker, in Goldsmith's *Good-nat'red Man*; you have always some stock horror, some conspiracy or sedition on hands. I wish they would make you a bishop, and then you would be quiet. Kitty Macguire, do ring the bell for dinner; what are the people about?'

'Won't you wait for the Chancellor?' asked Miss Macguire, while the Countess's *sortie* produced a momentary silence in all; for even Lord Knocklofty's solemn haughtiness was at times borne down by his wife's vehemence.

'Does the Chancellor dine here?' asked Lady Knocklofty, with a look of annoyance.

'He proposed to do so an hour back, when I met him on the circular road,' said Lord Knocklofty.

'So he told me,' said the Bishop. 'I rode into town with him. He doesn't see the row of last night in the same point of view as the Lord Lieutenant, who considers it as a mere street brawl. He says that he has long had his eye upon this O'Brien, who hoisted the seditious flag in the park yesterday.'

'Who the devil is he?' demanded Lord Knocklofty.

Lady Mary and the Archdeacon both opened their mouths at once; and the latter exclaimed, 'He is the mischievous young scamp, who gave my father the nick-name of the arch dæmon; the son of Terence O'Brien, the present Lord Arranmore. Your Lordship may remember the fuss which was made about this scape-grace twelve years ago, when I discovered that notwithstanding his name having been entered on the books of the diocesan school, he was, for the greater part of the year, actually under the tuition of a foreign priest in the isles of Arran: and this too in the face of the statute, which provided that the son of an attorney shall be bred in the established religion, and made it felony for any catholic priest to keep a school.'

'Well?' said Lord Knocklofty, impatiently.

'Well,' said the Archdeacon, 'a writ having been served, or rather sent by the proper officer to force this priest to appear before the constituted authorities of St Grellan, the people of the islands, followers of these O'Briens, and begotted papists, led on by one Shane, the son of the noted Mor ny Brien, and of one, the last of the Connaught rapparees, surrounded the priest's house for his protection: and this Shane, being pressed by one of the king's officers, murdered him on the spot; or rather caused his death, for the murdered man died within six months; and the fellow stood his trial, and was hanged at St Michael's Cross in Galway.'

'Well?' said Lord Knocklofty, still more impatiently.

'Well, my lord, the priest having escaped to the continent, and the boy having shortly afterwards disappeared, and his mother dying (a sister, by the way, of those old catamaran jacobites, the Miss Mac Taafs), Terence O'Brien came to Dublin to pursue his claims to the title; where he spent his time and fortune in haunting the law courts, and searching the record and rolls offices. The boy had been sent to Douay to be made a priest of;

but he suddenly reappeared at Trinity College, where he entered as a *filius nobilis*. As this happened just before I resigned my fellowship, I was struck with the name of Murrogh Mac Teig O'Brien on the books; and on further inquiry, I found that this youth had passed the last eight years of his life as a soldier of fortune; and has come from the continent warmed with the precepts of his old tutor, the *ci-devant* parish priest of St Grellan. For the Abbé O'Flaherty, you must know, my lord,' he added, turning to the Bishop, 'has become a French bishop, and is one of those who are called the constitutional clergy; renegades to their king and their God, who have declared that the property of the church is national property; and who have consented to the abolition of tithes. In a pamphlet dedicated to his friend Talleyrand, Bishop of Autun, he has advanced on the authority of scripture, that the clergy are the simple administrators of the church wealth; which was given for worship, and not to the priesthood. Such is the school, and such the precepts, to which the Irish university is indebted for its new honourable member.'

'*Le pauvre homme*,' said Lady Honoria, looking dramatically at the Archdeacon; who was perspiring at every pore at the horrors he was relating.

'And who is this courageous Bishop,' said Lady Knocklofty, 'who dares to sacrifice his own interests to the general good. What is his name? Good heavens, how I should like to know him.'

'What nonsense you talk, Albina,' said Lord Knocklofty.

'When in Ireland,' said the Archdeacon, 'he was called the Abbé O'Flaherty, and passed for a cousin of that famous, or rather infamous Count O'Flaherty, who, you may remember, my Lord, contrived to rob my father of a considerable part of his property, through the chicanery of Terence O'Brien; and who, received in Connaught as the champion of popery, ended by carrying off the foreign Abbess of St Bridget's, brought over from Italy by O'Brien's jesuit uncle, to reform the order in St Grellan.'

A general laugh followed this narrative.

'I was at Cambridge then,' said Lord Knocklofty; 'but I remember something of the matter.'

'Pray go on, Archdeacon,' said Lady Knocklofty, now interested and excited; 'carried off the Abbess?'

'Yes, Lady Knocklofty; or rather unfortunately, he did not carry her off, till he had scandalized the whole world, by taking her to the Abbey of Moycullen; where he had built apartments for the celebration of his orgies, which still attest, by their licentious pictures, the purposes for which they were fitted up.'

'What purposes?' asked Lady Honoria, demurely. 'What purposes, Archdeacon? pray tell us!'

'Lady Honoria,' said the Archdeacon, 'you will spare me the details.'

'Spare his blushes,' whispered Miss Macguire.

'Suffice it to say,' continued the Archdeacon solemnly, 'that all that was ever said of Cæsar Borgia and Heliogabalus, and all the profligate papists and pagans that ever lived, did not exceed the life led by the Count and his French friends; so at least I am told: for I was then a very young man, and such things were studiously kept from my knowledge by my father the late Archdeacon . . .'

'*Le pauvre innocent!*' whispered Lady Honoria to Lady Knocklofty.

'I am told that he actually assumed the habit of an Abbot, dressed up his companions in monk's tunics, and established a sort of licentious club, called the Monks of the Vine.'

'Something like the Monks of the Screw here in Dublin, I suppose,' said Lady Honoria.

'Oh, worse, worse a great deal, Lady Honoria. They exceeded in profligacy all that was ever heard of.'

'Had they any six-bottle men among them, like our Cherokees?' demanded Lord Kilcolman.

'Lord Kilcolman, I know not what they had: the proceedings at Moycullen were fortunately hid from the world. I believe the Count admitted but few persons at the abbey; though, when he went out, he was well received; for he was a most insinuating and winning man in his manners.'

'He was indeed!' said Lady Mary. 'I was then almost a child; but I remember he always put me in mind of Richardson's Lovelace.'

'And you, *par hasard*, might have been his Clarissa,' said Lady Honoria, 'if the mammas and papas had admitted him to *Beauregard*.'

'I assure you,' said Lady Mary, evasively, 'he was received and pushed on by the Clanrickards, the De Burghs, and other catholic nobility; though my dear father refused to visit him for many reasons.'

'But from the time,' continued the Archdeacon, 'when he abducted, or rather was suspected of abducting the Abbess (for it was given out that she was drowned, her veil having been found floating on the rocks at St Grellan at the back of the convent, and masses were said for her soul in spite of the penal statutes), he was cut by all.'

'Well,' said Lady Knocklofty, 'and how did the romance end?'

'Oh! the catholic church has a way of hushing up all its scandalous romances, as your ladyship calls this event. The Abbess was never heard of more. The whole circumstance was denied by those, whose interests required that the truth should not be revealed. The Monks of the Vine dispersed. The Count returned to France, and was either killed in a duel, or assassinated in the Bois de Boulogne; and his property was bequeathed in trust to some foreign agent, for purposes which, if inquired into, would, I doubt not, be found illegal.'

Here the announcement of the Lord Chancellor, and the order for dinner interrupted the conversation; and objects of more immediate importance at that season of the day, were discussed and digested, with a uniformity of opinion, unbroken by a single dissentient voice.

WILLIAM CARLETON

'Wildgoose Lodge'

I had read the anonymous summons, but, from its general import, I believed it to be one of those special meetings convened for some purpose affecting the usual objects and proceedings of the body; at least, the terms in which it was conveyed to me had nothing extraordinary or mysterious in them beyond the simple fact that it was not to be a general but a select meeting. This mark of confidence flattered me, and I determined to attend punctually. I was, it was true, desired to keep the circumstance entirely to myself; but there was nothing startling in this, for I had often received summonses of a similar nature. I therefore resolved to attend, according to the letter of my instructions, 'on the next night, at the solemn hour of midnight, to deliberate and act upon such matters as should then and there be submitted to my consideration'. The morning after I received this message, I arose and resumed my usual occupations; but from whatever cause it may have proceeded, I felt a sense of approaching evil hang heavily upon me. The beats of my pulse were languid, and an indefinable feeling of anxiety pervaded my whole spirit; even my face was pale, and my eye so heavy that my father and brothers concluded me to be ill; an opinion which I thought at the time to be correct, for I felt exactly that kind of depression which precedes a severe fever. I could not understand what I experienced; nor can I yet, except by supposing that there is in human nature some mysterious faculty by which, in coming calamities, the dread of some fearful evil is anticipated, and that it is possible to catch a dark presentiment of the sensations which they subsequently produce. For my part, I can neither analyse nor define it; but on that day I knew it by painful experience, and so have a thousand others in similar circumstances.

It was about the middle of winter. The day was gloomy and tempestuous almost beyond any other I remember; dark clouds rolled over the hills about me, and a close, sleet-like rain fell in slanting drifts that chased each other rapidly towards the earth on the course of the blast. The outlying cattle sought the closest and calmest corners of the fields for shelter; the trees and young groves were tossed about, for the wind was so unusually high that it swept in hollow gusts through them with that hoarse murmur which deepens so powerfully on the mind the sense of dreariness and desolation.

As the shades of night fell, the storm, if possible, increased. The moon was half gone, and only a few stars were visible by glimpses, as a rush of wind left a temporary opening in the sky. I had determined, if the storm should not abate, to incur any penalty rather than attend the meeting; but the appointed hour was distant, and I resolved to be decided by the future state of the night.

Ten o'clock came, but still there was no change; eleven passed, and on opening the door to observe if there were any likelihood of its clearing up, a blast of wind, mingled with rain, nearly blew me off my feet. At length it was approaching to the hour of midnight; and on examining a third time, I found it had calmed a little, and no longer rained.

I instantly got my oak stick, muffled myself in my greatcoat, strapped my hat about my ears, and as the place of meeting was only a quarter of a mile distant, I presently set out.

The appearance of the heavens was lowering and angry, particularly in that point where the light of the moon fell against the clouds from a seeming chasm in them, through which alone she was visible. The edges of this chasm were faintly bronzed, but the dense body of the masses that hung piled on each side of her was black and impenetrable to sight. In no other point of the heavens was there any part of the sky visible – a deep veil of clouds overhung the horizon – yet was the light sufficient to give occasional glimpses of the rapid shifting which took place in this dark canopy, and of the tempestuous agitation with which the midnight storm swept to and fro beneath it.

At length I arrived at a long slated house situated in a solitary part of the neighbourhood; a little below it ran a small stream, which was now swollen above its banks, and rushing with mimic roar over the flat meadows beside it. The appearance of the bare slated building in such a night was particularly sombre; and to those, like me, who knew the purpose to which it was usually devoted, it was, or ought to have been, peculiarly so. There it stood, silent and gloomy, without any appearance of human life or enjoyment about or within it. As I approached, the moon once more had broken out of the clouds, and shone dimly upon the wet, glittering slates and windows with a death-like lustre, that gradually faded away as I left the point of observation and entered the folding-door. It was the parish chapel.

The scene which presented itself here was in keeping not only with the external appearance of the house, but with the darkness, the storm, and the hour, which was now a little after midnight. About eighty persons were sitting in dead silence upon the circular steps of the altar. They did not seem to move; and as I entered and advanced, the echo of my footsteps rang through the building with a lonely distinctness, which added to the solemnity and mystery of the circumstances about me. The windows were secured with shutters on the inside; and on the altar a candle was lighted, which burned dimly amid the surrounding darkness, and lengthened the shadow of the altar itself, and those of six or seven persons who stood on its upper steps, until they mingled in the obscurity which shrouded the lower end of the chapel. The faces of the men who sat on the altar-steps were not distinctly visible, yet their prominent and more characteristic features were in sufficient relief, and I observed that some of the most malignant and reckless spirits in the parish were assembled. In the eyes of those who stood at the altar, and whom I knew to be invested with authority over the others, I could perceive gleams of some latent and ferocious purpose, kindled, as I soon observed, into a fiercer expression of vengeance by the additional excitement of ardent spirits, with which they had stimulated themselves to a point of determination that mocked at the apprehension of all future responsibility, either in this world or the next.

The welcome which I received on joining them was far different from the boisterous good-humour that used to mark our greetings on other occasions: just a nod of the head from this or that person, on the part of those who sat, with a *ghud dhemur tha thu?* in a suppressed voice, even below a common whisper; but from the standing group, who were evidently the projectors of the enterprise, I received a convulsive grasp of the hand, accompanied by a fierce and desperate look, that seemed to search my eye and countenance, to try if I were a person not likely to shrink from whatever they had resolved to execute. It is surprising to think of the powerful expression which a moment of intense interest or great danger is capable of giving to the eye, the features, and the slightest actions, especially in those whose station in society does not require them to constrain nature, by the force of social courtesies, into habits that conceal their natural emotions. None of the standing group spoke; but as each of them wrung my hand in silence, his eye was fixed on mine with an expression of drunken confidence and secrecy, and an insolent determination not to be gainsaid without peril. If looks could be translated with certainty, they seemed to say, 'We are bound upon a project of vengeance, and if you do not join us, remember that we can revenge.' Along with this grasp they did not forget to remind me of the common bond by which we were united, for each man gave me the secret grip of Ribbonism in a manner that made the joints of my fingers ache for some minutes afterwards.

There was one present, however – the highest in authority – whose actions and demeanour were calm and unexcited. He seemed to labour under no unusual influence whatever, but evinced a serenity so placid and philosophical that I attributed the silence of the sitting group, and the restraint which curbed in the outbreaking passions of those who stood, entirely to his presence. He was a schoolmaster, who taught his daily school in that chapel, and acted also, on Sunday, in the capacity of clerk to the priest – an excellent and amiable old man, who knew little of his illegal connections and atrocious conduct.

When the ceremonies of brotherly recognition and friendship were past, the captain (by which title I shall designate the last-mentioned person) stooped, and raising a jar of whiskey on the corner of the altar, held a wine-glass to its neck, which he filled, and, with a calm nod, handed it to me to drink. I shrunk back, with an instinctive horror at the profaneness of such an act, in the house, and on the altar, of God, and peremptorily refused to taste the proffered draught. He smiled mildly at what he considered my superstition, and added quietly, and in a low voice, 'You'll be wantin' it, I'm thinkin', afther the wettin' you got.'

'Wet or dry,' said I –

'Stop, man!' he replied, in the same tone; 'spake low. But why wouldn't you take the whiskey? Sure, there's as holy people to the fore as you; didn't they all take it? An' I wish we may never do worse nor dhrink a harmless glass o' whiskey to keep the cowld out, anyway.'

'Well,' said I, 'I'll jist trust to God and the consequences for the cowld, Paddy, *ma bouchal*; but a blessed dhrop of it won't be crossin' my lips, *avick*; so no more *gosther* about it – dhrink it yourself, if you like. Maybe you want it as much as I do; wherein I've the patthern of a good big coat upon me – so thick, your sowl, that if it was rainin' bullocks, a dhrop wouldn't get under the nap of it.'

He gave a calm but keen glance at me as I spoke.

'Well, Jim,' said he, 'it's a good comrade you've got for the weather that's in it; but, in the meantime, to set you a dacent patthern, I'll just take this myself'; saying which, with the jar still upon its side, and the forefinger of his left hand in its neck, he swallowed the spirits. 'It's the first I dhrank tonight,' he added; 'nor would I dhrink it now, only to show you that I've heart and spirit to do the thing that we're bound an' sworn to, when the proper time comes'; after which he laid down the glass, and turned up the jar, with much coolness, upon the altar.

During our conversation those who had been summoned to this mysterious meeting were pouring in fast; and as each person approached the altar he received from one to two or three glasses of whiskey, according as he chose to limit himself; but, to do them justice, there were not a few of those present who, in spite of their own desire, and the captain's express invitation, refused to taste it in the house of God's worship. Such, however, as were scrupulous he afterwards recommended to take it on the outside of the chapel door, which they did, as by that means the sacrilege of the act was supposed to be evaded.

About one o'clock they were all assembled except six; at least, so the captain asserted, on looking at a written paper.

'Now, boys,' said he, in the same low voice, 'we are all present except the thraitors whose names I am goin' to read to you; not that we are to count thim thraitors till we know whether or not it was in their power to come. Anyhow, the night's terrible; but, boys, you're to know that neither fire, nor wather is to prevint yees when duly summoned to attind a meeting – particularly whin the summons is widout a name, as you have been told that there is always something of consequence to be done thin.'

He then read out the names of those who were absent, in order that the real cause of their absence might be ascertained, declaring that they would be dealt with accordingly. After this, with his usual caution, he shut and bolted the door, and having put the key in his pocket, ascended the steps of the altar, and for some time traversed the little platform from which the priest usually addresses the congregation.

Until this night I have never contemplated the man's countenance with any particular interest; but as he walked the platform I had an opportunity of observing him more closely. He was slight in person, apparently not thirty, and, on a first view, appeared to have nothing remarkable in his dress or features. I, however, was not the only person whose eyes were fixed upon him at that moment; in fact, every one present observed him with equal interest, for hitherto he had kept the object of the meeting perfectly secret, and of course we all felt anxious to know it. It was while he traversed the platform that I scrutinized his features with a hope, if possible, to glean from them some evidence of what was passing within him. I could, however, mark but little, and that little was at first rather from the intelligence which seemed to subsist between him and those whom I have already mentioned as standing against the altar, than from any indication of his own. Their gleaming eyes were fixed upon him with an intensity of savage and demon-like hope which blazed out in flashes of malignant triumph, as, upon turning, he threw a cool but rapid glance at them, to intimate the progress he was making in the subject to which he devoted the undivided energies of his mind. But in the course of his meditation I could observe, on one or two occasions, a dark shade come over his countenance that contracted his brow into a deep furrow, and it was then, for the first time, that I saw the Satanic expression of which his face, by a very slight motion of its muscles, was capable. His hands, during this silence, closed and opened convulsively; his eyes shot out two or three baleful glances, first to his confederates, and afterwards vacantly into the deep gloom of the lower part of the chapel; his teeth ground against each other like those of a man whose revenge burns to reach a distant enemy; and finally, after having wound himself up to a certain determination, his features relapsed into their original calm and undisturbed expression.

At this moment a loud laugh, having something supernatural in it, rang out wildly from the darkness of the chapel: he stopped, and putting his open hand over his brows, peered down into the gloom, and said calmly, in Irish, *'Bee dhu husth; ha nihl anam inh –* Hold your tongue; it is not yet the time.'

Every eye was now directed to the same spot, but in consequence of its distance from the dim light on the altar, none could perceive the person from whom the laugh proceeded. It was by this time near two o'clock in the morning.

He now stood for a few moments on the platform, and his chest heaved with a depth of anxiety equal to the difficulty of the design he wished to accomplish.

'Brothers,' said he – 'for we are all brothers – sworn upon all that's blessed an' holy to obey whatever them that's over us, manin' among ourselves, wishes us to do – are you now ready, in the name of God, upon whose althar I stand, to fulfil yer oaths?'

The words were scarcely uttered, when those who had stood beside the altar during the night sprang from their places, and descending its steps rapidly, turned round, and raising their arms, exclaimed, 'By all that's sacred an' holy, we're willin'!'

In the meantime, those who sat upon the steps of the altar instantly rose, and following the example of those who had just spoken, exclaimed after them, 'To be sure – by all that's sacred an' holy, we're willin'!'

'Now, boys,' said the captain, 'aren't yees big fools for your pains? An' one of yees doesn't know what I mane.'

'You're our captain,' said one of those who had stood at the altar, 'an' has yer ordhers from higher quarthers; of coorse, whatever ye command upon us we're bound to obey you in.'

'Well,' said he, smiling, 'I only wanted to thry yees; an' by the oath yees tuck, there's not a captain in the country has as good a right to be proud of his min as I have. Well, yees won't rue it, maybe, when the right time comes; and for that same rason every one of yees must have a glass from the jar – thim that won't dhrink it in the chapel can dhrink it widout; an' here goes to open the door for them.'

He then distributed another glass to every man who would accept it, and brought the jar afterwards to the chapel door, to satisfy the scruples of those who would not drink within. When this was performed, and all duly excited, he proceeded:

'Now, brothers, you are solemnly sworn to obey me, and I'm sure there's no thraithur here that ud parjure himself for a thrifle; but I'm sworn to obey them that's above me, manin' still among ourselves; an' to show you that I don't scruple to do it, here goes!'

He then turned round, and taking the Missal between his hands, placed in upon the altar. Hitherto every word was uttered in a low, precautionary tone; but on grasping the book, he again turned round, and looking upon his confederates with the same Satanic expression which marked his countenance before, exclaimed, in a voice of deep determination:

'By this sacred an' holy book of God, I will perform the action which we have met this night to accomplish, be that what it may; an' this I swear upon God's book an' God's althar!'

On concluding he struck the book violently with his open hand.

At this moment the candle which burned before him went suddenly out, and the chapel was wrapped in pitchy darkness; the sound as if of rushing wings fell upon our ears; and fifty voices dwelt upon the last words of his oath with wild and supernatural tones, that seemed to echo and to mock what he had sworn. There was a pause, and an exclamation of horror from all present; but the captain was too cool and steady to be disconcerted. He immediately groped about until he got the candle, and proceeding calmly to a remote corner of the chapel, took up a half-burned turf which lay there, and after some trouble, succeeded in lighting it again. He then explained what had taken place; which indeed was easily done, as the candle happened to be extinguished by a pigeon which sat directly above it. The chapel, I should have observed, was at this time, like many country chapels, unfinished inside, and the pigeons of a neighbouring dovecote had built nests among the rafters of the unceiled roof; which circumstance also explained the rushing of the wings, for the birds had been affrighted by the sudden loudness of the noise. The mocking voices were nothing but the echoes, rendered naturally more awful by the scene, the mysterious object of the meeting, and the solemn hour of the night.

When the candle was again lighted, and these startling circumstances accounted for, the persons whose vengeance had been deepening more and more during the night rushed to the altar in a body, where each, in a voice trembling with passionate eagerness, repeated the oath; and as every word was pronounced, the same echoes heightened the wildness of the horrible ceremony by their long and unearthly tones. The countenances of these human tigers were livid with suppressed rage; their knit brows, compressed lips, and kindled eyes fell under the dim light of the taper with an expression calculated to sicken any heart not absolutely diabolical.

As soon as this dreadful rite was completed, we were again startled by several loud bursts of laughter, which proceeded from the lower darkness of the chapel; and the captain, on hearing them, turned to the place, and reflecting for a moment, said in Irish, '*Gutsho nish, avohelhee* – Come hither now, boys.'

A rush immediately took place from the corner in which they had secreted themselves all the night; and seven men appeared, whom we instantly recognized as brothers and cousins of certain persons who had been convicted some time before for breaking into the house of an honest poor man in the neighbourhood, from whom, after having treated him with barbarous violence, they took away such firearms as he kept for his own protection.

It was evidently not the captain's intention to have produced these persons until the oath should have been generally taken; but the exulting mirth with which they enjoyed the success of his scheme betrayed them, and put him to the necessity of bringing them forward somewhat before the concerted moment.

The scene which now took place was beyond all power of description; peals of wild, fiend-like yells rang through the chapel, as the party which stood on the altar, and that which had crouched in the darkness, met; wringing of hands, leaping in triumph, striking of sticks and firearms against the ground and the altar itself, dancing and cracking of fingers, marked the triumph of some hellish determination. Even the captain for a time was unable to restrain their fury; but at length he mounted the platform before the altar once more, and, with a stamp of his foot, recalled their attention to himself and the matter in hand.

'Boys,' said he, 'enough of this, and too much; an' well for us it is that the chapel is in a lonely place, or our foolish noise might do us no good. Let thim that swore so manfully jist now stand a one side, till the rest kiss the book, one by one.'

The proceedings, however, had by this time taken too fearful a shape for even the captain to compel them to a blindfold oath. The first man he called flatly refused to answer until he should hear the nature of the service that was required. This was echoed by the remainder, who, taking courage from the firmness of this person, declared generally that until they first knew the business they were to execute none of them would take the oath. The captain's lip quivered slightly, and his brow again became knit with the same hellish expression which I have remarked gave him so much the appearance of an embodied fiend; but this speedily passed away, and was succeeded by a malignant sneer, in which lurked, if there ever did in a sneer, 'a laughing devil', calmly, determinedly atrocious.

'It wasn't worth yer whiles to refuse the oath,' said he mildly; 'for the truth is, I had next to nothing for yees to do. Not a hand, maybe, would have to rise; only jist to look on; an' if any resistance would be made, to show yourselves; yer numbers would soon make them see that resistance would be no use whatever in the present case. At all evints, the oath of secrecy must be taken, or woe be to him that will refuse that; he won't know the day, nor the hour, nor the minute when he'll be made a spatchcock ov.'

He then turned round, and placing his right hand on the Missal, swore, 'In the presence of God, and before His holy altar, that whatever might take place that night he would keep secret from man or mortal, except the priest, and that neither bribery, nor imprisonment, nor death would wring it from his heart.'

Having done this, he again struck the book violently, as if to confirm the energy with which he swore, and then calmly descending the steps, stood with a serene countenance, like a man conscious of having performed a good action. As this oath did not pledge those who refused to take the other to the perpetration of any specific crime, it was readily taken by all present. Preparations were then made to execute what was intended; the half-burned turf was placed in a little pot; another glass of whiskey was distributed; and the door being locked by the captain, who kept the key as parish clerk and master, the crowd departed silently from the chapel.

The moment those who lay in the darkness during the night made their appearance at the altar, we knew at once the persons we were to visit; for, as I said before, they were related to the miscreants whom one of those persons had convicted, in consequence of their midnight attack upon himself and his family. The captain's object in keeping them unseen was that those present, not being aware of the duty about to be imposed on them, might have less hesitation about swearing to its fulfilment. Our conjectures were correct, for on leaving the chapel we directed our steps to the house in which this devoted man resided.

The night was still stormy, but without rain; it was rather dark, too, though not so as to prevent us from seeing the clouds careering swiftly through the air. The dense curtain which had overhung and obscured the horizon was now broken, and large sections of the sky were clear, and thinly studded with stars that looked dim and watery, as did indeed the whole firmament; for in some places black clouds were still visible, threatening a continuance of tempestuous weather. The road appeared washed and gravelly; every dyke was full of yellow water, and every little rivulet and larger stream dashed its hoarse music in our ears; every blast, too, was cold, fierce, and wintry, sometimes driving us back to a standstill, and again, when a turn in the road would bring it in our backs, whirling us along for a few steps with involuntary rapidity. At length the fated dwelling became visible, and a short consultation was held in a sheltered place between the captain and the two parties who seemed so eager for its destruction. The firearms were now loaded, and their bayonets and short pikes, the latter shod and pointed with iron, were also got ready. The live coal which was brought in the small pot had become extinguished; but to remedy this, two or three persons from a remote part of the country entered a cabin on the wayside, and under pretence of lighting their own and their comrades' pipes, procured a coal of fire – for so they called a lighted turf. From the time we left the chapel until this moment a profound silence had been maintained; a circumstance which, when I considered the number of persons present, and the mysterious and dreaded object of their journey, had a most appalling effect upon my spirits.

At length we arrived within fifty perches of the house, walking in a compact body, and with as little noise as possible; but it seemed as if the very elements had conspired to frustrate our design, for on advancing within the shade of the farm hedge, two or three persons found themselves up to the middle in water, and on stooping to ascertain more accurately the state of the place, we could see nothing but one immense sheet of it, spread like a lake over the meadows which surrounded the spot we wished to reach.

Fatal night! The very recollection of it, when associated with the fearful tempests of the elements, grows, if that were possible, yet more wild and revolting. Had we been engaged in any innocent or benevolent enterprise, there was something in our situation just then that had a touch of interest in it to a mind imbued with a relish for the savage beauties of nature. There we stood, about a hundred and thirty in number, our dark forms bent forward, peering into the dusky expanse of water, with its dim gleams of reflected light, broken by the weltering of the mimic waves into ten thousand fragments; whilst the few stars that overhung it in the firmament appeared to shoot through it in broken lines, and to be multiplied fifty-fold in the gloomy mirror on which we gazed.

Over us was a stormy sky, and around us a darkness through which we could only distinguish, in outline, the nearest objects, whilst the wind swept strongly and dismally upon us. When it was discovered that the common pathway to the house was inundated, we were about to abandon our object and return home. The captain, however, stooped down low for a moment, and almost closing his eyes, looked along the surface of the waters, and then raising himself very calmly, said, in his usual quiet tone, 'Yees needn't go back, boys; I've found a way; jist follow me.'

He immediately took a more circuitous direction, by which we reached a causeway that had been raised for the purpose of giving a free passage to and from the house during such inundations as the present. Along this we had advanced more than half way, when we discovered a breach in it, which, as afterwards appeared, had that night been made by the strength of the flood. This, by means of our sticks and pikes, we found to be about three feet deep and eight yards broad. Again we were at a loss how to proceed, when the fertile brain of the captain devised a method of crossing it.

'Boys,' said he, 'of coorse you've all played at leap-frog; very well, strip and go in, a dozen of you, lean one upon the back of another from this to the opposite bank, where one must stand facing the outside man, both their shoulders agin one another, that the outside man may be supported. Then we can creep over you, an' a dacent bridge you'll be, anyway.'

This was the work of only a few minutes, and in less than ten we were all safely over.

Merciful heaven! how I sicken at the recollection of what is to follow! On reaching the dry bank, we proceeded instantly, and in profound silence, to the house. The captain divided us into companies, and then assigned to each division its proper station. The two parties who had been so vindictive all the night he kept about himself; for of those who were present they only were in his confidence, and knew his nefarious purpose – their number was about fifteen. Having made these dispositions, he, at the head of about five of them, approached the house on the windy side, for the fiend possessed a coolness which enabled him to seize upon every possible advantage. That he had combustibles about him was evident, for in less than fifteen minutes nearly one-half of the house was enveloped in flames. On seeing this, the others rushed over to the spot where he and his gang were standing, and remonstrated earnestly, but in vain. The flames now burst forth with renewed violence, and as they flung their strong light upon the faces of the foremost group, I think hell itself could hardly present anything more Satanic than their countenances, now worked up into a paroxysm of infernal triumph at their own revenge. The captain's look had lost all of its calmness, every feature started out into distinct malignity; the curve in his brow was deep, and ran up to the root of the hair, dividing his face into two segments, that did not seem to have been designed for each other. His lips were half open, and the corners of his mouth a little brought back on each side, like those of a man expressing intense hatred and triumph over an enemy who is in the death-struggle under his grasp. His eyes blazed from beneath his knit eyebrows with a fire that seemed to be lighted up in the infernal pit itself. It is unnecessary and only painful to describe the rest of his gang. Demons might have been proud of such horrible visages as they exhibited; for they worked under all the power of hatred, revenge, and joy; and these passions blended into one terrible scowl, enough almost to blast any human eye that would venture to look upon it.

When the others attempted to intercede for the lives of the inmates, there were at least fifteen guns and pistols levelled at them.

'Another word,' said the captain, 'an' you're a corpse where you stand, or the first man who will dare to spake for them. No, no, it wasn't to spare them we came here. "No mercy" is the password for the night, an' by the sacred oath I swore beyant in the chapel, any one among yees that will attempt to show it will find none at my hand. Surround the house, boys, I tell ye, I hear them stirring. "No quarther – no mercy" is the ordher of the night.'

Such was his command over these misguided creatures, that in an instant there was a ring round the house to prevent the escape of the unhappy inmates, should the raging element give them time to attempt it; for none present durst withdraw themselves from the scene, not only from an apprehension of the captain's present vengeance or that of his gang, but because they knew that, even had they then escaped, an early and certain death awaited them from a quarter against which they had no means of defence. The hour now was about half past two o'clock. Scarcely had the last words escaped from the captain's lips, when one of the windows of the house was broken, and a human head, having the hair in a blaze, was descried, apparently a woman's, if one might judge by the profusion of burning tresses, and the softness of the tones, notwithstanding that it called, or rather shrieked, aloud for help and mercy. The only reply to this was the whoop from the captain and his gang of 'No mercy – no mercy!' and that instant the former and one of the latter rushed to the spot, and ere the action could be perceived, the head was transfixed with a bayonet and a pike, both having entered it together. The word mercy was divided in her mouth; a short silence ensued; the head hung down on the window, but was instantly tossed back into the flames!

This action occasioned a cry of horror from all present, except the gang and their leader, which startled and enraged the latter so much that he ran towards one of them, and had his bayonet, now reeking with the blood of its innocent victim, raised to plunge it in his body, when, dropping the point, he said in a piercing whisper that hissed in the ears of all, 'It's no use now, you know; if one's to hang, all will hang; so our safest way, you persave, is to lave none of them to tell the story. Ye may go now, if you wish; but it won't save a hair of your heads. You cowardly set! I knew if I had tould yees the sport, that none of yees, except my own boys, would come, so I jist played a thrick upon you; but remimber what you are sworn to, and stand to the oath ye tuck.'

Unhappily, notwithstanding the wetness of the preceding weather, the materials of the house were extremely combustible; the whole dwelling was now one body of glowing flame; yet the shouts and shrieks within rose awfully above its crackling, and the voice of the storm, for the wind once more blew in gusts and with great violence. The doors and windows were all torn open, and such of those within had escaped the flames rushed towards them, for the purpose of further escape, and of claiming mercy at the hands of their destroyers; but whenever they appeared, the unearthly cry of 'No mercy' rung upon their ears for a moment, and for a moment only, for they were flung back at the points of the weapons which the demons had brought with them to make the work of vengeance more certain.

As yet there were many persons in the house whose cry for life was strong as despair, and who clung to it with all the awakened powers of reason and instinct. The ear of man could hear nothing so strongly calculated to stifle the demon of cruelty and revenge within him as the long and wailing shrieks which rose beyond the elements in tones that were carried off rapidly upon the blast, until they died away in the darkness that lay behind the surrounding hills. Had not the house been in a solitary situation, and the hour the dead of night, any person sleeping within a moderate distance must have heard them, for such a cry of sorrow rising into a yell of despair was almost sufficient to have awakened the dead. It was lost, however, upon the hearts and ears that heard it; to them – though, in justice be it said, to only comparatively a few of them – it was as delightful as the tones of soft and entrancing music.

The claims of the surviving sufferers were now modified: they supplicated merely to suffer death by the weapons of their enemies; they were willing to bear that, provided they should be allowed to escape from the flames; but no – the horrors of the conflagration were calmly and malignantly gloried in by their merciless assassins, who deliberately flung them back into all their tortures. In the course of a few minutes a man appeared upon the side-wall of the house, nearly naked; his figure, as he stood against the sky in horrible relief, was so finished a picture of woe-begone agony and supplication that it is yet as distinct in my memory as if I were again present at the scene. Every muscle, now in motion by the powerful agitation of his sufferings, stood out upon his limbs and neck, giving him an appearance of desperate strength, to which by this time he must have been wrought up; the perspiration poured from his frame, and the veins and arteries of his neck were inflated to a surprising thickness. Every moment he looked down into the flames which were rising to where he stood; and as he looked, the indescribable horror which flitted over his features might have worked upon the devil himself to relent. His words were few.

'My child,' said he, 'is still safe; she is an infant, a young crathur that never harmed you nor any one – she is still safe. Your mothers, your wives, have young innocent childher like it. Oh, spare her! – think for a moment that it's one of your own! – spare it, as you hope to meet a just God; or if you don't, in mercy shoot me first – put an end to me before I see her burned!'

The captain approached him coolly and deliberately. 'You'll prosecute no one now, you bloody informer,' said he; 'you'll convict no more boys for takin' an ould gun an' pistol from you, or for givin' you a neighbourly knock or two into the bargain.'

Just then, from a window opposite him, proceeded the shrieks of a woman, who appeared at it with the infant in her arms. She herself was almost scorched to death; but with the presence of mind and humanity of her sex, she was about to put the little babe out of the window. The captain noticed this, and with characteristic atrocity, thrust, with a sharp bayonet, the little innocent, along with the person who endeavoured to rescue it, into the red flames, where they both perished. This was the work of an instant. Again he approached the man, 'Your child is a coal now,' said he, with deliberate mockery; 'I pitched it in myself, on the point of this' – showing the weapon – 'an' now is your turn' – saying which he clambered up, by the assistance of his gang, who stood with a front of pikes and bayonets bristling to receive the wretched man, should he attempt, in his despair, to throw himself from the wall. The captain got up, and placing the point of his bayonet against his shoulder, flung him into the fiery element that raged behind him. He uttered one wild and terrific cry as he fell back, and no more. After this, nothing was heard but the crackling of the fire and the rushing of the blast; all that had possessed life within were consumed, amounting either to eleven or fifteen persons.

When this was accomplished, those who took an active part in the murder stood for some time about the conflagration; and as it threw its red light upon their fierce faces and rough persons, soiled as they now were with smoke and black streaks of ashes, the scene seemed to be changed to hell, the murderers to spirits of the damned rejoicing over the arrival and the torture of some guilty soul. The faces of those who kept aloof from the slaughter were blanched to the whiteness of death; some of them fainted, and others were in such agitation that they were compelled to lean on their comrades. They became actually powerless with horror. Yet to such a scene were they brought by the pernicious influence of Ribbonism.

It was only when the last victim went down that the conflagration shot up into the air with most unbounded fury. The house was large, deeply thatched, and well furnished; and the broad red pyramid rose up with fearful magnificence towards the sky. Abstractedly it had sublimity, but now it was associated with nothing in my mind but blood and terror. It was not, however, without a purpose that the captain and his gang stood to contemplate its effect. 'Boys,' said he, 'we had betther be sartin that all's safe; who knows but there might be some of the sarpents crouchin' under a hape o' rubbish, to come out an' gibbet us tomorrow or next day; we had betther wait awhile, anyhow, if it was only to see the blaze.'

Just then the flames rose majestically to a surprising height. Our eyes followed their direction; and we perceived, for the first time, that the dark clouds above, together with the intermediate air, appeared to reflect back, or rather to have caught, the red hue of the fire. The hills and country about us appeared with an alarming distinctness; but the most picturesque part of it was the effect or reflection of the blaze on the floods that spread over the surrounding plains. These, in fact, appeared to be one broad mass of liquid copper; for the motion of the breaking waters caught from the blaze of the high waving column, as reflected in them, a glaring light, which eddied and rose and fluctuated as if the flood itself had been a lake of molten fire.

Fire, however, destroys rapidly. In a short time the flames sank – became weak and flickering – by and by they shot out only in fits – the crackling of the timbers died away – the surrounding darkness deepened – and, ere long, the faint light was overpowered by the thick volumes of smoke that rose from the ruins of the house and its murdered inhabitants.

'Now, boys,' said the captain, 'all is safe – we may go. Remember, every man of you, what you've sworn this night on the book an' altar of God – not on a heretic Bible. If you perjure yourselves, you may hang us; but let me tell you, for your comfort, that if you do, there is them livin' that will take care the lase of your own lives will be but short.'

After this we dispersed, every man to his own home.

Reader, not many months elapsed ere I saw the bodies of this captain, whose name was Patrick Devaun, and all those who were actively concerned in the perpetration of this deed of horror, withering in the wind, where they hung gibbeted near the scene of their nefarious villainy; and while I inwardly thanked Heaven for my own narrow and almost undeserved escape, I thought in my heart how seldom, even in this world, justice fails to overtake the murderer, and to enforce the righteous judgement of God – and 'whoso sheddeth man's blood, by man shall his blood be shed.'

This tale of terror is, unfortunately, too true. The scene of hellish murder detailed in it lies at Wildgoose Lodge in the county of Louth, within about four miles of Carrickmacross, and nine of Dundalk. No such multitudinous murder has occurred, under similar circumstances, except the burning of the Sheas in the county of Tipperary. The name of the family burned in Wildgoose Lodge was Lynch. One of them had, shortly before this fatal night, prosecuted and convicted some of the neighbouring Ribbonmen, who visited him with severe marks of their displeasure in consequence of his having refused to enrol himself as a member of their body.

The language of the story is partly fictitious; but the facts are pretty closely such as were developed during the trial of the murderers. Both parties were Roman Catholics. There were, if the author mistake not, either twenty-five or twenty-eight of those who took an active part in the burning hanged and gibbeted in different parts of the county of Louth. Devaun, the ringleader, hung for some months in chains, within about a hundred yards of his own house, and about half a mile from Wildgoose Lodge. His mother could neither go into or out of her cabin without seeing his body swinging from the gibbet. Her usual exclamation on looking at him was, 'God be good to the sowl of my poor marthyr!' The peasantry, too, frequently exclaimed, on seeing him, 'Poor Paddy!' – a gloomy fact that speaks volumes.

from *The Black Prophet*

6

A Rustic Miser and His Establishment

There is to be found in Ireland, and, we presume, in all other countries, a class of hardened wretches, who look forward to a period of dearth as to one of great gain and advantage, and who contrive, by exercising the most heartless and diabolical principles, to make the sickness, famine, and general desolation which scourge their fellow-creatures, so many sources of successful extortion and rapacity, and consequently of gain to themselves. These are country misers, or money-lenders, who are remarkable for keeping meal until the arrival of what is termed a hard year, or a dear summer, when they sell it out at enormous or usurious prices, and who, at all times and under all circumstances, dispose of it only at terms dictated by their own griping spirit, and the crying necessity of the unhappy purchasers.

The houses and places of such persons are always remarkable for a character in their owners of hard and severe saving, which at a first glance has the appearance of that rare virtue in our country called frugality – a virtue which, upon a closer inspection, is found to be nothing with them but selfishness sharpened up into the most unscrupulous avarice and penury.

About half-a-mile from the residence of the Sullivans, lived a remarkable man of this class, named Darby Skinadre. In appearance he was lank and sallow, with a long, thin, parched-looking face, and a miserable crop of yellow beard, which no one could pronounce as anything else than a 'dead failure'; added to this were two piercing ferret eyes, always sore and fiery, and with a tear standing in each, or trickling down his fleshless cheeks; so that, to persons disposed to judge only by appearances, he looked very like a man in a state of perpetual repentance for his transgressions, or, what was still farther from the truth, who felt a most Christian sympathy with the distresses of the poor. In his house, and about it, there was much, no doubt, to be commended, for there was much to mark the habits of the saving man. Everything was neat and clean, not so much from any innate love of neatness and cleanliness, as because these qualities were economical in themselves. His ploughs and farming implements were all snugly laid up, and covered, lest they might be injured by exposure to the weather; and his house was filled with large chests and wooden hogsheads, trampled hard with oatmeal, which, as they were never opened unless during a time of famine, had their joints and crevices festooned by innumerable mealy-looking cobwebs, which description of ornament extended to the dresser itself, where they might be seen upon most of the cold-looking shelves, and those neglected utensils that in other families are mostly used for food. His haggard was also remarkable for having in it, throughout all the year, a remaining stack or two of oats or wheat, or perhaps one or two large ricks of hay, tanned by the sun of two or three summers into a tawny hue – each or all kept in the hope of a failure and a famine.

In a room from the kitchen, he had a beam, a pair of scales, and a set of weights, all of which would have been vastly improved by a visit from the lord mayor, had our mealmonger lived under the jurisdiction of that civic gentleman. He was seldom known to use metal weights when disposing of his property; in lieu of these he always used round stones, which, upon the principle of the Scottish proverb, that 'many a little makes a muckle', he must have found a very beneficial mode of transacting business.

If anything could add to the iniquity of his principles, as a plausible but most unscrupulous cheat, it was the hypocritical prostitution of the sacred name and character of religion to his own fraudulent impositions upon the poor and the distressed. Outwardly, and to the eye of men, he was proverbially strict and scrupulous in the observation of its sanctions, but outrageously severe and unsparing upon all who appeared to be influenced either by a negligent or worldly spirit, or who omitted the least tittle of its forms. Religion and its duties, therefore, were perpetually in his mouth, but never with such apparent zeal and sincerity as when enforcing his most heartless and hypocritical exactions upon the honest and struggling creatures whom necessity or neglect had driven into his meshes.

Such was Darby Skinadre; and certain we are that the truth of the likeness we have given of him will be at once recognized by our readers as that of the roguish hypocrite, whose rapacity is the standing curse of half the villages of the country, especially during seasons of distress, or failure of crops.

Skinadre, on the day we write of, was reaping a rich harvest from the miseries of the unhappy people. In a lower room of his house, to the right of the kitchen as you entered it, he stood over his scales, weighing out with a dishonest and parsimonious hand, the scanty pittance which poverty enabled the wretched creatures to purchase from him; and in order to give them a favourable impression of his piety, and consequently of his justness, he had placed against the wall a delf crucifix, with a semi-circular receptacle at the bottom of it for holding holy water. This was as much as to say, 'how could I cheat you, with the image of our Blessed Redeemer before my eyes to remind me of my duty, and to teach me, as he did, to love my fellow-creatures?' And with many of the simple people, he actually succeeded in making the impression he wished; for they could not conceive it possible, that any principle, however rapacious, could drive a man to the practice of such sacrilegious imposture.

There stood Skinadre, like the very Genius of Famine, surrounded by distress, raggedness, feeble hunger, and tottering disease, in all the various aspects of pitiable suffering, hopeless desolation, and that agony of the heart which impresses wildness upon the pale check, makes the eye at once dull and eager, parches the mouth, and gives to the voice of misery tones that are hoarse and hollow. There he stood, striving to blend consolation with deceit, and, in the name of religion and charity, subjecting the helpless wretches to fraud and extortion. Around him was misery, multiplied into all her most appalling shapes. Fathers of families were there, who could read in each other's faces, too truly, the gloom and anguish that darkened the brow and wrung the heart. The strong man, who had been not long before a comfortable farmer, now stood dejected and apparently broken-down, shorn of his strength without a trace of either hope or spirit; so woefully shrunk away, too, from his superfluous apparel, that the spectators actually wondered to think that this was the large man, of such powerful frame, whose feats of strength had so often heretofore filled them with amazement. But, alas! what will not sickness and hunger do?

There, too, was the aged man – the grandsire himself – bent with a double weight of years and sorrow – without food until that late hour; forgetting the old pride that never stooped before, and now coming with the last feeble argument, to remind the usurer that he and his father had been school-fellows and friends, and that although he had refused to credit his son and afterwards his daughter-in-law, still, for the sake of old times, and of those who were now no more, he hoped he would not refuse to his grey hairs and tears, and for the sake of the living God besides, that which would keep life in his son and his daughter-in-law, and his famishing grandchildren, who had not a morsel to put in their mouths, nor the means of procuring it on earth – if *he* failed them.

And there was the widower, on behalf of his motherless children, coming with his worn and desolate look of sorrow, almost thankful to God that his Kathleen was not permitted to witness the many-shaped miseries of this woeful year; and yet experiencing the sharp and bitter reflection, that now, in all their trials – in his poor children's want and sickness – in their moanings by day and their cries for her by night, they have not the soft affection of her voice nor the tender touch of her hand to soothe their pain – nor has he that smile, which was ever his, to solace him now, nor that faithful heart to soothe him with its affection, or to cast its sweetness into the bitter cup of his affliction. Alas! no; he knows that that heart will beat for him and them no more; that that eye of love will never smile upon them again; and so he feels the agony of her loss superadded to all his other sufferings, and in this state he approaches the merciless usurer.

And the widow – emblem of desolation and dependence – how shall *she* meet and battle with the calamities of this fearful season? She out of whose heart these very calamities draw forth the remembrances of him she has lost, with such vividness that his past virtues are added to her present sufferings; and his manly love as a husband – his tenderness as a parent – his protecting hand and ever kind heart, crush her solitary spirit by their memory, and drag it down to the uttermost depths of affliction. Oh! bitter reflection! – 'if her Owen were now alive and in health, *she* would not be here; but God took him to himself, and now unless he – the miser – has compassion on her, she and her children – her Owen's children – must lie down and die! If it were not for *their* sakes, poor darlings, she would wish to follow *him* out of such a world; but now she and the Almighty are all that they have to look to, blessed be his name!'

Others there were whose presence showed how far the general destitution had gone into the heart of society, and visited many whose circumstances had been looked upon as beyond its reach. The decent farmer, for instance, whom no one had suspected of distress, made his appearance among them with an air of cheerfulness that was put on to baffle suspicion. Sometimes he laughed as if his heart were light, and again expressed a kind of condescending sympathy with some poor person or other, to whom he spoke kindly, as a man would do who knew nothing personally of the distress which he saw about him, but who wished to encourage those who *did* with the cheering hope that it must soon pass away. Then affecting the easy manner of one who was interesting himself for another person, he asked to have some private conversation with the usurer, to whom he communicated the immediate want that pressed upon himself and his family.

It is impossible, however, to describe the various aspects and claims of misery which presented themselves at Skinadre's house. The poor people flitted to and fro, silently and dejectedly, wasted, feeble, and sickly – sometimes in small groups of twos and threes, and sometimes a solitary individual might be seen hastening with earnest but languid speed, as if the life of some dear child or beloved parent, of a husband or wife, or perhaps the lives of a whole family, depended upon her or his arrival with food.

7

A Panorama of Misery

Skinadre, thin and mealy, with his coat off, but wearing a waistcoat to which were attached flannel sleeves, was busily engaged in the agreeable task of administering to their necessities. Such was his smoothness of manner, and the singular control which a long life of hypocrisy had given him over his feelings, that it was impossible to draw any correct distinction between that which he only assumed and that which he really felt. This consequently gave him an immense advantage over every one with whom he came in contact, especially the artless and candid, and all who were in the habit of expressing what they thought. We shall, however, take the liberty of introducing him to the reader, and allow honest Skinadre to speak for himself.

'They're beggars – thim three – that woman and her two childre; still my heart bleeds for them, bekase we should love our neighbours as ourselves; but I have given away as much meal in charity, an' me can so badly afford it, as would – I can't now, indeed, my poor woman! Sick – throth they look sick, an' you look sick yourself. Here, Paddy Lenaghan, help that poor woman and her two poor childre out of that half-bushel of meal you've got; you won't miss a handful for God's sake.'

This he said to a poor man who had just purchased some oatmeal from him; for Skinadre was one of those persons who, however he may have neglected works of mercy himself, took great delight in encouraging others to perform them.

'Troth it's not at your desire I do it, Darby,' replied the old man; 'but bekase she and they wants it, God help them. Here, poor creature, take this for the honour of God; and I'm only sorry, for both our sakes, that I can't do more.'

'Well, Jemmy Duggan,' proceeded the miser, addressing a new-comer, 'what's the news wid you? They're hard times, Jemmy; we all know that, an' feel it, too, and yet we live, most of us, as if there wasn't a God to punish us.'

'At all events,' replied the man, 'we feel what sufferin' is now, God help us! Between hunger and sickness, the counthry was never in sich a state widin the memory of man. What, in the name o' God, will become of the poor people I know not. The Lord pity them, an' relieve them!'

'Amen, amen, Jemmy! Well, Jemmy, can I do anything for you? But, Jemmy, in regard of that, the thruth is, we have brought all these scourges on us by our sins and our transgressions; thim that sins, Jemmy, must suffer.'

'There's no denyin' it, Darby; but you're axin' me can you do anything for me, and my answer to that is, that you can, if you like.'

'Ah! Jemmy, you wor ever an' always a wild, heedless, heerum-skeerum rake, that never was likely to do much good; little religion ever rested on you, an' now I'm afeard so sign's on it.'

'Well, well, who's widout sin? I'm sure I'm not. What I want is, to know if you'll credit me for a hundred of meal till the times mends a thrifle. I have the six o' them at home widout their dinner this day, and must go widout it if you refuse me. When the harvest comes round, I'll pay you.'

'Jemmy, you owe three half-years' rent; an' as for the harvest an' what it'll bring, only jist look at the day that's in it. It goes to my heart to refuse you, poor man; but, Jemmy, you see that you have brought this on yourself. If you had been an attentive, industrious man, and minded your religion, you wouldn't be as you are now. Six you have at home, you say?'

'Ay, not to speak of the woman an' myself. I know you won't refuse them, Darby, bekase if we're hard pushed now, it's a'most everybody's case as well as mine. Be what I may, you know I'm honest.'

'I don't doubt your honesty, Jemmy; but, Jemmy, if I sell my meal to a man that can pay and won't, or if I sell my meal to a man that would pay and can't, by which do I lose most? There it is, Jemmy – think o' that, now. Six in family, you say?'

'Six in family, wid the woman an' myself.'

'The sorra man livin' feels more for you than I do, an' I would let you have the meal if I could; but the truth is, I'm makin' up my rent – an', Jemmy, I lost so much last year by my own foolish good-nature, an' I gave away so much on trust, that now I'm brought to a hard pass myself. Throth I'll fret enough this night for havin' to refuse you. I know it was rash in me to make the promise I did; but still, God forbid that ever any man should be able to throw it in my face, and say that Darby Skinadre ever broke his promise.'

'What promise?'

'Why, never to sell a pound of meal on trust.'

'God help us, then! – for, what to do or where to go I don't know.'

'It goes to my heart, Jemmy, to refuse you – six in family, an' the two of yourselves. Throth it does, to my very heart itself; but stay, maybe we may manage it. You have no money, you say?'

'No money now, but won't be long so, plaise God.'

'Well, but hav'nt you value of any kind? – sure, God help them, they can't starve, poor creatures – the Lord pity them!'

Here he wiped away a drop of villainous rheum which ran down his cheek, and he did it with such an appearance of sympathy, that almost any one would have imagined it was a tear of compassion for the distresses of the poor man's family.

'Oh! no, they can't starve. Have you no value of any kind, Jemmy? – ne'er a beast now, or anything that way?'

'Why, there's a young heifer; but I'm strugglin' to keep it to help me in the rent. I was obliged to sell my pig long ago, for I had no way of feedin' it.'

'Well, bring me the heifer, Jemmy, an' I won't let the crathurs starve. We'll see what can be done when it comes here. An' now, Jemmy, let me ax you if you wint to hear mass last Sunday?'

'Troth I did'nt like to go in this trim. Peggy has a web of frieze half made this good while; it'll be finished some time, I hope.'

'Ah! Jemmy, Jemmy, it's no wondher the world's the way it is, for indeed there's little thought of God or religion in it. You passed last Sunday like a haythen, an' now see how you stand to-day for the same.'

'You'll let me bring some o' the meal home wid me now,' said the man; 'the poor cratures tasted hardly anything to-day yet, an' they wor cryin' whin I left home. I'll come back wid the heifer *full but*. Troth they're in outher misery, Darby.'

'Poor things! – an' no wondher, wid such a haythen of a father; but, Jemmy, bring the heifer here *first*, till I look at it; an' the sooner you bring it here the sooner they'll have relief, the crathurs.'

It is not our intention to follow up this iniquitous bargain any farther; it is enough to say that the heifer passed from Jemmy's possession into his, at about the fourth part of its value.

To those who had money he was a perfect honeycomb, overflowing with kindness and affection, expressed in such a profusion of warm and sugary words, that it was next to an impossibility to doubt his sincerity.

'Darby,' said a very young female, on whose face was blended equal beauty and sorrow, joined to an expression that was absolutely deathlike, 'I suppose *I* needn't ax you for credit?'

He shook his head.

'It's for the ould couple,' she added, 'an' not for myself. I wouldn't ax it for myself. I know my fault an' my sin, an' may God forgive myself in the first place, an' him that brought me to it, an' to the shame that followed it! But what would the ould couple do now widout me?'

'An' have you no money? Ah, Margaret Murtagh! sinful creature – shame, shame, Margaret. Unfortunate girl that you are, have you no money?'

'I have not, indeed; the death of my brother Alick left us as we are; *he's* gone from them now; but there was no fear of *me* goin' that *wished* to go. Oh, if God in his goodness to them had took me an' spared him, they wouldn't be sendin' to you this day for meal to keep life in them till things comes round.'

'Troth I pity them – from my heart I pity them, now that they're helpless an' ould –

especially for havin' sich a daughter as you are; but if it was my own father an' mother, God rest them, I couldn't give meal out on credit. There's not in the parish a poorer man than I am. I'm done wid givin' credit now, thank goodness; an' if I had been so long ago, it isn't robbed, an' ruined, an' beggared by rogues I'd be this day, but a warm, full man, able an' willin' too, to help my neighbours; an' it is not empty-handed I'd send away any messenger from your father or mother, as I must do, although my heart bleeds for them this minute.'

Here once more he wiped away the rheum, with every appearance of regret and sorrow. In fact, one would almost suppose that by long practice he had trained one of his eyes – for we ought to have said that there was one of them more sympathetic than the other – to shed its hypocritical tear at the right place, and in such a manner, too, that he might claim all the credit of participating in the very distresses which he refused to relieve, or by which he amassed his wealth.

The poor heart-broken looking girl, who by the way carried an unfortunate baby in her arms, literally tottered out of the room, sobbing bitterly, and with a look of misery and despair that it was woeful to contemplate.

'Ah, then, Harry Hacket,' said he, passing to another, 'how are you? an' how are you all over in Derrycloony, Harry? not forgettin' the ould couple?'

'Troth middlin' only, Darby. My fine boy, Dennis, is down wid this illness, an' I'm wantin' a barrel of meal from you till towards Christmas.'

'Come inside, Harry, to this little nest here, till I tell you something; an', by the way, let your father know I've got a new prayer that he'll like to larn, for it's he that's the pious man, an' attinds to his duties – may God enable him! an' every one that has the devotion in the right place; *amin a Chiernah!*'

He then brought Hacket into a little outshot behind the room in which the scales were, and, shutting the door, thus proceeded in a sweet, confidential kind of whisper –

'You see, Harry, what I'm goin' to say to you is what I'd not say to ever another in the parish, the divil a one – God pardon me for swearin' – *amin a Chiernah!* I'm ruined all out – smashed down, an' broke horse an' foot; there's the Slevins that wint to America, an' I lost more than thirty pounds by them.'

'I thought,' replied Hacket, 'they paid you before they went; they were always a daicent an' an honest family, an' I niver heard any one spake an ill word o' them.'

'Not a penny, Harry.'

'That's odd, then, bekase it was only Sunday three weeks that Murty Slevin, their cousin, if you rimimber, made you acknowledge that they paid you, at the chapel green.'

'Ay, an' I do acknowledge; bekase, Harry, one may as well spake charitably of the absent as not; it's only in private to you that I'm lettin' out the truth.'

'Well, well,' exclaimed the other, rather impatiently, 'what have they to do wid us?'

'Ay have they; it was what I lost by them an' others – see now don't be gettin' onpatient, I bid you – time enough for that when you're refused – that prevints me from bein' able to give credit as I'd wish. I'm not refusin' *you,* Harry; but achora, listen: you'll bring me your bill at two months, only I must charge you a thrifle for trust, for chances, or profit an' loss, as the schoolmaster says; but you're to keep it a saicret from livin' mortual, bekase if it 'ud get known in these times that I'd do sich a thing, I'd have the very flesh ait off o' my bones by others wantin' the same thing; bring me the bill, then, Harry, an' I'll fill it up myself, only *be dhe husth** about it.'

Necessity forces those who are distressed to comply with many a rapacious condition of the kind; and the consequence was that Hacket did what the pressure of the time compelled him to do, passed his bill to Skinadre at a most usurious price, for the food which was so necessary to his family.

It is surprising how closely the low rustic extortioner and the city usurer upon a larger scale resemble each other in the expression of their sentiments – in their habits of business – their plausibility – natural tact – and especially, in that hardness of heart and utter want of all human pity and sympathy, upon which the success of their black arts of usury and extortion essentially depends. With extortion in all its forms, Skinadre, for instance, was familiar. From those who were poor but honest he got a bill such as he exacted from Hacket, because he knew that, cost what it might to them, he was safe in their integrity. If dishonest, he still got a bill and relied upon the law and its cruel list of harassing and fraudulent expenses for security. From others he got property of all descriptions: from some, butter, yarn, a piece of frieze, a pig, a cow, or a heifer. In fact, nothing that possessed value came wrong to him, so that it is impossible to describe adequately the web of mischief which this blood-sucking old spider contrived to spread around him, especially for those whom he knew to be *too poor* to avail themselves of a remedy against his villainy.

'Molly Cassidy, how are you?' he said, addressing a poor-looking woman, who carried a parcel of some description rolled up under her cloak; 'how are all the family, achora?'

'Glory be to God for it, they can scarcely be worse,' replied the woman, in that spirit of simple piety and veneration for the Deity, which in all their misery characterizes the Irish people; 'but sure we're only sufferin' like others, an' indeed not so bad as many – there's Mick Kelly has lost his fine boy, Lanty; an' his other son, young Mick, isn't expected – an' all wid this sickness, that was brought on them, as it is everywhere, wid bad feedin'.'

'They're miserable times, Molly – at laist I find them so – for I dunna how it happens, but every one's disappointment falls upon me, till they have me a'most out of house an' home – troth it 'ud be no wondher I'd get hard-hearted some day, wid the way I'm thrated an' robbed by every one – ay, indeed – bekase I'm good-nathured, they play upon me.'

The poor creature gave a faint smile, for she knew the man's character thoroughly.

'I have a dish of butther here, Darby,' she said, 'an' I want meal instead of it.'

'Butther, Molly – why thin, Molly, sure it isn't to me you're bringin' butther – me that has so much of it lyin' on my hands here already. Sure, any way, it's down to dirt since the wars is over – butther is – if it was anything else but butther, Molly; but it's of no use – I've too much of it.'

* Hold your tongue.

'The sorra other thing I have, then, Mr Skinadre; but sure you'd betther look at it, an' you'll find it's what butther ought to be – firm, clane, an' sweet.'

'I can't take it, achora; there's no market for it now.'

'Here, as we're distressed, take it for sixpence a pound, and that's the lowest price – God knows if we worn't as we are, it isn't for that you'd get it.'

'Troth, I dar' say you're ill off – as who isn't in these times? – an' it's worse they're gettin' an' will be gettin' every day – throth, I say, my heart bleeds for you – but we can't dale – oh, no! – butther, as I said, is only dirt now.'

'For God's sake, then,' exclaimed the alarmed creature, 'take it for whatever you like.'

'It 'ud go hard wid me to see your poor family in a state of outher want,' he replied, 'an' it's not in my nature to be harsh to a strugglin' person – so whether I lose or gain, I'll allow you threepence a pound for it.'

A shade of bitterness came across her features at this iniquitous proposal; but she felt the truth of that old adage, in all its severity, that necessity has no law.

'God help us,' she exclaimed, 'threepence a pound for sich butther as this! – however, it's the will o' God, sure, an' it can't be helped – take it.'

'Ay, it's aisy said, take it; but not so aisy to say what 'ill I do wid it, when I have it; however, that's the man I am, an' I know how it'ill end wid me – sarvin' every one, workin' for every one, an' thinkin' of every one but myself, an' little thanks or gratitude for all – I know I'm not fit for sich a world – but still it's a consolation to be doin' good to our fellow-cratures when we can; an' that's what lightens my heart.'

A woman now entered, whose appearance excited general sympathy, as was evident from the subdued murmurs of compassion which were breathed from the persons assembled, as soon as she entered the room. There was something about her, which, in spite of her thin and worn dress, intimated a consciousness of a position, either then or at some previous time, above that of the common description of farmers' wives. No one could mistake her for a highly-educated woman, but there was in her appearance that decency of manner resulting from habits of independence and from moral feeling, which at a first glance, whether it be accompanied by superior dress or not, indicates something which is felt to entitle its proprietor to unquestionable respect. The miser, when she entered, had been putting away the dish of butter into the outshot we have mentioned, so that he had not yet an opportunity of seeing her, and ere he returned to the scales, another female possessing probably not less interest to the reader, presented herself – this was Mave or Mabel, the young and beautiful daughter of the pious and hospitable Jerry Sullivan.

Skinadre, on perceiving the matron who preceded her, paused for a moment, and looked at her with a wince in his thin features which might be taken for an indication of either pleasure or pain. He closed the sympathetic eye, and wiped it; but this not seeming to satisfy him, he then closed both, and blew his nose with a little skeleton mealy handkerchief, that lay on a sack beside him for the purpose.

'Hem – a-hem! why thin, Mrs Dalton, it isn't to my poor place I expected *you* would come.'

'Darby,' she replied, 'there is no use for any length of conversation between you and me – I'm here contrary to the wishes of my family – but I'm a mother, an' cannot look upon their destitution without feelin' that I shouldn't allow my pride to stand between them and death – we are starving, I mean – *they* are – and I'm come to you to ask for credit – if we are ever able to pay you, we will; if not, it's only one good act done to a family that often did many to you when they thought you grateful.'

'I'm the worst in the world – I'm the worst in the world,' replied Skinadre; 'but it wasn't till I knew that you'd be put out o' your farm that I offered for it, and now you've taken away my correcther, and spoke ill o' me everywhere, an' said I bid for it over your heads – ay, indeed; an' that it was your husband that set me up, by the way – oh, yes – an' supposin' it was – an' I'm not denyin' it – but is that any raison that I'd not bid for a good farm, when I knew that yez 'ud be put out of it?'

'I am now spakin' about the distress of our family,' said Mrs Dalton; 'you know that sickness has been among us, an' is among us – poor Tom is just able to be up, but that's all!'

'Troth an' it 'ud be well for you all, an' for himself, too, that he had been taken away afore he comes to a bad end, what he *will* come to, if God hasn't said it – I hope he feels the affliction he brought on poor Ned Murtagh and his family by the hand he made of his unfortunate daughter.'

'He does feel it. The death of her brother and their situation has touched his heart, and he's only waitin' for better health and better times to do her justice; but now, what answer do you give me?'

'Why this: I'm harrished by what I've done for every one – an' – an' the short and the long of it is, that I've neither male nor money to throw away. I couldn't afford it, and I can't. I'm a rogue, Mrs Dalton – a miser, an extortioner, an ungrateful knave, an' everything that's bad an' worse than another – an' for that raison, I say, I have neither male nor money to throw away. That's what I'd say if I was angry; but I'm *not* angry. I do feel for you an' them; still, I can't afford to do what you want, or I'd do it, for I like to do good for evil, bad as I am. I'm strivin' to make up my rent, an' to pay an unlucky bill that I have due to-morrow, and doesn't know where the money's to come from to meet both.

'Mave Sullivan, achora, what can I—'

Mrs Dalton, from her position in the room, could not have noticed the presence of Mave Sullivan, but even had she been placed otherwise, it would have been somewhat difficult to get a glimpse at the young creature's face. Deeply did she participate in the sympathy which was felt for the mother of her lover, and so naturally delicate were her feelings, that she had drawn up the hood of her cloak, lest the other might have felt the humiliation to which Mave's presence must have exposed her by the acknowledgement of their distress. Neither was this all the gentle and generous girl had to suffer. She experienced, in her own person, as well as Mrs Dalton did, the painful sense of degradation which necessity occasions, by a violation of that hereditary spirit of decent pride and independence which the people consider as the *prestige* of high respect, and which, even whilst it excites compassion and sympathy, is looked upon, to a certain extent, as diminished by even a temporary visitation of poverty. When the mealman, therefore addressed her, she unconsciously threw the hood of her cloak back, and disclosed to the spectators a face burning with blushes, and eyes filled with tears. The tears, however, were for the distress of Mrs Dalton and her family, and the blushes for the painful circumstances which compelled her at once to witness them, and to expose those which were felt under her own care-worn father's roof. Mrs Dalton, however, on looking round and perceiving what seemed to be an ebullition merely of natural shame, went over to her with a calm but mournful manner, that amounted almost to dignity.

'Dear Mave,' said she, 'there is nothing here to be ashamed of. God forbid that the struggle of an honest family with poverty should bring a blot upon either your good name or mine. It does not, nor it will not – so dry your tears, my darlin' girl – there are better times before us all, I trust. Darby Skinadre,' she added, turning to the miser, 'you are both hard-hearted and ungrateful, or you would remember, in our distress, the kindness we showed you and yours. If you can cleanse your conscience from the stain of ingratitude, it must be by a change of life.'

'Whatever stain may be on my ungrateful conscience,' he replied, turning up his red eyes, as it were with thanksgiving, 'there's not the stain of blood and murdher on it – that's one comfort.'

Mrs Dalton did not seem to hear him, neither did she look in the direction of where he stood. As the words were uttered, she had been in the act of extending her hand to Mave Sullivan, who had hers stretched out to receive it. There now occurred, however, a mutual pause. Her hand was withdrawn, as was that of Mave also, who had suddenly become pale as death.

'God bless you, my darlin' girl!' exclaimed Mrs Dalton, sighing, as if with some hidden sorrow – 'God bless you and yours, prays my unhappy heart this day!'

And with these words she was about to depart, when Mave, trembling and much agitated, laid her hand gently and timidly upon hers – adding, in a low, sweet, and tremulous voice –

'*My* heart is free from *that* suspicion – I can't tell why – but *I* don't believe it.'

And while she spoke, her small hand gradually caught that of Mrs Dalton, as a proof that she would not withhold the embrace on that account. Mrs Dalton returned her pressure, and at the same moment kissed the fair girl's lips, who sobbed a moment or two in her arms, where she threw herself. The other again invoked a blessing upon her head, and walked out, having wiped a few tears from her pale cheeks.

The miser looked upon this exhibition of feeling with some surprise; but as his was not a heart susceptible of the impressions it was calculated to produce, he only said, in a tone of indifference –

'Well, to be sure now, Mave, I didn't expect to see *you* shakin' hands wid and kissin' Condy Dalton's wife, at any rate – considherin' *all* that happened atween the families. However, it's good to be forgivin' – I hope it is – indeed, I know that; for it comes almost to a failin' in myself. Well, *achora*, what am I to do for *you?*'

'Will you let me speak to you inside, a minute?' she asked.

'Will I? Why, then, to be sure I will – an' who knows but it's my daughter-in-law I might have you yet, *avillish!* Yourself and Darby's jist about an age. Come inside, *ahagur.*'

Their dialogue was not of very long duration. Skinadre, on returning to the scales, weighed two equal portions of oatmeal, for one of which Mave paid him.

'I will either come or send for this,' she said, laying her hand upon the one for which she *had* paid. 'If I send any one, I'll give the token I mentioned.'

'Very well, *a-suchar* – very well,' he replied, 'it's for nobody livin' but yourself I'd do it; but sure now that I must begin to coort you for Darby, it won't be aisy to refuse you anything in raison.'

'Mind, then,' she observed, as she seized one of the portions, in order to proceed home – 'mind,' said she, laying her hand upon that which she was leaving behind her – 'mind it's for *this one* I have paid you.'

'Very well, achora – it makes no differ; sure a kiss o' them red, purty lips o' yours to Darby will pay the intherest for all.'

JOHN BANIM

from *The Croppy*

31

It was after the hour of noon, of a sultry summer day, that the first formidable insurgent throng of the County of Wexford, still preceded by their advance of horned cattle, set forward, shouting until, as Pistol would say, 'the welkin rang', to attack the town of Enniscorthy. They were followed, in numbers nearly equal to their own, by the clamorous women and children, many bearing the pikes of father, of husband, of brother, or of some other relative, to be handed to the insurgent soldier after he had expended his fire-arm ammunition, or even after his first musket-shot, if chance led him to close action: it was regularly stipulated that the weapon-bearer should always be at hand, prepared to effect the necessary change of arms.

At four o'clock, the town was in possession of the insurgents. Its garrison, of about three hundred men, gallantly defended themselves for more than three hours against the furious but irregular attacks of their untutored assailants.

The greater portion of Enniscorthy, or at least the more important portion, lies in a hollow: its thatched suburbs run up ascents that at every side inclose it. These had been fired by the destroying assaulters, while they contended for entrance into the better quarter of the town. They at last possessed themselves of that quarter; and we now speak of the ensuing half-hour, during which the majority of the shrieking inhabitants – the young, the old, – the wealthy, the needy – beauty and deformity, flew pell-mell, with the retreating garrison, through scorching flames, along the scarce less scorching and dusty road, to the capital of the county, the important town of Wexford. Hundreds of burning dwellings sent masses of fire to surcharge the already sultry atmosphere. Until, in the lower streets of Enniscorthy, overhung by clouds of smoke, and strewed with hot ashes, respiration became painful, and exertion difficult. And through dense vapour and glowing air, pealed the triumphant and deafening shouts of the ferocious visitors, as, trampling indifferently the heaped bodies of comrades and foes, they rushed on to plunder the abandoned houses, and to pour into their parched throats whatever liquor they could seize upon. Some wastefully and wantonly destroying property that they could not appropriate; others loading their attendant women with portable articles of value; others giving cause for the unheeded cry of supplication, distinctly heard amid the whoop of rude triumph, while they dragged trembling wretches from places of concealment, to be piked in the streets, already too deeply stained with blood.

All was shout, shriek, and clamour below; while overhead roared the ravenous flames, when Sir William Judkin, not an undistinguished leader in that day's battle, stood before the entrance-gate of the Castle of Enniscorthy.

Through every dungeon slit and window were presented the anxious faces of the prisoners, who, abandoned by their guards and turnkeys – Saunders Smyly amongst the foremost – yet had been left too well locked and bolted in to allow of their emancipating themselves from durance. Sir William scanned over with straining eye the countenances that appeared. At length his glance fixed ominously upon one.

'Two blows more, and it yields,' he cried to Shawn-a-Gow, who, wielding a great sledge, battered at the ponderous door; – 'quick! quick! I see him.'

The two prescribed blows followed, and door and lock and bolt gave way in shivers. There was a wild shout within, then a rush of the enfranchised captives, some hastening to enrol themselves, in revenge against their enemies, amongst the victorious insurgents; others to indulge in the general licentiousness. The pale-faced wretch upon whom Sir William had bent his baleful glance, came forward. On the threshold he started back, and, hastily pulling his hat over his brows, sought to mingle unobserved with the general throng. But the watchful eye of the Baronet instantly marked him out: as instantly the grasp of his former master was on his collar. The terrified man seemed confounded into nonentity.

'This is the fellow – this is Brown,' said Sir William, addressing Shawn-a-Gow – 'this is the Orange-traitor and informer!'

'Pitch him to us!' growled the stern smith.

'Oh, master, master! only listen to me!' gasped the victim, vainly endeavouring to sink upon his knees. But the strong arm of his indignant master upheld him. Then, swinging him round, he flung him towards Shawn-a-Gow, and he was dead ere he fell to the ground – four pikes had entered his shrinking body.

'Could iron is informer's hire,' remarked the father of Tom Delouchery, as he withdrew his reeking weapon. And he and his fellow-executioners hastily departed to rejoin the unbridled rioting, of which the fierce shouts reached them from every quarter, and which they had only left in obedience to the requests of so important a leader as the young Baronet.

'This done,' soliloquized Sir William, as, left alone with the body of his former servant, he wiped his brow from the stains of moisture, of dust, and of blood, – 'this done – this villain punished – I must now speed to seek my wife.'

His horse stood near. Actively and hastily mounting, he made his way, with as much speed as the intervening throngs would allow, to an inn at which he had heard Eliza Hartley and her aunt had put up on the previous night. Here additional excitement to his already exasperated mood awaited him. The inn had been invaded by an unbridled crowd of riotous insurgents. As he heard them shouting forth their clamours and threats for liquor, heavily clattering from room to room, and banging doors and breaking windows, obviously to exercise their newly acquired privilege of doing what they liked in a situation they had once never dreamt of attaining, the alarmed husband naturally shuddered at the idea, that his sensitive and unprotected bride might already have been exposed to the mercy of such boisterous intruders.

He flung himself from his jaded horse, burst through the rabble rout, and was very near experiencing a rough acceptance, only that he chanced to be recognized by one of their noisy set. He called loudly for the landlord, but was quickly answered that 'the murtherin' Orangeman took to the run, just in time to miss a reckonin' long scored against him, one that he would think worse of than the most robbin' reckonin' himself ever once scored against a lodger.' – From which Sir William inferred, that the conscious proprietor, being of the opposite party, had, along with almost all the other Protestant inhabitants of the town, joined or followed the garrison on their retreat to Wexford.

Thus, without a clue to guide him in his search after his bride, the young Baronet rushed from room to room, vainly calling upon her name. In a principal bed-room, after exploring many others, he found a group of 'pikemen', loud in ribald mirth, as they pressed forward and gaped over each other's shoulders, to view something held by the leader of their pillaging. Bursting on, Sir William snatched at his own miniature, the glass of which the man just then held up to view, brightening, or rather dimming it, with the sleeve of his rough frieze coat, as he cried out –

'By gonnies! an' sure my fort'n is made, for good-an'-all. I'll turn mysef into a gallanty showman – A penny apiece to see the raree-show, boys! – a penny apiece! –' He drew back his hand as Sir William endeavoured to seize the miniature with – 'Masther, asy, asy: every man's loock is his fort'n. D'you want to see the show for nothin', Sir?'

'That picture is mine, my good fellow; – give it me – give it –'

'Make that out, if you can. Didn't I find it here, afore it was lost?'

'Come, come!' flinging him money – 'give it now.'

'Here, then, faith, an' I wish you joy o' your bargain. By the pike in my hand, I wouldn't swap the half o' this for a score of 'em. As you're in the humour,' he continued, winking on his companions, 'who knows bud you'd buy another or two that fell in my way? Here's a glove wouldn't go on my thumb; an' here's a ring I'd give my sweetheart, only it's about a mile an' a half too narrow for Peg's little finger. Will you offer?'

'Double their value!' answered Sir William, his hand trembling with eagerness and dread as he recognized his bride's right-hand glove, and the wedding-ring he had, the previous morning put on her finger.

'Tare-an'-age!' resumed the collector of curiosities, 'maybe this, too, 'ud lie in your way? You can have it chape.' Exhibiting a child's rattle he had somewhere picked up.

A loud laugh at his waggery was interrupted by a sudden and expressive shout in the street, which caused all the men to stop and listen, and then seriously to question each other as to its cause.

'The Orangemen cum back again, I'll hould a groat!' said one. 'To see the fun' was resolved on, and forth they issued, shouting in answer to the challenge without.

The man from whom Sir William had got the miniature glove, and ring, was one of the last to leave the room. The Baronet seized him by the arm.

'See, now! Sure, I knew I'd put the temptation in you,' said the fellow, grinning broadly as he again held out the rattle.

'Where did you find the other things?' demanded Sir William.

'D' ye see the bed there?'

'The bed!'

'Yes – there I found 'em.'

Sir William stared for a time, seemingly unconscious of his situation, while his eyes rested on the bed. Suddenly he turned round his head to ask another question of his informant: the man was gone, and he remained alone in the chamber, or seemingly alone, as it proved to be. A rustling noise reached him from a press at one side. He sprang to the spot in all the eagerness of hope, and pulled open the folding-doors. A woman appeared within it, but not his wife. He seized her, and forced her from her concealment.

'Who are you? Do you belong to the house?'

'I'm only a poor innocent sarvant girl, Sir, that has no more harum in me nor the time I was born, Sir. I was only hiden from the Croppies, Sir.'

'Do you belong to the house?'

'I'm an honest father's an' mother's child, Sir, an' I'm an honest poor crather myself. I can show my charakther to you, Sir, undher the hand o' Misthress Malone, that sells the soap an' candles in Market-sthreet, an' there's one Misthress Maguire, that – '

'Answer my question! – Are you a servant of this house?'

'I was only follyin the childher, Sir, an' doin' a hand's turn, over-an'-hither.'

'Can you tell me who last occupied this sleeping-chamber?'

'It was a dauther of Sir Thomas Hartley, Sir. As purty a sowl as ever my two livin' eyes opened on. An' an ould lady wid her.'

'Do you know what has become of these ladies? When did you see them last?'

'Why, then, I'll tell you, Sir, an' nothin' bud the truth, all the same as if I was on my dyin' bed, an' they the last words I'd ever spake; or all the same as if a big Croppy had his pike to my breast this moment. Yestherday, Sir, it might be about one o'clock in the day, or maybe arlier, or maybe later, I won't be all out sartin, bud 'twas nigh hand from one, one way or th' other, becase – '

'Never mind the time! Be brief – quick, quick!'

'Well, then, Sir, out o' their carriage I seen them comin' yestherday at the dour. It wasn't long afther till I seen 'em get into it again, an' it dhruv off. I'm tould they went to beg an' pray for the life o' Sir Thomas, that was hanged last night, by candle-light, for bein' a Croppy. The carriage was away for an hour or more, when it came back to us again; an' the ladies got out at the dour a second time, Sir, houldin' down their heads as they went up-stairs. Then we soon hard a ring from their room. 'Here, Jinny,' says the misthress, spakin to me, Sir, 'pull your cap sthraight over your eyes, throw off the *prauskeen*,* rub your face in a great hurry, an' lave the child to me, an' run up to see what's wantin'.' 'Here, my honey,' says I, spakin' to the child, 'go to the mammy,' an' he set up the squall, Sir, bud – '

---

* Coarse apron.

'Silly creature! leave out this wretched stuff, and tell me of Miss Hartley.'

'I will, Sir. – I didn't think it was any hurt or harum, Sir –'

'Well, go on.'

'Yes, Sir. The rason it cum for me to go up, Sir, was becase the house was to and fro. The waither, Jack Sherry, gone to larn the news about the Croppies, an' the poor masther forced to be out sodgerin – So, Sir, in I came, an' I made my curtshy to the poor ladies. There was the nice, purty young crathur lyin' on the bed, an' her hands wringin' this way, an' the nice rosy colour gone from her cheeks, an' her lips as white as the cambric muslin, an' she moanin' an' sighin' so pitiful, Sir.'

Sir William Judkin here startled the narrator, breaking away from her, and rushing about the chamber like a maniac. After a pause, during which she eyed him in some misgiving, he commanded her to continue.

'I will, Sir. – "Would you be wantin' any thing at all, my ladies," says I, makin' my curtshy – "A glass of water, quick, good girl," says she, makin' answer. Down I went, an' brought it up, fresh an' sweet. The ould lady gave it to Miss Hartley, an' I went my ways, an' it didn't fall in my way to see 'em again. Bud, this mornin' as I hard, about seven o'clock, Sir, Capt'n Talbot ordhered the carriage to the dour.'

'Who?'

'Capt'n Talbot, Sir, indeed-an'-deed, Sir,' answered the girl, much terrified at the sudden start of her catechist. 'Sure we all thought the sight 'ud lave our eyes to see him, that people say, hanged her father wid his own hand, havin' any call to Miss Hartley, or to her comin' or goin', about her at all.'

'Had he previously gained admission to the ladies?'

'Why, then, I don't know, full out sart'n, Sir. Bud last night, as I was goin' up-stairs, in the dark, to look afther the child, an' he wakenin' in a great roar, Sir, at the same time, sorrow's in me, but I thought I saw Capt'n Talbot skulkin' by the side o' the dour, outside o' this room, Sir. Only I won't take it on me to say so, of a downright sartinty.'

'Hell and furies!'

'Oh, Sir, 'twas none o' my fault. I'm a poor crather of a girl, wid good carakthers –'

'And it was in his carriage that Miss Hartley left the inn?'

'Yes, Sir. An' he put up the step wid his own hands.'

'Who told you this?'

'Murtoch Kane, the stable-boy, Sir. An' sure, I b'lieve it's Murtoch got the horses ready.'

'Where is he to be found?'

'Below in the yard, Sir, he ought to be, if he hasn't left his work to join wid the Croppies.'

Sir William was hurrying away to seek the person named, when the terrified girl besought him to stop an instant, and just tell her if the Croppies wouldn't kill her. Having received a hasty assurance of safety, she offered to accompany him to the stable-yard.

It generally occurs, that when we are least in the vein to encounter thwarting circumstances, they rapidly present themselves to us. In his half-frenzied search after information, Sir William Judkin was again doomed to meet an interruption, which in his calmest mood would have irritated him.

Murtoch Kane was one of those vagabonds, to be met with about every inn, who, without any ostensible calling, are extremely ingenious in taxing travellers' purses for the performance of various petty services, always unsought, and most frequently unnecessary. It is needless to add that such characters seldom lay claim to morals or religion, and often excel in the indulgence of every grovelling vice and propensity. We would not pause, at this stage of our story, to characterize even slightly the individual in question, but that, added to the traits common to all his tribe, Murtoch Kane's name is still remembered in Enniscorthy as the principal executioner of insurgent vengeance, as the actual perpetrator of the greater number of cold-blooded murders, on the rocky hill which rises above the town, committed during fair-fighting elsewhere.

He was a ragged fellow, about twenty-six years of age, with a countenance of which the inherent malignity was disguised beneath a show of low humour, or rather of affected carelessness. As Sir William advanced towards the stable to seek him, he came staggering forward, evidently intoxicated, a faded green ribbon tied round his battered hat, a cockade at one side, and a pike in his hand.

The 'poor girl wid the good carakthers' pointed him out to Sir William as the object of his search, and the young Baronet accordingly accosted him as he staggered by.

'Stop, my man – a question.'

'For the Green or the Orange?' demanded Murtoch Kane.

'For the Green, and the Green for ever!'

'Hurrah, then! an' it's well you said it. This 'ud be through your backbone if you said any thing else. Mind what I tell you. I'd shake paws wid a mad-dog, bud the pike, the pike for the Orangeman! – Ay, an' they'll get it, right an' left, day an' night. Their pay-day is come, and who'd refuse 'em their long reckonin'?'

'Hearken! you helped to procure horses for Sir Thomas Hartley's daughter to leave Enniscorthy, last night?'

'Ay, they hanged him up by candle-light,' mistaking the question, 'an' the Orange murtherer that done the job, he tuck off the poor daughther. Oh!' he uttered a bellow, 'I'd give a gallon o' whiskey to lay one hand on that *skibbeah*,* Talbot.'

'If you dislike him so much, why did you assist him to carry away Miss Hartley?'

'Why did I? Who are you that's axin?'

'You saw the young lady enter the carriage?' questioned Sir William evasively; bent upon extracting information quietly from the intoxicated and unmanagable Murtoch.

'To be sure I did! What have you to say agin Sir Thomas's daughther?'

'Nothing. I am her friend, and, if possible, would rescue her from Talbot.'

'Oh, the decaivin Orange thief! Sure, I didn't know a word it was he was to go off by her side, until afther they tuck to the road. Then I overhard his crony, the black Orangeman that bribed me to stale out the horses, sayin' to another, as much as that it was all Talbot's job. Oh, murther!' he bellowed again.

'You can tell which road they went?'

'To be sure I can, if I like it. Oh! why didn't he just wait till the boys come in this mornin'!'

* Executioner.

'The road to Wexford, you say?' asked Sir William, at a venture.

'Yes, the road to Waxford town. What's that to you?'

'You are certain?' giving money.

'Sart'n, your grandaddy!' doggedly clutching the bribe; 'do you take me for a fool? Who says it wasn't to Waxford? Here's Murtoch Kane, that'll pike a score of Orangemen every day the sun gets up, an' who dares say it to him? Whoo!'

'Certainly not I, since you *are* so sure of the road Talbot took with Miss Hartley.'

'Sure! I wish I was as sure o' meetin' him, the Orange hangman, at the next turn o' the next sthreet. Hurrah for the bould Croppy boys! hurrah!' and he staggered off, yelling out –

> 'Rise up, my poor Croppies, you're long enough down,
> An' we'll pike all these Orangemen out o' the town,
> > Down, down, Orange, lie down!'

During this dialogue, it was with difficulty Sir William could keep in the boiling ferment of his blood, or bring his trembling lips to articulate the necessary questions. At length it seemed indeed certain that his bride was in the power of his detested rival. Nothing but an instinctive consciousness of the necessity of arming himself with information for the pursuit, had momentarily checked his turbulent fury. Now, he did not hesitate an instant in taking the only measures – though insanity itself might have hesitated in taking them – which his wild passions suggested. He sought his horse. The poor tired animal had found his unassisted way to a stable, and was eagerly snatching a mouthful of food. He dragged it from this needful indulgence, mounted, and again forcing his way through the rushing crowds of insurgents, and over the trampled bodies of slain, and through the yet flaming suburb, galloped towards Wexford.

But ere he had quite cleared the crowded streets of Enniscorthy, he became confusedly aware, from the explanatory clamour on every side, of the meaning of the continued shout which had attracted the notice and roused the curiosity of the first persons he had encountered at the inn. It was the expression of an agreement, on the part of the greater body of the victors, to evacuate the town, and take up their position on the rocky eminence above it, subsequently distinguished as the scene of Murtoch Kane's massacres, aided by other insurgents, who remaining there, either in cowardice, or for the satiation of highly excited revenge, perpetrated cruelties for which the mass of the peasant-army were not accountable. The reason urged by the leaders to the licentious mob for thus abandoning the conquered town were strong. Namely, the danger that a greater force than they had yet encountered might march upon Enniscorthy, and surprise them in the midst of their riot and disorder. Yet (Sir William, absorbed as he was by a private question, could not fail to notice the fact,) it proved no easy matter to induce the victors to give up their conquest, and the remaining spoils of their victory. And though at length the greater number yielded to the threats, the prayers, and the actual coercion of their nominal leaders, a sufficient body, acknowledging no command, remained behind to continue during the night the excesses begun in the heat of triumph.

The Baronet still pressed on his weary steed along the road to Wexford. We repeat, that even a madman might have shrunk from the course he was pursuing. Alone he approached a town in possession of the King's troops, and where a hundred eyes were ready to recognize him at a glance, as the rebel commander, Sir William Judkin. Yet it may be questioned if he once weighed, or even thought of the risk he ran. One purpose mastered and filled his mind: one passion possessed him. To encounter Talbot, even if he could not meet his wife, to force from him an account of her situation, and then to strike him dead at his feet. This was all that the despairing lover, husband, and rival, now lived for. Could he but once work his vengeance, the thought of instant destruction to himself after it, only called up a grim smile upon the features of Sir William.

Within three miles of his destined goal, his horse sank exhausted. Revengefully spurning the gasping beast, he bounded on a-foot.

The town wall of Wexford was standing in full preservation, so that none could gain ingress save through the archways, in which massive gates once stood, and which, at his approach, the panic-struck garrison were hastily barricading and blocking up. At the gate he was instantly recognized and apprehended. The large pistol he had seized the night before was still in his breast: he prepared to use it, – it was wrested from him, and his life had been forfeited on the spot, but that the identical yeoman-Captain he came to seek interfered to save him. Sir William struggled hard to leave the grasp of his captors and spring upon his rival. But Talbot coolly ordered him to be conveyed by main force to the prison of the town. Notwithstanding his continued resistance, in which he evinced the strength as well as the rage of a foaming madman, half-a-dozen of athletic yeomen dragged him through the streets. With brain on fire, and the blood boiling like melted ore through his veins, he was once more a captive, better secured than even in his last dungeon, under lock, bolt, bar, and a succession of formidable doors.

GERALD GRIFFIN

from *The Collegians*

3

How Mr Daly the Middleman Sat Down to Breakfast

The Dalys (a very respectable family in middle life) occupied, at the time of which we write, a handsome cottage on the Shannon side, a few miles from the suburban district above-mentioned.

They had assembled, on the morning of Eily's disappearance, a healthy and blooming household of all sizes, in the principal sitting room for a purpose no less important than that of dispatching breakfast. It was a favourable moment for any one who might be desirous of sketching a family picture. The windows of the room, which were thrown up for the purpose of admitting the fresh morning air, opened upon a trim and sloping meadow that looked sunny and cheerful with the bright green aftergrass of the season. The broad and sheety river washed the very margin of the little field, and bore upon its quiet bosom (which was only ruffled by the circling eddies that encountered the advancing tide) a variety of craft, such as might be supposed to indicate the approach to a large commercial city. Majestic vessels, floating idly on the basined flood, with sails half furled, in keeping with the languid beauty of the scene; lighters burthened to the water's edge with bricks or sand; large rafts of timber, borne onward towards the neighbouring quays under the guidance of a shipman's boat-hook; pleasure-boats, with gaudy pennons hanging at peak and topmast; or turf boats with their unpicturesque and ungraceful lading, moving sluggishly forward, while their black sails seemed gasping for a breath to fill them; such were the *incidents* that gave a gentle animation to the prospect immediately before the eyes of the cottage-dwellers. On the farther side of the river arose the Cratloe hills, shadowed in various places by a broken cloud, and rendered beautiful by the chequered appearance of the ripening tillage, and the variety of hues that were observable along their wooded sides. At intervals, the front of a handsome mansion brightened up in a passing gleam of sunshine, while the wreaths of blue smoke, ascending at various distances from amongst the trees, tended to relieve the idea of extreme solitude which it would otherwise have presented.

The interior of the cottage was not less interesting to contemplate than the landscape which lay before it. The principal breakfast table (for there were two spread in the room) was placed before the window, the neat and snow white damask cloth covered with fare that spoke satisfactorily for the circumstances of the proprietor, and for the housewifery of his helpmate. The former, a fair, pleasant-faced old gentleman in a huge buckled cravat and square-toed shoes, somewhat distrustful of the meagre beverage which fumed out of Mrs Daly's lofty and shining coffee-pot, had taken his position before a cold ham and fowl which decorated the lower end of the table. His lady, a courteous old personage, with a face no less fair and happy than her husband's, and with eyes sparkling with good nature and intelligence, did the honours of the board at the farther end. On the opposite side, leaning over the back of his chair with clasped hands in an attitude which had a mixture of abstraction and anxiety, sat Mr Kyrle Daly, the first pledge of connubial affection that was born to this comely pair. He was a young man already initiated in the rudiments of the legal profession; of a handsome figure; and in manner—but something now pressed upon his spirits which rendered this an unfavourable occasion for describing it.

A second table was laid in a more retired portion of the room, for the accommodation of the younger part of the family. Several well burnished goblets, or *porringers*, of *thick* milk flanked the sides of this board, while a large dish of smooth-coated potatoes reeked up in the centre. A number of blooming boys and girls, between the ages of four and twelve, were seated at this simple repast, eating and drinking away with all the happy eagerness of youthful appetite. Not, however, that this employment occupied their exclusive attention, for the prattle which circulated round the table frequently became so boisterous as to drown the conversation of the older people, and to call forth the angry rebuke of the master of the family.

The furniture of the apartment was in accordance with the appearance and manners of its inhabitants. The floor was handsomely carpeted, a lofty green fender fortified the fire-place, and supplied Mr Daly in his facetious moments with occasions for the frequent repetition of a favourite conundrum——'Why is that fender like Westminster

Abbey?' a problem with which he never failed to try the wit of any stranger who happened to spend a night beneath his roof. The wainscoted walls were ornamented with several of the popular prints of the day, such as Hogarth's Roast Beef – Prince Eugene – Schomberg at the Boyne – My Betterton playing Cato in all the glory of

Full wig, flower'd gown, and lacker'd chair

or the royal Mandane, in the person of Mrs Mountain, strutting among the arbours of her Persian palace in a lofty tête and hooped petticoat. There were also some family drawings, done by Mrs Daly in her school-days, of which we feel no inclination to say more than that they were very prettily framed. In justice to the fair artist it should also be mentioned that, contrary to the established practice, her sketches were never re-touched by the hand of her master; a fact which Mr Daly was fond of insinuating, and which no one, who saw the pictures, was tempted to call in question. A small book case, with the edges of the shelves handsomely gilded, was suspended in one corner of the room, and on examination might be found to contain a considerable number of works on Irish History – for which study Mr Daly had a national predilection, a circumstance much deplored by all the impatient listeners in his neighbourhood, and (some people hinted) in his own household; some religious books; and a few volumes on cookery and farming. The space over the lofty chimney-piece was assigned to some ornaments of a more startling description. A gun rack, on which were suspended a long shore gun, a brass barrelled blunderbuss, a cutlass, and a case of horse pistols, manifested Mr Daly's determination to maintain, if necessary, by force of arms, his claim to the fair possessions which his honest industry had acquired.

'Kyrle,' said Mr Daly, putting his fork into a breast of cold goose, and looking at his son – 'you had better let me put a little goose' [with an emphasis] 'on your plate. You know you are going a wooing to day.'

The young gentleman appeared not to hear him. Mrs Daly, who understood more intimately the nature of her son's reflections, deprecated, by a significant look at her husband, the continuance of any raillery upon so delicate a subject.

'Kyrle, some coffee?' said the lady of the house; but without being more successful in awakening the attention of the young gentleman.

Mr Daly winked at his wife.

'Kyrle!' he called aloud, in a tone against which even a lover's absence was not proof – 'Do you hear what your mother says?'

'I ask pardon sir – I was absent, I – what were you saying, mother?'

'She was saying,' continued Mr Daly with a smile, 'that you were manufacturing a fine speech for Anne Chute, and that you were just meditating whether you should deliver it on your knees, or out of brief, as if you were addressing the Bench in the Four Courts.'

'For shame, my dear! – Never mind him, Kyrle, I said no such thing. I wonder how you can say that, my dear, and the children listening.'

'Pooh! the little angels are too busy and too innocent to pay us any attention,' said Mr Daly, lowering his voice however. 'But speaking seriously, my boy, you take this affair too deeply to heart; and whether it be in our pursuit suit of wealth – or fame –

or even in love itself, an extreme solicitude to be successful is the surest means of defeating its own object. Besides, it argues an unquiet and unresigned condition. I have had a little experience, you know, in affairs of this kind,' he added, smiling and glancing at his fair helpmate, who blushed with the simplicity of a young girl.

'Ah, sir,' said Kyrle, as he drew nearer to the breakfast table with a magnanimous affectation of cheerfulness. 'I fear I have not so good a ground for hope as you may have had. It is very easy, sir, for one to be resigned to disappointment when he is certain of success.'

'Why, I was not bidden to despair, indeed,' said Mr Daly, extending his hand to his wife, while they exchanged a quiet smile, which had in it an expression of tenderness and of melancholy remembrance. 'I have, I believe, been more fortunate than more deserving persons. I have never been vexed with useless fears in my wooing days, nor with vain regrets when those days were ended. I do not know, my dear lad, what hopes you have formed, or what prospects you may have shaped out of the future, but I will not wish you a better fortune than that you may as nearly approach to their accomplishment as I have done, and that Time may deal as fairly with you as he has done with your father.' After saying this, Mr Daly leaned forward on the table with his temple supported by one finger, and glanced alternately from his children to his wife; while he sang in a low tone the following verse of a popular song:

> 'How should I love the pretty creatures,
>   While round my knees they fondly clung,
> To see them look their mother's features,
>   To hear them lisp their mother's tongue!
> And when with envy Time transported
>   Shall think to rob us of our joys –
> You'll in your girls again be courted,
>   And I——'

with a glance at Kyrle –

> 'And I go wooing with the boys.'

And this, thought young Kyrle, in the affectionate pause that ensued, this is the question which I go to decide upon this morning; whether my old age shall resemble the picture which I see before me, or whether I shall be doomed to creep into the winter of my life, a lonely, selfish, cheerless, money-hunting old bachelor. Is not this enough to make a little solicitude excusable, or pardonable at least?

'It is a long time now,' resumed Mr Daly, 'since I have had the pleasure of meeting Mrs Chute. She was a very beautiful but a very wild girl when I knew her. Nothing has ever been more inexplicable to me than the choice she made of a second husband. You never saw Anne's step-father, Tom Chute, or you would be equally astonished. You saw him, my love, did you not?'

Mrs Daly laughed and answered in the affirmative.

'It shewed indeed a singular taste,' said Mr Daly. 'They tell a curious story too, about the manner of their courtship.'

'What was that sir?' asked Kyrle, who felt a strong sympathetic interest in all stories connected with wooers and wooing.

'I have it, I confess, upon questionable authority – but you shall hear it, such as it is – Now, look at that young thief!' he added laughing, and directing Kyrle's attention to one of the children, a chubby young fellow, who, having deserted the potatoe-eating corps at the side-table, was taking advantage of the deep interest excited by the conversation, to make a sudden descent upon the contents of the japanned bread basket. Perceiving that he was detected, the little fellow relaxed his fingers, and drew back a little, glancing, from beneath his eye-lashes, a half dismayed and bashful look at the laughing countenance of his parent.

'Charles is not well to-day,' said the mother, in a compassionate tone, and cutting him a large wedge of her best home-made bread, which the lad began to demolish with a degree of rapidity that scarcely corroborated the assertion.

'But the story sir?' said Kyrle.

'But the story – Well, little Tom Chute, (he might have been better called little Tom-tit, only that he was not half so sprightly) was a very extraordinary man, for although he was small and fat, he was not merry, nor talkative. You would have pitied him to see him walking about a ball room with ruffles that looked like small buckles, and a queue half as long as himself, reminding one of the handle of a pump when the sucker is up – with the most forlorn aspect in the world, as if he were looking for a runaway wife. It was a curious anomaly in his character that although he – (Silence, there! my dear, will you speak to those children) – that although he always *looked* miserable in the midst of society, he really *was* so when out of it, as if the continued embarrassment and mortification which he experienced were a stimulus which he could not do without. Round, fat, shy, awkward, and oily, as he was, however, he tumbled his little rotund figure into the heart of Mrs Trenchard, who was at that time, though a widow, one of the leading belles in Munster. A fair friend was the first to disclose this rapturous secret to poor Tom, for he might have known Mrs Trenchard for a century without being able to make it out himself. He did not know whether he should be most frightened or pleased at the intelligence – but certain it is that in the warmth of his first feelings, he made a tender of his hand to the lady, and was instantly accepted. A dashing, handsome fellow who had been rejected by her some time before, and who knew Chute's irresolute temper, resolved to indemnify himself for the mortification he had received by throwing some embarrassment in the way of the nuptials, and effected it simply enough. It seems the lady's accomplishments were of a very general description, for besides playing the harpsichord to admiration, she could manage a horse with any hero of the County Club, and was known to join their hunting parties, and even to ride a steeple chase with eclat. Indeed it was generally admitted that she possessed more spirit than might have answered her purposes, or her husband's either. What fancy she could have taken to Tom Chute, I cannot for my life conceive. Well, this fellow met Tom going to her house one evening, as spruce as a water wagtail, with his queue poking up behind like the flag staff in the stern of a privateer. They got into conversation about the widow. "Beautiful creature, isn't she?" simpered Tom, blushing up to the eyes, for it was another funny foible of Tom's, to redden up like a rose whenever there was any discourse of ladies; even when nobody dreamed of any thing like raillery. "Beautiful creature, isn't she?" says Tom. "Beautiful indeed," replied the other. And Tom stood on his toes, threw out his right elbow and took snuff. "And accomplished, I think?" "And very sensible," says the other. "And lively," says Tom. "And high spirited," says the other. "So they say, her late husband found, poor man, to his cost." Tom dropped his jaw a little, and looked inquisitive. But the other, who saw that his business was done, declined all explanation, and hurried off with a concluding remark, that "the lady was unquestionably a capital *whip*". Well, Tom got a sudden attack of – I don't know what complaint, went home that night, and sent an apology to the widow. He was not seen near her house for a fortnight after, and a report reached her ears that he had some notion of quitting the country. But if he had, she put a stop to it. One morning when Tom was looking over his books, he was startled by the apparition of a tall woman in a riding dress, with a horsewhip in one hand, and a case of duelling pistols in the other. She nodded to Tom. "I understand," said she—'

At this moment, a potatoe peel, flung from the side-table, whisked past Mr Daly's nose, and with happier aim, lighted on that of Prince Eugene in the print before mentioned. The venerable, but too little venerated, story teller, who had been for the last few minutes endeavouring to raise his voice, so as to make it audible above the encreasing uproar of the young people, now turned round, at this unparalleled and violent aggression, and confronted the daring group in awful silence. Satisfied, however, with the sudden hush of terror which this action occasioned, and willing to reserve the burst of wrath for a future transgression, he turned again in silence; and directing the servant girl who was in the room, to take the potatoe peel off Prince Eugene's nose, he resumed the thread of his narrative.

'"I understand," said Mrs Trenchard – for it was no other than the widow – "that you intend leaving Ireland?" Tom stammered and hesitated. – "If my brother were living," continued the lady, "he would horsewhip you – but although he is not, Hetty Trenchard is able to fight her own way. Come, sir, my carriage is at the door below; either step into it with me this minute, or take one of those pistols, and stand at the other end of the room." Well, Tom looked as like a fool as any man in Ireland. He wouldn't fight, and he wouldn't be horsewhipped; so that the business ended in his going into the carriage and marrying the lady, some persons indeed insinuated that Tom was observed in the course of the day to chafe his shoulders two or three times with an expression of pain, as if his change of condition had been the result of a still harsher mode of reasoning than I have mentioned; but this part of the story is without foundation.'

'What a bold creature!' said the gentle Mrs Daly.

'And is it possible, sir,' asked Kyrle, 'that this amazon is the kind old lady whom Anne Chute attends with so much affection and tenderness in her infirmity?'

'Ah, ha! Kyrle, I see the nature of the bolt that has wounded you, and I like you the better for it, my boy. A good face is a pippin that grows on every hedge, but a good heart, that is to say, a well-regulated one, is the apple of the Hesperides, worth even the risk of ease and life itself.'

Kyrle assented to this sagacious aphorism with a deep sigh.

'Are the Cregans and they on terms now?' asked Mrs Daly.

'As much on terms as two families of such opposite habits can be. The Chutes invite the Cregans to a family dinner once or twice in the year, and the Cregans ask the Chutes to their Killarney cottage; both of which invitations are taken as *French compliments*, and never accepted. Cregan himself hates going to Castle Chute, because he has nobody there to make the jovial night with him, and young Hardress, (your friend, Kyrle) is too wild a lad to confine himself to mere drawing room society. Apropos, talk of—, 'tis a vulgar proverb, and let it pass; but there goes his trim pleasure boat, the *Nora Creina*, flying down the river, and there sits the youth himself, tiller in hand, as usual. Patcy, bring me the telescope; I think I see a female dress on board.'

The telescope was brought, and adjusted to the proper focus, while a dozen eager faces were collected about the small window, one over another, in the manner of those groups in painting called 'Studies of Heads'.

'That is he, indeed,' continued Mr Daly, resting the glass on the window-frame, and directing it towards the object of their attention – 'there is no mistaking that dark and handsome face, buried up as it is in his huge oiled penthouse hat, and there is his hunch-backed boatman, Danny Mann, or Danny the Lord, as the people call him since his misfortune, tending the foresheet in the bow. But that female – there is a female there, unquestionably, in a blue mantle, with the hood brought low over her eyes, sitting on the ballast. Who can she be?'

'Perhaps, Danny Mann's cousin, Cotch Coonerty?' said Mrs Daly.

'Or some western dealing woman who has come up to Limerick to purchase a reinforcement of pins, needles, whiskey, and Reading-made-easys, for her village counter, and is getting a free passage home from young master Hardress.'

'Like enough, like enough; it is just his way. – Hillo! the fellow is going to run down that fishing cot, I believe!'

A hoarse cry of 'Bear away! Hold up your hand!' was heard from the water, and reiterated with the addition of a few expletives, which those who know the energy of a boatman's dialect will understand without our transcribing them here. The pleasure-boat, however, heedless of those rough remonstrances, and apparently indisposed to yield any portion of her way, still held her bowsprit close to the wind, and sailed on, paying no more regard to the peril of the plebeian craft, than a French aristocrat of the vielle cour might be supposed to exhibit for that of a sans culottes about to be trodden down by his leaders in the Rue St Honoré. The fishermen, with many curses, backed water, and put about as rapidly as possible; but without being able to avoid the shock of the *Nora Creina*, who just touched their stern with sufficient force to make the cot dart forward nearly an oar's length through the water, and to lay the rowers sprawling on their backs in the bottom. Fortunately the wind, which had sprung up with the returning tide, was not sufficiently strong to render the concussion more dangerous.

'Like his proud mother in every feature,' said Mr Daly – 'Is it not singular that while we were speaking of the characters of the family, he could not pass our window without furnishing us with a slight specimen of his own. See how statelily the fellow turns round and contemplates the confusion he has occasioned. There is his mother's grandeur blended with the hair-brained wildness and idle spirit of his father.'

'Hardress Cregan's is the handsomest boat in the river,' said Patcy, a stout sunburnt boy – 'She beat all the Galway hookers from this to Beale. What a nice green hull! – and white sails and beautiful green colours flying over her peak and gaff-topsail! Oh! how I'd like to be steering her!'

Mr Daly winked at his wife, and whispered her that he had known Rear-Admirals come of smaller beginnings. Mrs Daly, with a little shudder, replied that she should not wish to see him a Rear-Admiral, the navy was so dangerous a service. Her husband, in order to sooth her, observed that the danger was not very near at hand.

In the meantime, Hardress Cregan became a subject of vehement debate at the side-table, to which the juvenile squadron had returned. One fair haired little girl declared that she was his 'pet'. A second claimed that distinction for herself.

'He gave me an O'Dell-cake when he was last here,' said one.

'And me a stick of peppermint.'

'He gave me a—' in a whisper – 'a kiss.'

'And me two.'

'He didn't –'

'He did.'

'I'll tell dadda it was you threw the potatoe peel while ago.'

'Ah ha, tattler-tell-tale!'

'Silence there! fie! fie! what words are these?' said Mrs Daly, 'come kiss and be friends, now, both of you and let me hear no more.'

The young combatants complied with her injunction, and, as the duelling paragraphs say, 'the affair terminated amicably'.

'But I was speaking,' Mr Daly resumed, 'of the family pride of the Cregans. It was once manifested by Hardress's father in a manner that might make an Englishman smile. When their little Killarney property was left to the Cregans, amongst many other additional pieces of display that were made on the occasion, it behoved Mr Barny Cregan to erect a family vault and monument in his parish churchyard. He had scarcely however given directions for its construction when he fell ill of a fever, and was very near enjoying the honour of hanselling the new cemetery himself. But he got over the fit, and made it one of his first cares to saunter out as far as the church, and inspect the mansion which had been prepared for his reception. It was a handsome Gothic monument occupying a retired corner of the churchyard, and shadowed over by a fine old sycamore. But Barny, who had no taste for the picturesque, was deeply mortified at finding his piece of sepulchral finery thrown so much into the shade. "What did I or my people do," he said to the architect, "that we should be sent skulking into that corner? I paid my money and I'll have my own value for it." The monument was accordingly got rid of, and a sporting, flashy one erected opposite the gateway with the Cregan crest and shield (in what herald's office it was picked up I cannot take upon me to say) emblazoned on the frontispiece. Here, it is to be hoped, the aspiring Barnaby and his posterity may one day rest in peace.'

'That would be a vain hope, I fear,' said Kyrle, 'at least so far as Mr Cregan is concerned, if it were true, as our peasantry believe, that the churchyard is frequently made a scene of midnight mirth and revel, by those whose earthly carousals are long concluded. But what relationship is there between that family and Mrs Chute?'

'She is step-sister to Mrs Cregan.'

'Indeed? So near?'

'Most veritable, therefore look to it. They tell a story –'

But the talkative old gentleman was interrupted in his anecdotical career by the entrance of a new actor on the scene.

*   *   *

18
How the Gentlemen Spent the Evening, which Proved Rather Warmer than Hardress Expected

'Peace!' said Hepton Connolly, with a face of drunken seriousness, 'peace be to the manes of poor Dalton!'

'Amen, with all my heart!' exclaimed Mr Cregan, 'although the cocks are well rid of him. But a better horseman never backed a hunter.'

'I drink him,' said Hyland Creagh, 'although I seldom care to toast a man who dies in his bed.'

'That's all trash and braggery, Creagh,' cried Connolly – 'we'll have you yet upon the flat of your back, and roaring for a priest into the bargain.'

'Upon my honour as a gentleman, I am serious,' said Creagh. 'They may talk of the field of battle and bloody breaches, forlorn hopes, and hollow squares, and such stuff; but what is the glory of a soldier after all! To drag through the fatigues of a whole campaign, with its concomitants of night-watches, marches in marshes, and bivouacs in rainy weather, and with no brighter prospect at the year's end, than that of making one among half a million of fighting fellows who are shot on a heap like larks. And, even then, you meet not hand to hand, but cloud to cloud, moving about in a flock, and waiting your turn to take your allowance of cold lead, and fill a pit with your neighbours. Glory? What glory is there in figuring in small types among a list of killed and wounded? the utmost distinction that a poor sub. can ever hope for. Why, a coward is no more ball proof than a gallant fellow, and both may often shine together upon the same list. No – my ambition should have a higher aim. While I live, let my life be that of a fearless fellow; and when I die, let my epitaph be found in a handsome paragraph, under the head of "Domestic Intelligence", in the county journal. "*Affair of honour*. Yesterday morning at five o'clock – meeting took place – Hyland Creagh, Esquire – attended by Blank Esquire – and Captain Blank attended by – Blank Esquire – regret to state – Mr Creagh – third fire – mortally wounded – borne from the ground. – The affair, we understand, originated in a dispute respecting a lovely and accomplished young lady, celebrated as a reigning toast in that quarter." '

'And grand-niece, we understand,' added Hardress, laughing 'to the unhappy old gentleman, whose fate we have just recorded.'

There was a laugh at Creagh.

'Nay, my young friend,' he said, adjusting his ruffles with the air of a Chesterfield – 'the journal that shall mention *that* circumstance must be dated many years hence.'

'Adad, not so far off neither, Creagh,' exclaimed Mr Cregan, 'and if you were to go out to-morrow morning, I should not like to see you go posting to the devil upon such a mission as that.'

'Talking of the devil,' said Hepton Connolly, 'did you hear, Creagh, that the priest is to have us all upon the altar next Sunday, on account of that little squib we had in the mountains the day of the races?'

'It may be,' said Creagh, with a supercilious smile; 'mais ce n'est pas mon affaire. I have not the honour to belong to his communion.'

'Oh,' cried Mr Cregan, 'true enough. *You* belong to the genteel religion.'

'There you have the whip hand of me,' said Connolly, 'for I am a papist. Well, Creagh, not meaning to impugn your gallantry now, I say this; a papist, to fight a duel, requires and possesses the courage of a protestant ten times over.'

'Pray will you oblige me with a reason for that pleasant speech?'

''Tis as clear as this glass. A protestant is allowed a wide discretionary range on most ethical, as well as theological points of opinion. A poor papist has none. The Council of Trent in its twenty-fifth session (I have it from the Bishop) excommunicates all duellists, and calls the practice an invention of the devil. And what can I say against it? I know something of the common law, and the rights of things, persons and so forth, but the canonical code to me is a fountain sealed. 'Tis something deeper than a cause before the petty sessions. 'Tis easier to come at Blackstone, or even Coke upon Lyttleton himself, than at Manochius, or Saint Augustine.'

'Well, but how you run on! You were talking about the courage of protestant and catholic.'

'I say a papist must be the braver man; for in addition to his chance of being shot through the brains on a frosty morning in this world (a cool prospect) it is no joke to be damned everlastingly in the next.'

'That never struck me before,' exclaimed Cregan.

'And if it had,' said Creagh, 'I confess I do not see what great disadvantage the reflection could have produced to our friend Connolly; for he knew, that whether he was to be shot yesterday in a duel, or physicked out of the world twenty years hence, that little matter of the other life will be arranged in precisely the same manner.'

'As much as to say,' replied Connolly, 'that now or then, the devil is sure of his bargain.'

'My idea precisely; but infinitely better expressed.'

'Very good, Creagh. I suppose it was out of a filial affection for the sooty old gentleman you took so much pains to send me to him the other morning.'

'You placed your honour in my hands, and I would have seen you raked fore and aft, fifty times, rather than let the pledge be tarnished. If you did go to the devil, it was my business to see that you met him with clean hands.'

'I feel indebted to you, Creagh.'

'I have seen a dozen shots exchanged on a lighter quarrel. I was present myself at the duel between Hickman and Leake, on a somewhat similar dispute. They fired fourteen shots each, and when their ammunition was exhausted, actually remained on the ground until the seconds could fetch a new supply from the nearest market-town.'

'And what use did they make of it when it came?'

'Give me time, and you shall hear. 'Twas Hickman's fire, and he put his lead an inch above Leake's right hip; (as pretty a shot as ever I saw in my life), Leake was not killed though, and he stood to his ground like a man. I never will forget the ghastly look he gave me, (I was his second), when he asked whether the laws of the duello would allow a wounded man a chair. I was confident they did, so long as he kept his feet upon the sod, and I said so. Well, the chair was brought. He took his seat somewhat in this manner, grasping the orifice of the wound closely with his disengaged hand. [Here the speaker moved his chair some feet from the table, in order to enact the scene with greater freedom]. There was a fatal steadiness in every motion. I saw Hickman's eye wink, and not without a cause. It winked again, and never opened after. The roof of his skull was literally blown away.'

'And the other fellow?' said Hardress.

'The other gentleman fell from his chair, a corpse, at the same moment; after uttering a sentiment of savage satisfaction, too horrible, too blasphemous, to think of, much less to repeat.'

'They were a murderous pair of ruffians,' said Hardress, 'and ought to have been impaled upon a cross-road.'

'One of them,' observed Hyland Creagh, sipping his punch, 'one of them was a cousin of mine.'

'Oh, and therefore utterly blameless, of course,' said Hardress with an ironical laugh.

'I don't know,' said Creagh; 'I confess I think it a hard word to apply to a gentleman who is unfortunate enough to die in defence of his honour.'

'Honour!' exclaimed Hardress, with indignant zeal, (for though he was no great devotee, he had yet some gleams of a half-religious virtue shining through his character;) 'Call you that honour? I say a duellist is a murderer, and worthy of the gallows, and I will prove it. The question lies in the justice or injustice of the mode of reparation. That cannot be a just one which subjects the aggressor and aggrieved to precisely the same punishment, if the duellist be the injured party, he is a suicide; and if he be the inflictor of the wrong, he is a murderer.'

'Ay, Hardress,' said his father, 'but there are cases – '

'Oh, I know what you mean, sir. Fine, delicate, thin-spun modes of insult, that draw on heavier assaults, and leave both parties labouring under the sense of injury. But they are murderers still. If I filled a seat in the legislature, do you think I would give my voice in favour of a law that made it a capital offence to call a man a scoundrel in the streets? And shall I dare to inflict with my own hand, a punishment that I would shudder to see committed to the hangman?'

'But if public war be justifiable,' said Connolly, 'why should not private?'*

'Aye,' exclaimed Hardress, 'I see you have got that aphorism of Johnson's, the fat moralist, to support you; but I say, shame upon the recreant, for as mean and guilty a compliance with the prejudices of the world as ever parasite betrayed. I stigmatize it as a wilful sin, for how can I esteem the author of *Rasselas* a fool?'

'Very hardly,' said Creagh, 'and pray what is your counter argument?'

---

* I am sorry the Author of *Guy Mannering* should have thought proper to adopt the same mode of reasoning. Will posterity remove that bar sinister from his literary escutcheon?

'This. Public war is never (when justifiable) a quarrel for sounds and conventual notions of honour. Public war is at best a social evil, and cannot be embraced without the full concurrence of society, expressed by its constituted authorities, and obtained only in obedience to the necessity of the case. But to private war, society has given no formal sanction, nor does it derive any advantage from the practice.'

'Upon my word,' said Creagh, 'you have some very curious ideas.'

'Well, Hardress,' exclaimed Connolly, 'if you have a mind to carry those notions into practice, I should recommend you to try it in some other country besides Ireland; you will never go through with it in this.'

'In every company and on every soil,' said Hardress, 'I will avow my sentiments. I never will fight a duel; and I will proclaim my purpose in the ears of all the duellists on earth.'

'But society, young gentleman – '

'I bid society defiance; at least that reckless, godless, heartless crew, to whom you wrongfully apply the term. The greater portion of those who bow down before this bloody error, is composed of slaves and cowards, who are afraid to make their own conviction the guide of their conduct.

> "Letting I *dare not*, wait upon *I would*.
> Like the poor cat in the adage."'

'I am sure,' said Creagh, 'I had rather shoot a man for doubting my word than for taking my purse.'

'Because you are as proud as Lucifer,' exclaimed Hardress. – 'Who but the great father of all injustice would say that he deserved to be shot for calling *you* a – (it is an unpleasant word to be sure) – a liar?'

'But he does more. He actually *does* strike at my life and property, for I lose both friends and fair repute, if I suffer such an insult to pass unnoticed.'

In answer to this plea, Hardress made a speech, of which (as the newspapers say) we regret that our space does not allow us to offer more than a mere outline. He contended that no consequences could justify a man in sacrificing his own persuasion of what was right to the error of his friends. The more general this error was, the more criminal it became to increase the number of its victims. The question was not whether society would disown or receive the passive gentleman, but whether society was in the wrong or in the right; and if the former, then he was bound to adopt the cause of justice at every hazard. He drew the usual distinction between moral and animal courage, and painted with force and feeling the heroism of a brave man encountering alone the torrent of general opinion, and taking more wounds upon his spirit than ever Horatius Coccles risked upon his person, he quoted the celebrated passage of the faithful seraph in Milton, alluded to the Athenian manners, and told the well-known story of Lucian Anacharsis, all which tended considerably more to exhaust the patience than to convince the understanding of his hearers.

'Finally,' said he, 'I denounce the system of private war, because it is the offspring of a barbarous pride. It was a barbarous pride that first suggested the expedient, and it is an intolerable pride that still sustains it. Talk of public war! The world could not exist if nation were to take up the sword against nation upon a point of honour, such as will call out for blood between man and man. The very word means pride. It is a measureless, bloody pride, that demands a reparation so excessive for every slight offence. Take any single quarrel of them all, and dissect its motive, and you will find every portion of it stained with pride, the child of selfishness – pride, the sin of the first devil – pride, the poor pitiful creature of folly and ignorance – pride, the——'

'Oh, trash and stuff, man,' exclaimed Connolly, losing patience, 'if you are going to preach a sermon choose another time for it. Come, Creagh, send the bowl this way, and let us drink. Here, young gentleman, stop spouting, and give us a toast. You'll make a fool of yourself, Hardress, if you talk in that manner among gentlemen.'

Without making any answer to this speech (which however he felt a little difficulty in digesting) Hardress proposed the health and future fame of young Kyrle Daly.

'With all my heart!' exclaimed both his father and Connolly.

'I'll not drink it,' said Creagh, putting in his glass.

Hardress was just as proud (to borrow his own simile) as Lucifer himself; and probably it was on this account he held the quality so cheap. It must be admitted, likewise, that his ambitious love of singularity formed but too considerable a part of his motive in the line of argument which he had followed up; and he was by no means prepared to perform the heroic part which he had described with so much enthusiasm. Least of all could he be expected to do so at the present moment; for while he was speaking, he had also been drinking, and the warmth of dispute, encreased by the excitement of strong drink, left his reason still less at freedom than it might have been under the dominion of an ordinary passion. He insisted upon Creagh's drinking his toast.

'I shall not drink it,' said Creagh; 'I consider him as an impertinent puppy.'

'He is my friend,' said Hardress.

'Oh, then of course,' said Fireball, with an ironical smile, (evidently intended as a retort) 'he is utterly blameless.'

To use a vulgar but forcible expression, the blood of Hardress was now completely up. He set his teeth for a moment, and then discharged the contents of his own glass at the face of the offender. The fire-eater, who, from long experience, was able to anticipate this proceeding, evaded by a rapid motion the degrading missile; and then quietly resuming his seat, 'Be prepared, sir,' he said, 'to answer this in the morning.'

'I am ready now,' exclaimed Hardress. 'Connolly, lend me your sword, and be my friend. Father, do you second that gentleman, and you will oblige me.'

Mr Barnaby Cregan rose to interfere, but in doing so, he betrayed a secret which had till that moment lain with himself; he was the first who fell.

'No, no swords,' said Connolly, 'there are a pretty pair of pistols over the chimney-piece. Let them decide the quarrel.'

It was so agreed. Hardress and Creagh took their places in the two-corners of the room, upon the understanding, that both were to approach step by step, and fire when they pleased. Hepton Connolly took his place out of harm's way in a distant corner, while Cregan crept along the floor, muttering in an indistinct tone. 'Drunk? aye, but not dead drunk. I call no man dead drunk while he lies on the high road, with sense enough to roll out of the way when a carriage is driving towards him.'

Hardress fired, after having made two paces. Creagh, who was unhurt, reserved his shot until he put the pistol up to the head of his opponent. Hardress never flinched, although he really believed that Creagh was about to shoot him.

'Come,' said he loudly, 'fire your shot and have done with it. I would have met you at the end of a handkerchief upon my friend's quarrel.'

Hyland Creagh, after enjoying for a moment the advantage he possessed, uncocked his pistol and laid it on the table.

'Hardress,' said he, 'you are a brave fellow. I believe I was wrong. I ask your pardon, and am ready to drink your toast.'

'Oh, well,' said Hardress, with a laugh; 'if that be the case, I cannot, of course, think of pursuing the affair any farther.' And he reached his hand to his opponent with the air of one who was exercising, rather than receiving, a kindness.

The company once more resumed their places at the table, somewhat sobered by this incident, which though not unusual at the period, was yet calculated to excite a little serious feeling. It was not long, however, before they made amends for what was lost in the way of intoxication. The immense blue jug, which stood inside the fender, was replenished to the brim, and the bowl flew round more rapidly than ever. Creagh told stories of the Hell-fire Club in the sweating and pinking days. Connolly overflowed with anecdotes of attornies outdone, of plates well won, of bailiffs maimed and beaten; and Cregan (whose tongue was the last member of his frame that became accessory to the sin of intoxication) filled up his share in the conversation, with accounts of cocks, and of ghosts, in the appearance of which last, he was a firm, though not a fearful believer. Hardress remained with the company until the sound of a vehicle, drawing up at the hall door, announced the return of his mother and cousin. He then left the room and hurried to his own apartment, in order to avoid meeting them under circumstances which he well supposed were not calculated to create any impression in his own favour.

We cannot better illustrate the habits of the period, than by transcribing an observation made in Mr Cregan's kitchen at the moment of the dispute above detailed. Old Nancy was preparing the mould candles for poor Dalton's wake, when she heard the shot fired in the dining parlour.

'Run into the gentlemen, Mike, eroo,' she exclaimed, without even laying aside the candle, which she was paring with a knife, in order to make it fit the socket more exactly. 'I lay my life the gentlemen are fighting a *jewel*.'

'It can't be a *jewel*,' said Mike the servant boy, who was courting slumber in a low chair before the blazing fire. 'It can't be a *jewel*, when there was only one shot.'

'But it isn't long from 'em, I'll be bail, till they'll fire another if they don't be hindered; for 'tis shot for shot with 'em. Run in, eroo.'

The servant stretched his limbs out lazily, and rubbed his eyes. 'Well,' said he, 'fair play all the world over. If one fired, you wouldn't have the other put up with it, without havin' his fair revinge?'

'But may be one of 'em is kilt already!' observed Nancy.

'E'then, d'ye hear this? Sure you know, well, that if there was any body shot, the master would ring the bell!'

This observation was conclusive. Old Nancy proceeded with her gloomy toil in silence, and the persuasive Mike, letting his head hang back from his shoulders, and crossing his hands upon his lap, slept soundly on, undisturbed by any idle conjectures on the cause of the noise which they had heard.

CHARLES LEVER

from *St Patrick's Eve*

At the time we speak of, intemperance was an Irish vice, and one which prevailed largely. Whisky entered into every circumstance and relation of life. It cemented friendships and ratified contracts; it celebrated the birth of the newly-born, it consoled the weeping relatives over the grave of the departed; it was a welcome and a bond of kindness, and, as the stirrup-cup, was the last pledge at parting. Men commemorated their prosperity by drink, and none dared to face gloomy fortune without it. Owen Connor had recourse to it, as to a friend that never betrayed. The easy circumstances, in comparison with many others, he enjoyed, left him both means and leisure for such a course; and few days passed without his paying a visit to the 'shebeen-house' of the village. If the old man noticed this new habit, his old prejudices were too strong to make him prompt in condemning it. Indeed, he rather regarded it as a natural consequence of their bettered fortune, that Owen should frequent these places; and as he never returned actually drunk, and always brought back with him the current rumours of the day, as gathered from newspapers and passing gossip, his father relied on such scraps of information for his evening's amusement over the fire.

It was somewhat later than usual that Owen was returning home one night, and the old man, anxious and uneasy at his absence, had wandered part of the way to meet him, when he saw him coming slowly forward, with that heavy weariness of step, deep grief and pre-occupation inspire. When the young man had come within speaking distance of his father, he halted suddenly, and looking up at him, exclaimed, 'There's sorrowful news for ye to-night, father!'

'I knew it! I knew it well!' said the old man, as he clasped his hands before him, and seemed preparing himself to bear the shock with courage. 'I had a dhrame of it last night; and 'tis death, wherever it is.'

'You're right there. The master's dead!'

Not another word was spoken by either, as side by side they slowly ascended the mountain-path. It was only when seated at the fire-side, that Owen regained sufficient collectedness to detail the particulars he had learned in the village. Mr Leslie had died of the cholera at Paris. The malady had just broken out in that city, and he was among its earliest victims. The terrors which that dreadful pestilence inspired, reached every remote part of Europe, and at last, with all the aggravated horrors of its devastating career, swept across Ireland. The same letter which brought the tidings of Mr Leslie's death, was the first intelligence of the plague. A scourge so awful needed not the fears of the ignorant to exaggerate its terrors; yet men seemed to vie with each other in their dreadful conjectures regarding it.

All the sad interest the landlord's sudden death would have occasioned under other circumstances was merged in the fearful malady of which he died. Men heard with almost apathy of the events that were announced as likely to succeed, in the management of the property; and only listened with eagerness if the pestilence were mentioned. Already its arrival in England was declared; and the last lingering hope of the devotee was, that the holy island of St Patrick might escape its ravages. Few cared to hear what a few weeks back had been welcome news – that the old agent was to be dismissed, and a new one appointed. The speculations which once would have been rife enough, were now silent. There was but one terrible topic in every heart and on every tongue – the Cholera.

The inhabitants of great cities, with wide sources of information available, and free conversation with each other, can scarcely estimate the additional degree of terror the prospect of a dreadful epidemic inspires among the dwellers in unfrequented rural districts. The cloud, not bigger than a man's hand at first, gradually expands itself, until the whole surface of earth is darkened by its shadow. The business of life stands still; the care for the morrow is lost; the proneness to indulge in the gloomiest anticipations common calamity invariably suggests, heightens the real evil, and disease finds its victims more than doomed at its first approach. In this state of agonizing suspense, when rumours arose to be contradicted, reasserted, and again disproved, came the tidings that the Cholera was in Dublin. The same week it had broken out in many other places; at last the report went, that a poor man, who had gone into the market of Galway to sell his turf, was found dead on the steps of the chapel. Then, followed the whole array of precautionary measures, and advices, and boards of health. Then, it was announced that the plague was raging fearfully – the hospitals crowded – death in every street.

Terrible and appalling as these tidings were, the fearful fact never realized itself in the little district we speak of, until a death occurred in the town close by. He was a shopkeeper in Oughterarde, and known to the whole neighbourhood. This solitary instance brought with it more of dreadful meaning than all the shock of distant calamity. The heart-rending wail of those who listened to the news smote many more with the cold tremour of coming death. Another case soon followed, a third, and a fourth succeeded, all fatal; and the disease was among them.

It is only when a malady, generally fatal, is associated with the terrors of contagion, that the measure of horror and dread flows over. When the sympathy which suffering sickness calls for is yielded in a spirit of almost despair, and the ministerings to the dying are but the prelude to the same state, then indeed death is armed with all his terrors. No people are more remarkable for the charities of the sick-bed than the poor Irish. It is with them less a sentiment than a religious instinct; and though they watched the course of the pestilence, and saw few, if any, escape death who took it, their devotion never failed them. They practised, with such skill as they possessed, every remedy in turn. They, who trembled but an hour before at the word when spoken, faced the danger itself with a bold heart; and, while the insidious signs of the disease were already upon them – while their wearied limbs and clammy hands bespoke that their own hour was come, they did not desist from their good offices, until past the power to render them.

It was spring-time, the season more than usually mild, the prospects of the year were already favourable, and all the signs of abundance rife in the land. What a contrast the scene without to that presented by the interior of each dwelling! There, death and dismay were met with at every step. The old man and the infant prostrated by the same stroke; the strong and vigorous youth who went forth to labour in the morning – at noon, a feeble, broken-spirited creature – at sunset, a corpse.

As the minds and temperaments of men were fashioned, so did fear operate upon them. Some, it made reckless and desperate, careless of what should happen, and indifferent to every measure of precaution; some, became paralysed with fear, and seemed unable to make an effort for safety, were it even attainable; others, exaggerating every care and caution, lived a life of unceasing terror and anxiety; while a few – they were unfortunately a very few – summoned courage to meet the danger in a spirit of calm and resolute determination; while in their reformed habits it might be seen how thoroughly they felt that their own hour might be a brief one. Among these was Owen Connor. From the day the malady appeared in the neighbourhood, he never entered the public-house of the village, but, devoting himself to the work of kindness the emergency called for, went from cabin to cabin rendering every service in his power. The poorest depended on him for the supply of such little comforts as they possessed, for at every market-day he sold a sheep or a lamb to provide them; the better-off looked to him for advice and counsel, following his directions as implicitly as though he were a physician of great skill. All recognized his devotedness in their cause, and his very name was a talisman for courage in every humble cabin around. His little ass-cart, the only wheeled vehicle that ever ascended the mountain where he lived, was seen each morning moving from door to door, while Owen brought either some small purchase he was commissioned to make at Oughterarde, or left with the more humble some offering of his own benevolence.

'There's the salt ye bid me buy, Mary Cooney; and here's fourpence out of it, – do ye all be well, still?'

'We are, and thank ye, Owen.'

'The Lord keep ye so! How's Ned Daly?'

'He's off, Owen dear; his brother James is making the coffin; poor boy, he looks very weak himself this morning.'

The cart moved on, and at length stopped at a small hovel built against the side of a clay ditch. It was a mere assemblage of wet sods with the grass still growing, and covered by some branches of trees and loose straw over them. Owen halted the ass at the opening of the miserable den, through which the smoke now issued, and at the same moment a man, stooping double to permit him to pass out into the open air, came forward: he was apparently about fifty years of age – his real age was not thirty; originally a well-formed and stout-built fellow, starvation and want had made him a mere skeleton. His clothes were, a ragged coat, which he wore next his skin, for shirt he had none, and a pair of worn corduroy trousers; he had neither hat, shoes, nor stockings; but still, all these signs of destitution were nothing in comparison with the misery displayed in his countenance. Except that his lip trembled with a convulsive shiver, not a feature moved – the cheeks were livid and flattened – the dull grey eyes had lost all the light of intelligence, and stared vacantly before him.

'Well, Martin, how is she?'

'I don't know, Owen dear,' said he, in a faltering voice; 'maybe 'tis sleeping she is.'

Owen followed him within the hut, and stooping down to the fire, lighted a piece of bogwood to enable him to see. On the ground, covered only by a ragged frieze coat, lay a young woman quite dead: her arm, emaciated and livid, was wrapped round a little child of about three years old, still sleeping on the cold bosom of its mother.

'You must take little Patsy away,' said Owen in a whisper, as he lifted the boy in his arms; '*she's* happy now.'

The young man fell upon his knees and kissed the corpse, but spoke not a word; grief had stupefied his senses, and he was like one but half awake. 'Come with me, Martin; come with me, and I'll settle every thing for you.' He obeyed mechanically, and before quitting the cabin, placed some turf upon the fire, as he was wont to do. The action was a simple one, but it brought the tears into Owen's eyes. 'I'll take care of Patsy for you till you want him. He's fond of me of ould, and won't be lonesome with me'; and Owen wrapped the child in his greatcoat, and moved forwards.

When they had advanced a few paces, Martin stopped suddenly and muttered, 'She has nothing to drink!' and then, as if remembering vaguely what had happened, added, 'It's a long sleep, Ellen dear!'

Owen gave the directions for the funeral, and leaving poor Martin in the house of one of the cottiers near, where he sat down beside the hearth, and never uttered a word; he went on his way, with little Patsy still asleep within his arms.

'Where are you going, Peggy?' asked Owen, as an old lame woman moved past as rapidly as her infirmity would permit: 'you're in a hurry this morning.'

'So I am, Owen Connor – these is the busy times wid me – I streaked five to-day, early as it is, and I'm going now over to Phil Joyce's. What's the matter wid yourself, Owen? sit down, avich, and taste this.'

'What's wrong at Phil's?' asked Owen, with a choking fulness in his throat.

'It's the little brother he has; Billy's got it, they say.'

'Is Mary Joyce well – did ye hear?'

'Errah! she's well enough now, but she may be low before night,' muttered the crone; while she added, with a fiendish laugh, 'her purty faytures won't save her now, no more nor the rest of us.'

'There's a bottle of port wine, Peggy; take it with ye, dear. 'Tis the finest thing at all, I'm tould, for keeping it off – get Mary to take a glass of it; but mind now, for the love o' ye, never say it was me gav it. There's bad blood between the Joyces and me, ye understand.'

'Ay, ay, I know well enough,' said the hag, clutching the bottle eagerly, while opening a gate on the roadside, she hobbled on her way towards Phil Joyce's cabin.

It was near evening as Owen was enabled to turn homewards; for besides having a great many places to visit, he was obliged to stop twice to get poor Patsy something to eat, the little fellow being almost in a state of starvation. At length he faced towards the mountain, and with a sad heart and weary step plodded along.

'Is poor Ellen buried?' said he, as he passed the carpenter's door, where the coffin had been ordered.

'She's just laid in the mould – awhile ago.'

'I hope Martin bears up better; – did you see him lately?'

'This is for him,' said the carpenter, striking a board with his hammer; 'he's at peace now.'

'Martin! sure he's not dead? – Martin Neale, I mean.'

'So do I too; he had it on him since morning, they say; but he just slipped away without a word or a moan.'

'O God, be good to us, but the times is dreadful!' ejaculated Owen.

'Some says it's the ind of the world's comin',' said an old man, that sat moving his stick listlessly among the shavings; 'and 'twould be well for most of us it was too.'

'Thrue for you, Billy; there's no help for the poor.'

No sentiment could meet more general acceptance than this – none less likely to provoke denial. Thrown upon each other for acts of kindness and benevolence, they felt from how narrow a store each contributed to another's wants, and knew well all the privations that charity like this necessitated, at the same time that they felt themselves deserted by those whose generosity might have been exercised without sacrificing a single enjoyment, or interfering with the pursuit of any accustomed pleasure.

There is no more common theme than the ingratitude of the poor – their selfishness and hard-heartedness; and unquestionably a life of poverty is but an indifferent teacher of fine feelings or gentle emotions. The dreary monotony of their daily lives, the unvarying sameness of the life-long struggle between labour and want, are little suggestive of any other spirit than a dark and brooding melancholy: and it were well, besides, to ask, if they who call themselves benefactors have been really generous, and not merely just? We speak more particularly of the relations which exist between the owner of the land and those who till it; and where benevolence is a duty, and not a virtue depending on the will: not that they, in whose behalf it is ever exercised, regard it in this light – very far from it! Their thankfulness for benefits is generally most disproportioned to their extent; but we are dissatisfied because our charity has not changed the whole current of their fortunes, and that the favours which cost us so little to bestow, should not become the ruling principle of their lives.

Owen reflected deeply on these things as he ascended the mountain-road. The orphan child he carried in his arms pressed such thoughts upon him, and he wondered why rich men denied themselves the pleasures of benevolence. He did not know that many great men enjoyed the happiness, but that it was made conformable to their high estate by institutions and establishments; by boards, and committees, and guardians; by all the pomp and circumstances of stuccoed buildings and liveried attendants. That to save themselves the burden of memory, their good deeds were chronicled in lists of 'founders' and 'life-subscribers', and their names set forth in newspapers; while to protect their finer natures from the rude assaults of actual misery, they deputed others to be the stewards of their bounty.

Owen did not know all this, or he had doubtless been less unjust regarding such persons. He never so much as heard of the pains that are taken to ward off the very sight of poverty, and all the appliances employed to exclude suffering from the gaze of the wealthy. All his little experience told him was, how much of good might be done within the sphere around him by one possessed of affluence. There was not a cabin around, where he could not point to some object claiming aid or assistance. Even in seasons of comparative comfort and abundance, what a deal of misery still existed; and what a blessing it would bring on him who sought it out, to compassionate and relieve it! So Owen thought, and so he felt too; not the less strongly that another heart then beat against his own, the little pulses sending a gush of wild delight through his bosom as he revelled in the ecstasy of benevolence. The child awoke, and looked wildly about him; but when he recognized in whose arms he was, he smiled happily, and cried, 'Nony, Nony,' the name by which Owen was known among all the children of the village and its neighbourhood.

'Yes, Patsy,' said Owen, kissing him, 'your own Nony! you're coming home with him to see what a nice house he has upon the mountain for you, and the purty lake near it, and the fish swimming in it.'

The little fellow clapped his hands with glee, and seemed delighted at all he heard.

'Poor darlin',' muttered Owen, sorrowfully; 'he doesn't know 'tis the sad day for him'; and as he spoke, the wind from the valley bore on it the mournful cadence of a death-cry, as a funeral moved along the road. 'His father's berrin'!' added he. 'God help us! how fast misfortune does be overtaking us at the time our heart's happiest! It will be many a day before he knows all this morning cost him.'

The little child meanwhile caught the sounds, and starting up in Owen's arms, he strained his eyes to watch the funeral procession as it slowly passed on. Owen held him up for a few seconds to see it, and wiped the large tears that started to his own eyes. 'Maybe Martin and poor Ellen's looking down on us now!' and with that he laid the little boy back in his arms and plodded forward.

It was but seldom that Owen Connor ascended that steep way without halting to look down on the wide valley, and the lake, and the distant mountains beyond it. The scene was one of which he never wearied; indeed, its familiarity had charms for him greater and higher than mere picturesque beauty can bestow. Each humble cabin with its little family was known to him; he was well read in the story of their lives; he had mingled in all their hopes and fears from childhood to old age; and, as the lights trembled through the dark night and spangled the broad expanse, he could bring before his mind's eye the humble hearths round which they sat, and think he almost heard their voices. Now, he heeded not these things, but steadily bent his steps towards home.

At last, the twinkle of a star-like light shewed that he was near his journey's end. It shone from the deep shadow of a little glen, in which his cabin stood. The seclusion of the spot was in Owen's eyes its greatest charm. Like all men who have lived much alone, he set no common store by the pleasures of solitude, and fancied that most if not all of his happiness was derived from this source. At this moment his gratitude was more than usual, as he muttered to himself, 'Thank God for it! we've a snug little place away from the sickness, and no house near us at all'; and with this comforting reflection he drew near the cabin. The door, contrary to custom at nightfall, lay open; and Owen, painfully alive to any suspicious sign, from the state of anxiety his mind had suffered, entered hastily.

'Father! where are you?' said he quickly, not seeing the old man in his accustomed place beside the fire; but there was no answer. Laying the child down, Owen passed into the little chamber which served as the old man's bedroom, and where now he lay stretched upon the bed in his clothes. 'Are ye sick, father? What ails ye, father dear?' asked the young man, as he took his hand in his own.

'I'm glad ye've come at last, Owen,' replied his father feebly. 'I've got the sickness, and am going fast.'

'No – no, father! don't be down-hearted!' cried Owen, with a desperate effort to suggest the courage he did not feel; for the touch of the cold wet hand had already told him the sad secret. ''Tis a turn ye have.'

'Well, maybe so,' said he, with a sigh; 'but there's a cowld feeling about my heart I never knew afore. Get me a warm drink, anyway.'

While Owen prepared some cordial from the little store he usually dispensed among the people, his father told him, that a boy from a sick house had called at the cabin that morning to seek for Owen, and from him, in all likelihood, he must have caught the malady. 'I remember,' said the old man, 'that he was quite dark in the skin, and was weak in his limbs as he walked.'

'Ayeh!' muttered Owen, 'av it was the "disease" he had, sorra bit of this mountain he'd ever get up. The strongest men can't lift a cup of wather to their lips, when it's on them; but there's a great scarcity in the glen, and maybe the boy eat nothing before he set out.'

Although Owen's explanation was the correct one, it did not satisfy the old man's mind, who, besides feeling convinced of his having the malady, could not credit his taking it by other means than contagion. Owen never quitted his side, and multiplied cares and attentions of every kind; but it was plain the disease was gaining ground, for ere midnight the old man's strength was greatly gone, and his voice sunk to a mere whisper. Yet the malady was characterized by none of the symptoms of the prevailing epidemic, save slight cramps, of which from time to time he complained. His case seemed one of utter exhaustion. His mind was clear and calm; and although unable to speak, except in short and broken sentences, no trait of wandering intellect appeared. His malady was a common one among those whose fears, greatly excited by the disease, usually induced symptoms of prostration and debility, as great, if not as rapid, as those of actual cholera. Meanwhile his thoughts were alternately turning from his own condition to that of the people in the glen, for whom he felt the deepest compassion. 'God help them!' was his constant expression. 'Sickness is the sore thing; but starvation makes it dreadful. And so Luke Clancy's dead! Poor ould Luke! he was seventy-one in Michaelmas. And Martin, too! he was a fine man.'

The old man slept, or seemed to sleep, for some hours, and on waking it was clear daylight. 'Owen, dear! I wish,' said he, 'I could see the Priest; but you mustn't lave me: I couldn't bear that now.'

Poor Owen's thoughts were that moment occupied on the same subject, and he was torturing himself to think of any means of obtaining Father John's assistance, without being obliged to go for him himself.

'I'll go, and be back here in an hour – ay, or less,' said he, eagerly; for terrible as death was to him, the thought of seeing his father die unanointed, was still more so.

'In an hour – where'll I be in an hour, Owen dear? the blessed Virgin knows well, it wasn't my fault – I'd have the Priest av I could – and sure, Owen, you'll not begrudge me masses, when I'm gone. What's that? It's like a child crying out there.'

''Tis poor Martin's little boy I took home with me – he's lost father and mother this day'; and so saying, Owen hastened to see what ailed the child. 'Yer sarvent, sir,' said Owen, as he perceived a stout-built, coarse-looking man, with a bull-terrier at his heels, standing in the middle of the floor; 'Yer sarvent, sir. Who do ye want here?'

'Are you Owen Connor?' said the man, gruffly.

'That same,' replied Owen, as sturdily.

'Then this is notice for you to come up to Mr Lucas's office in Galway before the twenty-fifth, with your rent, or the receipt for it, which ever you like best.'

'And who is Mr Lucas when he's at home?' said Owen, half-sneeringly.

'You'll know him when you see him,' rejoined the other, turning to leave the cabin, as he threw a printed paper on the dresser; and then, as if thinking he had not been formal enough in his mission, added, 'Mr Lucas is agent to your landlord, Mr Leslie; and I'll give you a bit of advice, keep a civil tongue in your head with him, and it will do you no harm.'

This counsel, delivered much more in a tone of menace than of friendly advice, concluded the interview, for having spoken, the fellow left the cabin, and began to descend the mountain.

Owen's heart swelled fiercely – a flood of conflicting emotions were warring within it; and as he turned to throw the paper into the fire, his eye caught the date, 16th March. 'St Patrick's Eve, the very day I saved his life,' said he, bitterly. 'Sure I knew well enough how it would be when the landlord died! Well, well, if my poor ould father doesn't know it, it's no matter. – Well, Patsy, acushla, what are ye crying for? There, my boy, don't be afeard, 'tis Nony's with ye.'

The accents so kindly uttered quieted the little fellow in a moment, and in a few minutes after he was again asleep in the old straw chair beside the fire. Brief as Owen's absence had been, the old man seemed much worse as he entered the room. 'God forgive me, Owen darling,' said he, 'but it wasn't my poor sowl I was thinking of that minit. I was thinking that you must get a letter wrote to the young landlord about this little place – I'm sure he'll never say a word about rent, no more nor his father; and as the times wasn't good lately—'

'There, there, father,' interrupted Owen, who felt shocked at the old man's not turning his thoughts in another direction; 'never mind those things,' said he; 'who knows which of us will be left? the sickness doesn't spare the young, no more than the ould.'

'Nor the rich, no more nor the poor,' chimed in the old man, with a kind of bitter satisfaction, as he thought on the landlord's death; for of such incongruous motives is man made up, that calamities come lighter when they involve the fall of those in station above our own. ''Tis a fine day, seemingly,' said he, suddenly changing the current of his thoughts; 'and elegant weather for the country; we'll have to turn in the sheep over that wheat; it will be too rank: ayeh,' cried he, with a deep sigh, 'I'll not be here to see it'; and for once, the emotions, no dread of futurity could awaken, were realized by worldly considerations, and the old man wept like a child.

'What time of the month is it?' asked he, after a long interval in which neither spoke; for Owen was not really sorry that even thus painfully the old man's thoughts should be turned towards eternity.

'Tis the seventeenth, father, a holy-day all over Ireland!'

'Is there many at the "station"? – look out at the door and see.'

Owen ascended a little rising ground in front of the cabin, from which the whole valley was visible; but except a group that followed a funeral upon the road, he could see no human thing around. The green where the 'stations' were celebrated was totally deserted. There were neither tents nor people; the panic of the plague had driven all ideas of revelry from the minds of the most reckless; and, even to observe the duties of religion, men feared to assemble in numbers. So long as the misfortune was at a distance, they could mingle their prayers in common, and entreat for mercy; but when death knocked at every door, the terror became almost despair.

'Is the "stations" going on?' asked the old man eagerly, as Owen re-entered the room. 'Is the people at the holy well?'

'I don't see many stirring at all, to-day,' was the cautious answer; for Owen scrupled to inflict any avoidable pain upon his mind.

'Lift me up, then!' cried he suddenly, and with a voice stronger, from a violent effort of his will. 'Lift me up to the window, till I see the blessed cross; and maybe I'd get a prayer among them. Come, be quick, Owen!'

Owen hastened to comply with his request; but already the old man's eyes were glazed and filmy. The effort had but hastened the moment of his doom; and, with a low faint sigh, he lay back, and died.

To the Irish peasantry, who, more than any other people of Europe, are accustomed to bestow care and attention on the funerals of their friends and relatives, the Cholera, in its necessity for speedy interment, was increased in terrors tenfold. The honours which they were wont to lavish on the dead – the ceremonial of the wake – the mingled merriment and sorrow – the profusion with which they spent the hoarded gains of hard-working labour – and lastly, the long train to the churchyard, evidencing the respect entertained for the departed, should all be foregone; for had not prudence forbid their assembling in numbers, and thus incurring the chances of contagion, which, whether real or not, they firmly believed in, the work of death was too widely disseminated to make such gatherings possible. Each had some one to lament within the limits of his own family, and private sorrow left little room for public sympathy. No longer then was the road filled by people on horseback and foot, as the funeral procession moved forth. The death-wail sounded no more. To chant the *requiem* of the departed, a few – a very few – immediate friends followed the body to the grave, in silence unbroken. Sad hearts, indeed, they brought, and broken spirits; for in this season of pestilence few dared to hope.

By noon, Owen was seen descending the mountain to the village, to make the last preparations for the old man's funeral. He carried little Patsy in his arms; for he could not leave the poor child alone, and in the house of death. The claims of infancy would seem never stronger than in the heart sorrowing over death. The grief that carries the sufferer in his mind's eye over the limits of this world, is arrested by the tender ties which bind him to life in the young. There is besides a hopefulness in early life – it is, perhaps, its chief characteristic – that combats sorrow, better than all the caresses of friendship, and all the consolations of age. Owen felt this now – he never knew it before. But yesterday, and his father's death had left him without one in the world on whom to fix a hope; and already, from his misery, there arose that one gleam, that now twinkled like a star in the sky of midnight. The little child he had taken for his own was a world to him; and as he went, he prayed fervently that poor Patsy might be spared to him through this terrible pestilence.

When Owen reached the carpenter's, there were several people there; some, standing moodily brooding over recent bereavements; others, spoke in low whispers, as if fearful of disturbing the silence; but all were sorrow-struck and sad.

'How is the ould man, Owen?' said one of a group, as he came forward.

'He's better off than us, I trust in God!' said Owen, with a quivering lip. 'He went to rest this morning.'

A muttered prayer from all around shewed how general was the feeling of kindness entertained towards the Connors.

'When did he take it, Owen?'

'I don't know that he tuk it at all; but when I came home last night he was lying on the bed, weak and powerless, and he slept away, with scarce a pain, till daybreak; then—'

'He's in glory now, I pray God!' muttered an old man with a white beard. 'We were born in the same year, and I knew him since I was a child, like that in your arms; and a good man he was.'

'Whose is the child, Owen?' said another in the crowd.

'Martin Neale's,' whispered Owen; for he feared that the little fellow might catch the words. 'What's the matter with Miles? he looks very low this morning.'

This question referred to a large powerful-looking man, who, with a smith's apron twisted round his waist, sat without speaking in a corner of the shop.

'I'm afeard he's in a bad way,' whispered the man to whom he spoke. 'There was a process-server, or a bailiff, or something of the kind, serving notices through the townland yesterday, and he lost a shoe off his baste, and would have Miles out, to put it on, tho' we all tould him that he buried his daughter – a fine grown girl – that mornin'. And what does the fellow do, but goes and knocks at the forge till Miles comes out. You know Miles Regan, so I needn't say there wasn't many words passed between them. In less nor two minutes – whatever the bailiff said – Miles tuck him by the throat, and pulled him down from the horse, and dragged him along to the lake, and flung him in. 'Twas the Lord's marcy he knew how to swim; but we don't know what'll be done to Miles yet, for he was the new agent's man.'

'Was he a big fellow, with a bull-dog following him?' asked Owen.

'No; that's another; sure there's three or four of them goin' about. We hear, that bad as ould French was, the new one is worse.'

'Well – well, it's the will of God!' said Owen, in that tone of voice which bespoke a willingness for all endurance, so long as the consolation remained, that the ill was not unrecorded above; while he felt that all the evils of poverty were little in comparison with the loss of those nearest and dearest. 'Come, Patsy, my boy!' said he at last, as he placed the coffin in the ass-cart, and turned towards the mountain; and, leading the little fellow by the hand, he set out on his way – 'Come home.'

It was not until he arrived at that part of the road from which the cabin was visible, that Owen knew the whole extent of his bereavement; then, when he looked up and saw the door hasped on the outside, and the chimney from which no smoke ascended, the full measure of his lone condition came at once before him, and he bent over the coffin and wept bitterly. All the old man's affection for him, his kind indulgence and forbearance, his happy nature, his simple-heartedness, gushed forth from his memory, and he wondered why he had not loved his father, in life, a thousand times more, so deeply was he now penetrated by his loss. If this theme did not assuage his sorrows, it at least so moulded his heart as to bear them in a better spirit; and when, having placed the body in the coffin, he knelt down beside it to pray, it was in a calmer and more submissive frame of mind than he had yet known.

It was late in the afternoon ere Owen was once more on the road down the mountain; for it was necessary – or at least believed so – that interment should take place on the day of death.

'I never thought it would be this way you'd go to your last home, father dear,' said Owen aloud, and in a voice almost stifled with sobs; for the absence of all his friends and relatives at such a moment, now smote on the poor fellow's heart, as he walked beside the little cart on which the coffin was laid. It was indeed a sight to move a sterner nature than his: the coffin, not reverently carried by bearers, and followed by its long train of mourners, but laid slant-wise in the cart, the spade and shovel to dig the grave beside it, and Patsy seated on the back of the ass, watching with infant glee the motion of the animal, as with careful foot he descended the rugged mountain. Poor child! how your guileless laughter shook that strong man's heart with agony!

It was a long and weary way to the old churchyard. The narrow road, too, was deeply rutted and worn by wheel-tracks; for, alas, it had been trodden by many, of late. The grey daylight was fast fading as Owen pushed wide the old gate and entered. What a change to his eyes did the aspect of the place present! The green mounds of earth which marked the resting-place of village patriarchs, were gone; and heaps of fresh-turned clay were seen on every side, no longer decorated, as of old, with little emblems of affectionate sorrow; no tree, nor stone, not even a wild flower, spoke of the regrets of those who remained. The graves were rudely fashioned, as if in haste – for so it was – few dared to linger there!

Seeking out a lone spot near the ruins, Owen began to dig the grave, while the little child, in mute astonishment at all he saw, looked on.

'Why wouldn't you stay out in the road, Patsy, and play there, till I come to you? This is a cowld damp place for you, my boy.'

'Nony! Nony!' cried the child, looking at him with an affectionate smile, as though to say he'd rather be near him.

'Well, well, who knows but you're right? if it's the will of God to take me, maybe you might as well go too. It's a sore thing to be alone in the world, like me now!' And as he muttered the last few words he ceased digging, and rested his head on the cross of the spade.

'Was that you, Patsy? I heard a voice somewhere.'

The child shook his head in token of dissent.

'Ayeh! it was only the wind through the ould walls; but sure it might be nat'ral enough for sighs and sobs to be here: there's many a one has floated over this damp clay.'

He resumed his work once more. The night was falling fast as Owen stepped from the deep grave, and knelt down to say a prayer ere he committed the body to the earth.

'Kneel down, darlin', here by my side,' said he, placing his arm round the little fellow's waist; ''tis the likes of you God loves best'; and joining the tiny hands with his own, he uttered a deep and fervent prayer for the soul of the departed. 'There, father!' said he, as he arose at last, and in a voice as if addressing a living person at his side; 'there, father: the Lord, he knows my heart inside me; and if walking the world barefoot would give ye peace or ease, I'd do it, for you were a kind man and a good father to me.' He kissed the coffin as he spoke, and stood silently gazing on it.

Arousing himself with a kind of struggle, he untied the cords, and lifted the coffin from the cart. For some seconds he busied himself in arranging the ropes beneath it, and then ceased suddenly, on remembering that he could not lower it into the grave unassisted.

'I'll have to go down the road for some one,' muttered he to himself; but as he said this, he perceived at some distance off in the churchyard the figure of a man, as if kneeling over a grave. 'The Lord help him, he has his grief too!' ejaculated Owen, as he moved towards him. On coming nearer he perceived that the grave was newly made, and from its size evidently that of a child.

'I ax your pardon,' said Owen, in a timid voice, after waiting for several minutes in the vain expectation that the man would look up; 'I ax your pardon for disturbing you, but maybe you'll be kind enough to help me to lay this coffin in the ground. I have nobody with me but a child.'

The man started and looked round. Their eyes met; it was Phil Joyce and Owen who now confronted each other. But how unlike were both to what they were at their last parting! Then, vindictive passion, outraged pride, and vengeance, swelled every feature and tingled in every fibre of their frames. Now, each stood pale, care-worn, and dispirited, wearied out by sorrow, and almost broken-hearted. Owen was the first to speak.

'I axed your pardon before I saw you, Phil Joyce, and I ax it again now, for disturbing you; but I didn't know you, and I wanted to put my poor father's body in the grave.'

'I didn't know he was dead,' said Phil, in a hollow voice, like one speaking to himself. 'This is poor little Billy here,' and he pointed to the mound at his feet.

'The heavens be his bed this night!' said Owen, piously; 'Good night!' and he turned to go away; then stopping suddenly, he added, 'Maybe, after all, you'll not refuse me, and the Lord might be more merciful to us both, than if we were to part like enemies.'

'Owen Connor, I ask your forgiveness,' said Phil, stretching forth his hand, while his voice trembled like a sick child's. 'I didn't think the day would come I'd ever do it; but my heart is humble enough now, and maybe 'twill be lower soon. Will you take my hand?'

'Will I, Phil? will I, is it? ay, and however ye may change to me after this night, I'll never forget this.' And he grasped the cold fingers in both hands, and pressed them ardently, and the two men fell into each other's arms and wept.

Is it a proud or a humiliating confession for humanity – assuredly it is a true one – that the finest and best traits of our nature are elicited in our troubles, and not in our joys? that we come out purer through trials than prosperity? Does the chastisement of Heaven teach us better than the blessings lavished upon us? or are these gifts the compensation sent us for our afflictions, that when poorest before man we should be richest before God? Few hearts there are which sorrow makes not wiser – none which are not better for it. So it was here. These men, in the continuance of good fortune, had been enemies for life; mutual hatred had grown up between them, so that each yearned for vengeance on the other; and now they walked like brothers, only seeking forgiveness of each other, and asking pardon for the past.

The old man was laid in his grave, and they turned to leave the churchyard.

'Won't ye come home with me, Owen?' said Phil, as they came to where their roads separated; 'won't ye come and eat your supper with us?'

Owen's throat filled up: he could only mutter, 'Not to-night, Phil – another time, plaze God.' He had not ventured even to ask for Mary, nor did he know whether Phil Joyce in his reconciliation might wish a renewal of any intimacy with his sister. Such was the reason of Owen's refusal; for, however strange it may seem to some, there is a delicacy of the heart as well as of good breeding, and one advantage it possesses – it is of all lands, and the fashion never changes.

Poor Owen would have shed his best blood to be able to ask after Mary – to learn how she was, and how she bore up under the disasters of the time; but he never mentioned her name: and as for Phil Joyce, his gloomy thoughts had left no room for others, and he parted from Owen without a single allusion to her. 'Good night, Owen,' said he, 'and don't forget your promise to come and see us soon.'

'Good night, Phil,' was the answer; 'and I pray a blessing on you and yours.' A slight quivering of the voice at the last word was all he suffered to escape him; and they parted.

JOSEPH SHERIDAN LE FANU

from *Uncle Silas*

17

An Adventure

For many days after our quarrel, Madame hardly spoke to me. As for lessons, I was not much troubled with them. It was plain, too, that my father had spoken to her, for she never after that day proposed our extending our walks beyond the precincts of Knowl.

Knowl, however, was a very considerable territory, and it was possible for a much better pedestrian than I to tire herself effectually, without passing its limits. So we took occasionally long walks.

After some weeks of sullenness, during which, for days at a time, she hardly spoke to me, and seemed lost in dark and evil abstraction, she once more, and somewhat suddenly, recovered her spirits, and grew quite friendly. Her gaieties and friendliness were not reassuring, and in my mind presaged approaching mischief and treachery. The days were shortening to the wintry span. The edge of the red sun had already touched the horizon as Madame and I, overtaken at the warren by his last beams, were hastening homeward.

A narrow carriage-road traverses this wild region of the park, to which a distant gate gives entrance. On descending into this unfrequented road I was surprised to see a carriage standing there. A thin, sly postilion, with that pert, turned-up nose which the old caricaturist Woodward used to attribute to the gentlemen of Tewkesbury, was leaning on his horses, and looked hard at me as I passed. A lady who sat within looked out, with an extra-fashionable bonnet on, and also treated us to a stare. Very pink and white cheeks she had, very black glossy hair and bright eyes, fat, bold, and rather cross, she looked – and in her bold way, she examined us curiously as we passed.

I mistook the situation. It had once happened before that an intending visitor at Knowl, had entered the place by that park road, and lost several hours in a vain search for the house.

'Ask him, Madame, whether they want to go to the house; I dare say they have missed their way,' whispered I.

'*Eh bien*, they will find again. I do not choose to talk to post-boys; *allons!*'

But I asked the man as we passed, 'Do you want to reach the house?'

By this time he was at the horses' heads, buckling the harness.

'Noa,' he said in a surly tone, smiling oddly on the winkers; but, recollecting his politeness, he added: 'Noa, thankee, misses, it's what they calls a pic-nic; we'll be takin' the road, now.'

He was smiling now on a little buckle with which he was engaged.

'Come – nonsense!' whispered Madame, sharply in my ear, and she whisked me by the arm, so we crossed the little stile at the other side.

Our path lay across the warren, which undulates in little hillocks. The sun was down by this time, blue shadows were stretching round us, colder in the splendid contrast of the burnished sunset sky.

Descending over these hillocks we saw three figures a little in advance of us, not far from the path we were tracing. Two were standing smoking and chatting at intervals. One tall and slim, with a high chimney-pot, worn a little on one side, and a white great-coat buttoned up to the chin. The other shorter and stouter, with a dark-coloured wrapper. These gentlemen were facing rather our way as we came over the edge of the eminence, but turned their backs on perceiving our approach. As they did so I remember so well each lowered his cigar suddenly, with the simultaneousness of a drill. The third figure sustained the pic-nic character of the group, for he was repacking a hamper. He stood suddenly erect as we drew near, and a very ill-looking person he was, low-browed, square-chinned, and with a broad, broken nose. He wore gaiters, and was a little bandy, very broad, and had a closely-cropped bullet head, and deep-set little eyes. The moment I saw him, I beheld the living type of the burglars and bruisers whom I had so often beheld with a kind of scepticism in *Punch*. He stood over his hamper and scowled sharply at us for a moment; then with the point of his foot he jerked a little fur cap that lay on the ground into his hand, drew it tight over his lowering brows, and called to his companions, just as we passed him – 'Hallo! mister. How's this?'

'All right,' said the tall person in the white great-coat, who as he answered shook his shorter companion by the arm, I thought angrily.

This shorter companion turned about. He had a muffler loose about his neck and chin. I thought he seemed shy and irresolute, and the tall man gave him a great jolt with his elbow, which made him stagger, and I fancied a little angry, for he said as it seemed a sulky word or two.

The gentleman in the white surtout, however, standing direct in our way, raised his hat with a mock salutation, placing his hand on his breast and forthwith began to advance with an insolent grin and an air of tipsy frolic.

'Jist in time, ladies; five minutes more and we'd a bin off. Thankee, Mrs Mouser, ma'am, for the honour of the meetin', and more particular for the pleasure of making your young lady's acquaintance – niece, ma'am? daughter, ma'am? granddaughter, by Jove, is it? Hallo! there, mild 'un, I say, stop packin'.' This was to the ill-favoured person with the broken nose. 'Bring us a couple o' glasses and a bottle o' curaçoa; what are you feard on, my dear? this is Lord Lollipop, here, a reg'lar charmer, wouldn't hurt a fly, hey Lolly? Isn't he pretty, Miss? and I'm Sir Simon Sugarstick – so called after old Sir Simon, ma'am; and I'm so tall and straight, Miss, and slim – ain't I? and ever so sweet, my honey, when you come to know me, just like a sugarstick; ain't I, Lolly, boy?'

'I'm Miss Ruthyn, tell them, Madame,' I said, stamping on the ground, and very much frightened.

'Be quaite, Maud. If you are angry they will hurt us; leave me to speak,' whispered the gouvernante.

All this time they were approaching from separate points. I glanced back, and saw the ruffianly-looking man within a yard or two, with his arm raised and one finger up, telegraphing, as it seemed, to the gentlemen in front.

'Be quaite, Maud,' whispered Madame, with an awful adjuration, which I do not care to set down. 'They are teepsy; don't seem 'fraid.'

I *was* afraid – terrified. The circle had now so narrowed that they might have placed their hands on my shoulders.

'Pray, gentlemen, wat you want? *weel* a you 'av the goodness to permit us to go on?'

I now observed for the first time, with a kind of shock, that the shorter of the two men, who prevented our advance, was the person who had accosted me so offensively at Church Scarsdale. I pulled Madame by the arm, whispering, 'Let us run.'

'Be quaite my dear Maud,' was her only reply.

'I tell you what,' said the tall man, who had replaced his high hat more jauntily than before on the side of his head, 'we've caught you now, fair game, and we'll let you off on conditions. You must not be frightened, Miss. Upon my honour and soul, I mean no mischief; do I, Lollipop? I call him Lord Lollipop, it's only chaff though; his name's Smith. Now, Lolly, I vote we let the prisoners go, when we just introduce them to Mrs Smith; she's sitting in the carriage, and keeps Mr S. here in precious good order, I promise you. There's easy terms for you, eh, and we'll have a glass o' curaçoa round, and so part friends. Is it a bargain? Come!'

'Yes, Maud, we must go – wat matter?' whispered Madame, vehemently.

'You shan't,' I said, instinctively terrified.

'You'll go with Ma'am, young 'un, won't you?' said Mr Smith, as his companion called him.

Madame was holding my arm, but I snatched it from her, and would have run; the tall man, however, placed his arms round me and held me fast with an affectation of playfulness, but his grip was hard enough to hurt me a good deal. Being now thoroughly frightened, after an ineffectual struggle, during which I heard Madame say, 'You fool, Maud, weel you come with me? See wat you are doing –' I began to scream, shriek after shriek, which the man attempted to drown with loud hooting, peals of laughter, forcing his handkerchief against my mouth, while Madame continued to bawl her exhortations to 'be quaite' in my ear.

'I'll lift her, I say?' said a gruff voice behind me.

But at this instant, wild with terror, I distinctly heard other voices shouting. The men who surrounded me were instantly silent, and all looked in the direction of the sound, now very near, and I screamed with redoubled energy. The ruffian behind me thrust his great hand over my mouth.

'It is the gamekeeper,' cried Madame. '*Two* gamekeepers – we are safe – thank Heaven!' and she began to call on Dykes by name.

I only remember, feeling myself at liberty – running a few steps – seeing Dykes' white furious face – clinging to his arm, with which he was bringing his gun to a level, and saying, 'Don't fire – they'll murder us if you do.'

Madame, screaming lustily, ran up at the same moment.

'Run on to the gate and lock it. I'll be wi' ye in a minute,' cried he to the other gamekeeper; who started instantly on this mission, for the three ruffians were already in full retreat for the carriage.

Giddy – wild – fainting – still terror carried me on.

'Now, Madame Rogers – s'pose you take young Misses on – I must run and len' Bill a hand.'

'No, no; you moste not,' cried Madame. 'I am fainting myself, and more villains they may be near to us.'

But at this moment we heard a shot, and muttering to himself and grasping his gun, Dykes ran at his utmost speed in the direction of the sound.

With many exhortations to speed, and ejaculations of alarm, Madame hurried me on toward the house, which at length we reached without further adventure.

As it happened, my father met us in the hall. He was perfectly transported with fury on hearing from Madame what had happened, and set out at once, with some of the servants, in the hope of intercepting the party at the park gate.

Here was a new agitation; for my father did not return for nearly three hours, and I could not conjecture what might be occurring during the period of his absence. My alarm was greatly increased by the arrival in the interval of poor Bill the under-gamekeeper, very much injured.

Seeing that he was determined to intercept their retreat, the three men had set upon him, wrested his gun, which exploded in the struggle, from him, and beat him savagely. I mention these particulars because they convinced everybody that there was something specially determined and ferocious in the spirit of the party, and that the fracas was no mere frolic, but the result of a predetermined plan.

My father had not succeeded in overtaking them. He traced them to the Lugton Station, where they had taken the railway, and no one could tell him in what direction the carriage and post-horses had driven.

Madame was, or affected to be, very much shattered by what had occurred. Her recollection and mine, when my father questioned us closely, differed very materially respecting many details of the *personnel* of the villainous party. She was obstinate and clear; and although the gamekeeper corroborated my description of them, still my father was puzzled. Perhaps he was not sorry that some hesitation was forced upon him, because although at first he would have gone almost any length to detect the persons, on reflection he was pleased that there was not evidence to bring them into a court of justice, the publicity and annoyance of which would have been inconceivably distressing to me.

Madame was in a strange state – tempestuous in temper, talking incessantly – every now and then in floods of tears, and perpetually on her knees pouring forth torrents of thanksgiving to Heaven for our joint deliverance from the hands of those villains. Notwithstanding our community of danger and her thankfulness on my behalf, however, she broke forth into wrath and railing whenever we were alone together.

'Wat fool you were! so disobedient and obstinate; if you 'ad done wat *I* say, then we should 'av been quaite safe; those persons they were tipsy, and there is nothing so dangerous as to quarrel with tipsy persons; I would 'av brought you quaite safe – the lady she seem so nice and quaite, and we should 'av been safe with her – there would 'av been nothing absolutely; but instead you would scream and pooshe, and so they grow quite wild, and all the impertinence and violence follow of course; and that a poor Bill – all his beating and danger to his life it is cause entairely by you.'

And she spoke with more real virulence than that kind of upbraiding generally exhibits.

'The beast!' exclaimed Mrs Rusk, when she, I, and Mary Quince were in my room together, 'with all her crying and praying, I'd like to know as much as she does, maybe, about them rascals. There never was sich like about the place, long as I remember it, till she came to Knowl, old witch! with them unmerciful big bones of hers, and her great bald head, grinning here, and crying there, and her nose everywhere. The old French hypocrite!'

Mary Quince threw in an observation, and I believe Mrs Rusk rejoined, but I heard neither. For whether the housekeeper spoke with reflection or not, what she said affected me strangely. Through the smallest aperture, for a moment, I had had a peep into Pandemonium. Were not peculiarities of Madame's demeanour and advice during the adventure partly accounted for by the suggestion? Could the proposed excursion to Church Scarsdale have had any purpose of the same sort? What was proposed? How was Madame interested in it? Were such immeasurable treason and hypocrisy possible? I could not explain nor quite believe in the shapeless suspicion that with these light and bitter words of the old housekeeper had stolen so horribly into my mind.

After Mrs Rusk was gone I awoke from my dismal abstraction with something like a moan and a shudder, with a dreadful sense of danger.

'Oh! Mary Quince,' I cried, 'do *you* think she really knew?'

'*Who?* Miss Maud.'

'Do you think Madame knew of those dreadful people? Oh, no – say you don't – you don't believe it – tell me she did not. I'm distracted, Mary Quince, I'm frightened out of my life.'

'There now, Miss Maud, dear – there now, don't take on so – why should she? – no sich a thing. Mrs Rusk, law bless you, she's no more meaning in what she says than the child unborn.'

But I was really frightened. I was in a horrible state of uncertainty as to Madame de la Rougierre's complicity with the party who had beset us at the warren, and afterwards so murderously beat our poor gamekeeper. How was I ever to get rid of that horrible woman? How long was she to enjoy her continual opportunities of affrighting and injuring me?

'She hates me – she hates me, Mary Quince; and she will never stop until she has done me some dreadful injury. Oh! will no one relieve me – will no one take her away? Oh, papa, papa, papa! you will be sorry when it is too late.'

I was crying and wringing my hands, and turning from side to side, at my wits' ends, and honest Mary Quince in vain endeavoured to quiet and comfort me.

18

A Midnight Visitor

The frightful warnings of Lady Knollys haunted me too. Was there no escape from the dreadful companion whom fate had assigned me? I made up my mind again and again to speak to my father and urge her removal. In other things he indulged me; here, however, he met me drily and sternly, and it was plain that he fancied I was under my Cousin Monica's influence, and also that he had secret reasons for persisting in an opposite course. Just then I had a gay, odd letter from Lady Knollys, from some country house in Shropshire. Not a word about Captain Oakley. My eye skimmed its pages in search of that charmed name. With a peevish feeling I tossed the sheet upon the table. Inwardly I thought how ill-natured and unwomanly it was.

After a time, however, I read it, and found the letter very good-natured. She had received a note from papa. He had 'had the impudence to forgive *her* for *his* impertinence'. But for my sake she meant, notwithstanding this aggravation, really to pardon him; and whenever she had a disengaged week, to accept his invitation to Knowl, from whence she was resolved to whisk me off to London, where, though I was too young to be presented at Court and come out, I might yet – besides having the best masters and a good excuse for getting rid of Medusa – see a great deal that would amuse and surprise me.

'Great news, I suppose, from Lady Knollys?' said Madame, who always knew who in the house received letters by the post, and by an intuition from whom they came. 'Two letters – you and your papa. She is quite well, I hope?'

'Quite well, thank you, Madame.'

Some fishing questions, dropt from time to time, fared no better. And as usual, when she was foiled even in a trifle, she became sullen and malignant.

That night, when my father and I were alone, he suddenly closed the book he had been reading and said –

'I heard from Monica Knollys to-day. I always liked poor Monnie; and though she's no witch, and very wrong-headed at times, yet now and then she does say a thing that's worth weighing. Did she ever talk to you of a time, Maud, when you are to be your own mistress?'

'No,' I answered, a little puzzled, and looking straight in his rugged, kindly face.

'Well, I thought she might – she's a rattle, you know – always *was* a rattle, and that sort of people say whatever comes uppermost. But that's a subject for me, and more than once, Maud, it has puzzled me.'

He sighed.

'Come with me to the study, little Maud.'

So, he carrying a candle, we crossed the lobby, and marched together through the passage, which at night always seemed a little awesome, darkly wainscoted, uncheered by the cross-light from the hall, which was lost at the turn, leading us away from the frequented parts of the house to that misshapen and lonely room about which the traditions of the nursery and the servants' hall had so many fearful stories to recount.

I think my father had intended making some disclosure to me on reaching this room. If so he changed his mind, or at least postponed his intention.

He had paused before the cabinet, respecting the key of which he had given me so strict a charge, and I think he was going to explain himself more fully than he had done. But he went on, instead, to the table where his desk, always jealously locked, was placed, and having lighted the candles which stood by it, he glanced at me, and said –

'You must wait a little, Maud; I shall have something to say to you. Take this candle and amuse yourself with a book meanwhile.'

I was accustomed to obey in silence. I chose a volume of engravings, and ensconced myself in a favourite nook in which I had often passed a half-hour similarly. This was a deep recess by the fireplace, fenced on the other side by a great old escritoire. Into this I drew a stool, and, with candle and book, I placed myself snugly in the narrow chamber. Every now and then I raised my eyes and saw my father either writing or ruminating, as it seemed to me, very anxiously at his desk.

Time wore on – a longer time than he had intended, and still he continued absorbed at his desk. Gradually I grew sleepy, and as I nodded, the book and room faded away, and pleasant little dreams began to gather round me, and so I went off into a deep slumber.

It must have lasted long, for when I wakened my candle had burnt out; my father, having quite forgotten me, was gone, and the room was dark and deserted. I felt cold and a little stiff, and for some seconds did not know where I was.

I had been wakened, I suppose, by a sound which I now distinctly heard, to my great terror, approaching. There was a rustling; there was a breathing. I heard a creaking upon the plank that always creaked when walked upon in the passage. I held my breath and listened, and coiled myself up in the innermost recess of my little chamber.

Sudden and sharp, a light shone in from the nearly closed study door. It shone angularly on the ceiling like a letter L reversed. There was a pause. Then some one knocked softly at the door, which after another pause was slowly pushed open. I expected, I think, to see the dreaded figure of the linkman. I was scarcely less frightened to see that of Madame de la Rougierre. She was dressed in a sort of grey silk, which she called her Chinese silk – precisely as she had been in the daytime. In fact I do not think she had undressed. She had no shoes on. Otherwise her toilet was deficient in nothing. Her wide mouth was grimly closed, and she stood scowling into the room with a searching and pallid scrutiny, the candle held high above her head at the full stretch of her arm.

Placed as I was in a deep recess, and in a seat hardly raised above the level of the floor, I escaped her, although it seemed to me for some seconds, as I gazed on this spectre, that our eyes actually met.

I sat without breathing or winking, staring upon the formidable image which with upstretched arm, and the sharp lights and hard shadows thrown upon her corrugated features, looked like a sorceress watching for the effect of a spell.

She was plainly listening intensely. Unconsciously she had drawn her lower lip altogether between her teeth, and I well remember what a deathlike and idiotic look the contortion gave her. My terror lest she should discover me amounted to positive agony. She rolled her eyes stealthily from corner to corner of the room, and listened with her neck awry at the door.

Then to my father's desk she went. To my great relief, her back was towards me. She stooped over it, with the candle close by; I saw her try a key – it could be nothing else – and I heard her blow through the wards to clear them.

Then, again, she listened at the door, candle in hand, and then with long tip-toe steps came back, and papa's desk in another moment was open, and Madame cautiously turning over the papers it contained.

Twice or thrice she paused, glided to the door, and listened again intently with her head near the ground, and then returned and continued her search, peeping into papers one after another, tolerably methodically, and reading some quite through.

While this felonious business was going on, I was freezing with fear lest she should accidentally look round and her eyes light on me; for I could not say what she might not do rather than have her crime discovered.

Sometimes she would read a paper twice over; sometimes a whisper no louder than the ticking of a watch; sometimes a brief chuckle under her breath, bespoke the interest with which here and there a letter or a memorandum was read.

For about half an hour, I think, this went on; but at the time it seemed to me all but interminable. On a sudden she raised her head and listened for a moment, replaced the papers deftly, closed the desk without noise, except for the tiny click of the lock, extinguished the candle, and rustled stealthily out of the room, leaving in the darkness the malign and hag-like face on which the candle had just shone still floating filmy in the dark.

Why did I remain silent and motionless while such an outrage was being committed? If, instead of being a very nervous girl, preoccupied with an undefinable terror of that wicked woman, I had possessed courage and presence of mind, I dare say I might have given an alarm, and escaped from the room without the slightest risk. But so it was; I could no more stir than the bird who, cowering under its ivy, sees the white owl sailing back and forward on its predatory cruise.

Not only during her presence, but for more than an hour after, I remained cowering in my hiding-place, and afraid to stir, lest she might either be lurking in the neighbourhood, or return and surprise me.

You will not be astonished, that after a night so passed I was ill and feverish in the morning. To my horror, Madame de la Rougierre came to visit me at my bedside. Not a trace of guilty consciousness of what had passed during the night was legible in her face. She had no sign of late watching, and her toilet was exemplary.

As she sat smiling by me, full of anxious and affectionate inquiry, and smoothed the coverlet with her great felonious hand, I could quite comprehend the dreadful feeling with which the deceived husband in the *Arabian Nights*, met his ghoul wife, after his nocturnal discovery.

Ill as I was, I got up and found my father in that room which adjoined his bedchamber. He perceived, I am sure, by my looks, that something unusual had happened. I shut the door, and came close beside his chair.

'Oh, papa, I have such a thing to tell you!' I forgot to call him 'Sir'. 'A secret; and you won't say who told you? Will you come down to the study?'

He looked hard at me, got up, and kissing my forehead, said – 'Don't be frightened, Maud; I venture to say it is a mare's nest; at all events, my child, we will take care that no danger reaches you; come, child.'

And by the hand he led me to the study. When the door was shut, and we had reached the far end of the room next the window, I said, but in a low tone, and holding his arm fast –

'Oh, sir, you don't know what a dreadful person we have living with us – Madame de la Rougierre, I mean. Don't let her in if she comes; she would guess what I am telling you, and one way or another I am sure she would kill me.'

'Tut, tut, child. You *must* know that's nonsense,' he said, looking pale and stern.

'Oh, no, papa. I am horribly frightened, and Lady Knollys thinks so too.'

'Ha! I dare say; one fool makes many. We all know what Monica thinks.'

'But I *saw* it, papa. She stole your key last night, and opened your desk, and read all your papers.'

'Stole my key!' said my father, staring at me perplexed, but at the same instant producing it. 'Stole it! Why here it is!'

'She unlocked your desk; she read your papers for ever so long. Open it now, and see whether they have not been stirred.'

He looked at me this time in silence, with a puzzled air; but he did unlock the desk, and lifted the papers curiously and suspiciously. As he did so he uttered a few of those inarticulate interjections which are made with closed lips, and not always intelligible; but he made no remark.

Then he placed me on a chair beside him, and sitting down himself, told me to recollect myself, and tell him distinctly all I had seen. This accordingly, I did, he listening with deep attention.

'Did she remove any paper?' asked my father, at the same time making a little search, I suppose, for that which he fancied might have been stolen.

'No; I did not see her take anything.'

'Well, you are a good girl, Maud. Act discreetly. Say nothing to any one – not even to your Cousin Monica.'

Directions which, coming from another person would have had no great weight, were spoken by my father with an earnest look and a weight of emphasis that made them irresistibly impressive, and I went away with the seal of silence upon my lips.

'Sit down, Maud, *there*. You have not been very happy with Madame de la Rougierre. It is time you were relieved. This occurrence decides it.'

He rang the bell.

'Tell Madame de la Rougierre that I request the honour of seeing her for a few minutes here.'

My father's communications to her were always equally ceremonious. In a few minutes there was a knock at the door, and the same figure, smiling, courtesying, that had scared me on the same threshold last night, like the spirit of evil, presented itself.

My father rose, and Madame having at his request taken a chair opposite, looking, as usual in his presence, all amiability, he proceeded at once to the point.

'Madame de la Rougierre, I have to request you that you will give me the key, now in your possession, which unlocks this desk of mine.'

With which termination he tapped his gold pencil-case suddenly on it.

Madame, who had expected something very different, became instantly so pale, with a dull purplish hue upon her forehead, that, especially when she had twice essayed with her white lips, in vain, to answer, I expected to see her fall in a fit.

She was not looking in his face; her eyes were fixed lower, and her mouth and cheek sucked in, with a strange distortion at one side.

She stood up suddenly, and staring straight in his face, she succeeded in saying, after twice clearing her throat –

'I cannot comprehend, Monsieur Ruthyn, unless you intend to insult me.'

'It won't do, Madame; I must have that *false key*. I give you the opportunity of surrendering it quietly here and now.'

'But who dares to say I possess such thing?' demanded Madame, who, having rallied from her momentary paralysis, was now fierce and voluble as I had often seen her before.

'You know, Madame, that you can rely on what I say, and I tell you that you were seen last night visiting this room, and with a key in your possession, opening this desk, and reading my letters and papers contained in it. Unless you forthwith give me that key, and any other false keys in your possession – in which case I shall rest content with dismissing you summarily – I will take a different course. You know I am a magistrate; – and I shall have you, your boxes, and places upstairs, searched forthwith, and I will prosecute you criminally. The thing is clear; you aggravate by denying; you must give me that key, if you please, instantly, otherwise I ring this bell, and you shall see that I mean what I say.'

There was a little pause. He rose and extended his hand towards the bell-rope. Madame glided round the table, extended her hand to arrest his.

'I will do everything, Monsieur Ruthyn – whatever you wish.'

And with these words Madame de la Rougierre broke down altogether. She sobbed, she wept, she gabbled piteously, all manner of incomprehensible roulades of lamentation and entreaty; coyly, penitently, in a most interesting agitation, she produced the very key from her breast, with a string tied to it. My father was little moved by this piteous tempest. He coolly took the key and tried it in the desk, which it locked and unlocked quite freely, though the wards were complicated. He shook his head and looked her in the face.

'Pray, who made this key? It is a new one, and made expressly to pick this lock.'

But Madame was not going to tell any more than she had expressly bargained for; so she only fell once more into her old paroxysm of sorrow, self-reproach, extenuation, and entreaty.

'Well,' said my father, 'I promised that on surrendering the key you should go. It is enough. I keep my word. You shall have an hour and a half to prepare in. You must then be ready to depart. I will send your money to you by Mrs Rusk; and if you look for another situation, you had better not refer to me. Now be so good as to leave me.'

Madame seemed to be in a strange perplexity. She bridled up, dried her eyes fiercely, and dropped a great courtesy, and then sailed away towards the door. Before reaching it she stopped on the way, turning half round, with a peaked, pallid glance at my father, and she bit her lip viciously as she eyed him. At the door the same repulsive pantomime was repeated, as she stood for a moment with her hand upon the handle. But she changed her bearing again with a sniff, and with a look of scorn, almost heightened to a sneer, she made another very low courtesy and a disdainful toss of her head, and so disappeared, shutting the door rather sharply behind her.

ANTHONY TROLLOPE

from *The Kellys and the O'Kellys*

23

Doctor Colligan

Doctor Colligan, the Galen of Dunmore, though a practitioner of most unprepossessing appearance and demeanour, was neither ignorant nor careless. Though for many years he had courted the public in vain, his neighbours had at last learned to know and appreciate him; and, at the time of Anty's illness, the inhabitants of three parishes trusted their corporeal ailments to his care, with comfort to themselves and profit to him. Nevertheless, there were many things about Doctor Colligan not calculated to inspire either respect or confidence. He always seemed a little afraid of his patient, and very much afraid of his patient's friends: he was always dreading the appearance at Dunmore of one of those young rivals, who had lately established themselves at Tuam on one side, and Hollymount on the other; and, to prevent so fatal a circumstance, was continually trying to be civil and obliging to his customers. He would not put on a blister, or order a black dose, without consulting with the lady of the house, and asking permission of the patient, and consequently had always an air of doubt and indecision.

Then, he was excessively dirty in his person and practice: he carried a considerable territory beneath his nails; smelt equally strongly of the laboratory and the stable; would wipe his hands on the patient's sheets, and wherever he went left horrid marks of his whereabouts: he was very fond of good eating and much drinking, and would neglect the best customer that ever was sick, when tempted by the fascination of a game of loo. He was certainly a bad family-man; for though he worked hard for the support of his wife and children, he was little among them, paid them no attention, and felt no scruple in assuring Mrs C. that he had been obliged to remain up all night with that dreadful Mrs Jones, whose children were always so tedious; or that Mr Blake was so bad after his accident that he could not leave him for a moment; when, to tell the truth, the Doctor had passed the night with the cards in his hands, and a tumbler of punch beside him.

He was a tall, thick-set, heavy man, with short black curly hair; was a little bald at the top of his head; and looked always as though he had shaved himself the day before yesterday, and had not washed since. His face was good-natured, but heavy and unintellectual. He was ignorant of everything but his profession, and the odds on the card-table or the race-course. But to give him his due, on these subjects he was not ignorant; and this was now so generally known that, in dangerous cases, Doctor Colligan had been sent for, many, many miles.

This was the man who attended poor Anty in her illness, and he did as much for her as could be done; but it was a bad case, and Doctor Colligan thought it would be fatal. She had intermittent fever, and was occasionally delirious; but it was her great debility between the attacks which he considered so dangerous.

On the morning after the hunt, he told Martin that he greatly feared she would go off, from exhaustion, in a few days, and that it would be wise to let Barry know the state in which his sister was. There was a consultation on the subject between the two and Martin's mother, in which it was agreed that the Doctor should go up to Dunmore House, and tell Barry exactly the state of affairs.

'And good news it'll be for him,' said Mrs Kelly; 'the best he heard since the ould man died. Av he had his will of her, she'd niver rise from the bed where she's stretched. But, glory be to God, there's a providence over all, and maybe she'll live yet to give him the go-by.'

'How you talk, mother,' said Martin; 'and what's the use? Whatever he wishes won't harum her; and maybe, now she's dying, his heart'll be softened to her. Any way, don't let him have to say she died here, without his hearing a word how bad she was.'

'Maybe he'd be afther saying we murdhered her for her money,' said the widow, with a shudder.

'He can hardly complain of that, when he'll be getting all the money himself. But, however, it's much betther, all ways, that Doctor Colligan should see him.'

'You know, Mrs Kelly,' said the Doctor, 'as a matter of course he'll be asking to see his sister.'

'You wouldn't have him come in here to her, would you? – Faix, Doctor Colligan, it'll be her death outright at once av he does.'

'It'd not be nathural, to refuse to let him see her,' said the Doctor; 'and I don't think it would do any harm: but I'll be guided by you, Mrs Kelly, in what I say to him.'

'Besides,' said Martin, 'I know Anty would wish to see him: he is her brother; and there's only the two of 'em.'

'Between you be it,' said the widow; 'I tell you I don't like it. You neither of you know Barry Lynch, as well as I do; he'd smother her av it come into his head.'

'Ah, mother, nonsense now; hould your tongue; you don't know what you're saying.'

'Well; didn't he try to do as bad before?'

'It wouldn't do, I tell you,' continued Martin, 'not to let him see her; that is, av Anty wishes it.'

It ended in the widow being sent into Anty's room, to ask her whether she had any message to send to her brother. The poor girl knew how ill she was, and expected her death; and when the widow told her that Doctor Colligan was going to call on her brother, she said that she hoped she should see Barry once more before all was over.

'Mother,' said Martin, as soon as the Doctor's back was turned, 'you'll get yourself in a scrape av you go on saying such things as that about folk before strangers.'

'Is it about Barry?'

'Yes; about Barry. How do you know Colligan won't be repating all them things to him?'

'Let him, and wilcome. Shure wouldn't I say as much to Barry Lynch himself? What do I care for the blagguard? – only this, I wish I'd niver heard his name, or seen his foot over the sill of the door. I'm sorry I iver heard the name of the Lynches in Dunmore.'

'You're not regretting the throuble Anty is to you, mother?'

'Regretting? – I don't know what you mane by regretting. I don't know is it regretting to be slaving as much and more for her than I would for my own, and no chance of getting as much as thanks for it.'

'You'll be rewarded hereafter, mother; shure won't it all go for charity?'

'I'm not so shure of that,' said the widow. 'It was your schaming to get her money brought her here, and, like a poor wake woman, as I was, I fell into it; and now we've all the throuble and the expinse, and the time lost, and afther all, Barry'll be getting everything when she's gone. You'll see, Martin; we'll have the wake, and the funeral, and the docthor and all, on us – mind my words else. Och musha, musha! what'll I do at all? Faix, forty pounds won't clear what this turn is like to come to; an' all from your dirthy undherhand schaming ways.'

In truth, the widow was perplexed in her inmost soul about Anty; torn and tortured by doubts and anxieties. Her real love of Anty and true charity was in state of battle with her parsimony; and then, avarice was strong within her; and utter, uncontrolled hatred of Barry still stronger. But, opposed to these was dread of some unforeseen evil – some tremendous law proceedings: she had a half-formed idea that she was doing what she had no right to do, and that she might some day be walked off to Galway assizes. Then again, she had an absurd pride about it, which often made her declare that she'd never be beat by such a 'scum of the 'arth' as Barry Lynch, and that she'd fight it out with him if it cost her a hundred pounds; though no one understood what the battle was which she was to fight.

Just before Anty's illness had become so serious, Daly called, and had succeeded in reconciling both Martin and the widow to himself; but he had not quite made them agree to his proposal. The widow, indeed, was much averse to it. She wouldn't deal with such a Greek as Barry, even in the acceptance of a boon. When she found him willing to compromise, she became more than ever averse to any friendly terms; but now the whole ground was slipping from under her feet. Anty was dying: she would have had her trouble for nothing; and that hated Barry would gain his point, and the whole of his sister's property, in triumph.

Twenty times the idea of a will had come into her mind, and how comfortable it would be if Anty would leave her property, or at any rate a portion of it, to Martin. But though the thoughts of such a delightful arrangement kept her in a continual whirlwind of anxiety, she never hinted at the subject to Anty. As she said to herself, 'a Kelly wouldn't demane herself to ask a brass penny from a Lynch'. She didn't even speak to her daughters about it, though the continual twitter she was in made them aware that there was some unusual burthen on her mind.

It was not only to the Kellys that the idea occurred that Anty in her illness might make a will. The thoughts of such a catastrophe had robbed Barry of half the pleasure which the rumours of his sister's dangerous position had given him. He had not received any direct intimation of Anty's state, but had heard through the servants that she was ill – very ill – dangerously – 'not expected', as the country people call it; and each fresh rumour gave him new hopes, and new life. He now spurned all idea of connexion with Martin; he would trample on the Kellys for thinking of such a thing; he would show Daly, when in the plenitude of his wealth and power, how he despised the lukewarmness and timidity of his councils. These and other delightful visions were floating through his imagination; when, all of a sudden, like a blow, like a thunderbolt, the idea of a *will* fell as it were upon him with a ton weight. His heart sunk low within him; he became white, and his jaw dropped. After all, there were victory and triumph, plunder and wealth, *his* wealth, in the very hands of his enemies! Of course the Kellys would force her to make a will, if she didn't do it of her own accord; if not, they'd forge one. There was some comfort in that thought: he could at any rate contest the will, and swear that it was a forgery.

He swallowed a dram, and went off, almost weeping to Daly.

'Oh, Mr Daly, poor Anty's dying: did you hear, Mr Daly – she's all but gone?' Yes; Daly had been sorry to hear that Miss Lynch was very ill. 'What shall I do,' continued Barry, 'if they say that she's left a will?'

'Go and hear it read. Or, if you don't like to do that yourself, stay away, and let me hear it.'

'But they'll forge one! They'll make out what they please, and when she's dying, they'll make her put her name to it; or they'll only just put the pen in her hand, when she's not knowing what she's doing. They'd do anything now, Daly, to get the money they've been fighting for so hard.'

'It's my belief,' answered the attorney, 'that the Kellys not only won't do anything dishonest, but that they won't even take any unfair advantage of you. But at any rate you can do nothing. You must wait patiently; you, at any rate, can take no steps till she's dead.'

'But couldn't she make a will in my favour? I know she'd do it if I asked her – if I asked her now – now she's going off, you know. I'm sure she'd do it. Don't you think she would?'

'You're safer, I think, to let it alone,' said Daly, who could hardly control the ineffable disgust he felt.

'I don't know that,' continued Barry. 'She's weak, and 'll do what she's asked: besides, *they'll* make her do it. Fancy if, when she's gone, I find I have to share everything with those people!' And he struck his forehead and pushed the hair off his perspiring face, as he literally shook with despair. 'I must see her, Daly. I'm quite sure she'll make a will if I beg her; they can't hinder me seeing my own, only, dying sister; can they, Daly? And when I'm once there, I'll sit with her, and watch till it's all over. I'm sure, now she's ill, I'd do anything for her.'

Daly said nothing, though Barry paused for him to reply. 'Only about the form,' continued he, 'I wouldn't know what to put. By heavens, Daly! you must come with me. You can be up at the house, and I can have you down at a minute's warning.' Daly utterly declined, but Barry continued to press him. 'But you must, Daly; I tell you I know I'm right. I know her so well – she'll do it at once for the sake – for the sake of – You know she is my own sister, and all that – and she thinks so much of that kind of thing. I'll tell you what, Daly; upon my honour and soul,' and he repeated the words in a most solemn tone, 'if you'll draw the will, and she signs it, so that I come in for the whole thing – and I know she will – I'll make over fifty – ay, seventy pounds a year for you for ever and ever. I will, as I live.'

The interview ended by the attorney turning Barry Lynch into the street, and assuring him that if he ever came into his office again, on any business whatsoever, he would unscrupulously kick him out. So ended, also, the connexion between the two; for Daly never got a farthing for his labour. Indeed, after all that had taken place, he thought it as well not to trouble his *ci-devant* client with a bill. Barry went home, and of course got drunk.

When Doctor Colligan called on Lynch, he found that he was not at home. He was at that very moment at Tuam, with the attorney. The doctor repeated his visit later in the afternoon, but Barry had still not returned, and he therefore left word that he would call early after breakfast the following morning. He did so; and, after waiting half an hour in the dining-room, Barry, only half awake and half dressed, and still half drunk, came down to him.

The doctor, with a long face, delivered his message, and explained to him the state in which his sister was lying; assured him that everything in the power of medicine had been and should be done; that, nevertheless, he feared the chance of recovery was remote; and ended by informing him that Miss Lynch was aware of her danger, and had expressed a wish to see him before it might be too late. Could he make it convenient to come over just now – in half an hour – or say an hour? – said the doctor, looking at the red face and unfinished toilet of the distressed brother.

Barry at first scarcely knew what reply to give. On his return from Tuam, he had determined that he would at any rate make his way into his sister's room, and, as he thought to himself, see what would come of it. In his after-dinner courage he had further determined, that he would treat the widow and her family with a very high hand, if they dared to make objection to his seeing his sister; but now, when the friendly overture came from Anty herself, and was brought by one of the Kelly faction, he felt himself a little confounded, as though he rather dreaded the interview, and would wish to put it off for a day or two.

'Oh, yes – certainly, Doctor Colligan; to be sure – that is – tell me, doctor, is she really so bad?'

'Indeed, Mr Lynch, she is very weak.'

'But, doctor, you don't think there is any chance – I mean, there isn't any danger, is there, that she'd go off at once?'

'Why, no, I don't think there is; indeed, I have no doubt she will hold out a fortnight yet.'

'Then, perhaps, doctor, I'd better put it off till to-morrow; I'll tell you why: there's a person I wish –'

'Why, Mr Lynch, to-day would be better. The fever's periodical, you see, and will be on her again to-morrow –'

'I beg your pardon, Doctor Colligan,' said Barry, of a sudden remembering to be civil, – 'but you'll take a glass of wine?'

'Not a drop, thank ye, of anything.'

'Oh, but you will'; and Barry rang the bell and had the wine brought. 'And you expect she'll have another attack to-morrow?'

'That's a matter of course, Mr Lynch; the fever'll come on her again to-morrow. Every attack leaves her weaker and weaker, and we fear she'll go off, before it leaves her altogether.'

'Poor thing!' said Barry, contemplatively.

'We had her head shaved,' said the doctor.

'Did you, indeed!' answered Barry. 'She was my favourite sister, Doctor Colligan – that is, I had no other.'

'I believe not,' said Doctor Colligan, looking sympathetic.

'Take another glass of wine, doctor? – now do,' and he poured out another bumper.

'Thank'ee, Mr Lynch, thank'ee; not a drop more. And you'll be over in an hour then? I'd better go and tell her, that she may be prepared, you know,' and the doctor returned to the sick room of his patient.

Barry remained standing in the parlour, looking at the glasses and the decanter, as though he were speculating on the manner in which they had been fabricated. 'She may recover, after all,' thought he to himself. 'She's as strong as a horse – I know her better than they do. I know she'll recover, and then what shall I do? Stand to the offer Daly made to Kelly, I suppose!' And then he sat down close to the table, with his elbow on it, and his chin resting on his hand; and there he remained, full of thought. To tell the truth, Barry Lynch had never thought more intensely than he did during those ten minutes. At last he jumped up suddenly, as though surprised at what had been passing within himself; he looked hastily at the door and at the window, as though to see that he had not been watched, and then went upstairs to dress himself, preparatory to his visit to the inn.

24
Anty Lynch's Bed-side. – Scene the First

Anty had borne her illness with that patience and endurance which were so particularly inherent in her nature. She had never complained; and had received the untiring attentions and care of her two young friends, with a warmth of affection and gratitude which astonished them, accustomed as they had been in every little illness to give and receive that tender care with which sickness is treated in affectionate families. When ill, they felt they had a right to be petulant, and to complain; to exact, and to be attended to: they had been used to it from each other, and thought it an incidental part of the business. But Anty had hitherto had no one to nurse her, and she looked on Meg and Jane as kind ministering angels, emulous as they were to relieve her wants and ease her sufferings.

Her thin face had become thinner, and was very pale; her head had been shaved close, and there was nothing between the broad white border of her nightcap and her clammy brow and wan cheek. But illness was more becoming to Anty than health; it gave her a melancholy and beautiful expression of resignation, which, under ordinary circumstances, was wanting to her features, though not to her character. Her eyes were brighter than they usually were, and her complexion was clear, colourless, and transparent. I do not mean to say that Anty in her illness was beautiful, but she was no longer plain; and even to the young Kellys, whose feelings and sympathies cannot be supposed to have been of the highest order, she became an object of the most intense interest, and the warmest affection.

'Well, doctor,' she said, as Doctor Colligan crept into her room, after the termination of his embassy to Barry; 'will he come?'

'Oh, of course he will; why wouldn't he, and you wishing it? He'll be here in an hour, Miss Lynch. He wasn't just ready to come over with me.'

'I'm glad of that,' said Anty, who felt that she had to collect her thoughts before she saw him; and then, after a moment, she added, 'Can't I take my medicine now, doctor?'

'Just before he comes you'd better have it, I think. One of the girls will step up and give it you when he's below. He'll want to speak a word or so to Mrs Kelly before he comes up.'

'Spake to me, docthor!' said the widow, alarmed. 'What'll he be spaking to me about? Faix. I had spaking enough with him last time he was here.'

'You'd better just see him, Mrs Kelly,' whispered the doctor. 'You'll find him quiet enough, now; just take him fair and asy; keep him down-stairs a moment, while Jane gives her the medicine. She'd better take it just before he goes to her, and don't let him stay long, whatever you do. I'll be back before the evening's over; not that I think that she'll want me to see her, but I'll just drop in.'

'Are you going, doctor?' said Anty, as he stepped up to the bed. He told her he was. 'You've told Mrs Kelly, haven't you, that I'm to see Barry alone?'

'Why, I didn't say so,' said the doctor, looking at the widow; 'but I suppose there'll be no harm – eh, Mrs Kelly?'

'You must let me see him alone, dear Mrs Kelly!'

'If Doctor Colligan thinks you ought, Anty dear, I wouldn't stay in the room myself for worlds.'

'But you won't keep him here long, Miss Lynch – eh? And you won't excite yourself? – indeed, you mustn't. You'll allow them fifteen minutes, Mrs Kelly, not more, and then you'll come up'; and with these cautions, the doctor withdrew.

'I wish he was come and gone,' said the widow to her elder daughter. 'Well; av I'd known all what was to follow, I'd niver have got out of my warm bed to go and fetch Anty Lynch down here that cowld morning! Well, I'll be wise another time. Live and larn, they say, and it's thrue, too.'

'But, mother, you ain't wishing poor Anty wasn't here?'

'Indeed, but I do; everything to give and nothin' to get – that's not the way I have managed to live. But it's not that altogether, neither. I'm not begrudging Anty anything for herself; but that I'd be dhriven to let that blagguard of a brother of hers into the house, and that as a frind like, is what I didn't think I'd ever have put upon me!'

Barry made his appearance about an hour after the time at which they had begun to expect him; and as soon as Meg saw him, one of them flew up-stairs, to tell Anty and give her her tonic. Barry had made himself quite a dandy to do honour to the occasion of paying probably a parting visit to his sister, whom he had driven out of her own house to die at the inn. He had on his new blue frock-coat, and a buff waistcoat with gilt buttons, over which his watch-chain was gracefully arranged. His pantaloons were strapped down very tightly over his polished boots; a shining new silk hat was on one side of his head; and in his hand he was dangling an ebony cane. In spite, however, of all these gaudy trappings, he could not muster up an easy air; and, as he knocked, he had that look proverbially attributed to dogs who are going to be hung.

Sally opened the door for him, and the widow, who had come out from the shop, made him a low courtesy in the passage.

'Oh – ah – yes – Mrs Kelly, I believe?' said Barry.

'Yes, Mr Lynch, that's my name; glory be to God!'

'My sister, Miss Lynch, is still staying here, I believe?'

'Why, drat it, man; wasn't Dr Colligan with you less than an hour ago, telling you you must come here, av you wanted to see her?'

'You'll oblige me by sending up the servant to tell Miss Lynch I'm here.'

'Walk up here a minute, and I'll do that errand for you myself. – Well,' continued she, muttering to herself – 'for him to ax av she war staying here, as though he didn't know it! There niver was his ditto for desait, maneness and divilry!'

A minute or two after the widow had left him, Barry found himself by his sister's bed-side, but never had he found himself in a position for which he was less fitted, or which was less easy to him. He assumed, however, a long and solemn face, and crawling up to the bed-side, told his sister, in a whining voice, that he was very glad to see her.

'Sit down, Barry, sit down,' said Anty, stretching out her thin pale hand, and taking hold of her brother's.

Barry did as he was told, and sat down. 'I'm so glad to see you, Barry,' said she: 'I'm so very glad to see you once more –' and then after a pause, 'and it'll be the last time, Barry, for I'm dying.'

Barry told her he didn't think she was, for he didn't know when he'd seen her looking better.

'Yes, I am, Barry: Doctor Colligan has said as much; and I should know it well enough myself, even if he'd never said a word. We're friends now, are we not? – Everything's forgiven and forgotten, isn't it, Barry?'

Anty had still hold of her brother's hand, and seemed desirous to keep it. He sat on the edge of his chair, with his knees tucked in against the bed, the very picture of discomfort, both of body and mind.

'Oh, of course it is, Anty,' said he; 'forgive and forget; that was always my motto. I'm sure I never bore any malice – indeed I never was so sorry as when you went away, and – '

'Ah, Barry,' said Anty; 'it was better I went then; maybe it's all better as it is. When the priest has been with me and given me comfort, I won't fear to die. But there are other things, Barry, I want to spake to you about.'

'If there's anything I can do, I'm sure I'd do it: if there's anything at all you wish done. – Would you like to come up to the house again?'

'Oh no, Barry, not for worlds.'

'Why, perhaps, just at present, you are too weak to move; only wouldn't it be more comfortable for you to be in your own house? These people here are all very well, I dare say, but they must be a great bother to you, eh? – so interested, you know, in everything they do.'

'Ah! Barry, you don't know them.'

Barry remembered that he would be on the wrong tack to abuse the Kellys. 'I'm sure they're very nice people,' said he; 'indeed I always thought so, and said so – but they're not like your own flesh and blood, are they, Anty? – and why shouldn't you come up and be – '

'No, Barry,' said she; 'I'll not do that; as they're so very, very kind as to let me stay here, I'll remain till – till God takes me to himself. But they're not my flesh and blood' – and she turned round and looked affectionately in the face of her brother – 'there are only the two of us left now; and soon, very soon you'll be all alone.' Barry felt very uncomfortable, and wished the interview was over: he tried to say something, but failed, and Anty went on – 'when that time comes, will you remember what I say to you now? – When you're all alone, Barry; when there's nothing left to trouble you or put you out – will you think then of the last time you ever saw your sister, and –'

'Oh, Anty, sure I'll be seeing you again!'

'No, Barry, never again. This is the last time we shall ever meet, and think how much we ought to be to each other! We've neither of us father or mother, husband or wife. – When I'm gone you'll be alone: will you think of me then – and will you remember, remember every day – what I say to you now?'

'Indeed I will, Anty. I'll do anything, everything you'd have me. Is there anything you'd wish me to give to any person?'

'Barry,' she continued, 'no good ever came of my father's will.' – Barry almost jumped off his chair as he heard his sister's words, so much did they startle him; but he said nothing. – 'The money has done me no good, but the loss of it has blackened your heart, and turned your blood to gall against me. Yes, Barry – yes – don't speak now, let me go on; – the old man brought you up to look for it, and, alas, he taught you to look for nothing else; it has not been your fault, and I'm not blaming you – I'm not maning to blame you, my own brother, for you are my own' – and she turned round in the bed and shed tears upon his hand, and kissed it. – 'But gold, and land, will never make you happy, – no, not all the gold of England, nor all the land the old kings ever had could make you happy, av the heart was bad within you. You'll have it all now, Barry, or mostly all. You'll have what you think the old man wronged you of; you'll have it with no one to provide for but yourself, with no one to trouble you, no one to thwart you. But oh, Barry, av it's in your heart that that can make you happy – there's nothing before you but misery – and death – and hell.' – Barry shook like a child in the clutches of its master – 'Yes, Barry; misery and death, and all the tortures of the damned. It's to save you from this, my own brother, to try and turn your heart from that foul love of money, that your sister is now speaking to you from her grave. – Oh, Barry! try and cure it. Learn to give to others, and you'll enjoy what you have yourself. – Learn to love others, and then you'll know what it is to be loved yourself. Try, try to soften that hard heart. Marry at once, Barry, at once, before you're older and worse to cure; and you'll have children, and love them; and when you feel, as feel you must, that the money is clinging round your soul, fling it from you, and think of the last words your sister said to you.'

The sweat was now running down the cheeks of the wretched man, for the mixed rebuke and prayer of his sister had come home to him, and touched him; but it was neither with pity, with remorse, nor penitence. No; in that foul heart there was no room, even for remorse; but he trembled with fear as he listened to her words, and, falling on his knees, swore to her that he would do just as she would have him.

'If I could but think,' continued she, 'that you would remember what I am saying –'

'Oh, I will, Anty: I will – indeed, indeed, I will!'

'If I could believe so, Barry – I'd die happy and in comfort, for I love you better than anything on earth'; and again she pressed his hot red hand – 'but oh, brother! I feel for you: – you never kneel before the altar of God – you've no priest to move the weight of sin from your soul – and how heavy that must be! Do you remember, Barry; it's but a week or two ago and you threatened to kill me for the sake of our father's money? you wanted to put me in a mad-house; you tried to make me mad with fear and cruelty; me, your sister; and I never harmed or crossed you. God is now doing what you threatened; a kind, good God is now taking me to himself, and you will get what you so longed for without more sin on your conscience; but it'll never bless you, av you've still the same wishes in your heart, the same love of gold – the same hatred of a fellow-creature.'

'Oh, Anty!' sobbed out Barry, who was now absolutely in tears, 'I was drunk that night; I was indeed, or I'd never have said or done what I did.'

'And how often are you so, Barry? – isn't it so with you every night? That's another thing; for my sake, for your own sake – for God's sake, give up the dhrink. It's killing you from day to day, and hour to hour. I see it in your eyes, and smell it in your breath, and hear it in your voice; it's that that makes your heart so black: – it's that that gives you over, body and soul, to the devil. I would not have said a word about that night to hurt you now; and, dear Barry, I wouldn't have said such words as these to you at all, but that I shall never speak to you again. And oh! I pray that you'll remember them. You're idle now, always: – don't continue so; earn your money, and it will be a blessing to you and to others. But in idleness, and drunkenness, and wickedness, it will only lead you quicker to the devil.'

Barry reiterated his promises; he would take the pledge; he would work at the farm; he would marry and have a family; he would not care the least for money; he would pay his debts; he would go to church, or chapel, if Anty liked it better; at any rate, he'd say his prayers; he would remember every word she had said to the last day of his life; he promised everything or anything, as though his future existence depended on his appeasing his dying sister. But during the whole time, his chief wish, his longing desire, was to finish the interview, and get out of that horrid room. He felt that he was mastered and cowed by the creature whom he had so despised, and he could not account for the feeling. Why did he not dare to answer her? She had told him he would have her money: she had said it would come to him as a matter of course; and it was not the dread of losing that which prevented his saying a word in his own defence. No; she had really frightened him: she had made him really feel that he was a low, wretched, wicked creature, and he longed to escape from her, that he might recover his composure.

'I have but little more to say to you, Barry,' she continued, 'and that little is about the property. You will have it all, but a small sum of money –'

Here Anty was interrupted by a knock at the door, and the entrance of the widow. She came to say that the quarter of an hour allowed by the doctor had been long exceeded, and that really Mr Barry ought to take his leave, as so much talking would be bad for Anty.

This was quite a god-send for Barry, who was only anxious to be off; but Anty begged for a respite.

'One five minutes longer, dear Mrs Kelly,' said she, 'and I shall have done; only five minutes – I'm much stronger now, and really it won't hurt me.'

'Well, then – mind, only five minutes,' said the widow, and again left them alone.

'You don't know, Barry – you can never know how good that woman has been to me; indeed all of them – and all for nothing. They've asked nothing of me, and now that they know I'm dying, I'm sure they expect nothing from me. She has enough; but I wish to leave something to Martin, and the girls'; and a slight pale blush covered her wan cheeks and forehead as she mentioned Martin's name. 'I will leave him five hundred pounds, and them the same between them. It will be nothing to you, Barry, out of the whole; but see and pay it at once, will you?' and she looked kindly into his face.

He promised vehemently that he would, and told her not to bother herself about a will: they should have the money as certainly as if twenty wills were made. To give Barry his due, at that moment, he meant to be as good as his word. Anty, however, told him that she would make a will; that she would send for a lawyer, and have the matter properly settled.

'And now,' she said, 'dear Barry, may God Almighty bless you – may He guide you and preserve you; and may He, above all, take from you that horrid love of the world's gold and wealth. Good bye,' and she raised herself up in her bed – 'good bye, for the last time, my own dear brother; and try to remember what I've said to you this day. Kiss me before you go, Barry.'

Barry leaned over the bed, and kissed her, and then crept out of the room, and down the stairs, with the tears streaming down his red cheeks; and skulked across the street to his own house, with his hat slouched over his face, and his handkerchief held across his mouth.

25

Anty Lynch's Bed-side. – Scene the Second

Anty was a good deal exhausted by her interview with her brother, but towards evening she rallied a little, and told Jane, who was sitting with her, that she wanted to say one word in private, to Martin. Jane was rather surprised, for though Martin was in the habit of going into the room every morning to see the invalid, Anty had never before asked for him. However, she went for Martin, and found him.

'Martin,' said she; 'Anty wants to see you alone, in private.'

'Me?' said Martin, turning a little red. 'Do you know what it's about?'

'She didn't say a word, only she wanted to see you alone; but I'm thinking it's something about her brother; he was with her a long long time this morning, and went away more like a dead man than a live one. But come, don't keep her waiting; and, whatever you do, don't stay long; every word she spakes is killing her.'

Martin followed his sister into the sick-room, and, gently taking Anty's offered hand, asked her in a whisper, what he could do for her. Jane went out; and, to do her justice sat herself down at a distance from the door, though she was in a painful state of curiosity as to what was being said within.

'You're all too good to me, Martin,' said Anty; 'you'll spoil me, between you, minding every word I say so quick.'

Martin assured her again, in a whisper, that anything and everything they could do for her was only a pleasure.

'Don't mind whispering,' said Anty; 'spake out; your voice won't hurt me. I love to hear your voices, they're all so kind and good. But Martin, I've business you must do for me, and that at once, for I feel within me that I'll soon be gone from this.'

'We hope not, Anty; but it's all with God now – isn't it? No one knows that betther than yourself.'

'Oh yes, I do know that; and I feel it is His pleasure that it should be so, and I don't fear to die. A few weeks back the thoughts of death, when they came upon me, nearly killed me; but that feeling's all gone now.'

Martin did not know what answer to make; he again told her he hoped she would soon get better. It is a difficult task to talk properly to a dying person about death, and Martin felt that he was quite incompetent to do so.

'But,' she continued, after a little, 'there's still much that I want to do, – that I ought to do. In the first place, I must make my will.'

Martin was again puzzled. This was another subject on which he felt himself equally unwilling to speak; he could not advise her not to make one; and he certainly would not advise her to do so.

'Your will, Anty? – there's time enough for that; you'll be sthronger you know, in a day or two. Doctor Colligan says so – and then we'll talk about it.'

'I hope there is time enough, Martin; but there isn't more than enough; it's not much that I'll have to say –'

'Were you spaking to Barry about it this morning?'

'Oh, I was. I told him what I'd do: he'll have the property now, mostly all as one as av the ould man had left it to him. It would have been betther so, eh Martin?' Anty never doubted her lover's disinterestedness; at this moment she suspected him of no dirty longing after her money, and she did him only justice. When he came into her room he had no thoughts of inheriting anything from her. Had he been sure that by asking he could have induced her to make a will in his favour, he would not have done so. But still his heart sunk a little within him when he heard her declare that she was going to leave everything back to her brother. It was, however, only for a moment; he remembered his honest determination firmly and resolutely to protect their joint property against any of her brother's attempts, should he ever marry her; but in no degree to strive or even hanker after it, unless it became his own in a fair, straightforward manner.

'Well, Anty; I think you're right,' said he. 'But wouldn't it all go to Barry, nathurally, without your bothering yourself about a will, and you so wake.'

'In course it would, at laist I suppose so; but Martin,' and she smiled faintly as she looked up into his face, 'I want the two dear, dear girls, and I want yourself to have some little thing to remember me by; and your dear kind mother, – she doesn't want money, but if I ask her to take a few of the silver things in the house, I'm sure she'll keep them for my sake. Oh, Martin! I do love you all so very – so very much!' and the warm tears streamed down her cheeks.

Martin's eyes were affected, too: he made a desperate struggle to repress the weakness, but he could not succeed, and was obliged to own it by rubbing his eyes, with the sleeve of his coat. 'And I'm shure, Anty,' said he, 'we all love you; any one must love you who knew you.' And then he paused: he was trying to say something of his own true personal regard for her, but he hardly knew how to express it. 'We all love you as though you were one of ourselves – and so you are – it's all the same – at any rate it is to me.'

'And I would have been one of you, had I lived. I can talk to you more about it now, Martin, than I ever could before, because I know I feel I am dying.'

'But you mustn't talk, Anty; it wakens you, and you've had too much talking already this day.'

'It does me good, Martin, and I must say what I have to say to you. I mayn't be able again. Had it plazed God I should have lived, I would have prayed for nothing higher or better than to be one of such a family as yourselves. Had I been – had I been' – and now Anty blushed again, and she also found a difficulty in expressing herself; but she soon got over it, and continued, 'had I been permitted to marry you, Martin, I think I would have been a good wife to you. I am very, very sure I would have been an affectionate one.'

'I'm shure you would – I'm shure you would, Anty. God send you may still: av you war only once well again there's nothing now to hindher us.'

'You forget Barry,' Anty said, with a shudder. 'But it doesn't matther talking of that now' – Martin was on the point of telling her that Barry had agreed, under certain conditions, to their marriage: but, on second thoughts, he felt it would be useless to do so; and Anty continued,

'I would have done all I could, Martin. I would have loved you fondly and truly. I would have liked what you liked, and, av I could, I would 've made your home quiet and happy. Your mother should have been my mother, and your sisthers my sisthers.'

'So they are now, Anty – so they are now, my own, own Anty – they love you as much as though they were.'

'God Almighty bless them for their goodness, and you too, Martin. I cannot tell you, I niver could tell you, how I've valued your honest thrue love, for I know you have loved me honestly and thruly; but I've always been afraid to spake to you. I've sometimes thought you must despise me, I've been so wake and cowardly.'

'Despise you, Anty? – how could I despise you, when I've always loved you?'

'But now, Martin, about poor Barry – for he is poor. I've sometimes thought, as I've been lying here the long long hours awake, that, feeling to you as I do, I ought to be laving you what the ould man left to me.'

'I'd be sorry you did, Anty. I'll not be saying but what I thought of that when I first looked for you, but it was never to take it from you, but to share it with you, and make you happy with it.'

'I know it, Martin: I always knew it and felt it.'

'And now, av it's God's will that you should go from us, I'd rather Barry had the money than us. We've enough, the Lord be praised; and I wouldn't for worlds it should be said that it war for that we brought you among us; nor for all County Galway would I lave it to Barry to say, that when you were here, sick, and wake, and dying, we put a pen into your hand to make you sign a will to rob him of what should by rights be his.'

'That's it, dear Martin; it wouldn't bless you if you had it; it can bless no one who looks to it alone for a blessing. It wouldn't make you happy – it would make you miserable, av people said you had that which you ought not to have. Besides, I love my poor brother; he is my brother, my only real relation; we've lived all our lives together; and though he isn't what he should be, the fault is not all his own. I should not sleep in my grave, av I died with his curse upon me; as I should, av he found, when I am gone, that I'd willed the property all away. I've told him he'd have it all – nearly all; and I've begged him, prayed to him, from my dying bed, to mend his ways; to try and be something betther in the world than what I fear he's like to be. I think he minded what I said when he was here, for death-bed words have a solemn sound to the most worldly; but when I'm gone he'll be all alone, there'll be no one to look afther him. Nobody loves him – no one even likes him; no one will live with him but those who mane to rob him; and he will be robbed, and plundered, and desaved, when he thinks he's robbing and desaving others.' Anty paused, more for breath than for a reply, but Martin felt that he must say something.

'Indeed, Anty, I fear he'll hardly come to good. He dhrinks too much, by all accounts; besides, he's idle, and the honest feeling isn't in him.'

'It's thrue, dear Martin; it's too thrue. Will you do me a great great favour, Martin' – and she rose up a little and turned her moist clear eye full upon him – 'will you show your thrue love to your poor Anty, by a rale lasting kindness, but one that'll be giving you much much throuble and pain? Afther I'm dead and gone – long long after I'm in my cold grave, will you do that for me, Martin?'

'Indeed I will, Anty,' said Martin, rather astonished, but with a look of solemn assurance; 'anything that I can do, I will: you needn't dread my not remembering, but I fear it isn't much that I can do for you.'

'Will you always think and spake of Barry – will you always act to him and by him, and for him, not as a man whom you know and dislike, but as my brother – your own Anty's only brother? – Whatever he does, will you thry to make him do better? Whatever troubles he's in, will you lend him your hand? Come what come may to him, will you be his frind? He has no frind now. When I'm gone, will you be a frind to him?'

Martin was much confounded. 'He won't let me be his frind,' he said; 'he looks down on us and despises us; he thinks himself too high to be befrinded by us. Besides, of all Dunmore he hates us most.'

'He won't when he finds you haven't got the property from him: but frindship doesn't depend on letting – rale frindship doesn't. I don't want you to be dhrinking, and ating, and going about with him. God forbid! – you're too good for that. But when you find he wants a frind, come forward, and thry and make him do something for himself. You can't but come together; you'll be the executhor in the will; won't you, Martin? and then he'll meet you about the property; he can't help it, and you must meet then as frinds. And keep that up. If he insults you, forgive it for my sake; if he's fractious and annoying, put up with it for my sake; for my sake thry to make him like you, and thry to make others like him.' Martin felt that this would be impossible, but he didn't say so – 'No one respects him now, but all respect you. I see it in people's eyes and manners, without hearing what they say. Av you spake well of him – at any rate kindly of him, people won't turn themselves so against him. Will you do all this, for my sake?'

Martin solemnly promised that, as far as he could, he would do so; that, at any rate as far as himself was concerned, he would never quarrel with him.

'You'll have very, very much to forgive,' continued Anty; 'but then it's so sweet to forgive; and he's had no fond mother like you; he has not been taught any duties, any virtues, as you have. He has only been taught that money is the thing to love, and that he should worship nothing but that. Martin, for my sake, will you look on him as a brother? – a wicked, bad, castaway brother; but still as a brother, to be forgiven, and, if possible, redeemed?'

'As I hope for glory in Heaven, I will,' said Martin; 'but I think he'll go far from this; I think he'll quit Dunmore.'

'Maybe he will; perhaps it's betther he should; but he'll lave his name behind him. Don't be too hard on that, and don't let others; and even av he does go, it'll not be long before he'll want a frind, and I don't know anywhere he can go that he's likely to find one. Wherever he may go, or whatever he may do, you won't forget he was my brother; will you, Martin? You won't forget he was your own Anty's only brother.'

Martin again gave her his solemn word that he would, to the best of his ability, act as a friend and brother to Barry.

'And now about the will.' Martin again endeavoured to dissuade her from thinking about a will just at present.

'Ah! but my heart's set upon it,' she said; 'I shouldn't be happy unless I did it, and I'm sure you don't want to make me unhappy, now. You must get me some lawyer here, Martin; I'm afraid you're not lawyer enough for that yourself.'

'Indeed I'm not, Anty; it's a trade I know little about.'

'Well; you must get me a lawyer; not to-morrow, for I know I shan't be well enough; but I hope I shall next day, and you may tell him just what to put in it. I've no secrets from you.' And she told him exactly what she had before told her brother. 'That'll not hurt him,' she continued; 'and I'd like to think you and the dear girls should accept something from me.'

Martin then agreed to go to Daly. He was on good terms with them all now, since making the last offer to them respecting the property; besides, as Martin said, 'he knew no other lawyer, and, as the will was so decidedly in Barry's favour, who was so proper to make it as Barry's own lawyer?'

'Good-bye now, Martin,' said Anty; 'we shall be desperately scolded for talking so long; but it was on my mind to say it all, and I'm betther now it's all over.'

'Good night, dear Anty,' said Martin, 'I'll be seeing you to-morrow.'

'Every day, I hope, Martin, till it's all over. God bless you, God bless you all – and you above all. You don't know, Martin – at laist you didn't know all along, how well, how thruly I've loved you. Good night,' and Martin left the room, as Barry had done, in tears. But he had no feeling within him of which he had cause to be ashamed. He was ashamed, and tried to hide his face, for he was not accustomed to be seen with the tears running down his cheeks; but still he had within him a strong sensation of gratified pride, as he reflected that he was the object of the warmest affection to so sweet a creature as Anty Lynch.

'Well, Martin – what was it she wanted?' said his mother, as she met him at the bottom of the stairs.

'I couldn't tell you now, mother,' said he; 'but av there was iver an angel on 'arth, it's Anty Lynch.' And saying so, he pushed open the door and escaped into the street.

'I wondher what she's been about now?' said the widow, speculating to herself – 'well, av she does lave it away from Barry, who can say but what she has a right to do as she likes with her own? – and who's done the most for her, I'd like to know?' – and pleasant prospects of her son's enjoying an independence flitted before her mind's eye. 'But thin,' she continued, talking to herself, 'I wouldn't have it said in Dunmore that a Kelly demaned hisself to rob a Lynch, not for twice all Sim Lynch ever had. Well – we'll see; but no good 'll ever come of meddling with them people. Jane, Jane,' she called out, at the top of her voice, 'are you niver coming down, and letting me out of this? – bad manners to you.'

Jane answered, in the same voice, from the parlour upstairs, 'Shure, mother, ain't I getting Anty her tay?'

'Drat Anty and her tay! – Well, shure, I'm railly bothered now wid them Lynches! –
Well, glory be to God, there's an end to everything – not that I'm wishing her anywhere
but where she is; she's welcome, for Mary Kelly.'

from *Phineas Finn*

I

Phineas Finn Proposes to Stand for Loughshane

Dr Finn, of Killaloe, in county Clare, was as well known in those parts, – the confines,
that is, of the counties Clare, Limerick, Tipperary, and Galway, – as was the bishop
himself who lived in the same town, and was as much respected. Many said that the
doctor was the richer man of the two, and the practice of his profession was extended
over almost as wide a district. Indeed the bishop, whom he was privileged to attend,
although a Roman Catholic, always spoke of their dioceses being conterminate. It will
therefore be understood that Dr Finn, – Malachi Finn was his full name, – had obtained
a wide reputation as a country practitioner in the west of Ireland. And he was a man
sufficiently well to do, though that boast made by his friends, that he was as warm a
man as the bishop, had but little truth to support it. Bishops in Ireland, if they live at
home, even in these days, are very warm men; and Dr Finn had not a penny in the
world for which he had not worked hard. He had, moreover, a costly family, five
daughters and one son, and, at the time of which we are speaking, no provision in the
way of marriage or profession had been made for any of them. Of the one son, Phineas,
the hero of the following pages, the mother and five sisters were very proud. The doctor
was accustomed to say that his goose was as good as any other man's goose, as far as
he could see as yet; but that he should like some very strong evidence before he allowed
himself to express an opinion that the young bird partook, in any degree, of the qualities
of a swan. From which it may be gathered that Dr Finn was a man of common-sense.

Phineas had come to be a swan in the estimation of his mother and sisters by reason
of certain early successes at college. His father, whose religion was not of that bitter
kind in which we in England are apt to suppose that all the Irish Roman Catholics
indulge, had sent his son to Trinity; and there were some in the neighbourhood of
Killaloe, – patients, probably, of Dr Duggin, of Castle Connell, a learned physician who
had spent a fruitless life in endeavouring to make head against Dr Finn, – who declared
that old Finn would not be sorry if his son were to turn Protestant and go in for a
fellowship. Mrs Finn was a Protestant, and the five Miss Finns were Protestants, and
the doctor himself was very much given to dining out among his Protestant friends on
a Friday. Our Phineas, however, did not turn Protestant up in Dublin, whatever his
father's secret wishes on that subject may have been. He did join a debating society, to
success in which his religion was no bar; and he there achieved a sort of distinction
which was both easy and pleasant, and which, making its way down to Killaloe, assisted
in engendering those ideas as to swanhood of which maternal and sisterly minds are so
sweetly susceptible. 'I know half a dozen old windbags at the present moment,' said the

doctor, 'who were great fellows at debating clubs when they were boys.' 'Phineas is not a boy any longer,' said Mrs Finn. 'And windbags don't get college scholarships,' said Matilda Finn, the second daughter. 'But Papa always snubs Phinny,' said Barbara, the youngest. 'I'll snub you, if you don't take care,' said the doctor, taking Barbara tenderly by the ear; – for his youngest daughter was the doctor's pet.

The doctor certainly did not snub his son, for he allowed him to go over to London when he was twenty-two years of age, in order that he might read with an English barrister. It was the doctor's wish that his son might be called to the Irish Bar, and the young man's desire that he might go to the English Bar. The doctor so far gave way, under the influence of Phineas himself, and of all the young women of the family, as to pay the usual fee to a very competent and learned gentleman in the Middle Temple, and to allow his son one hundred and fifty pounds per annum for three years. Dr Finn, however, was still firm in his intention that his son should settle in Dublin, and take the Munster Circuit, – believing that Phineas might come to want home influences and home connections, in spite of the swanhood which was attributed to him.

Phineas sat his terms for three years, and was duly called to the Bar; but no evidence came home as to the acquirement of any considerable amount of law lore, or even as to much law study, on the part of the young aspirant. The learned pundit at whose feet he he had been sitting was not especially loud in praise of his pupil's industry, though he did say a pleasant word or two as to his pupil's intelligence. Phineas himself did not boast much of his own hard work when at home during the long vacation. No rumours of expected successes, – of expected professional successes, – reached the ears of any of the Finn family at Killaloe. But, nevertheless, there came tidings which maintained those high ideas in the maternal bosom of whose mention has been made, and which were of such sufficient strength to induce the doctor, in opposition to his own judgement, to consent to the continued residence of his son in London. Phineas belonged to an excellent club, – the Reform Club, – and went into very good society. He was hand and glove with the Hon. Laurence Fitzgibbon, the eldest son of Lord Claddagh. He was intimate with Barrington Erle, who had been private secretary, – one of the private secretaries, – to the great Whig Prime Minister who was lately in but was now out. He had dined three or four times with that great Whig nobleman, the Earl of Brentford. And he had been assured that if he stuck to the English Bar he would certainly do well. Though he might fail to succeed in court or in chambers, he would doubtless have given to him some one of those numerous appointments for which none but clever young barristers are supposed to be fitting candidates. The old doctor yielded for another year, although at the end of the second year he was called upon to pay a sum of three hundred pounds, which was then due by Phineas to creditors in London. When the doctor's male friends in and about Killaloe heard that he had done so, they said that he was doting. Not one of the Miss Finns was as yet married; and, after all that had been said about the doctor's wealth, it was supposed that there would not be above five hundred pounds a year among them all, were he to give up his profession. But the doctor, when he paid that three hundred pounds for his son, buckled to his work again, though he had for twelve months talked of giving up the midwifery. He buckled to again, to the great disgust of Dr Duggin, who at this time said very ill-natured things about young Phineas.

At the end of the three years Phineas was called to the Bar, and immediately received a letter from his father asking minutely as to his professional intentions. His father recommended him to settle in Dublin, and promised the one hundred and fifty pounds for three more years, on condition that this advice was followed. He did not absolutely say that the allowance would be stopped if the advice were not followed, but that was plainly to be implied. That letter came at the moment of a dissolution of Parliament. Lord de Terrier, the Conservative Prime Minister, who had now been in office for the almost unprecedentedly long period of fifteen months, had found that he could not face continued majorities against him in the House of Commons, and had dissolved the House. Rumour declared that he would have much preferred to resign, and betake himself once again to the easy glories of opposition; but his party had naturally been obdurate with him, and he had resolved to appeal to the country. When Phineas received his father's letter, it had just been suggested to him at the Reform Club that he should stand for the Irish borough of Loughshane.

This proposition had taken Phineas Finn so much by surprise, that when first made to him by Barrington Erle it took his breath away. What! he stand for Parliament, twenty-four years old, with no vestige of property belonging to him, without a penny in his purse, as completely dependent on his father as he was when he first went to school at eleven years of age! And for Loughshane, a little borough in the county Galway, for which a brother of that fine old Irish peer, the Earl of Tulla, had been sitting for the last twenty years, – a fine, high-minded representative of the thorough-going Orange Protestant feeling of Ireland! And the Earl of Tulla, to whom almost all Loughshane belonged, – or at any rate the land about Loughshane, – was one of his father's staunchest friends! Loughshane is in county Galway, but the Earl of Tulla usually lived at his seat in county Clare, not more than ten miles from Killaloe, and always confided his gouty feet, and the weak nerves of the old countess, and the stomachs of all his domestics, to the care of Dr Finn. How was it possible that Phineas should stand for Loughshane? From whence was the money to come for such a contest? It was a beautiful dream, a grand idea, lifting Phineas almost off the earth by its glory. When the proposition was first made to him in the smoking-room at the Reform Club by his friend Erle, he was aware that he blushed like a girl, and that he was unable at the moment to express himself plainly, – so great was his astonishment and so great his gratification. But before ten minutes had passed by, while Barrington Erle was still sitting over his shoulder on the club sofa, and before the blushes had altogether vanished, he had seen the improbability of the scheme, and had explained to his friend that the thing could not be done. But to his increased astonishment, his friend made nothing of the difficulties. Loughshane, according to Barrington Erle, was so small a place, that the expense would be very little. There were altogether no more than 307 registered electors. The inhabitants were so far removed from the world, and were so ignorant of the world's good things, that they knew nothing about bribery. The Hon. George Morris, who had sat for the last twenty years, was very unpopular. He had not been near the borough since the last election, he had hardly done more than show himself in Parliament, and had neither given a shilling in the town nor got a place under Government for a single son of Loughshane. 'And he has quarrelled with his brother,' said Barrington

Erle. 'The devil he has!' said Phineas. 'I thought they always swore by each other.' 'It's at each other they swear now,' said Barrington; 'George has asked the Earl for more money, and the Earl has cut up rusty.' Then the negotiator went on to explain that the expenses of the election would be defrayed out of a certain fund collected for such purposes, that Loughshane had been chosen as a cheap place, and that Phineas Finn had been chosen as a safe and promising young man. As for qualification, if any question were raised, that should be made all right. An Irish candidate was wanted, and a Roman Catholic. So much the Loughshaners would require on their own account when instigated to dismiss from their service that thorough-going Protestant, the Hon. George Morris. Then 'the party', – by which Barrington Erle probably meant the great man in whose service he himself had become a politician, – required that the candidate should be a safe man, one who would support 'the party', – not a cantankerous, red-hot semi-Fenian, running about to meetings at the Rotunda, and such like, with views of his own about tenant-right and the Irish Church. 'But I have views of my own,' said Phineas, blushing again. 'Of course you have, my dear boy,' said Barrington, clapping him on the back. 'I shouldn't come to you unless you had views. But your views and ours are the same, and you're just the lad for Galway. You mightn't have such an opening again in your life, and of course you'll stand for Loughshane.' Then the conversation was over, the private secretary went away to arrange some other little matter of the kind, and Phineas Finn was left alone to consider the proposition that had been made to him.

To become a member of the British Parliament! In all those hot contests at the two debating clubs to which he had belonged, this had been the ambition which had moved him. For, after all, to what purpose of their own had those empty debates ever tended? He and three or four others who had called themselves Liberals had been pitted against four or five who had called themselves Conservatives, and night after night they had discussed some ponderous subject without any idea that one would ever persuade another, or that their talking would ever conduce to any action or to any result. But each of these combatants had felt, – without daring to announce a hope on the subject among themselves, – that the present arena was only a trial-ground for some possible greater amphitheatre, for some future debating club in which debates would lead to action, and in which eloquence would have power, even though persuasion might be out of the question.

Phineas certainly had never dared to speak, even to himself, of such a hope. The labours of the Bar had to be encountered before the dawn of such a hope could come to him. And he had gradually learned to feel that his prospects at the Bar were not as yet very promising. As regarded professional work he had been idle, and how then could he have a hope?

And now this thing, which he regarded as being of all things in the world the most honourable, had come to him all at once, and was possibly within his reach! If he could believe Barrington Erle, he had only to lift up his hand, and he might be in Parliament within two months. And who was to be believed on such a subject if not Barrington Erle? This was Erle's especial business, and such a man would not have come to him on such a subject had he not been in earnest, and had he not himself believed in success.

There was an opening ready, an opening to this great glory, – if only it might be possible for him to fill it!

What would his father say? His father would of course oppose the plan. And if he opposed his father, his father would of course stop his income. And such an income as it was! Could it be that a man should sit in Parliament and live upon a hundred and fifty pounds a year? Since that payment of his debts he had become again embarrassed, – to a slight amount. He owed a tailor a trifle, and a bootmaker a trifle, – and something to the man who sold gloves and shirts; and yet he had done his best to keep out of debt with more than Irish pertinacity, living very closely, breakfasting upon tea and a roll, and dining frequently for a shilling at a luncheon-house up a court near Lincoln's Inn. Where should he dine if the Loughshaners elected him to Parliament? And then he painted to himself a not untrue picture of the probable miseries of a man who begins life too high up on the ladder, – who succeeds in mounting before he has learned how to hold on when he is aloft. For our Phineas Finn was a young man not without sense, – not entirely a windbag. If he did this thing the probability was that he might become utterly a castaway, and go entirely to the dogs before he was thirty. He had heard of penniless men who had got into Parliament, and to whom had come such a fate. He was able to name to himself a man or two whose barks, carrying more sail than they could bear, had gone to pieces among early breakers in this way. But then, would it not be better to go to pieces early than never to carry any sail at all? And there was, at any rate, the chance of success. He was already a barrister and there were so many things open to a barrister with a seat in Parliament! And as he knew of men who had been utterly ruined by such early mounting, so also did he know of others whose fortunes had been made by happy audacity when they were young. He almost thought that he could die happy if he had once taken his seat in Parliament, – if he had received one letter with those grand initials written after his name on the address. Young men in battle are called upon to lead forlorn hopes. Three fall, perhaps, to one who gets through; but the one who gets through will have the Victoria Cross to carry for the rest of his life. This was his forlorn hope; and as he had been invited to undertake the work, he would not turn from the danger. On the following morning he again saw Barrington Erle by appointment, and then wrote the following letter to his father: –

Reform Club, Feb., 186–

My Dear Father,

I am afraid that the purport of this letter will startle you, but I hope that when you have finished it you will think that I am right in my decision as to what I am going to do. You are no doubt aware that the dissolution of Parliament will take place at once, and that we shall be in all the turmoil of a general election by the middle of March. I have been invited to stand for Loughshane, and have consented. The proposition has been made to me by my friend Barrington Erle, Mr Mildmay's private secretary, and has been made on behalf of the Political Committee of the Reform Club. I need hardly say that I should not have thought of such a thing with a less thorough promise of support than this gives me, nor should I think of it now had I not been assured that none of the expense of the election would fall upon me. Of course I could not have asked you to pay for it.

But to such a proposition, so made, I have felt that it would be cowardly to give a refusal. I cannot but regard such a selection as a great honour. I own that I am fond of politics, and have taken great delight in their study – ('Stupid young fool!' his father said to himself as he read this) – and it has been my dream for years past to have a seat in Parliament at some future time. ('Dream! yes; I wonder whether he has ever dreamed what he is to live upon.') The chance has now come to me much earlier than I have looked for it, but I do not think that it should on that account be thrown away. Looking to my profession, I find that many things are open to a barrister with a seat in Parliament, and that the House need not interfere much with a man's practice. ('Not if he has got to the top of his tree,' said the doctor.)

My chief doubt arose from the fact of your old friendship with Lord Tulla, whose brother has filled the seat for I don't know how many years. But it seems that George Morris must go; or, at least, that he must be opposed by a Liberal candidate. If I do not stand, some one else will, and I should think that Lord Tulla will be too much of a man to make any personal quarrel on such a subject. If he is to lose the borough, why should not I have it as well as another?

I can fancy, my dear father, all that you will say as to my imprudence, and I quite confess that I have not a word to answer. I have told myself more than once, since last night, that I shall probably ruin myself. ('I wonder whether he has ever told himself that he will probably ruin me also,' said the doctor.) But I am prepared to ruin myself in such a cause. I have no one dependent on me; and, as long as I do nothing to disgrace my name, I may dispose of myself as I please. If you decide on stopping my allowance, I shall have no feeling of anger against you! ('How very considerate!' said the doctor.) And in that case I shall endeavour to support myself by my pen. I have already done a little in the magazines.

Give my best love to my mother and sisters. If you will receive me during the time of the election, I shall see them soon. Perhaps it will be best for me to say that I have positively decided on making the attempt; that is to say, if the Club Committee is as good as its promise. I have weighed the matter all round, and I regard the prize as being so great, that I am prepared to run any risk to obtain it. Indeed, to me, with my views about politics, the running of such a risk is no more than a duty. I cannot keep my hand from the work now that the work has come in the way of my hand. I shall be most anxious to get a line from you in answer to this.

> Your most affectionate son,
> PHINEAS FINN

I question whether Dr Finn, when he read this letter, did not feel more of pride than of anger, – whether he was not rather gratified than displeased, in spite of all that his common-sense told him on the subject. His wife and daughters, when they heard the news, were clearly on the side of the young man. Mrs Finn immediately expressed an opinion that Parliament would be the making of her son, and that everybody would be sure to employ so distinguished a barrister. The girls declared that Phineas ought, at any rate, to have his chance, and almost asserted that it would be brutal in their father to stand in their brother's way. It was in vain that the doctor tried to explain that going into Parliament could not help a young barrister, whatever it might do for one thoroughly established in his profession; that Phineas, if successful at Loughshane, would at once abandon all idea of earning any income, – that the proposition, coming from so poor a man, was a monstrosity, – that such an opposition to the Morris family, coming from a son of his, would be gross ingratitude to Lord Tulla. Mrs Finn and the girls talked him down, and the doctor himself was almost carried away by something like vanity in regard to his son's future position.

Nevertheless he wrote a letter strongly advising Phineas to abandon the project. But he himself was aware that the letter which he wrote was not one from which any success could be expected. He advised his son, but did not command him. He made no threats as to stopping his income. He did not tell Phineas, in so many words, that he was proposing to make an ass of himself. He argued very prudently against the plan, and Phineas, when he received his father's letter, of course felt that it was tantamount to a paternal permission to proceed with the matter. On the next day he got a letter from his mother full of affection, full of pride, – not exactly telling him to stand for Loughshane by all means, for Mrs Finn was not the woman to run openly counter to her husband in any advice given by her to their son, – but giving him every encouragement which motherly affection and motherly pride could bestow. 'Of course you will come to us,' she said, 'if you do make up your mind to be member for Loughshane. We shall all of us be so delighted to have you!' Phineas, who had fallen into a sea of doubt after writing to his father, and who had demanded a week from Barrington Erle to consider the matter, was elated to positive certainty by the joint effect of the two letters from home. He understood it all. His mother and sisters were altogether in favour of his audacity, and even his father was not disposed to quarrel with him on the subject.

'I shall take you at your word,' he said to Barrington Erle at the club that evening.

'What word?' said Erle, who had too many irons in the fire to be thinking always of Loughshane and Phineas Finn, – or who at any rate did not choose to let his anxiety on the subject be seen.

'About Loughshane.'

'All right, old fellow; we shall be sure to carry you through. The Irish writs will be out on the third of March, and the sooner you're there the better.'

2

Phineas Finn is Elected for Loughshane

One great difficulty about the borough vanished in a very wonderful way at the first touch. Dr Finn, who was a man stout at heart, and by no means afraid of his great friends, drove himself over to Castlemorris to tell his news to the Earl, as soon as he got a second letter from his son declaring his intention of proceeding with the business, let the results be what they might. Lord Tulla was a passionate old man, and the doctor expected that there would be a quarrel; – but he was prepared to face that. He was under no special debt of gratitude to the lord, having given as much as he had taken in the long intercourse which had existed between them; – and he agreed with his son in thinking that if there was to be a Liberal candidate at Loughshane, no consideration of old pill-boxes and gallipots should deter his son Phineas from standing. Other considerations might very probably deter him, but not that. The Earl probably would be of a different opinion, and the doctor felt it to be incumbent on him to break the news to Lord Tulla.

'The devil he is!' said the Earl, when the doctor had told his story. 'Then I'll tell you what, Finn, I'll support him.'

'You support him, Lord Tulla!'

'Yes; – why shouldn't I support him? I suppose it's not so bad with me in the country that my support will rob him of his chance! I'll tell you one thing for certain, I won't support George Morris.'

'But, my lord –'

'Well; go on.'

'I've never taken much part in politics myself, as you know; but my boy Phineas is on the other side.'

'I don't care a — for sides. What has my party done for me? Look at my cousin, Dick Morris. There's not a clergyman in Ireland stauncher to them than he has been, and now they've given the deanery of Kilfenora to a man that never had a father, though I condescended to ask for it for my cousin. Let them wait till I ask for anything again.' Dr Finn, who knew all about Dick Morris's debts, and who had heard of his modes of preaching, was not surprised at the decision of the Conservative bestower of Irish Church patronage; but on this subject he said nothing. 'And as for George,' continued the Earl. 'I will never lift my hand again for him. His standing for Loughshane would be quite out of the question. My own tenants wouldn't vote for him if I were to ask them myself. Peter Blake' – Mr Peter Blake was the lord's agent – 'told me only a week ago that it would be useless. The whole thing is gone, and for my part I wish they'd disfranchise the borough. I wish they'd disfranchise the whole country, and send us a military governor. What's the use of such members as we send? There isn't one gentleman among ten of them. Your son is welcome for me. What support I can give him he shall have, but it isn't much. I suppose he had better come and see me.'

The doctor promised that his son should ride over to Castlemorris, and then took his leave, – not specially flattered, as he felt that were his son to be returned, the Earl would not regard him as the one gentleman among ten whom the county might send to leaven the remainder of its members, – but aware that the greatest impediment in his son's way was already removed. He certainly had not gone to Castlemorris with any idea of canvassing for his son, and yet he had canvassed for him most satisfactorily. When he got home he did not know how to speak of the matter otherwise than triumphantly to his wife and daughters. Though he desired to curse, his mouth would speak blessings. Before that evening was over the prospects of Phineas at Loughshane were spoken of with open enthusiasm before the doctor, and by the next day's post a letter was written to him by Matilda, informing him that the Earl was prepared to receive him with open arms. 'Papa has been over there and managed it all,' said Matilda.

'I'm told George Morris isn't going to stand,' said Barrington Erle to Phineas the night before his departure.

'His brother won't support him. His brother means to support me,' said Phineas.

'That can hardly be so.'

'But I tell you it is. My father has known the Earl these twenty years, and has managed it.'

'I say, Finn, you're not going to play us a trick, are you?' said Mr Erle, with something like dismay in his voice.

'What sort of trick?'

'You're not coming out on the other side?'

'Not if I know it,' said Phineas, proudly. Let me assure you I wouldn't change my views in politics either for you or for the Earl, though each of you carried seats in your breeches pockets. If I go into Parliament, I shall go there as a sound Liberal, – not to support a party, but to do the best I can for the country. I tell you so, and I shall tell the Earl the same.'

Barrington Erle turned away in disgust. Such language was to him simply disgusting. It fell upon his ears as false maudlin sentiment falls on the ears of the ordinary honest man of the world. Barrington Erle was a man ordinarily honest. He would not have been untrue to his mother's brother, William Mildmay, the great Whig Minister of the day, for any earthly consideration. He was ready to work with wages or without wages. He was really zealous in the cause, not asking very much for himself. He had some undefined belief that it was much better for the country that Mr Mildmay should be in power than that Lord de Terrier should be there. He was convinced that Liberal politics were good for Englishmen, and that Liberal politics and the Mildmay party were one and the same thing. It would be unfair to Barrington Erle to deny to him some praise for patriotism. But he hated the very name of independence in Parliament, and when he was told of any man, that that man intended to look to measures and not to men, he regarded that man as being both unstable as water and dishonest as the wind. No good could possibly come from such a one, and much evil might and probably would come. Such a politician was a Greek to Barrington Erle, from whose hands he feared to accept even the gift of a vote. Parliamentary hermits were distasteful to him, and dwellers in political caves were regarded by him with aversion as being either knavish or impractical. With a good Conservative opponent he could shake hands almost as readily as with a good Whig ally; but the man who was neither flesh nor fowl was odious to him. According to his theory of parliamentary government, the House of Commons should be divided by a marked line, and every member should be required to stand on one side of it or on the other. 'If not with me, at any rate be against me,' he would have said to every representative of the people in the name of the great leader whom he followed. He thought that debates were good, because of the people outside, – because they served to create that public opinion which was hereafter to be used in creating some future House of Commons; but he did not think it possible that any vote should be given on a great question, either this way or that, as the result of a debate; and he was certainly assured in his own opinion that any such changing of votes would be dangerous, revolutionary, and almost unparliamentary. A member's vote, – except on some small crotchety open question thrown out for the amusement of crotchety members, – was due to the leader of that member's party. Such was Mr Erle's idea of the English system of Parliament, and, lending semi-official assistance as he did frequently to the introduction of candidates into the House, he was naturally anxious that his candidates should be candidates after his own heart. When, therefore, Phineas Finn talked of measures and not men, Barrington Erle turned away in open disgust. But he remembered the youth and extreme rawness of the lad, and he remembered also the careers of other men.

Barrington Erle was forty, and experience had taught him something. After a few seconds, he brought himself to think mildly of the young man's vanity, – as of the vanity of a plunging colt who resents the liberty even of a touch. 'By the end of the first session the thong will be cracked over his head, as he patiently assists in pulling the coach up hill, without producing from him even a flick of his tail,' said Barrington Erle to an old parliamentary friend.

'If he were to come out after all on the wrong side,' said the parliamentary friend.

Erle admitted that such a trick as that would be unpleasant, but he thought that old Lord Tulla was hardly equal to so clever a stratagem.

Phineas went to Ireland, and walked over the course at Loughshane. He called upon Lord Tulla, and heard that venerable nobleman talk a great deal of nonsense. To tell the truth of Phineas, I must confess that he wished to talk the nonsense himself; but the Earl would not hear him, and put him down very quickly. 'We won't discuss politics, if you please, Mr Finn; because, as I have already said, I am throwing aside all political considerations.' Phineas, therefore, was not allowed to express his views on the government of the country in the Earl's sitting-room at Castlemorris. There was, however, a good time coming; and so, for the present, he allowed the Earl to ramble on about the sins of his brother George, and the want of all proper pedigree on the part of the new Dean of Kilfenora. The conference ended with an assurance on the part of Lord Tulla that if the Loughshaners chose to elect Mr Phineas Finn he would not be in the least offended. The electors did elect Mr Phineas Finn, – perhaps for the reason given by one of the Dublin Conservative papers, which declared that it was all the fault of the Carlton Club in not sending a proper candidate. There was a great deal said about the matter, both in London and Dublin, and the blame was supposed to fall on the joint shoulders of George Morris and his elder brother. In the meantime, our hero, Phineas Finn, had been duly elected member of Parliament for the borough of Loughshane.

The Finn family could not restrain their triumphings at Killaloe, and I do not know that it would have been natural had they done so. A gosling from such a flock does become something of a real swan by getting into Parliament. The doctor had his misgivings, – had great misgivings, fearful forebodings; but there was the young man elected, and he could not help it. He could not refuse his right hand to his son or withdraw his paternal assistance because that son had been specially honoured among the young men of his country. So he pulled out of his hoard what sufficed to pay off outstanding debts, – they were not heavy, – and undertook to allow Phineas two hundred and fifty pounds a year as long as the session should last.

There was a widow lady living at Killaloe who was named Mrs Flood Jones, and she had a daughter. She had a son also, born to inherit the property of the late Floscabel Flood Jones, of Floodborough, as soon as that property should have disembarrassed itself; but with him, now serving with his regiment in India, we shall have no concern. Mrs Flood Jones was living modestly at Killaloe, on her widow's jointure, – Floodborough having, to tell the truth, pretty nearly fallen into absolute ruin, – and with her lived her one daughter, Mary. Now, on the evening before the return of Phineas Finn, Esq., MP, to London, Mrs and Miss Flood Jones drank tea at the doctor's house.

'It won't make a bit of change in him,' Barbara Finn said to her friend Mary, up in some bedroom privacy before the tea-drinking ceremonies had altogether commenced.

'Oh, it must,' said Mary.

'I tell you it won't, my dear; he is so good and so true.'

'I know he is good, Barbara; and as for truth, there is no question about it, because he has never said a word to me that he might not say to any girl.'

'That's nonsense, Mary.'

'He never has, then, as sure as the blessed Virgin watches over us; – only you don't believe she does.'

'Never mind about the Virgin now, Mary.'

'But he never has. Your brother is nothing to me, Barbara.'

'Then I hope he will be before the evening is over. He was walking with you all yesterday and the day before.'

'Why shouldn't he, – and we that have known each other all our lives? But, Barbara, pray, pray never say a word of this to any one!'

'Is it I? Wouldn't I cut out my tongue first?'

'I don't know why I let you talk to me in this way. There has never been anything between me and Phineas, – your brother I mean.'

'I know whom you mean very well.'

'And I feel quite sure that there never will be. Why should there? He'll go out among great people and be a great man; and I've already found out that there's a certain Lady Laura Standish whom he admires very much.'

'Lady Laura Fiddlestick!'

'A man in Parliament, you know, may look up to anybody,' said Miss Mary Flood Jones.

'I want Phin to look up to you, my dear.'

'That wouldn't be looking up. Placed as he is now, that would be looking down; and he is so proud that he'll never do that. But come down, dear, else they'll wonder where we are.'

Mary Flood Jones was a little girl about twenty years of age, with the softest hair in the world, of a colour varying between brown and auburn, – for sometimes you would swear it was the one and sometimes the other; and she was as pretty as ever she could be. She was one of those girls, so common in Ireland, whom men, with tastes that way given, feel inclined to take up and devour on the spur of the moment; and when she liked her lion, she had a look about her which seemed to ask to be devoured. There are girls so cold-looking, – pretty girls, too, ladylike, discreet, and armed with all accomplishments, – whom to attack seems to require the same sort of courage, and the same sort of preparation, as a journey in quest of the north-west passage. One thinks of a pedestal near the Athenaeum as the most appropriate and most honourable reward of such courage. But, again, there are other girls to abstain from attacking whom is, to a man of any warmth of temperament, quite impossible. They are like water when one is athirst, like plovers' eggs in March, like cigars when one is out in the autumn. No one ever dreams of denying himself when such temptation comes in the way. It often happens, however, that in spite of appearances, the water will not come from the well, nor the egg from its shell, nor will the cigar allow itself to be lit. A girl of such appearance, so charming, was Mary Flood Jones of Killaloe, and our hero Phineas was not allowed to thirst in vain for a drop from the cool spring.

When the girls went down into the drawing-room Mary was careful to go to a part of the room quite remote from Phineas, so as to seat herself between Mrs Finn and Dr Finn's young partner, Mr Elias Bodkin, from Ballinasloe. But Mrs Finn and the Miss Finns and all Killaloe knew that Mary had no love for Mr Bodkin, and when Mr Bodkin handed her the hot cakes she hardly so much as smiled at him. But in two minutes Phineas was behind her chair, and then she smiled; and in five minutes more she had got herself so twisted round that she was sitting in a corner with Phineas and his sister Barbara; and in two more minutes Barbara had returned to Mr Elias Bodkin, so that Phineas and Mary were uninterrupted. They manage these things very quickly and very cleverly in Killaloe.

'I shall be off to-morrow morning by the early train,' said Phineas.

'So soon; – and when will you have to begin, – in Parliament, I mean?'

'I shall have to take my seat on Friday. I'm going back just in time.'

'But when shall we hear of your saying something?'

'Never probably. Not one in ten who go into Parliament ever do say anything.'

'But you will; won't you? I hope you will. I do so hope you will distinguish yourself; – because of your sister, and for the sake of the town, you know.'

'And is that all. Mary?'

'Isn't that enough?'

'You don't care a bit about myself, then?'

'You know that I do. Haven't we been friends ever since we were children? Of course it will be a great pride to me that a person whom I have known so intimately should come to be talked about as a great man.'

'I shall never be talked about as a great man.'

'You're a great man to me already, being in Parliament. Only think; – I never saw a member of Parliament in my life before.'

'You've seen the bishop scores of times.'

'Is he in Parliament? Ah, but not like you. He couldn't come to be a Cabinet Minister, and one never reads anything about him in the newspapers. I shall expect to see your name very often, and I shall always look for it. "Mr Phineas Finn paired off with Mr Mildmay." What is the meaning of pairing off?'

'I'll explain it all to you when I come back, after learning my lesson.'

'Mind you do come back. But I don't suppose you ever will. You will be going somewhere to see Lady Laura Standish when you are not wanted in Parliament.'

'Lady Laura Standish!'

'And why shouldn't you? Of course, with your prospects, you should go as much as possible among people of that sort. Is Lady Laura very pretty?'

'She's about six feet high.'

'Nonsense. I don't believe that.'

'She would look as though she were, standing by you.'

'Because I am so insignificant and small.'

'Because your figure is perfect, and because she is straggling. She is as unlike you as possible in everything. She has thick lumpy red hair, while yours is all silk and softness. She has large hands and feet, and –'

'Why, Phineas, you are making her out to be an ogress, and yet I know that you admire her.'

'So I do, because she possesses such an appearance of power. And after all, in spite of the lumpy hair, and in spite of large hands and straggling figure, she is handsome. One can't tell what it is. One can see that she is quite contented with herself, and intends to make others contented with her. And so she does.'

'I see you are in love with her, Phineas.'

'No; not in love, – not with her at least. Of all men in the world, I suppose that I am the last that has a right to be in love. I daresay I shall marry some day.'

'I'm sure I hope you will.'

'But not till I'm forty or perhaps fifty years old. If I was not fool enough to have what men call a high ambition I might venture to be in love now.'

'I'm sure I'm very glad that you've got a high ambition. It is what every man ought to have; and I've no doubt that we shall hear of your marriage soon, – very soon. And then, – if she can help you in your ambition, we – shall – all – be so – glad.'

Phineas did not say a word further then. Perhaps some commotion among the party broke up the little private conversation in the corner. And he was not alone with Mary again till there came a moment for him to put her cloak over her shoulders in the back parlour, while Mrs Flood Jones was finishing some important narrative to his mother. It was Barbara, I think, who stood in some doorway, and prevented people from passing, and so gave him the opportunity which he abused.

'Mary,' said he, taking her in his arms, without a single word of love-making beyond what the reader has heard, – 'one kiss before we part.'

'No, Phineas, no!' But the kiss had been taken and given before she had even answered him. 'Oh, Phineas, you shouldn't!'

'I should. Why shouldn't I? And, Mary, I will have one morsel of your hair.'

'You shall not; indeed, you shall not!' But the scissors were at hand, and the ringlet was cut and in his pocket before she was ready with her resistance. There was nothing further; – not a word more, and Mary went away with her veil down, under her mother's wing, weeping sweet silent tears which no one saw.

'You do love her; don't you, Phineas?' asked Barbara.

'Bother! Do you go to bed, and don't trouble yourself about such trifles. But mind you're up, old girl, to see me off in the morning.'

Everybody was up to see him off in the morning, to give him coffee and good advice, and kisses, and to throw all manner of old shoes after him as he started on his great expedition to Parliament. His father gave him an extra twenty pound note, and begged him for God's sake to be careful about his money. His mother told him always to have an orange in his pocket when he intended to speak longer than usual. And Barbara in a last whisper begged him never to forget dear Mary Flood Jones.

ROSA MULHOLLAND
'The Hungry Death'

I

It had been a wild night in Innisbofin, an Irish island perched far out among Atlantic breakers, as the bird flies to Newfoundland. Whoever has weathered an ocean hurricane will have some idea of the fury with which the tempest assaults and afflicts such lonely rocks. The creatures who live upon them, at the mercy of the winds and waves, build their cabins low, and put stones on the roof to keep the thatch from flying off on the trail of Mother Carey's chickens; and having made the sign of the cross over their threshold at night, they sleep soundly, undisturbed by the weird and appalling voices which have sung alike the lullaby and death-keen of all their race. In winter, rain or storm is welcome to rage round them, even though fish be frightened away, and food be scarce, but when wild weather encroaches too far upon the spring, then threats of the 'hungry death' are heard with fear in its mutterings.

Is any one to blame for this state of things? The people have a good landlord; but the greater part of the island is barren bog and rock. No shrub will grow upon it, and so fiercely is it swept by storm that the land by the northern and eastern coasts is only a picturesque wilderness, all life sheltering itself in three little thatched villages to the south. The sea is the treasury of the inhabitants, and no more daring hearts exist than those that fight these waves, often finding death in their jaws; but a want of even the rudest piers as defence against the Atlantic makes the seeking of bread upon the waters a perilous, and often an entirely impossible, exploit.

Bofin is of no mean size, and has a large population. Light-hearted and frugal, the people feel themselves a little nation, and will point out to you with pride the storied interest of their island. In early ages it was a seat of learning, witness the ruins of St Coleman's school and church; in Elizabeth's day the handsome masculine queen, Grace O'Malley, built herself a fort on a knoll facing the glories of the western sky; and on the straggling rocks which form the harbour Cromwell raised those blackened walls, still welded into the rock and fronting the foam. The island has a church, a school, a store where meal, oil, soap, ropes, etc., can be had, except when contrary winds detain the hooker which plies to and from Galway with such necessaries.

Foreign sailors, weather-bound in Bofin, are welcomed, and invited to make merry. Pipers and fiddlers come and go, and when times are good are kept busy making music for dancing feet. Even when the wolf is within a pace of the door laughter and song will ring about his ears, so long as the monster can be beaten back by one neighbour from another neighbour's threshold. But there comes a day when he enters where he will, and the bones of the people are his prey.

Last night's was a spring storm, and many a 'Lord have mercy on us!' went up in the silent hours, as the flooding rain that unearths the seedlings was heard seething on the wind; yet Bofin wakened out of its nightmare of terror green and gay, birds carolling in a blue sky, and the ring of the boat-maker's hammer suggesting peace and prosperity.

Through the dazzling sunshine a girl came rowing herself in a small boat that darted rapidly along the water. The oars made a quick, pleasant thud on the air, the larks sang in the clouds, and the girl poured out snatches of a song of her own in a plaintive and mellow voice. The tune was wild and mournful; the Irish words of the ever-recurring refrain might be freely translated thus:

> Fearful was her wooing,
> Ululu!
> All her life undoing.
> Ululu!
> When his face she sighted,
> Back she fell affrighted,
> Death and she were plighted,
> Ululu!

A strange song for such a gay, glittering morning! Thud, thud, went the oars, and the girl's kerchief fell back from her head as the firm elastic figure swayed with the wholesome exercise. Never was a fairer picture of health, strength, and beauty. Her thick, dark-red hair filled with the sunshine as a sponge fills with water; her red-brown eyes seemed to emit sparks of fire as the shadows deepened round them in the strong light. Two little round dimples fixed at the corners of the proud curved mouth whispered a tale of unusual determination lying at the bottom of a passionate nature. There was nothing to account for her curious choice of a song this brilliant morning, except the love of dramatic contrasts that exists in some eager souls. Suddenly she shipped her oars, and sat listening to the waves lapping the edges of the seaweed-fringed cliffs. 'I thought I heard some one calling me,' she muttered, looking up and down with a slight shudder but a bold gaze – 'Brigid, Brigid, Brigid!' then, with a little laugh, she dipped her oars again, burst into a lively song, so reeling with merriment that it was wonderful how she found breath for it, and her boat flew along the glittering waves like a gull.

Above the broad, shelving, shingly beach within the harbour stood the school, the store, and some of the best dwellings on the island, and high and dry on the dreaming shingle the boat-maker was at work with a knot of gossips around him. The sky over their heads was a soft vivid blue; the brown-fringed rocks loomed against a sea almost too dazzling to look upon; the dewy green fields lay like scattered emeralds among the rocks and hollows.

'Lord look to us!' said a man in a sou'wester hat, 'if the spring doesn't mend. Half my pratees was washed clane out o' the ground last night.'

'Whist, man, whist,' said the boat-maker cheerfully. 'Pick them up an' put them in again.'

'Bedad,' said an old fisherman, 'the fish has got down to the bottom of all etarnity. Ye might as well go fishin' for mermaids.'

'Aren't yez ashamed to grumble,' cried a hearty voice joining the group, 'an' sich a mornin' as this? I tell ye last night was the last o' the rain.'

'Ye have the hopes o' youth about ye, Coll Prendergast,' said the old fisherman, looking at the strong frame and smiling bronzed face of the young man before him. 'If yer words is not truth, it's the seaweed we'll be atin' afore next winther's out.'

'Faix, some of it doesn't taste so bad,' said Coll, laughing, 'an' a little of it dried makes capital tabaccy. But whist! if here isn't Brigid Lavelle, come all the way from West Quarter in her pretty canoe.'

The sound of oars had been heard coming steadily nearer, and suddenly Brigid's boat shot out from behind a mass of rock, making, with its occupant, such a picture on the glittering sea that the men involuntarily smiled as they shaded their eyes with their hands to look. Resting on her oars she smiled at them in return, while the sunshine gilded her perfect oval face, as brown as a berry, burnished the copper-hued hair rippling above her black, curved brows, and deepened the determined expression of her full red mouth. Her dress, the costume of the island, was only remarkable for the freshness and newness of its material – a deep crimson skirt of wool, with a light print bodice and short tunic, and a white kerchief thrown over the back of her head.

As she neared the shore Coll sprang into the water, drew her canoe close to the rocks, and, making it fast, helped her to land.

'That's a han'some pair,' said the old fisherman to the boat-maker. 'I hear their match is as good as made.'

'Coll's in luck,' said the other. 'A rich beauty is not for ivery man.'

'She's too proud, I'm thinking. Look at the airs of her now, an' him wet up to the knees in her sarvice.'

'Yer ould, man, an' ye forgot yer coortin'. Let the crature toss her head while she can.'

Brigid had proceeded to the store, where her purchases were soon made – a sack of meal, a can of oil, a little tea and sugar, and some white flour. The girl had a frown on her handsome brows as she did her business, and took but little notice of Coll, who busied himself gallantly with her packages. When all were stored in the boat, he handed her in, and stood looking at her, wondering if she would give him a smile in return for his attentions.

'Let me take the oars, Brigid. Ye'll be home in half the time.'

'No, thank ye,' she answered shortly. 'I'll row my own boat as long as I can.'

Coll smiled broadly, half amused and half admiring, and again sought for a friendly glance at parting, but in vain. The face that vanished out of his sight behind the cliff was cold and proud as though he had been her enemy. After he had turned and was striding up the beach the look that he had wanted to see followed him, shot through a rift in the rocks, where Brigid paused and peered with a tenderness in her eyes that altered her whole face. If Coll had seen that look this story might never have been written.

As the girl's boat sped past the cliffs towards home she frowned, thinking how awkward it was that she should have met Coll Prendergast on the beach. He must have known the errand that brought her to the store, and how dare he smile at her like that before he knew what answer she would give him? Coll's uncle and Brigid's father had planned a match between the young people, and the match-making was to be held that night at Brigid's father's house. Therefore had she come early in the morning in her boat to the store, to buy provisions for the evening's entertainment. Obedience to her father had obliged her to do this, but her own strong will revolted from the proceeding. She was proud, handsome, and an heiress, and did not like to be so easily won.

Brigid's father was sitting at the fire – a consumptive-looking man, with a wistful and restless eye.

'Father, I have brought very little flour. The hooker hasn't got in.'

'Sorra wondher, an' sich storms. 'Tis late in the year for things to be this ways.'

Brigid arranged her little purchases on the dresser and sat down at the table, but her breakfast – a few roasted potatoes and mug of buttermilk – remained untasted before her.

'Father, isn't you an' me happy as we are? Why need I marry in sich a hurry?'

'Because a lone woman's better with a husband, my girl.'

'I'm not a lone woman. Haven't I got you?'

'Not for long, avourneen machree. I'm readyin' to go this good while.'

'But I will hold you back,' cried Brigid, passionately, throwing her strong arms around his neck.

'You can't, asthoreen. I'm wanted yonder, and it's time I was gettin' on with my purgatory. An' there's bad times comin', an' I will not let you face them alone.'

'I could pack up my bundles and be off to America,' said Brigid, stoutly, dashing away tears.

'I will not have you wanderin' over the world like a stray bird,' said the father, emphatically; and Brigid knew there was nothing more to be said.

Lavelle's prosperity appeared before the world in a great deal of clean whitewash outside the house, and an interior more comfortable than is usual on the island. The cabin consisted of two rooms – the kitchen, with earthen floor and heather-lined roof, roosting-place for cocks and hens, and with its dresser, old and worm-eaten, showing a fair display of crockery; and the best room, containing a bed, a few pictures on sacred subjects, some sea-shells on the chimney-piece, an ornamental tray, an old gun, and an ancient, time-blackened crucifix against the wall, this last having been washed ashore one morning after the wreck of a Spanish ship. This was the finest house in Bofin, and Tim Lavelle, having returned from seeing the world and married late in life, had settled down in it, and on the most fertile bit of land on the island. It was thought he had a stockingful of money in the thatch, which would of course be the property of his daughter; so no wonder if the handsome Brigid has grown up a little spoiled with the knowledge of her own happy importance.

As she went about her affairs this morning she owned to herself that she would not be sorry to be forced to be Coll's wife in spite of her pride. True, he had paid her less court hitherto than any other young man on the island, and she longed to punish him for that; but what would become of her if she saw him married to another? Oh, if they had only left the matter to herself she could have managed it so much better – could have plagued him to her heart's content, and made him anxious to win her by means of the difficulties she would have thrown in his way. Had Coll been as poor as he seemed to be, with nothing but his boat and fishing-tackle, she would have been easier to woo, for then eagerness to bestow on him the contents of that stocking in the thatch would have swept away the stumbling-block of her pride. But his uncle had saved some money, which was to be given to Prendergast on the day of his marriage with her. It was a made-up match like Judy O'Flaherty's, while Brigid's proud head was crazed on the subject of being loved for her love's sake alone.

'I'll have to give him my hand tonight,' she said, folding her brown arms, and standing straight in the middle of the room she had been dusting and decorating. 'I be to obey father, an' I'll shame nobody afore the neighbours. But match-makin' isn't marryin'; and if it was to break my heart an' do my death I'll find means to plague him into lovin' me yet.'

Having made this resolve, she let down her long hair, that looked dark bronze while she sat in the corner putting on her shoes, and turned to gold as she walked through a sunbeam crossing the floor, and having brushed it out and twisted it up again in a coil round her head, she finished her simple toilet and went out to the kitchen to receive her visitors.

The first that arrived was Judy O'Flaherty, an old woman with a smoke-dried face, who sat down in the chimney corner and lit her pipe. Judy was arrayed in a large patchwork quilt folded like a shawl, being too poor to indulge in the luxury of a cloak. But the quilt, made of red and white calico patches, was clean, and the cap on her head was fresh and neat.

'I give ye joy of Coll Prendergast,' said Judy heartily. 'Ye ought to be the glad girl to get sich a match.'

'Why ought I be glad?' asked Brigid, angrily. 'It's all as one may think.'

'Holy Mother, girl! don't be sendin' them red sparks out o' yer eyes at me; where d' ye see the likes o' Coll, I'm askin', with his six feet if he's an inch, an' his eyes like the blue on the Reek afore nightfall!'

Brigid's heart leaped to hear him praised, and she turned away her face to hide the smile that curled her lips.

'An' yer match so aisy made for ye, without trouble to either o' ye. Not like some poor cratures, that have to round the world afore they can get one to put a roof over their heads or a bit in their mouths. It's me that knows. Sure wasn't I a wanderin' bein' doin' day's works in the mountains, and as purty a girl as you, Miss Brigid, on'y I hadn't the stockin' in the thatch, nor the good father to be settlin' for me. An' sore and tired an' spent I was when one night I heard a knock at the door o' the house I was workin' in, an' a voice called out: "Get up, Judy; here's a man come to marry you!" Maybe I didn't dress quick; an' who was there but a woman that knew my mother long ago, an' she had met a widow-man that wanted somebody to look after his childer. An' she brought him to me, an' wakened me out o' my sleep for fear he'd take the rue. An' we all sat o'r the fire for the rest o' the night to make the match, and in the first morning light we went down to Father Daly and got married. There's my marriage for ye, an' the rounds I had to get it, an' many a wan is like me. An' yet yer tossin' yer head at Coll, you that hasn't as much as the trouble o' bein' axed.'

The smile had gone off Brigid's face. This freedom from trouble was the very thing that troubled her. She would rather have had the excitement of being 'axed' a hundred questions. As they talked the sunshine vanished and the rain again fell in torrents. Brigid looked out of the door with a mischievous hope that the guests might be kept at home and the match-making postponed. Judy rocked herself and groaned:

'Oh, musha, the piatees, the piatees! Oh, Lord, look down with mercy on the poor!' then suddenly became silent and began telling her beads.

A slight lull in the storm brought the company in a rush to the door, with bursts of laughter, groans for the rain and the potatoes, shaking and drying of cloaks and coats, and squealing and tuning up of pipes. Among the rest came Coll, smiling and confident as ever, with an arch look in his eyes when they met Brigid's, and not the least symptom of fear or anxiety in his face. Soon the door was barred against the storm, the fish-oil lamp lighted, laughter, song, and dancing filled the little house, and the rotting potatoes and the ruinous rains were forgotten as completely as though the Bofin population had been goddesses and gods, with whose nectar and ambrosia no such thing as weather could dare to interfere.

'Faith, ye must dance with me, Brigid,' said Coll, after she had refused him half-a-dozen times.

'Why must I dance with you?'

'Oh, now, don't you know what's goin' on in there?' said Coll, roguishly, signing towards the room where father and uncle were arguing over money and land.

'I do,' said Brigid, with all the red fire of her eyes blazing out upon him. 'But, mind ye, this match-makin' is none o' my doin'.'

'Why then, avourneen?'

'I'm not goin' to marry a man that on'y wants a wife, an' doesn't care a pin whether it's me or another.'

'Bedad, I do care,' said Coll, awkwardly. 'I'm a bad hand at the speakin', but I care entirely.'

But Brigid went off and danced with another man.

Coll was puzzled. He did not understand her the least. He was a simple straightforward fellow, and had truly been in love with Brigid – a fact which his confident manner had never allowed her to believe. Latterly he had begun to feel afraid of her; whenever he tried to say a tender word, that red light in her eyes would flash and strike him dumb. He had hoped that when their 'match was made' she would have grown a little kinder; but it seemed she was only getting harsher instead. Well, he would try and hit on some way to please her; and, as he walked home that night, he pondered on all sorts of plans for softening her proud temper and satisfying her exacting mind.

On her side, Brigid saw that she had startled him out of his ordinary easy humour, and, congratulating herself on the spirit she had shown, resolved to continue her present style of proceeding. Not one smile would she give him, till she had, as she told herself, nearly tormented him to death. How close she was to keep to the letter of her resolution could not at this time be foreseen.

Every evening after this Coll travelled half the island to read some old treasured newspaper to the sickly Lavelle, and bringing various little offerings to his betrothed. Everything that Bofin could supply in the way of a love-gift was sought by him, and presented to her. Now it was a few handsome shells purchased from a foreign sailor in the harbour, or it was the model of a boat he had carved for her himself; and all this attention was not without its lasting effect. Unfortunately, however, while Brigid's heart grew more soft, her tongue only waxed more sharp, and her eyes more scornful. The more clearly she perceived that she would soon have to yield, the more haughty and capricious did she become. Had the young man been able to see behind outward appearances he would have been thoroughly satisfied, and a good deal startled at the vehemence of the devotion that had grown up and strengthened for him in that proud and wayward heart. As it was he felt more and more chilled by her continued coldness, and began to weary of a pursuit which seemed unlikely to be either for his dignity or his happiness.

Meanwhile the rain went on falling. The spring was bad, the summer was bad, potatoes were few and unwholesome, the turf lay undried and rotting on the bog. Distress began to pinch the cheerful faces of the islanders, and laughter and song were half-drowned in murmurs of fear. At the sight of so much sorrow and anxiety around her, Brigid's heart began to ache and to smite and reproach her for her selfish and unruly humours. One night, softened by the sufferings of others, she astonished herself by falling on her knees and giving humble thanks to heaven for the undeserved happiness that was awaiting her. She vowed that the next time Coll appeared she would put her hand in his, and let the love of her heart shine out in the smiles of her eyes. Had she kept this vow it might have been well with her, but her habit of vexing had grown all too strong to be cured in an hour. At the first sight of her lover's anxious face in the doorway all her passion for tormenting him returned.

It was an evening in the month of May; the day had been cold and wet, and as dark as January, but the rain had ceased, the clouds had parted, and one of those fiery sunsets burst upon the world that sometimes appear unexpectedly in the midst of stormy weather. In Bofin, where the sun drops down the heavens from burning cloud to cloud, and sinks in the ocean, the whole island was wrapped in a crimson flame. Brigid stood at her door, gazing at the wonderful spectacle of the heavens and sea, looking herself strangely handsome, with her bronze hair glittering in the ruddy sun light, and that dark shadow about her eyes and brows which, except when she smiled, always gave such a look of tragedy to her face. She was waiting for Coll, with softened lips and downcast eyes, and was so lost in her thoughts that she did not see him when he stood beside her.

He remained silently watching her for a few moments, thinking that if she would begin to look like that he would be ready to love her as well as he had ever loved her, and to forget that he had ever wearied of her harassing scorn. At this very moment Brigid was rehearsing within her mind a kind of little speech which was to establish a good understanding between them.

'I'm sorry I vexed you so often, for I love you true,' were the words she had meant to speak; but suddenly seeing Coll by her side, the habitual taunt flew involuntarily to her lips.

'You here again!' she said disdainfully. 'Then no one can say but you're the perseverinest man in the island!'

'Maybe I'm too perseverin',' said Coll, quietly, and, as Brigid looked at him with covert remorse, she saw something in his face that frightened her. His expression was a mixture of weariness and contempt. He was not hurt, or angry, or amused, as she had been accustomed to see him, but tired of her insolence, which was ceasing to give him pain. A sudden consciousness of this made Brigid turn sick at heart, and she felt that she had at last gone a little too far, that she had been losing him all this time while triumphantly thinking to win him. Oh, why could she not speak and say the word that she wanted to say? While this anguish came into her thoughts her brows grew darker than ever, and the warmth ebbed gradually out of her cheek. They went silently into the house, where Brigid took up her knitting, and Coll dropped into his seat beside Lavelle. The bad times, the rotting crops, the scant expectations of a harvest, were discussed by the two men while Brigid sat fighting with her pride, and trying to decide on what she ought to say or do. Before she had made up her mind, Coll had said good-evening abruptly, and gone out of the house.

The young fisherman's home was in Middle Quarter Village, a cluster of grey stone cabins close to the sea, and to reach it Coll had to cross almost the whole breadth of the island. He set out on his homeward walk with a weary and angry heart. Brigid's dark unyielding face followed him, and he was overwhelmed by a fit of unusual depression. He whistled as he went, trying to shake it off. Why should he fret about a woman who disliked him and who probably loved another whom her father disapproved? Let her do what she liked with herself and her purse. Coll would persecute her no more.

The red light had slowly vanished off the island, and the dark cliffs on the oceanward coast loomed large and black against the still lurid sky. Deep drifts of brown and purple flecked with amber swept across the bogs, and filled up the dreary horrors of the barren and irreclaimable land which Coll had to traverse on his way to the foam-drenched village where the fishermen lived. The heavens cooled to paler tints, a ring of yellow light encircled the island with its creeping shadows and ghost-like rocks. Twilight was descending when Coll heard a faint cry from the distance, like the call of a belated bird or the wail of a child in distress.

At first he thought it was the wind or a plover, but straining his eyes in the direction whence it came he saw a small form standing solitary in the middle of a distant hollow, a piece of treacherous bog, dangerous in the crossing except to knowing feet. Hurrying to the spot he found himself just in time to succour a fellow creature in distress.

Approaching as near as he could with ease to the person who had summoned him, he saw a very young girl standing gazing towards him with piteous looks. She was small, slight, poorly and scantily clad, and carried a creelful of sea-rack on her slight and bending shoulders. A pale after-gleam from the sky fell where she stood, young and forlorn, in the shadowy solitude, and lit up a face round and delicately pale, reminding one of a daisy, a wreath of wind-tossed yellow hair, and eyes as blue as forget-me-nots. Terror had taken possession of her, and she stretched out her hands appealingly to the strong man, who stood looking at her from the opposite side of the bog. Coll observed her in silence for a few moments. It seemed as if he had known her long ago, and that she belonged to him; yet if so, it was in another state of existence, for he assured himself that she was no one with whom he had any acquaintance. However that might be, he was determined to know more of her now, for, with her childlike, appealing eyes and outstetched hands, she went straight into Coll's heart, to nestle there like a dove of peace for evermore.

'Aisy, asthoreen,' cried Coll across the bog, 'I'm goin' to look after ye. Niver ye fear.'

He crossed the morass with a few rapid springs, and stood by her side.

'Give me the creel, avourneen, till I land it for ye safe.'

A few minutes and the burthen was deposited on the safe side of the bog, and then Coll came back and took the young girl in his arms.

'Keep a good hoult round my neck, machree.'

It was a nice feat for a man to pick his way through this bog, with even so small a woman as this in his arms. The girl clung to him in fear, as he swayed and balanced himself on one sure stone after another, slipping here and stumbling there, but always recovering himself before mischief could be done. At last the deed was accomplished – the goal was won.

'Ye were frightened, acushla,' said Coll, tenderly.

'I was feared of dhrownin' ye,' said the girl, looking wistfully in his face with her great, blue eyes.

'Sorra matther if ye had,' said Coll, laughingly, 'except that maybe ye 'd ha' been dhrowned too. Now, which ways are ye goin'? and maybe ye 'd be afther tellin' me who ye are?'

'I'm Moya Maillie,' said the girl; 'an' I live in Middle Quarter Village.'

'Why, yer niver little Moya that I used to see playing round poor Maillie's door that's dead an' gone! And how did ye grow up that ways in a night?'

'Mother says I'll niver grow up,' laughed Moya; 'but I'm sixteen on May mornin', and I'll be contint to be as I am.'

'Many a fine lady would give her fortune to be contint with that same,' said Coll, striding along with the creel on his shoulders, and glancing down every minute at the sweet white-flower-like face that flitted through the twilight at his side. Thus Brigid's repentance would now come all too late, for Coll had fallen in love with little Moya.

How he brought her home that night to a bare and poverty-stricken cabin in the sea-washed fishing village, and restored her like a stray lamb to her mother, need not be told. Her mother was a widow and the mother of seven, and Moya's willing labour was a great part of the family support. She mended nets for the fishermen, and carried rack for the neighbour's land, knitted stockings to be sent out to the great world and sold, and did any other task which her slender and eager hands could find to do. Coll asked himself in amazement how it was that having known her as a baby he had never observed her existence since then. Now an angel, he believed, had led her out into the dreary bog to stand waiting for his sore heart on that blessed day of days. And he would never marry any one but little Moya.

It was impossible they could marry while times were so bad, but, every evening after this, Moya might be seen perched on an old boat upon the shingle, busy with her knitting – her tiny feet, bare and so brown, crossed under the folds of her old worn red petticoat, with a faint rose-pink in her pale cheeks, and a light of extraordinary happiness in her childlike blue eyes. Coll lay on the shingle at her feet, and these two found an elysium in each other's company. There was much idleness perforce for the men of Bofin at this time, and Coll filled up his hours looking after the concerns of the Widow Maillie, carrying Moya's burdens, and making the hard times as easy for her as he could. When people would look surprised at him and ask: 'Arrah, thin, what about Brigid Lavelle?' Coll would answer: 'Oh, she turned me off long ago. Everybody knows that she could not bear the sight of me.'

In the meantime Brigid, at the other end of the island, was watching daily and hourly for Coll's reappearance. As evening after evening passed without bringing him, her heart misgave her more and more, and she mourned bitterly over her own harshness and pride. Oh, if he would only come again with that wistful, questioning look in his brave face, how kindly she would greet him, how eagerly put her hand in his grasp! As the rain rained on through the early summer evenings there would often come before sunset a lightening and a brightening all over the sky, and this was the hour at which Brigid used to look for her now ever-absent lover. Climbing to the top of the hill, she would peer over the sea-bounded landscape, with its dark stretches of bog, and strips and flecks of green, towards the grey irregular line of the fishing village, the smoke of which she could see hanging against the horizon. Her face grew paler and her eyes dull, but to no one, not even to her father, would she admit that she was pining for Coll's return. She had always lived much by herself, and had few gossiping friends to bring her news. At last, unable to bear the suspense any longer, she made an excuse of business at the store on the beach; and before she had gone far among the houses of that metropolis of the island, she was enlightened as to the cause of her lover's defection.

'So ye cast him off. So ye giv' him to little Moya Maillie,' were the words that greeted her wherever she turned. She smiled and nodded her head, as if heartily assenting to what was said, and content with the existing state of things; but as she walked away out of the reach of observing eyes, her face grew dark and her heart throbbed like to burst in her bosom. Almost mechanically she took her way home through the Middle Quarter Village, with a vague desire to see what was to be seen, and to hear whatever was to be heard. She passed among the houses without observing anything that interested her, but, as she left the village, by the sea-shore she came upon Coll and Moya sitting on a rock in the yellow light of a watery sunset, with a mist of sea-foam around them, and a net over their knees which they were mending between them. Their heads were close together, and Coll was looking in her face with the very look which, all these tedious days and nights, Brigid had been wearying to meet. She walked up beside them, and stood looking at them silently with a light in her eyes that was not good to behold.

'Brigid,' said Coll, when he could bear it no longer, 'for heaven's sake, are ye not satisfied yet?'

She turned from him, and fixed her strange glance on Moya.

'It was me before, an' it's you now,' she said shortly. 'He's a constant lover, isn't he?'

'I loved ye true, and ye scoffed and scorned me,' said Coll, gently, as the gleam of anguish and despair in her eyes startled him. 'I wasn't good enough for Brigid, but I'm good enough for Moya. We're neither of us as rich nor as clever as you, but we'll do for one another well enough.'

Brigid laughed a sharp, sudden laugh, and still looked at Moya.

'For heaven's sake, take that wicked look off her face,' cried Coll, hastily. 'What somdever way it is betune us three is yer own doin'; an', whether ye like it or not, it cannot now be helped.'

'I will never forgive either of you,' said Brigid, in a low, hard voice; and then, turning abruptly away, she set out on her homeward walk through the gathering shadows.

II

All through that summer the rain fell, and, when autumn came in Bofin, there was no harvest either of fuel or of food. The potato-seed had been for the most part washed out of the earth without putting forth a shoot, while those that remained in the ground were nearly rotted by a loathsome disease. The smiling little fields that grew the food were turned into blackened pits, giving forth a horrid stench. Winter was beginning again, the year having been but one long winter, with seas too wild to be often braved by even the sturdiest of the fishermen, and the fish seeming to have deserted the island. Accustomed to exist on what would satisfy no other race, and to trust cheerfully to Providence to send them that little out of the earth and out of the sea, the people bore up cheerfully for a long time, living on a mess of Indian-meal once a day, mingled with such edible sea-weed as they could gather off the rocks. So long as shopkeepers in Galway and other towns could afford to give credit to the island, the hooker kept bringing such scanty supplies as were now the sole sustenance of the impoverished population. But credit began to fail, and universal distress on the mainland gave back an answering wail to the hunger-cry of the Bofiners. It is hard for anyone who has never witnessed such a state of things to imagine the condition of ten or twelve hundred living creatures on a barren island girded round with angry breakers; the strong arms around them paralysed, first by the storms that dash their boats to pieces, and rend and destroy their fishing gear, and the devastation of the earth that makes labour useless, and later by the faintness and sickness which comes from hunger long endured, and the cold from which they have no longer a defence. Accustomed as they are to the hardships of recurring years of trial, the Bofiners became gradually aware that a visitation was at hand for which there had seldom been a parallel. Earth and sea alike barren and pitiless to their needs, whence could deliverance come unless the heavens rained down manna into their mouths? Alas! no miracle was wrought, and after a term of brave struggle, hope in Providence, cheerful pushing off of the terrible fears for the worst – after this, laughter, music, song faded out of the island; feet that had danced as long as it was possible now might hardly walk, and the weakest among the people began to die. Troops of children that a few months ago were rosy and sturdy, sporting on the sea-shore, now stretched their emaciated limbs by the fireless hearths, and wasted to death before their maddened mothers' eyes. The old and ailing vanished like flax before a flame. Digging of graves was soon the chief labour of the island, and a day seemed near at hand when the survivors would no longer have strength to perform even this last service for the dead.

Lavelle and his daughter were among the last to suffer from the hard times, and they shared what they had with their poor neighbours; but in course of time the father caught the fever which famine had brought in its train, and was quickly swept into his grave, while the girl was left alone in possession of their little property, with her stocking in the thatch and her small flock of 'beasts' in the field. Her first independent act was to despatch all the money she had left by a trusty hand to Galway to buy meal, in one of those pauses in the bad weather which sometimes allowed a boat to put off from the island. The meal arrived after long, unavoidable delay, and Brigid became a benefactor to numbers of her fellow-creatures. Late and early she trudged from village to village and from house to house, doling out her meal to make it go as far as possible, till her own face grew pale and her step slow, for she stinted her own food to have the more to give away. Her 'beasts' grew lean and dejected. Why should she feed them at the expense of human life? They were killed, and the meat given to her famishing friends. The little property of the few other well-to-do families in like manner melted away, and it seemed likely that 'rich' and poor would soon all be buried in one grave.

In the Widow Maillie's house the famine had been early at work. Five of Moya's little sisters and brothers had one by one sickened and dropped upon the cabin floor. The two elder boys still walked about looking like galvanized skeletons, and the mother crept from wall to wall of her house trying to pretend that she did not suffer, and to cook the mess of rank-looking sea-weed, which was all they could procure in the shape of food. Coll risked his life day after day trying to catch fish to relieve their hunger, but scant and few were the meals that all his efforts could procure from the sea. White and gaunt he followed little Moya's steps, as with the spirit of a giant she kept on toiling among the rocks for such weeds or shell-fish as could be supposed to be edible. When she fell Coll bore her up, but the once powerful man was not able to carry her now. Her lovely little face was hollow and pinched, the cheek-bones cutting through the skin. Her sweet blue eyes were sunken and dim, her pretty mouth purple and strained. Her beauty and his strength were alike gone.

Three of the boys died in one night, and it took Coll, wasted as he was, two days to dig a grave deep enough to bury them. Before that week was over all the children were dead of starvation, and the mother scarcely alive. One evening Coll made his way slowly across the island from the beach, carrying a small bag of meal which he had unexpectedly obtained. Now and again his limbs failed, and he had to lie down and rest upon the ground; but with long perseverance and unconquerable energy he reached the little fishing village at last. As he passed the first house, Brigid Lavelle, pallid and worn, the spectre of herself, came out of the door with an empty basket. Coll and she stared at each other in melancholy amazement. It was the first time they had met since the memorable scene on the rocks many months ago, for Coll's entire time had been devoted to the Maillies, and Brigid had persistently kept out of his way, striving, by charity to others, to quench the fire of angry despair in her heart. Coll would scarcely have recognized her in her present death-like guise, had it not been for the still living glory of her hair.

The sight of Coll's great frame, once so stalwart and erect, now stooping and attenuated, his lustreless eyes, and blue, cold lips, struck horror into Brigid's heart. She uttered a faint, sharp cry and disappeared. Coll scarcely noticed her, his thoughts were so filled with another; and a little further on he met Moya coming to meet him, walking with a slow, uneven step that told of the whirling of the exhausted brain. Half blind with weakness she stretched her hands before her as she walked.

'The hungry death is on my mother at last. Oh, Coll, come in and see the last o' her!'

'Whist, machree! Look at the beautiful taste o' male I am bringin' her. Hard work I had to carry it from the beach, for the eyes o' the cretures is like wolves' eyes, an' I thought the longin' o' them would have dragged it out o' my hands. An', Moya, there's help comin' from God to us. There's kind people out in the world that's thinkin' o' our needs. The man that has just landed with a sack, an' giv' me this, says there's a hooker full o' male on its road to us this day. May the great Lord send us weather to bring it here.'

'I'm 'feared – I'm 'feared it's too late for her,' sobbed Moya, clinging to him.

They entered the cabin where the woman lay, a mere skeleton covered with skin, with the life still flickering in her glassy eyes. Coll put a little of the meal, as it was, between her lips, while Moya hastened to cook the rest on a fire made of the dried roots of heather. The mother turned loving looks from one to the other, tried to swallow a little of the food to please them, gasped, shuddered a little, and was dead.

It was a long, hard task for Coll and Moya to bury her, and when this was done they sat on the heather clasping each other's wasted hands. The sky was dark; the storm was coming on again. As night approached a tempest was let loose upon the island, and many famishing hearts that had throbbed with a little hope at the news of the relief that was on its way to them, now groaned, sickened, and broke in despair. Louder howled the wind, and the sea raged around the dangerous rocks towards which no vessel could dare to approach. It was the doing of the Most High, said the perishing creatures. His scourge was in His hand. Might His ever blessed will be done!

That evening Moya became delirious, and Coll watched all night by her side. At morning light he fled out and went round the village, crying out desperately to God and man to send him a morsel of food to save the life of his young love. The suffering neighbours turned pitying eyes upon him.

'I'm 'feared it's all over with her when she can't taste the say-weed any more,' said one.

'Why don't ye go to Brigid Lavelle?' said another. 'She hasn't much left, poor girl; but maybe she'd have a mouthful for you.'

Till this moment Coll had felt that he could not go begging of Brigid; but, now that Moya's precious life was slipping rapidly out of his hands, he would suffer the deepest humiliation she could heap upon him, if only she would give him so much food as would keep breath in Moya's body till such time as, by Heaven's mercy, the storm might abate, and the hooker with the relief-meal arrive.

Brigid was alone in her house. A little porridge for some poor creature simmered on a scanty fire, and the girl stood in the middle of the floor, her hands wrung together above her head, and her brain distracted with the remembrance of Coll as she had seen him stricken by the scourge. All these months she had told her jealous heart that the Maillies were safe enough since they had Coll to take care of them. So long as there was a fish in the sea he would not let them starve, neither need he be in any danger himself. And so she had never asked a question about him or them. Now the horror of his altered face haunted her. She had walked through the direst scenes with courageous calm, but this one unexpected sight of woe had nearly maddened her.

A knock came to the door which at first she could not hear for the howling of the wind; but when she heard and opened there was Coll standing before her.

'Meal,' he said faintly – 'a little meal, for the love of Christ! Moya is dying.'

A spasm of anguish and tenderness had crossed Brigid's face at the first words; but at the mention of Moya her face darkened.

'Why should I give to you or Moya?' she said coldly. 'There's them that needs that help as much as ye.'

'But not more,' pleaded Coll. 'Oh, Brigid, I'm not askin' for myself. I fear I vexed ye, though I did not mean it. But Moya niver did any one any harm. Will you give me a morsel to save her from the hungry death?'

'I said I niver would forgive either o' ye, an' I niver will,' said Brigid, slowly. 'Ye broke my heart, an' why wouldn't I break yours?'

'Brigid, perhaps neither you nor me has much longer to live. Will ye go before yer Judge with sich black words on yer lips?'

'That's my affair,' she answered in the same hard voice, and then suddenly turning from him, shut the door in his face.

She stood listening within, expecting to hear him returning to implore her, but no further sound was heard; and, when she found he was gone, she dropped upon the floor with a shriek, and rocked herself in a frenzy of remorse for her wickedness.

'But I cannot help everyone,' she moaned; 'I'm starving myself, an' there's nothin' but a han'ful o' male at the bottom o' the bag.'

After a while she got up, and carried the mess of porridge to the house for which she had intended it, and all that day she went about, doing what charity she could, and not tasting any thing herself. Returning, she lay down on the heather, overcome with weakness, fell asleep, and had a terrible dream. She saw herself dead and judged; a black-winged angel put the mark of Cain on her forehead, and at the same moment Coll and Moya went, glorified and happy, hand in hand into heaven before her eyes. 'Depart from me, you accursed,' thundered in her ears; and she started wide awake to hear the winds and waves roaring unabated round her head.

Wet and shivering she struggled to regain her feet, and stood irresolute where to go. Dreading to return to her desolate home, she mechanically set her face towards the little church on the cliff above the beach. On her way to it she passed prostrate forms, dying or dead, on the heather, on the roadside, and against the cabin walls. A few weakly creatures, digging graves, begged from her as she went past, but she took no notice of anything, living or dead, making straight for the church. No one was there, and the storm howled dismally through the empty, barn-like building. Four bare, white-washed walls, and a rude wooden altar, with a painted tabernacle and cross – this was the church. On one long wall was hung a large crucifix, a white, thorn-crowned figure upon stakes of black-painted wood, which had been placed there in memory of a 'mission' lately preached on the island; and on this Brigid's burning eyes fixed themselves with an agony of meaning. Slowly approaching it she knelt and stretched out her arms, uttering no prayer, but swaying herself monotonously to and fro. After a while the frenzied pain of remorse was dulled by physical exhaustion, and a stupor was stealing over her senses when a step entering the church startled her back into consciousness. Looking round she saw that the priest of the island had come in, and was wearily dragging himself towards the altar.

Father John was suffering and dying with his people. He had just now returned from a round of visits among the sick, during which he had sped some departing souls on their journey, and given the last consolation of religion to the dying. His own gaunt face and form bore witness to the unselfishness which had made all his little worldly goods the common property of the famishing. Before he had reached the rails of the altar Brigid had thrown herself on her face at his feet.

'Save me, father, save me!' she wailed. 'The sin of murther is on my soul!'

'Nonsense, child! No such thing. It is too much that you have been doing, my poor Brigid! I fear the fever has crazed your brain.'

'Listen to me, father. Moya is dying, an' there is still a couple o' han'fuls o' male in the bag. Coll came an' asked me for her, an' I hated her because he left me, and I would not give it to him, an' maybe she is dead.'

'You refused her because you hated her?' said the priest. 'God help you, my poor Brigid. 'Tis true you can't save every life; but you must try and save this one.'

Brigid gazed up at him, brightly at first, as if an angel had spoken, and then the dark shadow fell again into her eyes.

The priest saw it.

'Look there, my poor soul,' he said, extending a thin hand towards the figure on the cross. 'Did He forgive His enemies, or did He not?'

Brigid turned her fascinated gaze to the crucifix, fixed them on the thorn-crowned face, and, uttering a wild cry, got up and tottered out of the church.

Spurred by terror lest her amend should come too late, and Moya be dead before she could reach her, she toiled across the heather once more, over the dreary bogs, and through the howling storm. Dews of suffering and exhaustion were on her brow as she carefully emptied all the meal that was left of her store into a vessel, and stood for a moment looking at it in her hand.

'There isn't enough for all of us,' she said, 'an' some of us be to die. It was always her or me, her or me; an' now it'll be me. May Christ receive me, Moya, as I forgive you.' And then she kissed the vessel and put it under her cloak.

Leaving the house, she was careless to close the door behind her, feeling certain that she should never cross the threshold again, and straining all her remaining strength to the task, she urged her lagging feet by the shortest way to the Middle Quarter Village. Dire were the sights she had to pass upon her way. Many a skeleton hand was outstretched for the food she carried; but Brigid was now deaf and blind to all appeals. She saw only Coll's accusing face, and Moya's glazing eyes staring terribly at her out of the rain-clouds. Reaching the Maillies' cabin, she found the door fastened against the storm.

Coll was kneeling in despair by Moya, when a knocking at the door aroused him. The poor fellow had prayed so passionately, and was in so exalted a state, that he almost expected to see an angel of light upon the threshold bring the food he had so urgently asked for. The priest had been there and was gone, the neighbours were sunk in their own misery; why should anyone come knocking like that, unless it were an angel bringing help? Trembling, he opened the door; and there was Brigid, or her ghost.

'Am I in time?' gasped she, as she put the vessel of food in his hand.

'Aye,' said Coll, seizing it. In his transport of delight he would have gone on his knees and kissed her feet; but before he could speak, she was gone.

Whither should she go now? was Brigid's thought. No use returning to the desolate and lonesome home where neither food nor fire was any longer to be found. She dreaded dying on her own hearthstone alone, and faint as she was she knew what was now before her. Gaining the path to the beach, she made a last pull on her energies to reach the whitewashed walls, above which her fading eyes just dimly discerned the cross. The only face she now wanted to look upon again was that thorn-crowned face which was waiting for her in the loneliness of the empty and wind-swept church. Falling, fainting, dragging herself on again, she crept within the shelter of the walls. A little more effort, and she would be at His feet. The struggle was made blindly, slowly, desperately, with a last rally of all the passion of a most impassioned nature; and at last she lay her length on the earthen floor under the cross. Darkness, silence, peace, settled down upon her. The storm raved around, the night came on, and when the morning broke, Brigid was dead.

Mildly and serenely that day had dawned, a pitiful sky looked down on the calamities of Bofin, and the vessel with the relief-meal sailed into the harbour. For many even then alive, the food came all too late, but to numbers it brought assuagement and salvation. The charity of the world was at work, and though much had yet to be suffered, yet the hungry death had been mercifully stayed. Thanks to the timely help, Moya lived for better times, and when her health was somewhat restored, she emigrated with Coll to America. Every night in their distant backwoods hut they pray together for the soul of Brigid Lavelle, who, when in this world, had loved one of them too well, and died to save the life of the other.

EMILY LAWLESS
from *Hurrish*

The Road to Jail

Mr Cavanagh, the 'resident' magistrate (so called because the only one of the magistrates *not* a permanent resident), had returned from Limerick the previous evening, and had been at once interviewed by Mr Higgins. Upon the evidence laid before him, he, to that gentleman's keen satisfaction, not only issued a warrant for Hurrish's arrest, but expressed himself in high terms of reprobation as to Mr O'Brien's unaccountable conduct in having hesitated to do so. Within as short a time, therefore, as was possible after his arrest, our hero found himself upon a car, with one well-armed policeman beside him, and two more upon the other side, bound for the assize town of Ennis, there to be lodged in jail to take his trial for murder – bail in a case of such gravity being, as a matter of course, refused.

He was not particularly alarmed for his own safety, and was able, therefore, to take the proceedings with a considerable amount of equanimity. He had had plenty of time to escape had he wished to do so, but had deliberately made up his mind against that course. Had he done so, beggary, pure and simple, would have stared his mother, the children, and Alley in the face. He had little or no money laid by, and as none of those left could have taken on the farm, of which he had only a yearly tenancy, within a very short time they would have had nothing to look to but the workhouse.

Over and above this, the mere fact of leaving Ireland – for life, as, under the circumstances, it must have been – would have been little less objectionable to him than death itself. He had never felt the faintest beckoning towards that delectable Land of Promise which lay upon the other side of the Atlantic. Had he not in his youth had the farm to look forward to, and had been forced to emigrate, his one thought day and night would have been to put together a sufficient sum of money and return to Ireland by the next ship. The only other alternative – that of remaining in the country *without* giving himself up – though a safe proceeding enough, is a remarkably uncomfortable one. Hurrish had seen others who had tried it, and knew its miseries. A week of such shuffling, skulking, shivering, night-wandering existence, would have driven him, he knew, into giving himself up to the police as a preferable alternative.

Going to jail – though a distinction, of course, in itself – was not, it is true, the precise form of distinction which he would have chosen, but then how few *are* entirely free to choose their own laurels? As to the danger of his incurring the further distinction of being hung, that was an idea to which he hardly gave a thought. He knew the situation well enough to feel pretty sure that the danger incurred in that direction was of the slightest. As for what an Englishman would probably have considered the safest thing to do – pleading manslaughter, or unavoidable homicide, and disclosing the whole circumstances as they really occurred, – that, save under seal of confession to his priest, was an idea which would never for an instant have visited his imagination. In his eyes – probably in those of his legal adviser also – it would have seemed an act of simple and reprehensible self-destruction.

The road from Tubbamina to Ennis is about as desolate a one as is to be found in the whole west of Ireland, which, it must be owned, is saying a good deal. Once the rocky hills of the Burren were left behind, the car entered upon a wide grey-green undulating tract, treeless, featureless, almost houseless, one low green or brown hill rising after another in endless succession as far as the eye could see. What cultivation there existed was of the most rudimentary type conceivable. Small, weedy-looking fields, divided from the road and from one another by dry walls of the lace-work variety, in some places by green dykes, with a fringe of willow or osmunda. Flakes of snow-white bog-cotton waved over dreary patches of swamp, and the dark heads of the reed mace crowded hollows from which turf had been cut and carted away. The houses, few and far between, were for the most part sunk below the level of the road. At one place three or four women were grubbing languidly at a sickly-looking plot of potatoes; at another two men were thatching, who turned and watched the car sullenly till it was out of sight. Then a mile or more without a creature save a stray cow on the road-side, or a sleepily-moving ass-cart. Suddenly they rattled around a sharp corner, and found themselves in the middle of a closely crowded cluster of houses, where the people all ran eagerly to the doors to see them go by, and the women spat, shrieked, and shook their fists passionately at the policemen. Another smaller but more prosperous-looking hamlet was passed, where a smart, newly-built chapel flaunted its cut-stone masonry and twirling weather-cock, and a sinister old castle looked blackly down from a windy green hill hard by. Just after leaving this village, in the middle of a particularly lonely bit of road, a wild-looking young fellow – a total stranger to Hurrish – sprang actively over a wall as they were passing, bounded up to the car, though they were going at a smart pace at the time, and asked him in rapid Irish whether he wanted a rescue. The three constables simultaneously pointed their guns at him, and told him to remain there at his peril. The young fellow, however, took no notice, but ran lightly on, his brimless felt hat falling back from his black curly head, his sunburnt face and wild hawk eyes fixed exclusively upon the prisoner: evidently he was good for another ten miles if need were. Hurrish, however, shook his head. It was not a rescue he wanted, but an acquittal, he explained. His unknown friend thereupon slackened speed suddenly, made a clutch at his hand to shake it, missed it, and disappeared immediately over another wall. From his appearance to his vanishing again there were scarcely three minutes.

When they got near to the outskirts of Ennis the car stopped at a police-station, and a short conference took place between the constables in charge and those within. Only one constable remained upon the car, and he appeared to be taking no particular heed of the prisoner. Hurrish, however, waited quietly. He had no idea of escaping. What would have been the use? It would only have been to begin the whole troublesome business over again. Better remain and see it out as it was.

A delicious brown trout-stream was sweeping under a bridge a little ahead of this point. A heron rose from its bank a few hundred yards lower down, spread its great sail-like wings, and flew away towards the west, its brown legs stretched stiffly out behind it. Hurrish followed it wistfully with his eyes as it grew gradually smaller and smaller, until it was lost to sight in the distance. A sudden yearning, a sudden wild, fierce desire for liberty, swept across him like thirst in a desert. He had hardly realized before that he was a prisoner, but now it seemed as if all at once he knew it. *He* could not turn back as the heron had done; *he* could not get home to his own house and his own people; he was a caged animal; a beast with a rope round its leg, – driven against his will as a sheep or a cow is driven to the market. To any one, but especially to so wild a son of the soil, the first realization of this fact has something in it that maddens. He looked suddenly round, first at the sleepy, vacant country, then up and down the road, and for a moment a thought of escape crossed his mind. Only for a moment. The hopelessness of the attempt rushed back upon him forcibly. He caught the eye of the constable, too, looking inquisitively at him across the well of the car. An impulse of self-respect made him relax the eagerness of the gaze, turn his head the other way, and resume his former air and attitude of indifference.

A minute after the other two constables returned, and directing the carman to take a detour which avoided the main street, got again upon the car and drove rapidly to the jail. Their way lay along a dirty but tolerably prosperous-looking street, where a number of peasant women were bargaining for the gorgeous crimson and magenta shawls and petticoats hung up in a tempting array along the outsides of the shops. It was market-day, and they were too eager to finish their purchases, and get back to their donkey-carts, to take much notice of the prisoner or his escort. Hurrish gazed at it all with the aching interest a man feels in the last things he beholds before the doors of a prison close behind him. Ennis, with its crowded market-place, – the centre of all the other smaller villages round about – its gorgeous new cathedral; its statue of the Liberator; its political pretension; its air of bustle and importance, – was London, Paris, Vienna, all at once to him, and this glimpse of fashion and brilliancy was not, even under the circumstances, without a pleasurable excitement.

He had not much time to enjoy it, however. The shops ceased; a line of stone walls, cold, high, and vacant-looking, took their place; they had arrived at the door of the jail. The three constables jumped down and took him by the arms. The door opened, and he was marched inside. Someone in authority advanced. Then, after a few minutes' delay, he was marched down a narrow passage, with iron-clamped doors on either side; one of these doors was unlocked, disclosing a narrow cell about the size of a bathing-box. Into this he was walked, and the next minute – almost before he had fairly realized what had happened – the door shut behind him with an emphatic bang.

He stood still for a moment, half-stunned, then stumbled over to the bed and sat down. It seemed as if the concussion of the door had shaken his ideas clean out of their usual courses. He felt numbed and stupefied, as if he had suddenly changed his identity with someone else, and had not got accustomed to the new one.

He was roused by a peculiar sensation of discomfort. The window of the cell was set in the outer wall of the prison, and a full blaze of daylight was pouring through it at that moment. It lit up every atom of the narrow space, glaring with immaculate whitewash, which reflected itself in twofold brilliancy at all the corners, and threw a responsive gleam upon the magnificently scoured boards. Hurrish felt dazed and giddy as a fish would have been, suddenly exposed to so brilliant an illumination. An unreasoning hatred for this glaring self-righteous place, into which he had been pushed, rose to his mind, and it was with some difficulty that he resisted rushing against the door and wounding himself in a vain effort to break through. Next to the whitewash, the worst offence – alas! poor Hurrish – was the ultra self-glorifying cleanliness! The ghastly cleanliness and whiteness together nearly made him sick. Out of doors he was used, of course, to light, but then no one out of doors is surrounded by a girdle of dazzling whiteness, a few feet from the end of his nose. How he yearned after his own brown weather-beaten cabin, with its smoke-obscured corners and multitudinous litter! Was there nothing else he could look at, he asked himself – *nothing*? If he had to stay staring at those sickening white walls for the next three weeks, he should go mad, and that would be very nearly as bad as being hung!

Suddenly the window itself caught his eye. It was high up in the wall, but by mounting upon a chair and pulling himself upwards, he was able, by sheer muscular effort, to get his nose and eyes over the ledge, and this he proceeded to do. It was strongly secured, but to his relief he found that it looked, not into the courtyard, but into the outer world. By stretching upwards he could even see a bit of the street below, and people passing and repassing. A black-faced beggar, with grimy professional clothes hanging on by a few alarmingly fragile ribbons, was leaning against the opposite wall, stretching out from time to time a mechanical hand for alms. An old woman, with a basket of apples before her, was squatting upon the ground, and at her feet a small fair-haired child, presumably her grandchild, was amusing itself by picking up fragments of apple-peel, and throwing them into the gutter. A feeling of unaccountable affection for these strange people filled Hurrish's mind, and the tears sprang into his eyes. The little girl was a pretty little creature, dressed in a single ragged garment, which left her small limbs and neck completely bare; against the grimy obscurity of the wall beyond, they looked wonderfully fresh and white. Suddenly a car came round the corner, imperiling the feet of the group. Hurrish, with an impulse of alarm, instinctively stretched out his hands as if to protect the child. A young man was seated on the car, – a slight active figure in a well-fitting suit of grey tweed. He was not really at all like Maurice Brady, still there was sufficient suggestion of resemblance to give Hurrish first a feeling of pleasure, to be immediately followed by a sudden bitter start of pain. Maurice Brady! That was the worst of all, – the only part of the misfortune that had overtaken him which *was* unendurable. He let himself drop from the window, and sat down again upon his pallet, his arms and legs falling despondently together, – a mere nerveless heap of dejected frieze!

When he had been first told that Maurice had denounced him, the intelligence had roused him to a fit of violent indignation – not against Maurice but his informant. He absolutely refused to give any credit whatever to the assertion. When, little by little, the truth of it, however, began to sink into his mind, it had produced a sort of torpor. He could not conceive it, – could not realize it, or get hold of the idea at all. All the time he was standing before the magistrate, all the time he was on the car, his thoughts kept recurring to it, and each time with the same dull sense of unreality. It was not merely painful or disagreeable, but it was inconceivable – a thing past imagination or finding out. If Maurice had attacked him, shot him, assaulted him in any way – *that* he could have understood, for a brother, after all, is a brother; but to denounce him to the police, to the Government! – 'th' *Inglish* Governmint!' – he kept repeating over and over to himself, as if it was in the very least likely that Maurice would have denounced him to the Spanish or the Dutch one!

Three or four hours after he had been in jail a warder brought him a large piece of bread, and some broth swimming with grease. He was very hungry, and ate with a good appetite. He tried to get into conversation with the man, but he turned away and shut the door without answering. Hurrish spun out the eating of his bread as long as he could, but all too soon it came to an end, and again vacuum stared him in the face. It seemed as if he had been already weeks in jail – as if all his previous life had been a dream, and this the reality. The punishment of imprisonment no doubt varies enormously, and to so wild a son of freedom – one to whom wind, rain, storm, all varieties of weather were welcome, but who had never yet spent an entire day in the house in his life – the misery must indeed have pretty nearly attained its maximum.

After a while he clambered up to the window again and resumed his gaze. It was his only link with the outer world, and as such he clung to it. Night came on, but still he remained. The figures below had by that time become mere phantoms, – still they were human phantoms, and moving ones. By the light of the one lamp at the corner, he saw a sooty object in coat and hat pass an equally sooty one in petticoats and a shawl; then both looked back, mutual recognitions ensued, and they stood for a while conversing amicably. A beggar was meanwhile bawling out a song, walking leisurely up and down the middle of the street, with his mouth wide open. Hurrish caught a stray word now and then – 'The mas-a-cree-in va-ga-bonds'. . . 'me dar-lint Paa-a-ady Wh-a-ck.' Suddenly a turnkey entered behind and roughly desired him to get down and go to bed. The lights were going to be put out. He got down, and, pulling off some of his clothes, threw himself upon the pallet. It was as hard as a brick floor, but that made very little difference, and within half an hour he was sound asleep, – and so his first day's experience of Ennis jail came to an end.

BRAM STOKER

from *Dracula*

I

Jonathan Harker's Journal
(Kept in shorthand)

3 May. Bistritz. Left Munich at 8.35 p.m. on 1st May, arriving at Vienna early next morning; should have arrived at 6.46, but train was an hour late. Buda-Pesth seems a wonderful place, from the glimpse which I got of it from the train and the little I could walk through the streets. I feared to go very far from the station, as we had arrived late and would start as near the correct time as possible. The impression I had was that we were leaving the West and entering the East; the most Western of splendid bridges over the Danube, which is here of noble width and depth, took us among the traditions of Turkish rule.

We left in pretty good time, and came after nightfall to Klausenburgh. Here I stopped for the night at the Hotel Royale. I had for dinner, or rather supper, a chicken done up some way with red pepper, which was very good but thirsty. (*Mem:* get recipe for Mina.) I asked the waiter, and he said it was called 'paprika hendl', and that, as it was a national dish, I should be able to get it anywhere along the Carpathians. I found my smattering of German very useful here; indeed, I don't know how I should be able to get on without it.

Having some time at my disposal when in London, I had visited the British Museum, and made search among the books and maps in the library regarding Transylvania; it had struck me that some foreknowledge of the country could hardly fail to have some importance in dealing with a noble of that country. I find that the district he named is in the extreme east of the country, just on the borders of three states, Transylvania, Moldavia, and Bukovina, in the midst of the Carpathian mountains; one of the wildest and least known portions of Europe. I was not able to light on any map or work giving the exact locality of the Castle Dracula, as there are no maps of this country as yet to compare with our own Ordnance Survey maps; but I found that Bistritz, the post town named by Count Dracula, is a fairly well-known place. I shall enter here some of my notes, as they may refresh my memory when I talk over my travels with Mina.

In the population of Transylvania there are four distinct nationalities: Saxons in the south, and mixed with them the Wallachs, who are the descendants of the Dacians; Magyars in the west, and Szekelys in the east and north. I am going among the latter, who claim to be descended from Attila and the Huns. This may be so, for when the Magyars conquered the country in the eleventh century they found the Huns settled in it. I read that every known superstition in the world is gathered into the horseshoe of the Carpathians, as if it were the centre of some sort of imaginative whirlpool; if so my stay may be very interesting. (*Mem.* I must ask the Count all about them.)

I did not sleep well, though my bed was comfortable enough, for I had all sorts of queer dreams. There was a dog howling all night under my window, which may have had something to do with it; or it may have been the paprika, for I had to drink up all the water in my carafe, and was still thirsty. Towards morning I slept and was wakened by the continuous knocking at my door, so I guess I must have been sleeping soundly then. I had for breakfast more paprika, and a sort of porridge of maize flour which they said was 'mamaliga', and egg-plant stuffed with forcemeat, a very excellent dish, which they call 'impletata'. (*Mem.* get recipe for this also.) I had to hurry breakfast, for the train started a little before eight, or rather it ought to have done so, for after rushing to the station at 7.30 I had to sit in the carriage for more than an hour before we began to move. It seems to me that the further East you go the more unpunctual are the trains. What ought they to be in China?

All day long we seemed to dawdle through a country which was full of beauty of every kind. Sometimes we saw little towns or castles on top of steep hills such as we see in old missals; sometimes we ran by rivers and streams which seemed from the wide stony margin on each side of them to be subject to great floods. It takes a lot of water, and running strong, to sweep the outside edge of a river clear. At every station there were groups of people, sometimes crowds, and in all sorts of attire. Some of them were just like the peasants at home or those I saw coming through France and Germany, with short jackets and round hats and home-made trousers; but others were very picturesque. The women looked pretty, except when you got near them, but they were very clumsy about the waist. They had all full white sleeves of some kind or other, and most of them had big belts with a lot of strips of something fluttering from them like the dresses in a ballet, but of course petticoats under them. The strangest figures we saw were the Slovaks, who are more barbarian than the rest, with their big cowboy hats, great baggy dirty-white trousers, white linen shirts, and enormous heavy leather belts, nearly a foot wide, all studded over with brass nails. They wore high boots, with their trousers tucked into them; and had long black hair and heavy black moustaches. They are very picturesque, but do not look prepossessing. On the stage they would be set down at once as some old Oriental band of brigands. They are, however, I am told, very harmless and rather wanting in natural self-assertion.

It was on the dark side of twilight when we got to Bistritz, which is a very interesting old place. Being practically on the frontier – for the Borgo Pass leads from it into Bukovina – it has had a very stormy existence, and it certainly shows marks of it. Fifty years ago a series of great fires took place, which made terrible havoc on five separate occasions. At the very beginning of the seventeenth century it underwent a siege of three weeks and lost 13,000 people, the casualties of war proper being assisted by famine and disease.

Count Dracula had directed me to go to the Golden Krone Hotel, which I found, to my great delight, to be thoroughly old-fashioned, for of course I wanted to see all I could of the ways of the country. I was evidently expected, for when I got near the door I faced a cheery-looking elderly woman in the usual peasant dress – white undergarment with long double apron, front and back, of coloured stuff fitting almost too tight for modesty. When I came close she bowed, and said, 'The Herr Englishman?' 'Yes,' I said, 'Jonathan Harker.' She smiled, and gave some message to an elderly man in white shirt-sleeves, who had followed her to the door. He went, but immediately returned with a letter:

MY FRIEND, Welcome to the Carpathians. I am anxiously expecting you. Sleep well tonight. At three tomorrow the diligence will start for Bukovina; a place on it is kept for you. At the Borgo Pass my carriage will await you and will bring you to me. I trust that your journey from London has been a happy one, and that you will enjoy your stay in my beautiful land. Your friend,

DRACULA

4 May. I found that my landlord had got a letter from the Count, directing him to secure the best place on the coach for me; but on making inquiries as to details he seemed somewhat reticent, and pretended that he could not understand my German. This could not be true, because up to then he had understood it perfectly; at least, he answered my questions exactly as if he did. He and his wife, the old lady who had received me, looked at each other in a frightened sort of way. He mumbled out that the money had been sent in a letter, and that was all he knew. When I asked him if he knew Count Dracula, and could tell me anything of his castle, both he and his wife crossed themselves, and, saying that they knew nothing at all, simply refused to speak further. It was so near the time of starting that I had no time to ask any one else, for it was all very mysterious and not by any means comforting.

Just before I was leaving, the old lady came up to my room and said in a very hysterical way:

'Must you go? Oh! young Herr, must you go?' She was in such an excited state that she seemed to have lost her grip of what German she knew, and mixed it all up with some other language which I did not know at all. I was just able to follow her by asking many questions. When I told her that I must go at once, and that I was engaged on important business, she asked again:

'Do you know what day it is?' I answered that it was the fourth of May. She shook her head as she said again:

'Oh, yes! I know that, I know that! but do you know what day it is?' On my saying that I did not understand, she went on:

'It is the eve of St George's Day. Do you not know that tonight, when the clock strikes midnight, all the evil things in the world will have full sway? Do you know where you are going, and what you are going to?' She was in such evident distress that I tried to comfort her, but without effect. Finally she went down on her knees and implored me not to go; at least to wait a day or two before starting. It was all very ridiculous, but I did not feel comfortable. However, there was business to be done, and I could allow nothing to interfere with it. I therefore tried to raise her up, and said, as gravely as I could, that I thanked her, but my duty was imperative, and that I must go. She then rose and dried her eyes, and taking a crucifix from her neck offered it to me. I did not know what to do, for, as an English Churchman, I have been taught to regard such things as in some measure idolatrous, and yet it seemed so ungracious to refuse an old lady meaning so well and in such a state of mind. She saw, I suppose, the doubt in my face, for she put the rosary round my neck, and said, 'For your mother's sake,' and went out of the room. I am writing up this part of the diary whilst I am waiting for the coach, which is, of course, late; and the crucifix is still round my neck. Whether it is the old lady's fear, or the many ghostly traditions of this place, or the crucifix itself, I do not know, but I am not feeling nearly as easy in my mind as usual. If this book should ever reach Mina before I do, let it bring my goodbye. Here comes the coach!

5 May. The Castle. The grey of the morning has passed, and the sun is high over the distant horizon, which seems jagged, whether with trees or hills I know not, for it is so far off that big things and little are mixed. I am not sleepy, and, as I am not to be called till I awake, naturally I write till sleep comes. There are many odd things to put down, and, lest who reads them may fancy that I dined too well before I left Bistritz, let me put down my dinner exactly. I dined on what they call 'robber steak' – bits of bacon, onion, and beef, seasoned with red pepper, and strung on sticks and roasted over the fire, in the simple style of the London cat's-meat! The wine was Golden Mediasch, which produces a queer sting on the tongue, which is, however, not disagreeable. I had only a couple of glasses of this, and nothing else.

When I got on the coach the driver had not taken his seat, and I saw him talking with the landlady. They were evidently talking of me, for every now and then they looked at me, and some of the people who were sitting on the bench outside the door – which they call by a name meaning 'word-bearer' – came and listened, and then looked at me, most of them pityingly. I could hear a lot of words often repeated, queer words, for there were many nationalities in the crowd; so I quietly got my polyglot dictionary from my bag and looked them out. I must say they were not cheering to me, for amongst them were 'Ordog' – Satan, 'pokol' – hell, 'stregoica' – witch, 'vrolok' and 'vlkoslak' – both of which mean the same thing, one being Slovak and the other Servian for something that is either were-wolf or vampire. (*Mem:* I must ask the Count about these superstitions.)

When we started, the crowd round the inn door, which had by this time swelled to a considerable size, all made the sign of the cross and pointed two fingers towards me. With some difficulty I got a fellow-passenger to tell me what they meant; he would not answer at first, but on learning that I was English he explained that it was a charm or guard against the evil eye. This was not very pleasant for me, just starting for an unknown place to meet an unknown man; but every one seemed so kind-hearted, and so sorrowful, and so sympathetic that I could not but be touched. I shall never forget the last glimpse which I had of the inn-yard and its crowd of picturesque figures, all crossing themselves, as they stood round the wide archway, with its background of rich foliage of oleander and orange trees in green tubs clustered in the centre of the yard. Then our driver, whose wide linen drawers covered the whole front of the box-seat – 'gotza' they call them – cracked his big whip over his four small horses, which ran abreast, and we set off on our journey.

I soon lost sight and recollection of ghostly fears in the beauty of the scene as we drove along, although had I known the language, or rather languages, which my fellow-passengers were speaking, I might not have been able to throw them off so easily. Before us lay a green sloping land full of forests and woods, with here and there steep hills, crowned with clumps of trees or with farmhouses, the blank gable end to the road. There was everywhere a bewildering mass of fruit blossom – apple, plum, pear, cherry; and as we drove by I could see the green grass under the trees spangled with the fallen petals. In and out amongst these green hills of what they call here the 'Mittel Land' ran the road, losing itself as it swept round the grassy curve, or was shut out by the straggling ends of pine woods, which here and there ran down the hillsides like tongues of flame. The road was rugged, but still we seemed to fly over it with a feverish haste. I could not understand then what the haste meant, but the driver was evidently bent on losing no time in reaching Borgo Pass. I was told that this road is in summer-time excellent, but that it had not yet been put in order after the winter snows. In this respect it is different from the general run of roads in the Carpathians, for it is an old tradition that they are not to be kept in too good order. Of old the Hospadars would not repair them, lest the Turk should think that they were preparing to bring in foreign troops, and so hasten the war which was always really at loading point.

Beyond the green swelling hills of the Mittel Land rose mighty slopes of forest up to the lofty steeps of the Carpathians themselves. Right and left of us they towered, with the afternoon sun falling full upon them and bringing out all the glorious colours of this beautiful range, deep blue and purple in the shadows of the peaks, green and brown where grass and rock mingled, and an endless perspective of jagged rock and pointed crags, till these were themselves lost in the distance, where the snowy peaks rose grandly. Here and there seemed mighty rifts in the mountains, through which, as the sun began to sink, we saw now and again the white gleam of falling water. One of my companions touched my arm as we swept round the base of a hill and opened up the lofty, snow-covered peak of a mountain, which seemed, as we wound on our serpentine way, to be right before us:

'Look! Isten szek!' – 'God's seat!' – and he crossed himself reverently. As we wound on our endless way, and the sun sank lower and lower behind us, the shadows of the evening began to creep round us. This was emphasized by the fact that the snowy mountain-top still held the sunset, and seemed to glow out with a delicate cool pink. Here and there we passed Cszeks and Slovaks, all in picturesque attire, but I noticed that goitre was painfully prevalent. By the roadside were many crosses, and as we swept by my companions all crossed themselves. Here and there was a peasant man or woman kneeling before a shrine, who did not even turn round as we approached, but seemed in the self-surrender of devotion to have neither eyes nor ears for the outer world. There were many things new to me: for instance, hay-ricks in the trees, and here and there very beautiful masses of weeping birch, their white stems shining like silver through the delicate green of the leaves. Now and again we passed a leiter-wagon – the ordinary peasant's cart, with its long, snake-like vertebra, calculated to suit the inequalities of the road. On this were sure to be seated quite a group of home-coming peasants, the Cszeks with their white, and the Slovaks with their coloured, sheepskins, the latter carrying lance-fashion their long staves, with axe at end. As the evening fell it began to get very cold, and the growing twilight seemed to merge into one dark mistiness the gloom of the trees, oak, beech, and pine, though in the valleys which ran deep between the spurs of the hills, as we ascended through the Pass, the dark firs stood out here and there against the background of late-lying snow. Sometimes, as the road was cut through the pine woods that seemed in the darkness to be closing down upon us, great masses of greyness, which here and there bestrewed the trees, produced a peculiarly weird and solemn effect, which carried on the thoughts and grim fancies engendered earlier in the evening, when the falling sunset threw into strange relief the ghost-like clouds which amongst the Carpathians seem to wind ceaselessly through the valley. Sometimes the hills were so steep that, despite our driver's haste, the horses could only go slowly. I wished to get down and walk up them, as we do at home, but the driver would not hear of it. 'No, no,' he said; 'you must not walk here; the dogs are too fierce'; and then he added, with what he evidently meant for grim pleasantry – for he looked round to catch the approving smile of the rest – 'and you may have enough of such matters before you go to sleep.' The only stop he would make was a moment's pause to light his lamps.

When it grew dark there seemed to be some excitement amongst the passengers, and they kept speaking to him, one after the other, as though urging him to further speed. He lashed the horses unmercifully with his long whip, and with wild cries of encouragement urged them on to further exertions. Then through the darkness I could see a sort of patch of grey light ahead of us, as though there were a cleft in the hills. The excitement of the passengers grew greater; the crazy coach rocked on its great leather springs, and swayed like a boat tossed on a stormy sea. I had to hold on. The road grew more level, and we appeared to fly along. Then the mountains seemed to come nearer to us on each side and to frown down upon us; we were entering on the Borgo Pass. One by one several of the passengers offered me gifts, which they pressed upon me with an earnestness which would take no denial; these were certainly of an odd and varied kind, but each was given in simple good faith, with a kindly word and a blessing, and that strange mixture of fear-meaning movements which I had seen outside the hotel at Bistritz – the sign of the cross and the guard against the evil eye. Then, as we flew along, the driver leaned forward, and on each side the passengers, craning over the edge of the coach, peered eagerly into the darkness. It was evident that something very exciting was either happening or expected, but though I asked each passenger, no one would give me the slightest explanation. This state of excitement kept on for some little time; and at last we saw before us the Pass opening out on the eastern side. There were dark, rolling clouds overhead, and in the air the heavy, oppressive sense of thunder. It seemed as though the mountain range had separated two atmospheres and that now we had got into the thunderous one. I was now myself looking out for the conveyance which was to take me to the Count. Each moment I expected to see the glare of lamps through the blackness; but all was dark. The only light was the flickering rays of our own lamps, in which the steam from our hard-driven horses rose in a white cloud. We could now see the sandy road lying white before us, but there was on it no sign of a vehicle. The passengers drew back with a sigh of gladness, which seemed to mock my own disappointment. I was already thinking what I had best do, when the driver, looking at his watch, said to the others something which I could hardly hear, it was spoken so quietly and in so low a tone; I thought it was 'An hour less than the time.' Then turning to me, he said in German worse than my own:

'There is no carriage here. The Herr is not expected after all. He will now come on to Bukovina, and return tomorrow or the next day; better the next day.' Whilst he was speaking the horses began to neigh and snort and plunge wildly, so that the driver had to hold them up. Then, amongst a chorus of screams from the peasants and a universal crossing of themselves, a calèche, with four horses, drove up behind us, overtook us, and drew up beside the coach. I could see from the flash of our lamps, as the rays fell on them, that the horses were coal-black and splendid animals. They were driven by a tall man, with a long brown beard and a great black hat, which seemed to hide his face from us. I could only see the gleam of a pair of very bright eyes, which seemed red in the lamplight, as he turned to us. He said to the driver:

'You are early tonight, my friend.' The man stammered in reply:

'The English Herr was in a hurry,' to which the stranger replied:

'That is why, I suppose, you wished him to go on to Bukovina. You cannot deceive me, my friend; I know too much, and my horses are swift.' As he spoke he smiled, and the lamplight fell on a hard-looking mouth, with very red lips and sharp-looking teeth, as white as ivory. One of my companions whispered to another the line from Bürger's *Lenore*:

'Denn die Todten reiten schnell.' ('For the dead travel fast.')

The strange driver evidently heard the words, for he looked up with a gleaming smile. The passenger turned his face away, at the same time putting out his two fingers and crossing himself. 'Give me the Herr's luggage,' said the driver; and with exceeding alacrity my bags were handed out and put in the calèche. Then I descended from the side of the coach, as the calèche was close alongside, the driver helping me with a hand which caught my arm in a grip of steel; his strength must have been prodigious. Without a word he shook his reins, the horses turned, and we swept into the darkness of the Pass. As I looked back I saw the steam from the horses of the coach by the light of the lamps, and projected against it the figures of my late companions crossing themselves. Then the driver cracked his whip and called to his horses, and off they swept on their way to Bukovina.

As they sank into the darkness I felt a strange chill, and a lonely feeling come over me; but a cloak was thrown over my shoulders, and a rug across my knees, and the driver said in excellent German:

'The night is chill, mein Herr, and my master the Count bade me take all care of you. There is a flask of slivovitz [the plum brandy of the country] underneath the seat, if you should require it.' I did not take any, but it was a comfort to know it was there all the same. I felt a little strangely, and not a little frightened. I think had there been any alternative I should have taken it, instead of prosecuting that unknown night journey. The carriage went at a hard pace straight along, then we made a complete turn and went along another straight road. It seemed to me that we were simply going over and over the same ground again; and so I took note of some salient point, and found that this was so. I would have liked to have asked the driver what this all meant, but I really feared to do so, for I thought that, placed as I was, any protest would have had no effect in case there had been an intention to delay. By-and-by, however, as I was curious to know how time was passing, I struck a match, and by its flame looked at my watch: it was within a few minutes of midnight. This gave me a sort of shock, for I suppose the general superstition about midnight was increased by my recent experiences. I waited with a sick feeling of suspense.

Then a dog began to howl somewhere in a farmhouse far down the road – a long, agonized wailing, as if from fear. The sound was taken up by another dog, and then another and another, till, borne on the wind which now sighed softly through the Pass, a wild howling began, which seemed to come from all over the country, as far as the imagination could grasp it through the gloom of the night. At the first howl the horses began to strain and rear, but the driver spoke to them soothingly, and they quieted down, but shivered and sweated as though after a runaway from sudden fright. Then, far off in the distance, from the mountains on each side of us began a louder and a sharper howling – that of wolves – which affected both the horses and myself in the same way – for I was minded to jump from the calèche and run, whilst they reared again and plunged madly, so that the driver had to use all his great strength to keep them from bolting. In a few minutes, however, my own ears got accustomed to the sound, and the horses so far became quiet that the driver was able to descend and to stand before them. He petted and soothed them, and whispered something in their ears, as I have heard of horse-tamers doing, and with extraordinary effect, for under his caresses they became quite manageable again, though they still trembled. The driver again took his seat, and shaking his reins, started off at a great pace. This time, after going to the far side of the Pass, he suddenly turned down a narrow roadway which ran sharply to the right.

Soon we were hemmed in with trees, which in places arched right over the roadway till we passed as through a tunnel; and again great frowning rocks guarded us boldly on either side. Though we were in shelter, we could hear the rising wind, for it moaned and whistled through the rocks, and the branches of the trees crashed together as we swept along. It grew colder and colder still, and fine, powdery snow began to fall, so that soon we and all around us were covered with a white blanket. The keen wind still carried the howling of the dogs, though this grew fainter as we went on our way. The baying of the wolves sounded nearer and nearer, as though they were closing round on us from every side. I grew dreadfully afraid, and the horses shared my fear; but the driver was not in the least disturbed. He kept turning his head to left and right, but I could not see anything through the darkness.

Suddenly, away on our left, I saw a faint flickering blue flame. The driver saw it at the same moment; he at once checked the horses and, jumping to the ground, disappeared into the darkness. I did not know what to do, the less as the howling of the wolves grew closer; but while I wondered the driver suddenly appeared again, and without a word took his seat, and we resumed our journey. I think I must have fallen asleep and kept dreaming of the incident, for it seemed to be repeated endlessly, and now looking back, it is like a sort of awful nightmare. Once the flame appeared so near the road, that even in the darkness around us I could watch the driver's motions. He went rapidly to where the blue flame arose – it must have been very faint, for it did not seem to illumine the place around it at all – and gathering a few stones, formed them into some device. Once there appeared a strange optical effect: when he stood between me and the flame he did not obstruct it, for I could see its ghostly flicker all the same. This startled me, but as the effect was only momentary, I took it that my eyes deceived me straining through the darkness. Then for a time there were no blue flames, and we sped onwards through the gloom, with the howling of the wolves around us, as though they were following in a moving circle.

At last there came a time when the driver went further afield than he had yet gone, and during his absence the horses began to tremble worse than ever and to snort and scream with fright. I could not see any cause for it, for the howling of the wolves had ceased altogether; but just then the moon, sailing through the black clouds, appeared behind the jagged crest of a beetling, pine-clad rock, and by its light I saw around us a ring of wolves, with white teeth and lolling red tongues, with long, sinewy limbs and shaggy hair. They were a hundred times more terrible in the grim silence which held them than even when they howled. For myself, I felt a sort of paralysis of fear. It is only when a man feels himself face to face with such horrors that he can understand their true import.

All at once the wolves began to howl as though the moonlight had had some peculiar effect on them. The horses jumped about and reared, and looked helplessly round with eyes that rolled in a way painful to see; but the living ring of terror encompassed them on every side, and they had perforce to remain within it. I called to the coachman to come, for it seemed to me that our only chance was to try to break out through the ring and to aid his approach. I shouted and beat the side of the calèche, hoping by the noise to scare the wolves from that side, so as to give him a chance of reaching the trap. How he came there, I know not, but I heard his voice raised in a tone of imperious command, and looking towards the sound, saw him stand in the roadway. As he swept his long arms, as though brushing aside some impalpable obstacle, the wolves fell back and back further still. Just then a heavy cloud passed across the face of the moon, so that we were again in darkness.

When I could see again the driver was climbing into the calèche and the wolves had disappeared. This was all so strange and uncanny that a dreadful fear came upon me, and I was afraid to speak or move. The time seemed interminable as we swept on our way, now in almost complete darkness, for the rolling clouds obscured the moon. We kept on ascending, with occasional periods of quick descent, but in the main always ascending. Suddenly I became conscious of the fact that the driver was in the act of pulling up the horses in the courtyard of a vast ruined castle, from whose tall black windows came no ray of light, and whose broken battlements showed a jagged line against the moonlit sky.

2

Jonathan Harker's Journal
(continued)

5 May. I must have been asleep, for certainly if I had been fully awake I must have noticed the approach to such a remarkable place. In the gloom the courtyard looked of considerable size, and as several dark ways led from it under great round arches it perhaps seemed bigger than it really is. I have not yet been able to see it by daylight.

When the calèche stopped the driver jumped down, and held out his hand to assist me to alight. Again I could not but notice his prodigious strength. His hand actually seemed like a steel vice that could have crushed mine if he had chosen. Then he took out my traps, and placed them on the ground beside me as I stood close to a great door, old and studded with large iron nails, and set in a projecting doorway of massive stone. I could see even in the dim light that the stone was massively carved, but that the carving had been much worn by time and weather. As I stood, the driver jumped again into his seat and shook the reins; the horses started forward, and trap and all disappeared down one of the dark openings.

I stood in silence where I was, for I did not know what to do. Of bell or knocker there was no sign; through these frowning walls and dark window openings it was not likely that my voice could penetrate. The time I waited seemed endless, and I felt doubts and fears crowding upon me. What sort of place had I come to, and among what kind of people? What sort of grim adventure was it on which I had embarked? Was this a customary incident in the life of a solicitor's clerk sent out to explain the purchase of a London estate to a foreigner? Solicitor's clerk! Mina would not like that. Solicitor – for just before leaving London I got word that my examination was successful; and I am now a full-blown solicitor! I began to rub my eyes and pinch myself to see if I were awake. It all seemed like a horrible nightmare to me, and I expected that I should suddenly awake, and find myself at home, with the dawn struggling in through the windows, as I had now and again felt in the morning after a day of overwork. But my flesh answered the pinching test, and my eyes were not to be deceived. I was indeed awake and among the Carpathians. All I could do now was to be patient, and to wait the coming of the morning.

Just as I had come to this conclusion I heard a heavy step approaching behind the great door, and saw through the chinks the gleam of a coming light. Then there was the sound of rattling chains and the clanking of massive bolts drawn back. A key was turned with the loud grating noise of long disuse, and the great door swung back.

Within stood a tall old man, clean shaven save for a long white moustache, and clad in black from head to foot, without a single speck of colour about him anywhere. He held in his hand an antique silver lamp, in which the flame burned without chimney or globe of any kind, throwing long quivering shadows as it flickered in the draught of the open door. The old man motioned me in with his right hand with a courtly gesture, saying in excellent English, but with a strange intonation:

'Welcome to my house! Enter freely and of your own will!' He made no motion of stepping to meet me, but stood like a statue, as though his gesture of welcome had fixed him into stone. The instant, however, that I had stepped over the threshold, he moved impulsively forward, and holding out his hand grasped mine with a strength which made me wince, an effect which was not lessened by the fact that it seemed as cold as ice – more like the hand of a dead than a living man. Again he said:

'Welcome to my house. Come freely. Go safely; and leave something of the happiness you bring!' The strength of the handshake was so much akin to that which I had noticed in the driver, whose face I had not seen, that for a moment I doubted if it were not the same person to whom I was speaking; so to make sure, I said interrogatively:

'Count Dracula?' He bowed in a courtly way as he replied:

'I am Dracula; and I bid you welcome, Mr Harker, to my house. Come in; the night air is chill, and you must need to eat and rest.' As he was speaking he put the lamp on a bracket on the wall, and stepping out, took my luggage; he had carried it in before I could forestall him. I protested, but he insisted:

'Nay, sir, you are my guest. It is late, and my people are not available. Let me see to your comfort myself.' He insisted on carrying my traps along the passage, and then up a great winding stair, and along another great passage, on whose stone floor our steps rang heavily. At the end of this he threw open a heavy door, and I rejoiced to see within a well-lit room in which a table was spread for supper, and on whose mighty hearth a great fire of logs flamed and flared.

The Count halted, putting down my bags, closed the door, and crossing the room, opened another door, which led into a small octagonal room lit by a single lamp, and seemingly without a window of any sort. Passing through this, he opened another door, and motioned me to enter. It was a welcome sight; for here was a great bedroom well lighted and warmed with another log fire, which sent a hollow roar up the wide chimney. The Count himself left my luggage inside and withdrew, saying, before he closed the door:

'You will need, after your journey, to refresh yourself by making your toilet. I trust you will find all you wish. When you are ready come into the other room, where you will find your supper prepared.'

The light and warmth and the Count's courteous welcome seemed to have dissipated all my doubts and fears. Having then reached my normal state, I discovered that I was half famished with hunger; so making a hasty toilet, I went into the other room.

I found supper already laid out. My host, who stood on one side of the great fireplace, leaning against the stonework, made a graceful wave of his hand to the table, and said:

'I pray you, be seated and sup how you please. You will, I trust, excuse me that I do not join you; but I have dined already, and I do not sup.'

I handed to him the sealed letter which Mr Hawkins had entrusted to me. He opened it and read it gravely; then, with a charming smile, he handed it to me to read. One passage of it, at least, gave me a thrill of pleasure:

'I much regret that an attack of gout, from which malady I am a constant sufferer, forbids absolutely any travelling on my part for some time to come; but I am happy to say I can send a sufficient substitute, one in whom I have every possible confidence. He is a young man, full of energy and talent in his own way, and of a very faithful disposition. He is discreet and silent, and has grown into manhood in my service. He shall be ready to attend on you when you will during his stay, and shall take your instructions in all matters.'

The Count himself came forward and took off the cover of a dish, and I fell to at once on an excellent roast chicken. This, with some cheese and a salad and a bottle of old Tokay, of which I had two glasses, was my supper. During the time I was eating it the Count asked me many questions as to my journey, and I told him by degrees all I had experienced.

By this time I had finished my supper, and by my host's desire had drawn up a chair by the fire and begun to smoke a cigar which he offered me, at the same time excusing himself that he did not smoke. I had now an opportunity of observing him, and found him of a very marked physiognomy.

His face was a strong – a very strong – aquiline, with high bridge of the thin nose and peculiarly arched nostrils; with lofty domed forehead, and hair growing scantily round the temples, but profusely elsewhere. His eyebrows were very massive, almost meeting over the nose, and with bushy hair that seemed to curl in its own profusion. The mouth, so far as I could see it under the heavy moustache, was fixed and rather cruel-looking, with peculiarly sharp white teeth; these protruded over the lips, whose remarkable ruddiness showed astonishing vitality in a man of his years. For the rest, his ears were pale and at the tops extremely pointed; the chin was broad and strong, and the cheeks firm though thin. The general effect was one of extraordinary pallor.

Hitherto I had noticed the backs of his hands as they lay on his knees in the firelight, and they had seemed rather white and fine; but seeing them now close to me, I could not but notice that they were rather coarse – broad, with squat fingers. Strange to say, there were hairs in the centre of the palm. The nails were long and fine, and cut to a sharp point. As the Count leaned over me and his hands touched me, I could not repress a shudder. It may have been that his breath was rank, but a horrible feeling of nausea came over me, which, do what I would, I could not conceal. The Count, evidently noticing it, drew back; and with a grim sort of smile, which showed more than he had yet done his protuberant teeth, sat himself down again on his own side of the fireplace. We were both silent for a while; and as I looked towards the window I saw the first dim streak of the coming dawn. There seemed a strange stillness over everything; but as I listened I heard as if from down below in the valley the howling of many wolves. The Count's eyes gleamed, and he said:

'Listen to them – the children of the night. What music they make!' Seeing, I suppose, some expression in my face strange to him, he added:

'Ah, sir, you dwellers in the city cannot enter into the feelings of the hunter.' Then he rose and said:

'But you must be tired. Your bedroom is all ready, and tomorrow you shall sleep as late as you will. I have to be away till the afternoon; so sleep well and dream well!' and, with a courteous bow, he opened for me himself the door to the octagonal room, and I entered my bedroom . . .

I am all in a sea of wonders. I doubt; I fear; I think strange things which I dare not confess to my own soul. God keep me, if only for the sake of those dear to me!

7 May. It is again early morning, but I have rested and enjoyed the last twenty-four hours. I slept till late in the day, and awoke of my own accord. When I had dressed myself I went into the room where we had supped, and found a cold breakfast laid out, with coffee kept hot by the pot being placed on the hearth. There was a card on the table, on which was written: 'I have to be absent for a while. Do not wait for me. – D.' So I set to and enjoyed a hearty meal. When I had done, I looked for a bell, so that I might let the servants know I had finished: but I could not find one. There are certainly odd deficiencies in the house, considering the extraordinary evidences of wealth which are round me. The table service is of gold, and so beautifully wrought that it must be of immense value. The curtains and upholstery of the chairs and sofas and the hangings of my bed are of the costliest and most beautiful fabrics, and must have been of fabulous value when they were made, for they are centuries old, though in excellent order. I saw something like them in Hampton Court, but there they were worn and frayed and moth-eaten. But still in none of the rooms is there a mirror. There is not even a toilet glass on my table, and I had to get the little shaving glass from my bag before I could either shave or brush my hair. I have not yet seen a servant anywhere, or heard a sound near the castle except the howling of wolves. When I had finished my meal – I do not know whether to call it breakfast or dinner, for it was between five and six o'clock when I had it – I looked about for something to read, for I did not like to go about the castle until I had asked the Count's permission. There was absolutely nothing in the room, book, newspaper, or even writing materials; so I opened another door in the room and found a sort of library. The door opposite mine I tried, but found it locked.

In the library I found, to my great delight, a vast number of English books, whole shelves full of them, and bound volumes of magazines and newspapers. A table in the centre was littered with English magazines and newspapers, though none of them were of very recent date. The books were of the most varied kind – history, geography, politics, political economy, botany, geology, law – all relating to England and English life and customs and manners. There were even such books of reference as the *London Directory*, the 'Red' and 'Blue' books, *Whitaker's Almanack*, the *Army and Navy Lists*, and – it somehow gladdened my heart to see it – the *Law List*.

Whilst I was looking at the books, the door opened, and the Count entered. He saluted me in a hearty way, and hoped that I had had a good night's rest. Then he went on:

'I am glad you found your way in here, for I am sure there is much that will interest you. These friends' – and he laid his hand on some of the books – 'have been good friends to me, and for some years past, ever since I had the idea of going to London, have given me many, many hours of pleasure. Through them I have come to know your great England; and to know her is to love her. I long to go through the crowded streets of your mighty London, to be in the midst of the whirl and rush of humanity, to share its life, its change, its death, and all that makes it what it is. But alas! as yet I only know your tongue through books. To you, my friend, I look that I know it to speak.'

'But, Count,' I said, 'you know and speak English thoroughly!' He bowed gravely.

'I thank you, my friend, for your all too flattering estimate, but yet I fear that I am but a little way on the road I would travel. True, I know the grammar and the words, but yet I know not how to speak them.'

'Indeed,' I said, 'you speak excellently.'

'Not so,' he answered. 'Well I know that, did I move and speak in your London, none there are who would not know me for a stranger. That is not enough for me. Here I am noble; I am *boyar*; the common people know me, and I am master. But a stranger in a strange land, he is no one; men know him not – and to know not is to care not for. I am content if I am like the rest, so that no man stops if he see me, or pause in his speaking if he hear my words, to say, "Ha, ha! a stranger!" I have been so long master that I would be master still – or at least that none other should be master of me. You come to me not alone as agent of my friend Peter Hawkins, of Exeter, to tell me all about my new estate in London. You shall, I trust, rest here with me a while, so that by our talking I may learn the English intonation; and I would that you tell me when I make error, even of the smallest, in my speaking. I am sorry that I had to be away so long today; but you will, I know, forgive one who has so many important affairs in hand.'

Of course I said all I could about being willing, and asked if I might come into that room when I chose. He answered: 'Yes, certainly,' and added:

'You may go anywhere you wish in the castle, except where the doors are locked, where of course you will not wish to go. There is reason that all things are as they are, and did you see with my eyes and know with my knowledge, you would perhaps better understand.' I said I was sure of this, and then he went on:

'We are in Transylvania; and Transylvania is not England. Our ways are not your ways, and there shall be to you many strange things. Nay, from what you have told me of your experiences already, you know something of what strange things here may be.'

This led to much conversation; and as it was evident that he wanted to talk, if only for talking's sake, I asked him many questions regarding things that had already happened to me or come within my notice. Sometimes he sheered off the subject, or turned the conversation by pretending not to understand; but generally he answered all I asked most frankly. Then as time went on, and I had got somewhat bolder, I asked him of some of the strange things of the preceding night, as, for instance, why the coachman went to the places where we had seen the blue flames. Was it indeed true that they showed where gold was hidden? He then explained to me that it was commonly believed that on a certain night of the year – last night, in fact, when all evil spirits are supposed to have unchecked sway – a blue flame is seen over any place where treasure has been concealed. 'That treasure has been hidden,' he went on, 'in the region through which you came last night, there can be but little doubt; for it was the ground fought over for centuries by the Wallachian, the Saxon, and the Turk. Why, there is hardly a foot of soil in all this region that has not been enriched by the blood of men, patriots or invaders. In old days there were stirring times, when the Austrian and the Hungarian came up in hordes, and the patriots went out to meet them – men and women, the aged and the children too – and waited their coming on the rocks above the passes, that they might sweep destruction on them with their artificial avalanches. When the invader was triumphant he found but little, for whatever there was had been sheltered in the friendly soil.'

'But how,' said I, 'can it have remained so long undiscovered, when there is a sure index to it if men will but take the trouble to look?' The Count smiled, and as his lips ran back over his gums, the long, sharp, canine teeth showed out strangely; he answered:

'Because your peasant is at heart a coward and a fool! Those flames only appear on one night; and on that night no man of this land will, if he can help it, stir without his doors. And, dear sir, even if he did he would not know what to do. Why, even the peasant that you tell me of who marked the place of the flame would not know where to look in daylight even for his own work. You would not, I dare be sworn, be able to find these places again?'

'There you are right,' I said. 'I know no more than the dead where even to look for them.' Then we drifted onto other matters.

'Come,' he said at last, 'tell me of London and of the house which you have procured for me.' With an apology for my remissness, I went into my own room to get the papers from my bag. Whilst I was placing them in order I heard a rattling of china and silver in the next room, and as I passed through, noticed that the table had been cleared and the lamp lit, for it was by this time deep into the dark. The lamps were also lit in the study or library, and I found the Count lying on the sofa, reading, of all things in the world, an English *Bradshaw's Guide*. When I came in he cleared the books and papers from the table; and with him I went into plans and deeds and figures of all sorts. He was interested in everything, and asked me a myriad questions about the place and its surroundings. He clearly had studied beforehand all he could get on the subject of the neighbourhood, for he evidently at the end knew very much more than I did. When I remarked this, he answered:

'Well, but, my friend, is it not needful that I should? When I go there I shall be all alone, and my friend Harker Jonathan – nay, pardon me, I fall into my country's habit of putting your patronymic first – my friend Jonathan Harker will not be by my side to correct and aid me. He will be in Exeter, miles away, probably working at papers of the law with my other friend, Peter Hawkins. So!'

We went thoroughly into the business of the purchase of the estate at Purfleet. When I had told him the facts and got his signature to the necessary papers, and had written a letter with them ready to post to Mr Hawkins, he began to ask me how I had come across so suitable a place. I read to him the notes which I had made at the time, and which I inscribe here:

'At Purfleet, on a by-road, I came across just such a place as seemed to be required, and where was displayed a dilapidated notice that the place was for sale. It is surrounded by a high wall, of ancient structure, built of heavy stones, and has not been repaired for a large number of years. The closed gates were of heavy old oak and iron, all eaten with rust.

'The estate is called Carfax, no doubt a corruption of the old *Quatre Face*, as the house is four-sided, agreeing with the cardinal points of the compass. It contains in all some twenty acres, quite surrounded by the solid stone wall above mentioned. There are many trees on it, which make it in places gloomy, and there is a deep, dark-looking pond or small lake, evidently fed by some springs, as the water is clear and flows away in a fair-sized stream. The house is very large and of all periods back, I should say, to mediaeval times, for one part is of stone immensely thick, with only a few windows high up and heavily barred with iron. It looks like part of a keep, and is close to an old chapel or church. I could not enter it, as I had not the key of the door leading to it from the house, but I have taken with my Kodak views of it from various points. The house has been added to, but in a very straggling way, and I can only guess at the amount of ground it covers, which must be very great. There are but few houses close at hand, one being a very large house only recently added to and formed into a private lunatic asylum. It is not, however, visible from the grounds.'

When I had finished, he said:

'I am glad that it is old and big. I myself am of an old family, and to live in a new house would kill me. A house cannot be made habitable in a day; and, after all, how few days go to make up a century. I rejoice also that there is a chapel of old times. We Transylvanian nobles love not to think that our bones may be amongst the common dead. I seek not gaiety nor mirth, not the bright voluptuousness of much sunshine and sparkling waters which please the young and gay. I am no longer young; and my heart, through weary years of mourning over the dead, is not attuned to mirth. Moreover, the walls of my castle are broken; the shadows are many, and the wind breathes cold through the broken battlements and casements. I love the shade and the shadow, and would be alone with my thoughts when I may.'

Somehow his words and his look did not seem to accord, or else it was that his cast of face made his smile look malignant and saturnine.

Presently, with an excuse, he left me, asking me to put all my papers together. He was some little time away, and I began to look at some of the books around me. One was an atlas, which I found opened naturally at England, as if that map had been much used. On looking at it I found in certain places little rings marked, and on examining these I noticed that one was near London on the east side, manifestly where his new estate was situated; the other two were Exeter, and Whitby on the Yorkshire coast.

It was the better part of an hour when the Count returned. 'Aha!' he said; 'still at your books? Good! But you must not work always. Come; I am informed that your supper is ready.' He took my arm, and we went into the next room, where I found an excellent supper ready on the table. The Count again excused himself, as he had dined out on his being away from home. But he sat as on the previous night, and chatted whilst I ate. After supper I smoked, as on the last evening, and the Count stayed with me, chatting and asking questions on every conceivable subject, hour after hour. I felt that it was getting very late indeed, but I did not say anything, for I felt under obligation to meet my host's wishes in every way. I was not sleepy, as the long sleep yesterday had fortified me; but I could not help experiencing that chill which comes over one at the coming of the dawn, which is like, in its way, the turn of the tide. They say that people who are near death die generally at the change to the dawn or at the turn of the tide; any one who has when tired, and tied as it were to his post, experienced this change in the atmosphere can well believe it. All at once we heard the crow of a cock coming up with preternatural shrillness through the clear morning air; Count Dracula, jumping to his feet, said:

'Why, there is the morning again! How remiss I am to let you stay up so long. You must make your conversation regarding my dear new country of England less interesting, so that I may not forget how time flies by us,' and, with a courtly bow, he left me.

I went into my own room and drew the curtains, but there was little to notice; my window opened into the courtyard, all I could see was the warm grey of quickening sky. So I pulled the curtains again, and have written of this day.

8 May. I began to fear as I wrote in this book that I was getting too diffuse; but now I am glad that I went into detail from the first, for there is something so strange about this place and all in it that I cannot but feel uneasy. I wish I were safe out of it, or that I had never come. It may be that this strange night-existence is telling on me; but would that that were all! If there were any one to talk to I could bear it, but there is no one. I have only the Count to speak with, and he! – I fear I am myself the only living soul within the place. Let me be prosaic so far as facts can be; it will help me to bear up, and imagination must not run riot with me. If it does I am lost. Let me say at once how I stand – or seem to.

I only slept a few hours when I went to bed, and feeling that I could not sleep any more, got up. I had hung my shaving glass by the window, and was just beginning to shave. Suddenly I felt a hand on my shoulder, and heard the Count's voice saying to me, 'Good morning.' I started, for it amazed me that I had not seen him, since the reflection of the glass covered the whole room behind me. In starting I had cut myself slightly, but did not notice it at the moment. Having answered the Count's salutation, I turned to the glass again to see how I had been mistaken. This time there could be no error, for the man was close to me, and I could see him over my shoulder. But there was no reflection of him in the mirror! The whole room behind me was displayed; but there was no sign of a man in it, except myself. This was startling, and, coming on top of so many strange things, was beginning to increase that vague feeling of uneasiness which I always have when the Count is near; but at that instant I saw that the cut had bled a little, and the blood was trickling over my chin. I laid down the razor, turning as I did so half round to look for some sticking plaster. When the Count saw my face, his eyes blazed with a sort of demoniac fury, and he suddenly made a grab at my throat. I drew away, and his hand touched the string of beads which held the crucifix. It made an instant change in him, for the fury passed so quickly that I could hardly believe that it was ever there.

'Take care,' he said, 'take care how you cut yourself. It is more dangerous than you think in this country.' Then seizing the shaving glass, he went on: 'And this is the wretched thing that has done the mischief. It is a foul bauble of man's vanity. Away with it!' and opening the heavy window with one wrench of his terrible hand, he flung out the glass, which was shattered into a thousand pieces on the stones of the courtyard far below. Then he withdrew without a word. It is very annoying, for I do not see how I am to shave, unless in my watch-case or the bottom of the shaving-pot, which is fortunately of metal.

When I went into the dining-room, breakfast was prepared; but I could not find the Count anywhere. So I breakfasted alone. It is strange that as yet I have not seen the Count eat or drink. He must be a very peculiar man! After breakfast I did a little exploring in the castle. I went out on the stairs and found a room looking towards the south. The view was magnificent, and from where I stood there was every opportunity of seeing it. The castle is on the very edge of a terrible precipice. A stone falling from the window would fall a thousand feet without touching anything! As far as the eye can reach is a sea of green tree-tops, with occasionally a deep rift where there is a chasm. Here and there are silver threads where the rivers wind in deep gorges through the forests.

But I am not in heart to describe beauty, for when I had seen the view I explored further; doors, doors, doors everywhere, and all locked and bolted. In no place save from the windows in the castle walls is there an available exit.

The castle is a veritable prison, and I am a prisoner!

3

Jonathan Harker's Journal
(continued)

When I found that I was a prisoner a sort of wild feeling came over me. I rushed up and down the stairs, trying every door and peering out of every window I could find; but after a little the conviction of my helplessness overpowered all other feelings. When I look back after a few hours I think I must have been mad for the time, for I behaved much as a rat does in a trap. When, however, the conviction had come to me that I was helpless I sat down quietly – as quietly as I have ever done anything in my life – and began to think over what was best to be done. I am thinking still, and as yet have come to no definite conclusion. Of one thing only am I certain: that it is no use making my ideas known to the Count. He knows well that I am imprisoned; and as he has done it himself, and has doubtless his own motives for it, he would only deceive me if I trusted him fully with the facts. So far as I can see, my only plan will be to keep my knowledge and my fears to myself, and my eyes open. I am, I know, either being deceived, like a baby, by my own fears, or else I am in desperate straits; and if the latter be so, I need, and shall need, all my brains to get through.

I had hardly come to this conclusion when I heard the great door below shut, and knew that the Count had returned. He did not come at once into the library, so I went cautiously to my own room and found him making the bed. This was odd, but only confirmed what I had all along thought – that there were no servants in the house. When later I saw him through the chink of the hinges of the door laying the table in the dining-room, I was assured of it; for if he does himself all these menial offices, surely it is proof that there is no one else to do them. This gave me a fright, for if there is no one else in the castle, it must have been the Count himself who was the driver of the coach that brought me here. This is a terrible thought; for if so, what does it mean that he could control the wolves, as he did, by only holding up his hand in silence. How was it that all the people at Bistritz and on the coach had some terrible fear for me? What meant the giving of the crucifix, of the garlic, of the wild rose, of the mountain ash? Bless that good, good woman who hung the crucifix round my neck! for it is a comfort and a strength to me whenever I touch it. It is odd that a thing which I have been taught to regard with disfavour and as idolatrous should in a time of loneliness and trouble be of help. Is it that there is something in the essence of the thing itself, or that it is a medium, a tangible help, in conveying memories of sympathy and comfort? Some time, if it may be, I must examine this matter and try to make up my mind about it. In the meantime I must find out all I can about Count Dracula, as it may help me to understand. Tonight he may talk of himself, if I turn the conversation that way. I must be very careful, however, not to awake his suspicion.

Midnight. I have had a long talk with the Count. I asked him a few questions on Transylvanian history, and he warmed up to the subject wonderfully. In his speaking of things and people, and especially of battles, he spoke as if he had been present at them all. This he afterwards explained by saying that to a *boyar* the pride of his house and name is his own pride, that their glory is his glory, that their fate is his fate. Whenever he spoke of his house he always said 'we', and spoke almost in the plural, like a king speaking. I wish I could put down all he said exactly as he said it, for to me it was most fascinating. It seemed to have in it a whole history of the country. He grew excited as he spoke, and walked about the room pulling his great white moustache and grasping anything on which he laid his hands as though he would crush it by main strength. One thing he said which I shall put down as nearly as I can; for it tells in its way the story of his race:

'We Szekelys have a right to be proud, for in our veins flows the blood of many brave races who fought as the lion fights, for lordship. Here, in the whirlpool of European races, the Ugric tribe bore down from Iceland the fighting spirit which Thor and Wodin gave them, which their Berserkers displayed to such fell intent on the seaboards of Europe, ay, and of Asia and Africa too, till the peoples thought that the werewolves themselves had come. Here, too, when they came, they found the Huns, whose warlike fury had swept the earth like a living flame, till the dying peoples held that in their veins ran the blood of those old witches, who, expelled from Scythia, had mated with the devils in the desert. Fools, fools! What devil or what witch was ever so great as Attila, whose blood is in these veins?' He held up his arms. 'Is it a wonder that we were a conquering race; that we were proud; that when the Magyar, the Lombard, the Avar, the Bulgar, or the Turk poured his thousands on our frontiers, we drove them back? Is it strange that when Arpad and his legions swept through the Hungarian fatherland he found us here when he reached the frontier; that the Honfoglalas was completed there? And when the Hungarian flood swept eastward, the Szekelys were claimed as kindred by the victorious Magyars, and to us for centuries was trusted the guarding of the frontier of Turkey-land; ay and more than that, endless duty of the frontier guard, for, as the Turks say, "water sleeps, and enemy is sleepless". Who more gladly than we throughout the Four Nations received the "bloody sword", or at its warlike call flocked quicker to the standard of the King? When was redeemed that great shame of my nation, the shame of Cassova, when the flags of the Wallach and the Magyar went down beneath the Crescent, who was it but one of my own race who as Voivode crossed the Danube and beat the Turk on his own ground? This was a Dracula indeed! Woe was it that his own unworthy brother, when he had fallen, sold his people to the Turk and brought the shame of slavery on them! Was it not this Dracula, indeed, who inspired that other of his race who in a later age again and again brought his forces over the great river into Turkey-land; who, when he was beaten back, came again, and again, and again, though he had to come alone from the bloody field where his troops were being slaughtered, since he knew that he alone could ultimately triumph? They said that he thought only of himself. Bah! What good are peasants without a leader? Where ends the war without a brain and heart to conduct it? Again, when, after the battle of Mohacs, we threw off the Hungarian yoke, we of the Dracula blood were amongst their leaders, for our spirit would not brook that we were not free. Ah, young sir, the Szekelys – and the Dracula as their heart's blood, their brains, and their swords – can boast a record that mushroom growths like the Hapsburgs and the Romanoffs can never reach. The warlike days are over. Blood is too precious a thing in these days of dishonourable peace; and the glories of the great races are as a tale that is told.'

It was by this time close on morning, and we went to bed. (*Mem:* this diary seems horribly like the beginning of the *Arabian Nights*, for everything has to break off at cockcrow – or like the ghost of Hamlet's father.)

12 May. Let me begin with facts – bare, meagre facts, verified by books and figures, and of which there can be no doubt. I must not confuse them with experiences which will have to rest on my own observation or my memory of them. Last evening when the Count came from his room he began by asking me questions on legal matters and on the doing of certain kinds of business. I had spent the day wearily over books, and, simply to keep my mind occupied, went over some of the matters I had been examined in at Lincoln's Inn. There was a certain method in the Count's inquiries, so I shall try to put them down in sequence; the knowledge may somehow or some time be useful to me.

First, he asked if a man in England might have two solicitors, or more. I told him he might have a dozen if he wished, but that it would not be wise to have more than one solicitor engaged in one transaction, as only one could act at a time, and that to change would be certain to militate against his interest. He seemed thoroughly to understand, and went on to ask if there would be any practical difficulty in having one man to attend, say, to banking, and another to look after shipping, in case local help were needed in a place far from the home of the banking solicitor. I asked him to explain more fully, so that I might not by any chance mislead him, so he said:

'I shall illustrate. Your friend and mine, Mr Peter Hawkins, from under the shadow of your beautiful cathedral at Exeter, which is far from London, buys for me through your good self my place at London. Good! Now here let me say frankly, lest you should think it strange that I have sought the services of one so far off from London instead of some one resident there, that my motive was that no local interest might be served save my wish only; and as one of London residence might, perhaps, have some purpose of himself or friend to serve, I went thus afield to seek my agent, whose labours should be only to my interest. Now, suppose I, who have much of affairs, wish to ship goods, say, to Newcastle, or Durham, or Harwich, or Dover, might it not be that it could with more ease be done by consigning to one in these ports?' I answered that certainly it would be most easy, but that we solicitors had a system of agency one for the other, so that local work could be done locally on instruction from any solicitor, so that the client, simply placing himself in the hands of one man, could have his wishes carried out by him without further trouble.

'But,' said he, 'I could be at liberty to direct myself. Is it not so?'

'Of course,' I replied; 'and such is often done by men of business, who do not like the whole of their affairs to be known by any one person.'

'Good!' he said, and then went on to ask about the means of making consignments and the forms to be gone through, and of all sorts of difficulties which might arise, but by forethought could be guarded against. I explained all these things to him to the best of my ability, and he certainly left me under the impression that he would have made a wonderful solicitor, for there was nothing that he did not think of or foresee. For a man who was never in the country, and who did not evidently do much in the way of business, his knowledge and acumen were wonderful. When he had satisfied himself on these points of which he had spoken, and I had verified all as well as I could by the books available, he suddenly stood up and said:

'Have you written since your first letter to our friend Mr Peter Hawkins, or to any other?' It was with some bitterness in my heart that I answered that I had not, that as yet I had not seen any opportunity of sending letters to anybody.

'Then write now, my young friend,' he said, laying a heavy hand on my shoulder; 'write to our friend and to any other; and say, if it will please you, that you shall stay with me until a month from now.'

'Do you wish me to stay so long?' I asked, for my heart grew cold at the thought.

'I desire it much; nay, I will take no refusal. When your master, employer, what you will, engaged that some one should come on his behalf, it was understood that my needs only were to be consulted. I have not stinted. Is it not so?'

What could I do but bow acceptance? It was Mr Hawkins's interest, not mine, and I had to think of him, not myself; and besides, while Count Dracula was speaking, there was that in his eyes and in his bearing which made me remember that I was a prisoner, and that if I wished it I could have no choice. The Count saw his victory in my bow, and his mastery in the trouble of my face, for he began at once to use them, but in his own smooth, resistless way:

'I pray you, my good young friend, that you will not discourse of things other than business in your letters. It will doubtless please your friends to know that you are well, and that you look forward to getting home to them. Is it not so?' As he spoke he handed me three sheets of notepaper and three envelopes. They were all of the thinnest foreign post, and looking at them, then at him, and noticing his quiet smile, with the sharp, canine teeth lying over the red under-lip, I understood as well as if he had spoken that I should be careful what I wrote, for he would be able to read it. So I determined to write only formal notes now, but to write fully to Mr Hawkins in secret, and also to

Mina, for to her I could write in shorthand, which would puzzle the Count, if he did see it. When I had written my two letters I sat quiet, reading a book whilst the Count wrote several notes, referring as he wrote them to some books on his table. Then he took up my two and placed them with his own, and put by his writing materials, after which, the instant the door had closed behind him, I leaned over and looked at the letters, which were face down on the table. I felt no compunction in doing so, for under the circumstances I felt that I should protect myself in every way I could.

One of the letters was directed to Samuel F. Billington, No. 7, The Crescent, Whitby, another to Herr Leutner, Varna; the third was to Coutts & Co, London, and the fourth to Herren Klopstock & Billreuth, bankers, Buda-Pesth. The second and fourth were unsealed. I was just about to look at them when I saw the door-handle move. I sank back in my seat, having just had time to replace the letters as they had been and to resume my book before the Count, holding still another letter in his hand, entered the room. He took up the letters on the table and stamped them carefully, and then turning to me, said:

'I trust you will forgive me, but I have much work to do in private this evening. You will, I hope, find all things as you wish.' At the door he turned, and after a moment's pause said:

'Let me advise you, my dear young friend – nay, let me warn you with all seriousness, that should you leave these rooms you will not by any chance go to sleep in any other part of the castle. It is old, and has many memories, and there are bad dreams for those who sleep unwisely. Be warned! Should sleep now or ever overcome you, or be like to do, then haste to your own chamber or to these rooms, for your rest will then be safe. But if you be not careful in this respect, then –' He finished his speech in a gruesome way, for he motioned with his hands as if he were washing them. I quite understood; my only doubt was as to whether any dream could be more terrible than the unnatural, horrible net of gloom and mystery which seemed closing round me.

Later. I endorse the last words written, but this time there is no doubt in question. I shall not fear to sleep in any place where he is not. I have placed the crucifix over the head of my bed – I imagine that my rest is thus freer from dreams; and there it shall remain.

When he left me I went to my room. After a little while, not hearing any sound, I came out and went up the stone stair to where I could look out towards the south. There was some sense of freedom in the vast expanse, inaccessible though it was to me, as compared with the narrow darkness of the courtyard. Looking out on this, I felt that I was indeed in prison, and I seemed to want a breath of fresh air, though it were of the night. I am beginning to feel this nocturnal existence tell on me. It is destroying my nerve. I start at my own shadow, and am full of all sorts of horrible imaginings. God knows that there is ground for any terrible fear in this accursed place! I looked out over the beautiful expanse, bathed in soft yellow moonlight till it was almost as light as day. In the soft light the distant hills became melted, and the shadows in the valleys and gorges of velvety blackness. The mere beauty seemed to cheer me; there was peace and comfort in every breath I drew. As I leaned from the window my eye was caught by something moving a storey below me, and somewhat to my left, where

I imagined, from the lie of the rooms, that the windows of the Count's own room would look out. The window at which I stood was tall and deep, stone-mullioned, and though weather-worn, was still complete; but it was evidently many a day since the case had been there. I drew back behind the stonework, and looked carefully out.

What I saw was the Count's head coming out from the window. I did not see the face, but I knew the man by the neck and the movement of his back and arms. In any case I could not mistake the hands which I had had so many opportunities of studying. I was at first interested and somewhat amused, for it is wonderful how small a matter will interest and amuse a man when he is a prisoner. But my very feelings changed to repulsion and terror when I saw the whole man slowly emerge from the window and begin to crawl down the castle wall over that dreadful abyss, *face down*, with his cloak spreading out around him like great wings. At first I could not believe my eyes. I thought it was some trick of the moonlight, some weird effect of shadow; but I kept looking, and it could be no delusion. I saw the fingers and toes grasp the corners of the stones, worn clear of the mortar by the stress of years, and by thus using every projection and inequality move downwards with considerable speed, just as a lizard moves along a wall.

What manner of man is this, or what manner of creature is it in the semblance of man? I feel the dread of this horrible place overpowering me; I am in fear – in awful fear – and there is no escape for me; I am encompassed about with terrors that I dare not think of . . .

15 May. Once more have I seen the Count go out in his lizard fashion. He moved downwards in a sidelong way, some hundred feet down, and a good deal to the left. He vanished into some hole or window. When his head had disappeared I leaned out to try and see more, but without avail – the distance was too great to allow a proper angle of sight. I knew he had left the castle now, and thought to use the opportunity to explore more than I had dared to do as yet. I went back to the room, and taking a lamp, tried all the doors. They were all locked as I had expected, and the locks were comparatively new; but I went down the stone stairs to the hall where I had entered originally. I found I could pull back the bolts easily enough and unhook the great chains; but the door was locked, and the key was gone! That key must be in the Count's room; I must watch should his door be unlocked, so that I may get it and escape. I went on to make a thorough examination of the various stairs and passages, and to try the doors that opened from them. One or two small rooms near the hall were open, but there was nothing to see in them except old furniture, dusty with age and moth-eaten. At last, however, I found one door at the top of a stairway which, though it seemed to be locked, gave a little under pressure. I tried it harder, and found that it was not really locked, but that the resistance came from the fact that the hinges had fallen somewhat, and the heavy door rested on the floor. Here was an opportunity which I might not have again, so I exerted myself, and with many efforts forced it back so that I could enter. I was now in a wing of the castle further to the right than the rooms I knew and a storey lower down. From the windows I could see that the suite of rooms lay along to the south of the castle, the windows of the end room looking out both west and south. On the latter side, as well as to the former, there was a great precipice. The castle was built on the corner of a great rock, so that on three sides it was quite impregnable, and great windows were placed here where sling, or bow, or culverin could not reach, and consequently light and comfort, impossible to a position which had to be guarded, were secured. To the west was a great valley, and then, rising far away, great jagged mountain fastnesses, rising peak on peak, the sheer rock studded with mountain ash and thorn, whose roots clung in cracks and crevices and crannies of the stone. This was evidently the portion of the castle occupied in bygone days, for the furniture had more air of comfort than any I had seen. The windows were curtainless, and the yellow moonlight, flooding in through the diamond panes, enabled one to see even colours, whilst it softened the wealth of dust which lay over all and disguised in some measure the ravages of time and the moth. My lamp seemed to be of little effect in the brilliant moonlight, but I was glad to have it with me, for there was a dread loneliness in the place which chilled my heart and made my nerves tremble. Still, it was better than living alone in the rooms which I had come to hate from the presence of the Count, and after trying a little to school my nerves, I found a soft quietude come over me. Here I am, sitting at a little oak table where in old times possibly some fair lady sat to pen, with much thought and many blushes, her ill-spelt love-letter, and writing in my diary in shorthand all that has happened since I closed it last. It is nineteenth century up-to-date with a vengeance. And yet, unless my senses deceive me, the old centuries had, and have, powers of their own which mere 'modernity' cannot kill.

Later: the morning of 16 May. God preserve my sanity, for to this I am reduced. Safety and the assurance of safety are things of the past. Whilst I live on here there is but one thing to hope for: that I may not go mad, if, indeed, I be not mad already. If I be sane, then surely it is maddening to think that of all the foul things that lurk in this hateful place the Count is the least dreadful to me: that to him alone I can look for safety, even though this be only whilst I can serve his purpose. Great God! merciful God! Let me be calm, for out of that way lies madness indeed. I begin to get new lights on certain things which have puzzled me. Up to now I never quite knew what Shakespeare meant when he made Hamlet say:

> 'My tablets! quick, my tablets!
> 'Tis meet that I put it down,' etc.

for now, feeling as though my own brain were unhinged or as if the shock had come which must end in its undoing, I turn to my diary for repose. The habit of entering accurately must help to soothe me.

The Count's mysterious warning frightened me at the time; it frightens me more now when I think of it, for in future he has a fearful hold upon me. I shall fear to doubt what he may say!

When I had written in my diary and had fortunately replaced the book and pen in my pocket I felt sleepy. The Count's warning came into my mind but I took a pleasure in disobeying it. The sense of sleep was upon me, and with it the obstinacy which sleep brings as outrider. The soft moonlight soothed, and the wide expanse without gave a sense of freedom which refreshed me. I determined not to return tonight to the gloom-haunted rooms, but to sleep here, where of old ladies had sat and sung and lived sweet lives whilst their gentle breasts were sad for their menfolk away in the midst of remorseless wars. I drew a great couch out of its place near the corner, so that, as I lay, I could look at the lovely view to east and south, and unthinking of and uncaring for the dust, composed myself for sleep.

I suppose I must have fallen asleep; I hope so, but I fear, for all that followed was startlingly real – so real that now, sitting here in the broad, full sunlight of the morning, I cannot in the least believe that it was all sleep. I was not alone. The room was the same, unchanged in any way since I came into it; I could see along the floor, in the brilliant moonlight, my own footsteps marked where I had disturbed the long accumulation of dust. In the moonlight opposite me were three young women, ladies by their dress and manner. I thought at the time that I must be dreaming when I saw them, for, though the moonlight was behind them, they threw no shadow on the floor. They came close to me and looked at me for some time, and then whispered together. Two were dark, and had high aquiline noses, like the Count, and great dark, piercing eyes, that seemed to be almost red when contrasted with the pale yellow moon. The other was fair, as fair as can be, with great, wavy masses of golden hair and eyes like pale sapphires. I seemed somehow to know her face, and to know it in connection with some dreamy fear, but I could not recollect at the moment how or where. All three had brilliant white teeth, that shone like pearls against the ruby of their voluptuous lips. There was something about them that made me uneasy, some longing and at the same time some deadly fear. I felt in my heart a wicked, burning desire that they would kiss me with those red lips. It is not good to note this down, lest some day it should meet Mina's eyes and cause her pain; but it is the truth. They whispered together, and then they all three laughed – such a silvery, musical laugh, but as hard as though the sound never could have come through the softness of human lips. It was like the intolerable, tingling sweetness of waterglasses when played on by a cunning hand. The fair girl shook her head coquettishly, and the other two urged her on. One said:

'Go on! You are first, and we shall follow; yours is the right to begin.' The other added:

'He is young and strong; there are kisses for us all.' I lay quiet, looking out under my eyelashes in an agony of delightful anticipation. The fair girl advanced and bent over me till I could feel the movement of her breath upon me. Sweet it was in one sense, honey-sweet, and sent the same tingling through the nerves as her voice, but with a bitter underlying the sweet, a bitter offensiveness, as one smells in blood.

I was afraid to raise my eyelids, but looked out and saw perfectly under the lashes. The fair girl went on her knees, and bent over me, fairly gloating. There was a deliberate voluptuousness which was both thrilling and repulsive, and as she arched her neck she actually licked her lips like an animal, till I could see in the moonlight the moisture shining on the scarlet lips and on the red tongue as it lapped the white sharp teeth. Lower and lower went her head as the lips went below the range of my mouth and chin and seemed about to fasten on my throat. Then she paused, and I could hear the churning sound of her tongue as it licked her teeth and lips, and could feel the hot breath on my neck. Then the skin on my throat began to tingle as one's flesh does when the hand that is to tickle it approaches nearer – nearer. I could feel the soft, shivering touch of the lips on the supersensitive skin of my throat, and the hard dents of two sharp teeth, just touching and pausing there. I closed my eyes in a languorous ecstasy and waited – waited with beating heart.

But at that instant another sensation swept through me as quick as lightning. I was conscious of the presence of the Count, and of his being as if lapped in a storm of fury. As my eyes opened involuntarily I saw his strong hand grasp the slender neck of the fair woman and with giant's power draw it back, the blue eyes transformed with fury, the white teeth champing with rage, and the fair cheeks blazing red with passion. But the Count! Never did I imagine such wrath and fury, even in the demons of the pit. His eyes were positively blazing. The red light in them was lurid, as if the flames of hell-fire blazed behind them. His face was deathly pale, and the lines of it were hard like drawn wires; the thick eyebrows that met over the nose now seemed like a heaving bar of white-hot metal. With a fierce sweep of his arm, he hurled the woman from him, and then motioned to the others, as though he were beating them back; it was the same imperious gesture that I had seen used to the wolves. In a voice which, though low and almost a whisper, seemed to cut through the air and then ring around the room, he exclaimed:

'How dare you touch him, any of you? How dare you cast eyes on him when I had forbidden it? Back, I tell you all! This man belongs to me! Beware how you meddle with him, or you'll have to deal with me.' The fair girl, with a laugh of ribald coquetry, turned to answer him:

'You yourself never loved; you never love!' On this the other women joined, and such a mirthless, hard, soulless laughter rang through the room that it almost made me faint to hear; it seemed like the pleasure of fiends. Then the Count turned, after looking at my face attentively, and said in a soft whisper:

'Yes, I too can love; you yourselves can tell it from the past. Is it not so? Well, now I promise you that when I am done with him you shall kiss him at your will. Now go! go! I must awaken him, for there is work to be done.'

'Are we to have nothing tonight?' said one of them, with a low laugh, as she pointed to the bag which he had thrown upon the floor, and which moved as though there were some living thing within it. For answer he nodded his head. One of the women jumped forward and opened it. If my ears did not deceive me there was a gasp and a low wail, as of a half-smothered child. The women closed round, whilst I was aghast with horror; but as I looked they disappeared, and with them the dreadful bag. There was no door near them, and they could not have passed me without my noticing. They simply seemed to fade into the rays of the moonlight and pass out through the window, for I could see outside the dim, shadowy forms for a moment before they entirely faded away. Then the horror overcame me, and I sank down unconscious.

4
Jonathan Harker's Journal
(continued)

I awoke in my own bed. If it be that I had not dreamt, the Count must have carried me here. I tried to satisfy myself on the subject, but could not arrive at any unquestionable result. To be sure, there were certain small evidences, such as that my clothes were folded and laid by in a manner which was not my habit. My watch was still unwound, and I am rigorously accustomed to winding it the last thing before going to bed, and many such details. But these things are not proof, for they may have been evidences that my mind was not as usual, and, from some cause or another, I had certainly been much upset. I must watch for proof. Of one thing I am glad: if it was the Count that carried me here and undressed me, he must have been hurried in his task, for my pockets are intact. I am sure this diary would have been a mystery to him which he would not have brooked. He would have taken or destroyed it. As I look round this room, although it has been to me so full of fear, it is now a sort of sanctuary, for nothing can be more dreadful than those awful women, who were – who *are* – waiting to suck my blood.

18 May. I have been down to look at that room again in daylight, for I must know the truth. When I got to the doorway at the top of the stairs I found it closed. It had been so forcibly driven against the jamb that part of the woodwork was splintered. I could see that the bolt of the lock had not been shot, but the door is fastened from the inside. I fear it was no dream, and must act on this surmise.

19 May. I am surely in the toils. Last night the Count asked me in the suavest tones to write three letters, one saying that my work here was nearly done, and that I should start for home within a few days, another that I was starting on the next morning from the time of the letter, and the third that I had left the castle and arrived at Bistritz. I would fain have rebelled, but felt that in the present state of things it would be madness to quarrel openly with the Count whilst I am so absolutely in his power; and to refuse would be to excite his suspicion and to arouse his anger. He knows that I know too much, and that I must not live, lest I be dangerous to him; my only chance is to prolong my opportunities. Something may occur which will give me a chance to escape. I saw in his eyes something of that gathering wrath which was manifest when he hurled that fair woman from him. He explained to me that posts were few and uncertain, and that my writing now would ensure ease of mind to my friends; and he assured me with so much impressiveness that he would countermand the later letters, which would be held over at Bistritz until due time in case chance would admit of my prolonging my stay, that to oppose him would have been to create new suspicion. I therefore pretended to fall in with his views, and asked him what dates I should put on the letters. He calculated a minute, and then said:

'The first should be June 12, the second June 19, and the third June 29.'

I know now the span of life. God help me!

28 May. There is a chance of escape, or at any rate of being able to send word home. A band of Szgany have come to the castle, and are encamped in the courtyard. These Szgany are gipsies; I have notes of them in my book. They are peculiar to this part of the world, though allied to the ordinary gipsies all the world over. There are thousands of them in Hungary and Transylvania, who are almost outside all law. They attach themselves as a rule to some great noble or *boyar*, and call themselves by his name. They are fearless and without religion, save superstition, and they talk only their own varieties of the Romany tongue.

I shall write some letters home, and shall try to get them to have them posted. I have already spoken to them through my window to begin an acquaintanceship. They took their hats off and made obeisance and many signs, which, however, I could not understand any more than I could their spoken language . . .

I have written the letters. Mina's is in shorthand, and I simply ask Mr Hawkins to communicate with her. To her I have explained my situation, but without the horrors which I may only surmise. It would shock and frighten her to death were I to expose my heart to her. Should the letters not carry, then the Count shall not yet know my secret or the extent of my knowledge . . .

I have given the letters; I threw them through the bars of my window with a gold piece, and made what signs I could to have them posted. The man who took them pressed them to his heart and bowed, and then put them in his cap. I could do no more. I stole back to the study, and began to read. As the Count did not come in, I have written here . . .

GEORGE MOORE

from *Esther Waters*

18

Her hair hung about her, her hands and wrists were shrunken, her flesh was soft and flabby, for suckling her child seemed to draw all strength from her, and her nervous depression increased from day to day, she being too weary and ill to think of the future; and for a whole week her physical condition held her to the exclusion of every other thought. Mrs Jones was very kind, charging her only ten shillings a week for her board and lodging; but this was a great deal when no more than two pounds five shillings remained between her and the workhouse, and this fact was brought home to her sternly when Mrs Jones came to her for the first week's money. Ten shillings gone; only one pound fifteen shillings left, and still she was so weak that she could hardly get up and down stairs. But if she were twice as weak, if she had to crawl along the street on her hands and knees, she must go to the hospital and implore the matron to find her a situation as wet-nurse. Well, it was raining heavily, and Mrs Jones said it was madness for her to go out in such weather, but go she must; and, though it was but a few hundred yards, she often thought she'd like to lie down and die. At the hospital disappointment awaited her. Why hadn't she called yesterday? Yesterday two ladies of title had come and taken two girls away. Such a chance might not occur for some time. 'For some time,' thought Esther. 'Very soon I shall have to apply for admission at the workhouse.' She reminded the matron of her promise, and returned home more dead than alive. Mrs Jones helped her to change her clothes, and bade her be of good heart. Esther looked at her hopelessly, and sitting down on the edge of her bed she put the baby to her breast.

Another week passed. She had been to the hospital every day, but no one had been to inquire for a wet-nurse. Her money was reduced to a few shillings, and she tried to reconcile herself to the idea that she might do worse than accept the harsh shelter of the workhouse. Her nature revolted against it; but she must do what was best for the child, and often asked herself how it would all end. And the more she thought, the more terrible did the future seem. Her miserable thoughts were interrupted by a footstep on the stairs. It was Mrs Jones, coming to tell her that a lady who wanted a wet-nurse had come from the hospital; and a lady dressed in a beautiful brown silk came in, and looked around the humble room, clearly shocked at its poverty. Esther, who was sitting on the bed, rose to meet the fine lady – a thin woman, with narrow temples, aquiline features, bright eyes, and a disagreeable voice.

'You are the young person who wants a situation as wet-nurse?'

'Yes, ma'am.'

'Are you married?'

'No, ma'am.'

'Is that your first child?'

'Yes, ma'am.'

'Ah! that's a pity. But it doesn't matter much, so long as you and your baby are healthy. Will you show it to me?'

'He is asleep now, ma'am,' Esther said, raising the bed-clothes. 'There never was a healthier child.'

'Yes, he seems healthy enough. You have a good supply of milk?'

'Yes, ma'am.'

'Fifteen shillings, and all found. Does that suit you?'

'I had expected a pound a week.'

'It is only your first baby. Fifteen shillings is quite enough. Of course, I only engage you subject to the doctor's approval. I'll ask him to call.'

'Very well, ma'am; I shall be glad of the place.'

'Then it is settled. You can come at once?'

'I must arrange to put my baby out to nurse, ma'am.'

The lady's face clouded. But following up another train of thought, she said:

'Of course, you must arrange about your baby, and I hope you'll make proper arrangements. Tell the woman in whose charge you leave it that I shall want to see it every three weeks. It will be better so,' she added, under her breath, 'for two have died already.'

'This is my card,' said the lady – 'Mrs Rivers, Curzon Street, Mayfair – and I shall expect you to-morrow afternoon – that is to say, if the doctor approves of you. Here is one and sixpence for your cab fare.'

'Thank you, ma'am.'

'I shall expect you not later than four o'clock. I hope you won't disappoint me. Remember, my child is waiting.'

And when Mrs Rivers left, Esther asked Mrs Jones what she was to do. She'd have to find somebody to look after her child. It was now just after two o'clock. Baby was asleep, and would want nothing for three or four hours, and Mrs Jones gave her the address of a respectable woman. But this woman was looking after twins, and could not undertake the charge of another baby. Esther visited many streets, always failing for one reason or another, till at last she found herself in Wandsworth, in a battered, tumbledown little street, no thoroughfare, only four houses, a coal-shed, and some broken wooden palings. In the area of No. 3 three mites were playing, and at Esther's call a short, fat woman came out of the kitchen, her dirty apron sloping over her high stomach, and her pale brown hair twisted into a knot at the top of her head.

'Well, what is it?'

'I came about putting a child out to nurse. You are Mrs Spires, ain't yer?'

'Yes, that's my name. May I ask who sent you?'

Esther told her, and then Mrs Spires asked her to step down into the kitchen.

'Them there children you saw in the area I looks after while their mothers are out washing or charing. They takes them 'ome in the evening. I only charges them fourpence a day, and it is a loss at that, for they takes a lot of minding. What age is yours?'

'Mine is only a month old. I've a chance to go out as wet-nurse if I can find a place to put him out to nurse. Will you look after my baby?'

'How much do you think of paying for him?'

'Five shillings a week.'

'And you a-going out as wet-nurse at a pound a week; you can afford more than that.'

'I'm only getting fifteen shillings a week.'

'Well, you can afford to pay six. I tell you the responsibility of looking after a hinfant is that awful nowadays that I don't care to undertake it for less.'

Esther hesitated, for she didn't like this woman.

'I suppose,' said the woman, altering her tone to one of mild interrogation, 'you would like your baby to have the best of everything, and not the drainings of any bottle that's handy?'

'I should like my child to be well looked after, and I must see him every three weeks.'

'Do you expect me to bring up the child to wherever the lady lives, and pay my bus fare, all out of five shillings a week? It can't be done!' Esther didn't answer. 'You ain't married, of course?' Mrs Spires said suddenly.

'No, I ain't; what about that?'

'Oh, nothing; there is so many of you, that's all. You can't lay yer 'and on the father and get a bit out of 'im?'

They stopped speaking. Esther looked round suspiciously, and noticing the look the woman said:

'Your baby will be well looked after 'ere; a nice warm kitchen, and I've no other babies for the moment; them children don't give no trouble, they plays in the area. You had better let me have the child; you won't do better than 'ere.'

Esther promised to think it over and let her know to-morrow. It took her many omnibuses to get home, and it was quite dark when she pushed the door to. The first thing that caught her ear was her child crying. 'What is the matter?' she cried, hurrying down the passage.

'Oh, is that you? You have been away a time. The poor child is that hungry he has been crying this hour or more. If I'd 'ad a bottle I'd 'ave given him a little milk.'

'Hungry, is he? Then he shall have plenty soon. It is nearly the last time I shall give the poor darling my breast.' She told Mrs Jones about Mrs Spires, and both women tried to arrive at a decision.

'Since you 'ave to put the child out to nurse, you might as well put him there as elsewhere; the woman will look after him as well as she can – she'll do that, if it is for the sake of the six shillings a week.'

'Yes, yes, I know; but I've always heard that children die that are put out to nurse. If mine died I never should forgive myself.'

She could not sleep; she lay with her arms about her baby, distracted at the thought of parting from him, and wondering what had she done that her baby should be separated from her? And of all what had the poor little darling done? He at least was innocent; yet he was to be deprived of his mother. And at midnight she threw her legs out of bed, lighted a candle, looked at him, took him in her arms, squeezed him to her bosom till he cried, and the thought came that it would be sweeter to kill him with her own hands than to be parted from him.

But the thought of murder went with the night, and she almost enjoyed the journey to Wandsworth. Her baby laughed and cooed, and was much admired in the omnibus, and the little street where Mrs Spires lived seemed different. A cart of hay was being unloaded, and this gave the place a pleasant rural air. Mrs Spires, too, was cleaner, tidier; Esther no longer disliked her; she had a nice little cot ready for the baby, and he seemed so comfortable in it that Esther did not feel the pain at parting which she had expected to feel. She would see him in a few weeks, and in those weeks she would be richer. It seemed quite wonderful to earn so much money in so short a time, and she returned thinking that her luck seemed to have turned at last; and so engrossed was she in thoughts and dreams of her good fortune that she nearly forgot to get out of her bus at Charing Cross, and had it not been for the attention of the conductor might have gone on, she did not know where – perhaps to Clerkenwell, or maybe to Islington. And when the second bus turned into Oxford Street she jumped out, not wishing to spend more money than she could help. Mrs Jones approved of all she had done, aided her to pack up her box, and sent her away full of the adventure and the prospect. She went wondering if the house she was going to was as grand as Woodview, and was much struck by the appearance of the maidservant who opened the door to her.

'Oh, here you are,' Mrs Rivers said. 'I have been anxiously expecting you; my baby is not at all well. Come up to the nursery at once. I don't know your name,' she said, turning to Esther.

'Waters, ma'am.'

'Emily, you'll see that Waters's box is taken to her room.'

'I'll see to it, ma'am.'

'Then come up at once, Waters. I hope you'll succeed better than the others.'

A tall, handsome gentleman stood at the door of a room full of beautiful things, and as they went past him Mrs Rivers said, 'This is the new nurse, dear.' Higher up, Esther saw a bedroom of soft hangings and bright porcelain. Then another staircase, and the little wail of a child caught on the ear, and Mrs Rivers said, 'The poor little thing; it never ceases crying. Take it, Waters, take it.'

Esther sat down, and soon the little thing ceased crying.

'It seems to take to you,' said the anxious mother.

'So it seems,' said Esther; 'it is a wee thing, not half the size of my boy.'

'I hope the milk will suit her, and that she won't bring it up. This is our last chance.'

'I daresay she will come round, ma'am. I suppose you weren't strong enough to suckle her yourself, and yet you looks 'ealthy.'

'I? No, I could not undertake to nurse it.' Then, glancing suspiciously at Esther, whose breast was like a little cup, Mrs Rivers said, 'I hope you have plenty of milk?'

'Oh, yes, ma'am; they said at the hospital I could bring up twins.'

'Your supper will be ready at nine. But that will be a long time for you to wait. I told them to cut you some sandwiches, and you'll have a glass of porter. Or perhaps you'd prefer to wait till supper? You can have your supper, you know, at eight, if you like?'

Esther took a sandwich and Mrs Rivers poured out a glass of porter. And later in the evening Mrs Rivers came down from her drawing-room to see that Esther's supper was all right, and, not satisfied with the handsome fare that had been laid before her child's nurse, she went into the kitchen and gave strict orders that the meat for the future was not to be quite so much cooked.

Something jarred, however; such constant mealing did not seem natural, and her self-respect was wounded; she hated her position in this house, and sought and found consolation in the thought that she was earning good money for her baby. She noticed, too, that she never was allowed out alone, and that her walks were limited to just enough exercise to keep her in health.

A fortnight passed, and one afternoon, after having put baby to sleep, she said to Mrs Rivers, 'I hope, ma'am, you'll be able to spare me for a couple of hours; baby won't want me before then. I'm very anxious about my little one.'

'Oh, nurse, I couldn't possibly hear of it; such a thing is never allowed. You can write to the woman, if you like.'

'I do not know how to write, ma'am.'

'Then you can get someone to write for you. But your baby is no doubt all right.'

'But, ma'am, you are uneasy about your baby; you are up in the nursery twenty times a day; it is only natural I should be uneasy about mine.'

'But, nurse, I've no one to send with you.'

'There is no reason why anybody should go with me, ma'am; I can take care of myself.'

'What! let you go off all the way to – where did you say you had left it – Wandsworth? – by yourself! I really couldn't think of it. I don't want to be unnecessarily hard – but I really couldn't – no mother could. But I don't want you to agitate yourself, and if you like I'll write myself to the woman who has charge of your baby. I cannot do more, and I hope you'll be satisfied.'

By what right, by what law, was she separated from her child? She was tired of hearing Mrs Rivers speak of 'my child, my child, my child', and of seeing this fine lady turn up her nose when she spoke of her own beautiful boy. And when Mrs Rivers came to engage her she said that it would be better for the baby to be brought to see her every three or four weeks, for two had died already. At the time she had not understood. She supposed vaguely, in a passing way, that Mrs Rivers had already lost two children. But yesterday the housemaid told her that that little thing in the cradle had had two wet-nurses before Esther, and that both their babies had died. It was then a life for a life. It was more.

For the children of two poor girls had been sacrificed so that this rich woman's child might be saved. Even that was not enough: the life of her beautiful boy was called for. And then other memories swept by. She remembered vague hints, allusions that Mrs Spires had thrown out; and, as in a dream darkly, it seemed to this ignorant girl that she was the victim of a far-reaching conspiracy; she experienced the sensation of the captured animal, and scanned the doors and windows, thinking of some means of escape.

At that moment a knock was heard and the housemaid came in.

'The woman who has charge of your baby has come to see you.'

Esther started up from her chair, and fat little Mrs Spires waddled into the room, the ends of her shawl touching the ground.

'Where is my baby?' said Esther. 'Why haven't you brought him?'

'Why, you see, my dear, the sweet little thing didn't seem as well as usual this afternoon, and I didn't like to bring 'im out, it being a long way and a trifle cold. But it is nice and warm in here. May I sit down?'

'Yes, there's a chair; but tell me what is the matter with him?'

'A little cold, dear – nothing to speak of. You must not worry yourself, it isn't worth while; besides, it's bad for you and the little darling in the cradle. May I have a look? A little girl, isn't it?'

'Yes, it is a girl.'

'And a beautiful little girl too. 'Ow 'ealthy she do look! I'll be bound you have made a difference in her. I suppose you are beginning to like her just as if she was your own?'

Esther did not answer.

'Yer know, all you girls are dreadful taken with your babies at first. But they is a awful drag on a girl who gets her living in service. For my part I do think it a providence that rich folk don't suckle their own. If they did, I dunno what would become of all you poor girls. The situation of wet-nurse is just what you wants at the time, and it is good money. I hope yer did what I told you and stuck out for a pound a week. Rich folk like these 'ere would think nothing of a pound a week, nor yet two, when they sees their child is suited.'

'Never mind about my money, that's my affair. Tell me what's the matter with my baby?'

''Ow yer do 'arp on it! I've told yer that 'e's all right; nothing to worry about, only a little poorly, but knowing you was anxious I thought it better to come up. I didn't know but what you might like to 'ave in the doctor.'

'Does he require the doctor? I thought you said it was nothing to worry about.'

'That depends on 'ow yer looks at it. Some likes to 'ave in the doctor, however little the ailing; then others won't 'ave anything to do with doctors – don't believe in them. So I thought I'd come up and see what you thought about it. I would 'ave sent for the doctor this morning – I'm one of those who 'as faith in doctors – but being a bit short of money I thought I'd come up and ask you for a trifle.'

At that moment Mrs Rivers came into the nursery and her first look went in the direction of the cradle, then she turned to consider curtseying Mrs Spires.

'This is Mrs Spires, the lady who is looking after my baby, ma'am,' said Esther; 'she has come with bad news – my baby is ill.'

'Oh, I'm sorry. But I daresay it is nothing.'

'But Mrs Spires says, ma'am—'

'Yes, ma'am, the little thing seemed a bit poorly, and I being short of money, ma'am, I had to come and see nurse. I knows right well that they must not be disturbed, and of course your child's 'ealth is everything; but if I may make so bold I'd like to say that the little dear do look beautiful. Nurse is bringing her up that well that yer must have every satisfaction in 'er.'

'Yes, she seems to suit the child; that's the reason I don't want her upset.'

'It won't occur again, ma'am, I promise you.'

Esther did not answer, and her white, sullen face remained unchanged. She had a great deal on her mind, and would have spoken if the words did not seem to betray her when she attempted to speak.

'When the baby is well, and the doctor is satisfied there is no danger of infection, you can bring it here – once a month will be sufficient. Is there anything more?'

'Mrs Spires thinks my baby ought to see the doctor.'

'Well, let her send for the doctor.'

'Being a bit short of money—'

'How much is it?' said Esther.

'Well, what we pays is five shillings to the doctor, but then there's the medicine he will order, and I was going to speak to you about a piece of flannel: if yer could let me have ten shillings to go on with.'

'But I haven't so much left. I must see my baby,' and Esther moved towards the door.

'No, no, nurse, I cannot hear of it; I'd sooner pay the money myself. Now, how much do you want, Mrs Spires?'

'Ten shillings will do for the present, ma'am.'

'Here they are; let the child have every attendance, and remember you are not to come troubling my nurse. Above all, you are not to come up to the nursery. I don't know how it happened, it was a mistake on the part of the new housemaid. You must have my permission before you see my nurse.' And while talking rapidly and imperatively Mrs Rivers, as it were, drove Mrs Spires out of the nursery. Esther could hear them talking on the staircase, and she listened, all the while striving to collect her thoughts. Mrs Rivers said when she returned, 'I really cannot allow her to come here upsetting you.' Then, as if impressed by the sombre look on Esther's face, she added: 'Upsetting you about nothing. I assure you it will be all right; only a little indisposition.'

'I must see my baby,' Esther replied.

'Come, nurse, you shall see your baby the moment the doctor says it is fit to come here. You can't expect me to do more than that.' Esther did not move, and thinking that it would not be well to argue with her, Mrs Rivers went over to the cradle. 'See, nurse, the little darling has just woke up; come and take her, I'm sure she wants you.'

Esther did not answer her. She stood looking into space, and it seemed to Mrs Rivers that it would be better not to provoke a scene. She went towards the door slowly, but a little cry from the cradle stopped her, and she said:

'Come, nurse, what is it? Come, the baby is waiting for you.'

Then, like one waking from a dream, Esther said: 'If my baby is all right, ma'am, I'll come back, but if he wants me, I'll have to look after him first.'

'You forget that I'm paying you fifteen shillings a week. I pay you for nursing my baby; you take my money, that's sufficient.'

'Yes, I do take your money, ma'am. But the housemaid has told me that you had two wet-nurses before me, and that both their babies died, so I cannot stop here now that mine's ill. Everyone for her own; you can't blame me. I'm sorry for yours – poor little thing, she was getting on nicely, too.'

'But, Waters, you won't leave my baby. It's cruel of you. If I could nurse it myself—'

'Why couldn't you, ma'am? You look fairly strong and healthy.'

Esther spoke in her quiet, stolid way, finding her words unconsciously.

'You don't know what you're saying, nurse; you can't. You've forgotten yourself. Next time I engage a nurse I'll try to get one who has lost her baby, and then there'll be no bother.'

'It is a life for a life – more than that, ma'am – two lives for a life; and now the life of my boy is asked for.'

A strange look passed over Mrs Rivers's face. She knew, of course, that she stood well within the law, that she was doing no more than a hundred other fashionable women were doing at the same moment; but this plain girl had a plain way of putting things, and she did not care for it to be publicly known that the life of her child had been bought with the lives of two poor children. But her temper was getting the better of her.

'He'll only be a drag on you. You'll never be able to bring him up, poor little bastard child.'

'It is wicked of you to speak like that, ma'am, though it is I who am saying it. It is none of the child's fault if he hasn't got a father, nor is it right that he should be deserted for that, and it is not for you to tell me to do such a thing. If you had made sacrifice of yourself in the beginning and nursed your own child such thoughts wouldn't have come to you. But when you hire a poor girl such as me to give the milk that belongs to another to your child, you think nothing of the poor deserted one. He is only a love-child, you say, and had better be dead and done with. I see it all now; I have been thinking it out. It is all so hidden up that the meaning is not clear at first, but what it comes to is this, that fine folks like you pays the money, and Mrs Spires and her like gets rid of the poor little things. Change the milk a few times, a little neglect, and the poor servant-girl is spared the trouble of bringing up her baby and can make a handsome child of the rich woman's little starveling.'

At that moment the baby began to cry; both women looked in the direction of the cradle.

'Nurse, you have forgotten yourself, you have talked a great deal of nonsense, you have said a great deal that is untrue. You accused me of wishing your baby were dead; indeed, I hardly know what wild remarks you did not indulge in. Of course, I cannot put up with such conduct – to-morrow you will come to me and apologize. In the meantime the baby wants you; are you not going to her?'

'I'm going to my own child.'

'That means that you refuse to nurse my baby?'

'Yes; I'm going straight to look after my own.'

'If you leave my house you shall never enter it again.'

'I don't want to enter it again.'

'I shall not pay you one shilling if you leave my baby. You have no money.'

'I shall try to manage without. I shall go with my baby to the workhouse. However bad the living may be there, he'll be with his mother.'

'If you go to-night my baby will die. She cannot be brought up on the bottle.'

'Oh, I hope not, ma'am. I should be sorry, indeed I should.'

'Then stay, nurse.'

'I must go to my baby, ma'am.'

'Then you shall go at once – this very instant.'

'I'm going this very instant, as soon as I've put on my hat and jacket.'

'You had better take your box with you. If you don't, I shall have it thrown into the street.'

'I daresay you're cruel enough to do that if the law allows you, only be careful that it do.'

19

The moment Esther got out of the house in Curzon Street she felt in her pocket for her money. She had only a few pence – enough for her bus fare, however, and her thoughts did not go further. She was absorbed by one desire, how to save her child – how to save him from Mrs Spires, whom she vaguely suspected; from the world, which called him a bastard, and denied to him the right to live. And she sat as if petrified in the corner of the bus, seeing nothing but a little street of four houses facing some hay-lofts, the low-pitched kitchen, the fat woman, the cradle in the corner. The intensity and the oneness of her desire seemed to annihilate time, and when she got out of the omnibus she walked with a sort of animal-like instinct straight for the house. There was a light in the kitchen just as she expected, and as she descended the four wooden steps into the area she looked to see if Mrs Spires was there. She was there, and Esther pushed open the door.

'Where's my baby?'

'Lord, 'ow yer did frighten me!' said Mrs Spires, turning from the range and leaning against the table, which was laid for supper. 'Coming like that into other folk's places without a word of warning – without as much as knocking at the door.'

'I beg your pardon, but I was anxious about my baby.'

'Was you indeed? It is easy to see it is the first one. There it is in the cradle there.'

'Have you sent for the doctor?'

'Sent for the doctor! I've to get my husband's supper.'

Esther took her baby out of the cradle. It woke up crying, and Esther said: 'You don't mind my sitting down a moment. The poor little thing wants its mother.'

'If Mrs Rivers saw you now a-nursing of yer baby?'

'I shouldn't care if she did. He's thinner than when I left him; ten days 'ave made a difference in him.'

'Well, yer don't expect a child to do as well without its mother as with her. But tell me, how did yer get out? You must have come away shortly after me.'

'I wasn't going to stop there and my child ill.'

'Yer don't mean to tell me that yer 'ave gone and thrown hup the situation?'

'She told me, if I went out, I should never enter her door again.'

'And what did you say?'

'Told her I didn't want to.'

'And what, may I ask, are yer thinking of doing? I 'eard yer say yer 'ad no money.'

'I don't know.'

'Take my advice, and go straight back and ask 'er to overlook it, this once.'

'Oh no, she'd never take me back.'

'Yes, she will. You suits the child, and that's all they thinks of.'

'I don't know what will become of me and my baby.'

'No more don't I. Yer can't stop always in the work'us, and a baby'll be a 'eavy drag on you. Can't you lay 'ands on 'is father some'ow?'

Esther shook her head, and Mrs Spires noticed that she was crying.

'I'm all alone,' she said; 'I don't know 'ow I'm ever to pull through.'

'Not with that child, yer won't – it ain't possible. You girls is all alike; yer thinks of nothing but yer babies for the first few weeks, then yer tires of them, the drag on yer is that 'eavy – I knows yer – and then yer begins to wish they 'ad never been born, or yer wishes they had died afore they knew they was alive. I don't say I'm not often sorry for them, poor little dears, but they takes less notice than you'd think for, and they're better out of the way, and that's a fact; it saves a lot of trouble hereafter. I often do think that to neglect them, to let them go off quiet, that I be their best friend; not wilful neglect, yer know, but what is a woman to do with ten or a dozen, and I often 'as as many? I am sure they'd thank me for it.'

Esther did not answer, but judging by her face that she had lost all hope, Mrs Spires was tempted to continue.

'There's that other baby in the far corner that was brought 'ere since you was 'ere by a servant-girl like yerself. She's out a-nursing of a lady's child, getting a pound a week, just as you was. Well, now, I asks 'ow she can 'ope to bring up that 'ere child – a weakly little thing that wants the doctor and all sorts of looking after. If that child was to live, it would be the ruin of that girl's life. Don't yer 'ear what I'm saying?'

'Yes, I hear,' said Esther, speaking like one in a dream; 'don't she care for her baby, then?'

'She used to care for them, but if they had all lived I should like to know where she'd be. There 'as been three of them – that's the third – so, instead of them a-costing 'er money, they brings 'er money. She 'as never failed yet to suit 'erself in a situation as wet-nurse.'

'And they all died?'

'Yes, they all died; and this little one don't look as if it was long for the world, do it?' said Mrs Spires, who had taken the infant from the cradle; and Esther looked at the poor wizened features, twitched with pain.

'It goes to my 'eart,' said Mrs Spires, 'it do indeed but, Lord, it is the best that could 'appen to 'em; who's to care for 'em? and there is 'undreds and 'undreds of them – ay, thousands and thousands every year – and they all dies like the early flies. It is 'ard, very 'ard, poor little dears, but they're best out of the way – they're only an expense and a disgrace.'

Mrs Spires talked on in a rapid, soothing, soporific voice. She had just finished pouring some milk in the baby's bottle and had taken down a jug of water from the dresser.

'But that's cold water,' said Esther, waking from the stupor of her despair; 'it will give the baby gripes for certain.'

'I've no 'ot water ready; I'll let the bottle stand afore the fire, that'll do as well.' Watching Esther all the while, Mrs Spires held the bottle a few moments before the fire, and then gave it to the child to suck. Very soon after a cry of pain came from the cradle.

'The little dear never was well; it wouldn't surprise me a bit if it died – went off before morning. It do look that poorly. One can't 'elp being sorry for them, though one knows there is no 'ouse for them 'ere. Poor little angels, and not even baptized. There's them that thinks a lot of getting that over. But who's to baptize the little angels?'

'Baptize them?' Esther repeated. 'That's not the way with the Lord's people'; and to escape from a too overpowering reality she continued to repeat the half-forgotten patter of the Brethren, 'You must wait until it is a symbol of living faith in the Lord!' And taking the baby in her hands for a moment, the wonder crossed her mind whether he would ever grow up and find salvation and testify to the Lord as an adult in voluntary baptism.

All the while Mrs Spires was getting on with her cooking. Several times she looked as if she were going to speak, and several times she checked herself. In truth, she didn't know what to make of Esther. Was her love of her child such love as would enable her to put up with all hardships for its sake; or was it the fleeting affection of the ordinary young mother, which, though ardent at first, gives way under difficulties? Mrs Spires had heard many mothers talk as Esther talked, but when the real strain of life was put upon them they had yielded to the temptation of ridding themselves of their burdens. So Mrs Spires could not believe that Esther was really different from the others, and if carefully handled she would do what the others had done. Still, there was something in Esther which kept Mrs Spires from making any distinct proposal. But it were a pity to let the girl slip through her fingers – five pounds were not picked up every day. There were three five-pound notes in the cradles; if Esther would listen to reason there would be twenty pounds. And once more greed set Mrs Spires's tongue flowing, and, representing herself as a sort of guardian angel, she spoke again about the mother of the dying child, pressing Esther to think what the girl's circumstances would have been if all her babies had lived.

'And they all died?' said Esther.

'Yes, and a good job, too,' said Mrs Spires, whose temper for the moment outsped her discretion. Was this penniless drab doing it on purpose to annoy her? A nice one indeed to high-and-mighty it over her. She would show her in mighty quick time she had come to the wrong shop. Just as Mrs Spires was about to speak out she noticed that Esther was in tears. Mrs Spires always looked upon tears as a good sign, so she resolved to give her one more chance. 'What are you crying about?' she said.

'Oh,' said Esther, 'I don't even know where I shall sleep to-night. I have only threepence, and not a friend in the world.'

'Now look 'ere, if you'll listen to reason I'll talk to you. Yer mustn't look upon me as a henemy. I've been a good friend to many a poor girl like you afore now, and I'll be one to you if you're sensible like. I'll do for you what I'm doing for the other girl. Give me five pounds—'

'Five pounds! I've only a few pence.'

''Ear me out. Go back to yer situation – she'll take you back: yer suits the child, that's all she cares about. Ask 'er for an advance of five pounds; she'll give it when she 'ears it is to get rid of yer child. They 'ates their nurses to be a-'ankering after their own; they likes them to be forgotten like; they asks if the child is dead very often, and won't engage them if it isn't. So believe me she'll give yer the money when yer tells 'er that it is to give the child to someone who wants to adopt it. That's what you 'as to say.'

'And you'll take the child off my hands for ever for five pounds?'

'Yes; and if you likes to go out again as wet-nurse, I'll take the second off yer 'ands too, and at the same price.'

'You wicked woman! Oh, this is awful!'

'Come, come. What do you mean by talking to me like that? And because I offered to find someone who would adopt your child.'

'You did nothing of the kind; ever since I've been in your house you have been trying to get me to give you up my child to murder as you are murdering those poor innocents in the cradles.'

'It is a lie, but I don't want no hargument with yer; pay me what you owe me and take yerself hoff. I want no more of yer, do you 'ear?'

Esther did not shrink before her as Mrs Spires expected. Clasping her baby more tightly, she said: 'I've paid you what I owe you; you've had more than your due. Mrs Rivers gave you ten shillings for a doctor which you didn't send for. Let me go.'

'Yes, when yer pays me.'

'What's all this row about?' said a tall, red-bearded man who had just come in; 'no one takes their babies out of this 'ere 'ouse before they pays. Come now, come now, who are yer getting at? If yer thinks yer can come here insulting of my wife, yer mistaken; yer've come to the wrong shop.'

'I've paid all I owe,' said Esther. 'You're no better than murderers, but yer shan't have my poor babe to murder for a five-pound note.'

'Take back them words, or else I'll do for yer; take them back,' he said, raising his fist.

'Help, help, murder!' Esther screamed. Before the brute could seize her she slipped past, but before she could scream again he laid hand on her at the door. Esther thought her last moment had come.

'Let 'er go, let 'er go!' cried Mrs Spires, clinging to her husband's arm. 'We don't want the perlice in 'ere.'

'Perlice! What do I care about the perlice? Let 'er pay what she owes.'

'Never mind, Tom; it is only a trifle. Let her go. Now then, take yer hook,' she said, turning to Esther; 'we don't want nothing to do with such as you.'

With a growl the man loosed his hold, and feeling herself free Esther rushed into the area and up the wooden steps. Some men drinking in a public-house frightened her and she ran on again, and to avoid the cabmen and the loafers in the next street she hastily crossed to the other side. Her heart beat violently, her thoughts were in disorder, and she walked on and on, stopping to ask the way, and then remembered there was no whither she might go unless the workhouse; no matter, any whither. All sorts of thoughts came upon her unsought till she came to the river, and saw vast water rolling. Was she to die, she and her child? Why she more than the next one? Why not go to the workhouse for the night? She didn't mind for herself, only she did not wish her boy to go there. But if God willed it . . .

She drew her shawl about her baby and tried once more to persuade herself into accepting the shelter of the workhouse. It seemed strange even to her that a pale, glassy moon should float high up in the sky, and that she should suffer; and then she looked at the lights that fell into the river from the Surrey shore, and wondered what had she done to deserve the workhouse? and of all, what had the poor, innocent child done to deserve it? If she once entered the workhouse she would remain there. She and her child paupers for ever. 'But what can I do?' she asked herself crazily, and sat down on one of the seats.

A young man coming home from an evening party looked at her as he passed, and she asked herself if she should run after him and tell him her story. Why should he not assist her? He could so easily spare it. Would he? But before she could decide to appeal to him he had called a passing hansom and was soon far away. Then looking at the windows of the great hotels, she thought of the folk there who could so easily save her from the workhouse if they knew. There must be many a kind heart behind those windows who would help her if she could only make known her trouble. But that was the hardship. She could not make known her trouble; she could not tell the misery. She couldn't understand it herself; why it had all come about she didn't know, for, after all—Her thoughts melted away and when she returned to herself she was thinking that she would be mistaken for a common beggar. Nowhere would she find anyone to listen to her, and in the delirium of her misery she asked herself would it not have been better, perhaps, if she had left him with Mrs Spires. What indeed had the poor little fellow to live for? A young man in evening dress came towards her, looking so happy and easy in life, walking with long, swinging strides. He stopped and asked her if she was out for a walk.

'No, sir; I'm out because I've no place to go.'

'How's that?'

She told him the story of the baby-farmer and he listened kindly, and she thought the needful miracle was about to happen. But he only complimented her on her pluck and got up to go. Then she understood that he did not care to listen to sad stories, and a vagrant came and sat down.

'The "copper",' he said, 'will be moving us on presently. It don't much matter; it's too cold to get to sleep, and I think it will rain. My cough is that bad.'

She might beg a night's lodging of Mrs Jones. But it was so far away that she didn't think she could walk so far. Mrs Jones might have left, then what would she do? The workhouse up there was much the same as the workhouse down here. Mrs Jones couldn't keep her for nothing, and there was no use trying for another situation as wet-nurse; the hospital would not recommend her again. So there was nothing for it but the workhouse. Her thoughts melted away, and she had been so near to sleep that it was almost a surprise to her to find herself on the Embankment. Her father, brothers, and sisters were on their way to Australia. But there was no use thinking of them, she and her baby were on their way to the workhouse, going to become paupers . . . The vagrant had fallen asleep. He knew all about the workhouse – should she ask him what it was like? He, too, was friendless. If he had a friend he would not be sleeping on the Embankment. Should she ask him? Poor chap, he was asleep. People were happy when they were asleep.

A full moon floated high up in the sky, and the city was no more than a faint shadow on the glassy stillness of the night; and she longed to float away with the moon out of sight of this world. Her baby grew heavy in her arms, and the vagrant, a bundle of rags thrown forward in a heap, slept at the other end of the bench. But she could not sleep, and the moon whirled on her miserable way. At last the glassy stillness was broken by the measured tramp of the policeman going his rounds, and in reply to her inquiry he directed her to Lambeth Workhouse. As she walked away she heard him rousing the vagrant and bidding him move onward.

'Home Sickness'

I

He told the doctor he was due in the bar-room at eight o'clock in the morning; the bar-room was in a slum in the Bowery; and he had only been able to keep himself in health by getting up at five o'clock and going for long walks in the Central Park.

'A sea-voyage is what you want,' said the doctor. 'Why not go to Ireland for two or three months? You will come back a new man.'

'I'd like to see Ireland again.'

And he began to wonder how the people at home were getting on. The doctor was right. He thanked him, and three weeks after he landed in Cork.

As he sat in the railway-carriage he recalled his native village, built among the rocks of the large headland stretching out into the winding lake. He could see the houses and the streets, and the fields of the tenants, and the Georgian mansion and the owners of it; he and they had been boys together before he went to America. He remembered the villagers going every morning to the Big House to work in the stables, in the garden, in the fields – mowing, reaping, digging, and Michael Malia building a wall; it was all as clear as if it were yesterday, yet he had been thirteen years in America; and when the train stopped at the station the first thing he did was to look round for any changes that might have come into it. It was the same blue limestone station as it was thirteen years ago, with the same five long miles between it and Duncannon. He had once walked these miles gaily, in little over an hour, carrying a heavy bundle on a stick, but he did not feel strong enough for the walk to-day, though the evening tempted him to try it. A car was waiting at the station, and the boy, discerning from his accent and his dress that Bryden had come from America, plied him with questions, which Bryden answered rapidly, for he wanted to hear who were still living in the village, and if there was a house in which he could get a clean lodging. The best house in the village, he was told, was Mike Scully's, who had been away in a situation for many years, as a coachman in the King's County, but had come back and built a fine house with a concrete floor. The boy could recommend the loft, he had slept in it himself, and Mike would be glad to take in a lodger, he had no doubt. Bryden remembered that Mike had been in a situation at the Big House. He had intended to be a jockey, but had suddenly shot up into a fine tall man, and had become a coachman instead; and Bryden tried to recall his face, but could only remember a straight nose and a somewhat dusky complexion.

So Mike had come back from King's County, and had built himself a house, had married – there were children for sure running about; while he, Bryden, had gone to America, but he had come back; perhaps he, too, would build a house in Duncannon, and—His reverie was suddenly interrupted by the carman.

'There's Mike Scully,' he said, pointing with his whip, and Bryden saw a tall, finely built, middle-aged man coming through the gates, who looked astonished when he was accosted, for he had forgotten Bryden even more completely than Bryden had forgotten him; and many aunts and uncles were mentioned before he began to understand.

'You've grown into a fine man, James,' he said, looking at Bryden's great width of chest. 'But you're thin in the cheeks, and you're very sallow in the cheeks too.'

'I haven't been very well lately – that is one of the reasons I've come back; but I want to see you all again.'

'And thousand welcome you are.'

Bryden paid the carman, and wished him 'God-speed'. They divided the luggage, Mike carrying the bag and Bryden the bundle, and they walked round the lake, for the townland was at the back of the domain; and while walking he remembered the woods thick and well-forested; now they were wind-worn, the drains were choked, and the bridge leading across the lake inlet was falling away. Their way led between long fields where herds of cattle were grazing; the road was broken – Bryden wondered how the villagers drove their carts over it, and Mike told him that the landlord could not keep it in repair, and he would not allow it to be kept in repair out of the rates, for then it would be a public road, and he did not think there should be a public road through his property.

At the end of many fields they came to the village, and it looked a desolate place, even on this fine evening, and Bryden remarked that the county did not seem to be as much lived in as it used to be. It was at once strange and familiar to see the chickens in the kitchen; and, wishing to re-knit himself to the old customs, he begged of Mrs Scully not to drive them out, saying they reminded him of old times.

'And why wouldn't they?' Mike answered, 'he being one of ourselves bred and born in Duncannon, and his father before him.'

'Now, is it truth ye are telling me?' and she gave him her hand, after wiping it on her apron, saying he was heartily welcome, only she was afraid he wouldn't care to sleep in a loft.

'Why wouldn't I sleep in a loft, a dry loft! You're thinking a good deal of America over here,' said he, 'but I reckon it isn't all you think it. Here you work when you like and you sit down when you like; but when you've had a touch of blood-poisoning as I had, and when you have seen young people walking with a stick, you think that there is something to be said for old Ireland.'

'You'll take a sup of milk, won't you? You must be dry,' said Mrs Scully.

And when he had drunk the milk Mike asked him if he would like to go inside or if he would like to go for a walk.

'Maybe resting you'd like to be.'

And they went into the cabin, and started to talk about the wages a man could get in America, and the long hours of work.

And after Bryden had told Mike everything about America that he thought of interest, he asked Mike about Ireland. But Mike did not seem to be able to tell him much. They were all very poor – poorer, perhaps, than when he left them.

'I don't think anyone except myself has a five-pound-note to his name.'

Bryden hoped he felt sufficiently sorry for Mike. But after all Mike's life and prospects mattered little to him. He had come back in search of health, and he felt better already; the milk had done him good, and the bacon and the cabbage in the pot sent forth a savoury odour. The Scullys were very kind, they pressed him to make a good meal; a few weeks of country air and food, they said, would give him back the health he had lost in the Bowery; and when Bryden said he was longing for a smoke, Mike said there was no better sign than that. During his long illness he had never wanted to smoke, and he was a confirmed smoker.

It was comfortable to sit by the mild peat fire watching the smoke of their pipes drifting up the chimney, and all Bryden wanted was to be left alone; he did not want to hear of anyone's misfortunes, but about nine o'clock a number of villagers came in, and Bryden remembered one or two of them – he used to know them very well when he was a boy; their talk was as depressing as their appearance, and he could feel no interest whatever in them. He was not moved when he heard that Higgins the stonemason was dead; he was not affected when he heard that Mary Kelly, who used to go to do the laundry at the Big House, had married; he was only interested when he heard she had gone to America. No, he had not met her there; America is a big place. Then one of the peasants asked him if he remembered Patsy Carabine, who used to do the gardening at the Big House. Yes, he remembered Patsy well. He had not been able to do any work on account of his arm; his house had fallen in; he had given up his holding and gone into the Poor-House. All this was very sad, and to avoid hearing any further unpleasantness, Bryden began to tell them about America. And they sat round listening to him; but all the talking was on his side; he wearied of it; and looking round the group he recognized a ragged hunchback with grey hair; twenty years ago he was a young hunchback, and, turning to him, Bryden asked him if he were doing well with his five acres.

'Ah, not much. This has been a poor season. The potatoes failed; they were watery – there is no diet in them.'

These peasants were all agreed that they could make nothing out of their farms. Their regret was that they had not gone to America when they were young; and after striving to take an interest in the fact that O'Connor had lost a mare and foal worth forty pounds, Bryden began to wish himself back in the slum. And when they left the house he wondered if every evening would be like the present one. Mike piled fresh sods on the fire, and he hoped it would show enough light in the loft for Bryden to undress himself by.

The cackling of some geese in the street kept him awake, and he seemed to realize suddenly how lonely the country was, and he foresaw mile after mile of scanty fields stretching all round the lake with one little town in the far corner. A dog howled in the distance, and the fields and the boreens between him and the dog appeared as in a crystal. He could hear Michael breathing by his wife's side in the kitchen, and he could barely resist the impulse to run out of the house, and he might have yielded to it, but he wasn't sure that he mightn't awaken Mike as he came down the ladder. His terror increased, and he drew the blanket over his head. He fell asleep and awoke and fell asleep again, and lying on his back he dreamed of the men he had seen sitting round the fireside that evening, like spectres they seemed to him in his dream. He seemed to have been asleep only a few minutes when he heard Mike calling him. He had come half-way up the ladder and was telling him that breakfast was ready. 'What kind of a breakfast will he give me?' Bryden asked himself as he pulled on his clothes. There were tea and hot griddle cakes for breakfast, and there were fresh eggs; there was sunlight in the kitchen, and he liked to hear Mike tell of the work he was going to be at in the farm – one of about fifteen acres, at least ten of it was grass; he grew an acre of potatoes, and some corn, and some turnips for his sheep. He had a nice bit of meadow, and he took down his scythe, and as he put the whetstone in his belt Bryden noticed a second scythe, and he asked Mike if he should go down with him and help him to finish the field.

'It's a long time since you've done any mowing, and it's heavier work than you think for. You'd better go for a walk by the lake.' Seeing that Bryden looked a little disappointed, he added, 'If you like you can come up in the afternoon and help me to turn the grass over.' Bryden said he would, and the morning passed pleasantly by the lake shore – a delicious breeze rustled in the trees, and the reeds were talking together, and the ducks were talking in the reeds; a cloud blotted out the sunlight, and the cloud passed and the sun shone, and the reed cast its shadow again in the still water; there was a lapping always about the shingle; the magic of returning health was sufficient distraction for the convalescent; he lay with his eyes fixed upon the castles, dreaming of the men that had manned the battlements; whenever a peasant driving a cart or an ass or an old woman with a bundle of sticks on her back went by, Bryden kept them in chat, and he soon knew the village by heart. One day the landlord from the Georgian mansion set on the pleasant green hill came along, his retriever at his heels, and stopped surprised at finding somebody whom he didn't know on his property. 'What, James Bryden!' he said. And the story was told again how ill-health had overtaken him at last, and he had come

331

home to Duncannon to recover. The two walked as far as the pine-wood, talking of the county, what it had been, the ruin it was slipping into, and as they parted Bryden asked for the loan of a boat.

'Of course, of course!' the landlord answered, and Bryden rowed about the islands every morning; and resting upon his oars looked at the old castles, remembering the prehistoric raiders that the landlord had told him about. He came across the stones to which the lake-dwellers had tied their boats, and these signs of ancient Ireland were pleasing to Bryden in his present mood.

As well as the great lake there was a smaller lake in the bog where the villagers cut their turf. This lake was famous for its pike, and the landlord allowed Bryden to fish there, and one evening when he was looking for a frog with which to bait his line he met Margaret Dirken driving home the cows for the milking. Margaret was the herdsman's daughter, and lived in a cottage near the Big House; but she came up to the village whenever there was a dance, and Bryden had found himself opposite to her in the reels. But until this evening he had had little opportunity of speaking to her, and he was glad to speak to someone, for the evening was lonely, and they stood talking together.

'You're getting your health again,' she said, 'and will be leaving us soon.'

'I'm in no hurry.'

'You're grand people over there; I hear a man is paid four dollars a day for his work.'

'And how much,' said James, 'has he to pay for his food and for his clothes?'

Her cheeks were bright and her teeth small, white and beautifully even; and a woman's soul looked at Bryden out of her soft Irish eyes. He was troubled and turned aside, and catching sight of a frog looking at him out of a tuft of grass he said: –

'I have been looking for a frog to put upon my pike line.'

The frog jumped right and left, and nearly escaped in some bushes, but he caught it and returned with it in his hand.

'It is just the kind of frog a pike will like,' he said. 'Look at its great white belly and its bright yellow back.'

And without more ado he pushed the wire to which the hook was fastened through the frog's fresh body, and dragging it through the mouth he passed the hooks through the hind-legs and tied the line to the end of the wire.

'I think,' said Margaret, 'I must be looking after my cows; it's time I got them home.'

'Won't you come down to the lake while I set my line?'

She thought for a moment and said: –

'No, I'll see you from here.'

He went down to the reedy tarn, and at his approach several snipe got up, and they flew above his head uttering sharp cries. His fishing-rod was a long hazel-stick, and he threw the frog as far as he could in the lake. In doing this he roused some wild ducks; a mallard and two ducks got up, and they flew toward the larger lake in a line with an old castle; and they had not disappeared from view when Bryden came toward her, and he and she drove the cows home together that evening.

They had not met very often when she said: 'James, you had better not come here so often calling to me.'

'Don't you wish me to come?'

'Yes, I wish you to come well enough, but keeping company isn't the custom of the country, and I don't want to be talked about.'

'Are you afraid the priest would speak against us from the altar?'

'He has spoken against keeping company, but it is not so much what the priest says, for there is no harm in talking.'

'But if you're going to be married there is no harm in walking out together.'

'Well, not so much, but marriages are made differently in these parts; there is not much courting here.'

And next day it was known in the village that James was going to marry Margaret Dirken.

His desire to excel the boys in dancing had caused a stir of gaiety in the parish, and for some time past there had been dancing in every house where there was a floor fit to dance upon; and if the cottager had no money to pay for a barrel of beer, James Bryden, who had money, sent him a barrel, so that Margaret might get her dance. She told him that they sometimes crossed over into another parish where the priest was not so averse to dancing, and James wondered. And next morning at Mass he wondered at their simple fervour. Some of them held their hands above their head as they prayed, and all this was very new and very old to James Bryden. But the obedience of these people to their priest surprised him. When he was a lad they had not been so obedient, or he had forgotten their obedience; and he listened in mixed anger and wonderment to the priest, who was scolding his parishioners, speaking to them by name, saying that he had heard there was dancing going on in their homes. Worse than that, he said he had seen boys and girls loitering about the roads, and the talk that went on was of one kind – love. He said that newspapers containing love stories were finding their way into the people's houses, stories about love, in which there was nothing elevating or ennobling. The people listened, accepting the priest's opinion without question. And their pathetic submission was the submission of a primitive people clinging to religious authority, and Bryden contrasted the weakness and incompetence of the people about him with the modern restlessness and cold energy of the people he had left behind him.

One evening, as they were dancing, a knock came to the door, and the piper stopped playing, and the dancers whispered: –

'Someone has told on us; it is the priest.'

And the awe-stricken villagers crowded round the cottage fire, afraid to open the door. But the priest said that if they didn't open the door he would put his shoulder to it and force it open. Bryden went towards the door, saying he would allow no one to threaten him, priest or no priest, but Margaret caught his arm and told him that if he said anything to the priest, the priest would speak against them from the altar, and they would be shunned by the neighbours.

'I've heard of your goings on,' he said – 'of your beer-drinking and dancing. I'll not have it in my parish. If you want that sort of thing you had better go to America.'

'If that is intended for me, sir, I'll go back to-morrow. Margaret can follow.'

'It isn't the dancing, it's the drinking I'm opposed to,' said the priest, turning to Bryden.

'Well, no one has drunk too much, sir,' said Bryden.

'But you'll sit here drinking all night,' and the priest's eyes went toward the corner where the women had gathered, and Bryden felt that the priest looked on the women as more dangerous than the porter. 'It's after midnight,' he said, taking out his watch.

By Bryden's watch it was only half-past eleven, and while they were arguing about the time Mrs Scully offered Bryden's umbrella to the priest, for in his hurry to stop the dancing the priest had gone out without his; and, as if to show Bryden that he bore him no ill-will, the priest accepted the loan of the umbrella, for he was thinking of the big marriage fee that Bryden would pay him.'

'I shall be badly off for the umbrella to-morrow,' Bryden said, as soon as the priest was out of the house. He was going with his father-in-law to a fair. His father-in-law was learning him how to buy and sell cattle. The country was mending, and a man might become rich in Ireland if he only had a little capital. Margaret had an uncle on the other side of the lake who would give twenty pounds, and her father would give another twenty pounds. Bryden had saved two hundred pounds. Never in the village of Duncannon had a young couple begun life with so much prospect of success, and some time after Christmas was spoken of as the best time for the marriage; James Bryden said that he would not be able to get his money out of America before the spring. The delay seemed to vex him, and he seemed anxious to be married, until one day he received a letter from America, from a man who had served in the bar with him. This friend wrote to ask Bryden if he were coming back. The letter was no more than a passing wish to see Bryden again. Yet Bryden stood looking at it, and everyone wondered what could be in the letter. It seemed momentous, and they hardly believed him when he said it was from a friend who wanted to know if his health were better. He tried to forget the letter, and he looked at the worn fields, divided by walls of loose stones, and a great longing came upon him.

The smell of the Bowery slum had come across the Atlantic, and had found him out in this western headland; and one night he awoke from a dream in which he was hurling some drunken customer through the open doors into the darkness. He had seen his friend in his white duck jacket throwing drink from glass into glass amid the din of voices and strange accents; he had heard the clang of money as it was swept into the till, and his sense sickened for the bar-room. But how should he tell Margaret Dirken that he could not marry her? She had built her life upon this marriage. He could not tell her that he would not marry her . . . yet he must go. He felt as if he were being hunted; the thought that he must tell Margaret that he could not marry her hunted him day after day as a weasel hunts a rabbit. Again and again he went to meet her with the intention of telling her that he did not love her, that their lives were not for one another, that it had all been a mistake, and that happily he had found out it was a mistake soon enough. But Margaret, as if she guessed what he was about to speak of, threw her arms about him and begged him to say he loved her, and that they would be married at once. He agreed that he loved her, and that they would be married at once. But he had not left her many minutes before the feeling came upon him that he could not marry her – that he must go away. The smell of the bar-room hunted him down. Was it for the sake of the money that he might make there that he wished to go back? No, it was not the money. What then? His eyes fell on the bleak country, on the little fields divided by bleak walls; he remembered the pathetic ignorance of the people, and it was these things that he could not endure. It was the priest who came to forbid the dancing. Yes, it was the priest. As he stood looking at the line of the hills the bar-room seemed by him. He heard the politicians, and the excitement of politics was in his blood again. He must go away from this place – he must get back to the bar-room. Looking up, he saw the scanty orchard, and he hated the spare road that led to the village, and he hated the little hill at the top of which the village began, and he hated more than all other places the house where he was to live with Margaret Dirken – if he married her. He could see it from where he stood – by the edge of the lake, with twenty acres of pasture land about it, for the landlord had given up part of his demesne land to them.

He caught sight of Margaret, and he called her to come through the stile.

'I have just had a letter from America.'

'About the money?'

'Yes, about the money. But I shall have to go over there.'

He stood looking at her, wondering what to say; and she guessed he would tell her that he must go to America before they were married.

'Do you mean, James, you will have to go at once?'

'Yes,' he said, 'at once. But I shall come back in time to be married in August. It will only mean delaying our marriage a month.'

They walked on a little way talking, and every step he took James felt that he was a step nearer the Bowery slum. And when they came to the gate Bryden said: –

'I must walk on or I shall miss the train.'

'But,' she said, 'you are not going now – you are not going to-day?'

'Yes, this morning. It is seven miles. I shall have to hurry not to miss the train.'

And then she asked him if he would ever come back.

'Yes,' he said, 'I am coming back.'

'If you are coming back, James, why don't you let me go with you?'

'You couldn't walk fast enough. We should miss the train.'

'One moment, James. Don't make me suffer; tell me the truth. You are not coming back. Your clothes – where shall I send them?'

He hurried away, hoping he would come back. He tried to think that he liked the country he was leaving, that it would be better to have a farmhouse and live there with Margaret Dirken than to serve drinks behind a counter in the Bowery. He did not think he was telling her a lie when he said he was coming back. Her offer to forward his clothes touched his heart, and at the end of the road he stood and asked himself if he should go back to her. He would miss the train if he waited another minute, and he ran on. And he would have missed the train if he had not met a car. Once he was on the car he felt himself safe – the country was already behind him. The train and the boat at Cork were mere formulae; he was already in America.

And when the tall skyscraper stuck up beyond the harbour he felt the thrill of home that he had not found in his native village, and wondered how it was that the smell of the bar seemed more natural than the smell of fields, and the roar of crowds more welcome than the silence of the lake's edge. He entered into negotiations for the purchase of the bar-room. He took a wife, she bore him sons and daughters, the bar-room prospered, property came and went; he grew old, his wife died, he retired from business, and reached the age when a man begins to feel there are not many years in front of him, and that all he has had to do in life has been done. His children married, lonesomeness began to creep about him in the evening and when he looked into the firelight, a vague, tender reverie floated up, and Margaret's soft eyes and name vivified the dusk. His wife and children passed out of mind, and it seemed to him that a memory was the only real thing he possessed, and the desire to see Margaret again grew intense. But she was an old woman, she had married, maybe she was dead. Well, he would like to be buried in the village where he was born.

There is an unchanging, silent life within every man that none knows but himself, and his unchanging, silent life was his memory of Margaret Dirken. The bar-room was forgotten and all that concerned it, and the things he saw most clearly were the green hillside, and the bog lake and the rushes about it, and the greater lake in the distance, and behind it the blue line of wandering hills.

OSCAR WILDE

from *The Picture of Dorian Gray*

2

As they entered they saw Dorian Gray. He was seated at the piano, with his back to them, turning over the pages of a volume of Schumann's *Forest Scenes*. 'You must lend me these, Basil,' he cried. 'I want to learn them. They are perfectly charming.'

'That entirely depends on how you sit to-day, Dorian.'

'Oh, I am tired of sitting, and I don't want a life-sized portrait of myself,' answered the lad, swinging round on the music-stool, in a wilful, petulant manner. When he caught sight of Lord Henry, a faint blush coloured his cheeks for a moment, and he started up. 'I beg your pardon, Basil, but I didn't know you had any one with you.'

'This is Lord Henry Wotton, Dorian, an old Oxford friend of mine. I have just been telling him what a capital sitter you were, and now you have spoiled everything.'

'You have not spoiled my pleasure in meeting you, Mr Gray,' said Lord Henry, stepping forward and extending his hand. 'My aunt has often spoken to me about you. You are one of her favourites, and, I am afraid, one of her victims also.'

'I am in Lady Agatha's black books at present,' answered Dorian, with a funny look of penitence. 'I promised to go to a club in Whitechapel with her last Tuesday, and I really forgot all about it. We were to have played a duet together – three duets, I believe. I don't know what she will say to me. I am far too frightened to call.'

'Oh, I will make your peace with my aunt. She is quite devoted to you. And I don't think it really matters about your not being there. The audience probably thought it was a duet. When Aunt Agatha sits down to the piano she makes quite enough noise for two people.'

'That is very horrid to her, and not very nice to me,' answered Dorian, laughing.

Lord Henry looked at him. Yes, he was certainly wonderfully handsome, with his finely-curved scarlet lips, his frank blue eyes, his crisp gold hair. There was something in his face that made one trust him at once. All the candour of youth was there, as well as all youth's passionate purity. One felt that he had kept himself unspotted from the world. No wonder Basil Hallward worshipped him.

'You are too charming to go in for philanthropy, Mr Gray – far too charming.' And Lord Henry flung himself down on the divan, and opened his cigarette case.

The painter had been busy mixing his colours and getting his brushes ready. He was looking worried, and when he heard Lord Henry's last remark he glanced at him, hesitated for a moment, and then said, 'Harry, I want to finish this picture to-day. Would you think it awfully rude of me if I asked you to go away?'

Lord Henry smiled, and looked at Dorian Gray. 'Am I to go, Mr Gray?' he asked.

'Oh, please don't, Lord Henry. I see that Basil is in one of his sulky moods; and I can't bear him when he sulks. Besides, I want you to tell me why I should not go in for philanthropy.'

'I don't know that I shall tell you that, Mr Gray. It is so tedious a subject that one would have to talk seriously about it. But I certainly shall not run away, now that you have asked me to stop. You don't really mind, Basil, do you? You have often told me that you liked your sitters to have some one to chat to.'

Hallward bit his lip. 'If Dorian wishes it, of course you must stay. Dorian's whims are laws to everybody, except himself.'

Lord Henry took up his hat and gloves. 'You are very pressing, Basil, but I am afraid I must go. I have promised to meet a man at the Orleans. Good-bye, Mr Gray. Come and see me some afternoon in Curzon Street. I am nearly always at home at five o'clock. Write to me when you are coming. I should be sorry to miss you.'

'Basil,' cried Dorian Gray, 'if Lord Henry Wotton goes I shall go too. You never open your lips while you are painting, and it is horribly dull standing on a platform and trying to look pleasant. Ask him to stay. I insist upon it.'

'Stay, Harry, to oblige Dorian, and to oblige me,' said Hallward, gazing intently at his picture. 'It is quite true, I never talk when I am working, and never listen either, and it must be dreadfully tedious for my unfortunate sitters. I beg you to stay.'

'But what about my man at the Orleans?'

The painter laughed. 'I don't think there will be any difficulty about that. Sit down again, Harry. And now, Dorian, get up on the platform, and don't move about too much, or pay any attention to what Lord Henry says. He has a very bad influence over all his friends, with the single exception of myself.'

Dorian Gray stepped up on the dais, with the air of a young Greek martyr, and made a little *moue* of discontent to Lord Henry, to whom he had rather taken a fancy. He was so unlike Basil. They made a delightful contrast. And he had such a beautiful voice. After a few moments he said to him, 'Have you really a very bad influence, Lord Henry? As bad as Basil says?'

'There is no such thing as a good influence, Mr Gray. All influence is immoral – immoral from the scientific point of view.'

'Why?'

'Because to influence a person is to give him one's own soul. He does not think his natural thoughts, or burn with his natural passions. His virtues are not real to him. His sins, if there are such things as sins, are borrowed. He becomes an echo of some one else's music, an actor of a part that has not been written for him. The aim of life is self-development. To realize one's nature perfectly – that is what each of us is here for. People are afraid of themselves, nowadays. They have forgotten the highest of all duties, the duty that one owes to oneself. Of course they are charitable. They feed the hungry, and clothe the beggar. But their own souls starve, and are naked. Courage has gone out of our race. Perhaps we never really had it. The terror of society, which is the basis of morals, the terror of God, which is the secret of religion – these are the two things that govern us. And yet—'

'Just turn your head a little more to the right, Dorian, like a good boy,' said the painter, deep in his work, and conscious only that a look had come into the lad's face that he had never seen there before.

'And yet,' continued Lord Henry, in his low, musical voice, and with that graceful wave of the hand that was always so characteristic of him, and that he had even in his Eton days, 'I believe that if one man were to live out his life fully and completely, were to give form to every feeling, expression to every thought, reality to every dream – I believe that the world would gain such a fresh impulse of joy that we would forget all the maladies of medievalism, and return to the Hellenic ideal – to something finer, richer, than the Hellenic ideal, it may be. But the bravest man amongst us is afraid of himself. The mutilation of the savage has its tragic survival in the self-denial that mars our lives. We are punished for our refusals. Every impulse that we strive to strangle broods in the mind, and poisons us. The body sins once, and has done with its sin, for action is a mode of purification. Nothing remains then but the recollection of a pleasure, or the luxury of a regret. The only way to get rid of a temptation is to yield to it. Resist it, and your soul grows sick with longing for the things it has forbidden to itself, with desire for what its monstrous laws have made monstrous and unlawful. It has been said that the great events of the world take place in the brain. It is in the brain, and the brain only, that the great sins of the world take place also. You, Mr Gray, you yourself, with your rose-red youth and your rose-white boyhood, you have had passions that have made you afraid, thoughts that have filled you with terror, day-dreams and sleeping dreams whose mere memory might stain your cheek with shame—'

'Stop!' faltered Dorian Gray, 'stop! you bewilder me. I don't know what to say. There is some answer to you, but I cannot find it. Don't speak. Let me think. Or, rather, let me try not to think.'

For nearly ten minutes he stood there, motionless, with parted lips, and eyes strangely bright. He was dimly conscious that entirely fresh influences were at work within him. Yet they seemed to him to have come really from himself. The few words that Basil's friend had said to him – words spoken by chance, no doubt, and with wilful paradox in them – had touched some secret chord that had never been touched before, but that he felt was now vibrating and throbbing to curious pulses.

Music had stirred him like that. Music had troubled him many times. But music was not articulate. It was not a new world, but rather another chaos, that it created in us.

Words! Mere words! How terrible they were! How clear, and vivid, and cruel! One could not escape from them. And yet what a subtle magic there was in them! They seemed to be able to give a plastic form to formless things, and to have a music of their own as sweet as that of viol or of lute. Mere words! Was there anything so real as words?

Yes; there had been things in his boyhood that he had not understood. He understood them now. Life suddenly became fiery-coloured to him. It seemed to him that he had been walking in fire. Why had he not known it?

With his subtle smile, Lord Henry watched him. He knew the precise psychological moment when to say nothing. He felt intensely interested. He was amazed at the sudden impression that his words had produced, and, remembering a book that he had read when he was sixteen, a book which had revealed to him much that he had not known before, he wondered whether Dorian Gray was passing through a similar experience. He had merely shot an arrow into the air. Had it hit the mark? How fascinating the lad was!

Hallward painted away with that marvellous bold touch of his, that had the true refinement and perfect delicacy that in art, at any rate, comes only from strength. He was unconscious of the silence.

'Basil, I am tired of standing,' cried Dorian Gray, suddenly. 'I must go out and sit in the garden. The air is stifling here.'

'My dear fellow, I am so sorry. When I am painting, I can't think of anything else. But you never sat better. You were perfectly still. And I have caught the effect I wanted – the half-parted lips, and the bright look in the eyes. I don't know what Harry has been saying to you, but he has certainly made you have the most wonderful expression. I suppose he has been paying you compliments. You mustn't believe a word that he says.'

'He has certainly not been paying me compliments. Perhaps that is the reason that I don't believe anything he has told me.'

'You know you believe it all,' said Lord Henry, looking at him with his dreamy, languorous eyes. 'I will go out to the garden with you. It is horribly hot in the studio. Basil, let us have something iced to drink, something with strawberries in it.'

'Certainly, Harry. Just touch the bell, and when Parker comes I will tell him what you want. I have got to work up this background, so I will join you later on. Don't keep Dorian too long. I have never been in better form for painting than I am to-day. This is going to be my masterpiece. It is my masterpiece as it stands.'

Lord Henry went out to the garden, and found Dorian Gray burying his face in the great cool lilac-blossoms, feverishly drinking in their perfume as if it had been wine. He came close to him, and put his hand upon his shoulder. 'You are quite right to do that,' he murmured. 'Nothing can cure the soul but the senses, just as nothing can cure the senses but the soul.'

The lad started and drew back. He was bareheaded, and the leaves had tossed his rebellious curls and tangled all their gilded threads. There was a look of fear in his eyes, such as people have when they are suddenly awakened. His finely chiselled nostrils quivered, and some hidden nerve shook the scarlet of his lips and left them trembling.

'Yes,' continued Lord Henry, 'that is one of the great secrets of life – to cure the soul by means of the senses, and the senses by means of the soul. You are a wonderful creation. You know more than you think you know, just as you know less than you want to know.'

Dorian Gray frowned and turned his head away. He could not help liking the tall, graceful young man who was standing by him. His romantic olive-coloured face and worn expression interested him. There was something in his low, languid voice that was absolutely fascinating. His cool, white, flower-like hands, even, had a curious charm. They moved, as he spoke, like music, and seemed to have a language of their own. But he felt afraid of him, and ashamed of being afraid. Why had it been left for a stranger to reveal him to himself? He had known Basil Hallward for months, but the friendship between them had never altered him. Suddenly there had come some one across his life who seemed to have disclosed to him life's mystery. And, yet, what was there to be afraid of? He was not a schoolboy or a girl. It was absurd to be frightened.

'Let us go and sit in the shade,' said Lord Henry. 'Parker has brought out the drinks, and if you stay any longer in this glare you will be quite spoiled, and Basil will never paint you again. You really must not allow yourself to become sunburnt. It would be unbecoming.'

'What can it matter?' cried Dorian Gray, laughing, as he sat down on the seat at the end of the garden.

'It should matter everything to you, Mr Gray.'

'Why?'

'Because you have the most marvellous youth, and youth is the one thing worth having.'

'I don't feel that, Lord Henry.'

'No, you don't feel it now. Some day, when you are old and wrinkled and ugly, when thought has seared your forehead with its lines, and passion branded your lips with its hideous fires, you will feel it, you will feel it terribly. Now, wherever you go, you charm the world. Will it always be so? . . . You have a wonderfully beautiful face, Mr Gray. Don't frown. You have. And Beauty is a form of Genius – is higher, indeed, than Genius, as it needs no explanation. It is of the great facts of the world, like sunlight or spring-time, or the reflection in dark waters of that silver shell we call the moon. It cannot be questioned. It has its divine right of sovereignty. It makes princes of those who have it. You smile? Ah! when you have lost it you won't smile . . . People say sometimes that Beauty is only superficial. That may be so. But at least it is not so superficial as Thought is. To me, Beauty is the wonder of wonders. It is only shallow people who do not judge by appearances. The true mystery of the world is the visible, not the invisible . . . Yes, Mr Gray, the gods have been good to you. But what the gods give they quickly take away. You have only a few years in which to live really, perfectly, and fully. When your youth goes, your beauty will go with it, and then you will suddenly discover that there are no triumphs left for you, or have to content yourself with those mean triumphs that the memory of your past will make more bitter than defeats. Every month as it wanes brings you nearer to something dreadful. Time is jealous of you, and wars against your lilies and your roses. You will become sallow, and hollow-cheeked, and dull-eyed. You will suffer horribly . . . Ah! realize your youth while you have it.

Don't squander the gold of your days, listening to the tedious, trying to improve the hopeless failure, or giving away your life to the ignorant, the common, and the vulgar. These are the sickly aims, the false ideals, of our age. Live! Live the wonderful life that is in you! Let nothing be lost upon you. Be always searching for new sensations. Be afraid of nothing . . . A new Hedonism – that is what our century wants. You might be its visible symbol. With your personality there is nothing you could not do. The world belongs to you for a season . . . The moment I met you I saw that you were quite unconscious of what you really are, of what you really might be. There was so much in you that charmed me that I felt I must tell you something about yourself. I thought how tragic it would be if you were wasted. For there is such a little time that your youth will last – such a little time. The common hill-flowers wither, but they blossom again. The laburnum will be as yellow next June as it is now. In a month there will be purple stars on the clematis, and year after year the green night of its leaves will hold its purple stars. But we never get back our youth. The pulse of joy that beats in us at twenty, becomes sluggish. Our limbs fail, our senses rot. We degenerate into hideous puppets, haunted by the memory of the passions of which we were too much afraid, and the exquisite temptations that we had not the courage to yield to. Youth! Youth! There is absolutely nothing in the world but youth!'

Dorian Gray listened, open-eyed and wondering. The spray of lilac fell from his hand upon the gravel. A furry bee came and buzzed round it for a moment. Then it began to scramble all over the oval stellated globe of the tiny blossoms. He watched it with that strange interest in trivial things that we try to develop when things of high import make us afraid, or when we are stirred by some new emotion for which we cannot find expression, or when some thought that terrifies us lays sudden siege to the brain and calls on us to yield. After a time the bee flew away. He saw it creeping into the stained trumpet of a Tyrian convolvulus. The flower seemed to quiver, and then swayed gently to and fro.

Suddenly the painter appeared at the door of the studio, and made staccato signs for them to come in. They turned to each other, and smiled.

'I am waiting,' he cried. 'Do come in. The light is quite perfect, and you can bring your drinks.'

They rose up, and sauntered down the walk together. Two green-and-white butterflies fluttered past them, and in the pear-tree at the corner of the garden a thrush began to sing.

'You are glad you have met me, Mr Gray,' said Lord Henry, looking at him.

'Yes, I am glad now. I wonder shall I always be glad?'

'Always! That is a dreadful word. It makes me shudder when I hear it. Women are so fond of using it. They spoil every romance by trying to make it last for ever. It is a meaningless word, too. The only difference between a caprice and a life-long passion is that the caprice lasts a little longer.'

As they entered the studio, Dorian Gray put his hand upon Lord Henry's arm. 'In that case, let our friendship be a caprice,' he murmured, flushing at his own boldness, then stepped up on the platform and resumed his pose.

Lord Henry flung himself into a large wicker armchair, and watched him. The sweep and dash of the brush on the canvas made the only sound that broke the stillness, except when, now and then, Hallward stepped back to look at his work from a distance. In the slanting beams that streamed through the open doorway the dust danced and was golden. The heavy scent of the roses seemed to brood over everything.

After about a quarter of an hour Hallward stopped painting, looked for a long time at Dorian Gray, and then for a long time at the picture, biting the end of one of his huge brushes, and frowning. 'It is quite finished,' he cried at last, and stooping down he wrote his name in long vermilion letters on the left-hand corner of the canvas.

Lord Henry came over and examined the picture. It was certainly a wonderful work of art, and a wonderful likeness as well.

'My dear fellow, I congratulate you most warmly,' he said. 'It is the finest portrait of modern times. Mr Gray, come over and look at yourself.'

The lad started, as if awakened from some dream. 'Is it really finished?' he murmured, stepping down from the platform.

'Quite finished,' said the painter. 'And you have sat splendidly to-day. I am awfully obliged to you.'

'That is entirely due to me,' broke in Lord Henry. 'Isn't it, Mr Gray?'

Dorian made no answer, but passed listlessly in front of his picture, and turned towards it. When he saw it he drew back, and his cheeks flushed for a moment with pleasure. A look of joy came into his eyes, as if he had recognized himself for the first time. He stood there motionless and in wonder, dimly conscious that Hallward was speaking to him, but not catching the meaning of his words. The sense of his own beauty came on him like a revelation. He had never felt it before. Basil Hallward's compliments had seemed to him to be merely the charming exaggerations of friendship. He had listened to them, laughed at them, forgotten them. They had not influenced his nature. Then had come Lord Henry Wotton with his strange panegyric on youth, his terrible warning of its brevity. That had stirred him at the time, and now, as he stood gazing at the shadow of his own loveliness, the full reality of the description flashed across him. Yes, there would be a day when his face would be wrinkled and wizen, his eyes dim and colourless, the grace of his figure broken and deformed. The scarlet would pass away from his lips, and the gold steal from his hair. The life that was to make his soul would mar his body. He would become dreadful, hideous, and uncouth.

As he thought of it, a sharp pang of pain struck through him like a knife, and made each delicate fibre of his nature quiver. His eyes deepened into amethyst, and across them came a mist of tears. He felt as if a hand of ice had been laid upon his heart.

'Don't you like it?' cried Hallward at last, stung a little by the lad's silence, not understanding what it meant.

'Of course he likes it,' said Lord Henry. 'Who wouldn't like it? It is one of the greatest things in modern art. I will give you anything you like to ask for it. I must have it.'

'It is not my property, Harry.'

'Whose property is it?'

'Dorian's, of course,' answered the painter.

'He is a very lucky fellow.'

'How sad it is!' murmured Dorian Gray, with his eyes still fixed upon his own portrait. 'How sad it is! I shall grow old, and horrible, and dreadful. But this picture will remain always young. It will never be older than this particular day of June . . . If it were only the other way! If it were I who was to be always young, and the picture that was to grow old! For that – for that – I would give everything! Yes, there is nothing in the whole world I would not give! I would give my soul for that!'

'You would hardly care for such an arrangement, Basil,' cried Lord Henry, laughing. 'It would be rather hard lines on your work.'

'I should object very strongly, Harry,' said Hallward.

Dorian Gray turned and looked at him. 'I believe you would, Basil. You like your art better than your friends. I am no more to you than a green bronze figure. Hardly as much, I dare say.'

The painter stared in amazement. It was so unlike Dorian to speak like that. What had happened? He seemed quite angry. His face was flushed and his cheeks burning.

'Yes,' he continued, 'I am less to you than your ivory Hermes or your silver Faun. You will like them always. How long will you like me? Till I have my first wrinkle, I suppose. I know, now, that when one loses one's good looks, whatever they may be, one loses everything. Your picture has taught me that. Lord Henry Wotton is perfectly right. Youth is the only thing worth having. When I find that I am growing old, I shall kill myself.'

Hallward turned pale, and caught his hand. 'Dorian! Dorian!' he cried, 'don't talk like that. I have never had such a friend as you, and I shall never have such another. You are not jealous of material things, are you? – you who are finer than any of them!'

'I am jealous of everything whose beauty does not die. I am jealous of the portrait you have painted of me. Why should it keep what I must lose? Every moment that passes takes something from me, and gives something to it. Oh, if it were only the other way! If the picture would change, and I could be always what I am now! Why did you paint it? It will mock me some day – mock me horribly!' The hot tears welled into his eyes; he tore his hand away, and, flinging himself on the divan, he buried his face in the cushions, as though he was praying.

'This is your doing, Harry,' said the painter, bitterly.

Lord Henry shrugged his shoulders. 'It is the real Dorian Gray – that is all.'

'It is not.'

'If it is not, what have I to do with it?'

'You should have gone away when I asked you,' he muttered.

'I stayed when you asked me,' was Lord Henry's answer.

'Harry, I can't quarrel with my two best friends at once, but between you both you have made me hate the finest piece of work I have ever done, and I will destroy it. What is it but canvas and colour? I will not let it come across our three lives and mar them.'

Dorian Gray lifted his golden head from the pillow, and with pallid face and tear-stained eyes looked at him, as he walked over to the deal painting-table that was set beneath the high curtained window. What was he doing there? His fingers were straying about among the litter of tin tubes and dry brushes, seeking for something. Yes, it was for the long palette-knife, with its thin blade of lithe steel. He had found it at last. He was going to rip up the canvas.

With a stifled sob the lad leaped from the couch, and, rushing over to Hallward, tore the knife out of his hand, and flung it to the end of the studio. 'Don't, Basil, don't!' he cried. 'It would be murder!'

'I am glad you appreciate my work at last, Dorian,' said the painter, coldly, when he had recovered from his surprise. 'I never thought you would.'

'Appreciate it? I am in love with it, Basil. It is part of myself. I feel that.'

'Well, as soon as you are dry, you shall be varnished, and framed, and sent home. Then you can do what you like with yourself.' And he walked across the room and rang the bell for tea. 'You will have tea, of course, Dorian? And so will you, Harry? Or do you object to such simple pleasures?'

'I adore simple pleasures,' said Lord Henry. 'They are the last refuge of the complex. But I don't like scenes, except on the stage. What absurd fellows you are, both of you! I wonder who it was defined man as a rational animal. It was the most premature definition ever given. Man is many things, but he is not rational. I am glad he is not, after all: though I wish you chaps would not squabble over the picture. You had much better let me have it, Basil. This silly boy doesn't really want it, and I really do.'

'If you let any one have it but me, Basil, I shall never forgive you!' cried Dorian Gray; 'and I don't allow people to call me a silly boy.'

'You know the picture is yours, Dorian. I gave it to you before it existed.'

'And you know you have been a little silly, Mr Gray, and that you don't really object to being reminded that you are extremely young.'

'I should have objected very strongly this morning, Lord Henry.'

'Ah! this morning! You have lived since then.'

There came a knock at the door, and the butler entered with a laden tea-tray and set it down upon a small Japanese table. There was a rattle of cups and saucers and the hissing of a fluted Georgian urn. Two globe-shaped china dishes were brought in by a page. Dorian Gray went over, and poured out the tea. The two men sauntered languidly to the table, and examined what was under the covers.

'Let us go to the theatre to-night,' said Lord Henry. 'There is sure to be something on, somewhere. I have promised to dine at White's, but it is only with an old friend, so I can send him a wire to say that I am ill, or that I am prevented from coming in consequence of a subsequent engagement. I think that would be a rather nice excuse: it would have all the surprise of candour.'

'It is such a bore putting on one's dress-clothes,' muttered Hallward. 'And, when one has them on, they are so horrid.'

'Yes,' answered Lord Henry, dreamily, 'the costume of the nineteenth century is detestable. It is so sombre, so depressing. Sin is the only real colour-element left in modern life.'

'You really must not say things like that before Dorian, Harry.'

'Before which Dorian? The one who is pouring out tea for us, or the one in the picture?'

'Before either.'

'I should like to come to the theatre with you, Lord Henry,' said the lad.

'Then you shall come; and you will come too, Basil, won't you?'

'I can't really. I would sooner not. I have a lot of work to do.'

'Well, then, you and I will go alone, Mr Gray.'

'I should like that awfully.'

The painter bit his lip and walked over, cup in hand, to the picture. 'I shall stay with the real Dorian,' he said, sadly.

'Is it the real Dorian?' cried the original of the portrait, strolling across to him. 'Am I really like that?'

'Yes; you are just like that.'

'How wonderful, Basil!'

'At least you are like it in appearance. But it will never alter,' sighed Hallward. 'That is something.'

'What a fuss people make about fidelity!' exclaimed Lord Henry. 'Why, even in love it is purely a question for physiology. It has nothing to do with our own will. Young men want to be faithful, and are not; old men want to be faithless, and cannot: that is all one can say.'

'Don't go to the theatre to-night, Dorian,' said Hallward. 'Stop and dine with me.'

'I can't, Basil.'

'Why?'

'Because I have promised Lord Henry Wotton to go with him.'

'He won't like you the better for keeping your promises. He always breaks his own. I beg you not to go.'

Dorian Gray laughed and shook his head.

'I entreat you.'

The lad hesitated, and looked over at Lord Henry, who was watching them from the tea-table with an amused smile.

'I must go, Basil,' he answered.

'Very well,' said Hallward; and he went over and laid down his cup on the tray. 'It is rather late, and, as you have to dress, you had better lose no time. Good-bye, Harry. Good-bye, Dorian. Come and see me soon. Come to-morrow.'

'Certainly.'

'You won't forget?'

'No, of course not,' cried Dorian.

'And . . . Harry!'

'Yes, Basil?'

'Remember what I asked you, when we were in the garden this morning.'

'I have forgotten it.'

'I trust you.'

'I wish I could trust myself,' said Lord Henry, laughing. 'Come, Mr Gray, my hansom is outside, and I can drop you at your own place. Good-bye, Basil. It has been a most interesting afternoon.'

As the door closed behind them, the painter flung himself down on a sofa, and a look of pain came into his face.

EDITH SOMERVILLE AND MARTIN ROSS
from *The Real Charlotte*

10

Washerwomen do not, as a rule, assimilate the principles of their trade. In Lismoyle, the row of cottages most affected by ladies of that profession was, indeed, planted by the side of the lake, but except in winter when the floods sent a muddy wash in at the kitchen doors of Ferry Row, the customers' linen alone had any experience of its waters. The clouds of steam from the cauldrons of boiling clothes ascended from morning till night, and hung in beads upon the sooty cobwebs that draped the rafters; the food and wearing apparel of the laundresses and their vast families mingled horribly with their professional apparatus, and, outside in the road, the filthy children played among puddles that stagnated under an iridescent scum of soap suds. A narrow strip of goose-nibbled grass divided the road from the lake shore, and at almost any hour of the day there might be seen a slatternly woman or two kneeling by the water's edge, pounding the wet linen on a rock with a flat wooden weapon, according to the immemorial custom of their savage class.

The Row ended at the ferry pier, and perhaps one reason for the absence of self-respect in the appearance of its inhabitants lay in the fact that the only passers-by were the country people on their way to the ferry, which here, where the lake narrowed to something less than a mile, was the route to the Lismoyle market generally used by the dwellers on the opposite side. The coming of a donkey-cart down the Row was an event to be celebrated with hooting and stone-throwing by the children, and, therefore, it can be understood that when, on a certain still, sleepy afternoon Miss Mullen drove slowly in her phaeton along the line of houses, she created nearly as great a sensation as she would have made in Piccadilly.

Miss Mullen had one or two sources of income which few people knew of, and about which, with all her loud candour, she did not enlighten even her most intimate friends. Even Mr Lambert might have been surprised to know that two or three householders in Ferry Row paid rent to her, and that others of them had money dealings with her of a complicated kind, not easy to describe, but simple enough to the strong financial intellect of his predecessor's daughter. No account books were taken with her on these occasions. She and her clients were equally equipped with the absolutely accurate business memory of the Irish peasant, a memory that in few cases survives education, but, where it exists, may be relied upon more than all the generations of ledgers and account books.

Charlotte's visits to Ferry Row were usually made on foot, and were of long duration, but her business on this afternoon was of a trivial character, consisting merely in leaving a parcel at the house of Dinny Lydon, the tailor, and of convincing her washerwoman of iniquity in a manner that brought every other washerwoman to the door, and made each offer up thanks to her most favoured saint that she was not employed by Miss Mullen.

The long phaeton was at last turned, with draggings at the horse's mouth and grindings of the fore-carriage: the children took their last stare, and one or two ladies whose payments were in arrear emerged from their back gardens and returned to their washing tubs. If they flattered themselves that they had been forgotten, they were mistaken; Charlotte had given a glance of grim amusement at the deserted washing tubs, and as her old phaeton rumbled slowly out of Ferry Row, she was computing the number of customers, and the consequent approximate income of each defaulter.

To the deep and plainly expressed chagrin of the black horse, he was not allowed to turn in at the gate of Tally Ho, but was urged along the road which led to Rosemount. There again he made a protest, but, yielding to the weighty arguments of Charlotte's whip, he fell into his usual melancholy jog, and took the turn to Gurthnamuckla with dull resignation. Once steered into that lonely road, Charlotte let him go at his own pace, and sat passive, her mouth tightly closed, and her eyes blinking quickly as she looked straight ahead of her with a slight furrow of concentration on her low forehead. She had the unusual gift of thinking out in advance her line of conversation in an interview, and, which is even less usual, she had the power of keeping to it. By sheer strength of will she could force her plan of action upon other people, as a conjurer forces a card, till they came to believe it was of their own choosing; she had done it so often that she was now confident of her skill, and she quite understood the inevitable advantage that a fixed scheme of any sort has over indefinite opposition. When the clump of trees round Gurthnamuckla rose into view, Charlotte had determined her order of battle, and was free to give her attention to outward circumstances. It was a long time since she had been out to Miss Duffy's farm, and as the stony country began to open its arms to the rich, sweet pastures, an often repressed desire asserted itself, and Charlotte heaved a sigh that was as romantic in its way as if she had been sweet and twenty, instead of tough and forty.

Julia Duffy did not come out to meet her visitor, and when Charlotte walked into the kitchen she found that the mistress of the house was absent, and that three old women were squatted on the floor in front of the fire, smoking short clay pipes, and holding converse in Irish that was punctuated with loud sniffs and coughs. At sight of the visitor the pipes vanished in the twinkling of an eye, and one of the women scrambled to her feet.

'Why, Mary Holloran, what brings you here?' said Charlotte, recognizing the woman who lived in the Rosemount gate lodge.

'It was a sore leg I have, yer honour, miss,' whined Mary Holloran; 'it's running with me now these three weeks, and I come to thry would Miss Duffy give me a bit o' a plashther.'

'Take care it doesn't run away with you altogether,' replied Charlotte facetiously; 'and where's Miss Duffy herself?'

'She's sick, the craythure,' said one of the other women, who, having found and dusted a chair, now offered it to Miss Mullen; 'she have a wakeness like in her head, and an impression on her heart, and Billy Grainy came afther Peggy Roche here, the way she'd mind her.'

Peggy Roche groaned slightly, and stirred a pot of smutty gruel with an air of authority.

'Could I see her, d'ye think?' asked Charlotte, sitting down and looking about her with sharp appreciation of the substantial excellence of the smoke blackened walls and grimy woodwork. 'There wouldn't be a better kitchen in the country,' she thought, 'if it was properly done up.'

'Ye can, asthore, ye can go up,' replied Peggy Roche, 'but wait a while till I have the sup o' grool hated, and maybe yerself'll take it up to herself.'

'Is she eating nothing but that?' asked Charlotte, viewing the pasty compound with disgust.

'Faith, 'tis hardly she'll ate that itself.' Peggy Roche rose as she spoke, and, going to the dresser, returned with a black bottle. 'As for a bit o' bread, or a pratie, or the like o' that, she couldn't use it, nor let it past her shest; with respects to ye, as soon as she'd have it shwallied it'd come up as simple and as pleashant as it wint down.' She lifted the little three-legged pot off its heap of hot embers, and then took the cork out of the black bottle with nimble, dirty fingers.

'What in the name of goodness is that ye have there?' demanded Charlotte hastily.

Mrs Roche looked somewhat confused, and murmured something about 'a wheeshy suppeen o' shperits to wet the grool'.

Charlotte snatched the bottle from her, and smelt it.

'Faugh!' she said, with a guttural at the end of the word that no Saxon gullet could hope to produce; 'it's potheen! that's what it is, and mighty bad potheen too. D'ye want to poison the woman?'

A loud chorus of repudiation arose from the sick-nurse and her friends.

'As for you, Peggy Roche, you're not fit to tend a pig, let alone a Christian. You'd murder this poor woman with your filthy fresh potheen, and when your own son was dying, you begrudged him the drop of spirits that'd have kept the life in him.'

Peggy flung up her arms with a protesting howl.

'May God forgive ye that word, Miss Charlotte! If 'twas the blood of me arrm, I didn't begridge it to him; the Lord have mercy on him –'

'Amen! amen! You would not, asthore,' groaned the other women.

'– but doesn't the world know it's mortial sin for a poor craythur to go into th' other world with the smell of dhrink on his breath!'

'It's mortal sin to be a fool,' replied Miss Mullen, whose medical skill had often been baffled by such winds of doctrine; 'here, give me the gruel. I'll go give it to the woman before you have her murdered.' She deftly emptied the pot of gruel into a bowl, and, taking the spoon out of the old woman's hand, she started on her errand of mercy.

The stairs were just outside the door, and making their dark and perilous ascent in safety, she stood still in a low passage into which two or three other doors opened. She knocked at the first of these, and, receiving no answer, turned the handle quietly and looked in. There was no furniture in it except a broken wooden bedstead; innumerable flies buzzed on the closed window, and in the slant of sunlight that fell through the dim panes was a box from which a turkey reared its red throat, and regarded her with a suspicion born, like her chickens, of long hatching. Charlotte closed the door and noiselessly opened the next. There was nothing in the room, which was of the ordinary low-ceiled cottage type, and after a calculating look at the broken flooring and the tattered wall-paper, she went quietly out into the passage again. 'Good servants' room,' she said to herself, 'but if she's here much longer it'll be past praying for.'

If she had been in any doubt as to Miss Duffy's whereabouts, a voice from the room at the end of the little passage now settled the matter. 'Is that Peggy?' it called.

Charlotte pushed boldly into the room with the bowl of gruel.

'No, Miss Duffy, me poor old friend, it's me, Charlotte Mullen,' she said in her most cordial voice: 'they told me below you were ill, but I thought you'd see me, and I brought your gruel up in my hand. I hope you'll like it none the less for that!'

The invalid turned her night-capped head round from the wall and looked at her visitor with astonished, bloodshot eyes. Her hatchety face was very yellow, her long nose was rather red, and her black hair thrust itself out round the soiled frill of her night-cap in dingy wisps.

'You're welcome, Miss Mullen,' she said, with a pitiable attempt at dignity; 'won't you take a cheer?'

'Not till I've seen you take this,' replied Charlotte, handing her the bowl of gruel with even broader *bonhomie* than before.

Julia Duffy reluctantly sat up among her blankets, conscious almost to agony of the squalor of all her surroundings, conscious even that the blankets were of the homespun, madder-dyed flannel such as the poor people use, and taking the gruel, she began to eat it in silence. She tried to prop herself in this emergency with the recollection that Charlotte Mullen's grandfather drank her grandfather's port wine under this very roof, and that it was by no fault of hers that she had sunk while Charlotte had risen; but the worn-out boots that lay on the floor where she had thrown them off, and the rags stuffed into the broken panes in the window, were facts that crowded out all consolation from bygone glories.

'Well, Miss Duffy,' said Charlotte, drawing up a chair to the bedside, and looking at her hostess with a critical eye, 'I'm sorry to see you so sick; when Billy Grainy left the milk last night he told Norry you were laid up in bed, and I thought I'd come over and see if there was anything I could do for you.'

'Thank ye, Miss Mullen,' replied Julia stiffly, sipping the nauseous gruel with ladylike decorum, 'I have all I require here.'

'Well, ye know, Miss Duffy, I wanted to see how you are,' said Charlotte, slightly varying her attack; 'I'm a bit of a doctor, like yourself. Peggy Roche below told me you had what she called "an impression on the heart", but it looks to me more like a touch of liver.'

The invalid does not exist who can resist a discussion of symptoms, and Miss Duffy's hauteur slowly thawed before Charlotte's intelligent and intimate questions. In a very short time Miss Mullen had felt her pulse, inspected her tongue, promised to send her a bottle of unfailing efficacy, and delivered an exordium on the nature and treatment of her complaint.

'But in deed and in truth,' she wound up, 'if you want my opinion, I'll tell you frankly that what ails you is you're just rotting away with the damp and loneliness of this place. I declare that sometimes when I'm lying awake in my bed at nights, I've thought of you out here by yourself, without an earthly creature near you if you got sick, and wondered at you. Why, my heavenly powers! ye might die a hundred deaths before anyone would know it!'

Miss Duffy picked up a corner of the sheet and wiped the gruel from her thin lips.

'If it comes to that, Miss Mullen,' she said with some resumption of her earlier manner, 'if I'm for dying I'd as soon die by myself as in company; and as for damp, I thank God this house was built by them that didn't spare money on it, and it's as dry this minyute as what it was forty years ago.'

'What! Do you tell me the roof's sound?' exclaimed Charlotte with genuine interest.

'I have never examined it, Miss Mullen,' replied Julia coldly, 'but it keeps the rain out, and I consider that suffeecient.'

'Oh, I'm sure there's not a word to be said against the house,' Charlotte made hasty reparation; 'but, indeed, Miss Duffy, I say – and I've heard more than myself say the same thing – that a delicate woman like you has no business to live alone so far from help. The poor Archdeacon frets about it, I can tell ye. I believe he thinks Father Heffernan'll be raking ye into his fold! And I can tell ye,' concluded Charlotte, with what she felt to be a certain rough pathos, 'there's plenty in Lismoyle would be sorry to see your father's daughter die with the wafer in her mouth!'

'I had no idea the people in Lismoyle were so anxious about me and my affairs,' said Miss Duffy. 'They're very kind, but I'm able to look afther my soul without their help.'

'Well, of course, everyone's soul is their own affair; but, ye know, when no one ever sees ye in your own parish church – well, right or wrong, there are plenty of fools to gab about it.'

The dark bags of skin under Julia Duffy's eyes became slowly red, a signal that this thrust had gone home. She did not answer, and her visitor rose, and moving towards the hermetically sealed window, looked out across the lawn over Julia's domain. Her roundest and weightiest stone was still in her sling, while her eye ran over the grazing cattle in the fields.

'Is it true what I hear, that Peter Joyce has your grazing this year?' she said casually.

'It is quite true,' answered Miss Duffy, a little defiantly. A liver attack does not predispose its victims to answer in a Christian spirit questions that are felt to be impertinent.

'Well,' returned Charlotte, still looking out of the window, with her hands deep in the pockets of her black alpaca coat, 'I'm sorry for it.'

'Why so?'

Julia's voice had a sharpness that was pleasant to Miss Mullen's ear.

'I can't well explain the matter to ye now,' Charlotte said, turning round and looking portentously upon the sick woman, 'but I have it from a sure hand that Peter Joyce is bankrupt, and will be in the courts before the year is out.'

When, a short time afterwards, Julia Duffy lay back among her madder blankets and heard the last sound of Miss Mullen's phaeton wheels die away along the lake road, she felt that the visit had at least provided her with subject for meditation.

*   *   *

30

One fine morning towards the end of August, Julia Duffy was sitting on a broken chair in her kitchen, with her hands in her lap, and her bloodshot eyes fixed on vacancy. She was so quiet that a party of ducks, which had hung uncertainly about the open door for some time, filed slowly in, and began to explore an empty pot or two with their long, dirty bills. The ducks knew well that Miss Duffy, though satisfied to accord the freedom of the kitchen to the hens and turkeys, had drawn the line at them and their cousins the geese, and they adventured themselves within the forbidden limits with the utmost caution, and with many side glances from their blinking, beady eyes at the motionless figure in the chair. They had made their way to a plate of potato skins and greasy cabbage on the floor by the table, and, forgetful of prudence, were clattering their bills on the delf as they gobbled, when an arm was stretched out above their heads, and they fled in cumbrous consternation.

The arm, however, was not stretched out in menace; Julia Duffy had merely extended it to take a paper from the table, and having done so, she looked at its contents in entire obliviousness of the ducks and their maraudings. Her misfortunes were converging. It was not a week since she had heard of the proclaimed insolvency of the man who had taken the grazing of Gurthnamuckla, and it was not half an hour since she had been struck by this last arrow of outrageous fortune, the letter threatening to process her for the long arrears of rent that she had felt lengthening hopelessly with every sunrise and sunset. She looked round the dreary kitchen that had about it all the added desolation of past respectability, at the rusty hooks from which she could remember the portly hams and flitches of bacon hanging; at the big fireplace where her grandfather's Sunday sirloin used to be roasted. Now cobwebs dangled from the hooks, and the old grate had fallen to pieces, so that the few sods of turf smouldered on the hearthstone. Everything spoke of bygone plenty and present wretchedness.

Julia put the letter into its envelope again and groaned a long miserable groan. She got up and stood for a minute, staring out of the open door with her hands on her hips, and then went slowly and heavily up the stairs, groaning again to herself from the exertion and from the blinding headache that made her feel as though her brain were on fire. She went into her room and changed her filthy gown for the stained and faded black rep that hung on the door. From a bandbox of tanned antiquity she took a black bonnet that had first seen the light at her mother's funeral, and tied its clammy satin strings with shaking hands. Flashes of light came and went before her eyes, and her pallid face was flushed painfully as she went downstairs again, and finding, after long search, the remains of the bottle of blacking, laboriously cleaned her only pair of boots. She was going out of the house when her eye fell upon the plate from which the ducks had been eating; she came back for it, and, taking it out with her, scattered its contents to the turkeys, mechanically holding her dress up out of the dirt as she did so. She left the plate on the kitchen window-sill, and set slowly forth down the avenue.

Under the tree by the gate, Billy Grainy was sitting, engaged, as was his custom in moments of leisure, in counting the coppers in the bag that hung round his neck. He looked in amazement at the unexpected appearance of his patroness, and as she approached him he pushed the bag under his shirt.

'Where are ye goin'?' he asked.

Julia did not answer; she fumbled blindly with the bit of stick that fastened the gate, and, having opened it, went on without attempting to shut it.

'Where are ye goin' at all?' said Billy again, his bleared eyes following the unfamiliar outline of bonnet and gown.

Without turning, she said, 'Lismoyle,' and as she walked on along the sunny road, she put up her hand and tried to wipe away the tears that were running down her face. Perhaps it was the excitement with which every nerve was trembling that made the three miles to Rosemount seem as nothing to this woman, who, for the last six months, had been too ill to go beyond her own gate; and probably it was the same unnatural strength that prevented her from breaking down, when, with her mind full of ready-framed sentences that were to touch Mr Lambert's heart and appeal to his sense of justice, she heard from Mary Holloran at the gate that he was away for a couple of days to Limerick. Without replying to Mary Holloran's exclamations of pious horror at the distance she had walked, and declining all offers of rest or food, she turned and walked on towards Lismoyle.

She had suddenly determined to herself that she would walk to Bruff and see her landlord, and this new idea took such possession of her that she did not realize at first the magnitude of the attempt. But by the time she had reached the gate of Tally Ho the physical power that her impulse gave her began to be conscious of its own limits. The flashes were darting like lightning before her eyes, and the nausea that was her constant companion robbed her of her energy. After a moment of hesitation she decided that she would go in and see her kinswoman, Norry the Boat, and get a glass of water from her before going farther. It wounded her pride somewhat to go round to the kitchen – she, whose grandfather had been on nearly the same social level as Miss Mullen's; but Charlotte was the last person she wished to meet just then. Norry opened the kitchen door, beginning, as she did so, her usual snarling maledictions on the supposed beggar, which, however, were lost in a loud invocation of her patron saint as she recognized her first cousin, Miss Duffy.

'And is it to leg it in from Gurthnamuckla ye done?' said Norry, when the first greetings had been exchanged, and Julia was seated in the kitchen, 'and you looking as white as the dhrivelling snow this minnit.'

'I did,' said Julia feebly, 'and I'd be thankful to you for a drink of water. The day's very close.'

'Faith ye'll get no wather in this house,' returned Norry in grim hospitality: 'I'll give ye a sup of milk, or would it be too much delay on ye to wait till I bile the kittle for a cup o' tay? Bad cess to Bid Sal! There isn't as much hot wather in the house this minute as'd write yer name!'

'I'm obliged to ye, Norry,' said Julia stiffly, her sick pride evolving a supposition that she could be in want of food; 'but I'm only after my breakfast myself. Indeed,' she added, assuming from old habit her usual attitude of medical adviser, 'you'd be the better yourself for taking less tea.'

'Is it me?' replied Norry indignantly. 'I take me cup o' tay morning and evening, and if 'twas throwing afther me I wouldn't take more.'

'Give me the cold wather, anyway,' said Julia wearily; 'I must go on out of this. It's to Bruff I'm going.'

'In the name o' God what's taking ye into Bruff, you that should be in yer bed, in place of sthreelin' through the counthry this way?'

'I got a letter from Lambert today,' said Julia, putting her hand to her aching head, as if to collect herself, 'and I want to speak to Sir Benjamin about it.'

'Ah, God help yer foolish head!' said Norry impatiently; 'sure ye might as well be talking to the bird above there,' pointing to the cockatoo, who was looking down at them with ghostly solemnity. 'The owld fellow's light in his head this long while.'

'Then I'll see some of the family,' said Julia; 'they remember my fawther well, and the promise I had about the farm, and they'll not see me wronged.'

'Throth, then, that's true,' said Norry, with an unwonted burst of admiration; 'they was always and ever a fine family, and thim that they takes in their hands has the luck o' God! But what did Lambert say t'ye?' with a keen glance at her visitor from under her heavy eyebrows.

Julia hesitated for a moment.

'Norry Kelly,' she said, her voice shaking a little; 'if it wasn't that you're me own mother's sister's child, I would not reveal to you the disgrace that man is trying to put upon me. I got a letter from him this morning saying he'd process me if I didn't pay him at once the half of what's due. And Joyce that has the grazing is bankrupt, and owes me what I'll never get from him.'

'Blast his sowl!' interjected Norry, who was peeling onions with furious speed.

'I know there's manny would be thankful to take the grazing,' continued Julia, passing a dingy pocket handkerchief over her forehead; 'but who knows when I'd be paid for it, and Lambert will have me out on the road before that if I don't give him the rent.'

Norry looked to see whether both the kitchen doors were shut, and then, putting both her hands on the table, leaned across towards her cousin.

'Herself wants it,' she said in a whisper.

'Wants what? What are you saying?'

'Wants the farm, I tell ye, and it's her that's driving Lambert.'

'Is it Charlotte Mullen?' asked Julia, in a scarcely audible voice.

'Now ye have it,' said Norry, returning to her onions, and shutting her mouth tightly.

The cockatoo gave a sudden piercing screech, like a note of admiration. Julia half got up, and then sank back into her chair.

'Are ye sure of that?'

'As sure as I have two feet,' replied Norry, 'and I'll tell ye what she's afther it for. It's to go live in it, and to let on she's as grand as the other ladies in the counthry.'

Julia clenched the bony, discoloured hand that lay on the table.

'Before I saw her in it I'd burn it over my head!'

'Not a word out o' ye about what I tell ye,' went on Norry in the same ominous whisper. 'Shure she have it all mapped this minnit, the same as a pairson'd be makin' a watch. She's sthriving to make a match with young Misther Dysart and Miss Francie, and b'leeve you me, 'twill be a quare thing if she'll let him go from her. Shure he's the gentlest crayture ever came into a house, and he's that innocent he wouldn't think how cute she was. If ye'd seen her, ere yestherday, follying him down to the gate, and she smilin' up at him as sweet as honey! The way it'll be, she'll sell Tally Ho house for a fortune for Miss Francie, though, indeed, it's little fortune himself'll ax!'

The words drove heavily through the pain of Julia's head, and their meaning followed at an interval.

'Why would she give a fortune to the likes of her?' she asked; 'isn't it what the people say, it's only for a charity she has her here?'

Norry gave her own peculiar laugh of derision, a laugh with a snort in it.

'Sharity! It's little sharity ye'll get from that one! Didn't I hear the old misthress tellin' her, and she sthretched for death – and Miss Charlotte knows well I heard her say it – "Charlotte," says she, and her knees, dhrawn up in the bed, "Francie must have her share." And that was the lasht word she spoke.' Norry's large wild eyes roved skywards out of the window as the scene rose before her. 'God rest her soul, 'tis she got the death aisy!'

'That Charlotte Mullen may get it hard!' said Julia savagely. She got up, feeling new strength in her tired limbs, though her head was reeling strangely, and she had to grasp at the kitchen table to keep herself steady. 'I'll go on now. If I die for it I'll go to Bruff this day.'

Norry dropped the onion she was peeling, and placed herself between Julia and the door.

'The divil a toe will ye put out of this kitchen,' she said, flourishing her knife; 'is it *you* walk to Bruff?'

'I must go to Bruff,' said Julia again, almost mechanically; 'but if you could give me a taste of sperrits, I think I'd be better able for the road.'

Norry pulled open a drawer, and took from the back of it a bottle containing a colourless liquid.

'Drink this to your health!' she said in Irish, giving some in a mug to Julia; 'it's potheen I got from friends of me own, back in Curraghduff.' She put her hand into the drawer again, and after a little search produced from the centre of a bundle of amorphous rags a cardboard box covered with shells. Julia heard, without heeding it, the clink of money, and then three shillings were slapped down on the table beside her. 'Ye'll go to Conolly's now, and get a car to dhrive ye,' said Norry defiantly; 'or howld on till I send Bid Sal to get it for ye. Not a word out o' ye now! Sure, don't I know well a pairson wouldn't think to put his money in his pocket whin he'd be hasting that way lavin' his house.'

She did not wait for an answer, but shuffled to the scullery door, and began to scream for Bid Sal in her usual tones of acrid ill-temper. As she returned to the kitchen, Julia met her at the door. Her yellow face, that Norry had likened by courtesy to the driven snow, was now very red, and her eyes had a hot stare in them.

'I'm obliged to you, Norry Kelly,' she said, 'but when I'm in need of charity I'll ask for it. Let me out, if you please.'

The blast of fury with which Norry was preparing to reply was checked by a rattle of wheels in the yard, and Bid Sal appeared with the intelligence that Jimmy Daly was come over with the Bruff cart, and Norry was to go out to speak to him. When she came back she had a basket of grapes in one hand and a brace of grouse in the other, and as she put them down on the table, she informed her cousin, with distant politeness, that Jimmy Daly would drive her to Bruff.

ROBERT TRESSELL

from *The Ragged-Trousered Philanthropists*

16

True Freedom

About three o'clock that afternoon, Rushton suddenly appeared and began walking silently about the house, and listening outside the doors of rooms where the hands were working. He did not succeed in catching anyone idling or smoking or talking. The nearest approach to what the men called 'a capture' that he made was, as he stood outside the door of one of the upper rooms in which Philpot and Harlow were working, he heard them singing one of Sankey's hymns – 'Work! for the night is coming'. He listened to two verses and several repetitions of the chorus. Being a 'Christian', he could scarcely object to this, especially as by peeping through the partly open door he could see that they were suiting the action to the word. When he went into the room they glanced round to see who it was, and stopped singing. Rushton did not speak, but stood in the middle of the floor, silently watching them as they worked, for about a quarter of an hour. Then, without having uttered a syllable, he turned and went out.

They heard him softly descend the stairs, and Harlow, turning to Philpot, said in a hoarse whisper:

'What do you think of the b—r, standing there watchin' us like that, as if we was a couple of bloody convicts? If it wasn't that I've got someone else beside myself to think of, I would 'ave sloshed the bloody sod in the mouth with this pound brush!'

'Yes; it does make yer feel like that, mate,' replied Philpot, 'but of course we mustn't give way to it.'

'Several times,' continued Harlow, who was livid with anger, 'I was on the point of turnin' round and sayin' to 'im, "What the bloody 'ell do you mean by standin' there watchin' me, you bloody, psalm-singin' swine?" It took me all my time to keep it in, I can tell you.'

Meanwhile, Rushton was still going about the house, occasionally standing and watching the other men in the same manner as he had watched Philpot and Harlow.

None of the men looked round from their work or spoke either to Rushton or to each other. The only sounds heard were the noises made by the saws and hammers of the carpenters who were fixing the frieze rails and dado rails or repairing parts of the woodwork in some of the rooms.

Cross placed himself in Rushton's way several times with the hope of being spoken to, but beyond curtly acknowledging the 'foreman's' servile 'Good hafternoon, sir', the master took no notice of him.

After about an hour spent in this manner Rushton went away, but as no one saw him go, it was not until some considerable time after his departure that they knew that he was gone.

Owen was secretly very disappointed. 'I thought he had come to tell me about the drawing-room,' he said to himself, 'but I suppose it's not decided yet.'

Just as the 'hands' were beginning to breathe freely again, Misery arrived, carrying some rolled-up papers in his hand. He also flitted silently from one room to another, peering round corners and listening at doors in the hope of seeing or hearing something which would give him an excuse for making an example of someone. Disappointed in this, he presently crawled upstairs to the room where Owen was working and, handing to him the roll of papers he had been carrying, said:

'Mr Sweater has decided to 'ave this work done, so you can start on it as soon as you like.'

It is impossible to describe, without appearing to exaggerate, the emotions experienced by Owen as he heard this announcement. For one thing it meant that the work at this house would last longer than it would otherwise have done; and it also meant that he would be paid for the extra time he had spent on the drawings, besides having his wages increased – for he was always paid an extra penny per hour when engaged on special work, such as graining or sign-writing or work of the present kind. But these considerations did not occur to him at the moment at all, for to him it meant much more. Since his first conversation on the subject with Rushton he had thought of little else than this work.

In a sense he had been *doing* it ever since. He had thought and planned and altered the details of the work repeatedly. The colours for the different parts had been selected and rejected and re-selected over and over again. A keen desire to do the work had grown within him, but he had scarcely allowed himself to hope that it would be done at all. His face flushed slightly as he took the drawings from Hunter.

'You can make a start on it tomorrow morning,' continued that gentleman. 'I'll tell Crass to send somone else up 'ere to finish this room.'

'I shan't be able to commence tomorrow, because the ceiling and walls will have to be painted first.'

'Yes: I know. You and Easton can do that. One coat tomorrow, another on Friday and the third on Saturday – that is, unless you can make it do with two coats. Even if it has to have the three, you will be able to go on with your decoratin' on Monday.'

'I won't be able to start it on Monday, because I shall have to make some working drawings first.'

'Workin' drorins!' ejaculated Misery with a puzzled expression. 'Wot workin' drorins? You've got them, ain't yer?' pointing to the roll of papers.

'Yes: but as the same ornaments are repeated several times, I shall have to make a number of full-sized drawings, with perforated outlines, to transfer the design to the walls,' said Owen, and he proceeded to laboriously explain the processes.

Nimrod looked at him suspiciously. 'Is all that really necessary?' he asked. 'Couldn't you just copy it on the wall, free-hand?'

'No; that wouldn't do. It would take much longer that way.'

This consideration appealed to Misery.

'Ah, well,' he sighed. 'I s'pose you'll 'ave to do it the way you said; but for goodness sake don't spend too much time over it, because we've took it very cheap. We only took it on so as you could 'ave a job, not that we expect to make any profit out of it.'

'And I shall have to cut some stencils, so I shall need several sheets of cartridge paper.'

Upon hearing of this additional expense, Misery's long visage appeared to become several inches longer; but after a moment's thought he brightened up.

'I'll tell you what!' he exclaimed with a cunning leer, 'there's lots of odd rolls of old wallpaper down at the shop. Couldn't you manage with some of that?'

'I'm afraid it wouldn't do,' replied Owen doubtfully, 'but I'll have a look at it and if possible I'll use it.'

'Yes, do!' said Misery, pleased at the thought of saving something. 'Call at the shop on your way home tonight, and we'll see what we can find. 'Ow long do you think it'll take you to make the drorin's and the stencils?'

'Well, today's Thursday. If you let someone else help Easton to get the room ready, I think I can get them done in time to bring them with me on Monday morning.'

'Wot do yer mean, "bring them with you"?' demanded Nimrod.

'I shall have to do them at home, you know.'

'Do 'em at 'ome! Why can't you do 'em 'ere?'

'Well, there's no table, for one thing.'

'Oh, but we can soon fit you out with a table. You can 'ave a pair of paperhanger's tressels and boards for that matter.'

'I have a lot of sketches and things at home that I couldn't very well bring here,' said Owen.

Misery argued about it for a long time, insisting that the drawings should be made either on the 'job' or at the paint-shop down at the yard. How, he asked, was he to know at what hour Owen commenced or left off working, if the latter did them at home?

'I shan't charge any more time than I really work,' replied Owen. 'I can't possibly do them here or at the paint-shop. I know I should only make a mess of them under such conditions.'

'Well, I s'pose you'll 'ave to 'ave your own way,' said Misery, dolefully. 'I'll let Harlow help Easton paint the room out, so as you can get your stencils and things ready. But for Gord's sake get 'em done as quick as you can. If you could manage to get done by Friday and come down and help Easton on Saturday, it would be so much the better. And when you do get a start on the decoratin', I shouldn't take too much care over it, you know, if I was you, because we 'ad to take the job for next to nothing or Mr Sweater would never 'ave 'ad it done at all!'

Nimrod now began to crawl about the house, snarling and grumbling at everyone.

'Now then, you chaps. *Rouse yourselves!*' he bellowed, 'you seem to think this is a 'orspital. If some of you don't make a better show than this, I'll 'ave to 'ave a Alteration! There's plenty of chaps walkin' about doin' nothin' who'll be only too glad of a job!'

He went into the scullery, where Crass was mixing some colour.

'Look 'ere, Crass!' he said. 'I'm not at all satisfied with the way you're gettin' on with the work. You must push the chaps a bit more than you're doin'. There's not enough being done, by a long way. We shall lose money over this job before we're finished!'

Cross – whose fat face had turned a ghastly green with fright – mumbled something about getting on with it as fast as he could.

'Well, you'll 'ave to make 'em move a bit quicker than this!' Misery howled, 'or there'll 'ave to be a *Alteration!*'

By an 'alteration' Crass understood that he might get the sack, or that someone else might be put in charge of the job, and that would of course reduce him to the ranks and do away with his chance of being kept on longer than the others. He determined to try to ingratiate himself with Hunter and appease his wrath by sacrificing someone else. He glanced cautiously into the kitchen and up the passage and then, lowering his voice, he said:

'They all shapes pretty well, except Newman. I would 'ave told you about 'im before, but I thought I'd give 'im a fair chance. I've spoke to 'im several times myself about not doin' enough, but it don't seem to make no difference.'

'I've 'ad me eye on 'im meself for some time,' replied Nimrod in the same tone. 'Anybody would think the work was goin' to be sent to a Exhibition, the way 'e messes about with it, rubbing it with glasspaper and stopping up every little crack! I can't understand where 'e gets all the glasspaper *from!*'

' 'E brings it 'isself!' said Crass hoarsely. 'I know for a fact that 'e bought two 'a'penny sheets of it, last week out of 'is own money!'

'Oh, 'e did, did 'e?' snarled Misery. 'I'll give 'im glasspaper! I'll 'ave a Alteration!'

He went into the hall, where he remained alone for a considerable time, brooding. At last, with the manner of one who has resolved on a certain course of action, he turned and entered the room where Philpot and Harlow were working.

'You both get sevenpence an hour, don't you?' he said.

They both replied to the affirmative.

'I've never worked under price yet,' added Harlow.

'Nor me neither,' observed Philpot.

'Well, of course you can please yourselves,' Hunter continued, 'but after this week we've decided not to pay more than six and a half. Things is cut so fine nowadays that we can't afford to go on payin' sevenpence any longer. You can work up till tomorrow night on the old terms, but if you're not willin' to accept six and a half you needn't come on Saturday morning. Please yourselves. Take it or leave it.'

Harlow and Philpot were both too much astonished to say anything in reply to this cheerful announcement, and Hunter, with the final remark, 'You can think it over,' left them and went to deliver the same ultimatum to all the other full-price men, who took it in the same way as Philpot and Harlow had done. Crass and Owen were the only two whose wages were not reduced.

It will be remembered that Newman was one of those who were already working for the reduced rate. Misery found him alone in one of the upper rooms, to which he was giving the final coat. He was at his old tricks. The woodwork of the cupboard he was doing was in a rather damaged condition, and he was facing up the dents with white-lead putty before painting it. He knew quite well that Hunter objected to any but very large holes or cracks being stopped, and yet somehow or other he could not scamp the work to the extent that he was ordered to; and so, almost by stealth, he was in the habit of doing it – not properly but as well as he dared. He even went to the length of occasionally buying a few sheets of glasspaper with his own money, as Crass had told Hunter. When the latter came into the room he stood with a sneer on his face, watching Newman for about five minutes before he spoke. The workman became very nervous and awkward under this scrutiny.

'You can make out yer time-sheet and come to the office for yer money at five o'clock,' said Nimrod at last. 'We shan't require your valuable services no more after tonight.'

Newman went white.

'Why, what's wrong?' said he. 'What have I done?'

'Oh, it's not wot you've *done*,' replied Misery. 'It's wot you've *not* done. That's wot's wrong! You've not done enough, that's all!' And without further parley he turned and went out.

Newman stood in the darkening room feeling as if his heart had turned to lead. There rose before his mind the picture of his home and family. He could see them as they were at this very moment, the wife probably just beginning to prepare the evening meal, and the children setting the cups and saucers and other things on the kitchen table – a noisy work, enlivened with many a frolic and childish dispute. Even the two-year-old baby insisted on helping, although she always put everything in the wrong place and made all sorts of funny mistakes. They had all been so happy lately because they knew that he had work that would last till nearly Christmas – if not longer. And now *this* had happened – to plunge them back into the abyss of wretchedness from which they had so recently escaped. They still owed several weeks' rent, and were already so much in debt to the baker and the grocer that it was hopeless to expect any further credit.

'My God!' said Newman, realizing the almost utter hopelessness of the chance of obtaining another 'job' and unconsciously speaking aloud. 'My God! How can I tell them? What *will* become of us?'

Having accomplished the objects of his visit, Hunter shortly afterwards departed, possibly congratulating himself that he had not been hiding his light under a bushel, but that he had set it upon a candlestick and given light unto all that were within that house.

As soon as they knew that he was gone, the men began to gather into little groups, but in a little while they nearly all found themselves in the kitchen, discussing the reduction. Sawkins and the other 'lightweights' remained at their work. Some of them got only fourpence halfpenny – Sawkins was paid fivepence – so none of these were affected by the change. The other two fresh hands – the journeymen – joined the crowd in the kitchen, being anxious to conceal the fact that they had agreed to accept the reduced rate before being 'taken on'. Owen also was there, having heard the news from Philpot.

There was a lot of furious talk. At first several of them spoke of 'chucking up', at once; but others were more prudent, for they knew that if they did leave there were dozens of others who would be eager to take their places.

'After all, you know,' said Slyme, who had – stowed away somewhere at the back of his head – an idea of presently starting business on his own account: he was only waiting until he had saved enough money, 'after all, there's something in what 'Unter says. It's very 'ard to get a fair price for work nowadays. Things *is* cut very fine.'

'Yes! We know all about that!' shouted Harlow. 'And who the bloody 'ell is it cuts 'em? Why, sich b—rs as 'Unter and Rushton! If this firm 'adn't cut *this* job so fine, some other firm would 'ave 'ad it for more money. Rushton's cuttin' it fine didn't *make* this job, did it? It would 'ave been done just the same if they 'adn't tendered for it at all! The only difference is that we should 'ave been workin' for some other master.'

'I don't believe the bloody job's cut fine at all!' said Philpot. 'Rushton is a pal of Sweater's and they're both members of the Town Council.'

'That may be,' replied Slyme; 'but all the same I believe Sweater got several other prices besides Rushton's – friend or no friend; and you can't blame 'im: it's only business. But pr'aps Rushton got the preference – Sweater may 'ave told 'im the others' prices.'

'Yes, and a bloody fine lot of prices they was, too, if the truth was known!' said Bundy. 'There was six other firms after this job to my knowledge – Pushem and Sloggem, Bluffum and Doemdown, Dodger and Scampit, Snatcham and Graball, Smeeriton and Leavit, Makehaste and Sloggitt, and Gord only knows 'ow many more.'

At this moment Newman came into the room. He looked so white and upset that the others involuntarily paused in their conversation.

'Well, what do *you* think of it?' asked Harlow.

'Think of what?' said Newman.

'Why, didn't 'Unter tell you?' cried several voices, whose owners looked suspiciously at him. They thought – if Hunter had not spoken to Newman, it must be because he was already working under price. There had been a rumour going about the last few days to that effect. 'Didn't Misery tell you? They're not goin' to pay more than six and a half after this week.'

'That's not what 'e said to me. 'E just told me to knock off. Said I didn't do enough for 'em.'

'Jesus Christ!' exclaimed Crass, pretending to be overcome with surprise.

Newman's account of what had transpired was listened to in gloomy silence. Those who – a few minutes previously – had been talking loudly of chucking up the job became filled with apprehension that they might be served in the same manner as he had been. Crass was one of the loudest in his expression of astonishment and indignation, but he rather overdid it and only succeeded in confirming the secret suspicion of the others that he had had something to do with Hunter's action.

The result of the discussion was that they decided to submit to Misery's terms for the time being, until they could see a chance of getting work elsewhere.

As Owen had to go to the office to see the wallpaper spoken of by Hunter, he accompanied Newman when the latter went to get his wages. Nimrod was waiting for them, and had the money ready in an envelope, which he handed to Newman, who took it without speaking and went away.

Misery had been rummaging amongst the old wallpapers, and had got out a great heap of odd rolls, which he now submitted to Owen, but after examining them the latter said that they were unsuitable for the purpose, so after some argument Misery was compelled to sign an order for some proper cartridge paper, which Owen obtained at a stationer's on his way home.

The next morning, when Misery went to the 'Cave', he was in a fearful rage, and he kicked up a terrible row with Crass. He said that Mr Rushton had been complaining of the lack of discipline on the job, and he told Crass to tell all the hands that for the future singing in working hours was strictly forbidden, and anyone caught breaking this rule would be instantly dismissed.

Several times during the following days Nimrod called at Owen's flat to see how the work was progressing and to impress upon him the necessity of not taking too much trouble over it.

KATHERINE CECIL THURSTON

from *The Fly on the Wheel*

ʃ

Very slowly Carey walked down the room to where a group of twelve or fourteen elderly women, arrayed in dark silk dresses and wearing lace caps, were gathered about their hostess, closely observant of the scene being enacted before them. Every guest in the ballroom, with his or her genealogical tree, was accurately known to each of these spectators, and a running fire of comment and criticism kept pace with their various actions. A little tremor of interest and curiosity passed over the group when Carey's approach was signalled, and glances of speculation were rapidly exchanged, heads brought closer together, and voices discreetly lowered.

With a man's innate sensitiveness to observation, he made haste to single out his hostess and shelter behind her greeting. Not that he had any affection for Mrs Michael Burke; on the contrary, it was a never-failing source of wonder to him how kindly, commonplace Michael could ever have chosen such a mate, for Mrs Burke was what, in her particular set, is known as 'very grand', which, literally translated, conveys the impression of a vast and unloveable superiority of manner, coupled with definite social ambitions. In his feeling of vague dislike Carey shared a common opinion, for not even Burke's own relations had ever, in the twenty odd years of his married life, arrived at the point of feeling at home with Mrs Michael. Her invitations to Fair Hill were never refused, for such invitations implied a certain social distinction, but the uncultured band of relatives never outgrew the nervous sense of the hostess's critical eye, and a sigh of relief invariably escaped them when the large iron gates, aggressive in their prosperous coating of white paint, clanged behind them and they were free to breathe their own less rarefied air.

This same consciousness of cold criticism fell now upon Carey as he clasped her long, thin hand, encased in a well-fitting black kid glove, for her actions and bearing could convey to a nicety the precise esteem in which a guest was held. As the daughter of a bank manager, she was obliged in the present instance to look askance at Carey's antecedents, though, as the wife of a successful trader, she granted him the meed of praise due to his self-earned position. In his case, circumstances balanced each other. He had been unfortunately brought up, but he had married well. Her fingers closed round his with a certain degree of cordiality, and her thin face relaxed into a smile.

'Good evening, Mr Carey! I have just been talking to your wife; she danced the first dance with my cousin, Surgeon-Major Cusacke. He's stationed at the Curragh, you know. Such a nice fellow! I must introduce you to each other.' She spoke in a high, clipped voice, from which the brogue had been carefully eliminated, – a voice that, in its studied precision, had something in common with his wife's.

The similarity struck Carey, flashing across his mind with a slight, sharp contempt. Usually, he was not a little proud of Daisy's social advantages, but this reflection of them in a woman who was antagonistic to him jarred upon his senses, still tingling from contact with elemental things. Dropping Mrs Burke's hand, he answered quickly and indifferently. 'Oh, Cusacke! I met him at the Tramore races last year.'

Mrs Burke was sensible of the little slight, but she prided herself on being a hostess and a woman of the world; and, whatever her silent criticism of his manners, she gave no outward expression of it.

'And what about yourself, Mr Carey? Are you going to play cards? Or can we persuade you to dance? There are plenty of pretty girls here – but the men are always wanted.'

Carey laughed. 'Old married men like me?'

She smiled the chilly smile that was thought the essence of good taste. 'Oh, you mustn't be running yourself down! Let me find a partner for you. But, of course, you know everybody here!'

'Indeed I don't! It makes me feel quite old seeing all these children who were in the nursery in my dancing days.'

'What nonsense! There's nobody here you don't know – unless, perhaps, Dan Costello's daughter. You remember the Costellos? Dan was with my father in the bank in Enniscorthy before he was moved here.'

'Oh, yes, I remember him. A dark, excitable little man.'

'Yes. The greatest fool that ever lived. If you made a king of Dan Costello, he'd be begging in the streets the week after! He hadn't a grain of sense.'

'Who was it he married?'

'Don't you remember? He ran away with a Miss Dysart of Derryvane. 'Twas the talk of the County Wexford for a year after. Her father cut her off without a penny; and, they say, she used to have to turn Dan's old coats for herself when he was done with them! But all the Wexford people are queer!'

Carey laughed. 'And what about the girl?'

'Oh, Isabel! Isabel is pretty. Perhaps you saw her, though. She was dancing the first dance.'

'I saw her, yes!' He was careful to answer indifferently.

'And what did you think of her? She's curious-looking, isn't she?'

He made no reply.

'Your wife and your sister-in-law admire her greatly. I must introduce you to her. I wonder where she's gone to!'

'She's half-way down the room, standing near the door.' Carey still kept his voice studiedly unconcerned, for he dreaded Mrs Michael Burke as we dread all powerful influences, the workings of which we do not understand.

'Oh, is she? We'll go and find her, then.' She excused herself to the nearest of the matrons, and sailed down the room, with Carey following in her wake.

As they drew near to Isabel Costello, she was standing by the wall, the centre of a group of men, her head thrown slightly backward, so that the light from the chandeliers fell full upon her rounded chin, her parted lips, and white, flawless teeth. More than ever, she suggested the young animal stretching itself to the warmth and comfort of the sun – to the caresses of life; and this subtle, indescribable impression came home to Carey interwoven with her physical being – lying like a shadow in the blackness of her hair, dancing like a will-o'-the-wisp in her hazel eyes.

At the moment that they paused beside her, she was holding up her programme, the pencil poised in her hand, her dancing eyes roving from one man's face to another, in transparent joy at the exercise of power. 'Well, I can't give it to you all!' she was saying in a clear voice. 'I can't give it to you all – unless I divide myself up into little bits! And, even then, only the person who got my feet would have a good dance!' She laughed, once more displaying her strong, white teeth.

'Isabel! Here's somebody I want to introduce to you!'

She turned at once at sound of Mrs Burke's voice, the laughter still on her lips.

'Mr Carey! Miss Costello! And don't dance too much, Isabel! Your aunt will be blaming me if you look washed-out to-morrow.'

A flash of amusement shot irresistibly from the girl's radiant eyes to Carey's, and involuntarily he responded to it, as he acknowledged the introduction; but the opening bars of the next waltz came swinging down the room as he bent his head, and before he could speak the little group of men became clamorous again.

'Well, Miss Costello, and who is to have the dance?'

'I asked first, you know!'

'Indeed you didn't, Jack! 'Twas I! Wasn't it, Miss Costello?'

'Well, I asked last. And the last shall be first, you know!' Owen Power pushed his way to the front with a confident smile.

Again Isabel looked from one face to the other. 'I tell you what I'll do!' she said suddenly. 'I'll give the dance to Mr Carey – and then none of you can be jealous!' Like a flash she wheeled round upon Stephen.

The demand in her glance was so strong, the whole onslaught so sudden, that no thought of resistance suggested itself to him. Without a word he stepped forward and put his arm round her waist, swinging her out into the circle of dancers that was rapidly filling the room.

It was five years or more since he had danced, but few Irishmen are awkward in an art that comes to them more or less naturally. He guided her carefully down the room, testing his powers, exercising his memory, anxious not to do himself discredit; then, as he gained the farther end, and passed the group of matrons, the spirit of the moment suddenly entered into him, as the music quickened and he felt the strong supple body of his partner brace itself in response. A thrill passed through him, dispersing a long apathy; his position and his responsibilities were momentarily submerged in the sense of sound and motion; his arm instinctively tightened, drawing the girl closer, and with one impulse they spun out into the centre of the room.

For several minutes they danced in silence; then at last they paused by the door where they had first met. They looked at each other, and she gave a breathless little laugh.

'How well you dance!'

'I don't! 'Twas you made me.'

She coloured with pleasure. 'Do I dance well, then?'

'Well? You dance wonderfully.'

'I learnt at the convent in Paris from a French teacher. We weren't supposed to learn waltzes, but she taught me. There's nothing so heavenly as dancing, is there?'

Carey looked at her, engrossed in some thought of his own.

Her face changed and darkened. 'But perhaps you didn't enjoy it?' she added, swift as lightning in her change of tone.

'Didn't I?' His eyes were still upon hers.

The blood rose quickly to her face, chasing away the shadows. 'Then perhaps it's only that you're trying to be nice to me, because it's my first dance?'

The tone of the voice, the utterance of the words, were charged with unconscious coquetry. The sense of exhilaration swept over Carey afresh, as though her light fingers had lifted the dry record of his days and her light breath had blown the dust from the pages.

'Could I be nice – even if I tried?' His tongue, unused to the tossing of words, brought out the question awkwardly – stupidly, it seemed to him; and he looked to see her lip curl.

But, so fine is the net by which fate snares, she liked the embarrassment in his voice; she liked his evident unfitness for the game of give and take. It was exciting to put it to the test – to step forward, sounding his interest – to retreat, daunted by the mystery that shrouds the unknown personality. Her feminine intuition recognized the essential – the man – in Carey, and her feminine instinct rose to meet it. Premature instinct, perhaps, in a girl of twenty! But mentally, as well as physically, the admixture of southern blood was marked by early development. As her body was built upon gracious lines, so her mind had already flowered, where others lay folded in the bud.

'You *are* nice – even without trying.' She felt her pulses throb at her own daring, and the sensation was delight.

Carey took a step forward. 'You'll have to justify that!' he said quickly. 'You'll have to give me another dance.'

Without a word, she handed him her programme; and as they bent over the little card, their heads close together, their shoulders all but touching, she was conscious that her heart was beating faster than it had beaten all the evening, exciting though the evening had been.

'Which would you like?'

'This!' He drew a line through a dance in the middle of the programme. 'And now, where will we go?'

As he handed her back the card, some crashing chords came down the room, indicating the end of the second waltz, and in response, half a dozen couples stopped at the door, and hurried out into the hall. The first to halt were his sister-in-law, Mary, and young Power; and as they passed, Mary's keen eyes swept over his face and Isabel's.

'Daisy waited ten minutes for you!' she remarked as she went by.

Isabel looked after her in surprise. 'Mary Norris didn't seem to know me!'

'Oh, you'll get used to that! It's a habit of Mary's to kiss people one day and cut them the next.'

Isabel's surprise was turned upon him. His tone, his expression, his bearing had all changed as if by magic. He had drawn back into a shell of reserve, as though in the moment of expansion some antagonistic influence had blown across his mind.

'Let us get out of this crowd,' he added in the same curt voice.

In the hall and on the stairs some chattering girls and their attendant youths had already found seats; but the hall door was open, offering a tempting view of dark trees and deserted pathways. Carey paused and looked towards it.

'I suppose you'd be afraid to go out?'

Isabel's momentary depression flared to excitement.

'Afraid? What would I be afraid of?'

'Oh, I don't know. Wet feet, I suppose. All girls' shoes are paper.'

She withdrew her fingers from his arm, and, with her head held high, led the way across the hall and out on to the gravelled pathway.

A little titter of laughter came from the stairs; she heard it and stopped.

'Were those people laughing at me?'

'No. Why?'

'No reason. Only I could kill any one who laughed at me!'

Carey looked at her through the darkness – her graceful figure bent slightly towards him, her muslin skirt held high above her white satin slippers. 'Do you always have such fiery sentiments?' he was drawn to ask.

'Oh, I feel things, yes!'

'Then I'm afraid you're going to dislike me, Miss Costello!'

There was no mistaking that his reason and his will forced him to snatch this opportunity, while his inclination stretched out detaining hands; and when such a conflict is waged in a man's mind, his expression is apt to be unnecessarily cold, his tone unnecessarily harsh.

At his words, Isabel's head went up again, with the action of a young deer scenting danger. 'Hate you? Why?'

'Let us walk on, and I'll try to tell you!'

In silence they turned and passed down the avenue – she brimming with uneasy curiosity, he girding himself to the attack.

'Do you mind if I smoke?'

'No, I don't.'

He took out a cigarette, and lighted it with the care of a man whose thoughts are upon other matters; then he threw the lighted match away into the undergrowth, where it flared for a moment and went out with a little splutter.

'Miss Costello, I had a letter the other day from my brother Frank.'

She stopped. 'From Frank?'

'Yes. He wrote – and told me.'

'Told you—?' Her voice faltered.

'Yes. Told me that you and he are engaged.'

'Oh,' she cried naïvely, 'and he never said a word to me about having written! I suppose he was afraid you'd be angry. Were you angry?'

Carey tightened the buckles of his armour. 'I was!' he said. 'Very angry.'

'And why?' Challenge and defiance leaped at him suddenly. He could feel her nerves quiver to her thought.

'Why? Oh, because a sensible man can't help being angry when he sees an act of folly; and this is folly, you know – utter folly.'

Isabel's muslin dress slipped from her fingers and trailed upon the ground. 'Why?'

'Oh, because Frank has no money, no influence – nothing in the world that could justify his marrying.'

She looked down. 'I suppose it wouldn't be so bad if the girl he wanted to marry had money of her own?' she asked in a very low voice.

Manlike, he walked into the trap. 'It certainly would make things more practicable.'

In a flash she was round upon him again, her pride and anger aflame, her sense of wounded dignity blazing in her eyes. 'Oh, I see! I see! I'm not good enough for your brother!'

Involuntarily he put out his hand. 'I never said that!'

She gave a sharp little laugh. 'Didn't you? It sounded very like it. I'm not good enough – not rich enough for him! He must wait till he can make a better match!' With a little gasp, her voice broke.

'But, my dear child—'

'I'm not a child! I'm twenty – and old enough to manage my own affairs. And I can tell you one thing! – I can tell you one thing, and that is that I'd rather die now than break off my engagement! I'd rather die now than break it off – even if I didn't care a pin for Frank!'

Carey looked at her passionate face, in which the eyes gleamed black and bright; and again he was stirred, as though a current of electricity had coursed along the rut of his commonplace life.

'Very well!' he said. 'Then I suppose we declare war? I have a will of my own, too, you know!'

She met his eyes, half curious, half amused. 'Yes,' she said with defiant seriousness. 'We do. We declare war!'

He bent his head in acceptance of the defiance; and, without another word, turned on his heel and began to walk slowly back towards the house, leaving her to follow as she pleased.

There was no chivalry in the action; it was a case of the elemental man following his instinct. But all human drama is built upon the primitive; and the fewer the stage accessories, the sooner the arrival of the psychological moment.

DANIEL CORKERY

'Nightfall'

His name was Reen, but they called him the Colonial: their way of pronouncing the word, however, could not easily be set down here. They had never used it, scarcely ever heard it until the newspapers during the Great War had dinned it into their ears. In New Zealand he had lived his many years. There he had landed in his young manhood, toiled upwards, found himself a wife, built his household, in course of years married off his three sons and his two daughters, all to the wrong people, it seemed; there at last he had buried his wife, upon which he had thrown in his hand, sold off everything, and made straight back to the rocks and the fields of his boyhood. Without warning one summer afternoon he drove into his sister's house in West Cork, a man still hardy, if grey-haired, erect enough, bright-eyed, and with the firm voice and free ways of one who had not won through without sweat and bitterness.

I

It was the quiet end of the farmer's year, a day in early October. The Renahans since morning had been building what they called the home rick. In the close beyond the cow sheds was its place from time out of mind. More than two months earlier, in August, before the corn was fit for cutting, they had built their main rick, also in its traditional place – where the pathway that wound up side of the *cummer* towards the hill-top was widest.

It was a gully for the north-west wind, this close of theirs, and they had been glad to put a crown on the day's work and get themselves within to the warmth and merriment, the fire and the card-playing. They were a large family on whom the scatter for America had not yet fallen. Even without the others who had been assisting in the work – Phil Cronin, the labouring boy; Pat Lehane, a neighbour of theirs, Kitty Mahony, a neighbour's daughter, and one of the Lynch boys – the Renahans of themselves were numerous enough to fill the flag-paved, lamp-lit kitchen with bright and noisy life. They were all in their characteristically careless working clothes, patched and repatched and unpatched, stained with mire or sulphate of copper, many-coloured, loose-fitting; and one could not but notice all this because of this Colonial relative of theirs sitting on the settle between Kitty Mahony and the blaze of the fire. How different he was from the others! This ingathering he had foreseen, perhaps had foreseen Kitty Mahony's visit, and had made himself ready for it – had shaved himself, had put on his newest clothes – he had many suits of them – chosen his heaviest watch chain, his best linen; his boots he had polished; and his thinnish hair, after drenching it with odorous oils, he had carefully brushed and creased. The others, all of them, had contented themselves with bending their long backs and washing their hands in the current of water that ran from between two rocks swiftly across the close. It was their way mostly to keep their tattered everyday caps on their heads, indoors or out; and their hair was anyhow. Kitty Mahony was the only one who had taken any care with herself before coming across the fields from her father's house; she, however, always looked clean and tidy. Everybody knew that she was to marry the eldest son of the house, Mat Renahan.

Phil Cronin and Pat Renahan, the second son, were trying to recapture a way of dancing the 'Blackbird' they had seen at Dunmanway *feis* the Sunday before, three days ago. Again and again they had tried it. They would break down, begin to argue, resume the clatter, and break down once more. The musician – the youngest of all the boys, Tim – as soon as the rhythm of their feet went into confusion, would at once take the fife from his lips, lean down over his knees, and without a word, again begin his teasing of the sheep dog which, with stiffened limbs, lay stretched between his feet on the flags.

The old Colonial gave his head a critical shake: 'No,' he said, 'that's not it; that's not a bit like it,' and he turned and put his lips almost against Kitty Mahony's shapely ear: 'They're clumsy, see? They're clumsy, you know.' 'Isn't their own way just as good?' she answered him, carelessly, without turning her head. In the dance she was taking but little interest. She was eager for her lover to return from Dunmanway: she had had no thought that he would not be in his own house before her that evening. Her eyes were firm on the open doorway, on the chilly luminous space of sky that lay beyond the firelit figures moving and dancing on the flags. Yet even these few words the old man was glad to hear: 'Yes, but they're clumsy all the time. They couldn't put any finish on it even if they had the steps, not what you'd call finish.'

But the dancers had resumed.

Every now and then the father, John Renahan, without a word would plod slowly, bulkily, heavy-footed across the room, disappearing into the dairy for something or other. Massive, silent, heavy-featured, he thought but little of disturbing the laughing group in the middle of the flags. He would hulk through them in a straight line like a surly bull making through a herd of milkers. Without breaking the rhythm they would draw aside, lifting up their chests. They were so used to his ways that they took no anger from them. Once again he entered from the close and passed through them without a word, without a sign. As he did so, the girl's thoughts took on sudden and passionate life. All those about her, the dancers, the others, were nothing to her either. They were there in that kitchen and he she would have there was elsewhere. 'I wish he'd come, oh, I wish he'd come' – her passion spoke within her so earnestly that she feared she had said the words aloud. She looked from one to another, turning her eyes only, and when she caught the annoying voice again in her ear she was almost relieved: 'There's a great change in everything, in everything. They're awkward.'

She nodded twice, and he was encouraged. He raised his voice this time, speaking to the whole room: 'You may give it up. You can't master it. You're that awkward.'

The dancers slackened off, and Pat Lehane, an onlooker leaning against the wall, took the pipe from his mouth: 'Of course we're awkward, and as you'd say, damn awkward too. And 'tisn't for want of instruction we're awkward. Our little priest, down from the Altar itself he's at us; and I'm afraid 'tis little improvement he's making in us. And the master, he says our equals for awkwardness isn't in Munster. And the returned Yanks, and they doing nothing at all themselves only strealing round, they're the worst of all. The awkward squad, that's what we are. The awkward squad that can't learn nothing.'

He was big, bony, high-coloured, with large flashing eyes, like an excited horse's, and a drooping moustache of strong hairs with dew drops pendulous at the tips of them; when speaking he threw up his head as if to give the voice free passage from the strong gristly throat. In gurgles and splashes it gushed from him; and the moods of his impetuous heart were felt in the uneven flow of it. 'The awkward squad that can't learn nothing,' and he threw his hand carelessly in the air as if there never could be question of amendment.

They were puzzled how to take him, but Tim, the musician, pointed his fife straight out at the dancers: 'The awkward squad,' he said, and throwing back his head, went into uncontrollable laughter. It was a way out. It took hold of them all; and the dancers began to look around for corners of seats to sink upon. The whole floor space in the centre of the room then lay vacant, the light falling on it.

Phil Cronin had already risen to get down the pack of cards when, whatever madness had seized on him, the old Colonial rose and stepped deliberately into the gaping space. 'Play it up, sonny,' he said to the boy, with such a motion of the hand as he might use to call a porter in a railway station.

The boy gave him a swift glance, tightened his fife with one firm twist, blew in the hole of it, and started the tune, his eyes looking straight out from under his brows at the waiting figure. Very erect he stood, silent, in the glow of the fire, his arms stiffly downwards, his head raised, and an inward expression on his features: he was listening, listening – delaying to let the music take full possession of him. As silently they all stared at him. Then he sprang out. With a lightness, even daintiness, with a restraint that puzzled them, he was tapping out the rhythm as he had learned it more than sixty years ago before decay had come upon the local traditions. But the onlookers were not impressed. They were soon aware how limited his steps were; and to them who had often seen prize dancers from Cork city or Limerick, where the dancing is even better, his style seemed old-fashioned and slow. And of course after a few minutes there was but little life left in the aged limbs. They sagged at the knees. Noticing this they took to encouraging him, whispering wondering remarks on his skill and timing. The old fool danced and danced, would dance until he dropped, it seemed, although by now his performance was little better than a sort of dull floundering.

Pat Lehane then took to letting yells of delight out of him as if he could not help it: 'Whew! Whew!' he cried: and soon the others were joining in. In the midst of the bedlam John Renahan, the father, entered in his silent way, made across the room, brushing almost against the floundering figure, whom, perhaps, the touch of a finger would now overturn. Silence fell upon them all. The fife still sang out, but not so boldly. The dancer floundered more helplessly than before. The tapping had become a sort of scraping and sliding.

As the father reached the door of the dairy room he looked along those ranged against the wall and without raising his voice said: ''Tis a shame for ye.'

Their eyes followed his rounded back as he went from them; then they looked at one another shyly. But the dancer held on. Somebody began to clap gently. They all took it up, and Pat Lehane reached his hand to the tottering figure and led Reen back to the settle.

The creature was trembling violently – one noticed it as he wiped his streaming face. His chest was heaving.

II

They heard the son of the house turning his horse and cart into the yard. Soon afterwards he entered, a bag of bran dragging heavily from his right arm.

As he sat eating his supper, he was given in whispers a glowing account of the Colonial's skill as a step-dancer. The Colonial himself, now in the centre of a little circle who, at the other side of the room, were shuffling and dealing the cards, let on not to hear what was being told to the young man. Yet they knew he was taking in every word of it. For all that whenever he played a card he raised his lips towards Kitty's ear, telling her that he was winning because she was there beside him.

When she saw that her lover had finished his meal she stood up from beside the Colonial. She could not further restrain herself. Her eyes were hot and flashing, her colour heightened. But the Colonial also stood up. He said with some huskiness in his voice, with some difficulty in making it carry: 'Maybe Mat is tired after his journey?'

Mat had been through three or four years of guerilla warfare, captaining his district. There were but few places in Munster he had not been in. He moreover had been in prison and following that in an internment camp. He had learned to shift for himself. From the colour in Kitty's cheeks, her angry eyes, her eager, parted lips, he guessed that the old man had been pestering her. He too took fire; yet he held himself in. He looked at him silently, and his smile broadened like the cold sunshine of a March day across a tract of bare countryside: 'Do I look tired?' he said.

Old Reen was confused: 'But if I went along with you, along with you, some of the way?'

The lover had put a cigarette between his lips. He leant across the table, stretching out his head until he had the tip of the cigarette above the chimney of the lamp that hung on the whitened wall. Kitty was standing uneasily in the middle of the floor. They heard the Colonial's voice again: 'My hat is upstairs.'

The cigarette had reddened: taking it from his lips Mat said nonchalantly: 'Up with you then.'

Stumbling in his eagerness Reen made up the stairs for the hat. He glowed to think what a surprising lot of things about dancing he would say to the two of them, things they could never have heard of. When he had disappeared, the lover impulsively flung open the door, held it open for the girl, put his arm about her shoulders passionately, and turned to those within: 'Give us half a mile start on that champion dancer of yours, half a mile – that's all we ask.'

They were gone, their spirits leaping within them.

When the Colonial came down with his new black hat in his hand, the roomful were very intent on their cards. He made straight out, pulling the door to behind him. Then the card playing ceased and there was a blank silence.

The father broke it saying: 'I wish to God that old idiot would go back to where he came from. And I don't like what that pair is after doing either. I don't like it at all.'

His words took the merriment out of the gathering. Soon afterwards all except the sons and daughters of the family, made out, but it was through the back door they went out. Their heavy boots were heard clamping up the rocky passage that led to the bohereen. That way they would not chance to come on a poor flustered creature groping in the darkness, making onward in sudden and reckless starts or standing still listening for any little stir that might let him know whether the lovers had gone east or west. Only in a dull way those neighbours felt that they should not care to come upon an old man so bothered in his thoughts. What a fool he was! – sixty-nine years of age, if a day, yet willing to let it slip from his memory that his life had been lived out, that his hair was grey, and that his arms would be empty for ever more. They gave no thought to the lovers. Yet, and for no reason it seemed, the spirits of the two of them as they made onwards began to leap with so astonishing an energy within them that their limbs for trembling could hardly keep the ground. Swifter and swifter they made on, whispering, wondering why they could no longer maintain their laughter.

JAMES STEPHENS
from *The Crock of Gold*

2

To the lonely house in the pine wood people sometimes came for advice on subjects too recondite for even those extremes of elucidation, the parish priest and the tavern. These people were always well received, and their perplexities were attended to instantly, for the Philosophers liked being wise and they were not ashamed to put their learning to the proof, nor were they, as so many wise people are, fearful lest they should become poor or less respected by giving away their knowledge. These were favourite maxims with them:

You must be fit to give before you can be fit to receive.

Knowledge becomes lumber in a week, therefore, get rid of it.

The box must be emptied before it can be refilled.

Refilling is progress.

A sword, a spade, and a thought should never be allowed to rust.

The Grey Woman and the Thin Woman, however, held opinions quite contrary to these, and their maxims also were different:

A secret is a weapon and a friend.

Man is God's secret, Power is man's secret, Sex is woman's secret.

By having much you are fitted to have more.

There is always room in the box.

The art of packing is the last lecture of wisdom.

The scalp of your enemy is progress.

Holding these opposed views it seemed likely that visitors seeking for advice from the Philosophers might be astonished and captured by their wives; but the women were true to their own doctrines and refused to part with information to any persons saving only those of high rank, such as policemen, gombeen men, and district and county councillors; but even to these they charged high prices for their information, and a bonus on any gains which accrued through the following of their advices. It is unnecessary to state that their following was small when compared with those who sought the assistance of their husbands, for scarcely a week passed but some person came through the pine wood with his brows in a tangle of perplexity.

In these people the children were deeply interested. They used to go apart afterwards and talk about them, and would try to remember what they looked like, how they talked, and their manner of walking or taking snuff. After a time they became interested in the problems which these people submitted to their parents and the replies or instructions wherewith the latter relieved them. Long training had made the children able to sit perfectly quiet, so that when the talk came to the interesting part they were entirely forgotten, and ideas which might otherwise have been spared their youth became the commonplaces of their conversation.

When the children were ten years of age one of the Philosophers died. He called the household together and announced that the time had come when he must bid them all good-bye, and that his intention was to die as quickly as might be. It was, he continued, an unfortunate thing that his health was at the moment more robust than it had been for a long time, but that, of course, was no obstacle to his resolution, for death did not depend upon ill-health but upon a multitude of other factors with the details whereof he would not trouble them.

His wife, the Grey Woman of Dun Gortin, applauded this resolution and added as an amendment that it was high time he did something, that the life he had been leading was an arid and unprofitable one, that he had stolen her fourteen hundred maledictions for which he had no use and presented her with a child for which she had none, and that, all things concerned, the sooner he did die and stop talking the sooner everybody concerned would be made happy.

The other Philosopher replied mildly as he lit his pipe:

'Brother, the greatest of all virtues is curiosity, and the end of all desire is wisdom; tell us, therefore, by what steps you have arrived at this commendable resolution.'

To this the Philosopher replied:

'I have attained to all the wisdom which I am fitted to bear. In the space of one week no new truth has come to me. All that I have read lately I knew before; all that I have thought has been but a recapitulation of old and wearisome ideas. There is no longer an horizon before my eyes. Space has narrowed to the petty dimensions of my thumb. Time is the tick of a clock. Good and evil are two peas in the one pod. My wife's face is the same for ever. I want to play with the children, and yet I do not want to. Your conversation with me, brother, is like the droning of a bee in a dark cell. The pine trees take root and grow and die. – It's all bosh. Good-bye.'

His friend replied:

'Brother, these are weighty reflections, and I do clearly perceive that the time has come for you to stop. I might observe, not in order to combat your views, but merely to continue an interesting conversation, that there are still some knowledges which you have not assimilated – you do not yet know how to play the tambourine, nor how to be nice to your wife, nor how to get up first in the morning and cook the breakfast. Have you learned how to smoke strong tobacco as I do? or can you dance in the moonlight with a woman of the Shee? To understand the theory which underlies all things is not sufficient. Theory is but the preparation for practice. It has occurred to me, brother, that wisdom may not be the end of everything. Goodness and kindliness are, perhaps, beyond wisdom. Is it not possible that the ultimate end is gaiety and music and a dance of joy? Wisdom is the oldest of all things. Wisdom is all head and no heart. Behold, brother, you are being crushed under the weight of your head. You are dying of old age while you are yet a child.'

'Brother,' replied the other Philosopher, 'your voice is like the droning of a bee in a dark cell. If in my latter days I am reduced to playing on the tambourine and running after a hag in the moonlight, and cooking your breakfast in the grey morning, then it is indeed time that I should die. Good-bye, brother.'

So saying, the Philosopher arose and removed all the furniture to the sides of the room so that there was a clear space left in the centre. He then took off his boots and his coat, and standing on his toes he commenced to gyrate with extraordinary rapidity. In a few moments his movements became steady and swift, and a sound came from him like the humming of a swift saw; this sound grew deeper and deeper, and at last continuous, so that the room was filled with a thrilling noise. In a quarter of an hour the movement began to noticeably slacken. In another three minutes it was quite slow. In two more minutes he grew visible again as a body, and then he wobbled to and fro, and at last dropped in a heap on the floor. He was quite dead, and on his face was an expression of serene beatitude.

'God be with you, brother,' said the remaining Philosopher, and he lit his pipe, focused his vision on the extreme tip of his nose, and began to meditate profoundly on the aphorism whether the good is the all or the all is the good. In another moment he would have become oblivious of the room, the company, and the corpse, but the Grey Woman of Dun Gortin shattered his meditation by a demand for advice as to what should next be done. The Philosopher, with an effort, detached his eyes from his nose and his mind from his maxim.

'Chaos,' said he, 'is the first condition. Order is the first law. Continuity is the first reflection. Quietude is the first happiness. Our brother is dead – bury him.' So saying, he returned his eyes to his nose, and his mind to his maxim, and lapsed to a profound reflection wherein nothing sat perched on insubstantiality, and the Spirit of Artifice goggled at the puzzle.

The Grey Woman of Dun Gortin took a pinch of snuff from her box and raised the keen over her husband:

'You were my husband and you are dead.
It is wisdom that has killed you.
If you had listened to my wisdom instead of to your own you would still be a
    trouble to me and I would still be happy.

Women are stronger than men – they do not die of wisdom.

They are better than men because they do not seek wisdom.

They are wiser than men because they know less and understand more.

Wise men are thieves – they steal wisdom from the neighbours.

I had fourteen hundred maledictions, my little store, and by a trick you stole them and left me empty.

You stole my wisdom and it has broken your neck.

I lost my knowledge and I am yet alive raising the keen over your body, but it was too heavy for you, my little knowledge.

You will never go out into the pine wood in the morning, or wander abroad on a night of stars. You will not sit in the chimney-corner on the hard nights, or go to bed, or rise again, or do anything at all from this day out.

Who will gather pine cones now when the fire is going down, or call my name in the empty house, or be angry when the kettle is not boiling?

Now I am desolate indeed. I have no knowledge, I have no husband, I have no more to say.'

'If I had anything better you should have it,' said she politely to the Thin Woman of Inis Magrath.

'Thank you,' said the Thin Woman, 'it was very nice. Shall I begin now? My husband is meditating and we may be able to annoy him.'

'Don't trouble yourself,' replied the other, 'I am past enjoyment and am, moreover, a respectable woman.'

'That is no more than the truth, indeed.'

'I have always done the right thing at the right time.'

'I'd be the last body in the world to deny that,' was the warm response.

'Very well, then,' said the Grey Woman, and she commenced to take off her boots. She stood in the centre of the room and balanced herself on her toes.

'You are a decent, respectable lady,' said the Thin Woman of Inis Magrath, and then the Grey Woman began to gyrate rapidly and more rapidly until she was a very fervour of motion, and in three-quarters of an hour (for she was very tough) she began to slacken, grew visible, wobbled, and fell beside her dead husband, and on her face was a beatitude almost surpassing his.

The Thin Woman of Inis Magrath smacked the children and put them to bed, next she buried the two bodies under the hearthstone, and then, with some trouble, detached her husband from his meditations. When he became capable of ordinary occurrences she detailed all that had happened, and said that he alone was to blame for the sad bereavement. He replied:

'The toxin generates the anti-toxin. The end lies concealed in the beginning. All bodies grow around a skeleton. Life is a petticoat about death. I will not go to bed.'

'A Glass of Beer'

It was now his custom to sit there. The world has its habits, why should a man not have his? The earth rolls out of light and into darkness as punctually as a business man goes to and from his office; the seasons come with the regularity of automata, and go as if they were pushed by an ejector; so, night after night, he strolled from the Place de l'Observatoire to the Pont St Michel, and, on the return journey, sat down at the same Café, at the same table, if he could manage it, and ordered the same drink.

So regular had his attendance become that the waiter would suggest the order before it was spoken. He did not drink beer because he liked it, but only because it was not a difficult thing to ask for. Always he had been easily discouraged, and he distrusted his French almost as much as other people had reason to. The only time he had varied the order was to request 'un vin blanc gommée', but on that occasion he had been served with a postage stamp for twenty-five centimes, and he still wondered when he remembered it.

He liked to think of his first French conversation. He wanted something to read in English, but was timid of asking for it. He walked past all the newspaper kiosks on the Boulevard, anxiously scanning the vendors inside – they were usually very stalwart, very competent females, who looked as though they had outgrown their sins but remembered them with pleasure. They had the dully-polished, slightly-battered look of a modern antique. The words 'M'sieu, Madame' rang from them as from bells. They were very alert, sitting, as it were, on tiptoe, and their eyes hit one as one approached. They were like spiders squatting in their little houses waiting for their daily flies.

He found one who looked jolly and harmless, sympathetic indeed, and to her, with a flourished hat, he approached. Said he, 'Donnez-moi, Madame, s'il vous plaît, le *Daily Mail.*' At the second repetition the good lady smiled at him, a smile compounded of benevolence and comprehension, and instantly, with a 'V'la M'sieu,' she handed him *The New York Herald.* They had saluted each other, and he marched down the road in delight, with his first purchase under his arm and his first foreign conversation accomplished.

At that time everything had delighted him – the wide, well-lighted Boulevard, the concierges knitting in their immense doorways, each looking like a replica of the other, each seeming sister to a kiosk-keeper or a cat. The exactly-courteous speech of the people and their not quite so rigorously courteous manners pleased him. He listened to the voluble men who went by, speaking in a haste so breathless that he marvelled how the prepositions and conjunctions stuck to their duty in so swirling an ocean of chatter. There was a big black dog with a mottled head who lay nightly on the pavement opposite the Square de l'Observatoire. At intervals he raised his lean skull from the ground and composed a low lament to an absent friend. His grief was respected. The folk who passed stepped sidewards for him, and he took no heed of their passage – a lonely, introspective dog to whom a caress or a bone were equally childish things: Let me alone, he seemed to say, I have my grief, and it is company enough. There was the very superior cat who sat on every window-ledge, winking at life. He (for in France all cats are masculine by order of philology) did not care a rap for man or dog, but he liked women and permitted them to observe him. There was the man who insinuated himself between the tables at the Café, holding out postcard-representations of the Panthéon, the Louvre, Notre-Dame, and other places. From beneath these cards his dexterous little finger would suddenly flip others. One saw a hurried leg, an arm that shone and vanished, a bosom that fled shyly again, an audacious swan, a Leda who was thoroughly enjoying herself and had never heard of virtue. His look suggested that he thought better of one than to suppose that one was not interested in the nude. 'M'sieu,' he seemed to say, with his fixed, brown-eyed regard, 'this is indeed a leg, an authentic leg, not disguised by even the littlest of stockings; it is arranged precisely as M'sieu would desire it.' His sorrow as he went away was dignified with a regret for an inartistic gentleman. One was *en garçon*, and yet one would not look at one's postcards! One had better then cease to be an artist and take to peddling onions and asparagus as the vulgar do.

It was all a long time ago, and now, somehow, the savour had departed from these things. Perhaps he had seen them too often. Perhaps a kind of public surreptitiousness, a quite open furtiveness, had troubled him. Maybe he was not well. He sat at his Café, three quarters down the Boulevard, and before him a multitude of grotesque beings were pacing as he sipped his bock.

Good manners decreed that he should not stare too steadfastly, and he was one who obeyed these delicate dictations. Alas! he was one who obeyed all dictations. For him authority wore a halo, and many sins which his heyday ought to have committed had been left undone only because they were not sanctioned by immediate social usage. He was often saddened when he thought of the things he had not done. It was the only sadness to which he had access, because the evil deeds which he had committed were of so tepid and hygienic a character that they could not be mourned for without hypocrisy; and now that he was released from all privileged restraints and overlookings and could do whatever he wished, he had no wish to do anything.

His wife had been dead for over a year. He had hungered, he had prayed for her death. He had hated that woman (and for how many years!) with a kind of masked ferocity. How often he had been tempted to kill her or to kill himself! How often he had dreamed that she had run away from him or that he had run away from her! He had invented Russian Princes, and Music Hall Stars, and American Billionaires with whom she could adequately elope, and he had both loved and loathed the prospect. What unending, slow quarrels they had together! How her voice had droned pitilessly on his ears! She in one room, he in another, and through the open door there rolled that unending recitation of woes and reproaches, an interminable catalogue of nothings, while he sat dumb as a fish, with a mind that smouldered or blazed. He had stood unseen with a hammer, a poker, a razor in his hand, on tiptoe to do it. A movement, a rush, one silent rush and it was done! He had revelled in her murder. He had caressed it, rehearsed it, relished it, had jerked her head back, and hacked, and listened to her entreaties bubbling through blood!

And then she died! When he stood by her bed he had wished to taunt her, but he could not do it. He read in her eyes – I am dying, and in a little time I shall have vanished like dust on the wind, but you will still be here, and you will never see me again. – He wished to ratify that, to assure her that it was actually so, to say that he would come home on the morrow night, and she would not be there, and that he would return home every night, and she would never be there. But he could not say it. Somehow the words, although he desired them, would not come. His arm went to her neck and settled there. His hand caressed her hair, her cheek. He kissed her eyes, her lips, her languid hands; and the words that came were only an infantile babble of regrets and apologies, assurances that he did love her, that he had never loved any one before, and never would love any one again . . .

Everyone who passed looked into the Café where he sat. Everyone who passed looked at him. There were men with sallow faces and wide black hats. Some had hair that flapped about them in the wind, and from their locks one gathered, with some distaste, the spices of Araby. Some had cravats that fluttered and fell and rose again like banners in a storm. There were men with severe, spade-shaped, most responsible-looking beards, and quizzical little eyes which gave the lie to their hairy sedateness – eyes which had spent long years in looking sidewards as a woman passed. There were men of every stage of foppishness – men who had spent so much time on their moustaches that they had only a little left for their finger-nails, but their moustaches exonerated them; others who were coated to happiness, trousered to grotesqueness, and booted to misery. He thought – In this city the men wear their own coats, but they all wear someone else's trousers, and their boots are syndicated.

He saw no person who was self-intent. They were all deeply conscious, not of themselves, but of each other. They were all looking at each other. They were all looking at him; and he returned the severe, or humorous, or appraising gaze of each with a look nicely proportioned to the passer, giving back exactly what was given to him, and no more. He did not stare, for nobody stared. He just looked and looked away, and was as mannerly as was required.

A negro went by arm in arm with a girl who was so sallow that she was only white by courtesy. He was a bulky man, and as he bent greedily over his companion it was evident that to him she was whiter than the snow of a single night.

Women went past in multitudes, and he knew the appearance of them all. How many times he had watched them or their duplicates striding and mincing and bounding by, each moving like an animated note of interrogation! They were long, and medium, and short. There were women of a thinness beyond comparison, sheathed in skirts as featly as a rapier in a scabbard. There were women of a monumental, a mighty fatness, who billowed and rolled in multitudinous, stormy garments. There were slow eyes that drooped on one as heavily as a hand, and quick ones that stabbed and withdrew, and glanced again appealingly, and slid away cursing. There were some who lounged with a false sedateness, and some who fluttered in an equally false timidity. Some wore velvet shoes without heels. Some had shoes, the heels whereof were of such inordinate length that the wearers looked as though they were perched on stilts and would topple to perdition if their skill failed for an instant. They passed and they looked at him; and from each, after the due regard, he looked away to the next in interminable procession.

There were faces also to be looked at: round chubby faces wherefrom the eyes of oxen stared in slow, involved rumination. Long faces that were keener than hatchets and as cruel. Faces that pretended to be scornful and were only piteous. Faces contrived to ape a temperament other than their own. Raddled faces with heavy eyes and rouged lips. Ragged lips that had been chewed by every mad dog in the world. What lips there were everywhere! Bright scarlet splashes in dead-white faces. Thin red gashes that suggested rat-traps instead of kisses. Bulbous, flabby lips that would wobble and shiver if attention failed them. Lips of a horrid fascination that one looked at and hated and ran to. Looking at him slyly or boldly, they passed along, and turned after a while and repassed him, and turned again in promenade.

He had a sickness of them all. There had been a time when these were among the things he mourned for not having done, but that time was long past. He guessed at their pleasures, and knew them to be without salt. Life, said he, is as unpleasant as a plate of cold porridge. Somehow the world was growing empty for him. He wondered was he outgrowing his illusions, or his appetites, or both? The things in which other men took such interest were drifting beyond him, and (for it seemed that the law of compensation can fail) nothing was drifting towards him in recompense. He foresaw himself as a box with nothing inside it, and he thought – It is not through love or fear or distress that men commit suicide: it is because they have become empty: both the gods and the devils have deserted them and they can no longer support that solemn stagnation. He marvelled to see with what activity men and women played the most savourless of games! With what zest of pursuit they tracked what petty interests. He saw them as ants scurrying with scraps of straw, or apes that pick up and drop and pick again, and he marvelled from what fount they renewed themselves, or with what charms they exorcized the demons of satiety.

On this night life did not seem worth while. The taste had gone from his mouth; his bock was water vilely coloured; his cigarette was a hot stench. And yet a full moon was peeping in the trees along the path, and not far away, where the country-side bowed in silver quietude, the rivers ran through undistinguishable fields chanting their lonely songs. The seas leaped and withdrew, and called again to the stars, and gathered in ecstasy and roared skywards, and the trees did not rob each other more than was absolutely necessary. The men and women were all hidden away, sleeping in their cells, where the moon could not see them, nor the clean wind, nor the stars. They were sundered for a little while from their eternal arithmetic. The grasping hands were lying as quietly as the paws of a sleeping dog. Those eyes held no further speculation than the eyes of an ox who lies down. The tongues that had lied all day, and been treacherous and obscene and respectful by easy turn, said nothing more; and he thought it was very good that they were all hidden, and that for a little time the world might swing darkly with the moon in its own wide circle and its silence.

He paid for his bock, gave the waiter a tip, touched his hat to a lady by sex and a gentleman by clothing, and strolled back to his room that was little, his candle that was three-quarters consumed, and his picture which might be admired when he was dead but which he would never be praised for painting; and, after sticking his foot through the canvas, he tugged himself to bed, agreeing to commence the following morning just as he had the previous one, and the one before that, and the one before that again.

JAMES JOYCE

'The Dead'

Lily, the caretaker's daughter, was literally run off her feet. Hardly had she brought one gentleman into the little pantry behind the office on the ground floor and helped him off with his overcoat than the wheezy hall-door bell clanged again and she had to scamper along the bare hallway to let in another guest. It was well for her she had not to attend to the ladies also. But Miss Kate and Miss Julia had thought of that and had converted the bathroom upstairs into a ladies' dressing-room. Miss Kate and Miss Julia were there, gossiping and laughing, and fussing, walking after each other to the head of the stairs, peering down over the banisters and calling down to Lily to ask her who had come.

It was always a great affair, the Misses Morkan's annual dance. Everybody who knew them came to it, members of the family, old friends of the family, the members of Julia's choir, any of Kate's pupils that were grown up enough and even some of Mary Jane's pupils too. Never once had it fallen flat. For years and years it had gone off in splendid style as long as anyone could remember; ever since Kate and Julia, after the death of their brother Pat, had left the house in Stoney Batter and taken Mary Jane, their only niece, to live with them in the dark gaunt house on Usher's Island, the upper part of which they had rented from Mr Fulham, the corn-factor on the ground floor. That was a good thirty years ago if it was a day. Mary Jane, who was then a little girl in short clothes, was now the main prop of the household for she had the organ in Haddington Road. She had been through the Academy and gave a pupils' concert every year in the upper room of the Antient Concert Rooms. Many of her pupils belonged to the better-class families on the Kingstown and Dalkey line. Old as they were, her aunts also did their share. Julia, though she was quite grey, was still the leading soprano in Adam and Eve's, and Kate, being too feeble to go about much, gave music lessons to beginners on the old square piano in the back room. Lily, the caretaker's daughter, did housemaid's work for them. Though their life was modest they believed in eating well; the best of everything: diamond-bone sirloins, three-shilling tea and the best bottled stout. But Lily seldom made a mistake in the orders so that she got on well with her three mistresses. They were fussy, that was all. But the only thing they would not stand was back answers.

Of course they had good reason to be fussy on such a night. And then it was long after ten o'clock and yet there was no sign of Gabriel and his wife. Besides they were dreadfully afraid that Freddy Malins might turn up screwed. They would not wish for worlds that any of Mary Jane's pupils should see him under the influence; and when he was like that it was sometimes very hard to manage him. Freddy Malins always came late but they wondered what could be keeping Gabriel: and that was what brought them every two minutes to the banisters to ask Lily had Gabriel or Freddy come.

– O, Mr Conroy, said Lily to Gabriel when she opened the door for him, Miss Kate and Miss Julia thought you were never coming. Good-night, Mrs Conroy.

— I'll engage they did, said Gabriel, but they forget that my wife here takes three mortal hours to dress herself.

He stood on the mat, scraping the snow from his goloshes, while Lily led his wife to the foot of the stairs and called out:

— Miss Kate, here's Mrs Conroy.

Kate and Julia came toddling down the dark stairs at once. Both of them kissed Gabriel's wife, said she must be perished alive and asked was Gabriel with her.

— Here I am as right as the mail, Aunt Kate! Go on up, I'll follow, called out Gabriel from the dark.

He continued scraping his feet vigorously while the three women went upstairs, laughing, to the ladies' dressing-room. A light fringe of snow lay like a cape on the shoulders of his overcoat and like toecaps on the toes of his goloshes; and, as the buttons of his overcoat slipped with a squeaking noise through the snow-stiffened frieze, a cold fragrant air from out-of-doors escaped from crevices and folds.

— Is is snowing again, Mr Conroy? asked Lily.

She had preceded him into the pantry to help him off with his overcoat. Gabriel smiled at the three syllables she had given his surname and glanced at her. She was a slim, growing girl, pale in complexion and with hay-coloured hair. The gas in the pantry made her look still paler. Gabriel had known her when she was a child and used to sit on the lowest step nursing a rag doll.

— Yes, Lily, he answered, and I think we're in for a night of it.

He looked up at the pantry ceiling, which was shaking with the stamping and shuffling of feet on the floor above, listened for a moment to the piano and then glanced at the girl, who was folding his overcoat carefully at the end of a shelf.

— Tell me, Lily, he said in a friendly tone, do you still go to school?

— O no, sir, she answered. I'm done schooling this year and more.

— O, then, said Gabriel gaily, I suppose we'll be going to your wedding one of these fine days with your young man, eh?

The girl glanced back at him over her shoulder and said with great bitterness:

— The men that is now is only all palaver and what they can get out of you.

Gabriel coloured as if he felt he had made a mistake and, without looking at her, kicked off his goloshes and flicked actively with his muffler at his patent-leather shoes.

He was a stout tallish young man. The high colour of his cheeks pushed upwards even to his forehead where it scattered itself in a few formless patches of pale red; and on his hairless face there scintillated restlessly the polished lenses and the bright gilt rims of the glasses which screened his delicate and restless eyes. His glossy black hair was parted in the middle and brushed in a long curve behind his ears where it curled slightly beneath the groove left by his hat.

When he had flicked lustre into his shoes he stood up and pulled his waistcoat down more tightly on his plump body. Then he took a coin rapidly from his pocket.

— O Lily, he said, thrusting it into her hands, it's Christmas-time, isn't it? Just . . . here's a little . . .

He walked rapidly towards the door.

— O no, sir! cried the girl, following him. Really, sir, I wouldn't take it.

– Christmas-time! Christmas-time! said Gabriel, almost trotting to the stairs and waving his hand to her in deprecation.

The girl, seeing that he had gained the stairs, called out after him:

– Well, thank you, sir.

He waited outside the drawing-room door until the waltz should finish, listening to the skirts that swept against it and to the shuffling of feet. He was still discomposed by the girl's bitter and sudden retort. It had cast a gloom over him which he tried to dispel by arranging his cuffs and the bows of his tie. He then took from his waistcoat pocket a little paper and glanced at the headings he had made for his speech. He was undecided about the lines from Robert Browning for he feared they would be above the heads of his hearers. Some quotation that they would recognize from Shakespeare or from the Melodies would be better. The indelicate clacking of the men's heels and the shuffling of their soles reminded him that their grade of culture differed from his. He would only make himself ridiculous by quoting poetry to them which they could not understand. They would think that he was airing his superior education. He would fail with them just as he had failed with the girl in the pantry. He had taken up a wrong tone. His whole speech was a mistake from first to last, an utter failure.

Just then his aunts and his wife came out of the ladies' dressing-room. His aunts were two small plainly dressed old women. Aunt Julia was an inch or so the taller. Her hair, drawn low over the tops of her ears, was grey; and grey also, with darker shadows, was her large flaccid face. Though she was stout in build and stood erect her slow eyes and parted lips gave her the appearance of a woman who did not know where she was or where she was going. Aunt Kate was more vivacious. Her face, healthier than her sister's, was all puckers and creases, like a shrivelled red apple, and her hair, braided in the same old-fashioned way, had not lost its ripe nut colour.

They both kissed Gabriel frankly. He was their favourite nephew, the son of their dead elder sister, Ellen, who had married T. J. Conroy of the Port and Docks.

– Gretta tells me you're not going to take a cab back to Monkstown to-night, Gabriel, said Aunt Kate.

– No, said Gabriel, turning to his wife, we had quite enough of that last year, hadn't we? Don't you remember, Aunt Kate, what a cold Gretta got out of it? Cab windows rattling all the way, and the east wind blowing in after we passed Merrion. Very jolly it was. Gretta caught a dreadful cold.

Aunt Kate frowned severely and nodded her head at every word.

– Quite right, Gabriel, quite right, she said. You can't be too careful.

– But as for Gretta there, said Gabriel, she'd walk home in the snow if she were let.

Mrs Conroy laughed.

– Don't mind him, Aunt Kate, she said. He's really an awful bother, what with green shades for Tom's eyes at night and making him do the dumb-bells, and forcing Eva to eat the stirabout. The poor child! And she simply hates the sight of it! . . . O, but you'll never guess what he makes me wear now!

She broke out into a peal of laughter and glanced at her husband, whose admiring and happy eyes had been wandering from her dress to her face and hair. The two aunts laughed heartily too, for Gabriel's solicitude was a standing joke with them.

– Goloshes! said Mrs Conroy. That's the latest. Whenever it's wet underfoot I must put on my goloshes. To-night even he wanted me to put them on, but I wouldn't. The next thing he'll buy me will be a diving suit.

Gabriel laughed nervously and patted his tie reassuringly while Aunt Kate nearly doubled herself, so heartily did she enjoy the joke. The smile soon faded from Aunt Julia's face and her mirthless eyes were directed towards her nephew's face. After a pause she asked:

– And what are goloshes, Gabriel?

– Goloshes, Julia! exclaimed her sister. Goodness me, don't you know what goloshes are? You wear them over your . . . over your boots, Gretta, isn't it?

– Yes, said Mrs Conroy. Guttapercha things. We both have a pair now. Gabriel says everyone wears them on the continent.

– O, on the continent, murmured Aunt Julia, nodding her head slowly.

Gabriel knitted his brows and said, as if he were slightly angered:

– It's nothing very wonderful but Gretta thinks it very funny because she says the word reminds her of Christy Minstrels.

– But tell me, Gabriel, said Aunt Kate, with brisk tact. Of course, you've seen about the room. Gretta was saying . . .

– O, the room is all right, replied Gabriel. I've taken one in the Gresham.

– To be sure, said Aunt Kate, by far the best thing to do. And the children, Gretta, you're not anxious about them?

– O, for one night, said Mrs Conroy. Besides, Bessie will look after them.

– To be sure, said Aunt Kate again. What a comfort it is to have a girl like that, one you can depend on! There's that Lily, I'm sure I don't know what has come over her lately. She's not the girl she was at all.

Gabriel was about to ask his aunt some questions on this point but she broke off suddenly to gaze after her sister who had wandered down the stairs and was craning her neck over the banisters.

– Now, I ask you, she said, almost testily, where is Julia going? Julia! Julia! Where are you going?

Julia, who had gone halfway down one flight, came back and announced blandly:

– Here's Freddy.

At the same moment a clapping of hands and a final flourish of the pianist told that the waltz had ended. The drawing-room door was opened from within and some couples came out. Aunt Kate drew Gabriel aside hurriedly and whispered into his ear:

– Slip down, Gabriel, like a good fellow and see if he's all right, and don't let him up if he's screwed. I'm sure he's screwed. I'm sure he is.

Gabriel went to the stairs and listened over the banisters. He could hear two persons talking in the pantry. Then he recognized Freddy Malins' laugh. He went down the stairs noisily.

– It's such a relief, said Aunt Kate to Mrs Conroy, that Gabriel is here. I always feel easier in my mind when he's here . . .Julia, there's Miss Daly and Miss Power will take some refreshment. Thanks for your beautiful waltz, Miss Daly. It made lovely time.

A tall wizen-faced man, with a stiff grizzled moustache and swarthy skin, who was passing out with his partner said:

– And may we have some refreshment, too, Miss Morkan?

– Julia, said Aunt Kate summarily, and here's Mr Browne and Miss Furlong. Take them in, Julia, with Miss Daly and Miss Power.

– I'm the man for the ladies, said Mr Browne, pursing his lips until his moustache bristled and smiling in all his wrinkles. You know, Miss Morkan, the reason they are so fond of me is–

He did not finish his sentence, but, seeing that Aunt Kate was out of earshot, at once led the three young ladies into the back room. The middle of the room was occupied by two square tables placed end to end, and on these Aunt Julia and the caretaker were straightening and smoothing a large cloth. On the sideboard were arrayed dishes and plates, and glasses and bundles of knives and forks and spoons. The top of the closed square piano served also as a sideboard for viands and sweets. At a smaller sideboard in one corner two young men were standing, drinking hop-bitters.

Mr Browne led his charges thither and invited them all, in jest, to some ladies' punch, hot, strong and sweet. As they said they never took anything strong he opened three bottles of lemonade for them. Then he asked one of the young men to move aside, and, taking hold of the decanter, filled out for himself a goodly measure of whisky. The young men eyed him respectfully while he took a trial sip.

– God help me, he said, smiling, it's the doctor's orders.

His wizened face broke into a broader smile, and the three young ladies laughed in musical echo to his pleasantry, swaying their bodies to and fro, with nervous jerks of their shoulders. The boldest said:

– O, now, Mr Browne, I'm sure the doctor never ordered anything of the kind.

Mr Browne took another sip of his whisky and said, with sidling mimicry:

– Well, you see, I'm like the famous Mrs Cassidy, who is reported to have said: *Now, Mary Grimes, if I don't take it, make me take it, for I feel I want it.*

His hot face had leaned forward a little too confidentially and he had assumed a very low Dublin accent so that the young ladies, with one instinct, received his speech in silence. Miss Furlong, who was one of Mary Jane's pupils, asked Miss Daly what was the name of the pretty waltz she had played; and Mr Browne, seeing that he was ignored, turned promptly to the two young men who were more appreciative.

A red-faced young woman, dressed in pansy, came into the room, excitedly clapping her hands and crying:

– Quadrilles! Quadrilles!

Close on her heels came Aunt Kate, crying:

– Two gentlemen and three ladies, Mary Jane!

– O, here's Mr Bergin and Mr Kerrigan, said Mary Jane. Mr Kerrigan, will you take Miss Power? Miss Furlong, may I get you a partner, Mr Bergin. O, that'll just do now.

– Three ladies, Mary Jane, said Aunt Kate.

The two young gentlemen asked the ladies if they might have the pleasure, and Mary Jane turned to Miss Daly.

— O, Miss Daly, you're really awfully good, after playing for the last two dances, but really we're so short of ladies to-night.

— I don't mind in the least, Miss Morkan.

— But I've a nice partner for you, Mr Bartell D'Arcy, the tenor. I'll get him to sing later on. All Dublin is raving about him.

— Lovely voice, lovely voice! said Aunt Kate.

As the piano had twice begun the prelude to the first figure Mary Jane led her recruits quickly from the room. They had hardly gone when Aunt Julia wandered slowly into the room, looking behind her at something.

— What is the matter, Julia? asked Aunt Kate anxiously. Who is it?

Julia, who was carrying in a column of table-napkins, turned to her sister and said, simply, as if the question had surprised her:

— It's only Freddy, Kate, and Gabriel with him.

In fact right behind her Gabriel could be seen piloting Freddy Malins across the landing. The latter, a young man of about forty, was of Gabriel's size and build, with very round shoulders. His face was fleshy and pallid, touched with colour only at the thick hanging lobes of his ears and at the wide wings of his nose. He had coarse features, a blunt nose, a convex and receding brow, timid and protruded lips. His heavy-lidded eyes and the disorder of his scanty hair made him look sleepy. He was laughing heartily in a high key at a story which he had been telling Gabriel on the stairs and at the same time rubbing the knuckles of his left fist backwards and forwards into his left eye.

— Good evening, Freddy, said Aunt Julia.

Freddy Malins bade the Misses Morkan good-evening in what seemed an off hand fashion by reason of the habitual catch in his voice and then, seeing that Mr Browne was grinning at him from the sideboard, crossed the room on rather shaky legs and began to repeat in an undertone the story he had just told to Gabriel.

— He's not so bad, is he? said Aunt Kate to Gabriel.

Gabriel's brows were dark but he raised them quickly and answered:

— O no, hardly noticeable.

— Now, isn't he a terrible fellow! she said. And his poor mother made him take the pledge on New Year's Eve. But come on, Gabriel, into the drawing-room.

Before leaving the room with Gabriel she signalled to Mr Browne by frowning and shaking her forefinger in warning to and fro. Mr Browne nodded in answer and, when she had gone, said to Freddy Malins:

— Now, then, Teddy, I'm going to fill you out a good glass of lemonade just to buck you up.

Freddy Malins, who was nearing the climax of his story, waved the offer aside impatiently but Mr Browne, having first called Freddy Malins' attention to a disarray in his dress, filled out and handed him a full glass of lemonade. Freddy Malins' left hand accepted the glass mechanically, his right hand being engaged in the mechanical readjustment of his dress. Mr Browne, whose face was once more wrinkling with mirth, poured out for himself a glass of whisky while Freddy Malins exploded, before he had well reached the climax of his story, in a kink of high-pitched bronchitic laughter and, setting down his untasted and overflowing glass, began to rub the knuckles of his left first backwards and forwards into his left eye, repeating words of his last phrase as well as his fit of laughter would allow him.

*   *   *

Gabriel could not listen while Mary Jane was playing her Academy piece, full of runs and difficult passages, to the hushed drawing-room. He liked music but the piece she was playing had no melody for him and he doubted whether it had any melody for the other listeners, though they had begged Mary Jane to play something. Four young men, who had come from the refreshment-room to stand in the doorway at the sound of the piano, had gone away quietly in couples after a few minutes. The only persons who seemed to follow the music were Mary Jane herself, her hands racing along the key-board or lifted from it at the pauses like those of a priestess in momentary imprecation, and Aunt Kate standing at her elbow to turn the page.

Gabriel's eyes, irritated by the floor, which glittered with beeswax under the heavy chandelier, wandered to the wall above the piano. A picture of the balcony scene in *Romeo and Juliet* hung there and beside it was a picture of the two murdered princes in the Tower which Aunt Julia had worked in red, blue and brown wools when she was a girl. Probably in the school they had gone to as girls that kind of work had been taught for one year his mother had worked for him as a birthday present a waistcoat of purple tabinet, with little foxes' heads upon it, lined with brown satin and having round mulberry buttons. It was strange that his mother had had no musical talent though Aunt Kate used to call her the brains carrier of the Morkan family. Both she and Julia had always seemed a little proud of their serious and matronly sister. Her photograph stood before the pierglass. She had an open book on her knees and was pointing out something in it to Constantine who, dressed in a man-o'-war suit, lay at her feet. It was she who had chosen the names for her sons for she was very sensible of the dignity of family life. Thanks to her, Constantine was now senior curate in Balbriggan and, thanks to her, Gabriel himself had taken his degree in the Royal University. A shadow passed over his face as he remembered her sullen opposition to his marriage. Some slighting phrases she had used still rankled in his memory; she had once spoken of Gretta as being country cute and that was not true of Gretta at all. It was Gretta who had nursed her during all her last long illness in their house at Monkstown.

He knew that Mary Jane must be near the end of her piece for she was playing again the opening melody with runs of scales after every bar and while he waited for the end the resentment died down in his heart. The piece ended with a trill of octaves in the treble and a final deep octave in the bass. Great applause greeted Mary Jane as, blushing and rolling up her music nervously, she escaped from the room. The most vigorous clapping came from the four young men in the doorway who had gone away to the refreshment-room at the beginning of the piece but had come back when the piano had stopped.

Lancers were arranged. Gabriel found himself partnered with Miss Ivors. She was a frank-mannered talkative young lady, with a freckled face and prominent brown eyes. She did not wear a low-cut bodice and the large brooch which was fixed in the front of her collar bore on it an Irish device.

When they had taken their places she said abruptly:

— I have a crow to pluck with you.

— With me? said Gabriel.

She nodded her head gravely.

— What is it? asked Gabriel, smiling at her solemn manner.

— Who is G. C.? answered Miss Ivors, turning her eyes upon him.

Gabriel coloured and was about to knit his brows, as if he did not understand, when she said bluntly:

— O, innocent Amy! I have found out that you write for *The Daily Express*. Now, aren't you ashamed of yourself?

— Why should I be ashamed of myself? asked Gabriel, blinking his eyes and trying to smile.

— Well, I'm ashamed of you, said Miss Ivors frankly. To say you'd write for a rag like that. I didn't think you were a West Briton.

A look of perplexity appeared on Gabriel's face. It was true that he wrote a literary column every Wednesday in *The Daily Express*, for which he was paid fifteen shillings. But that did not make him a West Briton surely. The books he received for review were almost more welcome than the paltry cheque. He loved to feel the covers and turn over the pages of newly printed books. Nearly every day when his teaching in the college was ended he used to wander down the quays to the second-hand booksellers, to Hickey's on Bachelor's Walk, to Webb's or Massey's on Aston's Quay, or to O'Clohissey's in the by-street. He did not know how to meet her charge. He wanted to say that literature was above politics. But they were friends of many years' standing and their careers had been parallel, first at the University and then as teachers: he could not risk a grandiose phrase with her. He continued blinking his eyes and trying to smile and murmured lamely that he saw nothing political in writing reviews of books.

When their turn to cross had come he was still perplexed and inattentive. Miss Ivors promptly took his hand in a warm grasp and said in a soft friendly tone:

— Of course, I was only joking. Come, we cross now.

When they were together again she spoke of the University question and Gabriel felt more at ease. A friend of hers had shown her his review of Browning's poems. That was how she had found out the secret: but she liked the review immensely. Then she said suddenly:

— O, Mr Conroy, will you come for an excursion to the Aran Isles this summer? We're going to stay there a whole month. It will be splendid out in the Atlantic. You ought to come. Mr Clancy is coming, and Mr Kilkelly and Kathleen Kearney. It would be splendid for Gretta too if she'd come. She's from Connacht, isn't she?

— Her people are, said Gabriel shortly.

— But you will come, won't you? said Miss Ivors, laying her warm hand eagerly on his arm.

— The fact is, said Gabriel, I have already arranged to go —

— Go where? asked Miss Ivors.

— Well, you know, every year I go for a cycling tour with some fellows and so —

— But where? asked Miss Ivors.

– Well, we usually go to France or Belgium or perhaps Germany, said Gabriel awkwardly.

– And why do you go to France and Belgium, said Miss Ivors, instead of visiting your own land?

– Well, said Gabriel, it's partly to keep in touch with the languages and partly for a change.

– And haven't you your own language to keep in touch with – Irish? asked Miss Ivors.

– Well, said Gabriel, if it comes to that, you know, Irish is not my language.

Their neighbours had turned to listen to the cross-examination. Gabriel glanced right and left nervously and tried to keep his good humour under the ordeal which was making a blush invade his forehead.

– And haven't you your own land to visit, continued Miss Ivors, that you know nothing of, your own people, and your own country?

– O, to tell you the truth, retorted Gabriel suddenly, I'm sick of my own country, sick of it!

– Why? asked Miss Ivors.

Gabriel did not answer for his retort had heated him.

– Why? repeated Miss Ivors.

They had to go visiting together and, as he had not answered her, Miss Ivors said warmly:

– Of course, you've no answer.

Gabriel tried to cover his agitation by taking part in the dance with great energy. He avoided her eyes for he had seen a sour expression on her face. But when they met in the long chain he was surprised to feel his hand firmly pressed. She looked at him from under her brows for a moment quizzically until he smiled. Then, just as the chain was about to start again, she stood on tiptoe and whispered into his ear:

– West Briton!

When the lancers were over Gabriel went away to a remote corner of the room where Freddy Malins' mother was sitting. She was a stout feeble old woman with white hair. Her voice had a catch in it like her son's and she stuttered slightly. She had been told that Freddy had come and that he was nearly all right. Gabriel asked her whether she had had a good crossing. She lived with her married daughter in Glasgow and came to Dublin on a visit once a year. She answered placidly that she had had a beautiful crossing and that the captain had been most attentive to her. She spoke also of the beautiful house her daughter kept in Glasgow, and of all the nice friends they had there. While her tongue rambled on Gabriel tried to banish from his mind all memory of the unpleasant incident with Miss Ivors. Of course the girl or woman, or whatever she was, was an enthusiast but there was a time for all things. Perhaps he ought not to have answered her like that. But she had no right to call him a West Briton before people, even in joke. She had tried to make him ridiculous before people, heckling him and staring at him with her rabbit's eyes.

He saw his wife making her way towards him through the waltzing couples. When she reached him she said into his ear:

– Gabriel, Aunt Kate wants to know won't you carve the goose as usual. Miss Daly will carve the ham and I'll do the pudding.

— All right, said Gabriel.

— She's sending in the younger ones first as soon as this waltz is over so that we'll have the table to ourselves.

— Were you dancing? asked Gabriel.

— Of course I was. Didn't you see me? What words had you with Molly Ivors?

— No words. Why? Did she say so?

— Something like that. I'm trying to get that Mr D'Arcy to sing. He's full of conceit, I think.

— There were no words, said Gabriel moodily, only she wanted me to go for a trip to the west of Ireland and I said I wouldn't.

His wife clasped her hands excitedly and gave a little jump.

— O, do go, Gabriel, she cried. I'd love to see Galway again.

— You can go if you like, said Gabriel coldly.

She looked at him for a moment, then turned to Mrs Malins and said:

— There's a nice husband for you, Mrs Malins.

While she was threading her way back across the room Mrs Malins, without adverting to the interruption, went on to tell Gabriel what beautiful places there were in Scotland and the beautiful scenery. Her son-in-law brought them every year to the lakes and they used to go fishing. Her son-in-law was a splendid fisher. One day he caught a fish, a beautiful big big fish, and the man in the hotel boiled it for their dinner.

Gabriel hardly heard what she said. Now that supper was coming near he began to think again about his speech and about the quotation. When he saw Freddy Malins coming across the room to visit his mother Gabriel left the chair free for him and retired into the embrasure of the window. The room had already cleared and from the back room came the clatter of plates and knives. Those who still remained in the drawing-room seemed tired of dancing and were conversing quietly in little groups. Gabriel's warm trembling fingers tapped the cold pane of the window. How cool it must be outside! How pleasant it would be to walk out alone, first along by the river and then through the park! The snow would be lying on the branches of the trees and forming a bright cap on the top of the Wellington Monument. How much more pleasant it would be there than at the supper-table!

He ran over the headings of his speech: Irish hospitality, sad memories, the Three Graces, Paris, the quotation from Browning. He repeated to himself a phrase he had written in his review: *One feels that one is listening to a thought-tormented music.* Miss Ivors had praised the review. Was she sincere? Had she really any life of her own behind all her propagandism? There had never been any ill-feeling between them until that night. It unnerved him to think that she would be at the supper-table, looking up at him while he spoke with her critical quizzing eyes. Perhaps she would not be sorry to see him fail in his speech. An idea came into his mind and gave him courage. He would say, alluding to Aunt Kate and Aunt Julia: *Ladies and Gentlemen, the generation which is now on the wane among us may have had its faults but for my part I think it had certain qualities of hospitality, of humour, of humanity, which the new and very serious and hypereducated generation that is growing up around us seems to me to lack.* Very good: that was one for Miss Ivors. What did he care that his aunts were only two ignorant old women?

A murmur in the room attracted his attention. Mr Browne was advancing from the door, gallantly escorting Aunt Julia, who leaned upon his arm, smiling and hanging her head. An irregular musketry of applause escorted her also as far as the piano and then, as Mary Jane seated herself on the stool, and Aunt Julia, no longer smiling, half turned so as to pitch her voice fairly into the room, gradually ceased. Gabriel recognized the prelude. It was that of an old song of Aunt Julia's – *Arrayed for the Bridal.* Her voice, strong and clear in tone, attacked with great spirit the runs which embellish the air and though she sang very rapidly she did not miss even the smallest of the grace notes. To follow the voice, without looking at the singer's face, was to feel and share the excitement of swift and secure flight. Gabriel applauded loudly with all the others at the close of the song and loud applause was borne in from the invisible supper-table. It sounded so genuine that a little colour struggled into Aunt Julia's face as she bent to replace in the music-stand the old leather-bound song-book that had her initials on the cover. Freddy Malins, who had listened with his head perched sideways to hear her better, was still applauding when every one else had ceased and talking animatedly to his mother who nodded her head gravely and slowly in acquiescence. At last, when he could clap no more, he stood up suddenly and hurried across the room to Aunt Julia whose hand he seized and held in both his hands, shaking it when words failed him or the catch in his voice proved too much for him.

– I was just telling my mother, he said, I never heard you sing so well, never. No, I never heard your voice so good as it is to-night. Now! Would you believe that now? That's the truth. Upon my word and honour that's the truth. I never heard your voice sound so fresh and so . . . so clear and fresh, never.

Aunt Julia smiled broadly and murmured something about compliments as she released her hand from his grasp. Mr Browne extended his open hand towards her and said to those who were near him in the manner of a showman introducing a prodigy to an audience:

– Miss Julia Morkan, my latest discovery!

He was laughing very heartily at this himself when Freddy Malins turned to him and said:

– Well, Browne, if you're serious you might make a worse discovery. All I can say is I never heard her sing half so well as long as I am coming here. And that's the honest truth.

– Neither did I, said Mr Browne. I think her voice has greatly improved.

Aunt Julia shrugged her shoulders and said with meek pride:

– Thirty years ago I hadn't a bad voice as voices go.

– I often told Julia, said Aunt Kate emphatically, that she was simply thrown away in that choir. But she never would be said by me.

She turned as if to appeal to the good sense of the others against a refractory child while Aunt Julia gazed in front of her, a vague smile of reminiscence playing on her face.

– No, continued Aunt Kate, she wouldn't be said or led by anyone, slaving there in that choir night and day, night and day. Six o'clock on Christmas morning! And all for what?

– Well, isn't it for the honour of God, Aunt Kate? asked Mary Jane, twisting round on the piano-stool and smiling.

Aunt Kate turned fiercely on her niece and said:

– I know all about the honour of God, Mary Jane, but I think it's not at all honourable for the pope to turn out the women out of the choirs that have slaved there all their lives and put little whipper-snappers of boys over their heads. I suppose it is for the good of the Church if the pope does it. But it's not just, Mary Jane, and it's not right.

She had worked herself into a passion and would have continued in defence of her sister for it was a sore subject with her but Mary Jane, seeing that all the dancers had come back, intervened pacifically:

– Now, Aunt Kate, you're giving scandal to Mr Browne who is of the other persuasion.

Aunt Kate turned to Mr Browne, who was grinning at this allusion to his religion, and said hastily:

– O, I don't question the pope's being right. I'm only a stupid old woman and I wouldn't presume to do such a thing. But there's such a thing as common everyday politeness and gratitude. And if I were in Julia's place I'd tell that Father Healey straight up to his face . . .

– And besides, Aunt Kate, said Mary Jane, we really are all hungry and when we are hungry we are all very quarrelsome.

– And when we are thirsty we are also quarrelsome, added Mr Browne.

– So that we had better go to supper, said Mary Jane, and finish the discussion afterwards.

On the landing outside the drawing-room Gabriel found his wife and Mary Jane trying to persuade Miss Ivors to stay for supper. But Miss Ivors, who had put on her hat and was buttoning her cloak, would not stay. She did not feel in the least hungry and she had already overstayed her time.

– But only for ten minutes, Molly, said Mrs Conroy. That won't delay you.

– To take a pick itself, said Mary Jane, after all your dancing.

– I really couldn't, said Miss Ivors.

– I am afraid you didn't enjoy yourself at all, said Mary Jane hopelessly.

– Ever so much, I assure you, said Miss Ivors, but you really must let me run off now.

– But how can you get home? asked Mrs Conroy.

– O, it's only two steps up the quay.

Gabriel hesitated a moment and said:

– If you will allow me, Miss Ivors, I'll see you home if you really are obliged to go.

But Miss Ivors broke away from them.

– I won't hear of it, she cried. For goodness sake go in to your suppers and don't mind me. I'm quite well able to take care of myself.

– Well, you're the comical girl, Molly, said Mrs Conroy frankly.

– *Beannacht libh*, cried Miss Ivors, with a laugh, as she ran down the staircase.

Mary Jane gazed after her, a moody puzzled expression on her face, while Mrs Conroy leaned over the banisters to listen for the hall-door. Gabriel asked himself was he the cause of her abrupt departure. But she did not seem to be in ill humour: she had gone away laughing. He stared blankly down the staircase.

At that moment Aunt Kate came toddling out of the supper-room, almost wringing her hands in despair.

– Where is Gabriel? she cried. Where on earth is Gabriel? There's everyone waiting in there, stage to let, and nobody to carve the goose!

– Here I am, Aunt Kate! cried Gabriel, with sudden animation, ready to carve a flock of geese, if necessary.

A fat brown goose lay at one end of the table and at the other end, on a bed of creased paper strewn with sprigs of parsley, lay a great ham, stripped of its outer skin and peppered over with crust crumbs, a neat paper frill round its shin and beside this was a round of spiced beef. Between these rival ends ran parallel lines of side-dishes: two little minsters of jelly, red and yellow; a shallow dish full of blocks of blancmange and red jam, a large green leaf-shaped dish with a stalk-shaped handle, on which lay bunches of purple raisins and peeled almonds, a companion dish on which lay a solid rectangle of Smyrna figs, a dish of custard topped with grated nutmeg, a small bowl full of chocolates and sweets wrapped in gold and silver papers and a glass vase in which stood some tall celery stalks. In the centre of the table there stood, as sentries to a fruit-stand which upheld a pyramid of oranges and American apples, two squat old-fashioned decanters of cut glass, one containing port and the other dark sherry. On the closed square piano a pudding in a huge yellow dish lay in waiting and behind it were three squads of bottles of stout and ale and minerals, drawn up according to the colours of their uniforms, the first two black, with brown and red labels, the third and smallest squad white, with transverse green sashes.

Gabriel took his seat boldly at the head of the table and, having looked to the edge of the carver, plunged his fork firmly into the goose. He felt quite at ease now for he was an expert carver and liked nothing better than to find himself at the head of a well-laden table.

– Miss Furlong, what shall I send you? he asked. A wing or a slice of the breast?

– Just a small slice of breast.

– Miss Higgins, what for you?

– O, anything at all, Mr Conroy.

While Gabriel and Miss Daly exchanged plates of goose and plates of ham and spiced beef Lily went from guest to guest with a dish of hot floury potatoes wrapped in a white napkin. This was Mary Jane's idea and she had also suggested apple sauce for the goose but Aunt Kate had said that plain roast goose without apple sauce had always been good enough for her and she hoped she might never eat worse. Mary Jane waited on her pupils and saw that they got the best slices and Aunt Kate and Aunt Julia opened and carried across from the piano bottles of stout and ale for the gentlemen and bottles of minerals for the ladies. There was a great deal of confusion and laughter and noise, the noise of orders and counter-orders, of knives and forks, of corks and glass-stoppers. Gabriel began to carve second helpings as soon as he had finished the first round without serving himself. Every one protested loudly so that he compromised by taking a long draught of stout for he had found the carving hot work. Mary Jane settled down quietly to her supper but Aunt Kate and Aunt Julia were still toddling round the table, walking on each other's heels, getting in each other's way and giving each other unheeded orders. Mr Browne begged of them to sit down and eat their suppers and so did Gabriel but they said there was time enough so that, at last Freddy Malins stood up and, capturing Aunt Kate, plumped her down on her chair amid general laughter.

When everyone had been well served Gabriel said, smiling:

– Now, if anyone wants a little more of what vulgar people call stuffing let him or her speak.

A chorus of voices invited him to begin his own supper and Lily came forward with three potatoes which she had reserved for him.

–Very well, said Gabriel amiably, as he took another preparatory draught, kindly forget my existence, ladies and gentlemen, for a few minutes.

He set to his supper and took no part in the conversation with which the table covered Lily's removal of the plates. The subject of talk was the opera company which was then at the Theatre Royal. Mr Bartell D'Arcy, the tenor, a dark-complexioned young man with a smart moustache, praised very highly the leading contralto of the company but Miss Furlong thought she had a rather vulgar style of production. Freddy Malins said there was a negro chieftain singing in the second part of the Gaity pantomime who had one of the finest tenor voices he had ever heard.

– Have you heard him? he asked Mr Bartell D'Arcy across the table.

– No, answered Mr Bartell D'Arcy carelessly.

– Because, Freddy Malins explained, now I'd be curious to hear your opinion of him. I think he has a grand voice.

– It takes Teddy to find out the really good things, said Mr Browne familiarly to the table.

– And why couldn't he have a voice too? asked Freddy Malins sharply. Is it because he's only a black?

Nobody answered this question and Mary Jane led the table back to the legitimate opera. One of her pupils had given her a pass for *Mignon*. Of course it was very fine, she said, but it made her think of poor Georgina Burns. Mr Browne could go back farther still, to the old Italian companies that used to come to Dublin – Tietjens, Ilma de Murzka, Campanini, the great Trebilli, Giuglini, Ravelli, Aramburo. Those were the days, he said, when there was something like singing to be heard in Dublin. He told too of how the top gallery of the old Royal used to be packed night after night, of how one night an Italian tenor had sung five encores to *Let me Like a Soldier Fall*, introducing a high C every time, and of how the gallery boys would sometimes in their enthusiasm unyoke the horses from the carriage of some great *prima donna* and pull her themselves through the streets to her hotel. Why did they never play the grand old operas now, he asked, *Dinorah*, *Lucrezia Borgia*? Because they could not get the voices to sing them: that was why.

– O, well, said Mr Bartell D'Arcy, I presume there are as good singers to-day as there were then.

– Where are they? asked Mr Browne defiantly.

– In London, Paris, Milan, said Mr Bartell D'Arcy warmly. I suppose Caruso, for example, is quite as good, if not better than any of the men you have mentioned.

– Maybe so, said Mr Browne. But I may tell you I doubt it strongly.

– O, I'd give anything to hear Caruso sing, said Mary Jane.

– For me, said Aunt Kate, who had been picking a bone, there was only one tenor. To please me, I mean. But I suppose none of you ever heard of him.

– Who was he, Miss Morkan? asked Mr Bartell D'Arcy politely.

– His name, said Aunt Kate, was Parkinson. I heard him when he was in his prime and I think he had then the purest tenor voice that was ever put into a man's throat.

– Strange, said Mr Bartell D'Arcy. I never even heard of him.

– Yes, yes, Miss Morkan is right, said Mr Browne. I remember hearing of old Parkinson, but he's too far back for me.

– A beautiful pure sweet mellow English tenor, said Aunt Kate with enthusiasm.

Gabriel having finished, the huge pudding was transferred to the table. The clatter of forks and spoons began again. Gabriel's wife served out spoonfuls of the pudding and passed the plates down the table. Midway down they were held up by Mary Jane, who replenished them with raspberry or orange jelly or with blancmange and jam. The pudding was of Aunt Julia's making and she received praises for it from all quarters. She herself said that it was not quite brown enough.

– Well, I hope, Miss Morkan, said Mr Browne, that I'm brown enough for you because, you know, I'm all brown.

All the gentlemen, except Gabriel, ate some of the pudding out of compliment to Aunt Julia. As Gabriel never ate sweets the celery had been left for him. Freddy Malins also took a stalk of celery and ate it with his pudding. He had been told that celery was a capital thing for the blood and he was just then under doctor's care. Mrs Malins, who had been silent all through the supper, said that her son was going down to Mount Melleray in a week or so. The table then spoke of Mount Melleray, how bracing the air was down there, how hospitable the monks were and how they never asked for a penny-piece from their guests.

– And do you mean to say, asked Mr Browne incredulously, that a chap can go down there and put up there as if it were a hotel and live on the fat of the land and then come away without paying a farthing?

– O, most people give some donation to the monastery when they leave, said Mary Jane.

– I wish we had an institution like that in our Church, said Mr Browne candidly.

He was astonished to hear that the monks never spoke, got up at two in the morning and slept in their coffins. He asked what they did it for.

– That's the rule of the order, said Aunt Kate firmly.

– Yes, but why? asked Mr Browne.

Aunt Kate repeated that it was the rule, that was all. Mr Browne still seemed not to understand. Freddy Malins explained to him, as best he could, that the monks were trying to make up for the sins committed by all the sinners in the outside world. The explanation was not very clear for Mr Browne grinned and said:

– I like that idea very much but wouldn't a comfortable spring bed do them as well as a coffin?

– The coffin, said Mary Jane, is to remind them of their last end.

As the subject had grown lugubrious it was buried in a silence of the table during which Mrs Malins could be heard saying to her neighbour in an indistinct undertone:

– They are very good men, the monks, very pious men.

The raisins and almonds and figs and apples and oranges and chocolates and sweets were now passed about the table and Aunt Julia invited all the guests to have either port or sherry. At first Mr Bartell D'Arcy refused to take either but one of his neighbours nudged him and whispered something to him upon which he allowed his glass to be filled. Gradually as the last glasses were being filled the conversation ceased. A pause followed, broken only by the noise of the wine and by unsettlings of chairs. The Misses Morkan, all three, looked down at the tablecloth. Some one coughed once or twice and then a few gentlemen patted the table gently as a signal for silence. The silence came and Gabriel pushed back his chair and stood up.

The patting at once grew louder in encouragement and then ceased altogether. Gabriel leaned his ten trembling fingers on the tablecloth and smiled nervously at the company. Meeting a row of upturned faces he raised his eyes to the chandelier. The piano was playing a waltz tune and he could hear the skirts sweeping against the drawing-room door. People, perhaps, were standing in the snow on the quay outside, gazing up at the lighted windows and listening to the waltz music. The air was pure there. In the distance lay the park where the trees were weighted with snow. The Wellington Monument wore a gleaming cap of snow that flashed westward over the white field of Fifteen Acres.

He began:

– Ladies and Gentlemen.

– It has fallen to my lot this evening, as in years past, to perform a very pleasing task but a task for which I am afraid my poor powers as a speaker are all too inadequate.

– No, no! said Mr Browne.

– But, however that may be, I can only ask you to-night to take the will for the deed and to lend me your attention for a few moments while I endeavour to express to you in words what my feelings are on this occasion.

– Ladies and Gentlemen. It is not the first time that we have gathered together under this hospitable roof, around this hospitable board. It is not the first time that we have been the recipients – or perhaps, I had better say, the victims – of the hospitality of certain good ladies.

He made a circle in the air with his arm and paused. Every one laughed or smiled at Aunt Kate and Aunt Julia and Mary Jane who all turned crimson with pleasure. Gabriel went on more boldly:

– I feel more strongly with every recurring year that our country has no tradition which does it so much honour and which it should guard so jealously as that of its hospitality. It is a tradition that is unique as far as my experience goes (and I have visited not a few places abroad) among the modern nations. Some would say, perhaps, that with us it is rather a failing then anything to be boasted of. But granted even that, it is, to my mind, a princely failing, and one that I trust will long be cultivated among us. Of one thing, at least, I am sure. As long as this one roof shelters the good ladies aforesaid – and I wish from my heart it may do so for many and many a long year to come – the tradition of genuine warm-hearted courteous Irish hospitality, which our forefathers have handed down to us and which we in turn must hand down to our descendants, is still alive among us.

A hearty murmur of assent ran round the table. It shot through Gabriel's mind that Miss Ivors was not there and that she had gone away discourteously: and he said with confidence in himself:

– Ladies and Gentlemen.

– A new generation is growing up in our midst, a generation actuated by new ideas and new principles. It is serious and enthusiastic for these new ideas and its enthusiasm, even when it is misdirected, is, I believe, in the main sincere. But we are living in a sceptical and, if I may use the phrase, a thought-tormented age: and sometimes I fear that this new generation, educated or hypereducated as it is, will lack those qualities of humanity, of hospitality, of kindly humour which belonged to an older day. Listening to-night to the names of all those great singers of the past it seemed to me, I must confess, that we were living in a less spacious age. Those days might, without exaggeration, be called spacious days: and if they are gone beyond recall let us hope, at least, that in gatherings such as this we shall still speak of them with pride and affection, still cherish in our hearts the memory of those dead and gone great ones whose fame the world will not willingly let die.

– Hear, hear! said Mr Browne loudly.

– But yet, continued Gabriel, his voice falling into a softer inflection, there are always in gatherings such as this sadder thoughts that will recur to our minds: thoughts of the past, of youth, of changes, of absent faces that we miss here tonight. Our path through life is strewn with many such sad memories: and were we to brood upon them always we could not find the heart to go on bravely with our work among the living. We have all of us living duties and living affections which claim, and rightly claim, our strenuous endeavours.

– Therefore, I will not linger on the past. I will not let any gloomy moralizing intrude upon us here to-night. Here we are gathered together for a brief moment from the bustle and rush of our everyday routine. We are met here as friends, in the spirit of good-fellowship, as colleagues, also to a certain extent, in the true spirit of *camaraderie*, and as the guest of – what shall I call them? – the Three Graces of the Dublin musical world.

The table burst into applause and laughter at this sally. Aunt Julia vainly asked each of her neighbours in turn to tell her what Gabriel had said.

– He says we are the Three Graces, Aunt Julia, said Mary Jane.

Aunt Julia did not understand but she looked up, smiling, at Gabriel, who continued in the same vein:

– Ladies and Gentlemen.

– I will not attempt to play to-night the part that Paris played on another occasion. I will not attempt to choose between them. The task would be an invidious one and one beyond my poor powers. For when I view them in turn, whether it be our chief hostess herself, whose good heart, whose too good heart, has become a byword with all who know her, or her sister, who seems to be gifted with perennial youth and whose singing must have been a surprise and revelation to us all to-night, or, last but not least, when I consider our youngest hostess, talented, cheerful, hard-working and the best of nieces, I confess, Ladies and Gentlemen, that I do not know to which of them I should award the prize.

Gabriel glanced down at his aunts and, seeing the large smile on Aunt Julia's face and the tears which had risen to Aunt Kate's eyes, hastened to his close. He raised his glass of port gallantly, while every member of the company fingered a glass expectantly, and said loudly:

– Let us toast them all three together. Let us drink to their health, wealth, long life, happiness and prosperity and may they long continue to hold the proud and self-won position which they hold in their profession and the position of honour and affection which they hold in our hearts.

All the guests stood up, glass in hand, and, turning towards the three seated ladies, sang in unison, with Mr Browne as leader:

> *For they are jolly gay fellows,*
> *For they are jolly gay fellows,*
> *For they are jolly gay fellows,*
> *Which nobody can deny.*

Aunt Kate was making frank use of her handkerchief and even Aunt Julia seemed moved. Freddy Malins beat time with his pudding-fork and the singers turned towards one another, as if in melodious conference, while they sang with emphasis:

> *Unless he tells a lie,*
> *Unless he tells a lie.*

Then, turning once more towards their hostesses, they sang:

> *For they are jolly gay fellows,*
> *For they are jolly gay fellows,*
> *For they are jolly gay fellows,*
> *Which nobody can deny.*

The acclamation which followed was taken up beyond the door of the supper-room by many of the other guests and renewed time after time, Freddy Malins acting as officer with his fork on high.

*   *   *

The piercing morning air came into the hall where they were standing so that Aunt Kate said:

– Close the door, somebody. Mrs Malins will get her death of cold.

– Browne is out there, Aunt Kate, said Mary Jane.

– Browne is everywhere, said Aunt Kate, lowering her voice.

Mary Jane laughed at her tone.

– Really, she said archly, he is very attentive.

– He has been laid on here like the gas, said Aunt Kate in the same tone, all during the Christmas.

She laughed herself this time good-humouredly and then added quickly:

– But tell him to come in, Mary Jane, and close the door. I hope to goodness he didn't hear me.

At that moment the hall-door was opened and Mr Browne came in from the doorstep, laughing as if his heart would break. He was dressed in a long green overcoat with mock astrakhan cuffs and collar and wore on his head an oval fur cap. He pointed down the snow-covered quay from where the sound of shrill prolonged whistling was borne in.

– Teddy will have all the cabs in Dublin out, he said.

Gabriel advanced from the little pantry behind the office, struggling into his overcoat and, looking round the hall, said:

– Gretta not down yet?

– She's getting on her things, Gabriel, said Aunt Kate.

– Who's playing up there? asked Gabriel.

– Nobody. They're all gone.

– O no, Aunt Kate, said Mary Jane. Bartell D'Arcy and Miss O'Callaghan aren't gone yet.

– Someone is strumming at the piano, anyhow, said Gabriel.

Mary Jane glanced at Gabriel and Mr Browne and said with a shiver:

– It makes me feel cold to look at you two gentlemen muffled up like that. I wouldn't like to face your journey home at this hour.

– I'd like nothing better this minute, said Mr Browne stoutly, than a rattling fine walk in the country or a fast drive with a good spanking goer between the shafts.

– We used to have a very good horse and trap at home, said Aunt Julia sadly.

– The never-to-be-forgotten Johnny, said Mary Jane, laughing.

Aunt Kate and Gabriel laughed too.

– Why, what was wonderful about Johnny? asked Mr Browne.

– The late lamented Patrick Morkan, our grandfather, that is, explained Gabriel, commonly known in his later years as the old gentleman, was a glue-boiler.

– O, now, Gabriel, said Aunt Kate, laughing, he had a starch mill.

– Well, glue or starch, said Gabriel, the old gentleman had a horse by the name of Johnny. And Johnny used to work in the old gentleman's mill, walking round and round in order to drive the mill. That was all very well; but now comes the tragic part about Johnny. One fine day the old gentleman thought he'd like to drive out with the quality to a military review in the park.

– The Lord have mercy on his soul, said Aunt Kate compassionately.

– Amen, said Gabriel. So the old gentleman, as I said, harnessed Johnny and put on his very best tall hat and his very best stock collar and drove out in grand style from his ancestral mansion somewhere near Back Lane, I think.

Every one laughed, even Mrs Malins, at Gabriel's manner and Aunt Kate said:

– O now, Gabriel, he didn't live in Back Lane, really. Only the mill was there.

– Out from the mansion of his forefathers, continued Gabriel, he drove with Johnny. And everything went on beautifully until Johnny came in sight of King Billy's statue: and whether he fell in love with the horse King Billy sits on or whether he thought he was back again in the mill, anyhow he began to walk round the statue.

Gabriel paced in a circle round the hall in his goloshes amid the laughter of the others.

– Round and round he went, said Gabriel, and the old gentleman, who was a very pompous old gentleman, was highly indignant. *Go on, sir! What do you mean, sir? Johnny! Johnny! Most extraordinary conduct! Can't understand the horse!*

The peals of laughter which followed Gabriel's imitation of the incident were interrupted by a resounding knock at the hall-door. Mary Jane ran to open it and let in Freddy Malins. Freddy Malins, with his hat well back on his head and his shoulders humped with cold, was puffing and steaming after his exertions.

– I could only get one cab, he said.

– O, we'll find another along the quay, said Gabriel.

– Yes, said Aunt Kate. Better not keep Mrs Malins standing in the draught.

Mrs Malins was helped down the front steps by her son and Mr Browne and, after many manœuvres, hoisted into the cab. Freddy Malins clambered in after her and spent a long time settling her on the seat, Mr Browne helping him with advice. At last she was settled comfortably and Freddy Malins invited Mr Browne into the cab. There was a good deal of confused talk, and then Mr Browne got into the cab. The cabman settled his rug over his knees, and bent down for the address. The confusion grew greater and the cabman was directed differently by Freddy Malins and Mr Browne, each of whom had his head out through a window of the cab. The difficulty was to know where to drop Mr Browne along the route and Aunt Kate, Aunt Julia and Mary Jane helped the discussion from the doorstep with cross-directions and contradictions and abundance of laughter. As for Freddy Malins he was speechless with laughter. He popped his head in and out of the window every moment, to the great danger of his hat, and told his mother how the discussion was progressing, till at last Mr Browne shouted to the bewildered cabman above the din of everybody's laughter:

– Do you know Trinity College?

– Yes, sir, said the cabman.

– Well, drive bang up against Trinity College gates, said Mr Browne, and then we'll tell you where to go. You understand now?

– Yes, sir, said the cabman.

– Make like a bird for Trinity College.

– Right, sir, cried the cabman.

The horse was whipped up and the cab rattled off along the quay amid a chorus of laughter and adieus.

Gabriel had not gone to the door with the others. He was in a dark part of the hall gazing up the staircase. A woman was standing near the top of the first flight, in the shadow also. He could not see her face but he could see the terracotta and salmonpink panels of her skirt which the shadow made appear black and white. It was his wife. She was leaning on the banisters, listening to something. Gabriel was surprised at her stillness and strained his ear to listen also. But he could hear little save the noise of laughter and dispute on the front steps, a few chords struck on the piano and a few notes of a man's voice singing.

He stood still in the gloom of the hall, trying to catch the air that the voice was singing and gazing up at his wife. There was grace and mystery in her attitude as if she were a symbol of something. He asked himself what is a woman standing on the stairs in the shadow, listening to distant music, a symbol of. If he were a painter he would paint her in that attitude. Her blue felt hat would show off the bronze of her hair against the darkness and the dark panels of her skirt would show off the light tones. *Distant Music* he would call the picture if he were a painter.

The hall-door was closed; and Aunt Kate, Aunt Julia and Mary Jane came down the hall, still laughing.

– Well, isn't Freddy terrible? said Mary Jane. He's really terrible.

Gabriel said nothing but pointed up the stairs towards where his wife was standing. Now that the hall-door was closed the voice and the piano could be heard more clearly. Gabriel held up his hand for them to be silent. The song seemed to be in the old Irish tonality and the singer seemed uncertain both of his words and of his voice. The voice, made plaintive by distance and by the singer's hoarseness, faintly illuminated the cadence of the air with words expressing grief:

> *O, the rain falls on my heavy locks*
> *And the dew wets my skin,*
> *My babe lies cold . . .*

O, exclaimed Mary Jane. It's Bartell D'Arcy singing, and he wouldn't sing all the night. O, I'll get him to sing a song before he goes.

– O, do, Mary Jane, said Aunt Kate.

Mary Jane brushed past the others and ran to the staircase but before she reached it the singing stopped and the piano was closed abruptly.

– O, what a pity! she cried. Is he coming down, Gretta?

Gabriel heard his wife answer yes and saw her come down towards them. A few steps behind her were Mr Bartell D'Arcy and Miss O'Callaghan.

– O, Mr D'Arcy, cried Mary Jane, it's downright mean of you to break off like that when we were all in raptures listening to you.

– I have been at him all the evening, said Miss O'Callaghan, and Mrs Conroy too and he told us he had a dreadful cold and couldn't sing.

– O, Mr D'Arcy, said Aunt Kate, now that was a great fib to tell.

– Can't you see that I'm as hoarse as a crow? said Mr D'Arcy roughly.

He went into the pantry hastily and put on his overcoat. The others, taken aback by his rude speech, could find nothing to say. Aunt Kate wrinkled her brows and made signs to the others to drop the subject. Mr D'Arcy stood swathing his neck carefully and frowning.

– It's the weather, said Aunt Julia, after a pause.

– Yes, everybody has colds, said Aunt Kate readily, everybody.

– They say, said Mary Jane, we haven't had snow like it for thirty years; and I read this morning in the newspapers that the snow is general all over Ireland.

– I love the look of snow, said Aunt Julia sadly.

– So do I, said Miss O'Callaghan. I think Christmas is never really Christmas unless we have the snow on the ground.

– But poor Mr D'Arcy doesn't like the snow, said Aunt Kate, smiling.

Mr D'Arcy came from the pantry, fully swathed and buttoned, and in a repentant tone told them the history of his cold. Every one gave him advice and said it was a great pity and urged him to be very careful of his throat in the night air. Gabriel watched his wife who did not join in the conversation. She was standing right under the dusty fanlight and the flame of the gas lit up the rich bronze of her hair which he had seen her drying at the fire a few days before. She was in the same attitude and seemed unaware of the talk about her. At last she turned towards them and Gabriel saw that there was colour on her cheeks and that her eyes were shining. A sudden tide of joy went leaping out of his heart.

– Mr D'Arcy, she said, what is the name of that song you were singing?

– It's called *The Lass of Aughrim*, said Mr D'Arcy, but I couldn't remember it properly. Why? Do you know it?

– *The Lass of Aughrim*, she repeated. I couldn't think of the name.

– It's a very nice air, said Mary Jane. I'm sorry you were not in voice to-night.

– Now, Mary Jane, said Aunt Kate, don't annoy Mr D'Arcy. I won't have him annoyed.

Seeing that all were ready to start she shepherded them to the door where good-night was said:

– Well, good-night, Aunt Kate, and thanks for the pleasant evening.

– Good-night, Gabriel. Good-night, Gretta!

– Good-night, Aunt Kate, and thanks ever so much. Good-night, Aunt Julia.

– O, good-night, Gretta, I didn't see you.

– Good-night, Mr D'Arcy. Good-night, Miss O'Callaghan.

– Good-night, Miss Morkan.

– Good-night, again.

– Good-night, all. Safe home.

– Good-night. Good-night.

The morning was still dark. A dull yellow light brooded over the houses and the river; and the sky seemed to be descending. It was slushy underfoot; and only streaks and patches of snow lay on the roofs, on the parapets of the quay and on the area railings. The lamps were still burning redly in the murky air and, across the river, the palace of the Four Courts stood out menacingly against the heavy sky.

She was walking on before him with Mr Bartell D'Arcy, her shoes in a brown parcel tucked under one arm and her hands holding her skirt up from the slush. She had no longer any grace of attitude but Gabriel's eyes were still bright with happiness. The blood went bounding along his veins; and the thoughts went rioting through his brain, proud, joyful, tender, valorous.

She was walking on before him so lightly and so erect that he longed to run after her noiselessly, catch her by the shoulders and say something foolish and affectionate into her ear. She seemed to him so frail that he longed to defend her against something and then to be alone with her. Moments of their secret life together burst like stars upon his memory. A heliotrope envelope was lying beside his breakfast-cup and he was caressing it with his hand. Birds were twittering in the ivy and the sunny web of the curtain was shimmering along the floor: he could not eat for happiness. They were standing on the crowded platform and he was placing a ticket inside the warm palm of her glove. He was standing with her in the cold, looking in through a grated window at a man making bottles in a roaring furnace. It was very cold. Her face, fragrant in the cold air, was quite close to his; and suddenly she called out to the man at the furnace:

– Is the fire hot, sir?

But the man could not hear her with the noise of the furnace. It was just as well. He might have answered rudely.

A wave of yet more tender joy escaped from his heart and went coursing in warm flood along his arteries. Like the tender fires of stars moments of their life together, that no one knew of or would ever know of, broke upon and illumined his memory. He longed to recall to her those moments, to make her forget the years of their dull existence together and remember only their moments of ecstasy. For the years, he felt, had not quenched his soul or hers. Their children, his writing, her household cares had not quenched all their souls' tender fire. In one letter that he had written to her then he had said: *Why is it that words like these seem to me so dull and cold? Is it because there is no word tender enough to be your name?*

Like distant music these words that he had written years before were borne towards him from the past. He longed to be alone with her. When the others had gone away, when he and she were in the room in the hotel, then they would be alone together. He would call her softly:

– Gretta!

Perhaps she would not hear at once: she would be undressing. Then something in his voice would strike her. She would turn and look at him . . .

At the corner of Winetavern Street they met a cab. He was glad of its rattling noise as it saved him from conversation. She was looking out of the window and seemed tired. The others spoke only a few words, pointing out some building or street. The horse galloped along wearily under the murky morning sky, dragging his old rattling box after his heels, and Gabriel was again in a cab with her, galloping to catch the boat, galloping to their honeymoon.

As the cab drove across O'Connell Bridge Miss O'Callaghan said:

– They say you never cross O'Connell Bridge without seeing a white horse.

– I see a white man this time, said Gabriel.

– Where? asked Mr Bartell D'Arcy.

Gabriel pointed to the statue, on which lay patches of snow. Then he nodded familiarly to it and waved his hand.

– Good-night, Dan, he said gaily.

When the cab drew up before the hotel Gabriel jumped out and, in spite of Mr Bartell D'Arcy's protest, paid the driver. He gave the man a shilling over his fare. The man saluted and said:

– A prosperous New Year to you, sir.

– The same to you, said Gabriel cordially.

She leaned for a moment on his arm in getting out of the cab and while standing at the curbstone, bidding the others good-night. She leaned lightly on his arm, as lightly as when she had danced with him a few hours before. He had felt proud and happy then, happy that she was his, proud of her grace and wifely carriage. But now, after the kindling again of so many memories, the first touch of her body, musical and strange and perfumed, sent through him a keen pang of lust. Under cover of her silence he pressed her arm closely to his side; and, as they stood at the hotel door, he felt that they had escaped from their lives and duties, escaped from home and friends and run away together with wild and radiant hearts to a new adventure.

An old man was dozing in a great hooded chair in the hall. He lit a candle in the office and went before them to the stairs. They followed him in silence, their feet falling in soft thuds on the thickly carpeted stairs. She mounted the stairs behind the porter, her head bowed in the ascent, her frail shoulders curved as with a burden, her skirt girt tightly about her. He could have flung his arms about her hips and held her still for his arms were trembling with desire to seize her and only the stress of his nails against the palms of his hands held the wild impulse of his body in check. The porter halted on the stairs to settle his guttering candle. They halted too on the steps below him. In the silence Gabriel could hear the falling of the molten wax into the tray and the thumping of his own heart against his ribs.

The porter led them along a corridor and opened a door. Then he set his unstable candle down on a toilet-table and asked at what hour they were to be called in the morning.

– Eight, said Gabriel.

The porter pointed to the tap of the electric-light and began a muttered apology but Gabriel cut him short.

– We don't want any light. we have light enough from the street. And I say, he added, pointing to the candle, you might remove that handsome article, like a good man.

The porter took up his candle again, but slowly for he was surprised by such a novel idea. Then he mumbled good night and went out. Gabriel shot the lock to.

A ghostly light from the street lamp lay in a long shaft from one window to the door. Gabriel threw his overcoat and hat on a couch and crossed the room towards the window. He looked down into the street in order that his emotion might calm a little. Then he turned and leaned against a chest of drawers with his back to the light. She had taken off her hat and cloak and was standing before a large swinging mirror, unhooking her waist. Gabriel paused for a few moments, watching her, and then said:

– Gretta!

She turned away from the mirror slowly and walked along the shaft of light towards him. Her face looked so serious and weary that the words would not pass Gabriel's lips. No, it was not the moment yet.

– You looked tired, he said.

– I am a little, she answered.

– You don't feel ill or weak?

– No, tired: that's all.

She went on to the window and stood there, looking out. Gabriel waited again and then, fearing that diffidence was about to conquer him, he said abruptly:

– By the way, Gretta!

– What is it?

– You know that poor fellow Malins? he said quickly.

– Yes. What about him?

– Well, poor fellow, he's a decent sort of chap, after all, continued Gabriel in a false voice. He gave me back that sovereign I lent him and I didn't expect it really. It's a pity he wouldn't keep away from that Browne, because he's not a bad fellow at heart.

He was trembling now with annoyance. Why did she seem so abstracted? He did not know how he could begin. Was she annoyed, too, about something? If she would only turn to him or come to him of her own accord! To take her as she was would be brutal. No, he must see some ardour in her eyes first. He longed to be master of her strange mood.

– When did you lend him the pound? she asked, after a pause.

Gabriel strove to restrain himself from breaking out into brutal language about the sottish Malins and his pound. He longed to cry to her from his soul, to crush her body against his, to overmaster her. But he said:

– O, at Christmas, when he opened that little Christmas card shop in Henry Street.

He was in such a fever of rage and desire that he did not hear her come from the window. She stood before him for an instant, looking at him strangely. Then, suddenly raising herself on tiptoe and resting her hands lightly on his shoulders, she kissed him.

– You are a very generous person, Gabriel, she said.

Gabriel, trembling with delight at her sudden kiss and at the quaintness of her phrase, put his hands on her hair and began smoothing it back, scarcely touching it with his fingers. The washing had made it fine and brilliant. His heart was brimming over with happiness. Just when he was wishing for it she had come to him of her own accord. Perhaps her thoughts had been running with his. Perhaps she had felt the impetuous desire that was in him and then the yielding mood had come upon her. Now that she had fallen to him so easily he wondered why he had been so diffident.

He stood, holding her head between his hands. Then, slipping one arm swiftly about her body and drawing her towards him, he said softly:

– Gretta dear, what are you thinking about?

She did not answer nor yield wholly to his arm. He said again, softly:

– Tell me what it is, Gretta. I think I know what is the matter. Do I know?

She did not answer at once. Then she said in an outburst of tears:

– O, I am thinking about that song, *The Lass of Aughrim.*

She broke loose from him and ran to the bed and, throwing her arms across the bed-rail, hid her face. Gabriel stood stock-still for a moment in astonishment and then followed her. As he passed in the way of the cheval-glass he caught sight of himself in full length, his broad, well-filled shirt-front, the face whose expression always puzzled him when he saw it in a mirror and his glimmering gilt-rimmed eyeglasses. He halted a few paces from her and said:

– What about the song? Why does that make you cry?

She raised her head from her arms and dried her eyes with the back of her hand like a child. A kinder note than he had intended went into his voice.

– Why, Gretta? he asked.

– I am thinking about a person long ago who used to sing that song.

– And who was the person long ago? asked Gabriel, smiling.

– It was a person I used to know in Galway when I was living with my grandmother, she said.

The smile passed away from Gabriel's face. A dull anger began to gather again at the back of his mind and the dull fires of his lust began to glow angrily in his veins.

– Someone you were in love with? he asked ironically.

– It was a young boy I used to know, she answered, named Michael Furey. He used to sing that song, *The Lass of Aughrim*. He was very delicate.

Gabriel was silent. He did not wish her to think that he was interested in this delicate boy.

– I can see him so plainly, she said after a moment. Such eyes as he had: big dark eyes! And such an expression in them – an expression!

– O then, you were in love with him?' said Gabriel.

– I used to go out walking with him, she said, when I was in Galway.

A thought flew across Gabriel's mind.

– Perhaps that was why you wanted to go to Galway with that Ivors girl? he said coldly.

She looked at him and asked in surprise:

– What for?

Her eyes made Gabriel feel awkward. He shrugged his shoulders and said:

– How do I know? To see him perhaps.

She looked away from him along the shaft of light towards the window in silence.

– He is dead, she said at length. He died when he was only seventeen. Isn't it a terrible thing to die so young as that?

– What was he? asked Gabriel, still ironically.

– He was in the gasworks, she said.

Gabriel felt humiliated by the failure of his irony and by the evocation of this figure from the dead, a boy in the gasworks. While he had been full of memories of their secret life together, full of tenderness and joy and desire, she had been comparing him in her mind with another. A shameful consciousness of his own person assailed him. He saw himself as a ludicrous figure, acting as a pennyboy for his aunts, a nervous well-meaning sentimentalist, orating to vulgarians and idealizing his own clownish lusts, the pitiable fatuous fellow he had caught a glimpse of in the mirror. Instinctively he turned his back more to the light lest she might see the shame that burned upon his forehead.

He tried to keep up his tone of cold interrogation but his voice when he spoke was humble and indifferent.

– I suppose you were in love with this Michael Furey, Gretta, he said.

– I was great with him at that time, she said.

Her voice was veiled and sad. Gabriel, feeling now how vain it would be to try to lead her whither he had purposed, caressed one of her hands and said, also sadly:

– And what did he die of so young, Gretta? Consumption, was it?

– I think he died for me, she answered.

A vague terror seized Gabriel at this answer as if, at that hour when he had hoped to triumph, some impalpable and vindictive being was coming against him, gathering forces against him in its vague world. But he shook himself free of it with an effort of reason and continued to caress her hand. He did not question her again for he felt that she would tell him of herself. Her hand was warm and moist: it did not respond to his touch but he continued to caress it just as he had caressed her first letter to him that spring morning.

– It was in the winter, she said, about the beginning of the winter when I was going to leave my grandmother's and come up here to the convent. And he was ill at the time in his lodgings in Galway and wouldn't be let out and his people in Oughterard were written to. He was in decline, they said, or something like that. I never knew rightly.

She paused for a moment and sighed.

– Poor fellow, she said. He was very fond of me and he was such a gentle boy. We used to go out together, walking, you know, Gabriel, like the way they do in the country. He was going to study singing only for his health. He had a very good voice, poor Michael Furey.

– Well; and then? asked Gabriel.

– And then when it came to the time for me to leave Galway and come up to the convent he was much worse and I wouldn't be let see him so I wrote a letter saying I was going up to Dublin and would be back in the summer and hoping he would be better then.

She paused for a moment to get her voice under control and then went on:

– Then the night before I left I was in my grandmother's house in Nuns' Island, packing up, and I heard gravel thrown up against the window. The window was so wet I couldn't see so I ran downstairs as I was and slipped out the back into the garden and there was the poor fellow at the end of the garden, shivering.

– And did you not tell him to go back? asked Gabriel.

– I implored of him to go home at once and told him he would get his death in the rain. But he said he did not want to live. I can see his eyes as well as well! He was standing at the end of the wall where there was a tree.

– And did he go home? asked Gabriel.

– Yes, he went home. And when I was only a week in the convent he died and he was buried in Oughterard where his people came from. O, the day I heard that, that he was dead!

She stopped, choking with sobs, and, overcome by emotion, flung herself face downward on the bed, sobbing in the quilt. Gabriel held her hand for a moment longer, irresolutely, and then, shy of intruding on her grief, let it fall gently and walked quietly to the window.

She was fast asleep.

Gabriel, leaning on his elbow, looked for a few moments unresentfully on her tangled hair and half-open mouth, listening to her deep-drawn breath. So she had had that romance in her life: a man had died for her sake. It hardly pained him now to think how poor a part he, her husband, had played in her life. He watched her while she slept as though he and she had never lived together as man and wife. His curious eyes rested long upon her face and on her hair: and, as he thought of what she must have been then, in that time of her first girlish beauty, a strange friendly pity for her entered his soul. He did not like to say even to himself that her face was no longer beautiful but he knew that it was no longer the face for which Michael Furey had braved death.

Perhaps she had not told him all the story. His eyes moved to the chair over which she had thrown some of her clothes. A petticoat string dangled to the floor. One boot stood upright, its limp upper fallen down: the fellow of it lay upon its side. He wondered at his riot of emotions of an hour before. From what had it proceeded? From his aunt's supper, from his own foolish speech, from the wine and dancing, the merry-making when saying good-night in the hall, the pleasure of the walk along the river in the snow. Poor Aunt Julia! She, too, would soon be a shade with the shade of Patrick Morkan and his horse. He had caught that haggard look upon her face for a moment when she was singing *Arrayed for the Bridal*. Soon, perhaps, he would be sitting in that same drawing-room, dressed in black, his silk hat on his knees. The blinds would be drawn down and Aunt Kate would be sitting beside him, crying and blowing her nose and telling him how Julia had died. He would cast about in his mind for some words that might console her, and would find only lame and useless ones. Yes, yes: that would happen very soon.

The air of the room chilled his shoulders. He stretched himself cautiously along under the sheets and lay down beside his wife. One by one they were all becoming shades. Better pass boldly into that other world, in the full glory of some passion, than fade and wither dismally with age. He thought of how she who lay beside him had locked in her heart for so many years that image of her lover's eyes when he had told her that he did not wish to live.

Generous tears filled Gabriel's eyes. He had never felt like that himself towards any woman but he knew that such a feeling must be love. The tears gathered more thickly in his eyes and in the partial darkness he imagined he saw the form of a young man standing under a dripping tree. Other forms were near. His soul had approached that region where dwell the vast hosts of the dead. He was conscious of, but could not apprehend, their wayward and flickering existence. His own identity was fading out into a grey impalpable world: the solid world itself which these dead had one time reared and lived in was dissolving and dwindling.

A few light taps upon the pane made him turn to the window. It had begun to snow again. He watched sleepily the flakes, silver and dark, falling obliquely against the lamplight. The time had come for him to set out on his journey westward. Yes, the newspapers were right: snow was general all over Ireland. It was falling on every part of the dark central plain, on the treeless hills, falling softly upon the Bog of Allen and, farther westward, softly falling into the dark mutinous Shannon waves. It was falling, too, upon every part of the lonely churchyard on the hill where Michael Furey lay buried. It lay thickly drifted on the crooked crosses and headstones, on the spears of the little gate, on the barren thorns. His soul swooned slowly as he heard the snow falling faintly through the universe and faintly falling, like the descent of their last end, upon all the living and the dead.

from *A Portrait of the Artist as a Young Man*

A great fire, banked high and red, flamed in the grate and under the ivytwined branches of the chandelier the Christmas table was spread. They had come home a little late and still dinner was not ready: but it would be ready in a jiffy, his mother had said. They were waiting for the door to open and for the servants to come in, holding the big dishes covered with their heavy metal covers.

All were waiting: Uncle Charles, who sat far away in the shadow of the window, Dante and Mr Casey, who sat in the easychairs at either side of the hearth, Stephen, seated on a chair between them, his feet resting on the toasted boss. Mr Dedalus looked at himself in the pierglass above the mantelpiece, waxed out his moustache ends and then, parting his coat tails, stood with his back to the glowing fire: and still from time to time he withdrew a hand from his coat tail to wax out one of his moustache ends. Mr Casey leaned his head to one side and, smiling, tapped the gland of his neck with his fingers. And Stephen smiled too for he knew now that it was not true that Mr Casey had a purse of silver in his throat. He smiled to think how the silvery noise which Mr Casey used to make had deceived him. And when he had tried to open Mr Casey's hand to see if the purse of silver was hidden there he had seen that the fingers could not be straightened out: and Mr Casey had told him that he had got those three cramped fingers making a birthday present for Queen Victoria.

Mr Casey tapped the gland of his neck and smiled at Stephen with sleepy eyes: and Mr Dedalus said to him:

– Yes. Well now, that's all right. O, we had a good walk, hadn't we, John? Yes . . . I wonder if there's any likelihood of dinner this evening. Yes. . . . O, well now, we got a good breath of ozone round the Head today. Ay, bedad.

He turned to Dante and said:

– You didn't stir out at all, Mrs Riordan?

Dante frowned and said shortly:

– No.

Mr Dedalus dropped his coat tails and went over to the sideboard. He brought forth a great stone jar of whisky from the locker and filled the decanter slowly, bending now and then to see how much he had poured in. Then replacing the jar in the locker he poured a little of the whisky into two glasses, added a little water and came back with them to the fireplace.

– A thimbleful, John, he said, just to whet your appetite.

Mr Casey took the glass, drank, and placed it near him on the mantelpiece. Then he said:

– Well, I can't help thinking of our friend Christopher manufacturing . . .

He broke into a fit of laughter and coughing and added:

– . . . manufacturing that champagne for those fellows.

Mr Dedalus laughed loudly.

– Is it Christy? he said. There's more cunning in one of those warts on his bald head than in a pack of jack foxes.

He inclined his head, closed his eyes, and, licking his lips profusely, began to speak with the voice of the hotel keeper.

— And he has such a soft mouth when he's speaking to you, don't you know. He's very moist and watery about the dewlaps, God bless him.

Mr Casey was still struggling through his fit of coughing and laughter. Stephen, seeing and hearing the hotel keeper through his father's face and voice, laughed.

Mr Dedalus put up his eyeglass and, staring down at him, said quietly and kindly:

— What are you laughing at, you little puppy, you?

The servants entered and placed the dishes on the table. Mrs Dedalus followed and the places were arranged.

— Sit over, she said.

Mr Dedalus went to the end of the table and said:

— Now, Mrs Riordan, sit over. John, sit you down, my hearty.

He looked round to where Uncle Charles sat and said:

— Now then, sir, there's a bird here waiting for you.

When all had taken their seats he laid his hand on the cover and then said quickly, withdrawing it:

— Now, Stephen.

Stephen stood up in his place to say the grace before meals:

Bless us, O Lord, and these Thy gifts which through Thy bounty we are about to receive through Christ our Lord. Amen.

All blessed themselves and Mr Dedalus with a sigh of pleasure lifted from the dish the heavy cover pearled around the edge with glistening drops.

Stephen looked at the plump turkey which had lain, trussed and skewered, on the kitchen table. He knew that his father had paid a guinea for it in Dunn's of D'Olier Street and that the man had prodded it often at the breast-bone to show how good it was: and he remembered the man's voice when he had said:

— Take that one, sir. That's the real Ally Daly.

Why did Mr Barrett in Clongowes call his pandybat a turkey? But Clongowes was far away: and the warm heavy smell of turkey and ham and celery rose from the plates and dishes and the great fire was banked high and red in the grate and the green ivy and red holly made you feel so happy and when dinner was ended the big plum pudding would be carried in, studded with peeled almonds and sprigs of holly, with bluish fire running around it and a little green flag flying from the top.

It was his first Christmas dinner and he thought of his little brothers and sisters who were waiting in the nursery, as he had often waited, till the pudding came. The deep low collar and the Eton jacket made him feel queer and oldish: and that morning when his mother had brought him down to the parlour, dressed for mass, his father had cried. That was because he was thinking of his own father. And Uncle Charles had said so too.

Mr Dedalus covered the dish and began to eat hungrily. Then he said:

— Poor old Christy, he's nearly lopsided now with roguery.

— Simon, said Mrs Dedalus, you haven't given Mrs Riordan any sauce.

Mr Dedalus seized the sauceboat.

– Haven't I? he cried. Mrs Riordan, pity the poor blind.

Dante covered her plate with her hands and said:

– No, thanks.

Mr Dedalus turned to Uncle Charles.

– How are you off, sir?

– Right as the mail, Simon.

– You, John?

– I'm all right. Go on yourself.

– Mary? Here, Stephen, here's something to make your hair curl.

He poured sauce freely over Stephen's plate and set the boat again on the table. Then he asked Uncle Charles was it tender. Uncle Charles could not speak because his mouth was full but he nodded that it was.

– That was a good answer our friend made to the canon. What? said Mr Dedalus.

– I didn't think he had that much in him, said Mr Casey.

– *I'll pay your dues, father, when you cease turning the house of God into a pollingbooth.*

– A nice answer, said Dante, for any man calling himself a catholic to give to his priest.

– They have only themselves to blame, said Mr Dedalus suavely. If they took a fool's advice they would confine their attention to religion.

– It is religion, Dante said. They are doing their duty in warning the people.

– We go to the house of God, Mr Casey said, in all humility to pray to our Maker and not to hear election addresses.

– It is religion, Dante said again. They are right. They must direct their flocks.

– And preach politics from the altar, is it? asked Mr Dedalus.

– Certainly, said Dante. It is a question of public morality. A priest would not be a priest if he did not tell his flock what is right and what is wrong.

Mrs Dedalus laid down her knife and fork, saying:

– For pity sake and for pity sake let us have no political discussion on this day of all days in the year.

– Quite right, ma'am, said Uncle Charles. Now Simon, that's quite enough now. Not another word now.

– Yes, yes, said Mr Dedalus quickly.

He uncovered the dish boldly and said:

– Now then, who's for more turkey?

Nobody answered. Dante said:

– Nice language for any catholic to use!

– Mrs Riordan, I appeal to you, said Mrs Dedalus, to let the matter drop now.

Dante turned on her and said:

– And am I to sit here and listen to the pastors of my church being flouted?

– Nobody is saying a word against them, said Mr Dedalus, so long as they don't meddle in politics.

– The bishops and priests of Ireland have spoken, said Dante, and they must be obeyed.

– Let them leave politics alone, said Mr Casey, or the people may leave their church alone.

– You hear? said Dante turning to Mrs Dedalus.

– Mr Casey! Simon! said Mrs Dedalus, let it end now.

– Too bad! Too bad! said Uncle Charles.

– What? cried Mr Dedalus. Were we to desert him at the bidding of the English people?

– He was no longer worthy to lead, said Dante. He was a public sinner.

– We are all sinners and black sinners, said Mr Casey coldly.

– *Woe be to the man by whom the scandal cometh!* said Mrs Riordan. *It would be better for him that a millstone were tied about his neck and that he were cast into the depth of the sea rather than that he should scandalise one of these, my least little ones.* That is the language of the Holy Ghost.

– And very bad language if you ask me, said Mr Dedalus coolly.

– Simon! Simon! said Uncle Charles. The boy.

– Yes, yes, said Mr Dedalus. I meant about the . . . I was thinking about the bad language of that railway porter. Well now, that's all right. Here, Stephen, show me your plate, old chap. Eat away now. Here.

He heaped up the food on Stephen's plate and served Uncle Charles and Mr Casey to large pieces of turkey and splashes of sauce. Mrs Dedalus was eating little and Dante sat with her hands in her lap. She was red in the face. Mr Dedalus rooted with the carvers at the end of the dish and said:

– There's a tasty bit here we call the pope's nose. If any lady or gentleman . . .

He held a piece of fowl up on the prong of the carving-fork. Nobody spoke. He put it on his own plate, saying:

– Well, you can't say but you were asked. I think I had better eat it myself because I'm not well in my health lately.

He winked at Stephen and, replacing the dishcover, began to eat again.

There was a silence while he ate. Then he said:

– Well now, the day kept up fine after all. There were plenty of strangers down too. Nobody spoke. He said again:

– I think there were more strangers down than last Christmas.

He looked round at the others whose faces were bent towards their plates and, receiving no reply, waited for a moment and said bitterly:

– Well, my Christmas dinner has been spoiled anyhow.

– There could be neither luck nor grace, Dante said, in a house where there is no respect for the pastors of the church.

Mr Dedalus threw his knife and fork noisily on his plate.

– Respect! he said. Is it for Billy with the lip or for the tub of guts up in Armagh? Respect!

– Princes of the church, said Mr Casey with slow scorn.

– Lord Leitrim's coachman, yes, said Mr Dedalus.

– They are the Lord's anointed, Dante said. They are an honour to their country.

– Tub of guts, said Mr Dedalus coarsely. He has a handsome face, mind you, in repose. You should see that fellow lapping up his bacon and cabbage of a cold winter's day. O Johnny!

He twisted his features into a grimace of heavy bestiality and made a lapping noise with his lips.

– Really, Simon, you should not speak that way before Stephen. It's not right.

– O, he'll remember all this when he grows up, said Dante hotly – the language he heard against God and religion and priests in his own home.

– Let him remember too, cried Mr Casey to her from across the table, the language with which the priests and the priests' pawns broke Parnell's heart and hounded him into his grave. Let him remember that too when he grows up.

– Sons of bitches! cried Mr Dedalus. When he was down they turned on him to betray him and rend him like rats in a sewer. Lowlived dogs! And they look it! By Christ, they look it!

– They behaved rightly, cried Dante. They obeyed their bishops and their priests. Honour to them!

– Well, it is perfectly dreadful to say that not even for one day in the year, said Mrs Dedalus, can we be free from these dreadful disputes!

Uncle Charles raised his hands mildly and said:

– Come now, come now, come now! Can we not have our opinions whatever they are without this bad temper and this bad language? It is too bad surely.

Mrs Dedalus spoke to Dante in a low voice but Dante said loudly:

– I will not say nothing. I will defend my church and my religion when it is insulted and spit on by renegade catholics.

Mr Casey pushed his plate rudely into the middle of the table and, resting his elbows before him, said in a hoarse voice to his host:

– Tell me, did I tell you that story about a very famous spit?

– You did not, John, said Mr Dedalus.

– Why then, said Mr Casey, it is a most instructive story. It happened not long ago in the county Wicklow where we are now.

He broke off and, turning towards Dante, said with quiet indignation:

– And I may tell you, ma'am, that I, if you mean me, am no renegade catholic. I am a catholic as my father was and his father before him and his father before him again when we gave up our lives rather than sell our faith.

– The more shame to you now, Dante said, to speak as you do.

– The story, John, said Mr Dedalus smiling. Let us have the story anyhow.

– Catholic indeed! repeated Dante ironically. The blackest protestant in the land would not speak the language I have heard this evening.

Mr Dedalus began to sway his head to and fro, crooning like a country singer.

– I am no protestant, I tell you again, said Mr Casey flushing.

Mr Dedalus, still crooning and swaying his head, began to sing in a grunting nasal tone:

> *O, come all you Roman catholics*
> *That never went to mass.*

He took up his knife and fork again in good humour and set to eating, saying to Mr Casey:

— Let us have the story, John. It will help us to digest.

Stephen looked with affection at Mr Casey's face which stared across the table over his joined hands. He liked to sit near him at the fire, looking up at his dark fierce face. But his dark eyes were never fierce and his slow voice was good to listen to. But why was he then against the priests? Because Dante must be right then. But he had heard his father say that she was a spoiled nun and that she had come out of the convent in the Alleghanies when her brother had got the money from the savages for the trinkets and the chainies. Perhaps that made her severe against Parnell. And she did not like him to play with Eileen because Eileen was a protestant and when she was young she knew children that used to play with protestants and the protestants used to make fun of the litany of the Blessed Virgin. *Tower of Ivory*, they used to say, *House of Gold!* How could a woman be a tower of ivory or a house of gold? Who was right then? And he remembered the evening in the infirmary in Clongowes, the dark waters, the light at the pierhead and the moan of sorrow from the people when they had heard.

Eileen had long white hands. One evening when playing tig she had put her hands over his eyes: long and white and thin and cold and soft. That was ivory: a cold white thing. That was the meaning of *Tower of Ivory*.

— The story is very short and sweet, Mr Casey said. It was one day down in Arklow, a cold bitter day, not long before the chief died. May God have mercy on him!

He closed his eyes wearily and paused. Mr Dedalus took a bone from his plate and tore some meat from it with his teeth, saying:

— Before he was killed, you mean.

Mr Casey opened his eyes, sighed and went on:

— He was down in Arklow one day. We were down there at a meeting and after the meeting was over we had to make our way to the railway station through the crowd. Such booing and baaing, man, you never heard. They called us all the names in the world. Well there was one old lady, and a drunken old harridan she was surely, that paid all her attention to me. She kept dancing along beside me in the mud bawling and screaming into my face: *Priesthunter! The Paris Funds! Mr Fox! Kitty O'Shea!*

— And what did you do, John? asked Mr Dedalus.

— I let her bawl away, said Mr Casey. It was a cold day and to keep up my heart I had (saving your presence, ma'am) a quid of Tullamore in my mouth and sure I couldn't say a word in any case because my mouth was full of tobacco juice.

— Well, John?

— Well. I let her bawl away, to her heart's content, *Kitty O'Shea* and the rest of it till at last she called that lady a name that I won't sully this Christmas board nor your ears, ma'am, nor my own lips by repeating.

He paused. Mr Dedalus, lifting his head from the bone, asked:

— And what did you do, John?

— Do! said Mr Casey. She stuck her ugly old face up at me when she said it and I had my mouth full of tobacco juice. I bent down to her and *Phth!* says I to her like that.

He turned aside and made the act of spitting.

— Phth! says I to her like that, right into her eye.

He clapped a hand to his eye and gave a hoarse scream of pain.

– *O Jesus, Mary and Joseph!* says she. *I'm blinded! I'm blinded and drownded!*

He stopped in a fit of coughing and laughter, repeating:

– *I'm blinded entirely.*

Mr Dedalus laughed loudly and lay back in his chair while Uncle Charles swayed his head to and fro.

Dante looked terrible angry and repeated while they laughed:

– Very nice! Ha! Very nice!

It was not nice about the spit in the woman's eye.

But what was the name the woman had called Kitty O'Shea that Mr Casey would not repeat? He thought of Mr Casey walking through the crowds of people and making speeches from a wagonette. That was what he had been in prison for and he remembered that one night Sergeant O'Neill had come to the house and had stood in the hall, talking in a low voice with his father and chewing nervously at the chinstrap of his cap. And that night Mr Casey had not gone to Dublin by train but a car had come to the door and he had heard his father say something about the Cabinteely road.

He was for Ireland and Parnell and so was his father: and so was Dante too for one night at the band on the esplanade she had hit a gentleman on the head with her umbrella because he had taken off his hat when the band played *God save the Queen* at the end.

Mr Dedalus gave a snort of contempt.

– Ah, John, he said. It is true for them. We are an unfortunate priestridden race and always were and always will be till the end of the chapter.

Uncle Charles shook his head, saying:

– A bad business! A bad business!

Mr Dedalus repeated:

– A priestridden Godforsaken race!

He pointed to the portrait of his grandfather on the wall to his right.

– Do you see that old chap up there, John? he said. He was a good Irishman when there was no money in the job. He was condemned to death as a whiteboy. But he had a saying about our clerical friends, that he would never let one of them put his two feet under his mahogany.

Dante broke in angrily:

– If we are a priestridden race we ought to be proud of it! They are the apple of God's eye. *Touch them not*, says Christ, *for they are the apple of My eye.*

– And can we not love our country then? asked Mr Casey. Are we not to follow the man that was born to lead us?

– A traitor to his country! replied Dante. A traitor, an adulterer! The priests were right to abandon him. The priests were always the true friends of Ireland.

– Were they, faith? said Mr Casey.

He threw his fist on the table and, frowning angrily, protruded one finger after another.

– Didn't the bishops of Ireland betray us in the time of the union when Bishop Lanigan presented an address of loyalty to the Marquess Cornwallis? Didn't the bishops and priests sell the aspirations of their country in 1829 in return for catholic emancipation?

Didn't they denounce the fenian movement from the pulpit and in the confession box? And didn't they dishonour the ashes of Terence Bellew MacManus?

His face was glowing with anger and Stephen felt the glow rise to his own cheek as the spoken words thrilled him. Mr Dedalus uttered a guffaw of coarse scorn.

— O, by God, he cried, I forgot little old Paul Cullen! Another apple of God's eye!

Dante bent across the table and cried to Mr Casey:

— Right! Right! They were always right! God and morality and religion come first.

Mrs Dedalus, seeing her excitement, said to her:

— Mrs Riordan, don't excite yourself answering them.

— God and religion before everything! Dante cried. God and religion before the world!

Mr Casey raised his clenched fist and brought it down on the table with a crash.

— Very well, then, he shouted hoarsely, if it comes to that, no God for Ireland!

— John! John! cried Mr Dedalus, seizing his guest by the coat sleeve.

Dante started across the table, her cheeks shaking. Mr Casey struggled up from his chair and bent across the table towards her, scraping the air from before his eyes with one hand as though he were tearing aside a cobweb.

— No God for Ireland! he cried. We have had too much God in Ireland. Away with God!

— Blasphemer! Devil! screamed Dante, starting to her feet and almost spitting in his face.

Uncle Charles and Mr Dedalus pulled Mr Casey back into his chair again, talking to him from both sides reasonably. He stared before him out of his dark flaming eyes, repeating:

— Away with God, I say!

Dante shoved her chair violently aside and left the table, upsetting her napkinring which rolled slowly along the carpet and came to rest against the foot of an easychair. Mrs Dedalus rose quickly and followed her towards the door. At the door Dante turned round violently and shouted down the room, her cheeks flushed and quivering with rage:

— Devil out of hell! We won! We crushed him to death! Fiend!

The door slammed behind her.

Mr Casey, freeing his arms from his holders, suddenly bowed his head on his hands with a sob of pain.

— Poor Parnell! he cried loudly. My dead king!

He sobbed loudly and bitterly.

Stephen, raising his terrorstricken face, saw that his father's eyes were full of tears.

From *Ulysses*

I was just passing the time of day with old Troy of the D. M. P. at the corner of Arbour hill there and be damned but a bloody sweep came along and he near drove his gear into my eye. I turned around to let him have the weight of my tongue when who should I see dodging along Stony Batter only Joe Hynes.

– Lo, Joe, says I. How are you blowing? Did you see that bloody chimneysweep near shove my eye out with his brush?

– Soot's luck, says Joe. Who's the old ballocks you were talking to?

– Old Troy, says I, was in the force. I'm on two minds not to give that fellow in charge for obstructing the thoroughfare with his brooms and ladders.

– What are you doing round those parts? says Joe.

– Devil a much, says I. There is a bloody big foxy thief beyond by the garrison church at the corner of Chicken Lane – old Troy was just giving me a wrinkle about him – lifted any God's quantity of tea and sugar to pay three bob a week said he had a farm in the county Down off a hop of my thumb by the name of Moses Herzog over there near Heytesbury street.

– Circumcised! says Joe.

– Ay, says I. A bit off the top. An old plumber named Geraghty. I'm hanging on to his taw now for the past fortnight and I can't get a penny out of him.

– That the lay you're on now? says Joe.

– Ay, says I. How are the mighty fallen! Collector of bad and doubtful debts. But that's the most notorious bloody robber you'd meet in a day's walk and the face on him all pockmarks would hold a shower of rain. *Tell him,* says he, *I dare him,* says he, *and I doubledare him to send you round here again or if he does,* says he, *I'll have him summonsed up before the court, so will I, for trading without a licence.* And he after stuffing himself till he's fit to burst! Jesus, I had to laugh at the little jewy getting his shirt out. *He drink me my teas. He eat me my sugars. Because he no pay me my moneys?*

For nonperishable goods bought of Moses Herzog, of 13 Saint Kevin's parade, Wood quay ward, merchant, hereinafter called the vendor, and sold and delivered to Michael E. Geraghty, Esquire, of 29 Arbour Hill in the city of Dublin, Arran quay ward, gentleman, hereinafter called the purchaser, videlicet, five pounds avoirdupois of first choice tea at three shillings per pound avoirdupois and three stone avoirdupois of sugar, crushed crystal, at three pence per pound avoirdupois, the said purchaser debtor to the said vendor of one pound five shillings and six pence sterling for value received which amount shall be paid by said purchaser to said vendor in weekly instalments every seven calendar days of three shillings and no pence sterling: and the said nonperishable goods shall not be pawned or pledged or sold or otherwise alienated by the said purchaser but shall be and remain and be held to be the sole and exclusive property of the said vendor to be disposed of at his good will and pleasure until the said amount shall have been duly paid by the said purchaser to the said vendor in the manner herein set forth as this day hereby agreed between the said vendor his heirs, successors, trustees and assigns of the one part and the said purchaser, his heirs, successors, trustees and assigns of the other part.

– Are you a strict t. t.? says Joe.

– Not taking anything between drinks, says I.

– What about paying our respects to our friend? says Joe.

– Who? says I. Sure, he's in John of God's off his head, poor man.

– Drinking his own stuff? says Joe.

– Ay, says I. Whisky and water on the brain.

– Come around to Barney Kiernan's, says Joe. I want to see the citizen.

– Barney mavourneen's be it, says I. Anything strange or wonderful, Joe?

– Not a word, says Joe. I was up at that meeting in the City Arms.

– What was that, Joe? says I.

– Cattle traders, says Joe, about the foot and mouth disease. I want to give the citizen the hard word about it.

So we went around by the Linenhall barracks and the back of the courthouse talking of one thing or another. Decent fellow Joe when he has it but sure like that he never has it. Jesus, I couldn't get over that bloody foxy Geraghty, the daylight robber. For trading without a licence, says he.

In Inisfail the fair there lies a land, the land of holy Michan. There rises a watchtower beheld of men afar. There sleep the mighty dead as in life they slept, warriors and princes of high renown. A pleasant land it is in sooth of murmuring waters, fishful streams where sport the gunnard, the plaice, the roach, the halibut, the gibbed haddock, the grilse, the dab, the brill, the flounder, the mixed coarse fish generally and other denizens of the aqueous kingdom too numerous to be enumerated. In the mild breezes of the west and of the east the lofty trees wave in different directions their first class foliage, the wafty sycamore, the Lebanonian cedar, the exalted planetree, the eugenic eucalyptus and other ornaments of the arboreal world with which that region is thoroughly well supplied. Lovely maidens sit in close proximity to the roots of the lovely trees singing the most lovely songs while they play with all kinds of lovely objects as for example golden ingots, silvery fishes, crans of herrings, drafts of eels, codlings, creels of fingerlings, purple seagems and playful insects. And heroes voyage from afar to woo them, from Eblana to Slievemargy, the peerless princes of unfettered Munster and of Connacht the just and of smooth sleek Leinster and of Cruachan's land and of Armagh the splendid and of the noble district of Boyle, princes, the sons of kings.

And there rises a shining palace whose crystal glittering roof is seen by mariners who traverse the extensive sea in barks built expressly for that purpose and thither come all herds and fatlings and first fruits of that land for O'Connell Fitzsimon takes toll of them, a chieftain descended from chieftains. Thither the extremely large wains bring foison of the fields, flaskets of cauliflowers, floats of spinach, pineapple chunks, Rangoon beans, strikes of tomatoes, drums of figs, drills of Swedes, spherical potatoes and tallies of iridescent kale, York and Savoy, and trays of onions, pearls of the earth, and punnets of mushrooms and custard marrows and fat vetches and bere and rape and red green yellow brown russet sweet big bitter ripe pomellated apples and chips of strawberries and sieves of gooseberries, pulpy and pelurious, and strawberries fit for princes and raspberries from their canes.

I dare him, says he, and I doubledare him. Come out here, Geraghty, you notorious bloody hill and dale robber!

And by that way wend the herds innumerable of bellwethers and flushed ewes and
shearling rams and lambs and stubble geese and medium steers and roaring mares and
polled calves and longwools and storesheep and Cuffe's prime springers and culls and
sowpigs and baconhogs and the various different varieties of highly distinguished swine
and Angus heifers and polly bullocks of immaculate pedigree together with prime
premiated milchcows and beeves: and there is ever heard a trampling, cackling, roaring,
lowing, bleating, bellowing, rumbling, grunting, champing, chewing, of sheep and pigs
and heavyhooved kine from pasturelands of Lush and Rush and Carrickmines and from
the streamy vales of Thomond, from M'Gillicuddy's reeks the inaccessible and lordly
Shannon the unfathomable, and from the gentle declivities of the place of the race of
Kiar, their udders distended with superabundance of milk and butts of butter and
rennets of cheese and farmer's firkins and targets of lamb and crannocks of corn and
oblong eggs, in great hundreds, various in size, the agate with the dun.

So we turned into Barney Kiernan's and there sure enough was the citizen up in the
corner having a great confab with himself and that bloody mangy mongrel, Garryowen,
and he waiting for what the sky would drop in the way of drink.

— There he is, says I, in his gloryhole, with his cruiskeen lawn and his load of papers,
working for the cause.

The bloody mongrel let a grouse out of him would give you the creeps. Be a corporal
work of mercy if someone would take the life of that bloody dog. I'm told for a fact
he ate a good part of the breeches off a constabulary man in Santry that came round
one time with a blue paper about a licence.

— Stand and deliver, says he.

— That's all right, citizen, says Joe. Friends here.

— Pass, friends, says he.

Then he rubs his hand in his eye and says he:

— What's your opinion of the times?

Doing the rapparee and Rory of the hill. But, begob, Joe was equal to the occasion.

— I think the markets are on a rise, says he, sliding his hand down his fork.

So begob the citizen claps his paw on his knee and he says:

— Foreign wars is the cause of it.

And says Joe, sticking his thumb in his pocket:

— It's the Russians wish to tyrannise.

— Arrah, give over your bloody codding, Joe, says I, I've a thirst on me I wouldn't
sell for half a crown.

— Give it a name, citizen, says Joe.

— Wine of the country, says he.

— What's yours? says Joe.

— Ditto MacAnaspey, says I.

— Three pints, Terry, says Joe. And how's the old heart, citizen? says he.

— Never better, *a chara*, says he. What Garry? Are we going to win? Eh?

And with that he took the bloody old towser by the scruff of the neck and, by Jesus,
he near throttled him.

The figure seated on a large boulder at the foot of a round tower was that of a broadshouldered deepchested stronglimbed frankeyed redhaired freely freckled shaggybearded widemouthed largenosed longheaded deepvoiced barekneed brawnyhanded hairylegged ruddyfaced sinewyarmed hero. From shoulder to shoulder he measured several ells and his rocklike mountainous knees were covered, as was likewise the rest of his body wherever visible, with a strong growth of tawny prickly hair in hue and toughness similar to the mountain gorse (*Ulex Europeus*). The widewinged nostrils, from which bristles of the same tawny hue projected, were of such capaciousness that within their cavernous obscurity the fieldlark might easily have lodged her nest. The eyes in which a tear and a smile strove ever for the mastery were of the dimensions of a goodsized cauliflower. A powerful current of warm breath issued at regular intervals from the profound cavity of his mouth while in rhythmic resonance the loud strong hale reverberations of his formidable heart thundered rumblingly causing the ground, the summit of the lofty tower and the still loftier walls of the cave to vibrate and tremble.

He wore a long unsleeved garment of recently flayed oxhide reaching to the knees in a loose kilt and this was bound about his middle by a girdle of plaited straw and rushes. Beneath this he wore trews of deerskin, roughly stitched with gut. His nether extremities were encased in high Balbriggan buskins dyed in lichen purple, the feet being shod with brogues of salted cowhide laced with the windpipe of the same beast. From his girdle hung a row of seastones which dangled at every movement of his portentous frame and on these were graven with rude yet striking art the tribal images of many Irish heroes and heroines of antiquity, Cuchulin, Conn of hundred battles, Niall of nine hostages, Brian of Kincora, the Ardri Malachi, Art MacMurragh, Shane O'Neill, Father John Murphy, Owen Roe, Patrick Sarsfield, Red Hugh O'Donnell, Red Jim MacDermott, Soggarth Eoghan O'Growney, Michael Dwyer, Francy Higgins, Henry Joy M'Cracken, Goliath, Horace Wheatley, Thomas Conneff, Peg Woffington, the Village Blacksmith, Captain Moonlight, Captain Boycott, Dante Alighieri, Christopher Columbus, S. Fursa, S. Brendan, Marshal MacMahon, Charlemagne, Theobald Wolfe Tone, the Mother of the Maccabees, the Last of the Mohicans, the Rose of Castille, the Man for Galway, The Man that Broke the Bank at Monte Carlo, The Man in the Gap, The Woman Who Didn't, Benjamin Franklin, Napoleon Bonaparte, John L. Sullivan, Cleopatra, Savourneen Deelish, Julius Caesar, Paracelsus, sir Thomas Lipton, William Tell, Michelangelo, Hayes, Muhammad, the Bride of Lammermoor, Peter the Hermit, Peter the Packer, Dark Rosaleen, Patrick W. Shakespeare, Brian Confucius, Murtagh Gutenberg, Patricio Velasquez, Captain Nemo, Tristan and Isolde, the first Prince of Wales, Thomas Cook and Son, the Bold Soldier Boy, Arrah na Pogue, Dick Turpin, Ludwig Beethoven, the Colleen Bawn, Waddler Healy, Angus the Culdee, Dolly Mount, Sidney Parade, Ben Howth, Valentine Greatrakes, Adam and Eve, Arthur Wellesley, Boss Croker, Herodotus, Jack the Giantkiller, Gautama Buddha, Lady Godiva, The Lily of Killarney, Balor of the Evil Eye, the Queen of Sheba, Acky Nagle, Joe Nagle, Alessandro Volta, Jeremiah O'Donovan Rossa, Don Philip O'Sullivan Beare. A couched spear of acuminated granite rested by him while at his feet reposed a savage animal of the canine tribe whose stertorous gasps announced that he was sunk in uneasy slumber, a supposition confirmed by hoarse growls and spasmodic movements which his master repressed from time to time by tranquillising blows of a mighty cudgel rudely fashioned out of paleolithic stone.

So anyhow Terry brought the three pints Joe was standing and begob the sight nearly left my eyes when I saw him land out a quid. O, as true as I'm telling you. A goodlooking sovereign.

– And there's more where that came from, says he.

– Were you robbing the poorbox, Joe? says I.

– Sweat of my brow, says Joe. 'Twas the prudent member gave me the wheeze.

– I saw him before I met you, says I, sloping around by Pill lane and Greek street with his cod's eye counting up all the guts of the fish.

Who comes through Michan's land, bedight in sable armour? O'Bloom, the son of Rory: it is he. Impervious to fear is Rory's son: he of the prudent soul.

– For the old woman of Prince's street, says the citizen, the subsidised organ. The pledgebound party on the floor of the house. And look at this blasted rag, says he. Look at this, says he. *The Irish Independent*, if you please, founded by Parnell to be the workingman's friend. Listen to the births and deaths in the *Irish all for Ireland Independent* and I'll thank you and the marriages.

And he starts reading them out:

– Gordon, Barnfield Crescent, Exeter; Redmayne of Iffley, Saint Anne's on Sea, the wife of William T. Redmayne, of a son. How's that, eh? Wright and Flint, Vincent and Gillett to Rotha Marion daughter of Rosa and the late George Alfred Gillett, 179 Clapham Road, Stockwell, Playwood and Ridsdale at Saint Jude's Kensington by the very reverend Dr Forrest, Dean of Worcester, eh? Deaths. Bristow, at Whitehall lane, London: Carr, Stoke Newington, of gastritis and heart disease: Cockburn, at the Moat house, Chepstow . . .

– I know that fellow, says Joe, from bitter experience.

– Cockburn. Dimsey, wife of David Dimsey, late of the admiralty: Miller, Tottenham, aged eightyfive: Welsh, June 12, at 35 Canning Street, Liverpool, Isabella Helen. How's that for a national press, eh, my brown son? How's that for Martin Murphy, the Bantry jobber?

– Ah, well, says Joe, handing round the boose. Thanks be to God they had the start of us. Drink that, citizen.

– I will, says he, honourable person.

– Health, Joe, says I. And all down the form.

Ah! Ow! Don't be talking! I was blue mouldy for the want of that pint. Declare to God I could hear it hit the pit of my stomach with a click.

And lo, as they quaffed their cup of joy, a godlike messenger came swiftly in, radiant as the eye of heaven, a comely youth, and behind him there passed an elder of noble gait and countenance, bearing the sacred scrolls of law, and with him his lady wife, a dame of peerless lineage, fairest of her race.

Little Alf Bergan popped in round the door and hid behind Barney's snug, squeezed up with the laughing, and who was sitting up there in the corner that I hadn't seen snoring drunk, blind to the world, only Bob Doran. I didn't know what was up and Alf kept making signs out of the door. And begob what was it only that bloody old pantaloon Denis Breen in his bath slippers with two bloody big books tucked under his oxter and the wife hotfoot after him, unfortunate wretched woman trotting like a poodle. I thought Alf would split.

— Look at him, says he. Breen. He's traipsing all round Dublin with a postcard someone sent him with u. p.: up on it to take a li . . .

And he doubled up.

— Take a what? says I.

— Libel action, says he, for ten thousand pounds.

— O hell! says I.

The bloody mongrel began to growl that'd put the fear of God in you seeing something was up but the citizen gave him a kick in the ribs.

— *Bi i dho husht*, says he.

— Who? says Joe.

— Breen, says Alf. He was in John Henry Menton's and then he went round to Collis and Ward's and then Tom Rochford met him and sent him round to the subsheriff's for a lark. O God, I've a pain laughing. U. p.: up. The long fellow gave him an eye as good as a process and now the bloody old lunatic is gone round to Green Street to look for a G. man.

— When is long John going to hang that fellow in Mountjoy? says Joe.

— Bergan, says Bob Doran, waking up. Is that Alf Bergan?

— Yes, says Alf. Hanging? Wait till I show you. Here, Terry, give us a pony. That bloody old fool! Ten thousand pounds. You should have seen long John's eye. U. p . . .

And he started laughing.

— Who are you laughing at? says Bob Doran. Is that Bergan?

— Hurry up, Terry boy, says Alf.

Terence O'Ryan heard him and straightway brought him a crystal cup full of the foaming ebon ale which the noble twin brothers Bungiveagh and Bungardilaun brew ever in their divine alevats, cunning as the sons of deathless Leda. For they garner the succulent berries of the hop and mass and sift and bruise and brew them and they mix therewith sour juices and bring the must to the sacred fire and cease not night or day from their toil, those cunning brothers, lords of the vat.

Then did you, chivalrous Terence, hand forth, as to the manner born, that nectarous beverage and you offered the crystal cup to him that thirsted, the soul of chivalry, in beauty akin to the immortals.

But he, the young chief of the O'Bergan's, could ill brook to be outdone in generous deeds but gave therefor with gracious gesture a testoon of costliest bronze. Thereon embossed in excellent smithwork was seen the image of a queen of regal port, scion of the house of Brunswick, Victoria her name, Her Most Excellent Majesty, by grace of God of the United Kingdom of Great Britain and Ireland and of the British dominions beyond the sea, queen, defender of the faith, Empress of India, even she, who bore rule, a victress over many peoples, the wellbeloved, for they knew and loved her from the rising of the sun to the going down thereof, the pale, the dark, the ruddy and the ethiop.

— What's that bloody freemason doing, says the citizen, prowling up and down outside?

— What's that? says Joe.

— Here you are, says Alf, chucking out the rhino. Talking about hanging. I'll show you something you never saw. Hangmen's letters. Look at here.

So he took a bundle of wisps of letters and envelopes out of his pocket.

— Are you codding? says I.

— Honest injun, says Alf. Read them.

So Joe took up the letters.

— Who are you laughing at? says Bob Doran.

So I saw there was going to be bit of a dust. Bob's a queer chap when the porter's up in him so says I just to make talk:

— How's Willy Murray those times, Alf?

— I don't know, says Alf. I saw him just now in Capel Street with Paddy Dignam. Only I was running after that . . .

— You what? says Joe, throwing down the letters. With who?

— With Dignam, says Alf.

— Is it Paddy? says Joe.

— Yes, says Alf. Why?

— Don't you know he's dead? says Joe.

— Paddy Dignam dead? says Alf.

— Ay, says Joe.

— Sure I'm after seeing him not five minutes ago, says Alf, as plain as a pikestaff.

— Who's dead? says Bob Doran.

— You saw his ghost then, says Joe, God between us and harm.

— What? says Alf. Good Christ, only five . . . What? . . . and Willy Murray with him, the two of them there near whatdoyoucallhim's . . . What? Dignam dead?

— What about Dignam? says Bob Doran. Who's talking about . . . ?

— Dead! says Alf. He is no more dead than you are.

— Maybe so, says Joe. They took the liberty of burying him this morning anyhow.

— Paddy? says Alf.

— Ay, says Joe. He paid the debt of nature, God be merciful to him.

— Good Christ! says Alf.

Begob he was what you might call flabbergasted.

In the darkness spirit hands were felt to flutter and when prayer by tantras had been directed to the proper quarter a faint but increasing luminosity of ruby light became gradually visible, the apparition of the etheric double being particularly lifelike owing to the discharge of jivic rays from the crown of the head and face. Communication was effected through the pituitary body and also by means of the orangefiery and scarlet rays emanating from the sacral region and solar plexus. Questioned by his earthname as to his whereabouts in the heavenworld he stated that he was now on the path of prālāyā or return but was still submitted to trial at the hands of certain bloodthirsty entities on the lower astral levels. In reply to a question as to his first sensations in the great divide beyond he stated that previously he had seen as in a glass darkly but that those who had passed over had summit possibilities of atmic development opened up to them. Interrogated as to whether life there resembled our experience in the flesh he stated that he had heard from more favoured beings now in the spirit that their abodes were equipped with every modern home comfort such as tālāfānā, ālāvātār, hātākāldā, wātāklāsāt and that the highest adepts were steeped in waves of volupcy of the very purest nature. Having requested a quart of buttermilk this was brought and evidently afforded relief. Asked if he had any message for the living he exhorted all who were still at the wrong side of Māyā to acknowledge the true path for it was reported in devanic circles that Mars and Jupiter were out for mischief on the eastern angle where the ram has power. It was then queried whether there were any special desires on the part of the defunct and the reply was: *We greet you, friends of earth, who are still in the body. Mind C. K. doesn't pile it on.* It was ascertained that the reference was to Mr Cornelius Kelleher, manager of Messrs H. J. O'Neill's popular funeral establishment, a personal friend of the defunct, who had been responsible for the carrying out of the interment arrangements. Before departing he requested that it should be told to his dear son Patsy that the other boot which he had been looking for was at present under the commode in the return room and that the pair should be sent to Cullen's to be soled only as the heels were still good. He stated that this had greatly perturbed his peace of mind in the other region and earnestly requested that his desire should be made known.

Assurances were given that the matter would be attended to and it was intimated that this had given satisfaction.

He is gone from mortal haunts: O'Dignam, sun of our morning. Fleet was his foot on the bracken: Patrick of the beamy brow. Wail, Banba, with your wind: and wail, O ocean, with your whirlwind.

– There he is again, says the citizen, staring out.

– Who? says I.

– Bloom, says he. He's on point duty up and down there for the last ten minutes.

And, begob, I saw his physog do a peep in and then slidder off again.

Little Alf was knocked bawways. Faith, he was.

– Good Christ! says he. I could have sworn it was him.

And says Bob Doran, with the hat on the back of his poll, lowest blackguard in Dublin when he's under the influence:

– Who said Christ is good?

– I beg your parsnips, says Alf.

– Is that a good Christ, says Bob Doran, to take away poor little Willy Dignam?

– Ah, well, says Alf, trying to pass it off. He's over all his troubles.

But Bob Doran shouts out of him.

– He's a bloody ruffian I say, to take away poor little Willy Dignam.

Terry came down and tipped him the wink to keep quiet, that they didn't want that kind of talk in a respectable licensed premises. And Bob Doran starts doing the weeps about Paddy Dignam, true as you're there.

– The finest man, says he, snivelling, the finest purest character.

The tear is bloody near your eye. Talking through his bloody hat. Fitter for him to go home to the little sleepwalking bitch he married, Mooney, the bumbailiff's daughter. Mother kept a kip in Hardwicke street that used to be stravaging about the landings Bantam Lyons told me that was stopping there at two in the morning without a stitch on her, exposing her person, open to all comers, fair field and no favour.

– The noblest, the truest, says he. And he's gone, poor little Willy, poor little Paddy Dignam.

And mournful and with a heavy heart he bewept the extinction of that beam of heaven.

Old Garryowen started growling again at Bloom that was skeezing round the door.

– Come in, come on, he won't eat you, says the citizen.

So Bloom slopes in with his cod's eye on the dog and he asks Terry was Martin Cunningham there.

– O, Christ M'Keown, says Joe, reading one of the letters. Listen to this, will you? And he starts reading out one.

> *7, Hunter Street, Liverpool.*
> *To the High Sheriff of Dublin, Dublin.*
> *Honoured sir i beg to offer my services in the above-mentioned painful case i hanged Joe Gann in Bootle jail on the* 12 *of February* 1900 *and i hanged . . .*

– Show us, Joe, says I.

– *. . . private Arthur Chace for fowl murder of Jessie Tilsit in Pentonville prison and i was assistant when . . .*

– Jesus, says I.

– *. . . Billington executed the awful murderer Toad Smith . . .*

The citizen made a grab at the letter.

– Hold hard, says Joe, *i have a special nack of putting the noose once in he can't get out hoping to be favoured i remain, honoured sir, my terms is five ginnese.*

> *H. Rumbold,*
> *Master Barber.*

– And a barbarous bloody barbarian he is too, says the citizen.

– And the dirty scrawl of the wretch, says Joe. Here, says he, take them to hell out of my sight, Alf. Hello, Bloom, says he, what will you have?

So they started arguing about the point, Bloom saying he wouldn't and couldn't and excuse him no offence and all to that and then he said well he'd just take a cigar. Gob, he's a prudent member and no mistake.

– Give us one of your prime stinkers, Terry, says Joe.

And Alf was telling us there was one chap sent in a mourning card with a black border round it.

– They're all barbers, says he, from the black country that would hang their own fathers for five quid down and travelling expenses.

And he was telling us there's two fellows waiting below to pull his heels down when he gets the drop and choke him properly and then they chop up the rope after and sell the bits for a few bob a skull.

In the dark land they bide, the vengeful knights of the razor. Their deadly coil they grasp: yea, and therein they lead to Erebus whatsoever wight hath done a deed of blood for I will on nowise suffer it even so saith the Lord.

So they started talking about capital punishment and of course Bloom comes out with the why and the wherefore and all the codology of the business and the old dog smelling him all the time I'm told those Jewies does have a sort of a queer odour coming off them for dogs about I don't know what all deterrent effect and so forth and so on.

– There's one thing it hasn't a deterrent effect on, says Alf.

– What's that? says Joe.

– The poor bugger's tool that's being hanged, says Alf.

– That so? says Joe.

– God's truth, says Alf. I heard that from the head warder that was in Kilmainham when they hanged Joe Brady, the invincible. He told me when they cut him down after the drop it was standing up in their faces like a poker.

– Ruling passion strong in death, says Joe, as someone said.

– That can be explained by science, says Bloom. It's only a natural phenomenon, don't you see, because on account of the . . .

And then he starts with his jawbreakers about phenomenon and science and this phenomenon and the other phenomenon.

The distinguished scientist Herr Professor Luitpold Blumenduft tendered medical evidence to the effect that the instantaneous fracture of the cervical vertebrae and consequent scission of the spinal cord would, according to the best approved traditions of medical science, be calculated to inevitably produce in the human subject a violent ganglionic stimulus of the nerve centres, causing the pores of the *corpora cavernosa* to rapidly dilate in such a way as to instantaneously facilitate the flow of blood to that part of the human anatomy known as the penis or male organ resulting in the phenomenon which has been denominated by the faculty a morbid upwards and outwards philoprogenitive erection *in articulo mortis per diminutionem capitis.*

So of course the citizen was only waiting for the wink of the word and he starts gassing out of him about the invincibles and the old guard and the men of sixtyseven and who fears to speak of ninetyeight and Joe with him about all the fellows that were hanged, drawn and transported for the cause by drumhead courtmartial and a new Ireland and new this, that and the other. Talking about new Ireland he ought to go and get a new dog so he ought. Mangy ravenous brute sniffling and sneezing all round the place and scratching his scabs and round he goes to Bob Doran that was standing Alf a half one sucking up for what he could get. So of course Bob Doran starts doing the bloody fool with him:

– Give us the paw! Give the paw, doggy! Good old doggy. Give us the paw here! Give us the paw!

Arrah! bloody end to the paw he'd paw and Alf trying to keep him from tumbling off the bloody stool atop of the bloody old dog and he talking all kinds of drivel about training by kindness and thoroughbred dog and intelligent dog: give you the bloody pip. Then he starts scraping a few bits of old biscuit out of the bottom of a Jacob's tin he told Terry to bring. Gob, he golloped it down like old boots and his tongue hanging out of him a yard long for more. Near ate the tin and all, hungry bloody mongrel.

And the citizen and Bloom having an argument about the point, the brothers Sheares and Wolfe Tone beyond on Arbour Hill and Robert Emmet and die for your country, the Tommy Moore touch about Sara Curran and she's far from the land. And Bloom, of course, with his knockmedown cigar putting on swank with his lardy face. Phenomenon! The fat heap he married is a nice old phenomenon with a back on her like a ballalley. Time they were stopping up in the *City Arms* Pisser Burke told me there was an old one there with a cracked loodheramaun of a nephew and Bloom trying to get the soft side of her doing the mollycoddle playing bézique to come in for a bit of the wampum in her will and not eating meat of a Friday because the old one was always thumping her craw and taking the lout out for a walk. And one time he led him the rounds of Dublin and, by the holy farmer, he never cried crack till he brought him home as drunk as a boiled owl and he said he did it to teach him the evils of alcohol and by herrings if the three women didn't near roast him it's a queer story, the old one, Bloom's wife and Mrs O'Dowd that kept the hotel. Jesus, I had to laugh at Pisser Burke taking them off chewing the fat and Bloom with his *but don't you see?* and *but on the other hand.* And sure, more be token, the lout I'm told was in Power's after, the blender's, round in Cope street going home footless in a cab five times in the week after drinking his way through all the samples in the bloody establishment. Phenomenon!

– The memory of the dead, says the citizen taking up his pintglass and glaring at Bloom.

– Ay, ay, says Joe.

– You don't grasp my point, says Bloom. What I mean is . . .

– *Sinn Fein!* says the citizen. *Sinn fein amhain!* The friends we love are by our side and the foes we hate before us.

The last farewell was affecting in the extreme. From the belfries far and near the funereal deathbell tolled unceasingly while all around the gloomy precincts rolled the ominous warning of a hundred muffled drums punctuated by the hollow booming of pieces of ordnance. The deafening claps of thunder and the dazzling flashes of lightning which lit up the ghastly scene testified that the artillery of heaven had lent its supernatural pomp to the already gruesome spectacle. A torrential rain poured down from the floodgates of the angry heavens upon the bared heads of the assembled multitude which numbered at the lowest computation five hundred thousand persons. A posse of Dublin Metropolitan police superintended by the Chief Commissioner in person maintained order in the vast throng for whom the York Street brass and reed band whiled away the intervening time by admirably rendering on their blackdraped instruments the matchless melody endeared to us from the cradle by Speranza's plaintive muse. Special quick excursion trains and upholstered charabancs had been provided for the comfort of our country cousins of whom there were large contingents. Considerable amusement was caused by the favourite Dublin streetsingers L-n-h-n and M-ll-g-n who sang *The Night before Larry was stretched* in their usual mirthprovoking fashion. Our two inimitable drolls did a roaring trade with their broadsheets among lovers of the comedy element and nobody who has a corner in his heart for real Irish fun without vulgarity will grudge them their hardearned pennies. The children of the Male and Female Foundling Hospital who thronged the windows overlooking the scene were delighted with this unexpected addition to the day's entertainment and a word of praise is due to the Little Sisters of the Poor for their excellent idea of affording the poor fatherless and motherless children a genuinely instructive treat. The viceregal houseparty which included many well-known ladies was chaperoned by Their Excellencies to the most favourable positions on the grand stand while the picturesque foreign delegation known as the Friends of the Emerald Isle was accommodated on a tribune directly opposite. The delegation, present in full force, consisted of Commendatore Bacibaci Beninobenone (the semi-paralysed *doyen* of the party who had to be assisted to his seat by the aid of a powerful steam crane), Monsieur Pierrepaul Petitépatant, the Grandjoker Vladinmire Poket-hankertscheff, the Archjoker Leopold Rudolph von Schwanzenbad-Hodenthaler, Countess Marha Virága Kisászony Putrápesthi, Hiram Y. Bomboost, Count Athanatos Karamelopulos, Ali Baba Backsheesh Rahat Lokum Effendi, Señor Hidalgo Caballero Don Pecadillo y Palabras y Paternoster de la Malora de la Malaria, Hokopoko Harakiri, Hi Hung Chang, Olaf Kobberkeddelsen, Mynheer Trik van Trumps, Pan Poleaxe Paddyrisky, Goosepond Prhklstr Kratchinabritchisitch, Herr Hurhausdirektorpräsident Hans Chuechli-Steuerli, Nationalgymnasiummuseumsanatoriumandsuspensoriumsor-dinaryprivatdocentgeneralhistoryspecialprofessordoctor Kriegfried Ueberallgemein. All the delegates without exception expressed themselves in the strongest possible het-erogeneous terms concerning the nameless barbarity which they had been called upon to witness. An animated altercation (in which all took part) ensued among F. O. T. E. I. as to whether the eighth or the ninth of March was the correct date of the birth of Ireland's patron saint. In the course of the argument cannonballs, scimitars, boomerangs, blunderbusses, stinkpots, meatchoppers, umbrellas, catapults, knuckle-dusters, sandbags, lumps of pig iron were resorted to and blows were freely exchanged. The baby policeman, Constable MacFadden, summoned by special courier from Booters-town, quickly restored order and with lightning promptitude proposed the seventeenth of the month as a solution equally honourable for both contending parties. The readywitted ninefooter's suggestion at once appealed to all and was unanimously accepted. Constable MacFadden was heartily congratulated by all the F.O.T.E.I., several of whom were bleeding profusely. Commendatore Beninobenone having been extricated from underneath the presidential armchair, it was explained by his legal adviser Avvocato Pagamimi that the various articles secreted in his thirtytwo pockets had been abstracted by him during the affray from the pockets of his junior colleagues in the hope of bringing them to their senses. The objects (which included several hundred ladies' and gentlemen's gold and silver watches) were promptly restored to their rightful owners and general harmony reigned supreme.

Quietly, unassumingly, Rumbold stepped on to the scaffold in faultless morning dress and wearing his favourite flower the *Gladiolus Cruentus*. He announced his presence by that gentle Rumboldian cough which so many have tried (unsuccessfully) to imitate – short, painstaking yet withal so characteristic of the man. The arrival of the world-renowned headsman was greeted by a roar of acclamation from the huge concourse, the viceregal ladies waving their handkerchiefs in their excitement while the even more excitable foreign delegates cheered vociferously in a medley of cries, *hoch, banzai, eljen, zivio, chinchin, polla kronia, hiphip, vive, Allah*, amid which the ringing *evviva* of the delegate of the land of song (a high double F recalling those piercingly lovely notes with which the eunuch Catalani beglamoured out greatgreatgrandmothers) was easily distinguishable.

It was exactly seventeen o'clock. The signal for prayer was then promptly given by megaphone and in an instant all heads were bared, the commendatore's patriarchal sombrero, which has been in the possession of his family since the revolution of Rienzi, being removed by his medical adviser in attendance, Dr Pippi. The learned prelate who administered the last comforts of holy religion to the hero martyr when about to pay the death penalty knelt in a most christian spirit in a pool of rainwater, his cassock above his hoary head, and offered up to the throne of grace fervent prayers of supplication. Hard by the block stood the grim figure of the executioner, his visage being concealed in a tengallon pot with two circular perforated apertures through which his eyes glowered furiously. As he awaited the fatal signal he tested the edge of his horrible weapon by honing it upon his brawny forearm or decapitated in rapid succession a flock of sheep which had been provided by the admirers of his fell but necessary office. On a handsome mahogany table near him were neatly arranged the quartering knife, the various finely tempered disembowelling appliances (specially supplied by the worldfamous firm of cutlers, Messrs John Round and Sons, Sheffield), a terracotta saucepan for the reception of the duodenum, colon, blind intestine and appendix etc when successfully extracted and two commodious milkjugs destined to receive the most precious blood of the most precious victim. The housesteward of the amalgamated cats' and dogs' home was in attendance to convey these vessels when replenished to that beneficent institution. Quite an excellent repast consisting of rashers and eggs, fried steak and onions, done to a nicety, delicious hot breakfast rolls and invigorating tea had been considerately provided by the authorities for the consumption of the central figure of the tragedy who was in capital spirits when prepared for death and evinced the keenest interest in the proceedings from beginning to end but he, with an abnegation rare in these our times, rose nobly to the occasion and expressed the dying wish (immediately acceded to) that the meal should be divided in aliquot parts among the members of the sick and indigent roomkeepers' association as a token of his regard and esteem. The *nec* and *non plus ultra* of emotion were reached when the blushing bride elect burst her way through the serried ranks of the bystanders and flung herself upon the muscular bosom of him who was about to be launched into eternity for her sake. The hero folded her willowy form in a loving embrace murmuring fondly *Sheila, my own*. Encouraged by this use of her christian name she kissed passionately all the various suitable areas of his person which the decencies of prison garb permitted her ardour to reach. She swore to him as they mingled the salt streams of their tears that she would cherish his memory, that she would never forget her hero boy who went to his death with a song on his lips as if he were but going to a hurling match in Clonturk park. She brought back to his recollection the happy days of blissful childhood together on the banks of Anna Liffey when they had indulged in the innocent pastimes of the young and, oblivious of the dreadful present, they both laughed heartily, all the spectators, including the venerable pastor, joining in the general merriment. That monster audience simply rocked with delight. But anon they were overcome with grief and clasped their hands for the last time. A fresh torrent of tears burst from their lachrymal ducts and the vast concourse of people, touched to the inmost core, broke into heartrending sobs, not the least affected being the aged prebendary himself. Big strong men, officers of the peace and genial giants of the royal Irish constabulary, were making frank use of their handkerchiefs and it is safe to say that there was not a dry eye in that record assemblage. A most romantic incident occurred when a handsome young Oxford graduate, noted for his chivalry towards the fair sex, stepped forward and, presenting his visiting card, bankbook and genealogical tree solicited the hand of the hapless young lady, requesting her to name the day, and was accepted on the spot. Every lady in the audience was presented with a tasteful souvenir of the occasion in the shape of a skull and crossbones brooch, a timely and generous act which evoked a fresh outburst of emotion: and when the gallant young Oxonian (the bearer, by the way, of one of the most timehonoured names in Albion's history) placed on the finger of his blushing *fiancée* an expensive engagement ring with emeralds set in the form of a fourleaved shamrock excitement knew no bounds. Nay, even the stern provostmarshal, lieutenantcolonel Tomkin-Maxwell ffrenchmullan Tomlinson, who presided on the sad occasion, he who had blown a considerable number of sepoys from the cannonmouth without flinching, could not now restrain his natural emotion. With his mailed gauntlet he brushed away a furtive tear and was overheard by those privileged burghers who happened to be in his immediate *entourage* to murmur to himself in a faltering undertone:

— God blimey if she aint a clinker, that there bleeding tart. Blimey it makes me kind of bleeding cry, straight, it does, when I sees her cause I thinks of my old mashtub what's waiting for me down Limehouse way.

So then the citizen begins talking about the Irish language and the corporation meeting and all to that and the shoneens that can't speak their own language and Joe chipping in because he stuck someone for a quid and Bloom putting in his old goo with his twopenny stump that he cadged off Joe and talking about the Gaelic league and the antitreating league and drink, the curse of Ireland. Antitreating is about the size of it. Gob, he'd let you pour all manner of drink down his throat till the Lord would call him before you'd ever see the froth of his pint. And one night I went in with a fellow into one of their musical evenings, song and dance about she could get up on a truss of hay she could my Maureen Lay, and there was a fellow with a Ballyhooly blue ribbon badge spiffing out of him in Irish and a lot of colleen bawns going about with temperance beverages and selling medals and oranges and lemonade and a few old dry buns, gob, flahoolagh entertainment, don't be talking. Ireland sober is Ireland free. And then an old fellow starts blowing into his bagpipes and all the gougers shuffling their feet to the tune the old cow died of. And one or two sky pilots having an eye around that there was no goings on with the females, hitting below the belt.

So howandever, as I was saying, the old dog seeing the tin was empty starts mousing around by Joe and me. I'd train him by kindness, so I would, if he was my dog. Give him a rousing fine kick now and again where it wouldn't blind him.

— Afraid he'll bite you? says the citizen, sneering.

— No, says I. But he might take my leg for a lamppost.

So he calls the old dog over.

— What's on you, Garry? says he.

Then he starts hauling and mauling and talking to him in Irish and the old towser growling, letting on to answer, like a duet in the opera. Such growling you never heard as they let off between them. Someone that has nothing better to do ought to write a letter *pro bono publico* to the papers about the muzzling order for a dog the like of that. Growling and grousing and his eye all bloodshot from the drouth is in it and the hydrophobia dropping out of his jaws.

All those who are interested in the spread of human culture among the lower animals (and their name is legion) should make a point of not missing the really marvellous exhibition of cynanthropy given by the famous old Irish red wolfdog setter formerly known by the *sobriquet* of Garryowen and recently rechristened by his large circle of friends and acquaintances Owen Garry. The exhibition, which is the result of years of training by kindness and a carefully thoughtout dietary system, comprises, among other achievements, the recitation of verse. Our greatest living phonetic expert (wild horses shall not drag it from us!) has left no stone unturned in his efforts to delucidate and compare the verse recited and has found it bears a *striking* resemblance (the italics are ours) to the ranns of ancient Celtic bards. We are not speaking so much of those delightful lovesongs with which the writer who conceals his identity under the graceful pseudonym of the Little Sweet Branch has familiarised the bookloving world but rather (as a contributor D. O. C. points out in an interesting communication published by an evening contemporary) of the harsher and more personal note which is found in the satirical effusions of the famous Raftery and of Donald MacConsidine to say nothing of a more modern lyrist at present very much in the public eye. We subjoin a specimen which has been rendered into English by an eminent scholar whose name for the moment we are not at liberty to disclose though we believe that our readers will find the topical allusion rather more than an indication. The metrical system of the canine original, which recalls the intricate alliterative and isosyllabic rules of the Welsh englyn, is infinitely more complicated but we believe our readers will agree that the spirit has been well caught. Perhaps it should be added that the effect is greatly increased if Owen's verse be spoken somewhat slowly and indistinctly in a tone suggestive of suppressed rancour.

> *The curse of my curses*
> *Seven days every day*
> *And seven dry Thursdays*
> *On you, Barney Kiernan,*
> *Has no sup of water*
> *To cool my courage,*
> *And my guts red roaring*
> *After Lowry's lights.*

So he told Terry to bring some water for the dog and, gob, you could hear him lapping it up a mile off. And Joe asked him would he have another.

– I will, says he, *a chara*, to show there's no ill feeling.

Gob, he's not as green as he's cabbagelooking. Arsing around from one pub to another, leaving it to your own honour, with old Giltrap's dog and getting fed up by the ratepayers and corporators. Entertainment for man and beast. And says Joe:

– Could you make a hole in another pint?

– Could a swim duck? says I.

– Same again, Terry, says Joe. Are you sure you won't have anything in the way of liquid refreshment? says he.

– Thank you, no, says Bloom. As a matter of fact I just wanted to meet Martin Cunningham, don't you see, about this insurance of poor Dignam's. Martin asked me to go to the house. You see, he, Dignam, I mean, didn't serve any notice of the assignment on the company at the time and nominally under the act the mortgagee can't recover on the policy.

– Holy Wars, says Joe laughing, that's a good one if old Shylock is landed. So the wife comes out top dog, what?

– Well, that's a point, says Bloom, for the wife's admirers.

– Whose admirers? says Joe.

– The wife's advisers, I mean, says Bloom.

Then he starts all confused mucking it up about the mortgagor under the act like the lord chancellor giving it out on the bench and for the benefit of the wife and that a trust is created but on the other hand that Dignam owed Bridgeman the money and if now the wife or the widow contested the mortgagee's right till he near had the head of me addled with his mortgagor under the act. He was bloody safe he wasn't run in himself under the act that time as a rogue and vagabond only he had a friend in court. Selling bazaar tickets or what do you call it royal Hungarian privileged lottery. True as you're there. O, commend me to an israelite! Royal and privileged Hungarian robbery.

So Bob Doran comes lurching around asking Bloom to tell Mrs Dignam he was sorry for her trouble and he was very sorry about the funeral and to tell her that he said and everyone who knew him said that there was never a truer, a finer than poor little Willy that's dead to tell her. Choking with bloody foolery. And shaking Bloom's hand doing the tragic to tell her that. Shake hands, brother. You're a rogue and I'm another.

– Let me, said he, so far presume upon our acquaintance which, however slight it may appear if judged by the standard of mere time, is founded, as I hope and believe, on a sentiment of mutual esteem, as to request of you this favour. But, should I have overstepped the limits of reserve let the sincerity of my feelings be the excuse for my boldness.

– No, rejoined the other, I appreciate to the full the motives which actuate your conduct and I shall discharge the office you entrust to me consoled by the reflection that, though the errand be one of sorrow, this proof of your confidence sweetens in some measure the bitterness of the cup.

– Then suffer me to take your hand, said he. The goodness of your heart, I feel sure, will dictate to you better than my inadequate words the expressions which are most suitable to convey an emotion whose poignancy, were I to give vent to my feelings, would deprive me even of speech.

And off with him and out trying to walk straight. Boosed at five o'clock. Night he was near being lagged only Paddy Leonard knew the bobby, 14 A. Blind to the world up in a shebeen in Bride street after closing time, fornicating with two shawls and a bully on guard, drinking porter out of teacups. And calling himself a Frenchy for the shawls, Joseph Manuo, and talking against the catholic religion and he serving mass in

Adam and Eve's when he was young with his eyes shut who wrote the new testament and the old testament and hugging and smugging. And the two shawls killed with the laughing, picking his pockets the bloody fool and he spilling the porter all over the bed and the two shawls screeching laughing at one another. *How is your testament? Have you got an old testament?* Only Paddy was passing there, I tell you what. Then see him of a Sunday with his little concubine of a wife, and she wagging her tail up the aisle of the chapel, with her patent boots on her, no less, and her violets, nice as pie, doing the little lady. Jack Mooney's sister. And the old prostitute of a mother procuring rooms to street couples. Gob, Jack made him toe the line. Told him if he didn't patch up the pot, Jesus, he'd kick the shite out of him.

So Terry brought the three pints.

– Here, says Joe, doing the honours. Here, citizen.

– *Slan leat*, says he.

– Fortune, Joe, says I. Good health, citizen.

Gob, he had his mouth half way down the tumbler already. Want a small fortune to keep him in drinks.

– Who is the long fellow running for the mayoralty, Alf? says Joe.

– Friend of yours, says Alf.

– Nannan? says Joe. The mimber?

– I won't mention any names, says Alf.

– I thought so, says Joe. I saw him up at that meeting now with William Field, M. P., the cattle traders.

– Hairy Iopas, says the citizen, that exploded volcano, the darling of all countries and the idol of his own.

So Joe starts telling the citizen about the foot and mouth disease and the cattle traders and taking action in the matter and the citizen sending them all to the rightabout and Bloom coming out with his sheepdip for the scab and a hoose drench for coughing calves and the guaranteed remedy for timber tongue. Because he was up one time in a knacker's yard. Walking about with his book and pencil here's my head and my heels are coming till Joe Cuffe gave him the order of the boot for giving lip to a grazier. Mister Knowall. Teach your grandmother how to milk ducks. Pisser Burke was telling me in the hotel the wife used to be in rivers of tears sometimes with Mrs O'Dowd crying her eyes out with her eight inches of fat all over her. Couldn't loosen her farting strings but old cod's eye was waltzing around her showing her how to do it. What's your programme today? Ay. Humane methods. Because the poor animals suffer and experts say and the best known remedy that doesn't cause pain to the animal and on the sore spot administer gently. Gob, he'd have a soft hand under a hen.

Ga Ga Gara. Klook Klook Klook. Black Liz is our hen. She lays eggs for us. When she lays her egg she is so glad. Gara. Klook Klook Klook. Then comes good uncle Leo. He puts his hand under black Liz and takes her fresh egg. Ga ga ga ga Gara. Klook Klook Klook.

– Anyhow, says Joe. Field and Nannetti are going over tonight to London to ask about it on the floor of the House of Commons.

– Are you sure, says Bloom, the councillor is going? I wanted to see him, as it happens.

— Well, he's going off by the mailboat, says Joe, tonight.

— That's too bad, says Bloom. I wanted particularly. Perhaps only Mr Field is going. I couldn't phone. No. You're sure?

— Nannan's going too, says Joe. The league told him to ask a question tomorrow about the commissioner of police forbidding Irish games in the park. What do you think of that, citizen? *The Sluagh na h-Eireann.*

Mr Cowe Conacre (Multifarnham. Nat): Arising out of the question of my honourable friend, the member for Shillelagh, may I ask the right honourable gentleman whether the Government has issued orders that these animals shall be slaughtered though no medical evidence is forthcoming as to their pathological condition?

Mr Allfours (Tamoshant. Con): Honourable members are already in possession of the evidence produced before a committee of the whole house. I feel I cannot usefully add anything to that. The answer to the honourable member's question is in the affirmative.

Mr Orelli (Montenotte. Nat): Have similar orders been issued for the slaughter of human animals who dare to play Irish games in the Phœnix park?

Mr Allfours: The answer is in the negative.

Mr Cowe Conacre: Has the right honourable gentleman's famous Mitchelstown telegram inspired the policy of gentlemen on the treasury bench? (O! O!)

Mr Allfours: I must have notice of that question.

Mr Staylewit (Buncombe. Ind.): Don't hesitate to shoot.

(Ironical opposition cheers.)

The speaker: Order! Order!

(The house rises. Cheers.)

— There's the man, says Joe, that made the Gaelic sports revival. There he is sitting there. The man that got away James Stephens. The champion of all Ireland at putting the sixteen pound shot. What was your best throw, citizen?

— *Na bacleis,* says the citizen, letting on to be modest. There was a time I was as good as the next fellow anyhow.

— Put it there, citizen, says Joe. You were and a bloody sight better.

— Is that really a fact? says Alf.

— Yes, says Bloom. That's well known. Do you not know that?

So off they started about Irish sport and shoneen games the like of the lawn tennis and about hurley and putting the stone and racy of the soil and building up a nation once again and all of that. And of course Bloom had to have his say too about if a fellow had a rower's heart violent exercise was bad. I declare to my antimacassar if you took up a straw from the bloody floor and if you said to Bloom: *Look at, Bloom. Do you see that straw? That's a straw.* Declare to my aunt he'd talk about it for an hour so he would and talk steady.

A most interesting discussion took place in the ancient hall of *Brian O'Ciarnain's* in *Sraid na Bretaine Bheag,* under the auspices of *Sluagh na h-Eireann,* on the revival of ancient Gaelic sports and the importance of physical culture, as understood in ancient Greece and ancient Rome and ancient Ireland, for the development of the race. The venerable president of this noble order was in the chair and the attendance was of large dimensions.

After an instructive discourse by the chairman, a magnificent oration eloquently and forcibly expressed, a most interesting and instructive discussion of the usual high standard of excellence ensued as to the desirability of the revivability of the ancient games and sports of our ancient panceltic forefathers. The wellknown and highly respected worker in the cause of our old tongue, Mr Joseph M'Carthy Hynes, made an eloquent appeal for the resuscitation of the ancient Gaelic sports and pastimes, practised morning and evening by Finn MacCool, as calculated to revive the best traditions of manly strength and power handed down to us from ancient ages. L. Bloom, who met with a mixed reception of applause and hisses, having espoused the negative the vocalist chairman brought the discussion to a close, in response to repeated requests and hearty plaudits from all parts of a bumper house, by a remarkably noteworthy rendering of the immortal Thomas Osborne Davis' evergreen verses (happily too familiar to need recalling here) *A nation once again* in the execution of which the veteran patriot champion may be said without fear of contradiction to have fairly excelled himself. The Irish Caruso-Garibaldi was in superlative form and his stentorian notes were heard to the greatest advantage in the timehonoured anthem sung as only our citizen can sing it. His superb highclass vocalism, which by its superquality greatly enhanced his already international reputation, was vociferously applauded by the large audience amongst which were to be noticed many prominent members of the clergy as well as representatives of the press and the bar and the other learned professions. The proceedings then terminated.

Amongst the clergy present were the very rev. William Delany, S. J., L. L. D.; the rt rev. Gerald Molloy, D. D.; the rev. P. J. Kavanagh, C. S. Sp.; the rev. T. Waters, C. C.; the rev. John M. Ivers, P. P.; the rev. P. J. Cleary, O. S. F.; the rev. L. J. Hickey, O. P.; the very rev. Fr. Nicholas, O. S. F. C.; the very rev. B. Gorman, O. D. C.; the rev. T. Maher, S. J.; the very rev. James Murphy, S. J.; the rev. John Lavery, V. F.; the very rev. William Doherty, D. D.; the rev. Peter Fagan, O. M.; the rev. T. Brangan, O. S. A.; the rev. J. Flavin, C. C.; the rev. M. A. Hackett, C. C.; the rev. W. Hurley, C. C.; the rt rev. Mgr M'Manus, V. G.; the rev. B. R. Slattery, O. M. I.; the very rev. M. D. Scally, P. P.; the rev. F. T. Purcell, O. P.; the very rev. Timothy canon Gorman, P. P.; the rev. J. Flanagan, C. C. The laity included P. Fay, T. Quirke, etc., etc.

– Talking about violent exercise, says Alf, were you at that Keogh-Bennett match?

– No, says Joe.

– I heard So and So made a cool hundred quid over it, says Alf.

– Who? Blazes? says Joe.

And says Bloom:

– What I meant about tennis, for example, is the agility and training of the eye.

– Ay, Blazes, says Alf. He let out that Myler was on the beer to run the odds and he swatting all the time.

– We know him, says the citizen. The traitor's son. We know what put English gold in his pocket.

– True for you, says Joe.

And Bloom cuts in again about lawn tennis and the circulation of the blood, asking Alf:

— Now don't you think, Bergan?

— Myler dusted the floor with him, says Alf. Heenan and Sayers was only a bloody fool to it. Handed him the father and mother of a beating. See the little kipper not up to his navel and the big fellow swiping. God, he gave him one last puck in the wind. Queensberry rules and all, made him puke what he never ate.

It was a historic and a hefty battle when Myler and Percy were scheduled to don the gloves for the purse of fifty sovereigns. Handicapped as he was by lack of poundage, Dublin's pet lamb made up for it by superlative skill in ringcraft. The final bout of fireworks was a gruelling for both champions. The welterweight sergeantmajor had tapped some lively claret in the previous mixup during which Keogh had been receivergeneral of rights and lefts, the artilleryman putting in some neat work on the pet's nose, and Myler came on looking groggy. The soldier got to business leading off with a powerful left jab to which the Irish gladiator retaliated by shooting out a stiff one flush to the point of Bennett's jaw. The redcoat ducked but the Dubliner lifted him with a left hook, the body punch being a fine one. The men came to handigrips. Myler quickly became busy and got his man under, the bout ending with the bulkier man on the ropes, Myler punishing him. The Englishman, whose right eye was nearly closed, took his corner where he was liberally drenched with water and, when the bell went, came on gamey and brimful of pluck, confident of knocking out the fistic Eblanite in jigtime. It was a fight to a finish and the best man for it. The two fought like tigers and excitement ran fever high. The referee twice cautioned Pucking Percy for holding but the pet was tricky and his footwork a treat to watch. After a brisk exchange of courtesies during which a smart upper cut of the military man brought blood freely from his opponent's mouth the lamb suddenly waded in all over his man and landed a terrific left to Battling Bennett's stomach, flooring him flat. It was a knockout clean and clever. Amid tense expectation the Portobello bruiser was being counted out when Bennett's second Ole Pfotts Wettstein threw in the towel and the Santry boy was declared victor to the frenzied cheers of the public who broke through the ringropes and fairly mobbed him with delight.

— He knows which side his bread is buttered, says Alf. I hear he's running a concert tour now up in the north.

— He is, says Joe. Isn't he?

— Who? says Bloom. Ah, yes, That's quite true. Yes, a kind of summer tour, you see. Just a holiday.

— Mrs B. is the bright particular star, isn't she? says Joe.

— My wife? says Bloom. She's singing, yes. I think it will be a success too. He's an excellent man to organise. Excellent.

Hoho begob, says I to myself, says I. That explains the milk in the cocoanut and absence of hair on the animal's chest. Blazes doing the tootle on the flute. Concert tour. Dirty Dan the dodger's son off Island bridge that sold the same horses twice over to the government to fight the Boers. Old Whatwhat. I called about the poor and water rate, Mr Boylan. You what? The water rate, Mr Boylan. You whatwhat? That's the bucko that'll organise her, take my tip. 'Twixt me and you Caddereesh.

Pride of Calpe's rocky mount, the ravenhaired daughter of Tweedy. There grew she to peerless beauty where loquat and almond scent the air. The gardens of Alameda knew her step: the garths of olives knew and bowed. The chaste spouse of Leopold is she: Marion of the bountiful bosoms.

And lo, there entered one of the clan of the O'Molloys, a comely hero of white face yet withal somewhat ruddy, his majesty's counsel learned in the law, and with him the prince and heir of the noble line of Lambert.

– Hello, Ned.

– Hello, Alf.

– Hello, Jack.

– Hello, Joe.

– God save you, says the citizen.

– Save you kindly, says J. J. What'll it be, Ned?

– Half one, says Ned.

So J. J. ordered the drinks.

– Were you round at the court? says Joe.

– Yes, says J. J. He'll square that, Ned, says he.

– Hope so, says Ned.

Now what were those two at? J. J. getting him off the grand jury list and the other give him a leg over the stile. With his name in Stubb's. Playing cards, hobnobbing with flash toffs with a swank glass in their eye, drinking fizz and he half smothered in writs and garnishee orders. Pawning his gold watch in Cummins of Francis street where no-one would know him in the private office when I was there with Pisser releasing his boots out of the pop. What's your name, sir? Dunne, says he. Ay, and done, says I. Gob, he'll come home by weeping cross one of these days, I'm thinking.

– Did you see that bloody lunatic Breen round there, says Alf. U. p. up.

– Yes, says J. J. Looking for a private detective.

– Ay, says Ned, and he wanted right go wrong to address the court only Corny Kelleher got round him telling him to get the handwriting examined first.

– Ten thousand pounds, says Alf laughing. God I'd give anything to hear him before a judge and jury.

– Was it you did it, Alf? says Joe. The truth, the whole truth and nothing but the truth, so help you Jimmy Johnson.

– Me? says Alf. Don't cast your nasturtiums on my character.

– Whatever statement you make, says Joe, will be taken down in evidence against you.

– Of course an action would lie, says J. J. It implies that he is not *compos mentis*. U. p. up.

– *Compos* your eye! says Alf, laughing. Do you know that he's balmy? Look at his head. Do you know that some mornings he has to get his hat on with a shoehorn?

– Yes, says J. J., but the truth of a libel is no defence to an indictment for publishing it in the eyes of the law.

– Ha, ha, Alf, says Joe.

– Still, says Bloom, on account of the poor woman, I mean his wife.

– Pity about her, says the citizen. Or any other woman marries a half and half.

– How half and half? says Bloom. Do you mean he . . .

– Half and half I mean, says the citizen. A fellow that's neither fish nor flesh.

– Nor good red herring, says Joe.

– That what's I mean, says the citizen. A pishogue, if you know what that is.

Begob I saw there was trouble coming. And Bloom explained he meant, on account of it being cruel for the wife having to go round after the old stuttering fool. Cruelty to animals so it is to let that bloody povertystricken Breen out on grass with his beard out tripping him, bringing down the rain. And she with her nose cockahoop after she married him because a cousin of his old fellow's was pew opener to the pope. Picture of him on the wall with his smashall sweeney's moustaches. The signor Brini from Summerhill, the eyetallyano, papal zouave to the Holy Father, has left the quay and gone to Moss street. And who was he, tell us? A nobody, two pair back and passages, at seven shillings a week, and he covered with all kinds of breastplates bidding defiance to the world.

– And moreover, says J. J., a postcard is publication. It was held to be sufficient evidence of malice in the testcase Sadgrove v. Hole. In my opinion an action might lie.

Six and eightpence, please. Who wants your opinion? Let us drink our pints in peace. Gob, we won't be let even do that much itself.

– Well, good health, Jack, says Ned.

– Good health, Ned, says J. J.

– There he is again, says Joe.

– Where? says Alf.

And begob there he was passing the door with his books under his oxter and the wife beside him and Corny Kelleher with his wall eye looking in as they went past, talking to him like a father, trying to sell him a secondhand coffin.

– How did that Canada swindle case go off? says Joe.

– Remanded, says J. J.

One of the bottlenosed fraternity it was went by the name of James Wought alias Saphiro alias Spark and Spiro, put an ad in the papers saying he'd give a passage to Canada for twenty bob. What? Do you see any green in the white of my eye? Course it was a bloody barney. What? Swindled them all, skivvies and badhachs from the county Meath, ay, and his own kidney too. J. J. was telling us there was an ancient Hebrew Zaretsky or something weeping in the witnessbox with his hat on him, swearing by the holy Moses he was stuck for two quid.

– Who tried the case? says Joe.

– Recorder, says Ned.

– Poor old sir Frederick, says Alf, you can cod him up to the two eyes.

– Heart as big as a lion, says Ned. Tell him a tale of woe about arrears of rent and a sick wife and a squad of kids and, faith, he'll dissolve in tears on the bench.

– Ay, says Alf. Reuben J. was bloody lucky he didn't clap him in the dock the other day for suing poor little Gumley that's minding stones for the corporation there near Butt bridge.

And he starts taking off the old recorder letting on to cry:

— A most scandalous thing! This poor hardworking man! How many children? Ten, did you say?

— Yes, your worship. And my wife has the typhoid!

— And a wife with typhoid fever! Scandalous! Leave the court immediately, sir. No, sir, I'll make no order for payment. How dare you, sir, come up before me and ask me to make an order! A poor hardworking industrious man! I dismiss the case.

And whereas on the sixteenth day of the month of the oxeyed goddess and in the third week after the feastday of the Holy and Undivided Trinity, the daughter of the skies, the virgin moon being then in her first quarter, it came to pass that those learned judges repaired them to the halls of law. There master Courtenay, sitting in his own chamber, gave his rede and master Justice Andrews sitting without a jury in the probate court, weighed well and pondered the claims of the first chargeant upon the property in the matter of the will propounded and final testamentary disposition *in re* the real and personal estate of the late lamented Jacob Halliday, vintner, deceased versus Livingstone, an infant, of unsound mind, and another. And to the solemn court of Green street there came sir Frederick the Falconer. And he sat him there about the hour of five o'clock to administer the law of the brehons at the commission for all that and those parts to be holden in and for the county of the city of Dublin. And there sat with him the high sanhedrim of the twelve tribes of Iar, for every tribe one man, of the tribe of Patrick and of the tribe of Hugh and of the tribe of Owen and of the tribe of Conn and of the tribe of Oscar and of the tribe of Fergus and of the tribe of Finn and of the tribe of Dermot and of the tribe of Cormac and of the tribe of Kevin and of the tribe of Caolte and of the tribe of Ossian, there being in all twelve good men and true. And he conjured them by Him who died on rood that they should well and truly try and true delivrance make in the issue joined between their sovereign lord the king and the prisoner at the bar and true verdict give according to the evidence so help them God and kiss the books. And they rose in their seats, those twelve of Iar, and they swore by the name of Him who is from everlasting that they would do His rightwiseness. And straightway the minions of the law led forth from their donjon keep one whom the sleuthhounds of justice had apprehended in consequence of information received. And they shackled him hand and foot and would take of him ne bail ne mainprise but preferred a charge against him for he was a malefactor.

— Those are nice things, says the citizen, coming over here to Ireland filling the country with bugs.

So Bloom lets on he heard nothing and he starts talking with Joe telling him he needn't trouble about that little matter till the first but if he would just say a word to Mr Crawford. And so Joe swore high and holy by this and by that he'd do the devil and all.

— Because you see, says Bloom, for an advertisement you must have repetition. That's the whole secret.

— Rely on me, says Joe.

— Swindling the peasants, says the citizen, and the poor of Ireland. We want no more strangers in our house.

— O I'm sure that will be all right, Hynes, says Bloom. It's just that Keyes you see.

— Consider that done, says Joe.

— Very kind of you, says Bloom.

— The strangers, says the citizen. Our own fault. We let them come in. We brought them. The adulteress and her paramour brought the Saxon robbers here.

— Decree *nisi*, says J. J.

And Bloom letting on to be awfully deeply interested in nothing, a spider's web in the corner behind the barrel, and the citizen scowling after him and the old dog at his feet looking up to know who to bite and when.

— A dishonoured wife, says the citizen, that's what's the cause of all our misfortunes.

— And here she is, says Alf, that was giggling over the *Police Gazette* with Terry on the counter, in all her warpaint.

— Give us a squint at her, says I.

And what was it only one of the smutty yankee pictures Terry borrows off of Corny Kelleher. Secrets for enlarging your private parts. Misconduct of society belle. Norman W. Tupper, wealthy Chicago contractor, finds pretty but faithless wife in lap of officer Taylor. Belle in her bloomers misconducting herself and her fancy man feeling for her tickles and Norman W. Tupper bouncing in with his peashooter just in time to be late after she doing the trick of the loop with officer Taylor.

— O Jakers, Jenny, says Joe, how short your shirt is!

— There's hair, Joe, says I. Get a queer old tailend of corned beef off of that one, what?

So anyhow in came John Wyse Nolan and Lenehan with him with a face on him as long as a late breakfast.

— Well, says the citizen, what's the latest from the scene of action? What did those tinkers in the cityhall at their caucus meeting decide about the Irish language?

O'Nolan, clad in shining armour, low bending made obeisance to the puissant and high and mighty chief of all Erin and did him to wit of that which had befallen, how that the grave elders of the most obedient city, second of the realm, had met them in the tholsel, and there, after due prayers to the gods who dwell in ether supernal, had taken solemn counsel whereby they might, if so be it might be, bring once more into honour among mortal men the winged speech of the seadivided Gael.

— It's on the march, says the citizen. To hell with the bloody brutal Sassenachs and their *patois*.

So J. J. puts in a word doing the toff about one story was good till you heard another and blinking facts and the Nelson policy putting your blind eye to the telescope and drawing up a bill of attainder to impeach a nation and Bloom trying to back him up moderation and botheration and their colonies and their civilisation.

— Their syphilisation, you mean, says the citizen. To hell with them! The curse of a goodfornothing God light sideways on the bloody thicklugged sons of whores' gets! No music and no art and no literature worthy of the name. Any civilisation they have they stole from us. Tonguetied sons of bastards' ghosts.

— The European family, says J. J. . . . .

— They're not European, says the citizen. I was in Europe with Kevin Egan of Paris.

You wouldn't see a trace of them or their language anywhere in Europe except in a *cabinet d'aisance*.

And says John Wyse:

– Full many a flower is born to blush unseen.

And says Lenehan that knows a bit of the lingo:

– *Conspuez les Anglais! Perfide Albion!*

He said and then lifted he in his rude great brawny strengthy hands the medher of dark strong foamy ale and, uttering his tribal slogan *Lamh Dearg Abu*, he drank to the undoing of his foes, a race of mighty valorous heroes, rulers of the waves, who sit on thrones of alabaster silent as the deathless gods.

– What's up with you, says I to Lenehan. You look like a fellow that had lost a bob and found a tanner.

– Gold cup, says he.

– Who won, Mr Lenehan? says Terry.

– *Throwaway*, says he, at twenty to one. A rank outsider. And the rest nowhere.

– And Bass's mare? says Terry.

– Still running, says he. We're all in a cart. Boylan plunged two quid on my tip *Sceptre* for himself and a lady friend.

– I had half a crown myself, says Terry, on *Zinfandel* that Mr Flynn gave me. Lord Howard de Walden's.

– Twenty to one, says Lenehan. Such is life in an outhouse. *Throwaway*, says he. Takes the biscuit and talking about bunions. Frailty, thy name is *Sceptre*.

So he went over to the biscuit tin Bob Doran left to see if there was anything he could lift on the nod, the old cur after him backing his luck with his mangy snout up. Old mother Hubbard went to the cupboard.

– Not there, my child, says he.

– Keep your pecker up, says Joe. She'd have won the money only for the other dog.

And J. J. and the citizen arguing about law and history with Bloom sticking in an odd word.

– Some people, says Bloom, can see the mote in others' eyes but they can't see the beam in their own.

– *Raimeis*, says the citizen. There's no-one as blind as the fellow that won't see, if you know what that means. Where are our missing twenty millions of Irish should be here today instead of four, our lost tribes? And our potteries and textiles, the finest in the whole world! And our wool that was sold in Rome in the time of Juvenal and our flax and our damask from the looms of Antrim and our Limerick lace, our tanneries and our white flint glass down there by Ballybough and our Huguenot poplin that we have since Jacquard de Lyon and our woven silk and our Foxford tweeds and ivory raised point from the Carmelite convent in New Ross, nothing like it in the whole wide world! Where are the Greek merchants that came through the pillars of Hercules, the Gibraltar now grabbed by the foe of mankind, with gold and Tyrian purple to sell in Wexford at the fair of Carmen? Read Tacitus and Ptolemy, even Giraldus Cambrensis. Wine, peltries, Connemara marble, silver from Tipperary, second to none, our far-famed horses even today, the Irish hobbies, with king Philip of Spain offering to pay customs duties for the right to fish in our waters. What do the yellowjohns of Anglia owe us for our ruined trade and our ruined hearths? And the beds of the Barrow and Shannon they won't deepen with millions of acres of marsh and bog to make us all die of consumption.

– As treeless as Portugal we'll be soon, says John Wyse, or Heligoland with its one tree if something is not done to reafforest the land. Larches, firs, all the trees of the conifer family are going fast. I was reading a report of lord Castletown's . . .

– Save them, says the citizen, and the giant ash of Galway and the chieftain elm of Kildare with a fortyfoot bole and an acre of foliage. Save the trees of Ireland for the future men of Ireland on the fair hills of Eire, O.

– Europe has its eyes on you, says Lenehan.

The fashionable international world attended *en masse* this afternoon at the wedding of the chevalier Jean Wyse de Neaulan, grand high chief ranger of the Irish National Foresters, with Miss Fir Conifer of Pine Valley. Lady Sylvester Elmshade, Mrs Barbara Lovebirch, Mrs Poll Ash, Mrs Holly Hazeleyes, Miss Daphne Bays, Miss Dorothy Canebrake, Mrs Clyde Twelvetrees, Mrs Rowan Greene, Mrs Helen Vinegadding, Miss Virginia Creeper, Miss Gladys Beech, Miss Olive Garth, Miss Blanche Maple, Mrs Maud Mahogany, Miss Myra Myrtle, Miss Priscilla Elderflower, Miss Bee Honeysuckle, Miss Grace Poplar, Miss O. Mimosa San, Miss Rachel Cedarfrond, the Misses Lilian and Viola Lilac, Miss Timidity Aspenall, Mrs Kitty Dewey-Mosse, Miss May Hawthorne, Mrs Gloriana Palme, Mrs Liana Forrest, Mrs Arabella Blackwood and Mrs Norma Holyoake of Oakholme Regis graced the ceremony by their presence. The bride who was given away by her father, the M'Conifer of the Glands, looked exquisitely charming in a creation carried out in green mercerised silk, moulded on an underslip of gloaming grey, sashed with a yoke of broad emerald and finished with a triple flounce of darkerhued fringe, the scheme being relieved by bretelles and hip insertions of acorn bronze. The maids of honour, Miss Larch Conifer and Miss Spruce Conifer, sisters of the bride, wore very becoming costumes in the same tone, a dainty *motif* of plume rose being worked into the pleats in a pinstripe and repeated capriciously in the jadegreen toques in the form of heron feathers of paletinted coral. Senhor Enrique Flor presided at the organ with his wellknown ability and, in addition to the prescribed numbers of the nuptial mass, played a new and striking arrangement of *Woodman, spare that tree* at the conclusion of the service. On leaving the church of Saint Fiacre *in Horto* after the papal blessing the happy pair were subjected to a playful crossfire of hazelnuts, beechmast, bayleaves, catkins of willow, ivytod, hollyberries, mistletoe sprigs and quicken shoots. Mr and Mrs Wyse Conifer Neaulan will spend a quiet honeymoon in the Black Forest.

– And our eyes are on Europe, says the citizen. We had our trade with Spain and the French and with the Flemings before those mongrels were pupped, Spanish ale in Galway, the winebark on the winedark waterway.

–And will again, says Joe.

–And with the help of the holy mother of God we will again, says the citizen, clapping his thigh. Our harbours that are empty will be full again, Queenstown, Kinsale, Galway, Blacksod Bay, Ventry in the kingdom of Kerry, Killybegs, the third largest harbour in the wide world with a fleet of masts of the Galway Lynches and the Cavan O'Reillys and the O'Kennedys of Dublin when the earl of Desmond could make a treaty with the emperor Charles the Fifth himself. And will again, says he, when the first Irish battleship is seen breasting the waves with our own flag to the fore, none of your Henry Tudor's harps, no, the oldest flag afloat, the flag of the province of Desmond and Thomond, three crowns on a blue field, the three sons of Milesius.

And he took the last swig out of the pint, Moya. All wind and piss like a tanyard cat. Cows in Connacht have long horns. As much as his bloody life is worth to go down and address his tall talk to the assembled multitude in Shanagolden where he daren't show his nose with the Molly Maguires looking for him to let daylight through him for grabbing the holding of an evicted tenant.

– Hear, hear to that, says John Wyse. What will you have?

– An imperial yeomanry, says Lenehan, to celebrate the occasion.

– Half one, Terry, says John Wyse, and a hands up. Terry! Are you asleep?

– Yes, sir, says Terry. Small whisky and bottle of Allsop. Right, sir.

Hanging over the bloody paper with Alf looking for spicy bits instead of attending to the general public. Picture of a butting match, trying to crack their bloody skulls, one chap going for the other with his head down like a bull at a gate. And another one: *Black Beast Burned in Omaha, Ga.* A lot of Deadwood Dicks in slouch hats and they firing at a sambo strung up on a tree with his tongue out and a bonfire under him. Gob, they ought to drown him in the sea after and electrocute and crucify him to make sure of their job.

– But what about the fighting navy, says Ned, that keeps our foes at bay?

– I'll tell you what about it, says the citizen. Hell upon earth it is. Read the revelations that's going on in the papers about flogging on the training ships at Portsmouth. A fellow writes that calls himself *Disgusted One.*

So he starts telling us about corporal punishment and about the crew of tars and officers and rearadmirals drawn up in cocked hats and the parson with his protestant bible to witness punishment and a young lad brought out, howling for his ma, and they tie him down on the buttend of a gun.

– A rump and dozen, says the citizen, was what that old ruffian sir John Beresford called it but the modern God's Englishman calls it caning on the breech.

And says John Wyse:

– 'Tis a custom more honoured in the breach than in the observance.

Then he was telling us the master at arms comes along with a long cane and he draws out and he flogs the bloody backside off of the poor lad till he yells meila murder.

– That's your glorious British navy, says the citizen, that bosses the earth. The fellows that never will be slaves, with the only hereditary chamber on the face of God's earth and their land in the hands of a dozen gamehogs and cottonball barons. That's the great empire they boast about of drudges and whipped serfs.

– On which the sun never rises, says Joe.

– And the tragedy of it is, says the citizen, they believe it. The unfortunate yahoos believe it.

They believe in rod, the scourger almighty, creator of hell upon earth and in Jacky Tar, the son of a gun, who was conceived of unholy boast, born of the fighting navy, suffered under rump and dozen, was scarified, flayed and curried, yelled like bloody hell, the third day he arose again from the bed, steered into haven, sitteth on his beamend till further orders whence he shall come to drudge for a living and be paid.

– But, says Bloom, isn't discipline the same everywhere? I mean wouldn't it be the same here if you put force against force?

Didn't I tell you? As true as I'm drinking this porter if he was at his last gasp he'd try to downface you that dying was living.

– We'll put force against force, says the citizen. We have our greater Ireland beyond the sea. They were driven out of house and home in the black 47. Their mudcabins and their shielings by the roadside were laid low by the batteringram and the *Times* rubbed its hands and told the whitelivered Saxons there would soon be as few Irish in Ireland as redskins in America. Even the grand Turk sent us his piastres. But the Sassenach tried to starve the nation at home while the land was full of crops that the British hyenas bought and sold in Rio de Janeiro. Ay, they drove out the peasants in hordes. Twenty thousand of them died in the coffinships. But those that came to the land of the free remember the land of bondage. And they will come again and with a vengeance, no cravens, the sons of Granuaile, the champions of Kathleen ni Houlihan.

– Perfectly true, says Bloom. But my point was . . .

– We are a long time waiting for that day, citizen, says Ned. Since the poor old woman told us that the French were on the sea and landed at Killala.

– Ay, says John Wyse. We fought for the royal Stuarts that reneged us against the Williamites and they betrayed us. Remember Limerick and the broken treatystone. We gave our best blood to France and Spain, the wild geese. Fontenoy, eh? And Sarsfield and O'Donnell, duke of Tetuan in Spain, and Ulysses Browne of Camus that was fieldmarshal to Maria Teresa. But what did we ever get for it?

– The French! says the citizen. Set of dancing masters! Do you know what it is? They were never worth a roasted fart to Ireland. Aren't they trying to make an *Entente cordiale* now at Tay Pay's dinnerparty with perfidious Albion? Firebrands of Europe and they always were?

– *Conspuez les Français*, says Lenehan, nobbling his beer.

– And as for the Prooshians and the Hanoverians, says Joe, haven't we had enough of those sausageeating bastards on the throne from George the elector down to the German lad and the flatulent old bitch that's dead?

Jesus, I had to laugh at the way he came out with that about the old one with the winkers on her blind drunk in her royal palace every night of God, old Vic, with her jorum of mountain dew and her coachman carting her up body and bones to roll into bed and she pulling him by the whiskers and singing him old bits of songs about *Ehren on the Rhine* and come where the boose is cheaper.

– Well! says J. J. We have Edward the peacemaker now.

– Tell that to a fool, says the citizen. There's a bloody sight more pox than pax about that boyo. Edward Guelph-Wettin!

– And what do you think, says Joe, of the holy boys, the priests and bishops of Ireland doing up his room in Maynooth in his Satanic Majesty's racing colours and sticking up pictures of all the horses his jockeys rode. The earl of Dublin, no less.

– They ought to have stuck up all the women he rode himself, says little Alf.

And says J. J.:

– Considerations of space influenced their lordships' decision.

– Will you try another, citizen? says Joe.

– Yes, sir, says he, I will.

– You? says Joe.

– Beholden to you, Joe, says I. May your shadow never grow less.

– Repeat that dose, says Joe.

Bloom was talking and talking with John Wyse and he quite excited with his dunducketymudcoloured mug on him and his old plumeyes rolling about.

– Persecution, says he, all the history of the world is full of it. Perpetuating national hatred among nations.

– But do you know what a nation means? says John Wyse.

– Yes, says Bloom.

– What is it? says John Wyse.

– A nation? says Bloom. A nation is the same people living in the same place.

– By God, then, says Ned, laughing, if that's so I'm a nation for I'm living in the same place for the past five years.

So of course everyone had a laugh at Bloom and says he, trying to muck out of it:

– Or also living in different places.

– That covers my case, says Joe.

– What is your nation if I may ask, says the citizen.

– Ireland, says Bloom. I was born here. Ireland.

The citizen said nothing only cleared the spit out of his gullet and, gob, he spat a Red bank oyster out of him right in the corner.

– After you with the push, Joe, says he, taking out his handkerchief to swab himself dry.

– Here you are, citizen, says Joe. Take that in your right hand and repeat after me the following words.

The muchtreasured and intricately embroidered ancient Irish facecloth attributed to Solomon of Droma and Manus Tomaltach og MacDonogh, authors of the Book of Ballymote, was then carefully produced and called forth prolonged admiration. No need to dwell on the legendary beauty of the cornerpieces, the acme of art, wherein one can distinctly discern each of the four evangelists in turn presenting to each of the four masters his evangelical symbol a bogoak sceptre, a North American puma (a far nobler king of beasts than the British article, be it said in passing), a Kerry calf and a golden eagle from Carrantuohill. The scenes depicted on the emunctory field, showing our ancient duns and raths and cromlechs and grianauns and seats of learning and maledictive stones, are as wonderfully beautiful and the pigments as delicate as when the Sligo illuminators gave free rein to their artistic fantasy long long ago in the time of the Barmecides. Glendalough, the lovely lakes of Killarney, the ruins of Clonmacnois, Cong Abbey, Glen Inagh and the Twelve Pins, Ireland's Eye, the Green Hills of Tallaght, Croagh Patrick, the brewery of Messrs Arthur Guinness, Son and Company (Limited), Lough Neagh's banks, the vale of Ovoca, Isolde's tower, the Mapas obelisk, Sir Patrick Dun's hospital, Cape Clear, the glen of Aherlow, Lynch's castle, the Scotch house,

Rathdown Union Workhouse at Loughlinstown, Tullamore jail, Castleconnel rapids, Kilballymacshonakill, the cross at Monasterboice, Jury's Hotel, S. Patrick's Purgatory, the Salmon Leap, Maynooth college refectory, Curley's hole, the three birthplaces of the first duke of Wellington, the rock of Cashel, the bog of Allen, the Henry Street Warehouse, Fingal's Cave – all these moving scenes are still there for us today rendered more beautiful still by the waters of sorrow which have passed over them and by the rich incrustations of time.

– Shove us over the drink, says I. Which is which?

– That's mine, says Joe, as the devil said to the dead policeman.

– And I belong to a race too, says Bloom, that is hated and persecuted. Also now. This very moment. This very instant.

Gob, he near burnt his fingers with the butt of his old cigar.

– Robbed, says he. Plundered. Insulted. Persecuted. Taking what belongs to us by right. At this very moment, says he, putting up his fist, sold by auction off in Morocco like slaves or cattles.

– Are you talking about the new Jerusalem? says the citizen.

– I'm talking about injustice, says Bloom.

– Right, says John Wyse. Stand up to it then with force like men.

That's an almanac picture for you. Mark for a softnosed bullet. Old lardyface standing up to the business end of a gun. Gob, he'd adorn a sweepingbrush, so he would, if he only had a nurse's apron on him. And then he collapses all of a sudden, twisting around all the opposite, as limp as a wet rag.

– But it's no use, says he. Force, hatred, history, all that. That's not life for men and women, insult and hatred. And everybody knows that it's the very opposite of that that is really life.

– What? says Alf.

– Love, says Bloom. I mean the opposite of hatred. I must go now, says he to John Wyse. Just round to the court a moment to see if Martin is there. If he comes just say I'll be back in a second. Just a moment.

Who's hindering you? And off he pops like greased lightning.

– A new apostle to the gentiles, says the citizen. Universal love.

– Well, says John Wyse, isn't that what we're told? Love your neighbours.

– That chap? says the citizen. Beggar my neighbour is his motto. Love, Moya! He's a nice pattern of a Romeo and Juliet.

Love loves to love love. Nurse loves the new chemist. Constable 14A loves Mary Kelly. Gerty MacDowell loves the boy that has the bicycle. M. B. loves a fair gentleman. Li Chi Han lovey up kissy Cha Pu Chow. Jumbo, the elephant, loves Alice, the elephant. Old Mr Verschoyle with the ear trumpet loves old Mrs Verschoyle with the turnedin eye. The man in the brown macintosh loves a lady who is dead. His Majesty the King loves Her Majesty the Queen. Mrs Norman W. Tupper loves officer Taylor. You love a certain person. And this person loves that other person because everybody loves somebody but God loves everybody.

– Well, Joe, says I, your very good health and song. More power, citizen.

– Hurrah, there, says Joe.

— The blessing of God and Mary and Patrick on you, says the citizen.

And he ups with his pint to wet his whistle.

— We know those canters, says he, preaching and picking your pocket. What about sanctimonious Cromwell and his ironsides that put the women and children of Drogheda to the sword with the bible text *God is love* pasted round the mouth of his cannon? The bible! Did you read that skit in the *United Irishman* today about that Zulu chief that's visiting England?

— What's that? says Joe.

So the citizen takes up one of his paraphernalia papers and he starts reading out:

— A delegation of the chief cotton magnates of Manchester was presented yesterday to His Majesty the Alaki of Abeakuta by Gold Stick in Waiting, Lord Walkup on Eggs, to tender to His Majesty the heartfelt thanks of British traders for the facilities afforded them in his dominions. The delegation partook of luncheon at the conclusion of which the dusky potentate, in the course of a happy speech, freely translated by the British chaplain, the reverend Ananias Praisegod Barebones, tendered his best thanks to Massa Walkup and emphasised the cordial relations existing between Abeakuta and the British Empire, stating that he treasured as one of his dearest possessions an illuminated bible, the volume of the word of God and the secret of England's greatness, graciously presented to him by the white chief woman, the great squaw Victoria, with a personal dedication from the august hand of the Royal Donor. The Alaki then drank a lovingcup of firstshot usquebaugh to the toast *Black and White* from the skull of his immediate predecessor in the dynasty Kakachakachak, surnamed Forty Warts, after which he visited the chief factory of Cottonopolis and signed his mark in the visitors' book, subsequently executing an old Abeakutic wardance, in the course of which he swallowed several knives and forks, amid hilarious applause from the girl hands.

— Widow woman, says Ned, I wouldn't doubt her. Wonder did he put that bible to the same use as I would.

— Same only more so, says Lenehan. And thereafter in that fruitful land the broadleaved mango flourished exceedingly.

— Is that by Griffith? says John Wyse.

— No, says the citizen. It's not signed Shanganagh. It's only initialled: P.

— And a very good initial too, says Joe.

— That's how it's worked, says the citizen. Trade follows the flag.

— Well, says J. J., if they're any worse than those Belgians in the Congo Free State they must be bad. Did you read that report by a man what's this his name is?

— Casement, says the citizen. He's an Irishman.

— Yes, that's the man, says J. J. Raping the women and girls and flogging the natives on the belly to squeeze all the red rubber they can out of them.

— I know where he's gone, says Lenehan, cracking his fingers.

— Who? says I.

— Bloom, says he, the courthouse is a blind. He had a few bob on *Throwaway* and he's gone to gather in the shekels.

— Is it that whiteyed kaffir? says the citizen, that never backed a horse in anger in his life.

— That's where he's gone, says Lenehan. I met Bantam Lyons going to back that horse only I put him off it and he told me Bloom gave him the tip. Bet you what you like he has a hundred shillings to five on. He's the only man in Dublin has it. A dark horse.

— He's a bloody dark horse himself, says Joe.

— Mind, Joe, says I. Show us the entrance out.

— There you are, says Terry.

Goodbye Ireland I'm going to Gort. So I just went round to the back of the yard to pumpship and begob (hundred shillings to five) while I was letting off my (*Throwaway* twenty to) letting off my load gob says I to myself I knew he was uneasy in his (two pints off of Joe and one in Slattery's off) in his mind to get off the mark to (hundred shillings is five quid) and when they were in the (dark horse) Pisser Burke was telling me card party and letting on the child was sick (gob, must have done about a gallon) flabbyarse of a wife speaking down the tube *she's better* or *she's* (ow!) all a plan so he could vamoose with the pool if he won or (Jesus, full up I was) trading without a licence (ow!) Ireland my nation says he (hoik! phthook!) never be up to those bloody (there's the last of it) Jerusalem (ah!) cuckoos.

So anyhow when I got back they were at it dingdong, John Wyse saying it was Bloom gave the idea for Sinn Fein to Griffith to put in his paper all kinds of jerrymandering, packed juries and swindling the taxes off of the Government and appointing consuls all over the world to walk about selling Irish industries. Robbing Peter to pay Paul. Gob, that puts the bloody kybosh on it if old sloppy eyes is mucking up the show. Give us a bloody chance. God save Ireland from the likes of that bloody mouseabout. Mr Bloom with his argol bargol. And his old fellow before him perpetrating frauds, old Methusalem Bloom, the robbing bagman, that poisoned himself with the prussic acid after he swamping the country with his baubles and his penny diamonds. Loans by post on easy terms. Any amount of money advanced on note of hand. Distance no object. No security. Gob he's like Lanty MacHale's goat that'd go a piece of the road with every one.

— Well, it's a fact, says John Wyse. And there's the man now that'll tell you about it, Martin Cunningham.

Sure enough the castle car drove up with Martin on it and Jack Power with him and a fellow named Crofter or Crofton, pensioner out of the collector general's, an orangeman Blackburn does have on the registration and he drawing his pay or Crawford gallivanting around the country at the king's expense.

Our travellers reached the rustic hostelry and alighted from their palfreys.

— Ho, varlet! cried he, who by his mien seemed the leader of the party. Saucy knave! To us!

So saying he knocked loudly with his swordhilt upon the open lattice.

Mine host came forth at the summons girding him with his tabard.

— Give you good den, my masters, said he with an obsequious bow.

— Bestir thyself, sirrah! cried he who had knocked. Look to our steeds. And for ourselves give us of your best for ifaith we need it.

— Lackaday, good masters, said the host, my poor house has but a bare larder. I know not what to offer your lordships.

– How now, fellow? cried the second of the party, a man of pleasant countenance, so servest thou the king's messengers, Master Taptun?

An instantaneous change overspread the landlord's visage.

– Cry you mercy, gentlemen, he said humbly. An you be the king's messengers (God shield His Majesty!) you shall not want for aught. The king's friends (God bless His Majesty!) shall not go afasting in my house I warrant me.

– Then about! cried the traveller who had not spoken, a lusty trencherman by his aspect. Hast aught to give us?

Mine host bowed again as he made answer:

– What say you, good masters, to a squab pigeon pasty, some collops of venison, a saddle of veal, widgeon with crisp hog's bacon, a boar's head with pistachios, a bason of jolly custard, a medlar tansy and a flagon of old Rhenish?

– Gadzooks! cried the last speaker. That likes me well. Pistachios!

– Aha! cried he of the pleasant countenance. A poor house and a bare larder, quotha! 'Tis a merry rogue.

So in comes Martin asking where was Bloom.

– Where is he? says Lenehan. Defrauding widows and orphans.

– Isn't that a fact, says John Wyse, what I was telling the citizen about Bloom and the Sinn Fein?

– That's so, says Martin. Or so they allege.

– Who made those allegations? says Alf.

– I, says Joe. I'm the alligator.

– And after all, says John Wyse, why can't a jew love his country like the next fellow?

– Why not? says J. J., when he's quite sure which country it is.

– Is he a jew or a gentile or a holy Roman or a swaddler or what the hell is he? says Ned. Or who is he? No offence, Crofton.

– We don't want him, says Crofter the Orangeman or presbyterian.

– Who is Junius? says J. J.

– He's a perverted jew, says Martin, from a place in Hungary and it was he drew up all the plans according to the Hungarian system. We know that in the castle.

– Isn't he a cousin of Bloom the dentist? says Jack Power.

– Not at all, says Martin. Only namesakes. His name was Virag. The father's name that poisoned himself. He changed it by deed poll, the father did.

– That's the new Messiah for Ireland! says the citizen. Island of saints and sages!

– Well, they're still waiting for their redeemer, says Martin. For that matter so are we.

– Yes, says J. J., and every male that's born they think it may be their Messiah. And every jew is in a tall state of excitement, I believe, till he knows if he's a father or a mother.

– Expecting every moment will be his next, says Lenehan.

– O, by God, says Ned, you should have seen Bloom before that son of his that died was born. I met him one day in the south city markets buying a tin of Neave's food six weeks before the wife was delivered.

– *En ventre sa mère*, says J. J.

– Do you call that a man? says the citizen.

– I wonder did he ever put it out of sight, says Joe.

– Well, there were two children born anyhow, says Jack Power.

– And who does he suspect? says the citizen.

Gob, there's many a true word spoken in jest. One of those mixed middlings he is. Lying up in the hotel Pisser was telling me once a month with headache like a totty with her courses. Do you know what I'm telling you? It'd be an act of God to take a hold of a fellow the like of that and throw him in the bloody sea. Justifiable homicide, so it would. Then sloping off with his five quid without putting up a pint of stuff like a man. Give us your blessing. Not as much as would blind your eye.

– Charity to the neighbour, says Martin. But where is he? We can't wait.

– A wolf in sheep's clothing, says the citizen. That's what he is. Virag from Hungary! Ahasuerus I call him. Cursed by God.

– Have you time for a brief libation, Martin? says Ned.

– Only one, says Martin. We must be quick. J. J. and S.

– You Jack? Crofton? Three half ones, Terry.

– Saint Patrick would want to land again at Ballykinlar and convert us, says the citizen, after allowing things like that to contaminate our shores.

– Well, says Martin, rapping for his glass. God bless all here is my prayer.

– Amen, says the citizen.

– And I'm sure he will, says Joe.

And at the sound of the sacring bell, headed by a crucifer with acolytes, thurifers, boatbearers, readers, ostiarii, deacons and subdeacons, the blessed company drew nigh of mitred abbots and priors and guardians and monks and friars: the monks of Benedict of Spoleto, Carthusians and Camaldolesi, Cistercians and Olivetans, Oratorians and Vallombrosans, and the friars of Augustine, Brigittines, Premonstratesians, Servi, Trinitarians, and the children of Peter Nolasco: and therewith from Carmel mount the children of Elijah prophet led by Albert bishop and by Teresa of Avila, calced and other: and friars brown and grey, sons of poor Francis, capuchins, cordeliers, minimes and observants and the daughters of Clara: and the sons of Dominic, the friars preachers, and the sons of Vincent: and the monks of S. Wolstan: and Ignatius his children: and the confraternity of the christian brothers led by the reverend brother Edmund Ignatius Rice. And after came all saints and martyrs, virgins and confessors: S. Cyr and S. Isidore Arator and S. James the Less and S. Phocas of Sinope and S. Julian Hospitator and S. Felix de Cantalice and S. Simon Stylites and S. Stephen Protomartyr and S. John of God and S. Ferreol and S. Leugarde and S. Theodotus and S. Vulmar and S. Richard and S. Vincent de Paul and S. Martin of Todi and S. Martin of Tours and S. Alfred and S. Joseph and S. Denis and S. Cornelius and S. Leopold and S. Bernard and S. Terence and S. Edward and S. Owen Caniculus and S. Anonymous and S. Eponymous and S. Pseudonymous and S. Homonymous and S. Paronymous and S. Synonymous and S. Laurence O' Toole and S. James of Dingle and Compostella and S. Columcille and S. Columba and S. Celestine and S. Colman and S. Kevin and S. Brendan and S. Frigidian and S. Senan and S. Fachtna and S. Columbanus and S. Gall and S. Fursey and S. Fintan and S. Fiacre and S. John Nepomuc and S. Thomas Aquinas and S. Ives of Brittany and S. Michan and S. Herman-Joseph and the three patrons of holy youth S. Aloysius Gonzaga and S. Stanislaus Kostka and S. John Berchmans and the saints Gervasius, Servasius and Bonifacius and S. Bride and S. Kieran and S. Canice of Kilkenny and S. Jarlath of Tuam and S. Finbarr and S. Pappin of Ballymun and Brother Aloysius Pacificus and Brother Louis Bellicosus and the saints Rose of Lima and of Viterbo and S. Martha of Bethany and S. Mary of Egypt and S. Lucy and S. Brigid and S. Attracta and S. Dympna and S. Ita and S. Marion Calpensis and the Blessed Sister Teresa of the Child Jesus and S. Barbara and S. Scholastica and S. Ursula with eleven thousand virgins. And all came with nimbi and aureoles and gloriae, bearing palms and harps and swords and olive crowns, in robes whereon were woven the blessed symbols of their efficacies, inkhorns, arrows, loaves, cruses, fetters, axes, trees, bridges, babes in a bathtub, shells, wallets, shears, keys, dragons, lilies, buckshot, beards, hogs, lamps, bellows, beehives, soupladles, stars, snakes, anvils, boxes of vaseline, bells, crutches, forceps, stags' horns, watertight boots, hawks, millstones, eyes on a dish, wax candles, aspergills, unicorns. And as they wended their way by Nelson's Pillar, Henry Street, Mary Street, Capel Street, Little Britain Street, chanting the introit in *Epiphania Domini* which beginneth *Surge, illuminare* and thereafter most sweetly the gradual *Omnes* which saith *de Saba venient* they did divers wonders such as casting out devils, raising the dead to life, multiplying fishes, healing the halt and the blind, discovering various articles which had been mislaid, interpreting and fulfilling the scriptures, blessing and prophesying. And last, beneath a canopy of cloth of gold came the reverend Father O'Flynn attended by Malachi and Patrick. And when the good fathers had reached the appointed place, the house of Bernard Kiernan and Co, limited, 8, 9 and 10 little Britain street, wholesale grocers, wine and brandy shippers, licensed for the sale of beer, wine and spirits for consumption on the premises, the celebrant blessed the house and censed the mullioned windows and the groynes and the vaults and the arrises and the capitals and the pediments and the cornices and the engrailed arches and the spires and the cupolas and sprinkled the lintels thereof with blessed water and prayed that God might bless that house as he had blessed the house of Abraham and Isaac and Jacob and make the angels of His light to inhabit therein. And entering he blessed the viands and the beverages and the company of all the blessed answered his prayers.

— *Adiutorium nostrum in nomine Domini.*

— *Que fecit cœlum et terram.*

— *Dominus vobiscum.*

— *Et cum spiritu tuo.*

And he laid his hands upon the blessed and gave thanks and he prayed and they all with him prayed:

— *Deus, cuius verbo sanctificantur omnia, benedictionem tuam effunde super creaturas istas: et præsta ut quisquis eis secundum legem et voluntatem Tuam cum gratiarum actione usus fuerit per invocationem sanctissimi nominis Tui corporis sanitatem et animæ tutelam Te auctore percipiat per Christum Dominum nostrum.*

— And so say all of us, says Jack.

— Thousand a year, Lambert, says Crofton or Crawford.

— Right, says Ned, taking up his John Jameson. And butter for fish.

I was just looking round to see who the happy thought would strike when be damned but in he comes again letting on to be in a hell of a hurry.

— I was just round at the courthouse, says he, looking for you. I hope I'm not . . .

— No, says Martin, we're ready.

Courthouse my eye and your pockets hanging down with gold and silver. Mean bloody scut. Stand us a drink itself. Devil a sweet fear! There's a jew for you! All for number one. Cute as a shithouse rat. Hundred to five.

— Don't tell anyone, says the citizen.

— Beg your pardon, says he.

— Come on boys, says Martin, seeing it was looking blue. Come along now.

— Don't tell anyone, says the citizen, letting a bawl out of him. It's a secret.

And the bloody dog woke up and let a growl.

— Bye bye all, says Martin.

And he got them out as quick as he could, Jack Power and Crofton or whatever you call him and him in the middle of them letting on to be all at sea up with them on the bloody jaunting car.

Off with you, says Martin to the jarvey.

The milkwhite dolphin tossed his mane and, rising in the golden poop, the helmsman spread the bellying sail upon the wind and stood off forward with all sail set, the spinnaker to larboard. A many comely nymphs drew nigh to starboard and to larboard and, clinging to the sides of the noble bark, they linked their shining forms as doth the cunning wheelwright when he fashions about the heart of his wheel the equidistant rays whereof each one is sister to another and he binds them all with an outer ring and giveth speed to the feet of men whenas they ride to a hosting or contend for the smile of ladies fair. Even so did they come and set them, those willing nymphs, the undying sisters. And they laughed, sporting in a circle of their foam: and the bark clave the waves.

But begob I was just lowering the heel of the pint when I saw the citizen getting up to waddle to the door, puffing and blowing with the dropsy and he cursing the curse of Cromwell on him, bell, book and candle in Irish, spitting and spatting out of him and Joe and little Alf round him like a leprechaun trying to peacify him.

— Let me alone, says he.

And begob he got as far as the door and they holding him and he bawls out of him:

— Three cheers for Israel!

Arrah, sit down on the parliamentary side of your arse for Christ' sake and don't be making a public exhibition of yourself. Jesus, there's always some bloody clown or other kicking up a bloody murder about bloody nothing. Gob, it'd turn the porter sour in your guts, so it would.

And all the ragamuffins and sluts of the nation round the door and Martin telling the jarvey to drive ahead and the citizen bawling and Alf and Joe at him to whisht and he on his high horse about the jews and the loafers calling for a speech and Jack Power trying to get him to sit down on the car and hold his bloody jaw and a loafer with a patch over his eye starts singing *If the man in the moon was a jew, jew, jew* and a slut shouts out of her:

— Eh, mister! Your fly is open, mister!

And says he:

— Mendelssohn was a jew and Karl Marx and Mercadante and Spinoza. And the Saviour was a jew and his father was a jew. Your God.

— He had no father, says Martin. That'll do now. Drive ahead.

— Whose God? says the citizen.

— Well, his uncle was a jew, says he. Your God was a jew. Christ was a jew like me.

Gob, the citizen made a plunge back into the shop.

— By Jesus, says he, I'll brain that bloody jewman for using the holy name. By Jesus, I'll crucify him so I will. Give us that biscuitbox here.

— Stop! Stop! says Joe.

A large and appreciative gathering of friends and acquaintances from the metropolis and greater Dublin assembled in their thousands to bid farewell to Nagyságos uram Lipóti Virag, late of Messrs Alexander Thom's, printers to His Majesty, on the occasion of his departure for the distant clime of Százharminczbrojúgulyás-Dugulás (Meadow of Murmuring Waters). The ceremony which went off with great *éclat* was characterised by the most affecting cordiality. An illuminated scroll of ancient Irish vellum, the work of Irish artists, was presented to the distinguished phenomenologist on behalf of a large section of the community and was accompanied by the gift of a silver casket, tastefully executed in the style of ancient Celtic ornament, a work which reflects every credit on the makers, Messrs Jacob *agus* Jacob. The departing guest was the recipient of a hearty ovation, many of those who were present being visibly moved when the select orchestra of Irish pipes struck up the wellknown strains of *Come back to Erin*, followed immediately by *Rakóczy's March*. Tarbarrels and bonfires were lighted along the coastline of the four seas on the summits of the Hill of Howth, Three Rock Mountain, Sugarloaf, Bray Head, the mountains of Mourne, the Galtees, the Ox and Donegal and Sperrin peaks, the Nagles and the Bograghs, the Connemara hills, the reeks of M'Gillicuddy, Slieve Aughty, Slieve Bernagh and Slieve Bloom. Amid cheers that rent the welkin, responded to by answering cheers from a big muster of henchmen on the distant Cambrian and Caledonian hills, the mastodontic pleasureship slowly moved away saluted by a final floral tribute from the representatives of the fair sex who were present in large numbers while, as it proceeded down the river, escorted by a flotilla of barges, the flags of the Ballast office and Custom House were dipped in salute as were also those of the electrical power station at the Pigeonhouse. *Visszontlátásra, kedvés baráton! Visszontlátásra!* Gone but not forgotten.

Gob, the devil wouldn't stop him till he got hold of the bloody tin anyhow and out with him and little Alf hanging on to his elbow and he shouting like a stuck pig, as good as any bloody play in the Queen's royal theatre.

— Where is he till I murder him?

And Ned and J. G. paralysed with the laughing.

— Bloody wars, says I, I'll be in for the last gospel.

But as luck would have it the jarvey got the nag's head round the other way and off with him.

— Hold on, citizen, says Joe. Stop.

Begob he drew his hand and made a swipe and let fly. Mercy of God the sun was in his eyes or he'd have left him for dead. Gob, he near sent it into the county Longford. The bloody nag took fright and the old mongrel after the car like bloody hell and all the populace shouting and laughing and the old tinbox clattering along the street.

The catastrophe was terrific and instantaneous in its effect. The observatory of Dunsink registered in all eleven shocks, all of the fifth grade of Mercalli's scale, and there is no record extant of a similar seismic disturbance in our island since the earthquake of 1534, the year of the rebellion of Silken Thomas. The epicentre appears to have been that part of the metropolis which constitutes the Inn's Quay ward and parish of Saint Michan covering a surface of fortyone acres, two roods and one square pole or perch. All the lordly residences in the vicinity of the palace of justice were demolished and that noble edifice itself, in which at the time of the catastrophe important legal debates were in progress, is literally a mass of ruins beneath which it is to be feared all the occupants have been buried alive. From the reports of eyewitnesses it transpires that the seismic waves were accompanied by a violent atmospheric perturbation of cyclonic character. An article of headgear since ascertained to belong to the much respected clerk of the crown and peace Mr George Fottrell and a silk umbrella with gold handle with the engraved initials, coat of arms and house number of the erudite and worshipful chairman of quarter sessions sir Frederick Falkiner, recorder of Dublin, have been discovered by search parties in remote parts of the island, respectively, the former on the third basaltic ridge of the giant's causeway, the latter embedded to the extent of one foot three inches in the sandy beach of Holeopen bay near the old head of Kinsale. Other eyewitnesses depose that they observed an incandescent object of enormous proportions hurtling through the atmosphere at a terrifying velocity in a trajectory directed south west by west. Messages of condolence and sympathy are being hourly received from all parts of the different continents and the sovereign pontiff has been graciously pleased to decree that a special *missa pro defunctis* shall be celebrated simultaneously by the ordinaries of each and every cathedral church of all the episcopal dioceses subject to the spiritual authority of the Holy See in suffrage of the souls of those faithful departed who have been so unexpectedly called away from our midst. The work of salvage, removal of *débris* human remains etc has been entrusted to Messrs Michael Meade and Son, 159, Great Brunswick Street, and Messrs T. C. Martin, 77, 78, 79 and 80, North Wall, assisted by the men and officers of the Duke of Cornwall's light infantry under the general supervision of H. R. H., rear admiral the right honourable sir Hercules Hannibal Habeas Corpus Anderson K.G., K.P., K.T., P.C., K.C.B., M.P., J.P., M.B., D.S.O., S.O.D., M.F.H., M.R.I.A., B.L., Mus. Doc., P.L.G., F.T.C.D., F.R.U.I., F.R.C.P.I. and F.R.C.S.I.

You never saw the like of it in all your born puff. Gob, if he got that lottery ticket on the side of his poll he'd remember the gold cup, he would so, but begob the citizen would have been lagged for assault and battery and Joe for aiding and abetting. The jarvey saved his life by furious driving as sure as God made Moses. What? O, Jesus, he did. And he let a volley of oaths after him.

– Did I kill him, says he, or what?

And he shouting to the bloody dog:

– After him, Garry! After him, boy!

And the last we saw was the bloody car rounding the corner and old sheepsface on it gesticulating and the bloody mongrel after it with his lugs back for all he was bloody well worth to tear him limb from limb. Hundred to five! Jesus, he took the value of it out of him, I promise you.

When, lo, there came about them all a great brightness and they beheld the chariot wherein He stood ascend to heaven. And they beheld Him in the chariot, clothed upon in the glory of the brightness, having raiment as of the sun, fair as the moon and terrible that for awe they durst not look upon Him. And there came a voice out of heaven, calling: *Elijah! Elijah!* And he answered with a main cry: *Abba! Adonai!* And they beheld Him even Him, ben Bloom Elijah, amid clouds of angels ascend to the glory of the brightness at an angle of fortyfive degrees over Donohoe's in Little Green Street like a shot off a shovel.

from *Finnegans Wake*

First she let her hair fal and down it flussed to her feet its teviots winding coils. Then, mothernaked, she sampood herself with galawater and fraguant pistania mud, wupper and lauar, from crown to sole. Next she greesed the groove of her keel, warthes and wears and mole and itcher, with antifouling butterscatch and turfentide and serpenthyme and with leafmould she ushered round prunella isles and eslats dun, quincecunct, allover her little mary. Peeld gold of waxwork her jellybelly and her grains of incense anguille bronze. And after that she wove a garland for her hair. She pleated it. She plaited it. Of meadowgrass and riverflags, the bulrush and waterweed, and of fallen griefs of weeping willow. Then she made her bracelets and her anklets and her armlets and a jetty amulet for necklace of clicking cobbles and pattering pebbles and rumbledown rubble, richmond and rehr, of Irish rhunerhinerstones and shellmarble bangles. That done, a dawk of smut to her airy ey, Annushka Lutetiavitch Pufflovah, and the lellipos cream to her lippeleens and the pick of the paintbox for her pommettes, from strawbirry reds to extra violates, and she sendred her boudeloire maids to His Affluence, Ciliegia Grande and Kirschie Real, the two chirsines, with respecks from his missus, seepy and sewery, and a request might she passe of him for a minnikin. A call to pay and light a taper, in Brie-on-Arrosa, back in a sprizzling. The cock striking mine, the stalls bridely sign, there's Zambosy waiting for Me! She said she wouldn't be half her length away. Then, then, as soon as the lump his back was turned, with her mealiebag slang over her shulder, Anna Livia, oysterface, forth of her bassein came.

Describe her! Hustle along, why can't you? Spitz on the iern while it's hot. I wouldn't miss her for irthing on nerthe. Not for the lucre of lomba strait. Oceans of Gaud, I mosel hear that! Ogowe presta! Leste, before Julia sees her! Ishekarry and washemeskad, the carishy caratimaney? Whole lady fair? Duodecimoroon? Bon a ventura? Malagassy? What had she on, the liddel oud oddity? How much did she scallop, harness and weights? Here she is, Amnisty Ann! Call her calamity electrifies man.

No electress at all but old Moppa Necessity, angin mother of injons. I'll tell you a test. But you must sit still. Will you hold your peace and listen well to what I am going to say now? It might have been ten or twenty to one of the night of Allclose or the nexth of April when the flip of her hoogly igloo flappered and out toetippit a bushman woman, the dearest little moma ever you saw, nodding around her, all smiles, with ems of embarras and aues to awe, between two ages, a judyqueen, not up to your elb. Quick, look at her cute and saise her quirk for the bicker she lives the slicker she grows. Save us and tagus! No more? Werra where in ourthe did you ever pick a Lambay chop as big as a battering ram? Ay, you're right. I'm epte to forgetting, Like Liviam Liddle did Loveme Long. The linth of my hough, I say! She wore a ploughboy's nailstudded clogs, a pair of ploughfields in themselves: a sugarloaf hat with a gaudyquiviry peak and a band of gorse for an arnoment and a hundred streamers dancing off it and a guildered pin to pierce it: owlglassy bicycles boggled her eyes: and a fishnetzeveil for the sun not to spoil the wrinklings of her hydeaspects: potatorings boucled the loose laubes of her laudsnarers: her nude cuba stockings were salmospotspeckled: she sported a galligo shimmy of hazevaipar tinto that never was fast till it ran in the washing: stout stays, the rivals, lined her length: her bloodorange bockknickers, a two in one garment, showed natural nigger boggers, fancyfastened, free to undo: her blackstripe tan joseph was sequansewn and teddybearlined, with wavy rushgreen epaulettes and a leadown here and there of royal swansruff: a brace of gaspers stuck in her hayrope garters: her civvy codroy coat with alpheubett buttons was boundaried round with a twobar tunnel belt: a fourpenny bit in each pocketside weighed her safe from the blowaway windrush; she had a clothespeg tight astride on her joki's nose and she kep on grinding a sommething quaint in her fiumy mouth and the rrreke of the fluve of the tail of the gawan of her snuffdrab siouler's skirt trailed ffiffty odd Irish miles behind her lungarhodes.

Hellsbells, I'm sorry I missed her! Sweet gumptyum and nobody fainted! But in whelk of her mouths? Was her naze alight? Everyone that saw her said the dowce little delia looked a bit queer. Lotsy trotsy, mind the poddle! Missus, be good and don't fol in the say! Fenny poor hex she must have charred. Kickhams a frumpier ever you saw! Making mush mullet's eyes at her boys dobelon. And they crowned her their chariton queen, all the maids. Of the may? You don't say! Well for her she couldn't see herself. I recknitz wharfore the darling murrayed her mirror. She did? Mersey me! There was a koros of drouthdropping surfacemen, boomslanging and plugchewing, fruiteyeing and flowerfeeding, in contemplation of the fluctuation and the undification of her filimentation, lolling and leasing on North Lazers' Waal all eelfare week by the Jukar Yoick's and as soon as they saw her meander by that marritime way in her grasswinter's weeds and twigged who was under her archdeaconess bonnet, Avondale's fish and Clarence's poison, sedges an to aneber, Wit-upon-Crutches to Master Bates: *Between our two southsates and the granite they're warming, or her face has been lifted or Alp has doped!*

But what was the game in her mixed baggyrhatty? Just the tembo in her tumbo or pilipili from her pepperpot? Saas and taas and specis bizaas. And where in thunder did she plunder? Fore the battle or efter the ball? I want to get it frisk from the soorce. I aubette my bearb it's worth while poaching on! Shake it up, do, do! That's a good old son of a ditch! I promise I'll make it worth your while. And I don't mean maybe. Nor yet with a goodfor. Spey me pruth and I'll tale you true.

Well, arundgirond in a waveney lyne aringarouma she pattered and swung and sidled, dribbling her boulder through narrowa mosses, the diliskydrear on our drier side and the vilde vetchvine agin us, curara here, careero there, not knowing which medway or weser to strike it, edereider, making chattahoochee all to her ain chichiu, like Santa Claus at the cree of the pale and puny, nistling to hear for their tiny hearties, her arms encircling Isolabella, then running with reconciled Romas and Reims, on like a lech to be off like a dart, then bathing Dirty Hans' spatters with spittle, with a Christmas box apiece for aisch and iveryone of her childer, the birthday gifts they dreamt they gabe her, the spoiled she fleetly laid at our door! On the matt, by the pourch and inunder the cellar. The rivulets ran aflod to see, the glashaboys, the pollynooties. Out of the paunschaup on to the pyre. And they all about her, juvenile leads and ingenuinas, from the slime of their slums and artesaned wellings, rickets and riots, like the Smyly boys at their vicereine's levee. Vivi vienne, little Annchen! Vielo Anna, high life! Sing us a sula, O, susuria! Ausone sidulcis! Hasn't she tambre! Chipping her and raising a bit of a chir or a jary every dive she'd neb in her culdee sacco of wabbash she raabed and reach out her maundy meerschaundize, poor souvenir as per ricorder and all for sore aringarung, stinkers and heelers, laggards and primelads, her furzeborn sons and dribblederry daughters, a thousand and one of them, and wickerpotluck for each of them. For evil and ever. And kiks the buch. A tinker's bann and a barrow to boil his billy for Gipsy Lee; a cartridge of cockaleekie soup for Chummy the Guardsman; for sulky Pender's acid nephew deltoïd drops, curiously strong; a cough and a rattle and wildrose cheeks for poor Piccolina Petite MacFarlane; a jigsaw puzzle of needles and pins and blankets and shins between them for Isabel, Jezebel and Llewelyn Mmarriage; a brazen nose and pigiron mittens for Johnny Walker Beg; a papar flag of the saints and stripes for Kevineen O'Dea; a puffpuff for Pudge Craig and a nightmarching hare for Techertim Tombigby; waterleg and gumboots each for Bully Hayes and Hurricane Hartigan; a prodigal heart and fatted calves for Buck Jones, the pride of Clonliffe; a loaf of bread and a father's early aim for Val from Skibereen; a jauntingcar for Larry Doolin, the Ballyclee jackeen; a seasick trip on a government ship for Teague O'Flanagan; a louse and trap for Jerry Coyle; slushmincepies for Andy Mackenzie; a hairclip and clackdish for Penceless Peter; that twelve sounds look for G. V. Brooke; a drowned doll, to face downwards for modest Sister Anne Mortimer; altar falls for Blanchisse's bed; Wildairs' breechettes for Magpeg Woppington; to Sue Dot a big eye; to Sam Dash a false step; snakes in clover, picked and scotched, and a vaticanned viper catcher's visa for Patsy Presbys; a reiz every morning for Standfast Dick and a drop every minute for Stumblestone Davy; scruboak beads for beatified Biddy; two appletweed stools for Eva Mobbely; for Saara Philpot a jordan vale tearorne; a pretty box of Pettyfib's Powder for Eileen Aruna to whiten her teeth and outflash Helen Arhone; a whippingtop for Eddy Lawless; for Kitty Coleraine of Butterman's Lane a penny wise for her foolish pitcher; a putty shovel for Terry the Puckaun; an apotamus mask for Promoter Dunne; a niester egg with a twicedated shell and a dynamight right for Pavl the Curate; a collera morbous for Mann in the Cloack; a starr and girton for Draper and Deane; for Will-of-the-Wisp and Barny-the-Bark two mangolds noble to sweeden their bitters; for Oliver Bound a way in his frey; for Seumas, thought little, a crown he feels big; a tibertine's pile with a Congoswood cross on the back for Sunny Twimjim; a praises be and spare me days for Brian the Bravo; penteplenty of pity with lubilashings of lust for Olona Lena Magdalena; for Camilla, Dromilla, Ludmilla, Mamilla, a bucket, a packet, a book and a pillow; for Nancy Shannon a Tuami brooch; for Dora Riparia Hopeandwater a cooling douche and a warmingpan; a pair of Blarney braggs for Wally Meagher; a hairpin slatepencil for Elsie Oram to scratch her toby, doing her best with her volgar fractions; an old age pension for Betty Bellezza; a bag of the blues for Funny Fitz; a *Missa pro Messa* for Taff de Taff; Jill, the spoon of a girl, for Jack, the broth of a boy; a Rogerson Crusoe's Friday fast for Caducus Angelus Rubiconstein; three hundred and sixtysix poplin tyne for revery warp in the weaver's woof for Victor Hugonot; a stiff steaded rake and good varians muck for Kate the Cleaner; a hole in the ballad for Hosty; two dozen of cradles for J.F.X.P. Coppinger; tenpounten on the pop for the daulphins born with five spoiled squibs for Infanta; a letter to last a lifetime for Maggi beyond by the ashpit; the heftiest frozenmeat woman from Lusk to Livienbad for Felim the Ferry; spas and speranza and symposium's syrup for decayed and blind and gouty Gough; a change of naves and joys of ills for Armoricus Tristram Amoor Saint Lawrence; a guillotine shirt for Reuben Redbreast and hempen suspendeats for Brennan on the Moor; an oakanknee for Conditor Sawyer and musquodoboits for Great Tropical Scott; a C3 peduncle for Karmalite Kane; a sunless map of the month, including the sword and stamps, for Shemus O'Shaun the Post; a jackal with hide for Browne but Nolan; a stonecold shoulder for Donn Joe Vance; all lock and no stable for Honorbright Merreytrickx; a big drum for Billy Dunboyne; a guilty goldeny bellows, below me blow me, for Ida Ida and a hushaby rocker, Elletrouvetout, for Who-is-silvier—Where-is-he?; whatever you like to swilly to swash, Yuinness or Yennessy, Laagen or Niger, for Festus King and Roaring Peter and Frisky Shorty and Treacle Tom and O. B. Behan and Sully the Thug and Master Magrath and Peter Cloran and O'Delawarr Rossa and Nerone MacPacem and whoever you chance to meet knocking around; and a pig's bladder balloon for Selina Susquehanna Stakelum. But what did she give to Pruda Ward and Katty Kanel and Peggy Quilty and Briery Brosna and Teasy Kieran and Ena Lappin and Muriel Maassy and Zusan Camac and Melissa Bradogue and Flora Ferns and Fauna Fox-Goodman and Grettna Greaney and Penelope Inglesante and Lezba Licking like Leytha Liane and Roxana Rohan with Simpatica Sohan and Una Bina Laterza and Trina La Mesme and Philomena O'Farrell and Irmak Elly and Josephine Foyle and Snakeshead Lily and Fountainoy Laura and Marie Xavier Agnes Daisy Frances de Sales Macleay? She gave them ilcka madre's daughter a moonflower and a bloodvein: but the grapes that ripe before reason to them that devide the vinedress. So on Izzy, her shamemaid, love shone befond her tears as from Shem, her penmight, life past befoul his prime.

My colonial, wardha bagful! A bakereen's dusind with tithe tillies to boot. That's what you may call a tale of a tub! And Hibernonian market! All that and more under one crinoline envelope if you dare to break the porkbarrel seal. No wonder they'd run from her pison plague. Throw us your hudson soap for the honour of Clane! The wee taste the water left. I'll raft it back, first thing in the marne. Merced mulde! Ay, and don't forget the reckitts I lohaned you. You've all the swirls your side of the current. Well, am I to blame for that if I have? Who said you're to blame for that if you have? You're a bit on the sharp side. I'm on the wide. Only snuffers' cornets drifts my way that the cracka dvine chucks out of his cassock, with her estheryear's marsh narcissus to make him recant his vanitty fair. Foul strips of his chinook's bible I do be reading, dodwell disgustered but chickled with chuckles at the tittles is drawn on the tattlepage. *Senior ga dito: Faciasi Omo! E omo fu fò.* Ho! Ho! *Senior ga dito: Faciasi Hidamo! Hidamo se ga facessà.* Ha! Ha! And *Die Windermere Dichter* and Lefanu (Sheridan's) old *House by the Coachyard* and Mill (J.) *On Woman* with *Ditto on the Floss.* Ja, a swamp for Altmuehler and a stone for his flossies! I know how racy they move his wheel. My hands are blawcauld between isker and suda like that piece of pattern chayney there, lying below. Or where is it? Lying beside the sedge I saw it. Hoangho, my sorrow, I've lost it! Aimihi! With that turbary water who could see? So near and yet so far! But O, gihon! I lovat a gabber. I could listen to maure and moravar again. Regn onder river. Flies do your float. Thick is the life for mere.

Well, you know or don't you kennet or haven't I told you every telling has a taling and that's the he and the she of it. Look, look, the dusk is growing! My branches lofty are taking root. And my cold cher's gone ashley. Fieluhr? Filou! What age is at? It saon is late. 'Tis endless now senne eye or erewone last saw Waterhouse's clogh. They took it asunder, I hurd thum sigh. When will they reassemble it? O, my back, my back, my bach! I'd want to go to Aches-les-Pains. Pingpong! There's the Belle for Sexaloitez! And Concepta de Send-us-pray! Pang! Wring out the clothes! Wring in the dew! Godavari, vert the showers! And grant thaya grace! Aman. Will we spread them here now? Ay, we will. Flip! Spread on your bank and I'll spread mine on mine. Flep! It's what I'm doing. Spread! It's churning chill. Der went is rising. I'll lay a few stones on the hostel sheets. A man and his bride embraced between them. Else I'd have sprinkled and folded them only. And I'll tie my butcher's apron here. It's suety yet. The strollers will pass it by. Six shifts, ten kerchiefs, nine to hold to the fire and this for the code, the convent napkins, twelve, one baby's shawl. Good mother Jossiph knows, she said. Whose head? Mutter snores? Deataceas! Wharnow are alle her childer, say? In kingdome gone or power to come or gloria be to them farther? Allalivial, allalluvial! Some here, more no more, more again lost alla stranger. I've heard tell that same brooch of the Shannons was married into a family in Spain. And all the Dunders de Dunnes in Markland's Vineland beyond Brendan's herring pool takes number nine in yangsee's hats. And one of Biddy's beads went bobbing till she rounded up lost histereve with a marigold and a cobbler's candle in a side strain of a main drain of a manzinahurries off Bachelor's Walk. But all that's left to the last of the Meaghers in the loup of the years prefixed and between is one kneebuckle and two hooks in the front. Do you tell me that now? I do in troth. Orara por Orbe and poor Las Animas! Ussa, Ulla, we're umbas all! Mezha, didn't you hear it a deluge of times, ufer and ufer, respund to spond? You deed, you deed! I need, I need! It's that irrawaddyng I've stoke in my aars. It all but husheth the lethest zswound. Oronoko! What's your trouble? Is that the great Finnleader himself in his joakimono on his statue riding the high horse there forehengist? Father of Otters, it is himself! Yonne there! Isset that? On Fallareen Common? You're thinking of Astley's Amphitheayter where the bobby restrained you making sugarstuck pouts to the ghostwhite horse of the Peppers. Throw the cobwebs from your eyes, woman, and spread your washing proper! It's well I know your sort of slop. Flap! Ireland sober is Ireland stiff. Lord help you, Maria, full of grease, the load is with me! Your prayers. I sonht zo! Madammangut! Were you lifting your elbow, tell us, glazy cheeks, in Conway's Carriga-curra canteen? Was I what, hobbledyhips? Flop! Your rere gait's creakorheuman bitts your butts disagrees. Amn't I up since the damp dawn, marthared mary allacook, with Corrigan's pulse and varicoarse veins, my pramaxle smashed, Alice Jane in decline and my oneeyed mongrel twice run over, soaking and bleaching boiler rags, and sweating cold, a widow like me, for to deck my tennis champion son, the laundryman with the lavandier flannels? You won your limpopo limp from the husky hussars when Collars and Cuffs was heir to the town and your slur gave the stink to Carlow. Holy Scamander, I sar it again! Near the golden falls. Icis on us! Seints of light! Zezere! Subdue your noise, you hamble creature! What is it but a blackburry growth or the dwyergray ass them four old codgers owns. Are you meanam Tarpey and Lyons and Gregory? I meyne now, thank all, the four of them, and the roar of them, that draves that stray in the mist and old Johnny MacDougal along with them. Is that the Poolbeg flasher beyant, pharphar, or a fireboat coasting nyar the Kishtna or a glow I behold within a hedge or my Garry come back from the Indes? Wait till the honeying of the lune, love! Die eve, little eve, die! We see that wonder in your eye. We'll meet again, we'll part once more. The spot I'll seek if the hour you'll find. My chart shines high where the blue milk's upset. Forgivemequick, I'm going! Bubye! And you, pluck your watch, forgetmenot. Your evenlode. So save to jurna's end! My sights are swimming thicker on me by the shadows to this place. I sow home slowly now by own way, moyvalley way. Towy I too, rathmine.

Ah, but she was the queer old skeowsha anyhow, Anna Livia, trinkettoes! And sure he was the quare old buntz too, Dear Dirty Dumpling, foosterfather of fingalls and dottergills. Gammer and gaffer we're all their gangsters. Hadn't he seven dams to wive him? And every dam had her seven crutches. And every crutch had its seven hues. And each hue had a differing cry. Sudds for me and supper for you and the doctor's bill for Joe John. Befor! Bifur! He married his markets, cheap by foul, I know, like any Etrurian Catholic Heathen, in their pinky limony creamy birnies and their turkiss indienne mauves. But at milkidmass who was the spouse? Then all that was was fair. Tys Elvenland! Teems of times and happy returns. The seim anew. Ordovico or viricordo. Anna was, Livia is, Plurabelle's to be. Northmen's thing made southfolk's place but howmulty plurators made eachone in person? Latin me that, my trinity scholard, out of eure sanscreed into oure eryan! *Hircus Civis Eblanensis!* He had buckgoat paps on him, soft ones for orphans. Ho, Lord! Twins of his bosom. Lord save us! And ho! Hey? What all men. Hot? His tittering daughters of. Whawk?

Can't hear with the waters of. The chittering waters of. Flittering bats, fieldmice bawk talk. Ho! Are you not gone ahome? What Thom Malone? Can't hear with bawk of bats, all thim liffeying waters of. Ho, talk save us! My foos won't moos. I feel as old as yonder elm. A tale told of Shaun or Shem? All Livia's daughtersons. Dark hawks hear us. Night! Night! My ho head halls. I feel as heavy as yonder stone. Tell me of John or Shaun? Who were Shem and Shaun the living sons or daughters of? Night now! Tell me, tell me, tell me, elm! Night night! Telmetale of stem or stone. Beside the rivering waters of, hitherandthithering waters of. Night!

PEADAR O'DONNELL
from *The Knife*

3

Even in the morning there had been no ripple of news. Sam Rowan had not been early in the market but Billy White had been there. Billy grew tired of the market; prices were poor and it was a mean, drizzly day that made the world feel its old age, and made the lives of things in it the off-shoots of old age. Other farmers might have to sell, for grass was short, but there was no reason why Billy should remain nibbling at buyers; he had grass for the stock. So he whisked them out of the market, and sent them off in the care of a servant man from his neighbourhood. Billy would take a walk round and see the market, and call at Dan Sweeney's too, and have a drink; whiskey was made for such a day as this.

He pushed his way through the fair, wedging cattle aside here and there with a jerk of his thigh. A sale was taking place down near the Bank, and a big, interested crowd hung around; like crows round a stook of oats, Billy thought, spat out, and went on his way. He pushed open the door and entered Sweeney's bar. Inside, the air was thick with smoke and fumes and talk; the talk buzzed in a fog. Billy's stubble jaws felt their way among faces to the counter, and again he used his thighs to wedge obstacles aside, and a man cursed. Sweeney nodded to Billy, and filled out a double Scotch. Without a word Billy swallowed it down, and rapped the glass on the counter before Sweeney, who refilled it.

Billy rested his elbow on the counter and looked round. Talk, talk, a milling of words; here and there a song wriggled its way amid the confusion. Angry words stabbed the babel, clung on the whirl of heedlessness and hilarity, and then melted down into maudlin murmurs. Billy gazed round him; his small eyes that showed little white, blank, uninterested, just seeing, his head jerking round and round on his neck as his gaze swung.

The bar door came in with a bang, and the noise nipped off suddenly. Two men continued to drone a song until their singing stood naked amid the silence, and then they sat down suddenly, spilling their beer over each other, laughing foolishly.

'Godfrey Dhu is buying the whole damn fair,' a man roared from the doorway.

Billy White struck his glass with his elbow and it spilled across the counter, emptying over into one of his boots. His head jerked forward towards the speaker, and then crouched, as though ducking a blow, between humped shoulders. He shot out his thigh, and a man stumbled; he dug into the crowd.

'Then by God it's true!' a voice gasped close to Billy's ear.

'What's true?' Billy barked.

'The Godfrey Dhus have bought Montgomerys.'

Billy White made a noise like an animal in pain, and stood stiff against the counter. 'The Godfrey Dhus, the Godfrey Dhus.' Recollection of The Knife and Nuala and the old man himself busy among the trees was rising in gusts of alarm in Billy White, until amid the roar he accepted in a riot of rage the truth of this news. He drove his fist into the roar around him, and found a man's face, and he was in the midst of the first group that was retched out of the bar in the great heave that tore the splintered door from its hinges.

The fair was leaping into rising billows of conflict and excitement. The servant men of the Lagan were building on the gathering down near the Bank, and the Orangemen, recognizing each other across spaces in the emptying market-place, moved into knots among the cattle, and then churning together drew near the roaring natives. The Godfrey Dhus were in front, silent beside a cart, with the servant men of the Lagan piled in behind them.

Billy White raced towards the Godfrey Dhus. He ran forward with an awkward jog, one clawed hand raised above his bare head, sweat beaded on his face, and blood from a cut lip dripping off his short whisker. He came on steadily, his jog settling into a purposeful stride with its queer swing. His eyes were on the old man, and when The Knife stepped forward Billy halted. Behind him the farmers of the Lagan pressed steadily, silent, this news groping into the forefront of each mind, flashing, whirling, until the fair became unreal, bizarre.

'Godfrey Dhu,' Billy White bellowed, but the servant men of the Lagan roared him down.

Breslin pushed out in front and stood a pace before Godfrey Dhu, glowering at Billy White; two enemies of a score of years. The Knife put a hand on Breslin's shoulder, and Sam Rowan walked to the front among the Orangemen. When The Knife raised his hand the market was silent.

'Is it true, Knife?'

'It's true, Sam.' And now a roar that was all challenge, the flinging of hats and of old threadbare caps: among the Orangemen a growl, here and there the sudden raising of a stick.

That scene burned deep into the minds of the Lagan. On one side the planter farmers, a solid crush of swarthy, big-bodied, well-coated men; opposing them the servant men of the Lagan, blue and grey eyes against shades of brown; fair skin against tawny, restless swaying bodies poised to spring, against a wall of stolid trunks. In front of the farmers, his small eyes blood-shot, his teeth bare, his jaws champing, his short legs wide apart, one hand clenched and held low, one raised and clawed, stood Billy White the Orangeman.

Blazing into Billy's eyes, his face thrust forward, his lips parted in a sneer, his fists pushed down along his sides by arms as stiff as ramrods, his knees bent to spring, stood Paddy Breslin, the Hibernian. Should these crowds clash, Billy and Paddy would meet first, Paddy with milling fist and butting head crashing into Billy's swinging boot and clawing hand.

Godfrey Dhu, nursing his secret of money from a dead brother's estate in Australia, had come into possession of a farm in the Lagan. Land in a compact planter district had always been disposed of by private treaty to British stock; it was part of the Orangemen's religion that the possession of soil must remain solid. This farm had passed to an absentee, and by some obscure process the absentee had let it slip into the hands of a Fenian, a papist; every native was both. Here in the market the crust of the centuries was burst; the past was boiling over, gushing out its lava of madness. Dazed, mystified, and angrier because of the mystery, the planters staggered under an eruption of boiling race hatred. One long, wild roar was ringing through the square from the servant men. Low growls from the sweating, compact, motionless Orangemen. Breslin and White, cheering and champing, straining forward. Should they meet this village will become a pit in a jungle of blind passion and men will rip one another to pieces.

Suddenly from among the natives a hand shot up commanding silence, and The Knife turned to the crowd behind him. Sam Rowan stepped to the front amid the Orangemen. His eye and The Knife's met, clear, hard looks, preoccupied; the concern of each was back on his own crowd. The Orangemen tramped past, slowly, without a word, with heavy, stamping feet. The natives were alone.

And Sam Rowan went home with the tidings which had preceded him to the fireside of the Black Rowans.

4

Nuala Godfrey Dhu was alone in the big house among the trees, and she sang as she worked in the kitchen. Being alone in this big house was an adventure, and her song was partly a challenge to the loneliness. The little cottage on the far-away slope of the hill had been without spaces, but here there was a sense of emptiness and silences. She stood by the dresser with a pile of delf in her arms and listened: the logs crackled in the wide fireplace, and, outside, beads of water plopped on a sheet of zinc under the trees. She put the delf in their place, and wondered what woman of the Montgomerys had arranged the delf in the kitchen; a quiet picturing that was sympathetic towards that wayward family. The Montgomerys were not popular among their stock; one of their breed had fought with the Americans in the War of Independence, and he had a place in history, but in the Lagan his name was only used to mock his folly. Thought of that rebel strain made the house friendly to Nuala: it took the emptiness out of the spaces.

'I'm going to like this place,' she thought, touching a plate into its place with her quick fingers.

She went upstairs to her room. Hugh and The Knife had cut down branches and now her window looked out over the broad fields, and in the distance the mountains, with shortened necks humped in the rain, cowered under leaking clouds. She smiled across at them; they reminded her, somehow, of little boys herding in the rain. She sang softly to herself as she worked, and her song now had no challenge.

It was when she was back in the kitchen that she grew restless. She went to the door, and looked out; the sky had cleared, but it was raw and she made a face at it. She went into her father's bedroom. She was still in there when she heard a shout; she paused for a moment in the bedroom door; it came again and she hurried out. She halted in the doorway, and frowned slightly. A man was coming across the open lawn; in the sunless light his face was without colour, and his hair curled on his forehead. He waved his cap to her. She stepped back into the kitchen and she was standing very erect when he came in.

'The whole fair went in a rage,' he said.

'Where's our folk?' she asked sharply.

'Comin', and half the countryside with them.'

She smiled at him now, and he came close; a whiff of whiskey came to her. 'You promised you'd stop it, James Burns,' she said.

'I'll do anything you ask me, Nuala,' he said: 'anything, but don't be a damned nun . . .'

The crash of a melodeon and voices sounded outside, and The Knife raced into the kitchen. His excitement passed at once to Nuala, and she grabbed him. They danced on to the street. Curran was singing:

'Ould Ireland will be free from the centre to the sea,
    Then hurray for liberty, says the Shan Van Vocht.'

Breslin was in front, his cap on a pitchfork. Godfrey Dhu, his coat thrown across his arm, his short legs making time with the best of them, came behind Breslin.

'Then hurray for liberty, says the Shan Van Vocht,'

and the singing ended in a cheer. There were girls among the crowd, and at sight of The Knife and Nuala men grabbed them. A spurt of dancing shaped itself into an eight-hand reel. Whoops rang out, and the roll of a drum joined in the whirl of sound, for the band instruments were being carried over to Godfrey Dhu's.

'And the Orange will decay, says the Shan Van Vocht.'

Godfrey Dhu signalled The Knife and Nuala aside. 'We must get something in; we must make a night of this.'

'You old codger,' Nuala said, 'I know what's in your mind. From this day on you'll have another big day to celebrate each year.'

'I never thought to be as worked up again about anything,' he said seriously. 'I'd paste a regiment of soldiers that'd look crooked at me this minute; I'm remembering things you children never knew. Let there be such a burst of noise and laughing and roaring as will crack the panes in every damn window of their's in the Lagan.' He shook his fist towards the lights in the plain. 'Childer, if She was only living for this day,' he added after a pause. 'And you will put word to Phil Burns and Denis Freel?'

'You'll go, Knife,' Nuala said.

He nodded.

He took his bicycle and set off leisurely and then suddenly he jerked down between the handle bars and cycled for all he could.

'And the Orange will decay, says the Shan Van Vocht,' buzzed in his mind.

LIAM O'FLAHERTY
from *Mr Gilhooley*

2

It was now a little after nine o'clock. Outside the Gaiety Theatre there was a ragged, thin loafer, a destitute one, watching the bright lights greedily, hoping to abstract from the lights some of the joy of the interior, where there was music and gay figures strutting on the stage and comfortable people lolling on plush-covered seats, eating chocolates and smiling.

Mr Gilhooley was quite drunk. His eyes stared fixedly. But in spite of his intoxication and the dullness in front of his eyes, he still felt bored and miserable. His increased intoxication had merely increased his misery instead of relieving it. No misery is as great as that of the lonely voluptuary who feels that his life is wrecked without any hope. Neither the misery of hunger, nor of homelessness, nor of disease. Because in all these miseries there is hope and a sense of righteousness. But in the misery of the bored voluptuary there is no hope nor sense of righteousness.

Mr Gilhooley looked at the bright lights of the theatre. It occurred to him to go in for an hour. He strutted aimlessly across the street and glanced at the bill. The loafer came up.

'Good thing on, sir,' he said. 'Hot stuff, I believe,' he added, subtly measuring the character of the tippled gentleman.

Mr Gilhooley stared contemptuously at the loafer with blurred eyes. He threw him a copper and walked away. He entered Grafton Street once more, and without troubling to think where he was going, he began to walk down towards College Green. The lights of the cinema struck his eyes, and he started slightly. Something pleasant occurred to him. He swallowed his breath and licked his lips slightly. He decided to enter the place.

This time he did not glance at the bill but entered rapidly, received an aluminium disc at the box office in exchange for his money, handed the disc to the door porter and passed through the hangings into the theatre.

The lights were turned low. Something was being exhibited on the screen. It was impossible to see whether the theatre was full or empty. Not a sound was heard from the audience if there was one. On the screen there were Americans dancing in a cabaret, while behind a curtain, on the screen, of course, a dark man was whispering to a half-naked woman.

A faint perfume reached Mr Gilhooley, as he stood breathing heavily with his hat in his hand, waiting for the attendant to lead him to a seat. This perfume was a curious feminine scent, which was familiar to him, for he was an habitué of the cinema for certain reasons; and that curious feminine scent is peculiar to the cinema. So many well-dressed women sitting in silence in the half-darkness. There was an air of mystery about it. An air of romance and of remoteness from actual life. With the mind drugged by the spectacle on the screen, the body hidden from observation by the darkness, yet in contact with others, eavesdropping on the absurd display of emotion exhibited on the screen, passions were aroused which in the cold air outside would bring a flush to the cheek.

The attendant flashed his torch on Mr Gilhooley, murmured, and led him along. Mr Gilhooley became very excited. He breathed still more heavily. A feeling of extraordinary passion pervaded his body. His movements were no longer under control of his brain. He could not see, and had he tried to speak at that moment his lips could have uttered no sound. Moisture filled his eyes. He was intoxicated with passion. To the degree that he had been miserable a minute ago, suddenly he had now become deliriously happy, plunged suddenly into that intoxication of the voluptuary by the environment, which suggested strange things to his imagination, and by the prospect of a subtle amusement to which he was addicted.

The attendant pointed with his lighted torch to a row of seats. People rose in a row, one after the other, slowly, to let Mr Gilhooley pass along. Blindly, without seeing anybody, guided by the forceful arm of the attendant, Mr Gilhooley found the entrance to the row. Then he pushed along, brushing against the knees and bodies of one man and three women. At last he dropped into a vacant seat, closed his eyes and remained perfectly still. His head was swimming. His mind was empty and as light as a feather. His body was rising into the air, as it were. It kept rising and vanishing. Then another body rose and vanished, leaving another body that rose and vanished to give place to another body that rose and vanished. Body after body kept rising and vanishing. But Mr Gilhooley kept on sitting there without moving, quite whole and substantial in spite of the numberless bodies that rose and vanished endlessly. And instead of being disturbed by these numberless bodies that rose out of himself and vanished, he kept laughing with great glee within himself, although his face was fixed and flabby. Gradually his breathing became more heavy. The bodies rose more slowly, vanished with difficulty and then ceased rising and vanishing. With a little snap stray ideas floated into his brain. A sort of mischievous idea began to ferment in his mind. His intoxication ceased to be formless and completely stupefied. His passions began to grow angry, as it were. His muscles wanted to take part in this peculiar form of debauchery. His intellect also began to make an effort to have a hand in it, giving it direction and suggesting methods and ideas. Mr Gilhooley opened one eye and stared straight in front of him at an indistinct object which was the back of a lady's brown fur coat. Then he moved his right knee about a quarter of an inch. It came in contact with something soft. A shock went through his whole body.

He turned slightly and saw a woman sitting on his right. She was a stout woman and, from the line of her sturdy face, a woman of middle-age. But her form, her age, her personality, were not of interest to his mind, nor to his body. His self-centred passion merely toyed with the subtlest form of lust, which does not depend on the object desired, but on the suggestions brought to bear on the object. He touched her knee again and it seemed there was a slight response, that nervous twitching of a muscle that is caused involuntarily, as if the muscle hit back to find out what hit it.

Mr Gilhooley became very calm suddenly. He slowly took off his coat, doubled it and drew it across his lap. He did this very slowly and it took him a considerable time to do it. While he was doing it, his mind was busy enjoying to the utmost the pleasure which he contemplated. Cunningly aware that the realization would not be as pleasant as this preparation, it delayed as much as possible the completion of the act of taking off the coat and of doubling it across the knees. The woman remained perfectly still. Although now and for a whole minute past, there had been ripples of laughter eddying through the audience at some buffoonery represented on the screen, the line of her face remained absolutely stiff and motionless. Her chin was raised and her bosom heaved irregularly, her prominent bust jutting out.

With his hand concealed beneath the folded overcoat, Mr Gilhooley swayed his knee over towards her knee again, until his hand touched her knee. It touched her with the fingers ever so gently. They remained motionless thus for over a minute. Mr Gilhooley, during this pause, did not feel any emotion at all. Everything, his body, his mind, everything was quite dead. Feeling was completely suspended. Then suddenly the fingers that touched her knee began to tremble. Imperceptibly they began to move along towards her thigh. His legs, then his arms, began to tremble. Shortly this trembling spread all over his body and he no longer knew whether his fingers were moving over her thigh, or indeed where he was. A minute passed, while the woman remained perfectly still, except that her bosom moved still more violently. The most extraordinary visions flashed across Mr Gilhooley's mind, became more and more exotic and unbelievable. He felt that . . .

There was a violent shock which sent a shiver down his spine. The woman had moved abruptly, drawing in a deep breath through her nostrils, like a gasp.

'God Almighty!' muttered Mr Gilhooley, clenching his teeth, drawing back his lower lip and becoming motionless.

The woman rose to her feet, making a considerable noise on purpose, as if making an effort to point out to the audience why she was going. He heard her say: 'Pardon,' in a gruff voice to whoever sat on the far side. And he heard the loud chorus of laughter that greeted some further buffoonery on the screen. Then her dress rustled against the seat in front as she passed out. Mr Gilhooley became terror-stricken. His body, disturbed in the middle of its debauch, exhausted by the vicious excitement of the nerves, was shivering with fear.

One, two, three, four, five . . . He kept counting, expecting at every moment to hear a disturbance caused by the lady coming along with an attendant and pointing him out. 'There he is. Seize him.' And the audience would cry: 'Pervert. Away with him. Lynch him.' He would be publicly ruined, disgraced.

The moments became minutes, while he sat there with his lower lip drawn back and his teeth clenched. Still nobody came. The audience, tired now of laughing, watched the buffoonery of their favourite screen buffoon with tears in their eyes, holding their exhausted stomachs. Mr Gilhooley's fear of detection lessened. Then it vanished. But as soon as his fear vanished it gave place to shame. Nothing could be more horrible than that shame.

It was so powerful that it became physical and he had to press his hands against his lungs to prevent himself crying out. He made his body rigid, planted his right heel on the carpet of the floor, stiffened his calf and pressed his elbows into his sides, while he drew in a deep breath through his clenched teeth. His eyes were popping out of his head. He was in the throes of the mania of guilt which follows in the wake of a perversion.

Terrified by the intensity of his feelings, thinking that he was going mad, that he was going to die, or that he was being stricken by that unknown form of paralysis with which the priest threatened them at school if they persisted in a certain practice, he used various subterfuges to allay his fear and calm his body. He told himself that in an hour at most he would have forgotten it. He told himself that thousands of others were committing acts far more disgraceful at the very moment. But these excuses had no effect on him, until his body of its own accord began to recover from the nervous effects of the debauch. Then his mental attitude to it also underwent a change. Instead of loathing for himself he now felt pity.

The misery of his life, the hopelessness of his future, his solitude, the grossness of the set of imbeciles in which he moved, regrets for the life of activity and of social utility which he had prematurely abandoned, mingled into a sort of shame, which was no longer entirely unpleasant. It had now become a sentimental pity for himself.

His mouth slowly fell open. Tears came into his eyes. He became maudlin. He began to sob in his throat. Tears trickled down his cheeks. The feeling of purity and of being cleansed of something foul, which penitents feel leaving the confessional, took possession of him. He fixed his tearful eyes on a spot in front, a little to the left. His vision formed a little red spot there. In that little red spot he saw his whole life, as he had lived it, futile, unhappy, vicious and degrading. Now there was no good in it, not even the great amount of useful work he had done, the many years of healthy, fierce labour under the hot suns of South America. In his penitential savagery he denied that too to himself. While on the other hand with a grovelling joy he formed a picture of the life he would like to lead in the future, of the life he *would* lead in the future. Something simple, an innocent country wife, children, a house in the country, pigs, cows, ploughed land, the music of a river, birds, new-mown hay, everything. He thought of the rabbit-farm which he had contemplated recently during similar fits of penitence. He thought of a bee-farm. 'Anything at all,' he mumbled, licking the salt tears that trickled into his mouth with his tongue, 'anything at all, provided it's simple and useful and . . . and healthy.'

Then he grew calmer. His mind underwent a further change. The grovelling penitence became repugnant to him, as gradually his body recovered its strength. His jaws set and his mind contemplated something at a distance: above his head, somewhere in the air, as is usual when a mind contemplates something abstract. There was pride and dignity in this contemplation and this attitude of his mind. There was also sincerity and truth in it, which there was not in the grovelling and despicable penitence of the former abject state.

He thought now of love. Love. Love. Love. He repeated the word several times. And as he repeated it, he was aware that he did not mean sensual love, but that ideal, pure love of which even the most degraded human beings are aware, which they treasure in their inmost hearts, perhaps unknown to themselves, their conception of that ultimate good which man calls God and which in moments of great pain comes to the surface of their consciousness, hurting them and making their souls cry out in anguish.

Soothed by this refreshing thought, his muscles became lax. His weary limbs stretched out limply. Trembling slightly and spasmodically, he closed his eyes and began to breathe gently through his half-open lips. His head swayed forward a little. He was beginning to fall asleep.

He thought of leaving the city, of settling in the country and changing his whole life. A picture formed in his mind. He could hear sounds. He could smell the summer, hawthorn bushes in bloom and the heavy perfume of clover fields, the drunkening perfume of summer with its sounds of sleepy insects, drugged with sap, murmuring in the hot fields. Cows lowed far away, and even though they were far away the sweet odour of their bodies, an odour of new milk, reached his nostrils. In an ivy-covered limestone hill over a river birds were twittering. He himself loafed on a stone fence at the cross-roads, smoking a clay pipe, yawning and conversing with the peasants about some idiotic subject. Soothed by the sounds and the torporous smells, he was falling asleep on the wall. Not on the wall, but in the cinema. He was very happy.

Just before he fell asleep he had a vision of God, a being with a white surplice around his body, girdled at the waist with a gold band, with enormous soft white limbs and a square head, smiling benignantly.

Moisture began to ooze from his forehead. He drew in a deep breath through his nostrils and then let it out in a deep, long snore. He was asleep.

'The Hawk'

He breasted the summit of the cliff and then rose in wide circles to the clouds. When their undertendrils passed about his outstretched wings, he surged straight inland. Gliding and dipping his wings at intervals, he roamed across the roof of the firmament, with his golden hawk's eyes turned down, in search of prey, toward the bright earth that lay far away below, beyond the shimmering emptiness of the vast blue sky.

Once the sunlight flashed on his grey back, as he crossed an open space between two clouds. Then again he became a vague, swift shadow, rushing through the formless vapour. Suddenly his fierce heart throbbed, as he saw a lark, whose dewy back was jewelled by the radiance of the morning light, come rising towards him from a green meadow. He shot forward at full speed, until he was directly over his mounting prey. Then he began to circle slowly, with his wings stiff and his round eyes dilated, as if in fright. Slight tremors passed along his skin, beneath the compact armour of his plumage – like a hunting dog that stands poised and quivering before his game.

The lark rose awkwardly at first, uttering disjointed notes as he leaped and circled to gain height. Then he broke into full-throated song and soared straight upward, drawn to heaven by the power of his glorious voice, and fluttering his wings like a butterfly.

The hawk waited until the songbird had almost reached the limit of his climb. Then he took aim and stooped. With his wings half-closed, he raked like a meteor from the clouds. The lark's warbling changed to a shriek of terror as he heard the fierce rush of the charging hawk. Then he swerved aside, just in time to avoid the full force of the blow. Half-stunned, he folded his wings and plunged headlong towards the earth, leaving behind a flutter of feathers that had been torn from his tail by the claws of his enemy.

When he missed his mark, the hawk at once opened wide his wings and canted them to stay his rush. He circled once more above his falling prey, took aim, and stooped again. This time the lark did nothing to avoid the kill. He died the instant he was struck; his inert wings unfolded. With his head dangling from his limp throat, through which his lovely song had just been poured, he came tumbling down, convoyed by the closely circling hawk. He struck earth on a patch of soft brown sand, beside a shining stream.

The hawk stood for a few moments over his kill, with his lewd purple tongue lolling from his open beak and his black-barred breast heaving from the effort of pursuit. Then he secured the carcass in his claws, took wing, and flew off to the cliff where his mate was hatching on a broad ledge, beneath a massive tawny-gold rock that rose, overarching, to the summit.

It was a lordly place, at the apex of a narrow cove, and so high above the sea that the roar of the breaking waves reached there only as a gentle murmur. There was no other sound within the semicircle of towering limestone walls that rose sheer from the dark water. Two months before, a vast crowd of other birds had lived on the lower edges of the cliffs, making the cove merry with their cries as they flew out to sea and back again with fish. Then one morning the two young hawks came there from the east to mate.

For hours the rockbirds watched them in terror, as the interlopers courted in the air above the cove, stooping past each other from the clouds down to the sea's edge, and then circling up again, wing to wing, winding their garland of love. At noon they saw the female draw the male into a cave, and heard his mating screech as he treaded her. Then they knew the birds of death had come to nest in their cove. So they took flight. That afternoon the mated hawks gambolled in the solitude that was now their domain, and at sundown the triumphant male brought his mate to nest on this lofty ledge, from which a pair of ravens had fled.

Now, as he dropped the dead lark beside her on the ledge, she lay there in a swoon of motherhood. Her beak rested on one of the sticks that formed her rude bed, and she looked down at the distant sea through half-closed eyes. Uttering cries of tenderness, he trailed his wings and marched around the nest on his bandy legs, pushing against her sides, caressing her back with his throat, and gently pecking at her crest. He had circled her four times, before she awoke from her stupor. Then she raised her head suddenly, opened her beak, and screamed. He screamed in answer and leaped upon the carcass of the lark. Quickly he severed its head, plucked its feathers, and offered her the naked, warm meat. She opened her mouth wide, swallowed the huge morsel in one movement, and again rested her beak on the stick. Her limp body spread out once more around the pregnant eggs, as she relapsed into her swoon.

His brute soul was exalted by the consciousness that he had achieved the fullness of the purpose for which nature had endowed him. Like a hound stretched out in sleep before a blazing fire, dreaming of the day's long chase, he relived the epic of his mating passion, while he strutted back and forth among the disgorged pellets and the bloody remains of eaten prey with which the rock was strewn.

Once he went to the brink of the ledge, flapped his wings against his breast, and screamed in triumph, as he looked out over the majestic domain that he had conquered with his mate. Then again he continued to march, rolling from side to side in ecstasy, as he recalled his moments of tender possession and the beautiful eggs that were warm among the sticks.

His exaltation was suddenly broken by a sound that reached him from the summit of the cliff. He stood motionless, close to the brink, and listened with his head turned to one side. Hearing the sound again from the summit, the same tremor passed through the skin within his plumage, as when he had soared, poised, above the mounting lark. His heart also throbbed as it had done then, but not with the fierce desire to exercise his power. He knew that he had heard the sound of human voices, and he felt afraid.

He dropped from the ledge and flew, close to the face of the cliff, for a long distance towards the west. Then he circled outward, swiftly, and rose to survey the intruders. He saw them from on high. There were three humans near the brink of the cliff, a short way east of the nest. They had secured the end of a stout rope to a block of limestone. The tallest of them had tied the other end to his body, and then attached a small brown sack to his waist belt.

When the hawk saw the tall man being lowered down along the face of the cliff to a protruding ledge that was on a level with the nest, his fear increased. He knew that the men had come to steal his mate's eggs; yet he felt helpless in the presence of the one enemy that he feared by instinct. He spiralled still higher and continued to watch in agony.

The tall man reached the ledge and walked carefully to its western limit. There he signalled to his comrades, who hauled up the slack of his rope. Then he braced himself, kicked the brink of the ledge, and swung out towards the west, along the blunt face of the cliff, using the taut rope as a lever. He landed on the eastern end of the ledge where the hawk's mate was sitting on her nest, on the far side of a bluff. His comrades again slackened the rope, in answer to his signal, and he began to move westward, inch by inch, crouched against the rock.

The hawk's fear vanished as he saw his enemy relentlessly move closer to the bluff. He folded his wings and dove headlong down to warn his mate. He flattened out when he came level with the ledge and screamed as he flew past her. She took no notice of the warning. He flew back and forth several times, screaming in agony, before she raised her head and answered him. Exalted by her voice, he circled far out to sea and began to climb.

Once more he rose until the undertendrils of the clouds passed about his outstretched wings and the fierce cold of the upper firmament touched his heart. Then he fixed his golden eyes on his enemy and hovered to take aim. At this moment of supreme truth, as he stood poised, it was neither pride in his power nor the intoxication of the lust to kill that stiffened his wings and the muscles of his breast. He was drawn to battle by the wild, sad tenderness aroused in him by his mate's screech.

He folded his wings and stooped. Down he came, relentlessly, straight at the awe-inspiring man that he no longer feared. The two men on the cliff top shouted a warning when they saw him come. The tall man on the ledge raised his eyes. Then he braced himself against the cliff to receive the charge. For a moment, it was the eyes of the man that showed fear, as they looked into the golden eyes of the descending hawk. Then he threw up his arms, to protect his face, just as the hawk struck. The body of the doomed bird glanced off the thick cloth that covered the man's right arm and struck the cliff with a dull thud. It rebounded and went tumbling down.

When the man came creeping round the bluff, the mother hawk stood up in the nest and began to scream. She leaped at him and tried to claw his face. He quickly caught her, pinioned her wings, and put her in his little sack. Then he took the eggs.

Far away below the body of the dead hawk floated, its broken wings outstretched on the foam-embroidered surface of the dark water, and drifted seaward with the ebbing tide.

K. ARNOLD PRICE

from *The New Perspective*

We speak very little now at table. That means we speak very little at all. We never did speak much. But in the past – in the pre-violin period – I believed that our thoughts ran in close grooves, that we had passed beyond the need for discussion; it did often seem that we shared a mood that flowed through time and silence until it reached a point where it mysteriously broke into word.

I have lost that belief.

I used to think we were special, Cormac and I.

I thought we had something others had not.

I think now that Cormac is special and I am not.

Cormac has a kind of intuitive friendliness for certain objects, forms and processes. People say to me: Your husband has taste.

And what is taste? Surely a love transforming itself into knowledge, an intuition whetting an appetite that prompts the most delicate of man's skills.

In thirty years Cormac has come to know more than he needs to know, that is, for his business, about the habitations of man, about the artifacts that he makes because he loves them.

In thirty years . . . indeed, why should there not be growth?

(But what have I done in thirty years?)

> *Qu'as-tu fait, toi que voilà,*
> *De ta jeunesse?*

What indeed. When I look back through that narrowing perspective it seems that I was always running; running after comrades, crying *Wait for me!* – or running ahead calling *Come on!*

But who or what was I running from or to?

A hasty girl. An unreflecting woman scratching the surface of the soil like a busy hen.

Cormac has taken new values into his life; or, more frightening, he is now pursuing activities that presume these values. For him there is music, there is the violin, and there are two people who play with him. That is all. And others seem to know this too. I have noticed that when friends come to spend the evening, no one says, *Play a tune for us, Cormac . . . Where is the violin, Cormac?* – likely enough, harmless enough, in a provincial town. Even Charlie, the compulsive gossip, never speaks of it.

Stringers will be Cormac's, a house suited to his tastes and pursuits. The day we move, I shall be an evicted tenant with 'no suitable alternative accommodation'. However judiciously Cormac furnishes the living rooms, I shall think of them as his.

This makes a real division between Cormac and me.

What am I saying? That *habitat* matters?

But of course it matters; the day, the hour and the place matter: but to what degree? Do I say: *I cannot love my love in Stringers?* And in Stringers will Cormac not love me as much as ever?

As *much* as *ever* screams the machine in Molloy's yard: as *much* as *ever* as *much as ever* as *much* as *ever* it squeals and I am shaken and pierced by the sound, by the metallic tongue that cannot know what unhappiness is.

In fact, did Cormac ever utter the word *love?*

He would say, Come on, we're late . . . Come on, I'm hungry . . . Come on, we've done enough . . . Come on, take off your pants . . .

Everyone seems to know that Cormac has bought Stringers for his own use.

Comments are various.

Oh, *Pattie!* says Julia, squeezing her eyes shut, Aren't you *thrilled?* I bet it was your idea!

But Margaret McLoughlin gives me a measuring look and says: Will you *like* it, Pattie? Living in the country? Do you think you will *like* it?

Grainne, of course, rolls her eyes as if she were about to say something witty and daring, and says: *Pattie!* You'll have to get that little car now, won't you, Pattie?

It's an investment, says Mr Molloy across the counter. It's a very choice place.

Yes, Mr Molloy.

(But, Mr Molloy: how would you know whether anything is choice or not choice?)

It's a good site, says Finnegan. The old house, of course is long past . . .

Ah, there's a terrible lot to do to it, says Charlie.

Cormac has done a good deal already, I say patiently.

He's going mad, says Charlie, with his gloating sadness, What do the two of you want with a laundry and a playroom?

A *playroom?*

Well, I call it a playroom. I suppose Cormac calls it a *utility* room. But what sort of utility will it be to you with the both of you out working all day?

I smile at Charlie. He, of course, never stops smiling.

You've given me an idea, I say, and walk away, hoping it is a good exit line.

In the evening I experiment cautiously with Cormac.

Have you any plans for the utility room, Cormac?

No, says Cormac, There's plenty of time for that.

Perhaps I could use it for my crafts –

Oh, are you taking up crafts, says Cormac, politely, just as if he were talking to an acquaintance.

There is no doubt if I said I were going to run a karate class his reaction would be the same.

I think it probable that in a few years the Baroque Ensemble will have come into being. I think, too, that it will grow in accomplishment as the Busato family grow up. It will be Cormac's abiding interest for the next thirty years.

An idea has been going about with me these last few days; it pops up while I am dealing with long-familiar library routine. I welcome it; it warms me a little; I need warming. Soon I will word it to Cormac; but at the right moment. For the present it is like the secret hope of a wished-for pregnancy.

It is something I can *do*.

The music room at Stringers will need a harpsichord. I will buy the harpsichord for Cormac. It will be my contribution to his new life. It will be a way of allying myself – the only way – with his new life, new perspective.

I feel nervous, *very* nervous, about proposing it to Cormac. But it must be soon or he will make some plan of his own.

————————

I heard my voice come out hoarse with agitation as I enquired: Does Mario Busato make instruments?

I don't know. He may do. He buys old violins and cellos and repairs them. But he makes his living, I imagine, selling records and guitars.

He doesn't make reproductions of old keyboard instruments?

I wouldn't know. I have no doubt that if Mario set his mind to it he could do it, and do it well.

Alas, Cormac was roaming about the room while he spoke, looking for something, probably matches. I didn't find it easy to talk to this moving object, but in desperation went on: When you begin playing in Stringers you will have to have a harpsichord –

Oh, yes, said Cormac, still searching. I have a scout looking out for one for me.

I got up then with my words prepared: When you do find one that is suitable, Cormac, I'll buy it. It will be my contribution to the Chamber Orchestra.

I stood waiting while he stooped over an open drawer, rattling the miscellaneous contents to and fro. I think I was panting. Supposing he didn't answer?

But he straightened up and turned round and said very pleasantly (but looking down at something he held in his palm): Not at all, I wouldn't let you do it. You must spend your money on yourself.

I walked up to him and seized him by the lapels.

But I *want* to do it, Cormac! I'd *like* to do it! It would give me a feeling I had a part in it –

No, no, you don't get any pleasure out of it. And when we begin to play at Stringers you'll have the chore of getting supper for us.

That's nothing, of course I'll get supper. I meant –

– And when we get into Stringers you'll find that there are plenty of things you'll need for the house –

But *you're* going to buy the furniture!

Yes, but . . . well, there are lots of small things you'll need . . . pots and pans, for instance, are expensive to day.

I dropped my hands from his lapels at that and turned away.

(*Pots and pans!*)

I said in a calm voice: Since Bob got married I seem to have spent nothing. My savings are just rotting.

No, they're not, they're producing interest.

I still feel terribly dashed. In fact, battered.

I am childish. The idea was childish.

I know money has nothing to do with the case. I could have afforded to buy the harpsichord, so there would be no sacrifice. And of course Cormac can afford to buy it too.

It was a stupid idea.

Nevertheless I feel battered. Cold. Chilled by reasonableness.

———————

There is imbalance between us now.

It is I who must set it right.

Some morning I shall wake up knowing what to say to Cormac.

There has been no virtue in me because for so many years I have done my duty, or what I conventionally believed was my duty. Now it would be ridiculous to believe I have any duty to Cormac. Cormac has found in music an interest that will last him his life.

I am free.

Free for what?

Sometimes I feel in a hysterical way that the days are running past me. At these times I make copious notes, as if by filling a note book I could control the mysterious forces of life. Perhaps if I keep quiet something will unfold in me. I must have some quiddity; everyone has. I shall say softly to myself: Sit still, my soul; there is nothing you need to *do*. You need not make notes. You can forget the clock. If you fall asleep sitting here and wake tomorrow morning, will it matter? No. And I must forget the word *use*. I need not be *useful*; that is *doing*.

I must try *being*.

It will be difficult.

How can I know what being is?

Shall I be an empty vessel, filling gradually with rubbish that will deaden all vibration?

*

I rehearse continually questions designed to probe and startle Cormac.
  I know it is no use to put them to him.
  I decide to be utterly unresponsive, inert, flaccid.
  I daren't.

Reciprocity: did he ever think about that; look for it; need it?

We'll live in these rooms, he said, referring to the four small rooms at the north end of Stringers.
  But of course Cormac will live as he does now, in his office, in the auction rooms, in his car, or, in the evenings, with his violin.
  A skilled sensualist, making money and making love with a casual competence, almost a negligence, as if he were only slightly involved.
  Perhaps he has remained rudimentary in feeling because I have never opposed him, never criticized him, or even made suggestions.

I thought we triumphed as home-makers. I thought we showed our skill as parents, living harmoniously without making or exacting sacrifice. Now I find that absurd. I brought up the boys, nearly bursting myself to be true mother *and* Cormac's girl, as well as keeping myself fresh (not merely efficient) in my profession. The strain, the consciousness of the triple life was always there. At home I had to keep a balance between Cormac and the boys, but the lurch of my heart was always towards Cormac, his loving never denied or curtailed, though sometimes postponed.
  I don't know that those years have left anything.
  Am I ennobled by motherhood? Of course not.
  Did I ever address Cormac as Daddy? Of course not.
  But for twenty-eight years I foolishly, oh, naively believed that Cormac loved me very much because he fucked me very often.
  And does so still.
  There may never have been love.
  This is what I have to face: there may never have been love.
  I must accept it while still accepting Cormac.

Praise all living, said Sappho or someone. Praise all living, the light and the dark.
  I am not big enough for that.

I am afraid of the years to come. Afraid that I shall get accustomed to a meagre existence. Acceptance is a tortoise sort of life. The tortoise lives to be about a hundred years old, but has spent perhaps a million years growing a carapace to do it. A toad, I believe, has sometimes been found alive imprisoned in a rock. This is survival, not life.
  My gazanias died. They were tender.

I am very healthy. I may live a long time.

KATE O'BRIEN

from *The Land of Spices*

In childhood she thought her father very beautiful. It always delighted her to come on the sight of him suddenly and realize, always with new pleasure, that he was different from other men, stronger and bigger, with curly, silky hair and eyes that shone like stars. And studying with him, or reciting poetry seated on his knee, she noticed that his face grew more beautiful as one drew nearer to it. This was not true of other faces, and she told him of it one evening, but he laughed at her impatiently.

He had many friends; most of his pupils sought his friendship, but unless they could be content with his austere and modest ways of entertainment and of pleasure they couldn't have it. Very early Anna learnt his passion for simplicity and quiet, and his need for long hours alone, in his study or the garden. Even if he were not working he often required, for many hours at a time, not to be spoken to by anyone save Marie-Jeanne. He liked also to sit in the Café Flamand at the bottom of the hill and talk with Monsieur Robert or with Armand. It was a very humble café a *bistro*, and he said it was his second home. He liked Helen to come and find him there, and join the talk with Monsieur Robert – although her mother did not think it a suitable practice. However, as everyone in the neighbourhood knew '*la petite Anglaise*', and as her father was the friend of all, provided only they gave themselves no airs, she came to no harm on her emancipated expeditions down the hill to the Café Flamand. And her mother smiled and said: 'Father is the Socrates of our suburb, darling. But I wonder what role he has in mind for you?'

Her mother died in the winter preceding Helen's twelfth birthday. There was a short illness which did not seem grave; then a night of hurrying messengers, night-lights and prayers. The little bell in the street when Père Bernard brought the Host; Marie-Jeanne's arms around her in the cold dawn; her father standing by the bedstead with bent head: 'Good-bye, dear Catherine.'

That was all.

Reverend Mother could remember that bereavement in its details now; could recall with love the warm grieving of Marie-Jeanne; could feel her father's pensive and uneasy sadness too, and the sustained quiet of the house. But in remembering herself of that time she could revive more clearly her own sense of remorse that grief should be so temperate than any remembrance of grief itself. She remembered feeling guiltily relieved, and shocked, to discover that life went on as before at Rue Saint Isidore when her mother was gone; she remembered her relief that rooms and habits remained as they had been. She had feared there would be changes, perhaps even a change of house, which she would have found insufferable, but might have thought correct, a gentle tribute to the lost one. But she was glad to see no thought of such sentimentality in her father's face. Yet she winced now, after many years, at realizing again how little he had loved her mother, and how much, how bitterly at the end, her mother had loved him.

She had never known anyone refuse him love, or at least the response of good will. Yet now, at the end of so good, and so bad, a life, he lay dying in forgotten solitude, with only two stranger nuns to minister to him, and old Marie-Jeanne to make him smile and give him courage.

But he would exclaim against her 'with only'. She could hear his protest: 'What else could a sane man want, Helen, except to die quietly in his own quiet house, at seventy-seven? With two good strangers to keep the dreadfulness of decay out of sight, and with a faithful good cook to make the last broth, and pray me off. With debts all paid and work all done, and knowing that a few friends down the hill will mourn, and will come to the funeral – Helen, what possible other way would you ask me to die?'

That is what he would say, generously. Stressing to the end the contentment of his days – although in fact they had been strung with punishment, which he detested, and never meted out. For, in fairness it could be said that fate had punished him just before he was awake to it, by letting him give up his fellowship and marry her mother before he had discovered what in fact existence meant or held for him. Thereafter, she guessed, in his first pain and excitement of self-discovery he fell into some offence against society, some stupid sin, which made it necessary, or at least wise, for him to live in exile. There were repetitive small punishments in this: the married state, undertaken in darkness and gracefully upheld, to the world at least, in light; the penalization in England, by chill silence or cold regrets, of his published work; the loss of background and early friends. And she too, in her turn, was to punish his sin. She, towards whom he was conscious of no iota of wrong or disillusion, was to turn in terror from his love, and from all he had thought and implanted, and leave him to the lonely years, to the days of loss and decline – alone, with Marie-Jeanne. Alone with the old *bonne* now, waiting for death, and laughing with tenderness while he waited, over '*ces beaux jours lointains de ton enfance*'.

The bell rang for Evening Meditation.

Reverend Mother rose, relieved by the obligation of obedience.

She folded Marie-Jeanne's letter and placed it with her father's in her desk.

'Not yet, Father,' she said gently. 'Not yet. There will be time.'

But throughout that evening and that night there was no time, or she believed that there was none, to read his letter.

'When *Quarant' Ore* has begun, I'll be ready to read his letter,' she assured herself.

It was as if she had to keep a kind of vigil for it. And indeed she might be said to have knelt immobile and seeking grace, all night, before her memories of him. Wrestling with her unresolved grief and fear.

While she sat in silence at supper and listened to a young novice's bad reading of the *Imitation*; while she laughed and sewed at Recreation, and led the Community at Night Prayers in the darkened tribune of the chapel; even when alone at last in her cell, at her own prie-dieu and as she prepared herself for sleep – she managed to hold him at bay, and even half forget that he was dying, that any one of the passing hours might certainly be his hour.

But when she was in her narrow bed at last, in darkness, she was assaulted by the necessity once more at last to relive a scene which, since entering religion, she had not allowed her conscious mind to rest on. By facing it at last, and asking God's mercy for him and for her hard, uncomprehending self, she might somehow help his dying hours, and bridge, at least to the easing of her own heart, the years of pain that left her now so far from him in his last hours of human need.

Some months after her mother's death, Reverend Mother at Place des Ormes had suggested to Henry Archer that it would be wise to allow Helen to become a boarder at the school. As it was necessary for him to be away from home often, and as he could not bear to impede Marie-Jeanne's legitimate freedom – she liked sometimes, for instance, to go home to Malines for a day and to come back drunk on the midnight train, and he wholly approved of these outings – he agreed to Reverend Mother's suggestion. But the separation was not a harsh one. Helen spent the whole of every Sunday at home, and often during the week was allowed to run down the curving, leafy street and spend an hour in the kitchen with Marie-Jeanne, or in the study or garden with her father. And he and Marie-Jeanne were also favourites at the convent, so that the gentle life of Rue Saint Isidore flowed all about the girl still, and was only enhanced, made clearer, by this slight lengthening of perspective.

The sense of companionship with her father deepened rapidly as she entered adolescence. She was considered a very pretty young girl, and she was happy and successful at school; also she loved the nuns, and was sincerely pious and believing. But she had no thought of taking the habit, and often laughed quite frankly over her lack of religious vocation. Indeed, on the contrary she sometimes thought, with real pleasure, that there was very much of her father in her. Beginning at this time, as she thought, to understand his terms, she often amused herself by thinking guiltily that she was, to some degree, 'a pagan'.

But his was a frugal, honourable paganism. She learnt many better things of him during girlhood than that he had, for her, a shattering charm. She learnt that he was an almost primly honest man, and that he was very kind in practical things. She learnt his mania for simple people – and though in later life she saw that this may have been a defence, a flight by one who had been hurt by the sophisticated and was afraid of them, may even have been, she thought with grief, an escape from the sterile, intellectualized devotion of her mother – yet it was to her a very sweet and pleasing characteristic. Sometimes in her religious life it occurred to her that it was probably his doing that she was more successful and at ease with lay-sisters than with choir nuns.

He took her on journeys of pleasure and instruction sometimes in vacation, and taught her how to travel, not at all as a young lady of her time and class should do, but as a person of frugal means who could not waste money on inessentials. He showed her how to be comfortable in third and fourth class carriages, and how to enjoy the chance food and chance company of journeys; he taught her to be unselfconscious, and to overcome the pudic suspicions and fears of young ladies in encounter with strange men.

Without mercy he fed and loaded her mind. She was free to read anything, but she had to read the works he prescribed and discussed with her. He took her all over Belgium and into Holland and the Rhineland in pursuit of art and architecture and history. He took her through Normandy one spring, through Brittany another. When she was sixteen he took her for eight weeks to Paris.

'This is going to be real work, Helen,' he warned her. And it was. Often she jibbed during those weeks, and asked for mercy.

'What for?' he would say.

'Oh, to loaf a bit, Daddy.'

'You haven't the right to, yet,' he would say. 'Wait till you've grown a soul to invite.'

'Information won't give me a soul!'

'No – but it may manure one, my darling. Anyway, believe me, there's no defence like a full mind.'

'Why should I need a defence?'

He laughed.

'Helen – I thought you were at least a *bit* of a theologian!'

But she was never afraid of him or afraid to resist him; and she was never bored by his exactions. Sometimes, if her interest in some picture, building or poem did not satisfy him, or if she would not read some book which he impatiently desired her to read, he lost his temper without a blush and abused her extravagantly.

'You remind me of Marie-Jeanne now,' she would say to him.

'Well, I could remind you of worse. Marie-Jeanne has a head on her shoulders.'

Still, it puzzled her that the only people he ever abused were herself, Marie-Jeanne and Monsieur Robert of the Café Flamand. She asked him why that was – because he was quite maddeningly gracious and gentle with the ordinary run of acquaintances.

'Well, there's nothing to get abusive over with those others; who wants to fight about inessentials? I'm fond of you three, so you have the power to get me shouting.'

She reflected sadly then that he had never shouted at her mother.

They walked miles each day in Paris, for economy's sake; they ate very well in *bistros*, talking with the *habitués* and taking down recipes at the dictation of *patronnes*, with which to infuriate Marie-Jeanne on their return to Brussels. They went, unflaggingly and as cheaply as they could, to theatres and concerts; once they went to a carefully chosen music-hall, but Helen did not really like it, and was troubled.

'I'm sorry, darling,' he said. 'That was a mistake. But you see, I'm terrified of your thinking I want you to be a prig.'

This was the summer of 1877, the year of the death of Thiers, early days of the Constitution of the Third Republic; edgy, nervous days with Marshal MacMahon, monarchical and clerical, still in the Presidency, the statue of Strasburg crêpe-hung in the Place de la Concorde, and Gambetta bitterly rallying all true republicans. It was a lively and instructive time in Paris, with 'much to be examined', Henry Archer said. And in the *bistros* they made friends with artisans and clerks who were eager to talk politics. So occasionally Henry gave Helen a rest, leaving her for an evening with the family of their hotel-keeper in Rue Saint Jacques, and went with his chance friends to political meetings or to spend some hours in informal café debate. Also, once or twice by day he allowed her to go shopping in charge of Madame of the hotel. But these separations were rare, and almost all their days in Paris were spent together. They went home in mid-September with no money left, but the richer by a great many second-hand books, a few modest purchases of clothes, some presents for Marie-Jeanne and a sense of great, reciprocal contentment.

'We'll do something cheap and boring next year – walk through the blessed old Ardennes perhaps – because the following summer you'll have left school; you'll be eighteen – and I think it will be time to tackle Italy. We must save up for that.'

'Oh, Daddy!'

'But mind you, if you found Paris hard work – and you are looking thin on it, Helen – I dare not think of the trouble you'll give me in Italy.'

They saved, happily and erratically, in the next two years, for that journey to Italy – which they were never to take.

Reverend Mother, trained to lie still in bed, composed as if to the restriction of a coffin, turned about now in sharp distress. She dreaded, almost madly, what lay in wait for the next movement of her thoughts, so she escaped a minute into the present, and prayed for him as he now was, prayed that the horny good love of Marie-Jeanne's old hands, so worn in work for him, would warm his dying hands in this dark hour and remind him, for as long as possible, of the human sympathy which he had always given, and needed, so abundantly. Marie-Jeanne would pray aloud, in her strong Flemish accent, her prayer of every occasion, which she had repeated over and over at her mistress's bedside, and repeated alike, all through life, when the pancakes went wrong or the stove smoked or her head ached after a day of pleasure at Malines: '*Que le nom du Seigneur soit béni. Que la volonté de Dieu, toujours juste, toujours aimable, soit exaltée pendant toute l'éternité.*' Reverend Mother knew that while human sound could reach her father, that old prayer of Marie-Jeanne's, which he loved to pick up and shout with her whenever he heard her beginning it, would make him smile with love, and trap him into his old chanting. So maybe – she smiled in the darkness – maybe he would go with the Christian words on his lips, tricked into Heaven by Marie-Jeanne.

But that was what Etienne Marot had said. She winced from the name that was so famous now, and that she could never hear pronounced in all these years without pain.

One sunny day she was reading in the summer-house, and Etienne was lying in the grass at Henry Archer's feet, his English lesson over. And Marie-Jeanne, overtaken by some misfortune in the kitchen, began her clamorous prayer, which her father took up in loud plain chant: '*Que la volonté de Dieu, toujours juste, toujours aimable . . .*'

Etienne laughed and chanted too. And then:

'Take care,' he said. 'Marie-Jeanne will trick you into Heaven yet, on that.'

'Ah, it isn't so easy,' her father had said. 'I honestly don't think God is as simple as Marie-Jeanne hopes.'

Etienne Marot, world-renowned and getting old. Since she was fifty-one this year, he would be sixty; living in New York now, very wealthy, very civilized. Once or twice in an illustrated paper sent to some sick nun or child, Reverend Mother had come upon photographs of his strange, melancholy face. One of the greatest violinists in the world, people had said for many years; and later, perhaps the greatest of musical conductors.

But she had known him as an obscure young man from a Brussels slum, an artisan's son, put to all conceivable shifts to achieve his goal of musicianship. A worker of incredible endurance, her father said. Certainly a young man sure of where he was going, so sure that, to be ready for the world, long before he gave his first concert in Brussels, he came to Henry Archer for lessons in English.

Quick-witted, graceful, shabby, and with that indifference to non-essentials which her father always sought in friends; ravenously eager for any crumb of culture that his

English tutor might bestow – and he was not stinted. And in return giving a world hitherto not open to Henry Archer – his world of music.

He became the friend of the house, even of Marie-Jeanne, who thought, and told him, that he was born too low to be on the level he was allowed with her master and young mistress, but that since Monsieur was mad and an angel, '*enfin, que la volonté de Dieu, si juste, si aimable . . .*'

Marie-Jeanne told Helen that there could be no doubt that Monsieur intended, later on, to marry her to Monsieur Etienne.

The *bonne* considered this an unwise plan on many counts since the young man was poor and low-born, and, she thought, a bit too sure of himself in a gentleman's house. However, she conceded his industry and that music was a very beautiful and satisfactory thing.

Helen thought nothing of this plan – and indeed did not believe in it. She had no intention of marrying anyone, for many years, and was sure that her father did not wish her to do so. Also, she could only laugh at the idea of his choosing a husband for her. Her father, so obsessed by the beauty of personal freedom, and the human obligation of non-interference! She said all this to Marie-Jeanne, who smiled and said that a father was a father, and knew his duty.

Helen was peculiarly happy just then. She had grown extremely attached to Place des Ormes; she worked well and her father became more than ever interested in her mental growth. He thought she showed some potentialities for scholarship, and talked of the possibility of her following the Modern History School in Brussels University. He explained that for her to do so would be unusual and perhaps embarrassing, but in spite of moments of panic, she was not daunted by his talk of the audacious step, and she began to look forward to her university studies as part of a wide, dreamy plan of life after her own heart.

She noticed beauty in her surroundings at this time. She was shy of the pleasure she took in the old slanting square, Place des Ormes, but in every weather and every light it pleased her. Its houses were shabbily baroque, grouped on three sides under elm-trees, behind wrought-iron gates. The stone fountain, shabby too, was ponderously beautiful. The cab that stood where the horse-tram stopped, on the west side, where the landscape fell towards Brussels, was nearly always there, for very few dwellers in Place des Ormes took cabs. Under rain or sun, and whether it was empty or mildly astir, Helen felt a significant melancholy in this square, in the stand-off shabbiness which even the trees expressed, and in the sharp descending curve of Rue Saint Isidore, so shabby and stand-offish too, with its smaller ancillary houses.

She admired much of Brussels, and had been enchanted by some of the places her father had taken her to visit; she thought and read very eagerly of what she would find in Italy, and *afterwards* Heaven knew where else under the sun – but again and again as her own suburb surprised her with undramatic variations of its character, she felt, as it were, an admonition in her heart, that beauty, the necessary root of the matter, was here in a particularly good, unassuming form. She sometimes thought, with a premonitory uneasiness not altogether welcome, that she would not feel again before any of the world's sights as sharp an æsthetic pleasure as these schoolday mornings and evenings gave her now in her own suburb.

One October afternoon she sat by the fountain with her father. They were waiting for the horse-tram to come up the hill, turn, get its breath, and take them down to Brussels, where they were meeting Etienne and would attend a concert. Helen was not feeling very much in the mood for Etienne, but she could not grudge him his right to take them to concerts. While they waited they bought ice-cream wafers from Matteotti, who was passing in his cart. And as they licked them up, her father talked of Siena to her, whence Matteotti came. He described the great square of the town, and went on to generalize about accidents of design, of perfection and its oddness and elusiveness.

'I expect you'll think me mad,' Helen said, 'but you know I think that this square, all this round here, is just what you're saying – accidentally perfect.'

He looked at her with attention.

'Are you saying that loosely? I mean, just the way a girl gushes, or do you mean anything?'

'Daddy, when do I gush? No, I mean that practically every day I think that this bit of Brussels is just one of those lucky things – perfect – and no one sees it, except me.'

He gave the quick, unsteady laugh that meant he was more moved than amused.

'Heaven bless your impudence! Why do you think your parents chose to live here – when they had Europe to choose from?'

'Why, have you always liked it as much as I do, Daddy?'

He looked about him.

'Since one must live somewhere, I've always liked this place enough to live and die in. And that's saying something. I think, like you, that it's perfect. Some obscure man, or men, designed this central bit about 1680. I suspect they were Spaniards, or sons of Spaniards. Anyway, never mind – they did everything right, even to the spacing of the trees, even to leaving this side open to the west. And the next century, following on with our little streets, behaved with its customary good sense. So there it is. I'm glad we agree about it, Helen. I often wondered if you liked it.'

'I don't believe I thought it out until just lately.'

'Your mother and I would have preferred to live in this square – but a whole house would have been crazy, though they are cheap – they are let in apartments now, of course, but some of them weren't when we first came. But we thought you ought to have a house, and a back door and so on.'

'I love our house. Still, Sainte Famille are lucky. Fancy having five of those exquisite houses to live in!'

'Aye – but fancy having to be a nun to live in them!'

She did not answer; she smiled towards the convent, pondering the suggestion he had raised.

'You're not thinking you wouldn't mind *being* a nun – are you, Helen?' he asked her sharply. 'If I thought that, I believe I'd turn tyrant and take you away from Sainte Famille right now.'

'No, Daddy,' she said. 'I don't want to be a nun. I do think it is a very good life, but – I don't want it.'

He smiled.

'Actually, you frightened me for a minute,' he said.

The tram was ready to start, and they mounted it.

Helen was not sure that she was quite truthful in saying to her father that she did not want a nun's life – but at least such untruth as she suspected was directed as much to deceive herself as him. For she was sometimes afraid of her own erratic, moody understanding of the rightness of the religious life, visitations of which she turned from with emphasis again and again. And she was glad of what she had always known without his own brief expression of it – her father's horror of such a vocation for her. In sympathy with him, and in proud desire to be the daughter he desired and saw in her, she shared his horror, and felt safe-guarded by his reliance on her, and his apparent need of her. Besides, instructed by him, steeped in his poets, she believed in human love, and felt in her English blood the rightness of compromise in the English mystics. And if love had somehow failed her father and mother, perhaps her love, and the development of her life on his principles of goodness, perhaps above all one day, her children would make up to him for whatever had gone wrong in a life which should have known completion in itself.

So, vaguely, she argued herself away from the threat of vocation. But perhaps her soul always knew that these arguments were beside the point, and that the issue was quite simple – that it lay between him and the only thing that measured up to him in her mind – the religious ideal. But all her *feelings* gave victory to him – and the other thing remained only an intellectual temptation, a shadow moving stealthily about her brain. And she was not afraid of it; it would pass, as her need and love of him could not. So it followed she would not be a nun, and when she said she did not want that life, she had spoken truly.

It was strange, after thirty-three years in religion, to lie in the dark in her cell and recall each foolish nuance of that adolescent flight towards life and her father, and away from God. Sharply indeed her course had been reversed. But perfection, or the sight of it, is nevertheless not to be won, as a child might know, by the clamour of egoism, the display of wounds, the reactions of vanity. It seemed indeed that spiritual victory can only be gained by those who have never lost it, who set out for purity already pure-intentioned. It was hardly fair to make the difficult thing impossibly difficult. 'The land of spices, something understood.' She remembered her mother smiling over that line one day not long before her death, and saying that whereas to her the image was odd and surprising, 'yet your father accepts it with his whole imagination – only, at the same time, he happens to have no real use for it. Isn't that ironic?'

Helen had been puzzled.

'All I mean, darling,' her mother went on, 'is that religious understanding is really a gift, like a singing voice – and can be wasted.'

Life among nuns had clarified this observation, and had made her ponder, sometimes amusedly, sometimes in sad longing, the poet's line.

Far off on the Grand Staircase a clock struck one. At half-past four the community rising bell would ring, as usual; and Sœur Antoine would knock on her door and call out: '*Loué soit Jésu*,' and she would answer, as all these years, from childhood at Place des Ormes: '*Béni soit le Seigneur à jamais.*' And another day, the first day of *Quarant' Ore*, would have begun.

But she could not seek sleep.

She struck a match and lighted a candle at her bedside. She felt that she must pray. She rose and put her black chapel cloak about her and knelt at her pri-dieu. She considered the Crucifix on the wall above her, and sought with her whole will to find the formal pattern of meditation.

But the past would not lie still.

And suddenly its last scene, the last scene of youth, of innocence, filled the austere dim cell.

It was June and brilliant weather. Helen's last term as a boarder at Place des Ormes. At the end of July she was going to Italy with her father and they would not return until mid-October, when his autumn classes, and her university studies, began. This brilliant prospect dissipated much of the sentimental melancholy she felt at giving up her schoolgirl life at Sainte Famille, yet she savoured the last term with particular affection.

One Saturday evening many of the girls who lived in Brussels had gone home for the week-end, and there was a pleasant sense of indolence through the convent. Helen, after having played some tennis, amused herself by helping Mère Alphonsine to arrange the flowers for the chapel. The next day was the Sunday within the Octave of Corpus Christi and Mère Alphonsine was dissatisfied with the colours of the roses Sœur Josèphe had sent in from the garden. She wanted more red ones, she said, and Sœur Josèphe said she couldn't have what wasn't there, and that she was never satisfied.

Helen said that unless Marie-Jeanne had taken them all to Malines that day, whither she had gone for her nephew's First Communion, there were red roses in the garden at Rue Saint Isidore. Mère Alphonsine commanded her to go and fetch them.

She went very happily, as she was, hatless and in tennis shoes. Glad of the sun and the lovely evening, and the chance of a word with Daddy, if he was at home.

The gate squeaked and let her in unwillingly, as usual. She never rang the front-door bell, even when Marie-Jeanne was at home to hear it; she always went straight through the garden to the ever-open kitchen door.

Her father's study was at the back of the house, above the kitchen. It had a long, wide balcony of wrought iron which ran full across the wall and ended in an iron staircase to the garden. This balcony made a pleasant, deep shade over the flagged space by the kitchen door, where Marie-Jeanne often sat to prepare vegetables, or to have a sleep. Traffic was free up and down these stairs; and Henry Archer was not formal about access to his study, even when he was working, even when he was having a silent and solitary mood.

Helen glanced in at the empty kitchen, scratched the cat behind the ears, and hoped that Marie-Jeanne wasn't getting too drunk at Malines. Then she ran up the iron stairs and along the balcony to the open window of her father's study.

She looked into the room.

Two people were there. But neither saw her; neither felt her shadow as it froze across the sun.

She turned and descended the stairs. She left the garden and went on down the curve of Rue Saint Isidore.

She had no objective and no knowledge of what she was doing. She did not see external things. She saw Etienne and her father, in the embrace of love.

*

Now in her dim and holy cell she could recall no more of the hours of that summer day. She did not know how long or where she walked, when she returned to Sainte Famille, or what she said of her lack of roses. She only remembered that later, after many days and very gradually, like an organism stirring again, distorted, after paralysis, her spirit moved and spoke again – unrecognizably.

She remembered her savage awareness of total change within, and the cunning which she used to hide it, and her delight in that cunning. She saw now that her self-control was like that of a mad woman, and that she might in fact have been mad. She slept hardly at all, for many nights. She remembered the long, bright, summer nights. She remembered the discipline with which she wept in her moonlit cubicle, without movement, without sob, drinking the tears. She remembered how the picture of Etienne and her father, stamped on her brain, became luridly vivid in those nights, and would not leave the stretched canvas of her eyelids. She remembered how it changed, became dreadful, became vast or savage or gargoyled or insanely fantastical; how it became a temptation, a curiosity, a threat, and sometimes no more than piteous, no more than dreary, sad. She remembered how she prayed to be delivered from it, to be blind, to be stupefied – and how it still moved and glittered evilly, faceless, nameless, and then again most violently identified – and every night at last, such sleep as she found came only through struggle with this image, and was broken by its glare.

She was cunning. Her normal health was so good that she could walk and talk and half-sleep in a blasting trance like this for many days without its telling very remarkably in her face or her behaviour. And by the time her frenzy, of which she could not allow a hint to appear to any living soul, might have become incontinent, she had grown up, she thought; she had seen what it all meant and what she had to do to escape from it for ever.

Within those days of enclosed insanity, she saw and understood, with much cold, true sense and mercilessness, the whole concealed shape and flame of her father's life. She saw what must have happened in Cambridge, and the woe to her mother, and the waste of love. She saw the source of that sensitiveness and oddness which marked him off; she saw the real meaning – or so she thought – of many observations, many actions and many friendships. With an anguish her frame could hardly bear – and in which now, after many years, the accusing nun saw jealousy as clearly as more honourable passions – she surveyed the two years of friendship with Etienne. Ah, blind, blind, blind! And she who believed she was the centre of her father's heart, who felt his love for her as sweet and certain as her own for him, who held him for a saint – by his own rules – but still, a saint!

So that was the sort of thing that the most graceful life could hide! That was what lay around, under love, under beauty. That was the flesh they preached about, the extremity of what the sin of the flesh might be. Here, at home, in her father, in the best person she had known or hoped to know.

She had absolutely no one to turn to; and she was innocent – and jealous. And would have freely died rather than say one word in any place, even in the Confessional, which might have betrayed the nature of her desolation. And there was no one old enough and detached enough to see her crisis, or approach it without seeking the specific facts.

Mère Générale was not in Brussels then, or even known to her. She was in Rouen, and not yet Mère Générale.

So alone the jealous, proud, fastidious and religious girl, just eighteen, steered herself through a brief, dark madness, and for ever away from what she saw as the devilry of human love. She did not have to harden her heart; as she came out of the first long convulsion of shock, and saw what she desired to do, she found to her pleasure that her heart was hard. She found, more specifically, that she hated her father. For many years she was to feel – without sign, without word – that hate.

It was a great defence, and made everything easy – even his shock and rage when she told him that she intended to be a nun. When she told him that she would not go to Italy, that she was sorry to disappoint him, but that she wished to enter the Order of Sainte Famille at the conclusion of the term.

The hatred held her up even against the contemptuous fury of Marie-Jeanne, and made her frozenly indifferent to the puzzled, half-pleased reaction of Etienne to the news her father seemed unable to hear.

She left him as she said; she entered the Convent on the 25th July, the Feast of Saint James. She did not heed the almost sacrilegious hatred in her heart; there would be time to work that out, and save her own soul – which now alone seemed the bearable use to make of life. She went into religion with a merciless heart. But her father, saying he would never forgive her, was dazed and sick with mercy for her, with sorrow and foreboding – and forgave her every day with every other thought and look and appeal.

But she could not bear him. She only desired to be out of sight of him, to be alone, and quit of all that he had stood for. And when, after she had left for Bruges, for her novitiate at Sainte Fontaine, he wrote one last despairing letter to her, and in his innocence told her that he was leaving Brussels for a little while, going to Vienna with Etienne, even then she felt no particular emotion – not even disgust. She turned indeed with a kind of delight to the life of loss and elimination.

But now he was dying; and she wished with her soul to reach him. There was no casuistry in her about sin, and she held him to be a sinner, one who had better have had a millstone about his neck; but she saw her own sin of arrogant judgment as the greater, in that it was her own, on which alone God sought her scorn. And she saw its insolence, not merely against God but against His creature.

'Father, forgive me,' she prayed. 'Father, forgive me – I know not what I did.'

She repeated the prayer. In her weariness she did not know whether she addressed it to Heaven or to her earthly father, whom now again at the eleventh hour she beheld, and felt in her heart with sudden sweetness, as he had been to her in childhood. She saw him all good again now, all wise and fatherly; she saw him as he had triumphantly shown himself so many happy years to her watching innocence; and also, looking up to the merciful Crucifix, she tried to see him as, his weary flesh forsaken, armed only with his humble, unexpecting spirit, he might appear to one who had borne all the sins of the world.

The faraway clock struck two.

She bowed her head into her hands, and began the Penitential Psalms. She offered them humbly for her father's waiting soul.

'*Domine, ne in furore . . .*'
She was still at prayer when Sœur Antoine passed by and cried '*Loué soit Jésu!*'

She was not alone again until three o'clock in the afternoon.

She came to her study desk exhausted but composed. Having accomplished and directed all the duties of the day, and the last the most exhausting, to sit in the Long Parlour and converse for more than an hour with the four priests who were her guests for lunch and who, pleased with what they had eaten and with the convent's excellent coffee, felt no desire to shorten a comfortable hour of leisure – yet, even this duty ended, she had returned to the chapel, to see the completed beauty of the Altar of Repose, and to make sure that the great feast was on its way in traditional hush and splendour.

She knelt awhile under the shadow of the Tribune.

The golden monstrance shone, like a fixed sun, against cloth of gold. Flowers stood in waves of red and purple, and blazing candles pressed about the Host like sentinels.

Like sentinels too the two young nuns who knelt on guard inside the rails; and almost as still, in their white veils, the Children of Mary who knelt without, below the step.

The silence was immeasurably peaceful.

Reverend Mother bent her head into her hands.

'He is at peace now,' she said peacefully. 'He is at peace. Oh God, forgive us both.'

She made the sign of the Cross, genuflected and left the chapel. So she came at last to her desk and was alone.

She opened his letter.

> Brussels, Rue Saint Isidore No. 4
> 18th April, 1912

MY DEAREST HELEN, –
This is the last letter I shall ever write to you, and it makes me happy that its chief message is nothing different from that which I know my first contained – my tender love and pride.

I may be gone when you read this – I have an idea that my days are numbered on the fingers of Marie-Jeanne's right hand. But if that is so, you will guess how easy death can be – since I write well enough, do I not? And my heart is light. I have in fact no pain – which is far more than I deserve. But I have always been given more than I deserved – and do not yet know, even on this last bed, whom to thank for that.

Do not grieve at my flippancy, I beg you. At least I am sure that if your God is there and acts according to your theology, I have a chance of meeting you again, and gladly acknowledging your rightness. For your God will hear your prayers, Helen – and I know that you will pray for me.

But – if we do not meet again – remember that I have loved you tenderly, and that, against my will, I have been proud of your successful, heroic life. I wished another kind of life for you, and even now, after thirty-three years of resignation, I still wonder, and so does Marie-Jeanne, why you turned away so sharply from that life. But you have been very patient with that monotonous wonder – and, I hope, will only smile to see it raised again in my very last letter.

I have instructed my lawyer, Charles Rodier – you remember his father? – to let you see my will. It is a very simple document. I leave my annuity of £200 to Marie-Jeanne and her heirs, without condition. She does not know this. I hope she will not get dangerously drunk when they tell her. Certain books I bequeath to St John's College, Cambridge; certain other belongings and small sums from my savings I bequeath to friends in Brussels, to Armand at the café, etc. This house, its contents, and my savings, subject to funeral expenses, to the Order of Sainte Famille without condition. My affairs are in order; there should be no delay or difficulty in execution of the will. I trust her wealth will not make Marie-Jeanne unhappy; I have asked Rodier to look after it for her, as I do not trust those nephews in Malines. She will be lonely without this house, etc. I wish you were in Brussels to comfort her. But '*que la volonté de Dieu, si juste, si aimable . . .*' Do you remember that, Helen?

Well, no more postponing. I must face this curious moment, my dear child. I must say farewell to you, forever. I do so from a full and grateful heart. All my life I have been proud of you and have seen in you a possible defence of my otherwise fruitless life. I thank you for all that you have been, my darling, and I wish you the deep spiritual happiness which you deserve and I am so wretchedly unable to understand.

The eleven years of your Irish exile have been the longest of my life. But in any case, I suppose that, if one dies old as I do, the last years seem very long. Still, it would have been good to have seen you again. Not that you are dim to my eyes, or to Marie-Jeanne's. But she and I, talking together, tend to see you from far off in the dear past, our own little girl, in your pinafore, with your long hair blowing about. You must forgive our sentimentality. We make each other happy with our stories of you, darling.

And now indeed farewell. My road has been long and peaceful, and you were its chief joy. The end is easy, and as I close my eyes for the last time I shall think of you and send my love.

> Your devoted father,
> HENRY ARCHER

In spite of his boast the writing was bad.

She fingered the pages of the letter dreamily. She would read it and reread it. There would be time. 'The end is easy, and as I close my eyes . . .' She knew that now he had done so, that the easy end had come and gone. She felt so peaceful in that realization that she smiled, as often in girlhood she had done over his letters, at their characteristic ease and innocence. Innocence – to the very end – of all the woe and pain that lay between them. Thank God. Thank God at least for that.

She sat and dreamt of him, half sleepy from her passionate vigil of the night, half puzzled by its onslaught, and the cold peace it left in her now.

A lay-sister came to her with a telegram.

Before she opened it she knew what it would tell her.
It was from Brussels, from Mère Générale.

'Chère enfant il est mort en paix à quatre heures du matin, assisté de Marie-Jeanne et des infirmières aucune souffrance il parlait de vous jusqu'au dernier moment courage et bonnes prières.'

from *The Anteroom*

2

Teresa Mulqueen had also heard the Mass bells ring, the hall clock strike, the distant dredger cough, sounds to which her day had always begun for thirty-seven years. So well did she know those sounds that often now, when in pain or in a morphia half-dream, she was uncertain whether she heard or only remembered them. But this morning, after a night which she must not let herself think about, there had suddenly been some real sleep and a lull. She was awake, and the pain was vague, hardly there at all, you might say. God was merciful.

She must use the chance to think – it wasn't often she felt as clear in the head as this. But first she would say her morning prayers. That was due to God, who had granted her this hour of blessed release. The least she might do was pray to Him sometimes when she could give her mind to what she was doing, for she knew that often lately she answered prayers that Sister Emmanuel said, and said some of her own, without being able to think at all of what they meant.

She fumbled about the counterpane for her rosary beads.

'Sister Emmanuel,' she croaked – she had hardly any voice nowadays – 'Sister Emmanuel, where did you put my beads from me this morning?'

Nurse Cunningham came to her bedside.

She was a pretty, firm-featured woman of thirty, who had recently been sent down from Dublin as day nurse to this case by the specialist in charge of it. Teresa would have preferred to see the holy old face of the Blue Nun who took care of her at night.

'Sister Emmanuel is gone for today, Mrs Mulqueen, and you've got to put up with me, I'm afraid. But here are your beads.' She put them into Teresa's hand and straightened her pillow skilfully. 'That better?' she asked, with a bright smile.

Teresa nodded. She did not resent the cheerfulness, although it exhausted her; she understood that it was trained into the young woman, but she thought of how the old nun would have given them to her in silence, or would maybe have gone on murmuring the sweet Latin of her Office while she did whatever had to be done to the pillow.

She fingered the silver cross.

'I believe in God, the Father Almighty . . .'

What feast of the Church was it today? 'Do you know whose feast it is, Nurse, by any chance?'

'It's Sunday, Mrs Mulqueen – the 31st of October – I don't know—'

'Well, now – the Eve of All Saints'. A glorious day; and tomorrow better still, and after that the Suffering Souls – I'm glad you reminded me. I'll say the Glorious Mysteries—'

She shut her eyes and let the brown beads slip through her worn-out fingers. First Glorious Mystery, the Resurrection. Our Father, who art in heaven – there had always been great fun in this house on the Eve of All Saints'. The girls used to come home from school for it and have a party; Danny used to be great at playing snap-apple with them. Well, this time there wouldn't be much fun – but only Dr Coyle coming from Dublin tomorrow night, she supposed, if he was to see her on Tuesday. She groaned a little in anxiety. She *must* have another operation. She had the strength for it, she knew she had. She could not leave her unprotected son – not yet, not yet. Not until she could see him somehow prepared to live without her. Dr Coyle must keep her alive no matter how. But she must say her rosary now. Hail, Mary, full of grace, the Lord is with thee . . . it was time some of them were coming in to say good morning to her, surely. Oh, Reggie, my son. But she must pray awhile, she must try to mind her prayers.

Beyond the draught screen that guarded her bedroom door she thought she heard a movement, but her senses did not function surely now beyond the immediate region of her bed. Yes, here was someone. Agnes, tall, light-footed, came and bent to kiss her.

'Good-morning, Mother.'

'Good-morning, child. I wondered when you were coming in to see me.'

'I'm afraid I'm late. I'm sorry, Mother.'

'It's to your father you should be saying that, and he waiting for his breakfast, I suppose. I don't know how this house is going at all these times.'

Teresa had always had an inclination to nag her youngest daughter, and now on her better days it revisited her. Agnes smiled at the good sign.

'It's going badly,' she said, with graciousness. Teresa looked pleased.

'You needn't tell me.'

'You're looking well,' the girl went on. She never inquired of Teresa herself about her nights, wanting to keep her mother's thoughts from them. Looking down at her now she felt the irony of the true thing she had said. Teresa did look better – but better than what? Not better than death, certainly, which was the only good thing left to want for her.

'Do you know the day it is?' she queried.

'The Eve of All Saints',' said Teresa proudly.

'Clever!' said Agnes, laughing at her. 'And I suppose you're thinking of getting up to play snap-apple?'

'Well, I was thinking it's a pity you'll have no fun tonight, child.'

Agnes laughed, almost too much.

'Snap-apple days are over,' she said. 'Do you realize I'm twenty-five?'

Teresa was exhausted by her own talkativeness. She closed her eyes. Twenty-five was young, she thought. When she was twenty-five she was carrying Reggie. A hot summer it was, and she felt wretched nearly all the time. It didn't seem long ago. How old was Reggie now? But the dear name, which was now the only one that never, in her sick dreams and fantasies, moved dissociate from a face and a meaning, stabbed hard with a clear and sane reminder of present grief. Reggie was thirty-five, wasted, unhappy, dangerous – dependent for his own decency and for his whole interest in life on his devotion to her – and she was leaving him – and God had not answered her yet or told her where he was to turn then, so that he would do no harm in his weakness, and yet might be a little happy, a little less than desolate. That was what she had to think about with whatever strength these interludes conferred – not silly nonsense about fun for Agnes. Agnes could look out for herself – but Reggie – what was to become of him when she was gone? God must hear and answer. Either He must save her life – never mind how middlingly, so that her son might have her shielding always – or He must provide another shield. And where could that be found – for a man unfit to love, unfit to marry? Oh, God must be implored, since He was merciful and died for sinners. God must let her live, like this, if necessary, for five years more, for ten years. To keep him safe, to keep him interested, to keep his misery from making misery. Teresa's eyes were closed, and Agnes, observing the passionate constriction of the withered and bitten brown mouth, knew where her thoughts were, knew the despairing prayer that that defeated frame was urging up to heaven. She saw her mother's dilemma, but, with impatience, did not see why Reggie could not be compelled to face his own.

The history of this dilemma was never mentioned in Roseholm, and to this day Agnes did not know how much or little of it her brothers and sisters understood. But during the last year it had become one of her duties to be in the house when Dr Curran called, and to hear what he had to say about her mother's condition and occasionally about her brother's. This general practitioner had been appointed to routine charge of Teresa by her specialist, Dr Coyle, of Merrion Square, Dublin – and recently he had taken charge of Reggie. It followed that in his professional conversations with Agnes he had had to mention many things about which no member of her family could have been explicit. At last, briefly but with exactitude, he had explained her brother's medical history to her.

Reggie was now thirty-five. Ten years ago, in 1870, he had been infected with syphilis, and for three years had spent long periods in nursing homes, until sufficiently cured to live uninterruptedly at home. But marriage and love were forbidden him henceforward, and seasonal doses of mercury, increased and decreased as considered necessary, and doing their specific work, also did harm. But a greater harm was wrought upon mind and spirit by the sustained humiliations and fears of his state of health, so that a native invalidism became a justified habit, until he gave up all pretense of doing any work, or leading the life of a normal man. But he was a shareholder in the rich firm from which his father's wealth was drawn, and had more than enough money for his pitifully restricted attempts at self-indulgence. The life which as a young man he had always coveted – of slippered, pottering *laissez-faire* – had become his ironically soon. He had always been good-natured, sentimental, sensual and coarsely amusing – but these attributes were of little purpose now. He had always been vain of his loose and swarthy good looks, and these were puffed and bloated now. He had always half desired to play the piano well – but now his thickened hands were more tentative than ever as he fooled at his eternal Chopin. As the years had deepened a misery which his lazy mind would no more than half confront, and then only that he might use it as a weapon in self-pity, he had found one good thing – the love which his mother Teresa had flung like a shield before him. This love, which in the first terrified months of his illness had given understanding and patience to a woman as prudish as she was holy, had been his courage and his hope. In his invalid years, when she was still well, she had devoted herself to his consolation and amusement, thereby compelling him to keep his wits bright for her, to keep his shrewdness on the move, to keep his piano open. Firmly, ruthlessly, without a word of pity or sentiment, she had built for her wasted son a life that was safe from life. She had built it with a concentration of purpose which had almost cost her the love of her other children, and had certainly caused the withdrawal of their confidence, since it was plain to them, who did not know its reason, where her true attention was. She had concentrated on Reggie almost to the extent of forgetting the existence of her husband, who understood, in part at least, her fierce devotion and made no complaint. Then disease had spread its dark wing over her, and for all her resistance, its shadow dimmed and shortened her view ahead from month to month. In her pain, in weary recoveries and distressed relapses, in delirium and half-dream, the bread which she had cast on the waters came back to her, for her son, for all he was worth, endeavoured to give her the courage and forgetfulness which she had resolutely found for him. He loved her now with an active anxiety which was both delight and anguish to her. He read to her, he gossiped and joked for hours by her fire, he played his bits of Chopin over and over, he sang in his weak, true tenor voice.

His love was almost heroism in its surrender of laziness to perpetual small exactions. But Reggie was not heroic enough to look beyond it. Though often terrified by the spectacle of his dying mother, he would not think of her as dead, and himself deprived of her in a world which she had both withheld from him and made endurable. For ten years there had been no future, but only this sheltered ambling from day to day. Nothing else was now imaginable – and that depended solely on his mother. Therefore such things as agony and delirium and near-death fantasies were only fantasies. She would live, since his life lived in her. She would live, because nothing else was bearable.

To Agnes, this situation of her brother, its long chain of small unselfishnesses founded on a mighty selfishness, was hideous. To her it seemed that the only way to love this tortured woman, her mother, was to set her free by making her feel, however wrongfully, that her work was done, that the strength she had put out had built something, and that the charge which she left reluctantly behind would be safe henceforward, because of her ten years of bulwarking. She was young and could not bear to see the eyes of a human being filmed against the consequences of himself. She could not bear the vast exactions of the sentimental. She wanted a quiet mind and a happy death for her mother – and only her brother barred them off.

'Where's Reggie?' Teresa asked, without opening her eyes. 'He's very long about coming in to say good-morning to me.'

Agnes moved her head in the direction of the screen. 'Here he is,' she said.

Teresa's eyes opened and grew bright as her son approached her. He was a large wreck of a man, and although he had the habit of moving with caution, a non-adjustment between his big, virile bones and his increasing flaccidity kept him clumsy. His flesh, uniformly red, was dry and flaky about his mouth and bulging neck, and sweaty on his forehead and hands. His hair, which Teresa remembered thick and dark and wavy, had receded completely from his temples and the top of his head, and was only a dusty straggle about his ears and the back of his skull. His eyes, well set, and once quite fine with a spark of impudent virility, were lashless and bloodshot, and the black brows above them thinned away to untidy tufts. His teeth were discoloured and broken; his hands thick, hot, and beautifully cared for. His whole appearance had an exaggerated, antiseptic immaculacy. He was a wreck, but still, in the tilt of his shoulders, and in the smile that now lit his face for Teresa, there were revealed the tatters of a commonplace charm, a departed power to please women.

He took his mother's hand and her rosary beads.

'Good-morning, Mother darling. You're looking grand today.'

'I'm feeling grand, my son.'

Agnes observed now, as often before, the change which came over her mother when Reggie was in the room, a change which was obviously a mighty and painful piece of acting. Teresa raised her voice almost to normal tone and energy for him; spoke in longer sentences when he was there, and attempted little jokes; really put up the appearance of a woman who was not so very desperately ill.

Reggie jingled the rosary beads up and down in his hand and laid them on her bedside table.

'Well, then, give Heaven a rest for a while, let you. Enjoy yourself, woman – there's plenty of time for praying.'

Teresa kept on smiling at him. Nurse Cunningham stepped up to the other side of the bed.

'Now, now, Mr Mulqueen – my patient isn't well enough to be bullied, you know,' she said good-temperedly.

There was a quality in this woman's voice which Agnes could not stand. With a smile to her mother she left the room.

'We've got to keep our patient especially well today, you know,' the nurse went on, 'with Dr Coyle coming tonight.'

Reggie's face clouded. Facts were things which he ignored as much as possible, and he had managed to wake and dress this morning without confronting this one of the specialist's coming. He could not bear her doctors, because they insisted that she was seriously ill.

'I can't see why *he* wants to come here plaguing you,' he said.

Teresa took her cue.

'I'm glad he is coming, if you want to know. Because, with the help of God, I'll be so well for him that he'll be able to put new heart into all of you.'

'Oh, Mother – is that true?'

'What'd be the good of saying it if it was a lie?'

He stared at her, loving the spurious conviction of her words. But it was too much comfort; it brought weak tears streaming down his face.

'Tch, tch,' said Teresa. 'There, there – you mustn't cry.' She tried to move a hand towards him, and he dropped on his knees and pressed his heavy head against the counterpane. She stroked his bald temple, where once the hair had been like heavy silk. 'There, there, don't cry. I'll be better soon. You'll see.'

Teresa knew that she was at the end of her long bluff, and that very soon even Reggie would not be deceived by these lies which, because of the actress effort they exacted, were nearly impossible to her now. Often, therefore, she played with the idea of telling him the truth – that her death was only a very little distant and that the interim must be, so far as her value to him was concerned, as increasingly like death as would make no matter. But again and again she funked such conversation. In her day she had been used to bully his weakness jocosely, or even firmly – and the method had served. But now such dregs of vigour as she had were always split in pity. And soon there would not be even that poor virtue with which to cosset him. The dark stretch was coming – when on flux and reflux, pain and morphia, she would be borne, stupefied and fantasia-maddened, into death. She would not even know him soon when he came whimpering; she would not hear his broken Chopin any more, or recognize the sad shuffle of his slippers.

Now, stroking his head faithfully, though the little movement roused up pain that had been sluggish, stroking his unhappy head, she pondered him. Amazing how he still drank up the nonsense that she talked about getting better! Amazing that he never caught a hint of her effort to assume a normally pitched voice for him, never dreamt that it was now almost impossible for her to stroke his head like that! He seemed to have no understanding at all of her disease and its relentless movement, or rather refused to understand it. As at first he had refused the realities of his own affliction. Coward! Ostrich! Yet she had no reproof to add to life's long vengeance on him. She only reproved herself in his regard. For she saw that her method of making his spoilt life livable had been a mistake. But no other had presented itself – she did not see how another could, or what was to become of him when she had wrung the very last possible allowance of days and nights from life. Oh, God! Oh, God! She groaned very softly in spite of herself.

Nurse Cunningham came to the bedside again.

'Really, Mr Mulqueen, this is too bad of you. Your mother was splendid until you came in upsetting her.'

Reggie stood up at once, both ashamed and reassured. Splendid was she, except for his stupidity?

'Oh, I'm sorry, Mother darling.' He dried his eyes.

'But I'm all right, son,' said Teresa.

He beamed at her.

'You see, Nurse, she isn't as upset as you make out.'

Nurse Cunningham smiled humouringly.

Reggie bent and kissed Teresa.

'Have a good rest this morning,' he said, 'and then we'll have a grand read of Miss Braddon in the afternoon.'

He tapped the book which lay on the little table.

'We will, my son,' said Teresa, smiling at him.

'Her Table Spread'

Alban had few opinions on the subject of marriage; his attitude to women was negative, but in particular he was not attracted to Miss Cuffe. Coming down early for dinner, red satin dress cut low, she attacked the silence with loud laughter before he had spoken. He recollected having heard that she was abnormal – at twenty-five, of statuesque development, still detained in childhood. The two other ladies, in beaded satins, made entrances of a surprising formality. It occurred to him, his presence must constitute an occasion: they certainly sparkled. Old Mr Rossiter, uncle to Mrs Treye, came last, more sourly. They sat for some time without the addition of lamplight. Dinner was not announced; the ladies by remaining on guard, seemed to deprecate any question of its appearance. No sound came from other parts of the Castle.

Miss Cuffe was an heiress to whom the Castle belonged and whose guests they all were. But she carefully followed the movements of her aunt, Mrs Treye; her ox-eyes moved from face to face in happy submission rather than expectancy. She was continually preoccupied with attempts at gravity, as though holding down her skirts in a high wind. Mrs Treye and Miss Carbin combined to cover her excitement; still, their looks frequently stole from the company to the windows, of which there were too many. He received a strong impression someone outside was waiting to come in. At last, with a sigh they got up: dinner had been announced.

The Castle was built on high ground, commanding the estuary; a steep hill, with trees, continued above it. On fine days the view was remarkable, of almost Italian brilliance, with that constant reflection up from the water that even now prolonged the too-long day. Now, in continuous evening rain, the winding wooded line of the further shore could be seen and, nearer the windows, a smothered island with the stump of a watch-tower. Where the Castle stood, a higher tower had answered the island's. Later a keep, then wings, had been added; now the fine peaceful residence had French windows opening on to the terrace. Invasions from the water would henceforth be social, perhaps amorous. On the slope down from the terrace, trees began again; almost, but not quite concealing the destroyer. Alban, who knew nothing, had not yet looked down.

It was Mr Rossiter who first spoke of the destroyer – Alban meanwhile glancing along the table; the preparations had been stupendous. The destroyer had come today. The ladies all turned to Alban: the beads on their bosoms sparkled. So this was what they had here, under their trees. Engulfed by their pleasure, from now on he disappeared personally. Mr Rossiter, rising a note, continued. The estuary, it appeared, was deep, with a channel buoyed up it. By a term of the Treaty, English ships were permitted to anchor in these waters.

'But they've been afraid of the rain!' chimed in Valeria Cuffe.

'Hush,' said her aunt, 'that's silly. Sailors would be accustomed to getting wet.'

But, Miss Carbin reported, that spring there *had* already been one destroyer. Two of the officers had been seen dancing at the hotel at the head of the estuary.

'So,' said Alban, 'you are quite in the world.' He adjusted his glasses in her direction.

Miss Carbin – blonde, not forty, and an attachment of Mrs Treye's – shook her head despondently. 'We were all away at Easter. Wasn't it curious they should have come then? The sailors walked in the demesne but never touched the daffodils.'

'As though I should have cared!' exclaimed Valeria passionately.

'Morale too good,' stated Mr Rossiter.

'But next evening,' continued Miss Carbin, 'the officers did not go to the hotel. They climbed up here through the trees to the terrace – you see, they had no idea. Friends of ours were staying here at the Castle, and they apologized. Our friends invited them in to supper . . .'

'Did they accept?'

The three ladies said in a breath: 'Yes, they came.'

Valeria added urgently, 'So don't you *think*—?'

'So tonight we have a destroyer to greet you,' Mrs Treye said quickly to Alban. 'It is quite an event; the country people are coming down from the mountains. These waters are very lonely; the steamers have given up since the bad times; there is hardly a pleasure-boat. The weather this year has driven visitors right away.'

'You are beautifully remote.'

'Yes,' agreed Miss Carbin. 'Do you know much about the Navy? Do you think, for instance, that this is likely to be the same destroyer?'

'*Will they remember?*' Valeria's bust was almost on the table. But with a rustle Mrs Treye pressed Valeria's toe. For the dining-room also looked out across the estuary, and the great girl had not once taken her eyes from the window. Perhaps it was unfortunate that Mr Alban should have coincided with the destroyer. Perhaps it was unfortunate for Mr Alban too.

For he saw now he was less than half the feast; unappeased, the party sat looking through him, all grouped at an end of the table – to the other, chairs had been pulled up. Dinner was being served very slowly. Candles – possible to see from the water – were lit now; some wet peonies glistened. Outside, day still lingered hopefully. The bushes over the edge of the terrace were like heads – you could have sworn sometimes you saw them mounting, swaying in manly talk. Once, wound up in the rain, a bird whistled, seeming hardly a bird.

'Perhaps since then they have been to Greece, or Malta?'

'That would be the Mediterranean fleet,' said Mr Rossiter.

They were sorry to think of anything out in the rain tonight.

'The decks must be streaming,' said Miss Carbin.

Then Valeria, exclaiming, 'Please excuse me!' pushed her chair in and ran from the room.

'She is impulsive,' explained Mrs Treye. 'Have *you* been to Malta, Mr Alban?'

In the drawing-room, empty of Valeria, the standard lamps had been lit. Through their ballet-skirt shades, rose and lemon, they gave out a deep, welcoming light. Alban, at the ladies' invitation, undraped the piano. He played, but they could see he was not pleased. It was obvious he had always been a civilian, and when he had taken his place on the piano-stool – which he twirled round three times, rather fussily – his dinner-jacket wrinkled across the shoulders. It was sad they should feel so indifferent, for he came from London. Mendelssohn was exasperating to them – they opened all four windows to let the music downhill. They preferred not to draw the curtains; the air, though damp, being pleasant tonight, they said.

The piano was damp, but Alban played almost all his heart out. He played out the indignation of years his mild manner concealed. He had failed to love; nobody did anything about this; partners at dinner gave him less than half their attention. He knew some spring had dried up at the root of the world. He was fixed in the dark rain, by an indifferent shore. He played badly, but they were unmusical. Old Mr Rossiter, who was not what he seemed, went back to the dining-room to talk to the parlour maid.

Valeria, glittering vastly, appeared in a window.

'Come *in*!' her aunt cried in indignation. She would die of a chill, childless, in fact unwedded; the Castle would have to be sold and where would they all be?

But – 'Lights down there!' Valeria shouted above the music.

They had to run out for a moment, laughing and holding cushions over their bare shoulders. Alban left the piano; they looked boldly down from the terrace. Indeed, there they were: two lights like arc-lamps, blurred by rain and drawn down deep in reflection into the steady water. There were, too, ever so many portholes, all lit up.

'Perhaps they are playing bridge,' said Miss Carbin.

'Now I wonder if Uncle Robert ought to have called,' said Mrs Treye. 'Perhaps we have seemed remiss – one calls on a regiment.'

'Patrick could row him out tomorrow.'

'He hates the water.' She sighed. 'Perhaps they will be gone.'

'Let's go for a row now – let's go for a row with a lantern,' besought Valeria, jumping and pulling her aunt's elbow. They produced such indignation she disappeared again – wet satin skirts and all – into the bushes. The ladies could do no more: Alban suggested the rain might spot their dresses.

'They must lose a great deal, playing cards throughout an evening for high stakes,' Miss Carbin said with concern as they all sat down again.

'Yet, if you come to think of it, somebody must win.'

But the naval officers who so joyfully supped at Easter had been, Miss Carbin knew, a Mr Graves, and a Mr Garrett: *they* would certainly lose. 'At all events, it is better than dancing at the hotel; there would be nobody of their type.'

'There is nobody there at all.'

'I expect they are best where they are . . . Mr Alban, a Viennese waltz?'

He played while the ladies whispered, waving the waltz time a little distractedly. Mr Rossiter, coming back, momentously stood: they turned in hope: even the waltz halted. But he brought no news. 'You should call Valeria in. You can't tell who may be round the place. She's not fit to be out tonight.'

'Perhaps she's not out.'

'She is,' said Mr Rossiter crossly. 'I just saw her racing past the window with a lantern.'

Valeria's mind was made up: she was a princess. Not for nothing had she had the dining-room silver polished and all set out. She would pace around in red satin that swished behind, while Mr Alban kept on playing a loud waltz. They would be dazed at all she had to offer – also her two new statues and the leopard-skin from the auction.

When he and she were married (she inclined a little to Mr Garrett) they would invite all the Navy up the estuary and give them tea. Her estuary would be filled up, like a regatta, with loud excited battleships tooting to one another and flags flying. The terrace would be covered with grateful sailors, leaving room for the band. She would keep the peacocks her aunt did not allow. His friends would be surprised to notice that Mr Garrett had meanwhile become an admiral, all gold. He would lead the other admirals into the Castle and say, while they wiped their feet respectfully: 'These are my wife's statues; she has given them to me. One is Mars, one is Mercury. We have a Venus, but she is not dressed. And wait till I show you our silver and gold plates . . .' The Navy would be unable to tear itself away.

She had been excited for some weeks at the idea of marrying Mr Alban, but now the lovely appearance of the destroyer put him out of her mind. He would not have done; he was not handsome. But she could keep him to play the piano on quiet afternoons.

Her friends had told her Mr Garrett was quite a Viking. She was so very familiar with his appearance that she felt sometimes they had already been married for years – though still, sometimes, he could not realize his good luck. She still had to remind him the island was hers too . . . Tonight, Aunt and darling Miss Carbin had so fallen in with her plans, putting on their satins and decorating the drawing-room, that the dinner became a betrothal feast. There was some little hitch about the arrival of Mr Garrett – she had heard that gentlemen sometimes could not tie their ties. And now he was late and would be discouraged. So she must now go half-way down to the water and wave a lantern.

But she put her two hands over the lantern, then smothered it in her dress. She had a panic. Supposing she should prefer Mr Graves?

She had heard Mr Graves was stocky, but very merry; when he came to supper at Easter he slid in the gallery. He would teach her to dance, and take her to Naples and Paris . . . Oh, dear, oh, dear, then they must fight for her; that was all there was to it . . . She let the lantern out of her skirts and waved. Her fine arm with bangles went up and down, up and down, with the staggering light; the trees one by one jumped up from the dark, like savages.

Inconceivably, the destroyer took no notice.

Undisturbed by oars, the rain stood up from the water; not a light rose to peer, and the gramophone, though it remained very faint, did not cease or alter.

In mackintoshes, Mr Rossiter and Alban meanwhile made their way to the boat-house, Alban did not know why. 'If that goes on,' said Mr Rossiter, nodding towards Valeria's lantern, 'they'll fire one of their guns at us.'

'Oh, no. Why?' said Alban. He buttoned up, however, the collar of his mackintosh.

'Nervous as cats. It's high time that girl was married. She's a nice girl in many ways, too.'

'Couldn't we get the lantern away from her?' They stepped on a paved causeway and heard the water nibble the rocks.

'She'd scream the place down. She's of age now, you see.'

'But if—'

'Oh, she won't do that; I was having a bit of fun with you.' Chuckling equably, Mrs Treye's uncle unlocked and pulled open the boat-house door. A bat whistled out.

'Why are we here?'

'She might come for the boat; she's a fine oar,' said Mr Rossiter wisely. The place was familiar to him; he lit an oil-lamp and, sitting down on a trestle with a staunch air of having done what he could, reached a bottle of whisky out of the boat. He motioned the bottle to Alban. 'It's a wild night,' he said. 'Ah, well, we don't have these destroyers every day.'

'That seems fortunate.'

'Well, it is and it isn't.' Restoring the bottle to the vertical, Mr Rossiter continued: 'It's a pity you don't want a wife. You'd be the better for a wife, d'you see, a young fellow like you. She's got a nice character; she's a girl you could shape. She's got a nice income.' The bat returned from the rain and knocked round the lamp. Lowering the bottle frequently, Mr Rossiter talked to Alban (whose attitude remained negative) of women in general and the parlourmaid in particular . . .

'*Bat!*' Alban squealed irrepressibly, and with his hand to his ear – where he still felt it – fled from the boat-house. Mr Rossiter's conversation continued. Alban's pumps squelched as he ran; he skidded along the causeway and balked at the upward steps. His soul squelched equally: he had been warned, he had been warned. He had heard they were all mad; he had erred out of headiness and curiosity. A degree of terror was agreeable to his vanity: by express wish he had occupied haunted rooms. Now he had no other pumps in this country, no idea where to buy them, and a ducal visit ahead. Also, wandering as it were among the apples and amphoras of an art school, he had blundered into the life room: woman revolved gravely.

'Hell,' he said to the steps, mounting, his mind blank to the outcome.

He was nerved for the jumping lantern, but half-way up to the Castle darkness was once more absolute. Her lantern had gone out; he could orientate himself – in spite of himself – by her sobbing. Absolute desperation. He pulled up so short that, for balance, he had to cling to a creaking tree.

'Hi!' she croaked. Then: 'You *are* there! I hear you!'

'Miss Cuffe—'

'How too bad you are! I never heard you rowing. I thought you were never coming—'

'Quietly, my dear girl.'

'Come up quickly. I haven't even seen you. Come up to the windows—'

'Miss Cuffe—'

'Don't you remember the way?' As sure but not so noiseless as a cat in the dark, Valeria hurried to him.

'Mr Garrett—' she panted. 'I'm Miss Cuffe. Where have you been? I've destroyed my beautiful red dress and they've eaten up your dinner. But we're still waiting. Don't be afraid; you'll soon be there now. I'm Miss Cuffe; this is my Castle—'

'Listen, it's I, Mr Alban—'

'Ssh, ssh, Mr Alban: *Mr Garrett has landed.*'

Her cry, his voice, some breath of the joyful intelligence, brought the others on to the terrace, blind with lamplight.

'Valeria?'

'Mr Garrett has landed!'

Mrs Treye said to Miss Carbin under her breath, 'Mr Garrett has come.'

Miss Carbin, half weeping with agitation, replied, 'We must go in.' But uncertain who was to speak next, or how to speak, they remained leaning over the darkness. Behind, through the windows, lamps spread great skirts of light, and Mars and Mercury, unable to contain themselves, stooped from their pedestals. The dumb keyboard shone like a ballroom floor.

Alban, looking up, saw their arms and shoulders under the bright rain. Close by, Valeria's fingers creaked on her warm wet satin. She laughed like a princess, magnificently justified. Their unseen faces were all three lovely, and, in the silence after the laughter, such a strong tenderness reached him that, standing there in full manhood, he was for a moment not exiled. For the moment, without moving or speaking, he stood, in the dark, in a flame, as though all three said: 'My darling . . .'

Perhaps it was best for them all that early, when next day first lightened the rain, the destroyer steamed out – below the extinguished Castle where Valeria lay with her arms wide, past the boat-house where Mr Rossiter lay insensible and the bat hung masked in its wings – down the estuary into the open sea.

from *The Last September*

7

Another thing Lady Naylor had noticed about the English was a disposition they had to be socially visible before midday.

Soon after ten, she had heard, Mrs Vermont and her friends were to be seen about the streets of Clonmore – from behind the still decently somnolent blinds of inhabitants – with gloves buttoned tight at the wrists, swinging coloured baskets. Before eleven, they would be seated behind the confectioner's window, deploring the coffee. Mrs Rolfe had once had Moriarty's shutters taken down for her specially – and she wishful, Moriarty said, to purchase the one pair of stockings only. A Mrs Peake, of the Gunners, demanded attention at the hairdresser's before ten. These unnatural practices were a strain on the town's normality; the streets had a haggard look, ready for anything. Really, as Lady Naylor said, almost English. She thought of the south of England as a kind of extension of Eastbourne, the north – serrated by factory chimneys, the middle – a blank space occupied by Anna Partridge. Only Danielstown's being out of dropping or popping in distance from Clonmore deprived her, as it transpired, of matutinal visits from Mrs Vermont and her friends.

Mrs Vermont, however, overcame difficulties, hired a Ford and had herself driven over one morning about eleven o'clock. She brought her great friend Mrs Rolfe; they were on their way to lunch at the Thompsons'. This she explained before they were out of the car; *she* knew what Mondays were, she did not want to alarm Lady Naylor – being so much with mother had made her considerate in these matters. Lady Naylor, as a matter of fact, would have minded them less at lunch time, one didn't notice people so much at meals, she discovered. When news of the dropping in came down to the kitchen, she groaned: 'My morning!' Nothing could have been worse.

Francie was lying down with 'a head'; Hugo was talking over old times with the coachman, who had been pensioned off and brooded all day in the harness-room, much at a loss. Lois, indirectly responsible for this outrage, was not to be found. She had not been herself at all, these last three days. Her aunt, after Gerald's departure, had made a point of saying: 'Well, I hope, of course, you have not made a mistake. But we all have to settle these things for ourselves, you know.' Francie never failed to inquire if she were getting on nicely with the Italian; her uncle agreed it was high time she went to that school of art. This morning she seemed to be nowhere; shouting did not produce her.

Laurence, always unfortunate, was surprised on the steps with Locke. 'Oh God,' he said as the Ford came round the bend of the lower avenue. He turned, too late, to escape; the girl wives were already shrieking and waving.

Betty said: 'Denise, this is Mr – (Oh dear, how awful!) This is Mrs Rolfe of the Gunners; my great friend, you know.'

'Good,' said Laurence. Denise glanced up, apprehensive, at all the windows. Laurence stood looking at them with resignation; he forgot to open the door of the car though they brimmed out over it.

'*May* we get out?' asked Betty, tittering up at him in the friendliest way from a perfect swirl of furs and red crêpe de Chine. On their knees, two little pairs of hands curled like loose chrysanthemums over their kid pochettes. He let them out and they ran up the steps shaking out their dresses. '*Oh*, what a brainy book!' cried Betty, pouncing. '– My dear, just look what he's reading – oh, you have got a brain! I mean, fancy reading . . .'

'You're at college, aren't you?' said Denise, fluttered.

'Sometimes,' said Laurence accurately. Opening his mouth very wide, he shouted for Lois. They shrieked and covered their ears. 'I expect,' he said finally, 'I had better go in and look for –'

'Don't go! I'm sure they will all come out . . . I did want Denise to see a lovely old Irish home.'

'Yes, we are quaint, really,' said Laurence, considering. 'And you oughtn't to miss the Trents; has she seen the Trents?'

'Well, I hardly know the Trents. Here, we always feel that Gerald is such a link.'

'Missing or otherwise,' Denise added.

'Exactly.' Betty smiled at him sidelong; but all the same it did seem a pity it should be Laurence that they had dropped in on with unintended accuracy. *This* was not at all what she had led Denise to expect. Laurence's not quite rudeness was, in fact, rather international – she supposed, Oxford. She said: 'I have a boy cousin at Reading University. That's quite near Oxford, isn't it?' Denise, plaintive, said that a wasp was bothering: Betty flapped with her pochette and the end of her fur. 'She's *terrified* of wasps!'

'So am I,' said Laurence, backing, 'absolutely *terrified* . . . I think I'd better go and – better get a –' He disappeared through the glass door, shutting it.

Denise said: 'Well, I do think people are extraordinary.' They both sat down and yawned. All these trees; it was quite extraordinary. 'Is that Lois's cousin?'

'More or less.'

'Well, I always did think she was an odd girl.'

'Ssh, there's Sir Richard writing in the library – Denise, *just* look through, sideways. He's such a type.'

'O-oh . . . yes. Is he a knight or a baronet?'

'Well, I don't see how he could have been knighted.'

'My dear, Ssssh!'

'He's deaf. Oh, darling, look at those little teeny black cows. Those are Kerry cows. They farm, you know; they have heaps of cattle.'

'I always meant to ask you: are there Kilkenny cats?'

'Really,' said Mrs Vermont, annoyed, as her friend yawned again and she felt her own jaw quiver, 'when one thinks these are the people we are defending! I wonder if they'll offer us any coffee. What I think about Irish hospitality: either they almost knock you down or they don't look at you. Or I tell you what, we might go out to the garden and get some plums. Only I would like you to see the drawing-room. I wish these were Livvy's people; the boys say her house smells – I hope you aren't bored, darling? – I mean, what I mean about Livvy; she does grow on you. I can't think what Gerald sees in this family, I must say. It isn't even as if Lois –'

'Of course, I always did think she was an odd girl.'

At this point Sir Richard, who was not deaf, came out in despair. He said this was too bad; he couldn't think what could have become of Lois. 'We might shout,' he said helplessly.

'Your nephew has been shouting.'

'Still,' said Sir Richard, and shouted again. 'How are you all getting on?' he said kindly, when he had recovered his breath.

Betty said with dignity: 'There may be going to be an offensive.'

'Sssh,' whispered Denise, pinching her elbow.

'Though I ought not really to tell you.'

'Never mind,' said Sir Richard, 'I don't suppose it will come to anything. Besides, now the days are drawing in – But this is too bad really; most unfortunate that my wife should not be here to receive you. She will be most distressed.'

'Oh, but we just dropped in. As I said to Denise, what is the good of being in Ireland if one isn't a bit unconventional?'

'She will be most distressed.'

'Don't bother! We've been admiring your darling cows.'

'I'll just go in and inquire,' said Sir Richard firmly and disappeared, shutting the glass door.

Denise said she would get the giggles: a seizure did seem to be imminent. 'Well, I must say, Gerald is well out of this family.'

'But my dear, *is* he?'

'Something's happened. He's *black* – even Timmy noticed. I said to Timmy: "You *must* find out" – Cause I think, don't you, that when men get together . . . You see, *I* can't – though I can't bear to see the boy suffer.'

'But I thought you said you –'

'Well, I've seen him in the distance and he didn't look like himself at all. But he hasn't been near us, or to the Club, or into the Fogartys'. And as I was saying to Mrs Fogarty –'

'It seems to me he's been treated rottenly. If it were one of our boys, my dear, I should be fur-rious.'

'All the same, I do want to *see* Lois . . .'

'What he sees in her, I cannot imagine. She's what I should call rather affected –'

'Sssh – Oh, hullo, Lois!' they cried in unison.

Lois, unbecomingly bright, came up from the beech walk.

'Oh, hullo,' she said. 'Splendid!'

'We've just been talking about you.'

'O-oh. *Can't* you stay to lunch?'

'No can do; we're off to the Thompsons'. My dear, aren't you thrilled about Livvy and David! Isn't it marvellous?'

'Thrilled, it's absolutely marvellous. *Do* stay to lunch – I mean,' she said agitatedly, 'do come back to tea? Oh no, we shall all be out. Oh, how rotten. Or come to tennis – no, I believe there won't be any more tennis; Laurence is going back to Oxford and the rain's washed all the marking off the court. Perhaps we could have a dance or something –'

The two young wives eyed her lightly and curiously; their looks ran over her form like spiders. They were so womanly, she could have turned and fled back down the beech walk. 'Donne ch'avete intelletto d'amore,' she thought to herself wildly. And the pause, the suspicion of some deformity that these ladies produced in her became so acute that she smiled more widely. She buttoned her cardigan up to the top, then unbuttoned it.

'Oh, but don't go *now*,' she said, but looked at the Ford, longingly.

'Oh, we must, we have been here hours, watching your darling cows.'

'I'm afraid they're very much in the distance. Does Aunt Myra –?'

'Oh, we'd hate to disturb her. Unless we might all run around the garden –?'

'It's locked and I've lost the key. I feel quite an outcast. That's what has been the matter the whole morning. Do have something to eat – have some biscuits?'

'Unless we just come into the drawing-room for one moment?'

'I always think drawing-rooms in the morning are so depressing.'

Denise said she did not see how the same room could be much different, but it was no good; Lois seemed determined to keep them out. From the way she shifted her feet and stared round you would have said she was expecting bad news momentarily; she talked so much that they hadn't a chance to express themselves. She went in for a tin of *petits beurres* and offered it with an odd air, rather propitiatory. Lady Naylor called from an upstairs window that this was too bad, that she was so much distressed, she would be down immediately. 'She spends whole mornings with the cook,' said Lois, 'I cannot think what they do. I believe they fence verbally. More biscuits?'

'No, we shall spoil our din-dins. Denise, we *must* go. I hear old Mr Thompson is a terrible ogre. Any messages in Clonmore, Lois? Any messages to Gerald?'

Lois thought she must blush, but did not; even her blood stood still.

'*I* should ask him,' said Denise, 'why he didn't send *you* a message. *I* think it was odd of him; I should be fur-rious.' Lois saw, with interest, a ripple of light down their dresses; they nudged each other. There must be something odd about her, really, if they had noticed; she must clearly be outside life.

'How is the gramophone?' she asked enthusiastically.

'Don't *ask*. Gerald is going to Cork to bring back a new one ... We thought we might all go too, it would be a rag.'

'Marvellous!'

'Look, I'll just run Denise in to have a look at the drawing-room.'

'I shouldn't, really. I haven't done the flowers.'

'Gerald says all your looking-glasses make him feel sleepy. He's a funny boy, in a way,' said Betty innocently. 'You don't think we ought to wait till we've seen your aunt? She won't be offended?'

'I shouldn't really; she's probably been delayed.' Lady Naylor did, in fact, arrive on the steps in time to make exclamations of despair as they drove away. 'Too bad, *too* bad!' she called. 'You must come again soon! ... Really, Lois, you might have found them some fruit or something. Fancy puffing them out with biscuits at this hour.'

'I tell you what I think it is about Lois,' said Betty cosily, nestling down in the car as the trees rushed over. '*I* think he's left her.'

Denise agreed. 'A boy needs keeping, if you know what I mean.' Betty also told her what she thought about the Naylor family: they were going down in the world. 'I should not be surprised if they never used that drawing-room,' she said viciously. 'It smells of damp. Myself, I do like a house to be bright and homy.'

The world did not stand still, though the household at Danielstown and the Thompsons' lunch party took no account of it. The shocking news reached Clonmore about eight o'clock. It crashed upon the unknowingness of the town like a wave that for two hours, since the event, had been standing and toppling, imminent. The news crept down streets from door to door like a dull wind, fingering the nerves, pausing. In the hotel bars heads went this way and that way, quick with suspicion. The Fogartys' Eileen, called to the door while she was clearing away the supper, cried, 'God help him!' and stumbled up to Mr Fogarty's door, blubbered. Mr Fogarty dropped his glass and stood bent some time like an animal, chin on the mantelpiece. Philosophy did not help; in his thickening brain actuality turned like a mill-wheel. His wife, magnificent in her disbelief, ran out, wisps blowing, round the square and through the vindictively silent town.

Barracks were closed, she could not get past the guards; for once she was at a loss, among strangers. She thought mechanically 'His mother,' and pressed her hands up under her vast and useless bosom. Trees in the square, uneasy, shifted dulled leaves that should already have fallen under the darkness. The shocking news, brought in at the barrack-gates officially, produced an abashed silence, hard repercussions, darkness of thought and a loud glare of electricity. In Gerald's room some new music for the jazz band, caught in a draught, flopped over and over. An orderly put it away, shocked. All night some windows let out, over the sandbags, a squeamish, defiant yellow.

Mrs Vermont heard when Timmy had just gone out; he was to be out all night with a patrol. She was to sleep alone, she could not bear it. Past fear, she ran to the Rolfes' hut. She spent the night there, sobbing, tearing off with her teeth the lace right round her handkerchief. Captain Rolfe kept bringing her hot whisky. 'I can't, I can't, not whisky: it's awful.' They all felt naked and were ashamed of each other, as though they had been wrecked. From the hut floor – where they had danced – the wicker furniture seemed to rise and waver.

'Percy, where did he – how was he –?'

'Through the head'

'Then it didn't –?'

'Oh, no. Probably instantaneous.'

'Oh, don't! Oh, Percy, how can you!'

Denise repeated: 'I can't believe it.' And while the others queerly, furtively stared, she tried to press from her hair the waves she had had put in that morning. 'You know, I can't believe it. Can you, Betty? It's so . . . extraordinary.'

'Why can't we all go home? Why did we stay here? Why don't we all go home? That's what I can't understand.'

'Percy, can *you* believe it? I mean, I remember him coming in and standing against this table –'

'Oh, don't – Percy, what became of *them*? Where did they go? Those devils!'

'Oh, got right away.'

'Didn't anyone hear anything, any firing? I mean, didn't it make a noise? . . . Couldn't they be tortured – why should they just be hanged or shot? Oh, I do think, I mean I do think when you think –'

'Well, we've got to get 'em, haven't we? Look, just try –'

'Oh, I can't, I tell you – Why can't we all go home?'

'Percy, leave her *alone*! O God, my head; I shall cut my hair off. I mean, he came in and stood there against that table. Why did they get just Gerald? – Oh, yes, I know there was the sergeant – but *he* won't die; I know he won't die . . . I can't believe it. Percy, *can* you believe it? Percy, say something!'

Betty sobbed: 'I should like to – Oh, I should like to – Those beasts, those beasts.'

'Look, you two girls go to bed.'

'Oh, how can we!'

'Oh, why isn't Timmie here! I mean, when I think of Timmie, and out all night – I can't understand the King, I can't understand the Government: *I* think it's awful.'

But they went to bed – Percy spent the night on two chairs – and lay in what seemed to both an unnatural contiguity, reclasping each other's fingers, talking of 'him', of 'you know who' and 'that boy' in the eager voices, low-pitched and breaking, kept as a rule to discuss the intimacies of their marriages. In the same moment they fell, dimly shocked at each other, asleep. Then Denise saw Lois clearly, standing affectedly on the Danielstown steps with a tin of biscuits, a room full of mirrors behind her. And Betty woke with surprise to hear herself say: 'What I mean is, it seems so odd that he shouldn't really have meant anything.'

They heard an early bugle shivering in the rain.

8

Mr Daventry arrived before the postman. He had not paid an unofficial visit since he had been in Ireland; it seemed to him odd there should be nothing to search for, nobody to interrogate. It was early, wet tarnished branches came cheerfully through the mist. He had come to the gate with a convoy on its way over to Ballyhinch; two lorries had ground into silence and waited for him at the gate, alarming the cottagers. He walked up the avenue lightly and rapidly: nothing, at the stage things had reached for him, mattered. And superciliously he returned the stare of the house.

He rang and made his demand. Lois came out slowly, dumb with all she must begin to say – for who could an anxious waiting officer be but Gerald? 'Really . . .' Lady Naylor had remarked, with a glance at the clock, advising her to put down her table napkin. And Francie, smiling, had covered up her egg for her.

'You?' she now said, while everything, the importance of everything, faintly altered. 'Come and have breakfast.'

He told her that there had been a catastrophe yesterday, west of Clonmore: a patrol with an officer and an NCO had been ambushed, fired on at a crossroads. The officer – Lesworth – was instantly killed, the NCO shot in the stomach. The enemy made off across country, they did not care for sustained fire, in spite of the hedges. The men did what they could for the sergeant.

'Will he die?'

'Probably.'

'And Gerald was killed.'

'Yes. Would you –?'

'I'm all right, thank you.'

'Right you are.' He turned round and stood with his back to her. She asked what time it had happened; he said about six o'clock. She thought how accurate Gerald was and how anxious, last time, he had been to establish just *when* she had been happy because of him, on what day, for how long. 'They'd been out all the afternoon?' They both saw the amazed white road and dust, displaced by the fall, slowly settling. 'As a matter of fact,' said Daventry, 'we are mostly ready for things. I don't suppose – if he knew at all – it mattered.' 'No, I don't suppose, to oneself, it ever would matter much.' But she thought of Gerald in the surprise of death. He gave himself up to surprise with peculiar candour.

'Thank you for coming.'

'I was passing this way anyhow.'

'But still, there was no reason why you should take the trouble.'

Daventry glanced at her, then at the gravel under his feet, without speculation. Cold and ironical, he was a stay; he was not expecting anything of her. He finally said: 'It seemed practical. Would you like me to – shall I just let the others know?' She nodded, wondering where to go, how long to stay there, how to come back. Her mind flooded with trivialities. She wondered who would go up to the tennis this afternoon, if there would be anyone left who did not know, who would expect him; she wondered what would become of the jazz band. She saw that for days ahead she must not deny humanity, she would have no privacy. 'As a matter of fact, they are expecting me back to breakfast.'

But at the thought of Francie's tender and proud smile, covering up her egg, she was enlightened and steadied by grief, as at the touch of finger-tips. She went into the house and up to the top to find what was waiting. Life, seen whole for a moment, was one act of apprehension, the apprehension of death. Daventry, staring after her in memory – she was, after all, a woman – went into the hall. Here, it pleased him to think of Gerald socially circumspect under the portraits.

He waited. The dining-room door swung open on a continued argument; they came out one by one, each, on the threshold, balanced a moment like a ball on a fountain by the shock of seeing him there. 'Lady Naylor?' he said to Francie. 'Oh, *no* –' she seemed appalled at the supposition. 'Isn't . . . Mr Lesworth here?' 'Not today.' Lady Naylor came last and stared hardest: really, the Army seemed to be inexhaustible. 'Oh, no –' she said quickly, as though to prevent something. He told her the circumstances. 'Oh – *no*,' she repeated, and turned in appeal to her husband. 'That is . . . that is too bad,' said Sir Richard and in despairing confusion touched her shoulder. He looked back into the dining-room at the chairs and plates and table, incredible in their survival.

The fact was, they did not at all care for the look of Mr Daventry. They felt instinctively that he had come here to search the house. Lady Naylor, still statuesque from the shock, made, even, a little disdainful gesture, a kind of: 'Here's everything.' He, unconscious of her impression of being brought to book, remained staring darkly and piercingly past her. Behind her, across the dark dining-room, he saw through a window the lawn striped with mist and sunshine. In Clonmore it had rained that morning: they seemed to have escaped that too. She said sharply: 'Where's Lois?'

'I'm afraid I don't know,' he replied, indifferent.

'She – you have –?'

'Oh yes.'

Her defence dropped; she said with heart-broken eyes on his face: 'You know, we knew him so well. He came out here so often to tennis. It seems queer that one can't – that one never – He was so –'

'Yes, he was, wasn't he?'

'His mother, he used to tell me about his mother. Who will write? I should like to write to her. Yes, I want very much to write to her. I think she might like – we did know him so well, you see – Richard, don't you think I –?'

But Sir Richard had slipped away quietly; he was an old man, really, outside all this, and did not know what to do. He was wondering also, about the Connors. Peter Connor's friends: they knew everything, they were persistent: it did not do to imagine . . .

Mr Daventry said that was all, he thought; he must go now. He took leave with unfriendly courtesy and went off abruptly, with an air that obliterated them, as though he had never been into their house at all. Then she exclaimed, recollecting herself: 'He must be unhappy; I ought to have said something.' There was so much to do now, more than would fit into a morning; she had some idea of postponing lunch. And hearing the postman, she half thought, terrified by a sense of exposure: 'Suppose there should be a – suppose he should have –'

But there was no letter for Lois from Gerald.

No one was on the steps to hear the news from the postman; he went away disappointed. Lady Naylor thought firmly: 'Now I must go and find Lois.' But she did not go; things seemed to delay her. She looked into the drawing-room to see whether something – she wasn't certain what – was there. Francie, red-eyed, looked guilty over the back of the sofa. They did not say anything. The room became so sharply painful that Lady Naylor almost exclaimed: 'Lois has not done the flowers!'

It was Laurence who, walking about the grounds unguardedly, was exposed to what they all dreaded. He came on Lois, standing beside a holly tree. She could have moved away, but seemed not so much rooted as indifferent.

'It's all right,' she explained, and added: 'I'm just thinking.'

His look became almost personal, as though he had recognized her. He said: 'I think I should. I expect – I don't know – one probably gets past things.'

'But look here, there are things that one can't – ' (She meant: He loved me, he believed in the British Empire.) 'At least, I don't want to.'

'Perhaps you are right,' he admitted, studying, with an effort of sight and of comprehension, some unfamiliar landscape.

'Well, don't stop, Laurence. You're going somewhere, aren't you?'

'Nowhere particular. Not if you – '

'No, I don't specially. Though if it has to be anyone, you.'

Taking this for what it was worth, he went on; brushing awkwardly past her against the laurels.

A fortnight later, Mrs Trent drove over, the very evening of her return from the North. She had been inexpressibly bored up there and wished to complain. Lady Naylor, delighted, came out to meet her; it was like old times again.

'The house feels empty. They've gone, you know.'

'Yes, dear me. I was sorry not to have seen the last of Hugo and poor little Francie. What about their bungalow?'

'Oh, that was just an idea; they are quite off it. Bungalows inland seem so pointless, cliffs are so windy and one cannot live on a flat coast. No, they think now of going to Madeira.'

'Then they won't unstore the furniture?'

'I don't think so; they never cared for it much.'

'It's a pity he never did go to Canada.' Mrs Trent looked round at the pleasant fields and lawns, the trees massive and tarnished, the windows that from their now settled emptiness seemed to have gained composure. Her sense of home-coming extended even to Danielstown. She went on: 'How's Richard? And listen: are you getting in your apples? – we haven't begun. They never seem to do anything while I'm away. And tell me; how's Lois?'

'Oh, gone, you know.'

'*Gone?* Oh, the school of art!'

'Oh, no,' said Lady Naylor, surprised. 'Tours. For her French, you know. And to such an interesting, cultivated family; she is really fortunate. I never have been happy about her French. As I said to her, there will be plenty of time for Italian.'

'Oh, that's splendid,' Mrs Trent said vaguely but warmly. 'Then of course you must feel quiet. She and Laurence travel over together?'

'She seemed so offended at being thought incompetent and he was worried at the idea of looking after her luggage, so we sent them over separately; he crossed Wednesday, she Friday. Both nights, I hear, it was rough ... Yes, it's been sad here, lately; we've been so much shocked and distressed about that unfortunate young Lesworth. I think I felt it particularly; he had been out here so much and seemed so glad to talk, and had come, in a way, to depend on one. Though it was a shock, too, for Lois. You see they had really played tennis so often and were beginning to be quite friends. She did not take it as hard as I feared, girls of her generation seem less sensitive, really ... I don't know, perhaps that is all for the best. And of course she has so many interests. But it was terrible, wasn't it? I still think: how terrible – But he did have a happy life. I wrote that to his mother; I said, it must always be some consolation to think how happy his life had been. He quite beamed, really; he was the life and soul of everything. And she wrote back – I did not think tactfully, but of course she would be distressed – that it was *her* first consolation to think he died in so noble a cause.'

Mrs Trent had for a moment an uneasy, exposed look. She said: 'It was heroic,' and glanced down awkwardly at her gloves. She missed a dog, she felt unstayed, there was no dog.

'Heroic,' said Lady Naylor, and scanned the skies with eager big-pupilled eyes that reflected the calm light. 'Although,' she added, half in surprise, 'he could not help it. But come in now and tell Richard about the North, he will be amused, though sorry that you were dull. To tell you the truth, we both rather feared you might be. Ah, don't mind the time, I'm sure it's early; come in, come in!'

But Mrs Trent could not; she was a punctilious person and wore a wrist-watch. She had not even sent round her dog-cart to the back; a man was walking the cob up and down the avenue. 'A flying visit,' said Lady Naylor mournfully, having prolonged the conversation by half an hour. Then Mrs Trent climbed briskly into the dog-cart and gathered the reins up; they sighed at each other their resignation at parting.

'Then we see you on Tuesday. Be sure and come early, before the Hartigans.' To the domestic landscape, Mrs Trent nodded an approving farewell. 'Every autumn, it strikes me this place looks really its best.'

'To tell you the truth, I really believe it does. There is something in autumn,' said Lady Naylor. She remained on the steps looking after the trap, her hands restlessly, lightly folded. Some leaves spun down from the gate with a home-coming air.

The two did not, however, again see Danielstown at such a moment, such a particular happy point of decline in the short curve of the day, the long curve of the season. Here, there were no more autumns, except for the trees. By next year light had possessed itself of the vacancy, still with surprise. Next year, the chestnuts and acorns pattered unheard on the avenues, that, filmed over with green already, should have been dull to the footsteps – but there were no footsteps. Leaves, fluttering down the slope with the wind's hesitation, banked formless, frightened, against the too clear form of the ruin.

For in February, before those leaves had visibly budded, the death – the execution, rather – of the three houses, Danielstown, Castle Trent, Mount Isabel, occurred in the same night. A fearful scarlet ate up the hard spring darkness; indeed, it seemed that an extra day, unreckoned, had come to abortive birth that these things might happen. It seemed, looking from east to west at the sky tall with scarlet, that the country itself was burning; while to the north the neck of mountain before Mount Isbael was frightfully outlined. The roads in unnatural dusk ran dark with movement, secretive or terrified; not a tree, brushed pale by wind from the flames, not a cabin pressed in despair to the bosom of night, not a gate too starkly visible but had its place in the design of order and panic. At Danielstown, half way up the avenue under the beeches, the thin iron gate twanged (missed its latch, remained swinging aghast) as the last unlit car slid out with the executioners bland from accomplished duty. The sound of the last car widened, gave itself to the open and empty country and was demolished. Then the first wave of a silence that was to be ultimate flowed back confidently to the steps. The door stood open hospitably upon a furnace.

Sir Richard and Lady Naylor, not saying anything, did not look at each other, for in the light from the sky they saw too distinctly.

SEAN O'FAOLAIN

'A Dead Cert'

Whenever Jenny Rosse came up to Dublin, for a shopping spree, or a couple of days with the Ward Union Hunt, or to go to the Opera, or to visit some of her widespread brood of relations in or around the city, or to do anything at all just to break the monotony of what she would then mockingly call 'my life in the provinces', the one person she never failed to ring was Oweny Flynn; and no matter how busy Oweny was in the courts or in his law chambers he would drop everything to have a lunch or a dinner with her. They had been close friends ever since he and Billy Rosse – both of them then at the King's Inns – had met her together twelve or thirteen years ago after a yacht race at the Royal Saint George. Indeed, they used to be such a close trio that, before she finally married Billy and buried herself in Cork, their friends were always laying bets on which of the two she would choose, and the most popular version of what happened in the end was that she let them draw cards for her. 'The first man,' she had cried gaily, 'to draw the ace of hearts!' According to this account the last card in the pack was Billy's, and before he turned it she fainted. As she was far from being a fainter, this caused a great deal of wicked speculation about which man she had always realized she wanted. On the other hand, one of her rivals said that she had faked the whole thing to get him.

This Saturday afternoon in October she and Oweny had finished a long, gossipy lunch at the Shelbourne, where she always stayed whenever she came up to Dublin. ('I hate to be tied to my blooming relatives!') They were sipping their coffee and brandy in two deep saddleback armchairs, the old flowery chintzy kind that the Shelbourne always provides. The lounge was empty and, as always after wine, Oweny had begun to flirt mildly with her, going back over the old days, telling her, to her evident satisfaction, how lonely it is to be a bachelor of thirty-seven ('My life trickling away into the shadows of memory!'), and what a fool he had been to let such a marvellous lump of a girl slip through his fingers, when, all of a sudden, she leaned forward and tapped the back of his hand like a dog pawing for still more attention.

'Oweny!' she said. 'I sometimes wish my husband would die for a week.'

For a second he stared at her in astonishment. Then, in a brotherly kind of voice, he said, 'Jenny! I hope there's nothing wrong between you and Billy?'

She tossed her red head at the very idea.

'I'm as much in love with Billy as ever I was! Billy is the perfect husband. I wouldn't change him for worlds.'

'So I should have hoped,' Oweny said, dutifully, if a bit stuffily. 'I mean, of all the women in the world you must be one of the luckiest and happiest that ever lived. Married to a successful barrister. Two splendid children. How old is Peter now? Eight? And Anna must be ten. There's one girl who is going to be a breaker of men's hearts and an engine of delight. Like,' he added, remembering his role, 'her beautiful mother. And you have that lovely house at Silversprings. With that marvellous view down the Lee . . .'

'You can't live on scenery!' she interposed tartly. 'And there's a wind on that river that'd cool a tomcat!'

'A car of your own. A nanny for the kids. Holidays abroad every year. No troubles or trials that I ever heard of. And,' again remembering his duty, 'if I may say so, every time we meet, you look younger, and,' he plunged daringly, 'more desirable than ever. So, for God's sake, Jenny Rosse, what the hell on earth are you talking about?'

She turned her head to look out pensively at the yellowing sun glittering above the last, trembling, fretted leaves of the trees in the Green, while he gravely watched her, admiring the way its light brought out the copper-gold of her hair, licked the flat tip of her cocked nose and shone on her freckled redhead's cheek that had always reminded him of peaches and cream, and 'No,' he thought, 'not a pretty woman, not pretty-pretty, anyway I never did care for that kind of prettiness, she is too strong for that, too much vigour, I'm sure she has poor old Billy bossed out of his life!' And he remembered how she used to sail her water-wag closer to the wind than any fellow in the yacht club, and how she used to curse like a trooper if she slammed one into the net, always hating to lose a game, especially to any man, until it might have been only last night that he had felt that aching hole in his belly when he knew that he had lost her forever. She turned her head to him and smiled wickedly.

'Yes,' she half agreed. 'Everything you say is true but . . .'

'But what?' he asked curiously, and sank back into the trough of his armchair to receive her reply.

Her smile vanished.

'Oweny! You know exactly how old I am. I had my thirty-fourth birthday party last week. By the way, I was very cross with you that you didn't come down for it. It was a marvellous party. All Cork was at it. I felt like the Queen of Sheba. It went on until about three in the morning. I enjoyed every single minute of it. But the next day, I got the shock of my life! I was sitting at my dressing table brushing my hair.' She stopped dramatically, and pointed her finger tragically at him as if his face were her mirror. 'When I looked out the window at a big red grain boat steaming slowly down the river, out to sea. I stopped brushing, I looked at myself, and there and then I said, "Jenny Rosse! You are in your thirty-fifth year. And you've never had a lover!" And I realized that I never could have a lover, not without hurting Billy, unless he obliged me by dying for a week.'

For fully five seconds Oweny laughed and laughed.

'Wait,' he choked, 'until the lads at the Club hear this one!'

The next second he was sitting straight up in his armchair.

'Jenny,' he said stiffly, 'would you mind telling me why exactly you chose to tell this to *me*?'

'Aren't you interested?' she asked innocently.

'Isn't it just a tiny little bit unfair?'

'But Billy would never know he'd been dead for a week. At most he'd just think he'd lost his memory or something. Don't you suppose that's what Lazarus thought? Oh! I see what you mean. Well, I suppose yes, I'd have betrayed Billy. That's true enough, isn't it?'

'I am not thinking of your good husband. I am thinking of the other unfortunate fellow when his week would be out!'

'What other fellow? Are you trying to suggest that I've been up to something underhand?'

'I mean,' he pressed on, quite angry now, 'that I refuse to believe that you are mentally incapable of realizing that if you ever did let any other man fall in love with you for even five minutes, not to speak of a whole week, you would be sentencing him to utter misery for the rest of his life.'

'Oh, come off it!' she huffed. 'You always did take things in high C. Why are you so bloody romantic? It was just an idea. I expect lots of women have it, only they don't admit it. One little, measly wild oat? It's probably something I should have done before I got married, but,' she grinned happily, 'I was too busy then having a good time. "In the morning sow thy seed and in the evening withhold not thine hand." Ecclesiastes. I learned that at Alexandra College. Shows you how innocent I was – I never knew what it really meant until I got married. Of course, you men are different. You think of nothing else.'

He winced.

'If you mean me,' he said sourly, 'you know damned well that I never wanted any woman but you.'

When she laid her hand on his he understood why she had said that about Billy dying for a week. But when he snatched his hand away and she gathered up her gloves with all the airs of a woman at the end of her patience with a muff, got up, and strode ahead of him to the levelling sun outside the hotel, he began to wonder if he really had understood. He even began to wonder if it was merely that he had upset her with all that silly talk about old times. A side-glance caught a look in her eyes that was much more mocking than hurt and at once his anger returned. She had been doing much more than flirting. She had been provoking him. Or had she just wanted to challenge him? Whatever she was doing she had manoeuvred him into a ridiculous position. Then he thought, 'She will drive to Cork tonight and I will never be certain what she really meant.' While he boggled she started talking brightly about her holiday plans for the winter. A cover-up? She said she was going to Gstaad for the skiing next month with a couple of Cork friends.

'Billy doesn't ski, so he won't come. We need another man. Would you like to join us? They are nice people. Jim Chandler and his wife. About our age. You'd enjoy them.'

He said huffily that he was too damned busy. And she might not know it but some people in the world have to earn their living. Anyway, he was saving up for two weeks' sailing in the North Sea in June. At which he saw that he had now genuinely hurt her. ('Dammit, if we really were lovers this would be our first quarrel!') He forced a smile.

'Is this goodbye, Jenny? You did say at lunch that you were going to drive home this evening? Shan't I see you again?'

She looked calculatingly at the sun winking coldly behind the far leaves.

'I hate going home – I mean so soon. And I hate driving alone in the dark. I think I'll just go to bed after dinner and get up bright and early on Sunday morning before the traffic. I'll be back at Silversprings in time for lunch.'

'If you are doing nothing tonight why don't you let me take you to dinner at the Yacht Club?'

She hesitated. Cogitating the long road home? Or what?

'Jenny! They'd all love to see you. It will be like old times. You remember the Saturday night crowds?'

She spoke without enthusiasm.

'So be it. Let's do that.'

She presented her freckled cheek for his parting kiss. In frank admiration he watched her buttocks swaying provocatively around the corner of Kildare Street.

Several times during the afternoon, back in his office, he found himself straying from his work to her equivocal words. Could there, after all, be something wrong between herself and Billy? Could she be growing tired of him? It could happen, and easily. A decent chap, fair enough company, silent, a bit slow, not brilliant even at his own job, successful only because of his father's name and connections, never any good at all at sport – he could easily see her flying down the run from the Egli at half a mile a minute, the snow leaping from her skis whenever she did a quick turn. But not Billy. He would be down in the valley paddling around like a duck among the beginners behind the railway – and he remembered what a hopeless sheep he had always been with the girls, who nevertheless seemed to flock around him all the time, perhaps (it was the only explanation he ever found for it) because he was the fumbling sort of fellow that awakens the maternal instinct in girls. At which he saw her not as a girl in white shorts dashing to and fro on the tennis courts, but as the mature woman who had turned his face into her mirror by crying at him along her pointing finger, 'You are in your thirty-fifth year!' How agile, he wondered, would she now be on the courts or the ski runs? He rose and stood for a long time by his window, glaring down at the Saturday evening blankness of Nassau Street, and heard the shouting from the playing fields of Trinity College, and watched the small lights of the buses moving through the bluing dusk, until he shivered at the cold creeping through the pane. He felt the tilt of time and the falling years, and in excitement understood her sudden lust.

As always on Saturday nights, once the autumn comes and the sailing is finished and every boat on the hard for another winter, the lounge and the bar of the Club were a cascade of noise. If he had been alone he would have at once added his bubble of chatter to it. Instead he was content to stand beside the finest woman in the crowd, watching her smiling proudly around her, awaiting attention from her rout (What was that great line? *Diana's foresters, gentlemen of the shade, minions of the moon?*) until, suddenly, alerted and disturbed, he found her eyes turning from the inattentive mob to look out broodily through the tall windows. The lighthouse on the pier's end was writing slow circles on the dusty water of the harbour. He said, 'Jenny, you are not listening to me!' She whispered crossly, 'But I don't know a single one of these bloody people!' He pointed out the commodore. Surely she remembered Tom O'Leary? She peered and said, 'Not *that* old man?' He said, 'How could you have forgotten?'

Tom had not forgotten her, as he found when he went to the bar to refresh their drinks.

'Isn't that Jenny Rosse you have there?' he asked Oweny. 'She's putting on weight, bedad! Ah, she did well for herself.'

'How do you mean?' Oweny asked, a bit shortly.

'Come off it. Didn't she marry one of the finest practices in Cork! Handsome is as handsome does, my boy! She backed a dead cert.'

Jealous old bastard! As he handed her the glass he glanced covertly at her beam. Getting a bit broad, alright. She asked idly, 'Who is that slim girl in blue, she is as brown as if she has been sailing all summer?' He looked and shrugged.

'One of the young set? I think she's George Whitaker's daughter.'

'That nice-looking chap in the black tie looks lost. Just the way Billy used always to look. Who is he?'

'Saturday nights!' he said impatiently. 'You know the way they bring the whole family. It gives the wives a rest from the cooking.'

It was a relief to lead her into the dining room and find her mood change like the wind to complete gaiety.

'So this,' she laughed, 'is where it all began. And look! The same old paintings. They haven't changed a thing.'

The wine helped, and they were safely islanded in their corner, even with the families baying cheerfully at one another from table to table, even though she got on his nerves by dawdling so long over the coffee that the maids had cleared every table but theirs. Then she revealed another change of mood.

'Oweny! Please let's go somewhere else for our nightcap.'

'But where?' he said irritably. 'Not in some scruffy pub?'

'Your flat?' she suggested, and desire spread in him like a water lily. It shrivelled when she stepped out ahead of him into the cold night air, looked up at the three-quarter moon, then at the Town Hall clock.

'What a stunning night! Oweny, I've changed my mind! Just give me a good strong coffee and I'll drive home right away.'

'So!' he said miserably. 'We squabbled at lunch. And our dinner was a flop.'

She protested that it had been a marvellous dinner; and wasn't it grand the way nothing had been changed?

'They even still have that old picture of the Duke of Windsor when he was a boy in the navy.'

He gave up. He had lost the set. All the way into town they spoke only once.

'We had good times,' she said. 'I could do it all over again.'

'And change nothing?' he growled.

Her answer was pleasing, but inconclusive—'Who knows?'

If only he could have her in the witness box, under oath, for fifteen minutes!

In his kitchenette, helping him to make the coffee, she changed gear again, so full of good spirits (because, he understood sourly, she was about to take off for home) that he thrust an arm about her waist, assaulted her cheek with a kiss as loud as a champagne cork, and said fervently (he had nothing to lose now), 'And I thinking how marvellous it would be if we could be in bed together all night!' She laughed mockingly, handed him the coffee pot – a woman long accustomed to the grappling hook – and led the way with the cups back into his living room. They sat on the small sofa before his coffee table.

'And I'll tell you another thing, Jenny!' he said. 'If I had this flat twelve years ago it might very easily have happened that you would have become my one true love! You would have changed my whole life!'

She let her head loll back on the carved moulding of the sofa, looking past him at the moon. Quickly he kissed her mouth. Unstirring she looked back into his eyes, whispered, 'I should not have let you do that,' returned her eyes to the moon, and whispered, 'Or should I?'

'Jenny!' he ordered. 'Close your eyes. Pretend you really are back twelve years ago.'

Her eyelids sank. He kissed her again, softly, wetly, felt her hand creep to his shoulder and impress his kiss, felt her lips open. Her hand fell weakly away. Desire climbed into his throat. And then he heard her moan the disenchanting name. He drew back, rose, and looked furiously down at her. She opened her eyes, stared uncomprehendingly around her, and looked up at him in startled recognition.

'So,' he said bitterly, 'he did not die even for one minute?'

She laughed wryly, lightly, stoically, a woman who would never take anything in a high key, except a five-barred gate or a double-ditch.

'I'm sorry, Oweny. It's always the same. Whenever I dream of having a lover I find myself at the last moment in my husband's arms.'

She jumped up, snatched her coat, and turned on him.

'Why the hell, Oweny, for God's sake, don't you go away and get married?'

'To have me dreaming about you, is that what you want?'

'I want to put us both out of pain!'

They glared hatefully at one another.

'Please drive me to the Shelbourne. If I don't get on the road right away, I'll go right out of the top of my head!'

They drove to the Green, she got out, slammed the car door behind her and without a word raced into the hotel. He whirled, drove hell for leather back to the Club, killed the end of the night with the last few gossipers, drank far too much and lay awake for hours staring sideways from his pillow over the grey, frosting roofs and countless yellow chimney pots of Dublin.

Past twelve. In her yellow sports Triumph she would tear across the Curragh at seventy-five and along the two straight stretches before and after Monasterevan. By now she has long since passed through Port Laoise and Abbeyleix where only a few lighted upper-storey windows still resist night and sleep. From that on, for hour after hour, south and south, every village street and small town she passes will be fast asleep, every roadside cottage, every hedge, field and tree, and the whole widespread, moonblanched country pouring past her headlights until she herself gradually becomes hedge, tree, field, and fleeting moon. Arched branches underlit, broken demesne walls, a closed garage, hedges flying, a grey church, a lifeless gate-lodge, until the black rock and ruin of Cashel comes slowly wheeling about the moon. A streetlamp falling on a blank window makes it still more blank. Cars parked beside a kerb huddle from the cold. In Cahir the boarded windows of the old granaries are blind with age. The dull square is empty. Her wheeling lights catch the vacant eyes of the hotel, leap the useless bridge, fleck the side of the Norman castle. She is doing eighty on the level uplands under the Galtee mountains, heedless of the sleep-wrapt plain falling for miles and miles away to her left.

Why is she stopping? To rest, to look, to light a cigarette, to listen? He can see nothing for her to see but a scatter of farmhouses on the plain; nothing to hear but one sleepless dog as far away as the moon it bays. He lights his bedside lamp. Turned half past two. He puts out his light and there are her kangaroo lights, leaping, climbing, dropping, winding, slowing now because of the twisting strain on her arms. She does not see the sleeping streets of Fermoy; only the white signpost marking the remaining miles to Cork. Her red taillights disappear and reappear before him every time she winds and unwinds down to the sleeping estuary of the Lee, even at low tide not so much a river as a lough – grey, turbulent and empty. He tears after her as she rolls smoothly westward beside its shining slobland. Before them the bruised clouds hang low over the city silently awaiting the morning.

She brakes to turn in between her white gates, her wheels spit back the gravel, she zooms upward to her house and halts under its staring windows. She switches off the engine, struggles out, stretches her arms high above her head with a long, shivering, happy, outpouring groan, and then, breathing back a long breath, she holds her breasts up to her windows. There is not a sound but the metal of her engine creaking as it cools, and the small wind whispering up from the river. She laughs to see their cat flow like black water around the corner of the house. She leans into the car, blows three long, triumphant horn blasts, and before two windows can light up over her head she has disappeared indoors as smoothly as her cat. And that, at last, it is the end of sleep, where, behind windows gone dark again, she spreads herself under her one true lover.

Neither of them hear the morning seagulls over the Liffey or the Lee. He wakes unrefreshed to the sounds of late church bells. She half opens her eyes to the flickering light of the river on her ceiling, rolls over on her belly, and stretching out her legs behind her like a satisfied cat, she dozes off again. He stares for a long time at his ceiling, hardly hearing the noise of the buses going by.

It is cold. His mind is clear and cold. I know now what she wants. But does she? Let her lie. She called me a romantic and she has her own fantasy. She has what she wanted, wants what she cannot have, is not satisfied with what she has got. I have known her for over twelve years and never known her at all. The most adorable woman I ever met. And a common slut! If she had married me I suppose she would be dreaming now of him? Who was it said faithful women are always regretting their own fidelity, never their husbands'? Die for a week? He chuckled at her joke. Joke? Or gamble? Or a dead cert? If I could make him die for a week it would be a hell of a long week for her. Will I write to her? I could telephone.

Hello, Jenny! It's me. I just wanted to be sure you got back safely the other night. Why wouldn't I worry? About anyone as dear and precious as you? Those frosty roads. Of course it was, darling, a lovely meeting. And we must do it again. No, nothing changes! That's a dead cert. Oh, and Jenny! I nearly forgot. About that skiing bit next month in Gstaad. Can I change my mind? I'd love to join you. May I? Splendid! Oh, no! Not for that long. Say . . . just for a week?

He could see her hanging up the receiver very slowly.

SEOSAMH MAC GRIANNA

'On the Empty Shore'

It was cold on the barren ridge, for it was within three weeks of All-Hallowtide. The air was cold, and the grey crags and the potato field under the lee of the hill were cold. And Cathal O Canann was cold as he traversed the field, hoking here and there. Cold, hungry, ragged, his old clothes torn and patched, hung in tatters around his big bare bones. It was an avid search he was making, like the wild ravenous search of an animal, and in spite of that, his every movement was sluggish. A long long time he spent from ridge to ridge, before he reckoned that he had what he needed, and that was not much, if he was satisfied with the dozen small potatoes that he had gathered in his cap, not one of which was as big as a hen's egg.

He went over to the house, a low cabin with weeds shooting from the thatch, and the walls green and damp from time. You would have known from the appearance of the house, and from the scum on the pools sleeping around the threshold that the day had departed when those walls had sheltered a joyous laughter-filled family. Bending down under the lintel Cathal went in – into the gloom, for there was only one window in the house, scarcely big enough to allow a human head to protrude from it. There was a bed in the corner, and the darkness thicker on it, because it was closed in with boards at the top and sides, and an unpractised eye would have looked at it twice before noticing that it held someone. A lank body lay under a red quilt, and a grey unkempt head and beard rested motionless on the pillow. Cathal stood over the figure in the bed.

'Art,' said he.

Art did not speak, and when Cathal laid his hand on him, he found out that the thought, the fear which had gripped his heart, was realized. Art was as cold as a rock.

Cathal went over, and hunkered down on a stool beneath the window. He put his elbows on his knees, his palm to his chin, and he sat there looking at the body. No tear came from him, no sob to his throat. He felt himself a little colder, a little emptier than before, and his heart a little sorer in his breast. If he and the man that was gone had ever spent a while happily in each other's company, he had forgotten it. He did not recall any of the old man's peculiar ways, his laugh, or the sound of his voice, or any word he had said, or any deed he had done, such as a friend would like to recall, the little remembrances which sadden the one that is left. He did not think of saying a prayer for the soul which had just torn itself painfully out of that wasted body. He had forgotten God, for it seemed that God had forgotten him a long time ago, ever since the blight came on the potatoes, since the beginning of the bad times. He sat there bruised in sorrow. His soul inside him was like a dark pool, which no stream entered or left, but lay there in a numbing stillness, under a sour coat of slime.

A noise was made on the old table by the wall. He started up, and he saw a noggin that had a trace of yellow stirabout in it lying on its side on the floor. He just got a glimpse of a dog fleeing across the house, a shaggy tawny animal, with its two sides hanging together.

Loneliness came on him now, the loneliness that comes on one who has a corpse in the house, the shiver of cold that comes from death, and makes people gather to wake the departed. But the time for wakes was no more. For as life was hardening, people were becoming distant with one another. In happy times people rejoice in their neighbours. In evil times they keep to themselves, and huckster up all their strength to fight the world. And of late people were dying in hundreds, melting away with hunger, falling to the fever. Some of them were getting Christian burial, some of them were lying in heaps in unhallowed clay. Cathal looked over at the green hillock on the far side of the river. There was a mound in the middle of it, and grass beginning to sprout from it. There the last three who had died in the place had been buried, White Michael's family. People had come west from the Great Height, and had thrown them down in a hurry. The cruel earth had no pity for them, that sterile, barren earth that was fated not to yield another crop until it had been manured throughout Ireland with human flesh and blood.

Cathal got a piece of rope, raised the corpse from the bed, and attached two loops to it, like the suspenders on a creel. When he was crossing the floor a lonesome cricket began to sing in some dark crevice, far back in the wall by the side of the hob.

Middle-aged labourers are heavy of heart, and heavy of step under a burden. Cathal was middle-aged, he was hungry, and he was carrying his own fate on his back, as he went up the speckled uneven rise that led to the old highway. Stagnant pools and boulders lay in his path, and it was with wet feet that he staggered to the road. It was an old twisted road with its banks rising high over the fields. In the ditch a ragged spindle-shanked boy was devouring a potato. When he saw Cathal approaching he made off in the direction of his parents' cabin. Cathal rested his back against the bank of the road, and paused. Away from him stretched the Barren Ridge, exposed to the north west wind, and lying behind it as far as the eye could see was a bleak moor. A long time he might have remained gazing at the land and the horizon, but that the work he had to do roused him.

He met no one for half a mile, until he turned down the road of the Big Hollow. In the hollow there was a man with a donkey carrying panniers, and they both gazed at him. The man with the donkey did not speak. Cathal trudged on slowly, growing smaller on the road, and the murmur of the stream that was between him and the end of his journey growing clearer.

He covered the first mile. As he came to the top of the Speckled Rise, a long cold headland extended before him, dotted with mean cabins near to him, but with no human habitation down on its point, there only the low shore, and a hem of white foam around it. He had to go the margin of that shore. Whilst he was in the hollow, he was sheltered from the wind, but when he mounted the height a cold blast blew on him. He felt it in a flood on his skin under his rags. Another rest was necessary when he had gained the top of the hill. He gave his back to the wind, and leaned against a rock, the cold corpse serving him for a shield against the sky.

At the crossroads he turned at the right hand. It was the longer way, but soup was being distributed at the Cairn. A drop would keep the life in him for another day. He was getting weak. Beads of sweat were breaking out on his skin, and he was feeling very empty inside. But he saw a vessel of soup, and a healthy steam and smell rising out of it that sent a flow of pleasure through his whole body. He quickened his step.

There was a throng of people at the Cairn. There was a cauldron at the side of the big house, and the attendants had just prepared the soup. A crowd had gathered around the cauldron, both young and old, spare hungry people, struggling and jostling, making for the food. The pity the strong once had for the weak had vanished. Men were brushing aside women and children.

Cathal went in among them, with the corpse on his back. No one took any notice of him. There were three or four backs swaying between him and the cauldron. He saw five or six hands crossing one another inside its mouth, vessels being struck against one another, and being spilt. A gaunt dark woman with fiery eyes lost her saucepan in the soup.

'My seven curses on you, thieving Caitriona!'

She made a lunge at the other woman. Cathal moved into her place, and reached his noggin in over the rim of the cauldron. Just then someone caught hold of the corpse on his back, and he was pulled out roughly from the crowd. He reeled five or six steps, and fell. He gathered himself up, and looked at the man that had jerked him out. He was a big heavy man with a brutish face. 'If you don't stay out, I'll stuff that corpse down into the cauldron,' he said.

'Take care your own turn doesn't come, Connor,' replied Cathal, and he went off.

More deeply crushed, more painful, weaker, he walked on. The world was blacker than ever. The cold was keener. He made for the point of the headland, and when he reached the last house, he went in.

'The blessing of God on us,' said a weak voice from the bed.

'Are you down too Michael?' asked Cathal.

'Cathal O Canann, is it you that is there? You have a sorrowful burden with you, man, a sorrowful burden!'

'Yes, indeed! I came in for the loan of a spade.'

'You'll find it at the gable, friend. A sorrowful burden – a sorrowful burden!'

Cathal went down to the graveyard on the sandy lawn. It was an old graveyard with the bones of ten generations lying in it, raked by the tempest. Tombstones in it were few, but there were many wooden crosses in it, most of them broken. And there were many mounds in it, that had no crosses at all, where the people who had died since the famine came had been thrown down in a hurry. Cathal searched for the corner where his father's cross stood, half-broken, with its head in the sand. He set to work, and dug a yard deep. He had not the courage to go down further. He took up the corpse that was like a bit of a stick, and laid it in the grave. It was very hard to throw a spadeful of sand on an uncovered corpse. It was hard to put the clay over that face, into the nostrils, through the beard. It was like killing someone. Slowly the trunk went out of sight. For a time the knees, which were drawn up a little, were visible above the sand, and the beard kept sticking up. It disappeared. The grave was filled, until it was a little mound like the other graves around it.

Cathal cast the spade from him, and flung himself down on the grave, with his two arms bent under his face, his body fixed to the ground in his agony.

A white seagull sailed on its wings above his head, crying and crying piteously. The sun came out from behind a cloud, and spread a weak watery light, that was like the spirit of fire and the spirit of frost commingled. It spread around over the covering of the dead, over fields of undug potatoes, over roads that were lonely, over houses where silence reigned.

Translated by Séamus Ó Néill

FRANCIS STUART

from *Black List, Section H*

58

After the second or third time with Halka it was as if they'd been lovemaking for years. She came in the late afternoons, between leaving the university and going to the Rundfunk, and as soon as they'd embraced, she took off her shoes and when he turned from locking the door was already stretched on the couch with her dress pulled up, delighting him by thus displaying the same impatience as his own.

Afterward they stayed on the couch while the water boiled on the much-patched electric ring in the corner for the black-market coffee H bought from Olga Mihailovich, and he read to her some of Keats's poems; raptly she listens, he reflected, his thoughts echoing the cadence of what he'd been reading out. Before she had to leave they made love again.

The first lovemaking in the afternoon involved the transition from the non-sexual world in which both had been caught up, but the second or third time they started from inside their sensual consciousness and, not having far to go, could take their time, savouring the eternal strangeness of the act.

In the hushed aftermath, where for a little while nothing is as it was before and objects are not quite set in their pre-orgasm outlines after their obscuration in the general physical melting, she took the used contraceptive and dangling it by the neck gave it one of her dark-eyed scrutinies before returning it to him to dispose of.

At the start of the winter semester, Olga Mihailovich glided in one evening and, with her ambiguous smile, offered him a piece of gold made up in a thick, crude-looking ring for one and a half thousand marks. The sum, large as it was, he could just afford to pay. And the next day, after withdrawing the amount from the American Express, as he counted the notes into her plump white hands, she suggested he might like a smaller room, the one next door that the young man whom Dominique's crying had disturbed had previously occupied.

Though the move was only a matter of a couple of yards, it was part of more subtle changes. It marked the end of his and Halka's honeymoon. There was no lessening of sexual intensity but, on recovering from the sensual trances, she began to take a closer look at him and what concerned him. She became jealous over some of the girls in his classes, 'brazen little witches', of Susan when she'd come around to fetch the rest of her things, 'what right has she to call you "darling"?' or of his not having told her something she considered important.

She sulked for a day or so, removed her few belongings, as well as a photo she'd given him, and only came around the second or third evening, white-faced and shadowy-browed. Then the wounds were healed in a bout of lovemaking which reached a delirious pitch in the ratio to the degree and duration of their estrangement.

A week or two after one such reconciliation she told him at the last minute of one of her visits when, having got into her overcoat, she'd turned to the wardrobe mirror, that she thought she was pregnant.

Lightheartedly, to reassure her, and hide his shock, H, from behind, laid his hand on her belly and boldly assured her, 'There's nothing there.' His touch excited them all the more for being made without sensual intent. He drew her back onto the couch and, still in her overcoat, made love to her over again.

As well as the physical contact, there was his reading aloud to her, mainly from Keats. Her enjoyment of this too was instinctive – she didn't always understand the poems – but he saw it as a bond of a different kind without which their relationship would have been even more precarious.

Though he didn't care for the overblown diction of many of the poems, what still fascinated H in Keats was his very personal sort of insights. Like himself, Keats was aware of intellectual limitations, which in H's case amounted to certain blind spots.

> What though I am not wealthy in the dower
> Of spanning wisdom, though I do not know
> The shiftings of the mighty winds that blow
> Hither and thither all the changing thoughts
> Of man, though no great ministering reason sorts

Out the dark mysteries of human souls
To clear conceiving; yet there ever rolls
A vast idea before me, and I glean
Therefrom my liberty: thence too I've seen
The end and aim of Poesy.

One Sunday Halka invited him home to lunch with her mother and sister. Because of what he'd heard of Frau Witebsk's strict Catholicism and of the rules she laid down for the girls for their meetings with men, H was doubtful about accepting.

'What will she think of you having a married admirer?'

'She won't think anything.'

'She's angry if you come home half an hour later than usual.'

'She's suspicious of soldiers and the sort of men she thinks Lise and I might pick up in cafés. She'll believe anything I tell her about what she imagines as the wonderful world of writers and university lecturers.'

None of this put H at ease. But when he arrived at the rather dark ground-floor flat he saw that Frau Witebsk wouldn't overawe him as his mother-in-law had. She was a small, prematurely white-haired woman in whom he noticed hints of Halka's innocence and passion.

All went well and H was touched by Frau Witebsk's apparent liking for, and even trust in, him. Halka's sister had evidently troubles enough of her own and kept silent most of the time. He came away wishing, for the first time seriously, that he wasn't married. Not for Halka's sake, though later they were to regret it because of the added dangers the lack of official sanction for being together exposed them to, but so that Frau Witebsk, dressed in her Sunday black, could go to church and see the priest pronounce the hallowed words over them that would efface some of the anxieties that marked her forehead and drew her mouth tight.

Suddenly the warring world intruded into the hidden life that H was living, not yet in the way of air raids or much reduced rations but involving him more closely. In answer to a phone call he went to see Dr Zimmermann who told him about a plan to broadcast to Ireland and asked him to contribute a weekly talk.

H guessed that the Herr Doktor, or his superiors, was afraid that America's entry into the conflict would influence Ireland to abandon her neutrality, though this seemed to H a very slight threat in the light of the powerful forces the Germans had managed to line up against them.

H returned to his room, aware that he wasn't going to refuse. For one thing, when he'd agreed to write talks soon after coming here he'd made the crucial decision even if he hadn't delivered them himself. In any case, what he told the professor in his study at Bad Godesberg before the war was his only criterion for deciding how far to go in his dissent.

Would it have been better to have had nothing to do with them now that he was here? Probably; but not simply in order to escape a formal guilt. He saw guilt in relation to the writer not so much as an involvement with malefactors as a sharing in universal attitudes for the sake of easing imagination's lonely ache. And it was not a question of how far these could be morally justified. Better the infected sovereign psyche than one that shared in a general righteousness that didn't belong to it.

59

What was he to say in these talks? And who would listen? Iseult and his mother-in-law? Molly's uncles? The Deasey brothers? Some of his former jailmates? He could condemn such Allied atrocities as he'd heard of – the indiscriminate bombing was only just beginning – but that would involve him in the same deception as the propagandists who presented the war as a moral conflict.

The harshest judgment passed on him would not be entirely undeserved even though he didn't accept the jurisdiction of the court. Could he express his belief that the only possible good that could now arise out of it was if it ended by bringing the whole structure, ideological, cultural, moral, crashing down about the heads of whoever was left with whole ones? Hardly.

Extract from H's wartime diary on a date in early 1942: 'An alert this afternoon as I was sitting reading at the window. So far the raids have been confined mostly to the city outskirts though a few incendiaries have dropped around the town, not yet on the block where I had the flat, unfortunately, which, if burnt out before the owners return would preclude trouble over the business of the china cabinet.

'After a few minutes saw what I took to be a solitary Russian plane flying slowly from the east and shining softly in the frosty light (a tiny silver cross horizontal against the pale sky and fringed around by ghostly pink and white rosettes). Watched it for five minutes or more till it turned south and slowly disappeared. Had it not been for Halka would have longed to be in it on its long, long homeward flight.'

H didn't want to end the war among the victors whoever they turned out to be. Russia in defeat would be infinitely preferable to a triumphant Nazi Germany, which still seemed a possible outcome.

From the radio on the folding table with the green baize top came, between the popular songs (Lala Anderson's lilting 'Lili Marlene', Zarah Leander's throaty sex moanings), the announcements of the defeat of Russian armies, at Bryansk and Taganrog, by the Don and Donetz. Other news came slipped under the door in the form of an occasional letter from home, with Iseult writing as if, for her, time had stood still, or even reversed itself to the days before their estrangement, his mother weaving a web of small local placidities, Kay with dutiful notes from the mould of the convent school to which she'd been sent, shy, clumsy ones from Ian, and Aunt Jenny's, which were the sharpest evocations of the past.

Along the hallway in late afternoon came the quick tap of Halka's wooden soles – he'd given her a duplicate key to the outside door – and, a scarf wound into a turban over her head and ears, her thin coat, into which her mother had sewn a rabbit-fur lining, smelling of icy winds, she'd appear in the warm room, where only a table lamp was burning.

To the excitement of her wintry apparition in the small haven, she added, while she undressed, odds and ends of her own news: increasing trouble between her sister and mother, a remark of her English professor about Blake that she wanted elucidated later, the welcome return of her period, the announcement of a gift for H in the way of a half-sheet of the ration coupons issued to soldiers on leave that her sister had got from her sergeant.

One night a week H went to the Rundfunkhaus with Halka and was directed to one of the soundproof cubicles where they sat before a microphone and waited for the red light to come on. Then she announced him and he read the talk from the script. Sometimes somebody from the Irische Redaktion came and listened, but they were mostly alone, and he doubted whether Dr Zimmermann or anybody else monitored what he said.

The talks were more difficult than he'd expected. He was supposed to be speaking to his own people, but who were they? He could try to stress the other reasons, beside material advantage, for Irish neutrality. One of these was that those who thought for themselves were free to come to certain conclusions about the war without feeling they were letting down their fellow countrymen who were taking the risks and doing the fighting.

They could question the Allied posture of moral grandeur, and in particular Churchill's, without giving comfort to the enemy. And they'd be able to dissociate themselves, in spirit, at least, from whoever proved the victors, and to forego participation in the celebrations ushering a peace that, not being the chastened kind born out of near-despair, would soon turn brash and complacent.

Dr Zimmermann asked H to come and see him and suggested he might not be laying enough stress on Hitler's war against communism – H had purposely never mentioned it – which, he said, must have much Irish support.

'Not from the sort of people I'm talking to,' H told him, 'some of them may be anti-British but none are anti-Russian.'

Dr Zimmermann said no more, though H saw he wasn't convinced but instead showed him a report from Dublin in an English magazine, *Picture Post*, saying that the Irish weren't impressed by the promises H was broadcasting from Germany.

'What promises?' H asked, though he knew there was no sense in resenting the paragraph.

'I thought you'd better see it,' Dr Zimmermann said. 'But don't let it worry you, you'll never have to give an account of yourself to these people.'

Zimmermann's other suggestion was that the talks should be given after ten o'clock when, he said, the Athlone station closed down, so that it couldn't be used as a guide to targets in Northern Ireland by German raiders, and H was glad for once to be able to agree.

On Saturdays he and Halka took the S-Bahn through suburbs of white stucco, red-and-green-roofed villas and neat lawns over which sprinklers were casting rainbow spray in the early morning sun and, further out, through sandy allotments with their wooden weekend shacks, screened by lilacs and silver birches, to several of which H imagined retiring with Halka. There they would live (on what?) far from the rest of the world and the war (was it over?) and, at the end of the hot day, after watering their beans and asparagus, lie on their couch by the frame window with the swallows darting and dipping against the clear, washed-out sky.

Not that he was taken in by this or other fantasies. The sight of the shacks behind their leafy screens – huts had always fascinated him – evoked a sensation of felicity that he couldn't resist enjoying for a few moments, but he knew it had little to do with what was in front of them. He also knew – but that was subconscious knowledge – that such a tranquil existence would be disastrous for them.

Iseult and the children were confidently waiting for him to return when the war was over. In an effort to make some sort of plan he told Halka that he'd bring her home with him and they'd all live together at Dineen.

'What about your wife? What would she say to that?'

'After the war a lot will be possible that wouldn't have been before.'

This might become true of those who would survive some of the worst horrors, but he knew that to imagine the post-war world as a place where fundamental changes would be general was an illusion.

Halka nodded – it was in the train on the way to the lakes that they first seriously discussed the future – and put her hand over his. 'I wouldn't mind as long as I could be with you. We'd go for walks alone together, wouldn't we?'

All was well, he needn't worry about what would happen if he survived the war; as long as he didn't ask himself how Iseult would take his going for walks with this girl, something he'd never done with her herself for years, or what it would feel like to be shut up in his room at night with Halka in the one downstairs that had been Miss Burnett's.

Once on the lake (Müggelsee or Sakrower See) the immediate sensations, of hot sun on his chest and arms, the plop of oar blades lifting leisurely and, finally, in a cove surrounded by rushes, her body, brown and crossed by the two paler sections usually hidden by her swim suit, stretched along the bottom of the boat that was gently rocking as he let himself down onto her, banished thought of the future. Late on these summer Saturday nights, back in his room from the Rundfunkhaus – her mother didn't know the exact hour of his broadcast – Halka still kept a scent of the hot tarry bottom of the boat where she'd lain sweaty and naked and, later, cool and smeared with sun lotion while they'd picnicked.

One of the passages Halka had him read to her and discuss was the letter in which Keats reflects on the purpose manifest in animals intent on their prey, and writes of the man who also 'hath a purpose and his eye is bright with it'. By 'purpose' Keats seemed to mean what H called obsession, and Keats's obsession with poetry enabled him in the end to give up his feverish desire for fame, for Fanny, even for 'a life of sensation', and live out his destined legend to his early and agonizing death.

H had his own 'vast ideas', even if he didn't mistake them as being of the same magnitude. And compared to them most of the news on which he commented in his talks were passing sensations soon overtaken by the next in the series.

Sometimes, by way of a change, he presented news items of his own. One of these was the recording of the deaths, in mysterious circumstances, of certain individualists embarrassing to the Allies: Cudahy, whom H had come across when he was American ambassador in Dublin and who, transferred to Brussels, had got himself into the news by welcoming the Germans there, had resigned, or been sacked, come to Berlin for an American paper, asked H to a drink at the Adlon and told him of an interview in which he'd warned Hitler not to continue to provoke Roosevelt by careless attacks on United States shipping, and had died suddenly in Switzerland shortly afterwards; a young

Englishman, whose name H had forgotten, who'd written a novel called *This Above All* that Kolbinsky had lent him, about the adventures of a soldier who'd deserted after Dunkirk, and had himself, as H had read in an old English newspaper in Zimmermann's office, been killed in a car accident in South America.

With the setting in of the long nights, the war loomed directly overhead out of the moonless sky and street after street crumbled into hillocks of white rubble that soon weathered into a gritty mud that sprouted weeds, between which paths were trodden and new landmarks appeared to replace the old: the floor of a room balanced between two solitary upright walls; a cellar that they passed on their way to the only restaurant in the neighbourhood still serving fish off the ration, gaping from under a pile of bricks from which came the stench of death and disinfectant. Then with the coming of another summer, women and girls, stocky and sallow-skinned, their hair bound in dusty scarfs, appeared from nowhere to shift the rubble. A colony of them, with their children and a few old men, lived in the only cluster of still standing but badly battered houses in the same street and, on the way back from the restaurant, passing them as they gathered in the warm dusk outside their dwellings – as formerly in their villages? – H imagined himself and Halka among these deserted Russians living in one of the rooms behind the boarded-up windows, fetching water from the hydrant down the street, cooking supper over a wood fire in the yard. In his fantasies they always hid, so that when the war ended they couldn't be found.

The constant disruption of the transport service and of the university schedules, the long queues outside shops and the delays everywhere, made it difficult for her mother to keep a close watch over Halka's comings and goings. So that when, on account of the air raids, Frau Witebsk went to stay with relations in East Prussia, it didn't, at least at first, cause any great change in their way of life except that sometimes when Halka came to his room from the Rundfunkhaus, instead of having to get up and dress again, she stayed the night.

One night H was having supper with her, her sister, and her sister's sergeant on night leave from his barracks, when a bomb burst a few yards away from the Witebsks' flat. The crockery jumped on the table, plaster showered down, the double-glass doors, long locked and stuffed with paper against draughts, flew open, the window panes broke behind the velvet curtains; this they only noted later. In the silence that was sucked back into the vacuum left by the roar they stood around the table on which Halka's birthday candle still burned – H didn't recall jumping up – waited a moment (for the house to cave in?) and then, not hurriedly but as if sleepwalking, made for the cellar, shepherded by the Feldwebel.

Those from other flats already sitting on benches hardly looked up as they entered, and H, once seated beside Halka, soon felt this reluctance to make any but the most circumspect movement as if the quiet between the explosions was too fragile to risk disturbing.

Here he was, her prophet, as she sometimes called him in the biblical terminology that came natural to her, and what could he say to her? It wasn't a matter of the death that comes from illness, old age, or even accident, in which the spirit is given a little time to make its retreat. It was destruction, utter and instantaneous, with no time for the psyche to sniff the oncoming of death and lay itself down in its own bed or whatever rags or straw it had gathered against that hour. This psyche, as the consciousness thought of itself, imagination's unique locale, its beautiful pattern of roots in the deoxyribonucleic acid, drawing up its 'vast ideas' from deep in the past, could it be annulled, reduced to a spot of slime on a collapsing wall?

Not that he felt any resentment against those who were doing the bombing. It was the apparent vulnerability of the nucleus at the core of the cosmic structure that appalled him.

Though apropos of the Allied bombing, an English airforce officer whom he met in a French transit camp after the war told him they hadn't been allowed to bomb the gas chambers in the concentration camps because the evidence of the enemy's guilt was far too valuable to destroy.

When the electric bulbs shining through the dust haze at the end of their cords had ceased to swing slowly, and the hunched shoulders began to straighten, the sweet tones of distant sirens (did they only sound faint after the explosion? or had the neighbouring ones been all destroyed?) gave the all clear.

Swiftly the sensations of living flowed back and before they were up the cellar stairs H was impelled by an urge to make love to Halka with the bodies that had been just restored to them. But wasn't this desire peculiar to his own kind of sexuality, that was stimulated by contrasts and incongruities, and something she wouldn't be likely to feel so soon after the shock of the raid? Better put it from his thoughts, be patient and let her come to herself in her own time.

With Lise and Kurt he was looking around for cracks in the walls and other signs of damage when he missed Halka who he thought had followed them into the living-room. Her sister said she was reheating the coffee that they'd been drinking with their interrupted meal, but he found her at the door of her room waiting.

'Come,' she said and beckoned him in.

FRANK O'CONNOR

'Guests of the Nation'

I

At dusk the big Englishman, Belcher, would shift his long legs out of the ashes and say, 'Well, chums, what about it?' and Noble and myself would say, 'All right, chum' (for we had picked up some of their curious expressions), and the little Englishman, Hawkins, would light the lamp and bring out the cards. Sometimes Jeremiah Donovan would come up and supervise the game, and get excited over Hawkins' cards, which he always played badly, and shout at him, as if he was one of our own, 'Ah, you divil, why didn't you play the tray?'

But ordinarily Jeremiah was a sober and contented poor devil like the big Englishman, Belcher, and was looked up to only because he was a fair hand at documents, though he was slow even with them. He wore a small cloth hat and big gaiters over his long pants, and you seldom saw him with his hands out of his pockets. He reddened when you talked to him, tilting from toe to heel and back, and looking down all the time at his big farmer's feet. Noble and myself used to make fun of his broad accent, because we were both from the town.

I could not at the time see the point of myself and Noble guarding Belcher and Hawkins at all, for it was my belief that you could have planted that pair down anywhere from this to Claregalway and they'd have taken root there like a native weed. I never in my short experience saw two men take to the country as they did.

They were passed on to us by the Second Battalion when the search for them became too hot, and Noble and myself, being young, took them over with a natural feeling of responsibility, but Hawkins made us look like fools when he showed that he knew the country better than we did.

'You're the bloke they call Bonaparte,' he says to me. 'Mary Brigid O'Connell told me to ask what you'd done with the pair of her brother's socks you borrowed.'

For it seemed, as they explained it, that the Second had little evenings, and some of the girls of the neighbourhood turned up, and, seeing they were such decent chaps, our fellows could not leave the two Englishmen out. Hawkins learned to dance 'The Walls of Limerick', 'The Siege of Ennis' and 'The Waves of Tory' as well as any of them, though he could not return the compliment, because our lads at that time did not dance foreign dances on principle.

So whatever privileges Belcher and Hawkins had with the Second they just took naturally with us, and after the first couple of days we gave up all pretence of keeping an eye on them. Not that they could have got far, because they had accents you could cut with a knife, and wore khaki tunics and overcoats with civilian pants and boots, but I believe myself they never had any idea of escaping and were quite content to be where they were.

It was a treat to see how Belcher got off with the old woman in the house where we were staying. She was a great warrant to scold, and cranky even with us, but before ever she had a chance of giving our guests, as I may call them, a lick of her tongue, Belcher had made her his friend for life. She was breaking sticks, and Belcher who had not been more than ten minutes in the house, jumped up and went over to her.

'Allow me, madam,' he said, smiling his queer little smile. 'Please allow me,' and he took the hatchet from her. She was too surprised to speak, and after that, Belcher would be at her heels, carrying a bucket, a basket or a load of turf. As Noble said, he got into looking before she leapt, and hot water, or any little thing she wanted, Belcher would have ready for her. For such a huge man (and though I am five foot ten myself I had to look up at him) he had an uncommon lack of speech. It took us a little while to get used to him, walking in and out like a ghost, without speaking. Especially because Hawkins talked enough for a platoon, it was strange to hear Belcher with his toes in the ashes come out with a solitary 'Excuse me, chum,' or 'That's right, chum.' His one and only passion was cards, and he was a remarkably good card player. He could have skinned myself and Noble, but whatever we lost to him, Hawkins lost to us, and Hawkins only played with the money Belcher gave him.

Hawkins lost to us because he had too much old gab, and we probably lost to Belcher for the same reason. Hawkins and Noble argued about religion into the early hours of the morning, and Hawkins worried the life out of Noble, who had a brother a priest, with a string of questions that would puzzle a cardinal. Even in treating of holy subjects, Hawkins had a deplorable tongue. I never met a man who could mix such a variety of cursing and bad language into any argument. He was a terrible man, and a fright to argue. He never did a stroke of work, and when he had no one else to argue with, he got stuck in the old woman.

He met his match in her, for when he tried to get her to complain profanely of the drought she gave him a great comedown by blaming it entirely on Jupiter Pluvius (a diety neither Hawkins nor I had ever heard of, though Noble said that among the pagans it was believed that he had something to do with the rain). Another day he was swearing at the capitalists for starting the German war when the old lady laid down her iron, puckered up her little crab's mouth and said: 'Mr Hawkins, you can say what you like about the war, and think you'll deceive me because I'm only a simple poor countrywoman, but I know what started the war. It was the Italian Count that stole the heathen divinity out of the temple of Japan. Believe me, Mr Hawkins, nothing but sorrow and want can follow people who disturb the hidden powers.'

A queer old girl, all right.

II

One evening we had our tea and Hawkins lit the lamp and we all sat into cards. Jeremiah Donovan came in too, and sat and watched us for a while, and it suddenly struck me that he had no great love for the two Englishmen. It came as a surprise to me because I had noticed nothing of it before.

Late in the evening a really terrible argument blew up between Hawkins and Noble about capitalists and priests and love of country.

'The capitalists pay the priests to tell you about the next world so that you won't notice what the bastards are up to in this,' said Hawkins.

'Nonsense, man!' said Noble, losing his temper. 'Before ever a capitalist was thought of people believed in the next world.'

Hawkins stood up as though he was preaching.

'Oh, they did, did they?' he said with a sneer. 'They believed all the things you believe – isn't that what you mean? And you believe God created Adam, and Adam created Shem, and Shem created Jehoshophat. You believe all that silly old fairytale about Eve and Eden and the apple. Well listen to me, chum! If you're entitled to a silly belief like that, I'm entitled to my own silly belief – which is that the first thing your God created was a bleeding capitalist, with morality and Rolls-Royce complete. Am I right, chum?' he says to Belcher.

'You're right, chum,' says Belcher with a smile, and he got up from the table to stretch his long legs into the fire and stroke his moustache. So, seeing that Jeremiah Donovan was going, and that there was no knowing when the argument about religion would be over, I went out with him. We strolled down to the village together, and then he stopped, blushing and mumbling, and said I should be behind, keeping guard. I didn't like the tone he took with me, and anyway I was bored with life in the cottage, so I replied by asking what the hell we wanted to guard them for at all.

He looked at me in surprise and said: 'I thought you knew we were keeping them as hostages.'

'Hostages?' I said.

'The enemy have prisoners belonging to us, and now they're talking of shooting them,' he said. 'If they shoot our prisoners, we'll shoot theirs.'

'Shoot Belcher and Hawkins?' I said.

'What else did you think we were keeping them for?' he said.

'Wasn't it very unforeseen of you not to warn Noble and myself of that in the beginning?' I said.

'How was it?' he said. 'You might have known that much.'

'We could not know it, Jeremiah Donovan,' I said. 'How could we when they were on our hands so long?'

'The enemy have our prisoners as long and longer,' he said.

'That's not the same thing at all,' said I.

'What difference is there?' said he.

I couldn't tell him, because I knew he wouldn't understand. If it was only an old dog that you had to take to the vet's, you'd try and not get too fond of him, but Jeremiah Donovan was not a man who would ever be in danger of that.

'And when is this to be decided?' I said.

'We might hear tonight,' he said. 'Or tomorrow or the next day at latest. So if it's only hanging round that's a trouble to you, you'll be free soon enough.'

It was not the hanging round that was a trouble to me at all by this time. I had worse things to worry about. When I got back to the cottage the argument was still on. Hawkins was holding forth in his best style, maintaining that there was no next world, and Noble saying that there was; but I could see that Hawkins had had the best of it.

'Do you know what, chum?' he was saying with a saucy smile. 'I think you're just as big a bleeding unbeliever as I am. You say you believe in the next world, and you know just as much about the next world as I do, which is sweet damn-all. What's heaven? You don't know. Where's heaven? You don't know. You know sweet damn-all! I ask you again, do they wear wings?'

'Very well, then,' said Noble. 'They do. Is that enough for you? They do wear wings.'

'Where do they get them then? Who makes them? Have they a factory for wings? Have they a sort of store where you hand in your chit and take your bleeding wings?'

'You're an impossible man to argue with,' said Noble. 'Now, listen to me –' And they were off again.

It was long after midnight when we locked up and went to bed. As I blew out the candle I told Noble. He took it very quietly. When we'd been in bed about an hour he asked if I thought we should tell the Englishmen. I didn't, because I doubted if the English would shoot our men. Even if they did, the Brigade officers, who were always up and down to the Second Battalion and knew the Englishmen well, would hardly want to see them plugged. 'I think so too,' said Noble. 'It would be great cruelty to put the wind up them now.'

'It was very unforeseen of Jeremiah Donovan, anyhow,' said I.

It was next morning that we found it so hard to face Belcher and Hawkins. We went about the house all day, scarcely saying a word. Belcher didn't seem to notice; he was stretched into the ashes as usual, with his usual look of waiting in quietness for something unforeseen to happen, but Hawkins noticed it and put it down to Noble being beaten in the argument of the night before.

'Why can't you take the discussion in the proper spirit?' he said severely. 'You and your Adam and Eve! I'm a Communist, that's what I am. Communist or Anarchist, it all comes to much the same thing.' And he went round the house, muttering when the fit took him: 'Adam and Eve! Adam and Eve! Nothing better to do with their time than pick bleeding apples!'

III

I don't know how we got through that day, but I was very glad when it was over, the tea things were cleared away, and Belcher said in his peaceable way: 'Well, chums, what about it?' We sat round the table and Hawkins took out the cards, and just then I heard Jeremiah Donovan's footsteps on the path and a dark presentiment crossed my mind. I rose from the table and caught him before he reached the door.

'What do you want?' I asked.

'I want those two soldier friends of yours,' he said, getting red.

'Is that the way, Jeremiah Donovan?' I asked.

'That's the way. There were four of our lads shot this morning, one of them a boy of sixteen.'

'That's bad,' I said.

At that moment Noble followed me out, and the three of us walked down the path together, talking in whispers. Feeney, the local intelligence officer, was standing by the gate.

'What are you going to do about it?' I asked Jeremiah Donovan.

'I want you and Noble to get them out; tell them they're being shifted again; that'll be the quietest way.'

'Leave me out of that,' said Noble, under his breath.

Jeremiah Donovan looked at him hard.

'All right,' he says. 'You and Feeney get a few tools from the shed and dig a hole by the far end of the bog. Bonaparte and myself will be after you. Don't let anyone see you with the tools. I wouldn't like it to go beyond ourselves.'

We saw Feeney and Noble go round to the shed and went in ourselves. I left Jeremiah Donovan to do the explanations. He told them that he had orders to send them back to the Second Battalion. Hawkins let out a mouthful of curses, and you could see that though Belcher didn't say anything, he was a bit upset too. The old woman was for having them stay in spite of us, and she didn't stop advising them until Jeremiah Donovan lost his temper and turned on her. He had a nasty temper, I noticed. It was pitch dark in the cottage by this time, but no one thought of lighting the lamp, and in the darkness the two Englishmen fetched their topcoats and said good-bye to the old woman.

'Just as a man makes a home of a bleeding place, some bastard at headquarters thinks you're too cushy and shunts you off,' said Hawkins, shaking her hand.

'A thousand thanks, madam,' said Belcher. 'A thousand thanks for everything' – as though he'd made it up.

We went round to the back of the house and down towards the bog. It was only then that Jeremiah Donovan told them. He was shaking with excitement.

'There were four of our fellows shot in Cork this morning and now you are to be shot as a reprisal.'

'What are you talking about?' snaps Hawkins. 'It's bad enough being mucked about as we are without having to put up with your funny jokes.'

'It isn't a joke,' said Donovan. 'I'm sorry, Hawkins, but it's true,' and begins on the usual rigmarole about duty and how unpleasant it is. I never noticed that people who talk a lot about duty find it much of a trouble to them.

'Oh, cut it out!' said Hawkins.

'Ask Bonaparte,' said Donovan, seeing that Hawkins wasn't taking him seriously. 'Isn't it true, Bonaparte?'

'It is,' I said, and Hawkins stopped.

'Ah, for Christ's sake, chum!'

'I mean it, chum,' I said.

'You don't sound as if you meant it.'

'If he doesn't mean it, I do,' said Donovan, working himself up.

'What have you against me, Jeremiah Donovan?'

'I never said I had anything against you. But why did your people take out four of your prisoners and shoot them in cold blood?'

He took Hawkins by the arm and dragged him on, but it was impossible to make him understand that we were in earnest. I had the Smith and Wesson in my pocket and I kept fingering it and wondering what I'd do if they put up a fight for it or ran, and wishing to God they'd do one or the other. I knew if they did run for it, that I'd never fire on them. Hawkins wanted to know was Noble in it, and when we said yes, he asked us why Noble wanted to plug him. Why did any of us want to plug him? What had he done to us? Weren't we all chums? Didn't we understand him and didn't he understand us? Did we imagine for an instant that he'd shoot us for all the so-and-so officers in the so-and-so British Army?

By this time we'd reached the bog, and I was so sick I couldn't even answer him. We walked along the edge of it in the darkness, and every now and then Hawkins would call a halt and begin all over again, as if he was wound up, about our being chums, and I knew that nothing but the sight of the grave would convince him that we had to do it. And all the time I was hoping that something would happen; that they'd run for it or that Noble would take over the responsibility from me. I had the feeling that it was worse on Noble than on me.

IV

At last we saw the lantern in the distance and made towards it. Noble was carrying it, and Feeney was standing somewhere in the darkness behind him, and the picture of them so still and silent in the bogland brought it home to me that we were in earnest, and banished the last bit of hope I had.

Belcher, on recognizing Noble, said: 'Hallo, chum,' in his quiet way, but Hawkins flew at him at once, and the argument began all over again, only this time Noble had nothing to say for himself and stood with his head down, holding the lantern between his legs.

It was Jeremiah Donovan who did the answering. For the twentieth time, as though it was haunting his mind, Hawkins asked if anybody thought he'd shoot Noble.

'Yes, you would,' said Jeremiah Donovan.

'No, I wouldn't, damn you!'

'You would, because you'd know you'd be shot for not doing it.'

'I wouldn't, not if I was to be shot twenty times over. I wouldn't shoot a pal. And Belcher wouldn't – isn't that right, Belcher?'

'That's right, chum,' Belcher said, but more by way of answering the question than of joining in the argument. Belcher sounded as though whatever unforeseen thing he'd always been waiting for had come at last.

'Anyway, who says Noble would be shot if I wasn't? What do you think I'd do if I was in his place, out in the middle of a blasted bog?'

'What would you do?' asked Donovan.

'I'd go with him wherever he was going, of course. Share my last bob with him and stick by him through thick and thin. No one can ever say of me that I let down a pal.'

'We've had enough of this,' said Jeremiah Donovan, cocking his revolver. 'Is there any message you want to send?'

'No, there isn't.'

'Do you want to say your prayers?'

Hawkins came out with a cold-blooded remark that even shocked me and turned on Noble again.

'Listen to me, Noble,' he said. 'You and me are chums. You can't come over to my side, so I'll come over to your side. That show you I mean what I say? Give me a rifle and I'll go along with you and the other lads.'

Noble answered him. We knew that was no way out.

'Hear what I'm saying?' he said. 'I'm through with it. I'm a deserter or anything else you like. I don't believe in your stuff, but it's no worse than mine. That satisfy you?'

Noble raised his head, but Donovan began to speak and he lowered it again without replying.

'For the last time, have you any messages to send?' said Donovan in a cold, excited sort of voice.

'Shut up, Donovan! You don't understand me, but these lads do. They're not the sort to make a pal and kill a pal. They're not the tools of any capitalist.'

I alone of the crowd saw Donovan raise his Webley to the back of Hawkins's neck, and as he did so I shut my eyes and tried to pray. Hawkins had begun to say something else when Donovan fired, and as I opened my eyes at the bang, I saw Hawkins stagger at the knees and lie out flat at Noble's feet, slowly and as quiet as a kid falling asleep, with the lantern-light on his lean legs and bright farmer's boots. We all stood very still, watching him settle out in the last agony.

Then Belcher took out a handkerchief and began to tie it about his own eyes (in our excitement we'd forgotten to do the same for Hawkins), and, seeing it wasn't big enough, turned and asked for the loan of mine. I gave it to him, and he knotted the two together and pointed with his foot at Hawkins.

'He's not quite dead,' he said. 'Better give him another.'

Sure enough, Hawkins's left knee was beginning to rise. I bent down and put my gun to his head; then recollecting myself, I got up again. Belcher understood what was in my mind.

'Give him his first,' he said. 'I don't mind. Poor bastard, we don't know what's happening to him now.'

I knelt and fired. By this time I didn't seem to know what I was doing. Belcher, who was fumbling a bit awkwardly with the handkerchiefs, came out with a laugh as he heard the shot. It was the first time I had heard him laugh and it sent a shudder down my back; it sounded so unnatural.

'Poor bugger!' he said quietly. 'And last night he was so curious about it all. It's very queer, chums, I always think. Now he knows as much about it as they'll ever let him know, and last night he was all in the dark.'

Donovan helped him to tie the handkerchiefs about this eyes. 'Thanks, chum,' he said. Donovan asked if there were any messages he wanted sent.

'No, chum,' he said. 'Not for me. If any of you would like to write to Hawkins's mother, you'll find a letter from her in his pocket. He and his mother were great chums. But my missus left me eight years ago. Went away with another fellow and took the kid with her. I like the feeling of a home, as you may have noticed, but I couldn't start another again after that.'

It was an extraordinary thing, but in those few minutes Belcher said more than in all the weeks before. It was just as if the sound of the shot had started a flood of talk in him and he could go on the whole night like that, quite happily, talking about himself. We stood around like fools now that he couldn't see us any longer. Donovan looked at Noble, and Noble shook his head. Then Donovan raised his Webley, and at that moment Belcher gave his queer laugh again. He may have thought we were talking about him, or perhaps he noticed the same thing I'd noticed and couldn't understand it.

'Excuse me, chums,' he said. 'I feel I'm talking the hell of a lot, and so silly, about my being so handy about a house and things like that. But this thing came on me suddenly. You'll forgive me, I'm sure.'

'You don't want to say a prayer?' asked Donovan.

'No, chum,' he said. 'I don't think it would help. I'm ready, and you boys want to get it over.'

'You understand that we're only doing our duty?' said Donovan.

Belcher's head was raised like a blind man's, so that you could only see his chin and the top of his nose in the lantern-light.

'I never could make out what duty was myself,' he said. 'I think you're all good lads, if that's what you mean. I'm not complaining.'

Noble, just as if he couldn't bear any more of it, raised his fist at Donovan, and in a flash Donovan raised his gun and fired. The big man went over like a sack of meal, and this time there was no need for a second shot.

I don't remember much about the burying, but that it was worse than all the rest because we had to carry them to the grave. It was all mad lonely with nothing but a patch of lantern-light between ourselves and the dark, and birds hooting and screeching all round, disturbed by the guns. Noble went through Hawkins's belongings to find the letter from his mother, and then joined his hands together. He did the same with Belcher. Then, when we'd filled in the grave, we separated from Jeremiah Donovan and Feeney and took our tools back to the shed. All the way we didn't speak a word. The kitchen was dark and cold as we'd left it, and the old woman was sitting over the hearth, saying her beads. We walked past her into the room, and Noble struck a match to light the lamp. She rose quietly and came to the doorway with all her cantankerousness gone.

'What did ye do with them?' she asked in a whisper, and Noble started so that the match went out in his hand.

'What's that?' he asked without turning round.

'I heard ye,' she said.

'What did you hear?' asked Noble.

'I heard ye. Do you think I didn't hear ye, putting the spade back in the houseen?'

Noble struck another match and this time the lamp lit for him.

'Was that what ye did to them?' she asked.

Then, by God, in the very doorway, she fell on her knees and began praying, and after looking at her for a minute or two Noble did the same by the fireplace. I pushed my way out past her and left them at it. I stood at the door, watching the stars and listening to the shrieking of the birds dying out over the bogs. It is so strange what you feel at times like that that you can't describe it. Noble says he saw everything ten times the size, as though there were nothing in the whole world but that little patch of bog with the two Englishmen stiffening into it, but with me it was as if the patch of bog where the Englishmen were was a million miles away, and even Noble and the old woman, mumbling behind me, and the birds and the bloody stars were all far away, and I was somehow very small and very lost and lonely like a child astray in the snow. And anything that happened to me afterwards, I never felt the same about again.

MOLLY KEANE

from *Two Days in Aragon*

38

It never occurred to Sylvia not to dress for dinner that evening when she feared her love lay newly murdered up in the heather. At 7.30 she took her bath with its accustomed drops of rose-geranium and washed herself with as much meticulous concentration as usual. She had felt cold as lead when she lay down in the hot water. When she got out and dried herself she was still cold and shivered as she walked across the passage, past all the tall mahogany doors, to her bedroom – her bedroom that had no more colour in it than the whites and greys and near-greens of river weeds, with all the distinction of such water flowers. Sylvia sat in front of her clear glass with its old nibbled frame of worn gilt and its pale golden bird posing in a leaf circle. In the glass she saw tears pouring down her clean chill cheeks, she saw a girl weeping in despair and hardly knew it was herself. She could know her love dead; her glass-cold little heart be shivered in pieces, but the pieces were still glass. Shock acts strangely. With Sylvia it delayed her yielding to despair although it left her without a movement towards hope. She was shut in a neat square box of despair and being Sylvia she moved with her usual grace and precision in this small dark place. She blew her nose and stuffed back the awful tears, but they flew up through her head again. She despised her own crying. I'll be good, I'll be good, she strained against the cruel evening air. Is it over? Yes. Yes. The tears went back. Four or six defeated her will and raced down her face and fell on her bare knees that were laced together, twisted up for strength to resist this crying. This was sorrow. Not to think of him. She didn't think of him. She thought backwards very quickly about a woman's face in church. What was she wearing? Make a list, don't lose hold. Hat, blouse, coat, skirt, shoes ... don't lose hold ... She brushed her hair back and back from the little peaks in which it grew down her forehead and above her ears. She would not look in the glass at her shaking mouth. She turned her back on the glass and put on her clean fine underclothes, her grey dress with its faint high-tied ribbon, her short string of river pearls. She picked up her work-bag and went down to the drawing-room to wait alone for dinner. As she waited she stitched at the flowers in her tapestry. It was as if she made a neat little wreath for a grave.

Frazer came in at five minutes to eight, he shut the door quietly and crossed over to where she was sitting.

'Will you have dinner at eight, Miss, or will you wait for Mrs Fox and Miss Grania?' He always spoke with the soft distinctness of a good servant, but this evening he breathed the words gently, as if he would rebuke his own voice for speaking at all, and if speak he must, the air should hardly be stirred by him.

'I won't wait beyond 8.15.'

Sylvia's voice sounded improperly natural, 'They may be very late.'

'Very good, Miss.'

She was left alone again, the perfect figure in such a room, as right as any of the marble reliefs that stooped with their garlands of pointed leaves in the plaques on the mantelpiece. Her strong small neck was bowed, her hands busy and steady as on the day before, when she had finished her swan's wing, and eaten her dinner with so much pleasure and good appetite.

To-night, as yesterday, the river and the April light were joined and took the indoor air together, sharpening the red in the coats of dead dull Fox soldiers and hunting men, dwelling and drowning in the pale round carpet, turning the white glaze on china milk-soft and luxurious to the eye, swelling light romantic and untruthful through the room. The air was burdened with ragged water scents. Broken river smells lifted the lilac on their strength as scent is built, so that lilac, doubly, terribly sweet filled the room too, and the rich heart-breaking songs of birds.

Sylvia sat on, her hands moving busily at her work. She thought with passionate liking of the silent grave herons, glad that she could not even see that lonely flight from their nest in a flat-topped cedar to the river below, they had no connection with sweet scents or rapturous songs. She could think of them.

The gong sounded and Frazer opened the drawing-room door and stood inside it with a murmur, dinner was served.

Dinner was eaten, soup, fish, cold lamb, a tiny savoury. Sylvia would show no silly signs of heartbreak through plates of untouched food. She ate steadily and went back to the drawing-room for her coffee, then the paper. After dinner she always read the paper. To-night, beyond any other night, there must be no change. The *Morning Post* of the day before was lying folded on the table by the sofa where it was always put. The fire, ten minutes lighted, gave out no heat. The curtains were not drawn and only one lamp near the fire was burning. Sylvia picked up the paper and sat down beside the light. She began to read the leading article, a furious indictment of England's weakness in the conduct of this Irish war. She read on in bitter agreement with all the *Morning Post* proposed to do to Rebels and Gunmen, read on until the door opened and she looked up to take her coffee from Frazer.

It was Killer Denny who stood there with his two boys, one on either side of him, and all three had guns in their hands.

'Good-evening,' Sylvia leaned out of her chair towards the fireplace.

'Don't touch that bell.'

'What do you want?' Sylvia asked as steadily as possible, for there is something unutterably alarming about three masked men with guns in their hands standing suddenly in your drawing-room on a spring evening. None the less so because you have just been reading that their country is at war with the government under which you live. None the less surprising because to-day they had killed your lover that to-night they should stand in your house with guns in their hands.

Sylvia was frightened, and because she was frightened she spoke boldly and rudely.

'Get out,' she said. 'Get out of this house at once.' How silly, how shrill.

Killer Denny laughed quite naturally.

'It's you who'll do the getting out, now see,' he said going up to her, 'and quick mind you, unless you want to burn along with your ancestral bloody home, now see.' He went to the fireplace. 'Not much heat out of that,' he said. 'We'll soon have a better blaze.'

He stood over Sylvia. He did not touch her. He did not put out a hand towards her. He looked at her out of his bold little dark eyes, bright as a rat's through his mask, and he turned his head on his strong neck and spat on the carpet.

'I've wanted to do that,' he said, 'for a long time.' When he had done it he was ashamed. It looked awful. It is one thing to burn a beautiful house, it is another thing to spit on its floor.

Sylvia was recovering some of her horrid poise.

'A childish thing to do,' she said, pulling her skirt closer to herself, 'childish and dirty, don't you think so, hardly what one expects from an officer of the IRA.'

He turned to his two men, 'Go and get the servants out, boys,' he said, 'and quick. Bring the lot in here.'

'There's a very old lady upstairs,' Sylvia said, 'may I go up and explain this little party to her? She may be rather alarmed, you know.'

'One of the servants can get her out. You stay where you are. We don't want any help from you.'

Sylvia sat back in her chair – was it any good arguing? was it any good doing anything? What did one save when houses were burnt? Silver? Jewellery? Papers?

'Could I collect a few personal belongings,' she said, frigidly, pompously.

'No.'

Suddenly she stood up, thin and straight in her grey dress as smoke in a frost.

'It's outrageous, it's awful, what good will you do to anybody by burning Aragon?' She looked wildly around the room. At the mantelpiece. At the dark glass. At the honey-coloured shells curling in the inlay of dark thin tables. At the china she had always seen, the gay-flowered coats of groups of Worcester and Chelsea. Suddenly she felt again the ache to touch that bright china gives to children, she cried out in their defence:

'You can't do it. Why are you doing this?'

Killer Denny followed her eyes to the Chelsea group.

'I had a great admiration for that ornament when I was a little fellow,' he said softly. 'Mrs O'Neill got me one day with it in my hand, she took it from me and she beat hell out of me.'

He picked it up again, a boy in a mulberry coat with a hen in a basket under his arm. He looked at the pretty silly thing and then dropped it on the flat stone before the fireplace, it broke, but not much, because it was tough and light.

'You'll have to try again,' Sylvia said.

He picked it up and held it in his hands, fitting the broken bits together.

'Nothing I do,' he said oddly, 'would divide me from that little boy.'

'I don't remember you.'

'One dirty pantry boy is very like another.' He put the broken figure back on the mantelpiece as the boys came in driving the whispering, terrified servants before them. Even in such a pass they felt very uncomfortable in the drawing-room. The housemaid thought the cook would take offence because she was pushed in before her, and the tweenie was miserably conscious that even such a disaster as this promised to be could not save her from a row because she had no cap on her head. Frazer was quite undone, pale and shaking and terrified for his northern blood.

'Out there, now.' Denny pointed through the window to the wall above the river, 'and if there's a word or a stir out of one of them, fire, boys.' It sounded very alarming.

'Can't we save anything,' Sylvia asked.

'Christ, God,' he swore, 'how much more time are we to waste? Till the soldiers are here, I suppose? Quick now, out with them.'

'But Aunt Pidgie,' Sylvia cried wildly, 'she is not here, let me get her.'

'Get out. I'll see to her, we don't want to burn old ladies, but we will if we're short of time. Out now the lot of you and keep quiet.'

Sylvia wanted to get a coat from the hall, but the boy in charge, the boy who had been captured by Nan, was too uncertain of himself to allow any leniency. Sylvia recognized early that he was far more likely to shoot one of them for disobedience than was his tough superior. He had the shaky manner in bullying that turns quickly to extremities for its support. It was better to hurry out into the garden, out into the chill evening and stand against a wall to watch the house burn.

Every few minutes she would say to the boy, 'What about the old lady? Why don't they bring her out?' And he would answer in the voice of an official in the customs: 'Captain Cussens will deal with that matter.'

She broke out of the line once crying desperately that she must find Aunt Pidgie, but she was halted, ordered back with such temper that she knew the foolishness of persistence. The wind that blew under the maids' aprons nipped her bare arms and roughed her neat hair. 'Mayn't we put our hands down?' Sylvia asked then, 'we haven't any arms and it is so tiring.'

'Captain Cussens' orders,' he answered, so they continued to stand like people in a game painted on a box lid, backs to the river, palms up towards the house.

Sylvia began to cry when she saw no sign of Aunt Pidgie being brought out. It was so terrifying not to know about her. By accident she might burn. No one's evil intention, but fluster and hurry and excitement would leave her helpless and unaccessible with Aragon burning round her. The burning house cutting off the way to the nursery, there would be no way of getting her out through the barred windows. Sylvia clapped her hands, and shouted, 'Aunt Pidgie!' 'Aunt Pidgie!' the cook shouted. The other servants were too timid. Afraid a little of their own voices or far more of their guard. Frazer grew pale and looked like a little frightened man, all butlerhood cast aside. 'Miss Sylvia, Miss Sylvia,' he whispered, 'do you want to get us all butchered?'

'If there's another word out of any of you,' the guard said, 'I'll fire.'

Sylvia was silenced. Indeed it was as well, for Miss Pidgie was sitting now with her ears stopped, so that she could not have heard a sound from the garden far below. She did not even hear the boys when they knocked at the door, calling and shaking the handle. She did not hear the steps going away or the shouts. It was Soo and the smoke that brought her to the window twenty minutes later.

'She's there, she's in there still,' Sylvia cried.

'Oh, my God, she's done for,' Frazer said. 'There's flames from the landing window, there's flames from the linen-room.'

'Ah, the poor little old dickens,' the boy said, horror in the light curious words.

It was then that Aunt Pidgie saw the three break from the line, Sylvia, Frazer and the boy with the gun. They ran towards the house calling confused reassuring words while the maids left behind sank down on their knees on the stones.

39

Burning curtains are madly beautiful, but there is something terrible about the sight of a flaming bed, as shocking as though a good comfortable hen was on fire. It is an unbearable sight, one would as soon look at a fat cosy bishop on his pyre.

It was through the open doors of the bedroom (left open to fan draughts) that Sylvia saw the fat beds blazing. Smoke poured out on to the stairs blinding and choking her. On the stairway going up to the nursery linen and blankets and pink eiderdowns had been pulled out and blazed in heaps and wreaths.

Frazer stood appalled. 'We'll never get her,' he said; it was like someone in a hunt saying: You can't go there. You can't get through there, wire, it's wired.

Sylvia said, 'It's only the linen burning, get some water, get the minimax.' Fraser and the boy stood coughing and doing nothing.

The two who had done the burning came running up the stairs. They had the savage desperate look of boys who had committed some outrage beyond their own believing, an outrage that has got beyond them and taken on a strength of its own.

'Outside,' they shouted, 'what the hell are you doing here?' The boy said, 'The old lady is above yet.'

'Come away, come away,' Frazer said. 'Do you want to be listening to her in her death?'

'There's no one in the house,' Denny said. 'God damn, didn't we try every door.'

'She's there, she was at the window.' Sylvia tore past him to the corner at the end of the corridor where a fire extinguisher was hung. As in all large houses there were perhaps three at extreme distance throughout the house, refilled last not less than ten years past.

'Get water, show them where to get water,' she shouted to Frazer. He put his hands over his eyes and ran coughing down the stairs and out of the house.

'Well, the old rat,' Denny looked down into the hall below, 'would you believe that, eh? Would you trust the sight of your sacred eyes?'

The boys had run down the corridor after Sylvia. They came back with cans of water in their hands like housemaids at their ordinary evening business.

'Yes, do, boys, and then fire down a spit and make a job of it.' He took the minimax from Sylvia. 'Go and put a coat on you,' he said. 'One spark and you're up in a blaze, now see. Give that here, and you chaps lift a carpet out of that room at the end, it's not burning.'

He cracked the knob of the extinguisher and sprayed the burning blankets on the stairs. They threw the carpet down and stamped out the curling flames. He shut the door of the burning linen-room and ran shouting up towards the nurseries.

'Keep the fire off the stairs, boys,' he called down behind him.

Sylvia came flying up from the hall, coated obedient to his order, she ran past the two on the stairs, past the awful roaring sound of the burning linen-room. He stood above her in the dark passage, white-faced, coughing, he had pulled off his mask and his hat, he was stooping down trying to get his breath.

'Aunt Pidgie, are you there?' Sylvia called at the nursery door. She twisted the handle. 'Open the door, Aunt Pidgie, quickly. It's all right. It's Sylvia. It's Sylvia, do you hear me?'

'Nan locked me up,' Aunt Pidgie spoke in a clear, trembling voice. 'All the doors are locked, Sylvia. I can't get out. There's no way out, Sylvia.'

'What does she say?' Killer Denny was whispering at Sylvia's shoulder, they were alone together with the terror and horror of Aunt Pidgie's certain death around them.

'Captain, Captain, this stair won't last,' the boys' voices came calling.

'She's locked in.'

The Killer pulled Sylvia gently away from the door and crashed his shoulder against it trying to burst it open. Then he said, 'Tell her to go back from it. I'll try to shoot the lock off.'

'Aunt Pidgie, do you hear me? Go into the night nursery.'

'The door's bolted,' came Aunt Pidgie's clear hopeless little voice again.

'Get away from this door, go over to the window. Get into the cupboard, Aunt Pidgie. We've got to shoot off the lock.'

He was profiled against the door, arm out, head sunk. Sylvia was close as a plaque to the wall behind him. He fired, once, twice. The shots crashed and echoed in the narrow place. The smell bit its way through the other smoke. He tried the door again. The wood was bruised and splintered but the beautifully made lock held firm. In the succeeding silence Aunt Pidgie's gnat's voice spoke.

'It's all right, Sylvia. Frazer says the soldiers are coming, he sees the lorries on the road across the river.'

'Do you hear that?' Sylvia whispered to the Killer, he was squeezing a splinter out of the ball of his thumb. He nodded and ran to the stairs.

Tears poured down Sylvia's face as she wrenched at the handle and flung herself on the door, she would have broken every bone in her body to get in. She was alone now. She knew that it was madness to stay here. She was doing no good. In a few minutes she herself would be more hopelessly trapped than Aunt Pidgie.

Sylvia was not in the least fond of Aunt Pidgie. She would have done this for her own dog as readily. With the same vain protectiveness of the strong towards the weak. All that was tough and cold and fair in her, all indeed that was least pleasant went to the sacrifice.

'Would Nan's big scissors help?' came Aunt Pidgie's voice again in most sensible suggestion.

'Yes, yes, shove it under the door.'

Sweat and tears running down her cheeks, Sylvia was struggling to drive the scissors through the splintered wood and somehow catch the lock when a hand was put on her arm and she looked up through her fallen hair and saw Denny.

'You came back. But you'll be caught.'

He gave her a direct look. A look that crossed fire and death and their opposite ways of living. A look straight from a tough guy to a tough girl. There was a streak of divine humour in the soft way he said:

'Ah, no. You'll get me off, now see, won't you?'

'I will,' Sylvia said, and the promise was given. She would do as much for his safety now as for Aunt Pidgie or for her dog's safety.

Then it was again, 'Stand back, Aunt Pidgie, say when you're in the cupboard.'

'One, two, three. Fire.'

Aunt Pidgie's voice came brave and oddly strong before the crash and echo of the gun. It was like a child playing soldiers afraid to be afraid of the bang.

This time more of the wood was shattered away. Denny picked cleverly and slowly at the bared lock. It was as if he had an afternoon before him to do a neat carpenter's job. His hands were as leisurely and as sure. Sylvia found herself forgetting the fire that was raging under them. He said to her, 'Go and keep water on the stairs where the boys were, if you can, and look out for yourself. The wall of that linen-room will go any minute.'

The hot crackle of fire was coming between the door he had shut and the jambs, the wall was like a plate out of the oven. Sylvia picked up the jugs the boys had left down when they had gone and ran down the passage to the bathroom, they had shut the bedroom doors, smoke came out flat underneath them and rose up in puffs. It poured up from the hall, the heat was terrifying, and what had she heard about putting wet cloths on your mouth in a fire? She had no cloths. She came heavily back with her jugs of water, sobbing out her coughs. She flung the water weakly, and it seemed to her pitiably, at the sizzling blistered door of the linen-room. She could hardly see as she set back down the wide end landing again towards the bathroom.

When she got back the door had fallen inwards. She looked into a hellish bowl of flame, of insupportable, impossible, raging flame. It was blown outwards to the stairs, through the door, like rain flat before a storm of wind. Sylvia put up her hands to save her face from the intense awful heat. She screamed upwards to the man she could not see:

'Come down, come down. It's too late, do you hear, come down.' There was no answer. She made an effort she did not know she had in her. She staggered up the six steps to where the fire would come through on to the stairs, and she poured her two cans of water on the steps, and screamed out again.

Then she saw him. He came down the dark corridor, and he carried in his arms a bundle as small as a six-year-old child, covered in a blanket. Aunt Pidgie's head against his shoulder showed out round through the blanket, like the drawing of some holy child underneath the mother's shawl. He stood for a moment at the head of that flight of stairs with the fire he had lighted belching towards it, then he tightened his grip on Aunt Pidgie and ran down into the smoke and flames.

Who can measure how intense the shock of burning is? He was trembling and crying and holding the wrist of his burnt hand while Sylvia squeezed the flame and scorch out of his clothes. Aunt Pidgie, out from under her blanket, was shaking but unsinged and obedient to orders.

They ran all three hand in hand down the wide staircase. 'Can we get through the kitchen way?' Sylvia asked. He nodded, coughing. They pushed through the heavy swing door that divided the hall from the back passages and suddenly the quiet was like that of a cold still well. The quiet of a dripping tunnel with a burning hot road at either end. The musty smell of back passages, plate powder and damp and firelessness, the smell of old pocket linings and empty wine cases was soothing to their throats. They felt real again. He said suddenly, and all the time they were running, 'I could do with a drink.'

'Yes,' Sylvia said, 'so could I.' In Frazer's pantry they found a bottle of whisky, the rows of clean tumblers in the cupboard looked sane and peaceful. It was worth waiting to get this, they needed this.

Sylvia said, 'We must keep Aunt Pidgie with us and they'll think we're all trapped up there. They'll be getting ladders.'

He said, 'But no one knows I'm with you.'

'Listen, I'm not bargaining.' Sylvia turned the cold tap into their whisky. 'But what have you done with Captain Purvis and Mr Craye?'

'My God,' he said, 'and I'd forgotten her, too.'

'Who?'

They drank, gulping in haste and looking at each other, a new distrust growing between them.

'I'd like a drop too,' said Aunt Pidgie.

'Yes, perhaps you do need it.' Sylvia measured it out like medicine.

'Ah, for God's sake, give her a drink,' he laughed.

'Who have you forgotten?'

'Listen, child, when I'm gone, away with you down the mountain avenue, and you'll find what I've forgotten.'

He would not say any more. She realized it was because he was afraid she would not help him. Sylvia grew a little afraid too. What would she find.

'What about the two officers?' she whispered.

'Safe back in barracks, when they should be cooling in the heather.'

They were growing apart, the bond of death and fear loosened.

'Thank God!'

'What about me now?' He looked at her closely, he did not trust her as he had done when she said, 'I will' in the darkness and the smoke.

Sylvia said, 'I'll get you out,' and looked at Aunt Pidgie, who had shrunk in importance now, shrunk back into the poor little old nuisance she really was. What a situation Aunt Pidgie had put her in.

'You'd want to hurry yourself,' he said roughly.

Sylvia said, 'Out through the stable yard would be the best.'

They were running again, Aunt Pidgie bundled along between them. In the yard she grew suddenly very weighty on their arms, her legs did not seem able to keep up with them. Once they pulled her back on to her feet which trailed behind like a dead duck's.

'Aunt Pidgie, are you all right?'

Aunt Pidgie shook her head peacefully. 'Put me on my nest,' she said, 'I'm a clocker. I'm broodie.'

'What are you talking about?'

'I'm a broodie birdie.'

Denny looked across her at Sylvia, there was laughter in his eyes. 'Blind,' he said.

Sylvia said, 'We'll shut her in a loose box. She'll be all right.' They opened one of the painted wooden stable doors and put her in. There was a heap of straw in one corner. There Aunt Pidgie nested contentedly.

'Don't move till I get back, Aunt Pidgie.'

'It takes twenty-one days,' Aunt Pidgie murmured, closing her eyes.

As she settled down they saw that her feet were bare. They had hurried her down the flagged passages and across the gravel on her bare feet and she had not said a word in complaint.

Sylvia felt a sudden pride in Aunt Pidgie. Again to-night those tortured little feet had their strange effect on cruel youth.

'Oh, Aunt Pidgie, your poor feet.'

Aunt Pidgie curled them away beneath her. 'Chook, chook,' she murmured drowsily. 'Chook, chook, chook.'

Sylvia saw the soldiers first. They came through the back door. They had rifles in their hands and they looked as foreign as men in uniforms always do.

'Get back, quick,' she said, 'get back with Aunt Pidgie.' She spoke without turning her head, and as she spoke a flood of determination to save him rose in her, the hunted creature must be saved. Danger is sacred; she was glad that her word bound her.

The soldiers, five of them, came running across the yard towards her.

'Any shinners 'ere, Miss?'

'They've cleared off.' How unsteady a lie makes the coldest voice.

'We've got orders to search the stables and out-offices.'

'For heaven's sake go up to the yard and get the long ladder, there's an old lady trapped upstairs.'

'Sorry, Miss, the poor old lady's done for. Terrible thing.'

'Butler says, floor went five minutes ago.'

'Quite a tragedy, Miss.'

'Yes, shocking, and the other old girl gone west on the drive. We were upset.'

'Who do you mean, not Nan?'

'That's it. That's what the young lady called her.'

Sylvia leaned against the high door of the loose box where Killer Denny crouched against the wall, his empty gun in his hand, and Aunt Pidgie stirred in her nest.

'Right,' she said, raising her head, 'get on with it, boys. Don't mind me. Careful of the chestnut mare at the end, she's a bit free with her heels. And leave this box alone, my young horse is here, he's half-cracked with the smoke and the smell.'

'Better get the 'orses out, I'd say.'

'The wind's all the other way. Send the stable boys down like good chaps when you're through. The horses will go handier with them.'

'Right, Miss, we'll carry on.'

They went down the line of boxes.

Sylvia went in to Denny.

'Woa, boy, steady, little man.' She spoke idiotic words of horse comfort and love, while Denny watched her with fierce bright eyes, the look of the cornered wolf was on him.

'Right, Miss,' they called, coming back.

'OK.'

'Thank you.'

'The beggars weren't going to 'ang around, were they? Do the dirty and run, that's them—'

'Quiet, old chap; quiet, little fellow,' Sylvia soothed the air.

Their voices faded across the yard. 'Quick,' she beckoned Denny. She went up the pigeon hole ladder to the lofts before him, her long dress catching and tearing as she climbed. They were up in the green, powdery dark of the lofts together. Sylvia went running ahead between the heaps of hay and straw, the carefully turned piles of oats, dark and blond. She knew the lofts in the particular way remembered from childhood. Knew the holes in the boards and the windows where the stable lads always undid the wire so that they could drop down on to the dung-heap below and short cut it into the village.

Yes, it was open. She knew it would be open. These things are unchanging.

'I'll be all right, now,' he said.

Suddenly she put out her hand.

'Thank you,' she said, 'and good luck.'

He held her hand in the smooth, dry grip of unnervous people.

'I didn't do Nan in,' he said, 'I don't know what's happened to her.'

'Hurry! Hurry!' Sylvia felt that even Nan's death was less important than his escape.

But when he went, dropping off the window-sill and disappearing into the night, she felt the hour empty, she was drained of all purpose. She was left with a sense of horror at what she had done and a sense of triumph in having done it. She had let a dangerous man go free, because he had chanced his life to save a cracked little old woman. He had nearly murdered her lover to-day and to-night she had his life in her hands and she had held it safe for him. Who would understand, no one, no one, least of all her lover. She sat in the dark, forgetting Aragon, forgetting Nan, crying over her secret she must never tell. Crying because her heart had shrunk so that there was not even room in it for relief and joy that her lover was safe. Because of what she had done, she had lessened her love to herself. Because of this past hour of peril with a tough stranger her importances were changed. She had played traitor to them and in their betrayal she had known an hour of truth. For that hour she had been closer, more obedient to one from whom by every law of her nature she was divided, than she had ever been to any man or woman in her life. And now the hour and the man were lost to her. Before she became once more the Sylvia of tennis parties and white hunting ties and blue habits, the Sylvia meet and right for her Norfolk lover (heir to a respectable old baronetcy) she must know tears for all that was lost to her. A bitter unreasoning grief that left her exhausted and unstrung.

PATRICK KAVANAGH

from *Tarry Flynn*

2

The silly attack on the girl at the cross-roads, though it was a fairly ordinary occurrence, appeared to have set Father Daly thinking – thinking that life in Dargan was in danger of boiling over in wild orgies of lust. And what did he decide to do but make arrangements for a big Mission to the parishioners by the Order of Redemptorists who were such specialists in sex sins.

Nothing could have appeared more pathetic to Tarry or Eusebius when the news got around. The parish was comprised of old unmarried men and women. For a mile radius from where Flynn's lived Tarry could only count four houses in which there were married couples with children.

From a devotion known as the Nine Fridays, Tarry was able to assess the number of old maids in the parish, for this devotion – which he had in his childhood practised – was the old unmarried girl's escape from the fruitless flower of virginity. On the first Friday of every month these old girls could be seen strolling home from the village church, their sharp tongues in keeping with their sharp noses. Tarry, when he reflected on this devotion, was glad that he had gone through it, for there was a story that anyone who had done so would never die unrepentant. That gave a man a great chance to have a good time.

The crooked old men sat up and took notice when they heard of the Mission; they began to dream themselves violent young stallions who needed prayer and fasting to keep them on the narrow path.

Mrs Flynn was glad to hear of the Mission too.

'I hope this'll stir up the pack of good-for-nothing geldings that's on the go in Dargan. And you'll have to go too,' she said to her son.

Petey Meegan from Miskin, across the hills, passing Flynn's house was in wonderful humour.

'I believe that the two men that's coming are the two toughest men in the Order,' said he, and his eyes began to dance under his bleary eyelids.

Old maids like Jennie Toole coming around were filled with the tales of awful things that young men had done to girls in that parish. 'It takes out,' she said to Mrs Flynn. She told how a certain girl was raped and another one half raped, while Mrs Flynn clicked her tongue, not looking at all displeased.

It was a story of life in a townland of death.

As far as Tarry could gather from his mother's talk about the Mission, she had hopes that the Missioners' condemnation of sex would have the effect of drawing attention to it.

He was paring her corn this morning before going out to finish the moulding of the potatoes when she said: 'It might stir them up . . . Easy now and don't draw blood. You'd never know the good it might do. I was talking to one of the McArdles there and I was telling him that he ought to be getting a woman. "Huh," says he, "what would I be doing with a woman? I have me pint and me fag," says he, "and I'm not going to bring in a woman." You ought to hurry with the praties before the ground gets too dry.'

He moulded the potatoes that day, his mind lifted to a new excitement by the thought of all the strange girls that would be coming to the Mission. It often worried him that a lot of other men might be as hypocritical as himself. He, when he analysed himself, knew that he went to religious events of this kind mainly to see the girls.

The clay was running through his mind.

He gloated over his potatoes and the fine job he was making of the moulding, though he was only using one horse. The clay was staying up nicely.

Molly came to the well several times that day but he was too engrossed in his work to take much notice of her.

The Holy Ghost was taking the Bedlam of the little fields and making it into a song, a simple song which he could understand. And he saw the Holy Spirit on the hills.

With the cynical side of himself, he realized that there was nothing unusual about the landscape. And yet what he imagined was hardly self-deception. The totality of the scene about him was a miracle. There might be something of self-deception in his imagination of the general landscape but there was none in his observation of the little flowers and weeds. These had God's message in them.

Filled with mystical thoughts he loosed out the horse that evening, threw the backrope and traces on the beam of the plough and let the mare out on the grass, and then went home to try out his ideas on his mother. In moments like these he was rapt to the silly heavens. Often, as now, he only said outlandish things to his mother to test them. Anything that stood up to her test would stand up to anything.

'Did you get finished?' said she.

'I did,' he said. He organized his will for a remarkable statement. 'The Holy Spirit is in the fields,' he said in even cold tones. He was unemotional, for these strange statements did not lend themselves to any human emotion.

The mother who had one shoe off and her foot on a stool did not seem to have heard. 'There's a curse o' God corn on that wee toe and it's starting to bother me again. I think we'll have a slash of rain. Get the razor blade and pare it for me.' He held the foot between his legs like a blacksmith shoeing a horse. 'Easy now,' she cried, 'and don't draw blood. Easy now, easy now. The Mission's opening next Sunday week, I hear. Aggie, run out and don't leave any feeding on the hens' dishes for Callan's ducks. Have you the pea out?'

'I have.'

After a while she quietly asked:

'What was that you said about the Holy something?'

'I said the Holy Spirit was in the fields.'

'Lord protect everyone's rearing,' she said with a twinkle that was half humorous and half terror in her eye. She knew that there was no madness on her side of the house – that was one sure five – but –

'Is it something to do with the Catholic religion you mean?'

'It has to do with every religion; it's beauty in Nature,' he said solemnly but also dispassionately.

It was a mad remark but it was said by a very sane man.

'You'll have to go to this Mission every evening, Tarry. I don't want to have the people talking, and it's talking they'd be. The last time there was a Mission in this parish . . .' She put her finger to her lip and began to consider . . . 'How many years ago would that be? It's either ten or eleven . . . the devil a go the Carlins ever went and their luck wasn't much the better of it . . . Did you scrape the dishes clane, Aggie? Oh, they had the devil's luck. You made a great job of that corn. I hadn't a foot to put under me.'

Tarry was moving out the door.

'And they couldn't have luck, people like them . . .'

He went as far as the road gate and returned.

'Are you back?' said the mother.

He was hoping to get some money for cigarettes but he said: 'I thought I left something here,' and he searched under the papers in the back window.

'Don't be throwing the *Messenger* on the ground and me not having it read,' said Aggie. 'It's rubbish.'

'That's the class of a man Tarry is,' said Aggie, 'always making little of religion.'

'I only said that the writing, the stories, in it were no good, that's all I said.'

'I suppose you'd take on to write better ones.'

'You keep your mouth shut, Aggie,' said the mother. 'But for God's sake and for everyone's sake don't let anyone outside hear you saying these things,' she addressed her son. 'The people that's going in this place are only waiting for the chance to carry stories to the Parochial House – like what happened over the Reilly one. What in the Name of the three gay fellas *are* you pouching for?'

'For nothing, I tell you.'

'There's a shilling there on the dresser and you can take it,' she said at last, 'but try and not to spend it. I like a man to have money in his pocket.'

He went out singing. The shilling made all the difference between a man who hated the parish and a lover of it.

Every evening himself and Eusebius went down the road, but since the stallion season opened Eusebius was disinclined to go too far away from the mouth of the Drumnay road lest he should miss a customer with a mare.

On this evening Tarry met his neighbour outside when he went to the gate the second time and together they walked slowly down the road.

'I'm going to ask you a thing I often had a mind to ask you before,' Tarry started out of nowhere, and puffed away at the long cigarette which he had the cunning to have lighted before Eusebius came on the scene.

'Yes?' said Eusebius with indifference, for he was listening for the distant sounds of neighing mares.

'Had you ever anything to do with a woman, Eusebius?'

'Good God, no.'

'Can I take that for the God's honest truth?'

'To be sure, man.'

Tarry was very much relieved to think of one man at least being so moral. Every moral man meant one rival less for him. Having satisfied himself as to the truth of Eusebius' reply he turned to other matters, and in a short time they were deep in the question of the moulding of the potatoes.

So the days went by and the corn grew taller and shot out, the potato-stalks closed the alleys and the turnips softened over the dry clay. And the Mission came round.

Every able-bodied man and woman in the parish was present at the opening of the Mission. Looking across the church Tarry and Eusebius, who were together, thought they never saw so many grey-headed and bald-headed men in one bunch, and all of them so alike in many ways. The same stoop, the same slightly roguish look in every eye, the look of old blackguards who are being flattered by bawdy suggestions; the same size generally and even similar sort of clothes. On the women's side of the church huddled as intense a crowd of barren virgins as had ever gathered together at the same time in that parish.

Up in the galleries there was a spattering of young girls and visitors from the local parishes and towns, but these could not lessen the terrible impact of the old bachelors and maids in the body of the church.

The two most passionate preachers in the Redemptorist Order in Dundalk had been called in to give the Mission. One of these made a tremendous sermon that evening. As it registered in Tarry's mind it was all about a boy who met a girl and as a result of the boy's behaviour the girl committed suicide. She was found in a well. And the preacher said with a cry that would tear the heart out of a stone: 'That man damned that girl's soul.'

For all its passion the sermon left Tarry indifferent. Compared to one of Father Daly's sermons it lacked that touch of humour, that appearance of not being too earnest, which is the real sign of sincerity.

The second Missioner was hearing Confessions during the sermon and the transformation he was effecting in the minds of the penitents was astonishing. Men who had forgotten what they were born for came out of the confessional, in the words of Charlie Trainor, 'ready to bull cows'. This was the effect the Mission was having on all minds.

Outside the church there were stalls set up where gay-coloured Rosaries and wild red religious pictures and statues were for sale. The women who owned these stalls were fantastic dealing women with fluent tongues and a sense of freedom which was unknown in Dargan. They were bohemians who had an easy manner with God – like poets or actresses.

Life was beginning in Dargan.

The sticky clay began to fall away from Tarry's feet and as he went home one evening with Eusebius he suggested that they should take a run round Dillon's, 'just for a cod'. The Dillons did not attend the Mission, but they must have liked it, for it provided them with new opportunities. When all the parish was at the Mission service in the evening they could almost do what they liked in the green fields along the road. Charlie set out to go to the Mission but it seemed that he went no farther than Dillon's house.

Ahead of Tarry and his neighbour walked the groups of old men and the lines of old maids. The conversation of the men was excited, even though they were talking about football and the big match that was being held in the village on the following Sunday.

'Should be a desperate gate, Hughie.'

'Twenty pound.'

'If it 'ill be trusting to it.'

And so on.

The women were gossiping about their hens, and some of the most hopeless old maids were discussing with sharp horror the doings of the Dillons. And everyone seemed to be going somewhere now, going somewhere with a purpose.

Dillon's house was a thatched cottage about a hundred yards in off the main road, half way between Dargan and Drumnay. The path up to the house continued as a short-cut across the hills which was used by the natives of Miskin and sometimes by the people of Drumnay. Seen from the road the house was a gay little house, trim, whitewashed, the real traditional Irish cabin.

The two boys without saying anything to each other both decided to take the short-cut. A couple of straggling old women looked after them as if taking notice and wondering why they were going that way. For once in his life Tarry felt no guilty conscience. He was pleasantly hysterical like a young girl at a wedding.

They were not talking about girls now:

'I put clay up to me spuds last week,' said Tarry, 'and they're doing terribly well.'

'The potash is your man,' said Eusebius.

'I only put on the bare hundred,' said Tarry, boastful of the soil of his farm.

'You did and the rest,' said Eusebius, but he was not thinking of potatoes.

'Stop a second,' said Tarry in a whisper.

They were standing still, surveying the corner of the field at the bottom of McArdle's hill in Miskin.

'It's him,' said Tarry.

'Isn't he the two ends of a hure?' said Eusebius.

Charlie was the man who was sneaking along the hedge in that corner, and the girl with him was Josie Dillon.

'As sure as there's an eye in a hawk,' said Eusebius.

'We'll watch him,' said Tarry.

When they came to the gable of Dillon's house they could see across the low boxwood hedge the little flower garden before the door, with rings of beautiful flowers. Around the doors and windows grew roses, wildish white roses and cream ones and red ones. And from within the house came the sound of laughter.

One of the girls came to the door and emptied the tea-pot. As she did so she managed to keep in touch with the conversation within. Those within were the older generations whose desires had come to rest. These did frequent the church, but were not vital in the local life, for nobody would consider them as capable of morality or immorality no more than they would the farm animals. They were looked upon as a people apart, and what they did did not reflect on the life of the ordinary people. There was a great-great grandmother in the house, the only great-great grandmother of the human race that Tarry had ever seen. There would have been a long line of her descendants if they hadn't been consumptive. There was a far-out relationship between the Dillons and the Reillys, and some people tried to make out that the Flynns had a drop of the same blood, but Tarry had proved to his own satisfaction that that relationship was no nearer than seventh cousin, and when he declared to the old men of the area that if all the seventh cousins were counted they would include every man, woman and child in Dargan and a lot more outside it, that kept the relationship theory from being developed.

While Tarry was taking in the beauty of the flowers, Eusebius had gone behind the house and peeped in the window.

'Jabus, do you know what?' he said, returning. 'I never saw such a house, shining like a kitten's eye, man, plates on the dresser and everything. Hell of a crowd in there drinking tay and porter. It's a dread.'

'Many of the younger ones in?'

'Only Mary.'

'My God!' Tarry sighed.

He had been developing a sort of pity for two of the youngest girls aged about thirteen and fifteen and he felt that these could be saved if taken in time. But if they couldn't be saved the next best thing would be for him to have them while they were virgins. He didn't tell his mind to Eusebius but led off with a few remarks to get the man's outlook.

'Would you say the two young ones are still all right, Eusebius?'

'How, like?'

'Would you say they had ever men with them?'

They had crossed the stile and were now coming up to one of Kerley's fields. They had to search for a hole in the hedge through which to pass, for apparently the old short-cut had been changed since last they went that way. They had to walk all along the field till they came to the railway. Eusebius was sampling the paling wire instead of replying to his companion's question. 'A few strands of that would come in very useful for fixing a cracked shaft of a cart,' said he.

A head bobbed up from among the long grass on the railway slope, and Tarry, knowing that they were running into the Dillons and their boy friends, urged on Eusebius to come away. He didn't want to see the two young ones with old blackguards. So long as he had some doubts about it he would have an escape but once he was sure – Eusebius didn't understand this at all.

'When we came this far –'

'There may be men waiting with mares for you to come back, Eusebius.'

'They'll know I'm at the Mission and wait. Come on, man.'

'Take your time a minute,' Tarry said, while he considered.

A girl's scream came from the direction of the railway bridge and Tarry's heart was shaken. None of the older Dillon girls would have screamed like that. He was late. He thought the worst. One virgin less for him to dream about.

Eusebius wouldn't wait any longer. He wanted, he said, to see what Charlie was up to, and he dashed down the railway slope and out of sight, calling on Tarry to come on as he disappeared under the long weeds and grass.

Tarry went home alone.

He hadn't the courage on this occasion, but he had plans. In matters of this description a man should plan ahead. No use rushing into something for which he might be sorry. Some other evening he would stay at home from the Mission and make a proper examination of conditions on the railway slope.

He went home in despair.

The mother was making tea when he arrived.

'You were born at meal time,' she said. 'I didn't expect you home yet awhile. I got a lift in Jemmy Kerley's trap – the devil must have broken a rib in him, for he's the narrow-gutted article, a bad garry that doesn't believe in putting too much weight on his springs. Who were you home with?'

'Nobody at all,' he said.

He went upstairs to his room to lie on his bed and read poems from one of the school books. He was looking for something that would console him about lost women, but the best he could find was a lyric by Byron.

We'll go no more a roving
So late into the night
Though the heart be still as loving
And the moon be still as bright.

He read, and as he read he was not reading the poem as if it were the work of another man: he had written that poem and was now saying it, impressing its romantic meaning on a lonely and beautiful virgin as they walked together then along the primrose bank at the top of Callan's hill.

The Mission was to continue for two weeks. Money was charged going in to it and on the first week all the respectable people had the job of holding the collecting boxes. Tarry had hopes that for the second week he would get one of these honorary jobs, and he went so far as to tell his mother that he didn't fancy the job at all. 'Can't you be like another and do it if you're asked – *if* you're asked. The devil the bit of me thinks you will.'

By the looks of her she would like him to be asked and was only casting doubt upon the suggestion to make the honour more honourable when it came.

On Sunday the curate, Father Markey, read out the list of those who were to hold the boxes and as name after name was announced and still not his, he was getting down-hearted. And when Charlie Trainor's name was announced he could hardly believe his ears. Were the priests blind or did they prefer a man who didn't care a damn for morals one way or the other? It looked very like it.

'You were lucky you wasn't offered one of them oul' jobs,' said Eusebius – who had also been called upon – rubbing the salt in.

'I sent word to Father Markey not to give me out,' Tarry said.

'Oh, I see,' said Eusebius in a manner that damaged Tarry's explanation.

Well, said he to himself one day as he was harnessing the mare in the stable, if they think that little of me I'll not go this evening at all. He stooped down under the belly of the animal to catch the girth strap and as he did he caught a glimpse of the morning sun coming down the valley; it glinted on the swamp and the sedge and flowers caught a meaning for him. That was his meaning. Having found it suddenly, the tying of the girth and the putting of the mare in the cart and every little act became a wonderful miraculous work. It made him very proud too and in some ways impossible. Other important things did not seem important at all.

When his mother came out to give him money for the stuff he was to buy in the shop, his mind was in the clouds.

'Now, don't forget,' said she up to him where he sat on his throne of the seat-board, 'don't forget the salt that I want for the churning.'

'No fear of me to forget,' he said as he took the money.

'I wish I could say that; the last time I sent you for it you forgot; you'd forget your head only it's tied to you. Another thing – if you meet one of them missioners – as you're likely to, for they do be out walking the roads – be nice to him and don't be carrying on with this nonsensical talk that you do be at sometimes . . . Mary, go in and keep the pot on the boil . . . Now, I'll hear if you say anything.'

'Lord God, but you're the innocent woman. Do you think I'd start to talk philosophy to every oul' cod I meet. Go on, mare.'

'Oul' cod, every oul' cod.' Mrs Flynn shook her head in disgust as she closed the gate behind him to keep Callan's straying animals from entering the street. On the way to the village shop he met Father Anthony who was the joker of the Mission. One of the priests sent to a parish was always a 'gay fella'. He cracked a joke on meeting Tarry, and Tarry pulled up. He didn't like this sort of joke when his mind was contemplating the lonely beauty of the landscape around him. He was somewhat abrupt with the monk and in his excitement said the wrong thing: he said the unusual thing, what he had often taken a vow against saying, and that made the monk suspicious. He didn't like to hear originality from a poor farmer and was disappointed to find his well-practised joke treated so indifferently.

Originality showed pride.

'Were you at your Confession yet?' asked the priest.

'I'm well within the walls of the Church,' said Tarry.

'What do you know about the Church?' said the monk a little angrily. 'What has a young country boy like you to do with these things? You must come and let me hear your Confession.'

He asked Tarry his name and where he lived, and finally his age. Asking his age Tarry always found was a sure sign that the man who asked was not friendly. There was always a touch of malice in such a question, it was being familiar. Whenever anyone asked him his age he put him down as an enemy. Considering that he was nearly thirty he would have preferred not being asked. He told the man he was twenty-five. The monk began to chastise Tarry for his outlook and was telling him that he was heading for the downward path when Charlie came by on a bicycle. With a smile like a full moon the monk saluted the calf-dealer and the joke he cracked was warmly enjoyed by Charlie.

Charlie had overheard the missioner's chastisement of Tarry and when they parted with the monk, Charlie, catching hold of the side-board of the cart while still keeping on his bicycle, ran alongside Tarry inquiring what the hell he was saying to the poor missioner.

'You wouldn't know,' said Tarry.

Charlie was very vexed. 'You're a desperate man to be making little of the priests like that, Flynn. We're all Catholics, aren't we?'

'I don't know so much about that, Charlie. Some of us are doubtful.'

'Oh, I see, you don't believe in religion.'

'No, but you do, Charlie,' Tarry sneered.

The way Charlie raised his eyebrows and pretended to be angry made Tarry mad; for he knew that this dishonest attitude was the stuff out of which ignorant bigotry is made. This encounter with the monk and the calf-dealer took most of the good out of his journey to the village which was usually such a pleasant holiday from the drag of his existence.

As he feared, his mother wasn't long hearing about the tiff. She heard it before the day was ended, though she did not accuse him of it till the day after. She talked as if she were terrified, but for all that there was humour in her terror which she couldn't conceal.

'What the devil's father did you say to him?' said she.

'Not one thing.'

'We'll be the talk of the country – like the Carlins. Did you hear that one of the missioners was up with them this evening, trying to get them to come out to the Mission?'

'They're not going?'

'Going, how are you . . . Give us up that long potstick from the door . . . O, going, aye! And you're taking pattern by them.'

Tarry was disgusted with the Carlins; they were liable to give the impression that having a respect for oneself was a sign of madness. If, in the cause of his self-esteem, *he* stayed at home from the chapel he'd be put down as a queer fellow. Not that he had any intention of missing the carnival spirit that was to be found around the church these days or of revolting against the Church – he had only intended staying away one evening. He would remain away that one evening – and he did. He ran over to the field to take a last look at a heifer that was due to calve and then went down the road as if he were going off to pray. Eusebius had to go off earlier, he being an official.

He crossed the hills into Miskin, intending to come out on the railway line. Passing Petey Meegan's house he saw the crooked old bachelor owner hurrying off up Kerley's hill on his way to hear more about sex.

The shadowy lane with the hedges that nearly met in the middle was filled with midges and flies buzzing over cow-dung. Here he was in another world. It was almost a year since he had gone up that lane and it evoked nostalgia. He remembered as a child coming home from second Mass on Sundays with Eusebius by this lane and how fairylike it seemed to him then. Old Petey's old father used to come out hobbling on his two sticks and like the Ancient Mariner try to get them to listen to his stories of the Sleeping Horsemen who were enchanted under a hill near Ardee. One day they would awaken to fight against the enemies of the Church. It was to be a deadly fight and the time would be the End of the World. There was an apocalyptic flavour about all those stories and the memory of them influenced the heavy-smelling fungi and flowers that grew in the dark ditches.

A great row was going on in McArdle's kitchen.

The four sons were arguing with their father and mother for money. These four sons were all over forty but they were treated as babies by their parents. That may have been why when they appeared at Drumnay cross-roads or in the discussions in Magan's pub they were so aggressive and spoke with airs of such domineering authority.

'I want a shilling for fags and I'll have to get it,' a powerful lamenting voice could be heard.

A pup screamed and ran under the table.

'Am I made of money? Am I made of money?' the father cried.

The mother was now crying quietly and Tarry hurried along, knowing that a family row is a most unhealthy affair for an outsider.

He had been hoping to run into the youngest of the Dillons. If the truth must be told, he had had his eye on those two young girls for years and was only waiting for them to get big enough. He didn't suspect that other men had had similar ambitions and even the affair of the earlier evening did not entirely disperse his hopes that they were still safe for him.

Crossing on to the railway line he was treading down the sleepers when Josie Dillon, who had had three children, came down the slope towards a well. She was smoking a cigarette, which she put out on seeing him. Was the girl afraid of him as of a priest? It looked like it, and he did not want to give that impression of himself, which was, in his opinion, a false impression. Yet the girl might have been right, for on taking a second look at her he knew that he just didn't associate with that class of person. She was the type of woman whom he often saw in the slums of the town of a fair day.

To find out about the sisters he would have to speak to her, so he spoke, much to her surprise, for he had often passed her by before with his head in the air. He only said it was a nice evening, and the girl took it for granted that he meant something else.

'Are you coming down the line?' she inquired.

'Good God! no,' he said. 'I'm late for the Mission as I am.'

He raced up the slope and out of her range as quickly as he could, praying as he ran that nobody saw him. Bad as he was, if he got the name of being seen with one of the Dillons he'd be ruined. Some men could take life easily. Some could dabble in sin, but it didn't fit into his life. He made a promise to the Sacred Heart that if he hadn't been seen he would go to the Mission every single evening, and to Confession on the next Saturday.

When he found out that nobody had seen him – if they had there would be talk – he was somewhat annoyed with himself for making rash promises – but he would keep them.

The little tillage fields and the struggle for existence broke every dramatic fall. A layer of sticky soil lay between the fires in the heart preventing a general conflagration. The Mission had lifted up the limp body of society in Dargan, but as soon as the pressure was relaxed it fell back again and the grass grew over the penitential sod.

With Tarry it was different. He believed that of all the people in the parish he alone took religion seriously. Too seriously, for being too serious meant that it was not integrated in his ordinary life. When the ordinary man went to Confession he rambled on with a list of harmless sins, ignoring all the ones that would have filled Tarry with remorse. When Tarry went to Confession that Saturday night he had the misfortune, contrary to his own well-thought-out arrangements, to mention unusual sins.

The Confessor was the monk he had met on the road.

'What sins do you remember since your last Confession?' the monk asked.

'I read books, father,' Tarry replied before he had time to think. He knew at once that he had made a mistake, for that started the monk off.

'What sort of books?'

Tarry did not want to admit that he only read school books and newspapers and it would appear that he was telling a lie if he didn't try to mention some books. So he said: 'Shaw, father.'

He had read about Shaw in the newspapers, but had never read a line of Shaw's.

'Have you a Rosary?' asked the Confessor.

Tarry had not but he said: 'Yes, father' in the hope of getting out of the confessional as quickly as possible. He had made it awkward enough as it was.

'You should read the *Messenger of the Sacred Heart*,' said the Confessor. 'Do you ever read the little *Messenger?*'

'Yes, father.'

'Continue to read it, my child; in that little book you will find all the finest literature written by the greatest writers. And give up this man, Shaw.'

In all he could not have been less than twenty minutes in the confessional and considering that there was a long impatient queue on both sides of the confessional – among whom were Charlie and Eusebius – and that that confessor had the reputation of being very quick and easy – which was why he had such queues waiting to tell their sins to him, no wonder that Tarry's lengthy period in the confession box caused such surprise.

'Shaw's a hard man,' remarked Charlie later, when they were standing outside Magan's shop. Charlie hadn't the faintest idea who Shaw was but he thought that by mentioning the name someone might reveal the secret behind it. No one knew, and Charlie was disappointed.

'You were a long time in the box with the priest, I hear,' said the mother when he got home. 'Did you kill a man or what? . . . You'll have to cut them yellow weeds in the Low Place the morrow and not have the fields a show to the world. What did you say that made him keep you?'

'It's a sin to tell a thing like that.'

'Whatever you do anyway, I wouldn't like to think of you knocking around Dillon's house, not that I'd ever believe you'd do anything, but you know the big-mouths that's about this place.'

'You needn't worry.'

The Mission came to an end with a brilliant display of lighted candles and the massed congregation of old men and women straightening their bent backs and vowing to renounce the World, the Flesh and the Devil. They promised to control their passions, and Tarry, as he watched the scene of self-abnegation from the gallery, got a queer creepy feeling in the nerves of his face which something that was ludicrous and pathetic always made him feel. Petey Meegan was thumping his breast and looking up towards the coloured window with an ecstatic gaze.

Old thin-faced, long-nosed Jenny Toole had a frightened look, thinking of the dangers she faced in a world of violent men.

The crowds went home and once again the clay hand was clapped across the mouth of Prophecy.

He cut the ragweeds and the thistles the following day. The yellow maggots wearing football jerseys which crept on the blossom fell to the ground. These maggots would become winged if they had lived long enough. Some day he, too, might grow wings and be able to fly away from this clay-stricken place. Ah, clay! It was out of clay that wings were made. He stared down at the dry little canyons in the parched earth and he loved that dry earth which could produce a miracle of wings.

SAMUEL BECKETT
from *Murphy*

6

Amor intellectualis quo Murphy se ipsum amat.

It is most unfortunate, but the point of this story has been reached where a justification of the expression 'Murphy's mind' has to be attempted. Happily we need not concern ourselves with this apparatus as it really was – that would be an extravagance and an impertinence – but solely with what it felt and pictured itself to be. Murphy's mind is after all the gravamen of these informations. A short section to itself at this stage will relieve us from the necessity of apologizing for it further.

Murphy's mind pictured itself as a large hollow sphere, hermetically closed to the universe without. This was not an impoverishment, for it excluded nothing that it did not itself contain. Nothing ever had been, was or would be in the universe outside it but was already present as virtual, or actual, or virtual rising into actual, or actual falling into virtual, in the universe inside it.

This did not involve Murphy in the idealist tar. There was the mental fact and there was the physical fact, equally real if not equally pleasant.

He distinguished between the actual and the virtual of his mind, not as between form and the formless yearning for form, but as between that of which he had both mental and physical experience and that of which he had mental experience only. Thus the form of kick was actual, that of caress virtual.

The mind felt its actual part to be above and bright, its virtual beneath and fading into dark, without however connecting this with the ethical yoyo. The mental experience was cut off from the physical experience, its criteria were not those of the physical experience, the agreement of part of its content with physical fact did not confer worth on that part. It did not function and could not be disposed according to a principle of worth. It was made up of light fading into dark, of above and beneath, but not of good and bad. It contained forms with parallel in another mode and forms without, but not right forms and wrong forms. It felt no issue between its light and dark, no need for its light to devour its dark. The need was now to be in the light, now in the half light, now in the dark. That was all.

Thus Murphy felt himself split in two, a body and a mind. They had intercourse apparently, otherwise he could not have known that they had anything in common. But he felt his mind to be bodytight and did not understand through what channel the intercourse was effected nor how the two experiences came to overlap. He was satisfied that neither followed from the other. He neither thought a kick because he felt one nor felt a kick because he thought one. Perhaps the knowledge was related to the fact of the kick as two magnitudes to a third. Perhaps there was, outside space and time, a non-mental non-physical Kick from all eternity, dimly revealed to Murphy in its correlated modes of consciousness and extension, the kick *in intellectu* and the kick *in re*. But where then was the supreme Caress?

However that might be, Murphy was content to accept this partial congruence of the world of his mind with the world of his body as due to some such process of supernatural determination. The problem was of little interest. Any solution would do that did not clash with the feeling, growing stronger as Murphy grew older, that his mind was a closed system, subject to no principle of change but its own, self-sufficient and impermeable to the vicissitudes of the body. Of infinitely more interest than how this came to be so was the manner in which it might be exploited.

He was split, one part of him never left this mental chamber that pictured itself as a sphere full of light fading into dark, because there was no way out. But motion in this world depended on rest in the world outside. A man is in bed, wanting to sleep. A rat is behind the wall at his head, wanting to move. The man hears the rat fidget and cannot sleep, the rat hears the man fidget and dares not move. They are both unhappy, one fidgeting and the other waiting, or both happy, the rat moving and the man sleeping.

Murphy could think and know after a fashion with his body up (so to speak) and about, with a kind of mental *tic douloureux* sufficient for his parody of rational behaviour. But that was not what he understood by consciousness.

His body lay down more and more in a less precarious abeyance than that of sleep, for its own convenience and so that the mind might move. There seemed little left of this body that was not privy to this mind, and that little was usually tired on its own account. The development of what looked like collusion between such utter strangers remained to Murphy as unintelligible as telekinesis or the Leyden Jar, and of as little interest. He noted with satisfaction that it existed, that his bodily need ran more and more with his mental.

As he lapsed in body he felt himself coming alive in mind, set free to move among its treasures. The body has its stock, the mind its treasures.

There were the three zones, light, half light, dark, each with its speciality.

In the first were the forms with parallel, a radiant abstract of the dog's life, the elements of physical experience available for a new arrangement. Here the pleasure was reprisal, the pleasure of reversing the physical experience. Here the kick that the physical Murphy received, the mental Murphy gave. It was the same kick, but corrected as to direction. Here the chandlers were available for slow depilation, Miss Carridge for rape by Ticklepenny, and so on. Here the whole physical fiasco became a howling success.

In the second were the forms without parallel. Here the pleasure was contemplation. This system had no other mode in which to be out of joint and therefore did not need to be put right in this. Here was the Belacqua bliss and others scarcely less precise.

In both these zones of his private world Murphy felt sovereign and free, in the one to requite himself, in the other to move as he pleased from one unparalleled beatitude to another. There was no rival initiative.

The third, the dark, was a flux of forms, a perpetual coming together and falling asunder of forms. The light contained the docile elements of a new manifold, the world of the body broken up into the pieces of a toy; the half light, states of peace. But the dark neither elements nor states, nothing but forms becoming and crumbling into the fragments of a new becoming, without love or hate or any intelligible principle of change. Here there was nothing but commotion and the pure forms of commotion.

Here he was not free, but a mote in the dark of absolute freedom. He did not move, he was a point in the ceaseless unconditioned generation and passing away of line.

Matrix of surds.

It was pleasant to kick the Ticklepennies and Miss Carridges simultaneously together into ghastly acts of love. It was pleasant to lie dreaming on the shelf beside Belacqua, watching the dawn break crooked. But how much more pleasant was the sensation of being a missile without provenance or target, caught up in a tumult of non-Newtonian motion. So pleasant that pleasant was not the word.

Thus as his body set him free more and more in his mind, he took to spending less and less time in the light, spitting at the breakers of the world; and less in the half light, where the choice of bliss introduced an element of effort; and more and more and more in the dark, in the will-lessness, a mote in its absolute freedom.

This painful duty having now been discharged, no further bulletins will be issued.

'First Love'

I associate, rightly or wrongly, my marriage with the death of my father, in time. That other links exist, on other levels, between these two affairs, is not impossible. I have enough trouble as it is in trying to say what I think I know.

I visited, not so long ago, my father's grave, that I do know, and noted the date of his death, of his death alone, for that of his birth had no interest for me, on that particular day. I set out in the morning and was back by night, having lunched lightly in the graveyard. But some days later, wishing to know his age at death, I had to return to the grave, to note the date of his birth. These two limiting dates I then jotted down on a piece of paper, which I now carry about with me. I am thus in a position to affirm that I must have been about twenty-five at the time of my marriage. For the date of my own birth, I repeat, my own birth, I have never forgotten, I never had to note it down, it remains graven in my memory, the year at least, in figures that life will not easily erase. The day itself comes back to me, when I put my mind to it, and I often celebrate it, after my fashion, I don't say each time it comes back, for it comes back too often, but often.

Personally I have no bone to pick with graveyards, I take the air there willingly, perhaps more willingly than elsewhere, when take the air I must. The smell of corpses, distinctly perceptible under those of grass and humus mingled, I do not find unpleasant, a trifle on the sweet side perhaps, a trifle heady, but how infinitely preferable to what the living emit, their feet, teeth, armpits, arses, sticky foreskins and frustrated ovules. And when my father's remains join in, however modestly, I can almost shed a tear. The living wash in vain, in vain perfume themselves, they stink. Yes, as a place for an outing, when out I must, leave me my graveyards and keep – you – to your public parks and beauty-spots. My sandwich, my banana, taste sweeter when I'm sitting on a tomb, and when the time comes to piss again, as it so often does, I have my pick. Or I wander, hands clasped behind my back, among the slabs, the flat, the leaning and the upright, culling the inscriptions. Of these I never weary, there are always three or four of such drollery that I have to hold on to the cross, or the stele, or the angel, so as not to fall. Mine I composed long since and am still pleased with it, tolerably pleased. My other writings are no sooner dry than they revolt me, but my epitaph still meets with my approval. There is little chance unfortunately of its ever being reared above the skull that conceived it, unless the State takes up the matter. But to be unearthed I must first be found, and I greatly fear those gentlemen will have as much trouble finding me dead as alive. So I hasten to record it here and now, while there is yet time:

> *Hereunder lies the above who up below*
> *So hourly died that he lived on till now.*

The second and last or rather latter line limps a little perhaps, but that is no great matter I'll be forgiven more than that when I'm forgotten. Then with a little luck you hit on a genuine interment, with real live mourners and the odd relict trying to throw herself into the pit. And nearly always that charming business with the dust, though in my experience there is nothing less dusty than holes of this type, verging on muck for the most part, nor anything particularly powdery about the deceased, unless he happened to have died, or she, by fire. No matter, their little gimmick with the dust is charming. But my father's yard was not amongst my favourites. To begin with it was too remote, way out in the wilds of the country on the side of a hill, and too small, far too small, to go on with. Indeed it was almost full, a few more widows and they'd be turning them away. I infinitely preferred Ohlsdorf, particularly the Linne section, on Prussian soil, with its nine hundred acres of corpses packed tight, though I knew no one there, except by reputation the wild animal collector Hagenbeck. A lion, if I remember right, is carved on his monument, death must have had for Hagenbeck the countenance of a lion. Coaches ply to and fro, crammed with widows, widowers, orphans and the like. Groves, grottoes, artificial lakes with swans, offer consolation to the inconsolable. It was December, I had never felt so cold, the eel soup lay heavy on my stomach, I was afraid I'd die, I turned aside to vomit, I envied them.

But to pass on to less melancholy matters, on my father's death I had to leave the house. It was he who wanted me in the house. He was a strange man. One day he said, Leave him alone, he's not disturbing anyone. He didn't know I was listening. This was a view he must have often voiced, but the other times I wasn't by. They would never let me see his will, they simply said he had left me such a sum. I believed then and still believe he had stipulated in his will that I be left the room I had occupied in his lifetime and for food to be brought me there, as hitherto. He may even have given this the force of condition precedent. Presumably he liked to feel me under his roof, otherwise he would not have opposed my eviction. Perhaps he merely pitied me. But somehow I think not. He should have left me the entire house, then I'd have been all right, the others too for that matter, I'd have summoned them and said, Stay, stay by all means, your home is here. Yes, he was properly had, my poor father, if his purpose was really to go on protecting me from beyond the tomb. With regard to the money it is only fair to say they gave it to me without delay, on the very day following the inhumation. Perhaps they were legally bound to. I said to them, Keep this money and let me live on here, in my room, as in Papa's lifetime. I added, God rest his soul, in the hope of melting them. But they refused. I offered to place myself at their disposal, a few hours every day, for the little odd maintenance jobs every dwelling requires, if it is not to crumble away. Pottering is still just possible, I don't know why. I proposed in particular to look after the hothouse. There I would have gladly whiled away the hours, in the heat, tending the tomatoes, hyacinths, pinks and seedlings. My father and I alone, in that household, understood tomatoes. But they refused. One day, on my return from stool, I found my room locked and my belongings in a heap before the door. This will give you some idea how constipated I was, at this juncture. It was, I am now convinced, anxiety constipation. But was I genuinely constipated? Somehow I think not. Softly, softly. And yet I must have been, for how otherwise account for those long, those cruel sessions in the necessary house? At such times I never read, any more than at other times, never gave way to revery or meditation, just gazed dully at the almanac hanging from a nail before my eyes, with its chromo of a bearded stripling in the midst of sheep, Jesus no doubt, parted the cheeks with both hands and strained, heave! ho! heave! ho!, with the motions of one tugging at the oar, and only one thought in my mind, to be back in my room and flat on my back again. What can that have been but constipation? Or am I confusing it with diarrhoea? It's all a muddle in my head, graves and nuptials and the different varieties of motion. Of my scanty belongings they had made a little heap, on the floor, against the door. I can still see that little heap, in the kind of recess full of shadow between the landing and my room. It was in this narrow space, guarded on three sides only, that I had to change, I mean exchange my dressing-gown and nightgown for my travelling costume, I mean shoes, socks, trousers, shirt, coat, greatcoat and hat, I can think of nothing else. I tried other doors, turning the knobs and pushing, or pulling, before I left the house, but none yielded. I think if I'd found one open I'd have barricaded myself in the room, nothing less than gas would have dislodged me. I felt the house crammed as usual, the usual pack, but saw no one. I imagined them in their various rooms, all bolts drawn, every sense on the alert. Then the rush to the window, each holding back a little, hidden by the curtain, at the sound of the street door closing behind me, I should have left it open. Then the doors fly open and out they pour, men, women and children, and the voices, the sighs, the smiles, the hands, the keys in the hands, the blessed relief, the precautions rehearsed, if this then that, but if that then this, all clear and joy in every heart, come let's eat, the fumigation can wait. All imagination to be sure, I was already on my way, things may have passed quite differently, but who cares how things pass, provided they pass. All those lips that had kissed me, those hearts that had loved me (it is with the heart one loves, is it not, or am I confusing it with something else?), those hands that had played with mine and those minds that had almost made their own of me! Humans are truly strange. Poor Papa, a nice mug he must have felt that day if he could see me, see us, a nice mug on my account I mean. Unless in his great disembodied wisdom he saw further than his son whose corpse was not yet quite up to scratch.

But to pass on to less melancholy matters, the name of the woman with whom I was soon to be united was Lulu. So at least she assured me and I can't see what interest she could have had in lying to me, on this score. Of course one can never tell. She also disclosed her family name, but I've forgotten it. I should have made a note of it, on a piece of paper, I hate to forget a proper name. I met her on a bench, on the bank of the canal, one of the canals, for our town boasts two, though I never knew which was which. It was a well situated bench, backed by a mound of solid earth and garbage, so that my rear was covered. My flanks too, partially, thanks to a pair of venerable trees, more than venerable, dead, at either end of the bench. It was no doubt these trees one fine day, aripple with all their foliage, that had sown the idea of a bench, in someone's fancy. To the fore, a few yards away, flowed the canal, if canals flow, don't ask me, so that from that quarter too the risk of surprise was small. And yet she surprised me. I lay stretched out, the night being warm, gazing up through the bare boughs interlocking high above me, where the trees clung together for support, and through the drifting cloud, at a patch of starry sky as it came and went. Shove up, she said. My first movement was to go, but my fatigue, and my having nowhere to go, dissuaded me from acting on it. So I drew back my feet a little way and she sat. Nothing more passed between us that evening and she soon took herself off, without another word. All she had done was sing, beneath her breath as to herself, and without the words fortunately, some old folk songs, and so disjointedly, skipping from one to another and finishing none, that even I found it strange. The voice, though out of tune, was not unpleasant. It breathed of a soul too soon wearied ever to conclude, that perhaps least arse-aching soul of all. The bench itself was soon more than she could bear and as for me, one look had been enough for her. Whereas in reality she was a most tenacious woman. She came back next day and the day after and all went off more or less as before. Perhaps a few words were exchanged. The next day it was raining and I felt in security. Wrong again. I asked her if she was resolved to disturb me every evening. I disturb you? she said. I felt her eyes on me. They can't have seen much, two eyelids at the most, with a hint of nose and brow, darkly, because of the dark. I thought we were easy, she said. You disturb me, I said, I can't stretch out with you there. The collar of my greatcoat was over my mouth and yet she heard me. Must you stretch out? she said. The mistake one makes is to speak to people. You have only to put your feet on my knees, she said. I didn't wait to be asked twice, under my miserable calves I felt her fat thighs. She began stroking my ankles. I considered kicking her in the cunt. You speak to people about stretching out and they immediately see a body at full length. What mattered to me in my dispeopled kingdom, that in regard to which the disposition of my carcass was the merest and most futile of accidents, was supineness in the mind, the dulling of the self and of that residue of execrable frippery known as the non-self and even the world, for short. But man is still today, at the age of twenty-five, at the mercy of an erection, physically too, from time to time, it's the common lot, even I was not immune, if that may be called an erection. It did not escape her naturally, women smell a rigid phallus ten miles away and wonder, How on earth did he spot me from there? One is no longer oneself, on such occasions, and it is painful to be no longer oneself, even more painful if possible than when one is. For when one is one knows what to do to be less so, whereas when one is not one is any old one irredeemably. What goes by the name of love is banishment, with now and then a postcard from the homeland, such is my considered opinion, this evening. When she had finished and my self been resumed, mine own, the mitigable, with the help of a brief torpor, it was alone. I sometimes wonder if that is not all invention, if in reality things did not take quite a different course, one I had no choice but to forget. And yet her image remains bound, for me, to that of the bench, not the bench by day, nor yet the bench by night, but the bench at evening, in such sort that to speak of the bench, as it appeared to me at evening, is to speak of her, for me. That proves nothing, but there is nothing I wish to prove. On the subject of the bench by day no words need be wasted, it never knew me, gone before morning and never back till dusk. Yes, in the daytime I foraged for food and marked down likely cover. Were you to inquire, as undoubtedly you itch, what I had done with the money my father had left me, the answer would be I had done nothing with it but leave it lie in my pocket. For I knew I would not be always young, and that summer does not last for ever either, nor even autumn, my mean soul told me so. In the end I told her I'd had enough. She disturbed me exceedingly, even absent. Indeed she still disturbs me, but no worse now than the rest. And it matters nothing to me now, to be disturbed, or so little, what does it mean, disturbed, and what would I do with myself if I wasn't? Yes, I've changed my system, it's the winning one at last, for the ninth or tenth time, not to mention not long now, not long till curtain down, on disturbers and disturbed, no more tattle about that, all that, her and the others, the shitball and heaven's high halls. So you don't want me to come any more, she said. It's incredible the way they repeat what you've just said to them, as if they risked faggot and fire in believing their ears. I told her to come just the odd time. I didn't understand women at that period. I still don't for that matter. Nor men either. Nor animals either. What I understand best, which is not saying much, are my pains. I think them through daily, it doesn't take long, thought moves so fast, but they are not only in my thought, not all. Yes, there are moments, particularly in the afternoon, when I go all syncretist, à la Reinhold. What equilibrium! But even them, my pains, I understand ill. That must come from my not being all pain and nothing else. There's the rub. Then they recede, or I, till they fill me with amaze and wonder, seen from a better planet. Not often, but I ask no more. Catch-cony life! To be nothing but pain, how that would simplify matters! Omnidolent! Impious dream. I'll tell them to you some day none the less, if I think of it, if I can, my strange pains, in detail, distinguishing between the different kinds, for the sake of clarity, those of the mind, those of the heart or emotional conative, those of the soul (none prettier than these) and finally those of the frame proper, first the inner or latent, then those affecting the surface, beginning with the hair and scalp and moving methodically down, without haste, all the way down to the feet beloved of the corn, the cramp, the kibe, the bunion, the hammer toe, the nail ingrown, the fallen arch, the common blain, the club foot, duck foot, goose foot, pigeon foot, flat foot, trench foot and other curiosities. And I'll tell by the same token, for those kind enough to listen, in accordance with a system whose inventor I forget, of those instants when, neither drugged, nor drunk, nor in ecstasy, one feels nothing. Next of course she desired to know what I meant by the odd time, that's what you get for opening your mouth. Once a week? Once in ten days? Once a fortnight? I replied less often, far less often, less often to the point of no more if she could, and if she could not the least often possible. And the next day (what is more) I abandoned the bench, less I must confess on her account than on its, for the site no longer answered my requirements, modest though they were, now that the air was beginning to strike chill, and for other reasons better not wasted on cunts like you, and took refuge in a deserted cowshed marked on one of my forays. It stood in the corner of a field richer on the surface in nettles than in grass and in mud than in nettles, but whose subsoil was perhaps possessed of exceptional qualities. It was in this byre, littered with dry and hollow cowclaps subsiding with a sigh at the poke of my finger, that for the first time in my life, and I would not hesitate to say the last if I had not to husband my cyanide, I had to contend with a feeling which gradually assumed, to my dismay, the dread name of love. What constitutes the charm of our country, apart of course from its scant population, and this without help of the meanest contraceptive, is that all is derelict, with the sole exception of history's ancient faeces. These are ardently sought after, stuffed and carried in procession. Wherever nauseated time has dropped a nice fat turd you will find our patriots, sniffing it up on all fours, their faces on fire. Elysium of the roofless. Hence my happiness at last. Lie down, all seems to say, lie down and stay down. I see no connexion between these remarks. But that one exists and even more than one, I have little doubt, for my part. But what? Which? Yes, I loved her, it's the name I gave, still give alas, to what I was doing then. I had nothing to go by, having never loved before, but of course had heard of the thing, at home, in school, in brothel and at church, and read romances, in prose and verse, under the guidance of my tutor, in six or seven languages, both dead and living, in which it was handled at length. I was therefore in a position, in spite of all, to put a label on what I was about when I found myself inscribing the letters of Lulu in an old heifer pat or flat on my face in the mud under the moon trying to tear up the nettles by the roots. They were giant nettles some full three foot high, to tear them up assuaged my pain, and yet it's not like me to do that to weeds, on the contrary, I'd smother them in manure if I had any. Flowers are a different matter. Love brings out the worst in man and no error. But what kind of love was this, exactly? Love-passion? Somehow I think not. That's the priapic one, is it not? Or is this a different variety? There are so many, are there not? All equally if not more delicious, are they not? Platonic love, for example, there's another just occurs to me. It's disinterested. Perhaps I loved her with a platonic love? But somehow I think not. Would I have been tracing her name in old cowshit if my love had been pure and disinterested? And with my devil's finger into the bargain, which I then sucked. Come now! My thoughts were all of Lulu, if that doesn't give you some idea nothing will. Anyhow I'm sick and tired of this name Lulu, I'll give her another, more like her, Anna for example, it's not more like her but no matter. I thought of Anna then, I who had learnt to think of nothing, nothing except my pains, a quick think through, and of what steps to take not to perish off-hand of hunger, or cold, or shame, but never on any account of living beings as such (I wonder what that means) whatever I may have said, or may still say, to the contrary or otherwise, on this subject. But I have always spoken, no doubt always shall, of things that never existed, or that existed if you insist, no doubt always will, but not with the existence I ascribe to them. Kepis, for example, exist beyond a doubt, indeed there is little hope of their ever disappearing, but personally I never wore a kepi. I wrote somewhere, They gave me . . . a hat. Now the truth is they never gave me a hat, I have always had my own hat, the one my father gave me, and I have never had any other hat than that hat. I may add it has followed me to the grave. I thought of Anna then, long long sessions, twenty minutes, twenty-five minutes and even as long as half an hour daily. I obtain these figures by the addition of other, lesser figures. That must have been my way of loving. Are we to infer from this I loved her with that intellectual love which drew from me such drivel, in another place? Somehow I think not. For had my love been of this kind would I have stooped to inscribe the letters of Anna in time's forgotten cowpats? To divellicate urtica *plenis manibus*? And felt, under my tossing head, her thighs to bounce like so many demon bolsters? Come now! In order to put an end, to try and put an end, to this plight, I returned one evening to the bench, at the hour she had used to join me there. There was no sign of her and I waited in vain. It was December already, if not January, and the cold was seasonable, that is to say reasonable, like all that is seasonable. But one is the hour of the dial, and another that of changing air and sky, and another yet again the heart's. To this thought, once back in the straw, I owed an excellent night. The next day I was earlier to the bench, much earlier, night having barely fallen, winter night, and yet too late, for she was there already, on the bench, under the boughs tinkling with rime, her back to the frosted mound, facing the icy water. I told you she was a highly tenacious woman. I felt nothing. What interest could she have in pursuing me thus? I asked her, without sitting down, stumping to and fro. The cold had embossed the path. She replied she didn't know. What could she see in me, would she kindly tell me that at least, if she could. She replied she couldn't. She seemed warmly clad, her hands buried in a muff. As I looked at this muff, I remember, tears came to my eyes. And yet I forget what colour it was. The state I was in then! I have always wept freely, without the least benefit to myself, till recently. If I had to weep this minute I could squeeze till I was blue, I'm convinced not a drop would fall. The state I am in now! It was things made me weep. And yet I felt no sorrow. When I found myself in tears for no apparent reason it meant I had caught sight of something unbeknownst. So I wonder if it was really the muff that evening, if it was not rather the path, so iron hard and bossy as perhaps to feel like cobbles to my tread, or some other thing, some chance thing glimpsed below the threshold, that so unmanned me. As for her, I might as well never have laid eyes on her before. She sat all huddled and muffled up, her head sunk, the muff with her hands in her lap, her legs pressed tight together, her heels clear of the ground. Shapeless, ageless, almost lifeless, it might have been anything or anyone, an old woman or a little girl. And the way she kept on saying, I don't know, I can't. I alone did not know and could not. Is it on my account you came? I said. She managed yes to that. Well here I am, I said. And I? Had I not come on hers? Here we are, I said. I sat down beside her but sprang up again immediately as though scalded. I longed to be gone, to know if it was over. But before going, to be on the safe side, I asked her to sing me a song. I thought at first she was going to refuse, I mean simply not sing, but no, after a moment she began to sing and sang for some time, all the time the same song it seemed to me, without change of attitude. I did not know the song, I had never heard it before and shall never hear it again. It had something to do with lemon trees, or orange trees, I forget, that is all I remember, and for me that is no mean feat, to remember it had something to do with lemon trees, or orange trees, I forget, for of all the other songs I have ever heard in my life, and I have heard plenty, it being apparently impossible, physically impossible short of being deaf, to get through this world, even my way, without hearing singing, I have retained nothing, not a word, not a note, or so few words, so few notes, that, that what, that nothing, this sentence has gone on long enough. Then I started to go and as I went I heard her singing another song, or perhaps more verses of the same, fainter and fainter the further I went, then no more, either because she had come to an end or because I was gone too far to hear her. To have to harbour such a doubt was something I preferred to avoid, at that period. I lived of course in doubt, on doubt, but such trivial doubts as this, purely somatic as some say, were best cleared up without delay, they could nag at me like gnats for weeks on end. So I retraced my steps a little way and stopped. At first I heard nothing, then the voice again, but only just, so faintly did it carry. First I didn't hear it, then I did, I must therefore have begun hearing it, at a certain point, but no, there was no beginning, the sound emerged so softly from the silence and so resembled it. When the voice ceased at last I approached a little nearer, to make sure it had really ceased and not merely been lowered. Then in despair, saying, No knowing, no knowing, short of being beside her, bent over her, I turned on my heel and went, for good, full of doubt. But some weeks later, even more dead than alive than usual, I returned to the bench, for the fourth or fifth time since I had abandoned it, at roughly the same hour, I mean roughly the same sky, no, I don't mean that either, for it's always the same sky and never the same sky, what words are there for that, none I know, period. She wasn't there, then suddenly she was, I don't know how, I didn't see her come, nor hear her, all ears and eyes though I was. Let us say it was raining, nothing like a change, if only of weather. She had her umbrella up, naturally, what an outfit. I asked if she came every evening. No, she said, just the odd time. The bench was soaking wet, we paced up and down, not daring to sit. I took her arm, out of curiosity, to see if it would give me pleasure, it gave me none, I let it go. But why these particulars. To put off the evil hour. I saw her face a little clearer, it seemed normal to me, a face like millions of others. The eyes were crooked, but I didn't know that till later. It looked neither young nor old, the face, as though stranded between the vernal and the sere. Such ambiguity I found difficult to bear, at that period. As to whether it was beautiful, the face, or had once been beautiful, or could conceivably become beautiful, I confess I could form no opinion. I had seen faces in photographs I might have found beautiful had I known even vaguely in what beauty was supposed to consist. And my father's face, on his death-bolster, had seemed to hint at some form of aesthetics relevant to man. But the faces of the living, all grimace and flush, can they be described as objects? I admired in spite of the dark, in spite of my fluster, the way still or scarcely flowing water reaches up, as though athirst, to that falling from the sky. She asked if I would like her to sing something. I replied no, I would like her to say something. I thought she would say she had nothing to say, it would have been like her, and so was agreeably surprised when she said she had a room, most agreeably surprised, though I suspected as much. Who has not a room? Ah I hear the clamour. I have two rooms, she said. Just how many rooms do you have? I said. She said she had two rooms and a kitchen. The premises were expanding steadily, given time she would remember a bathroom. Is it two rooms I heard you say? I said. Yes, she said. Adjacent? I said. At last conversation worthy of the name. Separated by the kitchen, she said. I asked her why she had not told me before. I must have been beside myself, at this period. I did not feel easy when I was with her, but at least free to think of something else than her, of the old trusty things, and so little by little, as down steps towards a deep, of nothing. And I knew that away from her I would forfeit this freedom.

There were in fact two rooms, separated by a kitchen, she had not lied to me. She said I should have fetched my things. I explained I had no things. It was at the top of an old house, with a view of the mountains for those who cared. She lit an oil-lamp. You have no current? I said. No, she said, but I have running water and gas. Ha, I said, you have gas. She began to undress. When at their wit's end they undress, no doubt the wisest course. She took off everything, with a slowness fit to enflame an elephant, except her stockings, calculated presumably to bring my concupiscence to the boil. It was then I noticed the squint. Fortunately she was not the first naked woman to have crossed my path, so I could stay, I knew she would not explode. I asked to see the other room which I had not yet seen. If I had seen it already I would have asked to see it again. Will you not undress? she said. Oh you know, I said, I seldom undress. It was the truth, I was never one to undress indiscriminately. I often took off my boots when I went to bed, I mean when I composed myself (composed!) to sleep, not to mention this or that outer garment according to the outer temperature. She was therefore obliged, out of common savoir faire, to throw on a wrap and light me the way. We went via the kitchen. We could just as well have gone via the corridor, as I realized later, but we went via the kitchen, I don't know why, perhaps it was the shortest way. I surveyed the room with horror. Such density of furniture defeats imagination. Not a doubt, I must have seen that room somewhere. What's this? I cried. The parlour, she said. The parlour! I began putting out the furniture through the door to the corridor. She watched, in sorrow I suppose, but not necessarily. She asked me what I was doing. She can't have expected an answer. I put it out piece by piece, and even two at a time, and stacked it all up in the corridor, against the outer wall. There were hundreds of pieces, large and small, in the end they blocked the door, making egress impossible, and *a fortiori* ingress, to and from the corridor. The door could be opened and closed, since it opened inwards, but had become impassable. To put it mildly. At least take off your hat, she said. I'll treat of my hat some other time perhaps. Finally the room was empty but for a sofa and some shelves fixed to the wall. The former I dragged to the back of the room, near the door, and next day took down the latter and put them out, in the corridor, with the rest. As I was taking them down, strange memory, I heard the word fibrome, or brone, I don't know which, never knew, never knew what it meant and never had the curiosity to find out. The things one recalls! and records! When all was in order at last I dropped on the sofa. She had not raised her little finger to help me. I'll get sheets and blankets, she said. But I wouldn't hear of sheets. You couldn't draw the curtain? I said. The window was frosted over. The effect was not white, because of the night, but faintly luminous none the less. This faint cold sheen, though I lay with my feet towards the door, was more than I could bear. I suddenly rose and changed the position of the sofa, that is to say turned it round so that the back, hitherto against the wall, was now on the outside and consequently the front, or way in, on the inside. Then I climbed back, like a dog into its basket. I'll leave you the lamp, she said, but I begged her to take it with her. And suppose you need something in the night, she said. She was going to start quibbling again, I could feel it. Do you know where the convenience is? she said. She was right, I was forgetting. To relieve oneself in bed is enjoyable at the time, but soon a source of discomfort. Give me a chamber-pot, I said. But she did not possess one. I have a close-stool of sorts, she said. I saw the grandmother on it, sitting up very stiff and grand, having just purchased it, pardon, picked it up, at a charity sale, or perhaps won it in a raffle, a period piece, and now trying it out, doing her best rather, almost wishing someone could see her. That's the idea, procrastinate. Any old recipient, I said, I don't have the flux. She came back with a kind of saucepan, not a true saucepan for it had no handle, it was oval in shape with two lugs and a lid. My stewpan, she said. I don't need the lid, I said. You don't need the lid? she said. If I had needed the lid she would have said, You need the lid? I drew this utensil down under the blanket, I like something in my hand when sleeping, it reassures me, and my hat was still wringing. I turned to the wall. She caught up the lamp off the mantelpiece where she had set it down, that's the idea, every particular, it flung her waving shadow over me, I thought she was off, but no, she came stooping down towards me over the sofa back. All family possessions, she said. I in her shoes would have tiptoed away, but not she, not a stir. Already my love was waning, that was all that mattered. Yes, already I felt better, soon I'd be up to the slow descents again, the long submersions, so long denied me through her fault. And I had only just moved in! Try and put me out now, I said. I seemed not to grasp the meaning of these words, nor even hear the brief sound they made, till some seconds after having uttered them. I was so unused to speech that my mouth would sometimes open, of its own accord, and vent some phrase or phrases, grammatically unexceptionable but entirely devoid if not of meaning, for on close inspection they would reveal one, and even several, at least of foundation. But I heard each word no sooner spoken. Never had my voice taken so long to reach me as on this occasion. I turned over on my back to see what was going on. She was smiling. A little later she went away, taking the lamp with her. I heard her steps in the kitchen and then the door of her room close behind her. Why behind her? I was alone at last, in the dark at last. Enough about that. I thought I was all set for a good night, in spite of the strange surroundings, but no, my night was most agitated. I woke next morning quite worn out, my clothes in disorder, the blanket likewise, and Anna beside me, naked naturally. One shudders to think of her exertions. I still had the stewpan in my grasp. It had not served. I looked at my member. If only it could have spoken! Enough about that. It was my night of love.

Gradually I settled down, in this house. She brought my meals at the appointed hours, looked in now and then to see if all was well and make sure I needed nothing, emptied the stew-pan once a day and did out the room once a month. She could not always resist the temptation to speak to me, but on the whole gave me no cause to complain. Sometimes I heard her singing in her room, the song traversed her door, then the kitchen, then my door, and in this way won to me, faint but indisputable. Unless it travelled by the corridor. This did not greatly incommode me, this occasional sound of singing. One day I asked her to bring me a hyacinth, live, in a pot. She brought it and put it on the mantelpiece, now the only place in my room to put things, unless you put them on the floor. Not a day passed without my looking at it. At first all went well, it even put forth a bloom or two, then it gave up and was soon no more than a limp stem hung with limp leaves. The bulb, half clear of the clay as though in search of oxygen, smelt foul. She wanted to remove it, but I told her to leave it. She wanted to get me another, but I told her I didn't want another. I was more seriously disturbed by other sounds, stifled giggles and groans, which filled the dwelling at certain hours of the night, and even of the day. I had given up thinking of her, quite given up, but still I needed silence, to live my life. In vain I tried to listen to such reasonings as that air is made to carry the clamours of the world, including inevitably much groan and giggle, I obtained no relief. I couldn't make out if it was always the same gent or more than one. Lovers' groans are so alike, and lovers' giggles. I had such horror then of these paltry perplexities that I always fell into the same error, that of seeking to clear them up. It took me a long time, my lifetime so to speak, to realize that the colour of an eye half seen, or the source of some distant sound, are closer to Giudecca in the hell of unknowing than the existence of God, or the origins of protoplasm, or the existence of self, and even less worthy than these to occupy the wise. It's a bit much, a lifetime, to achieve this consoling conclusion, it doesn't leave you much time to profit by it. So a fat lot of help it was when, having put the question to her, I was told they were clients she received in rotation. I could obviously have got up and gone to look through the keyhole. But what can you see, I ask you, through holes the likes of those? So you live by prostitution, I said. We live by prostitution, she said. You couldn't ask them to make less noise? I said, as if I believed her. I added, Or a different kind of noise. They can't help but yap and yelp, she said. I'll have to leave, I said. She found some old hangings in the family junk and hung them before our doors, hers and mine. I asked her if it would not be possible, now and then, to have a parsnip. A parsnip! she cried, as if I had asked for a dish of sucking Jew. I reminded her that the parsnip season was fast drawing to a close and that if, before it finally got there, she could feed me nothing but parsnips I'd be grateful. I like parsnips because they taste like violets and violets because they smell like parsnips. Were there no parsnips on earth violets would leave me cold and if violets did not exist I would care as little for parsnips as I do for turnips, or radishes. And even in the present state of their flora, I mean on this planet where parsnips and violets contrive to coexist, I could do without both with the utmost ease, the uttermost ease. One day she had the impudence to announce she was with child, and four or five months gone into the bargain, by me of all people! She offered me a side view of her belly. She even undressed, no doubt to prove she wasn't hiding a cushion under her skirt, and then of course for the pure pleasure of undressing. Perhaps it's just wind, I said, by way of consolation. She gazed at me with her big eyes whose colour I forget, with one big eye rather, for the other seemed riveted on the remains of the hyacinth. The more naked she was the more cross-eyed. Look, she said, stooping over her breasts, the haloes are darkening already. I summoned up my remaining strength and said, Abort, abort, and they'll blush like new. She had drawn back the curtain for a clear view of all her rotundities. I saw the mountain, impassible, cavernous, secret, where from morning to night I'd hear nothing but the wind, the curlews, the clink like distant silver of the stone-cutters' hammers. I'd come out in the daytime to the heather and gorse, all warmth and scent, and watch at night the distant city lights, if I chose, and the other lights, the lighthouses and lightships my father had named for me, when I was small, and whose names I could find again, in my memory, if I chose, that I knew. From that day forth things went from bad to worse, to worse and worse. Not that she neglected me, she could never have neglected me enough, but the way she kept plaguing me with *our* child, exhibiting her belly and breasts and saying it was due any moment, she could feel it lepping already. If it's lepping, I said, it's not mine. I might have been worse off than I was, in that house, that was certain, it fell short of my ideal naturally, but I wasn't blind to its advantages. I hesitated to leave, the leaves were falling already, I dreaded the winter. One should not dread the winter, it too has its bounties, the snow gives warmth and deadens the tumult and its pale days are soon over. But I did not yet know, at that time, how tender the earth can be for those who have only her and how many graves in her giving, for the living. What finished me was the birth. It woke me up. What that infant must have been going through! I fancy she had a woman with her, I seemed to hear steps in the kitchen, on and off. It went to my heart to leave a house without being put out. I crawled out over the back of the sofa, put on my coat, greatcoat and hat, I can think of nothing else, laced up my boots and opened the door to the corridor. A mass of junk barred my way, but I scrabbled and barged my way through it in the end, regardless of the clatter. I used the word marriage, it was a kind of union in spite of all. Precautions would have been superfluous, there was no competing with those cries. It must have been her first. They pursued me down the stairs and out into the street. I stopped before the house door and listened. I could still hear them. If I had not known there was crying in the house I might not have heard them. But knowing it I did. I was not sure where I was. I looked among the stars and constellations for the Wains, but could not find them. And yet they must have been there. My father was the first to show them to me. He had shown me others, but alone, without him beside me, I could never find any but the Wains. I began playing with the cries, a little in the same way as I had played with the song, on, back, on, back, if that may be called playing. As long as I kept walking I didn't hear them, because of the footsteps. But as soon as I halted I heard them again, a little fainter each time, admittedly, but what does it matter, faint or loud, cry is cry, all that matters is that it should cease. For years I thought they would cease. Now I don't think so any more. I could have done with other loves perhaps. But there it is, either you love or you don't.

Translated by the author

from *Malone Dies*

I shall soon be quite dead at last in spite of all. Perhaps next month. Then it will be the month of April or of May. For the year is still young, a thousand little signs tell me so. Perhaps I am wrong, perhaps I shall survive Saint John the Baptist's Day and even the Fourteenth of July, festival of freedom. Indeed I would not put it past me to pant on to the Transfiguration, not to speak of the Assumption. But I do not think so, I do not think I am wrong in saying that these rejoicings will take place in my absence, this year.

I have that feeling, I have had it now for some days, and I credit it. But in what does it differ from those that have abused me ever since I was born? No, that is the kind of bait I do not rise to any more, my need for prettiness is gone. I could die to-day, if I wished, merely by making a little effort, if I could wish, if I could make an effort. But it is just as well to let myself die, quietly, without rushing things. Something must have changed. I will not weigh upon the balance any more, one way or the other. I shall be neutral and inert. No difficulty there. Throes are the only trouble, I must be on my guard against throes. But I am less given to them now, since coming here. Of course I still have my little fits of impatience, from time to time, I must be on my guard against them, for the next fortnight or three weeks. Without exaggeration to be sure, quietly crying and laughing, without working myself up into a state. Yes, I shall be natural at last, I shall suffer more, then less, without drawing any conclusions, I shall pay less heed to myself, I shall be neither hot nor cold any more, I shall be tepid, I shall die tepid, without enthusiasm. I shall not watch myself die, that would spoil everything. Have I watched myself live? Have I ever complained? Then why rejoice now? I am content, necessarily, but not to the point of clapping my hands. I was always content, knowing I would be repaid. There he is now, my old debtor. Shall I then fall on his neck? I shall not answer any more questions. I shall even try not to ask myself any more. While waiting I shall tell myself stories, if I can. They will not be the same kind of stories as hitherto, that is all. They will be neither beautiful nor ugly, they will be calm, there will be no ugliness or beauty or fever in them any more, they will be almost lifeless, like the teller. What was that I said? It does not matter. I look forward to their giving me great satisfaction, some satisfaction. I am satisfied, there, I have enough, I am repaid, I need nothing more. Let me say before I go any further that I forgive nobody. I wish them all an atrocious life and then the fires and ice of hell and in the execrable generations to come an honoured name. Enough for this evening.

This time I know where I am going, it is no longer the ancient night, the recent night. Now it is a game, I am going to play. I never knew how to play, till now. I longed to, but I knew it was impossible. And yet I often tried. I turned on all the lights, I took a good look all round, I began to play with what I saw. People and things ask nothing better than to play, certain animals too. All went well at first, they all came to me, pleased that someone should want to play with them. If I said, Now I need a hunchback, immediately one came running, proud as punch of his fine hunch that was going to perform. It did not occur to him that I might have to ask him to undress. But it was not long before I found myself alone, in the dark. That is why I gave up trying to play and took to myself for ever shapelessness and speechlessness, incurious wondering, darkness, long stumbling with outstretched arms, hiding. Such is the earnestness from which, for nearly a century now, I have never been able to depart. From now on it will be different. I shall never do anything any more from now on but play. No, I must not begin with an exaggeration. But I shall play a great part of the time, from now on, the greater part, if I can. But perhaps I shall not succeed any better than hitherto. Perhaps as hitherto I shall find myself abandoned, in the dark, without anything to play with. Then I shall play with myself. To have been able to conceive such a plan is encouraging.

I must have thought about my time-table during the night. I think I shall be able to tell myself four stories, each one on a different theme. One about a man, another about a woman, a third about a thing and finally one about an animal, a bird probably. I think that is everything. Perhaps I shall put the man and the woman in the same story, there is so little difference between a man and a woman, between mine I mean. Perhaps I shall not have time to finish. On the other hand perhaps I shall finish too soon. There I am back at my old aporetics. Is that the word? I don't know. It does not matter if I do not finish. But if I finish too soon? That does not matter either. For then I shall speak of the things that remain in my possession, that is a thing I have always wanted to do. It will be a kind of inventory. In any case that is a thing I must leave to the very last moment, so as to be sure of not having made a mistake. In any case that is a thing I shall certainly do, no matter what happens. It will not take me more than a quarter of an hour at the most. That is to say it could take me longer, if I wished. But should I be short of time, at the last moment, then a brief quarter of an hour would be all I should need to draw up my inventory. My desire is henceforward to be clear, without being finical. I have always wanted that too. It is obvious I may suddenly expire, at any moment. Would it not then be better for me to speak of my possessions without further delay? Would not that be wiser? And then if necessary at the last moment correct any inaccuracies. That is what reason counsels. But reason has not much hold on me, just now. All things run together to encourage me. But can I really resign myself to the possibility of my dying without leaving an inventory behind? There I am back at my old quibbles. Presumably I can, since I intend to take the risk. All my life long I have put off this reckoning, saying, Too soon, too soon. Well it is still too soon. All my life long I have dreamt of the moment when, edified at last, in so far as one can be before all is lost, I might draw the line and make the tot. This moment seems now at hand. I shall not lose my head on that account. So first of all my stories and then, last of all, if all goes well, my inventory. And I shall begin, that they may plague me no more, with the man and woman. That will be the first story, there is not matter there for two. There will therefore be only three stories after all, that one, then the one about the animal, then the one about the thing, a stone probably. That is all very clear. Then I shall deal with my possessions. If after all that I am still alive I shall take the necessary steps to ensure my not having made a mistake. So much for that. I used not to know where I was going, but I knew I would arrive, I knew there would be an end to the long blind road. What half-truths, my God. No matter. It is playtime now. I find it hard to get used to that idea. The old fog calls. Now the case is reversed, the way well charted and little hope of coming to its end. But I have high hopes. What am I doing now, I wonder, losing time or gaining it? I have also decided to remind myself briefly of my present state before embarking on my stories. I think this is a mistake. It is a weakness. But I shall indulge in it. I shall play with all the more ardour afterwards. And it will be a pendant to the inventory. Aesthetics are therefore on my side, at least a certain kind of aesthetics. For I shall have to become earnest again to be able to speak of my possessions. There it is then divided into five, the time that remains. Into five what? I don't know. Everything divides into itself, I suppose. If I start trying to think again I shall make a mess of my decease. I must say there is something very attractive about such a prospect. But I am on my guard. For the past few days I have been finding something attractive about everything. To return to the five. Present state, three stories, inventory, there. An occasional interlude is to be feared. A full programme. I shall not deviate from it any further than I must. So much for that. I feel I am making a great mistake. No matter.

Present state. This room seems to be mine. I can find no other explanation to my being left in it. All this time. Unless it be at the behest of one of the powers that be. That is hardly likely. Why should the powers have changed in their attitude towards me? It is better to adopt the simplest explanation, even if it is not simple, even if it does not explain very much. A bright light is not necessary, a taper is all one needs to live in strangeness, if it faithfully burns. Perhaps I came in for the room on the death of whoever was in it before me. I enquire no further in any case. It is not a room in a hospital, or in a madhouse, I can feel that. I have listened at different hours of the day and night and never heard anything suspicious or unusual, but always the peaceful sounding of men at large, getting up, lying down, preparing food, coming and going, weeping and laughing, or nothing at all, no sounds at all. And when I look out of the window it is clear to me, from certain signs, that I am not in a house of rest in any sense of the word. No, this is just a plain private room apparently, in what appears to be a plain ordinary house. I do not remember how I got here. In an ambulance perhaps, a vehicle of some kind certainly. One day I found myself here, in the bed. Having probably lost consciousness somewhere, I benefit by a hiatus in my recollections, not to be resumed until I recovered my senses, in this bed. As to the events that led up to my fainting and to which I can hardly have been oblivious, at the time, they have left no discernible trace, on my mind. But who has not experienced such lapses? They are common after drunkenness. I have often amused myself with trying to invent them, those same lost events. But without succeeding in amusing myself really. But what is the last thing I remember, I could start from there, before I came to my senses again here? That too is lost. I was walking certainly, all my life I have been walking, except the first few months and since I have been here. But at the end of the day I did not know where I had been or what my thoughts had been. What then could I be expected to remember, and with what? I remember a mood. My young days were more varied, such as they come back to me, in fits and starts. I did not know my way about so well then. I have lived in a kind of coma. The loss of consciousness for me was never any great loss. But perhaps I was stunned with a blow, on the head, in a forest perhaps, yes, now that I speak of a forest I vaguely remember a forest. All that belongs to the past. Now it is the present I must establish, before I am avenged. It is an ordinary room. I have little experience of rooms, but this one seems quite ordinary to me. The truth is, if I did not feel myself dying, I could well believe myself dead, expiating my sins, or in one of heaven's mansions. But I feel at last that the sands are running out, which would not be the case if I were in heaven, or in hell. Beyond the grave, the sensation of being beyond the grave was stronger with me six months ago. Had it been foretold to me that one day I should feel myself living as I do to-day, I should have smiled. It would not have been noticed, but I would have known I was smiling. I remember them well, these last few days, they have left me more memories than the thirty thousand odd that went before. The reverse would have been less surprising. When I have completed my inventory, if my death is not ready for me then, I shall write my memoirs. That's funny, I have made a joke. No matter. There is a cupboard I have never looked into. My possessions are in a corner, in a little heap. With my long stick I can rummage in them, draw them to me, send them back. My bed is by the window. I lie turned towards it most of the time. I see roofs and sky, a glimpse of street too, if I crane. I do not see any fields or hills. And yet they are near. But are they near? I don't know. I do not see the sea either, but I hear it when it is high. I can see into a room of the house across the way. Queer things go on there sometimes, people are queer. Perhaps these are abnormal. They must see me too, my big shaggy head up against the window-pane. I never had so much hair as now, nor so long, I say it without fear of contradiction. But at night they do not see me, for I never have a light. I have studied the stars a little here. But I cannot find my way about among them. Gazing at them one night I suddenly saw myself in London. Is it possible I got as far as London? And what have stars to do with that city? The moon on the other hand has grown familiar, I am well familiar now with her changes of aspect and orbit, I know more or less the hours of the night when I may look for her in the sky and the nights when she will not come. What else? The clouds. They are varied, very varied. And all sorts of birds. They come and perch on the window-sill, asking for food! It is touching. They rap on the window-pane, with their beaks. I never give them anything. But they still come. What are they waiting for? They are not vultures. Not only am I left here, but I am looked after! This is how it is done now. The door half opens, a hand puts a dish on the little table left there for that purpose, takes away the dish of the previous day, and the door closes again. This is done for me every day, at the same time probably. When I want to eat I hook the table with my stick and draw it to me. It is on castors, it comes squeaking and lurching towards me. When I need it no longer I send it back to its place by the door. It is soup. They must know I am toothless. I eat it one time out of two, out of three, on an average. When my chamber-pot is full I put it on the table, beside the dish. Then I go twenty-four hours without a pot. No, I have two pots. They have thought of everything. I am naked in the bed, in the blankets, whose number I increase and diminish as the seasons come and go. I am never hot, never cold. I don't wash, but I don't get dirty. If I get dirty somewhere I rub the part with my finger wet with spittle. What matters is to eat and excrete. Dish and pot, dish and pot, these are the poles. In the beginning it was different. The woman came right into the room, bustled about, enquired about my needs, my wants. I succeeded in the end in getting them into her head, my needs and my wants. It was not easy. She did not understand. Until the day I found the terms, the accents, that fitted her. All that must be half imagination. It was she who got me this long stick. It has a hook at one end. Thanks to it I can control the furthest recesses of my abode. How great is my debt to sticks! So great that I almost forget the blows they have transferred to me. She is an old woman. I don't know why she is good to me. Yes, let us call it goodness, without quibbling. For her it is certainly goodness. I believe her to be even older than I. But rather less well preserved, in spite of her mobility. Perhaps she goes with the room, in a manner of speaking. In that case she does not call for separate study. But it is conceivable that she does what she does out of sheer charity, or moved with regard to me by a less general feeling of compassion or affection. Nothing is impossible, I cannot keep on denying it much longer. But it is more convenient to suppose that when I came in for the room I came in for her too. All I see of her now is the gaunt hand and part of the sleeve. Not even that, not even that. Perhaps she is dead, having predeceased me, perhaps now it is another's hand that lays and clears my little table. I don't know how long I have been here, I must have said so. All I know is that I was very old already before I found myself here. I call myself an octogenarian, but I cannot prove it. Perhaps I am only a quinquagenarian, or a quadragenarian. It is ages since I counted them, my years I mean. I know the year of my birth, I have not forgotten that, but I do not know what year I have got to now. But I think I have been here for some very considerable time. For there is nothing the various seasons can do to me, within the shelter of these walls, that I do not know. That is not to be learnt in one year or two. In a flicker of my lids whole days have flown. Does anything remain to be said? A few words about myself perhaps. My body is what is called, unadvisedly perhaps, impotent. There is virtually nothing it can do. Sometimes I miss not being able to crawl around any more. But I am not much given to nostalgia. My arms, once they are in position, can exert a certain force. But I find it hard to guide them. Perhaps the red nucleus has faded. I tremble a little, but only a little. The groaning of the bedstead is part of my life, I would not like it to cease, I mean I would not like it to decrease. It is on my back, that is to say prostrate, no, supine, that I feel best, least bony. I lie on my back, but my cheek is on the pillow. I have only to open my eyes to have them begin again, the sky and smoke of mankind. My sight and hearing are very bad, on the vast main no light but reflected gleams. All my senses are trained full on me, me. Dark and silent and stale, I am no prey for them. I am far from the sounds of blood and breath, immured. I shall not speak of my sufferings. Cowering deep down among them I feel nothing. It is there I die, unbeknown to my stupid flesh. That which is seen, that which cries and writhes, my witless remains. Somewhere in this turmoil thought struggles on, it too wide of the mark. It too seeks me, as it always has, where I am not to be found. It too cannot be quiet. On others let it wreak its dying rage, and leave me in peace. Such would seem to be my present state.

The man's name is Saposcat. Like his father's. Christian name? I don't know. He will not need one. His friends call him Sapo. What friends? I don't know. A few words about the boy. This cannot be avoided.

He was a precocious boy. He was not good at his lessons, neither could he see the use of them. He attended his classes with his mind elsewhere, or blank.

He attended his classes with his mind elsewhere. He liked sums, but not the way they were taught. What he liked was the manipulation of concrete numbers. All calculation seemed to him idle in which the nature of the unit was not specified. He made a practice, alone and in company, of mental arithmetic. And the figures then marshalling in his mind thronged it with colours and with forms.

What tedium.

*

He was the eldest child of poor and sickly parents. He often heard them talk of what they ought to do in order to have better health and more money. He was struck each time by the vagueness of these palavers and not surprised that they never led to anything. His father was a salesman, in a shop. He used to say to his wife, I really must find work for the evenings and the Saturday afternoon. He added, faintly, And the Sunday. His wife would answer, But if you do any more work you'll fall ill. And Mr Saposcat had to allow that he would indeed be ill-advised to forego his Sunday rest. These people at least are grown up. But his health was not so poor that he could not work in the evenings of the week and on the Saturday afternoon. At what, said his wife, work at what? Perhaps secretarial work of some kind, he said. And who will look after the garden? said his wife. The life of the Saposcats was full of axioms, of which one at least established the criminal absurdity of a garden without roses and with its paths and lawns uncared for. I might perhaps grow vegetables, he said. They cost less to buy, said his wife. Sapo marvelled at these conversations. Think of the price of manure, said his mother. And in the silence which followed Mr Saposcat applied his mind, with the earnestness he brought to everything he did, to the high price of manure which prevented him from supporting his family in greater comfort, while his wife made ready to accuse herself, in her turn, of not doing all she might. But she was easily persuaded that she could not do more without exposing herself to the risk of dying before her time. Think of the doctor's fees we save, said Mr Saposcat. And the chemist's bills, said his wife. Nothing remained but to envisage a smaller house. But we are cramped as it is, said Mrs Saposcat. And it was an understood thing that they would be more and more so with every passing year until the day came when, the departure of the first-born compensating the arrival of the new-born, a kind of equilibrium would be attained. Then little by little the house would empty. And at last they would be all alone, with their memories. It would be time enough then to move. He would be pensioned off, she at her last gasp. They would take a cottage in the country where, having no further need of manure, they could afford to buy it in cartloads. And their children, grateful for the sacrifices made on their behalf, would come to their assistance. It was in this atmosphere of unbridled dream that these conferences usually ended. It was as though the Saposcats drew the strength to live from the prospect of their impotence. But sometimes, before reaching that stage, they paused to consider the case of their first-born. What age is he now? asked Mr Saposcat. His wife provided the information, it being understood that this was of her province. She was always wrong. Mr Saposcat took over the erroneous figure, murmuring it over and over to himself as though it were a question of the rise in price of some indispensable commodity, such as butcher's meat. And at the same time he sought in the appearance of his son some alleviation of what he had just heard. Was it at least a nice sirloin? Sapo looked at his father's face, sad, astonished, loving, disappointed, confident in spite of all. Was it on the cruel flight of the years he brooded, or on the time it was taking his son to command a salary? Sometimes he stated wearily his regret that his son should not be more eager to make himself useful about the place. It is better for him to prepare his examinations, said his wife. Starting from a given theme their minds laboured in unison. They had no conversation properly speaking. They made use of the spoken word in much the same way as the guard of a train makes use of his flags, or of his lantern. Or else they said, This is where we get down. And their son once signalled, they wondered sadly if it was not the mark of superior minds to fail miserably at the written paper and cover themselves with ridicule at the viva voce. They were not always content to gape in silence at the same landscape. At least his health is good, said Mr Saposcat. Not all that, said his wife. But no definite disease, said Mr Saposcat. A nice thing that would be at his age, said his wife. They did not know why he was committed to a liberal profession. That was yet another thing that went without saying. It was therefore impossible he should be unfitted for it. They thought of him as a doctor for preference. He will look after us when we are old, said Mrs Saposcat. And her husband replied, I see him rather as a surgeon, as though after a certain age people were inoperable.

What tedium. And I call that playing. I wonder if I am not talking yet again about myself. Shall I be incapable, to the end, of lying on any other subject? I feel the old dark gathering, the solitude preparing, by which I know myself, and the call of that ignorance which might be noble and is mere poltroonery. Already I forget what I have said. That is not how to play. Soon I shall not know where Sapo comes from, nor what he hopes. Perhaps I had better abandon this story and go on to the second, or even the third, the one about the stone. No, it would be the same thing. I must simply be on my guard, reflecting on what I have said before I go on and stopping, each time disaster threatens, to look at myself as I am. That is just what I wanted to avoid. But there seems to be no other solution. After that mud-bath I shall be better able to endure a world unsullied by my presence. What a way to reason. My eyes, I shall open my eyes, look at the little heap of my possessions, give my body the old orders I know it cannot obey, turn to my spirit gone to rack and ruin, spoil my agony the better to live it out, for already from the world that parts at last its labia and lets me go.

I have tried to reflect on the beginning of my story. There are things I do not understand. But nothing to signify. I can go on.

Sapo had no friends – no, that won't do.

Sapo was on good terms with his little friends, though they did not exactly love him. The dolt is seldom solitary. He boxed and wrestled well, was fleet of foot, sneered at his teachers and sometimes even gave them impertinent answers. Fleet of foot? Well well. Pestered with questions one day he cried, Haven't I told you I don't know! Much of his free time he spent confined in school doing impositions and often he did not get home before eight o'clock at night. He submitted with philosophy to these vexations. But he would not let himself be struck. The first time an exasperated master threatened him with a cane, Sapo snatched it from his hand and threw it out of the window, which was closed, for it was winter. This was enough to justify his expulsion. But Sapo was not expelled, either then or later. I must try and discover, when I have time to think about it quietly, why Sapo was not expelled when he so richly deserved to be. For I want as little as possible of darkness in his story. A little darkness, in itself, at the time, is nothing. You think no more about it and you go on. But I know what darkness is, it accumulates, thickens, then suddenly bursts and drowns everything.

I have not been able to find out why Sapo was not expelled. I shall have to leave this question open. I try not to be glad. I shall make haste to put a safe remove between him and this incomprehensible indulgence, I shall make him live as though he had been punished according to his deserts. We shall turn our backs on this little cloud, but we shall not let it out of our sight. It will not cover the sky without our knowing, we shall not suddenly raise our eyes, far from help, far from shelter, to a sky as black as ink. That is what I have decided. I see no other solution. It is the best I can do.

At the age of fourteen he was a plump rosy boy. His wrists and ankles were thick, which made his mother say that one day he would be even bigger than his father. Curious deduction. But the most striking thing about him was his big round head horrid with flaxen hair as stiff and straight as the bristles of a brush. Even his teachers could not help thinking he had a remarkable head and they were all the more irked by their failure to get anything into it. His father would say, when in good humour, One of these days he will astonish us all. It was thanks to Sapo's skull that he was enabled to hazard this opinion and, in defiance of the facts and against his better judgment, to revert to it from time to time. But he could not endure the look in Sapo's eyes and went out of his way not to meet it. He has your eyes, his wife would say. Then Mr Saposcat chafed to be alone, in order to inspect his eyes in the mirror. They were palest blue. Just a shade lighter, said Mrs Saposcat.

Sapo loved nature, took an interest.

This is awful.

Sapo loved nature, took an interest in animals and plants and willingly raised his eyes to the sky, day and night. But he did not know how to look at all these things, the looks he rained upon them taught him nothing about them. He confused the birds with one another, and the trees, and could not tell one crop from another crop. He did not associate the crocus with the spring nor the chrysanthemum with Michaelmas. The sun, the moon, the planets and the stars did not fill him with wonder. He was sometimes tempted by the knowledge of these strange things, sometimes beautiful, that he would have about him all his life. But from his ignorance of them he drew a kind of joy, as from all that went to swell the murmur, You are a simpleton. But he loved the flight of the hawk and could distinguish it from all others. He would stand rapt, gazing at the long pernings, the quivering poise, the wings lifted for the plummet drop, the wild reascent, fascinated by such extremes of need, of pride, of patience and solitude.

I shall not give up yet. I have finished my soup and sent back the little table to its place by the door. A light has just gone on in one of the two windows of the house across the way. By the two windows I mean those I can see always, without raising my head from the pillow. By this I do not mean the two windows in their entirely, but one in its entirety and part of the other. It is in this latter that the light has just gone on. For an instant I could see the woman coming and going. Then she drew the curtain. Until to-morrow I shall not see her again, her shadow perhaps from time to time. She does not always draw the curtain. The man has not yet come home. Home. I have demanded certain movements of my legs and even feet. I know them well and could feel the effort they made to obey. I have lived with them that little space of time, filled with drama, between the message received and the piteous response. To old dogs the hour comes when, whistled by their master setting forth with his stick at dawn, they cannot spring after him. Then they stay in their kennel, or in their basket, though they are not chained, and listen to the steps dying away. The man too is sad. But soon the pure air and the sun console him, he thinks no more about his old companion, until evening. The lights in his house bid him welcome home and a feeble barking makes him say, It is time I had him destroyed. There's a nice passage. Soon it will be even better, soon things will be better. I am going to rummage a little in my possessions. Then I shall put my head under the blankets. Then things will be better, for Sapo and for him who follows him, who asks nothing but to follow in his footsteps, by clear and endurable ways.

Sapo's phlegm, his silent ways, were not of a nature to please. In the midst of tumult, at school and at home, he remained motionless in his place, often standing, and gazed straight before him with eyes as pale and unwavering as a gull's. People wondered what he could brood on thus, hour after hour. His father supposed him a prey to the first flutterings of sex. At sixteen I was the same, he would say. At sixteen you were earning your living, said his wife. So I was, said Mr Saposcat. But in the view of his teachers the signs were rather those of besottedness pure and simple. Sapo dropped his jaw and breathed through his mouth. It is not easy to see in virtue of what this expression is incompatible with erotic thoughts. But indeed his dream was less of girls than of himself, his own life, his life to be. That is more than enough to stop up the nose of a lucid and sensitive boy, and cause his jaw temporarily to sag. But it is time I took a little rest, for safety's sake.

I don't like those gull's eyes. They remind me of an old shipwreck, I forget which. I know it is a small thing. But I am easily frightened now. I know those little phrases that seem so innocuous and, once you let them in, pollute the whole of speech. *Nothing is more real than nothing.* They rise up out of the pit and know no rest until they drag you down into its dark. But I am on my guard now.

Then he was sorry he had not learnt the art of thinking, beginning by folding back the second and third fingers the better to put the index on the subject and the little finger on the verb, in the way his teacher had shown him, and sorry he could make no meaning of the babel raging in his head, the doubts, desires, imaginings and dreads. And a little less well endowed with strength and courage he too would have abandoned and despaired of ever knowing what manner of being he was, and how he was going to live, and lived vanquished, blindly, in a mad world, in the midst of strangers.

*

From these reveries he emerged tired and pale, which confirmed his father's impression that he was the victim of lascivious speculations. He ought to play more games, he would say. We are getting on, getting on. They told me he would be a good athlete, said Mr Saposcat, and now he is not on any team. His studies take up all his time, said Mrs Saposcat. And he is always last, said Mr Saposcat. He is fond of walking, said Mrs Saposcat, the long walks in the country do him good. Then Mr Saposcat wried his face, at the thought of his son's long solitary walks and the good they did him. And sometimes he was carried away to the point of saying, It might have been better to have put him to a trade. Whereupon it was usual, though not compulsory, for Sapo to go away, while his mother exclaimed, Oh Adrian, you have hurt his feelings!

We are getting on. Nothing is less like me than this patient, reasonable child, struggling all alone for years to shed a little light upon himself, avid of the least gleam, a stranger to the joys of darkness. Here truly is the air I needed, a lively tenuous air, far from the nourishing murk that is killing me. I shall never go back into this carcass except to find out its time. I want to be there a little before the plunge, close for the last time the old hatch on top of me, say goodbye to the holds where I have lived, go down with my refuge. I was always sentimental. But between now and then I have time to frolic, ashore, in the brave company I have always longed for, always searched for, and which would never have me. Yes, now my mind is easy, I know the game is won, I lost them all till now, but it's the last that counts. A very fine achievement I must say, or rather would, if I did not fear to contradict myself. Fear to contradict myself! If this continues it is myself I shall lose and the thousand ways that lead there. And I shall resemble the wretches famed in fable, crushed beneath the weight of their wish come true. And I even feel a strange desire come over me, the desire to know what I am doing, and why. So I near the goal I set myself in my young days and which prevented me from living. And on the threshold of being no more I succeed in being another. Very pretty.

The summer holidays. In the morning he took private lessons. You'll have us in the poorhouse, said Mrs Saposcat. It's a good investment, said Mr Saposcat. In the afternoon he left the house, with his books under his arm, on the pretext that he worked better in the open air, no, without a word. Once clear of the town he hid his books under a stone and ranged the countryside. It was the season when the labours of the peasants reach their paroxysm and the long bright days are too short for all there is to do. And often they took advantage of the moon to make a last journey between the fields, perhaps far away, and the barn or threshing floor, or to overhaul the machines and get them ready for the impending dawn. The impending dawn.

I fell asleep. But I do not want to sleep. There is no time for sleep in my time-table. I do not want – no, I have no explanations to give. Coma is for the living. The living. They were always more than I could bear, all, no, I don't mean that, but groaning with tedium I watched them come and go, then I killed them, or took their place, or fled. I feel within me the glow of that old frenzy, but I know it will set me on fire no more. I stop everything and wait. Sapo stands on one leg, motionless, his strange eyes closed.

The turmoil of the day freezes in a thousand absurd postures. The little cloud drifting before their glorious sun will darken the earth as long as I please.

Live and invent. I have tried. I must have tried. Invent. It is not the word. Neither is live. No matter. I have tried. While within me the wild beast of earnestness padded up and down, roaring, ravening, rending. I have done that. And all alone, well hidden, played the clown, all alone, hour after hour, motionless, often standing, spellbound, groaning. That's right, groan. I couldn't play. I turned till I was dizzy, clapped my hands, ran, shouted, saw myself winning, saw myself losing, rejoicing, lamenting. Then suddenly I threw myself on the playthings, if there were any, or on a child, to change his joy to howling, or I fled, to hiding. The grown-ups pursued me, the just, caught me, beat me, hounded me back into the round, the game, the jollity. For I was already in the toils of earnestness. That has been my disease. I was born grave as others syphilitic. And gravely I struggled to be grave no more, to live, to invent, I know what I mean. But at each fresh attempt I lost my head, fled to my shadows as to sanctuary, to his lap who can neither live nor suffer the sight of others living. I say living without knowing what it is. I tried to live without knowing what I was trying. Perhaps I have lived after all, without knowing. I wonder why I speak of all this. Ah yes, to relieve the tedium. Live and cause to live. There is no use indicting words, they are no shoddier than what they peddle. After the fiasco, the solace, the repose, I began again, to try and live, cause to live, be another, in myself, in another. How false all this is. No time now to explain. I began again. But little by little with a different aim, no longer in order to succeed, but in order to fail. Nuance. What I sought, when I struggled out of my hole, then aloft through the stinging air towards an inaccessible boon, was the rapture of vertigo, the letting go, the fall, the gulf, the relapse to darkness, to nothingness, to earnestness, to home, to him waiting for me always, who needed me and whom I needed, who took me in his arms and told me to stay with him always, who gave me his place and watched over me, who suffered every time I left him, whom I have often made suffer and seldom contented, whom I have never seen. There I am forgetting myself again. My concern is not with me, but with another, far beneath me and whom I try to envy, of whose crass adventures I can now tell at last, I don't know how. Of myself I could never tell, any more than live or tell of others. How could I have, who never tried? To show myself now, on the point of vanishing, at the same time as the stranger, and by the same grace, that would be no ordinary last straw. Then live, long enough to feel, behind my closed eyes, other eyes close. What an end.

The market. The inadequacy of the exchanges between rural and urban areas had not escaped the excellent youth. He had mustered, on this subject, the following considerations, some perhaps close to, others no doubt far from, the truth.

In his country the problem – no, I can't do it.

The peasants. His visits to. I can't. Assembled in the farmyard they watched him depart, on stumbling, wavering feet, as though they scarcely felt the ground. Often he stopped, stood tottering a moment, then suddenly was off again, in a new direction. So he went, limp, drifting, as though tossed by the earth. And when, after a halt, he started off again, it was like a big thistledown plucked by the wind from the place where it had settled. There is a choice of images.

I have rummaged a little in my things, sorting them out and drawing them over to me, to look at them. I was not far wrong in thinking that I knew them off, by heart, and could speak of them at any moment, without looking at them. But I wanted to make sure. It was well I did. For now I know that the image of these objects, with which I have lulled myself till now, though accurate in the main, was not completely so. And I should be sorry to let slip this unique occasion which seems to offer me the possibility of something suspiciously like a true statement at last. I might feel I had failed in my duty! I want this matter to be free from all trace of approximativeness. I want, when the great day comes, to be in a position to enounce clearly, without addition or omission, all that its interminable prelude had brought me and left me in the way of chattels personal. I presume it is an obsession.

I see then I had attributed to myself certain objects no longer in my possession, as far as I can see. But might they not have rolled behind a piece of furniture? That would surprise me. A boot, for example, can a boot roll behind a piece of furniture? And yet I see only one boot. And behind what pieces of furniture? In this room, to the best of my knowledge, there is only one piece of furniture capable of intervening between me and my possessions, I refer to the cupboard. But it so cleaves to the wall, to the two walls, for it stands in the corner, that it seems part of them. It may be objected that my button-boot, for it was a kind of button-boot, is in the cupboard. I thought of that. But I have gone through it, my stick has gone through the cupboard, opening the doors, the drawers, for the first time perhaps, and rooting everywhere. And the cupboard, far from containing my boot, is empty. No, I am now without this boot, just as I am now without certain other objects of less value, which I thought I had preserved, among them a zinc ring that shone like silver. I note on the other hand, in the heap, the presence of two or three objects I had quite forgotten and one of which at least, the bowl of a pipe, strikes no chord in my memory. I do not remember ever having smoked a tobacco-pipe. I remember the soap-pipe with which, as a child, I used to blow bubbles, an odd bubble. Never mind, this bowl is now mine, wherever it comes from. A number of my treasures are derived from the same source. I also discovered a little packet tied up in age-yellowed newspaper. It reminds me of something, but of what? I drew it over beside the bed and felt it with the knob of my stick. And my hand understood, it understood softness and lightness, better I think than if it had touched the thing directly, fingering it and weighing it in its palm. I resolved, I don't know why, not to undo it. I sent it back into the corner, with the rest. I shall speak of it again perhaps, when the time comes. I shall say, I can hear myself already, Item, a little packet, soft, and light as a feather, tied up in newspaper. It will be my little mystery, all my own. Perhaps it is a lakh of rupees. Or a lock of hair.

I told myself too that I must make better speed. True lives do not tolerate this excess of circumstance. It is there the demon lurks, like the gonococcus in the folds of the prostrate. My time is limited. It is thence that one fine day, when all nature smiles and shines, the rack lets loose its black unforgettable cohorts and sweeps away the blue for ever. My situation is truly delicate. What fine things, what momentous things, I am going to miss through fear, fear of falling back into the old error, fear of not finishing in time, fear of revelling, for the last time, in a last outpouring of misery, impotence and hate. The forms are many in which the unchanging seeks relief from its formlessness. Ah yes, I was always subject to the deep thought, especially in the spring of the year. That one had been nagging at me for the past five minutes. I venture to hope there will be no more, of that depth. After all it is not important not to finish, there are worse things than velleities. But is that the point? Quite likely. All I ask is that the last of mine, as long as it lasts, should have living for its theme, that is all, I know what I mean. If it begins to run short of life I shall feel it. All I ask is to know, before I abandon him whose life has so well begun, that my death and mine alone prevents him from living on, from winning, losing, joying, suffering, rotting and dying, and that even had I lived he would have waited, before he died, for his body to be dead. That is what you might call taking a reef in your sails.

My body does not yet make up its mind. But I fancy it weighs heavier on the bed, flattens and spreads. My breath, when it comes back, fills the room with its din, though my chest moves no more than a sleeping child's. I open my eyes and gaze unblinkingly and long at the night sky. So a tiny tot I gaped, first at the novelties, then at the antiquities. Between it and me the pane, misted and smeared with the filth of years. I should like to breathe on it, but it is too far away. It is such a night as Kasper David Friedrich loved, tempestuous and bright. That name that comes back to me, those names. The clouds scud, tattered by the wind, across a limpid ground. If I had the patience to wait I would see the moon. But I have not. Now that I have looked I hear the wind. I close my eyes and it mingles with my breath. Words and images run riot in my head, pursuing, flying, clashing, merging, endlessly. But beyond this tumult there is a great calm, and a great indifference, never really to be troubled by anything again. I turn a little on my side, press my mouth against the pillow, and my nose, crush against the pillow my old hairs now no doubt as white as snow, pull the blanket over my head. I feel, deep down in my trunk, I cannot be more explicit, pains that seem new to me. I think they are chiefly in my back. They have a kind of rhythm, they even have a kind of little tune. They are bluish. How bearable all that is, my God. My head is almost facing the wrong way, like a bird's. I part my lips, now I have the pillow in my mouth. I have, I have. I suck. The search for myself is ended. I am buried in the world, I knew I would find my place there one day, the old world cloisters me, victorious. I am happy, I knew I would be happy one day. But I am not wise. For the wise thing now would be to let go, at this instant of happiness. And what do I do? I go back again to the light, to the fields I so longed to love, to the sky all astir with little white clouds as white and light as snowflakes, to the life I could never manage, through my own fault perhaps, through pride, or pettiness, but I don't think so. The beasts are at pasture, the sun warms the rocks and makes them glitter. Yes, I leave my happiness and go back to the race of men too, they come and go, often with burdens. Perhaps I have judged them ill, but I don't think so, I have not judged them at all. All I want now is to make a last effort to understand, to begin to understand, how such creatures are possible. No, it is not a question of understanding. Of what then? I don't know. Here I go none the less, mistakenly. Night, storm and sorrow, and the catalepsies of the soul, this time I shall see that they are good. The last word is not yet said between me and – yes the last word is said. Perhaps I simply want to hear it said again. Just once again. No, I want nothing.

Translated by the author

'Company'

A voice comes to one in the dark. Imagine.

To one on his back in the dark. This he can tell by the pressure on his hind parts and by how the dark changes when he shuts his eyes and again when he opens them again. Only a small part of what is said can be verified. As for example when he hears, You are on your back in the dark. Then he must acknowledge the truth of what is said. But by far the greater part of what is said cannot be verified. As for example when he hears, You first saw the light on such and such a day. Sometimes the two are combined as for example, You first saw the light on such and such a day and now you are on your back in the dark. A device perhaps from the incontrovertibility of the one to win credence for the other. That then is the proposition. To one on his back in the dark a voice tells of a past. With occasional allusion to a present and more rarely to a future as for example, You will end as you now are. And in another dark or in the same another devising it all for company. Quick leave him.

Use of the second person marks the voice. That of the third that cankerous other. Could he speak to and of whom the voice speaks there would be a first. But he cannot. He shall not. You cannot. You shall not.

Apart from the voice and the faint sound of his breath there is no sound. None at least that he can hear. This he can tell by the faint sound of his breath.

Though now even less than ever given to wonder he cannot but sometimes wonder if it is indeed to and of him the voice is speaking. May not there be another with him in the dark to and of whom the voice is speaking? Is he not perhaps overhearing a communication not intended for him? If he is alone on his back in the dark why does the voice not say so? Why does it never say for example, You saw the light on such and such a day and now you are alone on your back in the dark? Why? Perhaps for no other reason than to kindle in his mind this faint uncertainty and embarrassment.

Your mind never active at any time is now even less than ever so. This is the type of assertion he does not question. You saw the light on such and such a day and your mind never active at any time is now even less than ever so. Yet a certain activity of mind however slight is a necessary complement of company. That is why the voice does not say, You are on your back in the dark and have no mental activity of any kind. The voice alone is company but not enough. Its effect on the hearer is a necessary complement. Were it only to kindle in his mind the state of faint uncertainty and embarrassment mentioned above. But company apart this effect is clearly necessary. For were he merely to hear the voice and it to have no more effect on him than speech in Bantu or in Erse then might it not as well cease? Unless its object be by mere sound to plague one in need of silence. Or of course unless as above surmised directed at another.

A small boy you come out of Connolly's Stores holding your mother by the hand. You turn right and advance in silence southward along the highway. After some hundred paces you head inland and broach the long steep homeward. You make ground in silence hand in hand through the warm still summer air. It is late afternoon and after some hundred paces the sun appears above the crest of the rise. Looking up at the blue sky and then at your mother's face you break the silence asking her if it is not in reality much more distant than it appears. The sky that is. The blue sky. Receiving no answer you mentally reframe your question and some hundred paces later look up at her face again and ask her if it does not appear much less distant than in reality it is. For some reason you could never fathom this question must have angered her exceedingly. For she shook off your little hand and made you a cutting retort you have never forgotten.

If the voice is not speaking to him it must be speaking to another. So with what reason remains he reasons. To another of that other. Or of him. Or of another still. To another of that other or of him or of another still. To one on his back in the dark in any case. Of one on his back in the dark whether the same or another. So with what reason remains he reasons and reasons ill. For were the voice speaking not to him but to another then it must be of that other it is speaking and not of him or of another still. Since it speaks in the second person. Were it not of him to whom it is speaking speaking but of another it would not speak in the second person but in the third. For example, He first saw the light on such and such a day and now he is on his back in the dark. It is clear therefore that if it is not to him the voice is speaking but to another it is not of him either but of that other and none other to that other. So with what reason remains he reasons ill. In order to be company he must display a certain mental activity. But it need not be of a high order. Indeed it might be argued the lower the better. Up to a point. The lower the order of mental activity the better the company. Up to a point.

You first saw the light in the room you most likely were conceived in. The big bow window looked west to the mountains. Mainly west. For being bow it looked also a little south and a little north. Necessarily. A little south to more mountain and a little north to foothill and plain. The midwife was none other than a Dr Hadden or Haddon. Straggling grey moustache and hunted look. It being a public holiday your father left the house soon after his breakfast with a flask and a package of his favourite egg sandwiches for a tramp in the mountains. There was nothing unusual in this. But on that particular morning his love of walking and wild scenery was not the only mover.

But he was moved also to take himself off and out of the way by his aversion to the pains and general unpleasantness of labour and delivery. Hence the sandwiches which he relished at noon looking out to sea from the lee of a great rock on the first summit scaled. You may imagine his thoughts before and after as he strode through the gorse and heather. When he returned at nightfall he learned to his dismay from the maid at the back door that labour was still in swing. Despite its having begun before he left the house full ten hours earlier. He at once hastened to the coachhouse some twenty yards distant where he housed his De Dion Bouton. He shut the doors behind him and climbed into the driver's seat. You may imagine his thoughts as he sat there in the dark not knowing what to think. Though footsore and weary he was on the point of setting out anew across the fields in the young moonlight when the maid came running to tell him it was over at last. Over!

You are an old man plodding along a narrow country road. You have been out since break of day and now it is evening. Sole sound in the silence your footfalls. Rather sole sounds for they vary from one to the next. You listen to each one and add it in your mind to the growing sum of those that went before. You halt with bowed head on the verge of the ditch and convert into yards. On the basis now of two steps per yard. So many since dawn to add to yesterday's. To yesteryear's. To yesteryears'. Days other than today and so akin. The giant tot in miles. In leagues. How often round the earth already. Halted too at your elbow during these computations your father's shade. In his old tramping rags. Finally on side by side from nought anew.

The voice comes to him now from one quarter and now from another. Now faint from afar and now a murmur in his ear. In the course of a single sentence it may change place and tone. Thus for example clear from above his upturned face, You first saw the light at Easter and now. Then a murmur in his ear, You are on your back in the dark. Or of course vice versa. Another trait its long silences when he dare almost hope it is at an end. Thus to take the same example clear from above his upturned face, You first saw the light of day the day Christ died and now. Then long after on his nascent hope the murmur, You are on your back in the dark. Or of course vice versa.

Another trait its repetitiousness. Repeatedly with only minor variants the same bygone. As if willing him by this dint to make it his. To confess, Yes I remember. Perhaps even to have a voice. To murmur, Yes I remember. What an addition to company that would be! A voice in the first person singular. Murmuring now and then, Yes I remember.

An old beggar woman is fumbling at a big garden gate. Half blind. You know the place well. Stone deaf and not in her right mind the woman of the house is a crony of your mother. She was sure she could fly once in the air. So one day she launched herself from a first floor window. On the way home from kindergarten on your tiny cycle you see the poor old beggar woman trying to get in. You dismount and open the gate for her. She blesses you. What were her words? God reward you little master. Some such words. God save you little master.

A faint voice at loudest. It slowly ebbs till almost out of hearing. Then slowly back to faint full. At each slow ebb hope slowly dawns that it is dying. He must know it will flow again. And yet at each slow ebb hope slowly dawns that it is dying.

Slowly he entered dark and silence and lay there for so long that with what judgement remained he judged them to be final. Till one day the voice. One day! Till in the end the voice saying, You are on your back in the dark. Those its first words. Long pause for him to believe his ears and then from another quarter the same. Next the vow not to cease till hearing cease. You are on your back in the dark and not till hearing cease will this voice cease. Or another way. As in shadow he lay and only the odd sound slowly silence fell and darkness gathered. That were perhaps better company. For what odd sound? Whence the shadowy light?

You stand at the tip of the high board. High above the sea. In it your father's upturned face. Upturned to you. You look down to the loved trusted face. He calls to you to jump. He calls, Be a brave boy. The red round face. The thick moustache. The greying hair. The swell sways it under and sways it up again. The far call again, Be a brave boy. Many eyes upon you. From the water and from the bathing place.

The odd sound. What a mercy to have that to turn to. Now and then. In dark and silence to close as if to light the eyes and hear a sound. Some object moving from its place to its last place. Some soft thing softly stirring soon to stir no more. To darkness visible to close the eyes and hear if only that. Some soft thing softly stirring soon to stir no more.

By the voice a faint light is shed. Dark lightens while it sounds. Deepens when it ebbs. Lightens with flow back to faint full. Is whole again when it ceases. You are on your back in the dark. Had the eyes been open then they would have marked a change.

Whence the shadowy light? What company in the dark! To close the eyes and try to imagine that. Whence once the shadowy light. No source. As if faintly luminous all his little void. What can he have seen then above his upturned face. To close the eyes in the dark and try to imagine that.

Another trait the flat tone. No life. Same flat tone at all times. For its affirmations. For its negations. For its interrogations. For its exclamations. For its imperations. Same flat tone. You were once. You were never. Were you ever? Oh never to have been! Be again. Same flat tone.

Can he move? Does he move? Should he move? What a help that would be. When the voice fails. Some movement however small. Were it but of a hand closing. Or opening if closed to begin. What a help that would be in the dark! To close the eyes and see that hand. Palm upward filling the whole field. The lines. The fingers slowly down. Or up if down to begin. The lines of that old palm.

*

There is of course the eye. Filling the whole field. The hood slowly down. Or up if down to begin. The globe. All pupil. Staring up. Hooded. Bared. Hooded again. Bared again.

If he were to utter after all? However feebly. What an addition to company that would be! You are on your back in the dark and one day you will utter again. One day! In the end. In the end you will utter again. Yes I remember. That was I. That was I then.

You are alone in the garden. Your mother is in the kitchen making ready for afternoon tea with Mrs Coote. Making the wafer-thin bread and butter. From behind a bush you watch Mrs Coote arrive. A small thin sour woman. Your mother answers her saying, He is playing in the garden. You climb to near the top of a great fir. You sit a little listening to all the sounds. Then throw yourself off. The great boughs break your fall. The needles. You lie a little with your face to the ground. Then climb the tree again. Your mother answers Mrs Coote again saying, He has been a very naughty boy.

What with what feeling remains does he feel about now as compared to then? When with what judgement remained he judged his condition final. As well inquire what he felt then about then as compared to before. When he still moved or tarried in remains of light. As then there was no then so there is none now.

In another dark or in the same another devising it all for company. This at first sight seems clear. But as the eye dwells it grows obscure. Indeed the longer the eye dwells the obscurer it grows. Till the eye closes and freed from pore the mind inquires, What does this mean? What finally does this mean that at first sight seemed clear? Till it the mind too closes as it were. As the window might close of a dark empty room. The single window giving on outer dark. Then nothing more. No. Unhappily no. Pangs of faint light and stirrings still. Unformulable gropings of the mind. Unstillable.

Nowhere in particular on the way from A to Z. Or say for verisimilitude the Ballyogan Road. That dear old back road. Somewhere on the Ballyogan Road in lieu of nowhere in particular. Where no truck any more. Somewhere on the Ballyogan Road on the way from A to Z. Head sunk totting up the tally on the verge of the ditch. Foothills to left. Croker's Acres ahead. Father's shade to right and a little to the rear. So many times already round the earth. Topcoat once green stiff with age and grime from chin to insteps. Battered once buff block hat and quarter boots still a match. No other garments if any to be seen. Out since break of day and night now falling. Reckoning ended on together from nought anew. As if bound for Stepaside. When suddenly you cut through the hedge and vanish hobbling east across the gallops.

For why or? Why in another dark or in the same? And whose voice asking this? Who asks, Whose voice asking this? And answers, His soever who devises it all. In the same dark as his creature or in another. For company. Who asks in the end, Who asks? And in the end answers as above? And adds long after to himself, Unless another still. Nowhere to be found. Nowhere to be sought. The unthinkable last of all. Unnamable. Last person. I. Quick leave him.

The light there was then. On your back in the dark the light there was then. Sunless cloudless brightness. You slip away at break of day and climb to your hiding place on the hillside. A nook in the gorse. East beyond the sea the faint shape of high mountain. Seventy miles away according to your Longman. For the third or fourth time in your life. The first time you told them and were derided. All you had seen was cloud. So now you hoard it in your heart with the rest. Back home at nightfall supperless to bed. You lie in the dark and are back in that light. Straining out from your nest in the gorse with your eyes across the water till they ache. You close them while you count a hundred. Then open and strain again. Again and again. Till in the end it is there. Palest blue against the pale sky. You lie in the dark and are back in that light. Fall asleep in that sunless cloudless light. Sleep till morning light.

Deviser of the voice and of its hearer and of himself. Deviser of himself for company. Leave it at that. He speaks of himself as of another. He says speaking of himself, He speaks of himself as of another. Himself he devises too for company. Leave it at that. Confusion too is company up to a point. Better hope deferred than none. Up to a point. Till the heart starts to sicken. Company too up to a point. Better a sick heart than none. Till it starts to break. So speaking of himself he concludes for the time being, For the time being leave it at that.

In the same dark as his creature or in another not yet imagined. Nor in what position. Whether standing or sitting or lying or in some other position in the dark. These are among the matters yet to be imagined. Matters of which as yet no inkling. The test is company. Which of the two darks is the better company. Which of all imaginable positions has the most to offer in the way of company. And similarly for the other matters yet to be imagined. Such as if such decisions irreversible. Let him for example after due imagination decide in favour of the supine position or prone and this in practice prove less companionable than anticipated. May he then or may he not replace it by another? Such as huddled with his legs drawn up within the semi-circle of his arms and his head on his knees. Or in motion. Crawling on all fours. Another in another dark or in the same crawling on all fours devising it all for company. Or some other form of motion. The possible encounters. A dead rat. What an addition to company that would be! A rat long dead.

Might not the hearer be improved? Made more companionable if not downright human. Mentally perhaps there is room for enlivement. An attempt at reflexion at least. At recall. At speech even. Conation of some kind however feeble. A trace of emotion. Signs of distress. A sense of failure. Without loss of character. Delicate ground. But physically? Must he lie inert to the end? Only the eyelids stirring on and off since technically they must. To let in and shut out the dark. Might he not cross his feet? On and off. Now left on right and now a little later the reverse. No. Quite out of keeping. He lie with crossed feet? One glance dispels. Some movement of the hands? A hand. A clenching and unclenching. Difficult to justify. Or raised to brush away a fly. But there are no flies. Then why not let there be? The temptation is great. Let there be a fly. For him to brush away. A live fly mistaking him for dead. Made aware of its error and renewing it incontinent. What an addition to company that would be! A live fly mistaking him for dead. But no. He would not brush away a fly.

You take pity on a hedgehog out in the cold and put it in an old hatbox with some worms. This box with the hog inside you then place in a disused hutch wedging the door open for the poor creature to come and go at will. To go in search of food and having eaten to regain the warmth and security of its box in the hutch. There then is the hedgehog in its box in the hutch with enough worms to tide it over. A last look to make sure all is as it should be before taking yourself off to look for something else to pass the time heavy already on your hands at that tender age. The glow at your good deed is slower than usual to cool and fade. You glowed readily in those days but seldom for long. Hardly had the glow been kindled by some good deed on your part or by some little triumph over your rivals or by a word of praise from your parents or mentors when it would begin to cool and fade leaving you in a very short time as chill and dim as before. Even in those days. But not this day. It was on an autumn afternoon you found the hedgehog and took pity on it in the way described and you were still the better for it when your bedtime came. Kneeling at your bedside you included it the hedgehog in your detailed prayer to God to bless all you loved. And tossing in your warm bed waiting for sleep to come you were still faintly glowing at the thought of what a fortunate hedgehog it was to have crossed your path as it did. A narrow clay path edged with sere box edging. As you stood there wondering how best to pass the time till bedtime it parted the edging on the one side and was making straight for the edging on the other when you entered its life. Now the next morning not only was the glow spent but a great uneasiness had taken its place. A suspicion that all was perhaps not as it should be. That rather than do as you did you had perhaps better let good alone and the hedgehog pursue its way. Days if not weeks passed before you could bring yourself to return to the hutch. You have never forgotten what you found then. You are on your back in the dark and have never forgotten what you found then. The mush. The stench.

Impending for some time the following. Need for company not continuous. Moments when his own unrelieved a relief. Intrusion of voice at such. Similarly image of hearer. Similarly his own. Regret then at having brought them about and problem how dispel them. Finally what meant by his own unrelieved? What possible relief? Leave it at that for the moment.

Let the hearer be named H. Aspirate. Haitch. You Haitch are on your back in the dark. And let him know his name. No longer any question of his overhearing. Of his not being meant. Though logically none in any case. Of words murmured in his ear to wonder if to him! So he is. So that faint uneasiness lost. That faint hope. To one with so few occasions to feel. So inapt to feel. Asking nothing better in so far as he can ask anything than to feel nothing. Is it desirable? No. Would he gain thereby in companionability? No. Then let him not be named H. Let him be again as he was. The hearer. Unnamable. You.

Imagine closer the place where he lies. Within reason. To its form and dimensions a clue is given by the voice afar. Receding afar or there with abrupt saltation or resuming there after pause. From above and from all sides and levels with equal remoteness at its most remote. At no time from below. So far. Suggesting one lying on the floor of a hemispherical chamber of generous diameter with ear dead centre. How generous? Given faintness of voice at its least faint some sixty feet should suffice or thirty from ear to any given point of encompassing surface. So much for form and dimensions. And composition? What and where clue to that if any anywhere. Reserve for the moment. Basalt is tempting. Black basalt. But reserve for the moment. So he imagines to himself as voice and hearer pall. But further imagination shows him to have imagined ill. For with what right affirm of a faint sound that it is a less faint made fainter by farness and not a true faint near at hand? Or of a faint fading to fainter that it recedes and not in situ decreases. If with none then no light from the voice on the place where our old hearer lies. In immeasurable dark. Contourless. Leave it at that for the moment. Adding only, What kind of imagination is this so reason-ridden? A kind of its own.

Another devising it all for company. In the same dark as his creature or in another. Quick imagine. The same.

Might not the voice be improved? Made more companionable. Say changing now for some time past though no tense in the dark in that dim mind. All at once over and in train and to come. But for the other say for some time past some improvement. Same flat tone as initially imagined and same repetitiousness. No improving those. But less mobility. Less variety of faintness. As if seeking optimum position. From which to discharge with greatest effect. The ideal amplitude for effortless audition. Neither offending the ear with loudness nor through converse excess constraining it to strain. How far more companionable such an organ than it initially in haste imagined. How far more likely to achieve its object. To have the hearer have a past and acknowledge it. You were born on an Easter Friday after long labour. Yes I remember. The sun had not long sunk behind the larches. Yes I remember. As best to erode the drop must strike unwavering. Upon the place beneath.

The last time you went out the snow lay on the ground. You now on your back in the dark stand that morning on the sill having pulled the door gently to behind you. You lean back against the door with bowed head making ready to set out. By the time you open your eyes your feet have disappeared and the skirts of your greatcoat come to rest on the surface of the snow. The dark scene seems lit from below. You see yourself at that last outset leaning against the door with closed eyes waiting for the word from you to go. To be gone. Then the snowlit scene. You lie in the dark with closed eyes and see yourself there as described making ready to strike out and away across the expanse of light. You hear again the click of the door pulled gently to and the silence before the steps can start. Next thing you are on your way across the white pasture afrolic with lambs in spring and strewn with red placentae. You take the course you always take which is a beeline for the gap or ragged point in the quickset that forms the western fringe. Thither from your entering the pasture you need normally from eighteen hundred to two thousand paces depending on your humour and the state of the ground. But on this last morning many more will be required. Many many more. The beeline is so familiar to your feet that if necessary they could keep to it and you sightless with error on arrival of not more than a few feet north or south. And indeed without any such necessity unless from within this is what they normally do and not only here. For you advance if not with closed eyes though this as often as not at least with them fixed on the momentary ground before your feet. That is all of nature you have seen. Since finally you bowed your head. The fleeting ground before your feet. From time to time. You do not count your steps any more. For the simple reason they number each day the same. Average day in day out the same. The way being always the same. You keep count of the days and every tenth day multiply. And add. Your father's shade is not with you any more. It fell out long ago. You do not hear your footfalls any more. Unhearing unseeing you go your way. Day after day. The same way. As if there were no other any more. For you there is no other any more. You used never to halt except to make your reckoning. So as to plod on from nought anew. This need removed as we have seen there is none in theory to halt any more. Save perhaps a moment at the outermost point. To gather yourself together for the return. And yet you do. As never before. Not for tiredness. You are no more tired now than you always were. Not because of age. You are no older now than you always were. And yet you halt as never before. So that the same hundred yards you used to cover in a matter of three to four minutes may now take you anything from fifteen to twenty. The foot falls unbidden in midstep or next for lift cleaves to the ground bringing the body to a stand. Then a speechlessness whereof the gist, Can they go on? Or better, Shall they go on? The barest gist. Stilled when finally as always hitherto they do. You lie in the dark with closed eyes and see the scene. As you could not at the time. The dark cope of sky. The dazzling land. You at a standstill in the midst. The quarter boots sunk to the tops. The skirts of the greatcoat resting on the snow. In the old bowed head in the old block hat speechless misgiving. Halfway across the pasture on your beeline to the gap. The unerring feet fast. You look behind you as you could not then and see their trail. A great swerve. Withershins. Almost as if all at once the heart too heavy. In the end too heavy.

Bloom of adulthood. Imagine a whiff of that. On your back in the dark you remember. Ah you you remember. Cloudless May day. She joins you in the little summerhouse. A rustic hexahedron. Entirely of logs. Both larch and fir. Six feet across. Eight from floor to vertex. Area twenty-four square feet to furthest decimal. Two small multicoloured lights vis-à-vis. Small stained diamond panes. Under each a ledge. There on summer Sundays after his midday meal your father loved to retreat with Punch and a cushion. The waist of his trousers unbuttoned he sat on the one ledge turning the pages. You on the other with your feet dangling. When he chuckled you tried to chuckle too. When his chuckle died yours too. That you should try to imitate his chuckle pleased and tickled him greatly and sometimes he would chuckle for no other reason than to hear you try to chuckle too. Sometimes you turn your head and look out through a rose-red pane. You press your little nose against the pane and all without is rosy. The years have flown and there at the same place as then you sit in the bloom of adulthood bathed in rainbow light gazing before you. She is late. You close your eyes and try to calculate the volume. Simple sums you find a help in times of trouble. A haven. You arrive in the end at seven cubic yards approximately. Even still in the timeless dark you find figures a comfort. You assume a certain heart rate and reckon how many thumps a day. A week. A month. A year. And assuming a certain lifetime a lifetime. Till the last thump. But for the moment with hardly more than seventy American billion behind you you sit in the little summerhouse working out the volume. Seven cubic yards approximately. This strikes you for some reason as improbable and you set about your sum anew. But you have not made much headway when her light step is heard. Light for a woman of her size. You open with quickening pulse your eyes and a moment later that seems an eternity her face appears at the window. Mainly blue in this position the natural pallor you so admire as indeed from it no doubt wholly blue your own. For natural pallor is a property you have in common. The violet lips do not return your smile. Now this window being flush with your eyes from where you sit and the floor as near as no matter with the outer ground you cannot but wonder if she has not sunk to her knees. Knowing from experience that the height or length you have in common is the sum of equal segments. For when bolt upright or lying at full stretch you cleave face to face then your knees meet and your pubes and the hairs of your heads mingle. Does it follow from this that the loss of height for the body that sits is the same as for it that kneels? At this point assuming height of seat adjustable as in the case of certain piano stools you close your eyes the better with mental measure to measure and compare the first and second segments namely from sole to kneepad and thence to pelvic girdle. How given you were both moving and at rest to the closed eye in your waking hours! By day and by night. To that perfect dark. That shadowless light. Simply to be gone. Or for affair as now. A single leg appears. Seen from above. You separate the segments and lay them side by side. It is as you half surmised. The upper is the longer and the sitter's loss the greater when seat at knee level. You leave the pieces lying there and open your eyes to find her sitting before you. All dead still. The ruby lips do not return your smile. Your gaze descends to the breasts. You do not remember them so big. To the abdomen. Same impression. Dissolve to your father's straining against the unbuttoned waistband. Can it be she is with child without your having asked for as much as her hand? You go back into your mind. She too did you but know has closed her eyes. So you sit face to face in the little summerhouse. With eyes closed and your hands on your pubes. In that rainbow light. That dead still.

Wearied by such stretch of imagining he ceases and all ceases. Till feeling the need for company again he tells himself to call the hearer M at least. For readier reference. Himself some other character. W. Devising it all himself included for company. In the same dark as M when last heard of. In what posture and whether fixed or mobile left open. He says further to himself referring to himself, When last he referred to himself it was to say he was in the same dark as his creature. Not in another as once seemed possible. The same. As more companionable. And that his posture there remained to be devised. And to be decided whether fast or mobile. Which of all imaginable postures least liable to pall? Which of motion or of rest the more entertaining in the long run? And in the same breath too soon to say and why after all not say without further ado what can later be unsaid and what if it could not? What then? Could he now if he chose move out of the dark he chose when last heard of and away from his creature into another? Should he now decide to lie and come later to regret it could he then rise to his feet for example and lean against a wall or pace to and fro? Could M be reimagined in an easy chair? With hands free to go to his assistance? There in the same dark as his creature he leaves himself to these perplexities while wondering as every now and then he wonders in the back of his mind if the woes of the world are all they used to be. In his day.

M so far as follows. On his back in a dark place form and dimensions yet to be devised. Hearing on and off a voice of which uncertain whether addressed to him or to another sharing his situation. There being nothing to show when it describes correctly his situation that the description is not for the benefit of another in the same situation. Vague distress at the vague thought of his perhaps overhearing a confidence when he hears for example, You are on your back in the dark. Doubts gradually dashed as voice from questing far and wide closes in upon him. When it ceases no other sound than his breath. When it ceases long enough vague hope it may have said its last. Mental activity of a low order. Rare flickers of reasoning of no avail. Hope and despair and suchlike barely felt. How current situation arrived at unclear. No that then to compare to this now. Only eyelids move. When for relief from outer and inner dark they close and open respectively. Other small local movements eventually within moderation not to be despaired of. But no improvement by means of such achieved so far. Or on a higher plane by such addition to company as a movement of sustained sorrow or desire or remorse or curiosity or anger and so on. Or by some successful act of intellection as were he to think to himself referring to himself, Since he cannot think he will give up trying. Is there anything to add to this esquisse? His unnamability. Even M must go. So W reminds himself of his creature as so far created. W? But W too is creature. Figment.

Yet another then. Of whom nothing. Devising figments to temper his nothingness. Quick leave him. Pause and again in panic to himself, Quick leave him.

Devised deviser devising it all for company. In the same figment dark as his figments. In what posture and if or not as hearer in his for good not yet devised. Is not one immovable enough? Why duplicate this particular solace? Then let him move. Within reason. On all fours. A moderate crawl torso well clear of the ground eyes front alert. If this no better than nothing cancel. If possible. And in the void regained another motion. Or none. Leaving only the most helpful posture to be devised. But to be going on with let him crawl. Crawl and fall. Crawl again and fall again. In the same figment dark as his other figments.

From ranging far and wide as if in quest the voice comes to rest and constant faintness. To rest where? Imagine warily.

Above the upturned face. Falling tangent to the crown. So that in the faint light it sheds were there a mouth to be seen he would not see it. Roll as he might his eyes. Height from the ground?

Arm's length. Force? Low. A mother's stooping over cradle from behind. She moves aside to let the father look. In his turn he murmurs to the newborn. Flat tone unchanged. No trace of love.

You are on your back at the foot of an aspen. In its trembling shade. She at right angles propped on her elbows head between her hands. Your eyes opened and closed have looked in hers looking in yours. In your dark you look in them again. Still. You feel on your face the fringe of her long black hair stirring in the still air. Within the tent of hair your faces are hidden from view. She murmurs, Listen to the leaves. Eyes in each other's eyes you listen to the leaves. In their trembling shade.

Crawling and falling then. Crawling again and falling again. If this finally no improvement on nothing he can always fall for good. Or have never risen to his knees. Contrive how such crawl unlike the voice may serve to chart the area. However roughly. First what is the unit of crawl? Corresponding to the footstep of erect locomotion. He rises to all fours and makes ready to set out. Hands and knees angles of an oblong two foot long width irrelevant. Finally say left knee moves forward six inches thus half halving distance between it and homologous hand. Which then in due course in its turn moves forward by as much. Oblong now rhomboid. But for no longer than it takes right knee and hand to follow suit. Oblong restored. So on till he drops. Of all modes of crawl this the repent amble possibly the least common. And so possibly of all the most diverting.

So as he crawls the mute count. Grain by grain in the mind. One two three four one. Knee hand knee hand two. One foot. Till say after five he falls. Then sooner or later on from nought anew. One two three four one. Knee hand knee hand two. Six. So on. In what he wills a beeline. Till having encountered no obstacle discouraged he heads back the way he came. From nought anew. Or in some quite different direction. In what he hopes a beeline. Till again with no dead end for his pains he renounces and embarks on yet another course. From nought anew. Well aware or little doubting how darkness may deflect. Withershins on account of the heart. Or conversely to shortest path convert deliberate veer. Be that as it may and crawl as he will no bourne as yet. As yet imaginable. Hand knee hand knee as he will. Bourneless dark.

*

Would it be reasonable to imagine the hearer as mentally quite inert? Except when he hears. That is when the voice sounds. For what if not it and his breath is there for him to hear? Aha! The crawl. Does he hear the crawl? The fall? What an addition to company were he but to hear the crawl. The fall. The rising to all fours again. The crawl resumed. And wonder to himself what in the world such sounds might signify. Reserve for a duller moment. What if not sound could set his mind in motion? Sight? The temptation is strong to decree there is nothing to see. But too late for the moment. For he sees a change of dark when he opens or shuts his eyes. And he may see the faint light the voice imagined to shed. Rashly imagined. Light infinitely faint it is true since now no more than a mere murmur. Here suddenly seen how his eyes close as soon as the voice sounds. Should they happen to be open at the time. So light as let be faintest light no longer perceived than the time it takes the lid to fall. Taste? The taste in his mouth? Long since dulled. Touch? The thrust of the ground against his bones. All the way from calcaneum to bump of philogenitiveness. Might not a notion to stir ruffle his apathy? To turn on his side. On his face. For a change. Let that much of want be conceded. With attendant relief that the days are no more when he could writhe in vain. Smell? His own? Long since dulled. And a barrier to others if any. Such as might have once emitted a rat long dead. Or some other carrion. Yet to be imagined. Unless the crawler smell. Aha! The crawling creator. Might the crawling creator be reasonably imagined to smell? Even fouler than his creature. Stirring now and then to wonder that mind so lost to wonder. To wonder what in the world can be making that alien smell. Whence in the world those wafts of villainous smell. How much more companionable could his creator but smell. Could he but smell his creator. Some sixth sense? Inexplicable premonition of impending ill? Yes or no? No. Pure reason? Beyond experience. God is love. Yes or no? No.

Can the crawling creator crawling in the same create dark as his creature create while crawling? One of the questions he put to himself as between two crawls he lay. And if the obvious answer were not far to seek the most helpful was another matter. And many crawls were necessary and the like number of prostrations before he could finally make up his imagination on this score. Adding to himself without conviction in the same breath as always that no answer of his was sacred. Come what might the answer he hazarded in the end was no he could not. Crawling in the dark in the way described was too serious a matter and too all-engrossing to permit of any other business were it only the conjuring of something out of nothing. For he had not only as perhaps too hastily imagined to cover the ground in this special way but rectigrade into the bargain to the best of his ability. And furthermore to count as he went adding half foot to half foot and retain in his memory the ever-changing sum of those gone before. And finally to maintain eyes and ears at a high level of alertness for any clue however small to the nature of the place to which imagination perhaps unadvisedly had consigned him. So while in the same breath deploring a fancy so reason-ridden and observing how revocable its flights he could not but answer finally no he could not. Could not conceivably create while crawling in the same create dark as his creature.

*

A strand. Evening. Light dying. Soon none left to die. No. No such thing then as no light. Died on to dawn and never died. You stand with your back to the wash. No sound but its. Ever fainter as it slowly ebbs. Till it slowly flows again. You lean on a long staff. Your hands rest on the knob and on them your head. Were your eyes to open they would first see far below in the last rays the skirt of your greatcoat and the uppers of your boots emerging from the sand. Then and it alone till it vanishes the shadow of the staff on the sand. Vanishes from your sight. Moonless starless night. Were your eyes to open dark would lighten.

Crawls and falls. Lies. Lies in the dark with closed eyes resting from his crawl. Recovering. Physically and from his disappointment at having crawled again in vain. Perhaps saying to himself, Why crawl at all? Why not just lie in the dark with closed eyes and give up? Give up all. Have done with all. With bootless crawl and figments comfortless. But if on occasion so disheartened it is seldom for long. For little by little as he lies the craving for company revives. In which to escape from his own. The need to hear that voice again. If only saying again, You are on your back in the dark. Or if only, You first saw the light and cried at the close of the day when in darkness Christ at the ninth hour cried and died. The need eyes closed the better to hear to see that glimmer shed. Or with adjunction of some human weakness to improve the hearer. For example an itch beyond reach of the hand or better still within while the hand immovable. An unscratchable itch. What an addition to company that would be! Or last if not least resort to ask himself what precisely he means when he speaks of himself loosely as lying. Which in other words of all the innumerable ways of lying is likely to prove in the long run the most endearing. If having crawled in the way described he falls it would normally be on his face. Indeed given the degree of his fatigue and discouragement at this point it is hard to see how he could do otherwise. But once fallen and lying on his face there is no reason why he should not turn over on one or other of his sides or on his only back and so lie should any of these three postures offer better company than any of the other three. The supine though most tempting he must finally disallow as being already supplied by the hearer. With regard to the sidelong one glance is enough to dispel them both. Leaving him with no other choice than the prone. But how prone? Prone how? How disposed the legs? The arms? The head? Prone in the dark he strains to see how best he may lie prone. How most companionably.

See hearer clearer. Which of all the ways of lying supine the least likely in the long run to pall? After long straining eyes closed prone in the dark the following. But first naked or covered? If only with a sheet. Naked. Ghostly in the voice's glimmer that bonewhite flesh for company. Head resting mainly on occipital bump aforesaid. Legs joined at attention. Feet splayed ninety degrees. Hands invisibly manacled crossed on pubis. Other details as need felt. Leave him at that for the moment.

Numb with the woes of your kind you raise none the less your head from off your hands and open your eyes. You turn on without moving from your place the light above you. Your eyes light on the watch lying beneath it. But instead of reading the hour of night they follow round and round the second hand now followed and now preceded by its shadow. Hours later it seems to you as follows. At 60 seconds and 30 seconds shadow hidden by hand. From 60 to 30 shadow precedes hand at a distance increasing from zero at 60 to maximum at 15 and thence decreasing to new zero at 30. From 30 to 60 shadow follows hand at a distance increasing from zero at 30 to maximum at 45 and thence decreasing to new zero at 60. Slant light now to dial by moving either to either side and hand hides shadow at two quite different points as for example 50 and 20. Indeed at any two quite different points whatever depending on degree of slant. But however great or small the slant and more or less remote from initial 60 and 30 the new points of zero shadow the space between the two remains one of 30 seconds. The shadow emerges from under hand at any point whatever of its circuit to follow or precede it for the space of 30 seconds. Then disappears infinitely briefly before emerging again to precede or follow it for the space of 30 seconds again. And so on and on. This would seem to be the one constant. For the very distance itself between hand and shadow varies as the degree of slant. But however great or small this distance it invariably waxes and wanes from nothing to a maximum 15 seconds later and to nothing again 15 seconds later again respectively. And so on and on. This would seem to be a second constant. More might have been observed on the subject of this second hand and its shadow in their seemingly endless parallel rotation round and round the dial and other variables and constants brought to light and errors if any corrected in what had seemed so far. But unable to continue you bow your head back to where it was and with closed eyes return to the woes of your kind. Dawn finds you still in this position. The low sun shines on you through the eastern window and flings all along the floor your shadow and that of the lamp left lit above you. And those of other objects also.

What visions in the dark of light! Who exclaims thus? Who asks who exclaims, What visions in the shadeless dark of light and shade! Yet another still? Devising it all for company. What a further addition to company that would be! Yet another still devising it all for company. Quick leave him.

Somehow at any price to make an end when you could go out no more you sat huddled in the dark. Having covered in your day some twenty-five thousand leagues or roughly thrice the girdle. And never once overstepped a radius of one from home. Home! So sat waiting to be purged the old lutist cause of Dante's first quarter-smile and now perhaps singing praises with some section of the blest at last. To whom here in any case farewell. The place is windowless. When as you sometimes do to void the fluid you open your eyes dark lessens. Thus you now on your back in the dark once sat huddled there your body having shown you it could go out no more. Out no more to walk the little winding back roads and interjacent pastures now alive with flocks and now deserted. With at your elbow for long years your father's shade in his old tramping rags and then for long years alone. Adding step after step to the ever mounting sum of those already accomplished. Halting now and then with bowed head to fix the score. Then on from nought anew. Huddled thus you find yourself imagining you are not alone while knowing full well that nothing has occurred to make this possible. The process continues none the less lapped as it were in its meaninglessness. You do not murmur in so many words, I know this doomed to fail and yet persist. No. For the first personal and a fortiori plural pronoun had never any place in your vocabulary. But without a word you view yourself to this effect as you would a stranger suffering say from Hodgkin's disease or if you prefer Percival Pott's surprised at prayer. From time to time with unexpected grace you lie. Simultaneously the various parts set out. The arms unclasp the knees. The head lifts. The legs start to straighten. The trunk tilts backward. And together these and countless others continue on their respective ways till they can go no further and together come to rest. Supine now you resume your fable where the act of lying cut it short. And persist till the converse operation cuts it short again. So in the dark now huddled and now supine you toil in vain. And just as from the former position to the latter the shift grows easier in time and more alacrious so from the latter to the former the reverse is true. Till from the occasional relief it was supineness becomes habitual and finally the rule. You now on your back in the dark shall not rise again to clasp your legs in your arms and bow down your head till it can bow down no further. But with face upturned for good labour in vain at your fable. Till finally you hear how words are coming to an end. With every inane word a little nearer to the last. And how the fable too. The fable of one with you in the dark. The fable of one fabling of one with you in the dark. And how better in the end labour lost and silence. And you as you always were.

Alone.

'Floodtide'

Mairead shook herself, made a fork of her first and ring-finger to rub the sleepclots from her eyes, felt the early-morning chill on her forearms. Her body took pleasure in her failure to rise. She curled herself back again on the warm side of the bed which Padraig had left a short while ago.

The month since she had come home, together with the three weeks since she had married, had left her out of practice. She thought of those ten years in America when she used to be out on the floor every single morning at the first clockwarning before daybreak for the sake of . . . for the sake of this day – a day when she could either rise or lie abed as she liked.

– Did ye get up yet? The quavering voice of her mother-in-law, it reached her from the far-room through the door which Padraig had left open behind him.

– We did, said Mairead, and rubbed some more sleep out of her eyes.

They said, she told herself, that Padraig wouldn't have the tenacity to wait for me until I'd be able to pay their passages over for my three sisters. It was said that since he was 'the only eye in the spud' he would give in to his mother and marry some other woman long ago . . . It was said that considering how young I was when I went over I'd forget him, marry beyond, and likely . . .

– Get up, Mairead. Lydon will be fit to be tied. The ebb won't wait for anybody . . .

She was jerked out of her daydream by the sharpness which she sensed for the first time in the old woman's voice. It proclaimed that the immemorial duel between a man's mother and his wife was about to begin. Having fastened on the bits of clothes that were nearest to her hand in the halfdark she remembered the rumour that was going the rounds, that the old woman was irked by the scant dowry which she had brought into the house. To wait ten years . . . Put up with a member of the American upper-class and the crumbs that fell from the table . . . Her shoe-lace broke in half in the second eyelet from the bottom . . . She felt the first tinge of bitterness.

– It's a long time since anyone got up so early in this house! Spring is at hand, at long last. Now Mairead, a splash of tea would make a gay young man of me.

Padraig had a fire down, the kettle hissing on the boil, while he brought a handful of oats out to the horse that stood already straddled at the door. With the gaiety in his voice, the love and affection that showed in his face as he named her, Mairead's irritation melted away. For the sake of all this she'd be well able to bear with the old woman's nagging. There'd never be an angry word between herself and Padraig, or if there was she herself would surely be to blame . . .

It wasn't quite bright as they left home. Down at the Beach Boreen Lydon's two daughters were seated on a pair of upturned basket-creels, while Lydon himself strode up and down at the edge of the shingle gnawing on his pipe.

– Upon my oath, he said, damn the wisp of seaweed I thought'd be cut on the Ridge today! I never yet saw a new-married couple destroyed by a desire to get up.

The pair of daughters smiled, and Mairead laughed aloud.

– It has ebbed a bit, said Padraig sheepishly.

– Ebbed a bit! And it almost at low-water! The spring-tide is at the second day of its strength, and unless we seize our chance, today and tomorrow, there'll be no such low-water again this year when it'll be possible to reap the deep seaweed beds of the Ridge.

– It's a spring-tide, said Mairead innocently. Having gone to America so early in life she had only a hazy knowledge of some of the home realities whose names were knit into the network of her memory.

– Spring-tide, said Lydon with the look of a bishop in whose presence an impudent blasphemy has been uttered. – The Spring-tide of the Feast of St Brigit! You're not acclimatized to the spring-tides yet, girl dear, and they're not exactly what's itching you.

He winked an eye at her and with a beck of his head drew her attention to Padraig who was on ahead, going down the shingle slope with Mairead's creel fixed into his own slung from his back.

At this point she didn't feel much like talk, it was enough to have to envisage her share of today's work which lay before her. For a week past the old couple had but the one tune, the Spring-tide. But she hadn't been a bit worried about going to the beach until she found herself now at the edge of the shingle.

She was born and grew up on 'Great Harbour's edge'. She had gathered periwinkles and sandeels, sloke, dulse, carrageen. The spring before she crossed over she had helped her father cut beach-crop. But she had gone before she was fully inured to the hardship of the shore. Soon her hands were wrinkled with washing, scouring, cooking, instead of acquiring the leathery skin of the sea-forager. Those ten years – years in which the sea would have injected its own bitterness into her blood and tempered her bones to its own mettle – she had spent them without setting eyes above ten times on saltwater.

But as they came then to the exposed margin of the ocean the salt wind in from the great waste sharpened her spirit.

– Aren't there many in the neighbourhood, she said to herself, many who spent even twenty years in America and are as used to this hardship today as if they had never left home? What's the hardship of the sea but part of the hardship I'll have to school myself again to? How is it worse than bog-hardship, field-hardship, the hardship of cattle and pigs, the hardship of bearing and rearing if God grants me family . . .

At the same time she would have preferred if that section of seaweed on the Ridge wasn't to be gathered in partnership with the Lydons. Would Nora and Caitín Lydon be mocking the ignoramus? Would the tale of her clumsiness come home to her mother-in-law? – How well it happened on my first day out that the Ridge had to be harvested in partnership! Pity it's not myself alone and Padraig.

She was determined to do her best for Padraig's sake, but she knew the best he'd allow her would be little enough for fear she'd overstrain herself from lack of practice in the job. If there were only two potatoes in the cow's tub it was – For God's sake, your back! from Padraig. Just now Mairead would rather he threw his shyness to the wind and wait to give her a helping hand. She was having great difficulty with the smooth and shifting stones of the shingle which were sliding under her feet and twice as quick to slip the more she tried to tread lightly over them.

– There's a vast difference between this and the streets of New York, said Lydon as they clattered down to the end of the shingle. – You should have put on hobnailed boots. You'd do better on the beach barefoot than in those light little toytoys.

– First thing to my hand this morning, said Mairead laughing, this time with an effort.

The sand, crisp and firm, on the ebb-strand was such a relief that she made a short dash towards a cluster of whelks and periwinkles which the tide had left stranded overnight. She inserted the toe of her shoe under them and struck Padraig with them on the calf of the leg. But he still didn't wait back for her.

She found it hard going at the place they called 'the footway' between high-water mark and the farthest line of the ebb. Every year, every generation, Lydons and Cades had planned to make a horse-track of this, but it remained 'intention good, performance poor'. She made a good deal of this uncouth passage by taking little leaps clean across the pools. Whenever she was faced with rugged outcrops of rock she slid sideways along them embracing a boulder. Her paps and the rockgrowths both suffered. Once a tentacle of sea-anemone kept her from falling. Once a little kingdom of periwinkles on a rockface went splashing down into the pool. The laughter of the work-party echoed in the clefts and fissures of the shore.

The Ridge was the farthest point out from land: a reef of rock, gapped, polished and bitten into by the ceaseless gnawing of the ocean. The Ridge was never entirely exposed; yet it could be harvested at the ebb of a spring-tide if one took the chance of a wetting. Padraig tucked the ends of his jacket of white homespun into his trouser-band and went to his hips in the narrow channel, but drew back again when he felt himself taken.

– We had better start on this black-weed here, Lydon said as if venting his ill-humour with the Cades in redirecting it against the slowness of the ebb. – Isn't that a nuisance now?

– Not worth our while killing ourselves with a year's growth, said Padraig, but since everyone else had begun he started himself. It pained Mairead to see the saltwater dripping from his clothes. She glanced towards him again and again so that the look in her eye might let him know how sorry she felt for him, but Padraig never once raised his head. She understood that since the spoils were to be divided equally between the two households, and seeing that there were three Lydons, Padraig was attempting to do two men's work. It didn't take her long to realize he was actually standing in for three: she herself was useless, might as well not be there at all. She was slipping on the slimy rockslabs, while the scabby one-year's growth was so tough that she skinned her knuckles trying to strip it from the rough coating of the stones. No matter how often she sharpened her hack-knife the result was the same. A stalk of seaweed sliced her finger. She stared at the blood dripping on the rock, loath to complain. Until Caitin Lydon noticed it and bound it with a strip of her calico bodice which the saltwater took neatly off again in no time. She felt her fingers numb, dark blue blotches appeared about the joints on the back of her hands. She had to begin rubbing the back of one hand in the crotch of the other. But she wasn't really shamed until she had to go wading.

Padraig glanced at her now and then out of the corner of his eye, vexation in his look, she thought – vexed that on account of the partnership she was obliged to do work which for his part he'd never ask her to do.

– The February bite is in the morning yet, said Caitin Lydon. I suppose you find the beach strange?

– Ah, not very, said Mairead. One has to get used to it I suppose.

– It's a sloppy sort of earning, said Nora Lydon. If I was in America, Lord, it's long 'ere I'd leave it. My passage is coming this summer.

– You're never without the hard and belittling word for the life at home, said Caitin to her young sister. But perhaps you may sigh for it some day.

Caitin spoke in the adult tone of a housewife, heir to the Lydon house, land and strand. But it seemed to Mairead that somewhat more than the mere defence of the homelife caused the sting in her voice. It was on the tip of Mairead's tongue to tell her about the shopkeeper in Brooklyn who had been pressing her to marry him until the day she left America; however, she refrained. It would be a matter for mockery in all the visiting-houses of the village that night. Did ever a slut or a slattern come back from America who hadn't some millionaire or other asking to marry her beyond?

By now the men had succeeded in getting out on the Ridge by going waist-deep in the water but the women stayed where they were until it had ebbed more in the channel.

Lydon, out on the Ridge, kept up a constant stream of orders back to his own daughters – strip the stones down to the skin – they wouldn't be reaped again for a couple of years. But Mairead was well aware he was aiming at her, though his eye never once lit on her. Soon the women moved out across the channel towards a red sand newly exposed near the last of the ebb. Mairead stood watching a crab that flopped about in a pool till he went in under a slanting stone. It gave her her best to dislodge the stone, but what came out of it but a tiny speckled fish that escaped her grasp and went into a cleft between two thighs of rock. Her heart jerked. She thought of the lusty appetite for crabs and rockfish she had when a girl. Her father had never come home from a seaweed-strand without bringing back some beach-gatherings. If Padraig wasn't so busy she'd ask him to collect her a hank of crabs and rockfish. The slab beside her was architected all over with limpets. She had a keen thought of the rare occasions she had served limpets and cockles as a tasty titbit in America, but she wouldn't give tuppence for that manner of serving compared with a batch of shellfish roasted on the embers. She began to long for the limpets. Maybe, too, they might sweeten the humour of the old woman at home. She thrust her blade in under the edge of a limpet that was slightly detached from the stone. She was reluctant at first to interfere between it and the rock. In spite of herself she was thinking of her mother-in-law going between herself and Padraig. But the limpet came away so readily with her that she had no further scruple. Pity I haven't a little can or a bucket, she thought. Then she remembered the apron she had on over her American dress, if she gathered it up and tied it behind it would hold a fine lot. She could put them in the creel when work on the beach was over. Bit by bit, she told herself, I am getting the knack of the shore.

– It's not worth bothering yourself with those limpets, Mairead, said Lydon. – There's twice the sustenance in the top-shore limpet than in the low-water one, and anyhow the limpet is never at his prime till he has taken three drinks of April water.

Though what he said was true, she took the hint that it wasn't to pick limpets she came but to cut seaweed.

She made her way out farther along with the two women. She was attracted by the little sand-pools left by the last of the ebb. Her thoughts were seduced by the faint thrum of the wave in the channel-mouth and the ripples of brine breaking in white flakes on the miniature strand made her happy in herself so that she lay into the work. Nor did she find it so piercingly difficult. Though the commonest weed here was the sawtooth wrack there was a lush growth of black-weed here and there on the backs of the jagged scarps, with patches of top-shore seaweed in among it and luxurious bunches of yellow-weed that were like golden tresses of hair in the rays of the morning sun. She was keener to go at them than she had been with the limpets a short while ago.

Now Lydon's tone began to grow sharp:

– Of course, ladies, ye don't imagine that old coarse-crop field of mine back up there is able to digest sawtooth wrack! Every single stalk of it will be still in the earth in its own shape next autumn. It isn't as if I'd ask you your business if it was sowing the loam at the bottom of the village I was. The tidewater is shallow enough now for you to come out here.

Caitin Lydon went out barefoot as far as a boulder under the Ridge. Nora took her boots off and got out on to another a slab. Mairead did likewise with her own boots. About to hoist up her skirt she hesitated once or twice and glanced shamefaced towards Lydon and Padraig. All she had under it was a transparent American petticoat. It surprised her at first how unconcerned the other pair were about hoisting a skirt, until she remembered they had never left home. Her feet shrank from the cold water, she went as gingerly as a cat crossing a patch of wet.

Suddenly she was afraid, the turbulent sea breaking in white spume over the lip of rock in the channel might sweep her legs from under her. The soles of her feet tingled on the gravelly bottom. She tensed her lips, it seemed to her the Lydons were grinning. She looked longingly out towards Padraig, he had his back to her, shearing as furiously as chance offered in the maw of the wave. He never as much as lifted his head . . .

She was out now on the exposed Ridge in face of the beds of strapwrack. The rank fronds of it excited her greed. She felt a lust to plunder. A desire to strip the rockfaces clean as a plate. She took pleasure in the squeak of the long ribbons of it letting go their hold and the hiss of the sheaves falling in the rock hollows. In spite of the chill and drench of the saltwater she felt a prick in her pulse, a prick ten years absent . . . She came to a gentle nook sheltered in under the backbone of the Ridge, where there was a feathery growth of carrageen on the cheek of the stone. How often that tuft of carrageen which Nora Sheain Liam brought to America had sent her thoughts bounding to 'Great Habour's edge', to the dear beach where lay her heart's desire . . . Again remembering her mother-in-law, she turned aside to pick the carrageen.

– Ladies, said Lydon, and now the ocean's urgency was in his voice, you are proving yourselves none too good. This reef isn't half-reaped yet. How shy you are of wetting yourselves! Saltwater never did harm to anybody.

Mairead gave up the carrageen, though the voice of Lydon caused her no irritation now. Now she felt sure she was fit to do her share, sure that the ocean's temper was getting under her own skin and through her veins the harsh reality was pulsing.

Again came the warning voice of Lydon:

– It's on the turn! Look, Carrigavackin almost submerged. Hadn't the ladies better begin drawing? They're more suited to that just now.

For the first time today Padraig raised his head and looked Mairead in the eye. He was on the verge of saying something, but shut his lips up tight again without speaking. Mairead understood, clearly he would forbid her that labour if he could. The strong bond of the partnership had inhibited the affection showing in his eye that moment. He needn't worry. She intended to show that though she might appear to be soft-spun there was a tough weft in her too. Since he was so good to her she was going to put herself to the limit for his sake.

They began filling from the part farthest out. They'd still be able to collect the nearer part until the tide had come well in.

For hands that had been ten years in the sweltering heat of a narrow kitchen it was pure refreshment to feel the stiff slime of the seaweed sticking to them as she stuffed the creel full to the brim. She had no great difficulty with the first creel in spite of the ruggedness of the passage while the brine streamed from the seaweed down along her back.

She put as much top-load on the second creel as did either of the Lydons. Very likely she wouldn't have slipped only that a sheaf of the top-load which overhung the edge of the creel slid off as she cleared the end of the Ridge. But though she slipped she wasn't injured. She grasped a rock which was right at her back and kept such a grip on the creel that only a few sheaves fell off the top. She would have preferred if the two Lydons had gone on instead of leaving their creels on the stones and coming back to help her gather the fallen sheaves. After the third creel it seemed to her that the Lydons were dawdling to allow her to keep up. The spreading-bank was nine or ten yards above highwater mark; the plod up there from the low-water edge seemed to grow longer with every creel. Like trying to teem out a fulltide, she thought.

She was sweating all over, felt the warm trickles of sweat tempering the chill of the saltwater. The strap began to raise blisters on her palms, the brine was biting into the crease of her fingers. Her back was bent stiff, and as for her legs, well, better forget them. They seemed to belong to someone else, not the legs of the one who had come down the boreen so quick and lithe that morning. Afraid every minute she'd turn an ankle. The soles had lifted clean from her light shoes. Every time she trod on a sharp pebble she clenched her foot, arching the instep against the shoe-laces. She was like a horse with a nail in the quick lifting her foot from a pointed periwinkle or a limpet shell. She was also ravenously hungry. She hadn't eaten much that morning. For ten years she had been in the habit of a cup of tea in the hand at eleven o'clock every day. But fasting was child's play in comparison with this excruciating work. In America there was a break or a change of occupation after every stint. But the selfsame journey, from low-water to the top of the beach, again and again . . .

Lydon's temper was shortening step by step with the rising tide.

– You are slow, ladies! It seems we'll have to leave this reef uncut and go drawing ourselves. If we're depending on you the floodtide will take a share of what we've already cut.

Once the men began drawing the pace grew fiercer. The rugged beach didn't cost them a thought, no more than it did Caitin Lydon who was able to keep up with them barefoot step for step. More often than not Padraig was emptying his creel on the spread-bank by the time the others had reached the tidemark, with Mairead still not beyond the edge of the sand.

There was no feeling left in her feet. Sometimes when she came to the upper edge of the sand she shut her eyes awhile so as not to be pierced by the prospect of the final stretch. She was dead to all sense of pain by now. She plodded along as if there was someone inside her goading her on. If her body was numb her mind was more so. Nothing occurred to her except disconnected scraps of thought . . . the partnership . . . if the seaweed was left to Padraig and myself . . . a body must become inured to the hardship . . . the floodtide . . .

She slackened now on the slope of the shingle without strength or will to open her eyes properly. First thing she knew she was into the tidemark, the heap of shells and periwinkles, oozy tangles of oarweed root, bits of board encrusted with barnacles, ringlets of wrack and trash-heaps of red seaweed which had come up with the full of the spring-tide from where it had been rotting during the neap. It was on a slimy strand of redweed she slipped. Quite aware of the feet sliding from under her, she let them go. A relief to let the strap of the creel slip from her grasp . . . Padraig refilled the creel, took it to the finish.

The eyes of the Lydon girls seemed to her to smile, in spite of what they had to say of . . . treacherous stones . . . too long a distance . . .

To think she had left the comfort of America for the sake of this. Yet Padraig wasn't to blame for it.

– No need for you to go down any more, Mairead, said Lydon. The three of us will gather what's left out there at a single go, and it'll no trouble to your boss-man to gather a little creel of the floating weed down at the channel. Padraig lad, hurry, the flood won't have a clump left.

But now Mairead was determined to go back down. How well they wouldn't ask Nora or Caitin Lydon to stay up here? She'd go down if only to spite them. If that floating weed contained only a single clump she'd make two halves of that clump! She had made her bed and she'd lie on it . . .

In spite of his striding haste she kept up with Padraig on the way down and when they reached low-tide mark she was no more out of breath than he was. It was some satisfaction that she had Padraig to herself for the first time since they had come to the beach. She gave up the idea of gathering her share of the floating weed into her own creel: there wasn't the full of a creel in it all told.

Floodtide was now so fiercely breaking in that it seemed to regret having been caught out that morning and intended to take full revenge for having bared at all. It pushed into the channel nuzzling the little piles of stones with its cold snout, sniffing into fissures with its nostrils hissing, feeling its way far up along the ebbway of red sand with its long greedy tentacles, making ravenous attacks on the cut swathes of weed not yet collected. It had already taken a few substantial heaps and Padraig was put to his knees trying to save a clump of strapweed from its gullet.

The rage and rapacity of the sea was in tune with Mairead's turbulent mood. The rush of the surf was an ease to her agonized spirit as it tousled the sawtooth wrack on the stones and broke them despondently, not having yet displaced the little pad of sand the ebb had left. But hardly had the little scattered rills of the first wave been absorbed by the sand when the thrust of the next wave was come to dislodge the wee strip once and for all. Mairead stood in a cold pool on bare-strand edge till the reflux of the wave which had taken the sand-pad drenched her up to the knees. A swimming-crab came out of a crevice and went foraging down the sloping shoulders of the wave. A periwinkle went from the rock as if in a game of tip-and-come with the upsurge of seawater which made a rush for the last gatherings of weed. Out went Mairead into the mouth of the surf to retrieve a clump – a glistening clump of yellow-weed.

– Out of my way! said Padraig and went to his thighs to snatch the last of the plunder from the devouring tide. Mairead straightened, her mind flared up at that voice. A harsh alien voice. A voice from a law of life other than the life of his complaining letters, other than the life of beguiling and sweethearting, alien to the life of the pillow. With the stab she got the little bladder of seaweed burst between her fingers and squirted a dull slime up in her cheek.

The dark shade she saw on Padraig's features at that moment was as strange and forbidding as the black streaks which the freshening wind was making in the bristling mane of the floodtide . . .

Translated by Eoghan Ó Tuairisc

MICHAEL MCLAVERTY
from *Call My Brother Back*

12

The end of the bonfire marked the end of the summer holidays. In a week's time Colm was back at the College; Clare went into her new class and already, in the evenings, was reading her new books with the help of her mother; Jamesy was still employed as message boy, and Alec had joined the Irish Republican Army. He sold the pigeons, for he had no time for them and no heart to work with them.

Colm took possession of the shed, scraped it out, swept the floor, and under the narrow glass window he got Jamesy to help him to make a shelf for his books.

For the first week after he went back to school he climbed every evening up the ladder to the shed. His mother had given him a stool; Jamesy had made a table for him out of old butter boxes; and so he was able to do his exercises and learn his lessons. Finished, he would stand for a while at the window which overlooked the yard-walls. From there he could see the men digging the brown clay in the pit, the glint of a shovel as it caught the sunlight, and the long line of bogies filled with clay moving slowly towards the sheds. Beyond was the white mountain lonin, and looking at it he often thought of the rocky pool at its end, the cold water forever gushing and tumbling into it, and the little drinking tin sitting on a flat stone. He knew every hollow on that mountain, saw them being filled with sun-shadow, and the whole mountain grow black and close at approaching rain. He would stand and think of Knocklayde and compare it with the mountain before him: the one barren and desolate, the other green and near. Then he would turn away, do some dumbbell exercises, pencil his height on the boards of the shed, and then out to the waste ground to play football until dark.

Sometimes when he would be leaving the shed for the evening he would see one of Alec's pigeons had returned and was looking for the entrance. He would then have to take the boards off the trap-door, spread newspapers over his books and let the pigeon in. In the morning Jamesy would tear two holes in a paper bag, put the pigeon inside, and take it back to its owner.

But Colm's seclusion didn't last long. Riots broke out again, and he left the quiet of the pigeon-shed for the noise and companionship of the kitchen, once again to listen to Mrs Heaney talking now about Theresa's newborn baby girl, showing his mother woollen coats that she had knitted for it, and all the time Clare pestering him with her sums. Tired of the chatter he would stand at the door and listen with a growing fear to the shots in another part of the city or a man just up from the town telling him about the number that were shot dead in Ballymacarret, and that curfew was being declared over the whole city.

'It must be near the end of the world,' said Mrs Heaney when she heard about the curfew and everyone to be in the house at half-past ten at night.

The first night of the curfew the MacNeills had gathered into the house early and Mrs Heaney had not come up for her usual chat. Alec slept in her house, for raids were now frequent and IRA suspects were being arrested and interned. Jamesy was making a scooter for the boy next door, Clare was in bed, and the mother was darning socks. They argued over the lighting of the gas, wondering if it were allowed to be lit during curfew. Jamesy went upstairs and looked out of the back-room window to see if the rest of the neighbours had their gas lit.

'Light up!' he shouted as he came running downstairs again.

'Quit the shouting,' Colm said to him when he came into the kitchen.

'Surely to goodness we can talk during curfew,' replied Jamesy cockily.

'S-s-s-h,' put in the mother, and they all hushed at once.

The armoured car rattled up the street and throbbed in the kitchen. Their eyes were alert and steady with fear as it passed the house; and then with suppressed delight they heard its noise fade in the distance. A lightness came over Colm, he gulped the air noisily, and felt a hollowness within him. Jamesy bent to the scooter again, and once when he hammered the wheel loudly Colm said irritably, 'Sure you can do that in the morning!'

'I'll do it now that I'm free and no other time,' and he gave the axle another whack with the hammer.

'Stop it, I tell you!' Colm shouted as Jamesy took a few nails from a box.

'Tell him to stop the hammering, Mother. You wouldn't know whether they were listening at the door and they'd think it was guns we were making.'

'And how could a child's scooter be guns?' Jamesy looked up at him, his face red from stooping.

'Put it away, I tell you, or I'll smash it in bits!'

'Try it on till ye see what you'll get.'

'Och, och,' intervened the mother, leaving down darning. 'Never since God made me did I see boys who fought so much. God knows there's enough fighting outside than you to be bringing it inside. Put everything away for the night and we'll say the rosary.'

They offered the prayers up for peace, for Alec's protection, and implored Our Blessed Lady to safeguard the house. Once Rover barked when they were at their prayers and Colm turned out the light and patted the dog's head. Then they knelt in silence, waiting any moment for the back-door to be battered or shots fired into the kitchen. But nothing happened, the dog went to sleep again, and the mother continued the prayers. When the rosary was ended Colm went off to bed.

He stood at the window of his room looking at the waste ground and the bits of broken delph catching the moonlight. Above the dark palings the trees were black and through the branches he saw thin clouds riding up the sky. It was very still, and he thought of the same moon glittering on the sea in Rathlin, filling the valleys with shadow, shining on the walls of his old home, and wetting the rock-face of his den with cold light. Inside the deserted house there would be the bare hearth, yellow straw in a corner, and a snail weaving its silver line across a mouldy sack . . . He felt weary and sick. He knelt on the bare boards and covered his face with his hands. He leaned forward on the bed-clothes, felt his warm breath flung back upon his cheeks and the dusty smell from the blankets. His mind wavered and fell into a dream, and it was Jamesy coming up to bed that wakened him.

'You're praying a lot tonight, Colm,' he remarked jovially. 'Are you doing a Novena?'

Colm did not answer. In silence and in the light of the moon they undressed, but, once in bed, Colm regretted his sullenness and felt the words form in his throat, the words that he had said to his brother for a long time – 'Good night, Jamesy.'

'Good night, Colm.'

13

A week afterwards the house was raided. It was Saturday. Alec had gone out after nine o'clock to Mrs Heaney's, and the rest had gone to bed before curfew. Then after midnight there came a loud knock at the front door. Colm jumped out of bed and went into his mother's room; the light from the street lamp shone through the curtained window, and he could see her gripping a coat in front of her. Clare was still asleep.

'What will we do, Mother?' he asked in a rising whisper.

'Wait till they knock again.'

He went to the window and peeped out. He saw the soldiers, their bayonets and helmets shining in the lamp light.

They knocked again. 'Open! Military!' a man ordered.

Jamesy came into the room, his teeth chattering.

'Get you two back to your bed and I'll open the door,' said the mother, going out on to the landing.

Colm and Jamesy sat up in the bed. They felt cold and couldn't keep their limbs from trembling. The door opened and they heard the clink of steel in the hall. Then a light made the shadow of the bannisters jig across the bedroom door. A military officer came into the room, an automatic pistol in one hand and an electric torch in the other. He lit the gas jet and looked at the two boys in bed.

'What is your age?' he asked Colm.

'Fifteen past,' Colm answered in a quaky voice.

'And yours?'

'Fourteen and a half,' replied Jamesy.

'You have an elder brother, haven't you? . . . Where is he?'

'He went down to the country for the week-end,' lied Jamesy, his courage gaining strength from the polite tones of the officer.

The officer turned to the chest of drawers, and a little soldier with his rifle and bayonet by his side looked over the rail of the bed and winked at Colm and Jamesy. They nervously smiled back at him. The officer gripped the two knobs of the top drawer and they came off in his hands.

'It always does that,' said Jamesy, and he hopped out of bed in his shirt, put his forefingers in the holes where the knobs had been, and pulled out the drawer.

The officer lifted up a few of the contents: old jerseys, patches for shirts, three yellow gritty candles tied with a scapular, and a few faded newspapers.

Outside on the landing a policeman was talking to the mother. He placed his hand gently on her shoulder, 'Now, like a good sensible woman, give me the gun now and there won't be a word about it.'

'What gun?' she raised her voice – 'There's no gun here!'

'S-s-s-h,' said the policeman, glancing into the room at the military officer as if it were a confidence trick between the woman and himself. He patted her on the shoulder and whispered:

'Give it to me now and it will be all right. There'll not be a word about it, not a word about it, I tell you.'

She shrugged her shoulders. The military officer came out and into the other room. He flashed his light round, and when he saw Clare asleep in the bed he turned down the stairs, and the policeman followed. As they were going out to the street the policeman turned back; they heard him search around the scullery and the kitchen. Then there was a noise of breaking glass; Rover started to bark and the policeman hurried from the house.

The lorry rattled down the street and soon everything was quiet except Rover who was sniffing loudly at the front door

The mother turned out the gas and in the dark sat on the edge of the boys' bed.

They remained for a while in silence and then they heard Rover's sharp claws on the oil-cloth of the stairs. He came into the room and walked round and round in the dark. No one spoke and he jumped on to the bed and licked the boys' faces.

The mother patted the dog and said: 'It's well Alec wasn't in or he'd have a hard bed tonight.'

'S-s-s-h!' replied Colm. 'I believe there's somebody downstairs.'

'Rover would have barked! Wait and I'll look.' The mother lit a candle and went down. Rover followed her.

In the kitchen her bare feet tramped on a piece of glass. She lit the gas and there on the wall were Alec's two pictures, *Thomas McDonagh* and *The Signing of the Republican Declaration*, smashed and torn. She called to Colm and Jamesy.

'It was the peeler did it! The time we heard him walking in the kitchen!' affirmed Jamesy.

They went back to bed, but were too excited to sleep, and in the morning they all arose earlier than usual. Alec came in for his breakfast and they all began telling him about the raid: Jamesy about the wee soldier that winked at them over the rail of the bed; Colm about Rover walking round and round like a dog in a fever; and the mother about the policeman plaguing her for a gun.

'What was he like? What way did he talk?' asked Alec.

'He talked, now, I'd think, like a south-of-Ireland man. He had a brogue anyway and a sweet tongue it was too.'

'Be God, but there's something rotten about the Southern character when they can breed so many peelers of that type! A nice not-a-word-about-it he'd have said if he'd been lucky enough to get a gun!' And as he took his breakfast he told them about fellows that were arrested last night. 'When I was coming up the street,' he said, 'I met the postman and he was telling me that six were arrested in the Kashmir Road.'

He had the same story to tell every morning, and when Colm was going to school he would see lorry loads of prisoners, brought in from the country, and singing rebel songs as they were conveyed to Crumlin Road Jail. People would shake their fists at them and sometimes groups of women at street corners would jeer and wave Union Jacks. Colm would rejoice secretly when he would hear the Crumlin Road echoing with the *Soldiers' Song*. Now and again he would stand too long and be late for school; he would try to sneak up behind the trees of the College avenue, and when he had entered the vestibule and thought all was safe, there would be a rustle of a soutane and the President would be before him: 'What's the meaning of this, Colm? Late again!' he would say in his sing-song voice; and if he were in good form he would let him off. 'Maybe you had to feed the baby; tut-tut, too bad, now! . . . Run on to your class like a good boy and don't let it occur again.'

BRYAN MACMAHON

'Exile's Return'

Far away the train whistled. The sound moved in rings through the rain falling on the dark fields.

On hearing the whistle the little man standing on the railway bridge gave a quick glance into the up-line darkness and then began to hurry downwards towards the station. Above the metal footbridge the lights came on weak and dim as he hurried onwards. The train beat him to the station; all rattle and squeak and bright playing cards placed in line, it drew in beneath the bridge. At the station's end the engine lurched uneasily: then it puffed and huffed, blackened and whitened, and eventually, after a loud release of steam, stood chained.

One passenger descended – a large man resembling Victor McLaglen. He was dressed in a new cheap suit and overcoat. A black stubble of beard littered his scowling jowls. The eyes under the cap were black and daft. In his hand he carried a battered attaché case tied with a scrap of rope. Dourly slamming the carriage door behind him, he stood glaring up and down the platform.

A passing porter looked at him, abandoned him as being of little interest, then as on remembrance glanced at him a second time. As he walked away the porter's eyes still lingered on the passenger. A hackney-driver, viewing with disgust the serried unprofitable door-handles, smiled grimly to himself at the sight of the big fellow. Barefooted boys grabbing cylinders of magazines that came hurtling out of the luggage van took no notice whatsoever of the man standing alone. The rain's falling was visible in the pocking of the cut limestone on the platform's edge.

Just then the little man hurried in by the gateway of the station. His trouser-ends were tied over clay-daubed boots above which he wore a cast-off green Army great-coat. A sweat-soiled hat sat askew on his poll. After a moment of hesitation he hurried forward to meet the swaying newcomer.

'There you are, Paddy!' the small man wheezed brightly, yet not coming too close to the big fellow.

The big fellow did not answer. He began to walk heavily out of the station. The little man moved hoppingly at his side, pelting questions to which he received no reply.

'Had you a good crossing, Paddy?' 'Is it true that the Irish Sea is as wicked as May Eve?' 'There's a fair share of Irish in Birmingham, I suppose?' Finally, in a tone that indicated that this question was closer to the bone than its fellows: 'How long are you away now, Paddy? Over six year, eh?'

Paddy ploughed ahead without replying. When they had reached the first of the houses of the country town, he glowered over his shoulder at the humpy bridge that led over the railway line to the open country: after a moment or two he dragged his gaze away and looked at the street that led downhill from the station.

'We'll have a drink, Timothy!' the big man said dourly.

'A drink, Paddy!' the other agreed.

The pub glittered in the old-fashioned way. The embossed wallpaper between the shelving had been painted lime-green. As they entered the bar, the publican was in the act of turning with a full pint-glass in his hand. His eyes hardened on seeing Paddy: he delayed the fraction of a second before placing the glass on the high counter in front of a customer.

Wiping his hands in a blue apron, his face working overtime, 'Back again, eh, Paddy?' the publican asked, with false cheer. A limp handshake followed.

Paddy grunted, then lurched towards the far corner of the bar. There, sitting on a high stool, he crouched against the counter. Timothy took his seat beside him, seating himself sideways to the counter as if protecting the big fellow from the gaze of the other customers. Paddy called for two pints of porter: he paid for his call from an old-fashioned purse bulky with English treasury notes. Timothy raised his full glass – its size tended to dwarf him – and ventured: 'Good health!' Paddy growled a reply. Both men tilted the glasses on their heads and gulped three-quarters of the contents. Paddy set down his glass and looked moodily in front of him. Timothy carefully replaced his glass on the counter, then placed his face closer to the other's ear.

'Yeh got my letter, Paddy?'

'Ah!'

'You're not mad with me?'

'Mad with *you*?' The big man's guffaw startled the bar.

There was a long silence.

'I got yer letter!' Paddy said abruptly. He turned and for the first time looked his small companion squarely in the face. Deliberately he set the big battered index finger of his right hand inside the other's collar-stud. As, slowly, he began to twist his finger, the collar-band tightened. When it was taut Paddy drew the other's face close to his own. So intimately were the two men seated that the others in the bar did not know what was going on. Timothy's face changed colour, yet he did not raise his hands to try to release himself.

'Yer swearin' 'tis true?' Paddy growled.

Gaspingly: 'God's gospel, it's true!'

'Swear it!'

'That I may be struck down dead if I'm tellin' you a word of a lie! Every mortal word I wrote you is true!'

'Why didn't you send me word afore now?'

'I couldn't rightly make out where you were, Paddy. Only for Danny Greaney comin' home I'd never have got your address. An' you know I'm not handy with the pen.'

'Why didn't you let me as I was – not knowin' at all?'

'We to be butties always, Paddy. I thought it a shame you to keep sendin' her lashin's o' money an' she to be like that! You're chokin' me, Paddy!'

As Paddy tightened still more, the button-hole broke and the stud came away in the crook of his index finger. He looked at it stupidly. Timothy quietly put the Y of his hand to his chafed neck. Paddy threw the stud behind him. It struck the timbered encasement of the stairway.

'*Ach!*' he said harshly. He drained his glass and with its heel tapped on the counter. The publican came up to refill the glasses.

Timothy, whispering: 'What'll you do, Paddy?'

'What'll I do?' Paddy laughed. 'I'll drink my pint,' he said. He took a gulp. 'Then, as likely as not, I'll swing for her!'

'Sssh!' Timothy counselled.

Timothy glanced into an advertising mirror: behind the picture of little men loading little barrels on to a little lorry he saw the publican with his eyes fast on the pair of them. Timothy warned him off with a sharp look. He looked swiftly around: the backs of the other customers were a shade too tense for his liking. Then suddenly the publican was in under Timothy's guard.

Swabbing the counter: 'What way are things over, Paddy?'

'Fair enough!'

'I'm hearin' great accounts of you from Danny Greaney. We were all certain you'd never again come home, you were doin' so well. How'll you content yourself with a small place like this, after what you've seen? But then, after all, home is home!'

The publican ignored Timothy's threatening stare. Paddy raised his daft eyes and looked directly at the man behind the bar. The swabbing moved swiftly away.

'Swing for her, I will!' Paddy said again. He raised his voice. 'The very minute I turn my back . . .'

'Sssh!' Timothy intervened. He smelled his almost empty glass, then said in a loud whisper: 'The bloody stout is casky. Let's get away out o' this!'

The word 'casky' succeeded in moving Paddy. It also nicked the publican's pride. After they had gone the publican, on the pretence of closing the door, looked after them. He turned and threw a joke to his customers. A roar of laughter was his reward.

Paddy and Timothy were now wandering towards the humpy bridge that led to the country. Timothy was carrying the battered case: Paddy had his arm around his companion's shoulder. The raw air was testing the sobriety of the big fellow's legs.

'Nothing hasty!' Timothy was advising. 'First of all we'll pass out the cottage an' go on to my house. You'll sleep with me tonight. Remember, Paddy, that I wrote that letter out o' pure friendship!'

Paddy lifted his cap and let the rain strike his forehead. 'I'll walk the gallows high for her!' he said.

'Calm and collected, that's my advice!'

'When these two hands are on her throat, you'll hear her squealin' in the eastern world!'

'Nothin' hasty, Paddy: nothin' hasty at all!'

Paddy pinned his friend against the parapet of the railway bridge. 'Is six years hasty?' he roared.

'For God's sake, let go o' me, Paddy! I'm the only friend you have left! Let go o' me!'

The pair lurched with the incline. The whitethorns were now on each side of them, releasing their raindrops from thorn to thorn in the darkness. Far away across the ridge of the barony a fan of light from a lighthouse swung its arc on shore and sea and sky. Wherever there was a break in the hedges a bout of wind mustered its forces and vainly set about capsizing them.

Paddy began to growl a song with no air at all to it.

'Hush, man, or the whole world'll know you're home,' Timothy said.

'As if to sweet hell I cared!' Paddy stopped and swayed. After a pause he muttered: 'Th' other fellah – is he long gone?'

Timothy whinnied. 'One night only it was, like Duffy's Circus.' He set his hat farther back on his poll and then, his solemn face tilted to the scud of the moon, said: 'You want my firm opinion, Paddy? 'Twas nothin' but a chance fall. The mood an' the man meetin' her. 'Twould mebbe never again happen in a million years. A chance fall, that's all it was, in my considered opinion.'

Loudly: 'Did you ever know me to break my word?'

'Never, Paddy!'

'Then I'll swing for her! You have my permission to walk into the witness-box and swear that Paddy Kinsella said he'd swing for her!'

He resumed his singing.

'We're right beside the house, Paddy. You don't want to wake your own children, do you? Your own fine lawful-got sons! Eh, Paddy? Do you want to waken them up?'

Paddy paused: 'Lawful-got is right! – you've said it there!'

'Tomorrow is another day. We'll face her tomorrow and see how she brazens it out. I knew well you wouldn't want to disturb your own sons.'

They lurched on through the darkness. As they drew near the low thatched cottage that was slightly below the level of the road, Timothy kept urging Paddy forward. Paddy's boots were more rebellious than heretofore. Timothy grew anxious at the poor progress they were making. He kept saying: 'Tomorrow is the day, Paddy! I'll put the rope around her neck for you. Don't wake the lads tonight.'

Directly outside the cottage, Paddy came to a halt. He swayed and glowered at the small house with its tiny windows. He drew himself up to his full height.

'She's in bed?' he growled.

'She's up at McSweeney's. She goes there for the sake of company. Half an hour at night when the kids are in bed – you'll not begrudge her that, Paddy?'

'I'll not begrudge her that!' Paddy yielded a single step, then planted his shoes still more firmly on the roadway. He swayed.

'The . . . ?' he queried.

'A girl, Paddy, a girl!'

A growl, followed by the surrender of another step.

'Goin' on six year, is it?'

'That's it, Paddy. Six year.'

Another step. 'Like the ma, or . . . the da?'

'The ma, Paddy. Mostly all the ma. Come on now, an' you'll have a fine sleep tonight under my roof.'

Paddy eyed the cottage. Growled his contempt of it, then spat on the roadway. He gave minor indications of his intention of moving forward. Then unpredictably he pounded off the restraining hand of Timothy, pulled violently away, and went swaying towards the passage that led down to the cottage.

After a fearful glance uproad, Timothy wailed: 'She'll be back in a minute!'

'I'll see my lawful-got sons!' Paddy growled.

When Timothy caught up with him the big fellow was fumbling with the padlock on the door. As on a thought he lurched aside and groped in vain in the corner of the window sill.

'She takes the key with her,' Timothy said. 'For God's sake leave it till mornin'.'

But Paddy was already blundering on the cobbled pathway that led around by the gable of the cottage. Finding the back door bolted, he stood back from it angrily. He was about to smash it in when Timothy discovered that the hinged window of the kitchen was slightly open. As Timothy swung the window open the smell of turf-smoke emerged. Paddy put his boot on an imaginary niche in the wall and dug in the plaster until he gained purchase of a sort. 'Gimme a leg!' he ordered harshly.

Timothy began clawing Paddy's leg upwards. Belabouring the small man's shoulders with boot and hand, the big fellow floundered through the open window. Spreadeagled on the kitchen table he remained breathing harshly for a full minute, then laboriously he grunted his way via a *súgán* chair to the floor.

'You all right, Paddy?'

A grunt.

'Draw the bolt of the back door, Paddy.'

A long pause followed. At last the bolt was drawn. 'Where the hell's the lamp?' Paddy asked as he floundered in the darkness.

'She has it changed. It's at the right of the window now.'

Paddy's match came erratically alight. He held it aloft. Then he slewed forward and removed the lamp-chimney and placed it on the table. ''Sall right!' he said, placing a match to the wick and replacing the chimney. Awkwardly he raised the wick. He began to look here and there about the kitchen.

The fire was raked in its own red ashes. Two *súgán* chairs stood one on each side of the hearth-stone. Delph glowed red, white, and green on the wide dresser. The timber of the chairs and the deal table were white from repeated scrubbings. Paddy scowled his recognition of each object. Timothy stood watching him narrowly.

'See my own lads!' Paddy said, focusing his gaze on the bedroom door at the rear of the cottage.

'Aisy!' Timothy counselled.

Lighting match held aloft, they viewed the boys. Four lads sleeping in pairs in iron-headed double-beds. Each of the boys had a mop of black hair and a pair of heavy eyebrows. The eldest slept with the youngest and the two middle-aged lads slept together. They sprawled anyhow in various postures.

Paddy had turned surprisingly sober. ''Clare to God!' he said. 'I'd pass 'em on the road without knowin' 'em!'

'There's a flamin' lad!' Timothy caught one of the middle-aged boys by the hair and pivoted the sleep-loaded head. Transferring his attention to the other of this pair: 'There's your livin' spit, Paddy!' Indicating the eldest: 'There's your own ould fellah born into the world a second time, devil's black temper an' all!' At the youngest: 'Here's Bren – he was crawlin' on the floor the last time you saw him. Ay! Bully pups all!'

'Bully pups all!' Paddy echoed loudly. The match embered in his fingers. When there was darkness: 'My lawful-got sons!' he said bitterly.

Timothy was in the room doorway. 'We'll be off now, Paddy!' he said. After a growl, Paddy joined him.

Timothy said: 'One of us'll have to go out by the window. Else she'll spot the bolt drawn.'

Paddy said nothing.

'You'll never manage the window twice.'

'I'll be after you,' Paddy said.

Timothy turned reluctantly away.

'Where's the . . . ?' Paddy asked. He was standing at the kitchen's end.

'The . . . ?'

'Yeh!'

'She's in the front room. You're not goin' to . . . ?' Paddy was already at the door of the other room.

'She sleeps like a cat!' Timothy warned urgently. 'If she tells the mother about me, the fat'll be in the fire!'

Paddy opened the door of the front room. Breathing heavily he again began fumbling with the match-box. Across the window moved the scudding night life of the sky. The matchlight came up and showed a quilt patterned with candle-wick. Then abruptly where the bed-clothes had been a taut ball there was no longer a ball. As if playing a merry game, the little girl, like jill-in-the-box, flax-curled and blue-eyed, sprang up.

'Who is it?' she asked fearlessly.

The matchlight was high above her. Paddy did not reply.

The girl laughed ringingly. 'You're in the kitchen, Timothy Hannigan,' she called out. 'I know your snuffle.'

'Holy God!' Timothy breathed.

'I heard you talking too, boyo,' she said gleefully as the matchlight died in Paddy's fingers.

''Tis me all right, Maag,' said Timmy, coming apologetically to the doorway of the room. 'Come on away!' he said in a whisper to Paddy.

'Didn't I know right well 'twas you, boyo!' Maag laughed. She drew up her knees and locked her hands around them in a mature fashion.

Another match sprang alive in Paddy's fingers.

'Who's this fellah?' Maag inquired of Timothy.

Timothy put his head inside the room. 'He's your . . . your uncle!'

'My uncle what?'

'Your uncle . . . Paddy!'

Paddy and Maag looked fully at one another.

Timothy quavered: 'You won't tell your mother I was here?'

'I won't so!' the girl laughed. 'Wait until she comes home!'

Timothy groaned. 'C'm'on away to hell outa this!' he said, showing a spark of spirit. Surprisingly enough, Paddy came. They closed the room door behind them.

'Out the back door with you,' Timothy said. 'I'll manage the lamp and the bolt.'

'Out, you!' Paddy growled. He stood stolidly like an ox.

Dubiously: 'Very well!'

Timothy went out. From outside the back door he called: 'Shoot the bolt quick, Paddy. She'll be back any minute.'

Paddy shot the bolt.

'Blow out the lamp, Paddy!' Timothy's head and shoulders were framed in the window.

After a pause Paddy blew out the lamp.

'Hurry, Paddy! Lift your leg!'

No reply.

'Hurry, Paddy, I tell you. What's wrong with you, man?'

Paddy gave a deep growl. 'I'm sorry now I didn't throttle you.'

'Throttle me! Is that my bloody thanks?'

'It was never in my breed to respect an informer.'

'Your breed!' Timothy shouted. 'You, with a cuckoo in your nest.'

'If my hands were on your throat . . .'

'Yehoo! You, with the nest robbed.'

'Go, while you're all of a piece. The drink has me lazy. I'll give you while I'm countin' five. One, two . . .'

Timothy was gone.

Paddy sat on the rough chair at the left of the hearth. He began to grope for the tongs. Eventually he found it. He drew the red coals of turf out of the ashes and set them together in a kind of pyramid. The flames came up.

The door of the front bedroom creaked open. Maag was there, dressed in a long white nightdress.

'Were you scoldin' him?'

'Ay!' Paddy answered.

'He wants scoldin' badly. He's always spyin' on my Mom.'

After a pause, the girl came to mid-kitchen.

'Honest,' she asked, 'are you my uncle?'

'In a class of a way!'

'What class of a way?' she echoed. She took a step closer.

'Are you cold, girlie?' Paddy asked.

'I am an' I am not. What class of a way are you my uncle?'

There was no reply.

'Mebbe you're my ould fellah back from England?' she stabbed suddenly.

'Mebbe!'

The girl's voice was shaken with delight. 'I knew you'd be back! They all said no, but I said yes – that you'd be back for sure.' A pause. A step nearer. 'What did you bring me?'

Dourly he put his hand into his pocket. His fingers encountered a pipe, a half-quarter of tobacco, a six-inch nail, a clotted handkerchief, and the crumpled letter from Timothy.

'I left it after me in the carriage,' he said limply.

Her recovery from disappointment was swift. 'Can't you get it in town a Saturday?' she said, drawing still closer.

'That's right!' he agreed. There was a short pause. Then: 'Come hether to the fire,' he said.

She came and stood between his knees. The several hoops of her curls were between him and the fire-light. She smelled of soap. His fingers touched her arms. The mother was in her surely. He knew it by the manner in which her flesh was sure and unafraid.

They remained there without speaking until the light step on the road sent her prickling alive. 'Mom'll kill me for bein' out of bed,' she said. Paddy's body stiffened. As the girl struggled to be free, he held her fast. Of a sudden she went limp, and laughed: 'I forgot!' she whispered. 'She'll not touch me on account of you comin' home.' She rippled with secret laughter. 'Wasn't I the fooleen to forget?'

The key was in the padlock. The door moved open. The woman came in, her shawl down from her shoulders. 'Maag!' she breathed. The girl and the man were between her and the firelight.

Without speaking the woman stood directly inside the door. The child said nothing but looked from one to the other. The woman waited for a while. Slowly she took off her shawl, then closed the door behind her. She walked carefully across the kitchen. A matchbox noised. She lighted the warm lamp. As the lamplight came up Paddy was seen to be looking steadfastly into the fire.

'You're back, Paddy?'

'Ay!'

'Had you a good crossin'?'

'Middlin!'

'You hungry?'

'I'll see . . . soon!'

There was a long silence. Her fingers restless, the woman stood in mid-kitchen.

She raised her voice: 'If you've anything to do or say to me, Paddy Kinsella, you'd best get it over. I'm not a one for waitin'!'

He said nothing. He held his gaze on the fire.

'You hear me, Paddy? I'll not live cat and dog with you. I know what I am. Small good your brandin' me when the countryside has me well branded before you.'

He held his silence.

'Sayin' nothin' won't get you far. I left you down, Paddy. Be a man an' say it to my face!'

Paddy turned: 'You left me well down,' he said clearly. He turned to the fire and added, in a mutter: 'I was no angel myself!'

Her trembling lips were unbelieving. 'We're quits, so?' she ventured at last.

'Quits!'

'You'll not keep firin' it in my face?'

'I'll not!'

'Before God?'

'Before God!'

The woman crossed herself and knelt on the floor. 'In the presence of my God,' she said, 'because you were fair to me, Paddy Kinsella, I'll be better than three wives to you. I broke my marriage-mornin' promise, but I'll make up for it. There's my word, given before my Maker!'

Maag kept watching with gravity. The mother crossed herself and rose.

Paddy was dourly rummaging in his coat-pocket. At last his fingers found what he was seeking. 'I knew I had it somewhere!' he said. He held up a crumpled toffee-sweet. 'I got it from a kid on the boat.'

Maag's face broke in pleasure: ''Twill do – till Saturday!' she said.

The girl's mouth came down upon the stripped toffee. Then, the sweet in her cheek, she broke away and ran across the kitchen. She flung open the door of the boys' bedroom.

'Get up outa that!' she cried out. 'The ould fellah is home!'

SAM HANNA BELL

from *December Bride*

8

With that urgency with which religious old age invests such matters, Martha still endeavoured to make the younger members of the household return to church. Hamilton had continued to go for a few Sabbaths after his father's death. Then one Sabbath morning he had gone out into the fields and from thence his attendance became more desultory, until now he and Frank contented themselves with driving Martha to the church and returning for her after the service. As time passed they did not even trouble to dress or shave themselves for these journeys.

On the homeward way the churchgoers would watch the Echlin trap pass, and pull down their mouths and say 'changed times at Rathard since ould Andra died', and others would maliciously add 'or since the Gomartins went up'. But most of her neighbours sympathized with Martha.

These whispers and glances did not escape the notice of the old woman, but the final humiliation was delivered by the Reverend Mr Sorleyson. One Sunday morning as she left the church, he drew her aside and asked her, kindly enough, to prevail on the Echlins to come back to the congregation. 'Aye, and my Sarah?' 'Of course,' exclaimed Mr Sorleyson after the faintest pause. 'Sarah, as well.' But the momentary hesitation in Sorleyson's voice went to the mother's heart like a knife.

When he left her she stood in the shelter of the hedge endeavouring to still the trembling in her legs. A dull burning pulsed in her cheeks and as she looked after the departing minister bitter tears flooded her eyes. 'Ah, Mr Sorleyson,' she whispered, 'could ye no leave the ninety and nine and go after that which is lost until ye find it! Sarah, Sarah, your mother's heart's sore for ye this day.' She dabbed her eyes with her black cotton gloves and walked slowly towards the church coach-house. The broad road before the coach-house was empty now, and when she looked into the Echlin's box in the stable two or three sparrows were quarrelling on the floor of it. 'They hae forgotten me,' she said, sitting down on the bench that ran along the wall. After a little while she arose and set out on the homeward road.

Hamilton, coming from the byre, saw the trap sitting in the close, its shafts in the air. An uneasy feeling made him hasten into the house. The hands of the clock pointed to twenty minutes past one. He hurried out to the stable and pushed open the top-door. Both horses stood in their stalls. 'Hell roast his sowl,' he muttered, 'he's forgotten the ould woman.' He went to the middle of the close and putting his hands to his mouth hallooed on his brother's name. He paused, expectant, as his shout rang over the empty fields. A few birds rose from the ridge of the stable and whirred away. Then he called on Sarah's name and as he listened he thought he heard a faint distant sound of laughter. He led out a horse, pulling cruelly on its mouth, and yoked it, single-handed, in the trap.

About two miles along the road he came on Martha seated on the ditch. He had to dismount and help her over to the trap. When she left the church she had vowed to herself that she would refuse to ride with them if they came to meet her. But now all her pride was gone; she had lost a glove somewhere and her fine buttoned boots, of which she was so proud, were coated with mud. Her face was drawn with weariness, and she had to press her lips together to keep from bursting outright into tears of misery and loneliness.

In a halting manner, and keeping his eyes fixed on the horse's ears, Hamilton tried to apologize for his brother's lapse. The old woman gathered from his remarks that Frank and Sarah had disappeared from the house.

'Did she lay the table?' Martha asked.

'I didna pay any heed,' answered Hamilton, touching up the horse.

'If it had been set you'd have noticed it,' she said briefly.

As they turned off the road into the loanen they saw the blue smoke of a replenished fire rise from the chimney of the farmhouse.

Frank stood leaning over the half-door of the stable with his back to them as they drew up in the close. Hamilton unloosed the horse and led it out of the shafts, slipping the brichen over his arm. As he heard his brother approach Frank unbolted the stable door and held it open, but Hamilton checked the horse on the threshold. 'What came intae ye?' he demanded, scowling at the other. Frank smiled, 'I forgot all about the ould one,' he answered. Although he smiled, his eyes were alert and he rocked gently on the balls of his feet. Hamilton stared at him for a moment then he spat contemptuously on the ground and led the horse into the stable. Frank loitered in the close until his brother appeared again, then without looking up or speaking, followed him into the house.

They sat down to the meal in silence. Frank, carefully watching the old woman, noted with apprehension that Sarah was doing the same. He had hoped that the two women would have had it out before he and Hamilton came in. As Sarah rose to bring the rennet dish to the table he suddenly turned to Martha and opening his lips was about to speak. At his gesture she looked up at him coldly and silently. At the sight of her faded eyes and indrawn lips the words died in his throat. He felt a sudden hatred for Sarah's mother with her cold reproachful look. As if he were bound to go when she said, go; and come when she said, come. To hell with ye, he said inwardly, you're nothing to me.

But his gesture stirred the old woman. Not content with knowing that her silence filled both the young people with remorse and anger she turned to her daughter. 'Where were ye, when I was at church?' she asked.

'We went over the fields to the head o' the brae,' answered the girl without raising her eyes from her plate.

'Weren't ye left tae look after the house?' demanded Martha.

'There now, Martha,' interrupted Frank angrily, 'the house didna run away.'

Martha ignored him. Her whole attention was fixed on her daughter. 'Since when hae ye taken to skiltin the fields on a Sabbath? Look at yourself – you're as tossed and through-other as if you'd been doing a day's work. What way's that to behave on the Sabbath?'

Sarah sprang up from the table. 'Lay me alone!' she cried. 'I'll go out in the fields when I want, Sunday or any other day!'

Martha had risen to her feet also, her face flushed and fingers plucking at her apron. Hamilton, who had been eating stolidly during all this talk, now rapped the table irritably with his spoon. 'Sit down, Martha,' he said, 'and let us get on wi' our dinner.'

Martha turned on him. 'Listen to me, Hamilton Echlin, and you Sarah, and you Frank. If there's not a change in this house I'm going the leave it and go back tae Banyil. God forgive me – I should ha' spoken out before. But I'm no going to see my daughter run about a heathen. If the memory o' your father won't send yous t'church, at least I'll see that *she* goes!'

'Don't meddle with me, Martha!' exclaimed Frank angrily. 'I can look after my own affairs. Hae ye forgotten already what my father brought ye here for?'

The old woman raised her hands to her head as if she had been struck. 'Wilt thou afflict the widow or fatherless child? If thou afflict them in any wise, and they cry at all unto me, I will surely hear their cry –' she intoned in a dull voice.

'Ah, give me none of your biblical cant!' cried Frank, beside himself with anger and shame at what he had said.

Hamilton struck the table with his open hand. 'That's mair than enough!' he shouted. He turned to Martha who had seated herself at the fire and was rocking backwards and forwards in her chair. 'Ye canna interfere wi' us, Martha. If you're no happy here, I'm sorry. It seems a wee thing tae leave us for. Nobody hinders ye going to church and after to-day I'll warrant ye that you'll no walk home again.' As he said this he looked at his brother, but Frank stood gazing sullenly out of the door. The younger brother's anger was really not so much at Martha's presumption as at the fear of being haltered again. Andrew had not been a tyrannical father but he had always commanded implicit obedience from his sons. In doing so he had been strengthened by affection and usage. But at his death, Frank had felt himself a free man, his own master. Without anything having been said between them, his word was as good as Hamilton's on the farm. And he possessed an undisputed delight which he hugged in secret glee, the enjoyment of Sarah. So when Martha, a stranger and a servant, upbraided him, it was like a stranger's hand on the neck of a wicked and restive horse.

Sarah stood with her hands clenched agonizingly together. She had never dreamt that her mother would jeopardize her comfortable life at Rathard for principles. She had forgotten easily and too soon that her mother was a spiritual and racial descendant of the two Margarets who, choking at their stakes in the rising waters of Solway, saw Christ and He wrestling. Martha's God was a terrible but hearkening God. Her every word and thought was weighed on His fingertip. Before a faith such as that, comfort and a hearth and a little folding of the hands burned away like so much dross. But to Sarah the novelty of her new position in life was too fresh for her not to appreciate the change for the better in her fortunes. They had come as servants and labourers to Rathard, and now she at least, had attained the position of mistress in the Echlin household. It was not avarice, but the fear of returning to a life of drudgery that filled her with hatred as she stood between the brothers, listening to the old woman.

'Will ye change your ways o' going, Sarah?' her mother asked.

'There's nothing wrong wi' my ways o' going,' the girl answered sullenly.

'Are ye going to do as your betters bid ye, and return to your church?' persisted Martha.

The girl raised her head sharply. 'My betters!' she exclaimed, her face flushing in anger. 'So that's it! Mr Sorleyson has been at ye – now isn't that the truth!'

'Aye, that's the truth. Your minister came down from his pulpit to beg wi' me that my daughter would come back. That's what I had to endure in my own church.' The old woman's voice grew bitter. 'He said that Frank and Hami would remember their father. God forgive them, they hae forgotten before the sod's healed over him.'

'Let us be, Martha,' said Hamilton uneasily, turning a cup in his hands. Frank stirred in the doorway but stood with his back to them, listening.

'It's your own affair,' said the old woman, rising. 'But I'll see to it that Sarah doesn't go that road.'

'Quit it!' shouted Sarah. 'Ye keep on talking o' me as if I was a helpless wean! Ye can go to your church if ye will, but you're no taking me!'

'Very well, then,' said her mother. 'We're leaving this house as soon as we can gather our wheen o' things thegither.'

The girl turned and clutched Hamilton's arm. 'Hami, will ye give me a job here?' she cried. Her eyes searched his face, and the man winced in her grasp.

He released his arm from her fingers and crossed to the fireplace. 'It's not for me tae interfere between you and your daughter, Martha. You're welcome tae bide here as long as ye wish, and I can't hinder ye if ye want to go, for you're neither blood nor kin tae us. You've done your work well, and if ye go we maun get another. But go or stay, singly or together, you're as free as the birds o' the air. That's my word.'

For a long time mother and daughter looked at each other. The girl's pale lips scarcely moved. 'I'm staying,' she said. The old woman turned away to the door of the lower room, leaning faintly for a moment on the handle.

She set about collecting her belongings with silent diligence. She accepted Frank's shame-faced offer of a wooden case for her linens. Of every three pieces she left one aside for Sarah, and the girl going down into her room in the dusk found them lying across the bed.

Martha's quiet determination to abide by her resolve with neither recrimination nor bitterness, succeeded in reducing her daughter to an anguish of spirit which in moments of weakness she thought almost too much to pay for her new life. Neither encouraged by an air of martyrdom on her mother's part, nor possessing herself that characteristic which in revolt and despair casts the whole burden of shame on the person who occasioned it, the girl was tormented by a superstitious belief that some day she would have to pay for her actions. She was fortified only by a secret stubborn shame and a hatred of subordination and its drudgery. Yet when at last Mrs Gomartin, with her few goods boxed and basketed, sat in the springcart, one backward glance would have brought her daughter into her arms. The old woman never looked round, and Sarah, through tear-blinded eyes, watched the small bowed figure nod and lurch beside Hamilton as they drove away.

FLANN O'BRIEN

'The Martyr's Crown'

Mr Toole and Mr O'Hickey walked down the street together in the morning.

Mr Toole had a peculiarity. He had the habit, when accompanied by another person, of saluting total strangers; but only if these strangers were of important air and costly raiment. He meant thus to make it known that he had friends in high places, and that he himself, though poor, was a person of quality fallen on evil days through some undisclosed sacrifice made in the interest of immutable principle early in life. Most of the strangers, startled out of their private thoughts, stammered a salutation in return. And Mr Toole was shrewd. He stopped at that. He said no more to his companion, but by some little private gesture, a chuckle, a shake of the head, a smothered imprecation, he nearly always extracted the one question most melodious to his ear: '*Who was that?*'

Mr Toole was shabby, and so was Mr O'Hickey, but Mr O'Hickey had a neat and careful shabbiness. He was an older and a wiser man, and was well up to Mr Toole's tricks. Mr Toole at his best, he thought, was better than a play. And he now knew that Mr Toole was appraising the street with beady eye.

'Gorawars!' Mr Toole said suddenly.

We are off, Mr O'Hickey thought.

'Do you see this hop-off-my-thumb with the stick and the hat?' Mr Toole said.

Mr O'Hickey did. A young man of surpassing elegance was approaching; tall, fair, darkly dressed; even at fifty yards his hauteur seemed to chill Mr O'Hickey's part of the street.

'Ten to one he cuts me dead,' Mr Toole said. 'This is one of the most extraordinary pieces of work in the whole world.'

Mr O'Hickey braced himself for a more than ordinary impact. The adversaries neared each other.

'*How are we at all, Sean a chara?*' Mr Toole called out.

The young man's control was superb. There was no glare, no glance of scorn, no sign at all. He was gone, but had left in his wake so complete an impression of his contempt that even Mr Toole paled momentarily. The experience frightened Mr O'Hickey.

'Who . . . who was *that?*' he asked at last.

'I knew the mother well,' Mr Toole said musingly. 'The woman was a saint.' Then he was silent.

Mr O'Hickey thought: there is nothing for it but bribery – again. He led the way into a public house and ordered two bottles of stout.

'As you know,' Mr Toole began, 'I was Bart Conlon's right-hand man. Bart, of course, went the other way in 'twenty-two.'

Mr O'Hickey nodded and said nothing. He knew that Mr Toole had never rendered military service to his country.

'In any case,' Mr Toole continued, 'there was a certain day early in twenty-one and orders come through that there was to be a raid on the Sinn Fein office above in Harcourt Street. There happened to be a certain gawskogue of a cattle jobber from the County Meath had an office on the other side of the street. And he was well in with a certain character be the name of Mick Collins. I think you get me drift?'

'I do,' Mr O'Hickey said.

'There was six of us,' Mr Toole said, 'with meself and Bart Conlon in charge. Me man the cattle jobber gets an urgent call to be out of his office accidentally on purpose at four o'clock, and at half-four the six of us is parked inside there with two machine guns, the rifles, and a class of a homemade bomb that Bart used to make in his own kitchen. The military arrived in two lurries on the other side of the street at five o'clock. That was the hour in the orders that come. I believe that man Mick Collins had lads working for him over in the War Office across in London. He was a great stickler for the British being punctual on the dot.'

'He was a wonderful organizer,' Mr O'Hickey said.

'Well, we stood with our backs to the far wall and let them have it through the open window and them getting down off the lurries. Sacred godfathers! I never seen such murder in me life. Your men didn't know where it was coming from, and a lot of them wasn't worried very much when it was all over, because there was no heads left in some of them. Bart then gives the order for retreat down the back stairs; in no time we're in the lane, and five minutes more the six of us upstairs in Martin Fulham's pub in Camden Street. Poor Martin is dead since.'

'I knew that man well,' Mr O'Hickey remarked.

'Certainly you knew him well,' Mr Toole said, warmly. 'The six of us was marked men, of course. In any case, fresh orders come at six o'clock. All hands was to proceed in military formation, singly, be different routes to the house of a great skin in the Cumann na mBan, a widow be the name of Clougherty that lived on the south side. We were all to lie low, do you understand, till there was fresh orders to come out and fight again. Sacred wars, they were very rough days them days; will I ever forget Mrs Clougherty! She was certainly a marvellous figure of a woman. I never seen a woman like her to bake bread.'

Mr O'Hickey looked up.

'Was she,' he said, 'was she . . . all right?'

'She was certainly nothing of the sort,' Mr Toole said loudly and sharply. 'By God, we were all thinking of other things in them days. Here was this unfortunate woman in a three-storey house on her own, with some quare fellow in the middle flat, herself on the ground floor, and six bloodthirsty pultogues hiding above on the top floor, every manjack ready to shoot his way out if there was trouble. We got feeds there I never seen before or since, and the *Independent* every morning. Outrage in Harcourt Street. The armed men then decamped and made good their escape. I'm damn bloody sure we made good our escape. There was one snag. We couldn't budge out. No exercise at all – and that means only one thing . . .'

'Constipation?' Mr O'Hickey suggested.

'The very man,' said Mr Toole.

Mr O'Hickey shook his head.

'We were there a week. Smoking and playing cards, but when nine o'clock struck, Mrs Clougherty come up, and, Protestant, Catholic, or Jewman, all hands had to go down on the knees. A very good . . . strict . . . woman, if you understand me, a true daughter of Ireland. And now I'll tell you a damn good one. About five o'clock one evening I heard a noise below and peeped out of the window. Sanctified and holy godfathers!'

'What was it – the noise?' Mr O'Hickey asked.

'What do you think, only two lurries packed with military, with my nabs of an officer hopping out and running up the steps to hammer at the door, and all the Tommies sitting back with their guns at the ready. Trapped! That's a nice word – *trapped!* If there was ever rats in a cage, it was me unfortunate brave men from the battle of Harcourt Street. God!'

'They had you at what we call a disadvantage,' Mr O'Hickey conceded.

'She was in the room herself with the teapot. She had a big silver satteen blouse on her; I can see it yet. She turned on us and gave us all one look that said: *Shut up, ye nervous lousers.* Then she roostered about a bit at the glass and walks out of the room with bang-bang-bang to shake the house going on downstairs. And I see a thing . . .'

'What?' asked Mr O'Hickey.

'She was a fine – now you'll understand me, Mr O'Hickey,' Mr Toole said carefully. 'I seen her fingers on the buttons of the satteen, if you follow me, and she leaving the room.'

Mr O'Hickey, discreet, nodded thoughtfully.

'I listened at the stairs. Jakers I never got such a drop in me life. She clatters down and flings open the hall door. This young pup is outside, and asks – awsks – in the law-de-daw voice, "Is there any men in this house?" The answer took me to the fair altogether. She puts on the guttiest voice I ever heard outside Moor Street and says, "Sairtintly not at this hour of the night; I wish to God there was. Sure, how could the poor unfortunate women get on without them, officer?" Well lookat. I nearly fell down the stairs on top of the two of them. The next thing I hear is, "Madam this and madam that" and "Sorry to disturb and I beg your pardon," "I trust this and I trust that," and then the whispering starts, and at the windup the hall door is closed and into the room off the hall with the pair of them. This young bucko out of the Borderers in a room off the hall with a headquarters captain of the Cumann na mBan! *Give us two more stouts there, Mick!*'

'That is a very queer one, as the man said,' Mr O'Hickey said.

'I went back to the room and sat down. Bart had his gun out, and we were all looking at one another. After ten minutes we heard another noise.'

Mr Toole poured out his stout with unnecessary care.

'It was the noise of the lurries driving away,' he said at last. 'She'd saved our lives, and when she come up a while later she said, "We'll go to bed a bit earlier tonight, boys; kneel down all." That was Mrs Clougherty the saint.'

Mr O'Hickey, also careful, was working at his own bottle, his wise head bent at the task.

'What I meant to ask you was this,' Mr O'Hickey said, 'that's an extraordinary affair altogether, but what has that to do with that stuck-up young man we met in the street, the lad with all the airs?'

'Do you not see it, man?' Mr Toole said in surprise. 'For seven hundred year, thousands – no, I'll make it millions – of Irish men and women have died for Ireland. We never rared jibbers; they were glad to do it, and will again. But that young man was *born* for Ireland. There was never anybody else like him. Why wouldn't he be proud?'

'The Lord save us!' Mr O'Hickey cried.

'A saint I called her,' Mr Toole said, hotly. 'What am I talking about – she's a martyr and wears the martyr's crown today!'

FLANN O'BRIEN

from *At Swim-Two-Birds*

Synopsis, being a summary of what has gone before, FOR THE BENEFIT OF NEW READERS: DERMOT TRELLIS, an eccentric author, conceives the project of writing a salutary book on the consequences which follow wrong-doing and creates for the purpose

THE POOKA FERGUS MACPHELLIMEY, a species of human Irish devil endowed with magical powers. He then creates

JOHN FURRISKEY, a depraved character, whose task is to attack women and behave at all times in an indecent manner. By magic he is instructed by Trellis to go one night to Donnybrook where he will by arrangement meet and betray

PEGGY, a domestic servant. He meets her and is much surprised when she confides in him that Trellis has fallen asleep and that her virtue has already been assailed by an elderly man subsequently to be identified as

FINN MACCOOL, a legendary character hired by Trellis on account of the former's venerable appearance and experience, to act as the girl's father and chastise her for her transgressions against the moral law; and that her virtue has also been assailed by

PAUL SHANAHAN, another man hired by Trellis for performing various small and unimportant parts in the story, also for running messages, &c. &c. Peggy and Furriskey then have a long discussion on the roadside in which she explains to him that Trellis's powers are suspended when he falls asleep and that Finn and Shanahan were taking advantage of that fact when they came to see her because they would not dare to defy him when he is awake. Furriskey then inquires whether she yielded to them and she replies that indeed she did not. Furriskey then praises her and they discover after a short time that they have fallen in love with each other at first sight. They arrange to lead virtuous lives, to simulate the immoral actions, thoughts and words which Trellis demands of them on pain of the severest penalties. They also arrange that the first of them who shall be free shall wait for the other with a view to marriage at the earliest opportunity. Meanwhile Trellis, in order to show how an evil man can debase the highest and the lowest in the same story, creates a very beautiful and refined girl called

SHEILA LAMONT, whose brother,

ANTONY LAMONT he has already hired so that there will be somebody to demand satisfaction off John Furriskey for betraying her – all this being provided for in the plot. Trellis creates Miss Lamont in his own bedroom and he is so blinded by her beauty (which is naturally the type of beauty nearest to his heart), that he so far forgets himself as to assault her himself. Furriskey in the meantime returns to the Red Swan Hotel where Trellis lives and compels all those working for him to live also. He (Furriskey) is determined to pretend that he faithfully carried out the terrible mission he was sent on. Now read on.

Further extract from Manuscript. Oratio recta: With a key in his soft nervous hand, he opened the hall door and removed his shoes with two swift spells of crouching on the one leg. He crept up the stairs with the noiseless cat-tread of his good-quality woollen socks. The door of Trellis was dark and sleeping as he passed up the stairs to his room.

There was a crack of light at Shanahan's door and he placed his shoes quietly on the floor and turned the handle.

The hard Furriskey, said Shanahan.

Here was Shanahan stretched at the fire, with Lamont on his left and the old greybeard seated beyond dimly on the bed with his stick between his knees and his old eyes staring far into the red fire like a man whose thought was in a distant part of the old world or maybe in another world altogether.

By God you weren't long, said Lamont.

Shut the door, said Shanahan, but see you're in the room before you do so. Shut the door and treat yourself to a chair, Mr F. You're quick off the mark all right. Move up there, Mr L.

It's not what you call a full-time occupation, said Furriskey in a weary way. It's not what you call a life sentence.

It is not, said Lamont. You're right there.

Now don't worry, said Shanahan in a pitying manner, there's plenty more coming. We'll keep you occupied now, don't you worry, won't we, Mr Lamont?

We'll see that he gets his bellyful, said Lamont.

You're decent fellows the pair of ye, said Furriskey.

He sat on a stool and extended his fan to the fire, the fan of his ten fingers.

You can get too much of them same women, he said.

Is that a fact, said Shanahan in unbelief. Well I never heard that said before. Come here, Mr Furriskey, did you . . .

O it was all right, I'll tell you sometime, said Furriskey.

Didn't I tell you it was all right? Didn't I?

You did, said Furriskey.

He took a sole cigarette from a small box.

I'll tell you the whole story sometime but not now, he said. He nodded towards the bed.

Is your man asleep or what?

Maybe he is, said Shanahan, but by God it didn't sound like it five minutes ago. Mr Storybook was wide awake.

He was wide awake, said Lamont.

Five minutes ago he was giving out a yarn the length of my arm, said Shanahan. Right enough he is a terrible man for talk. Aren't you now? He'd talk the lot of us into the one grave if you gave him his head, don't ask me how I know, look at my grey hairs. Isn't that a fact, Mr Lamont?

For a man of his years, said Lamont slowly and authoritatively, he can do the talking. By God he can do the talking. He has seen more of the world than you or me, of course, that's the secret of it.

That's true, said Furriskey, a happy fire-glow running about his body. He carefully directed the smoke of his cigarette towards the flames and up the chimney. Yes, he's an old man, of course.

His stories are not the worst though, I'll say that, said Lamont, there's always a head and a tail on his yarns, a beginning and an end, give him his due.

O I don't know, said Furriskey.

O he can talk, he can talk, I agree with you there, said Shanahan, credit where credit is due. But you'd want what you'd call a grain of *salo* with more than one of them if I know anything.

A pinch of salt? said Lamont.

A grain of *salo*, Mr L.

I don't doubt it, said Furriskey.

Relate, said hidden Conán, the tale of the Feasting of Dún na nGedh.

Finn in his mind was nestling with his people.

I mean to say, said Lamont, whether a yarn is tall or small I like to hear it well told. I like to meet a man that can take in hand to tell a story and not make a balls of it while he's at it. I like to know where I am, do you know. Everything has a beginning and an end.

It is true, said Finn, that I will not.

O that's right too, said Shanahan.

Relate then, said Conán, the account of the madness of King Sweeny and he on a madman's flight through the length of Erin.

That's a grand fire, said Furriskey, and if a man has that, he can't want a lot more. A fire, a bed, and a roof over his head, that's all. With a bite to eat, of course.

It's all very fine for you to talk, now, said Lamont, you had something for your tea to-night that the rest of us hadn't, eh, Mr Shanahan. Know what I mean?

Keep the fun clean, said Shanahan.

I beg, Mr Chairman, said Furriskey, to be associated with them sentiments. What's clean, keep it clean.

There was a concerted snigger, harmonious, scored for three voices.

I will relate, said Finn.

We're off again, said Furriskey.

The first matter that I will occupy with honey-words and melodious recital, said Finn, is the reason and the first cause for Sweeny's frenzy.

Draw in your chairs, boys, said Shanahan, we're right for the night. We're away on a hack.

Pray proceed, Sir, said Lamont.

Now Sweeny was King of Dal Araidhe and a man that was easily moved to the tides of anger. Near his house was the cave of a saint called Ronan – a shield against evil was this gentle generous friendly active man, who was out in the matin-hours taping out the wall-steads of a new sun-bright church and ringing his bell in the morning.

Good for telling, said Conán.

Now when Sweeny heard the clack of the clergyman's bell, his brain and his spleen and his gut were exercised by turn and together with the fever of a flaming anger. He made a great run out of the house without a cloth-stitch to the sheltering of his naked nudity, for he had run out of his cloak when his wife Eorann held it for restraint and deterrence, and he did not rest till he had snatched the beauteous light-lined psalter from the cleric and put it in the lake, at the bottom; after that he took the hard grip of the cleric's hand and ran with a wind-swift stride to the lake without a halting or a letting go of the hand because he had a mind to place the cleric by the side of his psalter in the lake, on the bottom, to speak precisely. But, evil destiny, he was deterred by the big storm-voiced hoarse shout, the shout of a scullion calling him to the profession of arms at the battle of Magh Rath. Sweeny then left the cleric sad and sorrowful over the godless battery of the king and lamenting his psalter. This, however, an otter from the murk of the lake returned to him unharmed, its lines and its letters unblemished. He then returned with joyous piety to his devotions and put a malediction on Sweeny by the uttering of a lay of eleven melodious stanzas.

Thereafter he went himself with his acolytes to the plain of Magh Rath for the weaving of concord and peace between the hosts and was himself taken as a holy pledge, the person of the cleric, that fighting should cease at sundown and that no man should be slain until fighting would be again permitted, the person of the cleric a holy hostage and exchange between the hosts. But, evil destiny, Sweeny was used to violating the guarantee by the slaughter of a man every morning before the hour when fighting was permitted. On the morning of a certain day, Ronan and his eight psalmists were walking in the field and sprinkling holy water on the hosts against the incidence of hurt or evil when they sprinkled the head of Sweeny with the rest. Sweeny in anger took a cast and reddened his spear in the white side of a psalmist and broke Ronan's bell whereupon the cleric uttered this melodious lay:

> My curse on Sweeny!
> His guilt against me is immense,
> he pierced with his long swift javelin
> my holy bell.
>
> The holy bell that thou hast outraged
> will banish thee to branches,
> it will put thee on a par with fowls —
> the saint-bell of saints with sainty-saints.
>
> Just as it went prestissimo
> the spear-shaft skyward,
> you too, Sweeny, go madly mad-gone
> skyward.
>
> Eorann of Conn tried to hold him
> by a hold of his smock
> and though I bless her therefore,
> my curse on Sweeny.

Thereafter when the hosts clashed and bellowed like stag-herds and gave three audible world-wide shouts till Sweeny heard them and their hollow reverberations in the sky-vault, he was beleaguered by an anger and a darkness, and fury and fits and frenzy and fright-fraught fear, and he was filled with a restless tottering unquiet and with a disgust for the places that he knew and with a desire to be where he never was, so that he was palsied of hand and foot and eye-mad and heart-quick and went from the curse of

Ronan bird-quick in craze and madness from the battle. For the nimble lightness of his
tread in flight he did not shake dewdrops from the grass-stalks and staying not for bog
or thicket or marsh or hollow or thick-sheltering wood in Erin for that day, he travelled
till he reached Ros Bearaigh in Glenn Earcain where he went into the yew-tree that was
in the glen.

In a later hour his kin came to halt beneath the tree for a spell of discourse and
melodious talk about Sweeny and no tidings concerning him either in the east or
the west; and Sweeny in the yew-tree above them listened till he made answer in this
lay:

> O warriors approach,
> warriors of Dal Araidhe,
> you will find him in the tree he is
> the man you seek.
>
> God has given me life here,
> very bare, very narrow,
> no woman, no trysting,
> no music or trance-eyed sleep.

When they noticed the verses from the tree-top they saw Sweeny in branches and
then they talked their honey-words, beseeching him that he should be trustful, and then
made a ring around the tree-bole. But Sweeny arose nimbly and away to Cell Riagain
in Tir Conaill where he perched in the old tree of the church, going and coming between
branches and the rain-clouds of the skies, trespassing and wayfaring over peaks and
summits and across the ridge-poles of black hills, and visiting in dark mountains,
ruminating and searching in cavities and narrow crags and slag-slits in rocky hidings,
and lodging in the clump of tall ivies and in the cracks of hill-stones, a year of time
from summit to summit and from glen to glen and from river-mouth to river till he
arrived at ever-delightful Glen Bolcain. For it is thus that Glen Bolcain is, it has four
gaps to the four winds and a too-fine too-pleasant wood and fresh-banked wells and
cold-clean fountains and sandy pellucid streams of clear water with green-topped
watercress and brooklime long-streamed on the current, and a richness of sorrels and
wood-sorrels, *lus-bian* and *biorragan* and berries and wild garlic, *melle* and *miodhbhun*, inky
sloes and dun acorns. For it was here that the madmen of Erin were used to come
when their year of madness was complete, smiting and lamming each other for choice
of its watercress and in rivalry for its fine couches.

In that glen it was hard for Sweeny to endure the pain of his bed there on the top
of a tall ivy-grown hawthorn in the glen, every twist that he would turn sending showers
of hawy thorns into his flesh, tearing and rending and piercing him and pricking his
blood-red skin. He thereupon changed beds to the resting of another tree where there
were tangles of thick fine-thorned briars and a solitary branch of blackthorn growing
up through the core of the brambles. He settled and roosted on its slender perch till it
bowed beneath him and bent till it slammed him to the ground, not one inch of him
from toe to crown that was not red-prickled and blood-gashed, the skin to his body

being ragged and flapping and thorned, the tattered cloak of his perished skin. He arose death-weak from the ground to his standing for the recital of this lay.

> A year to last night
> I have lodged there in branches
> from the flood-tide to the ebb-tide naked.
>
> Bereft of fine women-folk,
> the brooklime for a brother –
> our choice for a fresh meal
> is watercress always.
>
> Without accomplished musicians
> without generous women,
> no jewel-gift for bards –
> respected Christ, it has perished me.
>
> The thorntop that is not gentle
> has reduced me, has pierced me,
> it has brought me near death
> the brown thorn-bush.
>
> Once free, once gentle,
> I am banished for ever,
> wretch-wretched I have been
> a year to last night.

He remained there in Glen Bolcain until he elevated himself high in the air and went to Cluain Cille on the border of Tir Conaill and Tir Boghaine. He went to the edge of the water and took food against the night, watercress and water. After that he went into the old tree of the church where he said another melodious poem on the subject of his personal hardship.

After another time he set forth in the air again till he reached the church at Snámh-dá-én (or Swim-Two-Birds) by the side of the Shannon, arriving there on a Friday, to speak precisely; here the clerics were engaged at the observation of their nones, flax was being beaten and here and there a woman was giving birth to a child; and Sweeny did not stop until he had recited the full length of a further lay.

For seven years, to relate precisely, was Sweeny at the air travel of all Erin, returning always to his tree in charming Glen Bolcain, for that was his fortress and his haven, it was his house there in the glen. It was to this place that his foster-brother Linchehaun came for tidings concerning him, for he carried always a deep affection for Sweeny and had retrieved him three times from madness before that. Linchehaun went seeking him in the glen with shouts and found toe-tracks by the stream-mud where the madman was wont to appease himself by the eating of cresses. But track or trace of Sweeny he did not attain for that day and he sat down in an old deserted house in the glen till the labour and weariness of his pursuit brought about his sleep. And Sweeny, hearing his snore from his tree-clump in the glen, uttered this lay in the pitch darkness.

The man by the wall snores
a snore-sleep that's beyond me,
for seven years from that Tuesday at Magh Rath
I have not slept a wink.

O God that I had not gone
to the hard battle!
thereafter my name was Mad –
Mad Sweeny in the bush.

Watercress from the well at Cirb
is my lot at terce,
its colour is my mouth,
green on the mouth of Sweeny.

Chill chill is my body
when away from ivy,
the rain torrent hurts it
and the thunder.

I am in summer with the herons of Cuailgne
with wolves in winter,
at other times I am hidden in a copse –
not so the man by the wall.

And thereafter he met Linchehaun who came visiting to his tree and they parleyed there the two of them together and the one of them talkative and unseen in branches and prickle-briars. And Sweeny bade Linchehaun to depart and not to pursue or annoy him further because the curse of Ronan stopped him from putting his trust or his mad faith in any man.

Thereafter he travelled in distant places till he came at the black fall of a night to Ros Bearaigh and lodged himself in a hunched huddle in the middle of the yew-tree of the church in that place. But being besieged with nets and hog-harried by the caretaker of the church and his false wife, he hurried nimbly to the old tree at Ros Eareain where he remained hidden and unnoticed the length of a full fortnight, till the time when Linchehaun came and perceived the murk of his shadow in the sparse branches and saw the other branches he had broken and bent in his movements and in changing trees. And the two of them parleyed together until they had said between them these fine words following.

Sad it is Sweeny, said Linchehaun, that your last extremity should be thus, without food or drink or raiment like a fowl, the same man that had cloth of silk and of satin and the foreign steed of the peerless bridle, also comely generous women and boys and hounds and princely people of every refinement; hosts and tenants and men-at-arms, and mugs and goblets and embellished buffalo-horns for the savouring of pleasant-tasted fine liquors. Sad it is to see the same man as a hapless air-fowl.

Cease now, Linchehaun, said Sweeny, and give me tidings.

Your father is dead, said Linchehaun.

That has seized me with a blind agony, said Sweeny.

Your mother is likewise dead.

Now all the pity in me is at an end.

Dead is your brother.

Gaping open is my side on account of that.

She has died too your sister.

A needle for the heart is an only sister.

Ah, dumb dead is the little son that called you pop.

Truly, said Sweeny, that is the last blow that brings a man to the ground.

When Sweeny heard the sorry word of his small son still and without life, he fell with a crap from the middle of the yew to the ground and Linchehaun hastened to his thorn-packed flank with fetters and handcuffs and manacles and locks and black-iron chains and he did not achieve a resting until the lot were about the madman, and through him and above him and over him, roundwise and about. Thereafter there was a concourse of hospitallers and knights and warriors around the trunk of the yew, and after melodious tale they entrusted the mad one to the care of Linchehaun till he would take him away to a quiet place for a fortnight and a month, to the quiet of a certain room where his senses returned to him, the one after the other, with no one near him but the old mill-hag.

O hag, said Sweeny, searing are the tribulations I have suffered; many a terrible leap have I leaped from hill to hill, from fort to fort, from land to land, from valley to valley.

For the sake of God, said the hag, leap for us now a leap such as you leaped in the days of your madness.

And thereupon Sweeny gave a bound over the top of the bedrail till he reached the extremity of the bench.

My conscience indeed, said the hag, I could leap the same leap myself.

And the hag gave a like jump.

Sweeny then gathered himself together in the extremity of his jealousy and threw a leap right out through the skylight of the hostel.

I could vault that vault too, said the hag and straightway she vaulted the same vault. And the short of it is this, that Sweeny travelled the length of five cantreds of leaps until he had penetrated to Glenn na nEachtach in Fiodh Gaibhle with the hag at her hag's leaps behind him; and when Sweeny rested there in a huddle at the top of a tall ivy-branch, the hag was perched there on another tree beside him. He heard there the voice of a stag and he thereupon made a lay euologizing aloud the trees and the stags of Erin, and he did not cease or sleep until he had achieved these staves.

> Bleating one, little antlers,
> O lamenter we like
> delightful the clamouring
> from your glen you make.
>
> O leafy-oak, clumpy-leaved,
> you are high above trees,
> O hazlet, little clumpy-branch –
> the nut-smell of hazels.

O alder, O alder-friend,
delightful your colour,
you don't prickle me or tear
in the place you are.

O blackthorn, little thorny-one,
O little dark sloe-tree;
O watercress, O green-crowned,
at the well-brink.

O holly, holly-shelter,
O door against the wind,
O ash-tree inimical,
you spearshaft of warrior.

O birch clean and blessed,
O melodious, O proud,
delightful the tangle
of your head-rods.

What I like least in woodlands
from none I conceal it –
stirk of a leafy-oak,
at its swaying.

O faun, little long-legs,
I caught you with grips,
I rode you upon your back
from peak to peak.

Glen Bolcain my home ever,
it was my haven,
many a night have I tried
a race against the peak.

I beg your pardon for interrupting, said Shanahan, but you're after reminding me of something, brought the thing into my head in a rush.

He swallowed a draught of vesper-milk, restoring the cloudy glass swiftly to his knee and collecting little belated flavourings from the corners of his mouth.

That thing you were saying reminds me of something bloody good. I beg your pardon for interrupting, Mr Storybook.

In the yesterday, said Finn, the man who mixed his utterance with the honeywords of Finn was the first day put naked into the tree of Coill Boirche with nothing to his bare hand but a stick of hazel. On the morning of the second day thereafter . . .

Now listen for a minute till I tell you something, said Shanahan, did any man here ever hear of the poet Casey?

Who did you say? said Furriskey.

Casey. Jem Casey.

On the morning of the second day thereafter, he was taken and bound and rammed as regards his head into a black hole so that his white body was upside down and upright in Erin for the gazing thereon of man and beast.

Now give us a chance, Mister Storybook, yourself and your black hole, said Shanahan fingering his tie-knot with a long memory-frown across his brow. Come here for a minute. Come here till I tell you about Casey. Do you mean to tell me you never heard of the poet Casey, Mr Furriskey?

Never heard of him, said Furriskey in a solicitous manner.

I can't say, said Lamont, that I ever heard of him either.

He was a poet of the people, said Shanahan.

I see, said Furriskey.

Now do you understand, said Shanahan. A plain upstanding labouring man, Mr Furriskey, the same as you or me. A black hat or a bloody ribbon, no by God, not on Jem Casey. A hard-working well-made block of a working man, Mr Lamont, with the handle of a pick in his hand like the rest of us. Now say there was a crowd of men with a ganger all working there laying a length of gas-pipe on the road. All right. The men pull off their coats and start shovelling and working there for further orders. Here at one end of the hole you have your men crowded up together in a lump and them working away and smoking their butts and talking about the horses and one thing and another. Now do you understand what I'm telling you. Do you follow me?

I see that.

But take a look at the other end of the hole and here is my brave Casey digging away there on his own. Do you understand what I mean, Mr Furriskey?

Oh I see it all right, said Furriskey.

Right. None of your horses or your bloody blather for him. Not a bit of it. Here is my nabs saying nothing to nobody but working away at a pome in his head with a pick in his hand and the sweat pouring down off his face from the force of his work and his bloody exertions. That's a quare one!

Do you mind that now, said Lamont.

It's a quare one and one that takes a lot of beating. Not a word to nobody, not a look to left or right but the brain-box going there all the time. Just Jem Casey, a poor ignorant labouring man but head and shoulders above the whole bloody lot of them, not a man in the whole country to beat him when it comes to getting together a bloody pome – not a poet in the whole world that could hold a candle to Jem Casey, not a man of them fit to stand beside him. By God I'd back him to win by a canter against the whole bloody lot of them give him his due.

Is that a fact, Mr Shanahan, said Lamont. It's not every day in the week you come across a man like that.

Do you know what I'm going to tell you, Mr Lamont, he was a man that could give the lot of them a good start, pickaxe and all. He was a man that could meet them . . . and meet the best . . . and beat them at their own game, now I'm telling you.

I suppose he could, said Furriskey.

Now I know what I'm talking about. Give a man his due. If a man's station is high or low he is all the same to the God I know. Take the bloody black hats off the whole bunch of them and where are you?

That's the way to look at it, of course, said Furriskey.

Give them a bloody pick, I mean, Mr Furriskey, give them the shaft of a shovel into their hand and tell them to dig a hole and have the length of a page of poetry off by heart in their heads before the five o'clock whistle. What will you get? By God you could take off your hat to what you'd get at five o'clock from that crowd and that's a sure sharkey.

You'd be wasting your time if you waited till five o'clock if you ask me, said Furriskey with a nod of complete agreement.

You're right there, said Shanahan, you'd be waiting around for bloody nothing. Oh I know them and I know my hard Casey too. By Janey he'd be up at the whistle with a pome a yard long, a bloody lovely thing that would send my nice men home in a hurry, home with their bloody tails between their legs. Yes, I've seen his pomes and read them and . . . do you know what I'm going to tell you, I have loved them. I'm not ashamed to sit here and say it, Mr Furriskey. I've known the man and I've known his pomes and by God I have loved the two of them and loved them well, too. Do you understand what I'm saying, Mr Lamont? You, Mr Furriskey?

Oh that's right.

Do you know what it is, I've met the others, the whole lot of them. I've met them all and know them all. I have seen them and I have read their pomes. I have heard them recited by men that know how to use their tongues, men that couldn't be beaten at their own game. I have seen whole books filled up with their stuff, books as thick as that table there and I'm telling you no lie. But by God, at the heel of the hunt, there was only one poet for me.

On the morning of the third day thereafter, said Finn, he was flogged until he bled water.

Only the one, Mr Shanahan? said Lamont.

Only the one. And that one poet was a man . . . by the name . . . of Jem Casey. No 'Sir', no 'Mister', no nothing. Jem Casey, Poet of the Pick, that's all. A labouring man, Mr Lamont, but as sweet a singer in his own way as you'll find in the bloody trees there of a spring day, and that's a fact. Jem Casey, an ignorant God-fearing upstanding labouring man, a bloody navvy. Do you know what I'm going to tell you, I don't believe he ever lifted the latch of a school door. Would you believe that now?

I'd believe it of Casey, said Furriskey, and

I'd believe plenty more of the same man, said Lamont. You haven't any of his pomes on you, have you, Mr Shanahan?

Now take that stuff your man was giving us a while ago, said Shanahan without heed, about the green hills and the bloody swords and the bird giving out the pay from the top of the tree. Now that's good stuff, it's bloody nice. Do you know what it is, I liked it and liked it well. I enjoyed that certainly.

It wasn't bad at all, said Furriskey, I have heard worse, by God, often. It was all right now.

Do you see what I'm getting at, do you understand me, said Shanahan. It's good, very good. But by Christopher it's not every man could see it, I'm bloody sure of that, one in a thousand.

Oh that's right too, said Lamont.

You can't beat it, of course, said Shanahan with a reddening of the features, the real old stuff of the native land, you know, stuff that brought scholars to our shore when your men on the other side were on the flat of their bellies before the calf of gold with a sheepskin around their man. It's the stuff that put our country where she stands to-day, Mr Furriskey, and I'd have my tongue out of my head by the bloody roots before I'd be heard saying a word against it. But the man in the street, where does he come in? By God he doesn't come in at all as far as I can see.

What do my brave men in the black hats care whether he's in or out, asked Furriskey. What do they care? It's a short jump for the man in the street, I'm thinking, if he's waiting for that crowd to do anything for him. They're a nice crowd, now, I'm telling you.

Oh that's the truth, said Lamont.

Another thing, said Shanahan, you can get too much of that stuff. Feed yourself up with that tack once and you won't want more for a long time.

There's no doubt about it, said Furriskey.

Try it once, said Shanahan, and you won't want it a second time.

Do you know what it is, said Lamont, there are people who read that . . . and keep reading it . . . and read damn the bloody thing else. Now that's a mistake.

A big mistake, said Furriskey.

But there's one man, said Shanahan, there's one man that can write pomes that you can read all day and all night and keep reading them to your heart's content, stuff you'd never tire of. Pomes written by a man that is one of ourselves and written down for ourselves to read. The name of that man . . .

Now that's what you want, said Furriskey.

The name of that man, said Shanahan, is a name that could be christianed on you or me, a name that won't shame us. And that name, said Shanahan, is Jem Casey.

And a very good man, said Lamont.

Jem Casey, said Furriskey.

Do you understand what I mean, said Shanahan.

You haven't any of his pomes on you, have you, said Lamont. If there's one thing I'd like . . .

I haven't one *on* me if that's what you mean, Mr Lamont, said Shanahan, but I could give one out as quick as I'd say my prayers. By God it's not for nothing that I call myself a pal of Jem Casey.

I'm glad to hear it, said Lamont.

Stand up there and recite it man, said Furriskey, don't keep us waiting. What's the name of it now?

The name or title of the pome I am about to recite, gentlemen, said Shanahan with leisure priest-like in character, is a pome by the name of the 'Workman's Friend'. By God you can't beat it. I've heard it praised by the highest. It's a pome about a thing that's known to all of us. It's about a drink of porter.

Porter!

Porter.

Up on your legs man, said Furriskey. Mr Lamont and myself are waiting and listening. Up you get now.

Come on, off you go, said Lamont.

Now listen, said Shanahan clearing the way with small coughs. Listen now.

He arose holding out his hand and bending his knee beneath him on the chair.

> When things go wrong and will not come right,
> Though you do the best you can,
> When life looks black as the hour of night –
> A PINT OF PLAIN IS YOUR ONLY MAN.

By God there's a lilt in that, said Lamont.

Very good indeed, said Furriskey. Very nice.

I'm telling you it's the business, said Shanahan. Listen now.

> When money's tight and is hard to get
> And your horse has also ran,
> When all you have is a heap of debt –
> A PINT OF PLAIN IS YOUR ONLY MAN.

> When health is bad and your heart feels strange,
> And your face is pale and wan,
> When doctors say that you need a change,
> A PINT OF PLAIN IS YOUR ONLY MAN.

There are things in that pome that make for what you call *permanence*. Do you know what I mean, Mr Furriskey?

There's no doubt about it, it's a grand thing, said Furriskey. Come on, Mr Shanahan, give us another verse. Don't tell me that is the end of it.

Can't you listen? said Shanahan.

> When food is scarce and your larder bare
> And no rashers grease your pan,
> When hunger grows as your meals are rare –
> A PINT OF PLAIN IS YOUR ONLY MAN.

What do you think of that now?

It's a pome that'll live, called Lamont, a pome that'll be heard and clapped when plenty more . . .

But wait till you hear the last verse, man, the last polish-off, said Shanahan. He frowned and waved his hand.

Oh it's good, it's good, said Furriskey.

> In time of trouble and lousy strife,
> You have still got a darlint plan,
> You still can turn to a brighter life –
> A PINT OF PLAIN IS YOUR ONLY MAN!

Did you ever hear anything like it in your life, said Furriskey. A pint of plain, by God, what! Oh I'm telling you, Casey was a man in twenty thousand, there's no doubt about that. He knew what he was at, too true he did. If he knew nothing else, he knew how to write a pome. A pint of plain is your only man.

Didn't I tell you he was good? said Shanahan. Oh by Gorrah you can't cod me.

There's one thing in that pome, *permanence*, if you know what I mean. That pome, I mean to say, is a pome that'll be heard wherever the Irish race is wont to gather, it'll live as long as there's a hard root of an Irishman left by the Almighty on this planet, mark my words. What do you think, Mr Shanahan?

It'll live, Mr Lamont, it'll live.

I'm bloody sure it will, said Lamont.

A pint of plain, by God, eh? said Furriskey.

Tell us, my Old Timer, said Lamont benignly, what do you think of it? Give the company the benefit of your scholarly pertinacious fastidious opinion, Sir Storybook. Eh, Mr Shanahan?

from *The Third Policeman*

6

When I penetrated back to the day-room I encountered two gentlemen called Sergeant Pluck and Mr Gilhaney and they were holding a meeting about the question of bicycles.

'I do not believe in the three-speed gear at all,' the Sergeant was saying, 'it is a new-fangled instrument, it crucifies the legs, the half of the accidents are due to it.'

'It is a power for the hills,' said Gilhaney, 'as good as a second pair of pins or a diminutive petrol motor.'

'It is a hard thing to tune,' said the Sergeant, 'you can screw the iron lace that hangs out of it till you get no catch at all on the pedals. It never stops the way you want it, it would remind you of bad jaw-plates.'

'That is all lies,' said Gilhaney.

'Or like the pegs of a fairy-day fiddle,' said the Sergeant, 'or a skinny wife in the craw of a cold bed in springtime.'

'Not that,' said Gilhaney.

'Or porter in a sick stomach,' said the Sergeant.

'So help me not,' said Gilhaney.

The Sergeant saw me with the corner of his eye and turned to talk to me, taking away all his attention from Gilhaney.

'MacCruiskeen was giving you his talk I wouldn't doubt,' he said.

'He was being extremely explanatory,' I answered dryly.

'He is a comical man,' said the Sergeant, 'a walking emporium, you'd think he was on wires and worked with steam.'

'He is,' I said.

'He is a melody man,' the Sergeant added, 'and very temporary, a menace to the mind.'

'About the bicycle,' said Gilhaney.

'The bicycle will be found,' said the Sergeant, 'when I retrieve and restore it to its own owner in due law and possessively. Would you desire to be of assistance in the search?' he asked me.

'I would not mind,' I answered.

The Sergeant looked at his teeth in the glass for a brief intermission and then put his leggings on his legs and took a hold of his stick as an indication that he was for the road. Gilhaney was at the door operating it to let us out. The three of us walked out into the middle of the day.

'In case we do not come up with the bicycle before it is high dinner-time,' said the Sergeant, 'I have left an official memorandum for the personal information of Policeman Fox so that he will be acutely conversant with the *res ipsa*,' he said.

'Do you hold with rap-trap pedals?' asked Gilhaney.

'Who is Fox?' I asked.

'Policeman Fox is the third of us,' said the Sergeant, 'but we never see him or hear tell of him at all because he is always on his beat and never off it and he signs the book in the middle of the night when even a badger is asleep. He is as mad as a hare, he never interrogates the public and he is always taking notes. If rat-trap pedals were universal it would be the end of bicycles, the people would die like flies.'

'What put him that way?' I inquired.

'I never comprehended correctly,' replied the Sergeant, 'or got the real informative information but Policeman Fox was alone in a private room with MacCruiskeen for a whole hour on a certain 23rd of June and he has never spoken to anybody since that day and he is as crazy as tuppence-half-penny and as cranky as thruppence. Did I ever tell you how I asked Inspector O'Corky about rat-traps? Why are they not made prohibitive, I said, or made specialities like arsenic when you would have to buy them at a chemist's shop and sign a little book and look like a responsible personality?'

'They are a power for the hills,' said Gilhaney.

The Sergeant spat spits on the dry road.

'You would want a special Act of Parliament,' said the Inspector, 'a special Act of Parliament.'

'What way are we going?' I asked, 'or what direction are we heading for or are we on the way back from somewhere else?'

It was a queer country we were in. There was a number of blue mountains around us at what you might call a respectful distance with a glint of white water coming down the shoulders of one or two of them and they kept hemming us in and meddling oppressively with our minds. Half-way to these mountains the view got clearer and was full of humps and hollows and long parks of fine bogland with civil people here and there in the middle of it working with long instruments, you could hear their voices calling across the wind and the crack of the dull carts on the roadways. White buildings could be seen in several places and cows shambling lazily from here to there in search of pasture. A company of crows came out of a tree when I was watching and flew sadly down to a field where there was a quantity of sheep attired in fine overcoats.

'We are going where we are going,' said the Sergeant, 'and this is the right direction to a place that is next door to it. There is one particular thing more dangerous than the rat-trap pedal.'

He left the road and drew us in after him through a hedge.

'It is dishonourable to talk like that about the rat-traps,' said Gilhaney, 'because my family has had their boots in them for generations of their own posterity backwards and forwards and they all died in their beds except my first cousin that was meddling with the suckers of a steam thrashing-mill.'

'There is only one thing more dangerous,' said the Sergeant, 'and that is a loose plate. A loose plate is a scorcher, nobody lives very long after swallowing one and it leads indirectly to asphyxiation.'

'There is no danger of swallowing a rat-trap?' said Gilhaney.

'You would want to have good strong clips if you have a plate,' said the Sergeant, 'and plenty of red sealing-wax to stick it to the roof of your jaws. Take a look at the roots of that bush, it looks suspicious and there is no necessity for a warrant.'

It was a small modest whin-bush, a lady member of the tribe as you might say, with dry particles of hay and sheep's feathers caught in the branches high and low. Gilhaney was on his knees putting his hands through the grass and rooting like one of the lower animals. After a minute he extracted a black instrument. It was long and thin and looked like a large fountain-pen.

'My pump, so help me!' he shouted.

'I thought as much,' said the Sergeant, 'the finding of the pump is a fortunate clue that may assist us in our mission of private detection and smart policework. Put it in your pocket and hide it because it is possible that we are watched and followed and dogged by a member of the gang.'

'How did you know that it was in that particular corner of the world?' I asked in my extreme simplicity.

'What is your attitude to the high saddle?' inquired Gilhaney.

'Questions are like the knocks of beggarmen, and should not be minded,' replied the Sergeant, 'but I do not mind telling you that the high saddle is all right if you happen to have a brass fork.'

'A high saddle is a power for the hills,' said Gilhaney.

We were in an entirely other field by this time and in the company of white-coloured brown-coloured cows. They watched us quietly as we made a path between them and changed their attitudes slowly as if to show us all of the maps on their fat sides. They gave us to understand that they knew us personally and thought a lot of our families and I lifted my hat to the last of them as I passed her as a sign of my appreciation.

'The high saddle!' said the Sergeant, 'was invented by a party called Peters that spent his life in foreign parts riding on camels and other lofty animals – giraffes, elephants and birds that can run like hares and lay eggs the size of the bowl you see in a steam laundry where they keep the chemical water for taking the tar out of men's pants. When he came home from the wars he thought hard of sitting on a low saddle and one night accidentally when he was in bed he invented the high saddle as the outcome of his perpetual cerebration and mental researches. His Christian name I do not remember.

The high saddle was the father of the low handlebars. It crucifies the fork and gives you a blood rush in the head, it is very sore on the internal organs.'

'Which of the organs?' I inquired.

'Both of them,' said the Sergeant.

'I think this would be the tree,' said Gilhaney.

'It would not surprise me,' said the Sergeant, 'put your hands in under its underneath and start feeling promiscuously the way you can ascertain factually if there is anything there in addition to its own nothing.'

Gilhaney lay down on his stomach on the grass at the butt of a blackthorn and was inquiring into its private parts with his strong hands and grunting from the stretch of his exertions. After a time he found a bicycle lamp and a bell and stood up and put them secretly in his fob.

'That is very satisfactory and complacently articulated,' said the Sergeant, 'it shows the necessity for perseverance, it is sure to be a clue, we are certain to find the bicycle.'

'I do not like asking questions,' I said politely, 'but the wisdom that directed us to this tree is not taught in the National Schools.'

'It is not the first time my bicycle was stolen,' said Gilhaney.

'In *my* day,' said the Sergeant, 'half the scholars in the National Schools were walking around with enough disease in their gobs to decimate the continent of Russia and wither a field of crops by only looking at them. That is all stopped now, they have compulsory inspections, the middling ones are stuffed with iron and the bad ones are pulled out with a thing like the claw for cutting wires.'

'The half of it is due to cycling with the mouth open,' said Gilhaney.

'Nowadays,' said the Sergeant, 'it is nothing strange to see a class of boys at First Book with wholesome teeth and with junior plates manufactured by the County Council for half-nothing.'

'Grinding the teeth half-way up a hill,' said Gilhaney, 'there is nothing worse, it files away the best part of them and leads to a hob-nailed liver indirectly.'

'In Russia,' said the Sergeant, 'they make teeth out of old piano-keys for elderly cows but it is a rough land without too much civilization, it would cost you a fortune in tyres.'

We were now going through a country full of fine enduring trees where it was always five o'clock in the afternoon. It was a soft corner of the world, free from inquisitions and disputations and very soothing and sleepening on the mind. There was no animal there that was bigger than a man's thumb and no noise superior to that which the Sergeant was making with his nose, an unusual brand of music like wind in the chimney. To every side of us there was a green growth of soft ferny carpeting with thin green twines coming in and out of it and coarse bushes putting their heads out here and there and interrupting the urbanity of the presentation not unpleasingly. The distance we walked in this country I do not know but we arrived in the end at some place where we stopped without proceeding farther. The Sergeant put his finger at a certain part of the growth.

'It might be there and it might not,' he said, 'we can only try because perseverance is its own reward and necessity is the unmarried mother of invention.'

Gilhaney was not long at work till he took his bicycle out of that particular part of the growth. He pulled the briers from between the spokes and felt his tyres with red knowing fingers and furbished his machine fastidiously. The three of us walked back again without a particle of conversation to where the road was and Gilhaney put his toe on the pedal to show he was for home.

'Before I ride away,' he said to the Sergeant, 'what is your true opinion of the timber rim?'

'It is a very commendable invention,' the Sergeant said. 'It gives you more of a bounce, it is extremely easy on your white pneumatics.'

'The wooden rim,' said Gilhaney slowly, 'is a death-trap in itself, it swells on a wet day and I know a man that owes his bad wet death to nothing else.'

Before we had time to listen carefully to what he was after saying he was half-way down the road with his forked coat sailing behind him on the sustenance of the wind he was raising by reason of his headlong acceleration.

'A droll man,' I ventured.

'A constituent man,' said the Sergeant, 'largely instrumental but volubly fervous.'

Walking finely from the hips the two of us made our way home through the afternoon, impregnating it with the smoke of our cigarettes. I reflected that we would be sure to have lost our way in the fields and parks of bogland only that the road very conveniently made its way in advance of us back to the barrack. The Sergeant was sucking quietly at his stumps and carried a black shadow on his brow as if it were a hat.

As he walked he turned in my direction after a time.

'The County Council has a lot to answer for,' he said.

I did not understand his meaning, but I said that I agreed with him.

'There is one puzzle,' I remarked, 'that is hurting the back of my head and causing me a lot of curiosity. It is about the bicycle. I have never heard of detective-work as good as that being done before. Not only did you find the lost bicycle but you found all the clues as well. I find it is a great strain for me to believe what I see, and I am becoming afraid occasionally to look at some things in case they would have to be believed. What is the secret of your constabulary virtuosity?'

He laughed at my earnest inquiries and shook his head with great indulgence at my simplicity.

'It was an easy thing,' he said.

'How easy?'

'Even without the clues I could have succeeded in ultimately finding the bicycle.'

'It seems a very difficult sort of easiness,' I answered. 'Did you know where the bicycle was?'

'I did.'

'How?'

'Because I put it there.'

'You stole the bicycle yourself?'

'Certainly.'

'And the pump and the other clues?'

'I put them where they were finally discovered also.'

'And why?'

He did not answer in words for a moment but kept on walking strongly beside me looking as far ahead as possible.

'The County Council is the culprit,' he said at last.

I said nothing, knowing that he would blame the County Council at greater length if I waited till he had the blame thought out properly. It was not long till he turned in my direction to talk to me again. His face was grave.

'Did you ever discover or hear tell of the Atomic Theory?' he inquired.

'No,' I answered.

He leaned his mouth confidentially over to my ear.

'Would it surprise you to be told,' he said darkly, 'that the Atomic Theory is at work in this parish?'

'It would indeed.'

'It is doing untold destruction,' he continued, 'the half of the people are suffering from it, it is worse than the smallpox.'

I thought it better to say *something*.

'Would it be advisable,' I said, 'that it should be taken in hand by the Dispensary Doctor or by the National Teachers or do you think it is a matter for the head of the family?'

'The lock stock and barrel of it all,' said the Sergeant, 'is the County Council.'

He walked on looking worried and preoccupied as if what he was examining in his head was unpleasant in a very intricate way.

'The Atomic Theory,' I sallied, 'is a thing that is not clear to me at all.'

'Michael Gilhaney,' said the Sergeant, 'is an example of a man that is nearly banjaxed from the principle of the Atomic Theory. Would it astonish you to hear that he is nearly half a bicycle?'

'It would surprise me unconditionally,' I said.

'Michael Gilhaney,' said the Sergeant, 'is nearly sixty years of age by plain computation and if he is itself, he has spent no less than thirty-five years riding his bicycle over the rocky roadsteads and up and down the hills and into the deep ditches when the road goes astray in the strain of the winter. He is always going to a particular destination or other on his bicycle at every hour of the day or coming back from there at every other hour. If it wasn't that his bicycle was stolen every Monday he would be sure to be more than half-way now.'

'Half-way to where?'

'Half-way to being a bicycle himself,' said the Sergeant.

'Your talk,' I said, 'is surely the handiwork of wisdom because not one word of it do I understand.'

'Did you never study atomics when you were a lad?' asked the Sergeant, giving me a look of great inquiry and surprise.

'No,' I answered.

'That is a very serious defalcation,' he said, 'but all the same I will tell you the size of it. Everything is composed of small particles of itself and they are flying around in concentric circles and arcs and segments and innumerable other geometrical figures too numerous to mention collectively, never standing still or resting but spinning away and darting hither and thither and back again, all the time on the go. These diminutive gentlemen are called atoms. Do you follow me intelligently?'

'Yes.'

'They are lively as twenty leprechauns doing a jig on top of a tombstone.'

A very pretty figure, Joe murmured.

'Now take a sheep,' the Sergeant said. 'What is a sheep only millions of little bits of sheepness whirling around and doing intricate convolutions inside the sheep? What else is it but that?'

'That would be bound to make the beast dizzy,' I observed, 'especially if the whirling was going on inside the head as well.'

The Sergeant gave me a look which I am sure he himself would describe as one of *non-possum* and *noli-me-tangere*.

'That remark is what may well be called buncombe,' he said sharply, 'because the nerve-strings and the sheep's head itself are whirling into the same bargain and you can cancel out one whirl against the other and there you are – like simplifying a division sum when you have fives above and below the bar.'

'To say the truth I did not think of that,' I said.

'Atomics is a very intricate theorem and can be worked out with algebra but you would want to take it by degrees because you might spend the whole night proving a bit of it with rulers and cosines and similar other instruments and then at the wind-up not believe what you had proved at all. If that happened you would have to go back over it till you got a place where you could believe your own facts and figures as delineated from Hall and Knight's Algebra and then go on again from that particular place till you had the whole thing properly believed and not have bits of it half-believed or a doubt in your head hurting you like when you lose the stud of your shirt in bed.'

'Very true,' I said.

'Consecutively and consequentially,' he continued, 'you can safely infer that you are made of atoms yourself and so is your fob pocket and the tail of your shirt and the instrument you use for taking the leavings out of the crook of your hollow tooth. Do you happen to know what takes place when you strike a bar of iron with a good coal hammer or with a blunt instrument?'

'What?'

'When the wallop falls, the atoms are bashed away down to the bottom of the bar and compressed and crowded there like eggs under a good clucker. After a while in the course of time they swim around and get back at last to where they were. But if you keep hitting the bar long enough and hard enough they do not get a chance to do this and what happens then?'

'That is a hard question.'

'Ask a blacksmith for the true answer and he will tell you that the bar will dissipate itself away by degrees if you persevere with the hard wallops. Some of the atoms of the bar will go into the hammer and the other half into the table or the stone or the particular article that is underneath the bottom of the bar.'

'That is well-known,' I agreed.

'The gross and net result of it is that people who spent most of their natural lives riding iron bicycles over the rocky roadsteads of this parish get their personalities mixed up with the personalities of their bicycle as a result of the interchanging of the atoms of each of them and you would be surprised at the number of people in these parts who nearly are half people and half bicycles.'

I let go a gasp of astonishment that made a sound in the air like a bad puncture.

'And you would be flabbergasted at the number of bicycles that are half-human almost half-man, half-partaking of humanity'

Apparently there is no limit, Joe remarked. *Anything can be said in this place and it will be true and will have to be believed.*

I would not mind being working this minute on a steamer in the middle of the sea, I said, coiling ropes and doing the hard manual work. I would like to be far away from here.

I looked carefully around me. Brown bogs and black bogs were arranged neatly on each side of the road with rectangular boxes carved out of them here and there, each with a filling of yellow-brown brown-yellow water. Far away near the sky tiny people were stooped at their turfwork, cutting out precisely-shaped sods with their patent spades and building them into a tall memorial twice the height of a horse and cart. Sounds came from them to the Sergeant and myself, delivered to our ears without charge by the west wind, sounds of laughing and whistling and bits of verses from the old bog-songs. Nearer, a house stood attended by three trees and surrounded by the happiness of a coterie of fowls, all of them picking and rooting and disputating loudly in the unrelenting manufacture of their eggs. The house was quiet in itself and silent but a canopy of lazy smoke had been erected over the chimney to indicate that people were within engaged on tasks. Ahead of us went the road, running swiftly across the flat land and pausing slightly to climb slowly up a hill that was waiting for it in a place where there was tall grass, grey boulders and rank stunted trees. The whole overhead was occupied by the sky, serene, impenetrable, ineffable and incomparable, with a fine island of clouds anchored in the calm two yards to the right of Mr Jarvis's outhouse.

The scene was real and incontrovertible and at variance with the talk of the Sergeant, but I knew that the Sergeant was talking the truth and if it was a question of taking my choice, it was possible that I would have to forego the reality of all the simple things my eyes were looking at.

I took a sideways view of him. He was striding on with signs of anger against the County Council on his coloured face.

'Are you certain about the humanity of the bicycle?' I inquired of him. 'Is the Atomic Theory as dangerous as you say?'

'It is between twice and three times as dangerous as it might be,' he replied gloomily. 'Early in the morning I often think it is four times, and what is more, if you lived here for a few days and gave full play to your observation and inspection, you would know how certain the sureness of certainty is.'

'Gilhaney did not look like a bicycle,' I said. 'He had no back wheel on him and I did not think he had a front wheel either, although I did not give much attention to his front.'

The Sergeant looked at me with some commiseration.

'You cannot expect him to grow handlebars out of his neck but I have seen him do more indescribable things than that. Did you ever notice the queer behaviour of bicycles in these parts?'

'I am not long in this district.'

Thanks be, said Joe.

'Then watch the bicycles if you think it is pleasant to be surprised continuously,' he said. 'When a man lets things go so far that he is half or more than half a bicycle, you will not see so much because he spends a lot of his time leaning with one elbow on walls or standing propped by one foot at kerbstones. Of course there are other things connected with ladies and ladies' bicycles that I will mention to you separately some time. But the man-charged bicycle is a phenomenon of great charm and intensity and a very dangerous article.'

At this point a man with long coat-tails spread behind him approached quickly on a bicycle, coasting benignly down the road past us from the hill ahead. I watched him with the eye of six eagles, trying to find out which was carrying the other and whether it was really a man with a bicycle on his shoulders. I did not seem to see anything, however, that was memorable or remarkable.

The Sergeant was looking into his black notebook.

'That was O'Feersa,' he said at last. 'His figure is only twenty-three per cent.'

'He is twenty-three per cent bicycle?'

'Yes.'

'Does that mean that his bicycle is also twenty-three per cent O'Feersa?'

'It does.'

'How much is Gilhaney?'

'Forty-eight.'

'Then O'Feersa is much lower.'

'That is due to the lucky fact that there are three similar brothers in the house and that they are too poor to have a separate bicycle apiece. Some people never know how fortunate they are when they are poorer than each other. Six years ago one of the three O'Feersas won a prize of ten pounds in *John Bull*. When I got the wind of this tiding, I knew I would have to take steps unless there was to be two new bicycles in the family, because you will understand that I can steal only a limited number of bicycles in the one week. I did not want to have three O'Feersas on my hands. Luckily I knew the postman very well. The postman! Great holy suffering indiarubber bowls of brown stirabout!' The recollection of the postman seemed to give the Sergeant a pretext for unlimited amusement and cause for intricate gesturing with his red hands.

'The postman?' I said.

'Seventy-one per cent,' he said quietly.

'Great Scot!'

'A round of thirty-eight miles on the bicycle every single day for forty years, hail, rain or snowballs. There is very little hope of ever getting his number down below fifty again.'

'You bribed him?'

'Certainly. With two of the little straps you put around the hubs of bicycles to keep them spick.'

'And what way do these people's bicycles behave?'

'These people's bicycles?'

'I mean these bicycles' people or whatever is the proper name for them – the ones that have two wheels under them and a handlebars.'

'The behaviour of a bicycle that has a high content of humanity,' he said, 'is very cunning and entirely remarkable. You never see them moving by themselves but you meet them in the least accountable places unexpectedly. Did you never see a bicycle leaning against the dresser of a warm kitchen when it is pouring outside?'

'I did.'

'Not very far away from the fire?'

'Yes.'

'Near enough to the family to hear the conversation?'

'Yes.'

'Not a thousand miles from where they keep the eatables?'

'I did not notice that. You do not mean to say that these bicycles *eat food*?'

'They were never seen doing it, nobody ever caught them with a mouthful of steak. All I know is that the food disappears.'

'What!'

'It is not the first time I have noticed crumbs at the front wheels of some of these gentlemen.'

'All this is a great blow to me,' I said.

'Nobody takes any notice,' replied the Sergeant. 'Mick thinks that Pat brought it in and Pat thinks that Mick was instrumental. Very few of the people guess what is going on in this parish. There are other things I would rather not say too much about. A new lady teacher was here one time with a new bicycle. She was not very long here till Gilhaney went away into the lonely country on her female bicycle. Can you appreciate the immorality of that?'

'I can.'

'But worse happened. Whatever way Gilhaney's bicycle managed it, it left itself leaning at a place where the young teacher would rush out to go away somewhere on her bicycle in a hurry. Her bicycle was gone but here was Gilhaney's leaning there conveniently and trying to look very small and comfortable and attractive. Need I inform you what the result was or what happened?'

Indeed he need not, Joe said urgently. *I have never heard of anything so shameless and abandoned. Of course the teacher was blameless, she did not take pleasure and did not know.*

'You need not,' I said.

'Well, there you are. Gilhaney has a day out with the lady's bicycle and vice versa contrarily and it is quite clear that the lady in the case had a high number – thirty-five or forty, I would say, in spite of the newness of the bicycle. Many a grey hair it has put into my head, trying to regulate the people of this parish. If you let it go too far it would be the end of everything. You would have bicycles wanting votes and they would get seats on the County Council and make the roads far worse than they are for their own ulterior motivation. But against that and on the other hand, a good bicycle is a great companion, there is a great charm about it.'

'How would you know a man has a lot of bicycle in his veins?'

'If his number is over fifty you can tell it unmistakable from his walk. He will walk smartly always and never sit down and he will lean against the wall with his elbow out and stay like that all night in his kitchen instead of going to bed. If he walks too slowly or stops in the middle of the road he will fall down in a heap and will have to be lifted and set in motion again by some extraneous party. This is the unfortunate state that the postman has cycled himself into, and I do not think he will ever cycle himself out of it.'

'I do not think I will ever ride a bicycle,' I said.

'A little of it is a good thing and makes you hardy and puts iron on to you. But walking too far too often too quickly is not safe at all. The continual cracking of your feet on the road makes a certain quantity of road come up into you. When a man dies they say he returns to clay but too much walking fills you up with clay far sooner (or buries bits of you along the road) and brings your death half-way to meet you. It is not easy to know what is the best way to move yourself from one place to another.'

After he had finished speaking I found myself walking nimbly and lightly on my toes in order to prolong my life. My head was packed tight with fears and miscellaneous apprehensions.

'I never heard of these things before,' I said, 'and never knew these happenings could happen. Is it a new development or was it always an ancient fundamental?'

The Sergeant's face clouded and he spat thoughtfully three yards ahead of him on the road.

'I will tell you a secret,' he said very confidentially in a low voice. 'My great-grandfather was eighty-three when he died. For a year before his death he was a horse!'

'A horse?'

'A horse in everything but extraneous externalities. He would spend the day grazing in a field or eating hay in a stall. Usually he was lazy and quiet but now and again he would go for a smart gallop, clearing the hedges in great style. Did you ever see a man on two legs galloping?'

'I did not.'

'Well, I am given to understand that it is a great sight. He always said he won the Grand National when he was a lot younger and used to annoy his family with stories about the intricate jumps and the great height of them.'

'I suppose your great-grandfather got himself into this condition by too much horse riding?'

'That was the size of it. His old horse Dan was in the contrary way and gave so much trouble, coming into the house at night and interfering with young girls during the day and committing indictable offences, that they had to shoot him. The police were unsympathetic, not comprehending things rightly in these days. They said they would have to arrest the horse and charge him and have him up at the next Petty Sessions unless he was done away with. So my family shot him but if you ask me it was my great-grandfather they shot and it is the horse that is buried up in Cloncoonla Churchyard.'

The Sergeant then became thoughtful at the recollection of his ancestors and had a reminiscent face for the next half-mile till we came to the barracks. Joe and I agreed privately that these revelations were the supreme surprise stored for us and awaiting our arrival in the barracks.

When we reached it and the Sergeant led the way in with a sigh. 'The lock, stock and barrel of it all,' he said, 'is the County Council.'

MARY LAVIN

'Happiness'

Mother had a lot to say. This does not mean she was always talking but that we children felt the wells she drew upon were deep, deep, deep. Her theme was happiness: what it was, what it was not; where we might find it, where not; and how, if found, it must be guarded. Never must we confound it with pleasure. Nor think sorrow its exact opposite.

'Take Father Hugh,' Mother's eyes flashed as she looked at him. 'According to him, sorrow is an ingredient of happiness, a necessary ingredient, if you please.' And when he tried to protest she put up her hand. 'There may be a freakish truth in the theory for some people. But not for me. And not, I hope, for my children.' She looked severely at us three girls. We laughed. None of us had had much experience of sorrow. Bea and I were children and Linda only a year old when our father died suddenly after a short illness that had not at first seemed serious. 'I've known people to make sorrow a substitute for happiness,' Mother said.

Father Hugh protested again. 'You're not putting me in that class, I hope?'

Father Hugh, ever since our father died, had been the closest of anyone to us as a family, without being close to any one of us in particular, even to Mother. He lived in a monastery near our farm in County Meath, and he had been one of the celebrants at the Requiem High Mass our father's political importance had demanded. He met us that day for the first time, but he took to dropping in to see us, with the idea of filling the crater of loneliness left at our centre. He did not know that there was a cavity in his own life, much less that we would fill it. He and Mother were both young in those days, and perhaps it gave scandal to some that he was so often in our house, staying till late into the night and, indeed, thinking nothing of stopping all night if there was any special reason, such as one of us being sick. He had even on occasion slept there if the night was too wet for tramping home across the fields.

When we girls were young, we were so used to having Father Hugh around that we never stood on ceremony with him but in his presence dried our hair and pared our nails and never minded what garments were strewn about. As for Mother, she thought nothing of running out of the bathroom in her slip, brushing her teeth or combing her hair, if she wanted to tell him something she might otherwise forget. And she brooked no criticism of her behaviour. 'Celibacy was never meant to take all the warmth and homeliness out of their lives,' she said.

On this point, too, Bea was adamant. Bea, the middle sister, was our oracle. 'I'm so glad he has Mother,' she said, 'as well as her having him, because it must be awful the way most women treat them, priests, I mean, as if they were pariahs. Mother treats him like a human being, that's all.'

When it came to Mother's ears that there had been gossip about her making free with Father Hugh, she opened her eyes wide in astonishment. 'But he's only a priest,' she said.

Bea giggled. 'It's a good job he didn't hear that,' she said to me afterwards. 'It would undo the good she's done him. You'd think he was a eunuch.'

'Bea, do you think he's in love with her?' I said.

'If so, he doesn't know it,' Bea said firmly. 'It's her soul he's after. Maybe he wants to make sure of her in the next world.'

But thoughts of the world to come never troubled Mother. 'If anything ever happens to me, children,' she said, 'suddenly, I mean, or when you are not near me, or I cannot speak to you, I want you to promise you won't feel bad. There's no need. Just remember that I had a happy life and if I had to choose my kind of heaven I'd take it on this earth with you again, no matter how much you might at times annoy me.'

You see, according to Mother, annoyance and fatigue, and even illness and pain, could coexist with happiness. She had a habit of asking people if they were happy at times and in places that, to say the least of it, seemed to us inappropriate. 'But are you happy?' she'd probe as one lay sick and bathed in sweat, or in the throes of a jumping toothache. And once in our presence she made the inquiry of an old friend as he lay upon his deathbed. 'Why not?' she asked when we took her to task for it later. 'Isn't it more important than ever to be happy when you're dying? Take my own father, do you know what he said in his last moments? On his deathbed, he defied me to name a man who had enjoyed a better life. In spite of dreadful pain, his face radiated happiness.' Mother nodded her head comfortably. 'Happiness drives out pain, as fire burns out fire.'

Having no knowledge of our own to pit against hers, we thirstily drank in her rhetoric. Only Bea was sceptical. 'Perhaps you got it from him, like spots, or fever,' she said. 'Or something that could at least be slipped from hand to hand.'

'Do you think I'd have taken it if that were the case?' Mother cried. 'Then, when he needed it most?'

'Not there and then,' Bea said stubbornly. 'I meant as a sort of legacy.'

'Don't you think in that case,' Mother said, exasperated, 'he would have felt obliged to leave it to your grandmother?'

Certainly we knew that in spite of his lavish heart our grandfather had failed to provide our grandmother with enduring happiness. He had passed that job on to Mother. And Mother had not made too good a fist of it, even when Father was living and she had him, and later us children to help.

As for Father Hugh, he had given our grandmother up early in the game. 'God Almighty couldn't make that woman happy,' he said one day, seeing Mother's face, drawn and pale with fatigue, preparing for the nightly run over to her own mother's house that would exhaust her utterly. There were evenings after she came home from the County library where she worked, when we saw her stand with the car keys in her hand, trying to think which would be worse, to slog over there on foot, or take out the car again. And yet the distance was short. It was Mother's day that had been too long. 'Weren't you over to see her this morning?' Father Hugh demanded.

'No matter,' said Mother. She was no doubt thinking of the forlorn face our grandmother always put on when she was leaving.

'Don't say good night, Vera,' Grandmother would plead. 'It makes me feel too lonely. And you never can tell, you might slip over again before you go to bed.'

'Do you know the time?' Bea would ask impatiently if she happened to be with Mother. Not indeed that the lateness of the hour counted for anything, because in all likelihood Mother would go back, if only to pass by under the window and see that the lights were out, or stand and listen and make sure that as far as she could tell all was well.

'I wouldn't mind if she was happy,' Mother once said to us.

'And how do you know she's not?' we asked.

'When people are happy, I can feel it. Can't you?'

We were not sure. Most people thought our grandmother was a gay creature, a small birdy being who even at a great age laughed like a girl, and more remarkably sang like one, as she went about her day. But beak and claw were of steel. She'd think nothing of sending Mother back to a shop three times if her errands were not exactly right. 'Not sugar like that, that's too fine; it's not castor sugar I want. But not as coarse as that, either. I want an in-between kind.'

Provoked one day, my youngest sister, Linda, turned and gave battle. 'You're mean!' she cried. 'You love ordering people about.'

Grandmother preened, as if Linda had paid her a compliment. 'I was always hard to please,' she said. 'As a girl, I used to be called Miss Imperious.'

And Miss Imperious she remained as long as she lived, even when she was a great age. Her orders were then given a wry twist by the fact that as she advanced in age she took to calling her daughter Mother, as we did.

There was one great phrase with which our grandmother opened every sentence: '*if only*'. 'If only,' she'd say, when we came to visit her, 'if only you'd come earlier, before I was worn out expecting you.' Or if we were early, then she'd say, if only it was later, after she'd had a rest and could enjoy us, be able for us. And if we brought her flowers, she'd sigh to think that if only we'd brought them the previous day when she'd had a visitor to appreciate them or if only the stems were longer, or that we had picked a few green leaves, and included a few buds. Because she'd say disparagingly, the poor flowers we'd brought were already wilting. We used to feel we might just as well not have brought them. As the years went on Grandmother had a new bead to add to her rosary: if only her friends were not all dead. By their absence, they reduced to nil all real enjoyment in anything. Our own father, her son-in-law, was the one person who had ever gone close to pleasing her. But even here there had been a snag. 'If only he was my real son,' she used to say, with a sigh.

Mother's mother lived on through our childhood and into our early maturity, although she outlived the money our grandfather left her, and in our minds she was a complicated mixture of valiance and defeat. Courageous and generous within the limits of her own life, her simplest demand was yet enormous in the larger frame of Mother's life, and so we never could see her with the same clarity of vision with which we saw our grandfather, or our own father. Them we saw only through Mother's eyes.

'Take your grandfather,' she'd cry, and instantly we'd see him, his eyes turning upon us, yes, upon us, although in his day only one of us had been born: me. At another time, Mother would cry, 'Take your own father,' and instantly we'd see him, tall, handsome, young, and much more suited to marry one of us than poor bedraggled Mother. Most fascinating of all were the times Mother would say 'Take me.' By magic then, staring down the years, we'd see blazingly clear a small girl with black hair and buttoned boots, who, though plain and pouting, burned bright, like a star. 'I was happy, you see,' Mother said. And we'd strain hard to try and understand the mystery of the light that still radiated from her. 'I used to lean along a tree that grew out over the river,' she said, 'and look down through the grey leaves at the water flowing past below, and I used to think it was not the stream that flowed but me, spreadeagled over it, who flew through the air like a bird. That I'd found the secret.' She made it seem there might be such a secret, just waiting to be found. Another time she used to dream that she'd be a great singer.

'We didn't know you sang, Mother?'

She had to laugh. 'Like a crow,' she said.

Sometimes she used to think she'd swim the Channel.

'Did you swim that well, Mother?'

'Oh, not really, just the breast stroke,' she said. 'And only then by the aid of two pig bladders blown up by my father and tied around my middle. But I used to throb, yes, throb with happiness.'

Behind Mother's back, Bea raised her eyebrows.

What was it, we used to ask ourselves, that quality that she, we felt sure, misnamed? Was it courage? Was it strength, health, or high spirits? Something you could not give or take? A conundrum, or a game of catch-as-catch-can?

'I know what it was,' cried Bea one day. 'A sham.'

Whatever it was, we knew that Mother would let no wind of violence from within or without tear it from her. Although, one evening when Father Hugh was with us, our astonished ears heard her proclaim that there might be a time when one had to slacken hold on it, let it go for a moment, to catch at it again with a surer hand. In the way, we supposed, that the high-wire walker up among the painted stars of his canvas sky must wait to fling himself through the air until the bar he catches at has started to sway perversely from him. Oh no, no! That downward drag at our innards we could not bear, the belly swelling to the shape of a pear. Let happiness go by the board. 'After all, lots of people seem to make out without it,' Bea said. It was too tricky a business. And might it not be that one had to be born with a flair for it?

'A flair would not be enough,' Mother said when we once asked her. 'Take Father Hugh. He, if anyone, had a flair for it, a natural capacity. You've only to look at him when he's off guard with you children, or helping me in the garden. But he rejects happiness. He casts it from him.'

'That is simply not true, Vera,' said Father Hugh, overhearing her. 'It's just that I don't place an inordinate value on it like you. I don't think it's enough to carry one all the way. To the end, I mean – and after.'

'Oh, don't talk about the end when we're only in the middle,' said Mother. And, indeed, at that moment her own face shone with such happiness it was hard to believe that her earth was not her heaven. Certainly it was her constant contention that of happiness she had had a lion's share. This, however, we, in private, doubted. Perhaps there were times when she had had a surplus of it, when she was young, say, with her redoubtable father, whose love blazed circles around her, making winter into summer and ice into fire. Perhaps she did have a brimming measure in her early married years. By straining hard, we could find traces left in our minds from those days of milk and honey. Our father, while he lived, had cast a magic over everything, for us as well as for her. He held his love up over us like an umbrella and kept off the troubles that afterwards came down on us, pouring cats and dogs.

But if she did have more than the common lot of happiness in those early days, what use was that when we could remember so clearly how our father's death had ravaged her? And how could we forget the distress it brought on us when, afraid to let her out of our sight, Bea and I stumbled after her everywhere, through the woods and along the bank of the river, where, in the weeks that followed, she tried vainly to find peace.

The summer after Father died, we were invited to France to stay with friends, and when she went walking on the cliffs at Fécamp our fears for her grew frenzied, so that we hung on to her arm and dragged at her skirt, hoping that like leaded weights we'd pin her down if she went too near to the edge. But at night we had to abandon our watch, being forced to follow the conventions of a family still whole, a home still intact, and go to bed at the same time as the children of the house. It was at that hour, when the coast guard was gone from his rowing boat offshore, and the sand was as cold and grey as the sea, that Mother liked to swim. And when she had washed, kissed, and left us, our hearts almost died inside us and we'd creep out of bed again to stand in our bare feet at the mansard and watch as she ran down the shingle, striking out when she reached the water where, far out, wave and sky and mist were one, and the greyness closed over her. If we took our eyes off her for an instant, it was impossible to find her again.

'Oh, make her turn back, God please!' I prayed out loud one night.

Startled, Bea turned away from the window. 'She'll have to turn back sometime, won't she? Unless –?'

Locking our cold hands together, we'd stare out again. 'She wouldn't,' I whispered. 'It would be a sin.'

Secure in the deterring power of sin, we let out our breath. Then Bea's breath caught again. 'What if she went out so far she used up all her strength and couldn't swim back? It wouldn't be a sin then.'

'It's the intention that counts,' I said.

A second later, we could see the arm lift heavily up and wearily cleave down, and at last Mother was in the shallows, wading back to shore.

'Don't let her see us!' cried Bea. As if our chattering teeth would not give us away when she looked in at us before she went to her own room on the other side of the corridor, where later in the night the sound of her weeping would reach us.

What was it worth, a happiness bought that dearly?

But Mother had never questioned its worth. She told us once that on a wintry day she brought her own mother a snowdrop. 'It was the first one of the year,' she said, 'a bleak bud that had come up stunted before its time, and I meant it as a sign of Spring to come. But do you know what your grandmother said? 'What good are snowdrops to me now?' Such a thing to say! What good are snowdrops at all if they don't hold their value for us all our lives? Isn't that the whole point of a snowdrop? And that is the whole point of happiness, too. What good would it be if it could be erased without trace? Take me and those daffodils.' Stooping, she buried her face in a bunch that lay on the table waiting to be put in vases. 'If they didn't hold their beauty absolute and inviolable, do you think I could bear the sight of them after what happened when your father was in hospital?'

It was a fair question. When Father went to hospital, Mother went with him and stayed in a small hotel across the street so she could be with him all day from early to late. 'Because it was so awful for him, being in Dublin,' she said. 'You have no idea how he hated it.'

That he was dying neither of them realized. How could they know, as it rushed through the sky, that their star was a falling star? But one evening when she'd left him asleep Mother came back home for a few hours to see how we were faring, and it broke her heart to see the daffodils were out all over the place, in the woods, under the trees, and along the sides of the avenue. There had never been so many, and she thought how awful it was that Father was missing them. 'I know you send up little bunches to him, you poor dears,' she said. 'Sweet little bunches, too, squeezed tight as posies by your little fists. But stuffed into vases they can't really make up to him for not being able to see masses of them growing.' So on the way back to the hospital she stopped her car and pulled a great bunch of them, the full of her arms. 'They took up the whole back seat,' she said, 'and I was so excited at the thought of walking into his room and dumping them on his bed, you know just plomping them down so he could smell them, and feel them. I didn't mean them to be put in vases in his room, not all of them. It would have taken a rainwater barrel to hold them. Why, I could hardly see over them as I came up the steps; I kept tripping. But when I came into the hall, that nun – I told you about her – that nun came up to me, sprang out of nowhere it seemed, although I know now that she was waiting for me, knowing that somebody had to bring me to my senses. But the cruel way she did it. Reaching out she grabbed the flowers, letting lots of them fall. I remember some of them getting stood on. "Where are you going with those foolish flowers, you foolish woman?" she said. "Don't you know your husband is dying? Your prayers are all you can give him now." She was right. I was foolish. But I wasn't cured. And that Summer it was nothing but foolishness the way I dragged you children after me all over Europe. As if any one place was going to be different from another, any better, any less desolate. But there was great satisfaction in bringing you places your father and I had planned to bring you, although in fairness to him I must say that he would not perhaps have brought you so young. And he would not have had an ulterior motive. But above all, he would not have attempted those trips in such a dilapidated car.'

Oh, that car! It was a battered old red sports car, so depleted of accessories that when, eventually, we got a new car Mother still stuck out her hand on bends, and in wet weather jumped out to wipe the windscreen with her sleeve. And if fussed, she'd let down the window and shout at people, forgetting she now had a horn. How we ever fitted into it with all our luggage was a miracle.

'Oh. There was plenty of room, you were never lumpish, any of you,' Mother said proudly. 'But you were very healthy and very strong.' She turned to me. 'Think of how you got that car up the hill in Switzerland.'

'The Alps are not hills, Mother,' I pointed out coldly, as I had done at the time, when the car failed to make it on one of the inclines. Mother let it run back until it wedged against the rock face, and I had to get out and push till she got it going again in first gear. But when it got started it couldn't be stopped to pick me up until it reached the top, where they had to wait for me. And for a very long time.

'Ah, well,' Mother said, sighing wistfully at the thought of those trips. 'You got something out of them, I hope. All that travelling must have helped you with your geography and your history.'

We looked at each other and smiled, and then Mother herself laughed. 'Remember the time when we were in Italy, and it was Easter, and all the shops were chock-full of food? The butchers' shops had poultry and game hanging up outside the doors, fully feathered, and with their poor heads dripping blood, and in the windows they had poor little lambs and suckling pigs and young goats, all skinned and hanging by their hindfeet.' She shuddered. 'Continentals are so obsessed about food. I found it revolting. I had to hurry past. But Linda, who must have been only four then, dragged at me and stared and stared. You know how children at that age have a morbid fascination for what is cruel and bloody. Her face was flushed and her eyes were wide. I hurried her back to the hotel. But next morning she crept into my room, and pressed up close to me. "Can't we go back, just once, and look again at that shop?" she whispered. "The shop where they have the little children hanging up for Easter." She meant the young goats, of course, but I'd said *kids*, I suppose. How we laughed.' But here her face was grave. 'You were really very good children in general. Otherwise I would never have put so much effort into rearing you, because I wasn't a bit maternal. You brought out the best in me. I put an unnatural effort into you, of course, because I was taking my standards from your father, forgetting that his might not have remained so inflexible if he had lived to middle age and was beset by life, like other parents.'

'Well, the job is nearly over now, Vera,' said Father Hugh. 'And you didn't do so badly.'

'That's right, Hugh,' said Mother, and she straightened up, and put her hand to her back the way she sometimes did in the garden when she got up from her knees after weeding. 'I didn't go over to the enemy anyway. We survived.' Then a flash of defiance came into her eyes. 'And we were happy. That was the main thing.'

Father Hugh frowned. 'There you go again!' he said.

Mother turned on him. 'I don't think you realize the onslaughts that were made upon our happiness. The minute Robert died, they came down on me, cohorts of relatives, friends, even strangers, all draped in black, opening their arms like bats to let me pass into their company. "Life is a vale of tears," they said. "You are privileged to find it out so young." Ugh! After I staggered on to my feet and began to take hold of life once more, they fell back defeated. And the first day I gave a laugh, pouff, they were blown out like candles. They weren't living in a real world at all; they belonged to a ghostly world where life was easy: all one had to do was sit and weep. It takes effort to push back the stone from the mouth of the tomb and walk out.'

Effort. Effort. Ah, but that strange-sounding word could invoke little sympathy from those who had not learned yet what it meant. Life must have been hardest for Mother in those years when we older ones were at college, no longer children, yet still dependent on her. Indeed, we made more demands on her than ever then, having moved into new areas of activity and emotion. And friends came and went as freely as we did ourselves, so that the house was often like a hotel, and one where pets were not prohibited but took their places on chairs and beds, as regardlessly as the people. Anyway it was hard to have sympathy for someone who got things into such a state as Mother. All over the house there was clutter. Her study was like the returned-letter department of a post-office, with stacks of paper everywhere, bills paid and unpaid, letters answered and unanswered, tax returns, pamphlets, leaflets. If by mistake we left the door open on a windy day, we came back to find papers flapping through the air like frightened birds. Efficient only in that she managed eventually to conclude every task she began, it never seemed possible to outsiders that by Mother's methods anything whatever could be accomplished. In an attempt to keep order elsewhere she made her own room the clearing house into which the rest of us put everything: things to be given away, things to be mended, things to be stored, things to be treasured, things to be returned; even things to be thrown out. By the end of the year, the room resembled an obsolescence dump. And no one could help her; the chaos of her life was as personal as an act of creation. One might as well try to finish another person's poem.

As the years passed, Mother rushed around more hectically. And although Bea and I had married and were not at home any more, except at holiday time and for occasional weekends, Linda was noisier than the two of us put together had been, and for every follower we had brought home she brought twenty. The house was never still. Now that we were reduced to being visitors, we watched Mother's tension mount to vertigo, knowing that, like a spinning top, she could not rest till she fell. But now at the smallest pretext Father Hugh would call in the doctor and Mother would be put on the mail boat and dispatched to London. For it was essential that she get far enough away to make phoning home every night prohibitively costly.

Unfortunately, the thought of departure often drove a spur into her and she redoubled her effort to achieve order in her affairs. She would stay up until the early hours ransacking her desk. To her, as always, the shortest parting entailed a preparation as for death. And as if her end was at hand, we would all be summoned, to be given last minute instructions, although she never got time to speak a word to us, because five minutes before departure she would still be attempting to reply to letters that were the acquisition of weeks and would have taken whole days to answer.

'Don't you know the taxi is at the door, Vera?' Father Hugh would say, running his hand through his grey hair and looking very dishevelled himself. She had him at times as distracted as herself. 'You can't do any more. You'll have to leave the rest till you come back.'

'I can't, I can't!' Mother would cry. 'I'll have to cancel my plans.'

One day, Father Hugh opened the lid of her case, which was strapped up in the hall, and with a swipe of his arm he cleared all the papers on the top of the desk pell-mell into the suitcase. 'You can sort them on the boat,' he said, 'or the train to London.'

Thereafter, Mother's luggage always included an empty case to hold the unfinished papers on her desk. And years afterwards a steward on the Irish Mail told us she was a familiar figure, working away at letters and bills nearly all the way from Holyhead to Euston. 'She usually gave it up about Rugby or Crewe,' he said. 'She'd get talking to someone in the compartment.' He smiled. 'There was one day coming down the corridor of the train I was just in time to see her close up the window with a guilty look. I didn't say anything, but I think she'd emptied those papers of hers out the window.'

Quite likely. When we were children, even a few hours away from us gave her composure. And in two weeks or less, when she'd come home, the well of her spirit would be freshened. We'd hardly know her, her step so light, her eye so bright, and her love and patience once more freely flowing. But in no time at all the house would fill up once more with the noise and confusion of too many people and too many animals, and again we'd be fighting our corner with cats and dogs, bats, mice, bees and even wasps. 'Don't kill it!' Mother would cry if we raised a hand to an angry wasp. 'Just catch it, dear, and put it outside. Open the window and let it fly away!' But even this treatment could at times be deemed too harsh. 'Wait a minute. Close the window!' she'd cry. 'It's too cold outside. It will die. That's why it came in, I suppose. Oh dear, what will we do?' Life would be going full blast again.

There was only one place Mother found rest. When she was at breaking point and fit to fall, she'd go out into the garden, not to sit or stroll around but to dig, to drag up weeds, to move great clumps of corms or rhizomes, or indeed quite frequently to haul huge rocks from one place to another. She was always laying down a path, building a dry wall, or making compost heaps as high as hills. However jaded she might be going out, when dark forced her in at last her step had a spring of a daisy. So if she did not succeed in defining happiness to our satisfaction, we could see that whatever it was, she possessed it to the full when she was in her garden.

I said as much one Sunday when Bea and I had dropped round for the afternoon. Father Hugh was with us again. 'It's an unthinking happiness, though,' he cavilled. We were standing at the drawing-room window, looking out to where in the fading light we could see Mother on her knees weeding in the long border that stretched from the house right down to the woods. 'I wonder how she'd take it if she were stricken down and had to give up that heavy work,' he said. Was he perhaps a little jealous of how she could stoop and bend? He himself had begun to use a stick. I was often a little jealous of her myself, because although I was married and had children of my own, I had married young and felt the weight of living as heavy as a weight of years. 'She doesn't take enough care of herself,' Father Hugh said sadly. 'Look at her out there with nothing under her knees to protect her from the damp ground.' It was almost too dim for us to see her, but even in the drawing room it was chilly. 'She should not be let stay out there after the sun goes down.'

'Just you try to get her in then,' said Linda, who had come into the room in time to hear him. 'Don't you know by now that what would kill another person only seems to make Mother thrive?'

Father Hugh shook his head again. 'You seem to forget it's not younger she's getting.' He fidgeted and fussed, and several times went to the window to stare out apprehensively. He was really getting quite elderly.

'Come and sit down, Father Hugh,' Bea said, and to take his mind off Mother she turned on the light and blotted out the garden. Instead of seeing through the window, we saw into it as into a mirror, and there between the flower-laden tables and the lamps it was ourselves we saw moving vaguely. Like Father Hugh, we, too, were waiting for her to come in before we called an end to the day.

'Oh, this is ridiculous!' Father Hugh cried at last. 'She'll have to listen to reason.' And going over to the window he threw it open. 'Vera! Vera!' he called, sternly, so sternly that, more intimate than an endearment, his tone shocked us. 'She didn't hear me,' he said, turning back blinking at us in the lighted room. 'I'm going out to get her.' And in a minute he was gone from the room. As he ran down the garden path, we stared at each other, astonished; his step, like his voice, was the step of a lover. 'I'm coming, Vera!' he cried.

Although she never failed to answer him when he called, whatever about us, Mother had not moved. In the whole-hearted way she did everything, she was bent down close to the ground. It wasn't the light only that was dimming; her eyesight also was failing too, I thought, as instinctively I followed Father Hugh.

But halfway down the path I stopped. I had seen something he had not seen. Mother's hand that appeared to support itself in a forked branch of an old tree-peony she had planted as a bride, was not in fact gripping it but impaled upon it. And the hand that appeared to be grubbing in the clay in fact was sunk into the soft mould. 'Mother!' I screamed, and I ran forward, but when I reached her I covered my face with my hands. 'Oh Father Hugh,' I cried. 'Is she dead?'

It was Bea who answered, hysterically. 'She is! She is!' she cried, and she began to pound Father Hugh on the back with her fists, as if his pessimistic words had made this happen.

But Mother was not dead. And at first the doctor even offered hope of her pulling through. But from the moment Father Hugh lifted her up to carry her into the house we ourselves had no hope, seeing how effortlessly he, who was not strong, could carry her. When he put her down on her bed, her head hardly creased the pillow.

Mother lived for four hours. Like the days of her life, those four hours were packed tight with concern and anxiety. Partly conscious, partly delirious, she seemed to think the counterpane was her desk, and she scrabbled her fingers upon it as if trying to sort out a muddle of bills and correspondence. No longer indifferent now, we listened, anguished, to the distracted cries that had all our lifetime been so familiar to us. 'Oh, where is it? Where is it? I had it a minute ago. Where on earth did I put it?'

'Vera, Vera stop worrying,' Father Hugh pleaded, but she waved him away and went on sifting through the sheets as if they were sheets of paper. 'Oh, Vera,' he begged. 'Listen to me! Do you not know – '

Before he could say what he was going to say Bea pushed between them. 'You're not to tell her!' she commanded. 'Why frighten her?'

'But it ought not to frighten her,' said Father Hugh. 'This is what I was always afraid would happen, that she'd be frightened when it came to the end.'

At that moment, as if to vindicate him, Mother's hands fell idle on the coverlet, palm upward and empty. And turning her head she stared at each of us in turn, beseechingly. 'I cannot face it,' she whispered. 'I can't. I can't. I can't.'

'Oh, my God!' Bea said, and she started to cry.

'Vera. For God's sake listen to me!' Father Hugh cried, and pressing his face to hers, as close as a kiss, he kept whispering to her, trying to cast into the dark tunnel before her the powerful light of his own faith.

But it seemed to us that Mother must already be looking into God's exigent eyes. 'I can't!' she cried again. 'I can't face it.'

Then her mind came back from the stark world of the spirit to the world where her body was still detained, but even that world was now a whirling kaleidoscope of things which only she could see. Suddenly her eyes focused, and, catching at Father Hugh, she pulled herself up a little and pointed to something we could not see. 'What will be done with them?' Her voice was anxious. 'They ought to be put in water anyway,' she said, and, leaning over the edge of the bed, she pointed to the floor. 'Don't step on them,' she said sharply. Then, more sharply still, she addressed us all. 'Have them sent to the public ward,' she said peremptorily. 'Don't let that nun take them, she'll only put them on the altar. And God doesn't want them. He made them for us, not for Himself.'

It was the familiar rhetoric that all her life had characterized her utterances. For a moment we were mystified. Then Bea gasped. 'The daffodils!' she cried. 'Don't you remember? The day Father died.' And over Bea's face came the light that had so often blazed over Mother's. Leaning across the bed, she pushed Father Hugh aside. And, putting out her hands, she held Mother's face between her palms as tenderly as if it were the face of a child. 'It's all right, Mother. You don't have to face it. It's over.' Then she who had so fiercely forbade Father Hugh to do so blurted out the truth. 'You've finished with this world, Mother,' she said, and, confident that her tidings were joyous, her voice was strong.

Mother made the last effort of her life and grasped at Bea's meaning. She let out a sigh, and, closing her eyes, she sank back, and this time her head sank so deep into the pillow it seemed that it would have been dented had it been a pillow of stone.

MAEVE BRENNAN

'The Morning after the Big Fire'

From the time I was almost five until I was almost eighteen, we lived in a small house in a part of Dublin called Ranelagh. On our street, all of the houses were of red brick and had small back gardens, part cement and part grass, separated from one another by low stone walls over which, when we first moved in, I was unable to peer, although in later years I seem to remember looking over them quite easily, so I suppose they were about five feet high. All of the gardens had a common end wall, which was, of course, very long, since it stretched the whole length of our street. Our street was called an avenue, because it was blind at one end, the farthest end from us. It was a short avenue, twenty-six houses on one side and twenty-six on the other. We were No. 48, and only four houses from the main road, Ranelagh Road, on which trams and buses and all kinds of cars ran, making a good deal of noisy traffic.

Beyond the end wall of our garden lay a large tennis club, and sometimes in the summer, especially when the tournaments were on, my little sister and I used to perch in an upstairs back window and watch the players in their white dresses and white flannels, and hear their voices calling the scores. There was a clubhouse, but we couldn't see it. Our view was partly obstructed by a large garage building that leaned against the end wall of our garden and the four other gardens between us and Ranelagh Road. A number of people who lived on our avenue kept their cars in the garage, and the people who came to play tennis parked their cars there. It was a very busy place, the garage, and I had never been in there, although we bought our groceries in a shop that was connected with it. The shop fronted on Ranelagh Road, and the shop and the garage were the property of a red-faced, gangling man and his fat, pink-haired wife, the McRorys. On summer afternoons, when my sister and I went around to the shop to buy little paper cups of yellow water ice, some of the players would be there, refreshing themselves with ices and also with bottles of lemonade.

Early one summer morning, while it was still dark, I heard my father's voice, sounding very excited, outside the door of the room in which I slept. I was about eight. My little sister slept in the same room with me. 'McRory's is on fire!' my father was saying. He had been awakened by the red glare of the flames against his window. He threw on some clothes and hurried off to see what was going on, and my mother let us look at the fire from a back window, the same window from which we were accustomed to view the tennis matches. It was a really satisfactory fire, with leaping flames, thick, pouring smoke, and a steady roar of destruction, broken by crashes as parts of the roof collapsed. My mother wondered if they had managed to save the cars, and this made us all look at the burning building with new interest and with enormous awe as we imagined the big shining cars being eaten up by the galloping fire. It was very exciting. My mother hurried us back to our front bedroom, but even there the excitement could be felt, with men calling to one another on the street and banging their front doors after them as they raced off to see the fun. Since she had decided there was no danger to our house, my mother tucked us firmly back into bed, but I could not sleep, and as soon as it grew light, I dressed myself and trotted downstairs. My father had many stories to tell. The garage was a ruin, he said, but the shop was safe. Many cars had been destroyed. No one knew how the fire had started. Some of the fellows connected with the garage had been very brave, dashing in to rescue as many cars as they could reach. The part of the building that overlooked our garden appeared charred, frail, and empty because it no longer had much in the way of a roof and its insides were gone. The air smelled very burnt.

I wandered quietly out onto the avenue, which was deserted because the children had not come out to play and it was still too early for the men to be going to work. I walked up the avenue in the direction of the blind end. The people living there were too far from the garage to have been disturbed by the blaze. A woman whose little boy was a friend of mine came to her door to take in the milk.

'McRory's was burnt down last night!' I cried to her.

'What's that?' she said, very startled.

'Burnt to the ground,' I said. 'Hardly a wall left standing. A whole lot of people's cars burnt up, too.'

She looked back over her shoulder in the direction of her kitchen, which, since all the houses were identical, was in the same position as our kitchen. 'Jim!' she cried. 'Do you hear this? McRory's was burnt down last night. The whole place. Not a stick left . . . We slept right through it,' she said to me, looking as though just the thought of that heavy sleep puzzled and unsettled her.

Her husband hurried out to stand beside her, and I had to tell the whole story again. He said he would run around to McRory's and take a look, and this enraged me, because I wasn't allowed around there and I knew that when he came back he would be a greater authority than I. However, there was no time to lose. Other people were opening their front doors by now, and I wanted everyone to hear the news from me.

'Did you hear the news?' I shouted, to as many as I could catch up with, and, of course, once I had their ear, they were fascinated by what I had to tell. One or two of the men, hurrying away to work, charged past me with such forbiddingly closed faces that I was afraid to approach them, and they continued in their ignorance down toward Ranelagh Road, causing me dreadful anguish, because I knew that before they could board their tram or their bus, some officious busybody would be sure to treat them to my news. Then one woman, to whom I always afterward felt friendly, called down to me from her front bedroom window. 'What's that you were telling Mrs Pearce?' she asked me, in a loud whisper.

'Oh, just that McRory's was burnt to the ground last night. Nearly all the cars burnt up, too. Hardly anything left, my father says.' By this time I was being very offhand.

'You don't tell me,' she said, making a delighted face, and the next thing I knew, she was opening her front door, more eager for news than anybody.

However, my hour of glory was short. The other children came out – some of them were actually allowed to go around and view the wreckage – and soon the fire was mine no longer, because there were others walking around who knew more about it than I did. I pretended to lose interest, although I was glad when someone – not my father – gave me a lump of twisted, blackened tin off one of the cars.

The tennis clubhouse had been untouched, and that afternoon the players appeared, as bright and immaculate in their snowy flannels and linens as though the smoking garage yard and the lines of charred cars through which they had picked their way to the courts could never interfere with them or impress them. It was nearing tournament time, and a man was painting the platform on which the judge was to sit and from which a lady in a wide hat and a flowered chiffon dress would present cups and medals to the victors among the players. Now, in the sunshine, they lifted their rackets and started to play, and their intent and formal cries mingled with the hoarse shouts of the men at work in the dark shambles of the garage. My little sister and I, watching from our window, could imagine that the rhythmical thud of the ball against the rackets coincided with the unidentifiable sounds we heard from the wreckage, which might have been groans or shrieks as the building, unable to recover from the fire, succumbed under it.

It was not long before the McRorys put up another garage, made of silvery corrugated-metal stuff that looked garish and glaring against our garden wall; it cut off more of our view than the old building had. The new garage looked very hard and lasting, as unlikely to burn as a pot or a kettle. The beautiful green courts that had always seemed from our window to roll comfortably in the direction of the old wooden building now seemed to have turned and to be rolling away into the distance, as though they did not like the unsightly new structure and would have nothing to do with it.

My father said the odds were all against another fire there, but I remembered that fine dark morning, with all the excitement and my own importance, and I longed for another just like it. This time, however, I was determined to discover the blaze before my father did, and I watched the garage closely, as much of it as I could see, for signs that it might be getting ready to go up in flames, but I was disappointed. It stood, and still was standing, ugly as ever, when we left the house years later. Still, for a long time I used to think that if some child should steal around there with a match one night and set it all blazing again, I would never blame her, as long as she let me be the first with the news.

IRIS MURDOCH

from *The Red and the Green*

2

'What's on at the Abbey?'

'Some stuff by W. B. Yeats.'

'The Countess Cathleen man? I don't think we feel strong enough for that, do we. What about the Gaiety?'

'D'Oyly Carte. I believe it's *The Yeomen of the Guard.*'

'Well, we might go there. Only don't forget my furniture is arriving at Claresville on Thursday.'

It was about half an hour later and tea was nearly over. They were sitting round the low wickerwork table in the conservatory, while outside the garden was being caressed or playfully beaten by the light rain which drifted a little in the breeze from the sea. Rain in Ireland always seemed a different substance from English rain, its drops smaller and more numerous. It seemed now to materialize in the air rather than to fall through it, and, transformed into quick-silver, ran shimmering upon the surface of the trees and plants, to fall with a heavier plop from the dejected palms and the chestnut. This rain, this scene, the pattering on the glass, the smell of the porous concrete floor, never entirely dry, the restless sensation of slightly damp cushions, these things set up for Andrew a long arcade of memories. He shifted uneasily in his basket chair, wondering how long it took to develop rheumatism.

Christopher had lighted his pipe, Frances was sewing, Hilda, without occupation, was sitting very upright as if the organization of the party had suddenly fallen upon her. Her hair, a pale blonde striped with grey, rather scanty and silky, pulled well away from the face and banded by a black velvet ribbon, looked like a neat cap, and she appeared older than her age. Her face, lightly wrinkled or rather perhaps crumpled, was a uniform colour of soft parchmenty gold, and often gave the impression of being weather-beaten or sunburnt, although Hilda in fact shunned the open air. The large straight nose and rather stern dark-blue eyes completed the picture of a person of authority, although an inherent vagueness in Hilda's principles made her in practice a less commanding person than she seemed.

'I'm longing to see your house finished,' said Frances.

'Thank God you didn't buy that crumbling pile at Dundrum,' said Christopher. 'I'd have had to help you keep it upright, and it would have been a full-time job.'

What about me? thought Andrew, with a sudden pang, but then decided that he was being morbid.

'Kathleen said she'd find me a maid. I gather one has to pay ten shillings a week now.'

'And most of them would steal the cross off an ass's back and can't be trusted to cook anything but rashers and eggs!'

'Oh, I'm good at training servants. I had a perfect little jewel in London. And of course I shall have the telephone installed.'

'The telephone is fine here if you only want to talk to the exchange! Have I convinced you on the motor car question?'

'Yes, Christopher. I think after all it would be foolish to buy a motor car just now. There are too many difficulties. I hear Millie has just bought a Panhard. She is so extravagant.'

Andrew knew quite well that his mother was aware that she could not possibly afford a motor car.

'We might think in terms of a pony and trap, though. After all, one must get about. And when the war is over I shall certainly purchase a touring car. Andrew shall learn how to operate it.'

A Vauxhall Prince Henry, thought Andrew dreamily to himself. When the war was over he would have money to spend. It was nice to think that he had a rendezvous in the future with a Vauxhall Prince Henry.

'I think I shall always stick to my bike,' said Christopher. 'The bicycle is the most civilized conveyance known to man. Other forms of transport grow daily more nightmareish. Only the bicycle remains pure in heart.'

'I was very relieved Andrew didn't want to go into the Flying Corps,' said Hilda, speaking as if her son were not present.

'What's on tomorrow, Aunt Hilda?' asked Frances, revealing a long straight row of white teeth as she bit a length of thread off from the spool. Andrew's mother had always been content with this formal mode of address, which increased Andrew's nomenclaturial difficulties with Christopher, since to address him familiarly in Hilda's presence would seem a kind of disloyalty.

'*Tomorrow*, my dear,' said Hilda, with confiding eagerness she always evinced over any social plan, however trivial, 'tomorrow Andrew goes to tea at Blessington Street. I can't manage it, I've *got* to be at Claresville then to see the builder. You'll go with him, won't you?'

'I don't mind,' said Frances. 'I like to watch Cathal growing up. He looks entirely different now every time I see him.'

'He's such a big boy. It's hard to believe he's only fourteen. Children grow up so much more quickly nowadays. You'll go along too, Christopher?'

'Please not. That house depresses me. And Kathleen always makes me feel guilty!'

'I don't see why she should. But the house *is* gloomy, and there's always that curious smell on the stairs. Don't you think Kathleen has become awfully sour and self-absorbed just lately? And so dreadfully pious! Someone told me she goes to chapel every day.'

'She does it to spite Barney,' said Christopher, puffing his pipe, his gaze upon the quietly dripping palm trees.

Hilda, as usual, did not follow up a remark which made reference to her brother's religion. She went on, 'And on *Tuesday*, I know it's a terrible bore, but we *must* go and see Millie, I did promise. She's back from Rathblane now, it's her time for being in town. How do you think Millie is these days, Christopher? Going downhill?'

'Not specially,' said Christopher. 'She's been hunting like a maniac all the winter.'

'She certainly has plenty of energy,' Hilda conceded. 'I sometimes think she really might have been somebody if she'd been born a man.'

'Can't one be somebody if one's born a woman?' asked Frances.

'Well, hardly in that way, dear. Though in plenty of other ways which are just as important,' said Hilda vaguely.

'I think being a woman is like being Irish,' said Frances, putting aside her work and sitting up. At such moments she had an unconscious gesture of pushing back her hair to reveal her large brow. 'Everyone says you're important and nice, but you take second place all the same.'

'Come, come, women have always had Home Rule!' Christopher always jestingly set aside his daughter's sometimes rather ferocious attempts to turn conversation into serious channels.

'The emancipation question is certainly a grave one,' said Hilda. 'I am not at all hostile to the idea myself. But there are so many values – And I'm afraid that your Aunt Millicent's idea of emancipation is wearing trousers and firing a revolver in her own house.'

Christopher laughed. 'That's about it. But one must start somewhere! Will you be coming to Millie's, Frances?'

'No, thanks.'

Andrew had long been aware that Frances did not like Aunt Millicent, but he had never been able to make out why. Among the generalizations about women which passed freely around his regimental mess was one to the effect that women never like each other, since every woman regards every other woman as her rival. Andrew, while attending with interest to all such distillations of worldly wisdom on a subject which was still very mysterious to him, suspected that this one was over-simple. It was true that women, leading more isolated and emptier lives, were naturally, when opportunity offered, more frantically anxious to attract attention and more ruthless in their pursuit of the opposite sex than were men who had, after all, other interests, as well as more chances to know each other in an atmosphere of free fraternal co-operation. Or so it seemed to Andrew, who saw men as inherently dignified animals and women as inherently undignified animals. However, in his own experience, when he had noted a marked dislike of one woman for another there had usually been some reason for this other than the postulated general rivalry.

In the matter of dislike of Aunt Millicent, his mother for instance disliked her out of envy for her title and her money, and because she failed to further Hilda's social ambitions. While Aunt Kathleen disliked her because of Uncle Arthur. Kathleen had it seems been very attached to her brother Arthur and had, rightly or wrongly, felt him to be in some way slighted or belittled by Millie, who was in fact fairly universally said to have married Arthur for rather worldly reasons. Uncle Arthur's early death was also somehow vaguely felt to be Millie's fault. 'Poor Arthur,' Hilda used to say. 'Millie simply ate him. Kathleen never forgave her.' Frances' dislike, which could hardly be put down to loyalty to either Kathleen or Hilda, persons from whom to say the least she felt detached, could perhaps after all be more simply explained as the nervous envy felt by a young girl who, however much she might officially despise such values, recognized in an older person a kind of elegance and glitter which she could never hope to emulate. Or more simply still it might be that Frances had weighed Millie in some spiritual balance and found her wanting. Andrew noted, sometimes a little uneasily, that his fiancée was capable of making quite uncompromising moral judgements.

'I hear there is to be mixed bathing at the Kingstown baths,' said Hilda, pursuing some train of thought concerned with the enormities of the modern world. 'I cannot approve. Not with the bathing costumes people wear nowadays. Frances and I saw a girl at the Ladies Bathing Place at Sandycove who was showing nearly the whole of her legs. Do you remember, Frances?'

Frances smiled. 'She had very pretty legs.'

'I'm sure you have very pretty legs, my dear, but they're nobody's business but your own.'

Andrew, feeling an entirely private amused resentment at this judgement, suddenly found himself catching Christopher's eye. Christopher gave him a faint secretive smile. Distressed, Andrew dropped his gaze and pulled at his moustache. There was something curiously improper about catching Christopher's eye just then. It was almost like an exchange of winks. He felt suddenly mocked and threatened. He could never make Christopher out.

Christopher, perhaps to cover what he had apprehended of Andrew's embarrassment, went on at once, 'In fact nothing may come of the mixed bathing idea. Father Ryan has already protested about it. You and the Holy Romans see eye to eye on this, Hilda.'

'They're certainly very full of themselves these days,' said Hilda, 'protesting against this and demanding that. I expect it's the prospect of Home Rule. "Home Rule will be Rome Rule" may prove but too true. We must prepare ourselves.'

'Indeed,' said Christopher. 'And yet they've opposed it all along the line. It's the Church not the Castle that has really kept this country down. All the great Irish patriots have been Protestants, except for O'Connell. The Church was against the Fenians, against Parnell.'

'Oh well, *Parnell* –' said Hilda. The judgement was vast, vague, crushing.

Andrew here caught the eye of Frances, who was a devotee of the great man thus dismissed. He saw her draw breath to protest, decide not to, and half smile at him as if asking for approval, all in two seconds. He was pleased by the quick little exchange.

His mother was going on, 'I can't understand why recruiting is going so slowly in Ireland. I saw an article about it this morning.'

'I don't think it's going slowly. Irishmen are streaming into the British Army.'

'Well, yes, but so many remain behind. And the *attitude* of people. Last week I heard a man singing a song in German in the public street. And in Clery's yesterday I heard a woman say to another that Germany might win the war. She said it casually as if it were quite an ordinary thing to say!'

Christopher laughed. 'Of course, the English never ever for a second conceive that they can lose a war. It's one of their great strengths.'

'Why do you say "they", Christopher, and not "we"? You're English after all.'

'True, true. But having lived over here for so long I can't help seeing the dear old place a little bit from the outside.'

'Well, I think it's very disloyal to talk in that way about the Germans, as if they could possibly win. After all, England and Ireland are really one country.'

'So the English soldiers evidently think when they sing "It's a long way to Tipperary". But it's always easy for the top dog to extend his sense of identity over his inferiors. It's a different matter for the inferiors to accept the identification.'

'I can't understand this talk about inferiority. No one regards the Irish as inferior. They are loved and welcomed all over the world! And I can't stand this jumped-up Irish patriotism, it's so artificial. English patriotism is another thing. We have Shakespeare and the Magna Carta and the Armada and so on. But Ireland hasn't really had any history to speak of.'

'Your brother would hardly agree with this judgement.'

'I am not impressed by a few moth-eaten saints,' said Hilda with dignity.

'Ireland was a civilized country when England was still barbarous,' said Frances, tossing her hair back.

'My dear Frances, you are parroting your Uncle Barnabas,' said Hilda. 'You know very little about it.'

This, Andrew thought, was probably just. Frances was no scholar, and her views on politics, though often vehement, were extremely confused and discontinuous. Frances had always been very attached to Hilda's brother, and had never associated herself with the scandalized or mocking attitudes of the family towards the convert. Uncle Barnabas and her father between them had been her school and her university, and once for a short while she had helped her uncle with some aspect of his study of the early Irish Church. It was something, she used vaguely to say, about the date of Easter, and more Andrew could not gather. Long aware of a friendship between Frances and 'Barney', Andrew felt an undiminishing jealousy which he recognized to be both unworthy and irrational. He had never for a second been able to take his Uncle Barnabas seriously. While Christopher seemed to him, and rather formidably, a real scholar, he could not imagine Uncle Barnabas's toils as other than childish vanities, and Frances' muddled account of them seemed to confirm the view. 'Barney' shambled on the outskirts of the family caravan, an irredeemable figure of fun.

'And all this nonsense about reviving the Irish language,' Hilda was going on. 'With all due respect to you, Christopher . . .'

'Oh, but I entirely agree with you. Gaelic should be left to us scholars. One should be content to be born to the language of Shakespeare. And in fact the Irish have always written the best English.'

'The Anglo-Irish have.'

'True for you! Those aristocrats who think themselves superior both to the English and to the Irish!'

'And when you think of all the money we've poured into this country . . . The Irish farmers have never been better off.'

'Not everyone would agree with that,' said Christopher. 'I read an article in the *Irish Review* only yesterday saying that Alsace-Lorraine was far better off under German rule than Ireland under English rule.'

'That couldn't possibly be true. It's just Irish spite. I wonder why people think the Irish have such sunny characters? Don't they realize there's a war on? Now they've been promised Home Rule and everything they want they ought to be grateful.'

'Perhaps they don't feel they've got much to be grateful for,' said Frances. 'A million people died in the potato famine.'

'My dear Frances, that was regrettable but has nothing whatever to do with the present situation. You argue like a street-corner orator. There may have been some unfortunate things in the past, but they're all long ago now, and I'm sure England never purposely hurt Ireland, it was just economics.'

'There's something in what Hilda says,' said Christopher. 'Ireland had several bits of sheer historical bad luck, and one of them was that the potato famine coincided with the hey-day of Manchester free trade. In the eighteenth century England would have relieved the famine.'

'What were the other bits of bad luck, sir?' asked Andrew.

'Eighteen hundred and one and nineteen fourteen. It was very unfortunate that this war started just before Home Rule went through. Remember Churchill saying that if Belfast wouldn't submit to Home Rule the British fleet would teach them to? The Liberals were really exasperated with the North. A year or two of enforced religious toleration and everything would have settled down. Whereas now we shall have endless trouble. But the Act of Union was the big Irish disaster. English government in the eighteenth century was the most civilized government in history. Fear of the French put an end to eighteenth-century civilization. Perhaps it put an end to civilization. It certainly put an end to the Irish parliament. Ireland was really becoming an independent country, the great landowners thought of themselves as Irish. And of course that began to scare the English stiff. Hence the Act of Union and all our tears.'

'You think Ireland might have had a quite different history if it hadn't been for that?' said Andrew.

'I do. There was a real Irish culture at that time, a culture with its own brilliance and with international ties. Do you remember that monument I once showed you, Hilda, in St Patrick's Cathedral, which talks about "that exalted refinement which in the best period of our history characterized the Irish gentleman"? The date of that is twelve years after the Act of Union. Oh, they knew what had happened all right. If the Irish parliament had survived, Ireland wouldn't be the provincial backwater it is today.'

'Home Rule will make it even more provincial,' said Hilda.

'I fear it may,' said Christopher. 'And idiots like Pearse don't help when they invent a romantic Irish tradition which just ignores the English ascendancy. Ireland's real past *is* the ascendancy. Ireland should turn back to the eighteenth century, not to the Middle Ages. Goldsmith and Sterne would turn in their graves to hear the nonsense about Holy Ireland that's talked nowadays.'

'All that can't be quite right,' said Frances. 'I mean, you seem to be talking as if Ireland were just the grand people. You remember what Grattan said about *we* are not the people of Ireland. It's everyone having always been so poor that's awful. Compare the Irish countryside with the English countryside. There are no real towns and villages in Ireland. There are the same little featureless houses or hovels everywhere, and then nothing else till you come to the country mansions and the cathedrals of Christ the King.'

'Catholicism is the curse of this country,' said Hilda. 'If only Ireland had followed England at the Reformation.'

Christopher laughed. 'You mean the Irish, having rejected the most civilized religion in the world, Anglicanism, deserved their fate? That's arguable! But they were just that much farther away, and the Fitzgeralds and the O'Neills went on being Catholics and being warlords in a quiet way. As for Ireland being the grand people, it's unfortunately true that until lately history has been made by the grand people. Frances is really right, though. What this country lacks is a yeomanry. The Irish peasant remained primitive and remained poor.'

'Why?' asked Andrew.

'It's largely the same answer. No parliament. Think how important parliament was

669

in England from the very start. Ireland remained a country of overlords. The big estates were political prizes. Ireland was always a property being handed about. An insecure ruling class without a parliament is soon demoralized. And ever since the Irish princes sold out to Henry the Second there's been collusion between Irish gentry and English power. "Her faithless sons betrayed her", as the song says. Ireland's only hope of pulling herself out of feudalism was to develop a steady ruling class with its own culture and its own civilized organs of power, and that began to be possible in the eighteenth century, only the Act of Union wrecked it all just as it was becoming a reality. And by eighteen-fifteen standards in English political life had declined so much, England was so gross with triumph, there was no help for Ireland there.'

'So it looks as if the French are the villains of Europe,' said Andrew. 'A view I've long held!'

'Why do people in Ireland always talk about *history*?' said Hilda. 'My head's always swimming with dates when I'm over here. English people don't talk about English history all the time.'

'They don't have to ask the question, What went wrong?' said Christopher. 'For them nothing went wrong.'

'Well, I'm afraid Ireland is a thoroughly self-centred country.'

'All countries are, my dear Hilda. Only selfishness shows more in the unfortunate.'

'And now there's all this Trade Union nonsense and stopping the trams. It's so demoralizing. And all this playing at soldiers and marching about in green uniforms and so on. Even Barney got tied up with it at one time. Something ought to be done about it. People ought not to play at war when there's a real war on.'

Christopher blew out a curl of blue smoke and watched it rise to where the rain was running steadily and now almost silently along the glass roof of the conservatory. A soft salty mist was filling the garden, penetrating the curtain of the rain. There was a raw smell of the sea. Christopher spoke now with a more deliberate slowness, like one who feels he has been too vehement or is afraid of becoming so. 'After the Ulster Volunteers came into existence, and especially after they were armed, it was inevitable that there would be a similar movement down here. After all, it's the right of free men to prepare themselves to defend their freedom.'

'The British Navy will defend their freedom. It always has done!'

Andrew, who sensed that both Christopher and Frances were getting a bit tired of hearing from his mother, interposed in his most objective and manly manner, 'Wasn't it rather a mistake, sir, for the British Army not to recognize the Volunteers in the South? I gather General Mahon recommended it to Kitchener. Especially after the Ulster Volunteers were formed into a division.'

'Yes,' said Christopher. 'You'll find the Red Hand of Ulster in the British Army, but there's no sign of the Harp.'

'Kitchener is afraid to arm the Irish,' said Frances.

'I'm sure he's no such thing,' said Hilda. 'He told Mr Redmond and Lord Carson that he'd like to knock their heads together.'

'Do you agree,' said Andrew, adopting Christopher's slow tempo, 'with the people who say that Redmond ought to have demanded immediate Home Rule in exchange for Ireland's participation in the war?'

Christopher laughed. 'Good heavens no. I'm not an extremist. Home Rule is a certainty after the war. Or else a hundred thousand men back from the army will know the reason why!'

'Is it conceivable that the Castle would be so insane as to try to disarm the Volunteers?'

'No, no. The English will behave correctly. After all, people are watching them.'

'So you agree with Casement that the Irish question is an international question now, and not a local British matter any more?'

'Oh no! The notion of "joining Europe" is just another illusion. Poor old Ireland will always be a backwater. Imagine the most god-forsaken hole in the world and go on several hundred miles into the unknown and there you'll find Ireland!'

'I can't hear calmly about that man Casement,' said Hilda. 'To go over to the Germans and try to stab England in the back like that just when she's up against it . . .'

'It's the old story. "England's difficulty is Ireland's opportunity." Casement belongs to a classical tradition. And in a way I can't help admiring the fellow. It must be a lonely bitter business out there in Germany. He's a brave man and a patriot. He does it purely for love of Ireland. To love Ireland so much, to love anything so much, even if he's wrong-headed, is somehow noble.'

'He does it for love of gold, you may be sure,' said Hilda. 'It's the traitor mentality.'

Christopher thought for a moment. 'I think that word "traitor" ought to be removed from the language. It's just a muddled term of abuse. Casement's crime, or mistake, if it is one, is much more complex than anything that blunted word could name.'

'So you don't think there'll be any trouble in Ireland?' asked Andrew quickly before his mother could expostulate further.

'Trouble with the Sinn Feiners? No, I don't. And what could they make it with, hurley sticks? I was talking to Eoin MacNeill's brother about it all the other day. Eoin has quite returned to his Gaelic studies. He was never a firebrand leader in any case. The Volunteers are really just like Boy Scouts and James Connolly's lot, the Irish Citizen Army, are ten men and a dog. If the Germans actually invaded Ireland, a few hotheads might help them, but with the blockade that's an impossibility. And anyway, as I say, what trouble could the Irish make, even if they wanted to? They've got no arms and they're not insane. I saw a squad of Volunteers drilling the other day with ten-foot pikes. It was pathetic!'

Andrew laughed. 'Don't tell the Sinn Feiners, but our reserve squadron at Longford only has about a hundred rifles, and half of them are DP, drill purposes only. They'd probably explode if you tried to fire them!'

'Your lot at Longford had better look out then,' said Christopher. 'That place is a hot-bed of disaffection.'

'You shouldn't say things like that, Andrew,' said his mother. 'You never know who's listening.'

Andrew felt justly rebuked, and recalled suddenly to mind a rather unpleasant incident which had marked his arrival in Ireland. The one really constructive thing which he had managed to do when in France had been to get hold of a magnificent Italian rifle with telescopic sights. This extremely precious object had somehow or other disappeared at some point between the mail boat and Finglas. Christopher's gardener had sworn that the rifle had simply not been with the luggage when it arrived from the boat. Andrew now of course realized that it had been insane of him to take his eyes off it for a second in this gun-hungry country. Some time later he overheard Christopher saying casually that his gardener was connected with the Citizen Army. Andrew thought he would probably never know the truth of the matter: but he felt the disappearance of the rifle as a hostile act, upsetting and menacing.

'No, no,' Christopher was going on. 'I don't exactly see Ireland as explosive material. I agree with Bulmer Hobson. Ireland is a damp bog which will yet extinguish many a flaming torch and gunpowder barrel! The fact is the Irish are far more sentimental and emotional even than one imagines. It all ends in talk. This morning, for instance, when I was down in town I witnessed a curious little scene. I meant to tell you of it earlier. I was passing near Liberty Hall, you know, the Transport and General Workers' Union place, and I saw that some sort of ceremony was going on. There was a big crowd, and a girl in the Citizen Army uniform was climbing on the roof and unfurling a flag. It was a green flag with the Irish harp on it. And the ICA men were all drawn up in ranks presenting arms and the bugles were blowing and the pipe bands were playing and then everyone started cheering, and do you know, quite a lot of people in the crowd had tears in their eyes.'

Andrew was disturbed by this account; and he felt that Christopher had perhaps been more interested than he pretended to be. Frances had put down her sewing.

'But what did it mean?' said Andrew.

'Nothing. That's my point. The Irish are so used to personifying Ireland as a tragic female, any patriotic stimulus produces an overflow of sentiment at once.'

'"Did you see an old woman going down the path?" "I did not, but I saw a young girl, and she had the walk of a queen."'

'Precisely, Frances. St Teresa's Hall nearly fell down when Yeats first came out with that stuff. Though in fact if you recited the Dublin telephone directory in this town with enough feeling you'd have people shedding tears!'

'Well, I think it ought to be stopped,' said Hilda. 'I can't imagine how they can do it, with the town full of wounded soldiers, you'd think they'd be ashamed. And I'm very surprised indeed that Pat Dumay hasn't enlisted. I really must have a word about it with his mother. An able-bodied young fellow like that ought to be longing to get out to the Front. I have the impression that he's becoming a rather disagreeable young man.'

'I shouldn't say anything to Kathleen if I were you,' said Christopher. 'And I'd advise you not to show your opinion in any way to Pat himself.' As he said this, Christopher looked quickly at Andrew.

Andrew felt an immediate pang of annoyance and the familiar sense of a threat. As if he would be such a fool as to bait his cousin for not having enlisted.

'Well, you may be right,' said Hilda, getting up. The sea mist now shrouded the garden and enveloped the house, curling damply in through the interstices of the conservatory. The rain had stopped, but water now hung on the interior of the glass in rows of glittering beads which would suddenly start rolling, coalesce, and fall with a small splash on to the stiff linen tablecloth. Frances was packing up the tea-things. As they began to drift in towards the drawing-room, Andrew heard his mother saying to Christopher, 'I've been meaning to ask you for such a long time. What *exactly* did Wolfe Tone do?'

BENEDICT KIELY

'Homes on the Mountain'

The year I was twelve my father, my mother, my brother and myself had our Christmas dinner in the house my godmother's husband had built high up on the side of Dooish Mountain, when he and she came home to Ireland from Philadelphia.

That was a great godmother. She had more half-crowns in her patch pockets than there were in the Bank of England and every time she encountered me which, strategically, I saw was pretty often, it rained half-crowns. Those silver showers made my friend Lanty and myself the most popular boy bravados in our town. A curious thing was, though, that while we stood bobby-dazzler caramels, hazelnut chocolate, ice cream, cigarettes and fish and chips by the ton to our sycophants, we ourselves bought nothing but song-books. Neither of us could sing a note.

We had a splendid, patriotic taste in song-books, principally because the nearest newsagent's shop, kept by an old spinster in Devlin Street, had a window occupied by a sleeping tomcat, two empty tin boxes, bundles of pamphlets yellowed by exposure to the light, and all members of a series called Irish Fireside Songs. The collective title appealed by its warm cosiness. The little books were classified into Sentimental, Patriot's Treasury, Humorous and Convivial, and Smiles and Tears. Erin, we knew from Tom Moore and from excruciating music lessons at school, went wandering around with a tear and a smile blended in her eye. Because even to ourselves our singing was painful, we read together, sitting in the sunshine on the steps that led up to my father's house, such gems of the Humorous and Convivial as: 'When I lived in Sweet Ballinacrazy, dear, the girls were all bright as a daisy, dear.' Or turning to the emerald-covered Patriot's Treasury we intoned: 'We've men from the Nore, from the Suir and the Shannon, let the tyrant come forth, we'll bring force against force.'

Perhaps, unknown to ourselves, we were affected with the nostalgia that had brought my godmother and her husband back from the comfort of Philadelphia to the bleak side of Dooish Mountain. It was a move that my mother, who was practical and who had never been far enough from Ireland to feel nostalgia, deplored.

'Returned Americans,' she would say, 'are lost people. They live between two worlds. Their heads are in the clouds. Even the scrawny, black-headed sheep – not comparing the human being and the brute beast – know by now that Dooish is no place to live.'

'And if you must go back to the land,' she said, 'let it be the land, not rocks, heather and grey fields no bigger than pocket handkerchiefs. There's Cantwell's fine place beside the town going up for auction. Seventy acres of land, a palace of a dwelling-house, outhouses would do credit to the royal family, every modern convenience and more besides.'

For reasons that had nothing to do with prudence or sense Lanty and myself thought the Cantwell place an excellent idea. There were crab-apple trees of the most amazing fertility scattered all along the hedgerows on the farm; a clear gravel stream twisted through it; there were flat pastures made for football and, behind the house, an orchard that not even the most daring buccaneer of our generation had ever succeeded in robbing.

But there were other reasons – again nostalgic reasons – why my godmother's husband who was the living image of Will Rogers would build nowhere in Ireland except on the rough, wet side of Dooish, and there, on the site of the old home where he had spent his boyhood, the house went up. There wasn't a building job like it since the building of the Tower of Babel.

'Get a good sensible contractor from the town,' said my mother, 'not drunken Dan Redmond from the mountain who couldn't build a dry closet.'

But my godmother's husband had gone to school with Dan Redmond. They had been barefooted boys together and that was that, and there was more spent, according to my mother, on malt whisky to entertain Dan, his tradesmen and labourers, than would have built half New York. To make matters worse it was a great season for returned Americans and every one of them seemed to have known my godmother and her husband in Philadelphia. They came in their legions to watch the building, to help pass the bottle and to proffer advice. The acknowledged queen of this gathering of souls fluttering between two worlds was my Aunt Brigid, my mother's eldest sister. She was tiny and neat, precise in her speech, silver-haired, glittering with rimless spectacles and jet-black beads. In the States she had acquired a mania for euchre, a passion for slivers of chicken jelled in grey-green soup, a phonograph with records that included a set of the favourite songs of Jimmy Walker, and the largest collection of snapshots ever carried by pack mule or public transport out of Atlantic City.

Then there was a born American – a rarity in our parts in those days – a young man and a distant relative. Generous and jovial, he kissed every woman, young or old, calling them cousin or aunt; but it was suspected among wise observers that he never once in the course of his visit was able to see the Emerald Isle clearly. For the delegation, headed by my Aunt Brigid, that met him in Dublin set him straight away on the drink and when he arrived to view the building site – it was one of the few sunny days of that summer – he did so sitting on the dickey seat of a jaunting car and waving in each hand a bottle of whisky. The builder and his men and the haymakers in June meadows left their work to welcome him, and Ireland, as the song says, was Ireland through joy and through tears.

Altogether it was a wet season: the whisky flowed like water, the mist was low over the rocks and heather of Dooish and the moors of Loughfresha and Cornavara, the mountain runnels were roaring torrents. But miraculously the building was done; the returned Americans with the exception of Aunt Brigid, my godmother and her husband, went westwards again in the fall; and against all my mother's advice on the point of health, the couple from Philadelphia settled in for late November. The house-warming was fixed for Christmas Day.

*

'Dreamers,' my mother said. 'An American apartment on the groundwalls of an old cabin. Living in the past. Up where only a brave man would build a shooting lodge. For all they know or care there could be wolves still on the mountain. Magazines and gewgaws and chairs too low to sit on. With the rheumatism the mountain'll give them, they'll never bend their joints to sit down so low.'

Since the damp air had not yet brought its rheumatism we all sat down together in the house that was the answer to the exile's dream. Lamplight shone on good silver and Belfast linen. My godmother's man was proud to the point of tears.

'Sara Alice,' he said to my mother.

Content, glass in hand, he was more than ever like Will Rogers.

'Sara Alice,' he said. 'My mother, God rest her, would be proud to see this day.'

Practicality momentarily abandoned, my mother, moist-eyed and sipping sherry, agreed.

'Tommy,' he said to my father, 'listen to the sound of the spring outside.'

We could hear the wind, the voices of the runnels, the spring pouring clear and cool from a rainspout driven into a rock-face.

'As far as I recollect that was the first sound my ears ever heard, and I heard it all my boyhood, and I could hear it still in Girard Avenue, Philadelphia. But the voices of children used to be part of the sound of the spring. Seven of us, and me to be the youngest and the last alive. When my mother died and my father took us all to the States we didn't know when we were going away whether to leave the door open or closed. We left it open in case a travelling man might pass, needing shelter. We knocked gaps in the hedges and stone walls so as to give the neighbours' cattle the benefit of commonage and the land the benefit of the cow dung. But we left the basic lines of the walls so that nobody could forget our name or our claim to this part of the mountain.'

'In Gartan, in Donegal,' said my father, 'there's a place called the Flagstone of Loneliness where Saint Colmcille slept the night before he left Ireland under sentence of banishment. The exiles in that part used to lie down there the day before they sailed and pray to the saint to be preserved from the pangs of homesickness.'

My Aunt Brigid piped in a birdlike voice a bit of an exile song that was among her treasured recordings: 'A strange sort of sigh seems to come from us all as the waves hide the last glimpse of old Donegal.'

'Our American wake was held in Aunt Sally O'Neill's across the glen,' said my godmother's husband. 'Red Owen Gormley lilted for the dancers when the fiddlers were tired. He was the best man of his time at the mouth music.'

'He was also,' said my father, 'the first and last man I knew who could make a serviceable knife, blade and haft, out of a single piece of hardwood. I saw him do it, myself and wild Martin Murphy who was with me in the crowd of sappers who chained these mountains for the 1911 Ordnance Survey map. Like most of us, Martin drank every penny and on frosty days he would seal the cracks in his shoes with butter – a trick I never saw another man use. It worked too.'

'Aunt Sally's two sons were there at our American wake,' said my godmother's husband. 'Thady that was never quite right in the head and, you remember, Tommy, couldn't let a woman in the market or a salmon in the stream alone. John, the elder brother, was there with Bessy from Cornavara that he wooed for sixty years and never, I'd say, even kissed.'

The old people were silently laughing. My brother, older than myself, was on the fringe of the joke. As my godmother came and went I sniffed fine cooking. I listened to the mountain wind and the noise of the spring and turned the bright pages of an American gardening magazine. Here were rare blooms would never grow on Dooish Mountain.

'All dead now I suppose,' my father said to end the laughing.

'Bessy's dead now,' said my Aunt Brigid. 'Two years ago. As single as the day she was born. Like many another Irishman John wasn't overgiven to matrimony. But in the village of Crooked Bridge below, the postman told me that John and Thady are still alive in the old house on Loughfresha. Like pigs in a sty, he said. Pigs in a sty. And eight thousand pounds each, according to all accounts, in the Munster and Leinster Bank in the town.'

'God help us,' said my mother. 'I recall that house as it was when Aunt Sally was alive. It was beautiful.'

My father was looking out of the window, down the lower grey slopes of Dooish and across the deep glen towards Loughfresha and Cornavara.

'It won't rain again before dark or dinner,' he said. 'I haven't walked these hills since I carried a chain for His Majesty's Ordnance Survey. Who'd ever have thought the King of England would be interested in the extent of Cornavara or Dooish Mountain.'

'Get up you two boys,' he said, 'and we'll see if you can walk as well as your father before you.'

The overflow of the spring came with us as we descended the boreen. Winter rain had already rutted the new gravel laid by drunken Dan Redmond and his merry men. Below the bare apple-orchard the spring's overflow met with another runnel and with yet another where another boreen, overgrown with hawthorn and bramble, struggled upwards to an abandoned house.

'Some people,' said my father, 'didn't come back to face the mountain. Living in Philadelphia must give a man great courage.'

He walked between us with the regular easy step of an old soldier who, in days of half-forgotten wars, had footed it for ever across the African veldt.

'That was all we ever did,' he would say. 'Walk and walk. And the only shot I ever fired that I remember was at a black snake and I never knew whether I hit or missed. That was the Boer war for you.'

Conjoined, innumerable runnels swept under a bridge where the united boreens joined the road, plunged over rock in a ten-foot cataract, went elbowing madly between bare hazels down to the belly of the glen. White cabins, windows already lamp-lighted and candle-lighted for Christmas, showed below the shifting fringe of black grey mist.

'This house I knew well,' he said, 'this was Aunt Sally's. The Aunt was a title of honour and had nothing to do with blood relationship. She was stately, a widow, a great manager and aunt to the whole country. She had only the two sons.'

By the crossroads of the thirteen limekilns we swung right and descended the slope of the glen on what in a dry summer would have been a dust road. Now, wet sand shifted under our feet, loose stones rattled ahead of us, the growing stream growled below us in the bushes. To our left were the disused limekilns, lining the roadway like ancient monstrous idols with gaping toothless mouths, and as we descended the old man remembered the days when he and his comrades, veterans all, had walked and measured those hills; the limekilns in operation and the white dust on the grass and the roadside hedges; the queues of farm carts waiting for the loading. Fertilizers made in factories had ended all that. There was the place (he pointed across a field) where a tree, fallen on a mearing fence, had lain and rotted while the two farmers whose land the fence divided, swept away by the joy of legal conflict, had disputed in the court in the town the ownership of the timber. The case never reached settlement. Mountainy men loved law and had their hearts in twopence. And here was Loughfresha bridge. (The stream was a torrent now.) The gapped, stone parapet hadn't been mended since the days of the survey. And there was the wide pool where Thady O'Neill, always a slave to salmon, had waded in after a big fish imprisoned by low water, taken it with his bare hands after a mad struggle and, it was said, cured himself by shock treatment of premature arthritis.

Once across the bridge our ascent commenced. Black brooding roadside cattle looked at us with hostility. On a diagonal across a distant meadow a black hound-dog ran silently, swiftly up towards the mist, running as if with definite purpose – but what, I wondered, could a dog be doing running upwards there alone on a Christmas Day. The thought absorbed me to the exclusion of all else until we came to the falling house of John and Thady O'Neill.

'Good God in heaven,' said my father.

For a full five minutes he stood looking at it, not speaking, before he led his two sons, with difficulty, as far as the door.

Once it must have been a fine, long, two-storeyed, thatched farmhouse, standing at an angle of forty-five degrees to the roadway and built backwards into the slope of the hill. But the roof and the upper storey had sagged and, topped by the growth of years of rank decayed grass, the remnants of the thatched roof looked, in the Christmas dusk, like a rubbish heap a maniacal mass-murderer might pick as a burial mound for his victims.

'They won't be expecting us for our Christmas dinner,' said my brother.

To reach the door we went ankle-deep, almost, through plashy ground and forded in the half-dark a sort of seasonal stream. One small uncurtained window showed faintly the yellow light of an oil-lamp.

Knock, knock, knock went my father on the sagging door.

No dogs barked. No calves or cocks made comforting farmhouse noises. The wind was raucous in the bare dripping hazels that overhung the wreck of a house from the slope behind. An evil wizard might live here.

Knock, knock, knock went my father.

'Is there anybody there said the traveller,' said my brother, who had a turn for poetry.

'John O'Neill and Thady,' called my father. 'I've walked over from the Yankee's new house at Dooish and brought my two sons with me to wish you a happy Christmas.'

He shouted out his own name.

In a low voice he said to us, 'Advance, friends, and be recognized.'

My brother and myself giggled and stopped giggling as chains rattled and slowly, with a thousand creaks of aged iron and timber in bitter pain and in conflict with each other, the door opened. Now, years after that Christmas, I can rely only on a boyhood memory of a brief visit to a badly-lighted cavern. There was a hunched decrepit old man behind the opening door. Without extending his hand he shuffled backwards and away from us. His huge hobnailed boots were unlaced. They flapped around him like the feet of some strange bird or reptile. He was completely bald. His face was pear-shaped, running towards the point at the forehead. His eyes had the brightness and quickness of a rodent's eyes. When my father said, 'Thady, you remember me,' he agreed doubtfully, as if agreement or disagreement were equally futile. He looked sideways furtively at the kitchen table half-hidden in shadows near one damp-streaked yellow wall. For a tablecloth that table had a battered raincoat and when our knock had interrupted him Thady had, it would seem, been heeling over onto the coat a pot of boiled potatoes. He finished the task while we stood uncertainly inside the doorway. Then, as if tucking in a child for sleep, he wrapped the tails of the coat around the pile of steaming tubers. A thunderous hearty voice spoke to us from the corner between the hearth and a huge four-poster bed. It was a rubicund confident voice. It invited us to sit down, and my father sat on a low chair close to the hearth-fire. My brother and myself stood uncomfortably behind him. There was, at any rate, nothing for us to sit on. The smoky oil-lamp burned low but the bracket that held it was on the wall above the owner of the voice. So it haloed with a yellow glow the head of John O'Neill, the dilatory lover of Bessie of Cornavara who had gone unwed to the place where none embrace. It was a broad, red-faced, white-haired head, too large and heavy, it seemed, for the old wasted body.

'It's years since we saw you, Tommy,' said John.

'It's years indeed.'

'And all the wild men that had been in the army.'

'All the wild men.'

'Times are changed, Tommy.'

'Times are changed indeed,' said my father.

He backed his chair a little away from the fire. Something unpleasantly odorous fried and sizzled in an unlidded pot-oven. The flagged floor, like the roof, had sagged. It sloped away from the hearth and into the shadows towards a pyramid of bags of flour and meal and feeding stuffs for cattle.

'But times are good,' said John. 'The land's good, and the crops and cattle.'

'And the money plentiful.'

'The money's plentiful.'

'I'm glad to hear you say it,' said my father.

'The Yankee came back, Tommy.'

'He came back.'

'And built a house, I hear. I don't go abroad much beyond my own land.'

'He built a fine house.'

'They like to come back, the Yankees. But they never settle.'

'It could be that the change proves too much for them,' said my father.

Then after a silence, disturbed only by the restless scratching of Thady's nailed soles on the floor, my father said, 'You never married, John.'

'No, Tommy. Bessy died. What with stock to look after and all, a man doesn't have much time for marrying.'

'Thady was more of a man for the ladies than you ever were,' said my father to John.

Behind us there was a shrill hysterical cackle and from John a roar of red laughter.

'He was that. God, Tommy, the memory you have.'

'Memory,' said my father.

Like a man in a trance he looked, not at John or Thady, but into the red heart of the turf fire.

'There was the day, Thady,' he said, 'when Martin Murphy and myself looked over a whin hedge at yourself and Molly Quigley from Crooked Bridge making love in a field. Between you, you ruined a half-acre of turnips.'

The red laughter and the cackle continued.

'Tommy, you have the memory,' said John. 'Wasn't it great the way you remembered the road up Loughfresha?'

'It was great,' said my father. 'Trust an old soldier to remember a road.'

The odour from the sizzling pot-oven was thickening.

'Well, we'll go now,' said my father. 'We wouldn't have butted in on you the day it is only for old time's sake.'

'You're always welcome, Tommy. Anytime you pass the road.'

'I don't pass this road often, John.'

'Well, when you do you're welcome. Those are your two sons.'

'My two sons.'

'Two fine clean young men,' said John.

He raised a hand to us. He didn't move out of the chair. The door closed slowly behind us and the chains rattled. We forded the seasonal stream, my brother going in over one ankle and filling a shoe with water.

We didn't talk until we had crossed the loud stream at Loughfresha Bridge. In the darkness I kept listening for the haunted howl of the black hound-dog.

'Isn't it an awful way, Da,' I said, 'for two men to live, particularly if it's true they have money in the bank.'

'If you've money in the bank,' said my brother, who suffered from a sense of irony, 'it's said you can do anything you please.'

With a philosophy too heavy for my years I said, 'It's a big change from the house we're going to.'

'John and Thady,' said my brother, 'didn't have the benefit of forty-five years in Philadelphia.'

My father said nothing.

'What, I wonder,' I said, 'was cooking in the pot-oven?'

'Whatever it was,' said my brother, 'they'll eat it with relish and roll into that four-poster bed and sleep like heroes.'

The black brooding roadside cattle seemed as formidable as wild bison.

'Sixty years,' said my father to himself. 'Coming and going every Sunday, spending the long afternoons and evenings in her father's house, eating and drinking, and nothing in the nature of love transpiring.'

Like heroes I thought, and recalled from the song-books the heroic words: 'Side by side for the cause have our forefathers battled when our hills never echoed the tread of a slave; in many a field where the leaden hail rattled, through the red gap of glory they marched to their grave.'

Slowly, towards a lost lighted fragment of Philadelphia and our Christmas dinner, we ascended the wet boreen.

'Young love,' soliloquized the old man. 'Something happens to it on these hills. Sixty years and he never proposed nothing, good or bad.'

'In Carlow town,' said the song-books to me, 'there lived a maid more sweet than flowers at daybreak; their vows contending lovers paid, but none of marriage dared speak.'

'Sunday after Sunday to her house for sixty years,' said the old man. 'You wouldn't hear the like of it among the Kaffirs. It's the rain and the mist. And the lack of sunshine and wine. Poor Thady, too, was fond of salmon and women.'

'For I haven't a genius for work,' mocked the Humorous and Convivial, 'it was never a gift of the Bradies; but I'd make a most iligant Turk for I'm fond of tobacco and ladies.'

To the easy amusement of my brother and, finally, to the wry laughter of my father I sang that quatrain. Night was over the mountain. The falling water of the spring had the tinny sound of shrill, brittle thunder.

After dinner my godmother's husband said, 'Such a fine house as Aunt Sally O'Neill kept. Tables scrubbed as white as bone. Dances to the melodeon. I always think of corncrakes and the crowds gathered for the mowing of the meadows when I recall that house. And the churning. She had the best butter in the country. Faintly golden. Little beads of moisture showing on it.'

'We'll have a game of euchre,' said my Aunt Brigid.

'Play the phonograph,' said my godmother's husband.

He loathed euchre. So on the gramophone, high up on Dooish, we heard that boys and girls were singing on the sidewalks of New York.

I wondered where the hound-dog could possibly have been running to. In a spooky story I had once read the Black Hound of Kildare turned out to be the devil.

My godmother asked me to sing.

'But I can't sing,' I said.

'Then what do Lanty and yourself do with all the song-books?'

'We read them.'

Laughter.

'Read us a song,' said my brother.

So, because I had my back to the wall and also because once when visiting a convent with my mother I had sung, by request, 'Let Erin Remember', and received a box of chocolates from the Reverend Mother, I sang: 'Just a little bit of Heaven fell from out the sky one day, and when the angels saw it sure they said we'll let it stay; and they called it Ireland.'

That spring, following my heralding of the descent from Elysium of the Emerald Isle, there was a steady downpour of half-crowns.

JAMES PLUNKETT

'The Eagles and the Trumpets'

I

When the girl crossed from the library, the square was bathed in August sunshine. The folk from the outlying areas who had left their horses and carts tethered about the patriotic monument in the centre were still in the shops, and the old trees which lined either side emphasized the stillness of the morning. She went down a corridor in the Commercial Hotel and turned left into the bar. She hardly noticed its quaintness, the odd layout of the tables, its leather chairs in angles and corners, the long low window which looked out on the dairy yard at the back. After six years in the town she was only aware of its limitations. But the commercial traveller startled her. She had not expected to find anyone there so early. He raised his eyes and when he had stared at her gloomily for a moment, he asked, 'Looking for Cissy?'

One of the things she had never got used to was this easy familiarity of the country town. But she accepted it. One either accepted or became a crank.

'No,' she answered, 'Miss O'Halloran.'

'You won't see her,' he said. 'It's the first Friday. She goes to the altar and has her breakfast late.' He had a glass of whiskey in front of him and a bottle of Bass. He gulped half the whiskey and then added, 'I'll ring the bell for you.'

'Thank you.'

His greyish face with its protruding upper lip was vaguely familiar. Probably she had passed him many times in her six years without paying much attention. Now she merely wondered about his black tie. She heard the bell ringing remotely and after a moment Cissy appeared. The girl said:

'I really wanted Miss O'Halloran. It's a room for a gentleman tonight.' She hesitated. Then reluctantly she added, 'Mr Sweeney.' As she had expected, Cissy betrayed immediate curiosity.

'Not Mr Sweeney that stayed here last autumn?'

'Yes. He hopes to get in on the afternoon bus.'

Cissy said she would ask Miss O'Halloran. When she had gone to enquire, the girl turned her back on the traveller and pretended interest in an advertisement for whiskey which featured two dogs, one with a pheasant in its mouth. The voice from behind her asked:

'Boy friend?'

She had expected something like that. Without turning she said, 'You're very curious.'

'Sorry. I didn't mean that. I don't give a damn. Do you drink?'

'No, thank you.'

'I was going to offer you something better than a drink. Good advice.' The girl stiffened. She was the town librarian, not a chambermaid. Then she relaxed and almost smiled.

'If you ever do,' the voice added sadly, 'don't mix the grain with the grape. That's what happened to me last night.'

Cissy returned and said Mr Sweeney could have room seven. Miss O'Halloran was delighted. Mr Sweeney had been such a nice young man. Her eyes caught the traveller and she frowned.

'Mr Cassidy,' she said pertly, 'Miss O'Halloran says your breakfast's ready.'

The traveller looked at her with distaste. He finished his whiskey and indicated with a nod of his head the glass of Bass which he had taken in his hand.

'Tell Miss O'Halloran I'm having my breakfast,' he said. But Cissy was admiring the new dress.

'You certainly look pretty,' she said enviously.

'Prettiest girl in town,' the traveller added for emphasis.

The girl flushed. Cissy winked and said, 'Last night he told me I was.'

'Did I,' the traveller said, finishing his Bass with a grimace of disgust. 'I must have been drunk.'

On the first Friday of every month, precisely at eleven forty-five, the chief clerk put on his bowler hat, hung his umbrella on his arm and left to spend the rest of the day inspecting the firm's branch office. It was one of the few habits of the chief clerk which the office staff approved. It meant that for the rest of the day they could do more or less as they pleased. Sweeney, who had been watching the monthly ceremony from the public counter with unusual interest, turned around to find Higgins at his elbow.

'You're wanted,' he was told.

'Who?'

'Our mutual musketeer – Ellis. He's in his office.'

That was a joke. It meant Ellis was in the storeroom at the top of the building. Part of the duties assigned to Ellis was the filing away of forms and documents. The firm kept them for twenty-five years, after which they were burned. Ellis spent interminable periods in the storeroom, away from supervision and interference. It was a much-coveted position. Sweeney, disturbed in his day-dreaming, frowned at Higgins and said:

'Why the hell can't he come down and see me?' It was his habit to grumble. He hated the stairs up to the storeroom and he hated the storeroom. He disliked most of the staff, expecially the few who were attending night school classes for accountancy and secretarial management in order to get on in the job. Put into the firm at nineteen years of age because it was a good, safe, comfortable job with a pension scheme, and adequate indemnity against absences due to ill-health, he realized now at twenty-six that there was no indemnity against the boredom, no contributory scheme which would save his manhood from rotting silently inside him among the ledgers and the comptometer machines. From nine to five he decayed among the serried desks with their paper baskets and their telephones, and from five onwards there was the picture house, occasional women, and drink when there was money for it.

The storeroom was a sort of paper tomb, with tiers of forms and documents in dusty bundles, which exhaled a musty odour. He found Ellis making tea. A paper-covered book had been flung to one side. On the cover he could make out the words *Selected Poems*, but not whose they were. He was handed a cup with a chocolate biscuit in the saucer.

'Sit down,' Ellis commanded.

Sweeney, surprised at the luxury of the chocolate biscuit, held it up and inspected it with raised eyebrows.

Ellis offered milk and sugar.

'I pinched them out of Miss Bouncing's drawers,' he said deliberately.

Sweeney, secure in the knowledge that the chief clerk was already on his way across town, munched the biscuit contentedly and looked down into the street. It was filled with sunshine. Almost level with his eyes, the coloured flags on the roof of a cinema lay limp and unmoving, while down below three charwomen were scrubbing the entrance steps. He took another biscuit and heard Ellis saying conversationally, 'I suppose you're looking forward to your weekend in the country.'

The question dovetailed unnoticed in Sweeney's thought.

'I've been wanting to get back there since last autumn. I told you there was a girl . . .'

'With curly eyes and bright blue hair.'

'Never mind her eyes and her hair. I've tried to get down to see her twice but it didn't come off. The first time you and I drank the money – the time Dacey got married. The second, I didn't get it saved in time. But I'm going today. I've just drawn the six quid out of Miss Bouncing's holiday club.'

'What bus are you getting?'

'The half past two. His nibs has gone off so I can slip out.'

'I see,' Ellis said pensively.

'I want you to sign me out at five.'

They had done things like that for one another before. Turning to face him, Ellis said, 'Is there a later bus?'

'Yes. At half past eight. But why?'

'It's . . . well, it's a favour,' Ellis said uncertainly. With sinking heart Sweeney guessed at what was coming.

'Go on,' he invited reluctantly.

'I'm in trouble,' Ellis said. 'The old man was away this past two weeks and I hocked his typewriter. Now the sister's 'phoned me to tip me off he's coming home at half past two. They only got word after breakfast. If I don't slip out and redeem it there'll be stinking murder. You know the set-up at home.'

Sweeney did. He was aware that the Ellis household had its complications.

'I can give it back to you at six o'clock,' Ellis prompted.

'Did you try Higgins?' Sweeney suggested hopefully.

'He hasn't got it. He told me not to ask you but I'm desperate. There's none of the others I can ask.'

'How much do you need?'

'Four quid would do me – I have two.'

Sweeney took the four pound notes from his wallet and handed them over. They were fresh and stiff. Miss Bouncing had been to the bank. Ellis took them and said:

'You'll get this back. Honest. Byrne of the Prudential's to meet me in Slattery's at six. He owes me a fiver.'

Still looking at the limp flags on the opposite roof, Sweeney suggested, 'Supposing he doesn't turn up.'

'Don't worry,' Ellis answered him. 'He will. He promised me on his bended knees.' After a pause he diffidently added, 'I'm eternally grateful . . .'

Sweeney saw the weekend he had been aching for receding like most of his other dreams into a realm of tantalizing uncertainty.

'Forget it,' he said.

II

Sweeney, who was standing at the public counter, looked up at the clock and found it was half past two. Behind him many of the desks were empty. Some were at lunch, others were taking advantage of the chief clerk's absence. It only meant that telephones were left to ring longer than usual. To his right, defying the grime and the odd angles of the windows, a streak of sunlight slanted across the office and lit up about two square feet of the counter. Sweeney stretched his hand towards it and saw the sandy hairs on the back leap suddenly into gleaming points. He withdrew it shyly, hoping nobody had seen him. Then he forgot the office and thought instead of the country town, the square with its patriotic statue, the trees which lined it, the girl he had met on that autumn day while he was walking alone through the woods. Sweeney had very little time for romantic notions about love and women. Seven years knocking about with Ellis and Higgins had convinced him that Romance, like good luck, was on the side of the rich. It preferred to ride around in motor-cars and flourished most where the drinks were short and expensive. But meeting this strange girl among the trees had disturbed him. Groping automatically for the plausible excuse, he had walked towards her with a pleasurable feeling of alertness and wariness.

'This path,' he said to her, 'does it lead me back to the town?' and waited with anxiety for the effect. He saw her assessing him quickly. Then she smiled.

'It does,' she said, 'provided you walk in the right direction.'

He pretended surprise. Then after a moment's hesitation he asked if he might walk back with her. He was staying in the town, he explained, and was still finding his way about. As they walked together he found out she was the town librarian, and later, when they had met two or three times and accepted one another, that she was bored to death with the town. He told her about being dissatisfied too, about the office and its futility, about having too little money. One evening when they were leaning across a bridge some distance from the town, it seemed appropriate to talk rather solemnly about life. The wind ripped the brown water which reflected the fading colours of the sky, He said:

'I think I could be happy here. It's slow and quiet. You don't break your neck getting somewhere and then sit down to read the paper when you've got there. You don't have twenty or thirty people ahead of you every morning and evening – all queuing to sign a clock.'

'You can be happy anywhere or bored anywhere. It depends on knowing what you want.'

'That's it,' he said, 'but how do you find out? I never have. I only know what I don't want.'

'Money – perhaps?'

'Not money really. Although it has its points. It doesn't make life any bigger though, does it? I mean look at most of the people who have it.'

'Dignity?' she suggested quietly.

The word startled him. He looked at her and found she was quite serious. He wondered if one searched hard enough, could something be found to be dignified about. He smiled.

'Do you mean an umbrella and a bowler hat?'

He knew that was not what she meant at all, but he wanted her to say more.

'No,' she said, 'I mean to have a conviction about something. About the work you do or the life you lead.'

'Have you?' he asked.

She was gazing very solemnly at the water, the breeze now and then lifting back the hair from her face.

'No,' she murmured. She said it almost to herself. He slipped his arm about her. When she made no resistance he kissed her.

'I'm wondering why I didn't do that before,' he said when they were finished.

'Do you . . . usually?' she asked.

He said earnestly, 'For a moment I was afraid.'

'Of me?'

'No. Afraid of spoiling everything. Have I?'

She smiled at him and shook her head.

At five they closed their ledgers and pushed in the buttons which locked the filing cabinets. One after the other they signed the clock which automatically stamped the time when they pulled the handle. The street outside was hardly less airless than the office, the pavements threw back the dust-smelling August heat. Sweeney, waiting for Higgins and Ellis at the first corner, felt the sun drawing a circle of sweat about his shirt collar and thought wistfully of green fields and roadside pubs. By now the half past two bus would have finished its journey. The other two joined him and they walked together by the river wall, picking their way through the evening crowds. The tea-hour rush was beginning. Sweeney found the heat and the noise of the buses intolerable. A girl in a light cotton frock with long hair and prominent breasts brushed close to them. Higgins whistled and said earnestly: 'Honest to God, chaps. It's not fair. Not on a hot evening.'

'They're rubber,' Ellis offered with contempt.

'Rubber bedamned.'

'It's a fact,' Ellis insisted. 'I know her. She hangs them up on the bedpost at night.'

They talked knowledgeably and argumentatively about falsies until they reached Slattery's lounge. Then, while Ellis began to tell them in detail how he had smuggled the typewriter back into his father's study, Sweeney sat back with relief and tasted his whiskey. A drink was always welcome after a day in the office, even to hold the glass in his hand and lie back against his chair gave him a feeling of escape. Hope was never quite dead if he had money enough for that. But this evening it wasn't quite the same. He had hoped to have his first drink in some city pub on his way to the bus, a quick drink while he changed one of his new pound notes and savoured the adventure of the journey before him, a long ride with money in his pocket along green hedged roads, broken by pleasant half hours in occasional country pubs. When Higgins and Ellis had bought their rounds he called again. Whenever the door of the lounge opened he looked up hopefully. At last he indicated the clock and said, 'Your friend should be here.'

'Don't worry,' Ellis assured him, 'he's all right. He'll turn up.' Then he lifted his drink and added, 'Well – here's to the country.'

'The country,' Higgins sighed. 'Tomorrow to fresh fiends and pastors new.'

'I hope so,' Sweeney said. He contrived to say it as though it didn't really matter, but watching Ellis and Higgins he saw they were both getting uneasy. In an effort to keep things moving Higgins asked, 'What sort of a place is it?'

'A square with a statue in it and trees,' Sweeney said. 'A hotel that's fairly reasonable. Free fishing if you get on the right side of the Guards. You wouldn't think much of it.'

'No sea – no nice girls in bathing dresses. No big hotel with its own band?'

'Samuel Higgins,' Ellis commented. 'The man who broke the bank at Monte Carlo.'

'I like a holiday to be a real holiday,' Higgins said stoutly. 'Stay up all night and sleep all day. I like sophistication, nice girls and smart hotels. Soft lights and glamour and sin. Lovely sin. It's worth saving for.'

'We must write it across the doorway of the office,' Sweeney said.

'What?'

'Sin Is Worth Saving For.'

It had occurred to him that it was what half of them did. They cut down on cigarettes and scrounged a few pounds for their Post Office Savings account or Miss Bouncing's Holiday Club so that they could spend a fortnight of the year in search of what they enthusiastically looked upon as sin. For him sin abounded in the dusty places of the office, in his sweat of fear when the morning clock told him he was late again, in the obsequious answer to the official question, in the impulse which reduced him to pawing the hot and willing typist who passed him on the deserted stairs.

'I don't have to save for sin,' he commented finally.

'Oh – I know,' Higgins said, misunderstanding him. 'The tennis club is all right. So are the golf links on Bank Holiday. But it's nicer where you're not known.'

'View Three,' Ellis interjected. 'Higgins the hen butcher.'

'Last year there was a terrific woman who got soft on me because I told her I was a commercial pilot. The rest of the chaps backed me up by calling me Captain Higgins. I could have had anything I wanted.'

'Didn't you?'

'Well,' Higgins said, in a tone which suggested it was a bit early in the night for intimate details. 'More or less.' Then they consulted the clock again.

'It doesn't look as though our friend is coming,' Sweeney said.

'We'll give him 'til seven,' Ellis said. 'Then we'll try for him in Mulligan's or round in the Stag's Head.'

III

The girl watched the arrival of the bus from the entrance to the hotel. As the first passenger stepped off she smiled and moved forward. She hovered uncertainly. Some men went past her into the bar of the Commercial, the conductor took luggage from the top, the driver stepped down from his cabin and lit a cigarette. Townspeople came forward too, some with parcels to be delivered to the next town, some to take parcels sent to them from the city. He was not among the passengers who remained. The girl, aware of her new summer frock, her long white gloves, the unnecessary handbag, stepped back against the wall and bumped into the traveller.

'No boy friend,' he said.

She noticed he had shaved. His eyes were no longer bloodshot. But the sun emphasized the grey colour of his face with its sad wrinkles and its protruding upper lip. As the crowd dispersed he leaned up against the wall beside her.

'I had a sleep,' he said. 'Nothing like sleep. It knits up the ravelled sleeve of care. Who said that, I wonder?'

'Shakespeare,' she said.

'Of course,' he said, 'I might have guessed it was Shakespeare.'

'He said a lot of things.'

'More than his prayers,' the traveller conceded. Then he looked up at the sun and winced.

'God's sunlight,' he said unhappily. 'It hurts me.'

'Why don't you go in out of it?' she suggested coldly.

'I've orders to collect. I'm two days behind. Do you like the sun?'

'It depends.'

'Depends with me too. Depends on the night before. Mostly I like the shade. It's cool and it's easy on the eyes. Sleep and the shade. Did Shakespeare say anything about that, I wonder?'

'Not anything that occurs to me.' She wished to God he would go away.

'He should then,' the traveller insisted. 'What's Shakespeare for, if he didn't say anything about sleep and the shade?'

At another time she might have been sorry for him, for his protruding lip, his ashen face, the remote landscape of sorrow which lay behind his slow eyes. But she had her own disappointment. She wanted to go into some quiet place and weep. The sun was too strong and the noise of the awakened square too unsettling. 'Let's talk about Shakespeare some other time,' she suggested. He smiled sadly at the note of dismissal.

'It's a date,' he said. She saw him shuffling away under the cool trees.

*

When they left Slattery's they tried Mulligan's and in the Stag's Head Higgins said he could eat a farmer's arse, so they had sandwiches. The others had ham and beef but Sweeney took egg because it was Friday. There was a dogged streak of religion in him which was scrupulous about things like that. Even in his worst bouts of despair he still could observe the prescribed forms. They were precarious footholds which he hesitated to destroy and by which he might eventually drag himself out of the pit. After the Stag's Head Ellis thought of the Oval.

'It's one of his houses,' he said. 'We should have tried it before. What's the next bus?'

'Half eight.'

'Is it the last?'

'The last and ultimate bus. Aston's Quay at half past eight. Let's forget about it.'

'It's only eight o'clock. We might make it.'

'You're spoiling my drink.'

'You're spoiling mine too,' Higgins said, 'all this fluting around.'

'You see. You're spoiling Higgins' drink too.'

'But I feel a louser about this.'

'Good,' Higgins said pleasantly. 'Ellis discovers the truth about himself.'

'Shut up,' Ellis said.

He dragged them across the city again.

The evening was cooler. Over the western reaches of the Liffey barred clouds made the sky alternate with streaks of blue and gold. Steeples and tall houses staggered upward and caught the glowing colours. There was no sign of Byrne in the Oval. They had a drink while the clock moved round until it was twenty minutes to nine.

'I shouldn't have asked you,' Ellis said with genuine remorse.

'That's what I told you,' Higgins said. 'I told you not to ask him.'

'Byrne is an arch louser,' Ellis said bitterly. 'I never thought he'd let me down.'

'You should know Byrne by now,' Higgins said. 'He has medals for it.'

'But I was in trouble. And you both know the set-up at home. Christ if the old man found out about the typewriter . . .'

'Look,' Sweeney said, 'the bus is gone. If I don't mind, why should you? Go and buy me a drink.' But they found they hadn't enough money left between them, so they went around to the Scotch House where Higgins knew the manager and could borrow a pound.

IV

Near the end of his holiday he had taken her to a big hotel at a seaside resort. It was twenty miles by road from the little town, but a world away in its sophistication. They both cycled. Dinner was late and the management liked to encourage dress. A long drive led up to the imposing entrance. They came to it cool and fresh from the sea, their wet swimming togs knotted about the handlebars. It was growing twilight and he could still remember the rustle of piled leaves under the wheels of their bicycles. A long stone balustrade rose from the gravelled terrace. There was an imposing ponderousness of stone and high turrets.

'Glenawling Castle,' he said admiringly. She let her eyes travel from the large and shiny cars to the flag-mast some hundreds of feet up in the dusky air.

'Comrade Sweeney,' she breathed, 'cast your sweaty nightcap in the air.'

They walked on thick carpet across a foyer which smelled of rich cigar smoke. Dinner was a long, solemn ritual. They had two half bottles of wine, white for her, red for himself. When he had poured she looked at both glasses and said happily:

'Isn't it beautiful? I mean the colours.' He found her more astoundingly beautiful than either the gleaming red or the white.

'You are,' he said. 'Good God, you are.' She laughed happily at his intensity. At tables about them young people were in the minority. Glenawling Castle catered to a notable extent for the more elevated members of the hierarchy, Monsignors and Bishops who took a little time off from the affairs of the Church to play sober games of golf and drink discreet glasses of brandy. There were elderly business men with their wives, occasional and devastatingly bored daughters.

After dinner they walked in the grounds. The light had faded from the sky above them but far out to sea an afterglow remained. From the terrace they heard the sound of breakers on the beach below and could smell the strong, autumn smell of the sea. They listened for some time. He took her hand and said, 'Happy?'

She nodded and squeezed his fingers lightly.

'Are you?'

'No,' he said, 'I'm sad.'

'Why sad?'

'For the old Bishops and the Monsignors and the business men with their bridge-playing wives.'

They both laughed. Then she shivered suddenly in the cold breeze and they went inside again to explore further. They investigated a room in which elderly men played billiards in their shirt sleeves, and another in which the elderly women sat at cards. In a large lounge old ladies knitted, while in deep chairs an occasional Bishop read somnolently from a priestly book. Feeling young and a little bit out of place, they went into the bar which adjoined the ballroom. There were younger people here. He called for drinks and asked her why she frowned.

'This is expensive for you,' she said. She took a pound note from her bag and left it on the table.

'Let's spend this on drinks,' she suggested.

'All of it?'

She nodded gravely. He grinned suddenly and gave it to the attendant.

'Pin that on your chest,' he said, 'and clock up the damage until it's gone.'

The attendant looked hard at the note. His disapproval was silent but unmistakable.

'It's a good one,' Sweeney assured him. 'I made it myself.'

They alternated between the ballroom and the bar. In the bar she laughed a lot at the things he said, but in the ballroom they danced more or less silently. They were dancing when he first acknowledged the thought which had been hovering between them.

'I've only two days left.'

'One, darling.'

'Tomorrow and Saturday.'

'It's tomorrow already,' she said, looking at her watch. Now that it was said it was unavoidably necessary to talk about it.

'It's only about two hours by bus,' he said. 'I can get down to see you sometimes. There'll be weekends.'

'You won't though,' she said sadly.

'Who's going to stop me?'

'You think you will now but you won't. A holiday is a holiday. It comes to an end and you go home and then you forget.'

They walked through the foyer which was deserted now. The elderly ladies had retired to bed, and so had the somnolent churchmen with their priestly books.

'I won't forget,' he said when they were once again on the terrace. 'I want you too much.'

The leaves rustled again under their wheels, the autumn air raced past their faces coldly.

'That's what I mean,' she said simply. 'It's bad wanting anything too much.' Her voice came anonymously from the darkness behind him.

'Why?' he asked.

Their cycle lamps were two bars of light in a vast tunnel of darkness. Sometimes a hedge gleamed green in the light or a tree arched over them with mighty and gesticulating limbs.

'Because you never get it,' she answered solemnly.

V

Sweeney, looking through the smoke from Higgins and Ellis to the heavily built man whom he did not like, frowned and tried to remember what public house he was in. They had been in so many and had drunk so much. He was at that stage of drunkenness where his thoughts required an immense tug of his will to keep them concentrated. Whenever he succumbed to the temptation to close his eyes he saw them wandering and grazing at a remote distance from him, small white sheep in a landscape of black hills and valleys. The evening had been a pursuit of something which he felt now he would never catch up with, a succession of calls on some mysterious person who had always left a minute before. It had been of some importance, whatever he had been chasing, but for the moment he had forgotten why. Taking the heavily built man whom he didn't like as a focal point, he gradually pieced together the surroundings until they assumed first a vague familiarity and then a positive identity. It was the Crystal. He relaxed, but not too much, for fear of the woolly annihilation that might follow, and found Higgins and the heavily built man swopping stories. He remembered that they had been swopping stories for a long time. The heavily built man was a friend of Higgins'. He had an advertising agency and talked about the golf club and poker and his new car. He had two daughters – clever as hell. He knew the Variety Girls and had a fund of smutty stories. He told them several times they must come and meet the boys. 'Let's leave this hole,' he said several times, 'and I'll run you out to the golf club. No bother.' But someone began a new story. And besides, Sweeney didn't want to go. Every time he looked at the man with his neat suit and his moustache, his expensively fancy waistcoat and the pin in his tie, he was tempted to get up and walk away. But for Higgins' sake he remained and listened. Higgins was telling a story about a commercial traveller who married a hotel keeper's daughter in a small country town. The traveller had a protruding upper lip while the daughter, Higgins said, had a protruding lower lip. Like this, Higgins said. Then he said look here he couldn't tell the story if they wouldn't pay attention to him.

'This'll be good, boys,' the man said, 'this will be rich, I think I know this one. Go on.'

But Higgins said hell no they must look at his face. It was a story and they had to watch his face or they'd miss the point.

'Christ no,' Ellis said, 'not your face.'

Sweeney silently echoed the remark not because he really objected to Higgins' face but because it was difficult to focus it in one piece.

Well, Higgins said, they could all sugar off, he was going to tell the story and shag the lot of them.

'Now, now,' the man said, 'we're all friends here. No unpleasantness and no bickering, what?'

'Well,' Higgins continued, 'the father of the bride had a mouth which twisted to the left and the mother's mouth, funny enough, twisted to the right. So on the bridal night the pair went to bed in the hotel which, of course, was a very small place, and when the time came to get down to a certain important carry-on, the nature of which would readily suggest itself to the assembled company, no need to elaborate, the commercial traveller tried to blow out the candle. He held it level with his mouth but, of course, on account of the protruding upper lip, his breath went down the direction of his chin and the candle remained lit. Higgins stuck out his lip and demonstrated for their benefit the traveller's peculiar difficulty. '"Alice," said the traveller to his bride, "I'll have to ask you to do this." So her nibs had a go and, of course, with the protruding lower lip, her breath went up towards her nose, and lo and behold the candle was still lighting.' Again Higgins demonstrated. '"There's nothing for it, John, but call my father," says she. So the oul' fella is summoned and he has a go. But with his lips twisted to the left the breath goes back over his shoulder and the candle is still lighting away. "Dammit, this has me bet," says the father, "I'll have to call your mother," and after a passable delay the oul' wan appears on the scene but, of course, same thing happens, her breath goes over her right this time, and there the four of them stand in their nightshirts looking at the candle and wondering what the hell will they do next. So they send out for the schoolmaster, and the schoolmaster comes in and they explain their difficulty and ask him for his assistance and "Certainly," he says, "it's a great pleasure." And with that he wets his fingers and thumb and pinches the wick and, of course, the candle goes out.' Higgins wet his finger and thumb and demonstrated on an imaginary candle. 'Then the father looks at the other three and shakes his head. "Begod," says he, "did youse ever see the likes of that, isn't education a wonderful thing?"' The heavily built man guffawed and asserted immediately that he could cap that. It was a story about a commercial traveller too. But as he was about to start they began to call closing time and he said again that they must all come out to the golf club and meet the boys.

'Really,' he said, 'you'll enjoy the boys. I'll run you out in the car.'

'Who's game?' Higgins asked.

Ellis looked at Sweeney and waited. Sweeney looked at the heavily built man and decided he didn't dislike him after all. He hated him.

'Not me,' he said, 'I don't want any shagging golf clubs.'

'I don't care for your friend's tone,' the man began, his face reddening.

'And I don't like new cars,' Sweeney interrupted, rising to his feet.

'Look here,' the heavily built man said threateningly. Ellis and Higgins asked the stout man not to mind him.

'Especially new cars driven by fat bastards with fancy waistcoats,' Sweeney insisted. He saw Ellis and Higgins moving in between him and the other man. They looked surprised and that annoyed him further. But to hit him he would have had to push his way through them and it would take so much effort that he decided it was hardly worth it after all. So he changed his mind. But he turned around as he went out.

'With fancy pins in their ties,' he concluded. People moved out of his way.

They picked him up twenty minutes later at the corner. He was gazing into the window of a tobacconist shop. He was wondering now why he had behaved like that. He had a desire to lean his forehead against the glass. It looked so cool. There was a lonely ache inside him. He barely looked round at them.

'You got back quick,' Sweeney said.

'Oh, cut it out,' Ellis said, 'you know we wouldn't go without you.'

'I hate fat bastards with fancy pins,' Sweeney explained. But he was beginning to feel it was a bit inadequate.

'After all,' Higgins said, 'he was a friend of mine. You might have thought of that.'

'Sugar you and your friends.'

Higgins flushed and said, 'Thanks, I'll remember that.'

Pain gathered like a ball inside Sweeney and he said with intensity, 'You can remember what you sugaring well like.'

'Look,' Ellis said, 'cut it out – the pair of you.'

'He insulted my friend.'

'View four,' Ellis said, 'Higgins the Imperious.'

'And I'll be obliged if you'll cut this View two View three View four stuff . . .'

'Come on,' Ellis said wearily, 'kiss and make up. What we all need is another drink.'

It seemed a sensible suggestion. They addressed themselves to the delicate business of figuring out the most likely speak-easy.

VI

The last bus stayed for twenty minutes or so and then chugged out towards remoter hamlets and lonelier roads, leaving the square full of shadows in the August evening, dark under the trees, grey in the open spaces about the statue. The air felt thick and warm, the darkness of the sky was relieved here and there with yellow and green patches.

To the girl there was a strange finality about the departure of the bus, as though all the inhabitants had boarded it on some impulse which would leave the square empty for ever. She decided to have coffee, not in the Commercial where Cissy was bound to ask questions, but in the more formal atmosphere of the Imperial. She had hoped to be alone, and frowned when she met the traveller in the hallway. He said:

'Well, well. Now we can have our chat about Shakespeare.' She noticed something she had not observed earlier – a small piece of newspaper stuck on the side of his cheek where he had cut himself shaving. For some reason it made her want to laugh. She could see too that he was quite prepared to be rebuffed and guessed his philosophy about such things. Resignation and defeat were his familiars.

'I see you've changed your location,' she said, in a voice which indicated how little it mattered.

'So have you.'

'I was going to have coffee.'

'We can't talk Shakespeare over coffee,' he invited. 'Have a drink with me instead.'

'I wonder should I. I really don't know you,' she answered coolly.

'If it comes to that,' he said philosophically, 'who does?'

They went into the lounge. The lounge in the Imperial paid attention to contemporary ideas. There were tubular tables and chairs, a half moon of a bar with tube lighting which provided plenty of colour but not enough light. The drink was a little dearer, the beer, on such evenings in August, a little too warm. He raised his glass to her.

'I'm sorry about the boy friend,' he said. She put down her glass deliberately.

'I'd rather you didn't say things like that,' she said. 'It's not particularly entertaining. I'm not Cissy from the Commercial, you know.'

'Sorry,' he said repentantly, 'I meant no harm. It was just for talk's sake.'

'Then let's talk about you. Did you pick up your two days' orders?'

'No,' he said sadly, 'I'm afraid I didn't. I'm afraid I'm not much of a commercial traveller. I'm really a potter.'

'Potter?'

'Yes. I potter around from this place to that.'

She noticed the heavy upper lip quivering and gathered that he was laughing. Then he said:

'That's a little joke I've used hundreds of times. It amuses me because I made it up myself.'

'Do you often do that?'

'I try, but I'm not much good at it. I thought of that one, God knows how many years ago, when things began to slip and I was in bed in the dark in some little room in some cheap hotel. Do you ever feel frightened in a strange room?'

'I'm not often in strange rooms.'

'I am. All my life I've been. When I put out the light I can never remember where the door is. I suppose that's what makes me a pretty poor specimen of a traveller.'

'So you thought of a joke.'

'Yes.'

'But why?'

'It helps. Sometimes when you feel like that a joke has more comfort than a prayer.'

She saw what he meant and felt some surprise.

'Well,' she prompted. 'Why do you travel?'

'It was my father's profession too. He was one of the old stock. A bit stiff and ceremonious. And respected of course. In those days they didn't have to shoot a line. They had dignity. First they left their umbrella and hat in the hall stand. Then there was some polite conversation. A piece of information from the city. A glass of sherry and a biscuit. Now you've got to talk like hell and drive like hell. I suppose he trained me the wrong way.'

He indicated her glass.

'You'll have another?' he asked.

She looked again at his face and made her decision. She was not quite sure what it would involve, but she knew it was necessary to her to see it out.

'I think I will,' she said.

He asked her if she liked her work but she was not anxious to discuss herself at all. She admitted she was bored. After their third drink he asked her if she would care to drive out with him to Glenawling Castle. There were not likely to be people there who knew them and besides, there would be dancing. She hesitated.

'I know what you're thinking,' he said, 'but you needn't worry. I'm no he-man.' She thought it funny that that was not what had occurred to her at all. Then he smiled and added:

'With this lip of mine I don't get much opportunity to practise.'

They got into the car which took them up the hill from the square and over the stone bridge with its brown stream. The traveller looked around at her.

'You're a pretty girl,' he said warmly, 'prettiest I've met.'

She said coolly, 'Prettier than your wife?'

'My wife is dead.'

She glanced involuntarily at the black tie.

'Yes,' he said, 'a month ago.' He waited. 'Does that shock you?' he asked.

'I'm afraid it does.'

'It needn't,' he said. 'We were married for eighteen years, and for fifteen of that she was in a lunatic asylum. I didn't visit her this past eight or nine years. They said it was better. I haven't danced for years either. Do you think I shouldn't?'

'No,' she said after a pause. 'I think it might do you good. You might get over being afraid of strange rooms.'

'At forty-five?' he asked quietly.

His question kept the girl silent. She looked out at the light racing along the hedges, the gleaming leaves, the arching of trees.

VII

They eventually got into Annie's place. It was one of a row of tall and tottering Georgian houses. Ellis knew the right knock and was regarded with professional affection by the ex-boxer who kept the door. They went in the dark up a rickety stairs to a room which was full of cigarette smoke. They had to drink out of cups, since the girls and not the liquor were the nominal attraction. There was some vague tradition that Annie was entitled to serve meals too, but to ask for one was to run the risk of being thrown out by the ex-boxer. The smell of the whiskey in his cup made Sweeney shiver. He had had whiskey early in the evening and after it plenty of beer. Experience had taught him that taking whiskey at this stage was a grave mistake. But no long drinks were available and one had to drink. Ellis noted his silence.

'How are you feeling?' he asked with friendly solicitude.

'Like the Chinese maiden?' Higgins suggested amiably and tickled the plump girl who was sitting on his knee.

'No,' Sweeney said, 'like the cockle man.'

'I know,' Higgins said. 'Like the cockle man when the tide came in. We all appreciate the position of that most unfortunate gentleman.' He tickled the plump girl again. 'Don't we, Maisie?'

Maisie, who belonged to the establishment, giggled.

'You're a terrible hard root,' she said admiringly.

There were about a dozen customers in the place. One group had unearthed an old-fashioned gramophone complete with sound horn and were trying out the records. They quarrelled about whose turn it was to wind it and laughed uproariously at the thin nasal voices and the age of the records. Sweeney was noted to be morose and again Ellis had an attack of conscience.

'I feel a louser,' Ellis said.

'Look,' Sweeney said, 'I told you to forget it.'

'Only for me you could be down the country by now.'

'Only for me you could be out at the golf club,' Sweeney said, 'drinking with the best spivs in the country. You might even have got in the way of marrying one of their daughters.' The gramophone was asking a trumpeter what he was sounding now.

'God,' Maisie said, 'my grandfather used to sing that. At a party or when he'd a few jars aboard. I can just see him.'

'My God. Where?' Higgins asked in mock alarm.

'In my head – Smarty,' Maisie said. 'I can see him as if it was yesterday. Trumpet-eer what are yew sounding now – Is it the cawl I'm seeking?'

They looked in amazement at Maisie who had burst so suddenly into song. She stopped just as suddenly and gave a sigh of warm and genuine affection. 'It has hairs on it right enough – that thing,' she commented.

'What thing?' Higgins enquired salaciously and was rewarded with another giggle and a playful slap from Maisie.

'Maisie darling,' Ellis appealed, 'will you take Higgins away to some quiet place?'

'Yes,' Sweeney said. 'Bury his head in your bosom.' Maisie laughed and said to Higgins: 'Come on, sweetheart. I want to ask them to put that thing on the gramophone again.' As they went away the thought struck Sweeney that Mary Magdalene might have looked and talked like that and he remembered something which Ellis had quoted to him earlier in the week. He waited for a lull among the gramophone playing group and leaned forward. He said, groping vaguely:

'Last week you quoted me something, a thing about the baptism of Christ . . . I mean a poem about a painting of the baptism of Christ . . . do you remember what I mean?'

'I think I do,' Ellis said. Then quickly and without punctuation he began to rattle off a verse. 'A painter of the Umbrian School Designed upon a gesso ground The nimbus of the baptized God The wilderness is cracked and browned.'

'That's it,' Sweeney said. 'Go on.'

Ellis looked surprised. But when he found Sweeney was not trying to make a fool of him he clasped the cup tightly with both hands and leaned across the table. He moved it rhythmically in a small wet circle and repeated the previous verse. Then he continued with half-closed eyes:

> 'But through the waters pale and thin
> Still shine the unoffending feet . . .'

'The unoffending feet,' Sweeney repeated, almost to himself. 'That's what I wanted. Christ – that's beautiful.'

But the gramophone rasped out again and the moment of quietness and awareness inside him was shattered to bits. Higgins came with three cups which he let down with a bang on the table.

'Refreshment,' he said, 'Annie's own. At much personal inconvenience.'

Sweeney looked up at him. He had been on the point of touching something and it had been knocked violently away from him. That always happened. The cups and the dirty tables, the people drunk about the gramophone, the girls and the cigarette smoke and the laughter seemed to twist and tangle themselves into a spinning globe which shot forward and shattered about him. A new record whirled raspingly on the gramophone for a moment before a tinny voice gave out the next song.

> 'Have you got another girl at home
> Like Susie
> Just another little girl upon the family tree?
> If you've got another girl at home
> Like Susie . . .'

But the voice suddenly lost heartiness and pitch and dwindled into a lugubrious grovelling in the bass.

'Somebody wind the bloody thing,' Ellis screamed. Somebody did so without bothering to lift off the pick-up arm. The voice was propelled into a nerve-jarring ascent from chaos to pitch and brightness. Once again the composite globe spun towards him. Sweeney held his head in his hands and groaned. When he closed his eyes he was locked in a smelling cellar with vermin and excrement on the floor, a cellar in which he groped and slithered. Nausea tautened his stomach and sent the saliva churning in his mouth. He rose unsteadily.

'What is it?' Ellis asked.

'Sick,' he mumbled. 'Filthy sick.'

They left Higgins behind and went down into the street. Tenements with wide open doors yawned a decayed and malodorous breath, and around the corner the river between grimy walls was burdened with the incoming tide. Sweeney leaned over the wall.

'Go ahead,' Ellis said.

'I can't.'

'Stick your fingers down your throat.'

Sweeney did so and puked. He trembled. Another spasm gripped him. Ellis, who was holding him, saw a gull swimming over to investigate this new offering.

'It's an ill wind . . .' he said aloud.

'What's that?' Sweeney asked miserably, his elbows still on the wall, his forehead cupped in his hand.

'Nothing,' Ellis said. He smiled quietly and looked up at the moon.

VIII

'Do you mind if I ask you something?' the girl said. 'It's about your wife.'

'Fire ahead,' the traveller said gently.

They stood on the terrace in front of the hotel. Below them the sea was calm and motionless, but from behind them where the large and illuminated windows broke the blackened brick of the castle the sounds of the band came thinly.

'You haven't seen her for eight or nine years.'

'Fifteen,' the traveller corrected. 'You needn't count the few visits between.'

The girl formulated her next question carefully.

'When you married her,' the girl asked, 'did you love her?' The traveller's face was still moist after the dancing. She saw the small drops of sweat on his forehead while he frowned at the effort to recall the emotion of eighteen years before.

'I don't know,' he answered finally. 'It's funny. I can't exactly remember.'

The girl looked down at the pebbles. She poked them gently with her shoe.

'I see,' she said softly.

He took her hand. Then they both stood silently and watched the moon.

It rode in brilliance through the August sky. It glinted on the pebbled terrace. It stole through curtain chinks into the bedrooms of the sleeping Monsignors and Bishops, it lay in brilliant barrenness on the pillows of stiff elderly ladies who had no longer anything to dream about. Sweeney, recovering, found Ellis still gazing up at it, and joined him. It was high and radiant in the clear windy spaces of the sky. It was round and pure and white.

'*Corpus Domini Nostri*,' Sweeney murmured.

Ellis straightened and dropped his cigarette end into the water below.

'Like an aspirin,' he said, 'like a bloody big aspirin.'

BRIAN MOORE
from *Black Robe*

8

A lynx, moving as though at any moment the earth would shift beneath its paws, came with infinite caution into the clearing where last night's fire had been guttered by morning showers. Laforgue, who had waited since dawn, wondering if he dare venture outside his place of concealment, watched the lynx, his surrogate, as it moved closer to the empty kettle, its delicate nostrils leading it to the smell of food. Suddenly, the animal lifted its head, looking around as though it had heard something and was prepared to bolt. For a long moment it stood statue-still, then turned its head so that Laforgue could see its eyes, eyes which did not see him. Uneasy, as though threatened, the lynx crouched down, then cautiously began to make its way back in the direction from which it had come. As it did, Laforgue heard a noise like a sigh. The lynx stopped, transfixed, head thrown up. Vibrating like a harp string was a slender arrow embedded in its neck. At once, Laforgue ducked his head down into his hiding place. His ears, which a few days ago had been dulled by infection, now seemed to him like the ears of a Savage in their ability to detect the merest sound. When, again, he risked a look outside, a Savage, one of the strange painted faces of last night, bent over the lynx, removing the arrow. A second Savage crept from the trees and attached thongs to the dead animal's front paws. The first Savage lifted the animal up, placing it on the back of the one who had tied its paws. Both Savages moved away, going up the riverbank to the spot where the rapids, in a rush of white water, became unnavigable. Within seconds they were gone.

They are here and they are waiting. How long will they watch this place? How long before they decide to move on? They have killed a lynx and will want to eat it. For that, they must light a fire. If they light a fire, they will be sure to light it in some place where it cannot be seen. Where? They are waiting in a place where the trail from that first portage passes close by. They can also see the river. What will I do? What can I do?

The hours passed slowly. He watched the sun, fitfully present among high rolling clouds. He watched the river. For a time, he prayed. For a time he lay, staring at the little silver crucifix on the bead rosary his mother had given him on the day of his ordination as a priest. He thought of that day in the church of Saint Ouen, the solemn High Mass, the unseen choir singing the Kyrie high in the vaulted roof, his parents kneeling on prie-dieux just in front of the communion rail, their faces a mirror of their joy. How long ago that seemed, how odd, as though he had read of it in some book, or dreamed it, and now woke, half remembering what it was he dreamed. Would he ever again see Rouen, with its jumbled streets of crooked-timbered houses, the noisy, smelly fish markets he had played in as a child, or the ancient façade of Saint Ouen, its gable carved with the images of Judean kings and queens? An illimitable ocean separated him from that place, from that time; vertiginous walls of seas into which ships tumbled like paper boats. Was that other life a dream? Or was this a dream, this barbarous present in which he crouched in a hole beneath a tree trunk, alone, vulnerable as a lynx to an arrow in his throat?

Again, he crawled toward the opening and lifted his head into the light. He looked along the hidden path up which the Savages had dragged the lynx. He looked at the trees, high above the river. They are up there, hiding. They have lit no fire. They watch the trail and the river. Laforgue looked back at the river, curling into a bend. All was still. And then, closer, near the place where the Algonkin had landed yesterday, he saw two canoes drawn up on the riverbank. Coming up from them were Chomina, his wife and their little boy. Behind, his musket at the ready, as though to guard them, was Daniel. And lastly, the girl, Chomina's daughter. All of them looked around, looking for him.

At once Laforgue reached up from his hiding place and pulled himself to his feet. As he did, an eerie high-pitched yell struck into the silence. Ahead, he saw Chomina's party stop as if shot. Arrows hissed, some falling short, three finding a mark, one in Chomina's shoulder, one in his wife's neck, one in the bundle which his daughter carried on her back. At that moment Daniel's musket thundered. Seven painted Savages rushed out onto the trail, surrounding their victims, flailing at them with clubs. Laforgue saw Chomina turn to his wife as she fell, blood spurting from the arrow wound in her throat, saw Daniel on his knees, trying to protect his head and neck as the Savages with wild shrieks battered him down, saw the girl running with her little brother toward the canoes, saw four other Savages rush from the trees, pinioning her and tripping the child.

Laforgue stood, heart pounding. They had not seen him. Daniel's shot had felled one of the Savages, and now the Savage leader, wearing the mass vestments which he had donned last night, knelt by the fallen warrior, cradled him in his arms, then, with a cry of rage so terrible it made Laforgue quail, let the dead man fall back on the ground.

Rising, his silken robes bloodied from the dead man's wound, the Savage leader screamed to the others. Chomina's wife was dragged across the ground by one of her captors, while another ripped the arrow out of her neck. Laforgue saw them kick her and turn her over. The Savage leader, the embroidered gold cross on his vestments fouled with blood and dirt, uttered a second cry of rage, and at once the Savages fell on Chomina, Daniel and the girl, making them pass down a double line of warriors, each of whom struck at them with javelin or club. When Daniel, staggering, came in reach of the leader, the leader took a javelin, pulled Daniel's head back by his hair, then caught hold of Daniel's arm and held it up. With the point of his javelin he pierced Daniel's palm, laughing as the boy screamed in pain. Chomina, stumbling, fell to the ground. The Savages raised him up again, the better to beat him unconscious. The girl they punished with the staves of their javelins until they drew blood from her back and thighs. The little boy was the only member of the party they did not harm, one of them holding him by the hair as the child saw his mother bleeding from her dreadful arrow wound, his father bludgeoned senseless, his sister flayed. Again, the leader, brandishing Daniel's musket above his head, screamed an order. The Savages began to pass thongs over their captives' bodies, binding them, preparing to lead them to the canoes.

And in that moment, watching, Laforgue knew that Daniel, Chomina and Chomina's family all would die. And that he, if he crawled back into his hiding place, would escape their fate. But what is my life in the balance, if, by going forward now, I can confess Daniel, who is in a state of mortal sin, and, God willing, baptize the others before their last end?

He felt himself tremble. Deliberately slow, he began to walk toward the clearing. The painted Savages turned, their javelins poised, two of them threading their bows with arrows as he came toward the captives. The painted faces watched, impassive, as, pale and determined, a frail man in a long black robe, he knelt beside Chomina's wife and, wetting his fingers in the snow, began to say the words of baptism. He was too late. Tears came to his eyes as he saw her glazed pupils gaze past him at those heavens now forever denied her. Then, with a shriek of rage, the Savage leader came up behind him and clubbed him at the base of his skull. He fell forward, unconscious, and woke to hands passing thongs over his limbs. Within minutes, clubbed and bound, he stood with the others awaiting his fate.

The Savage strangers, silent now, loaded Laforgue's canoe with the remainder of the goods which Daniel earlier had strewn in the snow. Four warriors, coming from the trees, carried two canoes which Laforgue had not seen before, the canoes of the strangers. Within a minute all five canoes were launched in the waters of the lower rapids. With curses the painted Savages disposed of their captives, putting Daniel and Laforgue in one canoe and Chomina, his daughter and little son in the other. Then, with the Savage leader lifting his wet vestments up around his hips as he clambered aboard, and a second Savage, wearing Laforgue's spare cassock, pushing the leader's canoe to the front position, the strangers set out downriver. A light rain began to fall. Wincing, nursing his pierced hand, Daniel looked at Laforgue.

'We were coming back for you,' he said.

'I know.' Laforgue felt dizzy. The blow at the base of his skull had raised a large protrusion. 'Your hand,' he asked the boy. 'Did they break the bones?'

'No, I don't think so.'

'Chak, chak, chak, chak,' said one of the painted faces, mimicking the French speech. Turning, he spat in Laforgue's face. 'What is that dog talk, you hairy pig? What are you saying?'

'It is our tongue, the Norman tongue,' Laforgue said. Again, pain stabbed at the base of his skull.

'We speak your tongue,' Daniel said to the Savage. 'What people are you? You speak like Hurons.'

'Shut your hairy mouth,' the Savage said. 'If you cannot speak properly, then be silent, you prick.'

The Savage then called to the two others who paddled at the rear of the canoe. 'How is it that Normans can speak our tongue?'

'They talk like moose,' one of the Savages said, laughing. 'Algonkian moose. They will never sound like Iroquois.'

'Fucking right.'

Iroquois. Daniel looked at Laforgue. It was the danger Champlain had warned of. It was a sentence of death. Laforgue watched as Daniel, wincing, tried to lick his wounded hand. He leaned toward him. 'Let me confess you,' he whispered. 'Say an act of contrition.'

'Shut your fucking face,' the Savage shouted, turning, striking Laforgue across the nose, making his nose bleed.

'Say the words to yourself,' Laforgue whispered. 'Not aloud.'

Blood ran down his upper lip into his beard and mouth as he watched the boy close his eyes, watched his lips move in silent prayer. He felt a surge of joy. After a moment, Daniel opened his eyes, looked at him and nodded, as though to say he had finished. '*Ego te absolvo*,' Laforgue whispered, raising his hand in the sign of absolution. '*In nomine patris, et filii, et spiritus sancti.*'

The Savage who had struck him did not look back, for the canoes were now skimming at speed over rocky shallows, moving closer to shore. Laforgue, blood spilling down his chin onto his neck, nodded to Daniel to show that he had finished.

'Thank you,' the boy whispered. 'Forgive me, Father.'

'God is with us,' Laforgue said. 'It is He who forgives us.'

After paddling less than an hour, the Savages abruptly swung back toward shore, landing a few leagues downriver from the place where the Algonkin had first made camp. Here they hid the canoes and their contents high in the trees, then roped together their prisoners. Shouting, cursing, beating them with javelin staves, they set off along a narrow track through the forest. Within minutes, Laforgue and Daniel heard cries ahead. Four Savage women came through the trees wearing necklaces of beads, their bodies naked to the waist as for a ceremonial feast. They carried bark platters containing strips of cooked meat which they gave to the returning warriors. Gleeful, they danced around the prisoners, pulling at Laforgue's beard, striking Annuka, her father and Daniel, calling out, 'Let us caress them, let us caress them.'

'Later,' said the Savage leader, wolfing his meat and gesturing to the others to hasten on. And so, stumbling, bound, burdened, Chomina, his daughter and son, followed by Daniel and Laforgue, were led into an Iroquois village. Here were habitations of a sort Laforgue had never seen, dwellings laid out in a double row as in a village street with, at the end, a larger building, a communal house more than one hundred feet in length, built of strong saplings bent together to form an arched roof and covered with bark of oak and spruce. At the top of the arch was an open space to admit light and release the smoke of the fires.

As the warriors led their captives to this building, the party was surrounded by a large throng of men, women and children, all chanting at the tops of their voices. In the din Laforgue heard the beating of skin drums. At the entrance of the longhouse, a group of men, obviously leaders, stood waiting. They, like the warriors, had painted their faces. A few were heavily tattooed, their faces, backs and arms grotesquely traced in intricate arabesques. One of these tattooed figures, tall and gaunt, was adorned in such a profusion of coloured shells and beads, and wore a beaver coat of such splendour, that Laforgue assumed him to be the paramount leader. It was to this man that the warriors led their prisoners.

'Normans,' said the paramount chief.

'Travelling with Algonkin,' said the leader of the hunters. He held out Daniel's musket. 'Tarcha died of this.'

The paramount leader took the musket eagerly, examined it, then pulled the trigger. There was no explosion. He shook it in vexation, then looked at Laforgue. 'Bring them inside,' he said to the hunters.

'Yes, Kiotsaeton.'

The singing and drumming ceased. In a strange silence, the captives were led into the smoke-filled longhouse. Fires burned on the ground. Laforgue, looking up, saw rows of poles just under the vaulted roof. On them were suspended weapons, clothing, ornaments and skins. On a middle level were platforms running the length of the room and, as the captives were led to the fires, the villagers followed, scrambling up on these platforms to watch the spectacle.

'Strip them,' said Kiotsaeton.

At once, all the prisoners, including the little boy, were stripped naked. A cheer went up into the rafters as the older women came forward, singing. They took firebrands from the smoking fire and approached the paramount chief.

'May we caress the captives?' asked one of the women.

'Caress them,' said Kiotsaeton, 'but carefully. We must make them last.'

The women, gleeful, at once thrust their burning brands against the genitals of Chomina and Laforgue, causing them to double up in pain. They then burned Annuka's shoulder and thrust a flaming stick into Daniel's armpit. The crowd, wildly excited, yelled and shouted. 'Make them sing, make them sing their songs.'

'Sing,' commanded Kiotsaeton. 'Sing your war songs. And dance, you hairy dogs.'

Savage hands pulled the two Frenchmen forward and amid kicks and shoves they were forced to perform a clumsy dance. 'Sing,' Daniel cried to Laforgue. 'Sing or they will kill us.'

'*Ave Maria*,' Laforgue sang hoarsely, the words of the hymn lost in the yells of the exultant Iroquois, '*gratia plena, Dominus tecum . . .*'

He looked and saw Daniel singing the hymn, his good hand clutching his armpit where he had been burned. Men and women now scrambled down from the platform and, going to the fires, took up hot coals on platters. These they sprinkled on the captives, all the while laughing and yelling in excitement. Then, as the captives writhed and shrank from these tortures, the leader issued a new command. At once all were silent. He pointed to Chomina. 'Sing. Sing your war song.' He pointed to Annuka. 'Dance.'

Impassive, not looking at his captors, Chomina began to sing a war chant in a loud defiant voice. His daughter shuffled in a circle in a primitive dance step. Laforgue stared at the girl, his eyes misted by pain. That slender body which had aroused his lust now filled him with an infinite pity as her shoulders and narrow loins were kicked and pummelled by bystanders each time she stumbled and fell. *O Lord*, he prayed. *Grant me the chance to baptize her. Grant her eternal peace.*

And then, suddenly, the girl collapsed on the ground. The Savages fell silent; the only sound in the longhouse was Chomina's loud, monotonous war chant. Kiotsaeton and two other leaders went to the fires and spoke among themselves, then signalled to the waiting warriors. At once, a tall Savage, his head dyed red, his eyes horrid yellow circles, a strip of reddish fur hanging from a pigtail down his back, went up to Chomina's little boy, took him by the hair and, with a gesture callous as though he killed a fowl, swiftly slit his throat. Blood gurgled forth from the child's mouth. Daniel, anguished, tried to go toward him, but a Savage tripped him, spilling him on the ground. Chomina looked not at his dying son but up at the ceiling of the longhouse, singing a war chant as though he had seen nothing. And then, to his horror, Laforgue saw the child hacked to pieces with hatchets, its bloodied limbs thrown into a cooking kettle. He closed his eyes, as though unable to believe what he had witnessed.

Pandemonium filled the longhouse, a stamping, yelling, screaming din. The leader raised his hands for silence, then came up to Laforgue.

'Agnonha, who is Agnonha?'

'He is our leader, the leader of the French,' Laforgue replied.

'Then you are a dead man, you hairy fool. Agnonha is the cunt who killed our people. You will die, but not today. You will die slowly. We will caress you and caress you again. Today, we will give you a first caress. Take his hand.'

Two of the warriors at once seized and held Laforgue. Kiotsaeton took from his belt a razor-sharp clam shell. Taking Laforgue's left hand he pulled on the index finger; then, using the clam shell like a saw, cut to the bone. He sawed through the bone and pulled the skin and gristle free. He held up the finger joint. The crowd roared and cheered. He threw the piece of finger into the cooking kettle. In excruciating pain, Laforgue fell to his knees and then, in a scene so terrible that it surpassed horror or pity or forgiveness or rage, he saw three older women take from the cooking kettle the limbs of the dead child and pass them, parboiled, to the warriors who had captured Chomina's party. The warriors paraded up and down before Chomina and his daughter, eating the flesh as though it were succulent meat. Chomina stood, singing loudly, his eyes on the rafters. The girl vomited on the ground.

The women standing by the pot began to pass out parboiled flesh to other warriors. As they did, Kiotsaeton stepped forward and held up his arms. At once, the yelling died down.

'The prisoners must not die,' Kiotsaeton shouted. 'We will caress them again when the sun has risen. Give them food. Let the children caress them, but be careful. Give back their garments.'

Surrounded by smiling, jeering Savages, the captives were thrown their clothes, forced to dress, then pushed and pulled outside the longhouse. Children danced ahead of them as they were led to a smaller dwelling where a fire burned on a pit of live coals. There, the villagers left them alone, save for one warrior with club and hatchet and four young and gleeful children. Exhausted, the captives lay down on the bare earth. The children circled them. One little girl giggled, her hand over her mouth, almost in a parody of embarrassment. 'Take off your clothes,' she said.

'Which ones?' the guard asked.

'Those two. The hairy ones.'

'Take your fucking clothes off. Quick.' The guard, raising his club, gave Laforgue and Daniel each a blow on the shoulder. Wearily, both men removed their garments and stood naked once again.

'Dance,' cried a little boy. His companions, meanwhile, had gone to the rear of the habitation and returned now with sharpened sticks which they thrust into the flesh of the men's thighs.

Wearily, the captives began a shuffling dance.

'Sing,' cried one child.

They began the Ave Maria.

'Be quiet,' cried a second child.

They stopped singing. The first child, the one who had ordered them to sing, at once went to the fire and, picking up a burning brand, held it close to Daniel's penis. 'I told you to sing,' the child yelled.

Daniel began to sing.

'Stop!' cried the second child, approaching, also waving a burning brand. The guard laughed.

The little girl went up to Laforgue and pulled hard on his beard. 'What is this fucking shit on your face?' she cried. 'Are you a man or a hare?'

'All right, children,' the guard said indulgently. 'That's enough. We must let them rest. There will be more sport tomorrow. Now they must eat.'

'We will eat them,' cried a little boy.

'I will eat your foot,' the little girl screamed, dropping a hot coal on Daniel's foot.

'And I will eat one of your hands,' a second boy yelled.

'Now, children, now, children,' said the guard, laughing. 'Outside, go on.'

Yelling, giggling, the children ran out of the habitation. The two men, awkwardly, again put on their clothes. The guard bound their hands behind their backs, bound their feet so that they could only shuffle in a hobbled step. He bound Chomina and Annuka in a similar fashion, pausing to put his hand under the girl's skirt and fondle her. Then he brought pieces of some corn biscuit.

'Eat,' he said to the girl and gently held the biscuit to her lips. Like an automaton, the girl tried to chew, but vomited the biscuit on the floor. 'Never mind,' the guard said quietly. 'Later I will give you another piece.'

He then went to Chomina, who bit on the biscuit he offered as though he did not see him. The guard fed Laforgue and Daniel, then went back to the fire, where, squatting on his hunkers, he took out his pipe and began to smoke.

For the first time since the capture, Chomina seemed to rouse himself. He shuffled close to his daughter, and she laid her head in his lap. He sat, rocking, rocking. Daniel hobbled across the floor and lay at her feet, looking at her with agonized tenderness. At last, her sobbing and retching ceased and she said to her father, 'These aren't men. They're wolves.'

'No,' Chomina said. 'They are not wolves. They are men. They are afraid of each other.'

Laforgue, lying on the floor, turned to listen. 'What do you mean?' he asked.

'If an Iroquois sees another Iroquois show pity to a captive, he will make fun of him. The warrior must not show pity. Pity is a weakness.'

'They are wolves,' the girl said again.

'No, no.' Chomina looked down at her. 'Our people do the same if they capture enemies. So do the Montagnais and the Huron. An enemy must be made to cry out in pain. That is why they torture us. But, alone, the Iroquois is like you or me.' He nodded to the guard, who sat, his back to them, puffing on his pipe. 'He will not harm us.'.

'Will we die?' she asked.

Her father rocked her but did not reply.

'But why must we cry out?' Daniel whispered. 'Why?'

'If they can make us cry out, it means we cannot resist them. If we do not weep and plead for mercy, it means that when we die misfortunes will come upon them.'

'But if we do cry out,' Laforgue said. 'Does that mean that they stop the torture?'

Chomina looked at him. 'Don't you understand? If you cry out, then, when you die, they will possess your spirit.'

'But that's not true,' Laforgue said. 'If I die, I will go to paradise. You and your daughter will come with me to paradise if you let me baptize you. I can do it now.'

'Is that the water sorcery?'

'Yes. And all my God asks of you is that you believe in Him.'

'Leave me alone,' Chomina said bitterly. 'I saw you do the water sorcery to my wife. But she was dead when you did it. She could not believe in your god, because she had died already. And some nights ago you did it to a baby. But the baby was dead. The water sorcery will not bring me to paradise. The water sorcery kills.'

'You are wrong,' Laforgue said. 'Chomina, I am not lying to you. I will always be grateful to you. I can never repay you for coming back. But if you let me baptize you I swear that when you die you will go to paradise.'

'What paradise? A paradise for Normans?'

'No. For you. For all who are baptized.'

'But my people are not baptized with this water sorcery. Therefore they are not in your paradise. Why would I want to go to a paradise where there are none of my people? No, I will die and go to another country where our dead have gone. There I will meet my wife and my son. Your God shits on me and mine. My wife is dead because of you. My son is in the stomachs of the Iroquois. And the Iroquois will kill me slowly, day after day. It is you Normans, not the Iroquois, who have destroyed me, you with your greed, you who do not share what you have, who offer presents of muskets and cloth and knives and kettles to make us greedy as you are. And I have become as you, greedy for things. And that is why I am here and why we will die together.'

'You are right about our greed,' Laforgue said. 'But you are wrong about our God.'

'Leave him,' Daniel whispered. 'Be quiet, Father.'

And so they lay in the smoking habitation, silent, in pain, each alone in thought of what had happened that day and what lay ahead. In the opening of the roof, the sky darkened to night. And when, at last, Chomina saw that their guard was asleep, he began to whisper to his daughter. Daniel, licking the wound in his palm, heard their muted voices and crawled closer to listen. But as he did, Chomina turned and looked at him in the flames of the guttering fire, as though warning him to stay away.

It was much later when, exhausted from their wounds and sufferings, both Chomina and Laforgue slept, that Annuka, inching herself across the bare earth, came and lay, bound, against her bound lover. In the darkness, he could not see her face. 'Annuka,' he whispered. 'Your father is right. I have destroyed you.'

Her face came close. He felt her parched lips touch his cheek.

VAL MULKERNS

'Memory and Desire'

The television people seemed to like him and that was a new feeling he found exciting. Outside his own work circle he was not liked, on the whole, although he had a couple of lifelong friends he no longer cared for very much. The sort of people he would have wished to be accepted by found him arrogant, unfriendly, and not plain enough to be encouraged as an oddity. His wealth made him attractive only to the types he most despised. He was physically gross and clumsy with none of the social graces except laughter. Sometimes his jokes were good and communicable. More often they were obscure and left him laughing alone as though he were the last remaining inhabitant of an island.

Sometimes, indeed, he wondered if he spoke the same language as most other people, so frequently were they baffled if not positively repelled. He liked people generally, especially physically beautiful people who seemed to him magical as old gods. Sometimes he just looked at such people, not listening or pretending to listen to what they said, and then he saw the familiar expression of dislike and exclusion passing across their faces and he knew he had blundered again. Now for several weeks he had been among a closely knit group who actually seemed to find his company agreeable. He knew nothing about television and seldom watched it. But because his father's small glassmaking business had blossomed under his hand and become an important element in the export market, the television people thought a programme could be made out of his success story, a then-and-now sort of approach which seemed to him banal in the extreme. He had given his eventual consent because time so often hung on his hands now that expansion had progressed as far as was practical and delegation had left him with little to do except see his more lucrative contacts in Europe and the United States a couple of times a year.

The only work he would actually have enjoyed during these days was supervising the first efforts of young glassblowers. Two of the present half-dozen were grandsons of his father's original men. At a time when traditional crafts were dying out everywhere or falling into strange (and probably passing) hands, this pleased him. He tried to show signs of his approval while keeping the necessary distance right from the boys' first day at work, but this was probably one of the few places left in Ireland where country boys were shy and backward still, and their embarrassment had been so obvious that nowadays he confined himself to reports on them from the foreman. It had been different in his father's time. The single cutter and the couple of blowers had become personal friends of his father and mother, living in the loft above the workshop (kept warm in winter by the kiln) and eating with the family in the manner of medieval apprentice craftsmen.

During holidays from boarding school, they had become his friends too, gradually and naturally passing on their skills to him, and so listening without resentment to the new ideas on design he had in due course brought back with him from art school and from working spells in Sweden. Gradually over the years of expansion after his father's death he had grown away from the men. Now since the new factory had been built in Cork he knew very few of them any more.

The odd thing about the television people was that right from the beginning they had been unawed and called him Bernard, accepting that he had things to learn about their business and that he would stay with them in the same guesthouse, drink and live with them during the shooting of the film, almost as though they were his family and he an ordinary member of theirs. It had irritated and amused and baffled and pleased him in rapid progression and now he even found it hard to remember what his life had been like before them or how his days had been filled in. Their youth too had shocked him in the beginning; they seemed like children at play with dangerous and expensive toys. The director in particular (who was also the producer and therefore responsible for the whole idea) had in addition to a good-humoured boy's face an almost fatherly air of concern for his odd and not always biddable family. What was more remarkable, he could discipline them. The assistant cameraman who had got drunk and couldn't be wakened on the third day of the shooting had not done it again. When Eithne, the production assistant, had come down to breakfast one morning with a streaming cold and a raised temperature, Martin had stuffed a handful of her notes into the pocket of his jeans and sent her back up to bed, weeping and protesting that she was perfectly all right and not even her mother would dare to treat her like that.

Martin was very good with uncooperative fishermen, and with the farmer on whose land the original workshop still hung over the sea. A nearby hilly field had recently been sown with oats, and the farmer began with the strongest objection to a jeep laden with gear coming anywhere near it. He had agreed to it during preliminary negotiations, but shooting had in fact been delayed (delayed until more money became available) and that field, the farmer said, was in a delicate condition now. If they'd only come at the right time – Martin it was who finally talked him around with a guarantee against loss which would probably land him in trouble back in Dublin. But Martin (the Marvellous Boy was Bernard's private label for him) would worry about that one when he came to it and he advised Bernard to do the same about his fear of appearing ridiculous in some sequences. Not even half the stuff they were shooting would eventually be used, Martin said, and anyhow he'd give Bernard a preview at the earliest possible moment. Bernard stopped worrying again. Most of the time he had the intoxicating illusion of drifting with a strong tide in the company of excellent seamen and a captain who seemed to know his business.

The actual process of remembering was actually painful, of course. His only brother Tom had been swept away by a spring tide while fishing down on the rocks one day after school, and at first Bernard hadn't believed any reference to it would be possible when the script finally came to be written. Martin had come back to it casually again and again however, and finally one day of sharp March winds and flying patches of blue sky he had stood with Bernard on the headland near the roofless house.

'Let me show you what I have in mind,' Martin said gently, the south Kerry accent soft as butter. 'It will be very impressionistic, what I've in mind, a mere flash. A spin of sky and running tides, a moment. If you'd prefer, it won't need anything specific in the script. Just a reference to this friendly big brother mad about fishing, who knew about sea birds and seals and liked to be out by himself for hours on end. Maybe then, a single sentence about the nature of spring tides. The viewers generally won't know that spring tides have nothing to do with spring. You may say we're telling them about a successful glass industry, not about the sea, but the sea takes up a large part of your own early background and this piece is about you too. I'd write you a single sentence myself for your approval if you wouldn't mind – just to show you what I think would work – OK?'

' "These are pearls that were his eyes" – you could end like that, couldn't you?' Bernard heard himself sneering and almost at once regretted it. The director actually blushed and changed the subject. In a few seconds it was as if the moment had never happened, but it seemed to Bernard that a kind of bond had been perversely established.

Two days later a spring tide was running and he watched a few sequences being shot that might well be used for the passage he knew now he was going to write. He walked away from the crew when he found he could no longer watch the sort of sling from which the chief cameraman had been suspended above the cliffs to get some of the necessary angles. The whole thing could have been done better and more safely by helicopter but Martin had explained about the problems he had encountered after overrunning the budget for the last production. It wasn't of course that he wanted to make Bernard's backward look a cheaper affair; you often got a better end result (in his own experience) by using more ingenuity and less money: he thought he knew exactly how to do it. The somewhat unconvincing argument amused and didn't displease Bernard, who thought it more than likely that something less conventional might finally emerge. The last he saw of the crew was that crazy young man, clad as always when working in a cotton plaid shirt, suspending himself without benefit of the cameraman's sling to try to see exactly what the lens saw.

A fit of nervousness that had in it something of the paternal and something else not paternal at all made him walk the seven miles around to the next headland. He hadn't thought like a father for five years. For half of that isolated time he hadn't brought home casual male encounters either because nothing stable had ever emerged from them and more often than not he was put off by the jungle whiff of the predator and managed to change direction just in time. Now he tried to resist looking back at the pair of boys busy with their games which they apparently regarded as serious. The head cameraman was even younger than Martin. He had a fair freckled face and red hair so long that it would surely have been safer to tie it back in a girl's ponytail before swinging him out in that perilous contraption. Bernard turned his face again into the stiff wind and looked back at the receding insect wriggling above the foaming tide, man and technology welded together in the blasting sunlight. The weird shape drew back his eyes again and again until a rock they called the Billygoat's Missus cut it off and he was alone for (it seemed) the first time in several weeks.

For the first time as in a camera's framed eye he saw his own room at home. Tidy as a well-kept grave, it was full of spring light from the garden. There were daffodils on his desk. Spangles of light from the rocky pool outside danced on the Yeats canvas that took up most of one wall and struck sparks from the two early balloons which he treasured. Five poplars in a haze of young green marked the end of his garden. Beyond it, the sharp-breasted Great Sugarloaf and eventually the sea. The room had been tidy for five years now. No maddening litter of dropped magazines, no hairpins, no shoes kicked off and left where they fell: left for the woman next morning to carry to the appropriate place in the appropriate room because she was born to pick up the litter of other people's lives, paid for it as the only work she knew. One night in a fit of disgust he had kicked into the corner a black leather clog, left dead centre on the dark carpet awaiting the exact moment to catch his shin. Uncontrolled fits of violence he despised. Recovering quickly he had placed the shoes side by side outside the door as though this were an old-fashioned hotel with a dutiful boots in residence. She had come in laughing later on, both clogs held up incredulously in her hand, laughing and laughing, tossing them finally up in the air to fall where they might before she left the room. As perhaps she had done last night and would do again tomorrow. Wherever she was.

A rising wind drove before it into the harbour a flock of black clouds that had appeared from nowhere, and when drops of rain the size of old pennies began to lash down he sought refuge in the hotel which had been small and unpretentious in its comfort when he was a child. His father's clients had often stayed here. He had sometimes been sent on messages to them with his brother. Now the place had several stars from an international guide book and was famous both for its seafood and the prices that foreign gourmets were willing to pay for it.

He sat in the little bar full of old coastal maps and looked out at the sea; alone for the first time in two weeks he was no less content than in the casual company of the television people. Their young faces and their voices were still inside his head. As though on cue, Martin suddenly came through into the bar, also alone. The wind had made any more shooting too dangerous for today he said, and the girls had gone off to wash their hair. He had his fishing gear in the boot, but he doubted if he'd do much good today.

'Have lunch with me, then, and eat some fish instead,' Bernard invited, and was amused to see a flash of pure pleasure light up the director's face. Beer and a sandwich usually kept them going until they all sat down together at the end of the day.

'This place has got so much above itself even since the last time I was down here that I expect to be asked my business as soon as I set foot inside the door,' Martin grinned.

'They wouldn't do that in late March,' Bernard assured him. 'Neither the swallows nor the tourists have arrived yet, so I fancy even people in your state of sartorial decay would be encouraged.'

Martin took an imaginary clothes brush out of the jeans pocket (too tight to hold anything larger than a toothbrush) and began to remove stray hairs from that well-worn garment which had seaweedy stains in several places and looked slightly damp. The boy walked with a sort of spring, like a healthy cat, and there was no trace yet of the flab which his pint-drinking would eventually bring. He ate the bouillabaisse and the fresh baked salmon which followed with the relish of a child brought out from boarding school for the day and determined to take full advantage of it. He praised the Alsace wine which was apparently new to him and Bernard decided that one of the great remaining pleasures of money was never to have to worry about the cost of anything one suddenly wanted to do. Bernard listened abstractedly to a little house politics over the coffee and then at the end of the first cognac he spoke one unwary line about buying all those bandy little boss men for a next birthday present for Martin should he wish it. The sea-reflecting blue eyes opposite him narrowed coldly for a moment before they closed in a bellow of laughter and the moment passed, like the rain outside. The sea was too uneasy, however, in the whipping wind to yield anything, but Bernard remembered one good story about his dead brother on a long-ago trip to Kinsale. Martin made a note in biro on the back of the wrist which held his fishing rod and Bernard knew it would be transferred to the mounting heaps of papers back at the hotel. More and more in the course of the programme he was being his own production assistant.

Mr O'Connor had carried in a mountain of turf for the fire and Eithne rather liked to listen to the rattle of the rain outside by way of contrast. Her hair was dry by now but spread all over the hearthrug and she swung it back in a tickling blanket over the recumbent John D. who was still struggling with the *Irish Times* crossword.

'Give that over and sit up,' she said, fetching her eternal dice-throwing version of Scrabble which she had bought somewhere in Holland.

'I was just going to work out another angle for that last shot to put to Martin when he gets back.'

'Martin is probably half-way to France by now on an ebbing tide. We'll find his pathetic little bits and pieces in the morning.'

'Stop that!' John D. was superstitious as well as red-haired. He was nervous about things like that. 'All right, I'll give you three games and that's it.'

'Nice John D. Did you notice Bernard's face today when you were strung up over the cliff, by the way?'

'I had other things to worry about. Is "cadenza" allowed?'

'It's not English but I suppose it's in the *OED* like everything else – it's virtually been taken over, after all.'

'OK it's allowed.' John D. formed the word.

'But no *brio* or *allegro molto,*' Eithne warned.

'No *brio* or *allegro molto* – I haven't the makings of them anyhow. What sort of look did Bernard have on his unlovely mug?'

'A bit nervous for you, I think. I think that's why he walked away.'

'Arrogant bastard a lot of the time.' John D. swept up the dice after totting his score. 'Are capitalists human? You should put that theme to Martin some time.'

'More a Neville sort of line, surely? But I think you're wrong. He's shy and he's only just stopped being uneasy with us.'

'Just in time to say goodbye then,' said John D. with satisfaction. 'There's hardly a week in it, if the weather lifts a bit.'

'If,' Eithne said, scooping a single good score. It was her game, her thing, but the others always won. 'I think he's lonely, which only goes to show you money isn't everything.'

'You can be miserable in much more comfort though. He looks to me like a bod who's had it off wherever he pleased with one sex or t'other, despite his ugly mug. He has the brazen confidence you only get from too much money.'

'I think you're wrong and the death of his brother is still bothering him after all these years. It's something I just have a hunch about. And then of course his wife walked out on him a few years ago. Prime bitch they say she was too. He came home one night and found not as much as a hairclip left behind, and his baby gone too.'

'"Hunch" is not a permissible word all the same. Thirties slang,' said John D. with finality. 'Why wouldn't she walk out on him when he's probably given to buggery?'

'It's much more permissible than "cadenza". How about to hunch one's shoulders?'

'Go and ask Mr O'Connor if he has a dictionary then.'

'You go. My hair isn't dry yet.'

'Your hair is practically on fire, lady,' John D. said, settling himself comfortably on the hearthrug again. A car crunched in the sandy drive outside and Eithne gave a long sigh.

'Thank God. I couldn't have borne the smell of good country roast beef much longer.'

'There'll be frogs' eyes to follow.'

'At worst there'll be stewed apples, at best apple pie. Doesn't your nose tell you anything except whether a pint's good or bad?'

In out of the rain and the early dusk, Bernard was touched all over again by the sight of two apparent children playing a game beside the fire. He came over very willingly to join them when Eithne called and Martin went upstairs to look over his notes before dinner. He would call Evelyn on his way down, he said.

Later they all went in the pouring rain to the pub and listened while a couple of local Carusos rendered songs like 'Two Sweethearts' – one with hair of shining gold, the other with hair of grey – or the endless emigrant laments favoured by local taste. Whiskey chasing several pints made John D. a bit quarrelsome and he shouted for a song from Bernard just to embarrass him. To everybody's surprise, Bernard was not embarrassed. He stood up, supported only by two small Jamesons (the second of which he was still nursing) and gave the company a soft-voiced but not untuneful version of 'Carrigfergus' which was vociferously applauded by the locals and earned him delighted approval from the team. Eithne thought they ought maybe incorporate 'Carrigfergus' into the soundtrack, and John D. wanted to know why they couldn't all move up to Carrigfergus and let Bernard do his party piece with his back against the castle walls. This suggestion was received with the contempt it deserved, but Bernard wasn't discomfited.

That happened only when they got back to the guesthouse and he heard Martin telling Mrs O'Connor that they would almost certainly be finished shooting by the end of the week and would hardly stay over the weekend. The sinking of the heart was like what came long ago with the necessity of facing back to school after the long summer holidays. He felt ashamed of his emotion and unsure how to conceal it, so he went up early to his room. Normally they would hang about for hours yet, reading the newspapers they hadn't had time for during the day, swapping stories, doing crossword puzzles, discussing the next day's work. Usually he didn't contribute much to the conversation; like a silent member of a big family he was simply there, part of what was going on, perfectly content to sit up as long as they did.

Now there was something symbolic about hearing the murmur of their voices from downstairs. The script had still to be written and there would be consultations in Dublin about it, hopefully with Martin, but (give or take a few days from now) the thing was over. Next week they would all be busy taking somebody else through his mental lumber-room. The little family would re-form itself around another fire, and it would have nothing to do with him. And soon it would be April, breeding lilacs out of the dead land, mixing memory and desire. Time perhaps to go away; he had promised himself a few weeks in April. On the other hand, why not stay on here?

He let down the small dormer window and looked out over the water. This house echoed, in almost exact detail, that other, roofless, house; the murmur of voices, even, was like his sisters' voices before they settled down for the night, all together in the big back bedroom. His own small room above the harbour used to be shared with his brother. The rain had stopped now and there was almost no sound from the sea and he wasn't surprised when Martin came to his door to say the weather forecast had been very good for the south-west and they might get in a full day's shooting tomorrow.

'Come in and have a nightcap,' he invited, and Martin said he wouldn't stay long but happily didn't refuse the brandy when it was taken from the wardrobe.

'What will you do next?' Bernard asked, just for a moment unsure of how to begin.

'A bit of a break before I join Current Affairs for a short stint,' the boy smiled. 'Yours is the last programme in the present series. No more now until next season.'

'You mean you're going to take a holiday?' He strove to make his voice sound casual, although he was suddenly aware of the beating of his heart.

'Unless something untoward crops up, yes.'

'Why not join me in Greece, then, since that's where I'm heading next week or the week after? The place I have on Ios needs to be opened up after the winter and there's plenty of room I assure you. Also two local women waiting to cook and clean for us.' Bernard saw the refusal before it came; it was only a question of how it would be framed, how lightly he would be let down.

'It's a tempting offer, and there's nothing I'd enjoy more, all things being equal. Never been further than Corfu as a matter of fact. But my wife has organized a resident babysitter for the two boys and we're off on a busman's holiday to Canada as soon as I'm free. Laura is Canadian you know. I met her when I was training in London with the BBC. When we get back, maybe you'd come over for supper with us some evening? Laura's an unpredictable cook, but you'll agree that doesn't matter too much when you meet her. Is it a deal?'

He drained the glass and got up off Bernard's bed with the same catspring which was noticeable also in the way he walked.

'It's a deal. Many thanks. And maybe you'll both join me some time in Greece?'

Martin made the appropriate noises and didn't go at once, but started talking about a painter called Richard Dadd who (somebody had told him) had probably given Yeats his Crazy Jane themes. He hadn't seen the paintings himself at the Tate but Bernard had, so this kept them going until the door closed behind him, and on his youth, and on the hollow promise of knowing him as one knew every line of one's own hand. There was a lot of the night left and, fortunately, a lot of the brandy too.

The weather behaved as the weathermen said it would and the rest of the shooting went without a hitch. During this couple of weeks the year had turned imperceptibly towards summer, primroses in the land-facing banks, sea-pinks along the cliffs and an air about the television people that Bernard had seen before and couldn't quite place. Only when he went with them for the final day's shooting did he pin it down; a fairground the day after the circus. The television gear was more easily moved, of course; no long hours were needed for the pull-out. But the feeling was the same. They didn't believe him when he said he was staying on and they seemed shocked, which amused him, when he determinedly heaped presents on them the morning they were going: his Leica for Eithne who (incredibly) had never owned a camera of her own, a sheepskin jacket for John D. because his own was in flitters from the rocks, a silver brandy flask (circa 1840), a cigarette lighter and a gold biro scattered apparently at random among the rest. The vulgarity of the largesse amused Bernard himself because such behaviour was not usual and he didn't entirely understand his impulse. But he understood perfectly why he gave Martin his signed first edition of *The Winding Stair*, a volume which for a year or more had lived in the right-hand door-pocket of his car for no better reason than that he liked to have it there. He had bought it somewhere along the quays of Cork.

> 'Fair and foul are near of kin
> And fair needs foul,' I cried,
> 'My friends are gone and that's a truth
> Nor grave nor bed denied
> Learned in bodily loneliness,
> And in the heart's pride.'

A former owner had marked that with a small star in the margin, and Martin smiled slightly as he read it aloud in gratitude when the book fell open.

'I often have a disturbing feeling when I finish a job like this that I know –' he searched patiently for the words he wanted and his hesitation seemed to Bernard like comfort consciously given for some loss he could understand. 'That I know almost enough to begin over all over again. Properly.' He didn't smile at all when they shook hands so that the handgrip seemed warmer. 'Until soon, in Dublin,' were his last words, a rather childish farewell which would have left a pleasant glow behind if Bernard had not known by now that they would not meet again. The vanful of technology went on ahead of the boy's unreliable little red sports car, and watching from the drive of the guesthouse, Bernard had the feeling of the fairground again after the circus caravans have rolled away. It was peaceful, though, with the blue sea breathing quietly all around him and a few mares' tails of cloud slowly unravelling in the sky.

He was leaning over the wall considering how he would fill his remaining time when the guesthouse owner strolled by, indicating the blue boat which bobbed at the end of its mooring rope below them. 'You could take the aul' boat out fishing any day you had a fancy for it, Mr Golden. You're more than welcome to her any time though I wouldn't recommend today, mind you.'

'I'm much obliged to you, Stephen. I have all the gear I need in the boot of the car so I might do just that. But why not today?'

'She'll rise again from the south-west long before evening,' his host said positively. 'And she'll blow herself out if I'm not mistaken. 'Twould be a dangerous thing to go fishing out there today.'

'The weather men last night didn't mention any gales blowing up.'

'The weather men don't live around this Hook either,' O'Connor said drily. 'I've caught those same gentlemen out once or twice, and will again with the help of God.'

'You might be right at that, I suppose. But if I do go out, I'll only fish for a short while, I promise you.'

A pleasant man, Stephen O'Connor, a retired Civic Guard with an efficient wife to make a business out of the beautiful location of their house and her own hard work. Bernard remembered him vaguely from childhood, pedalling wet and fine around the coast roads, stopping here and there for a chat, missing nothing. It was he who had brought the news that Tom's body had been washed ashore somewhere near Kinsale. It was he who had in fact identified it. On remembering this Bernard toyed with the idea of having an actual conversation with this kindly man whose memories touched his own at one black juncture. The moment passed, however, and Stephen made a little more chat, lingering with natural courtesy just long enough for a guest to make up his mind whether or not further company would be welcome, and then he ambled contentedly in the direction of the greenhouse for a day's pottering. Old man, old man, if you never looked down again at a drowned face of my father's house it would be time enough for you. Forgive me, Stephen O'Connor.

The first warm sun of the year touched Bernard's eyes and he smiled, sitting up on the sea wall. No more Aprils, no more lilacs breeding out of the dead land, no more carnal awakenings. He felt peaceful then a little surprised that the image behind his closed eyelids was not of his brother or of the young Martin or even of the caravans pulling out. It was the small wilful face of his daughter in the act of breaking away when one tried to hold her. He didn't know where she was, or even how she looked now, whether she still mirrored her mother in every gesture. He had a perfect right to know for the mere trouble of enforcing it. He hadn't done that, at first put off by the refusal of maintenance, by the eternal sound of the phone ringing in an empty flat and by two or three unanswered letters. He hadn't made a very energetic effort to keep in touch. As one year became two or three and now five, it had always seemed too late, but it would be untrue to pretend he greatly cared. It was just that, not being able to understand why the child's face should be so vivid in his mind, he was bothered as by some minor irritation, a door that slammed somewhere out of sight, a dripping tap. It wasn't until he was actually aboard the boat starting up the engine in a freshening breeze that he realized why he couldn't rid himself of his daughter's face today, of all days.

ANTHONY CRONIN

from *The Life of Riley*

It seems to me now that things all round were not as good as they had been before my departure to Ardash. Perhaps the closing of The Warrens had something to do with it. I began to adventure more into other pubs, where I sometimes adopted a different persona and met a different class of person. I even occasionally visited the establishment where the regime intellectuals congregated. I caught a glimpse of the grocers' Secretary there once or twice, but I think my visits, apparalled as I then was, distressed him, for once when I came in he finished his drink and left the corner where he had been discoursing in Gaelic about that week's *New Statesman* immediately.

One morning, as I lay under my hearthrug in 'The Gurriers', I heard approaching down the garden from the direction of the house a voice which was vaguely familiar.

'And is it here he is, in this little housheen? Well I wouldn't put it past him to have found a plaisheen like this where the song of the birds would inveigle the song out of him.'

After a moment's cogitation I recognized this gibberish as belonging to a man called Ted O'Connell whom I had once or twice met in the Gaelic intellectuals' pub. He was, I knew, the boss of some state board or other: he administrated canals, or herrings, or limestone or something like that, and had the reputation of being wealthy and well-got in regime circles, but unfortunately, as I already knew, hard to touch.

As I wondered what had brought him to 'The Gurriers' his long and Celtic face appeared at the window and I could see that he was accompanied by my landlord and a rather lesser type of intellectual civil-servant.

I bade them enter. Cigarettes were produced and the conversation began. O'Connell expressed astonished, delighted admiration for the circumstances in which I lived. It was, he said, a sight for sore eyes to see me here in my fastness, behind my walls. He referred to my poetic solitude, an ideal circumstance for the creation of 'great spalpeens of poems', obviously unaware that I entertained guests day and night, and that two builders' labourers, a former rate-collector who was allegedly half-way through a gigantic novel about cattle-drovers, and another gentleman of uncertain profession who had been locked out by the whore with whom he was known to associate, had slept in my 'fastness' the night before, and indeed but lately departed for the pubs. He even used the phrase 'as snug as a bug in a rug' unblushingly, evidently unobservant of the fact that I was wrapped in one.

On our own removal to the pubs, however, it soon became apparent that behind the conversation lurked a moral imperative. They were all well-wishers, that was perfectly clear, and I shuddered in my broken shoes. The lesser civil-servant began by leading the conversation round to a friend of his, public relations officer for the gas-works or sewage system, I am not sure which. This was a sharp and talented man he declared, who wouldn't be a bit put out if he lost the job in the morning.

'Not a bit of him. Seumas could knock out a living as a free-lance journalist, starting tomorrow.'

The possibilities of living by the pen were discussed. It was agreed that in Ireland things were very difficult. We had been joined by an auctioneer, whose brother was editor of the *Tipperaryman* and often contributed articles to the *Irish Independent*.

'He was always a lad for the writin', but except for he had the ould job it wouldn't keep him in butter.'

This was to nobody's liking and the newcomer was soon reduced to a sulky silence. O'Connell held forth about the BBC and the possibilities inherent in the Irish Radio were canvassed.

'Did you ever send anything to *The Trumpet*, Paddy?' he asked. 'I'm sure you'd get a very sympathetic reception from Prunshios McGonaghy.'

I shook my head dumbly.

'The brother often reads it,' said the auctioneer. 'I don't know though if he ever sends his stuff there. Leastways I don't ever remember him mintionin' it. Of course he has stuff here and there and you'd never hear a word out of him about it. I only discovered meself by accidint that he had an aarticil in the *Irish Digest* that was taken out of one of the provincial papers. He's not one to boast, not like a lot of others that go in for the writin'.'

There was a stony silence. The rest of the company was afflicted by the greatest of conversational annoyances, a confusion as to levels.

O'Connell tried again. 'I had a wordeen with Prunshios the other day, Paddy,' he said. 'He's looking for somebody like you to do a few aartic . . . essays for him about a subject that's probably near to your own heart.'

I assumed a mask of interest and enquiry.

'Mind you he's a bit out of touch, but his heart is in the right place. He'll listen to what you have to say.'

'And what, might I ask,' I asked, 'would be the subject of these articles?'

'Well the fact of the matter is, Paddy, Prunshios is very interested in the younger generation, and he thinks, and I think, that you might be a spokesman for them. We old men, you know, with the best will in the world get a little bit out of touch and we don't know what you young fellows might be thinking. But we're anxious to learn. Oh, yes, we're anxious to learn all right. And you know, if you don't mind me saying so, I think it's your duty to tell us.'

The company took an assenting sip, adam's apples registering grave agreement.

'Begod I don't know but they think at all,' said the auctioneer. 'Only interested in women and the like of that, as far as I can see.' He congratulated himself by gesturing to the barman.

The day so far wasn't going too badly as days went, but I slipped in a sandwich on the auctioneer's round. There might well be agonies in store.

'I have a suspicion, Paddy, that there are a lot of things you'd be the better for getting off your chest. No use becoming too bitter, you know. I know you don't talk like my generation talked, nor Prunshios' either, for the matter of that, though our generations did a good job in their day. Oh they did a good job all right, and if you'll forgive me saying so, you young fellows should never forget it.'

'Well, by God,' said the auctioneer, 'you said a true word there. If you ask me these young fellows take a hell of a lot for granted. It wasn't them that bate the tans.'

'Oh well, be that as it may,' riposted my friend, 'I don't suppose they'd be found wanting either if the day ever came again. And for that matter Paddy here may well be serving the old sod better than you and I served it, though we did our bit. There's a time for everything in God's time, and, as Shakespeare himself says, God fulfils himself in many ways.'

He smiled benignly on the company, his long Celtic face full of goodwill, and urbanely and cheerfully ordered a drink in his turn, cracking a beneficent joke with the barman as he did so.

'You know,' he said, suddenly serious again, 'I often say this and as a matter of fact I was saying it to Prunshios himself only the day before yesterday when we were having a hand of cards together in the house of a mutual friend. There's more ways than one of serving your country, and Paddy here with his little poems and his intellect and his thoughts may well be striking a blow that future generations will think every bit as important as anything we ever did. I often feel we old fellows should have a bit more humility where the young are concerned. I'm not talking about understanding now, because to tell you the truth, Paddy, I don't pretend to understand a lot of the stuff that you young fellows are writing, but I think we ought to recognize our day is nearly done. Give the young their head. Let them think their own thoughts and say their own say. I'm not as young as I·was, but bejabers I'm not one of those old fellows that thinks the younger generation does not respect Ireland and the Irish ideal, ay and love it too, as much as we ever respected or loved it, though again I'm proud to say we all did our bit, and it wasn't a bad bit either.'

He smiled on the auctioneer. 'Eh Ned? Don't you think it's time we old fellows took a back seat and gave the young men of Ireland their head?'

'Take the back of my arse,' said the one enquired from. 'Take the back of my arse and boil it. It wasn't the like of the youth of today that won the battle of Ballanagheer.'

Silence washed in over this last remark, but my friend lost none of his urbanity and goodwill.

'You know,' he said, 'I've thought once or twice lately – and I know Prunshios agrees with me – that there may be a great wave coming, the like of the one that came thirty odd years ago.' He laid his hand on my arm. 'That it may be happening now, but that like the old men and the middle-aged men of those times, some of us may not be able to see what is happening, and that the youth may throw us aside as we threw the old fellows of those days. Don't get bitter, Paddy. Don't get bitter. Give us a chance. We're anxious to hear from you. We're anxious to help. We know you love your country. My God it makes my blood boil' . . . he did not deign to glance at the auctioneer . . . 'it makes my blood boil to hear men of my own generation, who should know how we were misunderstood, ay and maligned, by men who I am the first to say had done their bit in their own day, abuse the youth of today without taking the trouble of understanding what they're up to, without trying to find out what is their vision of the national ideal.' He smiled again. 'Well now that's where I think you should give us a bit of help. We were young fellows ourselves once upon a time you know.'

Apart from the anger that these insulting references to my alleged youth were causing me, I genuinely doubted that I could be any help. What, for example, was I up to? The plain fact of the matter was that I did not know. And what on earth was the national ideal? I accepted another drink and held my peace. My interlocutor continued.

'I was reading, you know, the other day a novel of O'Faolain's,' he said, the light of culture and civilization in his eye. 'Now O'Faolain is a man of my own generation almost. But you know his book is disillusioned. That's the only word for it, disillusioned. Now oddly enough I think that marks him out as a member of my generation, not of yours. For you know I believe that if there is one thing the youth of today are not, it's disillusioned. If there's one thing the youth of today are, it's' – for an instant I thought he was about to say illusioned, or perhaps deluded, but he avoided the trap. 'If there's one thing the youth of today are, it's too full of ideals. They may be unharnessed ideals. They may even be wrong ideals, though that's as may be, and it's maybe not for us old fellows to say. But I'll tell you something Paddy, when I saw the place you were living in this morning, the place you have chosen to write in, and to think in, and where may be the next revolution in Irish thought will come from, it made me feel very humble. Very humble indeed.'

'Well begod I don't know anything about that,' said the auctioneer, 'not having seen the apartment. But as far as humility goes, our friend here seems to have his share of it, for he's too humble to buy a drink anyway.'

The monopoly administrator seriously supplied the deficiency; while the auctioneer survived a paroxysm of self-congratulatory, bronchial laughter.

'I want you to promise me one thing, Paddy,' my friend continued. 'That you will ring up Prunshios McGonaghy. That you will think about what he has to say. And that when he asks you, as he will ask you, to write this article for him, that you will speak your piece like a man.'

Dumbly, glass in hand, I promised.

'I'm not sure Paddy, that we haven't made mistakes. Not at all sure. I'd be the first to admit that here is a very definite sense in which we might be said to have failed. Indeed yes. I remember, thirty-five years ago, Mellows saying to me: "Ted, have you ever envisaged the possibility of failure?" And you know it didn't strike me till long afterwards what he meant. When we were on hunger strike in nineteen hundred and thirty-three I was discussing with some of the boys what had happened to the national ideal, when it suddenly struck me that what Liam meant was that we might fail after we had won. And you know, to a man of my generation, that was a terrible thought.'

Comforting himself with another large whiskey, and magniloquently including the company in his gesture, my regime friend continued his, to me somewhat obscure, discourse.

'That's the thought that haunts me, Paddy, and troubles more than one man of my generation. And that's what only you can tell us. For our success or failure in terms of the national ideal depends to a great extent on how the young feel about Ireland. Oh I know all about the emigration figures and that sort of thing. That doesn't matter. That's only a matter of economic re-organization, and sooner or later we'll find the answer to that. What I want to know is, do you feel that your generation has come closer to the national ideal than ours, or not?'

He beamed on me gently but interrogatively.

'Begob I don't believe he'd even get close to an each-way treble from the looks of him, or a you-know-what on a starry night, unless he got his hair cut. I have a young fellow meself at the university goin' on to be a B.Comm. and 'jabers I don't know where he got half the notions he's picked up. 'Twasn't in the good Catholic household where he was reared anyway. The youth of today would be a sore disappointment to Rory and Liam and Cathal Brugha I'm thinkin'. God that young fellow of mine gives me the colic every time I look at him.'

Silently, seriously, albeit smilingly enduring, my administrator of inland waterways or otherwise continued to gaze at me interrogatively. I fell back on the only line of defence available.

'I think I'd rather answer that in writing,' I said.

'And spoken like a writer too,' he twinkled. 'I wouldn't doubt you. Oh, we'll get something worth reading when you and Prunshios get together. Now, remember I'll tell him you'll be ringing him up. And strictly entre nous as the saying goes, I don't think you'll find him ungenerous. And you won't mind me saying, Paddy, that there never was a poet yet – and I've known a few in my time, oh yes, I knew Fred Higgins and Colum and the lot – that wasn't the better for a few pounds in his pocket. Not that it stays there very long. Oh, I know the poets. Give us four more large ones there, Mick, like a good fellow.'

AIDAN HIGGINS

from *Balcony of Europe*

3

The hospital by the sea: That morning the bell had rung early, someone kept their finger on it. I dressed and went down and hammered open the stiff rainsoaked door. There was no one there. The lane was empty. I went back to bed again and must have dozed off. This strange dream came to me.

A Sunderland flying-boat of World War II was blundering slowly through clouds at no great altitude, and being fired at by citizens on the ground armed with antiquated rifles. I was discussing something with the coloured woman Guala Conroy in the studio. She was interested in one of my paintings and proposed hire purchase terms. There came a shout from the door: *Here it comes again!* I ran out and took up one of the heavy rifles, a Lee Enfield. I could see the shadowy bulk of it flying through clouds. It had a white fish-like belly. If I hit it I knew it would explode, a whale hit with a harpoon that carried a charge in its head. When I fired the dream ended. I didn't know whether I'd struck it or not, allowing for the altitude the dream-bullet had gone off on a trajectory well ahead of the flying-boat, passing high up through clouds, white as snow. I had certainly fired well ahead of the white belly; but it was me the bullet found – into me it struck.

When I woke again, there was the cold studio with its rafters and dirty sky-lights, the brown velvet curtains drawn; I had great difficulty in heating it. At one time it had been Dermot O'Brien's old studio.

Some warning there, a premonition, I felt uneasy, bad news was on the way. An hour later the studio bell rang again. I went down. In the open door a messenger in a crash helmet was taking a telegram from his leather satchel. He said, Ruttle? Yes, I replied, and took it from him. I read it inside, by the boat.

MA GONE TO HOSPITAL x COME OVER x DA. Dun Laoghaire.

The hospital was by the sea. It stood near the harbour and the yacht clubs, near the railway station. A bleak-looking edifice in grey stone.

The bus dropped me near the gate. Clouds hung low and I could see my breath in the air. Before midday it was already twilight. In the damp the snow had turned to slush and the slush to water soon after it reached the ground, forming irregular puddles in the hospital car-park. Nothing kept its shape. The name of the hospital was reflected upsidedown in pools of water. I saw the lame man going by and called to him but he did not hear me, chose not to hear me.

It was late autumn, in so far as there can be an autumn after no summer. For me it was already winter. Everything was grey, lead-coloured, not a stir of air, the low clouds releasing a drizzle of snow, the wettest autumn in those parts for seventeen years.

A doctor took me into a small well-heated room near the reception hall. He told me in effect that she was dying; her lungs were gone. We could but hope. (He meant there was no hope.) I could call him at any time. Any time, he repeated. We shook hands. He left. I went to her. She was in St Cecilia's, the female ward for the dying, near the service lift. I walked past the curtains for the last time.

Certainly she was dying. Her caved-in features and leaden colouring did not belong to the living. Her lower jaw had sunk. They had taken the bridge out. The flesh of her face had begun to collapse as the bones came through. If she lived through it, she would most likely be paralysed; opinion varied as to the severity of that paralysis, some holding out a little more hope than others, but none were sanguine. It was better, perhaps, that she should die knowing nothing and feeling nothing, go out in deep coma. The nuns were looking after her. They were dressed in white habits and moved about the ward, seldom speaking. In that hushed room the light was going. They moved past the windows, coifed and pale-faced sentinels of twilight, ghosts of this gloomy, fatal world. They did not represent the world, to be sure; they were the sexless gate-porters into the next. My mother was in good hands.

She, a great student of obituary notices, had feared death; first with religion, then without it, embracing it once more towards the end of her life. It's a strange Catholic fear, very Irish. A little light, a last feeble glow of intelligence about to be snuffed out, a little hard-won breath. It was hard-won all right, pulling her down. She was dying with each heart-beat; her sorrows and pleasures, shut up there for seventy-odd years would die with her. Something of me would die with her; I was watching part of my own death. It did not seem to belong to me, yet it was mine. Will my own death be like that, for another?

Now the long-brooded-upon, the long-feared, had caught up with her at last and soon there would be no more light, no more thought, no more pain, no more injections, no more breath. Knowing nothing of this, she was advancing step by step into darkness, going out in deep coma. She would know nothing of what had finished her – the cerebral haemorrhage, the night stroke. I took her hand. She was hardening already, tending towards the inertia of matter. I could not think of her dead, gone, no more, any more than I could think of myself dead. But nonetheless it was only too apparent that she was going.

Long ago, in the garden at Nullamore, she had sat on the rug and read Hans Andersen to Wally and myself. Red pulpy berries fell from the yew tree full of missel thrushes. She had been a beauty in her day. A local poet had composed a sonnet in her honour. The beauty sitting on the public bench by the Mall. Rhymester Jim McGinley had inscribed his little book of doggerel to her. Printed on poor quality paper, it had at one time been an object of wonder to me. Jim McGinley's verse was printed in the *Evening Mail*. The *Evening Mail* seemed to me a female newspaper, reserved and dull; it ran 'Mandrake the Magician'. The magician's cold, shaved features would never change, his coal-black hair and precise middle parting reminding me of my father. Cloaked, he was my father in tails. He had a gigantic Negro as body servant. The *Evening Herald* was masculine, with a red Crusader stamped as banner on the front page. It featured Inspector Wade, who also had an eagle nose, hair parted in the centre, a quiff like bow waves. His Negro was a detective called Donovan. The *Herald* was hot bread; the *Mail* was a glass of cold milk.

All that seems to have happened, if it ever happened, long ago, belonging to someone else's past, not mine. We sat under the oldest tree in the garden. Yew berries fell about us; there were ants crawling in the recently mowed lawn. The smell of fresh grass, the smell of the lime going in straight lines and at orderly right angles on the tennis court, the odour of grass decomposing behind the bamboos, this belonged to my childhood, and my sweet-faced mother reading there in a voice that breaks my heart. The straight white guide lines were the life I would follow, out in the world. The bamboos whispered of the advantages and pleasures that awaited me there.

She had reared us gently. Taught us to like books and paintings and such, all the things that my father had no interest in; he had the horses and the farm – those other things were beyond him. My parents were kind. Putting our interests before their own they pinched and saved, and gave us a boarding school and a college education that they could not comfortably afford; an education that dropped off me like water off a duck's back, my mother said. I took only what I wanted, the residue of my own exasperation with it, the hard drupe, and myself in the toils of it, not wanting it. Boarding school in the country, the Jesuit fiction of the world's order and essential goodness, stretching out ahead like the white guide lines. No.

They were of the country and loved the country, as I do, the lake areas around Sligo, the eleven lakes. In summer we went to a hotel in Bundoran, on a golf links. Before we were born, my taciturn brother and I, our parents had gone to Mulranny, I imagine because of sentimental associations. Later in Dublin they took to drink and followed the horses; bad habits I too have acquired. For my brother I cannot speak; he went his own sweet way.

I looked at the caved-in eyes, the bad colouring, the white hair soaked in sweat, arranged in an unfamiliar way, and hoped that she would not survive it, not continue to suffer, but rather go in sleep. I wished this for her who so dreaded death. The previous year had been a year of deaths. Too many too near to her. She had lived with my father in the damp place below street level, poorly enough towards the end and victimized him. Everything he did (and he did little) and everything he said (and he said much) annoyed her, yes and beyond all endurance. She was dying, as women sometimes die, of their man's equanimity. The days that could not change, would not change, refused to change, going like the English visitors in droves in both directions; the dying dying and the living living, yet sick of life, this life which is not life at all. Weddings up and down Dun Laoghaire, in the suburbs, brides with rice on their shoulders, issue. Funerals in Glasthule. Slow-moving and complacent-looking hearses, fleets owned by Fanagan and Creegan and others, moving in the narrow way, pedestrians doffing their hats. Droves 'in all directions', my mother said. She meant the ceaseless activity of the living into apparent life, and the dead into the ground. The boat train drawing out for Westland Row, tired Irish passengers gaping from the carriage windows in winter the level-crossing passed, rain on the tracks, the gate closing like the end of a yawn, my father huddled into his thin coat going home.

Your father, she said, as though disassociating herself from him. Your father, meaning: that abject fool. He went through a stage of dreaming winners, but it was too late. He still loved her in his way, but it was also too late. The life they had shared together had gone sour on them. Shortly before Christmas, her last Christmas in the year I am speaking of, my father won £24 with a tote treble on a shilling stake and bought himself a dark grey suit. My mother, knowing Olivia and I were going to Spain for a year or more, and feeling she would not survive another Irish winter, gave me, with a *contained* gesture, as a Christmas box, polaroid sunglasses. They were happy together for the last time. My father permitted himself, after a certain amount of Scotch, some broad but inoffensive jokes before Olivia. He was much taken with her. Crude, my mother sniffed, but Olivia laughed.

They had drifted apart over the years, as I from them, as my brother from them and me. We had never been what is called a united family, at least not since my childhood. My father, as a parent, had been anything any son could ever wish, and similarly my mother. My ever obliging father, none too astute in his dealings with people, particularly the fair sex, had given in to her too much and with predictable consequences. Each day more humiliations, which he pretended not to feel; she got in her digs, some sharp ones, *tela* followed by *estocada*, thrusts which he affected to turn aside, but which had, or should have hurt him deeply. Women were like that, tart, sharp-tongued, acid. Are they? Perhaps. At all events she lost any remaining respect she had for him; and, with that, restraint went too. She treated him like dirt. They disagreed, quarrelled incessantly; but it was all very one-sided.

She wiped the floor with him in company. It made any mutual assistance they might have given each other towards the end impossible. Each would die alone.

As a child I had a great fear of thunder, but never told my mother, who I think knew. Fear of thunderstorms around Sligo, apocalyptic lightning and the Garavogue gone green-grey, uncontrollable thunder crackling in the hills around Ben Bulben, my mother, pulling out more wool, looking over at me and saying, It's only God beating carpets in Heaven. Torrential rain fell, cutting small craters in the gravel. Seabirds flying inland, sign of a storm, my mother said, pointing with a knitting needle. Seagulls were floating in an air-current over Nullamore, staring down. I was nine. A pool, the colour of weak tea, was the gravel torn up. I sat on the window-seat looking out, feeling a sink of indescribable misery. I had no means to describe it, the world, myself, the world before myself. The world that would go on existing after myself, as if I had never been. I felt it all pouring out of me, this ignorance, the plug out and everything I had, which was precious little, running away. I was sitting in the window-seat and the rain was pouring down. And she whom I had come out of sat there knitting, saying without words, by her presence, by the way she yanked out the wool, *I am here, I am knitting, silly, don't you see? I am protecting you.* Perhaps she had an intuition of how awful I felt. Wait until you're forty, Dan. You'll see. (I did not.) I see my white bedroom with nobody in it. Go back and draw the sea-green Venetian blinds. Go back to the timid puritan you were. When I go, my mother said, true to her obsession, when I go, no one will miss me. No one will grieve for me. I'll grieve for you, Ma, I said. And the upper part of a great elm, struck by lightning, fell into the swollen Garavogue.

At five that morning the tide began to go out for her, it was the turning point, entering the third day of deep coma. My father had been visiting her day and night, haunting the hospital. He had seen her at eight that morning, and was convinced she would not survive the day. It was her last day. Sunday in Ireland. The streets were virtually deserted, the sky grey and overcast by mid-morning, threatening snow. As I was shaving the studio bell sounded below.

My father came in to say she was sinking fast, not expected to last the day. Oh, she's very bad, he said, shaking his head. Very bad, Dan. I'm afraid she's going on us. Get over to her quick. I'll try and get the other fellow.

I told him to stay in the studio and rest. If anything happened I would phone. He needed rest. I built up the fire and he sat before it in his overcoat. Then I left. It had begun to snow. At the Circle I recognized a heavy figure coming out of a newsagent with English Sunday papers tucked under his arm. He pretended not to see me and turned quickly away, going by the wall with short, quick, fussy steps, a furled umbrella in one gloved hand. He would not go to the hospital, only near it, to feel he was somewhere near her, but not to see her dying. Some intuition had warned Wally she was dying that morning. I let him go. There's love for you. I too turned away. There were no radio taxis about. The streets were white. I stood at the Dalkey and Dun Laoghaire bus stop and waited.

I reached the hospital before eleven. The house surgeon told me what he had to tell me. I went upstairs to sit by her until she died. When I reached the curtained bed I did not know what awaited me – a death's head, my poor mother transformed into some kind of horror. A dull heavy breathing came from behind the curtain; so she was still alive. I stood by the bed. A nurse came with a chair. I sat down. For two days death had been drawing closer and was now very near. It was doing terrible things to her; she was holding on with all her remaining strength, mumbling with pinched-in and discoloured lips, *For me? Is it for me this time?* Unmistakably it was for her. Death was already stirring in her. She had been relatively passive for two days, two days of more or less quiet dying; now giving way to this subdued turmoil. The weary breathing of a stubborn person ascending a hard hill. Her spirit was now engaged; before it was only her body fighting with the blow, the night stroke. A bird lost at a window. *For me? Is it this time for me?* The bridge of her nose was bruised on either side where the useless spectacles had pinched, or the mark of when she had fallen in George's Street. One windy night we had been out drinking hot toddies with the lame man. Now she was going up a steep hill, going on at all costs, puffing at it. It took all her strength and more, but she was obstinate, going at it, her nose pointed. My poor mother wearily persisting, her eyes sunk, her mouth collapsed, bitter and deprived, attempting the last impossible hill. Who may say what humiliations can be borne? What the body can endure? What the mind can stand? I sat by her, held her hand, called to her, felt her pulse where the feeblest lymph ebbed away, came fluttering back, uncertain, the blood that had given me life. I put into her hand her own rosary beads of mother-of-pearl, listening to her hard breathing, intermittent snoring, and wished her troubles ended. Her cheeks sagged and filled, loose on the bone, and a little white froth accumulated at the corner of her mouth. This sac wavered, agitated by the air brought up painfully from her lungs. It soon dried out and another began to form. Each breath dragged up with such painful and insistent effort disturbed the bedclothes where she lay on her side. Then another followed, hard as the preceding one, harsh as the one that followed, and the little scum wavered on the dry breath issuing from collapsed lungs, torn from deep inside her. All this interspersed with sighs such as a child might give, uncertain of what's happening. Then silence as though she were listening, harkening to something.

She had begun her death. I held her stiffening hand where *rigor mortis* had already started. Her hair was damp. All about her the ghosts moved, whispering. A moth burning in God's unsupportable fire. It was quiet in the ward, a feeling of the Sabbath in Ireland. The minute hand moved around the dial of the ward clock and the hour hand dragged after it. Time went by sadly and slowly. The nurse on duty made an entry in the Day Book and went past, her starched uniform rustling. The ward was warm and full of nuns. On the table by her bed stood a bowl of water with a white towel over it, cotton wool, a glass tumbler, a black leather prayer book, a priest's crucifix. She had received Extreme Unction.

The thin snow blown against the long windows soon melted and ran down the panes of glass, but it was close and humid in the ward. My mother was the only one dying. The gob of spittle hovered in the corner of her mouth. An old arthritic nun with a mushroom complexion under her white coif came and laid a hand as white and speckled as another mushroom on my mother's forehead. Her fingers lifted up my mother's eyelid. *Leave me alone*, the hazel eye said: *I am soon leaving you.* That famous fixed stare.

Her eyes were fixed on something moving within herself, something reflected there. World-weary flesh, unbend; eyes, look your last. I was offered rosary beads.

I took them in my hand, declined to kneel, for I wanted to watch her while she was still alive, so that if she opened her eyes it would be me she would first see, as she had been the first person I had seen with the light of intelligence in my life, looking down at me over the end of the cot and asking to be recognized. But her eyes would not open again, ever in this life. The dutiful nuns were kneeling around her saying a decade of the rosary.

They went at it sing-song, drifting with it. The termination of life, that bulk of sins at which their prayers were pointing, urging *Sanctify! Sanctify!* a thurible swung to and fro by a server, his mind far away – more lullaby than dirge, pleading and lamenting in high sweet voices.

Now, thought I, if she who dreaded all this were to open her eyes! They wanted to hurry her away. No more sensual fret, they chanted, lost in their dream; relieve her of her hard cross, oh Lord!

But her eyes did not open. The hard breathing went on. Now it would pause, as if she were listening, before continuing as before. A heavy sigh, and then another breath, and then the rattling in the throat, a snore, then another breath, pushing out her cheeks, and the pitiful effort to live began anew. Ledge by ledge she was climbing, turret by turret, looking in all the windows.

Relieve her of her sad cross, the chorus of nuns chanted, staring at her, lead her to the light, take from her her hard burden. Let her have respite from her labour, oh Lord!

But she was still down at the foot of the hill. Grown cynical in the face of innumerable setbacks, a deeply disappointed woman, she would carry her cynicism and disappointments with her, into whatever region she was bound for, eyes tight shut (here the laboured breathing faltered).

It went on a little, faltered again, slower, and then, quite abruptly, stopped dead. 'She's going,' the old nun announced, falling forward on her knees and dashing holy water into my mother's face. They began the prayers for the dying.

The prayers were urgent now, the nuns' voices raised, the thurible swinging faster, sending up clouds of incense. They were hunting my mother's spirit hither and thither, trying to tell her that it was not like that, that it was not like that at all; but it was eluding them, rising through the smoke of the incense, the snow melting down all the long windows and the ward quiet. The nuns' breaths going together as if to help her on her way. It seemed like something I had witnessed before, though performed in a more accomplished manner. This was a botched rehearsal for what had never happened, would never happen.

And true enough the harsh and troubled breathing did begin again, hesitantly at first, uncertain of its welcome (her spirit had flown over the abyss), and then as determined and rasping as before – the obstinate effort to scale the impossible hill. The candle in her limp hand tilted at a dangerous angle, dripped candle grease on the sheet folded back, and holy water rolled down her cheeks like tears. Nonplussed by this turn of events, the old nun watched her, felt her pulse. The breathing was weaker but still persisting. The Superior made a sign and the other nuns left the bedside, went about their chores. Then she too followed.

I looked at my mother, who had been only pretending to die. Her humour had always tended to be on the grim side, rarely if ever directed against herself. This was another of her grim jokes, but one against herself. She was obstinate and set in her aversions, had not expected much; and now she was dying at her own pace and in her own way. The nuns' prayers had not touched or even reached her; they would never reach her. She had always scoffed at nuns – their dubious piety and questionable humility. Nuns and male hairdressers, barbers. Like slugs, she had said.

The plea of those who had turned away from the world in order to pray for it. Their lullaby could not touch her or reach her. Drops of holy water rolled unheeded from the cavities of her eyes. The candle had been snuffed out and taken from her. It would not be much longer now. This was the pause before the end.

Presently the old nun came back, watching her, felt her pulse. She whispered something to the young nun who had looked after my mother. Then she went to another part of the ward where a strong female voice was calling.

I held her hand. It lay limply in mine, life all but extinct there.

I liked the young nun, liked her calm face and unhurried movements (Sister Alphonsus Ligoura, Sister of Mercy). A different sensibility there. Nuns, with shorn hair and vanity gone, were different.

I had found a prayer for the dying by Cardinal Newman near the glass bowl, the wadding and heavy crucifix. I asked her to read this prayer. She knelt down and began to read it in her white voice. I knelt with her, my mother was a little above us.

And my Guardian Angel whisper peace to me, the nun read. She finished the prayer. Again please, I said. And my mother, her face discoloured, her breath going slower but resigned to it at last, down at the bottom of her hill, listened. I was handing her back the copy of Hans Andersen that she had read to me when I was ill; yew berries were falling all around us. Missel thrushes were moving in the branches. She took it in hands that were not discoloured, saying brightly, Enough for one day I think. It had a pale blue cover, no illustrations, the dust jacket lost. *Enough for one day.* The tormented breathing stopped, this time for good, and she had gone upwards out of her ailing body, past the falling snow, the unavailing prayers of the Sisters of Mercy, the accumulated slush. Slowly from the corner of her mouth some pale matter flowed.

And the nuns were back in a flurry of kneeling and re-lighting of the candle. The Prayers for the Dying set out after my mother, the candle lit and thrust into her dead hand. When they had finished they blessed themselves, rose up and moved away, the old Kerry nun and another nun hid the bed with screens. I could hear them whispering behind it. Church gossip. Inside the ward it was warm. Only my mother was cold. Outside the snow whirled away, over the pubs where she had liked to drink, out over the yacht basin and the harbour. Out over Ireland's Eye.

The old Kerry nun offered me a cup of tea. It seemed to be the custom. A strange custom. I did not want it but took it without milk or sugar and swallowed it scalding hot. She questioned me about my father and family. I told her I was married, had no children of my own. There was another unmarried son, not on the premises but in the vicinity. Tactfully she made no comment. Woeful human love – that bondage. She was small and bent, reached only to my shoulder, had rough manners (the way she had lifted my mother's eyelid), a broad Kerry accent and a kind heart. I've seen all classes go, she said, and no two go the same way. And was it your first? the old nun asked. Yes, I said, the tea scalding my insides. Ah that's hard then, she said; it's worse when it's your own poor mammy. But sure God is good and He will be good to her, poor soul.

Behind her, the nuns filed silently by; the curtains blew inwards, and I saw a darkness, a shape on the bed.

I had not been able to weep; not then; not now when I think back on it. I don't know why. Going, I looked for the last time at where she lay. Her mouth had fallen open and she was all dark and angular and stiff. When a thing lies still, it will be still forever, is a truth that no man can deny. Death had fixed her in this inimical pose – dark and punished; she no longer resembled my mother. The jaw had fallen, the brown stockings stuck out, this I saw before the curtains fell to. Go on now, the old nun said at my elbow, don't be needlessly troubling yourself. You can do nothing for us here.

I let the curtain drop, blotting out that face that was not my mother's known face; that dark and monumental figure. She had her wish anyway, I said. And what was that? the old nun inquired, smelling of mould-mushroom. To die in Ireland, I said. The old Kerry nun gave me a sideways look, and the hand I held was almost as cold and unreceptive as my mother's. I thanked her and left.

Outside it was cold and overcast. The snow had stopped falling. I felt some relief. Pain and decay, pain and decay, something fishing just below the surface. It was like leaving the dentist's; decay in the system had to be removed; and now it was removed and one was glad to be rid of it. Something of myself had been removed with some pain and I was free to go on without it. The water in the harbour was the colour of lead. And there were the masts of the yachts, and there was the gutted church. I waited for a bus to take me back to the centre of town.

When I reached the studio my old man was sleeping in his overcoat, the sink blocked with his endless tea-leaves, the electric kettle out of order. No light. No fire. No matter. I made him tea and brought it to him, told him what had happened, that she was at peace. He sat wringing his hands and staring at me.

All had been done, everything was over. He had grown old in a few days. He lived in his overcoat, a gift, dreaming of summer like the flies, only emerging from a winter-long hibernation to lead a summer life hardly more purposeful than theirs, setting out each day for one or other of the bathing places. He expressed a wish to see her. Later, I told him – they said later; they are laying her out now. He stared at me. Drink your tea, Da, I said. He did so.

Later we would both go and see her; see how she was. A death-blow is a life-blow to some who, till they died, did not alive become; who, had they lived, had died, but when they died, vitality began.

My peevish elder brother was nowhere to be seen.

JOHN BRODERICK

from *The Trials of Father Dillingham*

9

Maurice sat in the old armchair in his bedroom, looked at his wrist watch, and slowly clenched and unclenched his fists. The La was out to dinner, Jim was working on his notes, and Eddie had not yet returned. It was exactly ten forty-seven. He held the watch with its thick leather strap against his ear and felt a strange sensation of comfort, as the minutes ticked on relentlessly. Here at least one knew where one was: time neatly and effectively divided into minutes, hours, days.

But when he took his hand away and let it fall on the arm of his chair, he immediately experienced a return of that sense of drowning, of being carried along on a deep, slow tide and sinking under it, which he had more than once become aware of recently whenever he was alone.

The room was absolutely silent. As he always woke up at exactly the same time each morning, even in his drinking days, he had never bought himself an alarm clock and to have one as an ornament would never have occurred to him. The fat tick-tock of a time-piece above a blazing fireplace, accompanied by the contented purring of a cat, and the bird-like chirrup of a cricket on the hearth were not sounds that appealed to him. He remembered that from his boyhood, when he had preferred to hide himself in the loft, or go on long solitary walks over the fields rather than join the circle round the fire. How often had he come back, drenched to the skin, in time to join the last decade of the rosary and to meet his mother's reproachful glance as she got up stiffly from her knees. There had never been any comfort for him at that fire and, as time went on, he avoided it more and more. His harsh early upbringing had done its work. It was designed to fit him for a life that was narrow, hard and fatalistic. He preserved those elements in his nature in an even more inflexible form when he left home, filled with vague but savage dissatisfaction with the way of life in which he had been reared. An old story. He could not have remained anyhow. There were two brothers older than he, and there was barely enough on the farm to keep the old people.

But in his case the reaction against his upbringing was made more violent by the discovery of something strange and alien in his nature; something for which the code he inherited made no provision.

He stood up and began to walk slowly about the flat. He had never bothered to furnish the front room, since he never entertained. It was carpetless and empty, except for a table in the corner piled with books. All his possessions were contained in the back room where he slept. Some coloured prints of places he had visited abroad with Eddie hung on the walls, but there were no souvenirs, no ornaments. A bed, a table, a couple of armchairs and a record player beside a pile of records in the corner were all that the room contained, apart from a few suits in the wardrobe and his linen in a chest of drawers. It was not particularly tidy but it was scrupulously clean, and The La had not been without justification when she claimed that he smelled of leather. Being in the business, he had more shoes than he needed. They were ranged in a make-shift rack under the window and, since some of them were brand new, there was always a faint scent of leather in the room.

He stopped and looked at his watch again. Time, freed of its arbitrary segments of minutes and hours, became a vast amorphous tide. The moment he thought of the second, of the smallest unit of time, it was gone, to be succeeded by another and then another. The present, when one tries to grasp it, does not seem to exist at all, except in theory. It can only be understood by the ticking of minutes. The past and the future had some sort of shape and validity and for him there was now little future. He could not shape it in his imagination, as others did. This new sense of the meaninglessness of the present, without clocks, appointments and the hum-drum activities of the daily round, produced a sense of terror. He felt beads of sweat gathering on his forehead and upper lip and a clammy film enveloped his body. He raised his wrist to his ear, and pressed the watch against it.

10

He was so preoccupied with the tiny sounds, so intent on keeping himself afloat, that he did not hear the quick steps on the stairs, or the door opening. Eddie rushed in.

'Maurice, are you all right?' The voice was quick and breathless, and it brought him back to life. He relaxed, sat down, leaned back and nodded.

'Why, what did you expect?'

'I didn't realize it was so late. And the traffic was awful.' In earlier times Eddie had often come back to find Maurice sitting alone like this, staring into space. Then he would have made a joke of it, asked him what the nightmare was. But now such questions were impossible. He was reduced to wariness and trivialities, and hated it.

Maurice held his watch up to his ear again instead of looking at it, a gesture which confused Eddie further. What did this mean?

'I know that,' said Maurice in a voice too gentle and calm to be natural. It sounded as if it came from far away. Eddie was frightened, and turned aside to take off his coat. He knew it was impossible for him to conceal anything from the other's piercing gaze. It was part of the mysterious affinity between them, transcending the physical attraction about which both of them had always been cautious, exercising a control upon it which had not always been easy. As a result the understanding between them became more acute: but there were times recently when Eddie wished that it were less so. He dreaded showing the anguish he felt.

He sat down and clasped his hands. Since Maurice first told him bluntly of his condition they had avoided any serious discussion of it. Eddie was so stunned that he had been unable to think of anything to say, and since then had strained every nerve to keep up appearances, hoping against hope that the whole thing would prove to be a false alarm. Even in his thoughts he fell back upon cliches. But he did not tell Maurice that he had gone secretly to Clarendon Street and given in money for masses to be said. In moments of crisis Eddie always reverted to the religion he had ceased to practise for many years and still clung to in his bones.

'I suppose you've been telling the holy Hugheses about me, and asking them to offer up the Rosary,' said Maurice with a sarcastic smile.

'I've been doing no such thing. I told them you had not been well, and were getting better.'

'Another lie. But then that's what keeps you going in that set-up. Lies. I don't know how you stick it. All those whining brats, and the little woman coping with a brave smile, I bet, while the man of the house hums and haws for fear he'd say anything contrary to the Constitution. A bloody polisman.' Whenever he was annoyed Maurice's Roscommon accent came out strong. 'Don't you know that the only good cop is a dead one? Trying to get all he can out of you. I bet you have to pay your way for the privilege of sitting with the elect. Christ Almighty.' He hardly raised his voice or moved a limb. Since his illness he seemed to be conserving his strength. The rough voice, the barely controlled savagery with which he once would have uttered such opinions were now lacking. And this new quietness was even more intimidating.

Eddie made no reply. They had been through all this before. The first time he visited the Hugheses, Maurice had given him a long, searching look on his return. Any suspicions he had that Hughes represented anything really dangerous for his friend were immediately dispelled.

'I won't go any more,' said Eddie simply. 'But there's no harm in them. In their own way they find things just as difficult as we do.'

'You don't have to stay away because of me,' grumbled Maurice, feeling more irritated than ever. 'It doesn't matter a damn anyhow, one way or the other.'

'That's quite right, it doesn't.'

'Then what are you yapping for? To hell with the Hugheses and all the rest of them.'

Eddie got up and looked around the barely furnished room. It was here that Maurice had hit him on the mouth, drawing blood, the first time he had made a tentative, ill-judged approach to intimacy. Here too, after many weeks of tense mutual trial, they had come together shyly and clumsily in what most of the world thought of as an unnatural and unmentionable love.

'All right Maurice, you've had it out on me.'

'Forget it,' said Maurice, running his hand over his thin face. Eddie took the opportunity to light a cigarette with trembling fingers. His fifth that evening. Ordinarily he smoked ten or twelve after supper. He sat down again and crossed his legs, feeling the pulse behind his knee racing.

'I know how you feel.' Maurice clasped his hands and pressed them against his chest. 'We're eejits to be talking like this. It isn't as if I was thinking much of that now. It's a bit late in the day. What I'm wondering about is how long I'll be able to go on working.' He lifted his thin shoulders as if he felt a sudden chill.

Eddie had often tried to think what he would say when this moment arrived – and always ended by putting it out of his mind. But now he felt curiously calm.

'Did Issacson say something?' He grasped his wrist to steady the hand which held the cigarette. His inner numbness did not extend to his fingers.

'No. But some day soon, he's going to tell me to lie up. I might have to go into hospital. And there's the expense. The insurance will cover things when it's all over.

But I haven't that much saved, about three hundred in the bank, as you know. God knows how long this damn thing will last.'

'You won't be going into any hospital,' said Eddie firmly. 'You'll stay here.'

'Oh.' Maurice raised his thick eyebrows. 'Have you been discussing this between you?'

'No,' declared Eddie, knowing well that that lie would not pass. 'You'll stay here. I'll look after you. You see I've never been as pessimistic about this as you.'

'My bitch of a sister-in-law bunged my auld father into the country-home when he began to wet the bed. The poor auld bastard never knew what hit him.' Maurice made an attempt to smile, baring his strong white teeth, but Eddie knew he was not angry. 'Of course you've discussed it, you and The La and Grace. And the fellow below.' He unclasped his hands and jerked his thumb at the floor, looking at Eddie narrowly. 'Have you noticed any change in him?'

'No, why?' Eddie thought he had; and knew what was coming.

'I'd say he isn't such a renegade priest as he pretends, especially since he came back from this tour. Not that he ever was, in my opinion. And I know what Grace and The La have in their heads. And you too, when it comes to the bit. It would make you all feel more comfortable if you got me fixed up in the end. This brings out a lot of hidden things in people, and I have a feeling that it'll bring them out in Dillingham more than anybody.'

'Yes, I *have* noticed a change in Jim.' Eddie tried to avoid a direct answer. 'He doesn't seem too happy about his new book.'

'Fuck his new book,' snarled Maurice. He got to his feet slowly, swayed for an instant, then recovered himself. 'But I want you to promise me that you'll let me leave this world in my own way. And you know what that means.'

Eddie crushed out his cigarette on an ash-tray near his elbow. He scattered sparks on the carpet and stamped on them with his toe. Then he raised his head and met that dark, implacable stare.

'I know.'

'And you mustn't ever regret it. They'll try to make you. I know them. But if you're thinking of accepting them, ever, you'll have to reject me now, and everything that has happened between us. Otherwise, even that has been a sham. Well?'

'I'll never deny that, Maurice. You needn't be afraid.'

There was a silence during which Eddie felt that the other man was trying to search his very soul. It was not the first time that Maurice had frightened him, but he had never felt so completely helpless before.

'I don't care much for the idea of pain, I needn't tell you. But they've got drugs now, haven't they? I don't want immortality and all that shit. I don't believe in it, and I never believed in it less than I do now.' He paused and slowly held out his hand. Eddie looked at it blindly, then held out his and felt it grasped in a hot dry grip that fastened round his fingers like a rope. 'You'll do for that,' the deep voice went on. 'So long as you live, I'll live. That's the only kind of survival I'm interested in.'

On Maurice's wrist Eddie could hear the large watch ticking. It was all he was aware of at that moment of committal.

WILLIAM TREVOR
'Kathleen's Field'

'I'm after a field of land, sir.'

Hagerty's tone was modest to the bank agent, careful and cautious. He was aware that Mr Ensor would know what was coming next. He was aware that he constituted a risk, a word Mr Ensor had used a couple of times when endeavouring to discuss the overdraft Hagerty already had with the bank.

'I was wondering, sir . . .' His voice trailed away when Mr Ensor's head began to shake. He'd like to say yes, the bank agent assured him. He would say yes this very instant, only what use would it be when Head Office wouldn't agree? 'They're bad times, Mr Hagerty.'

It was a Monday morning in 1948. Leaning on the counter, his right hand still grasping the stick he'd used to drive three bullocks the seven miles from his farm, Hagerty agreed that the times were as bad as ever he'd known them. He'd brought the bullocks in to see if he could get a price for them, but he hadn't been successful. All the way on his journey he'd been thinking about the field old Lally had spent his lifetime carting the rocks out of. The widow the old man had left behind had sold the nineteen acres on the other side of the hill, but the last of her fields was awkwardly placed for anyone except Hagerty. They both knew it would be convenient for him to have it; they both knew there'd be almost as much profit in that single pasture as there was in all the land he possessed already. Gently sloping, naturally drained, it was free of weeds and thistles, and the grass it grew would do you good to look at. Old Lally had known its value from the moment he'd inherited it. He had kept it ditched, with its gates and stone walls always cared for. And for miles around, no one had ever cleared away rocks like old Lally had.

'I'd help you if I could, Mr Hagerty,' the bank agent assured him. 'Only there's still a fair bit owing.'

'I know there is, sir.'

Every December Hagerty walked into the bank with a plucked turkey as a seasonal statement of gratitude: the overdraft had undramatically continued for seventeen years. It was less than it had been, but Hagerty was no longer young and he might yet be written off as a bad debt. He hadn't had much hope when he'd raised the subject of the field he coveted.

'I'm sorry, Mr Hagerty,' the bank agent said, stretching his hand across the width of the counter. 'I know that field well. I know you could make something of it, but there you are.'

'Ah well, you gave it your consideration, sir.'

He said it because it was his way to make matters easier for a man who had lent him money in the past: Hagerty was a humble man. He had a tired look about him, his spare figure stooped from the shoulders, a black hat always on his head. He hadn't removed it in the bank, nor did he in Shaughnessy's Provisions and Bar, where he sat in a corner by himself, with a bottle of stout to console him. He had left the bullocks in Cronin's yard in order to free himself for his business in the bank, and since Cronin made a small charge for this fair-day service he'd thought he might as well take full advantage of it by delaying a little longer.

He reflected as he drank that he hardly needed the bank agent's reminder about the times being bad. Seven of his ten children had emigrated, four to Canada and America, the three others to England. Kathleen, the youngest, now sixteen, was left, with Biddy, who wasn't herself, and Con, who would inherit the farm. But without the Lallys' field it wouldn't be easy for Con to keep going. Sooner or later he would want to marry the McKrill girl, and there'd always have to be a home for Biddy on the farm, and for a while at least an elderly mother and father would have to be accommodated also. Sometimes one or other of the exiled children sent back a cheque and Hagerty never objected to accepting it. But none of them could afford the price of a field, and he wasn't going to ask them. Nor would Con accept these little presents when his time came to take over the farm entirely, for how could the oldest brother be beholden like that in the prime of his life? It wasn't the same for Hagerty himself: he'd been barefoot on the farm as a child, which was when his humility had been learned.

'Are you keeping yourself well, Mr Hagerty?' Mrs Shaughnessy inquired, crossing the small bar to where he sat. She'd been busy with customers on the grocery side since soon after he'd come in; she'd drawn the cork out of his bottle, apologizing for her busyness when she gave it to him to pour himself.

'I am,' he said. 'And are you, Mrs Shaughnessy?'

'I have the winter rheumatism again. But thank God it's not severe.'

Mrs Shaughnessy was a tall, big-shouldered woman whom he remembered as a girl before she'd married into the shop. She wore a bit of make-up, and her clothes were more colourful than his wife's, although they were hidden now by her green shop overall. She had been flighty as a girl, so he remembered hearing, but in no way could you describe her as that in her late middle age; 'well-to-do' was the description that everything about Mrs Shaughnessy insisted upon.

'I was wanting to ask you, Mr Hagerty. I'm on the look-out for a country girl to assist me in the house. If they're any good they're like gold dust these days. Would you know of a country girl out your way?'

Hagerty began to shake his head and was at once reminded of the bank agent shaking his. It was then, while he was still actually engaged in that motion, that he recalled a fact which previously had been of no interest to him: Mrs Shaughnessy's husband lent people money. Mr Shaughnessy was a considerable businessman. As well as the Provisions and Bar, he owned a barber's shop and was an agent for the Property & Life Insurance Company; he had funds to spare. Hagerty had heard of people mortgaging an area of their land with Mr Shaughnessy, or maybe the farmhouse itself, and as a consequence being able to buy machinery or stock. He'd never yet heard of any unfairness or sharp practice on the part of Mr Shaughnessy after the deal had been agreed upon and had gone into operation.

'Haven't you a daughter yourself, Mr Hagerty? Pardon me now if I'm guilty of a presumption, but I always say if you don't ask you won't know. Haven't you a daughter not long left the nuns?'

Kathleen's round, open features came into his mind, momentarily softening his own. His youngest daughter was inclined to plumpness, but her wide, uncomplicated smile often radiated moments of prettiness in her face. She had always been his favourite, although Biddy, of course, had a special place also.

'No, she's not long left the convent.'

Her face slipped away, darkening to nothing in his imagination. He thought again of the Lallys' field, the curving shape of it like a tea-cloth thrown over a bush to dry. A stream ran among the few little ash trees at the bottom, the morning sun lingered on the heart of it.

'I'd never have another girl unless I knew the family, Mr Hagerty. Or unless she'd be vouched for by someone the like of yourself.'

'Are you thinking of Kathleen, Mrs Shaughnessy?'

'Well, I am. I'll be truthful with you, I am.'

At that moment someone rapped with a coin on the counter of the grocery and Mrs Shaughnessy hurried away. If Kathleen came to work in the house above the Provisions and Bar, he might be able to bring up the possibility of a mortgage. And the grass was so rich in the field that it wouldn't be too many years before a mortgage could be paid off. Con would be left secure, Biddy would be provided for.

Hagerty savoured a slow mouthful of stout. He didn't want Kathleen to go to England. *I can get her fixed up*, her sister, Mary Florence, had written in a letter not long ago. 'I'd rather Kilburn than Chicago,' he'd heard Kathleen herself saying to Con, and at the time he'd been relieved because Kilburn was nearer. Only Biddy would always be with them, for you couldn't count on Con not being tempted by Kilburn or Chicago the way things were at the present time. 'Sure, what choice have we in any of it?' their mother had said, but enough of them had gone, he'd thought. His father had struggled for the farm and he'd struggled for it himself.

'God, the cheek of some people!' Mrs Shaughnessy exclaimed, re-entering the bar. 'Tinned pears and ham, and her book unpaid since January! Would you credit that, Mr Hagerty?'

He wagged his head in an appropriate manner, denoting amazement. He'd been thinking over what she'd put to him, he said. There was no girl out his way who might be suitable, only his own Kathleen. 'You were right enough to mention Kathleen, Mrs Shaughnessy.' The nuns had never been displeased with her, he said as well.

'Of course, she would be raw, Mr Hagerty. I'd have to train every inch of her. Well, I have experience in that, all right. You train them, Mr Hagerty, and the next thing is they go off to get married. There's no sign of that, is there?'

'Ah, no, no.'

'You'd maybe spend a year training them and then they'd be off. Sure, where's the sense in it? I often wonder I bother.'

'Kathleen wouldn't go running off, no fear of that, Mrs Shaughnessy.'

'It's best to know the family. It's best to know a father like yourself.'

As Mrs Shaughnessy spoke, her husband appeared behind the bar. He was a medium-sized man, with grey hair brushed into spikes, and a map of broken veins dictating a warm redness in his complexion. He wore a collar and tie, which Mr Hagerty did not, and the waistcoat and trousers of a dark-blue suit. He carried a number of papers in his right hand and a packet of Sweet Afton cigarettes in his left. He spread the papers out on the bar and, having lit a cigarette, proceeded to scrutinize them. While he listened to Mrs Shaughnessy's further exposition of her theme, Hagerty was unable to take his eyes off him.

'You get in a country girl and you wouldn't know was she clean or maybe would she take things. We had a queer one once, she used eat a raw onion. You'd go into the kitchen and she'd be at it. "What are you chewing, Kitty?" you might say to her politely. And she'd open her mouth and you'd see the onion in it.'

'Kathleen wouldn't eat onions.'

'Ah, I'm not saying she would. Des, will you bring Mr Hagerty another bottle of stout? He has a girl for us.'

Looking up from his papers but keeping a finger in place on them, her husband asked her what she was talking about.

'Kathleen Hagerty would come in and assist me, Des.'

Mr Shaughnessy asked who Kathleen Hagerty was, and when it was revealed that her father was sitting in the bar with a bottle of stout, and in need of another one, he bundled his papers into a pocket and drew the corks from two further bottles. His wife winked at Hagerty. He liked to have a maid about the house, she said. He pretended he didn't, but he liked the style of it.

All the way back to the farm, driving home the bullocks, Hagerty reflected on that stroke of luck. In poor spirits he'd turned into Shaughnessy's, it being the nearest public house to the bank. If he hadn't done so, and if Mrs Shaughnessy hadn't mentioned her domestic needs, and if her husband hadn't come in when he had, there wouldn't have been one bit of good news to carry back. 'I'm after a field of land,' he'd said to Mr Shaughnessy, making no bones about it. They'd both listened to him, Mrs Shaughnessy only going away once, to pour herself half a glass of sherry. They'd understood immediately the thing about the field being valuable to him because of its position. 'Doesn't it sound a grand bit of land, Des?' Mrs Shaughnessy had remarked with enthusiasm. 'With a good hot sun on it?' He'd revealed the price old Lally's widow was asking; he'd laid every fact he knew down before them.

In the end, on top of four bottles of stout, he was poured a glass of Paddy, and then Mrs Shaughnessy made him a spreadable-cheese sandwich. He would send Kathleen in, he promised, and after that it would be up to Mrs Shaughnessy. 'But, sure, I think we'll do business,' she'd confidently predicted.

Biddy would see him coming, he said to himself as he urged the bullocks on. She'd see the bullocks and she'd run back into the house to say they hadn't been sold. There'd be long faces then, but he'd take it easy when he entered the kitchen and reached out for his tea. A bad old fair it had been, he'd report, which was nothing only the truth, and he'd go through the offers that had been made to him. He'd go through his conversation with Mr Ensor and then explain how he'd gone into Shaughnessy's to rest himself before the journey home.

On the road ahead he saw Biddy waving at him and then doing what he'd known she'd do: hurrying back to precede him with the news. As he murmured the words of a thanksgiving, his youngest daughter again filled Hagerty's mind. The day Kathleen was born it had rained from dawn till dusk. People said that was lucky for the family of an infant, and it might be they were right.

Kathleen was led from room to room and felt alarmed. She had never experienced a carpet beneath her feet before. There were boards or linoleum in the farmhouse, and linoleum in the Reverend Mother's room at the convent. She found the papered walls startling: flowers cascaded in the corners, and ran in a narrow band around the room, close to the ceiling. 'I see you admiring the frieze,' Mrs Shaughnessy said. 'I had the house redone a year ago.' She paused and then laughed, amused by the wonder in Kathleen's face. 'Those little borders,' she said. 'I think they call them friezes these days.'

When Mrs Shaughnessy laughed her chin became long and smooth, and the skin tightened on her forehead. Her very white false teeth – which Kathleen was later to learn she referred to as her 'delf' – shifted slightly behind her reddened lips. The laugh was a sedate whisper that quickly exhausted itself.

'You're a good riser, are you, Kathleen?'

'I'm used to getting up, ma'am.'

Always say ma'am, the Reverend Mother had adjured, for Kathleen had been summoned when it was known that Mrs Shaughnessy was interested in training her as a maid. The Reverend Mother liked to have a word with any girl who'd been to the convent when the question of local employment arose, or if emigration was mooted. The Reverend Mother liked to satisfy herself that a girl's future promised to be what she would herself have chosen for the girl; and she liked to point out certain hazards, feeling it her duty to do so. The Friday fast was not observed in Protestant households, where there would also be an absence of sacred reminders. Conditions met with after emigration left even more to be desired.

'Now, this would be your own room, Kathleen,' Mrs Shaughnessy said, leading her into a small bedroom at the top of the house. There was a white china wash-basin with a jug standing in it, and a bed with a mattress on it, and a cupboard. The stand the basin and the jug were on was painted white, and so was the cupboard. A net curtain covered the bottom half of a window and at the top there was a brown blind like the ones in the Reverend Mother's room. There wasn't a carpet on the floor and there wasn't linoleum either; but a rug stretched on the boards by the bed, and Kathleen couldn't help imagining her bare feet stepping on to its softness first thing every morning.

'There'll be the two uniforms the last girl had,' Mrs Shaughnessy said. 'They'd easily fit, although I'd say you were bigger on the chest. You wouldn't be familiar with a uniform, Kathleen?'

'I didn't have one at the convent, ma'am.'

'You'll soon get used to the dresses.'

That was the first intimation that Mrs Shaughnessy considered her suitable for the post. The dresses were hanging in the cupboard, she said. There were sheets and blankets in the hot press.

'I'd rather call you Kitty,' Mrs Shaughnessy said. 'If you wouldn't object. The last girl was Kitty, and so was another we had.'

Kathleen said that was all right. She hadn't been called Kitty at the convent, and wasn't at home because it was the pet name of her eldest sister.

'Well, that's great,' Mrs Shaughnessy said, the tone of her voice implying that the arrangement had already been made.

'I was never better pleased with you,' her father said when Kathleen returned home. 'You're a great little girl.'

When she'd packed some of her clothes into a suitcase that Mary Florence had left behind after a visit one time, he said it was hardly like going away at all because she was only going seven miles. She'd return every Sunday afternoon; it wasn't like Kilburn or Chicago. She sat beside him on the cart and he explained that the Shaughnessys had been generous to a degree. The wages he had agreed with them would be held back and set against the debt: it was that that made the whole thing possible, reducing his monthly repayments to a figure he was confident he could manage, even with the bank overdraft. 'It isn't everyone would agree to the convenience of that, Kathleen.'

She said she understood. There was a new sprightliness about her father; the fatigue in his face had given way to an excited pleasure. His gratitude to the Shaughnessys, and her mother's gratitude, had made the farmhouse a different place during the last couple of weeks. Biddy and Con had been affected by it, and so had Kathleen, even though she had no idea what life would be like in the house above the Shaughnessys' Provisions and Bar. Mrs Shaughnessy had not outlined her duties beyond saying that every night when she went up to bed she should carry with her the alarm clock from the kitchen dresser, and carry it down again every morning. The most important thing of all appeared to be that she should rise promptly from her bed.

'You'll listen well to what Mrs Shaughnessy says,' her father begged her. 'You'll attend properly to all the work, Kathleen?'

'I will of course.'

'It'll be great seeing you on Sundays, girl.'

'It'll be great coming home.'

A bicycle, left behind also by Mary Florence, lay in the back of the cart. Kathleen had wanted to tie the suitcase on to the carrier and cycle in herself with it, but her father wouldn't let her. It was dangerous, he said; a suitcase attached like that could easily unbalance you.

'Kathleen's field is what we call it,' her father said on their journey together, and added after a moment: 'They're decent people, Kathleen. You're going to a decent house.'

'Oh, I know, I know.'

But after only half a day there Kathleen wished she was back in the farmhouse. She knew at once how much she was going to miss the comfort of the kitchen she had known all her life, and the room along the passage she shared with Biddy, where Mary Florence had slept also, and the dogs nosing up to her in the yard. She knew how much she would miss Con, and her father and her mother, and how she'd miss looking after Biddy.

'Now, I'll show you how to set a table,' Mrs Shaughnessy said. 'Listen to this carefully, Kitty.'

Cork mats were put down on the tablecloth so that the heat of the dishes wouldn't penetrate to the polished surface beneath. Small plates were placed on the left of each mat, to put the skins of potatoes on. A knife and a fork were arranged on each side of the mats and a spoon and a fork across the top. The pepper and salt were placed so that Mr Shaughnessy could easily reach them. Serving spoons were placed by the bigger mats in the middle. The breakfast table was set the night before, with the cups upside down on the saucers so that they wouldn't catch the dust when the ashes were taken from the fireplace.

'Can you cut kindling, Kitty? I'll show you how to do it with the little hatchet.'

She showed her, as well, how to sweep the carpet on the stairs with a stiff hand-brush, and how to use the dust-pan. She explained that every mantelpiece in the house had to be dusted every morning, and all the places where grime would gather. She showed her where saucepans and dishes were kept, and instructed her in how to light the range, the first task of the day. The backyard required brushing once a week, on Saturday between four o'clock and five. And every morning after breakfast water had to be pumped from the tank in the yard, fifteen minutes' work with the hand lever.

'That's the WC you'd use, Kitty,' Mrs Shaughnessy indicated, leading her to a privy in another part of the backyard. 'The maids always use this one.'

The dresses of the uniforms didn't fit. She looked at herself in the blue one and then in the black. The mirror on the dressing-table was tarnished, but she could tell that neither uniform enhanced her in any way whatsoever. She looked as fat as a fool, she thought, with the hems all crooked, and the sleeves too tight on her forearms. 'Oh now, that's really very good,' Mrs Shaughnessy said when Kathleen emerged from her bedroom in the black one. She demonstrated how the bodice of the apron was kept in place and how the afternoon cap should be worn.

'Is your father fit?' Mr Shaughnessy inquired when he came upstairs for his six o'clock tea.

'He is, sir.' Suddenly Kathleen had to choke back tears because without any warning the reference to her father had made her want to cry.

'He was shook the day I saw him,' Mr Shaughnessy said, 'on account he couldn't sell the bullocks.'

'He's all right now, sir.'

The Shaughnessys' son reappeared then too, a narrow-faced youth who hadn't addressed her when he'd arrived in the dining-room in the middle of the day and didn't address her now. There were just the three of them, two younger children having grown up and gone away. During the day Mrs Shaughnessy had often referred to her other son and her daughter, the son in business in Limerick, the daughter married to a county surveyor. The narrow-faced son would inherit the businesses, she'd said, the barber's shop and the Provisions and Bar, maybe even the insurances. With a bout of wretchedness, Kathleen was reminded of Con inheriting the farm. Before that he'd marry Angie McKrill, who wouldn't hesitate to accept him now that the farm was improved.

Kathleen finished laying the table and went back to the kitchen, where Mrs Shaughnessy was frying rashers and eggs and slices of soda bread. When they were ready she scooped them on to three plates and Kathleen carried the tray, with a teapot on it as well, into the dining-room. Her instructions were to return to the kitchen when she'd done so and to fry her own rasher and eggs, and soda bread if she wanted it. 'I don't know will we make much of that one,' she heard Mrs Shaughnessy saying as she closed the dining-room door.

That night she lay awake in the strange bed, not wanting to sleep because sleep would too swiftly bring the morning, and another day like the day there'd been. She couldn't stay here: she'd say that on Sunday. If they knew what it was like they wouldn't want her to. She sobbed, thinking again of the warm kitchen she had left behind, the sheepdogs lying by the fire and Biddy turning the wheel of the bellows, the only household task she could do. She thought of her mother and father sitting at the table as they always did, her mother knitting, her father pondering, with his hat still on his head. If they could see her in the dresses they'd understand. If they could see her standing there pumping up the water they'd surely be sorry for the way she felt. 'I haven't the time to tell you twice, Kitty,' Mrs Shaughnessy said over and over again, her long, painted face not smiling in the least way whatsoever. If anything was broken, she'd said, the cost of it would have to be stopped out of the wages, and she'd spoken as though the wages would actually change hands. In Kathleen's dreams Mrs Shaughnessy kept laughing, her chin going long and smooth and her large white teeth moving in her mouth. The dresses belonged to one of the King of England's daughters, she explained, which was why they didn't fit. And then Mary Florence came into the kitchen and said she was just back from Kilburn with a pair of shoes that belonged to someone else. The price of them could be stopped out of the wages, she suggested, and Mrs Shaughnessy agreed.

When Kathleen opened her eyes, roused by the alarm clock at half past six, she didn't know where she was. Then one after another the details of the previous day impinged on her waking consciousness: the cork mats, the shed where the kindling was cut, the narrow face of the Shaughnessys' son, the greasy doorknobs in the kitchen, the impatience in Mrs Shaughnessy's voice. The reality was worse than the confusion of her dreams, and there was nothing magical about the softness of the rug beneath her bare feet: she didn't even notice it. She lifted her night-dress over her head and for a moment caught a glimpse of her nakedness in the tarnished looking-glass – plumply rounded thighs and knees, the dimple in her stomach. She drew on stockings and underclothes, feeling even more lost than she had when she'd tried not to go to sleep. She knelt by her bed, and when she'd offered her usual prayers she asked that she might be taken away from the Shaughnessys' house. She asked that her father would understand when she told him.

'The master's waiting on his breakfast, Kitty.'

'I lit the range the minute I was down, ma'am.'

'If you don't get it going by twenty to seven it won't be hot in time. I told you that yesterday. Didn't you pull the dampers out?'

'The paper wouldn't catch, ma'am.'

'If the paper wouldn't catch you'll have used a damp bit. Or maybe paper out of a magazine. You can't light a fire with paper out of a magazine, Kitty.'

'If I'd had a drop of paraffin, ma'am – '

'My God, are you mad, child?'

'At home we'd throw on a half cup of paraffin if the fire was slow, ma'am.'

'Never bring paraffin near the range. If the master heard you he'd jump out of his skin.'

'I only thought it would hurry it, ma'am.'

'Set the alarm for six if you're going to be slow with the fire. If the breakfast's not on the table by a quarter to eight he'll raise the roof. Have you the plates in the bottom oven?'

When Kathleen opened the door of the bottom oven a black kitten darted out, scratching the back of her hand in its agitation.

'Great God Almighty!' exclaimed Mrs Shaughnessy. 'Are you trying to roast the poor cat?'

'I didn't know it was in there, ma'am.'

'You lit the fire with the poor creature inside there! What were you thinking of to do that, Kitty?'

'I didn't know, ma'am – '

'Always look in the two ovens before you light the range, child. Didn't you hear me telling you?'

After breakfast, when Kathleen went into the dining-room to clear the table, Mrs Shaughnessy was telling her son about the kitten in the oven. 'Haven't they brains like turnips?' she said, even though Kathleen was in the room. The son released a half-hearted smile, but when Kathleen asked him if he'd finished with the jam he didn't reply. 'Try and speak a bit more clearly, Kitty,' Mrs Shaughnessy said later. 'It's not everyone can understand a country accent.'

The day was similar to the day before except that at eleven o'clock Mrs Shaughnessy said:

'Go upstairs and take off your cap. Put on your coat and go down the street to Crawley's. A half pound of round steak, and suet. Take the book off the dresser. He'll know who you are when he sees it.'

So far, that was the pleasantest chore she had been asked to do. She had to wait in the shop because there were two other people before her, both of whom held the butcher in conversation. 'I know your father,' Mr Crawley said when he'd asked her name, and he held her in conversation also, wanting to know if her father was in good health and asking about her brothers and sisters. He'd heard about the buying of the Lallys' field. She was the last uniformed maid in the town, he said, now that Nellie Broderick at Maclure's had had to give up because of her legs.

'Are you mad?' Mrs Shaughnessy shouted at her on her return. 'I should be down in the shop and not waiting to put that meat on. Didn't I tell you yesterday not to be loitering in the mornings?'

'I'm sorry, ma'am, only Mr Crawley – '

'Go down to the shop and tell the master I'm delayed over cooking the dinner and can you assist him for ten minutes.'

But when Kathleen appeared in the grocery Mr Shaughnessy asked her if she'd got lost. The son was weighing sugar into grey paper bags and tying string round each of them. A murmur of voices came from the bar.

'Mrs Shaughnessy is delayed over cooking the dinner,' Kathleen said. 'She was thinking I could assist you for ten minutes.'

'Well, that's a good one!' Mr Shaughnessy threw back his head, exploding into laughter. A little shower of spittle damped Kathleen's face. The son gave his half-hearted smile. 'Can you make a spill, Kitty? D'you know what I mean by a spill?' Mr Shaughnessy demonstrated with a piece of brown paper on the counter. Kathleen shook her head. 'Would you know what to charge for a quarter pound of tea, Kitty? Can you weigh out sugar, Kitty? Go back to the missus, will you, and tell her to have sense.'

In the kitchen Kathleen put it differently, simply saying that Mr Shaughnessy hadn't required her services. 'Bring a scuttle of coal up to the dining-room,' Mrs Shaughnessy commanded. And get out the mustard. Can you make up mustard?'

Kathleen had never tasted mustard in her life; she had heard of it but did not precisely know what it was. She began to say she wasn't sure about making some, but even before she spoke Mrs Shaughnessy sighed and told her to wash down the front steps instead.

'I don't want to go back there,' Kathleen said on Sunday. 'I can't understand what she says to me. It's lonesome the entire time.'

Her mother was sympathetic, but even so she shook her head. 'There's people I used to know,' she said. 'People placed like ourselves whose farms failed on them. They're walking the roads now, no better than tinkers. I have ten children, Kathleen, and seven are gone from me. There's five of them I'll maybe never see again. It's that you have to think of, pet.'

'I cried the first night. I was that lonesome when I got into bed.'

'But isn't it a clean room you're in, pet? And aren't you given food to eat that's better than you'd get here? And don't the dresses she supplies save us an expense again? Wouldn't you think of all that, pet?'

A bargain had been struck, her mother also reminded her, and a bargain was a bargain. Biddy said it sounded great, going out into the town for messages. She'd give anything to see a house like that, Biddy said, with the coal fires and a stairs.

'I'd say they were well pleased with you,' Kathleen's father said when he came in from the yard later on. 'You'd have been back here inside a day if they weren't.'

She'd done her best, she thought as she rode away from the farmhouse on Mary Florence's bicycle; if she'd done everything badly she would have obtained her release. She wept because she wouldn't see Biddy and Con and her father and mother for another week. She dreaded the return to the desolate bedroom which her mother had reminded her was clean, and the kitchen where there was no one to keep her company in the evenings. She felt as if she could not bear it, more counting of the days until Sunday and when Sunday came the few hours passing so swiftly. But she knew, by now, that she would remain in the Shaughnessys' house for as long as was necessary.

'I must have you back by half six, Kitty,' Mrs Shaughnessy said when she saw her. 'It's closer to seven now.'

Kathleen said she was sorry. She'd had to stop to pump the back tyre of her bicycle, she said, although in fact this was not true: what she'd stopped for was to wipe away the signs of her crying and to blow her nose. In the short time she had been part of Mrs Shaughnessy's household she had developed the habit of making excuses, and of obscuring her inadequacies beneath lies that were easier than the truth.

'Fry the bread like I showed you, Kitty. Get it brown on both sides. The master likes it crisp.'

There was something Mr Shaughnessy liked also, which Kathleen discovered when seven of her free Sunday afternoons had gone by. She was dusting the dining-room mantelpiece one morning when he came and stood very close to her. She thought she was in his way, and moved out of it, but a week or so later he stood close to her again, his breath warm on her cheek. When it happened the third time she felt herself blushing.

It was in this manner that Mr Shaughnessy rather than his wife came to occupy, for Kathleen, the central role in the household. The narrow-faced son remained as he had been since the day of her arrival, a dour presence, contributing little in the way of conversation and never revealing the fruits of his brooding silence. Mrs Shaughnessy, having instructed, had apparently played out the part she'd set herself. She came into the kitchen at midday to cook meat and potatoes and one of the milk puddings her husband was addicted to, but otherwise the kitchen was Kathleen's province now and it was she who was responsible for the frying of the food for breakfast and for the six o'clock tea. Mrs Shaughnessy preferred to be in the shop. She enjoyed the social side of that, she told Kathleen; and she enjoyed the occasional half glass of sherry in the bar. 'That's me all over, Kitty. I never took to housework.' She was more amiable in her manner, and confessed that she always found training a country girl an exhausting and irksome task and might therefore have been a little impatient. 'Kitty's settled in grand,' she informed Kathleen's father when he looked into the bar one fair-day to make a mortgage payment. He'd been delighted to hear that, he told Kathleen the following Sunday.

Mr Shaughnessy never said anything when he came to stand close to her, although on other occasions he addressed her pleasantly enough, even complimenting her on her frying. He had an easy way with him, quite different from his son's. He was more like his two other children, the married daughter and the son who was in Limerick, both of whom Kathleen had met when they had returned to the house for an uncle's funeral. He occasionally repeated a joke he'd been told, and Mrs Shaughnessy would laugh, her chin becoming lengthy and the skin tightening on her forehead. On the occasion of the uncle's funeral his other son and his daughter laughed at the jokes also, but the son who'd remained at home only smiled. 'Wait till I tell you this one, Kitty,' he'd sometimes say, alone with her in the dining-room. He would tell her something Bob Crowe, who ran the barber's shop for him, had heard from a customer, making the most of the anecdote in a way that suggested he was anxious to entertain her. His manner and his tone of voice denied that it had ever been necessary for him to stand close to her, or else that his practice of doing so had been erased from his memory.

But the scarlet complexion of Mr Shaughnessy's face and the spiky grey hair, the odour of cigarette smoke that emanated from his clothes, could not be so easily forgotten by Kathleen. She no longer wept from loneliness in her bedroom, yet she was aware that the behaviour of Mr Shaughnessy lent the feeling of isolation an extra, vivid dimension, for in the farmhouse kitchen on Sundays the behaviour could not be mentioned.

Every evening Kathleen sat by the range, thinking about it. The black kitten that had darted out of the oven on her second morning had grown into a cat and sat blinking beside her chair. The alarm clock ticked loudly on the dresser. Was it something she should confess? Was it a sin to be as silent as she was when he came to stand beside her? Was it a sin to be unable to find the courage to tell him to leave her alone? Once, in the village where the convent was, another girl in her class had pointed out a boy who was loitering with some other boys by the sign-post. That boy was always trying to kiss you, the girl said; he would follow you about the place, whispering to you. But although Kathleen often went home alone the boy never came near her. He wasn't a bad-looking boy, she'd thought, she wouldn't have minded much. She'd wondered if she'd mind the boys her sisters had complained about, who tried to kiss you when they were dancing with you. Pests, her sisters had called them, but Kathleen thought it was nice that they wanted to.

Mr Shaughnessy was different. When he stood close to her his breathing would become loud and unsteady. He always moved away quite quickly, when she wasn't expecting him to. He walked off, never looking back, soundlessly almost.

Then one day, when Mrs Shaughnessy was buying a new skirt and the son was in the shop, he came into the kitchen, where she was scrubbing the draining boards. He came straight to where she was, as if between them there was some understanding that he should do so. He stood in a slightly different position from usual, behind her rather than at her side, and she felt for the first time his hands passing over her clothes.

'Mr Shaughnessy!' she whispered. 'Mr Shaughnessy, now.'

He took no notice. Some part of his face was touching her hair. The rhythm of his breathing changed.

'Mr Shaughnessy, I don't like it.'

He seemed not to hear her; she sensed that his eyes were closed. As suddenly, and as quickly as always, he went away.

'Well, Bob Crowe told me a queer one this evening,' he said that same evening, while she was placing their plates of fried food in front of them in the dining-room. 'It seems there's a woman asleep in Clery's shop window above in Dublin.'

His wife expressed disbelief. Bob Crowe would tell you anything, she said.

'In a hypnotic trance, it seems. Advertising Odearest Mattresses.'

'Ah, go on now! He's pulling your leg, Des.'

'Not a bit of him. She'll stop there a week, it seems. The Guards have to move the crowds on.'

Kathleen closed the dining-room door behind her. He had turned to look at her when he'd said there was a woman asleep in Clery's window, in an effort to include her in what he was retailing. His eyes had betrayed nothing of their surreptitious relationship, but Kathleen hadn't been able to meet them.

'We ploughed the field,' her father said the following Sunday. 'I've never turned up earth as good.'

743

She almost told him then. She longed to so much she could hardly prevent herself. She longed to let her tears come and to hear his voice consoling her. When she was a child she'd loved that.

'You're a great girl,' he said.

Mr Shaughnessy took to attending an earlier Mass than his wife and son, and when they were out at theirs he would come into the kitchen. When she hid in her bedroom he followed her there. She'd have locked herself in the outside WC if there'd been a latch on the door.

'Well, Kitty and myself were quiet enough here,' he'd say in the dining-room later on, when the three of them were eating their midday dinner. She couldn't understand how he could bring himself to speak like that, or how he could so hungrily eat his food, as though nothing had occurred. She couldn't understand how he could act normally with his son or with his other children when they came on a visit. It was extraordinary to hear Mrs Shaughnessy humming her songs about the house and calling him by his Christian name.

'The Kenny girl's getting married,' Mrs Shaughnessy said on one of these mealtime occasions. 'Tyson from the hardware.'

'I didn't know she was doing a line with him.'

'Oh, that's been going on a long time.'

'Is it the middle girl? The one with the peroxide?'

'Enid she's called.'

'I wonder Bob Crowe didn't hear that. There's not much Bob misses.'

'I never thought much of Tyson. But, sure, maybe they're well matched.'

'Did you hear that, Kitty? Enid Kenny's getting married. Don't go taking ideas from her.' He laughed, and Mrs Shaughnessy laughed, and the son smiled. There wasn't much chance of that, Kathleen thought. 'Are you going dancing tonight?' Mr Crawley often asked her on a Friday, and she would reply that she might, but she never did because it wasn't easy to go alone. In the shops and at Mass no one displayed any interest in her whatsoever, no one eyed her the way Mary Florence had been eyed, and she supposed it was because her looks weren't up to much. But they were good enough for Mr Shaughnessy, with his quivering breath and his face in her hair. Bitterly, she dwelt on that; bitterly, she imagined herself turning on him in the dining-room, accusing him to his wife and son.

'Did you forget to sweep the yard this week?' Mrs Shaughnessy asked her. 'Only it's looking poor.'

She explained that the wind had blown in papers and debris from a knocked-over dustbin. She'd sweep it again, she said.

'I hate a dirty backyard, Kitty.'

Was this why the other girls had left, she wondered, the girls whom Mrs Shaughnessy had trained, and who'd then gone off? Those girls, whoever they were, would see her, or would know about her. They'd imagine her in one uniform or the other, obedient to him because she enjoyed his attentions. That was how they'd think of her.

'Leave me alone, sir,' she said when she saw him approaching her the next time, but he took no notice. She could see him guessing she wouldn't scream.

'Please, sir,' she said. 'Please, sir. I don't like it.'

But after a time she ceased to make any protestation and remained as silent as she had been at first. Twelve years or maybe fourteen, she said to herself, lying awake in her bedroom: as long as that, or longer. In her two different uniforms she would continue to be the outward sign of Mrs Shaughnessy's well-to-do status, and her ordinary looks would continue to attract the attentions of a grey-haired man. Because of the field, the nature of the farm her father had once been barefoot on would change. 'Kathleen's field,' her father would often repeat, and her mother would say again that a bargain was a bargain.

LELAND BARDWELL

'The Hairdresser'

Long ago they had painted the houses. Pale pastel shades – mauves, pinks, greys. The estate had expanded up Trevor's Hill, across the old sheep-field, curling back down like an anvil until it seemed the mountain had grown a second crust. Attempts to divert the streams had failed and water ran freely into the residents' gardens and rotted the foundations of the houses.

Paint cracked, window frames warped: there seemed no wisdom in the continuous building of new dwellings but after the last of the city clearances, the Local Authority brought out their trucks, their cranes, their earth-movers and packed them in the road that ran directly through the estate till it could run no more and ended, T-shaped beneath the higher slopes.

Electric wires, pylons blew down in the storms and were seldom repaired so the estate lay mostly in darkness during the winter. There were strange happenings behind those closed doors at night. Many of the middle-aged women whose husbands had taken off or been gaoled took in men – those who roamed the country homeless – with whom they shared their bed and welfare payments. Occasionally a daughter would return with a new brood. Those men came and went; domestic unease, lack of money, young children crowding and squabbling would drive them out after a few months.

The women did their best and it was not unusual to see a middle-aged woman perched on her roof, trying to pin over a piece of plastic or rope up a bit of guttering. Like many another family, Mona and her mother had one of the houses on the higher slopes. Victims of the worst winter weather, they spent hours, plastering, drying, mending window frames and replacing slates. With one difference, however: Mona was the only one in the estate who attended secondary school. A rather plain girl with dry ribbed hair and a boxy figure, she was something of a scholar. Her mother was a gaunt angular woman with fierce energy.

Unlike the other women she attracted a certain type of man, more chaotic, more unprincipled than the average. She responded passionately to these men and was thrown into despair when they left.

To Mona, her mother gave the recurring excuse that 'they were safer with a man about'. Mere excuse, of course, because the marauding gangs had 'cased' every house and in theirs there was little left to steal. To eke out their dole they had sold their furniture, their television, their kitchen appliances one by one. They now made do with the barest necessities. An old kitchen table, over which hung a thin plastic cloth, a few upright chairs, mattresses and one cupboard sufficed for their basic needs. Only Mona's room was spotless. Her fastidious nature forswore squalor, and to this room, as soon as she had cooked the dinner, she would retire, her lesson books spread before her, a stub of a candle lighting up the immediate circle on the floor and with her stiff hair tied back in a knot she would concentrate on her studies to the exclusion of all else.

For some weeks now a new man had established himself in their household. Although he combined all the complexities and evil ways of his forerunners he was as yet an unknown quantity to Mona. Her mother forever alert, listened to his speeches – he made speeches all day long, claiming an intellectual monopoly on every subject. This irked Mona, who had a fine mathematical brain and disagreed with many of his illogical conclusions. However, for the sake of her mother she held her peace.

Today she had decided to scrub the lino. As she scraped and picked between the cracks she could feel his gaze upon her as if it were a physical thing. She rose in confusion; there were rings on her knees from the muddy floor.

'Why don't you kneel on something?' he barked, looking down at her legs as if she were a yearling in the ring.

'Ah shut up,' she said; for once she lost her temper. 'If you'd shift your arse I'd get on more quickly.' He gazed at her angrily, his eyes still as glass; they were his most unsettling feature.

All this time her mother was sitting on the edge of her chair watching him, with the air of one who waits for her child to take its first few steps; she said nothing, nervously lighting one cigarette from the tip of another.

Mona went to the sink to wring out her cloth: she looked round at him, sizing him up once again. There was madness there, she felt, in this posture, his teeth grinding, the occasional bouts of pacing; he was leaning over, elbows on knees, his stained overcoat folded back like the open page of an almanac. His hands were gyrating as though he were shuffling a pack of cards. He had strangely delicate hands, his fingers tapered into neat girlish nails, yet he had huge tense shoulders. His face was stippled and pocked from long hours spent in the open. Yes, this man was not like the others – ruthless, fighting for survival – there were qualities within him, seams of impatience and rage that were beyond his control. Mona knew it was dangerous to answer him back; she wished she had held her tongue. Yet far from antagonizing her mother, his rages seemed to make her more submissive, more caressing, more loving than ever. Or perhaps she, too, sensed danger; Mona wasn't sure.

When they were alone she would try to warn her mother but the latter would touch her own brow with the hand of a lover and with her other hand take Mona's and say, 'Don't worry, darling. It will all be over one day.'

Winter crawled. Snow came, dried off and fell again. It was no longer possible to patch the roof so they caught the water in buckets placed under the worst of the leaks. One sleety February afternoon, Mona returning from her long journey back from school

– it was dole day and they had bought cider – she found them both slightly drunk. They sat by the fire – one more chair had been burnt – and there was a glow of frivolity between them. But on her entry he addressed her rudely, finishing up by shaking his fists and saying, 'You're a nasty piece of work.' Mona snapped back, 'You're a fucking creep, yourself.'

There was silence. The skin on her mother's cheeks darkened with fear but she rose – an animal hoisted from its lair – and slowly picked up the flagon. He automatically held out his glass but she ignored it and poured the cider into his eyes.

The kitchen exploded. Chairs, table, went flying, and they were both on the floor, his fingers, those mobile fingers, closing, closing on her mother's throat and Mona screaming, kicking him from behind till he fell back howling in his effort to wipe his eyes with his sleeve. In a second her mother was up, apologizing, begging for 'another chance'. But he was up too and heading for the door, his large frame bent like a sickle, his arms held stiffly from his body, he banged out of the house. The stricken women stood face to face as though waiting for a message that would never come. But her mother was already straining to go after him.

'Let him, mammy, let him go, for God's sake,' Mona grasped the wool of her mother's jersey.

'No, no, I must save him. Save him from the police,' and she slipped out of her jumper like a snake shedding its skin and she, too, ran out of the house.

The cold mountain air crept into the hall; gusts ran under the mat and up her legs as she shouldered shut the door. She stood for a while, knowing now that her life was beyond the ken of the two people out there. Who was she now? Mona the lucky one, she used to call herself, the only member of the family to forestall the fate that had swallowed up the rest of them. One brother killed in a hit-and-run, another in Mountjoy Gaol for armed robbery, a sister dead – from medical malpractice, another gone to England for an abortion, who never returned. Mona the lucky one who had long ago made a pact with herself: to work and work, to use her ability to study, to use her interests that lay beyond this hinterland, so that one day, one far off day, she could take her mother and herself away from this no-man's territory where rats and dogs got a better living than they did. Along with this pact she'd promised herself that she would never allow her neat parts to be touched by the opposite sex, never succumb to the martyrdom of sexual love. In all the other houses, mile upon mile, children had given birth to children and were already grandmothers in their thirties. But she, Mona, treaded a different path. Or did she? Should she not just pack her bags, go, too, into the recondite night, join the packs of boys and girls, small criminals, who got by by 'doing cheques' or robbing the rich suburbs on the other side of the city.

She climbed the stair, the re-lit candle dripping hot wax over her hand. In her room, her books, her friends, all stacked neatly, were suddenly strangers, strangers like the two people who had fled into the unyielding darkness. She went on her knees, taking each book and fondling it. The ones she cared for most, those on quantitive or applied mathematics, she held longingly, opening them, smoothing out the pages. But it was no use; they denied the half of her that was her pride. She threw them from her, went to the window, hoping to see her mother returning alone. But the street was dark, the houses down the hill, derelict as an unused railway station. She left the window open and sank down on the bed.

A little while later she heard them; they came into the hall. They spoke in low tones; the fight had been patched up and Mona knew that once again she'd get up, shop, make the dinner and act as if nothing had happened.

In the shop she would spend the few coins that she had, money that she earned from her better off student friends, the ones she helped with their homework; most of her mother's dole went on cigarettes and drink and lasted for about a day. So it was up to her to keep them from the edge of starvation.

She skirted the heaps of rubble, piles of sand that had been there for years. She used her memory to avoid the worst of the puddles and potholes. Even so her shoes filled up with icy water. The journey to the shop usually took about twenty minutes – it was over a mile away – and as it was nearly six Mona began to run.

The fierce cold of that day was the one thing that stuck in Mona's memory above all else. How dirty papers had flared up in front of her feet as she'd run the last few paces home; how the unending gale had pierced her chest and how she had clasped her inadequate coat collar round her chin. It had always been difficult to fit the yale into the keyhole and it seemed to take longer than usual as her white fingers grappled and twisted. But with the help of the wind the door blew in and a glass fell at the end of the passage – a glass of dead flowers – and water dripped quickly on to the floor. At first she had not seen her mother; the man had gone from the kitchen and Mona assumed they had gone upstairs to continue their moments of reparation.

So Mona had begun to unwrap the food before she saw the blood. In fact it was when she was about to throw the plastic wrapping into the rubbish bin that her eyes lit on the dark expanding pool. And before the horror had fully struck her her first thought had been that the body contains eight pints of blood – a gallon – and that this is what will now run over the floor, sink into the cracks of the lino, make everything black and slimy. Yes, he had slit her throat with the kitchen knife and left the body curled up half hidden by the piece of plastic cloth that hung down over the back of the table.

But the years had now passed. That murder had just become another legend in the estate, one of the many legends of killings and rapings. The football pitch, which had once been a place of recreation, had now become a graveyard for the people who died daily of diseases brought on by malnutrition and were bundled into the ground. There were thousands of dogs who crowded the 'funerals' and who, when night came, dug up the corpses and ate them. Soon the people had ceased to care and left the bodies unburied for the scavengers. Everyone pretended they had not eaten human flesh.

And what of Mona?

After her mother's murder the madman had disappeared and was never found – no doubt he had holed up with some other lonely woman. Mona had left school and gone to work in a better off suburb as a hairdresser's assistant. She had continued to live in the same house which was now neat and tidy, the roof well patched and the gutters straightened. She had no friends and seldom went out after dark. But as the country fell further and further into the well of poverty, the rich, behind their gun-towers and barbed wire, grasping to themselves their utopian 'freedom', jobs in the better suburbs folded one by one, so for want of something to do, Mona took over the old hardware shop and turned it into an establishment of her own. Nobody could pay so she accepted anything they could offer from watercress, which still proliferated on the hills – to bits of food stolen from the itinerants whose powers of survival were stronger than theirs.

People would do anything to get their hair fixed by Mona. It was the only entertainment left to them. Men, women and children flocked in happy to queue for hours, their absent expressions momentarily lit by narcissistic anticipation. Yes, there was nothing for them to do. The revolution that once people had hoped for had petered out in the nineties. The only way in which they might have expressed themselves would have been to fight the gangs of vigilantes who held the city in a grip of violence. But that would have meant a long trek into town and people were too underfed to face it. So Mona cut and dyed and permed from nine to six; the mathematician in her enjoyed the definition of a pleasant hairdo. She had grown gaunt, like her mother, and her strong brown eyes would survey her 'customers', assessing the sweep of their locks with the same fixed gaze as that which her mother had used to pin down her men-friends.

The smell from the football pitch would waft in while people admired their reflections in the mirror; at times the purple fissure and cracks enhanced or disguised their grey features, their hollow eye-sockets, their sagging skin.

But Mona didn't care about any of this but she cared, oh so deeply about her own expertise. If a person moved his head suddenly she'd get into a stifling rage. One day, she knew, she would kill one of her customers with the scissors, she would murder them as cold-bloodedly and as bloodily as her mother had been murdered. She'd clip them inch by inch, first the ears, then she'd shove the scissors up their nostrils and so on and so forth.

BRIAN FRIEL

'Foundry House'

When his father and mother died, Joe Brennan applied for their house, his old home, the gate lodge to Foundry House. He wrote direct to Mr Bernard (as Mr Hogan was known locally), pointing out that he was a radio-and-television mechanic in the Music Shop; that although he had never worked for Mr Hogan, his father had been an employee in the foundry for over fifty years; and that he himself had been born and reared in the gate lodge. Rita, his wife, who was more practical than he, insisted that he mention their nine children and the fact that they were living in three rooms above a launderette.

'That should influence him,' she said. 'Aren't they supposed to be one of the best Catholic families in the North of Ireland?' So, against his wishes, he added a paragraph about his family and their inadequate accommodation, and sent off his application. Two days later, he received a reply from Mrs Hogan, written on mauve scented notepaper with fluted edges. Of course she remembered him, she said. He was the small, round-faced boy with the brown curls who used to play with her Declan. And to think that he now had nine babies of his own! Where did time go? He could collect the keys from the agent and move in as soon as he wished. There were no longer any duties attached to the position of gatekeeper, she added – not since wartime, when the authorities had taken away the great iron gates that sealed the mouth of the avenue.

'Brown curls!' Rita squealed with delight when Joe read her the letter. 'Brown curls! She mustn't have seen you for twenty years or more!'

'That's all right now,' was all Joe could say. He was moved with relief and an odd sense of humility at his unworthiness. That's all right. That's all right.'

They moved into their new house at the end of summer. It was a low-set, solid stone building with a steep roof and exaggerated eaves that gave it the appearance of a gnome's house in a fairy tale. The main Derry–Belfast road ran parallel to the house, and on the other side the ground rose rapidly in a tangle of shrubs and wild rhododendron and decaying trees, through which the avenue crawled up to Foundry House at the top of the hill. The residence was not visible from the road or from any part of the town; one could only guess at its location somewhere in the green patch that lay between the new housing estate and the brassière factory. But Joe remembered from his childhood that if one stood at the door of Foundry House on a clear morning, before the smoke from the red-brick factories clouded the air, one could see through the trees and the undergrowth, past the gate lodge and the busy main road, and right down to the river below, from which the sun drew a million momentary flashes of light that danced and died in the vegetation.

For Joe, moving into the gate lodge was a homecoming; for Rita and the children, it was a changeover to a new life. There were many improvements to be made – there was no indoor toilet and no running water, the house was lit by gas only, and the windows, each made up a score of small, diamond-shaped pieces of glass, gave little light – and Joe accepted that they were inevitable. But he found himself putting them off from day to day and from week to week. He did not have much time when he came home from work, because the evenings were getting so short. Also, he had applied to the urban council for a money grant, and they were sending along an architect soon. And he had to keep an eye on the children, who looked on the grounds as their own private park and climbed trees and lit fires in the undergrowth and played their shrieking games of hide-and-seek or cowboys-and-Indians right up to the very front of the big house itself.

'Come back here! Come back!' Joe would call after them in an urgent undertone. 'Why can't you play down below near your own house? Get away down at once with you!'

'We want to play up here, Daddy,' some of them would plead. 'There are better hiding places up here.'

'The old man, he'll soon scatter you!' Joe would say. 'Or he'll put the big dog on you. God help you then!'

'But there is no old man. Only the old woman and the maid. And there is no dog, either.'

'No Mr Bernard? Huh! Just let him catch you, and you'll know all about it. No Mr

Bernard! The dog may be gone, but Mr Bernard's not. Come on now! Play around your own door or else come into the house altogether.'

No Mr Bernard! Mr Bernard always had been, Joe thought to himself, and always would be – a large, stern-faced man with a long white beard and a heavy step and a walking stick, the same ever since he remembered him. And beside him the Great Dane, who copied his master as best he could in expression and gait – a dour, sullen animal as big as a calf and as savage as a tiger, according to the men in the foundry. And Mrs Hogan? He supposed she could be called an old woman now, too. Well over sixty, because Declan and he were of an age, and he was thirty-three himself. Yes, an old woman, or at least elderly, even though she was twenty years younger than her husband. And not Declan now, or even Master Declan, but Father Declan, a Jesuit. And then there was Claire, Miss Claire, the girl, younger than Declan by a year. Fat, blue-eyed Claire, who had blushed every time she passed the gate lodge because she knew some of the Brennans were sure to be peering out through the diamond windows. She had walked with her head to one side, as if she were listening for something, and used to trail her fingers along the boxwood that fringed both sides of the avenue. 'Such a lovely girl,' Joe's mother used to say. 'So simple and so sweet. Not like the things I see running about this town. There's something good before that child. Something very good.' And she was right. Miss Claire was now Sister Claire of the Annuciation Nuns and was out in Africa. Nor would she ever be home again. Never. Sister Claire and Father Declan – just the two of them, and both of them in religion, and the big house up above going to pieces, and no one to take over the foundry when the time would come. Everything they could want in the world, anything that money could buy, and they turned their backs on it all. Strange, Joe thought. Strange. But right, because they were the Hogans.

They were a month in the house and were seated at their tea, all eleven of them, when Mrs Hogan called on them. It was now October and there were no evenings to speak of; the rich, warm days ended abruptly in a dusk that was uneasy with cold breezes. Rita was relieved at the change in the weather, because now the children, still unsure of the impenetrable dark and the nervous movements in the undergrowth, were content to finish their games when daylight failed, and she had no difficulty in gathering them for their evening meal. Joe answered the knock at the door.

'I'm so sorry to disturb you, Mr Brennan. But I wonder could you do me a favour?'

She was a tall, ungraceful woman, with a man's shoulders and a wasted body and long, thin feet. When she spoke, her mouth and lips worked in excessive movement.

Rita was at Joe's elbow. 'Did you not ask the woman in?' she reproved him. 'Come on inside, Mrs Hogan.'

'I'm sorry,' Joe stammered. 'I thought . . . I was about to . . .' How could he say he didn't dare?

'Thank you all the same,' Mrs Hogan said. 'But I oughtn't to have left Bernard at all. What brought me down was this. Mary – our maid, you know – she tells me that you have a tape-recording machine. She says you're in that business. I wonder could we borrow it for an afternoon? Next Sunday?'

'Certainly, Mrs Hogan. Certainly,' said Rita. 'Take it with you now. We never use it. Do we, Joe?'

'If Sunday suits you, I would like to have it then when Father Declan comes,' Mrs Hogan said. 'You see, my daughter, Claire, has sent us a tape-recording of her voice – these nuns nowadays, they're so modern – and we were hoping to have Father Declan with us when we play it. You know, a sort of family reunion, on Sunday.'

'Any time at all,' said Rita. 'Take it with you now. Go and get it, Joe, and carry it up.'

'No, no. Really. Sunday will do – Sunday afternoon. Besides, neither Bernard nor I know how to work the machine. We'll be depending on you to operate it for us, Mr Brennan.'

'And why wouldn't he?' said Rita. 'He does nothing on a Sunday afternoon, anyway. Certainly he will.'

Now that her request had been made and granted, Mrs Hogan stood irresolutely between the white gaslight in the hall and the blackness outside. Her mouth and lips still worked, although no sound came.

'Sunday then,' she said at last. 'A reunion.'

'Sunday afternoon,' said Rita. 'I'll send him up as soon as he has his dinner in him.'

'Thank you,' said Mrs Hogan. 'Thank you.' Her mouth formed an O, and she drew in her breath. But she snapped it shut again and turned and strode off up the avenue.

Rita closed the door and leaned against it. She doubled up with laughter. 'Lord, if you could only see your face!' she gasped between bursts.

'What do you mean, my face?'

'All scared-looking, like a child caught stealing!'

'What are you raving about?' he asked irritably.

'And she was as scared-looking as yourself.' She held her hand to her side. 'She must have been looking for the brown curls and the round face! And not a word out of you! Like a big, scared dummy!'

'Shut up,' he mumbled gruffly. 'Shut up, will you?'

Joe had never been inside Foundry House, had never spoken to Mr Bernard, and had not seen Declan since his Ordination. And now, as he stood before the hall door and the evil face on the leering knocker, the only introductory remark his mind would supply him was one from his childhood: 'My daddy says here are the keys to the workshop and that he put out the fire in the office before he left.' He was still struggling to suppress this senseless memory when Father Declan opened the door.

'Ah, Joe, Joe, Joe! Come inside. Come inside. We are waiting for you. And you have the machine with you? Good man! Good man! Great! Great!'

Father Declan was fair and slight, and his gestures fluttering and birdlike. The black suit accentuated the whiteness of his hair and skin and hands.

'Straight ahead, Joe. First door to the right. You know – the breakfast room. They live there now, Father and Mother. Convenient to the kitchen, and all. And Mother tells me you are married and have a large family?'

'That's right, Father.'

'Good man! Good man! Marvellous, too. No, no, not that door, Joe, the next one. No, they don't use the drawing room any more. Too large and too expensive to heat. That's it, yes. No, no, don't knock. Just go right in. That's it. Good man! Good man!'

One minute he was behind Joe, steering him through the hallway, and the next he had sped past him and was standing in the middle of the floor of the breakfast room, his glasses flashing, his arms extended in reception. 'Good man. Here we are. Joe Brennan, Mother, with the tape recorder.'

'So kind of you, Joe,' said Mrs Hogan, emerging from behind the door. 'It's going to be quite a reunion, isn't it?'

'How many young Brennans are there?' asked Father Declan.

'Nine, Father.'

'Good! Good! Great! Great!'

'Such healthy children too,' said Mrs Hogan. 'I've seen them playing on the avenue. And so . . . so healthy.'

'Have a seat, Joe. Just leave the recorder there. Anywhere at all. Good man. That's it. Fine!'

'You've had your lunch, Mr Brennan?'

'Yes, thanks, Mrs Hogan. Thank you all the same.'

'What I mean is, you didn't rush off without it?'

'Lucky for you, Joe,' the priest broke in. 'Because these people, I discover, live on snacks now. Milk and bananas – that sort of thing.'

'You'll find the room cold, I'm afraid, Mr Brennan.'

'If you have a power plug. I'll get this thing . . .'

'A power plug. A power plug. A power plug. A power plug.' The priest cracked his fingers each time he said the words and frowned in concentration.

'What about that thing there?' asked Mrs Hogan, pointing to the side of the mantelpiece.

'That's a gas bracket, Mother. No. Electric. Electric.' One white finger rested on his chin. 'An electric power plug. There must be one somewhere in the – ah! Here we are!' He dropped on his knees below the window and looked back exultantly over his shoulder. 'I just thought so. Here we are. I knew there must be one somewhere.'

'Did you find one?' asked Mrs Hogan.

'Yes, we did, didn't we, Joe? Will this do? Does your machine fit this?'

'That's grand, Father.'

'Good! Good! Then I'll go and bring Father down. He's in bed resting. Where is the tape, Mother?'

'Tape? Oh, the tape! Yes, there on the sideboard.'

'Fine! Fine! That's everything then. Father and I will be down in a minute. Good! Good!'

'Logs,' said Mrs Hogan to herself. Then, remembering Joe, she said to him, 'We burn our own fuel. For economy.' She smiled bleakly at him and followed her son from the room.

Joe busied himself with rigging up the machine and putting the new tape in position. When he was working in someone's house, it was part of his routine to examine the pictures and photographs around the walls, to open drawers and presses, to finger ornaments and bric-à-brac. But, here in Foundry House, a modesty, a shyness, a vague deference to something long ago did not allow his eyes even to roam from the work he was engaged in. Yet he was conscious of certain aspects of the room; the ceiling was high, perhaps as high as the roof of his own house, the fireplace was of black marble, the door handle was of cut glass, and the door itself did not close properly. Above his head was a print of horses galloping across open fields; the corner of the carpet was nibbled away. His work gave him assurance.

'There you are now, Mrs Hogan,' he said when she returned with a big basket of logs. 'All you have to do is turn this knob and away she goes.'

She ignored his stiff movement to help her with her load of logs, and knelt at the fireplace until she had built up the fire. Then, rubbing her hands down her skirt, she came and stood beside him.

'What was that, Mr Brennan?'

'I was saying that all you have to do is to turn this knob here to start it going, and turn it back to stop it. Nothing at all to it.'

'Yes?' she said, thrusting her lips forward, her mind a blank.

'That's all,' said Joe. 'Right to start, left to stop. A child could work it.' He tugged at the lapels of his jacket to indicate that he was ready to leave.

'No difficulty at all,' she repeated dreamily. Then suddenly alert again, 'Here they come. You sit there, Mr Brennan, on this side of the fire, Father Declan will sit here, and I will sit beside the table. A real family circle.'

'You'll want to listen to this by yourselves, Mrs Hogan. So if you don't mind . . .'

'Don't leave, Mr Brennan. You will stay, won't you? You remember Claire, our lovely Claire. You remember her, don't you? She's out in Africa, you know, and she'll never be home again. Never. Not even for a death. You'll stay, and hear her talking to us, won't you? Of course you will.' Her finger tips touched the tops of her ears. 'Claire's voice again. Talking to us. And you'll want to hear it too, won't you?'

Before he could answer, the door burst open. Mr Bernard had come down.

It took them five minutes to get from the door to the leather armchair beside the fire, and Joe was reminded of a baby being taught to walk. Father Declan came in first, backward, crouching slightly, his eyes on his father's feet and his arms outstretched and beckoning. 'Slow-ly. Slow-ly,' he said in a hypnotist's voice. 'Slow-ly. Slow-ly.' Then his father appeared. First a stick, then a hand, an arm, the curve of his stomach, then the beard, yellow and untidy, then the whole man. Since his return to the gate lodge, Joe had not thought of Mr Bernard beyond the fact that he was there. In his mind there was a twenty-year-old image that had never been adjusted, a picture which was so familiar to him that he had long since ceased to look at it. But this was not the image, this giant who had grown in height and swollen in girth instead of shrinking, this huge, monolithic figure that inched its way across the faded carpet, one mechanical step after the other, in response to a word from the black, weaving figure before him. Joe looked at his face, fleshy, trembling, coloured in dead purple and grey-black, and at the eyes, wide and staring and quick with the terror of stumbling or of falling or even of missing a syllable of the instructions from the priest. 'Lift again. Lift it. Lift it. Good. Good. Now down, down. And the right, up and up and up – yes – and now down.' The old man wore an overcoat streaked down the front with food stains, and the hands, one clutching the head of the stick, the other limp and lifeless by his side, were so big they had no contour. His breathing was a succession of rapid sighs.

Until the journey from door to armchair was completed, Mrs Hogan made fussy jobs for herself and addressed herself to no one in particular. 'The leaves are terrible this year. Simply terrible. I must get a man to sweep them up and do something with the rockery, too, because it has got out of hand altogether . . .'

'Slow-ly. Slow-ly. Left. Left. That's it . . . up yes. Yes. And down again. Down.'

'I never saw such a year for leaves. And the worst of it is the wind just blows them straight up against the hall door. Only this morning, I was saying to Mary we must make a pile of them and burn them before they smother us altogether. A bonfire – that's what we'll make.'

'Now turn. Turn. Turn. That's it. Right round. Round. Round. Now back. Good. Good.'

'Your children would enjoy a bonfire, wouldn't they, Mr Brennan? Such lively children they are too, and so healthy, so full of life. I see them, you know, from my bedroom window. Running all over the place. So lively and full of spirits.'

A crunch, a heavy thud, and Mr Bernard was seated, not upright but sideways over the arm of the chair, as he had dropped. His eyes blinked in relief at having missed disaster once more.

'Now,' said Mrs Hogan briskly, 'I think we're ready to begin, aren't we? This is Mr Brennan of the gate lodge, Daddy. He has given us the loan of his tape-recording machine and is going to work it for us. Isn't that kind of him?'

'How are you, Mr Hogan?' said Joe.

The old man did not answer, but looked across at him. Was it a sly, reproving look, Joe wondered, or was it the awkward angle of the old man's head that made it appear sly?

'Which of these knobs is it?' asked Father Declan, his fingers playing arpeggios over the recorder. 'On. This is it, isn't it? Yes. This is it.'

'The second one is for volume, Father,' said Joe.

'Volume. Yes. I see. Well, all set?'

'Ready,' said Mrs Hogan.

'Ready, Daddy?' asked Father Declan.

'Daddy's ready,' said Mrs Hogan.

'Joe?'

'Ready,' said Joe, because that was what Mrs Hogan had said.

'Here goes then,' said Father Declan. 'Come in, Claire. We're waiting.'

The recorder purred. The soft sound of the revolving spools spread up and out until it was heavy as the noise of distant seas. Mrs Hogan sat at the edge of her chair; Mr Bernard remained slumped as he had fallen. Father Declan stood poised as a ballet dancer before the fire. The spools gathered speed and the purring was a pounding of blood in the ears.

'It often takes a few seconds –' Joe began.

'Quiet!' snapped Mrs Hogan. 'Quiet, boy! Quiet!'

Then the voice came and all other sound died.

'Hello, Mammy and Daddy and Father Declan. This is Sister Claire speaking to the three of you from St Joseph's Mission, Kaluga, Northern Rhodesia. I hope you are all together when this is being played back, because I am imagining you all sitting before a great big fire in the drawing room at this minute, Daddy spread out and taking his well-earned relaxation on one side, and you, Mammy, sitting on the other side, and Declan between you both. How are you all? I wish to talk to each of you in turn – to Declan first, then to you, Mammy, and last, but by no means least, to my dear Daddy. Later in the recording, Reverend Mother, who is here beside me, will say a few words to you, and after that you will hear my school choir singing some Irish songs that I have taught them and some native songs they have taught me. I hope you will enjoy them.'

Joe tried to remember the voice. Then he realized that he probably had never heard Claire speak. This sounded more like reading than speaking, he thought – like a teacher reading a story to a class of infants, making her voice go up and down in pretended interest.

She addressed the priest first, and Joe looked at him – eyes closed, hands joined at the left shoulder, head to the side, feet crossed, his whole body limp and graceful as if in repose. She asked him for his prayers and thanked him for his letter last Christmas. She said that every day she got her children to pray both for him and for the success of his work, and asked him to send her the collection of Irish melodies – a blue-backed book, she said, which he would find either in the piano stool or in the glass bookcase beside the drawing-room window.

'And now you, Mammy. You did not mention your lumbago in your last letter, so I take it you are not suffering so much from it. And I hope you have found a good maid at last, because the house is much too big for you to manage all by yourself. There are many young girls around the mission here who would willingly give you a hand, but then they are too far away, aren't they? However, please God, you are now fixed up.'

She went on to ask about the garden and the summer crop of flowers, and told of the garden she had beside the convent and of the flowers she was growing. While her daughter spoke to her, Mrs Hogan worked her mouth and lips furiously, and Joe wondered what she was saying to herself.

'And now I come to my own Daddy. How are you, Daddy? I am sure you were very sorry when Prince had to be shot, you had him so long. And then the Prince before that – how long did you have him? I was telling Sister Monica here about him the other day, about the first Prince, and when I said he lived to be nineteen and a half, she just laughed in my face and said she was sure I was mistaken. But he was nineteen and a half, wasn't he? You got him on my sixth birthday, I remember, and although I never saw the second Prince – you got him after I had entered – I am quite sure he was as lovely as the first. Now, why don't you get yourself a third, Daddy? He would be company for you when you go on your rambles, and it would be nice for *you* to have him lying beside you on the office floor, the way the first Prince used to lie.'

Joe watched the old man. Mr Bernard could not move himself to face the recorder, but his eyes were on it, the large, startled eyes of a horse.

'And now, Daddy, before I talk any more to you, I am going to play a tune for you on my violin. I hope you like it. It is *The Gartan Mother's Lullaby*. Do you remember it?'

She began to play. The music was tuneful but no more. The lean tinny notes found a weakness in the tape or in the machine, because when she played the higher part of the melody, the only sound reproduced was a shrieking monotone. Joe sprang to his feet and worked at the controls but he could do nothing. The sound adjusted itself when she came to the initial melody again, and he went back to his seat.

It was then, as he turned to go back to the fire, that he noticed the old man. He had moved somehow in his armchair and was facing the recorder, staring at it. His one good hand pressed down on the sides of his chair and his body rocked backward and forward. His expression, too, had changed. The dead purple of his cheeks was now a living scarlet, and the mouth was open. Then, even as Joe watched, he suddenly levered himself upright in the chair, his face pulsating with uncontrollable emotion, the veins in his neck dilating, the mouth shaping in preparation for speech. He leaned forward, half pointing towards the recorder with one huge hand.

'*Claire!*'

The terrible cry – hoarse, breathy, almost lost in his asthmatic snortings – released Father Declan and Mrs Hogan from their concentration on the tape. They ran to him as he fell back into the chair.

Darkness had fallen by the time Joe left Foundry House. He had helped Father Declan to carry the old man upstairs to his bedroom and helped to undress him and put him to bed. He suggested a doctor, but neither the priest nor Mrs Hogan answered him. Then he came downstairs alone and switched off the humming machine. He waited for almost an hour for the others to come down – he felt awkward about leaving without making some sort of farewell – but when neither of them came, he tiptoed out through the hall and pulled the door after him. He left the recorder behind.

The kitchen at home was chaotic. The baby was in a zinc bath before the fire, three younger children were wrestling in their pyjamas, and the five elder were eating at the table. Rita, her hair in a turban and her sleeves rolled up, stood in the middle of the floor and shouted unheeded instructions above the din. Joe's arrival drew her temper to him.

'So you came back home at last! Did you have a nice afternoon with your fancy friends?'

He picked his steps between the wrestlers and sat in the corner below the humming gas jet.

'I'm speaking to you! Are you deaf?'

'I heard you,' he said. 'Yes, I had a nice afternoon.'

She sat resolutely on the opposite side of the fireplace, to show that she had done her share of the work; it was now his turn to give a hand.

'Well?' She took a cigarette from her apron pocket and lit it. The chaos around her was forgotten.

'Well, what?' he asked.

'You went up with the recorder, and what happened?'

'They were all there – the three of them.'

'Then what?'

'We played the tape through.'

'What's the house like inside?'

'It's very nice,' Joe said slowly. 'Very nice.'

She waited for him to continue. When he did not, she said, 'Did the grandeur up there frighten you, or what?'

'I was just thinking about them, that's all,' he said.

'The old man, what's he like?'

'Mr Bernard? Oh, Mr Bernard . . . he's the same as ever. Older, of course, but the same Mr Bernard.'

'And Father Declan?'

'A fine man. A fine priest. Yes, very fine.'

'Huh!' said Rita. 'It's not worth your while going out, for all the news you bring home.'

'The tape was lovely,' said Joe quickly. 'She spoke to all of them in turn – to Father Declan and then to her mother and then to Mr Bernard himself. And she played a tune on the violin for him, too.'

'Did they like it?'

'They loved it, loved it. It was a lovely recording.'

'Did she offer you anything?'

'Forced me to have tea with them, but I said no, I had to leave.'

'What room were they in?'

'The breakfast room. The drawing room was always draughty.'

'A nice room?'

'The breakfast room? Oh, lovely, lovely . . . Glass handle on the door and a beautiful carpet and beautiful pictures . . . everything. Just lovely.'

'So that's Foundry House,' said Rita, knowing that she was going to hear no gossipy details.

'That's Foundry House,' Joe echoed. 'The same as ever – no different.'

She put out her cigarette and stuck the butt behind her ear.

'They're a great family, Rita,' he said. 'A great, grand family.'

'So they are,' she said casually, stooping to lift the baby out of the bath. Its wet hands patterned her thin blouse. 'Here, Joe! A job for you. Dress this divil for bed.'

She set the baby on his knee and went to separate the wrestlers. Joe caught the child, closed his eyes, and rubbed his cheek against the infant's soft, damp skin. 'The same as ever,' he crooned into the child's ear. 'A great family. A grand family.'

EUGENE MCCABE

'Music at Annahullion'

She put her bike in the shed and filled a basket of turf. Curtains still pulled across Teddy's window. Some morning the gable'd fall, and he'd wake sudden. Course you had to pretend to Liam Annahullion was very special. 'See the depth of them walls' . . . 'Look at that door; they don't use timber like that now' . . . and 'feel that staircase, solid,

made to last.' Bit of a dose the way he went on; sure what was it only a mud and
stone lofted cottage, half thatched, half slated, with a leaning chimney and a cracked
gable.

'The finest view in Ireland,' Liam said a hundred times a year. High to the north by
Carn rock it was fine in spring and summer, very fine, but all you ever saw from this
door in winter was the hammered out barrels on the hayshed, the rutted lane, and a
bottom of rushes so high you'd be hard put at times to find the five cows. Liam went
on about 'the orchard' at the front put down by their grandfather, Matt Grue: a few
scabby trees in the ground hoked useless by sows, a half acre of a midden, but you
couldn't say that to his face.

One night Teddy said, 'Carried away auld cod: it's because he owns it.'

'Shush,' Annie said, pointing upstairs.

'A rotten stable, it'll fall before we're much older.'

'We grew up here, Teddy.'

'Signs on it we'll all die here. They'll plant it with trees when we're gone.'

'It's home.'

'Aye.'

Teddy talked like that when he came in late. He drank too much. His fingers were
tarry black from fags, the eyes burned out of his head. Even so you could look into his
eyes, you could have a laugh with Teddy. She called up the stairs as she closed the
kitchen door.

'Teddy, it's half-eleven.'

'Right.'

He gave a brattle of a cough and then five minutes later shouted down: 'Is there a
shirt?'

'Where it's always.'

'It's not.'

'Look again.'

She listened.

'Get it? In the low drawer?'

'It was under a sheet.'

'But you've got it?'

'I got it.'

'Thanks very much,' Annie said to herself. She hooked a griddle over the glow of
sods to warm a few wheaten scones. She could maybe mention it quiet like, give it time
to sink. He might rise to it after a while maybe, or again he might know what she was
up to and say nothing. He was always low over winter, got it tight to pay Liam the three
quid a week for board and keep. In the summer he had cash to spare, on hire through
the country with a 1946 Petrol Ferguson, cutting meadows, moulding spuds, buckraking,
drawing corn shigs to the thrasher. Sometimes he was gone a week.

'Knows all the bad weemen in the country,' Liam once said. 'Got a lot to answer for,
that bucko.'

Teddy came down and sat at the north window under an empty birdcage, his elbows
on the oilcloth. A tall stooped frame. He ate very little very slowly, put her in mind

often of some great grey bird; a bite, a look out the window, another bite. 'You were up at Reilly's?'

'We'd no butter.'

'Who was there?'

'George McAloon.'

'Wee blind George?'

'He's not that blind.'

Teddy lit a cigarette and looked out. He could see Liam stepping from ridge to ridge in the sloping haggard. The field had earthy welts running angle ways, like the ribs in a man's chest, hadn't felt the plough since the Famine or before.

'Anyone else?'

'Only Petey Mulligan the shopboy. He kep' sayin' "Jasus" every minute to see poor George nod and bless himself, and then he winked at me, much as to say "mad frigger, but we're wise" . . . too old-fashioned by half.'

Teddy was quiet for a minute and then said: 'Religion puts people mad.'

'No religion puts them madder.'

He thought about this. He hadn't confessed for near forty years, lay in bed of a Sunday with rubbishy papers Liam wouldn't use to light fires. Sometimes they had bitter arguments about religion and the clergy. Liam and Annie never missed Mass.

'It's a big question,' Teddy said.

Annie filled a tin basin from the kettle.

'I saw a piana at Foster's.'

'Aye?'

'In the long shed at the back of the garden.'

'What's it doin' there?'

'They've put a lot of stuff out.'

'What kind?'

'Horsetedder, cart wheels, pig troughs, beehives, auld churns, a grass harrow, stuff like that.'

'Useless?'

'Less or more.'

'Over from the auction.'

'Must be.'

'Odd place to leave a piana.'

'The very thing I thought.'

After a moment she said. 'It looks very good, shiny with two brass candle-sticks, like the one in the photo.'

'Auld I'd say?'

'Must be.'

'The guts of fifty years.'

'And maybe fifty along with that.'

Teddy went to the door and looked out. Annie said to his back, 'Pity to see a thing like that going to rack and loss.'

'If it's worth money,' Teddy said, 'some fly boy goin' the road'll cob it . . . maybe it's got no insides or it's rusted or seized up some way, must be something wrong with it or it would have gone in the auction.'

'If it come out of Foster's it's good, and it could come at handy money.'

Teddy looked round at her. 'Who'd want it?'

Annie shrugged.

'You want it, Annie?'

'A nice thing, a piana.'

'Everyone wants things.'

Teddy looked through stark apple trees towards the wet rushy bottom and the swollen river; rain again today.

'Who'd play it?'

'A body can pick out tunes with one finger, the odd visitor maybe, and you could put flowers on top of it, light candles at special times.'

Teddy was picking at his teeth with a tarry thumb: 'When one of us dies Annie?'

'Christmas, Easter, times like that.'

He went on picking his teeth with the tarry thumb.

'It's a bit daft, Annie.'

'Is it?'

There was a silence and Teddy looked round; when he saw her face he said, 'Don't go by me, but it's a dud I'd swear.'

'I'd say you're right.'

He took his cap from the top of the wireless.

'I'll see if there's letters.'

'Tell Liam there's tay.'

Annie saw him cross the yard, a scarecrow of a man, arms hung below his knees. Teddy wouldn't bother anyway. A Scotch collie bitch circled round him, yapping and bellycrawling. Guinea hens flapped to the roof of a piggery. She could see Liam blinding potholes in the rutted lane. Even in winter scutch grass clung to the middle ridge. Teddy stopped for a word; hadn't much to say to each other that pair, more like cold neighbours than brothers. Teddy went on down the road. Two years back Liam had put the post box on an ash tree near the gate . . . 'to keep Elliot the Postman away from about the place'.

'What's wrong with him?' Teddy had asked.

'Bad auld article,' Liam said.

'What way?'

'Handles weemen, or tries to, in near every house he goes to, anyway he's black Protestant.'

Teddy let on he didn't understand. 'Handles weemen? What weemen?'

Liam got redder.

'He'll not put a foot about this place.'

Annie thought about Joe Elliot, a rumpledy wee fellow, with a bate-in face, doggy eyes, and a squeaky voice. No woman in her right mind could let him next or near her without a fit of the giggles, but there was no arguing with Liam. He was proud and very private. Four or five signs about the farm forbade this and that. A 'Land Poisoned' sign had been kept up though there hadn't been sheep about Annahullion for twenty years. When stray hounds crossed the farm Liam fired at them. Every year in the *Anglo-Celt* he put a Notice prohibiting anyone from shooting or hunting.

'Jasus,' Teddy said, 'thirty wet sour acres and maybe a dozen starved snipe, who's he stopping? Who'd want to hunt or shoot about here? There's nothin' only us.'

Near the bridge there was a notice 'Fishing Strictly Forbidden'. The river was ten feet wide, the notice nailed to an alder in a scrub of stunted blackthorn that grew three yards out from the river bank When the water was low barbed-wire under the bridge trapped the odd carcass of dog and badger; sometimes you could see pram wheels, bicycle frames, tins and bottles. Liam once hooked a pike on a nightline. She had cooked it in milk. It tasted strong, oily. Teddy wouldn't touch it:

'I'd as lief ate sick scaldcrows, them auld river pike ates rats and all kinds of rubbish.'

Annie found it hard to stomach her portion. She fed the left-overs to the cat. Teddy swore later he saw the cat puke. Liam was dour for days. She heard him crossing the yard now and began pouring his tea; he blessed himself as he came across the floor, pulling off the cap.

'Half-eleven I'd say?'

'Nearer twelve,' Annie said.

Liam nodded and sucked at his tea.

'You could say mid-day.'

'Next or near, you could say that.'

Liam shook his head. Every day or so they had this exchange about Teddy.

'I'm never done tryin' to tell him,' Annie said. 'I get sick hearin' myself.'

'It's a pity of any man, he couldn't be tould often enough or strong enough.'

'True for you,' Annie said, and thought how neither of them ever dared a word, let alone hint. Teddy was his own man, paid steady for his room, helped about the yard or farm when he felt like it. Liam sucked his teeth. They were big and a bad fit, put you in mind of a horse scobing into a sour apple. He was squatter than Teddy, sturdier, slate-coloured eyes and tight reddish skin. He smiled seldom and no one had ever heard him laugh. Sometimes Annie heard him laugh alone about the yard and fields.

'Same as the Uncle Eddie,' Liam said, 'lazy and pagan and you know how he ended. In a bog-hole . . . drunk . . . drownded.'

Crabbed this morning, better leave it till evening.

'Teddy said you remarked a piana at Foster's.'

Oh God, Annie thought and said, 'I saw it from the road.'

Liam ate another scone before he said, 'Scrap.'

'I'd say.'

'Whole place was red out at the sale. Piana must have been lyin' about in a pig house or some of them auld rotten lofts.'

'That's what Teddy said, a dud.'

'He's right about that anyway.'

And that's that, Annie thought. Soon they'd all be pensioned, maybe then she could buy the odd thing. It was put up to her to run the house on the milk cheque. It could be a very small one in winter. She made up by crocheting, anything but approach Liam. All afternoon she thought of the piano. In the end she found herself crying as she kneaded bread. 'Yerra God,' she thought, 'I'm goin' astray in the head . . . an auld scrap piana, an' not a body in the house fit to play, and here I am all snivels over the head of it.' She blew her nose and put it out of her mind.

It was dark when Teddy got back. He smelled of whiskey and fags and his eyes looked bright, Liam didn't look up from the *Anglo-Celt*.

'Your dinner's all dried up,' Annie said.

'No odds,' Teddy said.

Liam switched on the wireless for the news. They all listened. When it was over Teddy said: 'I saw your piana, I made a dale for it.'

'Ah you're coddin', Teddy!'

'It's out of tune.'

'That's aisy fixed.'

'Woodworm in the back.'

'You can cure that too.'

'There's a pedal off.'

'What odds.'

From the way Liam held the paper she could tell he was cut. God's sake couldn't he let on for once in his life, his way of showing he kept the deeds. Teddy winked.

'Who sould it?' Liam asked.

'Wright, the Auctioneer. It was forgot at the sale, hid under a heap of bags in the coach house.'

'Cute boy, Wright.'

'He's all that.'

'How much?'

'Two notes, he give it away.'

'You paid him?'

'He's paid.'

'That's all right,' Liam said and went out.

They heard him rattling buckets in the boiler house.

'Pass no remarks,' Teddy said. 'If you want a thing, get it. What's he bought here all his years but two ton weight of the *Anglo-Celt*, one second-hand bird cage that no bird ever sang in, and a dose of holy pictures.'

'Horrid good of you, Teddy,' Annie said.

'Ah!'

'No, it was,' Annie said. 'If you'd waited to chaw it over with Liam you'd be that sick hearin' about it you'd as lief burn it as have it.'

'Liam's a cautious man.'

Next day Teddy took the tractor out and went off about three o'clock. Annie lit a fire in the parlour. It led off the kitchen at the end of the staircase. It was a long, narrow room smelling of turpentine, damp, and coats of polish on the parquetry lino. The white-painted boards, ceiling and wainscoting was yellow and spotty. Like the kitchen it had two windows at either end, a black horsehair chaise-lounge in one, a small table with a red chenille cover and potplant in the other. Two stiff armchairs faced the painted slate fireplace. On the mantelshelf there was a clock stopped since 1929, a china dog, and a cracked Infant of Prague. Annie looked at the photograph over the shelf: Teddy with a hoop, Liam wearing a cap and buttoned britches. Her mother had on a rucked blouse, a long skirt with pintucks at the bottom, high boots and gloves, and that was her with a blind doll on her mother's knee. Their father stood behind looking sideways. At the bottom of the photograph 'McEniff, Photographer, Dublin Road, Monaghan 1914' . . . some fairday long ago, no memory of it now. The rough-faced man and the soft young woman buried. She was now twenty years older than her mother was then, and she thought now how her mother in her last sickness had kept raving: 'the childer, the childer, where are my childer?' She remembered saying 'This is me; Annie, one of your childer.' Her mother had looked at her steady for a minute, then shook her head. Course she was old, dying of old age.

It was dark when they sat down to tea and Liam said, 'Long as he's not drunk . . . and lyin' in some ditch under the piana. That would be a square snippet for the *Celt*.'

'He'll be all right,' Annie said.

No noise for an hour but wind in the chimney, the hiss of thornlogs through turf, and the crackle of Liam's paper. She began to worry. Supposing he did cross a ditch, get buried or worse over the head of it. Then she heard the tractor, and went to the door. A single light was pulsing on the bonnet of the old Ferguson as it came into the yard. Teddy reversed to the front door and let the buck-rake gently to the ground. He untied the ropes and put the tractor away. Annie tested the keyboard in the dark windy yard. There was an odd note dumb. Guinea hens cackled and the collie bitch barked. Liam was watching from the door.

'What's wrong with them?'

'Damp,' Annie said. 'Nothing a good fire won't mend.' It was heavy, the castors seized or rusted.

'Like a coffin full of rocks,' Liam said.

'Time enough,' Teddy said. 'No hurry.'

They had a lot of bother getting it into the kitchen, Liam wouldn't let Annie help.

'Stand back woman, we're well fit.'

It seemed very big in the kitchen. Teddy sat down and lit a cigarette. Annie took down the Tilley lamp and went round the piano. Made from that thin shaved timber; damp had unstuck some of it. That could be fixed. The keys had gone yellow but the candle-sticks were very nice and the music stand was carved. God, it was lovely. She lifted the top lid and looked down into the frame. She could see something . . . a newspaper? She pulled it out, faded and flittered by mice. Liam came over.

'That's an auld one,' Teddy said from the hearth.

'The 7th November, 1936,' Liam read.

'The weight of forty years,' Annie said.

From where he was sitting Teddy could read an ad:

WHAT

LIES

AHEAD

FOR

YOU

Why not make the future certain?

'What's in it?'

Liam had put on his glasses . . . 'A Cavan man hung himself in an outhouse.'

'Aye?'

'Last thing he said to his wife was "Will I go to Matt Smith's or get the spade shafted?" . . . and the wife said "Damn the hair I care but the childer have wet feet . . . don't come back without boots".'

Liam looked up. 'Then he hung himself.'

'God help her,' Annie said. 'Women have a hard life.'

'God help *him*,' Liam said.

'Safer lave God out of it,' Teddy said.

'I must have bought that paper and read that maybe ten times . . . and it's all gone . . . forgot . . . Do *you* mind it, Annie?'

'No.'

'You, Ted?'

'It's like a lot of things you read, you couldn't mind them all.'

Liam put the paper aside. 'Better get this thing out of the way.'

He went to the parlour door, looked at it and looked at the piano. The two last steps of the staircase jutted across the parlour door. It was made from two heavy planks, each step dowelled into place. The whole frame was clamped to the wall with four iron arms. 'None of your fibby boxed in jobs,' Liam often said. 'That's solid, made to last.' He went to the dresser, got a ruler, measured, folded the ruler and said: 'Won't fit.'

'It'll be got in some way,' Annie said.

'How?'

'Let's try and we'll know.'

'If it doesn't fit, it doesn't fit. Damn thing's too big.'

Teddy took the rule and measured.

'We might jiggle it in,' he said, 'it's worth a try.'

'Won't fit,' Liam said.

Annie made tea and watched for an hour, measuring, lifting, forcing, levering, straining, Liam getting angrier and redder.

'For Christ's sake, don't pull agin me.'

'Where are you goin' now, up the friggin' stairs?'

'What in the name of Jasus are you at now?'

Finally he shouted, 'Have you no wit at all, the bloody thing's too big, the door's too small, the staircase is in the way, it won't fit or less you rip down them stairs.'

Annie tried not to listen. Teddy kept his voice low, but he was vexed and lit one fag off the other.

'Maybe we could strip her down,' he said, 'and lift in the insides, build her up again in the room.'

'Maybe we could toss the sidewall of the house,' Liam said, 'and drag her through, that's the only way.'

They said nothing for a while and then Annie said, 'I suppose it'll have to go out again?'

'Where else,' Liam said.

They got it out the door again and half lifted, half dragged it to the turf shed. Two castors broke off. The thrumming and jumble of notes set the guinea-hens clucking and flapping in the apple trees.

Liam went to bed early. Teddy sat at the hearth with Annie and drank more tea.

'It's only a couple of quid, Annie.'

'No odds,' she said.

He looked at her. He felt a bit of an eejit; maybe she did too.

'What odds what people say.'

'I don't give tuppence what people say . . . never wanted a thing so bad, dunno why, and to have it in the house.'

'If you're that strong for a piana, we'll get one, the same brass candlesticks, one that fits.'

'No.'

Teddy looked at her again. If she'd come out straight and say what was in her head; women never did. They never knew rightly what was in their heads.

'Two quid is nothing, Annie.'

'I told you, it's not the money.'

Teddy sat a while at the fire.

'I'll go up.'

He paused half-way up the stairs. 'It's only scrap, Annie, means nothin'.'

'I know.'

Annie dreamed that night that Liam had hung himself in the turf shed. Teddy cut him down and they laid him out in the parlour. She looked at the awful face on the piano, and then the face of the little boy in the photograph, and knelt. She felt her heart was breaking, she wanted to pray but all she could do was cry. 'What are you cryin' for, Annie?' Teddy was standing in the parlour door. 'Everything . . . all of us . . . I wish to God we were never born.'

When she woke up it was dark. She lit a candle, and prayed for a while. It was almost light again when she fell asleep. That morning she covered the piano with plastic fertilizer bags. The guinea-hens roosted on it all winter. Near dark one evening in February she saw a sick rat squeeze in where the pedal had broken off. By April varnish was peeling off the side. One wet day in July Teddy unscrewed the brass candlesticks. On and off she dreamed about it, strange dreams that made her unhappy. It was winter again and one evening she said, 'I'm sick to death lookin' at that thing in the turf shed. For God's sake get shut of it.'

She watched Teddy smash it with an axe. In ten minutes the rusted steel frame lay in the hen mess of the yard like the carcass of a skinned animal. Teddy slipped the buck-rake under it and drew it out of the yard. From under the empty birdcage Liam watched through the kitchen window. 'No wit, that man,' he said. 'Always bought foolish. His Uncle Eddie was identical.'

MARY BECKETT

'A Belfast Woman'

I mind well the day the threatening letter came. It was a bright morning, and warm, and I remember thinking while I was dressing myself that it would be nice if the Troubles were over so that a body could just enjoy the feel of a good day. When I came down the stairs the hall was dark but I could see the letter lying face down. I lifted it and just my name was on the envelope, 'Mrs Harrison' in red felt pen. I knew what it was. There was a page of an exercise book inside with 'Get out or we'll burn you out' all in red with bad printing and smeared. I just went in and sat at the kitchen table with the note in front of me. I never made myself a cup of tea even. It was a shock, though God knows I shouldn't have been surprised.

One of the first things I remember in my life was wakening up with my mother screaming downstairs when we were burned out in 1921. I ran down in my nightgown and my mother was standing in the middle of the kitchen with her hands up to her face screaming and screaming, and the curtains were on fire and my father was pulling them down and stamping on them with the flames catching the oilcloth on the floor. Then he shouted, 'Sadie, the children,' and she stopped screaming and said, 'Oh, God Michael, the children,' and she ran upstairs and came down with the baby in one arm and Joey under the other, and my father took Joey in his arms and me by the hand and we ran out along the street. It was a warm summer night and the fires were crackling all over the place and the street was covered with broken glass. It wasn't until we got into my grandmother's house that anybody noticed that I had nothing on but my nightie and nothing on my feet and they were cut. It was all burned, everything they had. My mother used to say she didn't save as much as a needle and thread. I wasn't able to sleep for weeks, afraid I'd be wakened by that screaming.

We stayed in my grandmother's house until 1935 and my grandmother was dead by that time and my father too, for he got TB like many another then. He used to say, 'When you have no house and no job sure what use are you?' and then he'd get fits of coughing. In 1935 when we got the letter threatening to burn us out I said to my mother, 'We'll gather our things and we'll go.' So we did, and like all the rest of them in our street we went up to Glenard to the new houses. When we showed our 'Get out or we'll burn you out' note they gave us a house and we'd enough out to get things fixed up. We got new jobs in another mill, my mother and Patsy and me. Only my mother never liked it there. She always said the air was too strong for her. It was cold right enough, up close to the mountains. But when I was getting married to William, and his aunt who was a Protestant gave him the key of her house in this street, my mother was in a terrible state – 'Don't go into that Protestant street, Mary, or you'll be a sorry girl'

– and she said we could live with her. But I didn't want William to pine like my poor father, so here we came and not a day's trouble until the note came.

Mind you, the second night we were here there was trouble in the Catholic streets across the road. We heard shots first and then the kind of rumbling, roaring noises of all the people out on the streets. I wanted to get up and run out and see what was wrong, but William held on to me in bed and he said, 'They don't run out on the street here. They stay in.' And it was true. They did. I was scared lying listening to the noise the way I never was when I was out with my neighbours. It turned out some poor young lad had stayed at home when he should have gone back to the British Army and they sent the police for him. He got out of the back window and ran down the entry and the police ran after him and shot him dead. They said their gun went off by accident but the people said they beat him up. When I went over the next day I saw him laid out in the wee room off the kitchen and his face had all big yellowy-greenish blotches on it. I never mentioned it to my new neighbours and they never mentioned it to me.

I couldn't complain about them. They were good decent people. They didn't come into the house for a chat or a loan of tea or milk or sugar like the neighbours in Glenard or North Queen Street but they were ready to help at any time. I didn't know the men much because they had work so they didn't stand around the corners the way I was used to. But when Liam was born they all helped and said what a fine baby he was. He was too. Nine pounds with black hair and so strong he could lift his head and look round at a week old. They were always remarking on his mottled skin – purply kind of measles when he'd be up out of the pram – and said it was the sign of a very strong baby. At that time I had never seen a baby with any other colour of skin – I suppose Catholic babies had to be strong to get by. But when Eileen was born a year and ten months later she was different. She had beautiful creamy skin. She was plump and perfect and I loved her more than Liam, God forgive me, and more than William and more than anybody in the world and I wanted everything to be right for her. I thought to myself, *If I was a Protestant now we'd have just the two and no more and I'd be able to look after them and do well for them.* So I didn't act fair with William at all.

Then I started having trouble. I looked as if I was expecting again and my stomach was hard and round but I had bleeding and I could feel no life so I was afraid. I went to the doctor and he said, 'No, Mrs Harrison, you're not pregnant. There is something here we shall have to look into.' And I said, 'Is it serious, doctor?' and he said, 'I can't tell you that, can I, until you go into hospital and have it investigated,' and I said, 'Do you mean an operation?' and he said, 'I do, Mrs Harrison.' I came home saying to myself, *It's cancer and who will rear my Eileen and Liam?* I remembered hearing it said that once they put the knife into you, you were dead in six months, so I made up my mind I'd have no operation and I'd last out as long as I could. Every year I was able to look after them would be a year gained and the bigger they were the better they d be able to do without me. But oh dear, it was terrible hard on everybody. I told William and my mother and Patsy there was nothing at all the matter with me but they knew to look at me it wasn't true. I was really wan and I was so tired I was ready to drop. I'd sit down by the fire at night when the children were in bed and my eyes would close, and if I opened them I'd see William staring at me with such a tortured look on his face I'd have to close them again so that I wouldn't go and lean my head against him and tell him the whole thing. I knew if I did that he'd make me go back to the doctor and I'd be done for. At times I'd see against my closed eyes the white long roots of the cancer growing all over my inside and I'd remember the first time William brought me to see his father in the country.

He had a fine labourer's cottage for he was a Protestant and was head plowman to some rich farmer down there. He was a good man. William's mother was a Catholic and she died when William was a wee boy but they brought him up a Catholic because it had been promised. He was cross-looking though, and I was a bit nervous of him. He had his garden all planted in rows and squares and he was digging clods in one corner and breaking them up fine and I could see all the long white roots and threads he was shaking the mud out of and he turned to us and he said, 'Sitfast and scutch! Sitfast and scutch! They're the plague of my life. No matter how much I weed there's more in the morning.' I told him about my grandfather and the big elderberry tree that grew behind the wee house he'd got in the country when he was burned out in Lisburn. It wasn't there when he went into the house and when he noticed it first it was only a wee bit of a bush but it grew so quickly it blocked out all the light from his back window. Then one summer it was covered with black slimy kind of flies so he cut it down to the stump, but it started growing again straightaway. One day when my father took Patsy and Joey and me down to visit him he had dug all round the stump and he was trying to pull it out with a rope. He told my father to pull with him. My father tried but then he leaned against the wall with his face pale and covered with sweat. My grandfather said, 'Are you finished, Michael?' and my father said, 'I'm clean done,' and my grandfather said, 'God help us all,' and brought us into the house and gave us lemonade. It was just after that my father went into the sanatorium and my mother was all the time bringing him bottles of lemonade. At the funeral I asked my grandfather if he got the stump out and he didn't know for a minute what I was talking about. Then he said, 'No, no. Indeed the rope's still lying out there. I must bring it in or it'll rot.' I never saw him again, never saw the wee house either. My mother never was one for the country.

She wasn't old herself when she died – not that much over fifty, but she looked an old woman. She wore a shawl at times and not many did that anymore. She was always fussing about my health and me going to the doctor but I managed fine without. I didn't look much. I had this swollen stomach and I got into the way of hiding it with my arms. But every year I got through I'd say to myself, wasn't I right to stick it out? When the war finished and the free health came, everybody thought I'd get myself seen to, and my mother was at me that she'd mind Liam and Eileen. Of course there were no more children but I kept those two lovely. There was no Protestant child better fed or better dressed than those two, and I always warned them to fight with nobody, never to get into trouble. If any of the children started to shout at them about being Catholics or Fenians or Teagues they were just to walk away, not to run, mind you, but just walk home. And Liam was the best boy ever. He wasn't great at his lessons but the masters said how pleasant and good he was. Eileen was inclined to be a bit bold and that was the cause of the only terrible thing I ever did. I can't believe even now how I came to do it. It was the week after my mother had died.

I blamed myself for what happened to my mother. I should have seen in time that she wasn't well and made her mind herself and she'd have lasted better. She came into my house one day with her shawl on and I was going to say I wished she'd wear a coat and not have my neighbours passing remarks, but she hung the shawl up on the back of the door and she looked poorly. She said she'd had a terrible pain in her chest and she had been to the doctor and he'd told her it was her heart. She was to rest and take tablets. She had other wee tablets to put under her tongue if she got a pain and she was not to go up hills. She looked so bad I put her to bed in the wee room off the kitchen. She never got up again. She had tense crushing pains and the tablets did no good. Sometimes the sip of Lourdes water helped her. The doctor said he could do nothing for her unless she went into hospital and she wouldn't hear of that. 'Ah no, no. I'm just done, that's all.' Every now and again she'd say this would never have happened if she hadn't been burned out of her home down near the docks and had to go half roads up the mountains with all the hills and the air too strong for her. 'And your father wouldn't ever have got consumption if he hadn't had to move in with my mother and spend his days at the street corner. You wouldn't remember it, Mary. You were too small,' she'd say and I never contradicted her, 'but we hadn't left as much as a needle and thread. The whole block went up. Nothing left.' She was buried from our house even though she kept saying she must go home. She had a horror of my Protestant neighbours even though she liked well enough the ones she met. But at her funeral, better kinder decenter neighbours you could not get. When it was over, all I could do was shiver inside myself as if my shelter had been taken away. William was good to me, always good to me, but I had to keep a bit of myself to myself with him. My mother never looked for anything from me. I'd tell her what I needed to tell her and she'd listen but she never interfered. And she was as proud of Liam and Eileen as I was. I'd see the way she looked at them.

The week after she died Eileen came home from school crying. She was ten years of age and she didn't often cry. She showed me the mark on her legs where the head teacher had hit her with a cane. A big red mark it was, right across the back of her legs. And she had lovely skin on her legs, lovely creamy skin. When I think of it I can still see that mark. I didn't ask her what happened. I just lifted my mother's shawl from where it was still hanging on the back of the kitchen door and I flung it round me and ran down to the school. I knocked on the door and she opened it herself, the head teacher, because most of the school had gone home. She took one look at me and ran away back into a classroom. I went after her. She ran into another room off it and banged the door. My arm stuck in through the glass panel and I pulled it out with a big deep cut from my wrist to my elbow. She didn't come out of the door and I never spoke to her at all. There were a couple of other teachers over a bit and a few children about but I couldn't say anything to anybody and they just stood. To stop the blood pouring so much I held my arm up out of my mother's shawl as I went back up the street. There was a woman standing at her door near the top of the street. She was generally at her door knitting, that woman. She had very clever children and some of them did well. One got to be a teacher; another was in the post office, which is about as far as a clever poor Catholic can get. She asked me what happened but when I couldn't answer she said, 'You'd need to get to the hospital, missus, I'll get my coat and go with you.' I didn't want to go to any hospital. I just wanted to go home and wash off all the blood but my head was spinning so I let myself be helped on the bus. They stitched it up and wanted me to stay in for the night but I was terrified they'd operate on me just when I was managing so well. I insisted I couldn't because the children were on their own and Mrs O'Reilly came with me right to the end of my own street. 'If your neighbours ask what happened, just tell them you fell off the bus,' she told me. 'You don't want them knowing all about your business.' I've heard she was from the west of Ireland.

When I went into the kitchen I was ready to drop but Eileen started screaming and crying and saying how ashamed of me she was and that she'd never go back to school again. Liam made me a cup of tea and stood looking worried at me. When William came in from work he helped me to bed and was kind and good but I could see by the cut of his mouth that he was shocked and offended at me. It took a long time to heal and the scar will never leave me. The story went around the parish in different ways. Some said I hit the teacher. Some said she knifed me. I was too ashamed ever to explain.

Eileen never was touched in school after that, though, and when she left she learned shorthand and typing and got an office job. She grew up lovely, and I used to think, watching her going out in the morning in the best of clothes with her hair shining, that she could have gone anywhere and done herself credit. She wasn't contented living where we did. At first I didn't understand what she wanted. I thought she wanted a better house in a better district. I didn't know how we could manage it but I made up my mind it would have to be done. I went for walks up round the avenues where there were detached houses with gardens and when I saw an empty house I'd peer in through the windows. Then one day a woman from the parish, who worked cleaning one of those houses, saw me and asked me in because the people of the house were out all day. Seeing it furnished with good solid shining furniture I knew we'd never manage it. In the sitting room there was an old-fashioned copper canopy over the fire and when I looked into it I could see the whole room reflected smaller like a fairy tale with flowers and books and pictures and plates on the wall. I knew it wasn't for us. How could I go in and out there? William and Liam wouldn't look right in their working clothes. Only Eileen would fit in. I was a bit sad but relieved because at no time could I see where the money would have come from. I told her that night when she came in but she looked at me all puzzled. 'But that wasn't what I meant, Mammy,' she said. 'I have to get away from everything here. There's no life for me here. I'm thinking of going to Canada.' That was before any trouble at all here. People now would say that was in the good times when you could get in a bus and go round the shops or into the pictures and nothing would have happened by the time you came home except that the slack would have burned down a bit on the fire.

Off she went anyway and got a job and wrote now and again telling us how well off she was. In no time at all she was married and was sending photographs, first of this lovely bungalow and then of her two wee girls with the paddling pool in her garden or at their swing when they were a bit bigger. I was glad she was doing so well. It was the kind of life I had reared her for and dreamed of for her, only I wished she and her children were not so far away. I kept inviting her home for a visit but I knew it would cost far too much money. Only I thought if she was homesick it would help her to know we wanted to see her too. Once the troubles came I stopped asking her.

Liam at that time was getting on well too. He was always such a nice pleasant big fellow that a plumber in the next street to ours asked him to join in his business at putting in fireplaces and hot-water pipes. Liam put in a lovely fireplace for me with a copper canopy like the one I'd seen years before and built me a bathroom and hot water and put in a sink unit for me till I was far better off than any of my neighbours, even though a lot of them had their houses very nice too. They were able to get paint from the shipyard of course, and marble slabs and nice bits of mahogany. He got married to a nice wee girl from the Bone and they got a house up in one of the nice streets in Ardoyne – up the far end in what they call now a mixed area. It's all gone, poor Liam's good way of living. When that street of houses up there was put on fire in 1972 his wife Gemma insisted on coming back to the Bone and squatting in an empty house. They did their best to fix it up but it's old and dark. Then when the murders got bad, his partner asked him not to come back to work anymore because he'd been threatened for working with a Catholic. I was raging when Liam told me, raging about what a coward the plumber was, but then as Liam said, you can't blame a man for not wanting to be murdered. So there he is – no work and no house and a timid wife and a family of lovely wee children. He had plenty to put up with. But where else could I go when I got the note? I sat looking round my shining kitchen and the note said, 'Get out or we'll burn you out,' and where could I go for help but to Liam?

Still I was glad William was dead before it happened. He would have been so annoyed. He felt so ashamed when the Protestants did something nasty. I could swallow my own shame every time the IRA disgraces us. I lived with it the same as I lived with the memory of my own disgrace when I went for the teacher and ripped my arm. But William had always been such a good upright man, he could never understand wickedness. Even the way he died showed it. He was a carter all his days, always in steady work, but for a while before he died they were saying to him that nobody had horses anymore and they were changing to a lorry. He could never drive a lorry. He was afraid he'd be on the dole. It wasn't the money he was worrying about, for I kept telling him it would make little difference to us – just the two of us, what did it matter? It was his pride that was upset. For years there was a big notice up on a corner shop at the bottom of the Oldpark Road. It said, 'Drivers, dismount. Don't overload your horses going up the hill.' He used to remark on it. It irked him if he didn't obey it. So one day in March when there was an east wind he collapsed on the hill and died the next day in hospital with the same disease as my mother.

There was a young doctor in the hospital asked me did I need a tranquillizer or a sleeping tablet or something to get over the shock. I told him no, that I never took any tablets, that I had had cancer when I was in my twenties and that I was still alive in my fifties with never a day in bed. He was curious and he asked me questions and then he said, 'Mrs Harrison, of course I can't be absolutely sure, but I'd say it was most unlikely you had cancer. Maybe you needed a job done on your womb. Maybe you even needed your womb removed but I would be very, very surprised if you had cancer. You wouldn't be here now if you had.' So I went in and knelt down at William's side. He still had that strained, worried look, even then. All I could think was: *Poor William. Poor William. Poor, poor, poor William.*

It wasn't that I was lonely without him for I'd kept him at a distance for a long time, but the days had no shape to them. I could have my breakfast, dinner, and tea whatever time I liked or I needn't have them at all. For a while I didn't bother cooking for myself, just ate tea and bread. Then Liam's wife, Gemma, said the butcher told her that I hadn't darkened his door since William died and that if I wouldn't cook for myself I'd have to come and have my dinner with them. So I thought to myself I wasn't being sensible and I'd only be a nuisance to them if I got sick, so I fixed everything to the clock as if there was no such thing as eternity. Until that morning the note came and then I just sat; I didn't know how long I stayed. I felt heavy, not able to move. Then I thought maybe Liam could get somebody with a van to take out my furniture and I could think later where to go. I took my rosary beads from under my pillow and my handbag with my money and my pension book and Eileen's letters and the photographs of her children and I shut the door behind me. There wasn't a soul in the street but there was nothing odd about that. You'll always know you're in a Protestant street if it's deserted. When I went across the road to get to Liam's house there were children playing and men at the corner and women standing at the doors in the sun and a squad of nervous-looking soldiers down at the other end.

Liam wasn't in but Gemma and the children were. The breakfast table wasn't cleared and Gemma was feeding the youngest. When he finished she stood him up on her lap and he reached over her shoulder trying to reach the shiny new handle Liam had put on the door. He was sturdy and happy and he had a warm smell of milk and baby powder. I wanted to hold him but I was afraid of putting her out of her routine. Sometimes I wonder if she has a routine – compared to the way I reared mine. Nothing was allowed to interrupt their feeding times and sleeping times. Maybe I was wrong and I'll never know what way Eileen managed hers. I would have liked to do the dishes too but I was afraid it might look like criticizing. After a wee while chatting Gemma got up to put the child in his pram and make us a cup of tea. 'You don't look great, Granny,' she said. 'Are you minding yourself at all?' I opened my bag and showed her the note.

She screamed and put her hands up to her face and the baby was startled and cried and bounced up and down in his pram with his arms up to be lifted. I said, 'Don't scream, Gemma. Don't ever scream, do you hear me?' and I unstrapped the baby and hugged him. She stared at me, surprised, and it stopped her.

'You'll have to come and stay here,' she said. 'We'll fit you in.' She gave a kind of a look round and I could see her thinking where on earth she could fit me in. Still, where could I go?

'All I wanted was for Liam to get a van and take out my stuff,' I explained. 'Maybe my sister Patsy would have more room than you.'

She took the baby and gave me my cup of tea. 'You'll come here,' she said. 'You'll count this your home and we'll be glad to have you.' She was a good kind girl, Gemma, and when Liam came in he was the same, only anxious to make me welcome, and he went off to get the van.

After a while Gemma said, 'Write to Eileen straightaway. She's the one you should be living with anyway – not all alone over yonder. All her money and her grand house. She's the one should have you.'

I laughed but it hurt me a bit to hear it said. 'What would I do in Eileen's grand house in Canada? How would I fit in?'

And Gemma said, 'You could keep her house all shining. She'd use you for that. Where would you see the like of your own house for polish! You'd do great for Eileen.' I looked round her own few bits and pieces – no look on anything, and a pile of children's clothes on the floor waiting to be washed and the children running in and out and knocking things over. Mary, my wee godchild, came and stood leaning against my knees, sucking her thumb. She was wearing one of the dresses I make for them. In the spring when I was fitting it on her I was noticing how beautiful her skin was with little pinprick freckles on the pink and white and I was thinking, *When she's so lovely what must Eileen's children be like?* Then she turned her head and looked at me and her eyes were full of love – for me! I couldn't get over it. Since then sometimes she'd just hold my hand. When Liam came back I said, 'Liam, I'm going home. I'm sorry about the bother. I just got frightened but you can cancel the van. I'm going home and I'm staying home. I've a Protestant house to the right of me and a Protestant house to the left of me. They'll not burn me out.' They argued with me and they were a bit upset but I knew they were relieved and I stuck to it.

Liam insisted on going back to the house with me, although since the murders started I had never let him come down my side of the road. There was a Land Rover with soldiers in it not far from my door and no flames, no smoke. But when I opened the door, such a mess. There was water spouting out of a broken pipe in the wall where they had pulled out my sink. The Sacred Heart statue and the wee red lamp were broken on the floor. My copper canopy was all dinged. The table had big hatchet marks on it. The cover on the couch was ripped and the stuffing pulled out. And filth. For months I thought I could get the smell of that filth. I wouldn't let Liam turn off the water until I had it washed away. We cleaned up a bit but Liam said he'd have to get help before he could do much and not to touch the electric because the water had got into it. He had been very quiet so I jumped when he shouted at the soldiers once he went out the door. They drove up very slowly and he was shouting and waving his arms and calling them names. One of them looked into the house and started to laugh. Liam yelled at him about me being a widow woman living alone and that they were here to protect me, but one of them said, 'You've got it wrong. We're here to wipe out the IRA.'

'Oh, Liam,' I said, 'go home. Go home before harm befalls you,' and he shook his fist at the soldiers and shouted, 'I'm going now but I'll be back and I won't be on my own then. Just look out. I'm warning you.'

He turned and ran off down the street and the soldier turned and looked after him and I thought he was lifting up his gun and I grabbed at his arm and the gun went off into the air and I begged, 'Don't shoot at him. Oh, don't shoot him.'

He said, 'Missus, I have no intention . . .' and then I fell against the wall and when I came to they were making me drink whiskey out of a bottle. It made me cough and splutter but it brought me round. They weren't bad to me, I must admit. When I was on my feet they corked up the bottle and put it back in the Land Rover and drove off.

Not one of my neighbours came out and all evening when I worked at tidying up, and all night when I sat up to keep watch, not one of them knocked at my door.

Next day Liam brought back two other lads and they fixed up the electricity and the water. It took a while to get everything decent again but they were in and out every day, sometimes three or four of them, and it never cost me a penny. Then a queer thing happened. My neighbours began moving out. The woman next door told me out of the side of her mouth that they had all been threatened. I didn't understand how a whole Protestant area could be threatened but out they all went. Of course I know they can always get newer better houses when they ask for them and indeed there was a lot of shooting and wrecking on the front of the road, but still I often wondered what was the truth of it. Maybe I'm better off not knowing. As they left, Catholics from across the road moved in – mostly older people – and I have good friends among them although it took us a while to get used to each other. I didn't take easy to people expecting to open my door and walk in at any hour of the day. They thought I was a bit stiff. I have no time for long chats and I never liked gossip. But Mrs Mulvenna, next door now, has a son in Australia – farther away than my Eileen and I think sons are even worse at writing home. I listen to her and I feel for her and I show her my photographs. I didn't tell her when Eileen wrote about how ashamed she was of us all and how she didn't like to let on she was Irish. I see talk like that in the papers too. It's not right to put the blame on poor powerless people. The most of us never did anything but stay quiet and put up with things the way they were. And we never taught our children to hate the others nor filled their heads with their wrongs the way it's said we did. When all the young people thought they could fix everything with marches and meetings I said it wouldn't work and they laughed at me. 'All you old ones are awful bitter,' they said and they jeered when Hannah in the shop and I were warning them, 'It'll all lead to shooting and burning and murder.'

Still, last November a man came round here trying to sell venetian blinds. Some of the houses have them but I said no, I liked to see out. I pointed to the sunset behind Divis – bits of red and yellow in the sky and a sort of mist all down the mountain that made it nearly see-through. The man looked at it for a minute and then he said, 'Do you know Belfast has the most beautiful sunsets in the whole world?' I said I didn't because I'd never been anyplace else to look at sunsets and he said, 'They tell me Belfast has the best and do you know why? It's because of all the smoke and dirt and dust and pollution. And it seems to me,' he said, 'it seems to me that if the dirt and dust and smoke and pollution of Belfast just with the help of the sun can make a sky like that, then there's hope for all of us.' He nodded and winked and touched his hat and went off and I went in and sat down at the table. And thinking of it I started to laugh, for it's true. There is hope for all of us. Well, anyway, if you don't die you live through it, day in day out.

JENNIFER JOHNSTON

from *The Captains and the Kings*

It was several days before Diarmid turned up again. The door stood open and he walked in without waiting for a yes or no. He dawdled his way through the hall. A grandfather clock that had stopped a few days after Nellie's death caught his fancy. He opened the case door and set the pendulum swinging. The figures on the face were brass and the ornate hands pointed permanently to twenty-five past three. There was a sound from the kitchen. Quickly he shut the clock. The pendulum moved slower without his helping hand. He went on down the passage to the kitchen.

The two men sat at the table, Mr Prendergast behind the paper, Sean, unprotected, chewing with great care. His teeth gave him trouble. They seemed to have shrunk in their sockets and sometimes it felt dangerous to eat. He looked over at the boy as he came in. The old man put the paper down on the floor.

'Well, well, well.'

'Hello.'

'Would you look what the wind blew in,' said Sean disagreeably.

Diarmid ignored him. 'I've brought you this.' Carefully he took from his pocket a large, luminous-looking duck egg. The shell was patterned like the moon's surface with ridges and bumps. He held it out towards Mr Prendergast.

'Well . . .' repeated the old man.

'Who'dya pinch that from?' Sean mopped round his plate with a piece of sliced loaf.

Mr Prendergast took the egg gingerly into his hand. It had a smear of mud or excrement on it.

'A duck egg.'

'Not a duck or a hen, if it comes to that, to be seen around your back yard, anyroad,' commented Sean through the bread and gravy.

'It's a present.'

'So I gather. I am most touched and grateful. I used to be very partial to duck's eggs. It's been a long time. Thank you, boy, hey.'

'Scallawag. It's a good larrup on the backside you need, not thanks.' Sean got up and carried his plate over to the sink. He dropped it in with a clatter.

'Never mind him.'

'Oh him; sure, why would I mind him?'

'You steal one flower out of my garden and you'll mind me. Or go bringing your friends up and galloping over the place. Let me warn you. Here and now.'

His eyes were really bad today, the old man thought; sunk right back into his head, rimmed with moist red. He must be coming up for one of his turns. As if the old man's thought had reached him the gardener groaned slightly, a disconcerting noise, and then took from his pocket a handkerchief of sorts and wiped, most carefully, one red slit and then the other. He examined the handkerchief with interest and groaned again before returning it to his pocket.

Diarmid paid no attention to the groans. 'You're not the boss around here, anyway.'

'"Mind the garden, Sean," the mistress said with her dying breath,' lied the gardener. The boy looked unimpressed.

Mr Prendergast put the egg down carefully on a saucer. 'I think we've had enough.'

'And mind it I will, 'till I drop in me tracks and there's some that appreciate what others do for them and some that don't.'

'Oh, I do. I couldn't have managed without you.'

The gardener smiled fiercely in the general direction of Diarmid, pulled his cap down over the sad, red, slits of eyes and went out into the garden. They watched him go down the steps in silence.

'He has turns. His life hasn't been all it might have been. You mustn't pay too much attention to him.'

'He's an old sod. I don't know how you stick him round the place.'

'Ah, well yes,' said the old man. 'How long . . . ?'

'I had in mind to stay till school was over. If it's all the same to you.'

'I have no plans.'

'Will I put the kettle on for coffee so?'

'That would be very kind.' He began to clear the table. 'What was your mother's reaction to my letter?'

'She said nothing to me at all but I heard her say to me Dad, "I might have saved the ink."' He lit the gas. 'They're in a right way, now. They don't know what to do with me at all.'

'They must be worried.'

'Worried in case they can't get rid of me. They think if they have me in the shop I'll be getting into trouble, dipping my hand in the till, adding up the bills wrong, eating and not earning.'

'I think you exaggerate.'

'They say as much to my face. My father should know the ropes, anyway. Doesn't he nick the petty cash himself a half a dozen times a day. She keeps him very short, I suppose he's not to be blamed.'

'And you?'

'Huh?'

He had to stand on his toes to reach the Nescafé tin which was on a shelf above the stove.

'You. Would you, ah, be carrying on like that?'

'I don't steal money.'

'Just things like duck eggs?' suggested the old man.

'Where will I find a spoon?'

Mr Prendergast handed him one out of the basin. The boy dried it carefully before measuring the powder into each cup.

'I'll take it back if you don't want it.'

'Oh, no. I didn't mean that. I was only making a dirty crack.' He looked at the boy frowning, as he worked the coffee and a little milk together with the spoon.

'You look like a little old man, frowning away there.'

The boy looked up at him and smiled. 'And you're behaving like a little boy, making dirty cracks.'

They both laughed.

'I only pinch things because I like them. Not because I need them. Isn't that all right?'

Mr Prendergast reached for the whiskey bottle and poured a small tot into each cup. 'It improves the taste. I refuse to make pronouncements on the rights and wrongs of stealing.' He put the bottle away and took a large bunch of keys from a hook near the door. He peered at the labels. The writing on some of them was so faded that it was impossible to read more than a letter here and there.

The kettle boiled and Diarmid filled the cups with water. The smell of warm whiskey rose with the steam.

'Bring the cups, boy. I've something to show you.'

The first flight of stairs had tarnished brass rods holding the carpet in place. Nellie used, once a week, to slide each one out from its slots and polish it golden and for a while the hall and stairway would smell of Brasso. She sang always as she did this job. Sometimes now, as the old man climbed the stairs, her voice came into his head. 'Come back to Erin, mavourneen, mavourneen. Come back, machree, to the land of your birth . . .' The cloth would squeak as she rubbed it up and down the rod and the smell of the polish flew up your nose and made you sneeze if you happened to be passing.

The top flight had only tacks which held the remaining rags of carpet to the floor. Up at the top, the long passage between the locked doors was lit by two half-moon windows, one at each end of the passage, perfectly symmetrical. Long creeper fronds tapped against them now, incessantly, impatiently, wanting in . . . The light in the passage was constant twilight. The smell was musty and all the time the tiny noises made by unused rooms brushed your ears. The end room on the right had been the nursery. Three windows to the south-west caught the afternoon sunlight in tangles of spiders' webs. Everywhere that dust could lie was filmed with grey. The chairs were sheeted. A large grey bear with one eye stared down from the top of a cupboard.

'It was the nursery. The playroom,' he explained, seeing the boy look puzzled. 'Look.' He opened a cupboard. Inside on the dusty shelves, neatly stacked as if only yesterday some creaking, crackling nanny had tidied them away, were boxes of soldiers and equipment. Each box was carefully labelled, spidery thin-nib, black writing, starting to fade now after many years. Black Watch, Lancers, Gurkhas, Field Artillery, Red Cross, Foot Guards, Dragoons, Légionnaires. Miscellaneous. 'My brother and I were great collectors.'

The boy moved to the cupboard and opened one of the boxes. He stared, fascinated, at the soldiers.

'We were very proud of them. Mind you, they're a bit out of date now. It must be almost sixty years.' He nodded to himself and whispered quietly '. . . or more'.

Diarmid was lining some men up along the edge of a shelf.

'. . . More. A bit more than sixty years since the last ones were bought. He was older than I.'

'What was his name?' He didn't sound really interested. He opened another box.

'Alexander. After my father.' The boy picked out a galloping horseman. 'That's an Uhlan. Ever heard of them?'

'No.'

'A very famous German regiment. There's a book downstairs. It will tell you all about them. We'll have a look later.

'Thanks. Where is he now?'

'Who?'

'Alexander. He must be very old. Or is he . . . ?' He paused discreetly.

'He's gone a long time ago.'

'Gone?'

'1915.'

'Oh.' He began to root in another box.

'I was on leave when we heard. It was in the summer. Nobody liked opening telegrams in those days. I was here, so we knew . . .'

'Knew what?'

'Knew it was he.'

'It might have been something else.'

'It never was.'

Mother and Father had been out, somewhere, couldn't recall, irrelevant, anyway, and the telegram had lain on a silver salver in the hall for several hours. He had gone to his room and lain, waiting, on his bed. Alexander's voice sang in his head – 'Röslein, röslein, röslein rot, röslein auf der heiden . . .' And as he heard the car door slam and his mother's laughter on the steps, the singing stopped. He ran down the passage to the bathroom and vomited into the basin.

'Your hands are shaking.'

'I must sit down a minute. It's . . . the stairs.'

The boy pulled the dust sheet off the nearest chair. A grey cloud rose into the air. Imperceptibly it settled again, this time also on the intruders. Mr Prendergast lowered himself into the chair. He clasped his shaking hands between his knees in the hope that the pressure would force the convulsive movements to stop. No thought of Alexander had entered his head for years and now it was as if the young man was there, inside his head, tearing down walls expertly built by time.

'Wer reitet so spät durch Nacht und Wind? Es ist der Vater mit seinem Kind . . .' As the walls fell, the song grew louder. The old man's fingers trembled now for the piano. He had never mastered the accompaniment then.

'No, no, boy.'

'I'm sorry. I'll try again.'

'You must practise. I keep telling you.'

'I do. But when you sing, it eludes me. Listen, I can do it.' He played a few phrases.

'It won't do. Honestly, Chas, it's terrible. Mother'll have to play.'

'Alec . . .'

'Not a word. Mother.'

When Mother moved it sounded as if someone was unwrapping a parcel of tissue paper. She came in from the garden at Alexander's call. She always came at Alexander's call.

'Well? What is it?'

'You must play for me. He is impossible.'

She swept Charles off the piano stool with a hand. 'You must practise more, my darling.' She sat down in his place and quickly began pulling her rings off and clattering them into a porcelain bowl on a table nearby, as if they were worthless pebbles. When her hands were bare she opened and closed her fingers several times and smiled up at her son. The old man felt the burn of jealousy in his stomach and remembered the smell of burning leaves that drifted past him as he stepped out of the window into the cool evening.

'It must have been autumn.'

'What?' Diarmid was staring up at him from the floor, where he was sitting surrounded by boxes.

'I'm sorry. I was very far away.'

'Sometimes I think you're a bit gone, you know.' He examined each man with care before putting it on the ground. 'I never seen soldiers as good as these before.'

'They don't make them like that nowadays. There's a shop in London that would give you a lot of money for these, in fact. If you go over to that cupboard by the window you'll find a book called . . . *Famous Battles* . . . something like that. It's full of maps and plans. We . . . he and I used to re-create them . . .' he gestured with his still shaking hands. 'All the floor was our battlefield. We used to take it in turns to have the winning army.'

'That would be a great idea.'

'Somewhere there's a box full of generals, field marshals. Even, if I remember aright, Le Petit Caporal himself.'

'Who's he when he's at home?'

'One of the greatest generals of all time. A rogue, mind you. A villain, rather. Alexander, Caesar and Napoleon Bonaparte. If you hand me down that box up there in the corner, I'll show you.'

The boy put the box on the old man's knee. He sat down on the floor again and watched Mr Prendergast's hands carefully as he picked his way through the great men of war.

'Yes, indeed, I suppose these probably have a considerable value nowadays. The Lord Protector. I'd forgotten we had him.' He held him out, warts and all, in his fingers towards the boy. 'Alexander had great admiration for Cromwell. It was one of the many subjects on which we differed.'

'Is that Cromwell? Can I see?'

'I thought that name might strike a chord in your peasant skull.' He handed Cromwell over to the boy.

'He was an ugly looking git, anyway. Why did your brother like him?'

'He liked efficiency and order. He thought that perfection could only be achieved through discipline.'

The boy thought about that. 'I suppose that's what's in the back of their minds when they larrup you at school.'

'I doubt it, boy. I doubt if much is in their heads at all.'

'I'd laugh to see Mr Moyne's face if he heard you say that.'

'There. That's Napoleon.' The Emperor stood, feet slightly apart, the hand stuck between the coat buttons, shoulders hunched, his peasant face brooding, in the palm of the old man's hand. 'He was a giant.'

The boy looked startled. 'A giant?'

'Metaphorically. A giant among men. He ruled almost all of Europe until one day he went too far.'

'What happened?'

'As a general, he overstretched his lines. As a man, he misjudged the character of his enemy. They were desperate and cunning. They lured him deeper and deeper into Russia, stretching his lines to the limits. They knew that, inevitably, Nature would be on their side. He thought he'd won the prize and then, literally overnight, they broke him. They say he got into his coach in Moscow and didn't get out until he reached Paris. That's romancing, of course. But he was lucky. Thousands and thousands never saw France again, let alone Paris.'

'Was that the end of him?'

'The beginning of the end. He was a hard man to finish off. Beaten in the end by an English army with an Irish general . . . a bit of help from the Germans.' He peered into the box. 'I don't recall that we had him.'

'And if he hadn't gone to Moscow, he'd have gone on ruling almost all of Europe?'

'I don't suppose so, really. It was just a matter of time. With time every tyrant's thinking becomes clouded. Had he thought more clearly he might have conquered Ireland, but he was preoccupied with things he thought were more important.'

'I might be a general.'

'You never can tell. It's an advantage to have been to school from time to time. Acquire some knowledge. It always comes in handy.'

'I can read, can't I? I can teach myself. What I want to know, not just what they decide they want me to know.'

'Unfortunately, we don't necessarily know what we need to know until it's too late. Like I said, if Napoleon had known more about the Russians, he'd never have gone all the way to Moscow. Into the trap.'

Diarmid took Napoleon from the old man and examined him closely. 'One thing I do know, anyway, is not to stretch my lines too far.' The old man laughed. 'I don't think much of his uniform.'

'He was never a flamboyant dresser.'

'That man downstairs, in the picture, was he a general?'

'No, alas. Merely a flamboyant dresser.'

'Flamboyant.' He tasted the word in his mouth, like a new piece of food.

'Peacocks,' suggested the old man.

The boy put Napoleon carefully on the shelf, not on the floor with the commonalty. 'I'll have a look at them all first and then, tell you what, we'll have smashing wars. Like you and he did.' He went back to the boxes.

Mr Prendergast watched him for a while then fell asleep, a sleep without dreams, without alarms. When he awakened, Diarmid was standing on a chair replacing some boxes on the top shelf. His face, hands and adolescent wrists were caught in the gilding sunshine. Benvenuto, thought the old man. Pure rascal.

'You snored,' said the boy.

'My wife always used to say so.'

'If my wife snores, I'll kick her out of bed. The noise coming out of Mam and Dada's room would waken the dead.' He stepped down from the chair. The old man saw that his face was streaked with dust.

'You're filthy, boy. What's the time? You'd better wash before you go home or your mother'll wonder what you've been up to.'

'Tomorrow will you show me that book?'

'What book is that?'

'The one about battles.'

'I suppose so.'

'I might come up a bit earlier.' The old man started to push himself up from the chair. 'You wouldn't mind, would you? Here, let me give you a hand.'

'I can manage, boy. I am not totally incapacitated yet. Though no doubt my time will come.'

'But would you mind?'

'What time you come? That's entirely up to you.'

'I could do a few things for you.'

'I don't think that . . .'

'Around the place, like.'

'It's very kind of you . . .'

'There's always things to do.'

The boy looked at Mr Prendergast and laughed as he watched him straighten himself carefully.

'We all grow old,' said the old man, with reasonable good humour.

'I won't.'

'Permit me to laugh this time.'

'What happened to him?' The boy nodded his head towards Napoleon. 'Did he die a hero's death?'

'No.'

'Oh.' The boy was taken aback.

'He was exiled. He spent the last six years of his life a prisoner.'

'He could have killed himself.'

'He could. You seem obsessed with the idea of people killing themselves. It is, as you know, a mortal sin.'

'It's always there for you to do. If you don't like the sort of life you have to live. Have to.'

'Your life is supposed to be in the holy hands of God, for Him to do what He likes with it. You are not supposed to take these decisions for yourself.'

'What's the time?'

The old man took his watch from his pocket. 'Getting on for five.'

'Mother of God, I'll be murdered. She'll ask me questions.' He put his hands over his ears, as if to protect them from the battery of shrill words.

'What'll you say?' He gave the boy a gentle shove towards the door.

'I'll think of something. I'm a great hand at inventing.'

They walked along the passage. A fly buzzed somewhere, caught irrevocably in a spider's web.

'I got kept in, Ma. I'm sorry I'm late.'

'Your tea's ruined. What were you up to this time? Nothing ordinary, I'll be bound.'

'It was spelling, Ma. I hadn't . . . I'd forgotten me stint.'

'The same old story. Wait till your father hears you were in trouble again and he'll give you what for.'

There was a distinct smell of mice, the old man thought. Perhaps a cat. But what, in the end of all, did it matter if the mice took over. When he was a child the passage had smelt of beeswax and friar's balsam. Both he and Alexander had been chesty and small lamps filled with friar's balsam had burned in their rooms during the winter. Somehow, even though the windows were wide open all through the summer months, the heavy smell had always lingered in the passage. He wondered why he had stayed on in this white elephant of a place after Clare's death. He should have taken something more compact, more suitable to his way of living. Sarah, at the time, had suggested that he move to London but the idea hadn't appealed to him. Didn't appeal to him now, either. Nor did the idea of the tentative and probably painful gestures that would have to be made if he and his daughter were to create even the most formal relationship.

'I think, in fact, I'd be safer to say I went along the river with Mick and never looked at the time. Mick is my friend, only I'd never trust him with my life.'

'Can you swim?' asked the old man.

They stood on the steps. There was a little breeze which lifted Diarmid's hair gently from his forehead and let it fall again. The rooks were having their afternoon fling and the sky seemed full of their ungainly bodies.

'I've never tried. We just fish a bit and throw stones. Skim, you know, if we can.' He skimmed an imaginary stone across the grass and through a rose bed.

'We used to swim in the lake.' He nodded over beyond the trees. 'In the summer we used to spend nearly all day down there. We had a boat and we used to take all our clothes off and dive in from it.'

The boy looked him up and down. The old man realized with embarrassment that he was trying to visualize what he must look like naked.

'A long time ago,' he said, in the direction of the rooks. 'We were boys.' Diarmid nodded. 'If I got Sean to cut the rushes back a bit in places, you and your friends could use it, if you wanted. With the summer coming on.'

'That would be great. I'll cut the rushes, though. I'd like to do that, if you want them cut.'

'I can always get Sean . . .'

'I'd like to.'

'You'll need a sickle.'

'I'll get one of them all right.'

'I'm sure if we asked Sean . . .'

'I wouldn't ask that git for anything if he was the last person left on earth.' He held out his hand. 'I've had a great afternoon.'

Formally and awkwardly they shook hands. Diarmid, with a wave of both arms, leapt down the five steps at once and ran down the avenue. At the bend he turned and waved again but the old man had gone into the house and closed the door. The boy whipped across the grass, bending low as he ran. He took his penknife from his pocket and cut three newly-opened rose buds. The outside petals were brilliant red and the hearts were yellow. As he went on down the avenue he examined them closely. Their smell was very sweet.

'Flamboyant,' he whispered and put them carefully inside his jacket.

'That one is here again.'

It was already eleven-thirty and Sean had only just arrived. He had brought the groceries from the village and left them on the kitchen table. Hearing the sound of the piano, he had put his head round the study door to announce this piece of information.

'I thought you weren't coming.'

'I'm not feeling too good.'

You could smell the drink from him. Each time he moved the smell intensified and then faded slightly until the next gesture. His clothes must have steeped all night in whiskey, thought the old man. He got up from the piano.

'Do you want a cup of tea?'

'I didn't like to let you down.'

'I appreciate that. I do, indeed.'

'I couldn't keep tea down.'

'Coffee, perhaps?'

'Nothing.' The humming of the wires always started gently but it inevitably filled his head with a sound that nothing could drown, not even alcohol. 'Couldn't bloody keep anything down at all.'

The old man looked out of the window. The haze that had covered the valley in the early morning had almost completely lifted and everything dazzled in the sun.

'We're really in for a heat-wave.' The gardener only grunted. His head was splitting. 'Well, if you won't have a cup of something . . .'

'Amn't I after telling you, that one is here again.'

'Who?'

'That Toorish boy. I seen him nipping through the rosiedandrons and I coming up the avenue.'

Mr Prendergast sighed. 'Just leave him, Sean. He'll do no harm.'

'I'm sorry I interfered.' He withdrew, his face sick and angry. By lunchtime he would be in a black mood and round about five he would grope his way from side to side down the avenue and along the road to his hovel, that was the only possible name for it, and that would be the last time that anyone would see of him for up to a week.

Sometimes it had even been two weeks and he would come back thin and crazy looking, his hands shaking so much that he was hardly able to lift the fork to his mouth. Nellie had always raged on and on at him as he sat there opposite her, desperately trying to eat, for the sake of peace, but the old man left him alone to recover his equilibrium as best he could.

Mr Prendergast took his blackthorn stick from the hall stand and went outside. It was safer to take it these days if he intended walking any distance at all. He walked slowly down the avenue and branched off along the path through the rhododendrons that led to the lake.

Diarmid had taken his trousers off and thrown them on the grass. He was standing up to his waist in water attacking the rushes. The sickle flashed like the sun on the water as it rose and fell.

'Good morning, boy.'

The boy looked up at him. 'It's muddy.'

'Always been like that round the edge. It's clear further out. Aren't you cold?'

'No. Look what I found.'

He moved slowly along the bank. Under the streaks of mud the old man could see that his legs were white, like they'd never before seen the light of day. He threw the sickle on to the grass and, stooping, gently pulled aside the rushes and uncovered a nest with three eggs in it.

'A moorhen,' said the old man.

'She went squawking away as if the devil was after her.' He laughed. 'Right enough, I near chopped the head off her.'

'She'll be back.'

The boy covered the nest again then climbed out of the water onto the grass. He shook like a dog and a thousand drops of shining water whirled away from him.

'Are you stopping?'

'Jaysus, no. I've only started.'

'You can have some lunch later, if you like. I doubt if Sean'll be wanting any today, so there'll be a chop going begging.'

'Great.'

Above them a lark's voice rose and fell in unphrased song. The old man looked pointlessly up to see if he could catch sight of the bird. He was many years too late.

'Like I said, I can't swim, though.' He bent down to poke some mud from between his toes.

'That's a bore.' Somehow he'd thought that all boys could swim. Everywhere he'd ever been, water had always seemed full of swimming children. He couldn't remember a time when he hadn't been able to swim. 'Old motor car tyres are a help.'

'Yeah. That's a great idea all right.' He picked up the sickle and slithered into the water again. 'Give me a shout when you want me up at the house. I'll carry on with this. It's a job you could be for ever doing.'

'Herculean. Don't overdo things, Hercules.'

He was glad of his stick on the way back to the house. He was constantly irritated by his increasing lack of mobility, by the discomfort he suffered in his bones. He was frightened, not of death, which now was so inevitable that it was like waiting for a visitor who never told the time of his arrival but you knew was on his way; rather, by the thought that one day he would be unable to get out of his bed and would be forced to lie, like Clare had done, wasting away. Imprisoned. He struck angrily at the grass with his stick. If he could strike the ground open and be swallowed, how splendid. No debris. Alexander had been hit by a shell. Very little debris there. Miscellaneous fragments, not worth gathering up. Mother had insisted that an empty coffin be buried with full pomp, here, in the churchyard. She had sent him packing the next day, unable to bear the sight of him. She had looked at him, he remembered, as if she'd thought that somehow it was his fault. Even a year later she still wore black. It was a colour that had always suited her. After the war was over, uniform in moth-balls, neatly folded into the black tin trunk in the attic, he had left home. 'A travelling man.' He'd once heard one of the maids describe him thus. 'Though I am old from wandering through hollow lands and hilly lands . . .' It didn't apply. He had merely been routed, weakling that he was, by a lady in black, whose diamonds flashed with grey splendour each time she moved her hands. The mica in the granite steps flashed ferociously up at him, baiting him. He wondered what Sarah had done with the rings. Clare had never worn them. Her hands had been too . . . no, it was her personality that had been colourless. She had been too retiring to control such jewels. They would have overpowered her. They had lain in their boxes until after her death. He had taken them from their velvet boxes and laid them all on the table in front of Sarah. She picked one up and slipped it onto her finger. In his head his mother's laughter glittered like the stones.

'Left of the Door'

Take the can, a stiff arm, take the can, fixing eyes high on walls, on doors. Creak of the can, your steps, rattle-and-click of the outer door. Step outside, sour May cold, slap of the wind, and stand stiff as a board. The spade left of the door. Eyes fixed, keeping the eyes at eye-level, reach, and gather the spade with the left hand, and turn, and past the kitchen window, dragging open the small gate, crossing the lane, and stepping on to the dung-heap. And advancing to the middle of the dung-heap, stand.

Looking away, leave down the can on a level spot. Do it quick. Grip the spade, and scrabble on the face of the dung-heap, root and scoop and hoke a spot, claw and tear. Drop the spade. Looking away, turn to the can. And take the can, and looking away, not looking away, spill it there, scorch of poor pink flesh-fish in the shit and the mess. Down the can, and grab the spade, and over it, cover it, maul and root dung back there, cover it, put more, that'll do, more, that'll do, leave it.

Take the can, spade and the can, turn away, stand up, lift your head, and fix on the sea, the stretch of it, the sea this day, rag where your chest was, and slap of the wind.

*

Step up on the dung-heap, and move to the middle. And stand and listen to yourself. Leave down the can on a level spot. Sprout looking up at you. Take the spade, and go to it, shoulder to the wind. Scoop, don't rush this, clear a basin in the dung-heap, give it shape, take time, you have time, your back a hard curve, face blind as the spade. Take your time. Leave down the spade. Turn to the can. Take the can, and care over what you're about, and watching, spill all into the basin, and look, and meet the whole slither and slop, blood and the mess and morsel raw on the dung. Turn away, and take the spade, and fill the basin, root on the cover of dung, and root more, and secure it, and then some more, and leave it now.

Lean on the spade, and fix on the stretch of sea.

Take the spade, and to it as they taught you, wield the spade, find a spot on the heap that will take the cut of the spade, moisture patch, and give it a rhythm, and make the small grave, know what you're about, good foot down and a foot by a foot, up on that, tidy it there, that'll do. Leave aside the spade. Go to the can. Stoop over it, and put in your hands. And lift out the sliver, slippery, and no weight, no weight at all, filmy man-woman of ours. Take it, dripping, and place in the one foot by one, set it there, scrap of her, lost bit. Go back to the can, and take the can, and again to the spot, and spill it all in. The dung drinks. The can aside. Pick up the spade. Sticky grip. 'Bye. And fill with care, using the spade as they taught you, finding the beat of it, letting the cut of the wind take your bones. Fill it, and fill it, and tend it, and more, and leave the spade aside. And down, and by the small heap, and feel it, and cry what you have for the was and the wasn't.

The can and the spade. Walk straight, child. Spade to the left of the door. Inside, the quiet, love, and the fire low.

EDNA O'BRIEN

from *The Country Girls*

14

We got in to Dublin just before six. It was still bright, and we carried our bags across the platform, stopping for a minute to let others pass by. We had never seen so many people in our lives.

Baba hailed a taxi and told the driver our new address. It was written on the label of her suitcase. We had got lodgings through an advertisement in the paper and our future landlady was a foreigner.

'Jesus, Cait, this is life,' Baba said, relaxing in the back seat, as she took out a hand mirror to look at herself. She brought a lock of hair down onto her forehead, and it looked well there, falling over one eyebrow.

I remember nothing of the streets we drove through. They were all too strange. At six the bells rang out from some church, which were followed by other bells, with other chimes, ringing from churches all over the city. The peals of the bells mingled together and were in keeping with the fresh spring evening, and there was a special comfort in their toll. I liked them already.

We passed a cathedral, whose dark stone was still wet from the afternoon rain, though the streets were dry. We were dizzy trying to see the clothes in the shop windows.

'Christ, there's a gorgeous frock in that window. Hey, sir,' she yelled, leaning forward in the seat.

The driver, without looking back, pushed a sliding window that separated the front of the car from the back.

'D'ju say something?' He had the singsong accent that is spoken in County Cork.

'Are you from Cork?' Baba said, sniggering. He pretended not to hear and closed the sliding window. Then, soon after, he turned to the left, drove down an avenue, and we were there. We got out and split the fare between us. We knew nothing about tipping. He left the cases on the footpath outside the gate. There was a motorbike against the railings, and inside, a narrow concrete path ran between two small squares of cut grass. Between the grass and the path was an oblong flower bed, at either side, and a few sallow snowdrops wilted in the damp clay. The house itself was red-brick, two-storey, with a bay window downstairs.

Baba gave a cheeky knock on the chromium knocker and rang the bell at the same time.

'Oh, God, Baba, don't be impatient like that.'

'None o' your cowardy-custard nonsense,' she said, winking at me. The lock of hair was very rakish. There were milk bottles beside the foot scraper and I heard someone come up the hallway.

The door was opened and we were greeted by a woman in thick-lensed glasses, who wore a brown knitted dress and knitted, hairy, grey stockings.

'Ah, you are the welcome,' she said, and called upstairs, 'Gustav, they're here.'

There were white mackintoshes on the hall stand and a coloured umbrella that reminded me of a postcard Miss Moriarty sent me from Rome. We took off our coats.

She was a low-sized woman, and was almost the width of the dining-room doorway. Her bottom was like the bottom of a woman in a funny postcard. It was a mountain in itself. We followed her into the dining room.

It was a small room crowded with walnut furniture. There was a piano in one corner, and next to it was a sideboard that had framed photographs on top of it, and opposite that was a china cabinet. It was stuffed with glasses, cups, mugs, and all sorts of souvenirs. Sitting at the table was a bald, middle-aged man eating a boiled egg. He held it in one hand and spooned the contents out with the other hand. He looked very funny holding the egg on his lap as if he wasn't supposed to be eating it. He greeted us in some foreign accent and went on with his tea. He was not handsome. His eyes were too close together and he looked somehow treacherous.

We sat down. The circular table was covered with a green velvet cloth that was tasselled at the edges, and there was a vase of multi-coloured everlasting anemones in the middle of the table.

Something about the room, perhaps the velvet cloth or the cluttered china cabinet or perhaps the period of the furniture, reminded me of my mother and of our house as it had once been.

Our landlady brought in two small plates of cooked ham, some buttered bread, and a small dish of jam.

'Gustav,' she called again, as she came in the dining room. I was a little afraid of her. Her voice was brutal and commandeering.

'Very good, my own make, homemade,' she said, putting a fancy spoon into the jam.

We ate quickly and ravenously, and when we had cleared the bread plate, we looked at one another and at the bald man opposite us. He had finished eating and was reading a foreign paper.

'Joanna,' he called, and she came in, drying her hands on her flowered apron. He said something in a foreign language to her. I supposed it was to ask for more bread.

'*Mein Gott* Almighty, save us! Country girls have big huge appetite,' she said, raising her hands in the air. They were fat hands and roughened from years of work. She had a marriage ring and an eternity ring. Poor Gustav.

She went out and the man continued reading.

Baba and I were certain that he didn't understand English. So while we were waiting for the bread, Baba did a little mime act. Bowing to me, she begged in a trembling voice, 'Oh, lady divine, will you pass me the wine?' I passed her the bottle of vinegar.

'Put on the tea cosy,' she said, and christened me 'lady supreme'. Then, in another voice, she pleaded, 'Oh, lady supreme, will you pass me the cream?' and I passed her the milk jug. Then she turned toward him, though he was hidden behind the paper, and said, 'You bald-headed scutter, will you pass me the butter?' and while we were grinning, his hand came out from behind the newspaper and slowly he pushed the empty butter dish in her direction. We laughed more and saw that his hands were shaking. He was laughing, too. It was a nice beginning.

Joanna brought back two more slices of bread and some small pieces of cake. It was cake with two colours. Half yellow, half chocolate. Mama called it marble cake, but Joanna had some other name for it. The pieces were cunningly cut. Each piece only a mouthful. The man opposite took two pieces, and Baba kicked me under the table as if to warn me to eat quickly. She stuffed her own mouth full.

Gustav came in and we stood up to shake hands with him. He was a small, pale-faced man with cunning eyes and an apologetic smile. His hands were white and refined-looking.

'No, ladies, stay be sitting,' he said humbly, too humbly. I preferred Joanna. Baba was delighted that he called us ladies, and she gave him one of her loganberry smiles.

'Up there shaving all the night. What you got your new shirt on for?' Joanna said, looking carefully at his shirt and the top of his waistcoat. He said that he was going down to the local.

'Just for a small time, Joanna,' he said.

'*Mein Gott!* I have two chickens to pluck and you not help me.' The smile never left his face.

'Nice, nice ladies,' he said, pointing to us, and Baba was fluttering her eyelashes at a furious rate.

'Oh yes, yes; eat, eat up,' Joanna said suddenly, remembering us. But there was nothing else to eat, as we had cleared the table.

I began to tidy up the things, and pile the plates on top of one another, but Baba said in my ear, 'Chrissake, we'll be doing it day and night if we begin once. Skivvies, that's what we'll be.' So I took her advice and followed her upstairs to the bedroom, where Gustav had put our cases.

It was a small room that looked out on the street. There was dark brown linoleum on the floor and a beaded lampshade over the electric bulb that hung from the ceiling.

I went over to the open window to smell the city air and see what it looked like. There were children down below, playing hopscotch, and picky beds. One boy had a mouth organ and he put it to his lips and played whenever he felt like it. Seeing me, they all stared up, and one, the biggest one, asked, 'What time is it?' I was smoking a cigarette and pretended not to hear him. 'Eh, miss, what time is it? Thirty-two degrees is freezing point, what's squeezing point?'

You could hear Baba laughing at the dressing table, and she told me for Chrissake to come in or we'd be thrown out. She said he was great gas, and we must get to know him.

The wardrobe was empty but we couldn't hang our clothes because we had forgotten to bring hangers. So we laid them across the big armchair in the corner of the room.

At the gate below a motorbike started up and went roaring down the avenue. Gustav was gone.

In the next room a man began to play a fiddle.

'Jesus,' Baba said, simply, and put her hands to her ears. She was walking around the room with her hands to her ears, swearing, when Joanna knocked and came in.

'Herman, he does to practise,' she said, smiling, when Baba pointed with her thumb toward the other room. 'Very talent. A musician. You like music?' And Baba said we adored music, and that we had come all the way to Dublin to hear a man playing a fiddle.

'Oh, nice. Good. Very nice,' and Baba made a gesture which told me that she thought Joanna was nuts. I was still unpacking, so Joanna came over and looked at my clothes. She asked me if my father was rich, and Baba chimed in and said he was a millionaire.

'A millionaire?' You could see her pupils get large behind her thick lenses.

'My charge too cheap then, hah?' she said, grinning at us. Her way of grinning was unfortunate. It was thick and stupid and made you hate her. But perhaps it was the glasses.

'No. Too dear,' Baba said.

'Dear? Darling? *Klein*? I not understand.'

'No. Too costly,' I said, catching my hair up with a ribbon and hoping before I consulted the mirror that it would make my face beautiful.

'You happy?' she asked, suddenly anxious, suddenly worried in case we should leave.

'We happy,' I said, for both of us, and she grinned. I liked her.

'I give you a present,' she said. We looked at one another in astonishment as she went out of the room.

She came back with a bottle of something yellow and two thimble-sized glasses. They were glasses such as the chemist had at home. They were for measuring medicines. She poured some of the thick yellow liquid into each glass.

'Your health here. Hah!' she said. We put the glasses to our lips.

'Good?' she asked, before we had tasted it at all.

'Good,' I said, lying. It was eggy and had a sharp spirit taste besides.

'Mine.' She put her hand across her stout chest. Her breasts were not defined; she was one solid front of outstanding chest.

'On the Continent we make our own. Parties, everything, we make our own.'

'God protect us from the Continent,' Baba said to me in Irish, and was smiling so that her two dimples showed.

I had put a jar of face cream and a small bottle of Evening in Paris perfume on the table, to make the room habitable, and Joanna went over to admire them. She took the lid off the cream jar and smelled it. Then she smelled the perfume.

'Nice,' she said, still smelling the contents of the dusky-blue perfume bottle.

'Have some,' I said, because we were under a compliment to her for the little drink.

'Expensive? Is it expensive?'

'Costs pounds,' Baba said, smirking into her glass. Baba was going to make a fool of Joanna, I could see that.

'Pounds. *Mein Gott!*' She screwed the metal cork back on the bottle and laid it down quickly. In case it should break.

'Tomorrow perhaps I have some. Tomorrow Sunday. You Catholics?'

'Yes. Are you?' Baba asked.

'Yes, but we on the Continent are not so rigid as you Irish.' She shrugged her shoulders to show a certain indifference. Her knitted dress was uneven at the tail and sagged at both sides. She went out and we heard her go downstairs.

'What will we do, Cait?' Baba asked as she lay full-length on the single bed.

'I don't know. Will we go to confession?' It was what we usually did on Saturday evenings.

'Confession. Christ, don't be such a drip, we'll go downtown. Oh, God, isn't it heaven?' She kicked her feet up in the air and hugged the pillow that was under the chenille bedspread.

'Put on everything you've got,' she said. 'We'll go to a dance.'

'So soon?'

'Christ, so soon! Soon, and we cooped up in that jail for three thousand years.'

'We don't know the way.' I wasn't really interested in dancing. At home I walked on the boys' toes and couldn't turn corners so well. Baba danced like a dream, spinning round and round until her cheeks were flushed and her hair blown every way.

'Go down and use your elegant English on Frau Buxomburger.'

'That's not nice,' I said, putting on my wistful face. The face Mr Gentleman liked best.

'Christ, she's gas, isn't she? I keep expecting that her old arse will drop off. Looks like one that's stuck on.'

'Ssh, ssh,' I said. I was afraid the fiddler would hear us, as he had stopped sawing.

'Go down and ask, and stop this ssh-ing business.'

Joanna was pouring a kettle of scalding water over a dead Rhode Island Red chicken. When the bird was completely wet she began to tear the feathers away. I was in the kitchen watching her, but she hadn't heard me because there was ceilidh music being played on the wireless.

The dead chicken reminded me of all our Sunday dinners at home. Hickey would wring a chicken's neck on Saturday morning, leave it outside the back door, and it would stir and make an effort to move itself for a long time after it was killed. Bull's-Eye, thinking it was alive, would bark at it and try to chase it away.

'*Mein Gott!* you give me a fright,' she said, turning around, as she held the chicken in one hand. I said I was very sorry and asked her the way downtown. She told me, but her instructions were very confusing and I knew that we would have to ask somebody else on the street.

When I came upstairs Baba had gone out to the bathroom, and without her the room was cheerless and empty. Outside in the avenue it was evening. The children were gone. The street was lonesome. A child's handkerchief blew on one of the spears of our railing. There were houses stretching across the plain of city, houses separated by church spires, or blocks of flats, ten and twenty storeys high. In the distance the mountains were a brown blur with clouds resting on them. They were not mountains really but hills. Gentle, memorable hills.

As I looked toward them, I thought of lambs being born in the cold and in the dark, of sheep farmers trudging down across the hills, and afterward I thought of the shepherds and their dogs stretching out in front of the fire, to doze for an hour until it was time to go out again and face the sharp wind. Our farm was not on the mountain, but four or five miles away there were mountains, where Hickey brought me once on the crossbar of his bicycle. He put a cushion on the bar, in case my bottom got sore. We went for a sheep dog. It was early spring, with lambs being born, and you could hear them bleating pitifully against the wind. We got the sheep dog. A handful of black and white fur, asleep in a box of hay. He grew up to be Bull's-Eye.

'Will you come a-waltzing, Matilda, with me; waltzing, Matilda,' Baba sang behind my back, and drew me into a waltz.

'What in the hell are you thinking about?' she asked. But she did not wait to hear.

'I've a smashing idea. I'll change my name. I'll be Barbara, pronounced "Baubra". Sounds terrific, doesn't it? Pity you're going to work in that damn shop. 'Twill cramp our style,' she said thoughtfully.

'Why?'

'Oh, every little country mohawk is in a bloody grocer's. We'll say you're at college if anyone asks.'

'But who's to ask?'

'Fellows; we'll have them swarming around us. And, mind you, Christ, if you take any fellow of mine, I'll give you something to cry about.'

'I won't,' I said, smiling, admiring the big wide sleeves of my blouse and wondering if he would notice it and wondering, too, when he and Mrs Gentleman would return home.

'Your cigarette, your cigarette,' I said to Baba. She had left it on the bedside table and it had burned a mark in from the edge. You could smell the burnt wood.

'*Mein Gott!* what you mean?' Joanna said, bursting in without knocking.

'My best table, my table,' she said, rushing over to examine the burn mark. I was crimson with fear.

'Smoking, young girls, it is forbid,' she said; there were tears in her eyes as she threw the cigarette into the fireplace.

'We must have an ashtray,' Baba said, and then she looked at the little bamboo table and got down on her knees to look under it.

'It's useless anyhow, it's reeking with worms,' she said to Joanna.

'What you mean?' Joanna was breathing terribly hard, as if she were going to erupt.

'Woodworm,' Baba said, and Joanna jumped and said it was impossible. But in the end Baba won and Joanna took the table away and brought it out to a shed in the yard.

'Please, ladies, not to lie on the good bedspreads, they are from the Continent, pure chenille,' she said imploringly, and I promised that we would be more careful.

'Now we have no table,' I said to Baba, when Joanna went out.

'So what?' she asked, as she took off her dress.

'Was it wormy?' I asked.

'How the hell would I know?' She began to spray deodorant under her arms. Her neck was not as white as mine. I was pleased.

We got ready quickly and went down into the neon fairyland of Dublin. I loved it more than I had ever loved a summer's day in a hayfield. Lights, faces, traffic, the enormous vitality of people hurrying to somewhere. A dark-faced woman in an orange silk thing went by.

'Christ, they're in their underwear here,' Baba said. The woman had enormous dark eyes, with dark shadows under them. She seemed to be searching the night and the crowd for something poignant. Something to equal the beauty of the shadows and her carved, cat-like face.

'Isn't she beautiful?' I said to Baba.

'She's like something dug up,' Baba said as she crossed over to look in the glass door of an ice-cream parlour.

A doorman opened it, and held it open. So there was nothing for us to do but to go in.

We had two large dishes of ice cream. It was served with peaches and cream, and the whole lot was decorated with flaked chocolate. There were songs pouring out of a metal box near our table. Baba tapped her feet and swayed her shoulders, keeping time with the melody. Afterward she put money in the slot herself and played the same songs over again.

'Jesus, we're living at last,' she said. She was looking around to see if there were any nice boys at the other tables.

'It's nice,' I said. I meant it. I knew now that this was the place I wanted to be. Forevermore I would be restless for crowds and lights and noise. I had gone from the sad noises, the lonely rain pelting on the galvanized roof of the chicken house; the moans of a cow in the night, when her calf was being born under a tree.

'Are we going dancing?' Baba asked. My feet were tired and I told her so. We went home and bought a bag of chips in a shop quite near our avenue. We ate them going along the pavement. The lights overhead were a ghastly green.

'Jesus, you look like someone with consumption,' Baba said as she handed me a chip.

'So do you,' I said. And together we thought of a poem that we had learned long ago. We recited it out loud:

> From a Munster Vale they brought her
> From the pure and balmy air,
> An Ormond Ullin's daughter
> With blue eyes and golden hair.
> They brought her to the city
> And she faded slowly there,
> For consumption has no pity
> For blue eyes and golden hair.

There were people looking at us, but we were too young to care. Baba blew into the empty chip bag until it was puffed out. Then she bashed it with her fist, and it burst, making a tremendous noise.

'I'm going to blow up this town,' she said, and she meant it, that first night in Dublin.

JULIA O'FAOLAIN

'Will You Please Go Now'

Lost among the demonstrators was a rain-sodden dog. Up and down it ran, rubbing against anonymous trousers and collecting the odd kick. It was a well-fed animal with a leather collar but was quickly taking on the characteristics of the stray: that festive cringe and the way such dogs hoop their spines in panic while they wag their shabby tails.

'Here boy! Come – ugh, he's all muddy. Down, sir, get away! Scram! Tss!'

People threw chocolate wrappers and potato-crisp packets which the dog acknowledged from an old habit of optimum while knowing the things were no good. It was tired and its teeth showed in a dampish pant as though it were laughing at its own dilemma.

Jenny Middleton, a mother of two, recognized the crowd's mood from children's parties.

'Don't tease him,' she said sharply to a dark-skinned young man who had taken the animal's forepaws in his hands and was forcing it to dance. The dog's dazed gash of teeth was like a reflection of the man's laugh. 'Here,' she said, more gently, 'let me see his tag. There's a loudspeaker system. It shouldn't be hard to find his owner.'

'I'll take him,' said the man at once, as though, like the dog, he had been obedience-trained and only awaited direction. 'I will ask them to announce that he has been found.'

Off he hared on his errand, like a boy-scout eager for merit. One hand on the dog's collar, he sliced through the crowd behind a nimbly raised shoulder. 'I'll be back,' he called to Jenny, turning to impress this on her with a sharp glance from yellowish, slightly bloodshot eyes.

He was the sort of man whom she would have avoided in an empty street – and, to be sure, she might have been wrong. He was friendly. Everyone at the rally was. Strangers cracked jokes and a group carrying an embroidered trade-union banner kept up a confident, comic patter. The one thing she wasn't sure she liked were the radical tunes which a bald old man was playing on his accordion. They seemed to her divisive, having nothing to do with the rally's purpose. When the musician's mate brought round the hat, she refused to contribute. 'Sorry,' she told him when he shook it in front of her. 'I've no change.' Turning, she was caught by the ambush of the dusky young man's grin. He was back, breathing hard and shaking rain from his hair.

'The dog will be OK,' he assured her. 'The authorities are in control.'

This confidence in hierarchy amused her. The next thing he said showed that it was selective.

'They,' he nodded furtively at the musicians, 'come to all rallies. I am thinking maybe they are the police? Musicians, buskers: a good disguise?' He had a shrill, excited giggle.

'There are plenty of ordinary police here,' she remarked, wondering whether he was making fun of her. She felt shy at having come here alone in her Burberry hat and mac. The hat was to protect her hair from torch drippings and was sensible gear for a torch-light procession. But then, might not sense be a middle-class trait and mark her out?

'Bobbies,' he said, 'are not the danger. I am speaking of the undercover police. The Special Branch. They have hidden cameras.'

'Oh.'

She eased her attention off him and began to read the graffiti on the struts of the bridge beneath which their section of the procession was sheltering. It was raining and there was a delay up front. Rumours or joke-rumours had provided explanations for this. The levity was so sustained as to suggest that many marchers were embarrassed at having taken to the streets. Old jokes scratched in concrete went back to her schooldays: *My mother made me a homosexual*, she read. *Did she?* goes the answer, conventionally written in a different hand. *If I get her some wool will she make me one too?* There was the usual Persian – or was it Arabic – slogan which she had been told meant *Stop killings in Iraq!* The man beside her could be an Arab. No. More likely an Indian.

'I know them,' he was saying of the secret police. 'We know each other. You see I myself come to all rallies. Every one in London.'

'Are you a journalist?'

'No. I come because I am lonely. Only at rallies are people speaking to me.'

Snap! She saw the trap-click of his strategy close in on her: his victim for the occasion. It was her hat, she thought and watched his eyes coax and flinch. It had singled her out. Damn! A soft-hearted woman, she had learned, reluctantly, that you disappointed people less if you could avoid raising their hopes. Something about him suggested that a rejection would fill him with triumph. He did not want handouts, conversational or otherwise, but must solicit them if he was to savour a refusal.

A graffito on the wall behind him said: *I thought Wanking was a town in China until I discovered Smirnov.* Don't *laugh*, she warned herself – yet, if she *could* think of a joke to tell him, mightn't it get her off his hook? Would Chinese laugh at the Smirnov joke, she wondered. Probably they wouldn't, nor Indians either. Wankers might. They were solitary and the solitary use jokes to keep people at bay.

'You see,' he was saying, 'I am a factory worker but also an intellectual. In my own country I was working for a newspaper but here in the factory I meet nobody to whom I can talk. Intellectuals in London are not inviting working men to their homes. I am starved for exchange of stimulating ideas.' His eye nailed a magazine she was carrying. 'You, I see, are an intellectual?'

'Goodness, no.' But the denial was a matter of style, almost a game which it was cruel to play with someone like him. She had never known an English person who would admit to being an intellectual. In India – Pakistan? – wherever he came from it would be a category which deserved honour and imposed duties. Denying membership must strike him as an effort to shirk such duties towards a fellow member in distress.

Her attempts to keep seeing things his way were making her nervous and she had twisted her sheaf of fliers and pamphlets into a wad. Am I worrying about *him*, she wondered, or myself? Perhaps even asking herself such a question was narcissistic? Objectivity too might be a middle-class luxury. How could a man like this afford it? He was a refugee, he was telling her now, a Marxist whose comrades back home were in prison, tortured or dead. Perhaps his party would take power again soon. Then he would go home and have a position in the new government. *Then* English intellectuals could meet him as an equal. He said this with what must have been intended as a teasing grin. She hadn't caught the name of his country and was embarrassed to ask lest it turn out to be unfamiliar. It would have to be a quite small nation, she reasoned, if he was hoping to be in its government. Or had *that* been a joke?

'We're moving.' She was relieved at the diversion.

The trade-union group started roaring the Red Flag with comic gusto and the procession ambled off. He was holding her elbow. Well, that, she supposed, must be solidarity. The rally was connected with an issue she cared about. She did not normally take to the streets and the etiquette of the occasion was foreign to her.

'*Let cowards mock,*' came the jovial Greater London bellow from up front, '*And traitors sneer . . .*'

'I'm as foreign here as he is,' she decided and bore with the downward tug at her elbow. He was small: a shrivelled man with a face like a tan shoe which hasn't seen polish in years. Dusky, dusty, a bit scuffed, he could be any age between thirty and forty-five. His fingers, clutching at her elbow bone, made the torch she had bought tilt and shed hot grease on their shoulders. She put up her left hand to steady it.

'You're married.' He nodded at her ring. 'Children?'

'Yes: two. Melanie and Robin. Melanie's twelve.'

The embankment was glazed and oozy. Outlines were smudged by a cheesy bloom of mist, and reflections from street-lights smeary in the mud for it was December and grew dark about four. Across the river, the South Bank complex was visible still. He remarked that you could sit all day in its cafeteria if you wanted and not be expected to buy anything. His room, out in the suburbs, depressed him so much that on Sundays he journeyed in just to be among the gallery- and theatre-goers, although he never visited such places himself.

'But galleries are cheap on Sundays,' she remonstrated. 'Maybe even free?'

He shrugged. Art – bourgeois art – didn't interest him. It was – he smiled in shame at the confession – the opulence of the cafeteria which he craved. 'Op*u*lence,' he said, stressing the wrong syllable so that she guessed that he had never heard the word pronounced. 'It is warm there,' he explained. 'Soft seats. Nice view of the river. Some of the women are wearing scent.'

On impulse and because it was two weeks to Christmas, she invited him to join her family for lunch on the 25th.

When the day came, she almost forgot him and had to tell Melanie to lay an extra place just before he was due to arrive. His name – he had phoned to test the firmness of her invitation – was Mr Rao. He called her Mrs Middleton and she found the formality odd after the mateyness of the rally when he had surely called her Jenny? Their procession, headed for Downing Steet, had been turned back to circle through darkening streets. Mounted police, came the word, had charged people in front. Several had been trampled. Maimed perhaps? No, that was rumour: a load of old rubbish. Just some Trots trying to provoke an incident. Keep calm. Then someone heard an ambulance. An old working man gibbered with four-letter fury but the banner-bearers were unfazed.

'Can't believe all you hear, Dad,' they told him.

Mr Rao tugged at Jenny's arm as though he had taken her into custody: the custody of the Revolution. 'You see,' he hissed, 'it is the system you must attack, root and branch, not just one anomaly. There are no anomalies. All are symptoms.' He was galvanized. Coils of rusty hair reared like antennae off his forehead. 'Social Democrats,' he shouted, 'sell the pass. They are running dogs of Capitalism. I could tell you things I have seen . . .' Fury restored him and she guessed that he came to rallies to revive a flame in himself which risked being doused by the grind of his working existence. He laughed and his eyes flicked whitely in the glow from the torches as he twitted the young men with the trade-union banner in their split allegiance. A Labour Government was loosing its police on the workers. 'Aha!' he hooted at their discomfiture. 'Do you see? Do you?' His laughter flew high and quavered like an exotic birdcall through the moist London night.

'You remember that demo I went to?' she reminded Melanie. 'Well, I met him there. He's a refugee and lonely at Christmas. A political refugee.'

'Sinister?' inquired her husband who'd come into the kitchen to get ice cubes, 'with a guerrillero grin and a bandit's moustache? Did he flirt with you?'

This sort of banter was irritating when one was trying to degrease a hot roasting pan to make sauce. She'd just remembered too that her mother-in-law, who was staying with them, was on a salt-free diet. Special vegetables should have been prepared. 'Did you lay the place for him?' she asked Melanie.

The girl nodded and rolled back her sleeve to admire the bracelet she'd got for Christmas. Posing, she considered her parents with amusement.

Jenny's husband was looking for something in the deep freeze. 'He did, didn't he?' he crowed. 'He flirted with you?'

She should have primed him, she realized. James was sensitive enough when things were pointed out to him but slow to imagine that other people might feel differently to the way he did. Mr Rao would be hoping for a serious exchange of ideas between men. Stress serious. He had been impressed when she told him that James, a senior civil servant, was chairman of a national committee on education. But now here was James wearing his sky-blue jogging suit with the greyhound on its chest – a Christmas present – all set to be festive and familial. He was a nimble, boyish man who prided himself on his youthfulness.

'Will Mr Rao disapprove of us?' he asked puckishly and tossed his lock of grey-blond hair off his forehead.

'Listen, he's a poor thing.' Jenny was peeved at being made to say this. 'Be careful with him, James. Can anyone see the soy sauce? I've burnt my hand. Thanks.' She spread it on the burn then went back to her roasting pan. Melanie, darling, could you do some quick, unsalted carrots for your grandmother? Please.'

'Better do plenty,' James warned. '*He* may be a vegetarian. Lots of Indians are.'

'God, do you think so? At Christmas.'

'Why not at Christmas? You'd think we celebrated it by drinking the blood of the Lamb.'

'People do,' said Melanie. 'Communion. There's the doorbell.'

'I'll go. Keep an eye on my pan.'

In the hall Jenny just missed putting her foot on a model engine which James had bought for five-year-old Robin and himself. An entire Southern Region of bright rails, switches, turntables and sidings was laid out and there was no sign of Robin. Did James dream of being an engine-driver, an aerial bomber or God? Or was it some sexual thing like everything else? Through the Art Nouveau glass of the door, she deduced that the blob in Mr Rao's purple hand must be daffodils, and wished that there was time to hide her own floral display which must minimize his gift.

'You were mean, horrible, appalling.'

'*He* is appalling.'

'Shsh! Listen, please, James, be nice. Try. Look, go back now, will you? They'll know we're whispering.'

'*I*'m not whispering.'

'Well you should be. He'll hear.'

'Jenny, you invited him. Try and control him. He has a chip a mile high on his . . .'

'Well, allow for it.'

'Why should I?'

'You're his host.'

'He's my guest.'

'God! Look, get the plum pud alight and take it in. I'll get the brandy butter.'

'If he suggests Robin eat this with his fingers, I'll . . .'

'Shush, will you? He doesn't understand children.'

'What does he understand? How to cadge money?'

'He didn't mean it that way.'

'He bloody did. Thinks the world owes him a living.'

'Well, doesn't it? Owe everyone I mean.'

'My dear Jenny . . .'

'Oh, all *right*. Here.'

She put a match to the brandy-soaked pudding so that blue flames sprang over its globe making it look like a scorched, transfigured human head. 'Go *on*. Take it while it's alight.' She pushed her husband in the direction of the dining-room and stood for a moment pulling faces at the impassive blankness of the kitchen fridge. Then she followed with the brandy butter.

Later, she came back to the kitchen to clean up. Vengefully, she let the men and her mother-in-law cope with each other over the coffee which their guest had at least not refused. He *had* refused sherry, also wine, also the pudding because it had brandy on it and had seemed to feel that it was his duty to explain why he did so and to point out the relativity of cultural values at the very moment when Robin's grandmother was telling the child how to pick fowl high.

'Only *two* fingers, Robin,' she'd been demonstrating daintily, 'never your whole hand and only pick up a *neat* bone.'

'We,' Mr Rao scooped up mashed chestnuts with a piece of bread, 'eat everything with our hands.' He laughed. 'There are millions of us.'

The anarchy of this so undermined Robin's sense of what might and might not be done on such an extraordinary day as Christmas that he threw mashed chestnuts at his grandmother and had to be exiled from the table. The older Mrs Middleton was unamused. Mr Rao bared his humourless, raking teeth.

'You are strict with your children,' he said, 'in imparting your class rituals. This is because as a people you still have confidence and prize cohesion. Maybe now you must relax?'

Nobody chose to discuss this. Doggedly, the family helped each other to sauce and stuffing and Mr Rao began to use his knife and fork like everyone else. A diffidence in him plucked at Jenny who saw that the incident with Robin had been meant as a joke: a humorous overture to the member of the family whom he had judged least likely to reject him. But now Robin himself was rejected, exiled to his room, and disapproval of Mr Rao hung unvoiced and irrefutable in the air. Seen by daylight, he was younger than she had supposed at the rally. His was a hurt, young face, puffy and unformed with bloodshot eyes and a soft, bluish, twitching mouth. He wanted to plead for Robin but could only talk in his magazine jargon. Perhaps he never spoke to people and knew no ordinary English at all? She imagined him sitting endlessly in the South Bank cafeteria reading political magazines and staring at the river.

'Pedagogical theory, you see . . .' he started and James, to deviate him – Robin's exile had to last at least ten minutes to placate his grandmother, interrupted with some remark about a scheme for facilitating adult education with which he was concerned.

'It's designed for people who didn't get a chance to go to university in the first instance,' said James. 'We give scholarships to deserving . . .'

'Could you give me one?' Mr Rao leaned across the table. 'Please. Could you? I am needing time to think and that factory work is destroying my brain. Have you worked ever on an assembly line?'

'You may certainly apply,' James told him. 'It's open to all applicants.'

'No.' Mr Rao spoke excitedly and a small particle of mashed chestnut flew from his mouth and landed on James's jogging suit. His words, spattering after it, seemed almost as tangible. 'No, no,' he denied, nervous with hope. 'You see I apply before for such things and never get them. Inferior candidates pass me by. Here in England, there is a mode, a ritual, you see. It is like the way you educate your son.' Mr Rao's mouth twisted like a spider on a pin. 'You teach him to give signals,' he accused. 'To eat the chicken *so* – and then his own kind will recognize and reward him. I give the wrong signals so I am always rejected.' He laughed sadly. 'Merit is not noted. In intellectual matters this is even more true. Examiners will take a working-class man only if they think he can be absorbed into their class. I cannot.'

'Then perhaps,' said James, 'you are an unsuitable applicant?'

'But the university,' pleaded Mr Rao, 'is not a caste system? Not tribal surely? You cannot afford to exclude people with other ways of being than your own. Even capitalism must inoculate itself with a little of the virus it fears. Intellectual life' – Mr Rao swung his fork like a pendulum – 'is a dialectical process. You must violate your rules,' he begged. 'Isn't that how change comes? Even in English law? First someone breaks a bad old law; then a judge condones the breaking and creates a precedent. I have read this. Now *you*,' Mr Rao pointed his fork at James, 'must break your bureaucratic rule. Give me a scholarship. Be brave,' he pleaded. The fork fell with a clatter but Mr Rao was too absorbed to care. 'Give,' he repeated, fixing James with feverish eyes as if he hoped to mesmerize him. The eyes, thought Jenny, looked molten and scorched like lumps of caramel when you burned a pudding. The fork was again swinging to and fro and it struck her that Mr Rao might not be above using hypnotism to try and make James acquiesce to his will.

She leaned over and took the fork from his fingers. He let it go. His energies were focused on James. The eyes were leeches now: animate, obscene. Melanie and her grandmother were collecting plates. They were outside the electric connection between the two men. Murmuring together, they seemed unaware of it. James's mouth tightened. Mr Rao, Jenny saw, was in for a rocket. But the man was conscious only of his own need. It was naked now. He was frightened, visibly sweating, his nails scratched at the table cloth. He wiped his face with a napkin.

'Men in lower positions must obey rules,' he told James. '*They* will not let me through. Only you can make an exception. Is not the spirit of your scheme to let the alienated back into society? I am such a man,' he said with dramatic intonation. 'I,' he said proudly, 'am needy, alienated, hard working and well read. Do you not believe I am intelligent? I could get references, but my referees,' he laughed his unhappy laugh, 'are tending to be in gaol: a minister of my country, the rector of my university. Oh, we had an establishment once.'

'Then perhaps,' said James, 'you understand about the need to eliminate personal appeals? Nepotism: the approach which corrupts a system. Did you,' asked James with contempt, 'pick my wife up at that rally because you knew who she was? Wait!' He held Jenny's hand to stop her talking. 'I'm quite well known. A number of people there could have recognized and pointed her out to you. A man like you is ruthless, isn't he? For a higher aim, to be sure.' James spoke with derision. 'No doubt you feel you matter more than other people?'

The stuffing had gone out of Mr Rao. His head sank. His mouth, a puffy wound mobile in his face, never settled on an emotion with confidence. Even now there was a twitch of humour in its gloom. 'Oh,' he said listlessly, 'many, many personal appeals are granted in this country. But it's like I said: I don't know the signals. I am an outsider here.' He stood up.

'Please!' Jenny wrenched her wrist from her husband's grip. 'Mr Rao! You're not going? There's pudding. The meal isn't over at all.'

But he had only stood up to welcome Robin who, released from his room by his grandmother, was returning in a haze of smiles and sulks. For the rest of the meal, attention was gratefully divided between the child and the food. It was Christmas, after all.

The dishwasher was on. Its noise drowned his approach and added urgency to the hand she felt landing on her arm.

'Jenny!' Mr Rao's shrewd, nervous face peered into hers. 'I go now. I am thanking you and . . .' Words, having betrayed him all day, seemed to be abandoning him utterly. 'Sorry,' he said as perfunctorily as Robin might have done. 'It is not true what your husband said.'

'Of course not. I'm sorry too – but I'm glad you came.' She smiled with a guilty mixture of sorrow and relief. After all, what more could she do? She gave him her hand.

He didn't take it. 'I appreciated this,' he said too eagerly. 'Being in a family. You know? Mine is a people who care a lot about family life. I miss it. That was why meeting little Robin, I . . .'

She thought he was apologizing. 'It's not important.'

'No, no. I know that with children things are always going wrong and being mended quickly. That is the joy of dealing with them. I miss children so much. Children and women – will you invite me again?'

She was astonished. Unaccountably, she felt a stab of longing to help him, to visit the unmapped regions where he lived: eager, vulnerable and alone, with no sense of what was possible any more than Robin had, or maybe great, mad saints. But how could she? The dishwasher had finished a cycle and begun another. It was so loud now that she could hardly hear what he was saying. He seemed to be repeating his question.

'We're going away for a while in January,' she began evasively. 'Skiing . . .' But evasion wouldn't do for this man. She looked him in the eye. 'I can't invite you,' she said. 'James and you didn't hit it off. You must realize that.'

'Will you meet me in town? I'll give you my number.'

'No.'

'Please.'

'Mr Rao . . .'

The wound of his mouth was going through a silent-movie routine: pleading, deriding, angry, all at once. 'The poor have no dignity,' he said, shocking her by this abrupt irruption of sound. 'They must beg for what others take.'

Suddenly, he had his arms around her and was slobbering, beseeching and hurting her in the hard grip of his hands. The sounds coming from him were animal: but like those of an animal which could both laugh and weep. One hand had got inside her blouse. 'A woman,' he seemed to be repeating, 'a family . . . woman . . .' Then a different cry got through to her: 'Mummy!'

Melanie, looking horrified, stood next to them. The dishwasher, now emptying itself with a loud gurgle, made it impossible to hear whether she had said anything else. Behind her stunned face bobbed her grandmother's which was merely puzzled. The older Mrs Middleton was a timorous lady, slow to grasp situations but constantly fearful of their not being as she would like.

'Mother!' yelled Melanie a second time.

Mr Rao, deafened by lust, loneliness or the noise of the dishwasher, was still clinging to Jenny and muttering incomprehensible, maybe foreign, sounds. She heaved him off and spoke with harsh clarity to his blind, intoxicated face.

'I'm sorry,' she said. 'I'm sorry. But will you please go now. Just leave.'

MAURICE LEITCH

from *Stamping Ground*

The band was playing a quickstep when she arrived at the Hall. She and Teresa Mullan. They could hear it coming out of the open windows. All the way up the street it had met them, getting louder and louder, *Cherokee*, old as the hills like the band, but it promised excitement, quicksteps always did somehow, and she imagined the Hall crammed and everyone dancing at a great rate. Teresa giggled with her and she gave her arm a quick squeeze as they ran up the steps together.

—Is there a big crowd, Bertie? She asked old man McCrory, a shade breathlessly.

He sat just inside the doorway; in front of him on a card-table the biscuit tin for the money and a big roll of pink tickets. He tore off two, saying—A brave few. But anyway, sure it won't be long in filling up, and in her haste to get in through that inner closed door to where the music thumped and couples spun she hardly took notice of what he said.

She might have known of course he would delude her with his double-talk, for when she and Teresa had pushed past and in, good money paid over and retreat cut off behind them, the Hall yawned, not a sinner on the bumpy glistening floor, just a few lost souls sitting in each corner and all staring at them in their finery. She clutched Teresa and they moved crabwise until the edge of a form brushed the back of her silk stockings. Why did people gape at you so? But then there was little refinement among this pitiful crew, she told herself, middle-aged, courting couples for the most part, down from the hills, by the look of them. And what made it worse of course was that this lot never got up to dance, were never known to, they just came for the supper and the chance to gawk, passing remarks to one another about the dancers behind their hands.

But now that she felt more composed in herself, she stared back; it was difficult to pick a target, because so many eyes from so many quarters were fastened on them, but she gave a fat woman, younger than the rest, red dress, and frizzed hair, as good as she got. She tried to be hurtful in her appraisal, gazing fixedly at the woman's perm, then at her frock with the cardigan draped over her bare shoulders in what she imagined was the height of sophistication, then down at the stockings, thick and a bilious tan, and last and worst of all the shoes – maroon patent with crossed straps.

She pretended to laugh then to Teresa, her hand cupping her mouth, gay and ladylike. *Oh, poor thing, such a get-up!* But Teresa looked at her as if she were crazy and edged along the bench. She could have strangled her. But then of course she might have known that Teresa would behave in that way. The place made her nervous, being what she was. Not that anyone would pass any remarks here, the Mullans being the only Catholic family for miles around, but there was always that wee uneasiness at finding herself inside the Orange Hall. Most of the time it seemed to her to be quite needless, something out of the dark ages, an old feeling running deep which she couldn't share or comprehend even, but there were other times when she forced herself to understand, especially when people around her, her 'own sort', talked about Catholics in that way they did. Her father, for instance . . .

She felt a sudden rush of loyalty for Teresa, her very best friend, sitting there beside her with her knees together, two hands clasped as if she were in church. Poor dote, maybe she did think, God help her wit, that there was something sacred about this place after all, you never could tell. How good she was, how clean and neat – not a bit like Catholics were supposed to be, always smelling fresh. Mrs Mullan kept them all well turned out, one couldn't deny it, even though there were seven of them. Made all their own clothes too, every stitch, down to their very vests. The Mullan children hated those because they were made out of flour-bags, oh, washed and ironed of course, and beautifully finished off on Mrs Mullan's treadle Singer, but one of them still had the blackbird on it, faint but recognizable; the brand was Early-Riser. They all had to wear it but the girls would cry bitterly whenever it came round to their turn. Teresa of course was the eldest – her own age – so perhaps she hadn't to any longer. Should she mention it, just to give them both a good giggle, anything to take their minds off this dreary place and these people? On second thoughts, no, she might be offended. She knew herself the shame of hand-me-downs. Some day she and Teresa Mullan would tell them all what to do with their cast-offs.

In one of her favourite day-dreams now she made room for her dear friend, for instead of just she alone riding in furs and luxury in the back of the big car she saw the two of them lying back and having the great laugh together. *Drive a little slower, Ponsonby,*

I wish to take a look at my old home. Teresa, darling, how did we ever put up with it as long as we did? How on earth did we? And she would advise her on what to wear, clothes and jewellery, perfume as well – she would be able to speak French by then – and tell her how to do her hair. Teresa would need all the advice she could get. Poor Teresa, it was awful to be as poor as she was and the eldest of a big family . . .

Just then, miracle of miracles, Frizzie Lizzie in the red frock rose to dance with her partner. They were the only couple on the floor and the man held her with his big hands, the two of them standing there, with that look of painful concentration on his face, waiting until he got on to the beat. It was an Olde-Tyme waltz; once settled into the rhythm, you revolved until you stopped from dizziness, round and round, spinning, held out, almost floating off the floor. It looked beautiful in the pictures, Cornel Wilde and Ann Blyth at the Palace Ball, but it never ever lived up to expectation. She usually refused, if someone asked her. Fright took hold because of the way the men became excited, the heat of their bodies, their eyes and faces, as they spun faster and faster, laughing at her cries.

The couple danced awkwardly, not looking at one another, around the edges of the floor. The man had a white carnation in his buttonhole. She supposed they had been to a wedding earlier in the day. The band played – a medley of three tunes – and not once did the woman in red nor the man holding her exchange a word or a smile. Each time they passed them sitting on their form against the back wall, they presented their faces in turn as they went past like two dead things.

A weight seemed to press on her. She couldn't even enjoy ridiculing them any longer. If she could only learn not to build things up so; far more sensible to anticipate the run of things, accept all that a dance in a place like this entailed – but that wasn't true – she was arguing with herself in her head as the music beat on for the engaged couple – not true at all, because she remembered times, indeed she did, when she could hardly wait for each dance to finish and the next begin, and in the same instant yearn for time to run slow almost to stopping-point. Nights when the band took on a lease of life, laughing among themselves at people rushing to dance, the men pushed out in a big lump at the door, eyeing every girl in the place, a hundred looks a minute, hungry for a whirl, a touch, anything, burning, half-mad.

—Sssst . . .

Teresa was whispering to her; she had something to say, something too good to keep to herself, despite her nervousness.

—The Well-Dressed Man. He's been seen again. Isn't it awful? Oh, Hetty, what would you do if he jumped out on you in one of them dark places?

—Well-Dressed Man indeed! He'd get the right dressing-down from me, I can tell you.

She put on a fierce face and voice for the other's benefit, but of course couldn't keep it up, had to giggle out loud at the poor dope and her expression.

Poor Teresa, she'd believe anything. Tell her any old string of rubbish about some ghost or banshee or other and she would sit by the fire quaking all night, afraid to budge, her eyes staring in her head. Catholics of course were well-known to be a superstitious crowd, always crossing themselves and muttering to a lot of statues. Mrs

Mullan would even turn the holy pictures to the wall if she heard bad language on the street.

The dance ended and the couple returned to their place along the wall. Then there was a lull as the band lit up cigarettes and talked among themselves. She wondered what time it was; she hadn't a watch, neither had Teresa.

—But, Hetty, would you really stand up to him? Would you?

She felt the plucking at her frock, the soft press of the other's arm on hers. Poor dote. Eyes big as plates and those freckles she was always trying to scrub off, and the party dress her mother had made her out of a length of blue and white curtain material that the doctor's wife didn't want.

—Now, listen to me and pay heed, just in case it ever happens to you, because it might, you never know – (she couldn't resist it, although it wasn't right) – All you have to do is stand your ground and defy them to do their worst. Because you know they're as scared as you are, maybe more so. Just stand there and look them straight in the eye and then say – she whispered it, giggling – Come one step further and I'll prune your Willy John for you with this knife I've got here.

Teresa's mouth opened and closed; her face went pale, then red, pale again. Oh so innocent, such a child. She had tried at times, to tell her a few things but always gave it up as a bad job. The shock would have been too much anyhow, for despite her head being stuffed with 'mortal sins', as she called them, she wouldn't know one if it came up and sat down next to her.

Inside her own handbag was the little notebook that Minnie Maitland had once given her when she had thought – they had both thought – she was leaving to go to the city to find a new life. Minnie had been full of embarrassment pressing it into her hand at the last minute, and although it had all been a false alarm, something of a joke as well, neither of them had referred to it again. It contained advice in Minnie's funny crabbed handwriting on how a young girl should take care of herself, about her periods and suchlike, and how she should never let any man 'fondle her in the wrong places'. If he did that he didn't love you, so Minnie said, or wrote, rather. She could never imagine Minnie saying any of those things, never. And it was funny, because reading the words – just like the writing in a school copybook – the shock was somehow greater, it seemed to dart into you more; she could remember it still, the feeling as she sat on the ditch that day on her way home. She couldn't help herself, she had to finish every word, perched there at the side of the road in a quiet private place. And then getting up with her eyes blinding, and her limbs stiff and damp, excited in a funny way, unsatisfied, as if she wanted to go on turning the pages on and on and on . . .

She felt affected now in that same way, here in the Hall, as the band played another number, lost to all around her, feeling, remembering . . .

Her legs quivered a little, a quick tremble underneath her smoothed-down frock. She touched her thighs just once. It stopped. The field earlier, the heat, smell and itch of the hay . . . All day she had repressed it; it went down like something under water, but she knew it would rise again – it did now. She felt sickish, stomach sliding, remembering the three touching her in 'the wrong places'. How little Minnie knew. She shut her eyes and ears like those three brass monkeys on her mantelpiece. Oh yes, it was all right for the likes of her going her own sheltered ways and writing down advice on how to behave oneself with 'the male sex'. No one had ever pulled her down in broad daylight with their rough hands tearing and tearing and fingers poking. She pressed her thighs tighter together as though to squeeze out the memory. What would it be like, she wondered, cutting it? Would it slice off clean, or would you have to saw at it like an old root?

—Ladies and Gentlemen, the next dance will be a Ladies' Choice.

The drummer was winking at the others in the band as much as to say, 'Some hope', then he rattled his sticks and they started to play 'Oh, Lady, Be Good'. There was the leader, who was blind, on the piano-keyed accordion; a fat, bald bus-conductor called Eddie Smith playing the fiddle – he sometimes sang; a saxophone player she hadn't seen before, and of course the drummer. A lot of girls thought he was the last word, clean-cut with dark, curly hair, a sort of John Garfield type, and he fancied himself no end. Some girls were easily pleased.

> I'm just a Babe who's lost in a wood,
> Oh, lady, be good
> To me.

Her feet jigged under the bench as the music swept on to an empty hall. Oh, how she loved dancing. The rhythm gave her goose flesh. It came and went on her skin and was delicious. Would Teresa ever dance with her, she wondered; it seemed a sin to sit this one out; she would lead and Teresa follow, but oh, what was the use, she knew what the answer would be. She seemed destined to be stuck with other people and their backward ways. They caged her in, indeed they did, not only the people but the place, this old Hall with its Lodge banners on the walls and dusty red, white and blue streamers looping and crossing above her head and outside the village and beyond that, the Valley itself, hills on either horizon. All the things tightened around her, tight wee place, tight wee people, tight, tight, *tight* . . .

Teresa was looking at her oddly again; she must have been saying it out loud. They all thought she was a bit mental anyway. They did. Wild, headstrong. She knew the words, knew what they thought of her – old Harper the teacher, women in the village, the Minister that time he rebuked her for laughing in church – her father, yes, him – wouldn't he have the pink fit if he knew she was wearing make-up and this dress?

Paint and powder, powder and paint. You're on the right road. A huer. Nothing surer. On the right road.

She must make certain to get back before he came home from Ballyclare. He always went on Saturday nights, riding there and back on his bicycle, a regular thing, winter and summer. Weather never deterred him. What would? She supposed he must look forward to his few bottles of stout, but she couldn't imagine him there in the company of other men, drinking and talking, laughing. Never. Couldn't imagine him doing anything like anyone else. Even . . .

That time she had burst in on him in the privy with his trousers down around his ankles. Luckily he was sitting sunk deep in the seat, covered that part of him. It still gave her a funny feeling. Shivers. His legs were so white and thin, like bleached sticks.

Were all men's the same? Horrible, pale and unhealthy looking. How could you love any man if his legs were like that? Beside yours in bed on the honeymoon. She couldn't understand why her brain should be so active tonight. Such strange thoughts. It was a funny thing really, all these people in this place, all with different secret ideas racing through their heads and no one to know but themselves.

—Knock, knock . . .

Teresa looked at her as if this time she had really gone mental.

She repeated it – a sudden whim, no rhyme or reason to it, just something that came to her lips, and daft, here with the band playing and the people around the walls with their straight faces.

—Who's there?

No laughing, just an agonized face. God wasn't Teresa Mullan a right drip!—Yvonne.

—Yvonne who?

—Yvonne your knickers, your da's coming.

Why did she say these things? *Why?* As soon as they came out they turned to ashes in her mouth. A foul taste.

She laughed, she had to do something. Those big, stupid cow-eyes. What a drip, what a drip. She wanted to nip her until she screamed. *What's 'pin' spelt backwards?* She must watch herself. The urge was almost more than she could control.

The band finished the number. They looked weary now. She supposed even they lost heart playing to an empty floor, taking it personally, no one to appreciate their music, rattle, bang and scrape though it was. Now they would start having longer breaks, deserting the stage with their instruments sitting about on the chairs for up to ten minutes at a time making the place seen even more forsaken than it was. On the face of the big drum was lettered in red, *The Merry Macks*. She should have paid more attention to the posters, *Music by the Merry Macks*, along the bottom in small print a warning of what to expect.

The band went out through a door at the side of the stage. She knew it led to a kitchen where the women were preparing the supper, laying out egg and ham sandwiches and pastries on bakers' trays, and boiling up the big brown pots of tea that scalded the roof of your mouth if you weren't careful. She didn't feel a bit hungry though, just resentful that still another part of the short night was to be further wasted on eating and drinking.

But then at that precise moment – her lowest point – a diversion, *the* diversion occurred. The door opened with some force and into the Hall came four young strangers. Laughing, all chewing gum, and unmistakably townies by their clothes, gaberdine suits and suede shoes with those thick crêpe soles – their faces fell the instant they saw the bare floor, the bandstand and what passed for a crowd sitting around the walls dumbly watching them. They hung there for a moment and she could almost read their thoughts.

She tried not to stare as brutally as everyone else, indeed she glanced off to the side a little trying to be aloof, but her heart thumped as she felt a hot wash of blood on her cheeks and neck. Teresa was gaping like any common fool and how she wished for a more sophisticated friend, particularly at a time like this, because wasn't the tall dark one in the nigger suit and the blue knitted tie the most gorgeous fellow she had ever seen. She wasn't looking; her eyes were settled for want of somewhere to land on a banner high up on one of the side walls. Queen Victoria was pictured handing a bible with a gold key on its bright open pages to a kneeling man. The man was bald; something which made the scene wrong. She couldn't fit a man like that into history somehow. But that was only a sideways leap away from what her attention really craved. Like all the rest of them, despise them as she would, she longed to stare at the four surveying the Hall and the prospects. She sat there with her hands pressed together, knees too, waiting for the dark good-looking one to notice her. She would know all right.

Then the door beside the stage opened and the band came out, still laughing among themselves. They seemed to spend their time laughing when they weren't playing, and even then they were always winking across to one another. She wondered what sort of a joke it was that could be stretched out all night between four grown men that way.

Events from that point on seemed to pick up speed, for no sooner had the band started to play again than three other newcomers arrived, but girls this time. She had seen them before, a trio of cheap specimens from Larne, smoking and laughing and sending their made-up eyes running around the Hall. *Hussies*, she thought, tightening in on herself, back stiff as a poker.

At her side, Teresa stared harder than ever, and she bit her lip with the effort not to leave a mark on her. She felt like going home that instant. Nothing seemed ever to go right, nothing. She just knew now if she stayed, her place would be in this corner all night beside Teresa Mullan, with her mouth open. For the first time she noticed the awful dress she was wearing. Worst of all, when she glanced down at her own, it seemed almost as dowdy. She wanted to tear it off and rip it into pieces, but not here – somewhere quiet and away where she could yell to her heart's content, like out in the fields deep in the country, and roll over and over in the grass, scoring the ground with her nails. It was the second time that day she had felt the urge, unexplained and a bit frightening. Maybe she was going mental, like all the people said she was, after all this time, catching up on her because if you believed something when people kept telling you you were often enough, it would happen.

A voice spoke to her.

—Would you like to dance?

She looked up, still with the mad fancies in her head, and it was *his* face looking down at her, and he had got rid of his chewing-gum and all she could think was that was nice of him.

Then they were dancing, without her even knowing whether she had said yes or not. She had this awful strong desire to close her eyes, make it all the more intense like the way it could be in bed underneath the bed-clothes, when everything was blotted out, and you could only smell, and hear your own blood pumping. It would just be the sound of the music and her hand in his with his right one pressing her gently in the small of her back. His palm felt dry and cool and he wasn't clutching or squeezing or trying to feel you through your thin dress an inch at a time up to the straps of your brassiere or down to the elastic of your knickers. The urge to dance blind was much greater now, to sharpen all of her experience into one hard little lump, something about the size of a boiled sweet. A strange nonsense, but she saw it like that. She would swallow it, have all of it in one go. A brandy-ball. She smiled to herself. The name always sounded indecent. A Minnie-word. And he must have felt her face move for he said quietly—What's the joke?

He wouldn't understand of course – who would? He would only think her a bit touched, like all the rest of them, but then again he might not; he looked different, felt and smelt too – some sort of lotion and a slight hint of drink, but not that awful Guinness smell, like sour milk, and the brown ring around the mouth.

It would be nice to say things straight out for a change – just once – the private things, and have someone listen all through to all of them, even the ones you daren't mention. Instead of which she found herself whispering to mirrors behind locked doors, or calling out in the middle of McGookin's wood, bad filthy things to the trees, shouting down into black holes in the trunks. When she was younger she used to post 'letters' through those same holes, thick wooden lips, rubbed smooth, the bark pulled back like real mouths.

—Well? Are you going to keep it all to yourself? What's the joke?

He hadn't that thin sing-song accent that townies had; something a shade better off, you could tell. She said:

—That's for me to know and you to find out, isn't it? And instantly wanted to die on the spot. The cleverness of it, head to one side, and the cheeky Miss Smartie-Pants grin. *What made her come out with it like that? What in God's name?*

And now the damage was done; she could tell that by his silence and the way he was dancing, holding her as if she had turned to a plank of wood. She felt she would trip over her own feet at any moment; the music blared in her ears as they went past the stage, suddenly extra loud, and she was positive that the drummer was winking and pointing them out to the rest of the band. *God*, she prayed, *let me not disgrace myself by falling, and let the dance end quickly, please Lord, I don't ask you for much, you know that, just this one thing . . .*

The first number ended and they stood side by side facing the platform, awkward like two sentries, and not as much as a look or a word between them and the drummer took his time before hitting the cymbals to start the second tune. And then the same grinning jack-ass was doing something smart with his drumsticks, *rat-tat-tat* on the round things that looked like coconuts, and before she knew what was afoot the other few dancers were thinning off the floor and they were left now forced to face one another and he was saying—Can you do the rumba?

Nothing in her life up to then, it seemed to her, had been so terrible as this moment. All eyes on her, thoughts like knives piercing her and how could she either go through with it or walk off the floor? How? All that ran through her head was—*They've got an awful lot of coffee in Brazil*, as the music brayed out reminding her all the more strongly of her humiliation, because it played only for them.

He took her hand then, but she still couldn't bring herself to look him in the face. He said—It's the same as the fox-trot, only slower. We'll help each other through it, and she was sure that she was in love with him already, as he took her and moved her strongly but gently off and into the rhythm.

It was as if they were in a bubble, floating free, in and around each other, all mixed up, legs and arms and cheeks touching. The 'sinful thoughts' that Minnie had warned her about rose in her thick and fast, but she wanted to hold them in her head, enjoying each to the full, sorry to feel it slide away before another took its place. She gave herself to them completely, the way she would give herself to him if he asked her. Right this minute if he asked her, she would leave with him, without a backward glance, or one single regret. *She would, she would, oh indeed she would . . .*

—Will you keep me the next dance?

The music still played, his voice seemed to come from very far away, and she came back to reality, blushing as she remembered what she had been thinking about.

—Oh yes – she said straight out, and she meant it, indeed had to hold back from saying, *every dance, if you like,* for there was still that tiny safeguard at the back of her mind, slipped away in there by Minnie at some time or other like a letter or a note behind a clock.

She held up her head now, looking about her proudly as they swept around the Hall. The tango was a dance she could do well. Its dash had always appealed to her and she was glad she had pestered old 'Cookie' Hughes who fancied himself as a ballroom expert to teach her its steps. *Jealousy, you conquered me, jealousy,* oh what lovely music it was and she had never heard an accordion played so well. Look at their faces, sour as crabs, as they rushed at her, then retreated, as he directed their pace so cleverly and manfully, just stopping short of the wall and all those feet on each run.

It was surprising how many people had come into the Hall by now. A night for them all to remember and talk about. The night Hetty Quinn bloomed before their very eyes. She began to look around her boldly, out and over his shoulder now, judging and observing.

Mr and Mrs 'Pooshie' Patton from Hillhead, never missed a hooley, he more of an old woman than she, panting home from his day's work to tell the latest bit of oily gossip (it was him they called 'Pooshie', not the wife); the Gourley sisters, two peroxide queens who'd never got over the times they'd had with the GI's, only officers were good enough for them in those days (some said they went out with darkies too) but Elmer and Byron and all the others never sent for them to go out to their big ranches, no sir-ee, they were still here in Tardree, with all their glamour and dyed hair. She gave them a pitying look as she sailed past; they'd never get a man now, never. And over there in a corner with all the young girls around him was the ageing village Romeo, Albert Higgins, who worked at the creamery. They said he wrote away to the Lonely Hearts advertisements in the paper. *Well set-up bachelor with own place, wishes to meet refined lady of similar means with a view to companionship and eventual matrimony.* They found out it was him when Sadie Brown replied to his Box No. in *The Belfast Telegraph.* It was hard to keep it to themselves; the letter he wrote back was such a scream. She whispered a bit of it to herself that she'd memorized before Sadie Brown lost her nerve and threw it into the river in pieces so that no one could ever put it together again. *A feeling for the finer things in life, reading, travel and listening to symphony concerts on the wireless . . .*

As she danced past all of them, she felt so superior, privileged, that all her life was before her and anything could happen. It lay in front of her, stretched out, a road that went on and on like the one in the school reader starting off thick and broad and disappearing into a point at the top of the page, curling and dipping with men and animals in fields along the way and farms and castles with enchanted woods and blue smoke rising out of the middle of them . . .

Someone standing near the door called out:

—Hello, Hetty, in a bold, loud voice, and she felt herself go stiff in his arms.

He noticed it because he said—Who's that? The boy friend, is it? and she said—Oh, it's nobody at all, but couldn't get herself to laugh and so make it convincing, and she thought, *oh, my God, I'm being punished for my pride*, because there he was, that creature Mack, grinning along with the other two.

She had her back to them now but knew they were watching and making cracks to one another, drunk too by the cut of them, and what must he be thinking as the tango rushed on to its close? All her schemes and dreams would die with the music, she felt certain of that now, all of them.

He said—Remember. The next dance is mine, but she knew he didn't mean it. What else could he say?

They parted and she went back to her place beside Teresa. Her head was full of heat and noise and Teresa was looking at her as if her face was on fire. It felt like it, but she was past caring. Straight ahead of her she gazed, neither to left nor right, hearing no one, hearing nothing. If she could only stay like that, untouched, unmoved, until she gathered enough strength to get up and go home on her own, and then creep into bed and burrow deep down beneath the blankets. That warm, lined cave seemed the only place left to her now holding out any last hope of comfort.

But Teresa was pulling at her, full of excitement. It was as if it had all been happening to Teresa and not to her.

—Oh, my God! he's coming over again! Hetty. *Hetty.*

She felt the tug moving her back and forth on the seat, but was too tired to resist or be annoyed, be anything other than a sack of potatoes. Who would want to dance with a sack of spuds, she asked herself in a daze, but he did, it seemed, and for the second time she was in his arms sweeping around the floor which someone had just sprinkled with white flakes of wax out of a tin a moment before. She watched it disappear beneath the feet of the dancers. It went like snow off a ditch, because there were many quick-stepping, all anxious to wipe out the memory of the tango. They bumped into her, but it hardly seemed to matter, she just hung her head and watched the feet coming and going down there as if they weren't attached to anything or anybody. An expression kept coming into her head, *the shock proved too much for her*, that Minnie used a lot. If she really did throw a fit here in the middle of Tardree Orange Hall, tearing out her hair by the roots and screeching, wouldn't it serve them all right – *them* being everybody, even her partner, for again she felt bruised and afflicted from all quarters that long weary live-long day.

Suddenly they stopped, or rather he halted for some reason, out on the edge of the floor. Someone was blocking their progress. Mack's hateful smiling face was there, fat moon-face; she saw his two cronies at his shoulder and he was saying in that polite voice that could never take her in for a moment—It's an Excuse-Me, and her partner with his arm holding her around the waist was considering and she knew so well that he was going to yield. She knew it.

In that instant she felt as if a red curtain was passing down over her eyes. The heat struck her and she started yelling without control. She could hear her own voice giving out loud and long, without any break in the things she was saying, as if it was some other person and not her that was scalding Mack McFarlane – and a part of her marvelled at the easy way they flowed out of her and from where she knew not, such a casting-up. She called him for all the names she could think of – *fat pig, dirty dog, scabby head, porridge-face* – things you could hear any day of the week in the school-yard and he only threw back his head, and laughed, enjoying it. But that made her all the more determined to sting, mad as a bee. Now she called him *a lowdown country shite*, and she felt her partner shrink away, but what did she care for any of them, they were all scum, the lot of them with their wee thing between their legs they were so proud of.

She said—And you would put it where I wouldn't put the end of my walking-stick, and that was a rare one, for the smile was going off his kisser now and his fine friends' for that matter too. (Their turn would come in a minute or two, never fear.) Sure had he ever told them how he used to sneak around the backs of the houses after dark to get a good dekko at daft Maisie Parkes getting ready for bed, had he told them that, because everyone knew that all Mack McFarlane was ever any good for was looking up the wee girls' clothes at school, and had he also told them about how he was never done tormenting her to go out with him, had he told his cronies that? It wasn't so completely accurate – perhaps he had asked her once or twice, once certainly, that day up at the old lime-kiln – but it hit hard, she could see that by his face. He moved at her, white as a sheet, and her partner said—Now push off, mac, not knowing it was his name and she shouted out too.

—Yes, push off, you fat fucker you! And she had used the word. It had slipped out unawares and the last one of her ladylike airs had flown along with it. But it still felt good saying it.

Then Frank Glass tried to butt in and she turned on him—And you can keep your trap shut, Frank Glass, because I have one or two home truths I could broadcast about you as well, you creepy wee book-worm you, and she had, that time she and Roberta Brownlees had spied on him down at the weir, playing with his thing, while he kept looking at a photograph in his other hand.

It was funny how they were all coming back to her, these things, and they were too good to waste. She must get them all out. She would make them sorry, that trio, they had ever taken their liberties with her. Her blood boiled and she stamped her foot, lost to all around her.

Frank Glass stuttered—There's someone at the door looking for you, and she knew it hadn't come out the way he wanted it to, for she cut the feet from him, you see. His dial was a picture, torn as he was between fright that she'd affront him and a grinning cleverness. She took her time about heeding what he'd said, expecting some trick or other, but then she looked and *oh God above*, her limbs turned to jelly, for it was *him* standing there with his old cap hanging off the side of his head, and under his arm a bloodstained, brown-paper parcel of butcher's meat from Ballyclare.

He hadn't seen her yet. His eyes, blurry with drink, were peering hard into each knot of people on the floor. *Oh, how could he do this to me*, was her first thought, and then terror took hold as she remembered the weight of his hand from the past. *Powder and paint, paint and powder*, as he whaled into her with the strap he sharpened his razor on. It hung under the stairs on a nail and her dearest wish was to take it from that place and hurl it into the deepest and fiercest part of the Moylena.

Never for one instant taking her eyes off him – oh, the picture of him swaying there with his old steak and sausages under his arm and his old eyes screwed up in the poor light – she moved back and away in among the dancers.

Her partner called out—Hetty! just once to her.

Later the sound of her name like that from him was to stay with her, but she had no choice but to go, no word to anyone, to him or even poor Teresa, still sitting there unawares; she just slid through the dancers looking for the side-door by the platform. It was lucky she hadn't a coat with her but it wouldn't have mattered anyway, she would have left it behind, such a panic was hammering in her breast.

When she reached the door, like a fool she looked back, just to make sure her escape was secure. She couldn't see him at first through the dancers, then suddenly a way was cleared between them, and he was looking straight at her down that long avenue. He raised his fist and the sodden parcel fell to the floor. She turned and ran down the steps in among the women making the tea in the back kitchen.

They called out after her as she gained the street door. Some of them knew her. All would know of her disgrace before that night was out. The whole world would know, the whole wide world, and she had nowhere to hide from them. She just ran and ran, mad, mental Hetty Quinn, down the village street under the moon like the wild thing she was.

JOHN MCGAHERN

from *The Barracks*

I

Mrs Reegan darned an old woollen sock as the February night came on, her head bent, catching the threads on the needle by the light of the fire, the daylight gone without her noticing. A boy of twelve and two dark-haired girls were close about her at the fire. They'd grown uneasy, in the way children can indoors in the failing light. The bright golds and scarlets of the religious pictures on the walls had faded, their glass glittered now in the sudden flashes of firelight, and as it deepened the dusk turned reddish from the Sacred Heart lamp that burned before the small wickerwork crib of Bethlehem on the mantelpiece. Only the cups and saucers laid ready on the table for their father's tea were white and brilliant. The wind and rain rattling at the window-panes seemed to grow part of the spell of silence and increasing darkness, the spell of the long darning-needle flashing in the woman's hand, and it was with a visible strain that the boy managed at last to break their fear of the coming night.

'Is it time to light the lamp yet, Elizabeth?' he asked.

He was overgrown for his age, with a pale face that had bright blue eyes and a fall of chestnut hair on the forehead. His tensed voice startled her.

'O Willie! You gave me a fright,' she cried. She'd been sitting absorbed for too long. Her eyes were tired from darning in the poor light. She let the needle and sock fall into her lap and drew her hand wearily across her forehead, as if she would draw the pain that had started to throb there.

'I never felt the night come,' she said and asked, 'Can you read what time it is, Willie?'

He couldn't see the hands distinctly from the fire-place. So he went quickly towards the green clock on the sideboard and lifted it to his face. It was ten past six.

The pair of girls came to themselves and suddenly the house was busy and full with life. The head was unscrewed off the lamp, the charred wicks trimmed, the tin of paraffin and the wide funnel got from the scullery, Elizabeth shone the smoked globe with twisted brown paper, Willie ran with a blazing roll of newspaper from the fire to touch the turned-up wicks into flame.

'Watch! Watch! Outa me way,' he cried, his features lit up with love of this nightly lighting. Hardly had Elizabeth pressed down the globe inside the steel prongs of the lamp when the girls were racing for the windows.

'My blind was down the first!' they shouted.

'No! My blind was down the first!'

'Wasn't my blind down the first, Elizabeth?' they began to appeal. She had adjusted the wicks down to a steady yellow flame and fixed the lamp in its place – one side of the delf on the small tablecloth. She had never felt pain in her breasts but the pulse in the side of her head beat like a rocking clock. She knew that the aspirin box in the black medicine press with its drawn curtains was empty. She couldn't send to the shop for more. And the girls' shouts tore at her patience.

'What does it matter what blind was down or not down? – only give me a little peace for once,' was on her lips when her name, her Christian name – Elizabeth – struck at her out of the child's appeal. She was nothing to these children. She had hoped when she first came into the house that they would look up to her as a second mother, but they had not. Then in her late thirties, she had believed that she could yet have a child of her own, and that, too, had come to nothing. At least, she thought, these children were not afraid of her, they did not hate her. So she gripped herself together and spoke pleasantly to them: they were soon quiet, laughing together on the shiny leatherette of the sofa, struggling for the torn rug that lay there.

Una was eleven, two years older than Sheila, almost beautiful, with black hair and great dark eyes. Sheila was like her only in their dark hair. She was far frailer, her features narrow and sensitive, changeable, capable of looking wretched when she suffered.

They were still playing with the rug when Elizabeth took clothes out of a press that stood on top of a flour bin in the corner and draped them across the back of a plain wooden chair she turned to the fire. They stopped their struggling to watch her from the sofa, listening at the same time to find there was no easing in the squalls of rain that beat on the slates and blinded windows.

'Daddy'll be late tonight?' Sheila asked with the child's insatiable and obvious curiosity.

'What do you think I'm airin' the clothes for, Sheila? Do you hear what it's like outside?'

'He might shelter and come home when it fairs?'

'It has no sound of fairin' to me – only getting heavier and heavier . . .'

They listened to the rain beat and wind rattle, and shivered at how lucky they were to be inside and not outside. It was wonderful to feel the warm rug on the sofa with their hands, the lamplight so soft and yellow on the things of the kitchen, the ash branches crackling and blazing up through the turf on the fire; and the lulls of silence were full of the hissing of the sap that frothed white on their sawed ends.

Elizabeth lowered the roughly made clothes-horse, a ladder with only a single rung at each end, hanging high over the fire, between the long black mantelpiece and the ceiling.

'Will you hold the rope for me?' she asked the boy and he held the rope that raised and lowered the horse while she lifted off a collarless shirt and felt it for dampness. She spread it on the back of a separate chair, the sleeves trailing on the hearth. He pulled up the horse again, hand over hand, and fastened the loop of the rope on its iron hook in the wall.

'Do you think he will be late tonight?' he asked.

'He's late already. You can never tell what hold-up he might have. Or he might have just taken shelter in some house. I don't know why he should have to go out at all on a night like this. It makes no sense at all! O never join the guards when you grow up, Willie!'

'I'll not,' he answered with such decision that she laughed.

'And what'll you be?'

'I'll not join the guards!'

They looked at each other. She knew he never trusted her, he'd never even confide his smallest dream in her. She seemed old to him, with her hair gone grey and the skin dried to her face. Not like the rich chestnut hair of his mother who had died, and the lovely face and hands that freckled in summer.

'It's time you all started your homework,' Elizabeth ordered. 'If your father sees a last rush at night there'll be trouble.'

They got their schoolbags and stood up the card-table close to the lamp on the laid table. There was the usual squabbling and sharpening of pencils before they gave themselves to the hated homework, envious of their stepmother's apparent freedom, aware of all the noises of the barracks. They heard Casey, the barrack orderly, open the dayroom and porch doors, and the rattle of his bucket as he rushed out for another bucket of turf: the draughts banging doors all over the house as he came in and the flapping of his raincoat as he shook it dry like a dog in the hallway, then his tongs or poker thudding at the fire after the door had closed.

'Will I be goin' up to sleep with Mrs Casey tonight?' Una lifted her head to ask.

'I don't know – your nightdress is ready in the press if you are,' she was answered.

'Guard Casey said this evenin' that I would,' the child pursued.

'You'll likely have to go up so. You'll not know for certain till your father comes home,' she was abruptly told. Elizabeth was tired to death, she could not bear more questions.

Casey's wife was childless and when barrack orderly fell to his turn and he had to sleep nights in the dayroom, on the official iron bed between the phone and the wall of the lock-up, Una would often have to go to sleep with her, for she couldn't be got to stay alone in the house on these nights. Una would get sweets or pennies, the slice of fruit cake and the glass of orange if she went and she didn't care whether Sheila had to sleep alone in their cold room or not, even when the smaller girl began to sob.

'What's wrong, Sheila?' Elizabeth was quick to notice.

'I'm afraid. I don't want to sleep on me own.'

'Oh, you're a small girl no longer, Sheila. Una mightn't be going yet at all. And even if she is we can leave the lamp lit! Shure you'll not be afraid then, Sheila?'

Elizabeth coaxed and she was quietened. They turned to work again at their exercises, Elizabeth kneading dough in a tin basin on the table beside them, her arms bare to the elbows and a white dusting of flour on the back of her hands and wrists.

It was their father's tyres they first heard going past on the loose gravel and, 'Daddy's home', they said to Elizabeth. He'd leave his high policeman's bicycle in the shed at the back and come in through the scullery.

His black cycling cape and pull-ups were shiny with wet when he came, his face chafed red with wind and rain. The narrow chinstrap held the cap firmly on his head, the medallion between the peak and the crown with its S twined through the Celtic G shining more vividly tonight against the darkened cloth. He carried his carbide bicycle lamp in his hand, big and silver, its blue jet of gas still burning, he left it to Willie to quench, quickly discarding his cycling clothes. The rain had penetrated the cape and pull-ups. There were dark patches of wet on the trousers, and on the tunic with its array of silver buttons, the three stripes of his rank on the sleeve.

'Wet to the bloody skin,' he complained. 'A terrible night to have to cycle about like a fool.'

The children were very still. He had an intense pity for himself and would fly into a passion of reproaches if he got any provocation. They watched him take off his tunic and boots. His socks left wet prints on the cement when he stood up.

'All the clothes are aired,' Elizabeth said as she gave them to him off the back of the chair. 'You'd better change quick.'

He changed in the dark hall that led down to the dayroom door at the bottom of the stairs and was soon back at the fire in his dry shirt and trousers. He towelled his face, then the back of his neck, then his feet. He pulled on socks and a pair of boots he didn't bother to lace.

'A terrible night,' he muttered at the fire. 'Not fit for a dog to be out in.'

'In what direction were you?' Elizabeth asked.

'Round be Derrada,' he answered.

He disliked talking about his police work in the house. He only answered Elizabeth because he needed to talk.

'And you'd never guess who I met?' he went reluctantly on.

'Who?'

'The bastard Quirke.'

'The Superintendent!' Her exclamation seemed a faint protest against the coarseness. 'What had him out, do you think?'

'He was lukin' for a chance he didn't get, you can be sure!'

He began to recount the clash, speaking with a slow, gloating passion and constant mimicry.

'He stopped in front of me and pulled down the window and asked, "Is that you, Reegan?"

' "That's me, sir," says I.

' "And is there some trouble?"

' "No, sir," says I.

' "And what has you out on a night like this?"

' "I'm out on patrol, sir," says I.

' "But are you mad, Reegan? Are you stone mad? No man in his senses would be out cycling on a night like this without grave reason. Good God, Reegan, don't you realize that all rules and regulations yield at a certain point to human discretion? Do you want to get your death, man, cycling about on a night like this?"

' "Aye, aye, sir," says I. "But I'll not get the sack, sir." '

No word was lost on the children who pretended to be busy with their exercises. It was an old feud between their father and Superintendent Quirke. They loved this savage mimicry and it frightened them. They heard him laugh fiendishly, 'That shuk him! That's what tuk the wind outa his sails! That's what shut him up, believe me!'

Then he repeated Quirke in a high, squeaky voice, the accent so outrageously exaggerated that it no longer resembled anything human.

' "Even regulations, Reegan, must yield at a certain point to human discretion – even the law! – even the law, Reegan! – must yield at a certain point to Human Discretion." '

'But you're only causing annoyance and trouble for yourself,' Elizabeth interrupted. 'You'll be only bringing him the more down on you. For the sake of a few words couldn't you let it go with him? What does it all matter?'

'You mean it'll be all the same in the end?' he asked shrewdly. 'We'll be all nice and quiet when we're dead and gone – and nothin'll matter then? Is that it?'

She did not answer. She felt she could care no longer. She knew he'd go his own way, he'd heed no one, opposition would make him only more determined.

'You never give a thought for anybody,' spun angrily over in her mind but she did not speak it. She feared she still loved him, and he seemed to care hardly at all, as if he had married a housekeeper. She watched him pull the jumper she had knitted for him over his head and draw on his old tunic, leaving the collar unclasped at the throat, the silver buckle on the belt swinging loosely on its black catches. It was more than four years now since she'd first met him, when she was home on convalescence from the London Hospital, worn out after nursing through the Blitz. She had come to the barracks to get some of her papers put in order. He happened to be on his own in the dayroom when she came. It was twelve, for the Angelus had rung as she left her bicycle against the barrack wall.

'It must have been a terror there in London durin' the bombin'?' he had asked, a conventional thing to ask anyone who had been there at the time and she smiled back the equally conventional, 'You get used to it after a time. You go on almost as if nothing was happening after the first few scares.'

'It's like a fella hangin', I suppose,' he laughed. 'He hasn't much of a choice. But what amazes me, though, is that one of those rich Americans didn't run off with a girl like you on us.'

She blushed hot at the flattery. He seemed so handsome to her in his blue uniform. He came to the door to see her out. She saw him watch from the barrack window as she cycled out the short avenue and turned left up the village.

The desire for such a day could drag one out of a sickness, it was so true to the middle of the summer. She felt so full of longing and happiness that she crossed from the shop to the chapel when she'd got the groceries for the house. The eternal medals and rosary beads were waiting on the spikes of the gate for whoever had lost them; the evergreens did not even sway in their sleep in the churchyard, where bees droned between the graves from dandelion to white clover; and the laurelled path between the brown flagstones looked so worn smooth that she felt she was walking on them again with her bare feet of school confession evenings through the summer holidays.

The midday glare was dimmed within, the church as cool as the stone touch of its holy water font, but she could get herself to say no formal prayer, all her habits and acceptances lost in an impassioned tumult of remembering.

A cart was rocking past on the road when she came out, its driver sunk deep in the hay on top of the load, a straw hat pulled down over his face. The way his body rolled to every rock and sway of the cart he could have been asleep in the sunshine. The reins hung slack. A cloud of flies swarmed about the mare's head and her black coat was stained with sweat all along the lines of the harness, but they rolled on as if they had eternity for their journey.

Whether he was ashamed or not to pass the shops so sleepily in the broad middle of the day, he started awake at the chapel gate and noticed Elizabeth.

'Powerful weather we're havin',' he shouted down, and it came to her as a prayer of praise, she never had such longing to live for ever.

She was helping her mother and brother on their small farm then, and they had opposed her marriage to Reegan from the beginning.

'There's three childer and his wife is barely cauld in the grave, remember. That's no aisy house to be walkin' into! An' what'll the neighbours say about it? Himself can be no angel neither, not if quarter of the accounts be true,' her brother had said one autumn night in the kitchen while their mother stirred the coals on the hearth and supported him by her half-silence.

'Take heed to what he says! Marryin' isn't something, believe me, that can be jumped into today and outa tomorrow. It's wan bed you have to sleep on whether it's hard or soft, wance you make it. An' remember, as he tauld you, it's no aisy house to be walkin' into, but I'm sayin' nothin'. It's for your God above to direct you!'

Elizabeth knew it would have suited them if she had stayed, stayed to nurse her crippled mother, the mother who had seemed so old when she died three months ago that not even her children had wept at the funeral, she meant as little as a flower that has withered in a vase behind curtains through the winter when it's discovered and lifted out on a day in spring.

And it would have suited her brother who'd never marry if she had to stop and keep house for him, but she did not stop. She married Reegan. She was determined to grasp at a life of her own desiring, no longer content to drag through with her repetitive days, neither happy nor unhappy, merely passing them in the wearying spirit of service; and the more the calls of duty tried to tie her down to this life the more intolerably burdened it became.

She'd not stay on this small farm among the hills, shut away from living by its pigsties and byres and the rutted lane that twisted out to the road between stone walls. She would marry Reegan, or she'd go back to London if she could ever forget the evening she came away from the operating theatre with Sister Murphy.

'I lit three candles today in St Anne's before the Blessed Virgin,' the frail Sister had said.

'Are you praying for something special? Or is there something worrying you, Brigid?' Elizabeth asked out of politeness.

'If I tell you, you'll not mention it to anybody, will you?'

'No. Why should I want to? But, maybe then it might be better not to tell me at all . . .'

'But you'll not mention it to anybody?'

'No! No!'

'I am praying to Her to send me a man – some nice, decent person.'

Elizabeth stared at her in astonishment, but this frail woman of more than fifty had never been more serious in her life. She had blurted it out with such sudden, confiding joy. It seemed obscene for a minute; yet, when Elizabeth thought, the desire itself was not ludicrous, no more than a young girl's, but only the ferocious ruthlessness of life had made it in time seem so. Hardly fifteen years separated the two women. Elizabeth had blanched before this vision of herself growing old and blind with the pain of ludicrous longing. She had few hesitations about marrying and she believed she loved Reegan. The children weren't hostile, even if they'd remained somewhat reserved. And for a time she was happy, extremely happy at first.

When Reegan had his clothes changed he felt new and clean before the fire, drowsily tired after miles of pedalling through the rain. He was in high good humour as he pulled his chair up to his meal on the table, but he wasn't easy until he had asserted himself against Elizabeth's, 'Couldn't you let it go for once with the Superintendent? You'll be only bringing him down on top of you?'

'When we're dead it'll be all the same,' he asserted. 'But bejasus we're not altogether in that state yet! It's still God for us all and may the devil take the hindmost. Isn't that right, Willie?'

Elizabeth said nothing. She gathered up his wet clothes and put them to dry. She listened to him talk with the three children.

'What did ye learn at school today?'

They were puzzled, nothing new or individual coming to their minds out of the long, grey rigmarole that had been drummed all day in school, one dry fact the same as the next.

'English, Irish . . .' Willie began, hesitant.

'And sums,' continued Reegan, laughing. 'Shure that tells nothin'. Did ye learn anything new? Did ye learn anything that ye didn't know yesterday?'

He saw by the boy's embarrassment that he'd be able to tell him nothing, so he turned to the girls, almost clumsily kind, 'Can the lassies tell me anything when this great fool of ours only goes to school to recreate himself?'

Neither could they think of anything. They had experienced nothing. All they'd heard was fact after fact. That nine nines were eighty-one. That the London they didn't know was built on the Thames they didn't know.

'Shure ye might as well be stoppin' at home and be givin' Elizabeth here a hand about the house,' he teased, rather gently, a merriment in his blue eyes.

'Do ye know why ye go to school at all?'

'To learn,' Willie ventured again, with renewed courage.

'To learn what?'

'Lessons.'

Reegan laughed. He felt a great sense of his superiority, not so much over the children, he took that for granted, but over everyone who had anything to do with them.

'You'll never get wit, Willie! Were you never tauld that you go to school to learn to think for yourself and not give two tuppenny curses for what anybody else is thinkin'?'

'And a lot of good that'd do them,' Elizabeth put in dryly; it shook Reegan, then amused him.

'A lot of good it did for any of us,' he laughed.

'We might as well have been learnin' our facts and figures and come out in every other way just as God sent us in — as long as we learned how to bow the knee and kiss the ring. If we had to learn how to do that we were right bejasus! And we'd have all got on like a house on fire! Isn't that right, Elizabeth?'

'That's perfectly right,' she agreed, glad he was happy.

He made the sign of the cross as he finished his meal. He'd never known mental prayer, so his lips shaped the words of the Grace as he repeated them to himself. He sat facing the fire again, beginning to feel how intimate he'd been with them ever since he came into the house tonight, his mind still hot after the clash with Quirke, and he fiercely wanted to be separate and alone again. The pain and frustration that the shame of intimacy brings started to nag him to desperation. He didn't want to talk any more, nor even read the newspaper. He would have to go down to Casey in the dayroom before ten and fill his report into the Patrol Book, but that could wait its turn. All he wanted now was to lounge before the fire and lose himself in the fantastic flaming of the branches: how they spat or leaped or burst in a shower of sparks, changing from pale red to white to shifting copper, taking on shapes as strange as burning cities. The children's steel nibs scratched in the silence when Elizabeth wasn't moving. She knew the mood he was in and lingered over the little jobs tonight, stirring the porridge for the morning and watching the cake brown in the oven, putting off the time when she'd take her darning or library book and sit with him, when the drowsy boredom of the hours before bedtime would begin.

Down the hallway the dayroom door opened and Casey's iron-shod boots rang on the cement. They thought he might be rushing out again into the rain for a bucket of turf, but the even, ponderous steps all policemen acquire came towards them in the kitchen. He tapped on the door and waited for the disturbed Reegan's, 'Come in', before he entered. He was over six feet, as tall as Reegan, but bald, and his face had the waxen pallor of candles. The eyes alone were bright, though all surface, without any resting-place. He carried the heavy Patrol Book under his arm.

'God bless all here,' he greeted.

'And you too, Ned,' they returned.

Reegan was glad of the disturbance. Minutes ago he'd wanted nothing but to be left alone, but he was more than glad by this time to be disturbed out of broodings that were becoming more lonely and desperate. He pulled his own chair to one side, eager to make room at the fire.

'Don't trouble to move yourself, Sergeant,' Casey assured, 'I'll work me way in all right, don't you worry. I just thought that if I carted you up the book it'd save you the trouble of comin' down.'

'That's powerful,' Reegan praised. 'I'd be down long ago only I couldn't tear meself away from the fire here.'

'And small blame to you! The devil himself wouldn't venture down to that joint on a night like this. I stuffed a few auld coats against the butt of the door but the draughts still go creepin' up the legs of yer britches like wet rats.

'God's truth,' he continued, 'I was gettin' the willies down there on me own: lukin' at the same bloody wonders all the evenin' in the fire and expectin' to be lifted outa me standin' at any minute be the phone!'

Then suddenly he felt he was complaining too much about himself and stopped and tried to turn the conversation with all the awkwardness of over-consciousness.

'And tell me, did you meet anything strange or startlin' on your travels, Sergeant?'

'Aye!' Reegan tried to joke. 'I met something all right – whether you can call it strange or startlin' or not is another matter.'

He was attempting a levity he didn't feel, it left greater feeling of anger and frustration behind it than violent speech.

'What did you meet with, Sergeant?'

'Did you ever hear of His Imperial Majesty, John James Quirke? Did you?'

'Jay,' Casey exclaimed in real amazement. 'You never met the Super, did you? What was takin' him out on an evenin' like this?'

Reegan began to recount the clash; and it had become more extravagant, more comic and vicious since the first telling. When he finished he shouted, 'That shuk him, believe me! That's what tuk the wind outa his sails!' and as he shouted he tried to catch Casey's face unaware, trying to read into his mind.

'Bejay, Sergeant, but he'll have it in for us from this on. He'll do nothing but wait his chance. You can sit on that for certain comfort. As sure as there's a foot on a duck, Sergeant!'

'But what do I care? Why should I care about the bastard?' Reegan ground back.

Elizabeth drifted from between them. She gathered the sagging fire together and heaped on fresh wood. The blast of heat on her face made her sway with sleep. She felt how ill she was – and still Reegan's voice stabbed into the quiet of the big barrack kitchen, harsh with mockery and violence.

She lifted the kettle and filled it from the bucket of spring water on the scullery table, cold and damp there, the table littered with cabbage leaves and the peelings of turnips that she'd been too tired to tidy away; if anything, the rain drummed more heavily on the low roof – sometimes it seemed as if it might never cease, the way it beat down in these western nights. She replaced the old raincoat of the children's against the bottom of the door as she came in and lowered the kettle so that it hung full in the flames.

Soon it would start to murmur over the blazing fire, then break into a steady hum, as if into song. She saw the lamplight, so softly golden on the dark blinds that were drawn against the night. And she could have cried out at Reegan for some peace.

Were their days not sufficiently difficult to keep in order as they were without calling in disaster? Quirke had the heavy hand of authority behind him and Reegan could only ruin himself. And if he got the sack! What then? What then?

Her women's days had no need of change. They were full and too busy, wanting nothing but to be loved. There was the shrill alarm clock at eight in the barracks morning and the raking of the ashes over the living coals close to midnight: between these two instants, as between tides, came the retreating nights of renewal and the chores of the days on which her strength was spent again, one always unfinished and two more eternally waiting, yet so colourless and small that only on a reel of film projected slowly could they be separated and named; and as no one noticed them they were never praised.

She cleared her throat as she stooped over the fire, reached for the hankie in the fold of her sleeve. It wasn't there. She spat softly, without thinking. The mucus hissed against the hot ashes. She shuddered as a tiny mushroom of the pale timber ash drifted up. How she'd always hated Reegan's spitting on the floor, then trying to rub it into the cement with a drag of his boot! Now she was no better! And to plague her, a vision of herself in London before the war flashed on her mind, a spring Sunday in London, when the light is grey and gentle as anything on earth. She had come out the great black hospital gates, a red tartan scarf thrown back on her shoulder; and turned right, up the marvellous width of Whitechapel Road, away from the crowds milling into the Lane, for it was the morning. Now she was spitting like any common slut in a barrack kitchen. It was with the abjection of a beaten animal that she lifted her knitting and sat down close to Casey and the three children, who had finished their exercises and come into the circle about the fire.

Reegan sat at the table, filling his report into the Patrol Book. They were silent as he wrote till Casey asked the children:

'Ye're finished the auld lessons?'

'All's finished,' they told him quietly.

'And ye have them all off?'

'Aye.'

'Well, that's the way to be. Be able to puzzle the schoolmaster.'

'I wouldn't be sure they're that well known,' said Elizabeth.

'Well, you'll get nothin' without the learnin' these days. Pass the exams. That's what gets people on. That and swindlin'. I didn't do much of either meself. More's the pity. And signs are on it!'

They laughed at Casey's rueful grin. He brought a wonderful ease with him sometimes into the house, the black hands of the clock would take wings. They loved to sit with him at the fire, listening to the talk, feeling the marvellous minutes melt like sweetness in the mouth for ever.

Reegan wrote quickly at the table, to the well-practised formula, and only when he came to describe the weather had he to pause. He wasn't sure of the wind's direction. He remembered catching his breath at the way it clawed at his face and chest as he turned downhill from Ardcare; and then a mile farther on of the same straight road it came behind him, making the bicycle shift like a boat in full sail, its course warped in some way by the solid beech trees behind the demesne wall.

'What way is the wind blowin', Ned? Is it from the south-west?'

'About that,' Casey pondered to answer. 'It was comin' from Moran's Bay when I was out for the turf. It seems about the only direction it knows how to blow from,' he added with a dry laugh.

Reegan was satisfied and turned back to finish his report but the wind's direction continued to amuse Casey.

'Where does the south-west wind come from, William Reegan?' he asked in the tones of a pompous schoolmaster.

'From the Atlantic Ocean,' Willie entered into the game, all the children's faces, and even Elizabeth's bright at the clown's face Casey had on for the performance.

'Very good, young Reegan! And can you tell me now what it gathers on its long journey across the oceans?'

'It gathers moisture,' Willie choked.

'Very right, my boy! I see you are one boy who comes to school to learn something other than villainy and rascality. And then as I have repeated day-in, day-out, while the hairs of me head turned grey, it strikes against the mountains, rises to a great height, and pisses down on the poor unfortunates who earn their daily bread by the sweat of their brows in this holy, catholic, and apostolic country of Ireland.'

There was a stifled roar of laughter as Reegan wrote, frowning to keep his concentration.

'You're a terrible man, Ned,' chaffed Elizabeth.

'But it's the God's truth!' he protested. 'You know what Cromwell said: Get roasted alive in hell or drownded and perished in Connaught.'

Naturally timid, the little comic success seemed to release him from the burden of himself. Everything was relaxed and easy as Reegan closed the Patrol Book and pulled his chair in among them, but even so Casey shirked asking for Una to spend the night with his wife, and he'd have to ask soon or it would be too late. Reegan could be moody and strange. At any time he might resent this constant call on Una. A refusal could shatter Casey's ease of mind for the whole night. His nervous fear came out in the painfully roundabout, 'The Missus was wonderin' if it'd be all right for Una to come up with me when I'm goin' up for the bit of supper, for to stop the night.'

Tonight he had no cause for fear.

'Shure she can go. But that's the woman's territory. Whatever she says,' deferred Reegan.

Elizabeth had no real say, though this social deference pleased her so, and she tried to catch Reegan's eyes with a smile of gratefulness as she assented, 'She can, of course. Her nightdress is ready there in the press.'

Una couldn't conceal her delight, though she tried. Nor could Sheila conceal her terror of the loneliness in the cold room. Both tried to suppress any expression of their feelings. They knew their places. They were simply pawns. And this world of their father and Casey and Elizabeth was as unknowable to them as the intolerable world of God is to the grown, if they have not dulled their sense of the mystery of life with the business or distractions of the day and the hour. All the two black-haired girls could do was sit there and wait, coming and going as they were willed.

'I don't like troublin' you all the time like this,' Casey shuffled.

Elizabeth stopped it. 'Don't be talkin' foolish. Una thinks she can't get up half quick enough. Isn't that right, Una?'

The dark child smiled and blushed. No more.

'We don't know what we'd do only for Una. We'd be lost. That woman of mine would go off her head if she had to stop all night in that house on her own.'

'And no one would blame her,' Elizabeth managed to end.

Casey's embarrassment was over. He was as happy as he could be. He looked at the clock and it was already nine. He had nothing more to do before he slept, nothing but the repetitions that had become more than his nature. He'd bring Una with him when he went for his supper; kiss his wife at the door when he left again for the barracks a half-hour later: she'd stand with her hand on the edge of the door until she had heard the white gate that led on to the avenue clang behind him, it was her habit. Then the rest of the night was plain sailing: bring down the mattress and blankets from upstairs and make up his bed beneath the phone, lock the door, put the key on the sill, take out his beads to say a decade of the rosary with his few night prayers, set the alarm for the morning, rake the fire, turn down the oil lamp on the wall before he got into bed. He was at least master of these repetitions, they had no power to disturb him, he knew them in his blood; and they ran there like a drug.

'What about a game of cards? It's ages since we had a game,' he said, now that he was no longer troubled. A pack of cards was found behind a statue of St Therese on the sideboard, the folding card-table fixed in the centre of the hearth. The cards were dealt and played. Elizabeth kept the scores on the inside of a torn Gold Flake packet. There was no tension in the play, no stakes, only the children excited as the night was cheated and hurried to its mid-hour.

From the outside the heavy porch door was shouldered open, small stones wedged beneath its bottom grinding on the concrete, the knocker clattering through the barracks. Steps lingered about the door of the dayroom before they came up the hall. They held their hands instinctively upright to listen.

'That's Jim's steps for sure,' Casey said before Brennan knocked and entered.

He was small for a policeman, the bare five feet nine of the regulations, his face thin, and the bones standing out. He looked overcome in the heavy woollen greatcoat.

'A terrible night that's in it,' he said.

'A terrible night.'

The voices echoed him, more or less in unison, the hoarse chant of a prayer.

'I saw the light turned low in the dayroom. I was thinkin' ye'd all be here.'

And he left his flashlamp down on the window-sill, his greatcoat and cap on the pedal sewing-machine just beneath. There was no further need of the cards. They were raked up and the green table lifted out.

'You let no grass grow under ye feet tonight, Jim?' he was asked, for it wasn't yet ten, and it was always later than ten when the policemen came to make their reports and sign themselves out for the night.

'I was makin' a bird cradle all the evenin' with the lads,' he explained. 'We just managed to make it a minute ago there. So I thought it might be as well to face out for here at wance and be finished with it for the night.'

They could see him on his knees in the kitchen of their rooms across the river, most of his eight children gathered round, building the cradle out of sallies and the cement-coloured rods of elder. When the snow came they'd set it on the street. And all through the hard weather they'd have cold thrushes and blackbirds.

'We got a great strong cradle med,' he added. 'None better in Ireland!'

The others smiled, Brennan's intense pride in everything that came into his possession was a barrack joke, it was artless as a child's.

'The best woman in Ireland to get a bargain,' he'd say when his wife came from town on a shopping Saturday; and when he came home himself with the little yellowed bundle of Early York in spring, the plants still knotted in their ragged belt of straw, he had already, 'A hundred of the best heads of cabbage in Ireland. Without question or doubt!'

'And how is Mrs Brennan's cold?' asked Elizabeth quietly.

'She's still coughin' away. A fierce rasp in her chest. But nothin'll get that woman of mine to stay up in bed,' he complained proudly.

'She'd be wiser to stop. Is she takin' anything for it?'

'She rubs on a bit of Vick at night. That's all I ever see her do. She always says a cauld has to run its course.'

'The bed's the only man,' advised Casey. 'It's the only place you can keep your temperature even. She needn't think that she can't be done without – the very best of us can be done without. So she's as well to take it aisy. Time and tide, they say, waits for no man, nor woman neither.'

It was the end, this litany of truisms, draining away whatever little life the conversation ever had. In the way women are so quick to sense, Elizabeth knew it was the time to do things. She got cups and saucers from the dresser, bread from the white enamelled bread box, tea out of a paper bag on the mantelpiece. They took the cups in their hands at the fire, and a plate of buttered soda bread was passed about.

Mullins came as they were eating. He was no older than the others, but red and swollen, a raw smell of porter on his breath, though he appeared more depressed than tipsy.

'A wild night!' he said. 'It seems I'm the last of the Mohicans.'

'But the last shall be first, remember,' Casey couldn't resist quoting. With his weak laugh it came like a sneer of derision. Mullins stiffened at the door with resentment.

'Aye!' he answered inarticulately back. 'And the first might be last.'

'Don't be standin' there, John. There's a cup of tea just waiting for you,' Elizabeth urged.

She pulled out a chair and Reegan, who had been taking less and less part in the conversation, just lying in a bored stupor in the chair, laughed, 'It's not who's first or last counts in this house. It's to be in time for the tay. That's what counts. And you couldn't have timed it nicer, John!' as the ungainly old policeman sat down.

It took all the hatred that the gibe brought. Mullins laughed so tipsily that the cup rocked over and back on his saucer.

'Bejasus!' he swore. 'It seems I med it on the eleventh hour, surely.'

Reegan began to tell his clash with Quirke to Brennan and Mullins, Casey forced to listen again; and the tones of violence had now taken the resonance of a constant theme repeating itself through the evening.

They listened nervously to his frustration and spleen wear itself to the end of its telling. When he finished Mullins burst out in drunken passion that, 'They can't ride roughshod over us these days. Them days are gone. They can try it on. But that's all – bejasus!'

'You'd be surprised what they can do,' Casey argued with unusual conviction. 'Things don't change that quick. They might luk different, that's all. But if you *wance* cross them they'll get rid of you, no matter whether they can or they can't. They'll find ways and means, don't worry. Who do you think the Chief Super's goin' to stand up for? For John Mullins or Mr Quirke? Power, let me tell you, always stands up for power.'

'But what do I care? What the hell do I care?' Reegan shouted and it was another argument.

Examples began to be quoted, old case histories dragged up for it to end as it began – with nothing proven, no one's convictions altered in any way, it becoming simply the brute clash of ego against ego, any care for tolerance or meaning or truth ground under their blind passion to dominate. And the one trophy they all had to carry away was a gnawing resentment of each other's lonely and passing world.

Even that resentment went quickly as a sudden liking can when Brennan steered the antagonism to a safe stop against the boy, 'What does young Willie think of all this? Will he join the Force when he grows up?'

'Not if he has any sense in his skull,' Reegan intervened. He spoke with the hotness of argument. The others were cooled and tired of it now.

'But do you think will he be the measurement?' Casey asked, preferring to ignore the challenge.

'We'll have to put a stone on his head, that's what we'll have to do soon with the way he's growin' up on us,' Mullins said kindly and then he laughed. 'But I'm afraid he'll never be *thick* enough.'

'Thirty-six inches across the chest, Willie, and a yard thick with solid ignorance like the fella from Connemara; then five feet nine inches against the wall in your stockin' feet and you're right for the Force, Willie. All the requirements laid down by the regulations.'

The pun was a favourite that never grew worn, always bringing back to them the six months they spent training in the Depot when they were nineteen or twenty, in the first days of the Irish Free State.

The British had withdrawn. The Capital was in a fever of excitement and change. New classes were forming, blacksmiths and clerks filling the highest offices in the turn of an hour. Some who had worried how their next loaf or day might come were attending ceremonial functions. There was a brand new tricolour to wave high; a language of their own to learn; new anthems of faith-and-fatherland to beat on the drum of the multitude; but most of all, unseen and savage behind these floral screens, was the struggle for the numbered seats of power.

These police recruits walking the Phoenix Park in the evenings, or on the lighted trams that went down past Phibsboro' to the music halls, what were their dreams? They knew that lightning promotion could come to the favoured. They saw the young girls stand to watch them from the pavements as they marched to Mass on Sunday mornings.

Now they sat and remembered, thirty years later, waiting to go to their homes in the rain.

'Some of the auld drill sergeants were a terror,' Casey comically mused as if he was enjoying bitterness itself. 'Do ye remember By Garrup?'

'Ah, Jasus,' Mullins swore. 'As if any mortal could forget him . . .

'"By Garrup, look at the creel of turf on Mullins's back," he used to roar, the auld bastard! "You're not on the bog now, Mullins – By Garrup! Head to the front! Right wheel! Chests out! Ye're not carryin' yeer auld dyin' grandmothers up the stairs on yeers backs now, By Garrup! Mark time! Lift the knees!"

'Oh, the auld bastard,' Mullins roared. They all joined him, loving few things better than these caricatures. The night that had hung about them like a responsibility seemed now too short, it was nearly wasted now and it seemed to be so quickly on the march.

'Do you mind Spats at the law classes,' Casey continued. 'The concate of the boyo!

'"A legal masterpiece, gentlemen of the jury, is the proper distribution of the proper quantity of ink on the proper number of white pages. That, gentlemen, is simply, solely and singularly the constitution of any masterpiece."'

'But wasn't he said to be wan of the cleverest men in Ireland?' Brennan interrupted suddenly. 'Wasn't he a BA and a barrister?'

The interruption annoyed Casey intensely. He had been a conductor for a few months on the Dublin trams before joining the police.

'A barrister! What's a barrister? A chancer of the first water,' he derided. 'Hundreds of them are walkin' round Dublin without a sole on their shoes. They'd hardly have even their tram fare!'

'But don't some of them make more than £5,000 a year?'

'Yes – some of them! – many are called, James, but few are chosen, as you and I should know at this stage of our existence,' Casey quoted in such a funereal and sanctified tone that it left no doubt about what he thought of Brennan's offering.

Brennan had been silent till then. He was a poor mimic. Neither could he sing. He had often tried, patrolling the roads alone, but catching the flat tones of his own voice he'd grow embarrassed and silent again. He envied Casey and Mullins their flow of talk, their ability to shine in company, and he did not know that those content to listen are rarest of all. He felt bored to distraction at having to sit silent for so long. He was determined to get a foothold in the conversation.

'Isn't it strange,' he said, 'that with all the men that ever went into the Depot none of them were exactly six feet?'

'That's right,' Mullins asserted. 'No man ever born was exactly six feet. It's because Jesus Christ was exactly six feet and no man since could be the same height. That's why it's supposed to be!'

He had taken the words out of Brennan's mouth, who twisted on the chair with annoyance and frustration.

'I often heard that,' Elizabeth joined, more to counteract Reegan's bored restlessness and silence than any wish of her own to speak.

'It's like the Blessed Virgin and Original Sin,' Brennan rushed out again and went on to quote out of the Catechism. *'The Blessed Virgin Mary by a singular privilege of grace was preserved free from original sin and that privilege is called her Immaculate Conception.'*

'Six feet is the ideal height for a man,' Mullins asserted again. 'Anything bigger is gettin' too big. While anything smaller is gettin' too small. It's the ideal height for a man.'

'Kelly, the Boy from Killann,' said Casey, 'was seven feet with some inches to spare.

'Seven feet was his height with some inches to spare
And he looked like a king in command,'

he quoted out of the marching song.

There was immediate feeling of blasphemy. The song connected up with Jesus Christ, though Casey had meant no harm, he said it just because it happened into his head and he'd decided to say something. In the subsequent uneasiness the time was noticed. It was five to eleven.

'There'll be murder,' Casey jumped. 'That woman of mine'll be expectin' me for this past hour.'

He put on his cap and coat in the dayroom. Elizabeth hurried Una so that she was waiting for him at the door. She wore wellingtons and had the parcel of her nightdress clasped inside her blue raincoat.

'It's time for any respectable man to be makin' home,' either Brennan or Mullins said and they went down to sign the books and left almost on the others' heels.

Reegan rose from the fire and pulled back the circle of chairs. His hair was tousled from scratching it with sleep, the collar of the tunic still unclasped, his feet loose in the boots.

'It's a good cursed job that those don't decide to come up many nights,' he complained. His face was ugly with resentment.

'Oh, it wasn't so much harm, was it?' Elizabeth pleaded. 'The nights are often long enough on us.'

'But were you listenin' to that rubbish? – Jesus Christ and Kelly, the Boy from Killann. Sufferin' duck, but did you hear that rubbish?'

He was shouting. Elizabeth had to gather herself together before answering quietly, 'It's only a saying that He was six feet tall. Does it matter very much? Did you never hear it?'

'Of course I heard it,' he cried, beside himself. 'I'm not deaf, unfortunately. If you listened long enough to everything said around here you'd soon hear the Devil himself talkin'.'

Then he grew quieter and said without passion, as if brooding, 'Surely you're not gettin' like the rest of them, girl?'

She drew closer. She felt herself no longer a woman growing old. She wasn't conscious of herself any more, of whatever beauty had been left her any more than her infirmities, for she was needed.

'No, but does it matter what they say?' she said. 'Hadn't the night to pass?'

The night had to pass, but not in that manner, was how he reacted. He turned towards the radio that stood on a small shelf of its own, some bills and letters scattered beside its wet battery, between the sideboard and curtained medicine press.

'Such rubbish to have to listen to,' he muttered. 'And in front of the childer . . . And the same tunes night-in, night-out, the whole bloody year round.'

He switched on the radio. The Sweepstake programme was ending. To soft music a honeyed voice was persuading, 'It makes no difference where you are – You can wish upon a star.'

It should all make you want to cry. You were lonely. The night was dark and deep. You must have some wish or longing. The life you lead, the nine to five at the office, the drudgery of a farm, the daily round, cannot be endured without hope.

'So now before you sleep make up your mind to buy a Sweepstake ticket and the first prize of £50,000 out of a total of £200,000 in prizes on this year's Grand National may be yours.'

The music rose for the young night. It was Venice, the voice intoned. There was moonlight on the sleeping canals as the power of longing was given full sway. A boy and a girl drift in their boat. There is a rustle of silken music from the late-night taverns. They clasp each other's hands in the boat. The starlight is in her hair and his face is lifted to hers in the moonlight. He is singing softly and his voice drifts across the calm water. It is Venice and their night of love . . .

In spite of themselves they felt half-engulfed by this induced flood of sentimentality and sick despair. Reegan switched it off as the speaking voice faded for a baritone to ease the boy's song of love into the music. The house was dead still.

'The news is long over,' he said. 'Are ye all ready for the prayers? We should have them said ages ago.'

He took a little cloth purse from his watch pocket and let the beads run into his palm. He put a newspaper down on the cement and knelt with his elbows on the table, facing his reflection in the sideboard mirror.

Elizabeth's and the children's beads were kept in an ornamental white vase on the dresser. Willie climbed on a chair to get them from the top shelf. Elizabeth's beads were a Franciscan brown, their own pale mother-of-pearl with silver crosses that they'd been given for their First Communion.

They blessed themselves together and he began:

'*Thou, O Lord, will open my lips*',

'*And my tongue shall announce Thy praise*,' they responded.

They droned into the *Apostles' Creed*. Then *Our Fathers* and *Hail Marys* and *Glory be to the Fathers* were repeated over and over in their relentless monotony, without urge or passion, no call of love or answer, the voices simply murmuring away in a habit or death, their minds not on what they said, but blank or wandering or dreaming over their own lives.

Elizabeth's fingers slipped heedlessly along the brown beads. No one noticed that she'd said eleven Hail Marys in her decade. She had tried once or twice to shake herself to attention and had lapsed back again.

She felt tired and sick, her head thudding, and she put her hands to her breasts more than once in awareness of the cysts there. She knelt with her head low between her elbows in the chair, changing position for any distraction, the words she repeated as intrusive as dust in her mouth while the pain of weariness obtruded itself over everything that made up her consciousness.

She knew she must see a doctor, but she'd known that months before, and she had done nothing. She'd first discovered the cysts last August as she dried herself at Malone's Island, a bathing-place in the lake, not more than ten minutes through the meadows; and she remembered her fright and incomprehension when she touched the right breast again with the towel and how the noise of singing steel from the sawmill in the woods pierced every other sound in the evening.

What the doctor would do was simple. He'd send her for a biopsy. She might be told the truth or she might not when they got the result back, depending on them and on herself. If she had cancer she'd be sent for treatment. She had been a nurse. She had no illusions about what would happen.

She had been only away from the house once since she was married. She shuddered at how miserable she'd been those three days, the first blight on her happiness.

A cousin had invited her to her wedding in Dublin. She'd no desire to go, but that she had been remembered so surprised her with delight that she told them about the letter at the dinner hour.

'You might as well take the chance when you get it. It mightn't be offered again. It'd be a break for you. It'd take you out of yourself for a few days,' she was pressed to go.

'But look at the cost! The train fare. The hotel. A wedding present for Nuala. And how on earth would I get past those shop windows full of things without spending every penny we have?' she laughed.

'Never you mind, girl. If the money's wanted it'll be always found,' Reegan said.

'Why don't you go, Elizabeth, when you get the chance?' Willie asked wonderingly.

'Who'd look after the place while I was away, Willie?'

'That's a poor excuse,' Reegan said. 'There's no fear of the auld barracks takin' flight while you're away, though more's the pity!'

'And what if some one ran away with you when I was gone?' she asked flirtatiously.

'Not a fear, girl,' he laughed. 'Every dog for his day but you, you girl, it's your day.'

She was flattered and satisfied. She would not go. Here they had need of her. What would she be at the wedding? A seat at the bottom of the breakfast-table, a relative who had married a widower in the country, a parable to those who had known her as a young girl.

'I think you should go, Elizabeth. I'd go if I was in your place, definitely,' Willie persuaded with obstinate persistence.

'But who'd cook and wash and bake and sew, Willie?'

'We would, Elizabeth. We'd stop from school in turn. We could buy loaves . . .'

'You only think you could, Willie,' she tried to laugh it off nervously.

'We'd manage somehow,' he enthused, heedless of his child's place in the house, he gestured excitedly with his hands and went on too quickly to be stopped.

'I think you'd be foolish to miss Dublin. Not many people ever get to Dublin. For the few days we'd be well able to manage. Shure, Elizabeth, didn't we manage for ages before you ever came?'

It fell as natural as a blessing, 'Didn't we manage for ages before you ever came?' And they'd manage, too, if she was gone. She stood with the shock. She must have been holding something for she remembered not to let it fall. Then she broke down.

She thought she'd never be able to climb the stairs to her room, the things of the house gathering in against her; she thanked God that the dayroom door wasn't open on her way.

She heard Reegan shout in the kitchen.

'Now do you see what you have done? Now do you see what you have done? Jesus Christ, can you not keep your mouth shut for wan minute of the day?'

Then the boy's terrified protest, 'I didn't mean anything! I didn't mean any harm, Daddy.'

Reegan's shouts again, 'Will you never understand? Will you never grow up? Will you never understand that women look on things different to men?'

She heard his feet follow her on the hollow stairs. She was sitting on the bed's edge when he came into the room. She could not lift her head. He'd look as unreal as all people pleading.

'The lad meant nothing. He was only thinkin' that we'd be able to give you a holiday at last. Shure you know yourself that we'd never be able to get on without you?'

He put his hands on her shoulders, she'd no wish to create a scene, she dried her face with her sleeve.

'I couldn't help it,' she said, looking at him with a nervous smile. 'But it doesn't matter. It was only that it came so sudden.'

'Would you like to go to the wedding? The lad was only wantin' to please you.'

'Maybe, I should go,' she had tried to look bright. She had not wanted to go. It had been simply easier to go than to stay then.

She felt the pain at last was easing. The rosary was droning to its end in the kitchen.

The decades were over. Reegan was sing-songing,

> Mystical Rose
> Tower of David
> Tower of Ivory
> House of Gold.

His face a mask without expression, staring as if tranced at its image in the big sideboard mirror, his fingers even now instinctively moving on the beads, the voice completely toneless that repeated Her praises, their continual 'Pray for us', like punctuating murmurs of sleep.

'The Dedication of the Christian Family,' began the last prayers, the trimmings.

Prayer for the Canonization of Blessed Oliver Plunkett – whose scorched head, they remembered reading on the leaflet, was on show in a church in Drogheda.

Prayers for all they were bound to pray for in duty, promise or charity.

Prayer for a happy death.

And the last prayer, the last terrible acknowledgment, the long iambic stresses relentlessly sledged:

O Jesus, I must die, I know not where nor when nor how, but if I die in mortal sin I go to hell for all eternity.

The newspapers were lifted, the beads and chairs returned to their places. They heard Casey come back from his supper. 'Rush! Rush!' Reegan said to the boy and girl. 'Off to bed! Ye'll be asleep all day in school tomorrow if you don't rush.'

Some red bricks had been set to warm at the fire. Willie slipped them into a pair of heavy woollen socks with the tongs. He lit the candles in their tin holders and they were ready to be kissed good night.

Sheila ran to Elizabeth. Reegan was sitting in front of the fire and the boy went close up to him, between his open knees. Hands came on his shoulders.

'Good night, Willie. God guard you.'

'Good night, Daddy.'

He lifted the hot bricks and said at the door, 'Good night, Elizabeth.'

'Good night, Willie.'

At last they were in the hall, their fluttering candles lighting up the darkness. Casey was coming down the stairs, a pile of the dark grey police blankets in his arms, the top and bottom edges braided with official green thread. He had to feel out his steps very carefully because of his load. They waited on him at the foot of the stairs with the candles.

'Ye're off to bed,' he said. 'Hot bricks and all to keep ye warm.'

'Good night, Guard Casey,' they answered simply.

He turned to them laughing, the whiteness of his bald head thrust over the pile of blankets into their candlelight.

> 'Good night,
> Sleep tight,
> And mind the fleas don't bite,'

he recited.

They smiled with polite servility, but it was the end of the night, and his pleasantness went through them like a shiver of cold. They watched him cruelly as he shaped sideways to manoeuvre his load of blankets through the dayroom door. They took his place on the stairs, the paint completely worn away in the centre of the steps, and even the wood shredding and a little hollowed by years of feet. They climbed without speaking a word. When they got near the top they could see their images with candles and bricks mounting into the night on the black shine of the window. It was directly at the head of the stairs, facing out on the huge sycamore between the house and the river. There was no sign of moon or star, only two children with candles reflected out of its black depth, raindrops slipping down the glass without, where the masses of wind struggled and reeled in the night.

Willie went with Sheila into her room. On nights like these they were never at ease with each other.

'Will you be afraid now, Sheila?' he asked.

'I'll leave the candle lit,' she said.

'And do you want the door open?'

He knew by the way she said 'Aye' that she was almost dumb with fear.

'Well, you want nothing else so?'

An importance had crept into his voice, the situation making him feel and act like a grown person.

'No,' Sheila said. 'Nothing.'

'Well, good night so, Sheila.'

'Good night, Willie.'

Downstairs Elizabeth strained Reegan's barley water into a mug with a little blue circle above its handle. He drank it sitting before the dying fire, blowing at it sometimes, for it was hot. He loved drawing out these last minutes. The thought of Quirke didn't trouble him any more than the thought of his own life and death. All things became remote and far away, speculations that might involve him one day, but they had no power over him now, and these minutes were his rest of peace.

'Is the cat out?' he asked.

'She didn't come in at all tonight,' Elizabeth answered.

'Are the hens shut in?'

'They are.'

'Do you want me to go out for anything?'

'No. There's nothing wanting.'

He rose, put the mug down on the table, and went and bolted the scullery door. She was setting the table for the morning when he came in.

'Don't stay long now,' he said on his way to bed, because she'd found it hard to sleep since she grew uneasy about her breasts, and often sat reading for hours in the stillness after he'd gone, books Willie brought her from the lending library in the school, a few books she'd brought with her from London and kept always locked in her trunk upstairs, books that'd grown in her life as if they'd been grafted there, that she'd sometimes only to handle again to experience blindingly.

'No. I won't be a minute after you. When I rake the fire.'

At the hall door he noticed the intense strained look on her face.

'You look tired out. You're killin' yourself workin' too hard.'

And then he asked as if he had been given vision, 'Are you sure you're feelin' well, girl?'

'Don't be foolish,' she tried to laugh. 'How could I work too hard with the few things that'd have to be done in this house! When I rake the fire I'll be in bed.'

'Don't be long so, that readin' at night'd drive a person crackers,' he said and left for his bed.

She put a few wet sods of turf on the fire, then covered it with ashes. She heard Casey noisily shifting his bed down in the dayroom, soon Reegan's boots clattered overhead on the ceiling and she blew out the lamp and followed him to their room.

'The Country Funeral'

After Fonsie Ryan called his brother he sat in his wheelchair and waited with growing impatience for him to appear on the small stairs and then, as soon as Philly came down and sat at the table, Fonsie moved his wheelchair to the far wall to wait for him to finish. This silent pressure exasperated Philly as he ate.

'Did Mother get up yet?' he asked abruptly.

'She didn't feel like getting up. She went back to sleep after I brought her tea.'

Philly let his level stare rest on his brother but all Fonsie did was to move his wheelchair a few inches out from the wall and then, in the same leaning rocking movement, let it the same few inches back, his huge hands all the time gripping the wheels. With his large head and trunk, he sometimes looked like a circus dwarf. The legless trousers were sewn up below the hips.

Slowly and deliberately Philly buttered the toast, picked at the rashers and egg and sausages, took slow sips from his cup, but his nature was not hard. As quickly as he had grown angry he softened towards his brother.

'Would you be interested in pushing down to Mulligan's after a while for a pint?'

'I have the shopping to do.'

'Don't let me hold you up, then,' Philly responded sharply to the rebuff. 'I'll be well able to let myself out.'

'There's no hurry. I'll wait and wash up. It's nice to come back to a clean house.'

'I can wash these things up. I do it all the time in Saudi Arabia.'

'You're on your holidays now,' Fonsie said. 'I'm in no rush but it's too early in the day for me to drink.'

Three weeks before, Philly had come home in a fever of excitement from the oil fields. He always came home in that high state of fever and it lasted for a few days in the distribution of the presents he always brought home, especially to his mother; his delight looking at her sparse filigreed hair bent over the rug he had brought her, the bright tassels resting on her fingers; the meetings with old school friends, the meetings with neighbours, the buying of rounds and rounds of drinks; his own fever for company after the months at the oil wells and delight in the rounds of celebration blinding him to the poor fact that it is not generally light but shadow that we cast; and now all that fever had subsided to leave him alone and companionless in just another morning as he left the house without further word to Fonsie and with nothing better to do than walk to Mulligan's.

Because of the good weather, many of the terrace doors were open and people sat in the doorways, their feet out on the pavement. A young blonde woman was painting her toenails red in the shadow of a pram in a doorway at the end of the terrace, and she did not look up as he passed. Increasingly people had their own lives here and his homecoming broke the monotony for a few days, and then he did not belong.

As soon as the barman in Mulligan's had pulled his pint he offered Philly the newspaper spread out on the counter that he had been reading.

'Don't you want it yourself?' Philly asked out of a sense of politeness.

'I must have been through it at least twice. I've the complete arse read out of it since the morning.'

There were three other drinkers scattered about the bar nursing their pints at tables.

'There's never anything in those newspapers,' one of the drinkers said.

'Still, you always think you'll come on something,' the barman responded hopefully.

'That's how they get your money,' the drinker said.

Feet passed the open doorway. When it was empty the concrete gave back its own grey dull light. Philly turned the pages slowly and sipped at the pint. The waiting silence of the bar became too close an echo of the emptiness he felt all around his life. As he sipped and turned the pages he resolved to drink no more. The day would be too hard to get through if he had more. He'd go back to the house and tell his mother he was returning early to the oil fields. There were other places he could kill time in. London and Naples were on the way to Bahrain.

'He made a great splash when he came home first,' one of the drinkers said to the empty bar as soon as Philly left. 'He bought rings round him. Now the brother in the wheelchair isn't with him any more.'

'Too much. Too much,' a second drinker added forcefully though it wasn't clear at all to what he referred.

'It must be bad when that brother throws in the towel, because he's a tank for drink. You'd think there was no bottom in that wheelchair.'

The barman stared in silent disapproval at his three customers. There were few things he disliked more than this 'behind-backs' criticism of a customer as soon as he left. He opened the newspaper loudly, staring pointedly out at the three drinkers until they were silent, and then bent his head to travel slowly through the pages again.

'I heard a good one the other day,' one of the drinkers cackled rebelliously. 'The only chance of travel that ever comes to the poor is when they get sick. They go from one state to the other state and back again to base if they're lucky.'

The other two thought this hilarious and one pounded the table with his glass in appreciation. Then they looked towards the barman for approval but he just raised his eyes to stare absently out on the grey strip of concrete until the little insurrection died and he was able to continue travelling through the newspaper again.

Philly came slowly back up the street. The blonde had finished painting her toenails – a loud vermilion – and she leaned the back of her head against a door jamb, her eyes closing as she gave her face and throat completely to the sun. The hooded pram above her outstretched legs was silent. Away, behind the area railings, old men wearing berets were playing bowls, a miniature French flag flying on the railings.

Philly expected to enter an empty room but as soon as he put his key in the door he heard the raised voices. He held the key still. His mother was downstairs. She and Fonsie were arguing. With a welcome little rush of expectancy, he turned the key. The two were so engaged with one another that they did not notice him enter. His mother was in her blue dressing gown. She stood remarkably erect.

'What's going on?' They were so involved with one another that they looked towards him as if he were a burglar.

'Your Uncle Peter died last night, in Gloria. The Cullens just phoned,' his mother said, and it was Philly's turn to look at his mother and brother as if he couldn't quite grasp why they were in the room.

'You'll all have to go,' his mother said.

'I don't see why we should have to go. We haven't seen the man in twenty years. He never even liked us,' Fonsie said heatedly, turning the wheelchair to face Philly.

'Of course we'll go. We are all he has now. It wouldn't look right if we didn't go down.' Philly would have grasped at any diversion, but the pictures of Gloria Bog that flooded his mind shut out the day and the room with amazing brightness and calm.

'That doesn't mean I have to go,' Fonsie said.

'Of course you have to go. He was your uncle as well as mine,' Philly said.

'If nobody went to poor Peter's funeral, God rest him, we'd be the talk of the countryside for years,' their mother said. 'If I know nothing else in the world I know what they're like down there.'

'Anyhow, there's no way I can go in this.' Fonsie gestured contemptuously to his wheelchair.

'That's no problem. I'll hire a Mercedes. With a jalopy like that you wouldn't think of coming yourself, Mother?' Philly asked suddenly with the humour and malice of deep knowledge, and the silence that met the suggestion was as great as if some gross obscenity had been uttered.

'I'd look a nice speck in Gloria when I haven't been out of my own house in years. There wouldn't be much point in going to poor Peter's funeral, God rest him, and turning up at my own,' she said in a voice in which a sudden frailty only served to point up the different shades of its steel.

'He never even liked us. There were times I felt if he got a chance he'd throw me into a bog hole the way he drowned the black whippet that started eating the eggs,' Philly said.

'He's gone now,' the mother said. 'He stood to us when he was needed. It made no difference whether he liked us or not.'

'How will you manage on your own?' Fonsie asked as if he had accepted he'd have to go.

'Won't Mrs O'Brien next door look in if you ask her and can't I call her myself on the phone? It'll be good for you to get out of the city for a change. None of the rest can be trusted to bring me back a word of anything that goes on,' she flattered.

'Was John told yet?' Philly interrupted, asking about their eldest brother.

'No. There'd be no use ringing him at home now. You'd have to ring him at the school,' their mother said.

The school's number was written in a notebook. Philly had to wait a long time on the phone after he explained the urgency of the call while the school secretary got John from the classroom.

'John won't take time off school to go to any funeral,' Fonsie said confidently as they waited.

To Fonsie's final disgust John agreed to go to the funeral at once. He'd be waiting for them at whatever time they thought they'd be ready to travel.

Philly hired the Mercedes. The wheelchair folded easily into its cavern-like boot. 'You'll all be careful,' their mother counselled as she kissed them goodbye. 'Everything you do down there will be watched and gone over. I'll be following poor Peter in my mind until you rest him with Father and Mother in Killeelan.'

John was waiting for them outside his front door, a brown hat in his hand, a gabardine raincoat folded on his arm, when the Mercedes pulled up at the low double gate. Before Philly had time to touch the horn John raised the hat and hurried down the concrete path. On both sides of the path the postage-stamp lawns showed the silver tracks of a mower, and roses were stacked and tied along the earthen borders.

'The wife doesn't seem to appear at all these days?' Philly asked, the vibrations of the engine shaking the car as they waited while John closed the gate.

'Herself and Mother never pulled,' Fonsie offered.

There was dull peace between the two brothers now. Fonsie knew he was more or less in Philly's hands for the next two days. He did not like it but the stupid death had moved the next two days out of his control.

'What's she like now?'

'I suppose she's much like the rest of us. She was always nippy.'

'I'm sorry for keeping you,' John said as he got into the back of the car.

'You didn't keep us at all,' Philly answered.

'It's great to get a sudden break like this. You can't imagine what it is to get out of the school and city for two or three whole days,' John said before he settled and was silent. The big Mercedes grew silent as it gathered speed through Fairview and the North Strand, crossing the Liffey at the Custom House, and turned into the one-way flow of traffic out along the south bank of the river. Not until they got past Leixlip, and fields and trees and hedges started to be scattered between the new raw estates, did they begin to talk, and all their talk circled about the man they were going to bury, their mother's brother, their Uncle Peter McDermott.

He had been the only one in the family to stay behind with his parents on Gloria Bog where he'd been born. All the rest had scattered. Their Aunt Mary had died young in Walthamstow, London; Martin died in Milton, Massachusetts; Katie, the eldest, had died only the year before in Oneida, New York. With Peter's death they were all gone now, except their mother. She had been the last to leave the house. She first served her time in a shop in Carrick-on-Shannon and then moved to a greengrocer's-cum-confectioner's on the North Circular Road where she met their unreliable father, a traveller for Lemons Sweets.

While the powerful car slowed through Enfield they began to recall how their mother had taken them back to Gloria at the beginning of every summer, leaving their father to his own devices in the city. They spent every summer there on the bog from the end of June until early September. Their mother had always believed that only for the clean air of the bog and the plain wholesome food they would never have made it through the makeshifts of the city winter. Without the air and the plain food they'd never, never have got through, she used to proclaim like a thanksgiving.

As long as her own mother lived it was like a holiday to go there every summer — the toothless grandmother who sat all day in her rocking chair, her shoulders shawled, the grey hair drawn severely back into a bun, only rising to gather crumbs and potato skins into her black apron, and holding it like a great cloth bowl, she would shuffle out on to the street. She'd wait until all her brown hens had started to beat and clamour around her and then with a quick laugh she'd scatter everything that the apron held. Often before she came in she'd look across the wide acres of the bog, the stunted birch trees, the faint blue of the heather, the white puffs of bog cotton trembling in every wind to the green slopes of Killeelan and walled evergreens high on the hill and say, 'I suppose it won't be long till I'm with the rest of them there.'

'You shouldn't talk like that, Mother,' they remembered their mother's ritual scold.

'There's not much else to think about at my age. The gaps between the bog holes are not getting wider.'

One summer the brown rocking chair was empty. Peter lived alone in the house. Though their mother worked from morning to night in the house, tidying, cleaning, sewing, cooking, he made it clear that he didn't want her any more, but she ignored him. Her want was greater than his desire to be rid of them and his fear of going against the old pieties prevented him from turning them away.

The old ease of the grandmother's time had gone. He showed them no welcome when they came, spent as little time in the house as possible, the days working in the fields, visiting other houses at night where, as soon as he had eaten, he complained to everybody about the burden he had to put up with. He never troubled to hide his relief when the day finally came at the end of the summer for them to leave. In the quick way of children, the three boys picked up his resentment and suffered its constraint. He hardly ever looked at Fonsie in his wheelchair, and it was fear that never allowed Fonsie to take his eyes from the back of his uncle's head and broad shoulders. Whenever Philly or John took him sandwiches and the Powers bottle of tea kept warm in the sock to the bog or meadow, they always instinctively took a step or two back after handing him the oilcloth bag. Out of loneliness there were times when he tried to talk to them but the constraint had so solidified that all they were ever able to give back were childish echoes of his own awkward questions. He never once acknowledged the work their mother had done in the house which was the way she had – the only way she had – of paying for their stay in the house of her own childhood. The one time they saw him happy was whenever her exasperation broke and she scolded him: he would smile as if all the days he had spent alone with his mother had suddenly returned. Once she noticed that he enjoyed these scolds, and even set to actively provoke them at every small turn, she would go more doggedly still than was her usual wont.

'What really used to get her dander up was the way he used to lift up his trousers by the crotch before he sat down to the table,' Fonsie said as the car approached Longford, and the brothers all laughed in their different ways.

'He looked as if he was always afraid he'd sit on his balls,' Philly said. 'He'll not have to worry about that any more.'

'His worries are over,' John said.

'Then, after our father died and she got that job in the laundry, that was the first summer we didn't go. She was very strange that summer. She'd take your head off if you talked. We never went again.'

'Strange, going down like this after all that,' John said vaguely.

'I was trying to say that in the house. It makes no sense to me but this man and Mother wouldn't listen,' Fonsie said. 'They were down my throat before I could open my mouth.'

'We're here now anyhow,' Philly said as the car crossed the narrow bridge at Carrick and they could look down at the Shannon. They were coming into country that they knew. They had suffered here.

'God, I don't know how she came here summer after summer when she wasn't wanted,' John said as the speeding car left behind the last curve of sluggish water.

'Well, she wasn't exactly leaving the Garden of Eden,' Philly said.

'It's terrible when you're young to come into a place where you know you're not wanted,' John said. 'I used to feel we were eating poor Peter out of house and home every summer. When you're a child you feel those sorts of things badly even though nobody notices. I see it still in the faces of the children I teach.'

'After all that we're coming down to bury the fucker. That's what gets me,' Fonsie said.

'He's dead now and belongs with all the dead,' Philly said. 'He wasn't all bad. Once I helped him drive cattle into the fair of Boyle. It was dark when we set out. I had to run alongside them in the fields behind the hedges until they got too worn out to want to leave the road. After we sold the cattle up on the Green he took me to the Rockingham Arms. He bought me lemonade and ginger snaps and lifted me up on the counter and said I was a great gosson to the whole bar even if I had the misfortune to be from Dublin.'

'You make me sick,' Fonsie said angrily. 'The man wasn't civilized. I always felt if he got a chance he'd have put me in a bag with a stone and thrown me in a bog hole like that black whippet.'

'That's exaggerating now. He never did and we're almost there,' John said as the car went past the church and scattered houses of Cootehall, where they had come to Mass on Sundays and bought flour and tea and sugar.

'Now, fasten your seat-belts,' Philly said humorously as he turned slowly into the bog road. To their surprise the deep pot-holes were gone. The road had been tarred, the unruly hedges of sally and hazel and briar cut back. Occasionally a straying briar clawed at the windscreen, the only hint of the old wildness. When the hedges gave way to the field of wild raspberry canes, Philly slowed the car to a crawl, and then stopped. Suddenly the bog looked like an ocean stretched in front of them, its miles of heather and pale sedge broken by the stunted birch trees, and high against the evening sun the dark evergreens stood out on the top of Killeelan Hill.

'He'll be buried there the day after tomorrow.'

The house hadn't changed, whitewashed, asbestos-roofed, the chestnut tree in front standing in the middle of the green fields on the edge of the bog; but the road was now tarred to the door, and all around the house new cattle sheds had sprung up.

Four cars were parked on the street and the door of the small house was open. A man shading his eyes with his hand came to the doorway as soon as the Mercedes came to a stop. It was Jim Cullen, the man who had telephoned the news of the death, smaller now and white-haired. He welcomed the three brothers in turn as he shook their hands. 'I'm sorry for your trouble. You were great to come all the way. I wouldn't have known any of you except for Fonsie. Your poor mother didn't manage to come?'

'She wasn't up to it,' Philly said. 'She hasn't left the house in years.'

As soon as they entered the room everybody stood up and came towards them and shook hands: 'I'm sorry for your trouble.' There were three old men besides Jim Cullen, neighbours of the dead man who had known them as children. Mrs Cullen was the older woman. A younger man about their own age was a son of the Cullens, Michael, whom they remembered as a child, but he had so grown and changed that his appearance was stranger to them than the old men.

'It's hard to think that Peter, God rest him, is gone. It's terrible,' Jim Cullen said as he led them into the bedroom.

The room was empty. A clock somewhere had not been stopped. He looked very old and still in the bed. They would not have known him. His hands were enormous on the white sheet, the beads a thin dark trickle through the locked fingers. A white line crossed the weathered forehead where he had worn a hat or a cap. The three brothers blessed themselves, and after a pause John and Philly touched the huge rough hands clasped together on the sheet. They were very cold. Fonsie did not touch the hands, turning the chair round towards the kitchen before his brothers left the side of the bed.

In the kitchen Fonsie and Philly drank whiskey. Mrs Cullen said it was no trouble at all to make John a cup of tea and there were platefuls of cut sandwiches on the table. Jim Cullen started to take up the story of Peter's death. He had told it many times already and would tell it many times again during the next days.

'Every evening before dark Peter would come out into that garden at the side. It can be seen plain from our front door. He was proud, proud of that garden though most of what it grew he gave away.'

'You couldn't have a better neighbour. If he saw you coming looking for help he'd drop whatever he was doing and swear black and blue that he was doing nothing at all,' an old man said.

'It was lucky,' Jim Cullen resumed. 'This woman here was thinking of closing up the day and went out to the door before turning the key, and saw Peter in the garden. She saw him stoop a few times to pull up a weed or straighten something and then he stood for a long time; suddenly he just seemed to keel over into the furrow. She didn't like to call and waited for him to get up and when he didn't she ran for me out the back. I called when I went into the garden. There was no sight or sound. He was hidden under the potato stalks. I had to pull them back before I was able to see anything. It was lucky she saw him fall. We'd have had to look all over the bog for days before we'd have ever thought of searching in the stalks.'

'Poor Peter was all right,' Philly said emotionally. 'I'll never forget the day he put me up on the counter of the Rockingham Arms.'

He was the only brother who seemed in any way moved by the death. John looked cautiously from face to face but whatever he found in the faces did not move him to speak. Fonsie had finished the whiskey he'd been given on coming from the room and appeared to sit in his wheelchair in furious resentment. Then, one by one, as if in obedience to some hidden signal or law, everybody in the room rose and shook hands with the three brothers in turn and left them alone with Jim and Maggie Cullen.

As soon as the house had emptied Jim Cullen signalled that he wanted them to come down for a minute to the lower room, which had hardly been used or changed since they had slept there as children: the bed that sank in the centre, the plywood wardrobe, the blue paint of the windowsill half flaked away and the small window that looked out on all of Gloria, straight across to the dark trees of Killeelan. First, Jim showed them a bill for whiskey, beer, stout, bread, ham, tomatoes, butter, cheese, sherry, tea, milk, sugar. He read out the words slowly and with difficulty.

'I got it all in Henry's. Indeed, you saw it all out on the table. It wasn't much but I wasn't certain if anybody was coming down and of course I'd be glad to pay it myself for poor Peter. You'll probably want to get more. When word gets out that you're here there could be a flood of visitors before the end of the night.' He took from a coat a large worn bulging wallet. 'Peter, God rest him, was carrying this when he fell. I didn't count it but there seems to be more than a lock of hundreds in the wallet.'

Philly took the handwritten bill and the wallet.

'Would Peter not have made a will?' John asked.

'No. He'd not have made a will,' Jim Cullen replied.

'How can we be sure?'

'That was the kind of him. He'd think it unlucky. It's not right but people like Peter think they're going to live for ever. Now that the rest of them has gone, except your mother, everything that Peter has goes to yous,' Jim Cullen continued as if he had already given it considerable thought. 'I ordered the coffin and hearse from Beirne's in Boyle. I did not order the cheapest – Peter never behaved like a small man when he went but – but he wouldn't like to see too much money going down into the ground either. Now that you're all here you can change all that if you think it's not right.'

'Not one thing will be changed, Jim,' Philly said emotionally.

'Then there's this key.' Jim Cullen held up a small key on a string. 'You'll find it opens the iron box in the press above in the bedroom. I didn't go near the box and I don't want to know what's in it. The key was around his poor neck when he fell. I'd do anything in the world for Peter.'

'You've done too much already. You've gone to far too much trouble,' Philly said.

'Far too much,' John echoed. 'We can't thank you enough.'

'I couldn't do less,' Jim Cullen replied. 'Poor Peter was one great neighbour. Anything you ever did for him he made sure you got back double.'

Fonsie alone did not say a word. He glowed in a private, silent resentment that shut out everything around him. His lips moved from time to time but they were speaking to some darkness seething within. It was relief to move out of the small cramped room. Mrs Cullen rose from the table as soon as they came from the room as if making herself ready to help in any way she could.

'Would you like to come with us to the village?' Philly asked.

'No, thanks,' Jim Cullen answered. 'I have a few hours' shuffling to do at home but then I'll be back.'

When it seemed as if the three brothers were going together to the village the Cullens looked from one to the other and Jim Cullen said, 'It'd be better if one of you stayed . . . in case of callers.'

John volunteered to stay. Philly had the car keys in his hand and Fonsie had already moved out to the car.

'I'll stay as well,' Mrs Cullen said. 'In case John might not know some of the callers.'

While Fonsie had been silent within the house, as soon as the car moved out of the open bog into that part of the lane enclosed by briars and small trees, an angry outpouring burst out like released water. Everything was gathered into the rushing complaint: the poor key with the string, keeling over in the potato stalks, the bloody wallet, the beads in the huge hands that he always felt wanted to choke him, the bit of cotton sticking out of the corner of the dead man's mouth. The whole thing was barbaric, uncivilized, obscene: they should never have come.

'Isn't it as good anyhow as having the whole thing swept under the carpet as it is in the city?' Philly argued reasonably.

'You mean we should bark ourselves because we don't keep a dog?'

'You make no effort,' Philly said. 'You never once opened your mouth in the house . . . In Dublin even when you're going to shop it takes you a half-hour to get from one end of a street to the next.'

'I never opened my mouth in the house and I never will. Through all those summers I never talked to anybody in the house but Mother and only when the house was empty. We were all made to feel that way – even Mother admitted that – but I was made to feel worse than useless. Every time I caught Peter looking at me I knew he was thinking that there was nothing wrong with me that a big stone and a rope and a deep bog hole couldn't solve.'

'You only thought that,' Philly said gently.

'Peter thought it too.'

'Well then, if he did – which I doubt – he thinks it no more.'

'By the way, you were very quick to pocket his wallet,' Fonsie said quickly as if changing the attack.

'That's because nobody else seemed ready to take it. But you take it if that's what you want.' Philly took the wallet from his pocket and offered it to Fonsie.

'I don't want it.' Fonsie refused the wallet roughly.

'We'd better look into it, then. We'll never get a quieter chance again in the next days.'

They were on a long straight stretch of road just outside the village. Philly moved the car in on to the grass margin. He left the engine running.

'There are thousands in this wallet,' Philly said simply after opening the wallet and fingering the notes.

'You'd think the fool would have put it in a bank where it'd be safe and earning interest.'

'Peter wouldn't put it in a bank. It might earn a tax inspector and a few awkward questions as well as interest,' Philly said as if he already was in possession of some of his dead uncle's knowledge and presence.

With the exception of the huge evergreens that used to shelter the church, the village had not changed at all. They had been cut down. Without the rich trees the church looked huge and plain and ugly in its nakedness.

'There's nothing more empty than a space you knew once when it was full,' Fonsie said.

'What do you mean?'

'Can you not see the trees?' Fonsie gestured irritably.

'The trees are gone.'

'That's what I mean. They were there and they're no longer there. Can you not see?'

Philly pressed Fonsie to come into the bar-grocery but he could not be persuaded. He said that he preferred to wait in the car. When Fonsie preferred something, with that kind of pointed politeness, Philly knew from old exasperations that it was useless to try to talk, and he left him there in silence.

'You must be one of the Ryans, then. You're welcome but I'm very sorry about poor Peter. You wouldn't be John, now? No? John stayed below in the house. You're Philly, then, and that's Fonsie out in the car. He won't come in? Your poor mother didn't come? I'm very sorry about Peter.' The old man with a limp behind the counter repeated each scrap of information after Philly as soon as it was given between his own hesitant questions and interjections.

'You must be Luke Henry, then?' Philly asked.

'The very man and still going strong. I remember you well coming in the summers. It must be at least ten years.'

'No. Twenty years now.'

'Twenty.' He shook his head. 'You'd never think. Terror how they go. It may be stiff pedalling for the first years but, I fear, after a bit, it is all freewheeling.' When Luke smiled his face became strangely boyish. 'What'll you have? On the house! A large brandy?'

'No, nothing at all. I just want to get a few things for the wake.'

'You'll have to have something, seeing what happened.'

'Just a pint, then. A pint of Guinness.'

'What will Fonsie have?'

'He's all right. He couldn't be got to come in out of the car. He's that bit upset,' Philly said.

'He'll have to have something,' Luke said doggedly.

'Well, a pint, then. I'll take it out to him myself. He's that bit upset.'

When Philly opened the door of the car and offered him Luke's pint, Fonsie said, 'What's this fucking thing for?'

'Nothing would do him but to send you out a drink when I said you wouldn't come in.'

'What am I supposed to do with it?'

'Put it in your pocket. Use it for hair oil. It's about time you came off your high horse and took things the way they are offered.' Fonsie's aggression was suddenly met with equal aggression, and before he had time to counter, Philly closed the car door, leaving him alone with the pint in his hand.

Back inside the bar Philly raised his glass. 'Good luck. Thanks, Luke.'

'To the man that's gone,' Luke said. 'There was no sides to poor Peter. He was straight and thick. We could do with more like him.'

Philly drank quickly and then started his order: several bottles of whiskey, gin, vodka, sherry, brandy, stout, beer, lemonade, orange, and loaves, butter, tea, coffee, ham and breasts of turkey. Luke wrote down each item as it was called. Several times he tried to cut down the order – 'It's too much, too much' he kept muttering – then, slowly, one by one, all the time checking the list, he placed each item on the counter, checking it against the list once more before packing everything into several cardboard boxes.

Philly pulled out a wad of money.

'No,' Luke refused the money firmly. 'We'll settle it all out here later. You'll have lots to bring back. Not even the crowd down in the bog will be able to eat and drink that much.' He managed a smile in which malice almost equalled wistfulness.

After they'd filled the boot with boxes, they stacked more in the back seat and on one side of the folded wheelchair. Luke shook Fonsie's hand as he helped to carry out the boxes to the car. 'I'm sorry for your trouble'; but if Fonsie made any response it was inaudible. When they finished, Philly lifted the empty pint glass from the dashboard and handed it to Luke with a wink. Luke raised the pint glass in a sly gesture to indicate that he was more than well acquainted with the strange ways of the world.

'In all my life I never had to drink a pint sitting on my own in a car outside a public house. There's no manners round here. The people are savages,' Fonsie complained as soon as the car moved.

'You wouldn't come in and Luke meant only the best,' Philly said gruffly.

'Of course, as usual you had to go and make a five- or six-course meal out of the whole business.'

'What do you mean?'

'I thought you'd never stop coming out of the pub with the boxes. The boot is full. The back seat is jammed. You must have enough to start a bar-restaurant yourself.'

'They can be returned,' Philly said defensively. 'Luke wouldn't even take money. We wouldn't want to be disgraced by running out of drink in the middle of the wake. Luke said, everybody said, there was never anything small about Uncle Peter. He wouldn't want anything to run short at his wake. The McDermotts were always big people.'

'They were in their shite,' Fonsie said furiously. 'He made us feel we were stealing bread out of his mouth. But that's you all over. Big, big, big,' he taunted. 'That's why people in Dublin are fed up with you. You always have to make the big splash. You live in a rathole in the desert for eighteen months, then you come out and do the big fellow. People don't want that. They want to go about their own normal lives. They don't want your drinks or big blow.'

There are no things more cruel than truths about ourselves spoken to us by another that are perceived to be at least half true. Left unsaid and hidden we feel they can be changed or eradicated, in time. Philly gripped Fonsie's shoulder in a despairing warning that he'd heard enough. They turned into the bog road to the house.

'We live in no rathole in the desert,' Philly said quietly. 'There's no hotel in Dublin to match where we live, except there's no booze, and sometimes that's no bad thing either.'

'That still doesn't take anything away from what I said.' Fonsie would not relent.

Without any warning, suddenly, they were out of the screen of small trees into the open bog. A low red sun west of Killeelan was spilling over the sedge and dark heather. Long shadows stretched out from the small birches scattered all over the bog.

'What are you stopping for?' Fonsie demanded.

'Just looking at the bog. On evenings like this I used to think it was on fire. Other times the sedge looked like gold. I remember it well.'

'You're talking through your drainpipe,' Fonsie said as the car moved on. 'All I remember of these evenings is poor Mother hanging out the washing.'

'Wouldn't she hang it out in the morning?'

'She had too much to do in the morning. It shows how little you were about the house. She used to wash all of Peter's trousers. They never were washed from one year to the next. She used to say they were fit to walk around on their own. Often with a red sun there was the frost. She thought it freshened clothes.'

To their surprise there were already six cars on the street as they drew close to the house.

'News must have gone out already that you've bought the world of booze,' Fonsie said as they drew up in front of the door, and his humour was not improved by having to sit in the car while all the boxes in the boot were carried into the house before the wheelchair could be taken out.

John was getting on famously with the people in the house who had come while his two brothers had been away. In fact, he got on better with strangers than with either of his brothers. He was a good listener. At school he had been a brilliant student, winning scholarships with ease all the way to university; but as soon as he graduated he disappeared into teaching. He was still teaching the same subjects in the same school where he had started, and appeared to dislike his work intensely though he was considered one of the best teachers in the school. Like most of his students and fellow teachers he seemed to live and work for the moment when the buzzer would end the school day.

'I don't want to be bothered,' was a phrase he used whenever new theories or educational practices came up in the classroom. 'They can go and cause trouble with their new ideas elsewhere. I just want to be left in peace.'

Their mother complained that his wife ran his whole life – she had been a nurse before they married – but others were less certain. They felt he encouraged her innate bossiness so that he could the better shelter unbothered behind it like a deep hedge. When offered the headship of the school, he had turned it down without consulting his wife. She had been deeply hurt when she heard of the offer from the wife of another teacher. She would have loved to have gone to the supermarket and church as the headmaster's wife. Her dismay forced her to ask him if it was true. 'You should at least have told me.' His admission that he'd refused the promotion increased her hurt. 'I didn't want to bother you,' he said so finally that she was silenced.

When the two brothers came back to the house, he gradually moved back into a corner, listening with perfect attention to anybody who came to him, while before he had been energetically welcoming visitors, showing them to the corpse room, getting them drinks and putting them at ease. Once Philly and Fonsie came into the house he turned it all over to them. The new callers lined up in front of them to shake their hands in turn.

'I'm sorry about poor Peter. I'm sorry for your trouble. Very sorry.'

'Thank you for coming. I know that. I know that well,' Philly answered equally ceremoniously, and his ready words covered Fonsie's stubborn silence.

Despite the aspersion Fonsie cast on the early mourners, very little was drunk or eaten that night. Maggie Cullen made sandwiches with the ham and turkey and tomatoes and sliced loaves. Her daughter-in-law cut the sandwiches into small squares and handed them around on a large oval plate with blue flowers around the rim. Tea was made in a big kettle. There were not many glasses in the house but few had to drink wine or whiskey from cups. Those that drank beer or stout refused all offers of cup or glass and drank from the bottles. Some who smoked had a curious, studious habit of dropping their cigarette butts carefully down the narrow necks of the bottles. Some held up the bottles like children to listen to the smouldering ash hiss in the beer dregs. By morning, butts could be seen floating in the bottoms of several of the bottles like trapped wasps.

All through the evening and night people kept coming to the house while others who had come earlier quietly left. First they shook hands with the three brothers, then went to the upper room, knelt by the bed; and when they rose they touched the dead hands or forehead in a gesture of leavetaking or communion, and then sat on one of the chairs by the bed. When new people came in to the room and knelt by the bed they left their chairs and returned to the front room where they were offered food and drink and joined in the free, unceasing talk and laughter. Almost all the talk was of the dead man. Much of it was in the form of stories. All of them showed the dead man winning out in life and the few times he had been forced to concede defeat it had been with stubbornness or wit. No surrender here, were his great words. The only thing he ever regretted was never having learned to drive a car. 'We always told him we'd drive him anywhere he wanted to go,' Jim Cullen said. 'But he'd never ask. He was too proud, and when we'd take him to town on Saturdays we'd have to make it appear that we needed him along for company; then he'd want to buy you the world of drink. When the children were young he'd load them down with money or oranges and chocolates. Then, out of the blue, he said to me once that he might be dead if he'd ever learned to drive: he'd noticed that many who drove cars had died, while a lot of those who had to walk or cycle like himself were still battering around.'

From the top of the dresser a horse made from matchsticks and mounted on a rough board was taken down. The thin lines of the matchsticks were cunningly spliced and glued together to suggest the shape of a straining horse in the motion of ploughing or mowing. A pig was found among the plates, several sheep that were subtly different from one another, as well as what looked like a tired old collie, all made from the same curved and spliced matchsticks.

'He was always looking for matches. Even in town on Saturdays you'd see him picking them up from the bar floor. He could do anything with them. The children loved the animals he'd give them. Seldom they broke them. Though our crowd are grown we still have several he made in the house. He never liked TV. That's what you'd find him at on any winter's night if you wandered in on your *ceilidh*. He could nearly make those matchsticks talk.'

It was as if the house had been sundered into two distinct and separate elements, and yet each reflected and measured the other as much as the earth and the sky. In the upper room there was silence, the people there keeping vigil by the body where it lay in the stillness and awe of the last change; while in the lower room that life was being resurrected with more vividness than it could ever have had in the long days and years it had been given. Though all the clocks in the house had now been silenced everybody seemed to know at once when it was midnight and all the mourners knelt except Fonsie and two very old women. The two rooms were joined as the Rosary was recited but as soon as the prayers ended each room took on again its separate entity.

Fonsie signalled to Philly that he wanted to go outside. Philly knew immediately that his brother wanted to relieve himself. In the city he never allowed any help but here he was afraid of the emptiness and darkness of the night outside the house and the strange ground. It was a clear moonlit night without a murmur of wind, and the acres of pale sedge were all lit up, giving back much of the light it was receiving, so that the places that were covered with heather melted into a soft blackness and the scattered shadows of the small birches were soft and dark on the cold sedge. High up and far off they could hear an aeroplane and soon they picked it out by the pulsing of its white nightlight as it crossed their stretch of sky. The tall evergreens within the pale stone wall on the top of Killeelan were dark and gathered together against the moonlight. As if to give something back to his brother for accompanying him into the night, Fonsie said as he was relieving himself in the shadowed corner of the house, 'Mother remembers seeing the first car in this place. She says she was ten. All of them from the bog rushed out to the far road to see the car pass. It's strange to think of people living still who didn't grow up with cars.'

'Maybe they were as well off,' Philly said.

'How could they be as well off?'

'Would Peter in there now be better off?'

'I thought it was life we were talking about. If they were that well off why had they all to do their best to get to hell out of the place?'

'I was only thinking that a lot of life never changes. If the rich could get the poor to die for them the rich would never die,' Philly said belligerently. It didn't take much or long for an edge to come between them, but before it could grow they went back into the house. Not until close to daylight did the crowd of mourners start to thin.

During all this time John had been the most careful of the three brothers. He had drunk less than either of the other two, had stayed almost as silent as Fonsie, and now he noticed each person's departure and accompanied them out to their cars to thank them for coming to Peter's wake as if he had been doing it all his life. By the time the last car left, the moon was still in the sky but was well whitened by the rising sun. The sedge had lost its brightness and taken on the dull colour of wheat. All that was left in the house with the dead man and his three nephews were the Cullens and a local woman who had helped with tea and sandwiches through the night. By that time they had all acquired the heady, vaguely uplifting spiritual feeling that comes in the early stages of exhaustion and is often strikingly visible in the faces of the old or sick.

In the same vague, absent, dreamlike way, the day drifted towards evening. Whenever they came to the door they saw a light, freshening wind moving over the sedge as if it were passing over water. Odd callers continued coming to the house throughout the day, and after they spent time with the dead man in the room they were given food and drink and they sat and talked. Most of their talk was empty and tired by now and had none of the vigour of the night before. Mrs Cullen took great care to ensure that the upper room was never left empty, that someone was always there by Peter's side on this his last day in the house. Shortly after five the hearse arrived and the coffin was taken in. It was clear that Luke had been right and that most of the drink Philly had ordered would have to be returned. Immediately behind the hearse was a late, brief flurry of callers. Shortly before six the body was laid in the coffin and, with a perfunctory little swish of beads, the undertaker began the decade of the Rosary. The coffin was closed and taken out to the hearse. Many cars had taken up position on the narrow road to accompany the hearse to the church.

After they left the coffin before the high altar in the church, some of the mourners crossed the road to Luke's Bar. There, Philly bought everybody a round of drinks but when he attempted to buy a second round both Luke and Jim Cullen stopped him. Custom allowed one round but no more. Instead he ordered a pint of stout for himself and Fonsie, and John shook his head to the offer of a second drink. Then when Philly went to pay for the two drinks Luke pushed the money back to him and said that Jim Cullen had just paid.

People offered to put the brothers up for the night but Fonsie especially would not hear of staying in a strange house. He insisted on going to the hotel in town. As soon as they had drunk the second pint and said their goodbyes Philly drove John and Fonsie to the Royal Hotel. He waited until they were given rooms and then prepared to leave.

'Aren't you staying here?' Fonsie asked sharply when he saw that Philly was about to leave him alone with John.

'No.'

'Where are you putting your carcass?'

'Let that be no worry of yours,' Philly said coolly.

'I don't think a more awkward man ever was born. Even Mother agrees on that count.'

'I'll see you around nine in the morning,' Philly said to John as they made an appointment to see Reynolds, the solicitor, before the funeral Mass at eleven.

Philly noticed that both the young Cullens and the older couple had returned from the removal by the two cars parked outside their house. Peter's house was unlocked and eerily empty, everything in it exactly as it was when the coffin was taken out. On impulse he took three bottles of whiskey from one of the boxes stacked beneath the table and walked with the bottles over to Cullen's house. They'd seen him coming from the road and Jim Cullen went out to meet him before he reached the door.

'I'm afraid you caught us in the act,' Mrs Cullen laughed. The four of them had been sitting at the table, the two men drinking what looked like glasses of whiskey, the women cups of tea and biscuits.

'Another half-hour and you'd have found us in the nest,' Jim Cullen said. 'We didn't realize how tired we were until after we came in from looking at our own cattle and Peter's. We decided to have this last drink and then hit off. We'll miss Peter.'

Without asking him, Mrs Cullen poured him a glass of whiskey and a chair was pulled out for him at the table. Water was added to the whiskey from a glass jug. He placed the three bottles on the table. 'I just brought over these before everything goes back to the shop.'

'It's far too much,' they responded. 'We didn't want anything.'

'I know that but it's still too little.' He seemed to reach far back to his mother or uncle for the right thing to say. 'It's just a show of something for all that you've done.'

'Thanks but it's still far too much.' They all seemed to be pleased at once and took and put the three bottles away. They then offered him a bed but he said he'd manage well enough in their old room. 'I'm used to roughing it out there in the oil fields,' he lied; and not many minutes after that, seeing Mrs Cullen stifle a yawn, he drank down his whiskey and left. Jim Cullen accompanied him as far as the road and stood there until Philly had gone some distance towards his uncle's house before turning slowly back.

In the house Philly went from room to room to let in fresh air but found that all the windows were stuck. He left the doors to the rooms open and the front door open on the bog. In the lower room he placed an eiderdown on the old hollowed bed and in the upper room he drew the top sheet up over where the corpse had lain until it covered both the whole of the bed and pillow. He then took the iron box from the cupboard and unlocked it on the table in the front room. Before starting to go through the box he got a glass and half filled it with whiskey. He found very old deeds tied with legal ribbon as he drank, cattle cards, a large wad of notes in a rubber band, a number of scattered US dollar notes, a one-hundred-dollar bill, some shop receipts ready to fall apart, and a gold wedding ring. He put the parchment to one side to take to the solicitor the next morning. The notes he placed in a brown envelope before locking the box and placing it back in the cupboard. He poured another large whiskey. On a whim he went and took down some of the matchstick figures that they had looked at the night before – a few of the sheep, a little pig, the dray-horse and cart, a delicate greyhound on a board with its neck straining out from the bent knees like a snake's as if about to pick a turning rabbit or hare from the ground. He moved them here and there on the table with his finger as he drank when, putting his glass down, his arm leaned on the slender suggestion of a horse, which crumpled and fell apart. Almost covertly he gathered the remains of the figure, the cart and scattered matches, and put them in his pocket to dispose of later. Quickly and uneasily he restored the sheep and pig and hound to the safety of the shelf. Then he moved his chair out into the doorway and poured more whiskey.

He thought of Peter sitting alone here at night making the shapes of animals out of matchsticks, of those same hands now in a coffin before the high altar of Cootehall church. Tomorrow he'd lie in the earth on the top of Killeelan Hill. A man is born. He dies. Where he himself stood now on the path between those two points could not be known. He felt as much like the child that came each summer years ago to this bog from the city as the rough unfinished man he knew himself to be in the eyes of others, but feelings had nothing to do with it. He must be already well out past halfway.

The moon of the night before lit the pale sedge. He could see the dark shapes of the heather, the light on the larger lakes of sedge, but he had no desire to walk out into the night. Blurred with tiredness and whiskey, all shapes and lives seemed to merge comfortably into one another as the pale, ghostly sedge and the dark heather merged under the moon. Except for the stirrings of animals about the house and a kittiwake calling sharply high up over the bog and the barking of distant dogs the night was completely silent. There was not even a passing motor. But before he lay down like a dog under the eiderdown in the lower room he remembered to set the alarm of his travelling clock for seven the next morning.

In spite of a throbbing forehead he was the first person in the dining-room of the Royal Hotel for breakfast the next morning. After managing to get through most of a big fry – sausages, black pudding, bacon, scrambled eggs and three pots of black coffee – he was beginning to feel much better when Fonsie and John came in for their breakfast.

'I wouldn't advise the coffee though I'm awash with the stuff,' Philly said as the two brothers looked through the menu.

'We never have coffee in the house except when you're back,' Fonsie said.

'I got used to it out there. The Americans drink nothing else throughout the day.'

'They're welcome to it,' Fonsie said.

John looked from one brother to the other but kept his silence. Both brothers ordered tea and scrambled eggs on toast.

'What did you two do last night?'

'I'm afraid we had pints, too many pints,' John answered.

'You had no pints, only glasses,' Fonsie said.

'It all totted up to pints and there were too many. This wild life doesn't suit me. How you are able to move around this morning I don't know.'

'That's nothing,' Fonsie said. 'And you should see yer man here when he gets going; then you'd have a chance to talk. It's all or nothing. There's never any turning back.'

As Philly was visibly discomforted, John asked, 'What did you do?'

'I thanked the Cullens.'

'More whiskey,' Fonsie crowed.

'Then I opened the iron box,' Philly ignored the gibe. 'I found the deeds. We'll need them for the lawyer in a few minutes. And there was another wad of money. There was sterling and dollars and a few Australian notes as well.'

'The sterling and dollars came from the brother and sister. They were probably sent to the mother and never cashed. God knows where the Australian came from,' John said.

'It all comes to thousands,' Philly said.

'When we used to go there you'd think we were starving him out of the place.'

'They probably didn't have it then.'

'Even if they did it would still have been the same. It's a way of thinking.'

'The poor fucker, it'd make you laugh,' Fonsie said. 'Making pigs and horses out of matchsticks in the night, slaving on the bog or running after cattle in the day, when he could have gone out and had himself a good time.'

'Maybe that was his way of having a good time,' John said carefully.

'It'll get some good scattering now,' Fonsie laughed at Philly.

'Are you sure?' Philly said sternly back. 'It all goes to Mother anyhow. She's the next of kin. Maybe you'll give it the scattering? I have lots for myself.'

'Mr Big again,' Fonsie jeered.

'It's time to go to see this lawyer. Do you want to come?'

'I have more sense,' Fonsie answered angrily.

The brown photos around the walls of the solicitor's waiting room as well as the heavy mahogany table and leather chairs told that the practice was old, that it had been passed from grandfather Reynolds to father to son. The son was about fifty, dressed in a beautifully cut dark pinstripe suit, his grey hair parted in the centre. His manner was soft and urbane and quietly watchful.

Philly had asked John to state their business, which he did with simple clarity. As he spoke Philly marvelled at his brother. Even if it meant saving his own life he'd never have been able to put the business so neatly without sidetracking or leaving something out.

'My advice would be to lose that money,' the solicitor said when he had finished. 'Strictly, I shouldn't be giving that advice but as far as I'm concerned I never heard anything about it.'

Both brothers nodded their understanding and gratitude.

'Almost certainly there's no will. I'd have it if there was. I acted for Peter in a few matters. There was a case of trespass and harassment by a neighbouring family called Whelan a few years back. None of it was Peter's fault. They were a bad lot and solved our little problem by emigrating *en masse* to the States. Peter's friend, Jim Cullen, bought their land.'

Philly remembered wild black-haired Marie Whelan who had challenged him to fight on the bog road during one of those last summers. John just nodded that he remembered the family.

'So everything should go to your mother as the only surviving next of kin. As she is a certain age it should be acted on quickly and I'll be glad to act as soon as I learn what it is your mother wants.' As he spoke he opened the deeds Philly gave John to hand over. 'Peter never even bothered to have the deeds changed into his name. The place is in your grandfather's name and this document was drawn up by my grandfather.'

'Would the place itself be worth much?' Philly's sudden blunt question surprised John. Out of his quietness Mr Reynolds looked up at him sharply.

'I fear not a great deal. Ten or eleven thousand. A little more if there was local competition. I'd say fourteen at the very most.'

'You can't buy a room for that in the city and there's almost thirty acres with the small house.'

'Well, it's not the city and I do not think Gloria Bog is ever likely to become the Costa Brava.'

Philly noticed that both the solicitor and his brother were looking at him with withdrawn suspicion if not distaste. They were plainly thinking that greed had propelled him to stumble into the inquiry he had made when it was the last thing in the world he had in mind. Before anything further could be said, the solicitor was shaking both their hands at the door and nodding over their shoulders to the receptionist behind her desk across the hallway to take their particulars before showing them out.

In contrast to the removal of the previous evening, when the church had been full to overflowing, there were only a few dozen people at the funeral Mass. Eight cars followed the hearse to Killeelan, and only the Mercedes turned into the narrow laneway behind the hearse. The other mourners abandoned their cars at the road and entered the lane on foot. Blackthorn and briar scraped against the windscreen and sides of the Mercedes as they moved behind the hearse's slow pace. At the end of the lane there was a small clearing in front of the limestone wall that ringed the foot of Killeelan Hill. There was just enough space in the clearing for the hearse and the Mercedes to park on either side of the small iron gate in the wall. The coffin was taken from the hearse and placed on the shoulders of John and Philly and the two Cullens. The gate was just wide enough for them to go through. Fonsie alone stayed behind in the front seat of the Mercedes and watched the coffin as it slowly climbed the hill on the four shoulders. The coffin went up and up the steep hill, sometimes swaying dangerously, and then anxious hands of the immediate followers would go up against the back of the coffin. The shadows of the clouds swept continually over the green hill and brown varnish of the coffin. Away on the bog they were a darker, deeper shadow as the clouds travelled swiftly over the pale sedge. Three times the small snail-like cortège stopped completely for the bearers to be changed. As far as Fonsie could see – he would have needed binoculars to be certain – they were the original bearers, his brothers and the two Cullens, who took up the coffin the third and last time and carried it through the small gate in the wall around the graveyard on the hilltop. Then it was only the coffin itself and the heads of the mourners that could be seen until they were lost in the graveyard evergreens. In spite of his irritation at this useless ceremony, that seemed only to show some deep love of hardship or enslavement – they'd be hard put to situate the graveyard in a more difficult or inaccessible place except on the very top of a mountain – he found the coffin and the small band of toiling mourners unbearably moving as it made its low stumbling climb up the hill, and this deepened further his irritation and the sense of complete uselessness.

Suddenly he was startled by the noise of a car coming very fast up the narrow lane and braking to a stop behind the hearse. A priest in a long black soutane and white surplice with a purple stole over his shoulders got out of the car carrying a fat black breviary. Seeing Fonsie, he saluted briskly as he went through the open gate. Then, bent almost double, he started to climb quickly like an enormous black-and-white crab after the coffin. Watching him climb, Fonsie laughed harshly before starting to fiddle with the car radio.

After a long interval the priest was the first to come down the hill, accompanied by two middle-aged men, the most solid looking and conventional of the mourners. The priest carried his surplice and stole on his arm. The long black soutane looked strangely menacing between the two attentive men in suits as they came down. Fonsie reached over to turn off the rock and roll playing on the radio as they drew close, but, in a sudden reversal, he turned it up louder still. The three men looked towards the loud music as they came through the gate but did not salute or nod. They got into the priest's car and, as there was no turning place between the hearse and the Mercedes, it proceeded to back out of the narrow lane. Then in straggles of twos and threes, people started to come down the hill. The two brothers and Jim Cullen were the last to come down. As soon as Philly got into the Mercedes he turned off the radio.

'You'd think you'd show a bit more respect.'

'The radio station didn't know about the funeral.'

'I'm not talking about the radio station,' Philly said.

'That Jim Cullen is a nice man,' John said in order to steer the talk away from what he saw as an imminent clash. 'He's intelligent as well as decent. Peter was lucky in his neighbour.'

'The Cullens,' Philly said as if searching for a phrase. 'You couldn't, you couldn't if you tried get better people than the Cullens.'

They drove straight from Killeelan to the Royal for lunch. Not many people came, just the Cullens among the close neighbours and a few far-out cousins of the dead man. Philly bought a round for everyone and when he found no takers to his offer of a second round he did not press.

'Our friend seems to be restraining himself for once,' Fonsie remarked sarcastically to John as they moved from the bar to the restaurant.

'He's taking his cue from Jim Cullen. Philly is all right,' John said. 'It's those months and months out in the oil fields and then the excitement of coming home with all that money. It has to have an effect. Wouldn't it be worse if he got fond of the money?'

'It's still too much. It's not awanting,' Fonsie continued doggedly through a blurred recognition of all that Philly had given to their mother and to the small house over the years, and it caused him to stir uncomfortably.

The set meal was simple and good: hot vegetable soup, lamb chops with turnip and roast potatoes and peas, apple tart and cream, tea or coffee. While they were eating, the three gravediggers came into the dining-room and were given a separate table by one of the river windows. Philly got up as soon as they arrived to ensure that drinks were brought to their table.

When the meal ended, the three brothers drove back behind the Cullens' car to Gloria Bog. There they put all that was left of the booze back into the car. The Cullens accepted what food was left over but wouldn't hear of taking any more of the drink. 'We're not planning on holding another wake for a long time yet,' they said half humorously, half sadly. John helped with the boxes, Fonsie did not leave the car. As soon as Philly gave Jim Cullen the keys to the house John shook his hand and got back into the car with Fonsie and the boxes of booze, but still Philly continued talking to Jim Cullen outside the open house. In the rear mirror they saw Philly thrust a fistful of notes towards Jim Cullen. They noticed how large the old farmer's hands were as they gripped Philly by the wrist and pushed the hand and notes down into his jacket pocket, refusing stubbornly to accept any money. When John took his eyes from the mirror and the small sharp struggle between the two men, what met his eyes across the waste of pale sedge and heather was the rich dark waiting evergreens inside the back wall of Killeelan where they had buried Peter beside his father and mother only a few hours before. The colour of laughter is black. How dark is the end of all of life. Yet others carried the burden in the bright day on the hill. His shoulders shuddered slightly in revulsion and he wished himself back in the semi-detached suburbs with rosebeds outside in the garden.

'I thought you'd never finish,' Fonsie accused Philly when the big car began to move slowly out the bog road.

'There was things to be tidied up,' Philly said absently. 'Jim is going to take care of the place till I get back,' and as Fonsie was about to answer he found John's hands pressing his shoulders from the back seat in a plea not to speak. When they parked beside the door of the bar there was just place enough for another car to pass inside the church wall.

'Not that a car is likely to pass,' Philly joked as he and John carried the boxes in. When they had placed all of them on the counter they saw Luke reach for a brandy bottle on the high shelf.

'No, Luke,' Philly said. 'I'll have a pint if that's what you have in mind.'

'John'll have a pint, then, too.'

'I don't know,' John said in alarm. 'I haven't drunk as much in my life as the last few days. I feel poisoned.'

'Still, we're unlikely to have a day like this ever again,' Philly said as Luke pulled three pints.

'I don't think I'd survive many more such days,' John said.

'Wouldn't it be better to bring Fonsie in than to have him drinking out there in the car? It'll take me a while to make up all this. One thing I will say,' he said as he started to count the returned bottles. 'There was no danger of anybody running dry at Peter's wake.'

Fonsie protested when Philly went out to the car. It was too much trouble to get the wheelchair out of the boot. He didn't need drink. 'I'll take you in.' Philly offered his stooped neck and carried Fonsie into the bar like a child as he'd done many times when they were young and later when they were on certain sprees. He set him down in an armchair in front of the empty fireplace and brought his pint from the counter. It took Luke a long time to make up the bill, and when he eventually presented it to Philly, after many extra countings and checkings, he was full of apologies at what it had all come to.

'It'd be twice as much in the city,' Philly said energetically as he paid.

'I suppose it'd be as much anyhow,' Luke grumbled happily with relief and then at once started to draw another round of drinks which he insisted they take.

'It's on the house. It's not every day or year brings you down.'

Fonsie and Philly drank the second pint easily. John was already fuddled and unhappy and he drank reluctantly.

'I won't say goodbye.' Luke accompanied them out to the car when they left. 'You'll have to be down again before long.'

'It'll not be long till we're down,' Philly answered firmly for all of them.

In Longford and Mullingar and Enfield Philly stopped on their way back to Dublin. John complained each time, but it was Philly who had command of the car. Each time he carried Fonsie into the bars – and in all of them the two drank pints – John refused to have anything in Mullingar or Longford but took a reluctant glass in Enfield.

'What'll you do if you have an accident and get breathalysed?'

'I'll not have an accident. And they can send the summons all the way out to the Saudis if I do.'

He drove fast but steadily into the city. He was silent as he drove. Increasingly, he seemed charged with an energy that was focused elsewhere and had been fuelled by every stop they had made. In the heart of the city, seeing a vacant place in front of Mulligan's where he had drunk on his own in the deep silence of the bar a few short mornings before, he pulled across the traffic and parked. Cars stopped to blow hard at him but he paid no attention as he parked and got out.

'We'll have a last drink here in the name of God before we face back to the mother,' Philly said as he carried Fonsie into the bar. There were now a few dozen early evening drinkers in the bar. Some of them seemed to know the brothers, but not well. John offered to move Fonsie from the table to an armchair but Fonsie said he preferred to remain where he was. John complained that he hadn't asked for the pint when the drinks were brought to the table.

'Is it a short you want, then?'

'No. I have had more drink today than I've had in years. I want nothing.'

'Don't drink it, then, if you don't want,' he was told roughly.

'Well, Peter, God rest him, was given a great send-off,' Philly said with deep satisfaction as he drank. 'I thank God I was back. I wouldn't have been away for the world. The church was packed for the removal. Every neighbour around was at Killeelan.'

'What else have they to do down there? It's the one excuse they have to get out of their houses,' Fonsie said.

'They honour the dead. That's what they do. People still mean something down there. They showed the respect they had for Peter.'

'Respect, my arse. Everybody is respected for a few days after they conk it because they don't have to be lived with any more. Oh, it's easy to honour the dead. It doesn't cost anything and gives them the chance to get out of their bloody houses before they start to eat one another within.'

An old argument started up, an argument they had had many times before without resolving anything, the strength of their difference betraying the hidden closeness.

Philly and Fonsie drained their glasses as John took the first sip from his pint and he looked uneasily from one to the other.

'You have it all crooked,' Philly said as he rose to get more drink from the counter. John covered his glass with his palm to indicate that he wanted nothing more. When Philly came back with the two pints he started to speak before he had even put the glasses down on the table: he had all the blind dominating passion of someone in thrall to a single idea.

'I'll never forget it all the days of my life, the people coming to the house all through the night. The rows and rows of people at the removal passing by us in the front seat of the church grasping our hands. Coming in that small lane behind the hearse; then carrying Peter up that hill.'

Fonsie tried to speak but Philly raised his glass into his face and refused to be silenced.

'I felt something I never felt when we left the coffin on the edge of the grave. A rabbit hopped out of the briars a few yards off. He sat there and looked at us as if he didn't know what was going on before he bolted off. You could see the bog and all the shut houses next to Peter's below us. There wasn't even a wisp of smoke coming from any of the houses. Everybody gathered around, and the priest started to speak of the dead and the Mystery and the Resurrection.'

'He's paid to do that and he was nearly late. I saw it all from the car,' Fonsie asserted. 'It was no mystery from the car. Several times I thought you were going to drop the coffin. It was more like a crowd of apes staggering up a hill with something they had just looted. The whole lot of you could have come right out of the Dark Ages, without even a dab of make-up. I thought a standard of living had replaced the struggle for survival ages ago.'

'I have to say I found the whole ceremony moving, but once is more than enough to go through that experience,' John said carefully. 'I think of Peter making those small animals out of matchsticks in the long nights on the bog. Some people pay money for that kind of work. Peter just did it out of some need.'

Philly either didn't hear or ignored what John said.

'It's a godsend they don't let you out often,' Fonsie said. 'People that exhibit in museums are a different kettle. Peter was just killing the nights on the bloody bog.'

'I'll never forget the boredom of those summers, watching Peter foot turf, making grabs at the butterflies that tossed about over the sedge. Once you closed your hand they always escaped,' John said as if something long buried in him was drawn out. 'I think he was making things out of matchsticks even then but we hardly noticed.'

'Peter never wanted us. Mother just forced us on him. He wasn't able to turn us away,' Fonsie said, the talk growing more and more rambling and at odds.

'He didn't turn us away, whether he wanted to or not,' Philly asserted truculently. 'I heard Mother say time and time again that we'd never have got through some of the winters but for those long summers on the bog.'

'She'd have to say that since she took us there.'

'It's over now. With Peter it's all finished. One of the things that made the last days bearable for me was that everything we were doing was being done for the last time,' John said with such uncharacteristic volubility that the two brothers just stared.

'I'll say amen to that,' Fonsie said.

'It's far from over but we better have a last round for the road first.' Philly drained his glass and rose, and again John covered his three-quarter-full glass with his palm. 'As far as I can make out nothing is ever over.'

'Those two are tanks for drink, but they don't seem to have been pulling lately,' a drinker at the counter remarked to his companion as Philly passed by shakily with the pair of pints. 'The pale one not drinking looks like a brother as well. There must have been a family do.'

'You'd wonder where that wheelchair brother puts all that drink,' the other changed.

'He puts it where we all put it. You don't need legs, for God's sake, to take drink. Drink only gets down as far as your flute.'

'Gloria is far from over,' Philly said as he put the two pints down on the table. 'Nothing is ever over. I'm going to take up in Peter's place.'

'You can't be that drunk,' Fonsie said dismissively.

'I'm not sober but I was never more certain of anything in my born life.'

'Didn't the lawyer say it'd go to Mother? What'll she do but sell?'

'I'm not sure she'll want to sell. She grew up there. It was in her family for generations.'

'I'm sure. I can tell you that now.'

'Well, it's even simpler, then. I'll buy the place off Mother,' Philly announced so decisively that Fonsie found himself looking at John.

'I'm out of this,' John said. 'What people do is their own business. All I ask is to be let go about my own life.'

'I've enough money to buy the place. You heard what the lawyer said it was worth. I'll give Mother its price and she can do with it what she likes.'

'We're sick these several years hearing about all you can buy,' Fonsie said angrily.

'Well, I'll go where people will not be sick, where there'll be no upcasting,' Philly said equally heatedly.

'What'll you do there?' John asked out of a desire to calm the heated talk.

'He'll grow onions.' Fonsie shook with laughter.

'I can't be going out to the oil fields for ever. It'll be a place to come home to. You saw how the little iron cross in the circle over the grave was eaten with rust. I'm going to have marble put up. Jim Cullen is going to look after Peter's cattle till I get back in six months and everything will be settled then.'

'You might even get married there,' Fonsie said sarcastically.

'It's unlikely but stranger things have happened, and I'll definitely be buried there. Mother will want to be buried there some day.'

'She'll be buried with our father out in Glasnevin.'

'I doubt that. Even the fish go back to where they came from. I'd say she's had more than enough of our poor father in one life to be going on with. John here has a family, but it's about time you gave where you're going yourself some thought,' Philly spoke directly to Fonsie.

'If I were to go I'd want to go where there was people and a bit of life about, not on some God-forsaken hill out in the bog with a crow or a sheep or a bloody rabbit.'

'There's no *if* in this business, it's just *when*. I'm sorry to have to say it, but it betrays a great lack of maturity on your part,' Philly said with drunken severity.

'You can plant maturity out there in the bog, for all I care, and may it grow into an ornament.'

'We better be going,' John said.

Philly rose and took Fonsie into his arms. In spite of his unsteadiness he carried him easily out to the car. Fonsie was close to tears. He had always thought he could never lose Philly. The burly block of exasperation would always come and go from the oil fields. Now he would go out to bloody Gloria Bog instead. As he was put in the car, his tears turned to rage.

'Yes, you'll be a big shot down there at last,' he said. 'They'll be made up. They'll be getting a Christmas present. They'll be getting one great big lump of a Christmas present.'

'Look,' John said soothingly. 'Mother will be waiting. She'll want to hear everything. And I have another home I have to go to yet.'

'I followed it all on the clock,' the mother said. 'I knew the Mass for Peter was starting at eleven and I put the big alarm clock on the table. At twenty past twelve I could see the coffin going through the cattle gate at the foot of Killeelan.'

'They were like a crowd of apes carrying the coffin up the hill. I could see it all from the car. Several times they had to put up hands as if the coffin was going to fall off the shoulders and roll back down the hill.'

'Once it did fall off. Old Johnny Whelan's coffin rolled halfway down the hill and broke open. They had to tie the boards together with the ropes they use for lowering into the grave. Some said the Whelans were drunk, others said they were too weak with hunger to carry the coffin. The Whelans were never liked. They are all in America now.'

'Anyhow, we buried poor Peter,' Philly said, as if it was at last a fact.

SEAMUS DEANE

from *Reading in the Dark*

Grandfather

December 1948

Brother Regan was lighting a candle in his dark classroom at the foot of the statue of the Blessed Virgin. Regan permitted no overhead lights when he gave his Christmas address in primary school. Regan was small, neat, economical. He had been at Una's funeral earlier that year, along with several other Christian Brothers from the primary school.

'Boys,' he said.

After he said 'Boys', he stopped for a bit and looked at us. Then he dropped his eyes and kept them down until he said, more loudly again,

'*Boys*.'

He had complete silence this time.

'Some of you here, one or two of you, perhaps, know the man I am going to talk about today. You may not know you know him, but that doesn't matter.

'More than twenty-five years ago, during the troubles in Derry, this man was arrested and charged with the murder of a policeman. The policeman had been walking home one night over Craigavon Bridge. It was a bleak night, November, nineteen hundred and twenty-two. The time was two in the morning. The policeman was off duty; he was wearing civilian clothes. There were two men coming the other way, on the other side of the bridge. As the policeman neared the middle of the bridge, these two men crossed over to his side. They were strolling, talking casually. They had their hats pulled down over their faces and their coat collars turned up for it was wet and cold. As they passed the policeman, one of them said, "Goodnight," and the policeman returned the greeting. And then suddenly he found himself grabbed from behind and lifted off his feet. He tried to kick but one of the men held his legs. "This is for Neil McLaughlin," said one. 'May you rot in the hell you're going to, you murdering . . ."'

Regan shook his head rather than say a swear word. Then he went on.

'They lifted him to the parapet and held him there for a minute like a log and let him stare down at the water – seventy, eighty feet below. Then they pushed him over and he fell, with the street lights shining on his wet coat until he disappeared into the shadows with a splash. They heard him thrashing, and he shouted once. Then he went under. His body was washed up three days later. No one saw his assailants.

'They went home and said nothing. A week later, a man was arrested and charged with the murder. He was brought to trial. But the only evidence the police had was that he was the friend and workmate of Neil McLaughlin, who had been murdered by a policeman a month before. The story was that, before McLaughlin died on the street where he had been shot, coming out of the newspaper office where he worked, he had whispered the name of his killer to this man who had been arrested. And this man had been heard to swear revenge, to get the policeman – let's call him Billy Mahon – in revenge for his friend's death. There was no point in going to the law, of course, justice would never be done; everyone knew that, especially in those early years. So maybe the police thought they could beat an admission out of him, but he did not flinch from his story. That night, he was not even in the city. He had been sent by his newspaper to Letterkenny, twenty miles away, and he had several witnesses to prove it. The case was thrown out. People were surprised, even though they believed the man to be innocent. Innocence was no guarantee for a Catholic then. Nor is it now.

'Well, I wasn't even in the city in those days. But one of the priests, with whom I have since become friends, was then a young curate. He told me the story of the accused man. This man was prominent in local sporting circles and he helped in various ways to raise money for the parish building fund. One night, in the sacristy of the Long Tower Church, just down the road from here, he told the priest that he had not been to confession in twenty years. He had something on his conscience that no penance could relieve. The priest told him to trust in God's infinite mercy. He offered to hear the man's confession; he offered to find someone else, a monk he knew down in Portglenone, to whom the man could go, in case he did not want to confess to someone he knew. But no, he wouldn't go. No penance, he said, would be any use, because, in his heart, he could not feel sorrow for what he had done. But he wanted to tell someone, not as a confession, but in confidence.

'So he told the priest about being arrested. He told him about the beatings he had been given – rubber truncheons, punches, kicks, threats to put him over the bridge. He told how he had resisted these assaults and never wavered.

'The priest told him that such steadiness in sticking to his story was a testimony to the strength a person gets from knowing he is in the right.

'He looked at the priest in amazement. And then he said these words, words the priest never forgot.

' "D'ye think that's what I wanted to tell you? The story of my innocence? For God's sake, Father, can't you see? I wasn't innocent. I was guilty. I killed Mahon and I'd kill him again if he came through the door this minute. That's why I can't confess. I have no sorrow, no resolve not to do it again. No pity. Mahon shot my best friend dead in the street, for nothing. He was a drunken policeman with a gun, looking for a Catholic to kill, and he left that man's wife with two young children and would have got off scot-free for the rest of his days; probably got promoted for sterling service. And Neil told me as he lay there, with the blood draining from him, that Mahon did it. 'Billy Mahon, Billy Mahon, the policeman,' that's what he said. And even then I had to run back into the doorway and leave his body there in the street because they started shooting down the street from the city walls. And I'm not sorry I got Mahon and I told him what it was for before I threw him over that bridge and he knew, just too late, who I was when I said goodnight to him. It was goodnight all right. One murdering . . ." ' – Regan bowed his head – ' "less."

'Boys, in the story the priest told to me, and that I have now just told to you, look what happened. A man went to the grave without confessing his sin. And think of all the things that were done in that incident. The whole situation makes men evil. Evil men make the whole situation. And these days, similar things occur. Some of you boys may feel like getting involved when you leave school, because you sincerely believe you will be on the side of justice, fighting for the truth. But, boys, let me tell you, there is a judge who sees all, knows all and is never unjust; there is a judge whose punishments and rewards are beyond the range of human imagining; there is a Law greater than the laws of human justice, far greater than the law of revenge, more enduring than the laws of any state whatsoever. That judge is God, that Law is God's Law, and the issue at stake is your immortal soul.

'We live, boys, in a world that will pass away. The shadows that candle throws upon the walls of this room are as insubstantial as we are. Injustice, tyranny, freedom, national independence are realities that will fade too, for they are not ultimate realities, and the only life worth living is a life lived in the light of the ultimate. I know there are some who believe that the poor man who committed that murder was justified, and that he will be forgiven by an all-merciful God for what he did. That may be. I fervently hope that it is so, for who would judge God's mercy? But it is true, too, of the policeman: he may have been as plagued by guilt as his own murderer; he may have justified himself too; he may have refused sorrow and known no peace of mind; he may have forgiven himself or he may have been forgiven by God. It is not for us to judge. But it is for us to distinguish, to see the difference between wrong done to us and equal wrong done *by* us; to know that our transient life, no matter how scarred, how broken, how miserable it may be, is also God's miracle and gift; that we may try to improve it, but we may not destroy it. If we destroy it in another, we destroy it in ourselves. Boys, as you leave another year behind, you come that much closer to entering a world of wrong, insult, injury, unemployment, a world where the unjust hold power and the ignorant rule. But there is an inner peace nothing can reach; no insult can violate, no corruption can deprave. Hold to that; it is what your childish innocence once was and what your adult maturity must become. Hold to that. I bless you all.'

And he raised his hand and made the sign of the Cross above our heads and crossed the room, blew out the candle as the bell rang wildly in the chapel tower, and asked that the lights be switched on. He left in silence with the candle smoking heavily behind him at the foot of the statue, stubby in its thick drapery of wax.

'That was your grandfather,' said McShane to me. 'I know that story too. He worked at the newspaper office and he was McLaughlin's friend. My father told me all about it.'

I derided him. I had heard the story too, but I wasn't going to take it on before everyone else. Not if my mother's father was involved. Did Regan know? Was it really my grandfather who had done that, the little man who sat around in his simmet vest all day long, looking sick and scarcely saying a word? Anyway, it was just folklore. I had heard something of it when I was much younger and lay on the landing at night listening to the grown-ups talking in the kitchen below and had leaned over the banisters and imagined it was the edge of the parapet and that I was falling, falling down to the river of the hallway, as deaf and shining as a log.

MARY LELAND
from *The Killeen*

7

'There will be trouble.' Bina put down the *Cork Examiner* and rested it, half-folded, on her knees. At the other side of the fire Fr Costello emerged from his abstraction, a haze engendered by the warmth, Bina's silence, and a consciousness of what was going on upstairs.

'No, really, there can't be any doubt about it. Maybe not yet, a few years perhaps, but there must be trouble in Europe, an outbreak of some kind.' Having stated this certainty Bina was prepared to take up the newspaper again, but Fr Costello's reply halted her.

'Whose side would we be on, do you think?' It was less of a question than a comment. He was not really interested in the possibility of a war in Europe, being still scarred from the war in Ireland.

'What "we" are we talking about, Fr Costello?' Bina raised the end of the question to a challenge. 'Do you mean the Irish government? Or the Irish people? I have no doubts about that. De Valera will either side with England or stay neutral. It will be easier for him to be neutral if England isn't drawn into it, but from what I know' – she bowed her head at him – 'I know it isn't much – of English policies in Europe I feel sure that country will be heavily involved, may even instigate the final confrontation. That will be De Valera's real dilemma; can he really support the British, no matter who the enemy is? I don't think he can, you know, even if he goes on the way he's started.' She rattled the paper and went on. 'But I can answer for the Irish people. Their choice would be Germany. It would have to be.'

The priest envied her certainty even when he didn't share it. All her certainties. She sat here opposite him, legs in ribbed stockings set square under the long tweed skirt, the solidity of her presence a guarantee of utter self-confidence. She discussed Europe with the same efficient assurance she gave to her acid consideration of the Irish parliament, to household management, or to the affairs and gossip of the parish around St Luke's.

'Not that it's my business,' she would say sometimes (he had heard her once outside St Patrick's Church on a Sunday morning); 'not that it's my business, it's not my parish. But one must try to help people settle things properly.'

It was the *properly* that mattered. 'Properly' according to Miss Bina Mulcahy was not always what suited the objects of her concern, but then she didn't live in the parish and she didn't have to hear their mutterings. Yet there was no doubt, and she herself would not have doubted it for a second, that the Misses Mulcahy were regarded here in St Luke's with the same classless awe as they were in the South Parish. Inevitably upright, well-bred if not well-born, propertied, Catholic, educated and powerful. And martyred.

Apart from his son, the Mulcahy sisters were the only living blood relatives of Maurice Mulcahy, hero and martyr, dead in the Curragh military prison camp, on hunger strike. A Republican victim of other Republicans. Sisters of his father, their political lineage was impeccable for eternity.

Fr Costello's mother and the mother of Maurice Mulcahy had been sisters; that made him a cousin of the martyr, reduced his acceptability to his Bishop and in Cork committed his immediate prospects of preferment to an atmosphere of public sympathy and an intermediate series of chaplaincies. His day would come; even the Bishop, in careful nuances, indicated that his day would come. He was simply experiencing a period of adjustment. The fire roasting his trouser-legs gave out an added warmth, reminding him of places where he would be welcome, where Earnán would have been welcome.

'She has agreed, she is still in agreement, is she?' He inclined his head sideways and upwards towards the door and the stairs.

'Absolutely.' Miss Bina spoke with resolution. 'That's why we have Dr Douglass with her. Otherwise a midwife would have done. Dr Douglass has a woman waiting to take the child and later will take charge of it herself. When it is older, not needing so much care. She is a busy woman, God bless her.'

Fr Costello wondered if Miss Bina did not wonder why he was asking. He had no need to do so; he had been privy to all the plans. So why was he asking, now, when it was all happening? There was no sound in the hall, nothing came from overhead to indicate the turmoil blocked into one small room. The house was calm. He was here only to recognize the child and to baptize it in a quick and necessary ritual. With that out of the way he need have no more dealings with the infant until it was old enough to be educated, and even then he knew that the Misses Mulcahy could be trusted there, they knew what would be required for and from the education of such a child.

Miss Bina's paper rustled again; to forestall another international forecast the priest moved his chair back from the fire by pressing his feet hard on the floor and his lower spine against the studded leather back. The anticipated squeaking shuffle cut across what Miss Bina had been about to say, and Fr Costello asked instead: 'Julia is up there, is she?'

Miss Bina did not answer at once. Julia was up there. Miss Bina did not approve, but perhaps, in these very particular circumstances, she should make some allowances in the name of Christian Charity.

'Yes, poor girl, she is so kind. No one is beneath her compassion. A foolish poor girl she is, as we know. But very kind.'

Fr Costello was not at all sure that Julia Mulcahy, *née* Watson, was foolish. Most distinctly she was not poor, and although she was discreet about her wealth, this, combined with his uneasy suspicion of more intelligence and certainly more education than her husband's aunts wished to credit, made him carefully civil in his dealings with her. Again in this he admired the aunts, whose assumptions could only be called presumptions by people who felt for Julia's gentility. They treated this composed relic of the dead man with dismissive courtesy. They used the house as if it were their own – but then, Julia allowed that. Thinking about her now, Fr Costello suddenly thought that perhaps Julia could behave like that because it didn't matter, her own secret life was contained elsewhere.

So much of her life had been public. There was still intense, if muted, public interest in her well-being, and in that of her son, the two-year-old boy the Mulcahys had tried to call Maurice, Julia and her husband had christened Robert Patrick and Julia, determinedly unromantic, always called Pat.

He wondered what could be happening up there. He knew what was happening. For the first time in his life he wondered, nearly, what it was like, the steady waiting time punctured by gasping, tearing pains, the rhythms building with moans and cries, the bursting out with floods of blood and liquids. Yet the house was silent, as if all this sequence of agony and shameful relief and soiled sheets and blood and ordure could be absorbed by the very walls.

The silence grew loud in his ears. His pulse throbbed with heat and the picture grew from the fireplace, a picture more confused and tortured because it was the flesh of imagination. The female legs splayed out, held down by rigorous hands, the black gap between suddenly gushing with blood and birth. Horrible! But he was excited in some way he could not relish, and with a creeping sense of sin he tried to remember the face of the mother, the girl he had last seen leaning against the slate steps in the nuns' garden, her body relaxed and tired as she sat, waiting and still, high up above him when he left the convent cemetery. As he watched her she had stirred, looked down, and she had seen him.

Brown hair waved around her face. She was not conveniently pretty. It was hard to describe the distinctive features which made her appearance memorable. He had pretended all those first months that she had been cheaply attractive but, taking this long look and now embracing what he had seen, he knew that wasn't true. Her face was the face of many Irish girls, healthy, some people might say 'bonny': a white forehead met the brown curls, her deeply lashed eyes were grey under delicate arched brows. The skin of her cheeks had a faint, sunny flush to them, and her mouth was wide, and full, and pale. Then, as he watched her, she shivered and her skirt tightened around the curve of her stomach and he felt distaste rise in his throat. He had turned away to where Julia Mulcahy was waiting inside the porch of the convent, where Margaret was to be met and taken away. To here and now.

'England's difficulty is Ireland's opportunity!' Miss Bina's rejoicing tones reminded him of the great world outside. The world itself was festering; like Miss Bina, like her sister Lou, like Dr Douglass and other men and women scattered in groups large and small through the country, his conviction was that Ireland could be kept pure, unsoiled by what was happening outside. That purity would itself eventually produce a nation strong, inviolable, racially untarnished, Catholic from Bantry to Belfast, the envy of whatever Europe would emerge from the rearrangements now being dreamed, discussed, or witnessed, in Berlin, Paris, London and Rome, even in Madrid.

'I never told her, and that nun swore *she* never told her that I have any connection with the child. Do you think, will Julia tell her?' His question was lightly asked, but anxious.

'Not at all! Julia knows very little about it all, she's not a curious girl, you know. And even if she did know, what difference could it make? Wouldn't all the world see that it is right for a child born in these circumstances to be guarded by his own uncle?'

No nonsense to Miss Bina. She didn't think much of the priest's anxiety on that matter. Earnán was gone, the child was, or would be, here, its mother incapable of caring for it. The choice was between an orphanage or Miss Bina's 'arrangements'. Naturally her plans must be the best since they included the concern of a priest who was also a relative, a doctor who was also a woman, and herself. Seeing the priest subside more easily in his chair, she went back to the Continent, carefully searching the references to Germany for further signs that the rise of National Socialism offered some helpful guidelines for aspirant and dedicated Irish nationalists.

The high ceiling above them suddenly strummed with hasty steps, then there was silence again.

'How long has it been now?' he asked nervously.

'Only since yesterday afternoon. For a first child that's not so long, I believe. And she's a grand healthy girl. Julia gave her every attention. She should have kept her below in the kitchen like I advised her, but no, she's too kind . . .'

The unspoken rebuke trailed away. Fr Costello was counting the hours. Then – 'In sorrow shalt thou bring forth children!' he muttered, reminding himself how justified, in this case, such punishment was.

'The situation here, of course, is bad enough. And it can only get worse, now that he's taken over! Coming like a saviour to his people – as if the entire population of the nation had gone down on their knees to beg him to forget his promises and enter parliament and guide a state so young that it isn't even out of swaddling bonds. De Valera!'

Miss Bina pronounced the name with relish, shortening the second syllable in a ridiculous emphasis.

'We can all see now what's happening with the soldiers he was so friendly with, once upon a time. He's not going to fight for a republic – and it could be done now, you know. It could be done now.'

She hit her hand off the padded wood under her arm. Her voice rose. The priest shared her disillusionment, but not her anger. His purpose could not be reduced; he brought the sanction of his church to the drive for unity, for Catholic unity which would be a barrier to alien vices like socialism. He had no need for anger. His staff of life was controlled hate.

'Well, there may not be many the likes of Maurice and Earnán this minute, but they'll come, you mark my words! Maurice has left a legend behind him, Earnán is working to get the Irish in America behind us. The day has to come, Father. My only hope now is that it will come when I can see it, watch it happening.'

She was calm again. Fr Costello agreed with her on so many things there was no need for speech. Now he heard the footsteps on the lower stairs, the hand on the door. When it opened, Miss Lou stood there, trailing a thin reek of chloroform.

'All over. A boy, a grand big child. She's asleep, Doctor saw to that. Bring your things, Father, come on.'

The three of them left the room together and went upstairs, to baptize the baby.

BERNARD MAC LAVERTY

'Life Drawing'

After darkness fell and he could no longer watch the landscape from the train window, Liam Diamond began reading his book. He had to take his feet off the seat opposite and make do with a less comfortable position to let a woman sit down. She was equine and fifty and he didn't give her a second glance. To take his mind off what was to come, he tried to concentrate. The book was a study of the Viennese painter Egon Schiele who, it seemed, had become so involved with his thirteen-year-old girl models that he ended up in jail. Augustus John came to mind: 'To paint someone you must first sleep with them', and he smiled. Schiele's portraits – mostly of himself – exploded off the page beside the text, distracting him. All sinew and gristle and distortion. There was something decadent about them, like Soutine's pictures of hanging sides of beef.

Occasionally he would look up to see if he knew where he was but saw only the darkness and himself reflected from it. The streetlights of small towns showed more and more snow on the roads the farther north he got. To stretch, he went to the toilet and noticed the faces as he passed between the seats. Like animals being transported. On his way back he saw a completely different set of faces, but he knew they looked the same. He hated train journeys, seeing so many people, so many houses. It made him realize he was part of things whether he liked it or not. Seeing so many unknown people through their back windows, standing outside shops, walking the streets, moronically waving from level crossings, they grew amorphous and repulsive. They were going about their static lives while he had a sense of being on the move. And yet he knew he was not. At some stage any one of those people might travel past his flat on a train and see him in the act of pulling his curtains. The thought depressed him so much that he could no longer read. He leaned his head against the window and although he had his eyes closed he did not sleep.

The snow, thawed to slush and refrozen quickly, crackled under his feet and made walking difficult. For a moment he was not sure which was the house. In the dark he had to remember it by number and shade his eyes against the yellow glare of the sodium street lights to make out the figures on the small terrace doors. He saw Fifty-six and walked three houses farther along. The heavy wrought-iron knocker echoed in the hallway as it had always done. He waited, looking up at the semicircular fan-light. Snow was beginning to fall, tiny flakes swirling in the corona of light. He was about to knock again or look to see if they had got a bell when he heard shuffling from the other side of the door. It opened a few inches and a white-haired old woman peered out. Her hair was held in place by a net a shade different from her own hair colour. It was one of the Miss Harts but for the life of him he couldn't remember which. She looked at him, not understanding.

'Yes?'

'I'm Liam,' he said.

'Oh, thanks be to goodness for that. We're glad you could come.'

Then she shouted over her shoulder, 'It's Liam.'

She shuffled backwards, opening the door and admitting him. Inside she tremulously shook his hand, then took his bag and set it on the ground. Like a servant, she took his coat and hung it on the hall stand. It was still in the same place and the hallway was still a dark electric yellow.

'Bertha's up with him now. You'll forgive us sending the telegram to the College but we thought you would like to know,' said Miss Hart. If Bertha was up the stairs then she must be Maisie.

'Yes, yes, you did the right thing,' said Liam. 'How is he?'

'Poorly. The doctor has just left – he had another call. He says he'll not last the night.'

'That's too bad.'

By now they were standing in the kitchen. The fireplace was black and empty. One bar of the dished electric fire took the chill off the room and no more.

'You must be tired,' said Miss Hart, 'it's such a journey. Would you like a cup of tea? I tell you what, just you go up now and I'll bring you your tea when it's ready. All right?'

'Yes, thank you.'

When he reached the head of the stairs she called after him,

'And send Bertha down.'

Bertha met him on the landing. She was small and withered and her head reached to his chest. When she saw him she started to cry and reached out her arms to him saying,

'Liam, poor Liam.'

She nuzzled against him, weeping. 'The poor old soul,' she kept repeating. Liam was embarrassed feeling the thin arms of this old woman he hardly knew about his hips.

'Maisie says you have to go down now,' he said, separating himself from her and patting her crooked back. He watched her go down the stairs, one tottering step at a time, gripping the banister, her rheumatic knuckles standing out like limpets.

He paused at the bedroom door and for some reason flexed his hands before he went in. He was shocked to see the state his father was in. He was now almost completely bald except for some fluffy hair above his ears. His cheeks were sunken, his mouth hanging open. His head was back on the pillow so that the strings of his neck stood out.

'Hello, it's me, Liam,' he said when he was at the bed. The old man opened his eyes flickeringly. He tried to speak. Liam had to lean over but failed to decipher what was said. He reached out and lifted his father's hand in a kind of wrong handshake.

'Want anything?'

His father signalled by a slight movement of his thumb that he needed something. A drink? Liam poured some water and put the glass to the old man's lips. Arcs of scum had formed at the corners of his sagging mouth. Some of the water spilled on to the sheet. It remained for a while in droplets before sinking into dark circles.

'Was that what you wanted?' The old man shook his head. Liam looked around the room, trying to see what his father could want. It was exactly as he had remembered it. In twenty years he hadn't changed the wallpaper, yellow roses looping on an umber trellis. He lifted a straight-backed chair and drew it up close to the bed. He sat with his elbows on his knees, leaning forward.

'How do you feel?'

The old man made no response and the question echoed around and around the silence in Liam's head.

Maisie brought in tea on a tray, closing the door behind her with her elbow. Liam noticed that two red spots had come up on her cheeks. She spoke quickly in an embarrassed whisper, looking back and forth between the dying man and his son.

'We couldn't find where he kept the teapot so it's just a tea-bag in a cup. Is that all right? Will that be enough for you to eat? We sent out for a tin of ham, just in case. He had nothing in the house at all, God love him.'

'You've done very well,' said Liam. 'You shouldn't have gone to all this trouble.'

'If you couldn't do it for a neighbour like Mr Diamond – well? Forty-two years and there was never a cross word between us. A gentleman we always called him, Bertha and I. He kept himself to himself. Do you think can he hear us?' The old man did not move.

'How long has he been like this?' asked Liam.

'Just three days. He didn't bring in his milk one day and that's not like him, y'know. He'd left a key with Mrs Rankin, in case he'd ever lock himself out again – he did once, the wind blew the door shut – and she came in and found him like this in the chair downstairs. He was frozen, God love him. The doctor said it was a stroke.'

Liam nodded, looking at his father. He stood up and began edging the woman towards the bedroom door.

'I don't know how to thank you, Miss Hart. You've been more than good.'

'We got your address from your brother. Mrs Rankin phoned America on Tuesday.'

'Is he coming home?'

'He said he'd try. She said the line was as clear as a bell. It was like talking to next door. Yes, he said he'd try but he doubted it very much.' She had her hand on the door knob. 'Is that enough sandwiches?'

'Yes thanks, that's fine.' They stood looking at one another awkwardly. Liam fumbled in his pocket. 'Can I pay you for the ham . . . and the telegram?'

'I wouldn't dream of it,' she said. 'Don't insult me now, Liam.' He withdrew his hand from his pocket and smiled his thanks to her.

'It's late,' he said, 'perhaps you should go now and I'll sit up with him.'

'Very good. The priest was here earlier and gave him . . .' she groped for the word with her hands.

'Extreme Unction?'

'Yes. That's twice he has been in three days. Very attentive. Sometimes I think if our ministers were half as good . . .'

'Yes, but he wasn't what you could call gospel greedy.'

'He was lately,' she said.

'Changed times.'

She half turned to go and said, almost coyly,

'I'd hardly have known you with the beard.' She looked up at him, shaking her head in disbelief. He was trying to make her go, standing close to her but she skirted round him and went over to the bed. She touched the old man's shoulder.

'I'm away now, Mr Diamond. Liam is here. I'll see you in the morning,' she shouted into his ear. Then she was away.

Liam heard the old ladies' voices in the hallway below, then the slam of the front door. He heard the crackling of their feet over the frozen slush beneath the window. He lifted the tray off the chest of drawers and on to his knees. He hadn't realized it, but he was hungry. He ate the sandwiches and the piece of fruit cake, conscious of the chewing noise he was making with his mouth in the silence of the bedroom. There was little his father could do about it now. They used to have the most terrible rows about it. You'd have thought it was a matter of life and death. At table he had sometimes trembled with rage at the boys' eating habits, at their greed as he called it. At the noises they made, 'like cows getting out of muck'. After their mother had left them he took over the responsibility for everything. One night, as he served sausages from the pan Liam, not realizing the filthy mood he was in, made a grab. His father in a sudden downward thrust jabbed the fork he had been using to cook the sausages into the back of Liam's hand.

'Control yourself.'

Four bright beads of blood appeared as Liam stared at them in disbelief.

'They'll remind you to use your fork in future.'

He was sixteen at the time.

The bedroom was cold and when he finally got round to drinking his tea it was tepid. He was annoyed that he couldn't heat it by pouring more. His feet were numb and felt damp. He went downstairs and put on his overcoat and brought the electric fire up to the bedroom, switching on both bars. He sat huddled over it, his fingers fanned out, trying to get warm. When the second bar was switched on there was a clicking noise and the smell of burning dust. He looked over at the bed but there was no movement.

'How do you feel?' he said again, not expecting an answer. For a long time he sat staring at the old man, whose breathing was audible but quiet – a kind of soft whistling in his nose. The alarm clock, its face bisected with a crack, said twelve-thirty. Liam checked it against the red figures of his digital watch. He stood up and went to the window. Outside the roofs tilted at white snow-covered angles. A faulty gutter hung spikes of icicles. There was no sound in the street, but from the main road came the distant hum of a late car that faded into silence.

He went out on to the landing and into what was his own bedroom. There was no bulb when he switched the light on so he took one from the hall and screwed it into the shadeless socket. The bed was there in the corner with its mattress of blue stripes. The lino was the same, with its square pock-marks showing other places the bed had been. The cheap green curtains that never quite met on their cord still did not meet.

He moved to the wall cupboard by the small fireplace and had to tug at the handle to get it open. Inside, the surface of everything had gone opaque with dust. Two old radios, one with a fretwork face, the other more modern with a tuning dial showing such places as Hilversum, Luxembourg, Athlone; a Dansette record player with its lid missing and its arm bent back, showing wires like severed nerves and blood vessels; the empty frame of the smashed glass picture was still there; several umbrellas, all broken. And there was his box of poster paints. He lifted it out and blew off the dust.

It was a large Quality Street tin and he eased the lid off, bracing it against his stomach muscles. The colours in the jars had shrunk to hard discs. Viridian green, vermilion, jonquil yellow. At the bottom of the box he found several sticks of charcoal, light in his fingers when he lifted them, warped. He dropped them into his pocket and put the tin back into the cupboard. There was a pile of magazines and papers and beneath that again he saw his large Winsor and Newton sketchbook. He eased it out and began to look through the work in it. Embarrassment was what he felt most, turning the pages, looking at the work of this schoolboy. He could see little talent in it, yet he realized he must have been good. There were several drawings of hands in red pastel which had promise. The rest of the pages were blank. He set the sketchbook aside to take with him and closed the door.

Looking round the room, it had to him the appearance of nakedness. He crouched and looked under the bed, but there was nothing there. His fingers coming in contact with the freezing lino made him aware how cold he was. His jaw was tight and he knew that if he relaxed he would shiver. He went back to his father's bedroom and sat down.

The old man had not changed his position. He had wanted him to be a lawyer or a doctor but Liam had insisted, although he had won a scholarship to the university, on going to art college. All that summer his father tried everything he knew to stop him. He tried to reason with him,

'*Be* something. And you can carry on doing your art. Art is OK as a sideline.'

But mostly he shouted at him. 'I've heard about these art students and what they get up to. Shameless bitches prancing about with nothing on. And what sort of a job are you going to get? Drawing on pavements?' He nagged him every moment they were together about other things. Lying late in bed, the length of his hair, his outrageous appearance. Why hadn't he been like the other lads and got himself a job for the summer? It wasn't too late because he would willingly pay him if he came in and helped out in the shop.

One night, just as he was going to bed, Liam found the old framed print of cattle drinking. He had taken out the glass and had begun to paint on the glass itself with small tins of Humbrol enamel paints left over from aeroplane kits he had never finished. They produced a strange and exciting texture which was even better when the paint was viewed from the other side of the pane of glass. He sat stripped to the waist in his pyjama trousers painting a self-portrait reflected from the mirror on the wardrobe door. The creamy opaque nature of the paint excited him. It slid on to the glass, it built up, in places it ran scalloping like cinema curtains, and yet he could control it. He lost all track of time as he sat with his eyes focused on the face staring back at him and the painting he was trying to make of it. It became a face he had not known, the holes, the lines, the spots. He was in a new geography.

His brother and he used to play a game looking at each other's faces upside down. One lay on his back across the bed, his head flopped over the edge, reddening as the blood flooded into it. The other sat in a chair and stared at him. After a time the horror of seeing the eyes where the mouth should be, the inverted nose, the forehead gashed with red lips, would drive him to cover his eyes with his hands. 'It's your turn now,' he would say, and they would change places. It was like familiar words said over and over again until they became meaningless, and once he ceased to have purchase on the meaning of a word it became terrifying, an incantation. In adolescence he had come to hate his brother, could not stand the physical presence of him, just as when he was lying upside down on the bed. It was the same with his father. He could not bear to touch him and yet for one whole winter when he had a bad shoulder he had to stay up late to rub him with oil of wintergreen. The old boy would sit with one hip on the bed and Liam would stand behind him, massaging the stinking stuff into the white flesh of his back. The smell, the way the blubbery skin moved under his fingers, made him want to be sick. No matter how many times he washed his hands, at school the next day he would still reek of oil of wintergreen.

It might have been the smell of the Humbrol paints or the strip of light under Liam's door – whatever it was, his father came in and yelled that it was half-past three in the morning and what the hell did he think he was doing, sitting half-naked drawing at this hour of the morning? He had smacked him full force with the flat of his hand on his bare back and, stung by the pain of it, Liam had leapt to retaliate. Then his father had started to laugh, a cold snickering laugh. 'Would you? Would you? Would you indeed?' he kept repeating with a smile pulled on his mouth and his fists bunched to knuckles in front of him. Liam retreated to the bed and his father turned on his heel and left. Thinking the incident over, Liam knotted his fists and cursed his father. He looked over his shoulder into the mirror and saw the primitive daub of his father's hand, splayed fingers outlined across his back. He heard him on the stairs and when he came back into the bedroom with the poker in his hand he felt his insides turn to water. But his father looked away from him with a sneer and smashed the painting to shards with one stroke. As he went out of the door he said,

'Watch your feet in the morning.'

He had never really 'left home'. It was more a matter of going to art college in London and not bothering to come back. Almost as soon as he was away from the house his hatred for his father eased. He simply stopped thinking about him. Of late he had wondered if he was alive or dead – if he still had the shop. The only communication they had had over the years was when Liam sent him, not without a touch of vindictiveness, an invitation to some of the openings of his exhibitions.

Liam sat with his fingertips joined, staring at the old man. It was going to be a long night. He looked at his watch and it was only a little after two.

He paced up and down the room, listening to the tick of snow on the window-pane. When he stopped to look down, he saw it flurrying through the haloes of the street lamps. He went into his own bedroom and brought back the sketchbook. He moved his chair to the other side of the bed so that the light fell on his page. Balancing the book on his knee, he began to draw his father's head with the stick of charcoal. It made a light hiss each time a line appeared on the cartridge paper. When drawing he always thought of himself as a wary animal drinking, the way he looked up and down, up and down, at his subject. The old man had failed badly. His head scarcely dented the pillows, his cheeks were hollow and he had not been shaved for some days. Earlier, when he had held his hand it had been clean and dry and light like the hand of a girl. The bedside light deepened the shadows of his face and highlighted the rivulets of veins on his temple. It was a long time since he had used charcoal and he became engrossed in the way it had to be handled and the different subtleties of line he could get out of it. He loved to watch a drawing develop before his eyes.

His work had been well received and among the small Dublin art world he was much admired – justly he thought. But some critics had scorned his work as 'cold' and 'formalist' – one had written, 'Like Mondrian except that he can't draw a straight line'

– and this annoyed him because it was precisely what he was trying to do. He felt it was unfair to be criticized for succeeding in his aims.

His father began to cough – a low wet bubbling sound. Liam leaned forward and touched the back of his hand gently. Was this man to blame in any way? Or had he only himself to blame for the shambles of his life? He had married once and lived with two other women. At present he was on his own. Each relationship had ended in hate and bitterness, not because of drink or lack of money or any of the usual reasons but because of a mutual nauseating dislike.

He turned the page and began to draw the old man again. The variations in tone from jet black to pale grey, depending on the pressure he used, fascinated him. The hooded lids of the old man's eyes, the fuzz of hair sprouting from the ear next the light, the darkness of the partially open mouth. Liam made several more drawings, absorbed, working slowly, refining the line of each until it was to his satisfaction. He was pleased with what he had done. At art school he had loved the life class better than any other. It never ceased to amaze him how sometimes it could come just right, better than he had hoped for; the feeling that something was working through him to produce a better work than at first envisaged.

Then outside he heard the sound of an engine followed by the clinking of milk bottles. When he looked at his watch he was amazed to see that it was five-thirty. He leaned over to speak to his father.

'Are you all right?'

His breathing was not audible and when Liam touched his arm it was cold. His face was cold as well. He felt for his heart, slipping his hand inside his pyjama jacket, but could feel nothing. He was dead. His father. He was dead and the slackness of his dropped jaw disturbed his son. In the light of the lamp his dead face looked like the open-mouthed moon. Liam wondered if he should tie it up before it set. In a Pasolini film he had seen Herod's jaw being trussed and he wondered if he was capable of doing it for his father.

Then he saw himself in his hesitation, saw the lack of any emotion in his approach to the problem. He was aware of the deadness inside himself and felt helpless to do anything about it. It was why all his women had left him. One of them accused him of making love the way other people rodded drains.

He knelt down beside the bed and tried to think of something good from the time he had spent with his father. Anger and sneers and nagging was all that he could picture. He knew he was grateful for his rearing but he could not *feel* it. If his father had not been there somebody else would have done it. And yet it could not have been easy – a man left with two boys and a business to run. He had worked himself to a sinew in his tobacconist's, opening at seven in the morning to catch the workers and closing at ten at night. Was it for his boys that he worked so hard? The man was in the habit of earning and yet he never spent. He had even opened for three hours on Christmas Day.

Liam stared at the dead drained face and suddenly the mouth held in that shape reminded him of something pleasant. It was the only joke his father had ever told and to make up for the smallness of his repertoire he had told it many times; of two ships passing in mid-Atlantic. He always megaphoned his hands to tell the story.

'Where are you bound for?' shouts one captain.

'Rio – de – Janeir – io. Where are you bound for?'

And the other captain, not to be outdone, yells back,

'Cork – a – lork – a – lor – io.'

When he had finished the joke he always repeated the punch-line, laughing and nodding in disbelief that something could be so funny.

'Cork a – lorka – lorio.'

Liam found that his eyes had filled with tears. He tried to keep them coming but they would not. In the end he had to close his eyes and a tear spilled from his left eye on to his cheek. It was small and he wiped it away with a crooked index finger.

He stood up from the kneeling position and closed the sketchbook, which was lying open on the bed. He might work on the drawings later. Perhaps a charcoal series. He walked to the window. Dawn would not be up for hours yet. In America it would be daylight and his brother would be in shirtsleeves. He would have to wait until Mrs Rankin was up before he could phone him – and the doctor would be needed for a death certificate. There was nothing he could do at the moment, except perhaps tie up the jaw. The Miss Harts when they arrived would know everything that ought to be done.

ITA DALY

'Such Good Friends'

Although it all happened over two years ago, I still cannot think about Edith without pain. My husband tells me I am being silly and that I should have got over it long ago. He says my attitude is one of self-indulgence and dramatization and that it is typical of me to over-react in this way. I have told no one but Anthony, and I think that this is a measure of the hurt I suffered, not to be able even to mention it to anyone else. I don't think I am over-reacting – though I admit that I have a tendency to get very excited when I discover a new friend or a potential friend. This may sound as if I am wallowing in permanent adolescence, but even if this were so, the knowledge still wouldn't stop me being overcome with joy if I should meet someone whom I felt to be truly sympathetic.

It may be that I feel like this because I have had so few real friends in my life. I do not say this with any suggestion of self-pity; I am aware that such affinity of spirit is a very rare commodity and so, when there is a possibility of finding it, why, there is every reason to be excited. And it is something I have only ever found with members of my own sex.

Not that I have ever had any shortage of men friends. I have a certain bold physical appeal which seems to attract them, and before I was married, I always had four or five men hovering around, waiting to take me out. I don't deny that this gave me a satisfaction – it was sexually stimulating and very good for one's ego – but I have never felt the possibility of a really close relationship with any of these men. Even Anthony, to whom I have been married for five years, and of whom I am genuinely fond, even he spends half the time not knowing what I am talking about, and indeed, I am the same with him. Men on the whole are unsubtle creatures. You feed them, bed them, and bolster their egos, and they are quite content. They demand nothing more from a relationship, and for them physical intimacy is the only kind that matters. They don't seem to feel a need for this inner communion, they are happy to jog along as long as their bodies are at ease. I do not bare my soul to men. I tried to once with Anthony in the early days of our marriage, and, poor dear, he became upset and was convinced that I must be pregnant. Pregnant women are known to suffer from all sorts of strange whims.

You may by now think that I do not like men, but you would be quite wrong. I do like them and I am sure that living with one must be so much easier than living with a member of one's own sex. They are easy to please, and easy to deceive, and it is on the whole therapeutic to spend one's days and nights with someone who sees life as an uncomplicated game of golf, with the odd rough moments in the bunker. All I point out are their limitations, and I do so knowing that these views may be nothing more than an eccentricity on my part.

However, to return to Edith. I first met her during a bomb scare when that spate of bomb scares was going on, a little over two years ago. Before my marriage I had been studying law. I passed my first two exams and then I left to get married. About a year later I decided I would try to get a job as a solicitor's clerk, for I found I was bored doing nothing all day long and I thought it might be a good idea to keep my hand in, so to speak. It would make it easier if I ever decided to go back to College and attempt to qualify.

The firm where I got my job had its offices on the top floor of an old house in Westmoreland Street. The offices had a Dickensian air of shabbiness and dust, although I knew the firm to be a thriving one. It consisted of Mr Kelly Senior, Mr Kelly Junior, and Mr Brown. Along with five typists and myself of course. Mr Brown was a downtrodden man of the people, who was particularly grateful to Mr Kelly Senior for having lifted him from the lowly status of clerk to the heights of a fully fledged solicitor. He spent his days trotting round after the boss, wringing his hands and looking worried, and, as far as I could see, making a general nuisance of himself. Mr Kelly *père et fils* were tall dour Knights of Columbanus. They had crafty grey eyes in emaciated grey faces and they always dressed in clerical grey three piece suits. One day, Mr Kelly *fils* caused quite a sensation when he ventured in wearing a yellow striped shirt, but this break with tradition must not have met with approval, for next day, and thereafter, he was back to the regulation policeman's blue.

The typists in the office were nice girls. I had little to do with them, as I had my own room, and only saw one of them when I had any work to give to her. In the beginning, as I was the only other female in the office, I did try joining them for morning coffee. However, it was not a success. They were not at their ease, and neither was I. I didn't know what to say to them, and they were obviously waiting for me to leave until they could resume their chatter of boyfriends and dances and pop music. There was only about six years difference in our ages, yet I felt like another generation. It was because of this lack of contact that I hardly noticed Edith's existence, although she had been in the office nearly six weeks. That was, until the day of the bomb scare.

We were cursed with bomb scares that winter and particularly irritated by this one, the third in the same week. We filed out of the building, silently, as people were doing on either side of us. The novelty had worn off and these regular sorties into the winter afternoons were beginning to get under people's skin. It was bitterly cold, and I thought I might as well go and have a drink. It seemed more sensible than standing around in the raw air, making small talk. I crossed over the bridge and turned down towards a little pub that I had discovered on such a previous occasion. I sat sipping a hot whiskey, enjoying the muggy warmth, when I happened to glance across at the girl sitting opposite me. She looked familiar in some vague way, and just as I was wondering if she was from the office, she caught my glance and smiled back at me. Yes, now I remembered, she was one of the typists all right, and now that she had seen me I felt obliged to go over and join her. I hadn't wanted to – I had been looking forward to a nice quiet drink without the effort of conversation. But I couldn't be so obviously rude.

'You're with Kelly and Brown,' I began, sitting down beside her.

Her smile was diffident, almost frightened.

'Yes, that's right. And you're Mrs Herbert. I know because the other girls told me – I haven't been long there myself. My name is Edith Duggan,' she added and held out her hand, rather formally I thought. We sat side by side, both of us ill-at-ease. I was wondering what I could talk about, and then I saw, lying open in front of her, a copy of *The Great Gatsby*. Good – at least this could be a common theme.

'Please call me Helen,' I said. 'Any friend of Gatsby's is a friend of mine. Do you like Scott Fitzgerald?'

'Oh I love him, I think he's great. He's marvellous.'

Her whole face lit up, and it was then I realized what a good-looking girl she was. As I have mentioned before, I have a certain showy attractiveness myself. I know I am not basically good-looking, and I depend heavily for effect on my skilful use of paints. But I have red hair and green eyes, and with a bold make-up I am very much the sort of woman that men stop to look at in the street. I could see now that Helen was not at all like this. She was small and slight, with a tiny face half hidden under a heavy weight of dark brown hair. You would pass her by and not look at her, but if you did stop to take a second look you would realize that her features, though small, were exquisitely proportioned, that her skin had a translucent sheen and that her eyes – her eyes were deep and soft and tranquil. I was the one getting all the barman's looks, but I could see at a glance that Edith was much the finer of us. She was such a charming girl too, shy and low spoken, yet with none of the gaucherie and bluster that so often accompany shyness.

But though I was pleased by her good looks and her charm, it was not these that excited me. What excited me was a realization that here was someone to whom I could speak. Right from the beginning, from my remark about Fitzgerald, I think we both were aware that we were instantly communicating. We talked that day, long into the afternoon, and the more we talked the more we found we wanted to say. It was not only that we shared values and views and interests, but there was a recognition, on both our parts I thought, of an inner identification, a oneness. I knew that I would never have to pretend to Edith, that she would always understand what I was trying to say. I knew that a bond and a sympathy had been established between us and that I could look forward with joy to the times that we would talk and laugh and cry together. I had found a friend.

Do women love their husbands, I sometimes wonder? Do I love Anthony? I know that I like him, that I am grateful to him, that I feel the constant desire to protect him. But love? How can you love somebody you are so apart from? We live together comfortably, but so distinctly. Anthony wants it so, although if I told him this he would be incredulous. I have come to realize as I lie in bed at night, or at the first light of dawn, with his supple body, wracked by pleasure, lying in my arms, that Anthony is undergoing his most profound experience. His body shudders, and his isolation is complete. Sometimes I am amazed by the exclusivity of his passion, although I know well that this sort of pleasure is something that you cannot share. I know, for I am no stranger to pleasure myself; I have felt a tingling in the loins, a heat in the bowels. But I have always kept a weather eye out and asked – is there nothing more? Anthony's capitulation to his body is so complete, and his gratitude to me afterwards so overwhelming, that I know that, for him, this is where we touch, this is where he reaches me. And I am left in the cold outside.

But not once I had met Edith. Anthony should have been grateful to Edith, for with her coming I stopped harassing him. He didn't have to watch me in the evenings, sitting bleakly in our elegant drawing-room, upsetting his innocent enjoyment of the evening papers. I didn't suddenly snap at him for no reason, or complain of being bored, or depressed or lonely. Edith became my source of pleasure. Soon we were having lunch together every day, and I would drive her home in the evenings after work. She soon confessed to me that she had been unhappy in the office before she met me, for the other girls were as unwilling to accept her as they had been me, although in both instances, to be fair, I think it was a sensible recognition on the typists' part of our essential difference. We just had nothing to share with them.

For a start, she was older than they were. She had been a third year philosophy student at the University, she told me. A most successful student, apparently, who had hoped to pursue an academic career. She had been working away quite happily, looking forward to her finals, when one day her mother, who had gone quite innocently in search of matches, had found a packet of contraceptive pills in Edith's handbag. It was not, Edith told me, the implication that she was sleeping with a man or men that had so shocked her parents. It was the deliberateness of the act. Young girls did from time to time fall from grace, and it was wrong and they should be punished accordingly. But that anyone, particularly a daughter whom they had reared so carefully, could arm herself with these pills before-hand – that sort of calculation denoted a wickedness and evil of a far more serious order. She was thrown out of the house that very evening and told never to darken the door again.

'The thing I regret most,' Edith said, 'was hurting them. You cannot expect them to understand, the way they were brought up themselves. It's natural that they'd react like that. But I do love them, and I really didn't want to cause them pain. They'll come round, I'm sure. I'll just have to give them a few months, and then everything will be all right I hope. I'll just have to be a lot more careful. But I do miss them, you know – particularly Mammy.'

I had known Edith about six weeks when she introduced me to Declan. She had mentioned him several times, and I gathered that they intended to get married as soon as Declan qualified. He was an engineering student. What a surprise I got the first time I saw him. I couldn't understand, and never did understand afterwards, how someone of Edith's delicacy and intelligence could fall in love with such a slob. And he *was* a slob, a lumbering six-foot-two, with a red face and a slack mouth and a good-humoured, apparently unlimited amount of self-confidence. The night I met him, he had come round after work to collect Edith, and she asked me to stay and have a drink with them. He took us to a rather draughty and gloomy pub, and having bought our drinks, sat opposite me and fixed me with a disapproving eye.

'What,' he asked, 'do you think of the situation in South Africa?'

I later discovered that being a swimming champion all through his school days and most of his college days, Declan had come late to the world of ideas. But not at all abashed by his late start, he was now determined, it appeared, to make up for lost time. I found his zeal rather wearying, I must admit, and I resented the off-hand way he dismissed Edith's comments. I wondered what would happen when he discovered Women's Lib. With a bit of luck he might offer to liberate Edith by refusing to marry her.

In the meantime I realized that Edith would not take kindly to any criticism I might voice and that I had better be careful to simulate some sort of enthusiasm. So next day when she asked me what I thought, I told her I found him very interesting, and that I'd like them both to come to dinner soon and meet Anthony. We decided on the next night, and I said I'd come and collect them as Declan didn't have a car. I planned my dinner carefully and told Anthony to provide an exceptional claret – it was a special occasion. At these times, I'm pleased to be married to a wine merchant, for Anthony can produce the most miraculous bottles, guaranteed to revive any social disaster. I did want Edith to be happy, to like my home and my dinner and my husband. I didn't want to impress her – I knew anyway that the trappings of wealth would leave her unmoved – but I wanted to offer her something, to share whatever I had with her. I was afraid she might be bored.

But I needn't have worried. The evening was a tremendous success and Anthony and Declan seemed to take to one another straight away. Anthony is a most tolerant man, and cannot understand my own violent reactions towards people. I don't think he notices them very much. Once he has had a good meal and with a decent cigar in his hand, he is prepared to listen to all kinds of nonsense all night long. I was amused that evening at the interest he seemed to be showing in Declan's lengthy monologues, nodding his head intelligently and throwing in a 'Really – How interesting' every now and again. Afterwards he told me he thought Declan a 'rather solemn but quite decent chap'.

I blessed his tolerance that night, for I thought it might provide a solution to a problem I saw looming. I had no interest in being lectured to by Declan, and on the other hand, if I saw as much of Edith as I wanted to, if I could take her to films, concerts, even perhaps on holiday, then I knew Declan would begin to resent me and feel perhaps that I was monopolizing Edith. But if I could manage to arrange these foursomes, then Anthony would keep Declan happy, and I would have Edith to myself.

And how happy I was at this prospect. The more I saw of Edith, the more I admired and loved her. She had a quietness and repose about her which I found particularly attractive – I am such a strident person myself. I always look for the limelight and though I have tried to cure myself of this fault, I know I am as bad as ever. But Edith actually preferred to listen. And when she listened, you knew that she was actually considering what you were saying, and not simply waiting for an opportunity to get in herself. I talked a lot to Edith, more, I think, than I had ever talked to anyone in my life. The pleasure I got from our conversation was enormous. The world suddenly seemed to be full of things and people and ideas to discuss. I asked for no other stimulant than the excitement generated by our talk, and I looked forward to our meetings with a sense of exhilaration. I loved to buy things for her too. I have always liked giving people gifts, but through being married to Anthony my sense of pleasure had become dulled. Mind you, I don't think it was Anthony, most men would be the same. You can buy a man only a certain number of shirts, and after that – what is there? But with Edith the possibilities were endless. She dressed quite badly – I don't think she ever thought about the way she looked. But I, who saw all the possibilities of her beauty, felt like a creator when I thought of dressing her. A scarf to bring out the purity of her skin, a chiffon blouse to emphasize that fragile line of her neck – the changes I could make in her appearance! Of course I had to be careful not to offend her, as I knew that one so sensitive might be made to feel uncomfortable by all these gifts. So sometimes I would pretend that I had bought something for myself and it didn't fit and she would be doing me a favour by taking it. Or I would accept a pound for a leather bag which had cost me fifteen, saying that I had picked it up cheaply but that the colour wasn't right.

Creating this new Edith re-awoke all my interest in clothes and make-up. I seemed to have been dressing myself and putting on my face for so long that I felt I could do it in my sleep, and I had some time ago grown bored with myself. Besides, presenting my rather obvious persona to the world was a straightforward task, and the subtleties which I used in dressing Edith would have been lost on me. And as Edith saw her new self emerging, she grew interested too. I wondered how this would affect her attitude towards Declan. As she began to realize what a beautiful girl she was, might she not also realize what a slob Declan was, and get rid of him? Not that I thought very much about Declan any more. He was by now busy preparing for his final examinations and when he did have time to go out with Edith he seemed quite happy for them to come and have dinner with us, or at Anthony's club. Anthony had even interested him in wine, and as they sat sniffing their glasses and delicately tasting, we sat giggling over ours, having quaffed too much of the stuff in a most unconnoisseur-like fashion. Edith and I both agreed that we knew little about wine, but knew what we liked. Sometimes, when Declan was studying, I'd go round to Edith's flat for supper, and we'd get through a bottle of plonk enjoying it just as much as any rare Burgundy. This formed a bond between us and gave us a nice comfortable sense of vulgarity, of which Delcan would have disapproved for intellectual reasons and Anthony for social.

I was happy. It is a state you have to be in to recognize. Before I met Edith, it had never occurred to me that I was unhappy. I knew that I was bored a lot of the time and often lonely. I felt that something was missing from my life and various well-meaning girlfriends had told me from time to time that what I wanted was a baby. Instinctively I knew however that this was not so. I have always rebelled at the idea of becoming a mother; I could never see myself, baby at breast, looking out placidly at the world. Now I knew that my reservations had been right: I would probably have made a very bad mother, and I would not have fulfilled myself. All I needed all that time was a friend. A real friend.

But it seems to be a rule of life that, having achieved a measure of happiness, clouds begin to float across one's Eden. I don't know when things started going wrong with Edith and myself, for my state of happiness had begun to blur my perceptions, and I wasn't as conscious as I should have been of all Edith's reactions. Then little by little I noticed changes in her. She started to make excuses about not coming out to the house with me. When I'd ask her to go to a concert or lecture she'd say no thank you, she was doing something else. She grew irritable too, and would cut me off short when I'd begin to talk about something. Then she took to avoiding me in the office or so it seemed to me, and she started bringing sandwiches in at lunch time, saying that she had no time to go out to lunch as she was doing extra work for Mr Kelly.

When I was certain that I had not been imagining Edith's attitude, when I could no longer fool myself that everything was as it had been, I grew very upset. What upset me most, I think, was that I could not offer an explanation for her behaviour. I knew I was not the most tactful person in the world, but I had felt that Edith and I were so close that there was no need for pretence; and anyway I couldn't remember having said anything so awful that she would stop wanting to see me because of it.

One afternoon I became so worried that I burst into tears in the office. Mr Kelly junior was with me at the time, and I think I frightened the poor man out of his wits, for he told me that I looked tired and to go home at once and not to bother coming in the next day, which was Friday. That weekend I did a lot of thinking. Away from the office I grew calm, and I began to think that things would sort themselves out if I could remain calm. Maybe I had been seeing too much of Edith, and if I left her alone for a while she would probably recover her equilibrium and everything would be all right again.

When I returned to the office, I stuck to my resolution. I remained perfectly friendly towards Edith, but I stopped asking her to come places with me, and I began to have my lunch half-an-hour earlier than the rest of the office. It was so difficult, this calm indifference, but I knew it was the only way. Then one morning as I was taking my coat off, one of the typists rushed into my room.

'Isn't it awful, have you heard?' she said.

'No, what is it, what's happened?'

'Edith Duggan's mother was killed last night. Run over by a bus as she was crossing the road. She died instantly. Edith, the poor thing, went to bits, I believe. They couldn't get her to stop crying.'

God, how awful. I felt quite sick. What must Edith be feeling? I knew she had loved her mother . . . and that she should have been killed before they could be reconciled

... The guilt she must be feeling, added to the pain. I must go to her, I knew. I put my coat back on and got her home address from one of the girls, and left without even telling Mr Kelly where I was going.

The house was a shabby semi-detached with a few sad flowers struggling for life in the patch of green outside. A man I took to be Edith's father answered the door. He showed me in to the little front room and there I saw Edith, sitting white-faced and stiff, staring at nothing. She looked up and gave me a wintry smile.

'Edith, what can I say – ' I began, but she interrupted me with a shake of her head.

'I know. It's all right really. I understand. It was good of you to come.'

The words sounded so small and distant in that front parlour.

'Oh, Edith, my poor, poor Edith.' I ran towards her and put my arms around her, kissing her, kissing her to comfort her. Suddenly she tore at my arms and flung herself from me. She ran behind the sofa and stood there, trembling.

'Get out of here,' she shouted. 'Leave me alone. Go away you – you monster.'

I tried to say something, but she began to scream some incoherent phrases about the girls in the office and how stupid she'd been and how could I have come there then. I could still hear the screams as I made my way down the path.

She didn't come back to the office. Anthony suggested that she had probably been reconciled with her father and was now staying at home to mind the family. I worried about her, for it seemed to me that the shock of her mother's death must have unhinged her mind. How else could I explain the dreadful things she shouted that day in her front room?

Then about a month later, as I was walking down Grafton Street one afternoon, I saw her coming towards me. She saw me too, and as we drew level I put out my hand. She looked at me, directly into my eyes, with a cold hostility.

'Hello Helen,' she said, and she sounded quite calm. 'I'm glad I've met you like this. You see, I want you to realize that I meant what I said that day. I wasn't hysterical or anything like that. I do not wish to see you ever again.' Then she stepped aside and walked on down towards O'Connell Street.

I felt my stomach heave as she walked away. I felt I could never get home, that I would have to stand there, in Grafton Street, rooted to the spot in horror. I twisted and turned, like an animal in a cage, not wanting to face the fact that Edith's shouted obscenities were the result of no temporary derangement. When I did get home and told Anthony, he refused to discuss it. He said that the only thing to do was to put the whole business out of my mind, forget about it completely. But how could I forget? How can I shrug off the pain and the pleasure, as if it had never happened? I can find no way of doing that, no way of wiping out the profound sense of loss I am left with. You see, we were such good friends, Edith and I. Such good friends.

JOHN BANVILLE

from *Birchwood*

Summer ended officially with the lighting of a fire in the drawing room. Rain fell all day, big sad drops drumming on the dead leaves, and smoke billowed back down the chimneys, where rooks had nested. The house seemed huge, hollow, all emptiness and echo. In the morning Granny Godkin was discovered in the hall struggling with an umbrella which would not open. She was going down to the summerhouse, rain or no rain, and when they tried to restrain her she shook her head and muttered, and rattled the umbrella furiously. In the last weeks, after her brief vibrant interval of fanged gaiety when the prospect appeared of a peasant revolt, she had become strangely withdrawn and vague, wandering distractedly about the house, sighing and sometimes even quietly weeping. She said there was no welcome for her now at Birchwood – a remark I wish to stress, for reasons which I will presently disclose – and spent more and more time down at the lake despite the autumnal damp. Often Michael and I would see her sitting motionless by the table in the summerhouse, her head inclined and her eyes intently narrowed, listening to the subtle shifts and subsidences within her, the mechanism of her body winding down.

'But you'll catch your death,' Mama cried. 'It's teeming.'

'What?' the old woman snapped. 'What? Leave me alone.'

'But –'

'Let me *be*, will you.'

Mama turned to my father. 'Joe, can you not . . . ? She'll get her death . . .' As always when she spoke to him now her voice dwindled hopelessly, sadly, and in silence her eyes, moist with tenderness and despair, followed him as he shrugged indifferently and turned away wearily to shut himself into the drawing room.

'*Curse you, will you open*,' Granny Godkin snarled, and thwacked the brolly like a whip. Mama, with her pathetic faith in reason, opened wide the front door to show the old woman the wickedness of the weather. 'Look, look how bad it is. You'll be drenched.'

Granny Godkin paused, and grinned slyly, wickedly, and glanced up sideways at Mama.

'You worry?' she whispered. 'Heh!'

The grin became a skeletal sneer, and she glared about her at the hall, and suddenly the umbrella flew open, a strange glossy black blossom humming on its struts, and when I think of that day it is that black flower dipping and bobbing in the gloomy hall which recalls the horror best. The old woman thrust it before her out the door, where a sudden gust of wind snatched it up and she was swept down the steps, across the lawn, and I ducked into the library to avoid Mama's inevitable, woebegone embrace.

Aunt Martha waited for me, huddled in an armchair by the empty fireplace with a shawl around her shoulders, gazing blankly at a book open in her lap and gnawing a raw carrot. She hardly looked at me, but flung the carrot into the grate and began to whine at once.

'Where have you been? I'm waiting this hour. Do you think I've nothing better to do? Your father says you're to learn Latin, I don't know why, god only knows, but there you are. Look at this book. Amo amas amat, love. Say it, amo, come on. Amo, I love.'

I sat and looked at her with that serene silent stare which never failed to drive her into a frenzy. She slapped the primer shut and bared her teeth, an unpleasant habit she had when angry, just like Papa.

'You know you really are a horrible little boy, do you know that, do you? Why do you hate me? I spend half my life in this house trying to give you some kind of an education, and all you do is gawp and grin – O yes, I've seen you grinning, you you you . . .' She clapped a hand to her forehead and closed her eyes. 'O, I, I must . . . Look, come, try to learn something, look at this lovely language, these words, Gabriel, please, for me, for your Mama, you're a dear child. Now, amo, I love . . .'

But she shut the book again, and with a low moan looked fretfully around the room, searching for something to which she might anchor her fractured attention. It occurred to me that my presence made hardly any difference to her, I mean she would have carried on like this whether I was there or not, might even have talked all that nonsense to the empty air. They were all fleeing into themselves, as fast as they could flee, all my loved ones. At the dinner table now I could gaze at any or all of them without ever receiving in return an inquiring glance, or an order to eat up and stop staring, or even a sad smile from Mama. Even Michael had since that day at the summerhouse become silent and preoccupied, had begun to avoid me, and I felt sure that he knew some secret which involved me and which I was not to know. I was like a lone survivor wandering among the wreckage, like Tiresias in the city of plague.

Papa insinuated himself into the room, slipped in at the door and tiptoed to the window without looking at us, and there stood gazing out at the dripping trees, rocking slowly on his heels, a gloomy ghost. Aunt Martha appeared not to have noticed him. She tapped my knee peremptorily with her fist.

'You must learn, Gabriel, it's no good to –'

The room shook. There was no sound, but instead a sensation of some huge thing crumpling, like a gargantuan heart attack, that part of an explosion that races out in a wave ahead of the blast and buckles the silence. But the blast did not arrive, and Aunt Martha looked at the ceiling, and Papa glanced at us querulously over his shoulder, and we said nothing. Perhaps we had imagined it, like those peals of thunder that wrench us out of sleep on calm summer nights. The world is full of inexplicable noises, yelps and howls, the echoes of untold disasters.

'It's no good to just sit and say nothing, Gabriel,' said Aunt Martha. 'You must learn things, we all had to learn, and it's not so difficult. Mensa is a table, see? Mensa . . .'

While she talked, Papa made his way across the room by slow degrees, casually, his lips pursed, until he stood behind her chair looking down over her shoulder at the book and jingling coins in his pocket. She fell silent, and sat very still with her head bent over the page, and Papa hummed a tune and walked out of the room, and she put down the primer and followed him, and I was left alone, wondering where and when all this had happened before.

I picked up the book she had dropped and thumbed glumly through it. The words lay dead in ranks, file beside file of slaughtered music. I rescued one, that verb to love, and, singing its parts in a whisper, I lifted my eyes to the window. Nockter, his elbows sawing, knees pumping, came running across the lawn. It was so perfect a picture of bad news arriving, this little figure behind the rainstippled glass looming out of wind and violence, that at first I took it to be no more than a stray fancy born of boredom. I looked again. He slipped on the grass, frantically backpedalling an imaginary bicycle, and plunged abruptly arse over tip out of my view amid a sense of general hilarity. I waited, and sure enough a few moments later the house quivered with the first groundswell of catastrophe. Nockter appeared in my window again, limping back the way he had come, with my father now by his side, his coattails flying. Next came poor Mama, struggling against the wind and, last of all, in a pink dressing gown, Aunt Martha. They dived into the wood, one after another, but when they were gone the shaking and shuddering of the stormtossed garden seemed an echo of their tempestuous panic. Michael entered quietly behind me.

'What's up?' he asked.

I did not know, and hardly cared. It was not for me to question this splendid spectacle of consternation in the adult camp. I was not a cruel child, only a cold one, and I feared boredom above all else. So we clasped our hands behind our backs and gazed out into the rain, awaiting the next act. Soon they came back, straggling despondently in reverse order, Aunt Martha, Mama, and then Nockter and my father. They passed by the window with downcast eyes.

'We should . . .' Michael began. He eyed me speculatively, biting bits off a thumbnail. 'Do you think she's . . . ?'

The hall. I remember it so well, that scene, so vividly. My father was stooped over the phone, rattling the cradle with a frenzied forefinger and furiously shaking the earpiece, but the thing would not speak to him. His hair was in his eyes, his knees trembled. Mama, with one hand on her forehead and the other stretched out to the table behind her for support, leaned backwards in a half swoon, her lips parted and eyelids drooping, her drenched hair hanging down her back. Nockter sat, caked with mud from his fall, on the edge of a little chair, looking absurdly stolid and calm, almost detached. The front door stood open. Three dead leaves were busy chasing each other round and round on the carpet. I saw all this in a flash, and no doubt that precise situation took no more than an instant to swell and flow into another, but for me it is petrified forever, the tapping finger, Mama's dripping hair, those leaves. Aunt Martha, in her ruined pink frilly, was slowly ascending the stairs backwards. The fall of her foot on each new step shook her entire frame as the tendons tugged on a web of connections, and her jaws slackened, her chest heaved, while out of her mouth there fell curious little high-pitched grunts, which were so abrupt, so understated, that I imagined them as soft furry balls of sound falling to the carpet and lodging in the nap. Up she went, and up, until there were no more steps, and she sat down on the highest one with a bump and buried her face in her hands, and at last an ethereal voice in the phone answered Papa's pleas with a shrill hoot.

My memory is curious, a magpie with a perverse eye, it fascinates me. Jewels I remember only as glitter, and the feel of glass in my beak. I have filled my nest with dross. What does it mean? That is a question I am forever asking, what can it mean?

There is never a precise answer, but instead, in the sky, as it were, a kind of jovian nod, a celestial tipping of the wink, *that's all right, it means what it means.* Yes, but is that enough? Am I satisfied? I wonder. That day I remember Nockter falling, Mama running across the garden in the rain, that scene in the hall, all those things, whereas, listen, what I should recall to the exclusion of all else is the scene in the summerhouse that met Michael and me when we sneaked down there, the ashes on the wall, that rendered purplish mass in the chair, Granny Godkin's two feet, all that was left of her, in their scorched button boots, and I do remember it, in a sense, as words, as facts, but I cannot see it, and there is the trouble. Well, perhaps it is better thus. I have no wish to make unseemly disclosures about myself, and I can never think of that ghastly day without suspecting that somewhere inside me some cruel little brute, a manikin in my mirror, is bent double with laughter. Granny! Forgive me.

We missed her, in a way. When Granda Godkin died it was like the shamefaced departure of a ghost who no longer frightens. That tiresome clank of bones was no more to be heard in the hall, the wicked laughter on the landing was silenced. The space he had occupied closed in, making a little more room for the rest of us, and we stretched ourselves and heaved a small sigh, and were secretly relieved. But when the old woman was so unceremoniously snuffed out something fretful entered the house. Now there was always something wrong with the stillness. Our chairs seemed to vibrate, a ceaseless tremor under our backsides would not let us sit, and we went wandering from room to room like old dogs sniffing moodily after their dead master. The house seemed incomplete, as often a room did when Mama, on one of her restless days, shifted out of it a piece of furniture which had stood in the same place for so long that it was only noticed in its absence. Birchwood was diminished, there is no denying it.

The arranging of her funeral gave rise to some moments of bleak comedy. That was really awful, for we could not in decency laugh. How was she to be buried, anyway? Were we to call in the undertakers to scrape what little was left of her out of the chair, off the walls? No no, if the ghastly manner of her death got out the town would burst with merriment. Well then, were we to do it ourselves? God forbid! An unspeakable vision arose of the family donning dungarees and gumboots and trooping off to the summerhouse with buckets and trowels. Never had the euphemism *the remains* seemed more apt.

The situation itself was bad enough, but it was made doubly difficult by the virtual impossibility of talking about it. Apart from the unmentionable horror of the old woman's death, each of us was tonguetied by the fact that we were convinced that the others knew exactly how she had died, that it was ridiculously obvious, that our own bafflement was laughable. We became very cunning in our efforts to quiz each other. The fishing! How we sighed, and played with our fingers, and glared solemnly out of windows during those awful plummeting silences between casts. *The poor thing, it must have been terrible – to go like that!* Yes, terrible. *Do you think . . . ?* No no, no, I wouldn't . . . *Still, she must have known . . .* O there's no doubt – *But still* – Yes? Yes? *Exactly!* And at the end, no wiser, we parted morosely, guiltily, furious with ourselves.

Doc McCabe was the only one to offer an explanation, and although it was too scandalous and too simple in its way for my family to accept, I think he may have been right. He arrived in the afternoon, huffing and puffing, trailing rainwater behind him from the ends of his cape, an overweight tweedy ball of irritation. He had attended two hysterical and protracted births that day, and now he pronounced himself banjaxed. Before anyone could speak he lumbered over to my chair, wrenched my jaws open and glared down my throat.

'Touch of the grippe. Be over it in a day or two. Well?'

The constraint in the atmosphere at last made an impression on him, and he looked around at the rest of them with his eyebrows quivering. Apparently he had not heard of Granny Godkin's departure. We marched down to the summerhouse, the tribe leading their medicine man to the evil spirit. The rain stopped and the sun appeared abruptly. We waited outside on the porch in an embarrassed silence while he went in to investigate. After what seemed an age the door opened and he backed out slowly, his head bent, fingers to his lips. He was intrigued.

'*Extraordinary*. Upon my word, I've never come across anything like it . . .' He found the bereaved family watching him with a suitably muted air of expectation, and he coughed and turned away abruptly, humming and hawing under his breath. We trooped back to the house, and there, in the dining room, swilling tea, his curiosity got the better of him again, and he had trouble preventing himself from grinning enthusiastically as he mused upon that strange death.

'Most extraordinary, really. I've read of one or two similar cases, you know, in America, if I remember rightly, but I never thought' – he scoffed at his lack of foresight – 'dear me, I never thought that here . . . that Birchwood . . .' He looked about with a newfound air of respect at this humble and familiar place that had produced such a marvel. 'Not a mark anywhere, only the chair. Can't have been a fire, discount that absolutely. Those smuts on the wall . . .' Aunt Martha let fall a muffled sob, and the old boy glanced at her apologetically. 'But it's terrible, of course, very sad, it must have been a great shock, indeed yes, ahem.'

He put down his cup, and with a promise to *tip the wink* to the coroner he prepared to depart. Papa tackled him in the hall.

'Well you think then, Doctor . . . ? I mean . . . ?'

'Eh?' He cast a wary eye over Papa's shoulder at Aunt Martha's puffed tear-stained face. 'Well of course until I examine it further . . . I may have to call in some people from Dublin. At the moment, however, I can see no other explanation . . . after all . . .'

'Yes?'

The old shammer sniffed, and fussed with the collar of his cape. He turned to the door, paused, and cast one bloodshot eye back over his shoulder at us.

'*Spontaneous combustion*,' he said faintly, dived out on the step, and with a last embarrassed grunt was gone. As I say, he may have been right, she may have just . . . burst, but I cannot rid myself of the notion that the house itself had something to do with it. Birchwood had grown weary of her, she saw that herself. Did it assassinate her? Extraordinary, as the Doc observed.

He did speak to the coroner, and a vague verdict of death by misadventure was returned, but for this service he expected to be allowed to conduct the people he had called in from Dublin, old cronies of his, around the scene of the disaster, and was greatly incensed when Papa refused entry to him and his band of ghouls. However, he kept our secret from the town. In a week or two there was hardly anything of the incident left, except Josie's mournful sobbing at odd hours of the day and night, for she came up trumps and surprised us all by displaying genuine grief for the old woman's passing. By the way, we settled the business of the funeral very neatly, and buried Granny Godkin's feet in a full-sized coffin. Despite the needless expense, the craftiness of the ruse pleased Papa enormously.

from *The Book of Evidence*

So I am driving away from the village, in the Humber Hawk, with a foolish grin on my face. I felt, for no good reason, that I was escaping all my problems, I pictured them dwindling in space and time like the village itself, a quaint jumble of things getting steadily smaller and smaller. If I had stopped for a moment to think, of course, I would have realized that what I was leaving behind me was not my tangled troubles, as I fondly imagined, but, on the contrary, a mass of evidence, obvious and unmistakable as a swatch of matted hair and blood. I had skipped Ma Reck's without paying for my lodgings, I had bought a burglar's kit in the village shop, and now I had as good as stolen a car – and all this not five miles from what would soon come to be known as the scene of the crime. The court will agree, these are hardly the marks of careful premeditation. (Why is it that every other thing I say sounds like the sly preamble to a plea of mitigation?) The fact is, I was not thinking at all, not what could really be called thinking. I was content to sail through sun and shade along these dappled back roads, one hand on the wheel and an elbow out the window, with the scents of the countryside in my nostrils and the breeze whipping my hair. Everything would be well, everything would work itself out. I do not know why I felt so elated, perhaps it was a form of delirium. Anyway, I told myself, it was only a madcap game I was playing, I could call it off whenever I wished.

Meanwhile here was Whitewater, rising above the trees.

An empty tour bus was parked at the gate. The driver's door was open, and the driver was lounging in the stepwell, sunning himself. He watched me as I swung past him into the drive. I waved to him. He wore tinted glasses. He did not smile. He would remember me.

Afterwards the police could not understand why I showed so little circumspection, driving up brazenly like that, in broad daylight, in that unmistakable motor car. But I believed, you see, that the matter would be entirely between Behrens and me, with Anna perhaps as go-between. I never imagined there would be anything so vulgar as a police investigation, and headlines in the papers, and all the rest of it. A simple business transaction between civilized people, that's what I intended. I would be polite but firm, no more than that. I was not thinking in terms of threats and ransom demands, certainly not. When later I read what those reporters wrote – the Midsummer Manhunt, they called it – I could not recognize myself in their depiction of me as a steely, ruthless character. Ruthless – me! No, as I drove up to Whitewater it was not police I was thinking of, but only the chauffeur Flynn, with his little pig eyes and his boxer's meaty paws. Yes, Flynn was a man to avoid.

Halfway up the drive there was

God, these tedious details.

Halfway up there was a fork in the drive. A wooden arrow with HOUSE written on it in white paint pointed to the right, while to the left a sign said STRICTLY PRIVATE. I stopped the car. See me there, a big blurred face behind the windscreen peering first this way, then that. It is like an illustration from a cautionary tract: the sinner hesitates at the parting of the ways. I drove off to the left, and my heart gave an apprehensive wallop. Behold, the wretch forsakes the path of righteousness.

I rounded the south wing of the house, and parked on the grass and walked across the lawn to the garden room. The french window was open. Deep breath. It was not yet noon. Far off in the fields somewhere a tractor was working, it made a drowsy, buzzing sound that seemed the very voice of summer, I hear it still, that tiny, distant, prelapsarian song. I had left the rope and the hammer in the car, and brought with me the twine and the roll of wrapping paper. It struck me suddenly how absurd the whole thing was. I began to laugh, and laughing stepped into the room.

The painting is called, as everyone must know by now, *Portrait of a Woman with Gloves*. It measures eighty-two centimetres by sixty-five. From internal evidence – in particular the woman's attire – it has been dated between 1655 and 1660. The black dress and broad white collar and cuffs of the woman are lightened only by a brooch and gold ornamentation on the gloves. The face has a slightly Eastern cast. (I am quoting from the guidebook to Whitewater House.) The picture has been variously attributed to Rembrandt and Frans Hals, even to Vermeer. However, it is safest to regard it as the work of an anonymous master.

None of this means anything.

I have stood in front of other, perhaps greater paintings, and not been moved as I am moved by this one. I have a reproduction of it on the wall above my table here – sent to me by, of all people, Anna Behrens – when I look at it my heart contracts. There is something in the way the woman regards me, the querulous, mute insistence of her eyes, which I can neither escape nor assuage. I squirm in the grasp of her gaze. She requires of me some great effort, some tremendous feat of scrutiny and attention, of which I do not think I am capable. It is as if she were asking me to let her live.

She. There is no she, of course. There is only an organization of shapes and colours. Yet I try to make up a life for her. She is, I will say, thirty-five, thirty-six, though people without thinking still speak of her as a girl. She lives with her father, the merchant (tobacco, spices, and, in secret, slaves). She keeps house for him since her mother's death. She did not like her mother. Her father dotes on her, his only child. She is, he proclaims, his treasure. She devises menus – father has a delicate stomach – inspects the kitchen, she even supervises his wine cellar. She keeps an inventory of the household linen in a little notebook attached to her belt by a fine gold chain, using a code of her own devising, for she has never learned to read or write. She is strict with the servants, and will permit no familiarities. Their dislike she takes for respect. The house is not enough to absorb her energies, she does good works besides: she visits the sick, and is on the board of visitors of the town's almshouse. She is brisk, sometimes impatient, and there are mutterings against her among the alms-folk, especially the old women. At times, usually in spring and at the beginning of winter, everything becomes too much for her. Notice the clammy pallor of her skin: she is prey to obscure ailments. She takes to her bed and lies for days without speaking, hardly breathing, while outside in the silvery northern light the world goes about its busy way. She tries to pray, but God is distant. Her father comes to visit her at evening, walking on tiptoe. These periods of prostration frighten him, he remembers his wife dying, her terrible silence in the last weeks. If he were to lose his daughter too – But she gets up, wills herself to it, and very soon the servants are feeling the edge of her tongue again, and he cannot contain his relief, it comes out in little laughs, roguish endearments, a kind of clumsy skittishness. She considers him wryly, then turns back to her tasks. She cannot understand this notion he has got into his head: he wants to have her portrait painted. I'm old, is all he will say to her, I am an old man, look at me! And he laughs, awkwardly, and avoids her eye. My portrait? she says, mine? – I am no fit subject for a painter. He shrugs, at which she is first startled, then grimly amused: he might at least have attempted to contradict her. He seems to realize what is going through her mind, and tries to mend matters, but he becomes flustered, and, watching him fuss and fret and pluck at his cuffs, she realizes with a pang that it's true, he has aged. Her father, an old man. The thought has a touch of bleak comedy, which she cannot account for. You have fine hands, he says, growing testy, annoyed both at himself and her, your mother's hands – we'll tell him to make the hands prominent. And so, to humour him, but also because she is secretly curious, she goes along one morning to the studio. The squalor is what strikes her first of all. Dirt and daubs of paint everywhere, gnawed chicken bones on a smeared plate, a chamber-pot on the floor in the corner. The painter matches the place, with that filthy smock, and those fingernails. He has a drinker's squashed and pitted nose. She thinks the general smell is bad until she catches a whiff of his breath. She discovers that she is relieved: she had expected someone young, dissolute, threatening, not this pot-bellied old soak. But then he fixes his little wet eyes on her, briefly, with a kind of impersonal intensity, and she flinches, as if caught in a burst of strong light. No one has ever looked at her like this before. So this is what it is to be known! It is almost indecent. First he puts her standing by the window, but it does not suit, the light is wrong, he says. He shifts her about, grasping her by the upper arms and walking her backwards from one place to another. She feels she should be indignant, but the usual responses do not seem to function here. He is shorter than her by a head. He makes some sketches, scribbles a colour note or two, then tells her to come tomorrow at the same time. And wear a darker dress, he says. Well! She is about to give him a piece of her mind, but already he has turned aside to another task. Her maid, sitting by the door, is biting her lips and smirking. She lets the next day pass, and the next, just to show him. When she does return he says nothing about the broken appointment, only looks at her black dress – pure silk, with a broad collar of Spanish lace – and nods carelessly, and she is so vexed at him it surprises her, and she is shocked at herself. He has her stand before the couch. Remove your gloves, he says, I am to emphasize the hands. She hears the note of amused disdain in his voice. She refuses. (*Her* hands, indeed!) He insists. They engage in a brief, stiff little squabble, batting icy politenesses back and forth between them. In the end she consents to remove one glove, then promptly tries to hide the hand she has bared. He sighs, shrugs, but has to suppress a grin, as she notices. Rain streams down the windows, shreds of smoke fly over the rooftops. The sky has a huge silver hole in it. At first she is restless, standing there, then she seems to pass silently through some barrier, and a dreamy calm comes over her. It is the same, day after day, first there is agitation, then the breakthrough, then silence and a kind of softness, as if she were floating away, away, out of herself. He mutters under his breath as he works. He is choleric, he swears, and clicks his tongue, sending up sighs and groans. There are long, fevered passages when he works close up against the canvas, and she can only see his stumpy legs and his old, misshapen boots. Even his feet seem busy. She wants to laugh when he pops his head out at the side of the easel and peers at her sharply, his potato nose twitching. He will not let her see what he is doing, she is not allowed even a peek. Then one day she senses a kind of soundless, settling crash at his end of the room, and he steps back with an expression of weary disgust and waves a hand dismissively at the canvas, and turns aside to clean his brush. She comes forward and looks. For a second she sees nothing, so taken is she by the mere sensation of stopping like this and turning: it is as if – as if somehow she had walked out of herself. A long moment passes. The brooch, she says, is wonderfully done. The sound of her own voice startles her, it is a stranger speaking, and she is cowed. He laughs, not bitterly, but with real amusement and, so she feels, a curious sort of sympathy. It is an acknowledgement, of – she does not know what. She looks and looks. She had expected it would be like looking in a mirror, but this is someone she does not recognize, and yet knows. The words come unbidden into her head: Now I know how to die. She puts on her glove, and signals to her maid. The painter is speaking behind her, something about her father, and money, of course, but she is not listening. She is calm. She is happy. She feels numbed, hollowed, a walking shell. She goes down the stairs, along the dingy hall, and steps out into a commonplace world.

Do not be fooled: none of this means anything either.

I had placed the string and the wrapping-paper carefully on the floor, and now stepped forward with my arms outstretched. The door behind me opened and a large woman in a tweed skirt and a cardigan came into the room. She halted when she saw me there, with my arms flung wide before the picture and peering wildly at her over my shoulder, while I tried with one foot to conceal the paper and the ball of twine on the floor. She had blue-grey hair, and her spectacles were attached to a cord around her neck. She frowned. You must stay with the party, she said loudly, in a cross voice – really, I don't know how many times I have to say it. I stepped back. A dozen gaudily dressed people were crowding in the doorway behind her, craning to get a look at me. Sorry, I heard myself say meekly, I got lost. She gave an impatient toss of the head and strode to the middle of the room and began at once to speak in a shouted singsong about Carlin tables and Berthoud clocks, and weeks later, questioned by the police and shown my photograph, she would deny ever having seen me before in her life. Her charges shuffled in, jostling surreptitiously in an effort to stay out of her line of sight. They took up position, standing with their hands clasped before them, as if they were in church, and looked about them with expressions of respectful vacancy. One grizzled old party in a Hawaiian shirt grinned at me and winked. I confess I was rattled. There was a knot in the pit of my stomach and my palms were damp. All the elation I had felt on the way here had evaporated, leaving behind it a stark sense of foreboding. I was struck, for the first time, really, by the enormity of what I was embarked on. I felt like a child whose game has led him far into the forest, and now it is nightfall, and there are shadowy figures among the trees. The guide had finished her account of the treasures in the room – the picture, *my* picture, was given two sentences, and a misattribution – and walked out now with one arm raised stiffly above her head, still talking, shepherding the party behind her. When they had gone I waited, staring fixedly at the doorknob, expecting her to come back and haul me out briskly by the scruff of the neck. Somewhere inside me a voice was moaning softly in panic and fright. This is something that does not seem to be appreciated – I have remarked on it before – I mean how timorous I am, how easily daunted. But she did not return, and I heard them tramping away up the stairs. I set to work again feverishly. I see myself, like the villain in an old three-reeler, all twitches and scowls and wriggling eyebrows. I got the picture off the wall, not without difficulty, and laid it flat on the floor – shying away from that black stare – and began to tear off lengths of wrapping-paper. I would not have thought that paper would make so much noise, such scuffling and rattling and ripping, it must have sounded as if some large animal were being flayed alive in here. And it was no good, my hands shook, I was all thumbs, and the sheets of paper kept rolling back on themselves, and I had nothing to cut the twine with, and anyway the picture, with its thick, heavy frame, was much too big to be wrapped. I scampered about on my knees, talking to myself and uttering little squeaks of distress. Everything was going wrong. Give it up, I told myself, oh please, please, give it up now, while there's still time! but another part of me gritted its teeth and said, no you don't, you coward, get up, get on your feet, do it. So I struggled up, moaning and snivelling, and grasped the picture in my arms and staggered with it blindly, nose to nose, in the direction of the french window. Those eyes were staring into mine, I almost blushed. And then – how shall I express it – then somehow I sensed, behind that stare, another presence, watching me. I stopped, and lowered the picture, and there she was, standing in the open window, just as she had stood the day before, wide-eyed, with one hand raised. This, I remember thinking bitterly, this is the last straw. I was outraged. How dare the world strew these obstacles in my path. It was not fair, it was just not fair! Right, I said to her, here, take this, and I thrust the painting into her arms and turned her about and marched her ahead of me across the lawn. She said nothing, or if she did I was not listening. She found it hard going on the grass, the picture was too heavy for her, and she could hardly see around it. When she faltered I prodded her between the shoulder-blades. I really was very cross. We reached the car. The cavernous boot smelled strongly of fish. There was the usual jumble of mysterious implements, a jack, and spanners and things – I am not mechanically minded, or handed, have I mentioned that? – and a filthy old pullover, which I hardly noticed at the time, thrown in a corner with deceptive casualness by the hidden arranger of all these things. I took out the tools and threw them behind me on to the grass, then lifted the painting from the maid's arms and placed it face-down on the worn felt matting. This was the first time I had seen the back of the canvas, and suddenly I was struck by the antiquity of the thing. Three hundred years ago it had been stretched and sized and left against a lime-washed wall to dry. I closed my eyes for a second, and at once I saw a workshop in a narrow street in Amsterdam or Antwerp, smoky sunlight in the window, and hawkers going by outside, and the bells of the cathedral ringing. The maid was watching me. She had the most extraordinary pale, violet eyes, they seemed transparent, when I looked into them I felt I was seeing clear through her head. Why did she not run away? Behind her, in one of the great upstairs windows, a dozen heads were crowded, goggling at us. I could make out the guide-woman's glasses and the American's appalling shirt. I think I must have cried aloud in rage, an old lion roaring at the whip and chair, for the maid flinched and stepped back a pace. I caught her wrist in an iron claw and, wrenching open the car door, fairly flung her into the back seat. Oh, why did she not run away? When I got behind the wheel, fumbling and snarling, I caught a whiff of something, a faint, sharp, metallic smell, like the smell of worn pennies. I could see her in the mirror, crouched behind me as in a deep glass box, braced between the door and the back of the seat, with her elbows stuck out and fingers splayed and her face thrust forward, like the cornered heroine in a melodrama. A fierce, choking gust of impatience surged up inside me. Impatience, yes, that was what I felt most strongly – that, and a grievous sense of embarrassment. I was mortified. I had never been so exposed in all my life. People were looking at me – she in the back seat, and the tourists up there jostling at the window, but also, it seemed, a host of others, of phantom spectators, who must have been, I suppose, an intimation of all that horde who would soon be crowding around me in fascination and horror. I started the engine. The gears shrieked. In my agitation I kept getting ahead of myself and having to go back and repeat the simplest actions. When I had got the car off the grass and on to the drive I let the clutch out too quickly, and the machine sprang forward in a series of bone-shaking lurches, the bonnet going up and down like the prow of a boat caught in a wash and the shock absorbers grunting. The watchers at the window must have been in fits by now. A bead of sweat ran down my cheek. The sun had made the steering-wheel almost too hot to hold, and there was a blinding glare on the windscreen. The maid was scrabbling at the door handle, I roared at her and she stopped at once, and looked at me wide-eyed, like a rebuked child. Outside the gate the bus driver was still sitting in the sun. When she saw him she tried to get the window open, but in vain, the mechanism must have been broken. She pounded on the glass with her fists. I spun the wheel and the car lumbered out into the road, the tyres squealing. We were shouting at each other now, like a married couple having a fight. She pummelled me on the shoulder, got a hand around in front of my face and tried to claw my eyes. Her thumb went up my nose, I thought she would tear off the nostril. The car was going all over the road. I trod with both feet on the brake pedal, and we sailed in a slow, dragging curve into the hedge. She fell back. I turned to her. I had the hammer in my hand. I looked at it, startled. The silence rose around us like water. Don't, she said. She was crouched as before, with her arms bent and her back pressed into the corner. I could not speak, I was filled with a kind of wonder. I had never felt another's presence so immediately and with such raw force. I saw her now, really saw her, for the first time, her mousy hair and bad skin, that bruised look around her eyes. She was quite ordinary, and yet, somehow, I don't know – somehow radiant. She cleared her throat and sat up, and detached a strand of hair that had caught at the corner of her mouth.

You must let me go, she said, or you will be in trouble.

It's not easy to wield a hammer in a motor car. When I struck her the first time I expected to feel the sharp, clean smack of steel on bone, but it was more like hitting clay, or hard putty. The word *fontanel* sprang into my mind. I thought one good bash would do it, but, as the autopsy would show, she had a remarkably strong skull – even in that, you see, she was unlucky. The first blow fell just at the hairline, above her left eye. There was not much blood, only a dark-red glistening dent with hair matted in it. She shuddered, but remained sitting upright, swaying a little, looking at me with eyes that would not focus properly. Perhaps I would have stopped then, if she had not suddenly launched herself at me across the back of the seat, flailing and screaming. I was dismayed. How could this be happening to me – it was all so *unfair*. Bitter tears of self-pity squeezed into my eyes. I pushed her away from me and swung the hammer in a wide, backhand sweep. The force of the blow flung her against the door, and her head struck the window, and a fine thread of blood ran out of her nostril and across her cheek. There was blood on the window, too, a fan-shaped spray of tiny drops. She closed her eyes and turned her face away from me, making a low, guttural noise at the back of her throat. She put a hand up to her head just as I was swinging at her again, and when the blow landed on her temple her fingers were in the way, and I heard one of them crack, and I winced, and almost apologized. Oh! she said, and suddenly, as if everything inside her had collapsed, she slithered down the seat on to the floor.

There was silence again, clear and startling. I got out of the car and stood a moment, breathing. I was dizzy. Something seemed to have happened to the sunlight, everywhere I looked there was an underwater gloom. I thought I had driven only a little way, and expected to see the gates of Whitewater, and the tour bus, and the driver running towards me, but to my astonishment the road in both directions was empty, and I had no idea where I was. On one side a hill rose steeply, and on the other I could see over the tops of pine trees to far-off, rolling downs. It all looked distinctly improbable. It was like a hastily painted backdrop, especially that smudged, shimmering distance, and the road winding innocently away. I found I was still clutching the hammer. With a grand sweep of my arm I flung it from me, and watched it as it flew, tumbling slowly end over end in a long, thrilling arc, far, far out over the blue pine-tops. Then abruptly I bent forward and vomited up the glutinous remains of the breakfast I had consumed an age ago, in another life.

I crawled back into the car, keeping my eyes averted from that crumpled thing wedged behind the front seat. The light in the windscreen was a splintered glare, I thought for a second the glass was smashed, until I put a hand to my face and discovered I was crying. This I found encouraging. My tears seemed not just a fore-token of remorse, but the sign of some more common, simpler urge, an affect for which there was no name, but which might be my last link, the only one that would hold, with the world of ordinary things. For everything was changed, where I was now I had not been before. I trembled, and all around me trembled, and there was a sluggish, sticky feel to things, as if I and all of this – car, road, trees, those distant meadows – as if we had all a moment ago struggled mute and amazed out of a birthhole in the air. I turned the key in the ignition, bracing myself, convinced that instead of the engine starting something else would happen, that there would be a terrible, rending noise, or a flash of light, or that slime would gush out over my legs from under the dashboard. I drove in second gear along the middle of the road. Smells, smells. Blood has a hot, thick smell. I wanted to open the windows, but did not dare, I was afraid of what might come in – the light outside seemed moist and dense as glair, I imagined it in my mouth, my nostrils.

I drove and drove. Whitewater is only thirty miles or so from the city, but it seemed hours before I found myself in the suburbs. Of the journey I remember little. That is to say, I do not remember changing gears, accelerating and slowing down, working the pedals, all that. I see myself moving, all right, as if in a crystal bubble, flying soundlessly through a strange, sunlit, glittering landscape. I think I went very fast, for I recall a sensation of pressure in my ears, a dull, rushing blare. So I must have driven in circles, round and round those narrow country roads. Then there were houses, and housing estates, and straggling factories, and supermarkets big as aircraft hangers. I stared through the windscreen in dreamy amazement. I might have been a visitor from another part of the world altogether, hardly able to believe how much like home everything looked and yet how different it was. I did not know where I was going, I mean I was not going anywhere, just driving. It was almost restful, sailing along like that, turning the wheel with one finger, shut off from everything. It was as if all my life I had been clambering up a steep and difficult slope, and now had reached the peak and leaped out blithely into the blue. I felt so free. At the first red traffic light the car drifted gently to a stop as if it were subsiding into air. I was at the junction of two suburban roads. On the left there was a little green rise with a chestnut tree and a neat row of new houses. Children were playing on the grassy bank. Dogs gambolled. The sun shone. I have always harboured a secret fondness for quiet places such as this, unremarked yet cherished domains of building and doing and tending. I leaned my head back on the seat and smiled, watching the youngsters at play. The lights changed to green, but I did not stir. I was not really there, but lost somewhere, in some sunlit corner of my past. There was a sudden rapping on the window beside my ear. I jumped. A woman with a large, broad, horsy face – she reminded me, dear God, of my mother! – was peering in at me and saying something. I rolled down the window. She had a loud voice, it sounded very loud to me, at any rate. I could not understand her, she was talking about an accident, and asking me if I was all right. Then she pressed her face forward and squinnied over my shoulder, and opened her mouth and groaned. Oh, she said, the poor child! I turned my head. There was blood all over the back seat now, far too much, surely, for just one person to have shed. For a mad instant, in which a crafty spark of hope flared and died, I wondered if there *had* been a crash, which somehow I had not noticed, or had forgotten, if some overloaded vehicle had ploughed into the back of us, flinging bodies and all this blood in through the rear window. I could not speak. I had thought she was dead, but there she was, kneeling between the seats and groping at the window beside her, I could hear her fingers squeaking on the glass. Her hair hung down in bloodied ropes, her face was a clay mask streaked with copper and crimson. The woman outside was gabbling into my ear about telephones and ambulances and the police – the police! I turned to her with a terrible glare. Madam! I said sternly (she would later describe my voice as *cultured* and *authoritative*), will you please get on about your business! She stepped back, staring in shock. I confess I was myself impressed, I would not have thought I could muster such a commanding tone. I rolled up the window and jammed the car into gear and shot away, noticing, too late, that the lights had turned to red. A tradesman's van coming from the left braked sharply and let out an indignant squawk. I drove on. However, I had not gone more than a street or two when suddenly an ambulance reared up in my wake, its siren yowling and blue light flashing. I was astonished. How could it have arrived so promptly? In fact, this was another of those appalling coincidences in which this case abounds. The ambulance, as I would later learn, was not looking for me, but was returning from – yes – from the scene of a car crash, with – I'm sorry, but, yes – with a dying woman in the back. I kept going, haring along with my head down, my nose almost touching the rim of the wheel. I do not think I could have stopped, locked in fright as I was. The ambulance drew alongside, swaying dangerously and trumpeting like a frenzied big beast. The attendant in the passenger seat, a burly young fellow in shirt-sleeves, with a red face and narrow sideburns, looked at the blood-streaked window behind me with mild, professional interest. He conferred briefly with the driver, then signalled to me, with complicated gestures, nodding and mouthing, to follow them. They thought I was coming from the same crash, ferrying another victim to hospital. They surged ahead. I followed in their wake, befuddled with alarm and bafflement. I could see nothing but this big square clumsy thing scudding along, whooshing up dust and wallowing fatly on its springs. Then abruptly it braked and swung into a wide gateway, and an arm appeared out of the side window and beckoned me to follow. It was the sight of that thick arm that broke the spell. With a gulp of demented laughter I drove on, past the hospital gate, plunging the pedal to the floor, and the noise of the siren dwindled behind me, a startled plaint, and I was free.

I peered into the mirror. She was sitting slumped on the seat with her head hanging and her hands resting palm upwards on her thighs.

Suddenly the sea was on my left, far below, blue, unmoving. I drove down a steep hill, then along a straight cement road beside a railway track. A pink and white hotel, castellated, with pennants flying, rose up on my right, enormous and empty. The road straggled to an end in a marshy patch of scrub and thistles, and there I stopped, in the midst of a vast and final silence. I could hear her behind me, breathing. When I turned she lifted her sibyl's fearsome head and looked at me. *Help me*, she whispered. *Help me.* A bubble of blood came out of her mouth and burst. *Tommy!* she said, or a word like that, and then: *Love.* What did I feel? Remorse, grief, a terrible – no no no, I won't lie. I can't remember feeling anything, except that sense of strangeness, of being in a place I knew but did not recognize. When I got out of the car I was giddy, and had to lean on the door for a moment with my eyes shut tight. My jacket was bloodstained, I wriggled out of it and flung it into the stunted bushes – they never found it, I can't think why. I remembered the pullover in the boot, and put it on. It smelled of fish and sweat and axle-grease. I picked up the hangman's hank of rope and threw that away too. Then I lifted out the picture and walked with it to where there was a sagging barbed-wire fence and a ditch with a trickle of water at the bottom, and there I dumped it. What was I thinking of, I don't know. Perhaps it was a gesture of renunciation or something. Renunciation! How do I dare use such words. The woman with the gloves gave me a last, dismissive stare. She had expected no better of me. I went back to the car, trying not to look at it, the smeared windows. Something was falling on me: a delicate, silent fall of rain. I looked upwards in the glistening sunlight and saw a cloud directly overhead, the merest smear of grey against the summer blue. I thought: I am not human. Then I turned and walked away.

SHANE CONNAUGHTON

'Topping'

The road was dry, dusty and pock-marked with pot-holes. You had to keep swerving to avoid them. When you didn't you could feel the jagged edges dunting the rim of the front wheel.

'Keep into the side,' his father shouted back at him.

It was easier along the side but his bicycle gathered speed there and that was dangerous. The brakes weren't good. In fact he only had half a one. A worn-down block of rubber which did little more than clean one side of the back wheel. Crashing into his father was a nightmare to be avoided at all costs.

He didn't even have a bell. And the saddle was no good either. It kept tipping forward and he had to reach between his legs to adjust it back into position. He stayed in the middle of the road and let the pot-holes serve as brakes. 'Sure isn't that what they're for?' he heard one of the Guards joke to his father. 'Have you ever met a Cavan man yet with brakes on his bicycle?'

It was a lost part of the world, this. No tarred roads, no running water in the houses, no electric light and outside lavatories full of brown and wet and newspaper. The clinging smell of Elsan and when the lavatory was full burying the contents down the bottom of the garden.

He knew his mother wasn't happy here.

His father rode on in front, pressing with measured energy on the pedals, letting the exercise do him good.

Earlier he had watched him eating his dinner in the same mechanical way. His jaws pedalling up and down on the roast chicken, potatoes, carrots, cabbage and two helpings of rhubarb pie. Grinding out the goodness. A short nap and then this trip out to see the football match was just what the digestive system needed. Routine and a well-regulated stomach were the keys to long life. And eventually Heaven. His father had read as much in the *Garda Review*.

As they rode along, hedges, hills, dandelions and swampy fields skirted the way. Cattle, standing in the half-dried mud of gateways, stared at them. A pair of cackling magpies flitted across the road and landed on a rusty barrel lying abandoned in the middle of the field.

'Well, there's two of them in it anyway,' his father said. One for sorrow, two for joy . . .

His father had two big fists. They gripped the handlebars raw and red. Even in warm weather they looked cold. The knuckles crinkled with tight skin, like a chicken's leg. The rubber grips on the handlebar ends were lost in the coil of his fingers.

His feet were big too. He wore boots, the long laces double-wrapped round the uppers and tied in a knotted bow just below the second hole from the top. 'Always give the ankle a bit of leeway.'

His trouser ends were folded neat and clipped up on the calf so the knee action wouldn't round out the regulation-sharp seams.

His dark blue uniform moved through the countryside like a cloud. The truncheon in its black leather sheath belted to the tunic. The truncheon had grooves round the top and a loop of brown leather through which you put your hand so it couldn't be snatched away. His father had shown him how to grip it.

The truncheon was heavy and shone like chestnut.

They came out from the hills and into a flat stretch. To the right towards the Six Counties the land was even, green and healthy-looking. To the left, though, there was only mile after mile of rushy fields, marsh, lakes and bog. 'By cripes,' muttered his father, 'they knew what they were doing when they drew that Border.'

Suddenly he slowed down. There was something ahead. The boy drawing level with him, deliberately steered into a pot-hole rather than pass him out.

They were going so slowly now the spokes no longer blurred.

In the distance, on a piece of grass between the road and the hedge, something was hanging. It looked like a brown sheet.

'Fecking tinkers,' said his father, 'and just inside my sub-district.'

They drew nearer the encampment. The brown sheet was a piece of canvas flung across hoops of some kind to form a tent.

A turf fire smouldered at its entrance. A green and yellow painted spring-cart was upended at the back of the tent, the graceful shafts curving to the sky. A horse was tethered to the wheel.

A young stout woman squatted in front of the fire, poking life into it with a cabbage stalk.

His father got off his bike and stood looking at her. She refused to look up. Flames spurted.

The horse moved its rump against the cart, shifting its weight from a hind leg. The boy looked at the woman but looked quickly away in case she caught his eye.

As his father continued staring at her her face became sullen. But she wouldn't look up and recognize his existence. She had seen them approaching. The uniform. The peaked cap. The silver buttons. She knew well they were there. Arresting her peace with hostile eyes.

His father nodded a few times, whistling quietly as he did so, then remounted his bicycle and pedalled on.

The boy surprised by the move was left stranded for a few seconds. The tinker woman looked up at him. Her brown eyes books of knowledge beyond his power.

A man's face peeped from the slit entrance to the tent.

The boy jumped on his bike and rode quickly along the verge.

Why had his father left the tinkers alone?

Down a laneway they saw a whitewashed house with a window box of red flowers. The nearby sheds were whitewashed too. It had to be a Protestant house. Cleanliness was part of their religion.

Onto the hills on the left, through a gap in the hedge, tore a pack of beagles. Strung out in line they snaked across the fields trumpeting their mad hunger into the air. Behind them pounded shouting men in wellington boots and carrying sticks.

'God help the poor hare if them savages catch him. The two-legged ones!' Like a belch the jibe came from deep within his father: the words flung with a sharp sideways flick of the head at the backs of the ragged mob of hunters. They watched the last of them disappear behind a clump of withered trees. The boy knew expressing contempt was exercise. His father got rid of bile that way. He looked down at the road flying beneath his wheels. It sped out between his legs like a river in spate.

There was a thick black line on his white sock. Oil. The chain wasn't cased. His mother would scold him. But her words wouldn't hurt.

In bed with his mother was the warmest place in the world. Hay. Honey.

'Out the hell outa the way! Ye mangy beggars!' roared his father. Goats tethered in pairs wandered in the middle of the road. Like wet blackcurrants faeces spilled from under their tails. Cupfuls of them. The thick smell from their coarse-haired bodies could almost be tasted.

'Their stink has me stunk, Daddy.'

'And they call this the county of little hills and lakes,' shouted his father, as they steered through the scattering herd, 'the county of goats and pot-holes is the right title.'

Soon they left the pock-marked road behind and with a final rattle bumped up onto the tarred main road linking Cavan, Clones and the North. Turning right they headed towards the Border and the football field. He pedalled up to his father's shoulder. His father with a grin on the side of his mouth glanced at him.

A contest.

They stopped pedalling and free-wheeled.

Which bike would be the last to wobble to a halt?

His father's was heavier, had bigger wheels and was well looked-after. He oiled it regularly and wiped it down with a cloth especially if it had been out in the rain. The rims shone, the wheels ran true, the spokes were tight, the cranks glistened, the reflector gleamed and the bell was bright as the belt buckle on his uniform. 'Tin Lizzie', he called it.

'I've looked after her. So she looks after me.'

'How old is she, Daddy?'

'She was old when I bought her. And that's thirty years ago. That'll give you some idea. A Rudge. You couldn't beat her with a drumstick.'

They free-wheeled along, his father gaining momentum, the boy beginning to drop behind.

He didn't mind losing. In fact he had to. Because if his father lost at anything he would bring a mood down on the world thick as tar.

In the silent Border countryside above the gentle ticking of turning wheels they could hear the distant baying of the pack of beagles.

He looked again at the oil mark on his sock.

White ankle-socks. The tinker woman wore ankle-socks too. Green ones. Her legs were brown with dirt and weather. She belonged to the man in the tent. A slit of white eyes, alert and dangerous. Green ankle-socks.

The mudguards rattled as he wobbled to a halt.

'I've lost Daddy.'

'Ah-hah ya boya,' his father shouted back in triumph. He was pleased.

'If we can't fight a war, any little victory will do. That's what your grandfather used to say RIP.'

They reached the Border. A slight difference in level and texture of the tarmacadam was all that indicated they were passing into what was supposed to be a foreign country. But further along they came to a row of iron spikes stuck across the road. It was a measure aimed at the IRA. But the locals had bulldozed between the hedge and the nearest spike, making a deep rutted muddy path wide enough for the use of cars, lorries and tractors. His father dismounted and looked at the spikes. Then he reached out and with his hands tested their strength. The boy did the same.

Rusty flakes on the brown girders. Railway lines sticking up from hell. For the next mile the Border zig-zagged crazily so that one minute his father would announce they were in the North, the next minute the South.

'Whilst grass is green and water runs, as long as that Border is there, this country will never be at peace,' declaimed his father and went on to repeat it a number of times. As if repetition would turn the words into a political fact so blatant even a fool could see it.

Peace. Why weren't his mother and father at peace? Why did he thump his mother's bedroom door at night, trying to get into her? What kind of peace was that? And why when they sat to eat was his hand under the table on her knee, her ankle trapped in the twist of his great black boots? Once when his spoon fell on the floor and he went under the table to retrieve it, he saw her hand trying to push his hand away from her flesh. Why?

They rode on but his bicycle bell fell off and went hopping into the ditch. They searched but couldn't find it, his father lashing at the long grass and nettles, tramping them down with brute force. The boy knew his father was angry. He valued things like bent nails, odd buttons, buckets without handles, sewing needles with the eyes snapped off . . . bicycle bells.

'There it is, Daddy!'

His father bent to pick it up but it was only a stone.

'Ah, get away out of that, you nigget'

He flung the stone into the ditch and looked at the countryside and the sky above it.

'What on God's earth did I do to deserve being sent here to this cursed hole? Civilization as far away as the dark side of the stars!'

'Mammy's not happy here either.'

'How do you know?'

'Ah . . . she . . . she told me.'

His father glared at him, his eyes bright as the badge on his cap.

'Did she indeed?'

'And I'm not happy as well.'

'Why not?'

How could you tell anyone why you were unhappy? Especially your father!

'Because . . . because this bloody bike is breaking my heart.'

'This WHAT bike?'

'This . . . RUSTY bike.'

'Don't get too big for your boots, me buck. I heard what you said. There's nothing wrong with that bike. It's the way you ride it.'

'But it's falling to bits, Daddy.'

'It's a poor jockey blames his horse. When I was your age I had to WALK everywhere.'

'I'd prefer to walk.'

'Get on that bike! Move!'

Tears came into his eyes and, though he knew it was dangerous, he heard himself shouting at his father.

'I want to go home to Mammy!'

He expected a crack from his father's fist but instead his father looked steadily at him and said, as if challenging him, 'So do I. So do I!'

Why should he want to go home? He turned away from his father's eyes and stared into the ditch. Right at the bottom water seeped through the weeds and a dandelion clock took off and floated above their heads. Getting on the bikes they rode towards the football pitch. When they got there the rival supporters were gathered on opposite sides of the field. The teams were out, the visitors in red, Butlershill in blue and yellow hoops.

Though people spoke to his father they stood away from him. Beside the uniform they felt they couldn't swear at the players with customary abandon.

His father stood in front of his bike, his rump resting on the crossbar. Everyone else slung their bikes in tangled heaps on the ground. The match started and almost immediately a fight broke out. Punches and kicks were swopped and soon spectators had joined in, some of them rolling about in the mud in their Sunday suits seemingly trying to strangle one another.

The boy looked down at the streak of oil on his sock.

'Arrest them, Sergeant,' a man shouted.

'Arrest the bloody referee,' shouted a woman, 'he's the one started it.'

But his father grinned at them, took off his cap, breathed over the silver badge, wiped it with his sleeve and returning the cap to his head said, 'When they get fed up they'll stop of their own accord.'

They did.

Up the other end of the field away from the game the boy saw a hare carefully hopping along, stopping every few yards, ears cocked, checking the distant clamour of the crowd. Some other boys had noticed it too and gave chase. The hare sprung above the long grass and with swift lanky bounds made for a gap in the far hedge.

'Come on,' said his father, 'this standard of football is too bad to be true.'

They rode homewards, a brooding look on his father's face.

Nearing the spikes across the road they saw an Army jeep blocking the bulldozed pathway.

Soldiers looked out at them, rifles resting between their knees.

'Cripes,' said his father, 'it's the British.'

Standing by the jeep was an officer. He was tall, handsome, blond-haired and round his neck wore a red cravat. Drawing level with him the officer saluted his father, who saluted back.

'Grand day now,' said his father.

'Topping,' replied the officer. A soldier winked at the boy.

'Everything alright your side, Sergeant?'

'Yes. Thank God. Why wouldn't they be?'

They didn't await a reply but rode swiftly out of Fermanagh, his father pleased at his religious and political swipe at the Forces of the Queen.

When they came onto the pot-holed road the boy dropped behind. He had noticed his father was looking grim, muttering, churning himself into a temper. He would now look for an excuse to explode it.

Before they even got to them he knew they were going to stop at the tinker's encampment.

His father was pedalling with purpose, making for somewhere definite. And it wasn't home. Tea wouldn't be ready for another hour at least. It had to be the tinkers. What was he going to do to them?

When the upturned cart was in sight his father slowed down, pulling on the brakes with a jerk of his shoulders. When a little nearer he swung his right leg to the same side as his left and, standing on one pedal, scootered to an eventual stop.

The fire this time was well banked round with turf and on the busy flames rested a black pan of sausages and rashers. The tinker woman squatted by the fire, her hand on the pan handle.

'Smells good,' said his father, surprising her with his easy tone, so that she looked up at him. 'Where's your man?'

'He's not here,' replied the woman. The boy looked at her green ankle-socks. His father rested his bicycle against the cart and was about to look into the tent when the man came out.

'He's here now,' said his father, with laconic sarcasm.

The tinker wore brown boots, a faded brown suit, an open-necked shirt and a hat.

His face was tight, compact, chiselled, attractive, shifty. His skin was very white and on his upper lip was a pencil-thin moustache.

His dancing eyes flickered from the uniform to the frying pan. The smoke curving up the side of the pan went straight into the still air. Silence was a tactic of his father's, during which he sized up his quarry. The woman stared into the pan, the man shifted from foot to foot.

'What ails you?' queried the tinker.

'Where did you get that turf?'

The tinker swung towards the fire. The flames spurted. So that was it. Stolen turf. What harm was it, thought the boy to himself, even if it was stolen.

'Sure the bog's full of it,' said the woman, echoing his thoughts.

On the other side of the hedge was a brown stretch of water, reedy, treacherous-looking bogland.

The banks were too poor and unformed for turf to be harvested in the normal way. Mud was shovelled out from wet holes, spread on the banks, cut into rough shapes with the back of the hand and left to dry. The sods were much bigger and not as neat as cut turf but the local people claimed there was 'ojus burning' in them.

His father stepped towards the tinker.

The horse turned its head and stared at the uniform.

'The farmer gave me it,' said the tinker, gesturing towards the whitewashed house in the distance.

'Did he now? We'll go and ask him.'

The tinker looked at the woman. She took the pan from the flames.

The boy was left alone with her.

She put the pan on the ground. The sizzling faded. Squatting down she pressed her dress between her legs and stared at the boy with cold fury, trying to hurt him because of his father.

He tried to look away but her eyes held him tight. She bounced up and down on her hunkers, her thumb in her mouth. Staring at him. Her eyes big as moons. He clung to his bicycle unable to move out of her gaze. Panic gripped him. He tried to lick his lips but his tongue was dry. He was conscious of his eyes blinking and then to his amazement he felt his grip loosen and saw his bike clatter to the road, one of the handlebars resting in a pot-hole puddle.

In a trance he hauled the bike up and tried to stare at the front wheel but his eyes were pulled towards the woman's.

'Do you eat sweets?'

'I do,' he whispered.

'Pity I haven't got any,' and she rocked over and back with laughter. He felt ashamed and angry. If his father didn't return soon he was going to jump on the bike and cycle like mad for home.

The woman's attention was diverted to the horse which had pulled at its tether and begun to urinate.

It gushed out from under its tail onto the grass verge and flooded into the road, foam swirling on top.

'Good girl, Dolly,' said the woman.

A she. Like her. Like his mother. Not like him.

Getting up she went to the back of the tent and came back with a bucket, soap and a creamery can. She poured water from the can into the bucket. Kicking off her shoes she lifted a foot onto the rim of the creamery can and began to peel away her ankle-sock with the hook of her thumb. When half off she scratched her heel before rolling the sock away completely. Admiring her neat foot she wiggled her toes and searched between them with her fingers. Unlike her legs her feet were white and clean.

As she took off her other sock, her dress fell back along her thigh so that the boy saw the far flesh and curved moon of her rump.

White like her feet. Like flour.

He looked at the horse and back to the woman.

She began to wash her socks. Green soapy suds in her mashing fingers. Flies buzzing round the dying foam on the roadway.

'What the hell are you looking at?'

Not knowing where they came from or why, the boy heard the words 'Not much', coming out of his mouth. The woman's eyes narrowed, but then she smiled at him.

'Well, aren't you the spoilt wee pup?'

His father often said that to him. Spoilt. But he only said it when his mother was listening. It was like a secret word; the use of which they knew would start a row.

When his mother hugged him she was warm through her clothes, her apron, even through an overcoat. His father's uniform was cold and smelt of ink.

The tinker woman looked warm. As a cake coming out of the oven. She continued washing the socks, ignoring him for some time, as she rinsed, squeezed and then hung them on a bush.

They were a lighter green than the velvet green in a magpie's tail. Lighter than ivy. Than moss. Grass green.

She squatted back down on her hunkers by the fire. He found he wasn't afraid of her now. Her face, her hair, her dress, her white feet were pleasant to look at.

'Where are you from?' he asked shyly, but with a growing feeling of superiority. She laughed, her teeth flashing in her open mouth.

'Give us a kiss and I'll tell you. Just a little one, like you give your mammy.'

The last two words she rolled round her mouth, curdling them, before spitting them out with a venom that cut straight into him.

A surge of panic gripped him again and once more he was on the point of jumping on his bike and making for home. But he was powerless to move. Besides what would his father say if he disappeared just like that?

He noticed his fists gripping the handlebars, knuckles glistening with tension.

He felt dizzy and believed he was at any moment going to faint.

The woman stood up.

'Give that to me!' she commanded.

He had no idea what she meant. Now she was pointing at him.

With dread at the consequences, when his father found out, he feared she was going to take his bicycle. That's what tinkers did! They even committed murder!!

His legs were weakening and but for the bike propping him up he would have clattered down into a heap on the roadside.

'It's streaky black,' he heard her saying, but didn't understand, 'I'll wash it for you.'

She stood looking at him, waiting for him to obey her, impatient at his stupidity.

'Your sock,' she shouted, 'I'll wash it for you.'

'Wash it? It?' The words burbled silently round his head. Then they hit him. Now he realized. She wanted to wash his oil-streaked sock.

Never. Never. His mother wouldn't be pleased. A tinker woman wash his sock? He'd be a laughing-stock. Oh no. Never. He couldn't.

But, as if outside his body, he watched himself laying down his bike, going on one knee, untying his shoe, taking off his ankle-sock and handing it to her. If his father came back now and saw him standing with one foot bare, and the wife of the tinker he was about to arrest washing his sock, there'd be ructions when he got home.

He looked up the road towards the whitewashed house. They were coming back. And there was his sock in the bucket of suds. He'd never get it back in time. His stomach churned and he noticed he was dancing from one foot to the other. She had the oily part of the sock in a washingboard grip of knuckles and fingers and was rubbing another part of the sock against it, trying to get rid of the stain.

He could only think of how wet the sock looked and how it would be impossible to dry it, iron it and get it back on before his father reached them.

The woman looked at him and followed his gaze. But she didn't hurry when she saw the men approaching. With a soapy hand she flicked the hair from the side of her face revealing a big ear-ring, smiled at the boy and carried on washing. His father and the tinker were now only about fifty yards away.

He slipped his foot into his shoe and tried to hide his naked ankle by holding it close to his other leg.

The woman flung the suddy water over the hedge, poured fresh water and began to rinse the sock just as the men reached them.

His father looked grim. Now the woman had the sock by the toe and was whirling it through the clear water. Almost playing with it.

Surely his father must have noticed.

'I'm taking your man into the barracks with me,' he said to the woman. Maybe he hadn't.

'But his tea's ready,' said the woman with limp defiance.

'He'll be back,' said his father, 'when I'm done with him.' He went to her, took the bucket of water from her and dowsed the fire with a sizzling splash.

The woman was furious. She tore at his face with her eyes, the boy's ankle-sock dangling from her fingers.

Her man went into the tent. His father took four half-burnt sods from the quenched fire, put two on the carrier of his bike and handed two to the boy.

'You bring these,' he ordered. 'And don't lose them – they're evidence.'

The tinker came rushing out of the tent, and going to the horse, untied it and leaped on its back.

The sleepy animal taken by surprise staggered about in the middle of the road not knowing what was going on. A quick crack on its neck with the halter and a couple of heels in the belly brought it to the required reality and, in a cloud of dust galloped away, the tinker clutching down his hat with one hand.

His father swung his leg over his bike, his great boot momentarily hanging in the air as he adjusted himself on the saddle; then ramming down hard on the pedal, head down, back crouched, rode after the tinker.

The tinker rode flat out only to be awkward. Not to escape. He knew he couldn't.

Once again the boy was alone with the woman.

She stood for a moment looking after the boy's father, then at the dowsed fire, then at the boy. Lifting up her dress to reveal her knees she sunk to the ground.

'God blast his face with warts and wrinkles and that he may die roarin'. And that's my solemn curse this day,' she roared to the sky.

The boy knew why she had bared her knees. His mother told him once that with love or curses you had to have flesh. Now he knew what she meant. Partly anyway.

'My sock, please,' he said to the woman.

Her eyes narrowed, and breathing heavily after the effort of cursing she seemed about to attack him but then with a weary sigh she sunk to her hunkers and just looked at him, almost in an appealing way.

She still held onto his sock.

He was worried. He didn't want to be left too far behind. He wanted to show his father how capable he was by bringing his share of the evidence swiftly and safely to the Station.

But he couldn't arrive without his ankle-sock. He would have to, somehow, get it back from her.

'How would you like to join the tinkers?' the woman asked, her teeth smiling, shining.

His heart thumped up inside him. He sloped his bicycle at an angle the better to get his leg quickly across the bar. He would have to go home without the sock and think of some lie to tell on the way. And later in bed with his mother tell the truth.

'Where the hell do you think you're going?' shouted the woman.

The boy was sure she was going to capture him. Murder him. Kiss him. And keep him forever.

He moved off but the front wheel went into a pot-hole, stopping him dead. He struggled for balance but the bike lurched over and he had to scramble off, the jolt knocking the two sods of turf onto the road.

Holding the bike with one hand he bent to pick them up with the other. One of the sods crumbled to pieces. He began to cry. Little anguished whimpers of fear and anger.

He stuffed some of the pieces into his pockets and managed to secure the other sod on his carrier.

As he mounted the bike again he couldn't resist looking at the woman.

A breeze was sifting through her hair and tucking her dress about her body. She coiled his sock into the ball of her fist and flung it at him. It hit him right between the eyes and fell down onto his crossbar and then to the road.

Her face was fierce and proud and sad.

The green ankle-socks flapped drying on the hedge.

'Come back nice boy. Come back angel.'

He managed to get moving, his legs growing stronger the further he got from her. But even a long way away he thought he could hear her hysterical laughter following him along the wind.

When he got near the Station he saw the tinker's horse tied to the barracks gate. It had assumed its lazy-leg posture of the encampment.

He went into the day room with his 'evidence'. His sense of achievement diminished by the loss of his sock.

But neither his father nor the tinker was there.

He put the turf on the table. Then he heard muffled groans and raised voices. Startled, he went into the hallway to listen. Silence. Frightened, he tip-toed along the tiled corridor and though he had decided to get out of the barracks, instinctively he stopped at the cell door. He knew they were in there. Behind the massive door, all bolts, locks and hinges.

A big bunch of keys dangled from a keyhole. Rooted to the spot he listened in the terrifying silence. Why weren't they making a noise now? His neck was craned at an unnatural angle, the tension hurting.

A strangulated cry of temper tore through the thick wooden door. That was his father.

'You broke into that lock-up shop, didn't you, come on, admit it. And you can go.'

The boy ran outside. The horse looked up, pointing its ears forward.

His father was beating the tinker. It wasn't fair. He'd missed his tea and now he was being beaten! And his woman was nice.

The Station was a large yellow-coloured pebbledashed bungalow with separate entrances to the married quarters and barracks. The outhouses were separate too and the vegetable gardens divided by a high wall.

His father didn't allow him at the back of the police quarters; but he raced round, got a ladder from an outhouse and put it up against the outer wall of the cell.

The tinker was screaming.

A slit in the wall let daylight into the cell. Peering in he could see his father's cap and another head with a bald spot on it. That was Guard McMurray.

'You broke in there and anything you couldn't take you stood on! Butter, cameras, bread, radios, eggs . . . didn't you?' shouted his father.

For a split second he saw the tinker's face. Blood came from his nose. This wasn't fair. It just wasn't. He wanted to shout 'Stop', but he couldn't. He heard himself shout 'Hello', instead. He felt foolish.

The bodies in the slit of light stopped swirling and he saw his father flash a look up at him.

'It's going to rain, Daddy,' he said, surprised at his calmness and the stupidity of the remark.

There were murmurs from Guard McMurray and he heard the cell door banging open.

Getting down from the ladder he ran to the front of the building. To keep a distance between himself and his father he went out the gate and sat on the opposite side of the road.

Minutes later the tinker came out. He had his hat in his hand. He untied his horse, got on it, but not as nimbly as before and throwing a sideways glance at the boy galloped away.

His father came out and walked towards the married quarters. The boy called out to him.

'I left the evidence on the table, Daddy.'

His father stared over at him.

'Come here you.'

The boy was afraid but he knew he had to go.

His father took him gently by the hand and they walked in together. His mother had the tea ready. The boy sat into the table, keeping his naked ankle well under. So far no one had noticed.

His father chewed his food methodically. Masticating, he called it.

His mother played with crumbs in silence. Staring down at the willow-patterned plate.

The silence was broken by his father grumbling out from deep within his thoughts.

'"Topping", he said to me, the beggar. "Topping".'

The boy laughed. His father looked at him.

'You tell your mammy what happened to your ankle-sock. You spoilt wee pup you.'

His mother glanced up, her moon eyes flashing fire.

Squirming away from them, he slid to the floor.

Under the table his mother's ankle was entwined in his father's boots and his hand gripped her knee, the dress pushed up along her thigh. He sat back up at the table.

On the mantelpiece was a picture of God. His eyes watched them and the clock ticked the silence away.

DERMOT HEALY

from *A Goat's Song*

II

The News at Six

Along with geese and apples and Catholics, Maisie Ruttle brought fiction into Jonathan Adams' life. On the mantelpiece, leaning against a clock shaped like a windmill, were copies of Dickens, Thackeray, Balzac – novels belonging to an earlier generation on Maisie's side. Jonathan Adams was a widely read man, but unlike his wife or daughters he did not read fiction. Fiction contained inaccuracies, untruths, generalizations, assumptions. The real world was a poor metaphor for what might happen in the hereafter, but at least it was more true than fiction.

The language of the imagination offered licentious freedom. It acquired trappings, idols, delusions, false promises, too much madness. Not till Matti Bonner died did

Jonathan Adams rediscover fiction. And this was his attempt at trying to recall Matti Bonner's life. That life, which he had presumed he was familiar with, now grew strange.

He could not place his hand on the facts. Yet throughout his life Jonathan Adams at heart was a reader. The real world, with its physical discomforts, could not accommodate the shocking facts that remained to the fore in his brain. He wanted knowledge of God, and though he baulked at attributing to Him human qualities, this he did, in the full awareness of the fragility of human knowledge when faced with the *Uncognoscibility of the Absolute*, as John Stuart Mill called it.

For Jonathan Adams reality was scripture. It was the sacred history of a people finding their God. So, though Jonathan might wish to transcend history, he grew to love its bare inviolable physicality. As a reader, like many of his age, he had turned to autobiographies, to biography, to see how others had succeeded in dealing with their demons. He had entered again that boyish period of life when the mind selects figures: the numbers on opposing sides in the siege of Derry; the numbers on opposing sides in the Battle of the Boyne; the number of languages spoken when we were given the gift of tongues. Is life not tuned more to the ear than to the eye? How many royals died of choking on fish bones? How many royals were afflicted by small gullets? How many Napoleons existed? How many Jews? How many gypsies? How many Ulstermen died at the Somme? What was the number of Presbyterians that travelled in the Famine ships to America? He traced Carson's lineage and counted the number of homosexual politicians in Britain. He estimated the number of Catholics in the world. How many Protestants died at the hands of the Godfathers of the Roman Church in the Inquisition? How many Ulster Protestants died, were tortured, had their breasts sheared off by blood-thirsty Catholics on 23 October 1641, the feast of Ignatius Loyola, founder of the Jesuits? 30,000? 40,000? 50,000? Who was Roger Casement? What are Rome's finances? How war-worthy were Russian tanks? Did the Russians actually try to send messages through space by means of brain waves? Was it true that Communism only flourished in Catholic countries? How many Jews died so that their blood could be shipped to the front to keep the German Army going? He read magazines on American rifles, on wild pheasants in Ireland. Articles on Paisley. Biographies of American presidents, histories of the Boer War, the Second World War. Geese. Peel and the Law and Order Bill of 1852.

'You must read *Pride and Prejudice*,' said Maisie, 'that at least.'

'No,' replied the Sergeant.

He gave her no moral or high-minded reason. Sometimes he might counter with the weak excuse that *fiction was the outcome of idleness*, that it was *fantasy rather than fiction*, but the real reason was that he had a fine memory which could not be induced to recall an imagined narrative. He read fiction as a child, but in the aftermath it remained a blur. Fiction was the shameful stories prisoners made up to escape prison. It was created to obscure guilt. Fiction for him was irreligious, the act of imagination itself was a door opening onto the void. His mind baulked at characters who entered the first line of a novel but did not reside in the real world. In truth, what did not come from the Bible was fiction.

Yet, he was addicted to mythology. Here there was no author, the author had been erased through time. And so the characters thrived, they became real. The New Testament, though it was told through Matthew, Mark, Luke and John, presented no problem. The author was Jesus, and he was not of this world.

The Old Testament was the history of memory itself.

At school, Jonathan Adams had been an outstanding Biblical scholar. The story of the Bible was for him like a roll call of everything that existed in nature and in himself.

The name Abraham sounded like an Indian gong that called the people to morning prayer. It was a wide primal landscape. It was a name given by simple men to a simple man. Abraham was one of the first words breathed by men. As men were naming the colours and the plants and the animals, they were naming each other. In the word Abraham were deserts, famine, emigration ships. In his private world, as he drove or walked, here and there, when he lay down before sleep, lines from the Book of Job would stir in Jonathan Adams' mind and haunt his subconscious.

It was the people's book. They had named the flowers and the rain. They had re-created the world being made before their very eyes in a language given them by God. The movements of the tribes were poems. The translations of the Bible by Wycliffe into English, Luther into German, Calvin into French had extended and enriched all those languages more than ever poetry or drama or fiction had. And yet the story was intended for simple men. *Their ears did not sleep.* They were simple exact words.

At Pentecost, the gift of first fruits, he could actually hear that sound from heaven fill the room they were in. He imagined the eleven tongues of fire leaping over the heads of the 120 members of the congregation. The words the Holy Spirit gave them were words of law. As the Spirit gave utterance, the people named the world.

And when the world was created the angels shouted for joy!

The people had named the oak and the ash. The parts of the body, the brain. And they named the places where they had stood. They had named the ancient places of Ireland. Places were not a statistic. They were where language stood still, where people had settled before they moved on. But Jonathan Adams, and his people, had come to stay. And he himself, though he did not know it then, was to become one of his most uncherished statistics. Already fate was preparing that path for him.

Meanwhile, he read, he wrote out summonses, he cycled to his barracks through Ulster's quiet years, he felt safe as a policeman.

It was being a policeman saved Jonathan Adams from continuing as an evangelist. Sometimes when he listened to Willy he was shocked and enthralled by his brother's lack of intellectualism, the lack of humility. His shameless oratory made the Sergeant wince. Jonathan Adams did not want to hear the words read out. The policeman in him did not want to hear raised voices. And it was being a policeman brought Jonathan Adams face to face with an element in himself he would rather never have encountered.

When the Civil Rights march on 5 October 1968 passed through the city of Derry it was met by a police baton-charge. Jonathan Adams, along with other elder policemen, had been called up from various counties in the North for the day. Not only because of a shortfall in numbers but also because outsiders would not be recognized. The air was rank with bigotry and acrimonious shouts like 'In the name of God let us through'. The whole affair, the police thought, would be restricted to a small side street, and here it was proposed that Law and Order would make its stand on a genuine footing. The police had been told beforehand that the march had not been properly endorsed by the Civil Rights movement, that it was directly Republican, directly IRA. This was the perfect chance to settle old grievances.

First the Catholics parleyed, then became adamant. But the route they wished to take was closed to them. Then it started. It was a hectic violent day.

Jonathan Adams clouted with euphoria to the right and left of him.

That was the night, in the aftermath of the march that did not take place, that the riots started in the Catholic Bogside area of the city. But by then the old timers had been removed from the scene, the young local police took over, and Jonathan Adams, battle-worn and fiercely satisfied, had returned home to Fermanagh. The following morning he began three days' leave with his wife and daughters.

They drove at break of day into the west through Ballyshannon. With a sense of pride Jonathan Adams flashed his identity card as they entered the Republic. The guard, with a knowing nod, leaned in and said: 'That was a bad doing, yesterday.' 'What did he mean?' asked Maisie as they drove through the uplifted barrier. 'I don't know. Every last man of them is a Republican,' said the Sergeant, 'but they don't frighten me.' Then the family was undecided as to what to do. Because the girls wanted to see Yeats' grave they turned south and drove along the coast to Sligo. From Sligo, they drove out west to Achill Island. They stopped there for the night in the Valley House Hotel.

'What's thon island I can see from here?' Sergeant Adams asked.

'What's that you're saying?' asked the man.

'What is that island over there?'

'That's Mullet peninsula,' the manager told him. 'It's where the Playboy of the Western World came from.'

The intention was to spend the next night somewhere in Galway, but Jonathan Adams was drawn to explore the isolated peninsula to the north, and so at noon the following day they entered Belmullet town after a long drive through the unpopulated bogland of Erris. The Nephin Beg range of mountains which had been shrouded the day before in mist, now rose clear and pure.

An old Fair Day was in progress in the town. Cattle and sheep and chickens were being bartered. Gypsies sold socks, gates and radios. A man swallowed lit cigarettes and brought them back up again still burning. Dogs fought. Goats butted the sideboards of carts. Men sat on steps eating sandwiches. Cows shat on pavements. Men sat on tractors licking ice-cream cones. It was like watching some medieval pageant. They drove from Erris Head in Broad Haven Bay down to Blacksod in the south, amazed at the isolation, the white sandy roads that ran by the sea; the Inishkea Islands, holy, absolute; the wind-glazed violent cliffs; the meteorological station; the endless bogs; the rips and cracks through the huge dunes; the black curraghs; the lighthouse that sat perched on Eagle Island like a castle in a fairy story; the piers, the harbour, the sea.

'What's the island beyant?' asked Jonathan Adams of a man who was oiling his Honda 50. He straightened up with a grimace.

'They are a great bike,' said the man, 'if you look after them.' He wiped his hands on his trousers, looked at the Honda and then looked at the island. 'That'd be Inishglora,' he said, and felt his wet nose with his thumb and forefinger. 'The Isle of Purity.'

'Oh.'

'That's right. Yes indeed.' He grimaced again. 'It's where Brendan landed.'

He saw that this remark did not signify anything to the Adams family.

'Brendan the navigator,' he explained, 'the lad who discovered America – like the rest of us. Except that he was the first. Though of course that may not be true.' The family and himself stood looking out, with the Honda up on its stand, and the car engine running. 'And it's where the Children of Lir are buried, God bless them.' He felt his nose again. 'And there you have it.'

'Thanking you,' said the Sergeant, humbly.

'And what part of the world do ye hail from?'

'Fermanagh,' said Jonathan.

'Oh, but they're giving you a hard time,' said the man, and he shook his head sadly. 'The sooner you drive them to feck out of there the better.'

Sheepishly, they got into the car, the man slapped the roof and they drove on. And the man stood there, his hands on the grips of the Honda, looking out on Inishglora as if he were seeing it for the first time.

They booked into a bed-and-breakfast a few mile out the road in Corrloch. From her window there Maisie Adams saw that a large cut-stone house opposite was for sale. She was intrigued to hear from their landlady that the price of the property was only £1,200. Next morning, despite her husband's entreaties, Maisie arranged a viewing of the house with the auctioneer.

'The lighthouse men lived here,' he explained. 'They're known locally as The Dwellings.'

'Such huge rooms,' said Maisie.

'This one is mine,' said Sara.

But Jonathan Adams, treating the whole affair as foolishness, kept up only a desultory conversation with the auctioneer. And as the man pointed out what came with the property the Sergeant merely nodded, not wanting to enter into any false dealings. Yes, it was a fine house, he agreed, indeed it had a wonderful view. This being as far as manners and prudence would allow.

Afterwards, Jonathan Adams went down to the hotel in Belmullet for a coffee. They served him in the bar where he sat uncomfortably among the drinkers. First the Angelus rang out, then came the news from RTE on the black-and-white TV. The Sergeant took no notice till he heard sounds and names that gradually grew familiar. He looked up with terror and saw they were re-running an account of the march. This came as a shock to Jonathan Adams. He had seen no TV men there, nor was he used to them. It showed the Catholics gathering in Duke Street. Then the chaotic start of the march. The shouts for the police to give way were raised. With great religious zeal the Catholics called to the policemen. Within seconds a protester was being batoned. What happened next was seen by Jonathan Adams with blinding clarity. To the left of the picture could be seen a grey-haired policeman, hatless, chasing after a youth. When he lost him among the other marchers, he turned and batoned a middle-aged man who was already pouring blood.

The crowd in the bar shouted 'bastards'.

On the TV the old policeman had found his hat. As he put it on, he looked round for someone else to hit. Seeing no one he turned back and hit the screaming man again. A woman crouched low as she pulled her man away. The old policeman charged past the camera. Then, wild-eyed and wielding a baton, he stared remorselessly straight at the lens. Jonathan Adams had become a witness to himself. He saw the mad look of fury in his own eye. He looked round the bar but no one was taking any notice of him. His chin began shaking. Then he shook uncontrollably.

'Bastards,' said someone.

Jonathan Adams slipped away.

Next morning at six they left Mayo without breakfast. They were on the road in the dark. He brooked no complaints. And this time he kept his head down as they crossed the border lest anyone might recognize him. Everywhere this RTE film of the confrontation was being viewed. He was terrified. He could not wait to get back to the safety of his own home. He drove furiously, in his mind's eye watching himself right his hat and turn back to strike the man who was down and screaming.

Jonathan Adams had become a part of history. Whenever a documentary of those troubled years in Ireland was made, that clip from the Telefís Éireann file would be shown. Word went out through the police that the cameraman responsible should be dealt with. But by now, TV men were coming from all over the world.

That evening on Ulster Television, as his family sat round after dinner, the news turned to the riots in Derry. Again, in slow motion, the Catholics collected in Duke Street. Again they began to move forward. Again they implored, hysterically, in the name of God, to be let through. Jonathan Adams stood up and switched off the TV. He said nothing. He left the room. Catherine switched the TV back on. In his kitchen, Jonathan Adams heard the eerie voices call out again. He thought it was fiction, but it was reality. He could envisage the whole scene, the heads, the hatred, the jerky movements. He came in shaking with wrath. The TV was switched off again.

'I don't want ye to look at that,' he roared.

He unplugged the TV and put it into his car.

By the following day it was obvious that everyone in the village, including Matti Bonner, had seen Jonathan Adams on the news the night before. He sent the TV back to the company he had hired it from. He phoned his superiors to see if they could bring forward his retirement. In the barracks, young Saunderson joked: 'Ye still have it in ye, Sergeant.'

'Mind your own business, sonny,' said Sergeant Adams.

He was terrified. Terrified and angry. The seal on his privacy had been broken. Sleepless nights followed. Each night the same set of images swam again before his mind, and he succumbed to such fear that he spent the night at the foot of the stairs, a loaded revolver in his hand, facing the door.

Then the girls learned at school how their father had been teaching manners to the popeheads.

'Everyone saw you on television,' Catherine said, when she came in from school.

He was sitting in his uniform in the kitchen. He looked at Maisie and then at Catherine, and then he went up to his room and prayed. He called on God to give him peace. They were calling him a bigot, but he was a patriot. He was not by nature a violent man. The camera could not tell the history that led to that moment when he had become one of those statistics he despised.

The camera did not hear orders. The camera did not hear the chants of hate. It did not remember that wherever the Mass was said soon men were burning upon the stake. It selected its own branch of history. But why had he retaliated like that? And why had the young policemen held back? Had they seen the camera? Had the Fenians known the whole time that this would appear on TV and so deliberately driven the police to it? It was the old fogies like himself who had struck out, not knowing that they were being filmed. The young fellows had known.

It was them that went up under cover of darkness to the Bogside.

In the light of day he had become the author of his own misfortune. Jonathan Adams cursed the cameraman. He cursed the police that had used him and his stupidity. He remembered going up together with other policemen in the minibus from Fermanagh on the fatal day. They had stopped off at a seaside town for dinner at a hotel. All the talk that day was of how they would put a stop to Rome. We'll show them! Hey! Now he felt that the same policemen had thrown him to the lions. After he turned on Saunderson for mentioning that escapade, his appearance on the TV was never mentioned. But sometimes, out of the corner of his eye, he caught them smiling. There was no escape.

The whole of the world had seen him.

Because someone had knocked off his hat, Jonathan Adams had started a war.

CLARE BOYLAN

from *Holy Pictures*

6

Wertzsberger, wine merchant; Buchalter, baker; Weinronk, baker. The Jews lived in a network of narrow streets around South Circular Road which was known as Little Israel. It was a foreign territory, connected to the ordinary city only by the pavements beneath and the sky overhead.

'Wertzsberger.' Nan mouthed the strange-sounding names as she dawdled along Clanbrassil Street. She stopped to watch her green-tunicked reflection in a window piled with bread that was brown and shiny as conkers. She felt that a part of her had escaped. 'Weinronk.' She was on her way to see Shyster, the Jew.

His real name was Schweitzer. No one knew his first name. He wheeled a creaking pram filled with old clothes and terrible noises. Corner boys chased him but the small children were respectful because the bigger ones said that the pram was filled with devils. At night the children were haunted by a memory of the muffled squawk and cackle of spirits.

There were about five thousand Jews living in Dublin.

They had come without money, without professions, without English. They found things to sell. All of them were tallymen or *vickla*. Shyster sold secondhand clothes and another thing, a most useful commodity. It was his combination of trades that made him a legend and attracted Nellie to add him to her store of 'God's demented'.

He wheeled his pram through the streets where children were put to sit on the step because there was no space in overcrowded rooms. He beckoned to the littlest ones: 'Come and see my babies. Babies for the oven. Babies for the dinner table.' Bristling with dread and interest the children pushed one another forward. Shyster lifted away layers of sweat-smelling wool, lifeless cotton. He had a delicate wrist movement. He might have sold lace or linen. The infants pressed forward, reassured by familiar smells in the clothing. Inside, the demons rattled.

The bottom layer was a gentleman's tweed overcoat. It bubbled with hidden activity. Shyster smiled at the children. He whipped away the greenish tweed. Bundles of rusty life, raisin-eyed, razor-beaked, flew up into the stricken faces. Screaming and bumping into each other, clawing the air for mothers who were nowhere to be seen, the children raced away. The small sirens of their voices could still be heard when they had vanished from sight.

It was different when he wheeled his pram into town where there were grown-ups, paying customers. There he would employ his best English for a phrase learnt by heart. 'Hens, two and sixpence. Used clothing, no infection.'

'But sometimes . . .' Nellie's eye bore into her wonderfully frightened audience. 'A squawk was heard from under the pickins' that was like no hen ever heard by mortal ears. It was the cry of a young child.'

There was an ordinary explanation. Shyster kept the hens beneath the clothes to stop them from flying away.

Nan was fourteen. She wasn't afraid. At any rate – she felt in her pocket the half-crown and forced herself to walk on – she was more afraid of father than of Nellie's Jew. She pulled herself away from the tempting shops and turned into a maze of smaller streets. Little red-brick houses, like toy houses, had front doors on the street. They all looked the same. Nan did not know where to go. 'Excuse me,' she said to a young woman sitting in a dark hall with the front door left open. She was about twenty-five with dark, half-sleeping eyes. She came forward slowly. 'You tell your mama I sell her a nice quilt, only a shilly a week,' she said urgently. Nan ran away.

Soon she got used to these overtures. People tried to sell her boots, shawls – even money. At last one of them told her that Shyster lived on Abel Street. You could recognize the house by its yellow door. This fact alone shocked her. The rich painted their front doors in white. Ordinary people used dark green or black or a wood stain. No one used yellow, like a tinker's caravan.

When she found the house she was surprised by the beauty of the door. It was the bright yellow of a buttercup. The letter box gleamed like gold. She lifted the flap and let it go with a small sound. Someone raised the flap from the inside by poking at it with a finger. The door was drawn slowly back.

All she had seen through the slit of the letter box were two brown eyes, warily considering. Now, in the widening gap of the door, she was introduced to a fantastic sight, the dining-room where a large table was spread with a snowy cloth. Eight candles as translucent as Sister Immaculata's fingers stretched from a stand of gleaming silver and there was wine on the table and sparkling glasses. It was fit for a palace.

The door had been opened by a wild-looking man whose long nose ploughed a raging black beard. There was so much to see that she could not take it all in at once. It was not until the man spoke very softly – 'come in, child' – and beckoned with fingers so delicate that they might have sold lace or linen, that she realized and stepped back, unnerved.

'Shyster!'

Behind him a plump girl of twelve or thirteen, with pink in her cheeks and brown ringlets, laughed delightedly.

'Poor Ivor,' she said. 'You must not tease him.'

'Ivor?'

'My brother,' the girl said. 'Ivor Schweitzer!' She took Nan's hand and drew her into the mysterious splendour.

It was the first time she had been inside a Jewish house. She expected to feel some faint sense of danger for she had been warned by the nuns that one's faith could be threatened by keeping company with people of misguided persuasions. Apart from the beautiful dining table, the house was disappointingly ordinary. The furniture was shabby and badly matched. The squares of carpet did not reach the edges of the stone floor.

A woman came from the kitchen, followed by a girl of perhaps fifteen. They both had the dark, curling hair and pink plump faces of the younger girl. The woman looked large and firm as a gentleman's armchair in her green velvet dress.

'Good girl, Gicki!' she beamed on Nan's companion. 'You have brought the little goyim.' She smiled at Nan. 'You like rice pudding?'

'Yes.'

'Good child. You know what is to do?' Her English was not fluent.

Nan hesitated. 'No.'

It caused them to laugh. They threw back their heads and showed the solidity of their teeth. This made Nan nervous. She turned to Shyster but he looked angry and left them. The women glanced at one another guiltily and stemmed their mirth with rounded hands.

Nan took her hand from her pocket and held out the half-crown. 'I've come to buy a hen,' she said.

The three who looked so alike were taken by a fresh seizure of laughter until the oldest one, wiping tears from her eyes, said, 'Hush, my darlings, we shall be eating the cold food in the darkness. The Shiksa wants a hen.'

The girl who had greeted Nan explained: 'It is the Sabbath.'

'I don't know very much . . .' Nan said doubtfully. The girls began to giggle again but their mother stopped them. 'We have to be very quiet,' she said.

'Because of the Sabbath,' Nan said.

'No. Because of our brother, Sam.'

'Is he ill?'

'Oh, no! He is learning to be a surgeon.' They led Nan into the tiny kitchen and shut the door so that they could talk.

'I am Gickla,' the youngest said.

'I'm Nan.'

'I'm Becca,' said the elder sister.

'We not work on Sabbath,' their mother explained.

'All food is prepared yesterday. The little Shiksa comes to light our fire and our stove and our candles.'

'Today she did not come,' said Becca.

'So you have come instead,' Gickla explained.

Nan found it hard to concentrate. Her attention was pulled by the glamour of the tiny room. Every available space between stove and window and table and sink and cooker was taken up with pictures of film stars cut out from magazines. Some of them were brown and grease-spattered but they smiled with radiant happiness and uniqueness in their furs and jewels and shiny top hats.

'You like them?' Gickla noticed Nan's rapt stare. 'We are mad about the movies.'

'You all go? Together?' Nan was envious.

'No.' The mother looked regretful. 'Papa passed away. The boys are religious. There is only us ladies.'

Nan's heart struggled with excitement and envy while she lit the jets on the stove and then the oven and the coal fire and finally set a dewy bud of flame on each of the five white candles.

'Is that all?' she said then.

'Sit down. Sit down,' said Mrs Schweitzer. 'You want some rice pudding. Gickla, get the child some rich pudding.'

Nan sat at the kitchen table and Gickla brought the pudding in a large tin dish and Becca set out a small pudding bowl and a spoon. There were raisins in the pudding, and pieces of cherry. Nan spooned it slowly into her mouth and felt the pieces of fruit between her teeth, while the two girls fixed her with their moist brown eyes and told her about all the men and women who had become famous on the screen and the films they had seen, which were quite unlike the matinées, where true love triumphed and the audience wept.

It was a grown-up world, but an adult world quite different to any Nan had ever glimpsed. She could not picture it. She wanted them to go slowly, to point out the people in the photographs, to break down the words, like Sister Immaculata. When her head was whirling with a glittering, dancing swarm of these beautiful grown-up people, they began to tell her about the Four Horsemen.

This was a wonderful thing at the Scala Cinema, a moving picture with sound. The voices of Rudolph Valentino and Alice Terry did not actually speak out of the screen.

It was a man who came out beforehand. He was draped in heavy robes. He stood in front of the curtains and delivered, in sepulchral tones, a prologue about death and pestilence. The film, which was called *The Four Horsemen of the Apocalypse*, was about this sort of thing.

When the audience had been whipped up into a stew of fear the picture began. They sat back, thinking they could relax, that the ordeal was over. Worse was to come.

Loudspeakers had been set up at the back of the cinema giving off startling noises to simulate the sound of firing cannons. The audience, feeling itself under fire from all quarters, panicked. There were riots in the cinema. Many people fainted and had to be carried away. The film was a huge success. Men and women queued for three and a half hours before it was due to commence.

By the time Gickla finished speaking Nan realized that she had barely eaten a spoonful of the delicious pudding. She was too excited to swallow. She went to the cinema every Saturday with the Tallons but it was always the Thomas Street Picture House, which they called The Tommo, or the Phoenix Picture House on Ellis Quay, known as The Feno. It was twopence into the Tommo. The Feno was the cheapest. On Saturdays it was a penny and this was known as the penny rush. It was rough. A man kept the queue in order with a whip.

They did not show proper films at the matinées, but cartoons and serials. The children's serials were not really thrilling. It was difficult to work up a proper sense of fear over the girl tied to the railway track for she was always freed in time for the following week's episode.

Nan had never been to a real film in one of the adult cinemas. 'How much is it to get in?' she demanded.

'A *shilling*,' Becca taunted.

'Mama took us both on Becca's birthday,' said Gickla.

A shilling. Nan and Mary got twopence for the tram fare to school. When there was time they walked, but when school was over they were so hungry they had to spend their money on an eccles cake at a bakery in the city. Father was generous when in a good mood, but he handed out sweets or brought home ice-cream; he rarely gave money, and he disapproved violently of the cinema, calling it licentious filth, which the children associated in their minds with dirty hair. It was true that the matinée queues rang out with the taint of unwashed bodies.

She never had as much as a shilling at once. Today she had half a crown in her pocket but that was for the hen. The hen! She had almost forgotten father's hen.

She took the money from her pocket and put it on the table. The dimpled faces looked amused. It was as if they had never known anything but material comfort. Rich, sweet, greasy smells, rising from the stove, reinforced this impression. 'My father sent me,' Nan said. 'I have to buy a hen.'

Mrs Schweitzer arched a thick black eyebrow. 'Ivor not sell his hens on the Sabbath,' she said.

'I'm sorry,' Nan said. 'I forgot.' She put the money back in her pocket.

The woman watched the vanishing coin in alarm. 'Perhaps,' she said slowly, 'if you leave money on table and pick a hen yourself, it not amount to the same thing.'

'Come,' Gickla said sharply. She fetched a metal bowl and filled it with yellow meal and Nan followed her to the yard. The concrete path had a net roof to keep cats away. The ground had a sandy covering of grain out of which a few hens picked fastidious feet. There were dozens of hens dozing like fat cabbages and a couple that lurched toward the children, squinting dangerously and giving abuse. Gickla threw a fistful of grain into the air and the birds jostled and squawked and dropped foolish faces.

'There!' Gickla set down the bowl and wiped her hands. 'I cannot sell you a hen but I can make it easy for you to choose.'

'They all look the same,' Nan said.

'Don't be silly. Use your eyes. See how they fight for the food. That one is a fool. She pecks at her sister's eyes instead of the grain. This one just eats and gets fat and lays brown eggs. Choose for yourself. I only advise.'

But Nan's attention had been caught by a thin bird that neither dozed nor quarrelled but watched from a sad, glassy eye.

'Gickla?' A thought had struck her. 'You and your sister wear nice dresses but Shyster – Ivor – is dressed in rags.'

Gickla frowned and threw another handful of seeds to the birds. 'We dress to suit our purpose.'

'I don't understand.'

She offered Nan a sideways smile, like the photographs of the women in films. 'You think perhaps he should wear a three-piece suit with a silk handkerchief and a gold fob watch to sell old clothes to the poor. He dresses for his business.'

'I'm sorry.'

Gickla laughed. 'You are always sorry. We are merely poor. Mama makes our dresses from the best cast-offs. All our money goes to make Sam a surgeon. Becca and me went barefoot until we were twelve but now that men notice us we must wear nice dresses so that we will have husbands.'

She put her hands on her hips and stuck out her plump chest. 'See! Already there are grown-up men calling to see me.' She laughed. 'Mama always sells them something.'

Nan looked away. She watched the thin, isolated bird. It flinched when some big bossy bird jutted its neck in an ill-tempered manner.

'I'll take that one,' she pointed. 'What's its name?'

Gickla looked at her with amusement. 'Betty.' She waded through the angry feathery mass. Birds rose around her ankles, barking in fright. She picked up the little docile hen firmly, holding its wings to its breast. 'Have you brought a scarf?'

'A scarf?'

'You have to wrap her up to carry her home.'

'I'll hold her under my arm.' She held out a tentative hand. 'Here, Betty.' The bird pecked feebly at her fingers.

'Do as you like,' said Gickla. 'If you hold her under your arm, she will do her business in your pocket.'

She borrowed Gickla's woollen headsquare and it occurred to her as the dark child tied the angry bird up like Dick Whittington's bundle that perhaps Gickla was using it as an excuse to see her again. Gickla was more clever than she was. She held her bundle tightly as she said goodbye to the women. She could feel the hen's feet stamping exploratively through the cloth. Every so often it emitted an impatient grunt. 'You wash my scarf if that hen does her business,' Gickla admonished.

'You get your mama to take you to the Scala,' Becca smiled. 'You tell your mama I sell her a most beautiful model coat in navy repp, only a shilling a week.'

Nan watched the closed bedroom door that belonged to the brothers, where Sam studied to be a surgeon and Shyster sulked because the women laughed and sold hens on the Sabbath.

'Goodbye,' she said regretfully.

'Come back soon!' A trio of plump hands waved.

'Oh, I will.'

She ran then, clutching the warm, struggling bird, holding it with care in case it should lay an egg.

It began to rain. By the time she reached Portobello Bridge Nan's gymslip was soaked through and the drenched hen shrank in the scarf like a piece of stewed meat. Nan heard the church bell ring out seven times. She was late.

For a while the warm rain came down in lumps like the drops of sanctifying grace that fell from the Holy Ghost and then it stopped and the mildewed mountains and the toy villages, the stout-coloured river and the grey people were lit up pink by a violent blood-orange sun.

There was a brief illusion of silence after the blankety hissing of the rain and then the streets spat out sharp noises. Tram tracks glistened like eels as they writhed out from under the rattling cars. The tyres of bicycles sucked the wet cobbles. Iron wheels of horse-drawn goods vans made the noise of a boy running a stick along a railing. 'He can't kill me, he can't kill me, he can't kill me,' tapped out the sedate hooves of a little pony with bald patches. She ducked her head and ran, ignoring the sulky 'parp' of a Cluly's horn as its wet sporty driver sped past at fifteen miles an hour, splashing her with mud.

When she got home Mary was sitting on the front step, her lank plaits plastered to her cheeks from rain, her face green with fright.

'They're all gone out and I can't get in,' she shrilled accusingly. 'I've been sitting here for hours and hours and I'm afraid Hammer'll come and get me.'

'Where's everyone gone?' Nan said.

'Father never came home and Nellie's gone home. Mother's at her sodality.' She wiped her nose with her sleeve.

'Never mind,' Nan said. 'Look what I've got.' She pulled back a corner of the scarf to show the hen which grunted unhappily.

Mary's face brightened. 'You went to see Shyster?'

'Oh, it was nothing much. He wasn't very interesting. Let's go and fry ourselves up some rashers and bread and black pudding.'

'And tomatoes. Oh, *let's*.'

When they had washed up after their tea and had changed their clothes and dried the hen in a towel, they went to find a suitable house for the bird. They decided on the coal-house. Bertie, being a coward, would not bother it. They pulled out the pile of sacking from the back and spread it over the coal dust.

'There should be straw,' Mary said.

'I suppose so. And grain for her to eat.'

'Last Christmas's crib is still in the Indian room. There's some straw in that,' Mary said. She stood up, wiping coal dust from her hands on the front of her dress in a business-like manner.

'I'll get some scraps and a dish of water,' Nan said. 'I'll try some stale bread and rasher skins. Oh, I wish we had asked mother to buy porridge for Etta Gorman.'

Mary hurried to the house and climbed the stairs. She went to her parents' bedroom and reached into one of father's army boots. The key of the Indian room was kept hidden in his boots. It was a secret. She peered out the window at the dusty violet evening in case her mother or father should be returning, but there was no one. She crept to the return landing and let herself into the room. As always, she held her breath when she went in.

The Indian room was a foreign city, deserted. There were pieces of brass and strange lumps of carved furniture, a sly little stone goddess, with twisted legs. Men in splendid uniforms gazed dully out of beige photographs and a grinning sword was anchored to the wall. The floor was occupied by a single bed, a wardrobe and a big leather trunk filled with father's mementoes. Over the trunk was flung the withered skin of a tiger.

The crib was not to be seen. She looked under the bed but there was only an immaculate flowery china bowl.

The wardrobe revealed father's uniform from the horse regiment and a pair of riding boots. She thought it must be in the trunk. She pulled away the tiger skin and dust rose in a musty snarl. She unfastened the straps from their stout metal buckles. She pushed. The trunk was locked. She stood for a moment, dreaming, then went back to the wardrobe. She took out the boots. The legs were very long. Her arm went in all the way before she could reach the toe. The cold ring of a little iron key skidded into her grasp.

Before opening the trunk she examined her conscience. She was soon to make her first confession and she was militant against sin. There was nothing in the 'thou shalt nots' about opening things that were locked. She ground the key against its spring and pushed up the creaking lid. She looked in. A lot of queer things started happening. She felt as if she was a musical instrument, being played. Her free hand plucked at her gymslip and there was a pricking feeling in her armpit.

Her teeth bit deep into her lower lip. She was looking at a framed photograph of smiling teeth in a dark brown face, a girl.

There was a bunch of dried flowers, some women's clothing, bright and shapeless, an embroidered shawl. On top of these things was a small bunch of old letters, addressed in weak green ink and one letter separate, its ink still bright as mint cordial. Her hand shook when she lifted out the letter. 'Thou shalt not,' said a voice in her head. She supported the lid of the trunk with an aching shoulder and used two hands for the letter. A smell of perfumed dust, like the scent of Benediction, climbed into her nose.

There was no address, but a date in the spring. 'Mr Cantwell,' said the looped green words, 'at long last I have found you. Soon I come. Make ready, for you belong to me. Your obedient, Mumtaz.'

Mary put the letter back in its envelope. She let down the lid of the trunk and fastened the straps. She ground the little key in its lock and returned it to the black riding boot. She locked the door of the Indian room and brought that key back to its secret boot. Slowly she walked down the darkening stairway and went outside to where Nan was feeding the hen.

'You've been crying,' Nan said. 'Crybaby. You're afraid of the dark.'

Mary's wet face was blank and Nan felt sorry. 'There,' she said, pulling her limp school hankie from her blazer pocket. 'Dry your eyes and I'll tell you the most interesting thing you've ever heard.'

She told her about the Four Horsemen, the figure in robes who warned of plague and pestilence, the firing cannons, the fainting women, all of which could be witnessed at the Scala for a shilling.

'A shilling,' Mary said.

Nan turned her attention to the hen who had spread her wings on the dirty sacking to finish drying them. She pecked cautiously at a piece of brown bread. 'Perhaps Betty has laid an egg by now.' She climbed in over the makeshift bedding, and lifted the hen. There was nothing.

'*Betty?*' Mary said.

'Betty. That's her name.'

'You can't call her Betty. Hens in books are always called Betty. She's our hen. She's special. She's beautiful. Besides, Betty is too like Bertie. Neither would know which was being called.'

'Betty's her name,' Nan maintained stubbornly.

'I shall call her Elizabeth,' Mary said fiercely. 'After the young queen.'

'Night in Tunisia'

That year they took the green house again. She was there again, older than him and a lot more venal. He saw her on the white chairs that faced the tennis-court and again in the burrows behind the tennis-court and again still down on the fifteenth hole where the golf-course met the mouth of the Boyne. It was twilight each time he saw her and the peculiar light seemed to suspend her for an infinity, a suspended infinite silence, full of years somehow. She must have been seventeen now that he was fourteen. She was fatter, something of an exhausted woman about her and still something of the girl whom adults called mindless. It was as if a cigarette between her fingers had burnt towards the tip without her noticing. He heard people talking about her even on her first day there, he learnt that underneath her frayed blouse her wrists were marked. She was a girl about whom they would talk anyway since she lived with a father who drank, who was away for long stretches in England. Since she lived in a green corrugated-iron house. Not even a house, a chalet really, like the ones the townspeople built to house summer visitors. But she lived in it all the year round.

They took a green house too that summer, also made of corrugated iron. They took it for two months this time, since his father was playing what he said would be his last stint, since there was no more place for brassmen like him in the world of three-chord showbands. And this time the two small bedrooms were divided differently, his sister taking the small one, since she had to dress on her own now, himself and his father sharing the larger one where two years ago his sister and he had slept. Every night his father took the tenor sax and left for Mosney to play with sixteen others for older couples who remembered what the big bands of the forties sounded like. And he was left alone with his sister who talked less and less as her breasts grew bigger. With the alto saxophone which his father said he could learn when he forgot his fascination for three-chord ditties. With the guitar which he played a lot, as if in spite against the alto saxophone. And with the broken-keyed piano which he played occasionally.

When it rained on the iron roof the house sang and he was reminded of a green tin drum he used to hand when he was younger. It was as if he was inside it.

He wandered round the first three days, his sister formal and correct beside him. There was one road made of tarmac, running through all the corrugated houses towards the tennis-court. It was covered always with drifts of sand, which billowed while they walked. They passed her once, on the same side, like an exotic and dishevelled bird, her long yellow cardigan coming down to her knees, covering her dress, if she wore any. He stopped as she passed and turned to face her. Her feet kept billowing up the sand, her eyes didn't see him, they were puffy and covered in black pencil. He felt hurt. He remembered an afternoon three years ago when they had lain on the golf links, the heat, the nakedness that didn't know itself, the grass on their three backs.

'Why don't you stop her?' he asked his sister.

'Because,' she answered. 'Because, because.'

He became obsessed with twilights. Between the hour after tea when his father left and the hour long after dark when his father came home he would wait for them, observe them, he would taste them as he would a sacrament. The tincture of the light fading, the blue that seemed to be sucked into a thin line beyond the sea into what the maths books called infinity, the darkness falling like a stone. He would look at the long shadows of the burrows on the strand and the long shadows of the posts that held the sagging tennis-nets on the tarmac courts. He would watch his sister walking down the road under the eyes of boys that were a little older than him. And since he hung around at twilight and well into the dark he came to stand with them, on the greens behind the clubhouse, their cigarette-tips and their laughter punctuating the dark. He played all the hits on the honky-tonk piano in the clubhouse for them and this compensated for his missing years. He played and he watched, afraid to say too much, listening to their jokes and their talk about girls, becoming most venal when it centred on her.

*

He laughed with them, that special thin laugh that can be stopped as soon as it's begun.

There was a raft they would swim out to on the beach. His skin was light and his arms were thin and he had no Adam's apple to speak of, no hair creeping over his togs, but he would undress all the same with them and swim out. They would spend a day on it while the sun browned their backs and coaxed beads of resin from the planks. When they shifted too much splinters of wood shot through their flesh. So mostly they lay inert, on their stomachs, their occasional erections hidden beneath them, watching on the strand the parade of life.

It galled his father what he played.

'What galls me,' he would say, 'is that you could be so good.'

But he felt vengeful and played them incessantly and even sang the tawdry lyrics. Some day soon, he sang, I'm going to tell the Moon about the crying game. And maybe he'll explain, he sang.

'Why don't you speak to her?' he asked his sister when they passed her again. It was seven o'clock and it was getting dark.

'Because,' she said. 'Because I don't.'

But he turned. He saw her down the road, her yellow cardigan making a scallop round her fattening buttocks.

'Rita,' he called. 'Rita.'

She turned. She looked at him blankly for a moment and then she smiled, her large pouting lips curving the invitation she gave to any boy that shouted at her.

He sat at the broken-keyed piano. The light was going down over the golf-links and his sister's paperback novel was turned over on the wooden table. He heard her in her room, her shoes knocking off the thin wooden partition. He heard the rustling of cotton and nylon and when the rustles stopped for a moment he got up quickly from the piano and opened the door. She gave a gasp and pulled the dress from the pile at her feet to cover herself. He asked her again did she remember and she said she didn't and her face blushed with such shame that he felt sorry and closed the door again.

The sea had the movement of cloth but the texture of glass. It flowed and undulated, but shone hard and bright. He thought of cloth and glass and how to mix them. A cloth made of glass fibre or a million woven mirrors. He saw that the light of twilight was repeated or reversed at early morning.

He decided to forget about his sister and join them, the brashness they were learning, coming over the transistors, the music that cemented it. And the odd melancholy of the adulthood they were about to straddle, to ride like a Honda down a road with one white line, pointless and inevitable.

His father on his nights off took out his Selmer, old loved talisman that was even more shining than on the day he bought it. He would sit and accompany while his father stood and played – 'That Certain Feeling', 'All The Things You Are', the names that carried their age with them, the embellishments and the filled-in notes that must have been something one day but that he had played too often, that he was too old now to get out of. And to please his father he would close his eyes and play, not knowing how or what he played and his father would stop and let him play on, listening. And he would occasionally look and catch that look in his listening eyes, wry, sad and loving, his pleasure at how his son played only marred by the knowledge of how little it meant to him. And he would catch the look in his father's eyes and get annoyed and deliberately hit a bum note to spoil it. And the sadness in the eyes would outshine the wryness then and he would be sorry, but never sorry enough.

He soon learnt that they were as mistrustful of each other as he was of them and so he relaxed somewhat. He learnt to turn his silence into a pose. They listened to his playing and asked about his sister. They lay on the raft, watched women on the strand, their eyes stared so hard that the many shapes on the beach became one, indivisible. It made the sand-dunes and even the empty clubhouse redundant. Lying face down on the warm planks, the sun burning their backs with an aching languor. The blaring transistor, carried over in its plastic bag. Her on the beach, indivisible, her yellow cardigan glaring even on the hottest days. He noticed she had got fatter since he came. Under them on the warm planks the violent motions of their pricks. She who lived in the chalet all the year round.

The one bedroom and the two beds, his father's by the door, his by the window. The rippled metal walls. The moon like water on his hands, the bed beside him empty. Then the front door opening, the sound of the saxophone case laid down. His eyes closed, his father stripping in the darkness, climbing in, long underwear and vest. The body he'd known lifelong, old and somewhat loved, but not like his Selmer, shining. They get better with age, he said about instruments. His breath scraping the air now, scraping over the wash of the sea, sleeping.

The tall thin boy put his mouth to the mouth of the french letter and blew. It expanded, huge and bulbous, with a tiny bubble at the tip.

'It's getting worked up,' he said.

He had dark curling hair and dark shaven cheeks and a mass of tiny pimples where he shaved. The pimples spread from his ears downwards, as if scattered from a pepper-canister. His eyes were dark too, and always a little closed.

'We'll let it float to England,' he said, 'so it can find a fanny big enough for it.'

They watched it bobbing on the waves, brought back and forwards with the wash. Then a gust of wind lifted it and carried it off, falling to skim the surface and rising again, the bubble towards the sky.

He had walked up from the beach and the french letter bound for England. He had seen her yellow cardigan on the tennis-court from a long way off, above the strand. He was watching her play now, sitting on the white wrought-iron seat, his hands between his legs.

She was standing on the one spot, dead-centre of the court, hardly looking at all at her opponent. She was hitting every ball cleanly and lazily and the sound that came from her racquet each time was that taut twang that he knew only came from a good shot. He felt that even a complete stranger would have known, from her boredom, her ease, that she lived in a holiday town with a tennis-court all the year round. The only sign of effort was the beads of sweat round her lips and the tousled blonde curls round her forehead. And every now and then when the man she was playing against managed to send a shot towards the sidelines, she didn't bother to follow it at all. She let the white ball bounce impotent towards the wire mesh.

He watched the small fat man he didn't recognize lose three balls for every ball won. He relished the spectacle of a fat man in whites being beaten by a bored teenage girl in sagging high-heels. Then he saw her throw her eyes upward, throw her racquet down and walk from the court. The white ball rolled towards the wire mesh.

She sat beside him. She didn't look at him but she spoke as if she had known him those three years.

'You play him. I'm sick of it.'

He walked across the court and his body seemed to glow with the heat generated by the slight touch of hers. He picked up the racquet and the ball, placed his foot behind the white line and threw the ball up, his eye on it, white, skewered against the blue sky. Then it came down and he heard the resonant twang as his racquet hit it and it went spinning into the opposite court but there was no-one there to take it. He looked up and saw the fat man and her walking towards a small white car. The fat man gestured her in and she looked behind at him once before she entered.

As the car sped off towards Mornington he swore she waved.

The car was gone down the Mornington road. He could hear the pop-pop of the tennis-balls hitting the courts and the twang of them hitting the racquets as he walked, growing fainter. He walked along the road, past the tarmac courts and past the grass courts and past the first few holes of the golf-course which angled in a T round the tennis-courts. He walked past several squares of garden until he came to his. It wasn't really a garden, a square of sand and scutch. He walked through the gate and up the path where the sand had been trodden hard to the green corrugated door. He turned the handle in the door, always left open. He saw the small square room, the sand fanning across the line from the doorstep, the piano with the sheet-music perched on the keys. He thought of the midday sun outside, the car with her in the passenger seat moving through it, the shoulders of the figure in the driver's seat. The shoulders hunched and fat, expressing something venal. He thought of the court, the white tennis-ball looping between her body and his. Her body relaxed, vacant and easeful, moving the racquet so the ball flew where she wished. His body worried, worrying the whole court. He felt there was something wrong, the obedient ball, the running man. What had she lost to gain that ease, he wondered. He thought of all the jokes he had heard and of the act behind the jokes that none of those who told the jokes experienced. The innuendoes and the charged words like the notes his father played, like the melodies his father willed him to play. The rich full twang as the ball met her racquet at the centre.

He saw the alto saxophone on top of the piano. He took it down, placed it on the table and opened the case. He looked at the keys, remembering the first lessons his father had taught him when it was new-bought, months ago. The keys unpressed, mother-of-pearl on gold, spotted with dust. He took out the ligature and fixed the reed in the mouthpiece. He put it between his lips, settled his fingers and blew. The note came out harsh and childish, as if he'd never learnt. He heard a shifting movement in the inside room and knew that he'd woken his father.

He put the instrument back quickly and made for the tiny bathroom. He closed the door behind him quietly, imagining his father's grey vest rising from the bed to the light of the afternoon sun. He looked into the mirror that closed on the cabinet where the medicine things were kept. He saw his face in the mirror looking at him, frightened, quick glance. Then he saw his face taking courage and looking at him full-on, the brown eyes and the thin fragile jawline. And he began to look at his eyes as directly as they looked at him.

'You were playing,' his father said, in the living-room, in shirtsleeves, in uncombed afternoon hair, 'the alto –'
    'No,' he said, going for the front door, 'you were dreaming –'

And on the raft the fat asthmatic boy, obsessed more than any with the theatre on the strand, talking about 'it' in his lisping, mournful voice, smoking cigarettes that made his breath wheeze more. He had made classifications, rigid as calculus, meticulous as algebra. There were girls, he said, and women, and in between them what he termed lady: the lines of demarcation finely and inexorably drawn. Lady was thin and sat on towels, with high-heels and suntan-lotions, without kids. Woman was fat, with rugs and breasts that hung or bulged, with children. Then there were girls, his age, thin, fat and middling, nyloned, short-stockinged –

He lay on his stomach on the warm wood and listened to the fat boy talking and saw her walking down the strand. The straggling, uncaring walk that, he decided, was none of these or all of these at once. She was wearing flat shoes that went down at the heels with no stockings and the familiar cardigan that hid what could have classified her. She walked to a spot up the beach from the raft and unrolled the bundled towel from under her arm. Then she kicked off her shoes and pulled off her cardigan and wriggled out of the skirt her cardigan had hidden. She lay back on the towel in the yellow bathing suit that was too young for her, through which her body seemed to press like a butterfly already moulting in its chrysalis. She took a bottle then and shook it into her palm and began rubbing the liquid over her slack exposed body.

He listened to the fat boy talking about her – he was local too – about her father who on his stretches home came back drunk and bounced rocks off the tin roof, shouting, 'Hewer.'

'What does that mean,' he asked.

'Just that,' said the asthmatic boy: 'Rhymes with sure.'

He looked at her again from the raft, her slack stomach bent forward, her head on her knees. He saw her head lift and turn lazily towards the raft and he stood up then, stretching his body upwards, under what he imagined was her gaze. He dived, his body imagining itself suspended in air before it hit the water. Underwater he held his breath, swam through the flux of tiny bubbles, like crotchets before his open eyes.

'What did you say she was,' he asked the fat boy, swimming back to the raft.

'Hewer,' said the fat boy, more loudly.

He looked towards the strand and saw her on her back, her slightly plump thighs towards the sky, her hands shielding her eyes. He swam to the side of the raft then and gripped the wood with one hand and the fat boy's ankle with the other and pulled. The fat boy came crashing into the water and went down and when his head came up, gasping for asthmatic breath, he forced it down once more, though he didn't know what whore meant.

His father was cleaning the alto when he came back.

'What does hewer mean?' he asked his father.

His father stopped screwing in the ligature and looked at him, his old sideman's eyes surprised, and somewhat moral.

'A woman,' he said, 'who sells her body for monetary gain.'

He stopped for a moment. He didn't understand.

'That's tautology,' he said.

'What's that?' his father asked.

'It repeats,' he said, and went into the toilet.

He heard the radio crackle over the sound of falling water and heard a rapid-fire succession of notes that seemed to spring from the falling water, that amazed him, so much faster than his father ever played, but slow behind it all, melancholy, like a river. He came out of the toilet and stood listening with his father. Who is that, he asked his father. Then he heard the continuity announcer say the name Charlie Parker and saw his father staring at some point between the wooden table and the wooden holiday-home floor.

He played later on the piano in the clubhouse with the dud notes, all the songs, the trivial mythologies whose significance he had never questioned. It was as if he was fingering through his years and as he played he began to forget the melodies of all those goodbyes and heartaches, letting his fingers take him where they wanted to, trying to imitate that sound like a river he had just heard. It had got dark without him noticing and when finally he could just see the keys as question-marks in the dark, he stopped. He heard a noise behind him, the noise of somebody who has been listening, but who doesn't want you to know they are there. He turned and saw her looking at him, black in the square of light coming through the door. Her eyes were on his hands that were still pressing the keys and there was a harmonic hum tiny somewhere in the air. Her eyes rose to his face, unseeing and brittle to meet his hot, tense stare. He still remembered the rough feel of the tartan blanket over them, three of them, the grass under them. But her eyes didn't, so he looked everywhere but on them, on her small pinched chin, ridiculous under her large face, on the yellow linen dress that was ragged round her throat, on her legs, almost black from so much sun. The tiny hairs on them glistened with the light behind her. He looked up then and her eyes were still on his, keeping his fingers on the keys, keeping the chord from fading.

He was out on the burrows once more, he didn't know how, and he met the thin boy. The thin boy sat down with him where they couldn't be seen and took a condom from his pocket and masturbated among the bushes. He saw how the liquid was caught by the anti-septic web, how the sand clung to it when the thin boy threw it, like it does to spittle.

He left the thin boy and walked down the beach, empty now of its glistening bodies. He looked up at the sky, from which the light was fading, like a thin silver wire. He came to where the beach faded into the mouth of a river. There was a statue there, a Virgin with thin fingers towards the sea, her feet layered with barnacles. There were fishermen looping a net round the mouth. He could see the dim line of the net they pulled and the occasional flashes of white salmon. And as the boat pulled the net towards the shore he saw how the water grew violent with flashes, how the loose shoal of silver-and-white turned into a panting, open-gilled pile. He saw the net close then, the fishermen lifting it, the water falling from it, the salmon laid bare, glutinous, clinging, wet, a little like boiled rice.

He imagined the glistening bodies that littered the beach pulled into a net like that. He imagined her among them, slapping for space, panting for air, he heard transistors blare Da Doo Run Run, he saw suntan-lotion bottles crack and splinter as the Fisher up above pulled harder. He imagined his face like a lifeguard's, dark sidelocks round his muscular jaw, a megaphone swinging from his neck, that crackled.

He saw the thin band of light had gone, just a glow off the sea now. He felt frightened, but forced himself not to run. He walked in quick rigid steps past the barnacled Virgin then and down the strand.

'Ten bob for a touch with the clothes on. A pound without.'
   They were playing pontoon on the raft. He was watching the beach, the bodies thicker than salmon. When he heard the phrase he got up and kicked the dirt-cards into the water. He saw the Queen of Hearts face upwards in the foam. As they made for him he dived and swam out a few strokes.
   'Cunts,' he yelled from the water. 'Cunts.'

*

On the beach the wind blew fine dry sand along the surface, drawing it in currents, a tide of sand.

His sister laid the cups out on the table and his father ate with long pauses between mouthfuls. His father's hand paused, the bread quivering in the air, as if he were about to say something. He looked at his sister's breasts across a bowl of apples, half-grown fruits. The apples came from monks who kept an orchard. Across the fields, behind the house. He imagined a monk's hand reaching for the unplucked fruit, white against the swinging brown habit. For monks never sunbathed.

When he had finished he got up from the table and idly pressed a few notes on the piano.

'Why do you play that,' his father asked. He was still at the table, between mouthfuls.

'I don't know,' he said.

'What galls me,' said his father, 'is that you could be good.'

He played a bit more of the idiotic tune that he didn't know why he played.

'If you'd let me teach you,' his father said, 'you'd be glad later on.'

'Then why not wait till later on and teach me then.'

'Because you're young, you're at the age. You'll never learn as well as now, if you let me teach you. You'll never feel things like you do now.'

He began to play again in defiance and then stopped.

'I'll pay you,' his father said.

His father woke him coming in around four. He heard his wheezing breath and his shuffling feet. He watched the grey, metal-coloured light filling the room that last night had emptied it. He thought of his father's promise to pay him. He thought of the women who sold their bodies for monetary gain. He imagined all of them on the dawn golf-course, waking in their dew-sodden clothes. He imagined fairways full of them, their monetary bodies covered with fine drops of water. Their dawn chatter like birdsong. Where was that golf-course, he wondered. He crept out of bed and into his clothes and out of the door, very quietly. He crossed the road and clambered over the wire fence that separated the road from the golf-course. He walked through several fairways, across several greens, past several fluttering pennants with the conceit in his mind all the time of her on one green, asleep and sodden, several pound notes in her closed fist. At the fourteenth green he stopped and saw that the dull metal colour had faded into morning, true morning. He began to walk back, his feet sodden from the dew.

DESMOND HOGAN

'Memories of Swinging London'

Why he went there he did not know, an instinctive feel for a dull façade, an intuition born out of time of a country unbeknownst to him now but ten years ago one of excessive rain, old stone damaged by time and trees too green, too full.

He was drunk, of course, the night he stumbled in there at ten o'clock. It had been three weeks since Marion had left him, three weeks of drink, of moronic depression, three weeks of titillating jokes with the boys at work.

Besides it had been raining that night and he'd needed shelter.

She was tired after a night's drama class when he met her, a small nun making tea with a brown kettle.

Her garb was grey and short and she spoke with a distinctive Kerry accent but yet a polish at variance with her accent.

She'd obviously been to an elocution class or two, Liam thought cynically, until he perceived her face, weary, alone, a makeshift expression of pain on it.

She'd failed that evening with her lesson, she said. Nothing had happened, a half dozen boys from Roscommon and Leitrim had left the hall uninspired.

Then she looked at Liam as though wondering who she was speaking to anyway, an Irish drunk, albeit a well-dressed one. In fact he was particularly well-dressed that evening, wearing a neatly cut grey suit and a white shirt, spotless but for some dots of Guinness.

They talked with some reassurance when he was less drunk. He sat back as she poured tea.

She was from Kerry she said, West Kerry. She'd been a few months in Africa and a few months in the United States but this was her first real assignment, other than a while as domestic science teacher in a Kerry convent. Here she was all of nurse, domestic and teacher. She taught young men from Mayo and Roscommon how to move; she had become keen on drama while going to college in Dublin. She'd pursued this interest while teaching domestic science in Kerry, an occupation she was ill-qualified for, having studied English literature in Dublin.

'I'm a kind of social worker,' she said, 'I'm given these lads to work with. They come here looking for something. I give them drama.'

She'd directed Eugene O'Neill in West Kerry, she'd directed Arthur Miller in West Kerry. She'd moulded young men there but a different kind of young men, bank clerks. Here she was landed with labourers, drunks.

'How did you come by this job?' Liam asked.

She looked at him, puzzled by his directness.

'They were looking for a suitable spot to put an ardent Sister of Mercy,' she said.

There was a lemon iced cake in a corner of the room and she caught his eye spying it and she asked him if he'd like some, apologizing for not offering him some earlier. She made quite a ceremony of cutting it, dishing it up on a blue-rimmed plate.

He picked at it.

'And you,' she said, 'what part of Ireland do you come from?'

He had to think about it for a moment. It had been so long. How could he tell her about limestone streets and dank trees? How could he convince her he wasn't lying when he spun yarns about an adolescence long gone?

'I come from Galway,' he said, 'from Ballinasloe.'

'My father used to go to the horse fair there,' she said. And then she was off again about Kerry and farms, until suddenly she realized it should be him that should be speaking.

She looked at him but he said nothing.

He was peaceful. He had a cup of tea, a little bit of lemon cake left.

'How long have you been here?' she asked.

'Ten years.'

He was unforthcoming with answers.

The aftermath of drink had left his body and he was sitting as he had not sat for weeks, consuming tea, peaceful. In fact, when he thought of it, he hadn't been like this for years, sitting quietly, untortured by memories of Ireland but easy with them, memories of green and limestone grey.

She invited him back and he didn't come back for days. But as always in the case of two people who meet and genuinely like one another they were destined to meet again.

He saw her in Camden Town one evening, knew that his proclivity to Keats and Byron at school was somehow justified. She was unrushed, carrying vegetables, asked him why he had not come. He told her he'd been intending to come, that he was going to come. She smiled. She had to go she said. She was firm.

Afterwards he drank, one pint of Guinness. He would go back he told himself.

In fact it was as though he was led by some force of persuasion, easiness of language which existed between him and Sister Sarah, a lack of embarrassment at silence.

He took a bus from his part of Shepherd's Bush to Camden Town. Rain slashed, knifing the evening with black. The first instinct he had was to get a return bus but unnerved he went on.

Entering the centre the atmosphere was suddenly appropriated by music, Tchaikovsky, *Swan Lake*. He entered the hall to see a half dozen young men in black jerseys, blue trousers, dying, quite genuinely like swans.

She saw him. He saw her. She didn't stop the procedure, merely acknowledged him and went on, her voice reverberating in the hall, to talk of movement, of the necessity to identify the real lines in one's body and flow with them.

Yes, he'd always recall that, 'The real lines in one's body.' When she had stopped talking she approached him. He stood there, aware that he was a stranger, not in a black jersey.

Then she wound up the night's procedure with more music, this time Beethoven, and the young men from Roscommon and Mayo behaved like constrained ballerinas as they simulated dusk.

Afterwards they spoke again. In the little kitchen.

'Dusk is a word for balance between night and day,' she said. 'I asked them to be relaxed, to be aware of time flowing through them.'

The little nun had an errand to make.

Alone, there, Liam smoked a cigarette. He thought of Marion, his wife gone north to Leeds, fatigued with him, with marriage, with the odd affair. She had worked as a receptionist in a theatre.

She'd given up her job, gone home to Mummy, left the big city for the northern smoke. In short her marriage had ended.

Looking at the litter-bin Liam realized how much closer to accepting this fact he'd come. Somehow he'd once thought marriage to be for life but here it was, one marriage dissolved and nights to fill, a body to shelter, a life to lead.

A young man with curly blond hair entered. He was looking for Sister Sarah. He stopped when he saw Liam, taken aback. These boys were like a special battalion of guards in their black jerseys. He was an intruder, cool, English almost, his face, his features relaxed, not rough or ruddy. The young man said he was from Roscommon. That was near Liam's home.

He spoke of farms, of pigs, said he'd had to leave, come to the city, search for neon. Now he'd found it. He'd never go back to the country. He was happy here, big city, many people, a dirty river and a population of people which included all races.

'I miss the dances though,' the boy said, 'the dances of Sunday nights. There's nothing like them in London, the cars all pulled up and the ballroom jiving with music by Big Tom and the Mainliners. You miss them in London but there are other things that compensate.'

When asked by Liam what compensated most for the loss of fresh Sunday night dancehalls amid green fields the boy said, 'The freedom.'

Sister Sarah entered, smiled at the boy, sat down with Liam. The boy questioned her about a play they were intending to do and left, turning around to smile at Liam.

Sarah — her name came to him without the prefix now — spoke about the necessity of drama in schools, in education.

'It is a liberating force,' she said. 'It brings out' — she paused — 'the swallow in people.'

And they both laughed, amused and gratified at the absurdity of the description.

Afterwards he perceived her in a hallway alone, a nun in a short outfit, considering the after-effects of her words that evening, pausing before plunging the place into darkness.

He told her he would return and this time he did, sitting among boys from Roscommon and Tipperary, improvising situations. She called on him to be a soldier returning from war and this he did, embarrassedly, recalling that he too was a soldier once, a boy outside a barracks in Ireland, beside a bed of crocuses. People smiled at his shattered innocence, at this attempt at improvisation. Sister Sarah reserved a smile. In the middle of a simulated march he stopped.

'I can't. I can't,' he said.

People smiled, let him be.

He walked to the bus stop, alone. Rain was edging him in, winter was coming. It hurt with its severity tonight. He passed a sex shop, neon light dancing over the instruments in the window. The pornographic smile of a British comedian looked out from a newsagent's.

He got his bus.

Sleep took him in Shepherd's Bush. He dreamt of a school long ago in County Galway which he attended for a few years, urns standing about the remains of a Georgian past.

At work people noticed he was changing. They noticed a greater serenity. An easiness about the way he was holding a cup. They virtually chastised him for it.

Martha McPherson looked at him, said sarcastically, 'You look hopeful.'

He was thinking of Keats in the canteen when she spoke to him, of words long ago, phrases from mouldering books at school at the beginning of autumn.

His flat was tidier now; there was a space for books which had not hitherto been there. He began a letter home, stopped, couldn't envisage his mother, old woman by a sea of bog.

Sister Sarah announced plans for a play they would perform at Christmas. The play would be improvised, bit by bit, and she asked for suggestions about the content.

One boy from Leitrim said, 'Let's have a play about the tinkers.'

Liam was cast for a part as tinker king and bit by bit over the weeks he tried, tried to push off shyness, act out little scenes.

People laughed at him. He felt humiliated, twisted inside. Yet he went on.

His face was moulding, clearer than before, and in his eyes was a piercing darkness. He made speeches, trying to recall the way the tinkers spoke at home, long lines of them on winter evenings, camps in country lanes, smoke rising as a sun set over distant steeples.

He spoke less to colleagues, more to himself, phrasing and rephrasing old questions, wondering why he had left Ireland in the first place, a boy, sixteen, lonely, very lonely on a boat making its way through a winter night.

'I suppose I left Ireland,' he told Sister Sarah one night, 'because I felt ineffectual, totally ineffectual. The priests at school despised my independence. My mother worked as a char. My father was dead. I was a mature youngster who liked women, had one friend at school, a boy who wrote poetry.

'I came to England seeking reasons for living. I stayed with my older brother who worked in a factory.

'My first week in England a Greek homosexual who lived upstairs asked me to sleep with him. That ended my innocence. I grew up somewhere around then, became adult very, very young.'

1966, the year he left Ireland.

Sonny and Cher sang 'I've got you, babe'.

London was readying itself for blossoming, the Swinging Sixties had attuned themselves to Carnaby Street, to discothèques, to parks. Ties looked like huge flowers, young hippies sat in parks. And in 1967, the year 'Sergeant Pepper's Lonely Hearts Club Band' appeared, a generation of young men and horned-rimmed glasses looking like John Lennon. 'It was like a party,' Liam said, 'a continual party. I ate, drank at this feast.

'Then I met Marion. We married in 1969, the year Brian Jones died. I suppose we spent our honeymoon at his funeral. Or at least in Hyde Park where Mick Jagger read a poem in commemoration of him. "Weep no more for Adonais is not dead."'

Sister Sarah smiled. She obviously liked romantic poetry too, she didn't say anything, just looked at him, with a long slow smile. 'I understand,' she said, though what she was referring to he didn't know.

Images came clearer now, Ireland, the forty steps at school, remnants of a Georgian past, early mistresses, most of all the poems of Keats and Shelley.

Apart from the priests, there had been things about school he'd enjoyed, the images in poems, the celebration of love and laughter by Keats and Shelley, the excitement at finding a new poem in a book.

She didn't say much to him these days, just looked at him. He was beginning to fall into place, to be whole in this environment of rough and ready young men.

Somehow she had seduced him.

He wore clean, cool, casual white shirts now, looked faraway at work, hair drifting over his forehead as in adolescence. Someone noticed his clear blue eyes and remarked on them, Irish eyes, and he knew this identification as Irish had not been so absolute for years.

'"They came like swallows and like swallows went,"' Sister Sarah quoted one evening. It was a fragment from a poem by Yeats, referring to Coole Park, a place not far from Liam's home, where the legendary Irish writers convened, Yeats, Synge, Lady Gregory, O'Casey, a host of others, leaving their mark in a place of growth, of bark, of spindly virgin trees. And in a way now Liam associated himself with this horde of shadowy and evasive figures; he was Irish. For that reason alone he had strength now. He came from a country vilified in England but one which, generation after generation, had produced genius, and observation of an extraordinary kind.

Sister Sarah made people do extraordinary things, dance, sing, boys dress as girls, grown men jump over one another like children. She had Liam festoon himself in old clothes, with paper flowers in his hat.

The story of the play ran like this:

Two tinker families are warring. A boy from one falls in love with a girl from the other. They run away and are pursued by Liam who plays King of the Tinkers. He eventually finds them but they kill themselves rather than part and are buried with the King of the Tinkers making a speech about man's greed and folly.

No one questioned that it was too mournful a play for Christmas; there were many funny scenes, wakes, fights, horse-stealing, and the final speech, words of which flowed from Liam's mouth, had a beauty, an elegance which made young men from Roscommon who were accustomed to hefty Irish showband singers stop and be amazed at the beauty of language.

Towards the night the play was to run Sister Sarah became a little irritated, a little tired. She'd been working too hard, teaching during the day. She didn't talk to Liam much and he felt hurt and disorganized. He didn't turn up for rehearsal for two nights running. He rang and said he was ill.

He threw a party. All his former friends arrived and Marion's friends. The flat churned with people. Records smashed against the night. People danced. Liam wore an open-neck collarless white shirt. A silver cross was dangling, one picked up from a craft shop in Cornwall.

In the course of the party a girl became very, very drunk and began weeping about an abortion she'd had. She sat in the middle of the floor, crying uproariously, awaiting the arrival of someone.

Eventually, Liam moved towards her, took her in his arms, offered her a cup of tea. She quietened. 'Thank you,' she said simply.

The crowds went home. Bottles were left everywhere. Liam took his coat, walked to an all-night café and, as he didn't have to work, watched the dawn come.

She didn't chastise him. Things went on as normal. He played his part, dressed in ridiculous clothes. Sister Sarah was in a lighter mood. She drank a sherry with Liam one evening, one cold December evening. As it was coming near Christmas she spoke of festivity in Kerry. Cross-road dances in Dún Caoin, the mirth of Kerry which had never died. She told Liam how her father would take her by car to church on Easter Sunday, how they'd watch the waters being blessed and later dance at the cross-roads, melodions playing and the Irish fiddle.

There had been nothing like that in Liam's youth. He'd come from the Midlands, dull green, statues of Mary outside factories. He'd been privileged to know defeat from an early age.

'You should go to Kerry some time,' Sister Sarah said.

'I'd like to,' Liam said, 'I'd like to. But it's too late now.'

Yet when the musicians came to rehearse the music Liam knew it was not too late. He may have missed the west of Ireland in his youth, the simplicity of a Gaelic people but here now in London, melodions exploding, he was in an Ireland he'd never known, the extreme west, gullies, caves, peninsulas, roads winding into desecrated hills and clouds always coming in. 'Imagine,' he thought, 'I've never even seen the sea.'

He told her one night about the fiftieth anniversary of the 1916 revolution which had occurred before he left, old priests at school fumbling with words about dead heroes, bedraggled tricolours flying over the school and young priests, beautiful in the extreme, reciting the poetry of Patrick Pearse.

'When the bombs came in England,' Liam said, 'and we were blamed, the ordinary Irish working people, I knew they were to blame, those priests, the people who lied about glorious deeds. Violence is never, ever glorious.'

He met her in a café for coffee one day and she laughed and said it was almost like having an affair. She said she'd once fancied a boy in Kerry, a boy she was directing in *All My Sons*. He had bushy blond hair, kept Renoir reproductions on his wall, was a bank clerk. 'But he went off with another girl,' she said, 'and broke my heart.'

He met her in Soho Square Gardens one day and they walked together. She spoke of Africa and the States, travelling, the mission of the modern church, the redemption of souls lost in a mire of nonchalance. On Tottenham Court Road she said goodbye to him.

'See you next rehearsal,' she said.

He stood there when she left and wanted to tell her she'd awakened in him a desire for a country long forgotten, an awareness of another side of that country, music, drama, levity but there was no saying these things.

When the night of the play finally arrived he acted his part well. But all the time, all the time he kept an eye out for her.

Afterwards there were celebrations, balloons dancing, Irish bankers getting drunk. He sat and waited for her to come to him and when she didn't rose and looked for her.

She was speaking to an elderly Irish labourer.

He stood there, patiently, for a moment. He wanted her to tell him about Christmas lights in Ireland long ago, about the music of O'Riada and the southern going whales. But she persevered in speaking to this old man about Christmas in Kerry.

Eventually he danced with her. She held his arm softly. He knew now he was in love with her and didn't know how to put it to her. She left him and talked to some other people.

Later she danced again with him. It was as though she saw something in his eyes, something forbidding.

'I have to go now,' she said as the music still played. She touched his arm gently, moved away. His eyes searched for her afterwards but couldn't find her. Young men he'd acted with came up and started clapping him on the back. They joked and they laughed. Suddenly Liam found he was getting sick. He didn't make for the lavatory. He went instead to the street. There he vomited. It was raining. He got very wet going home.

At Christmas he went to midnight mass in Westminster Cathedral, a thing he had never done before. He stood with women in mink coats and Irish charwomen as the choir sang 'Come all ye faithful'. He had Christmas with an old aunt and at midday rang Marion. They didn't say much to one another that day but after Christmas she came to see him.

One evening they slept together. They made love as they had not for years, he entering her deeply, resonantly, thinking of Galway long ago, a river where they swam as children.

She stayed after Christmas. They were more subdued with one another. Marion was pregnant. She worked for a while and when her pregnancy became too obvious she ceased working.

She walked a lot. He wondered at a woman, his wife, how he hadn't noticed before how beautiful she looked. They were passing Camden Town one day when he recalled a nun he'd once known. He told Marion about her, asked her to enter with him, went in a door, asked for Sister Sarah.

Someone he didn't recognize told him she'd gone to Nigeria, that she'd chosen the African sun to boys in black jerseys. He wanted to follow her for one blind moment, to tell her that people like her were too rare to be lost but knew no words of his would convince her. He took his wife's hand and went about his life, quieter than he had been before.

MARY DORCEY

'A Country Dance'

On the arm of your chair, your hand for a moment is still; the skin smooth and brown against the faded, red velvet. I touch it lightly with mine. 'Maybe what she needs is more time,' I say.

The air is dense with cigarette smoke, my eyes are tired. You stare past me and begin again to fidget with a silver bracelet on your wrist. I make my tone persuasive: 'Time to regain her identity, a sense of independence, and . . .'

The words are swept from me in a sudden upswell of sound as last orders are called. The climax of the night, and so much left unsaid, undone. Every man in the room is on his feet, shoving for place at the bar, the voices bluff, seductive, as they work for one last round.

'Here, John, two large ones . . .'

'Pat, good man, four more pints . . .'

You ignore them, your gaze holding mine, your attention caught once more by the hope of her name.

'What did you say about independence?'

'I said you need it, need to cultivate it,' something perverse in me all at once, wanting to disappoint you. Your eyes drop, slide to the fireplace where the coal burns with a dim red glow.

'Ah, I thought it was Maeve you meant.'

And what matters after all which way I put it? In these stories aren't all the characters interchangeable? The lights are turned up full now, the evening over. And you as much in the dark as when we started. If I had used less tact; if I had said straight out what everyone thinks, would it have made a difference? I twist the stub of my last cigarette into the glass ashtray. No, whatever I say you will hear what you choose. Your misery safely walled beyond the reach of logic, however much you may plead with me to advise, console. If you were not fully certain of this, would you have asked me here tonight?

'Time, ladies and gents, please – have you no homes to go to?' The barman turns, the great wash of his belly, supported just clear of the crotch, tilts towards us. He swipes a greasy cloth across the tabletop, forcing us to lift our drinks: 'Come on now, girls.'

I take another sip of my whiskey and replace the glass emphatically on the cardboard coaster. You clasp your pint to your chest, swilling the dregs in languid circles.

'I don't think I can bear it much longer.'

I look at you, your dark eyes have grown sullen with pain, under the clear skin of your cheek a nerve twitches. Years ago, I would have believed you. Believed your hurt unlooked for – believed even in your will to escape it. Now, too many nights like this one have altered me. Too many nights spent in comforting others, watching while each word of sympathy is hoarded as a grain of salt to nourish the wound. On the blackness of the window I watch beads of rain glance brilliant as diamonds, each one falling distinct, separate, then merging – drawn together in swift streams to the ground. Why try to impose reason? Let you have your grand passion, the first taste of self-torment – never so sweet or keen again.

'Look, will you have another drink?' I say in a last attempt to cheer you, 'they might give us one yet.'

Instantly your face brightens. 'Thanks, but you've bought enough,' you say, and add lightly as if you'd just thought of it, 'Did you see someone has left a pint over there – will I get it?'

Without waiting for a reply, you slide your narrow hips in their scarlet jeans between our table and the bar. You reach for the pint of Harp and a half-finished cocktail. The barman swings round. 'Have you got twenty Marlboros?' you ask to distract him. While he roots on a shelf above the till, you slip the drinks over to me and turn back with a smile. Seeing it, placated, he tosses the cigarettes in the air, beating you to the catch. 'What has such a nice looking girl alone at this hour?' he asks, his voice oiled, insistent. You stand and say nothing. Your smile ransom enough. 'Go home to your bed,' he says, and throws the pack along the wet counter.

'Jesus, the things you have to do around here for a drink.' You fling yourself down on the seat beside me, close so that our knees and shoulders touch.

'You don't have to,' I say.

'Is that right?' you answer and raise one skeptical eyebrow. You pick up the cocktail glass and hold it to your nose. 'Is it gin or what?'

'I don't know and I certainly don't want it.'

Fishing a slice of stale lemon from the clouded liquid, you knock it back and reach for the Harp.

'Easy on,' I say, 'you'll be pissed at this rate.'

You take no notice, your head thrown back, drinking with total concentration. I watch Pat, the young barboy, guide customers to the door. A big woman, her pink dress stretched tight across her thighs, is hanging on his arm. She tells him what a fine looking lad he is, and laughs something caressively in his ear.

'Ah, wouldn't I love to, Molly, but what would Peter have to say?' Slapping her flanks with the flat of his hand, he winks across at me, and slams the door behind her. Outside, in the carpark, someone is singing in a drunken baritone: 'Strangers in the night, exchanging glances, wondering in the night . . .'

'At this stage of the evening,' I say, 'everyone is wondering.'

'About what?' you ask. You run your fingers idly through your long hair, puzzled but incurious.

'Nothing,' I reply. 'A silly joke – just the crowd outside singing.'

You have noticed no singing, much less the words that accompany it. Your gaze is fixed resolutely on the uncleared tables – you have spotted one more in the corner. It's obvious now that you have no intention of going home sober, but we cannot sit here all night and I do not want Paddy to catch you lifting leftovers.

'Well, if you want to stay on,' I say smiling at you, as though it were the very thing I wanted myself, 'why don't we finish what we have in comfort, next door?' I look towards the hallway and an unmarked wooden door on the far side. You are on your feet at

937

once, gathering our glasses, not caring where we go so long as there is a drink at the end of it.

A thin Persian carpet covers the floor of the residents' lounge. On the dim papered walls hang red, satin shaded lamps with frayed gold fringing, and three framed prints – hunting scenes – men and animals confused in the dark oils. A few of the regulars have drawn armchairs up to the fire. Pipe tobacco and the scent of cloves from their hot whiskeys hang together in the air. A man is kneeling over the coal bucket, struggling to open the tongs. He has the red face and shrunken thighs of the habitual toper. 'What the bloody fuck is wrong with this yoke anyway?' he says.

'Here, let me,' leaving him the tongs, you lift the bucket and empty half its contents into the grate. You rattle the poker through the bars, shifting the live coals from front to back. Dust crackles. After a moment, shoots of yellow flame break from the new untouched black.

'Nothing like a good fire,' the man announces, rubbing together his blue-veined hands, 'I always like to build up a good fucking fire.'

His eyes follow the line of your flank, taut and curved as you bend to the hearth. His tongue slides over his bottom lip. 'Always like to build up a good fire,' he repeats as though it were something witty.

He looks towards me, suddenly conscious of my presence, and gives a deferential nod. 'Excuse the language,' he calls over. He has placed me then as protector, older sister. And why not after all? Is it not the role I have adopted since that first day I met you in Grafton Street, walking blinded by tears, after one of your quarrels? Did I not even then, that first moment laying eyes on you, want to protect you, from Maeve – from yourself – from that reckless vulnerability of yours, that touched some hidden nerve in me? But it was not protection you wanted, it was empathy. You wanted me to look on, with everyone else, impassive, while you tormented yourself struggling to retain a love that had already slipped into obligation. Though you would not see it – you would see nothing but your own desire. Night after night, following her, watching; your wide, innocent eyes stiff with pain, while she ignored you or flirted with someone else. Waiting because at the end of the evening she might turn, and on an impulse of guilt ask you to go home with her.

'The last one, I think, do you want it?' You hand me an almost full pint of Guinness – brown, sluggish, the froth gone from it. I accept with a wry smile, why not – nothing worse than being empty-handed among drunks, and you clearly will not be hurried.

'Are they residents?' you ask with vague curiosity, looking towards the threesome on the opposite side of the fire.

'No, just regulars,' I say, and none more regular than Peg Maguire. Peg who is here every night with one man or another, drinking herself into amiability. A woman with three children who might be widowed or separated – no one asks. With her blonde hair piled above her head, lipstick a little smudged at the corners, her white coat drawn tight about her as though she were just on the point of departure, Peg – shrewd, jaunty – always careful to maintain the outward show. 'But you know country hotels: once the front door is shut you could stay forever.' I should not have said that, of course, it encourages you. You will have to stay over with me now, I suppose, you are long past driving.

I take a deep draught of the bitter stout, letting it slip quickly down my throat, and to keep this first lightness of mood, I ask you about the college. You are bored, dismissive. Second year is worse than first, you tell me – the life drawing is hopeless, you have only one male model and he wears a g-string; afraid of getting it on in front of women. 'Anyway, I haven't been there for a week – too stoned,' you add as if that exonerated you. Tossing your head back to sweep the hair from your face. For which of us, I wonder, do you present this elaborate disdain.

'You'll come to a sorry end,' I warn you. 'All this dope and sex at nineteen destroys the appetite.' I have made you smile, a slow, lilting smile, that draws your lips from white, perfect teeth.

'Is that what happened to you?' you ask.

'Perhaps it is. I would say I have decayed into wisdom. A forty-hour week and a regular lover – no unfulfilled lust masquerading as romance.'

'Don't tell me you are not romantic about Jan,' you look at me intently, your eyes at once teasing and solemn, 'when anyone can see you're mad about her.'

'That's one way of putting it, I suppose. At least the feeling is mutual so there is no aggravation.'

'And what about Liz?' you ask. 'Was it not very hard on her?'

'Oh, Liz had other interests,' I say. 'There was no heartache there.'

I have shocked you. You want fervour and longing, not this glib detachment. Should I tell you I am posing, or am I? Is there anything I cherish more than my independence? You lean forward, the cigarette at your mouth, gripped between thumb and forefinger, urging some story of need or rejection.

'You know, it is possible for people to care for each other without tearing their souls out,' I hear my voice, deliberately unemotional. 'All this strife and yearning is a myth invented to take our minds off the mess around us. Happiness distracts no one.' And what is it that impels me to disillusion you? Is it only that this intensity of yours so clearly hurts no one but yourself? With impatience you fan the trail of blue smoke from your face and cut me short.

'Ah, you are always so cynical. You would think thirty is middle age the way you go on. Anyway it's different for you. You have your work – something you really care about. It's all different.'

And so, maybe it is. What answer could I give you that would not be twisting the knife?

You stare into the fire, blazing now. The flames bouncing up the chimney throw great splashes of light about the room. Dance on the red brown of your hair. You have finished your cigarette. Your hands in your lap are curiously still – palms upturned. My own lean, fidgeting. I look about the room, at the rubber plant in the corner, the gilt-framed mirror above the mantelpiece – from it my eyes stare back at me, to my surprise still bright and sharp; a gleaming blue. I notice the faint tracing of lines at the corners. First signs. Give up the fags for good next week – get a few early nights. I look towards you. Your lips are at the rim of your glass, sipping at it, stretching it out. Do you dread going home so much?

'You can stay over with me, you know. Anna is in town – you can have her bed. Maybe you would come jogging in the morning – do you good.'

Roused for a moment, you regard me slowly, from shoulders to thigh, appraising me. 'Aw, I'm not in your shape,' you say. 'I wouldn't last more than a mile.'

'Well, you can walk while I run,' I answer, but your gaze has slipped back to the fire, watching the leap of the flames as if they held some private message. We sit in silence, lulled by the heat and alcohol until I break it to ask – 'What are you thinking?' Foolish question, as though you would tell me. But you do, holding my eyes to yours, you answer slowly: 'I was wondering if I might ring Maeve – she could be . . .'

'At this hour? You are incorrigible.' I do not try to hide my irritation. 'I thought you said you were going to keep away for a week . . .'

You begin to smile again. For a moment I wonder if you are playing with me. Then your face shuts, suddenly, as though a light had been switched off. 'You are right, of course. I'd forgotten.'

And why should I strain to follow these moods? If it were not that you look so forlorn, huddled in your chair, like an animal shut out in the rain.

'You are inconsolable, aren't you?' I say, hoping to tease you out of it. 'Tell me, have you not, even for five minutes, been attracted to another woman?'

You turn away abruptly, as though I had struck you, and ask over-loudly: 'Do you think we can get something to take away?'

'Is it a drink you want?' one of Peg's friends calls over. He has been listening to us for some time, his gaze flickering between us like a snake's tongue. 'I'll get you a drink,' he offers.

'It's all right thanks,' I say quickly.

'No, no, I insist. Name your poison, girls.' His speech is slurred. Conscious of it he repeats each sentence. 'Pat will give us a bottle – no trouble.' He hauls himself up from his chair, clutching the mantelpiece. Peg grabs at his arm.

'Pat has gone off hours ago – don't bother yourself.'

'No bother. Got to get these lassies a drink. Can't send them home thirsty,' he rolls a watering eye at us.

'And what would you know about thirst – you've never been dry long enough to have one.' Peg is an old friend and wants no trouble with me. 'Sit down, Frank, and don't be annoying the girls.'

'Who's annoying anyone, Peg Maguire – certainly not you – not if you were the last bloody woman on earth.'

We have set them bickering between themselves now. Time to go. But you are edgy, persistent. 'Is there really no chance of another drink?' you ask Peg. She lowers her voice and gives you a conspiratorial look.

'What is it you want – would a six-pack do? If you come with us to the Mountain View, I'll get you something there. They've a disco with late closing.'

'The very thing,' Frank roars. 'A disco tit. Let's all go. Two such lovely young women need . . .' he staggers to his feet once more and begins to sing, 'I could have danced all night – I could have danced all night and still have begged for more. I could have spread my wings,' he wheels his arms in a jagged circle almost knocking Peg's glass, 'and done a thousand things, I'd never done . . .'

'Will you for God's sake hold on to yourself,' Peg snaps furiously, and pushes him forward.

'Are you right then, girls,' she nods towards us. 'I'll give you the lift down and you can walk back. It's only ten minutes.'

Well, that has done it. There will be no stopping you now. We will not get home, 'till you are soused. And why should I try to deter you? Have I anything better to offer? All the tired virtues. Useless. I should be exasperated by you, dragging me all over the country as if a pint of stout were the holy grail. But something about you halts me. As you move to the door, something exaggerated in you – the turn of your shoulders, your head thrown back as though pulling from harness. Defiance and vulnerability in every line. Something more than youth. Something more than me as I was before I learnt – and who was it who finally taught me? – the hard-won pleasures of realism and self-sufficiency. Yet if I had the power to bestow them on you, this very instant, would I want to?

In the unlit carpark we find Peg's Fiat and pile in – Frank pulling me towards his knee: 'If you were the only girl in the world and I was the only boy.' Rain slashes at the windscreen, one wiper stuck halfway across it. Peg seems to drive by ear. Wet fir trees arching over us make a black tunnel of the road. The road to God knows where. I recognize none of it, letting myself be carried forward – lapsing into the heedless collective will. All needs converging in the simple drive for one more drink. 'Nothing else would matter in the world today . . .' Frank's whiskey breath encircles us. We reach tall, silver gates, pass them, and sluice through rain-filled craters in the drive, the wind snapping at our wheels. A furious night – clouds blown as fast as leaves across the sky. Lights ahead – the tall Georgian house bright in welcome. Braking almost on the front steps, Peg jumps out, leaving the door wide: 'I'll put in a word for you.' We follow, our faces lowered from the rain. In the hallway with the bouncer, her blonde head bent to his ear, she is confidential, explaining that we want only a takeaway – no admission. Solemn as a mother entrusting her daughters. Then she turns back to the car and her boys waiting outside. She throws a wicked grin at me over her shoulder – why? – 'Enjoy yourselves girls,' and she is off.

Out of the night – into a frenzy of light and sound. We push through the black swing doors. Red and purple light, great shafts of it, beat against the walls and floor. The music hammers through my chest, shivering my arms. A man and woman locked together, move in a tight circle at the centre of the room. In the corner, beside a giant speaker, two girls on stiletto heels dance an old-fashioned jive. We push through the wall of shoulders at the bar, country boys shy of dancing. 'Two large bottles of stout,' I order. The barman reaches for pint glasses and shoves them under the draught tap. 'Bottles – to take away,' I call across to him. But it is useless, he has already moved to the far end of the counter to measure out whiskey.

'We will just have to drink them here,' you say, putting your mouth close to my ear so that I feel the warmth of your breath. So be it – at least we are in from the rain for a while.

We choose a corner table, as far from the speakers as possible, but still I have to shout to make you hear me.

'It's easier if you whisper,' you say, bringing your lips to my ear once more, in demonstration.

'You are used to these places, I suppose.' It is years since I have sat like this. Though so little has altered. The lights and music more violent maybe, the rest unchanging. Nobody really wants to be here, it seems. Young women dressed for romance display themselves – bringing their own glamour. The men stand banded in council, shoulders raised as a barrier, until they have drunk enough. The faces are bored or angry. Each one resenting his need, grudging submission to this ritual fever.

You finish half your pint at one go and offer the glass to me. I down the remainder and together we start on the next, laughing. A rotating light on the ceiling spins a rainbow of colours; blue, red, gold, each thrust devouring the last. Smoke hangs in heavy green clouds about us. As though it were the fumes of marijuana, I breathe it deep into my lungs and feel suddenly a burst of dizzy gaiety . . . the absurdity of it all – that we should be here. And back to me come memories of years ago – adolescence, when it might have been the scene of passion, or was it even then absurd? The pace slows and three couples move to the centre of the floor. 'I don't want to talk about it – how you broke my heart.' The voice of Rod Stewart rasps through the speakers in an old song. But a favourite of yours. We have danced to it once before – in the early hours at Clare's party two weeks ago, when Maeve had left without you. You stand beside me now and in pantomime stretch your hand. 'Will you dance with me?' You walk ahead on to the floor. Under the spotlight your white shirt is luminous – your eyes seem black. You rest your hands on your hips, at the centre of the room, waiting.

'If you stay here just a little bit longer – if you stay here – won't you listen to my heart . . .' We step into each other's arms. Our cheeks touch. I smell the scent of your shirt – the darkness of your hair. Your limbs are easy, assured against mine. Your hands familiar, hold me just below the waist. We turn the floor, elaborately slow, in one movement, as though continuing something interrupted. The music lapping thigh and shoulder. 'The stars in the sky don't mean nothing to you – they're a mirror.' Round we swing, round; closer in each widening circle. Lost to our private rhythm. The foolish words beating time in my blood.

I open my eyes. The music has stopped. Behind you I see a man standing; his eyes riveted to our bodies, his jaw dropped wide as though it had been punched. In his maddened stare I see reflected what I have refused to recognize through all these weeks. Comfort, sympathy, a protective sister – who have I been deceiving? I see it now in his eyes. Familiar at once in its stark simplicity. Making one movement of past and future. I yield myself to it; humbled, self-mocking. Quick as a struck match.

As if I had spoken aloud, with a light pressure of my hand, you return to consciousness and walk from the floor.

I follow, my skin suddenly cold. I want as quickly as possible to be gone from the spotlight. I have remembered where we are: a Friday night country dance, surrounded by drunken males who have never before seen two women dance in each other's arms. All about the room they are standing still, watching. As we cross the empty space to our table no one moves. I notice for the first time Brid Keane from the post office: she is leaning against the wall, arms folded, her face contorted in a look of such disgust, it seems for a moment that she must be putting it on.

'Let's get out of here – as soon as you've finished your drink,' I whisper.

'What – do you want another drink?' Your voice rises high above the music that has begun again. I stare at you in amazement – is it possible that you haven't noticed, that you don't yet know what we've done? Can you be so naïve or so drunk that you haven't realized whose territory we are on?

And then someone moves from the table behind and pushes into the seat opposite us. Squat, red-faced, his hair oiled across his forehead. He props an elbow on the table, and juts his head forward, struggling to focus his eyes. His pink nylon shirt is open, a white tie knotted about the neck.

'Fucking lesbians,' he says at last. 'Are you bent or what?' The breath gusting into my face is sour with whiskey. We look towards the dancers writhing under a strobe light and ignore him.

'Did you not hear me?' he asks, shoving his face so close to me, I see the sweat glisten on his upper lip. 'I said are you bent – queers?' He drives his elbow against mine so that the stout spills over my glass.

A familiar anger rips through me, making my legs tremble. I press my nails into the palm of my hand and say nothing. I will not satisfy him so easily.

'What were you saying about the music?' I throw you a smile.

'I asked you a question,' he says. 'Will you give me a bloody answer.' He runs the words together as though speed were his only hope of completing them.

'I said it's lousy,' you reply, 'about ten years out of date.'

He looks from me to you and back again with baffled irritation and his voice grows querulous. He asks: 'Look, would one of you lesbians give me a dance.'

A friend has joined him now, leaning over the back of your chair, a grin on his lips sly and lascivious.

'Will you not answer me?' the first one shouts, 'or are you fucking deaf?'

Drawing my shoulders up, I turn and for the first time look directly into his eyes. 'No,' I say with warning deliberation, 'we are not deaf, yes, we are lesbians and no, we will not give you a dance.'

He stares at us stupefied, then falls back into his seat, breath hissing from his chest as though a lung had burst. 'Jesus, fucking, Christ.'

You give a whoop of laughter, your eyes wide with delight. It seems you find him hugely amusing. Then you're on your feet and across the room in search of the toilet or God knows another drink.

I have my back turned to him when I feel the pink-sleeved arm nudging mine again. 'Hey, blondie – you've gorgeous hair,' he says, giving an ugly snigger. 'Did anyone ever tell you that?' It is a moment before I recognize the smell of singed hair. I reach my hand to the back of my head and a cigarette burns my fingertips. With a cry of pain, I grab hold of the one lock across his forehead and wrench hard enough to pull it from the roots. He stretches his arm to catch hold of mine but I tear with all my force. 'You fucking cunt!' he screams.

Suddenly someone catches hold of us from behind and pulls us roughly apart. It's the bouncer – a big red-haired man in a grey suit. When he sees my face he steps back aghast. He had plainly not expected a woman.

'I don't know what you two want,' his voice is cold, contemptuous, 'but whatever it is you can settle it between you – outside.' He drops the hand on my shoulder, wheels round and walks back to his post at the door. At the sight of him my opponent is instantly subdued. He shrinks back into his seat as though he had been whipped, then slowly collapses on to the table, head in his arms.

You return carrying another drink. I wait until you are sitting down to whisper: 'We have to get out of here, Cathy – they're half savage. That one just tried to set fire to my hair.'

'The little creep!' you exclaim, your eyes sparking with indignation. 'Oh, he's easily handled – but the rest of them, look.'

At the bar a group of six or seven are standing in a circle drinking. Big farm boys in tweed jackets – older than the others and more sober. Their gaze has not left us, I know, since we walked off the dance floor, yet they have made no move. This very calm is what frightens me. In their tense vigilance, I feel an aggression infinitely more threatening than the bluster of the two next us. Hunters letting the hounds play before closing in?

'I think they might be planning something,' I say, and, as if in response to some prearranged signal, one of them breaks from the group and slowly makes his way to our table.

His pale, thin face stares into mine, he makes a deep bow and stretches out his hand. 'Would one of you ladies care to dance?'

I shake my head wearily. 'No, thanks.'

He gives a scornful shrug of the shoulders and walks back to his companions. A moment later another one sets out. When he reaches us, he drops to one knee before you and for the benefit of those watching, loudly repeats the request. When you refuse him he retreats with the same show of disdain.

'They can keep this going all night,' I say, 'building the pressure. With their mad egotism anything is better than being ignored.' And I know also what I do not say, that we have to put up with it. They have us cornered. Under all the theatrics lies the clear threat that if we dare to leave, they can follow, and once outside, alone in the dark, they will have no need for these elaborate games.

'What can we do?' you ask, twisting a strand of hair about your finger, your eyes attentive at last.

'I'll go off for a few minutes. Maybe if we separate, if they lose sight of us, they might get distracted.'

Five minutes later, pushing my way through the crowd to our table, I find you chatting with the one in the pink shirt and his mate, smoking and sharing their beer like old drinking pals. How can you be so unconcerned? I feel a sudden furious irritation. But you look up at me and smile warningly. 'Humour them,' I read in the movement of your lips. And you may be right. They have turned penitent now, ingratiating: 'We never meant to insult you, honest, love. We only wanted to be friendly.' His head lolling back and forth, he stabs a finger to his chest: 'I'm Mick, and this is me mate Gerry.'

All right then, let us try patience. At least while we are seen talking to these two the others will hold off.

'You know, blondie, I think you're something really special,' with the deadly earnest of the drunk, Mick addresses me. 'I noticed you the second you walked in. I said to Gerry – didn't I Gerry? Blondie, would you not give it a try with me? I know you're into women – your mate explained – and that's all right with me – honest – that's cool, you know what I mean? But you never know 'till you try, do you? Might change your life. Give us a chance, love.' He careens on through his monologue, long past noticing whether I answer or not. On the opposite side I hear Gerry, working on you with heavy flattery, admiring your eyes (glistening now – with drink or anger – dark as berries), praising the deep red of your lips – parted at the rim of your glass. And you are laughing into his face and drinking his beer. Your throat thrown back as you swallow, strong and naked.

Mick has collapsed, his head on the table drooping against my arm. 'Just one night,' he mutters into my sleeve, 'that's all I'm asking – just one night. Do yourself a favour.' His words seep through my brain, echoing weirdly, like water dripping in a cave. Drumming in monotonous background to the movements of your hands and face. Half turned from me, I do not hear what you answer Gerry, but I catch your tone; languorous, abstracted, I watch you draw in the spilt froth on the table. Your eyes lowered, the lashes black along your cheek, one finger traces the line of a half moon. Behind you I see the same group watching from the bar; patient, predatory. My blood pounds – fear and longing compete in my veins.

And then all at once, the music stops. Everyone stands to attention, silent. The disc-jockey is making an announcement: the offer of a bottle of whiskey, a raffle, the buying of tickets – gripping them as the music and dance never could. This is our moment, with Gerry moving to the bar to buy cigarettes and Mick almost asleep, slumped backwards, his mouth dropped open. I grasp your hand beneath the table, squeezing it so that you may feel the urgency and no one else, and look towards the green exit sign. We are across the floor, stealthy and cautious as prisoners stepping between the lights of an armed camp. At the door at last, 'Fucking whoores – you needn't trouble yourselves to come back,' the bouncer restraining fury in the slam of the swing doors behind us.

And we are out.

Out in the wet darkness. The wind beating escape at our backs. I catch your hand. 'Run and don't stop.' Our feet scatter the black puddles, soaking our shins. The fir trees flapping at our sides beckon, opening our path to the gates. So much further now. The moon will not help – hidden from us by sheets of cloud – withholding its light. We run blind, my heart knocking at my ribs; following the track only by the sting of gravel through my thin soles. 'Come on – faster.' The gates spring towards us out of nowhere – caught in a yellow shaft of brightness. A car rounds the bend behind us, the water flung hissing from its tyres. We dodge under the trees, the drenched boughs smacking my cheek. The headlights are on us, devouring the path up to and beyond the open gates. The window rolled down, I hear the drunken chanting – like the baying of hounds: 'We're here because we're queer because we're here because we're . . .' 'Great fucking crack, lads . . .' Gone. Past us. Pitched forward in the delirium of the chase – seeing nothing to left or right. A trail of cigarette smoke in the air.

'All right – we can go on now,' you say, laughing – drawing me out from cover. 'Do you think it was them?'

'Yes, or worse. We had better be gone before the next lot.'

We run on again, through the wide gates to the main road. The alcohol is washing through me now, spinning my head. My heart is beating faster than ever, though the fear has left me. You are beginning to tire. 'We are almost there,' I urge you, marvelling that you can still stand, let alone run. The rain darts in the gutter, the leaves slithering under our feet. Jumping a pool I slip towards you. Your arm outflung steadies me. You're laughing again – the long looping kind you do not want to stop. 'You're worse than I am,' you say.

The moon all at once throws open the night before us, scattering in sequins on the tarred road, silver on the hanging trees. I see the house massed and still in its light.

'We are home,' I say.

You slow your pace and let go of my hand. Your eyes under the white gleam of the moon are darker than ever – secretive.

'Are you laughing at me?' I ask, to capture your attention.

'I'm not – really,' you answer, surprised.

I lift the latch of the gate, softly so as to wake no one. How am I to keep this? To keep us from slipping back into the everyday: the lighted, walled indoors – all the managed, separating things. And what is it I fear to lose? Any more than my desire – dreaming yours. Any more than a drunken joy in escape?

The cat comes through a gap in the hedge, whipping my shins with her tail. I lift her to me and she gives a low, rough cry.

'She's been waiting for you,' you tell me.

I turn the key in the kitchen door. You step inside and stand by the window, the moonlight falling like a pool of water about your feet. I gaze at your shoes for no reason; at the pale, wet leather, muddied now.

'Well, that looked bad for a moment,' I say, putting my arm round you, not knowing whether it is you or myself I am consoling. 'Were you not frightened at all?'

'Oh yes, I was,' you answer, leaning into me, pulling me close. 'Yes.'

And so, I have been right. So much more than comfort. I slide my lips down your cheek, still hesitant, measuring your answer. And you lift your open mouth to meet mine. I have imagined nothing, then. Everything. All this long night has been a preparation – an appeal. You untie the belt of my raincoat. I feel your hands, still cold from the night rain, along my sides: 'I'm freezing. Are you?'

'Yes.'

'Are there beds anywhere in this house?'

'We might find one.'

You laugh. I take your hand and silently, as though fearful of waking someone, we cross the hall together and climb the wooden staircase.

The room is dark but for a shaft of moonlight which falls across the double bed, with its silver and wine red quilt, that waits at the centre of the floor. I light a candle by the window. You sit on the cane chair and unlace your sneakers, slowly, knot by knot. Then stand and drop your clothes – red jeans and white shirt – in a ring about them. I turn back the sheets and step towards you. Downstairs the phone sounds, cracking the darkness like a floodlight. It rings and rings and will not stop. 'I had better answer it,' I say and move to the door.

'Who was it?' When I return, you are sitting propped against the pillow, easy as though you spent every night here. I cannot tell you that it was Jan, feeling amorous, wanting to chat, imagining me alone.

'Jan . . .' I begin, but you do not wait to hear. Reaching your hand behind my head you pull my mouth towards you. I feel, but do not hear the words you speak against my lips.

The rain drives at the window, shivering the curtains. The wind blown up from the sea sings in the stretched cables. Your body strains to mine, each movement at once a repetition and discovery. Your mouth, greedy and sweet, sucks the breath from my lungs. I draw back from your face, your long dark hair and look in your eyes: you are laughing again – a flame at the still black centre. Your tongue seals my eyelids shut. Your hands, travelling over me, startle the skin as if they would draw it like a cover from muscle and bone. We move – bound in one breath – muscle, skin and bone. I kiss you from forehead to thigh. Kiss the fine secret skin beneath your breast, the hard curve of your belly.

The wind moans through the slates of the roof. The house shifts. Beneath us the sea crashes on the stones of the shore. Your voice comes clear above them beating against mine, high above the wind and rain. Spilling from the still centre – wave after wave. And then, a sudden break; a moment's straining back as though the sea were to check for one instant – resisting – before its final drop to land. But the sea does not.

You lie quiet above me. I taste the salt of tears on my tongue.

'Are you crying? What is it?'

'No. I'm not,' you answer gently, your head turned from me. Maybe so. Maybe so. I close my arms about you, stroking the silk of your back, finding no words. But it does not matter. Already you have moved beyond me into sleep. I lie still. Clouds have covered the moon, blackening the window of sky. I cannot see your face. Your body is heavy on mine, your breath on my cheek. I soothe myself with its rhythm. The rain has ceased. I hear once more the small night sounds of the house: the creak of wood in floorboards and rafters, the purr of the refrigerator. Then suddenly there comes a loud crash – the noise of cup or plate breaking on the kitchen's tiled floor. My breath stops – you do not stir. I hear the squeal of a window swung on its hinge. A dull thud. Footsteps?

Before my eyes a face rises: mottled cheeks, beads of sweat along the lip. A wild fear possesses me that he or his friends have followed us, come here to this house in search of us. I slide gently from under you. I creep to the door and stand listening for a moment, breath held, before opening it. Silence . . . Nothing but the hum of the 'fridge. And then . . . a soft, triumphal cry. Of course – the cat. How well I know that call. Elsie has caught a rat or bird and brought it home through the window. In the morning there will be a trail of blood and feathers on the carpet. Time enough to deal with it tomorrow.

I go back to bed. Lifting the sheet I press near to your warmth, my belly fitting exactly in the well of your back. I breathe the strange, new scent of you. A shudder goes through my limbs. I reach my hand and gently gather the weight of your breast. I feel the pulsing through the fine veins beneath the surface. You stir, sighing, and press your thighs against mine. You murmur something from sleep – a word, or name. Someone's name.

My arms slacken. I taste your tears, again, on my lips. In the morning what will we say to each other? Drunk as you were it will be easy to forget, to pretend the whole thing an accident. No need then to prepare an attitude – for Maeve (when she calls, as she will, as before, thanking me for taking care of you), for Jan – for ourselves. The night is fading at the window. The bare branch of the sycamore knocks on the wall behind us. Words echo in my mind, the words of the song we danced to, foolish, mocking: 'The stars in the sky mean nothing to you – they are a mirror.' And to me? What was it I said this evening about romantic illusion? I reach out my hand for the candlestick on the table. As I lift it, the flame flares golden. My movement has woken you. You regard me, for an instant, startled. How childish you look, your forehead smooth, your eyes washed clear. Was it only your hurt that set a cord between us – that lent you the outline of maturity? 'I thought I heard a noise downstairs,' you say.

'Yes, but it was nothing,' I kiss your eyes shut. 'Only the cat with a bird,' I answer as you move into sleep, your cheek at my shoulder. 'Nothing.'

Far out to sea, a gull cries against the coming of light. For a little longer night holds us beyond the grasp of speech. I lean and blow the candle out.

HUGO HAMILTON

'Nazi Christmas'

It began with the man in the fish shop saying 'Achtung!' and all the customers turning around to look at us. Even the people outside under the row of naked turkeys and hanging pheasants stared in through the window. We were exposed. Germans. War criminals using Ireland as a sanctuary. There was a chance they might have overlooked the whole thing if it wasn't for the man in the fish shop trying out some more of his German. All the stuff he had picked up from films like *Von Ryan's Express* and *The Great Escape*.

'Guten Morgen,' he said leaning over the counter, then leaning back with an explosive laugh that acted as a trademark for his shop. Our mother was shy of these friendly, red-faced Irishmen. She smiled at all the people in the shop and they smiled back silently. That was the thing about Ireland. They were all so friendly.

'We haff ways of making you talk,' he said to us whenever we refused to perform for the benefit of his customers and say a few words of German. Like our mother, we were too shy and unable to respond to these contortions of language.

'Halt! We must not forgetten der change.' There was something about us that made people laugh, or whisper, or stop along the street quite openly to ask the most bizarre questions; something that stuck to us like an electronic tag.

It was as though the man in the fish shop had let out this profane secret about us. The word was out. Our assumed identity as Irish children was blown. Everywhere we went, the German past floated on the breeze after us. 'Heil Hitler!' we heard them shout, on the way to Mass, on the way to school, on the way back from the shops. Our mother told us to ignore them. We were not Nazis.

When we were on our own they jumped out behind us or in front of us howling their warcries. It was all 'Donner und Blitzen', and 'Achtung! Get the Krauts'. We lacked the Irish instinct for blending in with the crowd, that natural expertise of human camouflage. It didn't help that Eichmann went on trial for war crimes when I was around five years old. So I was called Eichmann, or sometimes Göring. My older brother usually went under Hitler or Himmler, and the greeting 'Sieg Heil!' was generally accompanied by a neat karate chop on the back of the neck.

It didn't help either that on those shopping trips into town before Christmas, our mother talked to us in German on the bus. Just when we began to enjoy the comfort of anonymity, she would say 'Lass das sein' ('Stop that') in a harsh German tone and the passengers would turn around to stare again. But once we saw the lights in the city and the vast toy departments it was easy to forget. On the way home she told stories and sang Christmas songs like 'O Tannenbaum' with the shopping bags stacked on the seats beside us and the winter sky lighting up pink beyond the roofs of the houses. It was a sign that the angels were baking. And at home there was always the smell of baking.

When we got home there were sweets laid out in the hallway, on the stairs, sometimes across our pillows at night, and when we asked how they got there she said: 'the angels'. She made 'marzipan potatoes', small marzipan marbles coated with cinnamon. On the morning of the sixth of December we came down to find a plate for each of us filled with sweets and a glazed 'Männeken' – a little man with raisin eyes that lasted for ever. The St Nicholas plates stood on the *Truhe* in the hall, a large oak trunk made in 1788 to store vestments. It was part of her heirloom from Kempen. Everything inside our house was German.

Everything outside was Irish, or imported from Britain. The other houses all had coloured fairy-lights on Christmas trees in the windows. We envied those coloured lights. At the same time we knew we were the only house with real candles, almost like a sign to the outside, a provocation. Most of our clothes and our toys came in parcels from German relatives.

The snow seemed to be a German invention too. Thick flakes fell in Ireland that Christmas and made our mother think of home. There was never any snow again at Christmas; perhaps afterwards in January but never on Christmas Day itself. Somehow Ireland had committed itself more towards the milder Mediterranean climate. With the undercurrent of the Gulf Stream, people here had grown a variety of palm tree that leaned towards the tropical; palm trees that formed the centrepiece of front gardens and patios. Guest houses along the coast expanded the subtropical illusion by hanging nameplates like Santa Maria or Stella Maris from their palms.

Snow was another import which remained mostly in the imagination, on Christmas cards, on top of Christmas cakes, in the form of cotton wool on the roof of the crib. But that year the snow was real; full white snow that took away the seaside appearance and transformed the streets into a fairy-tale of winter. It was our Christmas. Our father put on his favourite Christmas record of the Cologne Children's Choir and the house was filled with the bells of Cologne Cathedral ringing out across the sea to Dublin. There was the taste of German food, pretzels and *Lebkuchen* and exotic gifts from Germany.

We might as well have been in Kempen where our mother came from, kneeling in front of the crib as we prayed and sang in German with the white candles reflected in my father's glasses and the smell of pine merging with the smell of *Glühwein* in the front room.

Later, we went out to build a snowman in the front garden and it was only when we entered a snowball fight with other children in the street that we realized we were back in Ireland; where children had scooped snow from the low walls or where the cars had skidded and exposed the raw street underneath. We went from one garden to the next looking for new untouched sheets of snow, where the street was still under a dream. And when all the other children disappeared inside for Christmas dinner, we decided to go to the football field to see how deep the snow was there.

It seemed like a good idea until we were ambushed in the lane by a gang of boys we had never seen before. Amelia and I ran away into the field through the opening in the barbed-wire fence, but they had caught Karl and pushed him against the wall. One of them held a stick across his neck. 'You Nazi bastard,' they said.

Amelia and I shouted to let him go. She threatened to tell on them but it was a frail plea. We were trapped.

'Get them,' one of them said and three or four of the boys ran into the field after us. There was no point in screaming for help either because nobody would hear.

'You Nazi bastard,' they said again to Karl. Then they twisted his arm up behind his back and made him walk towards the field where Amelia and I had already been caught behind a line of eucalyptus trees. One of them was forcing snow up Amelia's jumper and she was whining with the effort to fight him off.

Karl said nothing. He had already put into action his plan of inner defiance and was determined to give them nothing but silence, as though they didn't exist, as though they would soon get tired and go away. Amelia stopped resisting and they stopped putting snow under her jacket because she wasn't contributing to the fun. We were told to line up with our backs against the wall of the football field.

The leader of the gang had no fear of the cold. While the other boys blew into their cupped red hands for warmth, he calmly picked up more snow and caked it into a flat icy disc in his palms. We kept repeating in our heads the maxims our mother had taught us: 'The winner yields. Ignore them.' I tried to look as though standing against the wall was exactly what I wanted to be doing at that very moment.

'What will we do with these Nazi fuckers?' the leader asked, holding his stony white disc up to our faces. 'Put them on trial,' somebody said.

They formed a circle around us and discussed how they would proceed with this. There was no point in thinking of escape. One of the boys was pushing a discoloured piece of brown snow towards Karl with the tip of his shoe, whispering to him: 'I'm going to make you eat that.' Amelia started crying again but Karl told her to be quiet.

'OK, Nazi,' the leader said. 'What have you got to say for yourselves?'

'Don't indulge them,' Karl said to us. 'Don't indulge them,' they all mocked and for some of them it was the sign to start speaking in a gibberish of German. 'Gotten, blitzen . . . Himmel.' Another boy started dancing around, trampling a circle in the snow with 'Sieg Heils' until Amelia could no longer contain a short, nervous smile. For the leader it was a sign to hurl his snowball. It hit me in the eye with a flash of white; a hard lump of icy stone that immediately made me hold my face. I was close to tears but I didn't want to let Karl down and give them the satisfaction.

'The Nazi Brothers,' he then announced. 'Guilty or not guilty?'

'Guilty,' they all shouted and they laughed and collected more snow. The trees were being pushed by the wind. Above the white landscape of the football field the sky was darkening and it looked as though it would snow again. Low on the grey sky there were flashes of white or silver seagulls.

'We have to go home now,' Amelia said with a sudden burst of self-righteousness as she moved forward to go. But she was held back. 'You're going nowhere, you SS whore.'

All of it meant little to us. It was as though the terms were being invented there and then, as though they came from somebody's perverse imagination. One of them said something about concentration camps, and gas chambers. Whenever I asked my mother about the Nazis I saw a look in her eyes somewhere between confusion and regret.

'Execute them,' they all shouted. They were looking for signs that one of us might break. The only hope for us was that they might get bored with it all. That they too might be numb with the cold.

The sentence became obvious as they quietly began an industry of snowball-making. Somebody mentioned the 'firing squad'. Some of them laughed and Amelia once more began to cry. They crouched down and collected mounds of snowballs, enough to start another war. Somebody reminded everyone to pack them hard. One of them included the discoloured piece of snow in his armoury and when they all had heaps of white cannonballs ready beside their feet, we waited for the order and watched the leader of the gang mutely raise his hand.

It seemed like an endless wait in which it was possible to think of all kinds of random, irrelevant things like Christmas cake, and marzipan potatoes and the peculiar skull-shaped design of the plum pudding as well as other even more irrelevant things like the three little dials of the gas meter under the stairs, until the hand eventually came down and the piercing shout brought with it a hail of blinding white fire. Karl put his hands up to his eyes. 'It's only snow.'

CARLO GÉBLER

from *The Cure*

Bridget lay in bed. The door was ajar and she heard their voices in the kitchen, her father's, Michael's, Joanna's and John Dunne's. Why on earth had Michael asked him up? He was a horrible, vile man. When all this was over, she might just tell Michael what happened the day she was reading *Kidnapped*. She heard the squeak of the crane swinging over the fire.

They were making a concoction. If she could just manage a mouthful, that was all, Michael said. A little cup's worth and he would be happy.

The unmistakable herb smell wafted through. She was trembling and shaking. Just one mouthful. Surely she could manage to get that much down and keep it there. One swig and it would be over.

Think of it like the cod liver oil, she told herself, that she had when she was a child. It had a hideous flavour but, once swallowed, that was it – over. It always came presented on a big spoon which was kept in the house expressly for medicine. The handle was long and freckled, the end of the spoon lightly buckled and the rim sharp. There was always a taste of metal on the tongue as it went in, and if she kept her mouth too closed when the spoon was withdrawn, it sometimes cut her lip.

The burnt herb smell was growing stronger. It reminded her of something, she thought. No, that was a useless way to think. She had to push her mind in a different direction. She must not think bad. She must think good. She remembered her conversation with Joanna in the afternoon. That was better. Maybe her cousin was right. She hadn't given the herbs a chance before. For all she knew they were a miracle cure. One go and they might restore her completely. Wouldn't that be wonderful?

In her mind's eye she saw herself the next morning . . . She awoke. She stretched herself in bed. There was no pain, not in her arms, her elbows, her knees, her throat. She coughed and her throat was clear. She touched her upper lip. It was dry. Then her forehead. It was cool. She threw the covers back and reached her legs on to the floor. Slowly she stood. She felt strong and light. She was better. It was over.

They came through the door now, Dunne first and Michael following. He was carrying a saucepan over which he was cutting the sign of the cross in the air.

'Where's Joanna?'

'She'll stay outside,' Dunne murmured.

'This room's too small,' said Michael.

Dunne closed the door. Old Boot Polish was freshly shaven and his fifty-year-old face was pink and glistening. However, it was only a matter of seconds before his sour smell was all around her, mixed with the herbs. The time she looked after him when he was sick, she remembered, she had had to burn a good many of his clothes because they were too filthy to wash. Michael set the saucepan down, produced a cup from his pocket, dipped it in.

He lifted the dripping cup out slowly. Dunne wiped the edges with a cloth.

One cupful, that was all, and then it would be over, she told herself.

She reached forward. Michael put the cup into her hands. The porcelain was warm. She looked down. The liquid was black with bubbles and bits floating.

One cupful, she could knock it back in a gulp.

She swallowed and exhaled. That way she kept the odour at bay.

They were watching her, their eyes bearing down.

Slowly she raised her arms.

The rim was at her lip.

She dropped her tongue down to make a space behind her teeth.

Think of it as a raw egg. Hadn't she had plenty of those in her time?

She counted inwardly. One, two, three.

This was it.

One, two . . .

She tipped her head back and threw in the liquid. For a moment she didn't know what was happening. Then she had this overwhelming sense of the concoction being everywhere – up her nose, down her throat and in her mouth . . .

It was like the one time she went to the sea and she went into the water. A wave smacked her in the face and there was salt suddenly everywhere, the bitter, bitter taste of salt as she had never before tasted it. It was in her mouth, up her nose, in her eyes in her ears, in every nook and cranny of her head and body. It overwhelmed her.

Dazed, panic-stricken, grimacing, spluttering, retching, she tried to stagger towards where she thought the beach was. Then, bending and falling forward, she went on coughing and gasping while a length of mucus dropped from her nose and she spat with all her vigour. None the less, the salty taste remained for minutes afterwards . . .

But this was not seawater, cold and at least clear. This was warm, with solids in it which were slimy, and it was not going to go over the back of her tongue, it was not going to pour down her throat. It was a filthy brown-black mess, in fact it was privy mess, she thought, and as she made the fatal connection she spat forward with all her might. She immediately felt the milky stuff through her nightdress. It was warm for a second but then it quickly went cold. Then she heard the cup landing and smashing on the floor.

Blinking through the tears in her eyes, she glimpsed the towel Dunne had draped over his arm. She lunged and pulled it to herself and started dragging its rough bumpy surface over her lips and her tongue. She wanted to scour away the taste of the concoction which remained.

'Bridget,' Michael shouted. 'What have you done?'

Joanna was suddenly at the door.

'Go out, Joanna,' he said.

'Stay,' she called. Her voice was muffled through the towel. She saw Dunne was pushing her cousin away and now he was closing the door.

'There's a whole pan here,' said Michael. 'You will have it.'

'I can't. I won't,' she said angrily.

'You will.'

'I won't.'

'You must,' said Dunne solemnly.

'I won't,' she shouted back at him fiercely. She rubbed the towel against her tongue. The damn concoction was like a stain; she would never get it out.

'Give me water,' she said. 'Give me a drink of water for God's sake.'

'Get a spoon,' she heard Michael saying now.

What was this? she wondered. Oh yes, she thought, that old trick. That was the way Joanna's parents made her take Ganey's medicine for her sore gums, wasn't it? Well, they weren't going to get her with that one. No way.

'Yes,' she heard Old Boot Polish replying, eagerly if she wasn't mistaken, and then she followed the sound of his footfalls as he turned and moved from the bed.

Opening back the sickroom door and stepping into the kitchen, the first thing John Dunne saw was Joanna Burke sitting at the table.

'What are you doing?' he demanded. He was intentionally abrupt. This was, he thought, the only answer to the brazen manner in which she was staring up at him.

However, then, which was typical, she ignored the question and called past him through the doorway, 'Are you all right in there?' to Bridget on the bed.

'Joanna,' Bridget called back to her but before anything further could be said, he slammed the door smartly behind himself and scowled.

'Hello, John. How are you? How's Bridgie doing?' Joanna asked cheerfully.

He shook his head and thought to himself how very disagreeable he had always found Joanna Burke.

He strode over to the hearth, nodded to Pat sitting there in his chair and thrust the poker into the middle of the hottest embers in the grate. As he squatted he felt the heat on his face and on his eyes. It was even in his mouth as he breathed in.

He riddled the poker from side to side. Red coals dropped silently through the grate and plopped into the grey ash below, glowed momentarily and lost their colour.

John Dunne resented Joanna Burke. Bridget would have been his friend, he thought, but Joanna was jealous and would not let her. As he stared into the fire, he remembered the winter he was sick and how Bridget came down to him once and sometimes twice a day. She made the fire; she washed the sheets; she cleaned the house and trimmed the lamp; she fed the chickens; she fetched the eggs; she made him soups and broths; she read to him. He could tell that she liked him. Then, one day and for no good reason, Joanna appeared down at his house with Bridget and from that day forward he was never alone with Bridgie again. That was when he realized Joanna was jealous of him.

To thank Bridget for caring for him when he was sick he had bought her a pair of ear-rings. They were the long, dangling type – a gold hoop and a piece of glass etched with the profile of a young woman. Bridget was shy and awkward when he presented the small package wrapped in brown paper. However, she touched his hand after she opened the box, and he could tell she was pleased.

But he never saw his present again after that. Once, he asked Bridget about them; this was one evening when she was outside her house, returning with a basket of turf, and he had gone out to help her. She told him they were lost. She even added some nonsense about fairies, he remembered now, staring at the sooty chimney-back and the sparks floating upwards.

He knew that it was Joanna who had turned Bridget against him. But then, given her jealous and possessive nature, he told himself, it really should come as no surprise to him that she acted like this.

He jiggled the poker again. In the middle of his palm he felt how the handle was starting to warm up. It was a good fire all right.

His thoughts turned to Bridget lying inside on her bed. When he was sick she cared for him and now he was repaying her for looking after him. And when she was restored, she would thank him and Michael for helping her to get better, and maybe this time she might even buy him a gift.

The next thought followed and, as it did, he smiled. Oh no, she would not of course thank Joanna, because her so-called best friend was doing nothing.

Involuntarily, he glanced over his shoulder at Joanna. She had remained sitting at the table. As usual he saw she was wearing her long mournful face, her large cow-like eyes were dull and she had adopted her usual slovenly position, elbows on table, head lolling on her hands. And she was waiting to complain about what he and Michael were doing to help Bridget. He just knew it.

John Dunne turned back to the fire. She did not like him and he felt quite entitled to dislike her in return. She was an irritating, nosy busybody, and he would have been very happy never to set eyes on her ever again. Indeed, just the idea of staying in the kitchen with her for even one second longer was repulsive.

He hurried back across the floor towards the sickroom.

From her bed Bridget saw the door swinging open and then John Dunne's flushed face. He looked furious. His red skin looked as if it were stretched as tight as the skin of a drum over the bones of his face. It was obviously something Joanna had said. She would ask her later. It was funny that. She was frightened and angry, yet somewhere within, there was a part of her that was calm. She was watching, thinking, calculating how to get through this.

'I won't take Ganey's stuff,' she bellowed.

Her father would hear that, she thought. And Joanna too. It was about time they stirred themselves. But then she heard the door closing. What were they doing out in the kitchen?

'Yes, you will take it,' she heard Michael shouting now. 'If I bring sickness into my father's house, he'll never leave this earth.'

What was he going on about? She was the one who was sick. Not him. She was the one who was sick and she was not going. No, she couldn't, of course she couldn't, feeling as she did, hot, weak, feverish. She could barely cross the room, let alone make the – what was it? – eight-mile journey to Ballynure. Wasn't that obvious? she wondered.

'But I'm not going,' she shouted up at him.

'Yes, you are,' he shouted back. His voice was steely. They were talking at cross-purposes now. She meant the wake but he was back on the herbs again, she realized. Anyway, no, she wasn't taking them. She had tried the concoction and it was revolting. No one could swallow muck like that. Well, children maybe, ten-year-olds, like Joanna, who were made to, she thought. But not her. She simply could not. It was impossible.

'Did you get the spoon?' Michael's chin floated above her as he spoke across the bed.

She swivelled her eyes right. John Dunne's shining red chin, mirror of Michael's, pointed back from the other side of her bed.

'The spoon, sorry,' she heard Old Boot Polish apologizing. 'I forgot.'

The sickroom door scraped back and John Dunne went out again.

'Where do you keep your spoons, Pat?' His voice coming from the kitchen was oily, she thought. He sounded polite but that was just put on to impress her father.

'In the base of the dresser,' came the voice of her father. He was suitably impressed of course and his usual obliging self. Why didn't he lie? she wondered. And what had he been doing for the last half an hour?

Sitting in his chair by the fire, she told herself.

Well, get up, Pat, she thought. Get up. Get in here.

No, that was a ridiculous hope. He was an old man, frightened and cowed.

But what about Joanna, her cousin and her friend? Why didn't she do something? Where was her courage?

She held her breath and she strained her ears. Come on, Joanna, she thought. But there was only silence. Not a word from her.

Now she heard the sound of a hinge creaking. That, she guessed, was the dresser door opening. Now sounds of rummaging followed, then the door banging shut. Old Boot Polish had found the spoon. Any second he would be back in the room and the whole business of the cure was going to start again. She had to prepare. She had to close her mouth as firmly as it would shut.

'Hey!' she heard. That exclamation was in Joanna's voice. At last, her cousin had spoken.

'What's going on?' she heard Joanna continuing. But that was not Joanna's normal, angry voice, she thought. Her cousin sounded – what?

'What do you think you're doing?' She heard Joanna again, louder than before.

Yes, now she had it. She knew what it was. Her cousin sounded frightened. So what was happening? Was Old Boot Polish hitting her?

She listened but there were no sounds of blows exchanged or screams of pain. No, all she could hear were hurrying feet, and the noise of bodies in motion.

Now Boot Polish was at the door. He got in and slammed it behind himself. Then she heard the key turning in the lock.

A second later Joanna was on the other side of the sickroom door. She was kicking and banging and rattling the handle.

'Open this door,' she heard Joanna shouting.

'Go away,' said Old Boot Polish gruffly, but with what sounded to her like a smirk in his voice.

'Unlock this at once.' It was Joanna again. 'Don't worry, Bridget. I'll be in there in a moment.'

'No, you won't.' Dunne was laughing now.

Ferocious banging on the door continued as Joanna shouted, 'Let me in. Let me give Bridget the herbs. You know it'll be a lot easier if I do it. She'll take from me what she won't from you.'

That's it, you tell them, Joanna.

'Leave us to our business, Joanna.' It was Michael speaking this time.

Now Old Boot Polish was turning from the door and she suddenly understood her cousin's tone of voice. In one hand he had the wooden spoon but in the other he was carrying the poker.

Oh my God. Her heart trembled. What was he doing with that thing in her bedroom?

'Look at this, Bridget,' he said.

The black tip of the poker was waving in the air. Then suddenly Old Boot Polish jabbed it against the orange box in the corner. She heard the wood hiss as it blackened and saw a coil of smoke rising.

It was hot. Oh God. Her heart raced faster. The poker had been in the fire and he had gone back to fetch it with the spoon. Oh God. Old Boot Polish was mad. Michael too. What possessed them? She was suffering from a fever, for God's sake. She was sick with bronchitis and they were . . .

No, she interrupted this thought. She had to remain calm and keep her thinking cool. She had to avoid the end of the poker. Absolutely. At all costs.

Old Boot Polish came up to the bed. She watched as he passed the wooden spoon across and then as Michael dipped it into the saucepan.

'One drink, Bridget, and then you'll be better.'

The spoon was slowly floating through the air towards her. It dipped below the level of her chin and she could see the black concoction delicately balanced in the bowl at the end of the handle.

Joanna was banging again outside. 'Let me in. Do you hear me?'

'I wish she'd shut up.' It was Old Boot Polish this time. She saw his knee coming up over the side of the bed. It came down on to her chest and he started pushing down on her. She felt herself sinking into the mattress.

She started to wriggle. If she could get under the bedclothes she could get away from the spoon and the poker. But movement was difficult. The knee was pressing down on her chest very hard. Very, very hard.

'See this?' Dunne was shouting at her.

She saw it all right, the point of the poker hovering six inches from her face.

'If you don't cooperate, you're going to get a taste of this.'

She had to keep wriggling. The spoon was getting closer. She had to struggle, to wriggle. Dunne's knee was pressing down harder than ever. But she could feel her strength coming. God knows where it's coming from, she thought, but yes she could feel her body was slipping out from under Dunne's knee. If she could get out from under Old Boot Polish, and then pull the covers over her head and shove herself down into the bottom of the bed, she'd be safe for a while. They would have to drag her back up.

'I'm warning you,' she heard Dunne shouting. He lowered the poker another inch. His eyes were gleaming. She had seen them gleaming like that before. Knew them only too well. She should have told Michael what had happened when she was reading *Kidnapped.* If she had told him, Old Boot Polish wouldn't be here in the house now, let alone in her bedroom. It had been cowardly. She should have spoken. If Michael knew what she knew, then he'd understand what Old Boot Polish was up to. He wasn't there to give the herbs. Damn, why hadn't she told Michael? Well, it was too late now and there was no point in fretting. She had to concentrate. She had one objective and one only. She had to get away from the poker.

She wrenched downwards, almost escaping from under Dunne's knee. However, then he caught her neck and started pushing down there. That hurt even more than when he was pressing on her chest.

Suddenly, the poker point was right in front of her eyes. She could feel the hotness of the metal on her face.

'I'm warning you,' she heard.

It was coming; what she dreaded and feared, it was happening. She opened her mouth. Her intention was to shout 'Joanna, Joanna.' She was going to shout with such urgency that her cousin would have to break down the door. That was when she felt it, the poker point on her forehead. It was like a drop of hot lead plopping on to her skin. For a second there was no pain and then the pain started. She opened her mouth. She heard a scream coming out. It was the loudest scream she had ever screamed. 'Joanna,' she screamed at the top of her lungs, 'Joanna, Joanna . . .'

From the other side of the door in the kitchen, Joanna heard Bridget calling out 'Joanna, Joanna . . .' Then she heard the bed-head thumping against the wall, the bed-springs groaning, a chair crashing, and finally a wordless scream . . . This all happened in a matter of seconds.

'Open this door,' Joanna shouted, beating her fists on the door.

She put her eye to the keyhole. Blocked. She plucked a hairpin from the back of her head and frantically poked with it.

'Get a cork,' Michael shouted inside, 'to hold her mouth open.'

'The cork'll be useless,' Dunne argued back, 'she'll just bite on to it and stop us getting the herbs into her.'

The barrel of the key slid back, the key dropped and at last Joanna saw inside. The bolster had split. Feathers were floating about. Bridget was somewhere hidden in the tangled bedclothes. Michael, holding spoon and saucepan, was towering above her. Dunne was on the bed, brandishing the poker, his knee across Bridget's neck.

Dunne turned. She saw him staring back furiously at her eye. Then with a horrible cry he leapt from the bed and sprang towards her. He was like a wild animal. Joanna jumped up, terrified, and fell back on to the floor.

'It's kill or cure. Do you understand, Joanna Burke?' John Dunne shouted at her through the keyhole. She heard him ramming the key back in and twisting it half a turn. He did this, she realized at once, so that she could not poke it out again.

'You're animals,' she shouted back through the wood as she struggled to her feet. 'This is no cure!'

She snatched her coat from the hook where it hung. She saw Pat was still sitting in his chair, crying quietly now into his handkerchief and moaning.

She bolted out of the door and through the gate and hurried on down the lane.

DAVID PARK

from *The Healing*

From his bedroom window he watched the two men get out of their car. They were dressed in dark suits and one wore a dog-collar. They were checking the number of the house against a piece of paper. As the minister stood looking towards the front door he smoothed the wrinkles out of his jacket, while the man who had been driving checked carefully that all the car doors were locked. They both looked hesitant and nervous but there was something official about their appearance. The minister glanced up at the bedroom window and smiled at him, but he stepped back into the room and waited for the sound of the bell. It rang twice before his mother scurried down the hall and opened the door, then with an instinctive lightness of step he moved to the landing and listened to the voices which filtered into the silence, disturbing the little cloud of stillness which had settled over the house.

He missed the first few words of the introductions, but one man was a colonel and the other some sort of army chaplain. They were both English and their accents sounded high and strange, belonging to some world in which he had never been. His mother took them into the living-room and he heard her offering them a cup of tea. He moved onto the top stair and crouched close and hard like a knot that someone had pulled tight. The water gushed into the kettle and cups clinked against saucers as his mother clock-worked mechanically in the kitchen, preparing the tea tray. Sometimes he caught a glimpse of her as she opened cupboards near the door. In the living-room, the men spoke to each other in low voices. His mother looked a little flustered and a jerky hand flicked away a wisp of hair which fell across her forehead. Sometimes her hand did it even when there was no hair out of place. When she carried the tray through she glanced up at him and smiled, then rolled her eyes. The little secret message made him feel close to her and although he felt safe where he was, he wanted to help her through the coming moments, and so he bumped noiselessly down the stairs like a child and followed her into the living-room.

Both men stood up and shook his hand. He was too close to them to risk looking into their faces, but he knew they had been at his father's funeral. When they spoke to him he nodded his head, then sat down in a corner of the room while his mother answered their questions on his behalf as she poured the tea.

'Samuel likes to keep his own counsel these days,' she said.

They nodded blandly in return to signal that they understood whatever she said and then they complimented her on how well the house was looking.

'Still a long way to go,' she said jauntily. 'Plenty of jobs that need doing to keep Samuel and me busy.'

'It must be quite a change for you living in the city,' the chaplain said, balancing his biscuit on the rim of the saucer.

'Well, I was born here, you know. Of course, things have changed a lot, though I suppose it's the same everywhere.'

They both agreed with her as if anxious to concur with everything she said. Occasionally his mother looked towards him and smiled with her eyes. The two men talked in turn, steering the conversation into safe areas, and helping each other out when it lapsed into silence. The colonel had black, shiny hair and an angular face. Sometimes, his left eyelid twitched a little and each time it did he drummed his knee with his index finger. The chaplain was an older, grey-haired man with a plump red face and watery eyes. When he was listening, he angled his head a little to the side, as if to show he was carefully taking in everything that was said, and nodded constantly.

After an appropriate time they gently edged towards the purpose of their visit. It was the colonel who led off, speaking in his clipped tones but trying to sound friendly and personal.

'You're probably wondering why we've called, Mrs Anderson. We've come because we know that these are difficult times for you and your family and we know how easy it is after – after things have moved on a little to think that you've been forgotten about. And also to offer any practical help that we can, or assist with any pressing financial worries that you might have.'

The chaplain angled his head further to the side and smiled reassuringly at her, as the colonel continued.

'We know that the pain of your loss will endure long after the media attention has faded. And unfortunately we know, too, from other equally painful experiences that very often the bereaved feel their plight is forgotten by the very society their husbands sought to serve.'

His mother stared impassively forward and said nothing.

'We feel it's important in situations like these that those who have lost husbands or sons do not feel that their sacrifice has been – passed over, or –'

'Or taken lightly,' finished the chaplain. 'Indeed, these are difficult times but you know, as I visit homes which mourn the loss of a loved one, I am struck by the dignity and strength with which they seek to rebuild their lives.'

His watery eyes were fixed on her, but still she said nothing. It was the colonel who spoke.

'Your husband was a very brave man, and I know from everyone I've spoken with that he was highly respected by all those who served with him. The turnout at the funeral was very impressive and I know he showed the same fine qualities in his private life.'

His mother wreathed her hand with a handkerchief.

'My husband was the very best of men. All he lived for was his family and his church. He did no harm to a living soul and wished no one in the world any ill. And they killed him for it, killed him without a thought or a care and I can't ever forget that or forgive it.'

Both his hands gripped the bottom of his chair and he rocked himself gently, trying to spin an invisible cocoon of silence. He longed to push his palms against his ears to block out the screams rising within him; rock, rock, cradle his soul into sweet fields of forgetfulness, but each new word pulled his senses tighter. Rock, rock . . . block out the screams which were trying to prise him open.

'I know you meant well coming here, but please don't tell me that my husband did not die in vain because I know it's a lie. Thomas died in vain, all right, because it didn't change anything. They keep right on killing and nobody does anything to stop them. The Government doesn't care about men like my husband because if they did, they'd have done something a long time ago.'

She flicked away a wisp of hair which had fallen forward onto her forehead and her knuckles whitened as she squeezed the handkerchief into the palm of her hand.

'Please, Mrs Anderson, don't upset yourself. I understand how you must feel and really, believe me, we didn't come here to upset you or to cause you distress,' said the chaplain, his voice dropping to a whisper.

'I know you didn't, but there's one other thing I want to tell you,' his mother insisted. 'I let the army give Thomas a military funeral out of respect to his wishes, but if it had been my decision alone, we would've laid him to rest in private – buried him quietly and decently without the hypocrisy. All the ceremony and all those words which no one listens to anymore. Too many empty words and condemnations from people who've been saying the same things for twenty years.'

The colonel sat back stiffly on the chair, his face colouring with embarrassment, searching for some avenue of escape.

'I can understand why you feel this way, Mrs Anderson,' persisted the chaplain. 'Sometimes I feel not very different from the way you do – I've walked in too many funeral processions, spoken to too many people suffering in the way your family is, not to have had very similar thoughts.'

'Are our lives worth less than English lives? Do the people sitting in government really care about what happens here to the likes of us?' his mother asked, her voice breaking with bitterness.

'I assure you, Mrs Anderson,' the colonel said, 'that the authorities have the highest regard for the people of this Province, and the loyalty and devotion to their country which has led so many of them to make the ultimate sacrifice, is not something which is taken lightly. And because we're talking here in private, I may say that there are many of us who share your frustrations. There are many people in uniform who would welcome only too readily the opportunity to take these people out of existence. But you know as well as I do, that these decisions rest in the hands of politicians, not in the hands of soldiers.'

His mother stared forlornly into the cup she was holding. He wanted to go to her, but like some animal frightened of breaking cover, he hid deeper in himself. His mother stood up. She had something more to say.

'You were right about feeling forgotten about – we feel it, all right. Two minutes on the headlines and then swept aside by some other bit of news. A couple of days later who even remembered his name? And the people who forget are the lucky ones. We would forget too, but we can't, and we'll remember it every day for the rest of our lives.'

She started to put plates back on the tray. The two men looked at each other and the colonel started to say something but the chaplain cut across him.

'Thank you for the tea, Mrs Anderson. It was good to have this opportunity to meet you and your son. And please remember, if there's any way at all that we can be of any help, don't hesitate to get in touch.'

DAVID PARK

He handed her a small card but she looked away. He set it gently on the fireplace and then both men said goodbye and made their own way down the hall. His mother followed, and as they left he climbed the stairs to his room to watch them go. He heard her close the front door and carry the tray into the kitchen. Outside, the chaplain stood staring up at the leaden sky while the other man was on his knees on the pavement checking the underside of the car. Then he stood up, unlocked the door and brushed both hands clean.

For the rest of the day his mother cleaned the house with a frantic determination. He helped as best he could, clearing out the fire and vacuuming the hall and stairs. He cleaned places that he knew his mother had cleaned the day before and would clean the next day. When he came back to the living-room he saw that the card had gone. Sometimes his mother sang as she worked, the music synchronizing with her mechanical movements as she dusted and polished. At times in her darting, frenetic movements she looked like a little automaton that had been wound too tightly. Not long before bedtime she started to bake, as if afraid to leave any minute of the day unfilled with activity, and when she kissed him goodnight she had a stripe of flour on her cheek.

That night before sleeping he stared down into the black pool where yellow lights criss-crossed the darkness like neon necklaces. Sometimes a light flickered like a candle flame blown by the wind. As he closed the curtains he ran his hands down their join, anxious to make sure there was no chink, no little spy hole through which eyes could peer, then pulled the quilt tightly about him. He no longer read before going to sleep. It did not help and sometimes it got mixed into the dreams and made them worse. His hand fingered the still unfamiliar texture of wallpaper and his eyes searched its pattern for the legion of faces that had lurked in the crevices of his old room, but so far none had emerged. But it gave him no feeling of safety because he knew that they waited somewhere else for him, brooding remorselessly in the shadows and planning the right moment to reach out for him.

Sleep was now the great unpredictable part of his life. Sometimes it was his friend, drowning him in a deep sea of oblivion and carrying him safely through to the morning, but sometimes it deceived him, whispering to him to trust it, to give himself to it, and when he had placed his soul in its hands, it took it greedily and carried him to that place he could not bear to go. He had tried many different things to break its power; focusing his mind on a safe, warm moment of the past, repeating a talismanic word over and over until his mind grew numb and dead, holding a small stone in his hand. Once he had even tried prayer but his words floated away aimlessly like thistledown. At other times he invented a new persona for himself and constructed a safer, better story of his life, painting in details like a child colouring a book.

It carried him now, a little boat tugged by swirling currents, rudderless and drifting into dangerous seas. It steered him through the weak, watery eyes of the chaplain into a chain of caverns where the flapping wings of bats beat in serried flurries and sharp-edged images cut him to the bone. In his dreams he saw the colonel on his knees checking the undercarriage of his car, his mother's face whitened with flour like the face of a ghost. The images washed over him, carrying him deeper into the great echoing chambers

962

of his heart where his mother's words – 'every day for the rest of our lives' – reverberated eternally.

The voyage was always different but the destination never changed. It took him to his father. Tall and strong in his dark blue overalls, bits of grass in his hair after a day of silage cutting. Only the big field left to do and the clear blue skies of a summer's evening stretching still and unbroken. Hedgerows alive with colour and blossom, and everywhere, everywhere, the sweet smell of cut grass. He helped his father with many jobs but he liked this one more than any of them. He liked it because it had a start and a finish and when it was done, and the last bale safely stored it felt as if you had really done something big. Sometimes when the weather was likely to change, his father and his uncles would work through the night, their tractor lights shooting moth-filled shafts of light into darkness. But tonight, on this still summer's evening with the sun slowly sinking red, it was only the two of them. Sometimes when he had promised not to tell his mother, he was allowed to drive the tractor, his father perched behind him in the cab, his hand resting on his shoulder and his eye keeping the steering line straight.

The grass is already cut and raked by the machine into ridged furrows, curving round the field like the graded rings of a giant shell. And everywhere lingers the sweet smell of cut grass, the fresh sap of summer lacing the night. Black smoke belches from the tractor and crows fly overhead, then land in the tractor's wake to search through the freshest swathe. As the sun ignites the tops of the hedgerows on the horizon, his father loads the machine which gathers the cut grass. Soon its long red neck spews grass into the baler, firing it in fiercely like a ceaseless torrent of rain bleeding across the sun. In the glow of the setting sun it looks like a dragon breathing fire. He stands watching it. It seems to fill very quickly and when it can take no more his father stops the tractor and climbs down, taking a minute's rest before he drives the filled baler away.

They must have been waiting for him to get out of the tractor. They must have been standing in the hedgerow, watching and waiting for this moment. They both walk across the ridged furrows of grass, moving steadily, not running. He sees them before his father does, but he looks at them with only slight curiosity. When his father registers them they are close enough for their faces to be seen. In his dreams their faces change so often he no longer remembers what they look like and in his dreams something happens to time. Everything slows and freeze-frames – his father staring and then tightening, shouting at him to run, but his words are strangled in his throat as the first shots hit him in the chest. But no sound from their handguns, only the flapping of the birds' wings as they scatter skyward in a sudden black cloud, as the two men run forward, firing more shots, their feet kicking up grass. Shooting into his father's body as it jerks as if in a fit, and then crumples like a child's on the bed of sharp-spiked stubble. Shooting until the guns are jammed or empty. Only one of them looks at him, and only for a second, looks at him with nothing in his eyes, then they both turn and run to the hedge bounding the road. He falls to his knees beside his father's head, afraid to touch him, and his hand feels the warm blood seeping into the grass. Blood on the grass, red as the setting sun being swallowed by the dark ridge of the horizon. He screams, a raw scream of pain and terror. Screams and screams, until every part of him is locked rigid in it.

The scream was still in his throat when he jerked upright in the bed, his eyes wide and staring. Every day for the rest of his life – eyes with nothing in them, bloodied grass in his father's hair, a black cloud of birds beating across the dying sky. His whole body still shuddered as he felt the warm stream of his urine spread slowly across the plastic sheet.

SEBASTIAN BARRY

from *The Whereabouts of Eneas McNulty*

A fresh recruit by the wisdom and mercy of headquarters in the Phoenix Park is never let serve in his own town and especially so in the new world of guerrilla war and reprisal, for a policeman is a target now, like one of those wooden ducks in the fairground going round and round on the wooden hill. Every recruited man is suspected by both sides of informing, one way or another, and a man is rendered greater innocence by being posted to an unfamiliar town. So Eneas finds himself in Athlone with the bright peaked cap and the shining boots and the black suit. For a brace of months he is drilled and perfected in the barracks square. Out at six they are in their greatcoats, the peaks on the caps as black as blackbirds' feathers, and rain or shine the boots making the crippled cobbles ring, and they wheel and stamp and take the orders as the one animal. A hundred boys in similar coats, and the fresh reds of the dawn cluttering up the lower gaps between the buildings. The name for a raw boy is a shoofly, and each man aims to be a constable, but the name among the historical-minded people of the town is the peelers, the polis. At end of training each man gets his gun and bullets. All about the barracks the countryside is boiling with sedition and treachery and hatred according to the sergeant, William Doyle of Leitrim, of Leitrim in these latter years, but an Athlone boy in times gone by, so he will tell you. As such a useful man to herd his men about the dangerous districts.

And indeed ferocious events are afoot in the sacred web of fields and rainy towns. It isn't just murders and such or killings, you couldn't call them that. Wherever an RIC man uses a gun and wounds or kills in a skirmish, some man in his uniform is taken and God help him in the dark hedges and isolated farms. Such a man might be gutted with a big knife and his entrails fed to the homely pig in front of him, and the last leaks of life drained out of him then slowly and silently with terrible swipes.

Next thing the RIC is augmented, as the official word goes, with an Auxiliary Force and now the merry dance gets wilder back and forth. For these are men as strange and driven as the Irish heroes themselves. They're quaffing long bottles of beer and whisky at every juncture and resting-spot, and visiting themselves upon guilty and innocent alike with the fierce passion and separateness of lions. Perhaps this isn't an easy matter for recruits like Eneas, jostled in the very police barracks by these haunted faces.

They have come back most of them from the other war and what haunts them now is the blood and torn matter of those lost, bewildering days. Many of the Auxiliaries are decorated boys, boys that ran out into no-man's-land and took positions that only bodiless gods could have, and rescued men from the teeth of slaughter and saw sights worse than the drearest nightmares. And they have come back altered for ever and in a way more marked by atrocity than honoured by medals. They are half nightmare themselves, in their uniforms patched together from army and RIC stores, some of them handsome and elegant men, with shining accents, some terrible dark boys from the worst back-alleys of England, but all with the blank light of death and drear unimportance of being alive in their eyes. As ancient as old stories. And every auxiliary has the strength of four ordinary men you would think, as if death and fearlessness were an elixir.

And they are visited upon the countryside lethally and notoriously. Reprisals are daily sorrows, daily sad persons are found in ditches of a morning and no matter what allegiance was in their hearts at any daybreak. Because they are broken, bloody, vanished hearts now, auxiliary and guerrilla alike. Eneas's principal duty is the finding and motoring of these remnants back to the coroner's premises in Athlone town.

The king of the Auxiliaries is the man called the Reprisal Man and Eneas knows him by no other name. It's said generally that he comes from the dark north of England and killed seven Germans in a bomb hole somewhere in the muddy wastes of the Somme. He's a person as big and real as one of the cowboys in the flicks – Athlone has its passionate cinema too. How he does it nobody can tell on his poor wages but the man is never but spick and span and the crease straight and ridged in the old trews from stores. A hero in other places no doubt, but a tongue of pure avenging fire in the backroads of the lands about the town. This is a fella never to be seen with and if the rule of thumb among the recruits and indeed the RIC men in general is to stay clear of the Auxiliaries, or the Tans as they are called by the people, an article of faith is to avoid the Reprisal Man like the devil himself. To be spotted in the company of such as he either in hours of duty or relaxing in the bars of the town would be noted on some black-list of marked men.

Even the sergeant Doyle stays away from him and Doyle is a policeman of the old school, loyal as a child to the kings and queens of England, Scotland and Ireland and the princes of Wales also. His father was a simple cabinkeeper in Leitrim after losing the huxter's shop in Athlone when the sergeant was only a scrap. His grandfather died, it was said, during the hunger of the forties in the old century, killed by a mob for feeding Indian grain meant for paupers to his fattening pig. This isn't information that Eneas gets from the sergeant, but the sort of thing you'll get whispered to you by the older men less useful than the sergeant, less promoted.

Well, the whole business is mightily complicated one way and another and Eneas in his heart cannot say that he enjoys the policing he is set to do. He had had in mind the more usual duties of the RIC, in days more peaceful, when he joined, and never had the ambition to be a carter of corpses or a young fella atop a cart weeping from bewilderment. No man fool or sage could get used to the scenes of murder, because they are ever changing and unnatural. Indeed older men long years in the force have taken their own lives in answer to the crushing horror of the times, and rakes of others in the country generally are said to be housed now in the county homes and the asylums.

They were unfit for such sights. Eneas tries many a stratagem to water down what he sees, to satisfy his heart that it is a passing matter, but truth to tell each dead soul afflicts him. The trouble and sorrow of being a peeler is a revelation to him.

Doyle is the man who tries to keep his men true and indeed safe. No constable walks alone now through the streets of Athlone, and many a homespun speech issues forth from Doyle's lips on the topics of duty and order and loyalty and God. God is the chief superintendent, right enough, or even a commissioner.

Bit by bit Eneas understands that a fella by the name of Mick Collins is the big man behind the wild lads willing to kill for the lovely trout of freedom. No decent description of him exists in police files, but a field of stories growing fast with brambles and tares attaches to the name. And yet the name rises immaculate and bright as a sovereign from the mire of events that muddy all normal men. It's a mystery. Eneas could call Collins the enemy except in his private mind he does not. If he had a picture of him maybe he could. He sees the Reprisal Man every so often stomping through the wooden corridors of the barracks or passing up the street in a Crossley tender like a savage prince, and it seems to Eneas that that same Reprisal Man is more his enemy than the invisible Mick Collins. But both are men of blood no doubt. Eneas's head rackets with warring notions. He's adrift on the shallow sea of his homeland.

At first he tries to get home to his Mam and Pappy every furlough but the cat's cradle of Sligo talk is against him. His Pappy is stopped in the street and talked to by O'Dowd, the auctioneer, one of Collins's men it may be, but a proper bowsie, according to Old Tom McNulty. Yes, a proper bowsie, a scam merchant and the son of a boxty cooker from over Strandhill way, an unkempt boiler of a fella that used mash up spuds for the trippers and their kids hungry after the salt sea and the wild playing. So it is a mighty affront for Old Tom to be stopped by the son of O'Dowd the boxty man and at the same time the words he says to Old Tom are precise and calm.

'Let your son keep out of Sligo, man, if he wants to keep his ability to walk.'

There's no misunderstanding that song and Eneas keeps to barracks when other men are able to catch motor-buses or trains or go on the long walk and lift-cadging home to towns and rural places, and no word said against them, as yet. But Eneas knows that the stint at sea is held against him also, the stint at sea and maybe also his old friendship with Jonno Lynch, which might be a useful thing to a policeman bent on gathering intelligence. Eneas is not bent on anything except daily life but O'Dowd's imagination and the imaginations of a score of worried men in Sligo are afire with conspiracy and secrecy.

At any rate something occurs that puts such straightforward matters in the halfpenny place. There's a right old hooley of a series of tit-for-tat jobs between the Roscommon rebels and the Tans, with the RIC mixed in somewhere too. And the doings of the rebels are further tangled by betrayals in their own number as the curious war grows in months like a terrible child, and certain quaint advantages are to be got out of the situation. Sometimes now Eneas carts back creatures done in by their own comrades, mightily done in. And fellas say now that it's like the old famine days when some of the worst cruelty was visited on the poor of Ireland by them that were slightly less poor, and Doyle's ould grandfather is darkly cited. When a strong farmer was content to see his rentless neighbour driven off to fever, death or America, if he could only get a hoult of the vacated farm, and attach it to his own. If this is not the bedevilment of Irish historical goings-on, Eneas doesn't know what is, or so he says plainly to his companions, though indeed the matter is not quite so clear as that in his head.

Well, he's going up the town one night in Athlone with Sergeant Doyle himself as a companion, and they've been idly drinking in the old Great Western Hotel where the proprietor is above politics and beneath neutrality. It has become a policeman and soldier's drinking spot but no matter, the two are well watered now but not drunk as such and climbing the little hill past the curious pewter of the black river and the mossy walls of the Cathedral. And there's a little stone-covered alleyway there that would bring you up conveniently to the sacristy if you were a priest, and there are two dark men in the gap there that get a good hold on Doyle and a penknife to his throat. And Eneas hangs back from jumping at the men or trying to get his gun out of his cut-down holster because he piercingly sees how honed and steeled the knife is, as thin as the leg of a sandpiper.

'Come in, you bugger, out of the light,' says one of the men, 'or I'll tear out the gullet of your sergeant.'

So Eneas steps in carefully, into the holy dark, where priests and priests' messengers have often darted, and Doyle says not a word, for fear of inciting a regretful move. These are clearly some of the bould men themselves, some of the heroes of Athlone, the dark men of freedom. Some of Jonno Lynch's crowd, or the Athlone branch anyhow. They have an air about them fretful and desperate, not like policemen or soldiers but like hunters, fellas that go out after hares with big long streels of dogs in the blessed autumns. Townies with guns – nothing worse, nothing more dangerous to the peace of the countryside. And Eneas is silent, as indeed his training recommends. For an attacker is like a snake that strikes at movement, at history, at words.

'We're taking you for the job done on Stephen Jackson,' says the same man, 'just so you know why we're doing this to you.'

And Eneas knows who Jackson is or was and so does Doyle, because Eneas took Jackson to the coroner's icy room with bullets of the Reprisal Man in his cold head.

'I don't know nothing about that,' says Doyle in his Leitrim accent.

'Ah, you do, and you did,' says the man.

'It's the feckin Tans you want,' says Doyle, simply.

'Jaysus, that'll be the day, the day we get him, the long bollocks that he is. The Reprisal Man, in all his glory. That'll be the day of history, the time we get that shite. But he's no easy sparrow like yourselves. We'll get him too some day, some day. In the meantime, your ticket's come good, Doyle, and we know you're mixed up in it.'

'I hadn't got a finger in it,' says Doyle. 'I never even met the man.'

'Arra,' says the murdering man, 'isn't that a big fib. Ha? Didn't you go to school with the fella, up with the brothers in Mount Temple? Aren't you on the old register there, and anyway, don't I know you knew him, because he told me himself, with his dying breath. Said he'd know your skin on a board. After the Reprisal Man put bullets in his face at point-blank range and the poor bastard came running down Cook Street with his life leaking from his ears, blind from blood and pain, and into my arms like a boy, oh yes, and the last thing he said was it must have been yourself put his name in the Big Man's way, because you were pals in the school on the hill with the Brothers.'

And Eneas looks at Doyle to see if this could be accurate, at least about the schooling together, and he can see from Doyle's simple face that there's no lie in it.

'We've been waiting for you to make something of your old associations, you hooer's melt, ye. And didn't your grandfather make his money in the hungry days, you poor witless cunt, ye?'

'That's just an ould story, men,' says Doyle. Now Eneas smells a strange smell, a smell he's smelt once or twice only, and it's the stink of fear that rises from a man when he's in mortal dread.

'You had a hand in it as sure as cowshite, and if you didn't, aren't you peeler enough for our intentions?'

And Doyle hangs now in the man's arms, as if every grain of energy's gone out of him. And his face acquires a complete deep look of stupidity and gracelessness. Eneas himself stares like a calf. No course of action presents itself. A few people even going home late in their raincoats pass up the street but he doesn't feel inspired to call out to them, with the thin knife sparking at Doyle's scraggled throat. The four of them know something is going to happen, they are united at least in that certainty. It could be the flicks or a dark penny dreadful, the way the four of them know all that. And their different histories, their different childhoods, their different ages and faces and hopes even, their different souls sullied up by different matters, all seem to tend towards the same event, this cold and shadowy event in the little granite slipway of the cathedral priests.

'Say goodnight, Doyle,' says the speaking man, and never a word from the other. 'May God forgive me.'

And he takes a snug gun from his coat of darkness and places it up against the bullocky face of Doyle no doubt just as the Reprisal Man did with Stephen Jackson, Doyle's childhood companion in the roistering schoolyard, and he prints the O of the little barrel against the right cheekbone and fires into the suddenly flashing face. And places the gun a second time into the left cheekbone, or where it might well be if the blood and splinters and scraps of flesh were cleaned off, and fires again and Eneas looks into the face of the killer and it has the set effort in it of a person struggling for precision in a world of vagueness and doubt, struggling with a physical task in a world of Godless souls and wormy hearts.

'Will I do this poor bastard too?' says the trembling killer to his friend, turning the little gun on Eneas.

'One's enough for the night,' says the other man. 'One's enough. The whole town will be stirring now. That's McNulty, the Sligoman. Let Sligo look after him, if they want. I'm not killing a simpleton like that. Look at the gawmy stare of him. Look at the stare of him.'

So he looks at Eneas for a second, the killer man, as if having been bidden to do so, he is honour-bound to do it, to fulfil every article of talk and action. For the freedom of Ireland and the Republic so earnestly wished for.

'Oh, let's feckin run for it,' says the assassin, weary as a donkey.

Then off indeed, truthful and exact, they run like they are kids hooering out of an orchard and the apples bubbling from their ganseys and banging on the metalled roads. And Eneas is left there standing indeed like a gom, like a remnant, like an oddment. Couldn't they have shot him too, for the look of things? For courtesy even? He thinks that and in another corner of his head he knows it is a daft thought. He feels a tremendous love as long as an English mile for the poor corpse in the lane. He knew him but slightly, yet all the purposes of that ordinary life, the tobacco, the papers, the idle talk, the dreams of promotion that never came true, afflict Eneas in the darkness. He wants to kneel down and embrace the dead man, soothe him, do something to send him up safe and sound to his Maker. But he stirs not a muscle. He finds he is frozen by terror. And Doyle is at his feet, simple as a song, all ruined and wrecked like Humpty Dumpty. Doyle is at his stupid feet, his bloody feet familiar and square, cased brightly in their police-issue boots.

PATRICK MCCABE

from *The Butcher Boy*

I woke up the next morning and went round to the slaughterhouse but it was too early I was waiting for near two hours before Leddy came how long are you here he says a good while Mr Leddy I said. Its near time you'd show your face around here or where in the hell were you! Oh I says I was off rambling. Rambling he says, you'd do well to ramble in your own time Brady I've a mind to kick you rambling down that road. Well says I you won't have to worry for that's the end of it it'll be all over now shortly. He pulled on his apron and says they have a half ton of shite round at that hotel you were supposed to collect it and they have my heart scalded now get round there today and fuckingwell see about it. Right so Mr Leddy I said.

Then we started into the killing and we were working right through till dinnertime. Then he wiped his hands on his apron and says I'm away to my dinner take that cart round now. And make sure and tell them tell them you'll collect on time next week. I will indeed Mr Leddy I says. When he was gone off down the town I took the captive bolt pistol down off the nail where it was hanging and got the butcher's steel and the knife out of the drawer. There was a bucket of old slops and pig meal or something lying by the door so I just stuck them into that and went away off with the cart whistling. So Traynor's daughter had been talking to Our Lady again, eh? They were all talk about her going to appear on the Diamond. I heard two old women on about it. We should be very proud says one of them its not every town the Mother Of God comes to visit. Indeed it is not says the other one I wonder missus will there be angels. I wouldn't know about that now but sure what odds whether there is or not so long as she saves us from the end of the world what do we care? Now you said it missus now you said it. Everywhere you went: Not long now.

I went by Doctor Roche's house it was all painted up with big blue cardboard letters spread out on the grass: AVE MARIA WELCOME TO OUR TOWN. I was wondering could

I mix them up to make THIS IS DOCTOR ROCHE THE BASTARD'S HOUSE, but I counted them and there wasn't enough letters and anyway they were the wrong ones.

Tell Leddy to collect this brock on time or its the last he'll get from us says the kitchen man and stands there looking at me like I was stealing something off him. I will indeed I said and started shovelling it into the cart. I shovelled and whistled away and made sure there wasn't a scrap left so there'd be no more complaining. Then off I went again on my travels. Everybody was all holy now, we're all in this together people of the town, bogmen taking off their caps to women, looking into prams and everything. This is the holiest town in the world they should have put that up on a banner.

There was a nice altar on the Diamond. There was three angels flying over it just in front of the door of the Ulster Bank.

I never saw the town looking so well. It looked like the brightest, happiest town in the whole world.

I went round the back swinging my meal bucket. I could see the neighbour's curtain twitching whistle whistle hello there Mr Neighbour its me Francie with my special delivery for Mrs Nugent. Then away she went from the windows so I knocked on Mrs Nugent's door and out she came wearing her blue housecoat. Hello Mrs Nugent I said is Mr Nugent in I have a message for him from Mr Leddy. She went all white and stood there just stuttering I'm sorry she said my husband isn't here he's gone to work oh I said that's all right and with one quick shove I pushed her inside she fell back against something. I twisted the key in the lock behind me. She had a white mask of a face on her and her mouth a small o now you know what its like for dumb people who have holes in their stomachs Mrs Nugent. They try to cry out and they can't they don't know how. She stumbled trying to get to the phone or the door and when I smelt the scones and seen Philip's picture I started to shake and kicked her I don't know how many times. She groaned and said please I didn't care if she groaned or said please or what she said. I caught her round the neck and I said: You did two bad things Mrs Nugent. You made me turn my back on my ma and you took Joe away from me. Why did you do that Mrs Nugent? She didn't answer I didn't want to hear any answer I smacked her against the wall a few times there was a smear of blood at the corner of her mouth and her hand was reaching out trying to touch me when I cocked the captive bolt. I lifted her off the floor with one hand and shot the bolt right into her head *thlok* was the sound it made, like a goldfish dropping into a bowl. If you ask anyone how you kill a pig they will tell you cut its throat across but you don't you do it longways. Then she just lay there with her chin sticking up and I opened her then I stuck my hand in her stomach and wrote PIGS all over the walls of the upstairs room.

I made sure to cover her over good and proper with the brock there was plenty of it they wouldn't be too pleased if they saw me with Mrs Nugent in the bottom of the cart then I lifted the shafts and off I went on my travels again there was more hymns and streams of people up and down Church Hill with prayerbooks. Who did I meet then only your man with the bicycle and the raincoat thrown over the handlebars. He was all friendly this time he was a happy man Our Lady was coming he said. I haven't seen you this long time he says are you still collecting the tax? No I said that's all finished I'm wheeling carts now. You never thought you'd see the day the Mother of God would be coming to this town, eh? he says and looked at me as much as to say it was me arranged the whole thing. No, I did not, I said, its a happy time for the town and no mistake. A happy happy time he says and reached in his pocket to take out his tobacco puff puff what will we talk about now nothing I said the best of luck now I'm away off round to the yard right he says no rest for the wicked that's right I says no rest for anyone only Mrs Nugent in the bottom of this cart. But he didn't hear me saying that.

I left down the cart for a minute and went in to buy some fags the women were there over by the sugar only without Mrs Connolly. I got the fags and I says to the women its a pity Mrs Connolly isn't here I wanted to talk to her about what I said sure I was only codding! I said. What would I go and say the like of that to her for! Me and Mrs Connolly are old friends! Didn't I get a prize off her for doing a dance! A lovely juicy apple! I lit up a fag and puffed it ha ha they said ah sure don't be worrying your head Francie they said we all do things we regret don't we ladies. Yes I said especially Mrs Nugent and laughed through the smoke. Then they said: What? But I said: Oh nothing.

One of them twisted the strap of her handbag round her little finger and said there was no use in people bearing grudges at a special time like this. Now you said it I said, you never spoke a truer word.

Well ladies, I said, I must be off about my business there's no rest for the wicked indeed there is not Francie said the woman with three heads laughing away like in the old days. I had gone through that fag already and the shop was full of smoke I was puffing it all out that fast so what did I do only light another one. Francie Brady – I smoke one hundred cigarettes a day! Yes its true! Francie Brady says! No, it isn't. Only when I'm wheeling Mrs Nooge around. I stuck a little finger in the air and pulled on the fag like something out of the pictures. I say ladies – good day, I said and that started them off into the laughing again. Master Algernon Carruthers and his Nugent cart. OK Nooge let's ride I said, the Francie Brady Deadwood stage is pulling out. The drunk lad went by with another saint in a barrow and ducked down when he seen me.

Stop thief! Come back with that saint! I says and started into the laughing again. Stop that man! He's going to sell that poor saint for drink! Whistling away on I went my old man's a dustman he wears a dustman's hat. I don't know where all the songs came out of. Well its one for the money. I am a little baby pig I'll have you all to know. Yes this is the Baby Pig Show broadcasting on Raydeeoh Lux-em-Bourg!

Hello my good man. Fine weather we're having. What did you order? Two pounds of chump steak?

Or was it a half pound of Mrs Nugent?

Sorry folks, Mrs Nugent's not for sale! She's off on her travels with her old pal Francie Brady. I was passing by Mary's sweetshop so in I went and got a quarter of sweets clove drops. I came in to say hello to my old friend Mary I said will you ever forget them old days Mary! Twenty years in Camden Town! What about that! What do you say we go inside and you can give us a song on the piano!

I lit another fag and went on talking away but Mary said nothing just scooped the sweets into the bag with a silver shovel and then twisted it the way she did spin twist and there it was a little knobbly bag of best clove drops yes indeed. Then she went and sat down by the window again looking out across the square. Look at that Mary! The same old clove drops! I said but she still didn't say anything just smiled if you could call it a smile. I knew who she was thinking about. She was thinking about Alo that's who she was thinking about. Don't worry Mary I said, your troubles are over Mary – Francie Brady the Time Lord is here!

But soon as I said it I felt stupid and I tried to think of something completely different to say but I could think of nothing so I just put the sweets in my pocket and went out the bell jingle jingle and the door closing behind me. Mary had the same face as ma used to have sitting staring into the ashes it was funny that face it slowly grew over the other one until one day you looked and the person you knew was gone. And instead there was a half-ghost sitting there who had only one thing to say: All the beautiful things of this world are lies. They count for nothing in the end.

Even if that was true I still went round the lane where the kids were this might be my last chance I said. Sure enough there they were setting toy tea-things on an orange box and clumping around in the enormous shoes. Can I play I said. How can you play if you're big one of them said, clear off! There was a young lad sailing lollystick rafts out into the middle of a puddle. I said to him: What would you do if you won a hundred million billion trillion dollars?

Without thinking he looked at me and said: I'd buy a million Flash Bars. Well fuck me, I laughed, then off I went again and left him churning up the water with his stick and whistling some tune he was making up as he went along.

Where the hell were you says Leddy when I got back to the slaughterhouse yard. Oh, tricking about I says, well trick about in your own time he says I have to go on up to the shop, you take over here. Right, I said, that suits me, and I left down the barrow beside the Pit of Guts and asked Leddy where he'd put the lime. Clear off Grouse! I shouted and he tore off through the gate with a string of intestines. I got the shovel and slit open the bag of lime there was warm tears in my eyes because I could do nothing for Mary.

I'd say it was a good laugh when Mr Nugent Ready Rubbed came home that evening. Brr that's a cold one yoo-hoo! I'm home what's for tea dear? Dear oh dear that wife of mine she's so busy she hears nothing. The smell of scones and the black and white tiles polished so you could see your face in them. O she's probably just gone out to the shop for something never mind let's see what's on the telly. Here is The News. News. Mm, isn't it quiet around here since Philip went to boarding school? Mm, isn't it quiet around here since my Mrs went to heaven he'd soon be saying but he didn't know that. I wonder what it will be – rashers and eggs maybe or one of her special steak and kidney pies! But poor old Mr Nugent he'd have a long wait before he got one of them again. Ah yes, it was sad. And that is the end of the news. Hmm. Tick tock. I wonder where she could be. I wonder where my wife could be? Hello next door neighbour did you see my wife? No, to tell you the God's honest truth now I didn't. Oh dear said Mr Nooge. Tick tick and walking round the kitchen the silence wasn't so nice now over and over again just where is Mrs Nugent the invisible woman? Tick tock and I don't care about Maltan Ready Rubbed, where is my wife! Look at that old Mr Nugent and his big red eyes! Maltan Ready Rubbed – Its The Best Boo Hoo Hoo! That wouldn't look so good on the television. I wonder would she be upstairs? Do you think she might have gone upstairs and fallen asleep next door neighbour? Why yes she could have couldn't she? Let's go and investigate shall we? Good idea says Mr Nugent and off they go taking the stairs two at a time but then when they open the door what do they see all over the walls oh no Mr Nugent hardly able to stand and the next door neighbour don't look don't look!

Well she doesn't seen to be in there anyway ha ha perhaps the police might know why don't we ring up let me do it Mr Nugent. Sweaty fingerprints all over the telephone hello is that Sergeant Sausage I mean is that the police station?

I was whistling away when I looked up and seen Sausage and four or five bogmen police coming across the yard I never seen them before they weren't from the town. One of them kept looking over the whole time sizing me up trying to catch my eye to tell me *by Chrisht you're for it now boy!* but I just went on skinning and whistling. I don't know what I was whistling I think it was the tune from *Voyage to the Bottom of the Sea.* Leddy was standing in the doorway wiping his hands with a rag then looking over at me with a chalky old face on him. I heard the sergeant saying: *The neighbours seen him going in round the back of the house this morning.*

Next thing what does Leddy do only lose the head. Before the sergeant could stop him he had a hold of me and gives me this push I fell back against the fridge door *I hope to Chrisht they give you everything that's coming to you! I should never have let you darken the door of the place only I let myself be talked into it on account of your poor mother!* he says standing there shaking with his fists opening and closing. He tried to push me again but I managed to get a hold of his arm I looked right into his eyes and he knew what I was saying to him, Mr Leddy from the Cutting Up Pigs University you better watch who you're pushing Bangkok you were never in Bangkok in your life and you better watch what you're saying about my father plucking my mother or you'll get the same Nugent got would you like that Pig Leddy – Leddy the Pig Man would you fuckingwell like that!

Then I burst out laughing in his face he was so shocked – looking I thought he was going to say O please Francie I'm sorry I didn't mean to say all that it was a slip of the tongue.

What could I say? Such a daft place!

Mr Nugent was shivery and everything I knew he couldn't bear to look at me. Where is she, said Sausage and the bullneck bogmen got a grip of me two on either side. They had me now all right I wasn't fit to move a muscle. Oh I said, this must be the end of the world. I hope the Blessed Virgin comes along to save me!

Where is she? says Sausage again.

Maltan Ready Rubbed Flake, that's the one!, I said to Mr Nugent and I got a thump in the ribs. Then they said right turn this place inside out and that's what they did. They turned it upside down. Those bogmen cops. You could fry a rasher on their necks. How many rashers was that? Four. No – let's make it two rashers and two eggs instead if you don't mind!

I wonder is she in behind this half-a-cow? No, she doesn't appear to be. What about under this septic tank? No, no sign of her. Then they got hysterical. They had to take Mr Nugent away. What have you done with her? I said who and they got worse. They gave me a beating and took me for a drive all round the town. What had they draped across the chickenhouse only THE TOWN WELCOMES OUR LADY. I said to them: She must be going to land on the chickenhouse roof and they stuck the car to the road with a screech of brakes by Christ I'll tear that blasphemous tongue out of your head with my bare hands says Sausage. But he didn't, then we were off again where to, the river. Is she out here? Who, I said again. After all that they took me back to the station and gave me the father and mother of a kicking. In the middle of it all what does one of the bullnecks say: Let me have a crack at him and I'll knock seven different kinds of shite out of him!

That finished me off altogether. I started saying it the way he said it. Seven different kinds of shoite! For fuck's sake!

The way they do it they put a bar of soap in a sock and I don't know how many times they gave it to me it leaves no marks. But it still knocks seven different kinds of shite out!

Where is she said Sausage, shaking. Castlebar Sausages – they're the best! I said. Hear them sizzle in the pan – Sergeant Sausage says!

Then they got fed up and said fuck him into the cell we'll get it out of him in the morning. I could hear them playing cards. Foive o' trumps! and all this. That's the besht keeerd you've played thish ayvnin'! I stuck my ear to the wall so as I wouldn't miss any of it. I heard them saying: I wouldn't turn my back on that treacherous fucker not for a second!

They kept me in the cell the whole of the next day they were waiting for the detective to come down from Dublin. I could hear them all going by in the street come over here you bastard I shouts to the drunk lad through the bars you owe me two and six the fucker away off then running like the clappers. Hello Mrs Connolly I shouted look where they have me now! Your man with the bicycle, I shouts over: This is what I get for not paying my pig toll tax! It serves me right!

Ha ha he says and nearly drove the bicycle into a wall. Who appears at the window of the cell then only Mickey Traynor and McCooey the miracle worker. I'm praying for you son, says McCooey. He had Maria Goretti propped up against a couple of haybales on the back of the cart he said she was going to bleed at the apparition. Then he says I hear there's been bad trouble in the town this past few days. How are you my son, he says, I'm praying for your immortal soul, never fear. Through the bars I could see Goretti gawking up at the sky with her hands joined. Observe her beautiful eyes, McCooey'd say, Observe the beautiful saint's eyes and then two red red rubies of blood would appear and roll down her white cheeks. Its sad Mr McCooey, I said. What, my son, he said, this vale of tears in which we are all but wanderers searching for home? No, I said, fat old bastards like you wasting all that tomato sauce. O Jesus Mary and Joseph says Mickey and reaches out in case he faints. You're a bad and wicked and evil man and you broke your mother's heart didn't even go to the poor woman's funeral! I said to him what the fuck would you know about it Traynor what do you know you couldn't even fix the television could you well what are you talking about! Do you hear me Traynor? Fuck you! Fuck you and your daughter and The Blessed Virgin! I didn't mean to say that Traynor made me say it the whole street heard me there they were all looking and crossing themselves oh Jesus Mary and Joseph then in came the bullnecks and the detective they gave me another kicking and says we're going for a drive after and you'd better start opening your mouth Brady or by Christ you'll get what's coming to you. I fell into a sort of sleep then after that and I heard Mrs Connolly and them all saying the rosary for me outside in the square. I looked up and there was Buttsy and Devlin looking in between the bars. You better pray they hang you says Buttsy what we're going to do to you we'll string you up like the pig you are. He was all smart but then he starts screeching *what have you done to my sister* till Devlin had to take him away. I said good riddance and read the *Beano* I got one of the children to get me in Mary's shop. General Jumbo he had some army, tiny little robot men he controlled using this wrist panel of buttons made for him by his friend Mr Professor. I used to think: I wouldn't mind having one of them that controlled all the people in the town. I'd march them all out to the river and click!, stop right at the edge. Then just when they were saying: Phew that was a lucky one we nearly went in there, Hi-yah! I'd press the button – in you go youse bastards aiee! and the whole lot of them into the water.

The next time Sausage came in on his own turning the cap round on his lap looking at me with these sad eyes why does there have to be so many sad things in the world Francie I'm an old man I'm not able for this any more. When I seen them eyes, I said to myself, poor old Sausage its not fair. All right Sausage I said I'll show you where she is thanks Francie he said, I knew you would. Its gone on long enough. There's been enough unhappiness and misery. There has indeed sergeant I said.

The new detective was in the front of the car, Fabian of the Yard I called him after the fellow in the pictures, and I was hemmed in between two of the bullnecks in the back.
Sausage was all proud now that things had worked out and he hadn't made a cod of himself in front of Fabian. It'll be all over shortly now Francie he says you're doing the right thing. I know Sergeant I said. When we turned into the lane he drove slowly to

avoid the children what were they at now selling comics on a table it was a comic sale. They stood there looking after us I seen tassels pointing look Brendy its him!

We stopped at the chickenhouse and Fabian says you two men stay out here at the front just in case you can't be too careful. Right they said and me and the sergeant and him and the other two went inside. The fan was humming away and it made me sad. The chicks were still scrabbling away who are all these coming with Francie?

We waded through the piles of woodchips as we went along and I said to them it isn't far its just down here at the back. Fabian wasn't sure of where he was going it was so dark and when he walked into the light hanging in front of his face it went swinging back and forth painting the big shadows on the walls and the ceilings. I think the chicks must have known what was going to happen for they started burbling and getting excited. I said fuck who put that there and made on to trip and fall down. Watch yourself says Sausage its very dark and when Fabian came over to help me up I had the chain in my hand it had been lying there under the pallets where it always was. I swung it once and Fabian cried out but that was all I needed I tore into the back room and bolted the door. I didn't waste any time I threw the chain there and flung open the window and got out then ran like fuck.

I don't know where all the policemen came from but they were combing the country for me high up and low down. I could see them moving out across the fields and shouting to each other: Any luck? and Have you searched the other side of the woods yet?

It was a good laugh listening to all this I could see everything from inside the hide and old Sausage would he have kicked kicked himself stupid if he knew that he was standing right beside me twice.

They brought more police in you could hear them poking about night noon and morning and the sniffer dogs wuff wuff on the bank of the river time was running out for the deadly Francie Brady! Oh no it wasn't it was running out for fed-up Fabian and his men for all they had found was a dead cat in the ditch and you could hardly take that back to Scotland Yard. Well done Detective Fabian! You didn't catch Brady but you did catch this – a maggot-ridden old moggy! Congratulations!

In the end they said he has to be in the river so out the frogmen police went and dragged it there was reporters and Buttsy and Devlin and half the town all waiting to see me coming up covered in weeds and dirt but all they got this time was an iron bedstead and half a mattress. They came back a few times after that poking bits of sticks in bushes and muttering to themselves ah fuck this he's gone then they just slowly drifted away and then there was only me and the river hiss hiss. Hey fish! I said, youse are lucky youse didn't tell youse bastards! then out I went onto the main road there wasn't a sinner to be seen so off I went towards the town whistle whistle I was back in action. There was an old farmer humming away to himself and his bike lying up against the ditch. Tick tick tick and off I went and soon as I turned the corner wheee freewheeling away down the hill round the lane by the back of the houses in I went da-dan! I'm home! What's this ma used to say? I've so much tidying to do I don't know where to start. I rubbed my brow and stood there with my hands on my hips. I just don't know! Such a smell there was in the place! Not only had Grouse Armstrong been in but every dirty mongrel in the town. Everywhere you looked there was dog poo! In the corners, smeared on the walls. I gathered up as much of it as I could and put it all in a big pile in the middle of the kitchen. Well, I said, at least that's a start! Now – what about those mouldy old books! I lifted up one of them. What's this? *The Glory That was Greece*! To Benny 1949.

I turned a few of the pages and it all broke up in bits in my hands. I threw them all on the pile one after the other. There was a heap of clothes lying in the corner. A handful of earwigs fell out of the pocket of da's Al Capone coat. There was skirts and odd shoes and all sorts of things. I threw them all on. Then I went out to the scullery and got plates and knives and any other things that were lying around. I wiped my hands. Dear oh dear this is hard work I said. And I haven't even touched the upstairs yet! I didn't bother going through the drawers I just turned them upside down. There was letters and calendars and bills and stuff like that. Then I went upstairs and got the bedclothes and anything that was left in the wardrobes. What about us? said the pictures on the walls. Oops, I said, silly me! I nearly went and forgot all about you didn't I?

There was one of da pressing the mouthpiece to his lips. On you go, I says. Then the Sacred Heart with his two fingers up and the thorny heart burning outside his chest. Do you remember all the prayers we used to say in the old days Francie? He says. Oh now Sacred Heart I says, will I ever forget them? May the curse of Christ light upon you this night you rotten cunting bitch – do you remember that one?

I do, He says, raising His eyes to heaven, then off he goes what about this I says John F. Kennedy the man himself. What about me says Pope John the twenty third do I have to be dumped to? I'm sorry Holy Father I have to or else I'll get into trouble with the rest so on you go it'll not be long now. I had a hard job carrying the telly over I wanted it on the top but I managed it. The guts was still hanging out of it, wires and bulbs all over the place. The records were still under the stairs but I only wanted one I threw the rest away. I plugged in the gramophone it was working as good as ever then I carried it out to the scullery and put it near the sink. Right says I, now we're in business.

I got the paraffin from the coalhouse and threw it round everywhere but mostly on the pile. Spin spin goes your head with the smell of it here we go I says and then what happens.

No matches! No fucking matches! Oh for fuck's sake! I said.

When I got out into the street I couldn't believe it what's going on now I says. It was like the bit in *Gone with the Wind* where they burn the city. Fellows with halves of legs and some with none at all only a bit of a stump. Traynor's daughter was bucking away on the Diamond between two nuns, with her mouth all suds. The drunk lad was directing traffic with a new tie on him. *This way to the Mother of God, my friends!* They were far too busy waiting for her to be bothered about me running round for matches. I went into the shop thank you very much Mary I says its goodbye now I'm afraid but she didn't say anything she just sat there.

When I got back to the house I locked all the doors and then I lit a couple of matches. Soon as they fell on the heap up she went whumph!

I put on the record then I went in and lay down on the kitchen floor I closed my eyes and it was just like ma singing away like she used to.

> In that fair city where I did dwell
> A butcher boy I knew right well
> He courted me my life away
> But now with me he will not stay

> I wish I wish I wish in vain
> I wish I was a maid again
> But a maid again I ne'er will be
> Till cherries grow on an ivy tree.

> He went upstairs and the door he broke
> He found her hanging from a rope
> He took a knife and he cut her down
> And in her pocket these words he found

> Oh make my grave large wide and deep
> Put a marble stone at my head and feet
> And in the middle a turtle dove
> That the world may know I died for love.

I was crying because we were together now. Oh ma I said the whole house is burning up on us then a fist made of smoke hit me a smack in the mouth its over says ma its all over now.

AIDAN MATHEWS

'In the Dark'

The lights had gone out all over the O Muirithe household, and Harry and Joan were obliged to talk to one another. At the end of a difficult day, this was the last straw. Indeed, it was the short one. After all, they had been married for twenty-seven years, and were naturally speechless.

'The bastards,' said Harry. 'The bloody bastards. They said eight o'clock. They swore it.'

'I know,' said Joan. 'I know they did.'

'Zone B. No risk after eight. You can't believe daylight out of them.'

'It's only ten past.'

'I tell you this,' said Harry. 'The next house we buy, it's going to be . . .'

'Within spitting distance of a hospital,' said Joan.

'Within spitting distance,' said Harry. 'So near, so close you can hear the doctors putting in stitches, and the static on the set in the television lounge of the geriatric ward.'

(Harry had been to visit his father once when the old man became prematurely senile and had spent was it four years in just such an institution, rambling on about the toy-train in the park and the baby wallabies in the zoo sticking their heads out of their mother's pouches; but it was the static on the set which had always angered his son to the point where he had walked away in a pet. This, by the way, is a digression, the first of four, and you are quite at liberty to ignore them utterly. For my own part, I shall play fair, and indicate each one by the use of the parenthesis.)

'. . . of the geriatric ward.'

'And the nurses at their tea-break,' said Joan.

'And the nurses at their tea-break,' said Harry. 'Scraping out the last bit of strawberry yoghurt.'

'Next year,' said Joan.

'Next year,' Harry said.

There was a long silence. The battery clock on the mantelpiece ticked, as battery clocks do; and the curtains stirred, but only slightly.

'I could light a fire.'

But that was typical of Joan: trying to look on the bright side.

'I wouldn't bother.'

'Not for the heat. For the light. It'd be nice for Johnny and Avril.'

'You wouldn't see your nose under the stairs. You'd crack your skull open.'

Joan was hurt by this. Not that she noticed. She was as used to being hurt as to being fifty.

'I would have missed my bus if I'd stayed to set it,' she said. 'I had to be out by eight.'

'Am I complaining? Have I uttered a single syllable of recrimination? You shouldn't have to set it. Let Johnny set it.'

'You try asking Johnny to set it. Set it, my foot. Johnny wouldn't even know how to roll a newspaper.'

'Don't ask him. Tell him. Order him. Asking gets you nowhere. Telling gets you nowhere. This world is about the boot. Get the boot in. Look, where are those other candles? These two are useless. They're wobbly. They'd set the whole place on fire. You have to soften the bottom ends first. Soften the bottom end of one of them with the flame off the other. Then you sort of wedge it into the saucer till the wax hardens again. Are you with me?'

'I'm not a fool,' Joan said. 'Don't talk to me as if I were a fool.'

'I'm not saying you're a fool. I'm not suggesting you're a fool. I'd never have thought of going to the church. I thought the candles were electric nowadays. At least they were the last time I was there. So you did well. I hand it to you.'

'Now you're patronizing me,' Joan said. 'Please don't patronize me.'

Harry had meant well. He had meant well and he had been misunderstood. It was the story of his life. The story of his life could be summed up in the one word 'misunderstanding'. But he would be patient. He would not retaliate. 'Have you taken your Melleril?' he asked gently. 'Or did you forget again?' And then, before Joan could answer, he was noisily rummaging among the remaining candles.

'Here,' he said. 'What about this one?'

'What one?'

'Here. Where's your hand? That one.'

Joan smelled it.

'Harry, it's that awful scented kind. I can't stand them.'

'But it'll give us more light. And we need more light. Those piddly ones are for shrines.'

'The shrine of St Jude,' Joan said, which was, all considered, an excellent riposte; that is, if you know your saints, and Harry didn't. But it was still worth saying, and I personally regard it as a high point in the story. Harry lit a match. It struck the third time round, lighting their faces in a quite uncomplimentary fashion, and filling the room with their shadows.

'Harry, that scented smell makes me sick,' said Joan.

'Well, I'm not just going to squat here in total darkness. I've been working since I woke up. Surely to Christ I can . . .'

'I've been working too,' said Joan. 'Ever since I came in from work I've been working. I did the washing by hand. I went out again, to get the candles. In the rain.'

'Violins,' said Harry softly. 'Violins.'

'This is just hell. They never strike when it's summer. They do it when it gets dark.'

Harry had moved quietly out of the small circle of light in which she was sitting. He knew perfectly well why he was doing it too, but it was not revenge. It was a matter of principle. He still felt misunderstood.

'Harry? Harry? Where are you?'

'Nigeria,' he said. 'Where do you think I am?'

'Are you sure you're all right?'

Harry managed a small wheeze. He even tried to prolong it, but his lungs were clear. In any event, it achieved the desired effect.

'Are you breathless?'

'A bit. A bit breathless. It'll pass.'

'Sit down, Harry. Sit down and hold your head in your hands.'

(Harry's father had died on a ventilator, and Harry had persuaded Joan that the ailment was hereditary. He had almost persuaded himself. Ventolin inhalers were scattered strategically round about the whole house, and they served to inhibit outbreaks of marital discord. After all, Harry might not be here tomorrow, and words spoken in wrath might well be regretted. It was still only five years since her husband had taken the bus from the funeral parlour to add to the pathos of his father's removal, and had sat staring at 'Charley's Angels' without uttering a sentence, letting the barbecue chicken grow cold on his lap: Joan had forgotten none of this, and was easily panicked.)

'. . . and hold your head in your hands.'

'I am holding my head in my hands.'

'When do you think we'll have light, Harry?'

'When we reach the end of the tunnel. And not before.'

'This is hell.'

There was a long silence. The battery clock on the mantelpiece was still ticking; and the curtains stirred, but only slightly.

'What we need,' Harry decided, 'is someone like Mussolini. Benito would have known what to do. Line up the ringleaders. Shoot 'em down. Finito. That's the only thing that would bring these fellows to their senses. Make them tighten their belts. Both barrels. No bloody strikes in those days.'

Joan was relieved. Harry hadn't wheezed once.

'I wouldn't mind if they were paid badly,' she said.

'Yes, sirree,' Harry said. 'There's a lot to be said for a man like Mussolini.'

'You're just cross because you're missing your programme.'

'I was waiting for that,' said Harry.

'I don't know why you race home to watch that eejit.'

'I don't race anywhere. I haven't the energy. I work too hard.'

'And he's not even funny,' said Joan.

'My God, if I had to choose between Benny Hill and . . . and Mother Teresa, I know who I'd plumb for.'

'Just bottoms and sniggers,' she said. 'And the two of you sitting there, tittering. You're as bad as Johnny.'

'I've made up my mind,' said Harry, who hadn't. 'I *am* going to smoke.'

'You can't, Harry. Not now. Not after three weeks.'

'I can't have a hot meal,' Harry said. 'I can't watch Benny Hill. I can't have a normal conversation about normal things. The least I can do is smoke myself silly.'

'You mustn't give in.'

'Give me one good reason.'

'You'll live longer.'

'Jesus Christ,' said Harry with a ferocity which almost surprised him. 'That's the best bloody reason for taking them up.'

Noise in the hallway startled Joan.

'Harry, stop it, they're coming. And make an effort for me. Don't call her Shelley. Please. It's very unkind.'

But Harry was not about to lower his voice.

'Well, I liked Shelley. She was good for Johnny. Besides, she was a doctor. This one's a nurse. Next time round, I suppose he'll be dating the porter.'

Johnny's voice called out from the darkness of the doorway.

'Dr and Mrs Livingstone, I presume?'

Then Avril's, more timidly.

'Hello, Mr O Moorithe.'

'Shelley,' Harry said.

'Avril,' she replied. The girl was obviously dense: there wasn't a hint of malice in her voice.

'Force of habit,' Harry said to the darkness. 'Mea culpa.'

'Don't mind my Pater, Avril,' Johnny said. 'His nerves are shot. He's off the fags.'

But Avril ignored him. Shelley would have shown more spunk.

'Hi, Mrs O Moorithe.'

'Hello, love. Mind where you stand. I have a tray on the floor somewhere.'

'I can't stand the way she says it,' Harry said to Johnny in an audible undertone. 'O Moorithe. Can you not get her to pronounce it the right way? Shelley never had any difficulty, but then Shelley . . .'

'It has to do with the way you part your lips,' Johnny said. 'I'll work on it later.'

(Johnny was not ordinarily insolent; indeed, he lacked a capacity to do otherwise than dislike his father, a circumstance which chose him for this fiction, since in fiction the facts must fit that fabulous domain we poormouth as the ordinary world. But he'd been studying late in the National Library, and Avril had arrived to collect him at least an hour after the agreed time. He had pretended irritation, feeling little if any; so Avril had told him that, later in the evening, she would dress in her nurse's uniform and allow him to spank her across his lap with a rolled-up newspaper. He had had an erection ever since, and feared no one, not even his father.)

'Isn't this gas?' said Avril to Joan. 'I bet there'll be tons of babies in nine months time.'

'Don't be putting ideas in his head,' Joan said. But she liked Avril; it was a feminine thought and, besides, the girl worked, or had once worked, in the neo-natal unit.

There was a long silence. The battery clock could not prevent itself ticking gently and gingerly; and the curtains stirred in the lightest of breezes.

'You could have set a fire,' said Johnny.

'You could have set one,' said Joan. The darkness made her confident.

'Missed your programme, Dad?'

But Harry ignored him.

'I tell you this for nothing, Avril. I don't know how you feel, but I was saying to Johnny's mother that Mussolini had the right idea.'

'What was that?' said Avril.

'My father is about to deliver himself of a political apophthegm,' said Johnny. 'Stand well clear.'

'Johnny's father is just being difficult,' said Joan.

'What is that dreadful smell?' said Johnny, sniffing the darkness.

'I think it's lovely,' Avril said. 'I think it's churchy, sort of.'

'Bring in the troops,' Harry said. 'Pick four men at random. You, you, you, you. Out to the factory gates. Bayonet practice. Now that's my kind of crash course in industrial relations.'

'More crash than course,' said Johnny.

But Avril disagreed.

'I think it's a wonderful idea, Mr O Moorithe. After all, the working classes are getting ideas above their station. They think they can hold the country up to ransom.'

'How right you are, Avril,' Harry said warmly. 'How right you are.'

'But wouldn't it be a better idea to cut off their arms and legs first?'

(Avril was no more impudent than Johnny. I have known her a long time and have always found her to be easily cowed and crestfallen, with a complex of sorts about her skin, which is so fair it tans badly even with minimal exposure on the sunbed in the solarium. But that very afternoon she had been taking a quite handsome patient's blood pressure in the Admission Ward, and the back of his hand had grazed against the watch strap which she wore on her left breast. It was only a moment, a matter of seconds. But it had been deliberate. Of that she was sure. And the surety solaced her.)

'Well,' said Harry, managing another slight wheeze. 'That puts me in my place, doesn't it?'

The silence lengthened like a strip of chewing-gum between a child's fingers. The battery clock went on ticking with a desperate self-consciousness, like a man breaking wind in company; and the curtains twitched, but only just.

'I'll put . . . the kettle on,' said Joan.

'Momma,' Johnny said. 'No electricity. Ergo, no tea.'

'I wasn't thinking. I must be . . . tired.'

'We should be going,' Avril said. She was sorry now.

'And let the two of you get back to . . . to . . .' said Johnny, whose erection was beginning to subside.

'We were just chatting,' said Harry.

'We were . . . reminiscing,' Joan said.

'That's the great thing about power cuts,' said Harry. 'They give you time to talk. You're not just sitting like a zombie in front of the goggle box. And when you go to bed, you can't even remember what you were watching. No, your mother and I were talking. Looking back. There's so much to look back at. And to look forward to, of course.'

'We were remembering your blanket, Johnny. Johnny had a blanket, Avril. He was only a toddler at the time. People kept showering him with toys, you know the sort of cuddly bears people buy. But he couldn't be bothered with any of them. All he wanted was his dirty old blanket. He wouldn't sleep without it. He even took it to Montessori in his satchel.'

'And the games he used to play,' said Harry. 'With his marbles and his toy soldiers. He'd line them up at one end of the room and aim at them with his marble from the other end. You should have seen the skirting board. Chips here, chips there, chips everywhere. Great years. The best years. We were looking back . . . at it all.'

'You can spend hours . . . looking back,' said Joan.

'Ages. A lifetime.'

'We didn't even notice it was getting . . .'

'Dark all around us.'

'We were so engrossed,' Joan said.

Johnny was furious. Furious, yet contrite too. His erection had collapsed.

'Well,' he said, 'we don't want to break up the party. Or is it a seance?' Blankets and marbles. How could they do this to him? And what chance was there now of Avril's stretching herself across his lap in her nurse's uniform? Bugger all. She would want to talk about his childhood.

'Tell him off, Mrs O Moorithe,' Avril said. 'He needs a good clip on his ear.'

'Your predecessor set a high standard when it came to that sort of thing,' Harry said.

'Pater,' said Johnny, 'missing Benny Hill is no excuse for rudeness.'

'Do you watch Benny Hill, Mr O Moorithe?' said Avril.

'Who,' he replied, 'is Benny Hill?'

'Oh, you'd love him. He's a panic. A bit saucy, but he makes you laugh. Johnny says he's a dirty old man, but I like him.'

Harry decided Avril was all right. But Johnny's despair had deepened.

'What are we doing here, standing in the darkness?' he said.

'Power cuts make you queer,' his mother said.

'Andiamo,' Johnny decided. 'Avril Airlines announce a flight departure.'

'Where are you off to?' Harry said. He wanted Avril to go on talking about Benny Hill. In a strange way, he found it rather arousing.

'We're off to *The Seventh Heaven*,' Johnny said.

'I'd go there like a shot if I knew where to find it,' said Harry.

'I should have rang my folks,' Avril said.

'Ring from the club.'

'Stay a bit,' Harry said. 'It's early. Please.'

'Sure what's your hurry?' Joan said.

The truth is, Harry was a little afraid of being left alone with Joan. Why had she started all that nonsense about blankets and cuddly toys? And Joan was a little more than afraid of being left alone with Harry. By now, the ice-cubes would have melted in the freezer, and Harry hated his whiskey without at least three ice-cubes.

'There'll be lights any minute now,' said Harry. 'You'll see. You could even watch that programme you were talking about.'

But Johnny stood his ground.

'Adieu, farewell, remember us.'

'I suppose I'd better . . .' Avril said.

'Do stay,' said Joan. And she prayed for the lights to come on; she prayed against the darkness which was so bewildering.

'A firm and final Ciao,' Johnny said. It delighted him to hear his parents begging. Openly begging. His erection began to stir again.

'Wear your safety belts,' his father said, giving up and giving in.

'We'll take every precaution,' Johnny said. He could get a newspaper at the corner shop. Unless it were closed because of the power cut. Anyhow, there were dozens of newsagents along the route to the club.

'See you,' said Avril, who had seen neither of them.

'That's right,' Johnny said. 'We'll see you in a different light in future.'

And the two of them left, just like that.

When the hall door slammed shut, there was a short silence. I am not going to talk about the battery clock or the curtains because that point has been well and truly established, and you can imagine it for yourself. After all, we are in this together.

'So,' said Joan.

'Well?'

'Hmm?'

'Nothing,' said Harry.

'Nice child.'

'I should have rang.'

'Who?' said Joan.

'Rang. It's wrong. It should be rung.'

'What?'

'Never mind.'

He had not thought of the whiskey or the ice-cubes yet. Perhaps there was still time.

'She's very confident,' Joan said.

'I like her.'

'That's a bit of a U-turn.'

'She's very . . . feminine.'

Joan was thunderstruck. Harry had always doted on Shelley, though he tended to mistake her surname and call her Winters instead of Brennan.

'Is there a full moon tonight?' she asked him.

Harry came clean. One tends to do that in the darkness.

'I liked what she said about Benny Hill. It was natural.'

'I think we're all going mad,' Joan said.

But Harry had made up his mind, the way Joan made up her face: slowly and deliberately.

'Yes,' he said. 'She's more natural than Shelley.'

It was more than a decision. It was a conviction. Harry felt he owed himself a drink. A double, at that. And why not? Who was there to see? So he edged along the sofa in the general direction of the kitchen.

'Damn it, damn it, Harry, look at that! You've knocked the candle! It must have dripped wax all over the carpet.'

'So what?' said Harry. 'It'll come off.'

'It'll come off? All on its ownie own, I suppose?'

'Would you ever calm down?' Harry shouted.

'It won't just "come off",' Joan sobbed. 'I'll get it off. On my hands and knees, that's how.'

'Isn't there a pill you could take?' said Harry. He had just remembered that the freezer would be off and the ice-cubes melted. What was a whiskey without an ice-cube? A gin without a tonic, that was what.

'And it stinks the whole house,' Joan said. She was weeping now. It was so bloody typical. She made the effort for strangers. For her own husband it was a different matter. All hell broke loose once the hall door heaved to.

'Blankets,' Harry spat. 'What in Christ's name were you doing talking about blankets?'

'You were worse,' she wept. 'You were worse with your marbles.'

'Eight o'clock,' Harry said between clenched teeth. 'Eight o'clock. The bastards. They said eight o'clock we'd be out of danger.'

'I know,' Joan shouted at him. 'I know.'

'Mussolini was right. Shoot every last manjack. To hell with them. To hell with the whole lot of them.'

And the lights came on. Delicate white lace curtains blew in the air of the open window; and from the kitchen, above the hum of the peach-coloured fridge, Harry and Joan could hear the fragile sound of the battery clock, with a noise like matchsticks breaking. For a brief moment, husband and wife looked at each other: the man with the stained moustache and the tiny crack in the lens of his spectacles; the woman in her housecoat with needle and thread stuck into the linen lapel, and the bright, brown hair with grey at its roots. For as long as the moment lasted, they longed for the darkness. But it passed, as all unendurable things must. Light was one thing, illumination another. That was a word to be kept strictly for Christmas.

'Well, glory be,' said Joan.

'The power of prayer,' said Harry.

'Just like that.'

'All's well that ends well.'

'I'd better go round the house,' said Joan anxiously. 'I left lights on all over the place.'

'May light perpetual shine upon us!' said Harry. It would only take an hour or so for the cubes to congeal again. 'What time is it?'

'Ten to nine,' said Joan.

'Goodo. I'll get the last ten minutes of Benny Hill. And there's Dallas at ten. Is it tonight is Dallas night?'

'Don't you know well it is?'

'We're set so. Crisis averted.'

'Right as rain.'

'Right as rain,' Harry agreed.

'High and dry,' said Joan, as she turned off the overhead light and one of the side-lamps.

'High and dry,' Harry repeated. 'Or is it home and dry? I'm always getting the two of them mixed up.'

Joan banged the window shut, and the curtains stood stock-still. Harry was pressing the buttons on the television remote control. The noise of the stations swelled above the sound of the battery clock.

MARY MORRISSY

'The Cantilever Principle'

'Trussed-up', my father was saying, 'like a chicken. Oven-ready!' He beamed at me, grateful for my indulgence – I had heard the story several times over – then turned back to Sam.

'They daubed this stuff on me, like washing-up liquid. Rubbed it on neat – all over!'

'By the prettiest nurse, no doubt, Jack!' Uncle Sam winked extravagantly.

They were like boys again, gleeful with reprieve. Sam, snowy-haired, with a grizzled jaw, and my father, propped up on the pillows, his face ripe and waxy as a windfallen apple. The danger had passed. We were safely allowed our gaiety. Indeed, it was necessary because we had so nearly lost him. We lost my mother – early. For years he had measured time by her death. That was, he would say, puckering his brow, that was just before we lost your mother. That was his word for it. Lost.

I cannot remember her now except as a collection of sensations cut adrift – the smell of cold cream, the steady thump of another heart, a benign shape leaning over me as a prelude to embrace. He was generous with details of her. They had met at a tea dance at the Metropole. She was a good deal younger than him. He had been accused of cradle-snatching. They had walked out together for eight months. Her family did not approve. After they were married his landlady let her move in. Then there was the flat by the canal before they bought a home – here. This other world that they belonged to, grey and grainy, the one before I was born, this was where I was convinced my mother was lost. I identified the year as 1947, the worst winter on record, and pictured her wandering in a blizzard in the wrap-around coat and angora beret she wore in those long-ago holiday snaps. These seemed always to be taken in winter, at the edge of cliffs, my mother's hair wild around her face, her teeth chattering with cold through a brave smile. My father, it has to be said, looks pretty goofy in these pictures. The short-back-and-sides haircut, his large ears, a gormless sort of smile. He has improved with age. Whereas she seems perfect then, for then, as if she somehow knew . . . but, no, that's ascribing premonition to mere candour for the camera.

Of her death he would not speak. A brain haemorrhage. My only guide is Mrs Parfitt. He had left for work. And where was I? Somewhere out of the picture. My mother is sitting over the debris of breakfast things. It is a wan April morning aching to be spring. She is gazing out the kitchen window, elbows propped on the table, one hand clasping a cup of luke-warm tea. Suddenly there is an intruder who strikes her one blow on the temple sending everything spinning. The cup leaps from her hand, a plate slides off the edge of the table. She tries to rise but her arm buckles beneath her, crumpling the waxed folds of the oiled cloth and rattling the teapot. Her last view is of the mocking darkness of its spout. My father finds her at lunchtime, face bathed in milk, crumbs in her hair, dried blood around her ear. He thinks she has passed out or, comically, has fallen asleep. He leaves her be and calls a neighbour – the inner workings of women are no business of his. *She* knows.

'She's dead, Mr Eustace,' Mrs Parfitt says, 'your wife is dead.' Here, she says, here at this very table.

Without a mother, not only death, but birth, too, was a mystery. We found you in a basket on the canal, my father used to say. I liked the 'we' in this; for the first time it included me. And it beat those stories about cabbage leaves. I could imagine this. The pair of them walking along the towpath near the gasworks and finding a Moses basket in the green, scummy water by the bank. My mother (wearing the same hat and coat; there are no costume changes for her) lifts me out carefully.

'Ah look,' she says, 'look at the wee mite.'

I am wearing a long white christening robe.

'John, just look.'

She hoists me up on her shoulder and turns around so that he is looking directly into my eyes. Was it then it started – this fierce, reluctant attachment?

She swings around, her voice brimming with excitement and says: 'Shall we keep her?' as if it's the most reckless, daring adventure they have ever considered.

My father says yes.

Hospital time is different. Elongated. It was – is – high summer but already the recent gusty, blue-bright days and cool, lilac evenings belong to a carefully delineated past. Even the heartbreaking sunsets, melancholy and grand, which accompanied my vigil, now seem like the fevered reproduction of some long distant memory. A by-pass. Appropriate surgery for the man. My father, the engineer. Bridges were his thing. During school holidays we made pilgrimages to them. I remember a misty January evening standing reverentially by the Forth Bridge which rose like a giant brontosaurus out of the still waters.

'The cantilever principle,' my father said importantly. 'See, the three spans.' He pointed, one hand on my shoulder. 'They each stand separately but when projected towards each other they form a bridge. Stress against stress.'

I was terrified that he would die.

'Don't worry,' Sam had said, 'he's a hardy one.' But the warning signs, once glimpsed, will never go away. His breathlessness, the alarming puce of his cheeks, the panic in his eye. I had seen them all and knew the cold, hard dread they induced in me. I grew to hate him for his frailty. I despised him when he gasped for air. I turned away, ashamed, when he clutched his chest in pain. I told myself he was pretending, doing it for effect, and that sympathy would only make him weaker. He had deceived me. His robust good health all these years had been a sham. He had secretly been cultivating the germ of his own death.

Intensive Care. My father adrift somewhere while all around him gadgets did his struggling for him. There was a bleeping green monitor and the noisy shuffling of a ventilator. Narrow tubes snaked in under the bedclothes and a bulbous bag of intravenous drip stood sentry at the bedhead. It reminded me of the pictures of bridges he collected, all huge beams and girders and in between the steel and metal latticework, a tiny train trapped.

The hardware hid him from me; all his fear and helplessness put on hold.

'It's quite normal,' one of the nurses assured me, 'we keep them heavily sedated. Lessens the likelihood of rejection.'

For days I sat by his bedside or paced up and down the phlegm-coloured corridors. The light there was dull and dead as if it, too, had been etherized. And the noise – like the muted clamour of a penitentiary. The wheeling and droning of cleaners, the rattle of trolleys shivering with instruments, the clangour of bed pans, gave way to periods of forsaken quiet. At night, after visiting hour, it seemed as if we were on board a ghostly liner, abandoned and adrift. Sometimes I would go to the Day Room. A television with the sound turned down was perched high on a ledge. Animated faces on the screen mouthed messages to the silent room. Several patients would be slumped in the leatherette armchairs which broke wind when they sat down. Their slippers chafed the shiny lino.

Some of them had crude crosses in gentian violet daubed on their faces to mark where they'd been treated. It was also a cancer hospital.

That must have been what he had. My friend. That's what I thought of him as, although we never spoke. He was in the ward opposite the intensive care unit, his bed just inside the door. He was a young man, the same age as me, perhaps. He lay on the bed in pyjama bottoms and a dressing gown, open and stranded around his waist. There was, to look at him, no sign of illness except for the shaved rectangle at his temple. Beneath the hurtful ridge of his brow his eyes were sunken, fogged-looking, slow to register, and yet, I had the feeling that I was being watched intensely. He was stricken on one side. Above his head like a noose, a tubular triangle hung. With one arm he used this to manoeuvre himself in the bed. He moved his good leg constantly, grinding his heel against the bedclothes like the restless kicking of a baby. Everything about him was like a baby. The awful trustfulness of his gaze. The little identity tag around his wrist with those bare details with which he had come into the world – his name, his date of birth. He seemed utterly defenceless and alone.

And yet, he was not alone. A woman, Miriam (I gave her a name, but never him), came daily, kissing him on the forehead before settling down in a chair beside his bed. She moved with what seemed like exaggerated care as if any sudden gesture might startle him. He watched her silently, following her about wonderingly with his eyes. He would grasp her hand, rubbing his fingers on her knuckles as if touch were new to him. I could hear her speak soothingly to him.

Intimacy is shocking in a hospital, absurd amidst the starch and clatter, and *their* tenderness, especially, seemed alien. But I couldn't take my eyes off them. She drew things from a crowded tote bag like a conjurer desperate to please. She brought flowers which she carefully arranged in a jug beside the bed. Once she sellotaped a child's drawing to the side of his locker. She fed him, handing him a cup with a straw in it to drink from. She wiped his mouth. She peeled fruit for him – oranges, bananas – holding them up in front of him before clamping his fingers firmly around them. It was like watching a mother and child. I felt as I do when women breastfeed in public. The fear of other people's nakedness.

I never wanted to know any more about him except what I could learn from watching. Perhaps I knew the bargain I was about to make. His life for one I valued more.

'And at last Pharaoh made a proclamation to the whole of his people: Whenever a male child is born, cast it into the river, keep only the girls alive. And now one of the descendants of Levi wooed and married a woman of his own clan, who conceived and bore him a son. So winning were the child's looks that for three months she kept him hidden away; then, unable to conceal him any longer, she took a little basket of reeds, which she smeared with clay and pitch, and in this put her baby son down among the bulrushes on the river bank . . .'

On the third day there was a change in my father's condition. I detected this only by a certain change in the atmosphere, an added grim bustle in the room. The nurses, usually chatty and given to small talk, instead conferred with one another at the door casting anxious glances in my direction. They made what seemed to be futile adjustments to the equipment, picked up my father's lumpen hand to get a pulse with an air of resignation, leafed through his charts as if searching for some clue to his condition they'd overlooked. I didn't ask them, of course, what they thought was wrong. I was too afraid. 'Not responding,' was a phrase I overheard.

Meanwhile in the ward opposite, my friend was celebrating. He was in a wheelchair by the bed, a rug thrown over his legs. Above him, hanging from the curtain rails was an array of balloons and streamers, and Miriam was stringing together a loop of cards behind his bed. It was his birthday. In the afternoon visiting hour, a gang of people arrived. They drew up in a circle around him. Some perched on the bed, others stood. There was the popping of corks and a rush of paper cups to catch the foaming champagne. There were bursts of raucous laughter, an air of triumph.

'Come on,' someone called out to one of the nurses, 'join the party!'

'Ye'll all be thrown out,' she warned mockingly.

A loud 'awh' from the group.

I couldn't see him in the midst of them but I imagined him there smiling jaggedly, drunk with memory. When the visitors' bell rang at four they wheeled him recklessly out of the ward and down the corridor towards the Day Room, whooping and singing – 'Happy birthday to you, happy birthday to you, happy birthday dear . . .' The swing doors closed behind them.

Three a.m. Condition, stable. They had told me to go home but I wouldn't. I didn't trust them. I was a nuisance, I knew that, prowling around, nervously alert from lack of sleep and haunted by unspoken fears. Even Sam had got irritated.

'Don't do the martyr on us. For God's sake, go home. There's nothing you can do here,' he had said when he left at midnight. He was right; there was nothing I could do – there or anywhere else. But I thought that any sudden movement of mine might precipitate disaster. As long as I was there, nothing could happen to him.

There is something sacred about those early hours of the morning. A hush. It isn't difficult to see why death comes then, how it gains easeful entry when the defences of the world are down. The graveyard hours. If Dad makes it through these, I thought, he will make it through another day. It was then I remembered my friend. I slipped out of Intensive Care and crossed the corridor. He too was sleeping. It was a warm night and he had thrown off all the bedclothes except for a sheet swaddled around his groin. In the blue light his limbs looked startlingly beautiful; there were perfect half-moons on all his fingernails.

A breeze sighed softly at the open window. I thought of wind among rushes. It would be easy now to push him forth out into the calm waters of the night in this, the easeful hour. I laid my hand on his pillow. There would be no struggle. In his slumber he would barely notice the gentle rocking of the basket. He was the boy-child, the one who must be sacrificed. And, in return, my father would be saved. Take him, I urged the darkness, take *him*.

By the next morning my father was awake, in a different ward, the hardware all removed. He smiled sheepishly at me as I came in, as if he'd been away on a drunken binge.

'I'm sorry,' he said weakly, 'for giving you a fright.'

'You had us worried, you old dog,' Sam said, 'we'd thought you'd given up the ghost. Isn't that right, Kate?'

For days, almost a week, I dared not see my friend. It was easy to avoid him. His ward was on the floor below and I did not have to pass it now. Only when my father could leave his bed did I have the courage to venture down. I walked along the familiar corridor, halting at his doorway. The bed was empty, the locker cleared. The child's drawing had been torn roughly from its spot leaving only a corner scrap. The coverlet on the bed did not even bear the outline of his body.

'Gone, my dear,' a nurse said as she bustled past.

I did not – could not – ask what she meant by gone.

I watch out for him on the street now. Certain men remind me of him. I see them in pubs, on trains, in buses, and my heart leaps. I am about to rush up to them when they turn around and reveal themselves as imposters. Anyway, I know it's all in vain. I know the price that's been exacted. I *know* that I will never see him again.

RODDY DOYLE

from *The Snapper*

On the Tuesday morning after Larrygogan joined the family, in the middle of week eleven, Sharon got an awful fright when she was climbing out of bed, just waking up. Her period had started.

– Oh no!—Oh God—

She'd been robbed.

But then she remembered: she'd read in the book that this could happen. It wasn't a real period. It probably wasn't a real period.

She stayed at home in bed and waited. She lay there, afraid to move too much. She tried to remember the Hail Mary but she couldn't get past Hello Be Thy Name, and anyway, she didn't believe in it, not really; so she stopped trying to remember the rest of it. It was just something to do. She wanted to turn on her side but she was afraid to. She just lay there and she started saying Please please please please all the time to herself. She kept everything else out of her mind. She concentrated on that.

– Please please please please.

The book was right. It didn't last long. It wasn't the same. It wasn't a real period at all. She was still pregnant.

– Aah! Jaysis!!

Veronica put the skirt on the table and got up to see what was wrong in the hall. But before she got to the door Jimmy Sr came hopping into the kitchen with one of his leather slippers in his hand.

– What happened? said Veronica.

– The dog's after shitein' in the fuckin' hall an' I fuckin' stood in it, that's wha' happened.

– On the floor?

– No. On the fuckin' ceilin'. Jesus!

He hopped over to the sink and put the slipper under the tap. Veronica came back from the hall.

– It's comin' off alrigh', Jimmy Sr told her.

– What about the carpet?

– The twins'll be cleanin' tha', don't worry. An' the sink here.

– It's disgusting, said Veronica.

Jimmy Sr inspected the slipper. It was grand and clean again. He threw it on the floor and stepped into it.

– Ah, he's only a pup, he said.

– He'll have to go. They're not training him properly.

– Give him a chance, Veronica. You'll be expectin' the poor little bollix to eat with a knife an' fork next.

Veronica gave up and got back to the skirt. She was just finishing Linda's and then she had Tracy's to do.

Jimmy Sr saw the twins out in the back. They were trying to get Larrygogan to catch a burst plastic football but Larrygogan was having problems staying upright. If the ball landed on him Jimmy Sr thought it would kill him. The grass needed cutting. Larrygogan kept disappearing in it.

Jimmy Sr opened the back door.

– Get in here, you-is!

Sharon woke up and she knew she was going to be sick.

She was hunched down at the toilet bowl. There was sweat, getting cold, on her face. She shivered. More puke, not much now – hardly any – rushed into her mouth.

– Yu – hh—!

It dropped into the water and she groaned. She squeezed her eyes shut. She wiped them, then her nose, and her eyes again. She stood up carefully. She was cold.

– Are yeh alrigh' in there, Sharon?

It was Jimmy Sr.

– Yeah, she said. – Ou' in a minute.

– No hurry, Jimmy Sr assured her. – I was in already.

Sharon rubbed her arms. A wave of horribleness ran through her.

She gagged. She really felt terrible, and weak. She leaned against the wall. It was cool; nice. She knew she wasn't going to be sick again. This morning.

She thought about nothing.

– Are yeh stayin' in there, or wha'?

It was the other Jimmy.

Sharon unlocked the door.

– What's your fuckin' hurry? she said.

Jimmy Jr looked at her face.

– Wha' were you drinkin' last nigh'? he asked.

Sharon passed him. She was going back to bed. That was where she wanted to be. The twins looked at her.

– Are yeh not well, Sharon? Linda asked her.

– No, said Sharon.

– That'll be the flu, said Linda.

Tracy agreed with her.

– There's a bug goin' around, she said. – Cover yourself up properly.

They went downstairs to get a cup of tea and a bit of dry toast for Sharon. Sharon rubbed her legs. Only her forehead was cold now.

Well, she was pregnant now alright. She pressed her stomach gently: still nothing, but she was on her way. She smiled, but she hoped to God it wasn't going to be like this every morning.

When she took her hand away from her stomach – probably because she didn't feel sick any more – she noticed that her skin there was kind of sore, a bit like sunburn but not nearly as bad. She pressed again: yeah, the same. She tried her tits.

– Ouw! –

She'd been half-aware of that soreness for a few days but it was only now, because she'd just been sick, that she paid proper attention and linked it to being pregnant. They used to get a bit sore before her periods, but now – God, it was all starting to happen.

She'd have to tell her friends now; no, soon.

Jesus.

Tracy ran in.

– Ma said to say if yeh keep not goin' to work you'll be sacked an' jobs don't grow on trees.

– Tell her I'll be down in a little while.

Linda came in. She had Larrygogan with her.

– Larrygogan wants to say Howyeh.

She brought him over to Sharon's bed so he could lick Sharon's face. Sharon lifted her head for him.

– Hiyeh, Larry.

He stared at her. Linda put him right up to Sharon's nose.

– Kiss her, she said.

Nothing happened.

– Kiss her, will yeh.

– Give us a kiss, Larry, said Sharon.

– Daddy said we're to call him his whole name so he'll know who he is, said Tracy.

– He kisses us, Linda told Sharon. – Tracy, doesn't he?

– Yeah.

– He doesn't really know me yet, that's all, said Sharon. – Bring him back down now, will yeh.

– Okay. Come on, Larrygogan.

Linda ran out.

– Tracy, will yeh tell Mammy I'm gettin' up now, said Sharon.

She sat up.

– Ah, said Tracy. – Do yeh not have the flu?

– No.

– Ah janey.

She sounded very disappointed.

– Wha'? said Sharon.

– I wanted to catch it off yeh, an' so did Linda.

Sharon laughed.

– Why?

– Don't want to do the majorettes annymore, said Tracy. – It's stupid.

– I thought yis liked it.

– No. We used to. But it's stupid.

– Why is it? Sharon asked.

– It's just stupid, said Tracy. – She won't let us be in the front.

– Why won't she?

– Don't know.—She hates us. It's prob'ly cos Daddy called her a wagon at tha' meetin'.

Sharon laughed. She got out of bed.

– He didn't really call Miss O'Keefe a wagon, she told Tracy. – He was only messin' with yeh.

Tracy continued.

– Nicola 'Malley's in the front an' she's nearly always droppin' her stick an' me an' Linda only drop ours sometimes.

– It's not fair, sure it's not, said Sharon.

Tracy followed her into the bathroom.

– No, she agreed. – The last time Nicola 'Malley threw her stick through the fuckin' window.

Sharon nearly bit the top off her toothbrush.

– Tracy!

– It just came ou'.—She did though, Sharon.

– An' is she still in the front row?

– Yeah. It's not fair.—An' the music's stupid.

They were back in the bedroom.

– What is it? Sharon asked.

– Don't know. A woman singin' Moll-ee My Irish Moll-ee, or somethin'. Miss O'Keefe thinks it's brilliant but it's thick.

Jimmy Sr shouted from downstairs.

– Are yeh ready for a lift, Sharon?

– Nearly.

– Make it snappy, will yeh.

He strolled back into the kitchen. Veronica was the only one still in there.

– Cummins is comin' ou' to have a look at the plasterin' this mornin' an' we've still got one o' the rooms to do, Jimmy Sr told her.

– Did you mention about a job for Leslie to him? Veronica asked him.

– Not yet. I will but. Today.

– Mm, said Veronica.

– I will now, Jimmy Sr assured her. – Scout's honour. Is he up yet?

– Not at all.

– We'll have to put a stop to tha'.

He picked up his sandwiches.

– Wha' are they? he asked.

– It's a surprise.

– It's not Easy Slices, is it?

Veronica turned to the sink.

– Is it? It is. Ah Jaysis, Veronica! How many times –!?

Linda came in from the back.

– Does the dog like sandwiches, does he? Jimmy Sr asked her.

And he lobbed the tinfoil pack out the door into the back garden.

It was the thirteenth week of Sharon's pregnancy and the middle of May, but it was cold.

– It's fuckin' freezin', said Jimmy Sr, and he was right.

Any time now, Sharon knew, and the real swelling would start. But she kept putting off telling the girls. Twice in the last week she'd gone down to the Hikers and she was definitely going to tell them. But she didn't. She couldn't.

She could've told them she was pregnant. That wouldn't have been too bad, not all that embarrassing really. But it was the big question that would come after that – WHO? – that was what she couldn't face.

But she'd have to tell them sooner or later and, judging by what she'd been reading, it would have to be sooner.

She struggled through her book. She read forward into the weeks ahead. Parts of it terrified her. She learned that the veins in her rectum might become painful. She was sure she felt a jab just after she'd read that.

She might get varicose veins. Or nosebleeds. Better than iffy rectum veins, she thought. Oedema sounded shocking. She could see herself filling up with water and bouncing around. Larrygogan would claw her and she'd have a puncture.

All these things were bad but when she read about eclampsia she went to the toilet and got sick. She shook and shivered for ages after it. She read it again: protein in the urine – blurred vision – severe headaches – hospital – swelling of face and fingers – she read it very slowly this time   —eclampsia   —convulsions   —coma   ——death. She was going to catch it, she knew it. She always got the flu and colds when they were going around. She didn't mind the protein in her urine, or even the blurred vision so much. It was the word Convulsions that got to her.

So much could go wrong. Even when it was okay there seemed to be nothing but secretions and backache and constipation. And she'd thought there was no more to it than getting bigger and then having it and maybe puking a few times along the way.

Still, nothing was going wrong so far. The book said there might be vomiting in the mornings, and there was – not every morning though. The book said her breasts would be tender. She'd always thought that that was another word for Good when you were talking about meat but she looked for it in Darren's dictionary and that was what her tits were alright. They were still the same colour though. Her nipples were the same colour as well, although it was hard to tell for sure. They changed colour every day in the bathroom mirror.

She started doing sit-up exercises and touching her toes when she got home from work. They'd make carrying the extra weight easier. As well as that the exercises helped to squeeze water from the pore spaces in her blood vessels. But the book didn't say what happened to the water after that. Sometimes she forgot about the exercises though, and sometimes she just didn't feel like it; she was too knackered. Anyway, she was tall and quite strong and she always walked straight, so she didn't think the exercises mattered that much. She really did them because she wanted to do everything right, and the book said she should do them.

She was drinking a lot of milk. She was eating oranges. She kept reminding herself to go to a chemist's and get vitamin pills. She was eating All-Bran four times a week.

— What's tha' stuff like, Sharon? Jimmy Sr asked her one morning she'd the time to eat her breakfast sitting down.

— Horrible, said Sharon.

— Does it work?

— Sort of, yeah.

— Ah well, that's the main thing, isn't it?—You don't need it, sure yeh don't?

He was talking under the table to Larrygogan.

She kept eating the celery and the carrots. The right food was hard and boring and it took ages to eat but Sharon thought she was doing things the right way, and that pleased her. And excited her. She felt as if she was getting ready, packing to go somewhere — for good. And that frightened her a bit.

She felt her stomach. It was harder and curved, becoming like a shell or a wall.

She'd definitely have to tell the girls.

It was Tuesday morning. It was raining. There was war going on downstairs in the kitchen.

Linda and Tracy put the table between themselves and their mother.

— What's wrong now? Jimmy Sr wanted to know. — Can a man not eat his bit o' breakfast in peace?

— It's stupid, Ma, said Linda.

— Yeah, said Tracy.

— Mammy! said Veronica.

— Mammy, said Linda. — It's stupid.

— I don't care, said Veronica. — I spent hours making those skirts for you two little rips —

— They're stupid, said Linda.

She hadn't meant to say that. She knew she'd made a mistake but she hated those skirts, especially her own one.

Veronica roared.

— Aaah!

The hours she'd wasted; cutting, clipping, sewing, making mistakes, starting again.
Jimmy Sr threw his knife and fork onto the plate.

— Wha' kind of a fuckin' house is this at all? he asked the table.

He looked at Veronica. She was deciding if she'd throw the marmalade at the twins.

— A man gets up in the mornin', said Jimmy Sr. — an' — an' —

— Oh shut up, said Veronica.

— I will not shut up, said Jimmy Sr. — A man gets up —

— Hi-dee-hi, campers, Jimmy Jr greeted them all when he came into the kitchen.

— Fuck off, Jimmy Sr shouted.

Jimmy Jr looked down at Jimmy Sr.

— Do yeh not love me annymore, Daddy?

— Yeh sarcastic little prick, yeh, said Jimmy Sr. — If —

— Stop that language, said Veronica.

— I'm only startin', said Jimmy Sr.

— Miss O'Keefe said yeh should be ashamed of yourself, Linda told Jimmy Sr.

This interested Jimmy Sr.

— What? said Veronica.

Darren came in and sat down and started eating Sugar-Puffs.

— They're ours, said Tracy.

— So? said Darren.

— When did, eh, Miss O'Keefe say tha' to yis? Jimmy Sr asked.

— Last week.

— Yeah, said Tracy.

— WHY did she say it? Veronica asked.

— Yeh took the words righ' ou' of me mouth, said Jimmy Sr.

— When Tracy said wha' you said, Linda told him.

— You said it as well! said Tracy.

— I did not!

— Girls, girls, said Jimmy Sr. — Wha' happened? Exactly.

He looked at Veronica. She looked away.

— She told everyone to say wha' our mammies an' our daddies said to each other tha' mornin'.

— Oh my God! said Veronica.

Jimmy Jr started laughing. Darren was listening now as well.

— An' it was real borin' cos they were all sayin' things like Good mornin' dear an' Give us the milk.—An' Tracy said wha' you said to Mammy.

She looked at Tracy. Tracy was going to kill her.

Veronica sat down.

— An' would yeh by any chance remember wha' I said to your mammy? Jimmy Sr asked.

— Yeah.

— Well? What was it?

— Yeh pointed ou' the window—at the rainin' —

She pointed at the window.

— An' then yeh said—

Jimmy Jr laughed. He remembered.

– Go on, said Jimmy Sr.

– You said It looks like another fuck of a day.

Jimmy Jr howled. So did Darren. Jimmy Sr tried not to.

Veronica put her hands to her face and slowly dragged her fingers down over her cheeks. Her mouth was open.

– Oh sweet Jesus, she said then, to no one.

Sharon came in.

– Hiyis, said Sharon. – What're yis laughin' at?

– There's Sharon, said Jimmy Sr. – How are yeh, Sharon?

– Grand.

– Good.—Good.

He started laughing.

– Serves her righ', the nosey brasser.

Jimmy Jr, Darren and the twins laughed. Jimmy Sr grinned at Veronica.

– Listen, he said to the twins. – If she asks yis again today tell her –

– No!

That was Veronica.

The Rabbittes laughed.

– What're yis laughin' at? Sharon still wanted to know.

– You, said Jimmy Jr.

Sharon gave him a dig.

– Mammy, you can give the skirts to the poor people, said Linda.

This tickled Jimmy Sr.

– What's this? said Jimmy Jr.

– None o' your business, said Jimmy Sr.

– What poor people? said Veronica.

– The Ethiopians, said Jimmy Jr.

Linda and Tracy giggled.

– I think that's a lovely idea, Linda, said Jimmy Sr. – Fair play to yeh.

– Stop encouraging them, said Veronica.

– Stop? said Jimmy Sr, shocked. – Well now, I hope Miss O'Keefe doesn't hear abou' this. My God, wha'. The twins's mother won't let them show a bit o' charity to those less fortunate than –

– Stop that!

Darren was in stitches. He loved it when his da talked like that.

– I'm sure there's a couple o' piccaninnies –

– Daddy!

The boys laughed, cheering on Jimmy Sr. The twins were still giggling, and looking at their mammy.

—in a refugee camp somewhere that'd love a couple o' red lurex majorette's dresses. An' the sticks as well.

– You're not fit to be a father, said Veronica.

– Not now maybe, Jimmy Sr admitted.

He patted his gut.

– I used to be though, wha'.

He winked at Veronica. She growled at him. Jimmy Sr looked at the boys and raised his eyes to heaven.

– Women, wha'.

He lowered the last of his tea. Then he heard something, a scraping noise.

– What's tha'?

– Larrygogan, said Tracy. – He wants to come in.

Linda opened the door. Larrygogan, even smaller than usual because his hair was stuck down by the rain, was standing on the step.

– Come on, Larrygogan, said Linda.

Larrygogan couldn't make it. He fell back twice. They laughed.

– The poor little sappo, said Jimmy Sr.

Linda picked him up and carried him in and put him down on the floor. He skidded a bit on the lino, then shook himself and fell over.

Then he barked.

The Rabbittes roared laughing. Jimmy Sr copied Larrygogan.

– Yip! Yip!

He looked at his watch.

– Oh good shite!

He was up, and grabbed his sandwiches.

– Are yeh righ', Sharon?—Wha' are they, he asked Veronica.

– Corned beef.

– Yippee.—Good luck now. See yeh tonigh'.

He wondered if he should kiss Veronica on the cheek or something because they were both in a good mood at the same time. But no, he decided, not with the boys there. They'd slag him.

– Da, can I've a bike for me birth'y? Darren asked him.

– Yeh can in your hole, said Jimmy Sr.

– Ah, Da!

– Forget it, Sunshine.

Jimmy Sr waited for Sharon to go out into the hall first.

– Good girl.

He followed her.

– Hang on a sec, he said, at the front door.

He gave Sharon the keys of the van.

– Let yourself in.

Les thought it was a heart attack. He tried to scream, but he couldn't.

Jimmy Sr's hand was clamped tight over Les's face. He waited till Les was awake and knew what was happening.

– That's the front o' me hand, Jimmy Sr told Les.

He pushed Les's head deeper into the pillow.

– If yeh don't get up for your breakfast tomorrow like I told yeh you'll get the back of it. D'yeh follow?

Jimmy Sr took his hand off Les's face.

– Now get up, yeh lazy get, an' don't be upsettin' your mother.

He stopped at the door.

– I want to talk to you tonigh', righ'.

Downstairs, Jimmy Jr and Darren heard a snort. They looked and saw their mother crying. It was terrible. She was wiping tears from her eyes before they could get to her cheeks.

But she wasn't crying. She was laughing. She tried to explain why.

– They're not –

She started laughing again.

– They're not corned beef at all.

A giggle ran through her, and out.

– They're Easy Slices.

They didn't know what she was on about but they laughed with her anyway.

DERMOT BOLGER

from *The Journey Home*

From then on Pascal Plunkett rarely went anywhere in the daytime without me driving him in his BMW. In the fields beyond St Margaret's he had received planning permission to build two small terraces of houses. To reach them I had to turn off a narrow country lane and manoeuvre the car down a mud track with the tyre marks of earth movers deeply scored into its surface.

When Plunkett was in his office I spent my time out of the men's way in the garage forecourt cleaning the spattered mud from the car. Some days I still took lunch in the canteen there, a litany of licking noises trailing me as I left the room. But mostly I ate at the bar in Mother Plunkett's Cabin while he drank his ritual two neat Paddies from the fresh bottle placed at his elbow which he then topped with water before going over the previous night's takings with the manager. The pub was in two sections: the bar in front paved with flagstones like a scene from *The Quiet Man*, with old black-and-white photographs of Kerry lining the walls; the door of the cabaret lounge at the back was in the shape of a horseshoe and the green carpet had a design of gold stetsons and wagon wheels.

I was surely the worst driver he could have chosen. My only experience had been at dawn in Shay's Triumph Herald and frequently in those early weeks the BMW would cut out at traffic lights or I'd finally have to get out and let him park it in some narrow space. My inexperience with everything amused him: those inept sagas of reversing and stalling were the first occasions I had seen him in good humour. I'd watch him in the mirror letting me sweat until he decided to show me how to do it. Surprisingly he was a good teacher, better than Shay. I would think of the business clients he was keeping late as he sat beside me in the front until I had got the procedure perfect. A fortnight after I began driving him, in a sudden burst of confidence I came too quickly out of the driveway of Mother Plunkett's Cabin and had to swerve up on to the ditch to avoid an oncoming car. I slammed on the brakes and glanced nervously in the rear-view mirror. Pascal Plunkett was looking delightedly back at the furious motorist who had stopped behind us and was climbing out of his car. He hit me on the shoulder.

'Would you look at the sour face on that cunt. Drive on young Francy and stick to the road this time.'

All the way back into the garage he kept chuckling to himself and impersonating the motorist's indignant face until by the time we pulled into the forecourt I too was bent over the wheel with laughter. When he went inside I realized with a chill that for the first time since going to work for him I had enjoyed my morning.

I was spending less time in the garage and people elsewhere were getting used to me. In Plunkett Stores I glowered at the baby-faced manager who fidgeted nervously whenever I was there, terrified that I was discussing him with Plunkett. One evening my mother told me she had been there and he had insisted on pushing the trolley for her around the shelves. The men in the pub and on the building site were more casual and I began to make friends among them. I carried on a nervous but intense flirtation with the receptionist in the auctioneer's. The only place I hated was the undertaker's where some evenings when I walked in my mother would look up with pride from where she knelt with her bucket and scrubbing brush. My wages were better than in the Voters' Register but still not enough for her to give up work or stop making that weekly journey from his office to the post office and back. It was something she never mentioned though once I saw her across the street waiting for me to leave the forecourt before sneaking into his office.

Sometimes I gripped the wheel of his car with anger when I remembered my mother's face that day; yet in a curious way I had begun to admire Pascal. It was like he was a river in torrent and I wasn't strong enough to resist being swept along by the current. Since the confrontation in the canteen I had done everything he had asked without question, and he in turn had never raised his voice to me. I was seeing a side of his character which few people knew. As I drove along he would mimic with a vicious accuracy those people who managed his businesses. I saw how much he played along in the role which others had cast him in. He would storm off the building site, shouting back angrily at the foreman, and slam the car door, shouting for me to drive on. When we reached the tarmacadam I'd glance in the mirror and find his eyes waiting to spot mine, alive with amusement as though looking for applause for his performance.

He was gaining my trust slowly, introducing me to his empire, ensuring that everyone treated me with respect. I was like a fish, cautiously moving out from under a rock, and he was an angler gaining my trust, luring me further and further out. I had been driving him for a month when he orchestrated my next compromise. It was a morning in March and I was sitting in the car waiting for him to finish a meeting with two of his men, O'Brien and Flynn. They drifted from premises to premises, occasionally bouncers in the Abbey, sometimes even standing in for chauffeurs at the undertaker's. But mostly they just came and went after a few words with Plunkett. They were tough men whom I rarely spoke to. Even to be in the same room as them made me feel nervous. They came out of the garage and had climbed in the back of the car before I realized what was happening. I turned around.

'You're driving us today, Francis,' O'Brien said. 'Take a left at the lights there and just keep going straight.'

I drove towards Ballymun, listening to them casually discussing football behind me and admiring the women on the footpath. At the roundabout by the shopping centre they told me to go left and then turn in, across a rubble-strewn car-park till we stopped outside one of the tower blocks.

'Will you be long?' I asked.

'You're coming with us kid,' O'Brien replied, and when I hesitated he half-pulled me from the car.

Neither man spoke as we waited for the lift in the hallway. Two women came out with prams and we got in. It smelt of urine, the walls covered with IRA slogans, a crude picture of a penis painted on the inside of the doors.

'Time to earn your keep kid,' O'Brien said. 'Just like the rest of us.' From inside his pocket he produced a small pistol and pushed it into my hand. I was shaking so much I couldn't hold it. Flynn bent down to pick it up.

'I don't like it,' he said to O'Brien. 'Fucking working with kids. There's no need for him or for a shooter here.'

'You take your money, you take your instructions,' O'Brien replied sourly, taking the gun from me. He opened it to show me that it was empty, gripped my right hand firmly and placed it between my fingers. The lift stopped. He put his body in front of mine in case anybody was looking and stepped out into the empty corridor.

'Listen to me,' he said. 'There's nobody going to get hurt unless you fuck up. You just hold it inside your jacket so they can see a bulge. All you have to do is stand at the door and pretend to look tough – if that's possible. If the boss says you're to come along it's nothing to do with us.'

The lift behind me was closing. If I had run I might have reached it. I didn't. I turned and walked between them.

When the young woman opened the door slightly at his knock, O'Brien put his weight against it so that she fell back on to the floor. She scrambled up in her dressing-gown. She looked maybe twenty-two or three, still pretty but her face had lost its glow like a cake gone stale in a shop window. Her husband sat in a string vest and jeans on the sofa, his moustache making him look older.

'Ah Jesus lads,' he said. 'Could you not pick somebody rich to rob?'

His wife backed away towards the sofa. He rose and put his hand protectively about her shoulder.

'If there's robbers here don't look in this corner,' Flynn said. 'I'm just collecting for what we're owed. Ask your missis.'

She kept her head down while her husband looked at her.

'Oh God,' she said. 'Oh God.'

'What money? Jesus Christ Maria, what money do you owe them?'

His hands were shaking her now. She shook him off and stared into his face.

'Open your eyes Mick will you. Where do you think the money came from when Sharon was sick? You kept saying you'd be back at work when you were better. It wasn't much, Mick – only three loans of a hundred when we were desperate. Remember the time I told you the welfare gave me for the ESB. The fuckers gave me nothing. Nothing. I'd nowhere else to go. It's been eight months since you worked Mick. She was sick, you were sick. I kept thinking I could pay it back from the housekeeping when you got your job back.'

The man seemed to have forgotten us. It looked as if he was about to strike her. Then he stared at Flynn.

'I didn't know mate. Honest I didn't. I had a fall, off a scaffold. Been on disability ever since. You'll get it back, every penny. Just as soon as I'm well.'

O'Brien walked over to the small play-pen in the corner, set back a few inches from the wall that was discoloured by damp. The tiny girl inside it looked up at him with curious brown eyes. He looked back at me as though waiting for a nod from his boss, then picked the child up by the leg. He walked towards the balcony door with the screaming child. Her mother tried to run towards them but Flynn pushed her back on to the sofa and produced a steel bar from inside his coat. O'Brien turned the key on the door and stepped out into the air. He held the frantic child by one leg over the balcony and said in a calm voice:

'I'm going to count to fifty. After that you won't need to worry about her being sick again. Move once from that sofa and it'll be so much daughter under the bridge.'

The woman kept screeching her child's name like a prayer. The father just sat there, hands crossed over his chest like a laid-out corpse. Inside my jacket I gripped the gun. I was leaning against the door. If I'd tried to stand by myself I think I would have fallen. At thirty the woman ceased screaming and took her eyes off the balcony to stare desperately at me. I didn't want to look at her but I couldn't lower my eyes. We stared at each other as the count continued, our eyes filled with terror and disbelief. She was pleading with me, knowing there was no mercy in the two men. At fifty we both closed our eyes. O'Brien walked quietly back in and replaced the child in the play-pen.

'Twelve o'clock tomorrow. Don't be late,' he said, making his way towards the door. Flynn followed him. The woman had begun to sob. The men left the room and I was left staring at her. She looked up.

'Go on!' she screamed. 'Go on you bastard!'

No one spoke in the lift on the way down. O'Brien reached in and took the pistol from my jacket. The doors opened.

'A messy business,' Flynn said, almost to himself. 'No need for shooters or half of that carry on, whatever the fuck Plunkett's at.'

I had the car door open when it came over me. I raced down towards the tower block wall and vomited violently at the side of the steps. The men waited inside the car. My hands were so unsteady it took me several minutes to start the engine. We were almost at the garage when O'Brien spoke.

'I've two little ones myself,' he said. 'She was never safer than in my arms. Even if he told me to I wouldn't have dropped her.'

When I got home that night I climbed into bed. My sisters had moved in with my mother, my brothers into their room and I had the box-room to myself. I could hear children playing on the street outside. All I wanted to do was sleep, to stop trembling and forget that young woman's face. I felt dirty, as if my body was consumed by leprosy.

If I reached beneath the bedclothes I'd feel my skin peeling and rotten. I wanted to be back there, still with that gun in my hand, only loaded this time; wanted to aim it at O'Brien and Flynn; wanted to return to the garage, climb those wooden steps and aim it again at the wrinkled skin on Plunkett's face. In the darkness I could feel my finger squeezing the trigger and see his head explode in slow motion, splattering blood over the white wall behind him. I pulled that trigger again and again and still I couldn't feel clean.

I heard my mother listening out on the landing, anxious that I had eaten no dinner. I pulled the blankets over my face in case she came in. I told myself that I had a choice: I could flee the country, I could go to the police and tell them everything. But I knew I couldn't, knew that even the couple in the flat wouldn't back me up. And if I left I knew my mother's eyes, my sisters' voices would follow me anywhere I went. I tried to recall the figure who'd wandered through the night-time streets with Shay, but it was someone so different from the person who lay sweating in bed that it was too painful to think about. I woke next morning with sore eyes and a twisted feeling in my stomach. My sister Lisa was in the room holding a breakfast tray.

'Mummy says I'm to give you this and thank you for the lovely new dress and the shoes you bought for me. Well, she bought them, but you paid for them.'

She paused and peered more closely at me.

'Your eyes look real cranky, like an old fellow's.'

I got dressed, avoided my mother, closed the front door quietly and walked to Plunkett Motors.

I drove him in silence to the building site and the pub. At three o'clock that afternoon Eddie came out and told me to go to the office. Pascal Plunkett had a brown envelope on his desk. He counted out twenty ten-pound notes and ten fives and laid one of each in front of me.

'Don't be fooled by sob stories,' he said. 'That's the first lesson. People can always get it when they need to. That's yours, take it.'

'I don't want it.'

'You were there. You were a part of it. Whether you like it or not Francy you've earned it.'

We stared at each other, like those old games of statues in the Voters' Register, only this time it was deadly serious. In the end it was I who lowered my eyes and picked the money up. At the door I turned and asked bitterly why, if he was such a tough man, hadn't he got the full three hundred back. Pascal's laugh was different from the one I knew in the car.

'I did Francy, but sure I loaned her back fifty. We don't want to lose a good customer, do we?'

He was still laughing when I closed the door. Later that evening I put the fifteen pounds in a collection box for old people in my local newsagents. The girls behind the counter were stunned into silence but it didn't make me feel any less cheap as I walked on through the darkness towards the place I once called home.

At home I had grown more sullen. My sisters began to avoid me whereas once they had tumbled into my lap when I returned. At times I ventured back out to the pubs and snooker halls where Shay had reigned but I always felt uncomfortable, knowing that to people there I had been Shay's friend and nothing else. Sometimes I just walked the streets; sometimes I drank. Occasionally I hid in doorways to avoid meeting people from the Voters' Register and having to talk about the past.

Plunkett could sense the change in me. He knew how isolated I had become. I had grown to hate the hours lingering in the garage forecourt away from the men, and was happy when he suggested a more flexible arrangement. I began to come in at noon to drive him to Mother Plunkett's Cabin. Often, after the rounds of premises and the visits to offices in the city, I would find myself back in the Abbey for the last hour of opening time, drinking at the bar while the awful strains of a local talent contest came through the wall of the lounge. By now I too had acquired a briefcase and kept receipt books and invoices in it to remind him of them. But basically my job was still to drive. I'd finish each night by unsteadily driving those last two miles into the countryside, and having deposited him in his hallway I would return through dark half-built lanes to my mother's house and wake next morning, hung-over and sullen.

In working hours Plunkett was often silent in the car but he mellowed with drink each evening. Once as I drove him home we came to a garda check-point. I had rolled the window down nervously, knowing that I'd been sitting with Plunkett over a bottle of whiskey since eight that evening, when he leaned forward from the back seat and spoke in a more cultured accent:

'You are halting the Junior Minister for Justice on state business. Take down that guard's number, driver.'

Afterwards he invited me in for a last drink and giggled like a schoolboy as he imitated the guard's embarrassed and frightened apologies. He had made himself sound exactly like the minister and, as I discovered, the minister, when he lost his temper, sounded exactly like him. Although Patrick Plunkett rarely came to the garage itself, often in the evenings he would appear at the house. The two brothers would go into the drawing-room, leaving me to sit in the kitchen with the government driver and listen to the low murmur of voices.

Although the minister's name never appeared on any business documents it became obvious to me that he was a silent partner in all of Pascal's ventures. Sitting in that kitchen waiting for them to emerge, I began to piece together a thumb-nail sketch of their lives from what I had heard there and from what my mother had told me.

Patrick had been two years a national schoolteacher in the suburb when his elder brother returned from England in the early sixties with capital and ambition. Soon he had Patrick selling encyclopaedias to the parents of his pupils, checking up on their home backgrounds to give Pascal leads for his new business of selling door to door. In those days the two brothers were inseparable. Although Pascal was a year older, my mother said they looked like twins. At dances girls had problems telling them apart. But soon they were rarely to be seen at dances. They moved into lodgings with an old bachelor on the North Road where the light in the living-room was still burning no matter how late you passed the house.

By 1966 Pascal had opened the garage and found others to go from door to door for him. The fiftieth anniversary of the Easter Rising that year was the making of them. From his native Mayo they dragged up their grandfather, Eoin, who had been thirty-eight during the rising and was eighty-eight then. They brought him around the estates to meet the people. One night when we were drinking heavily, Pascal described him to me. Eoin had come to Dublin in 1916 looking for work and joined with Connolly's men only on the morning of the rising. He had stuck to his new leader's side and even helped to carry Connolly down when he was shot on the roof of the GPO. Before arriving in Dublin he had known nothing, but he came out of the internment camp in Wales a confirmed socialist. Wounded six times in the War of Independence, he had not died. Pascal used to repeat this bitterly. If only his grandfather had been killed I think he felt they could have both won seats.

After the dust had settled in 1923 he was still a socialist and still spoke out as one. They gave him medals reluctantly and eventually a pension, but he was not there in the carve up of jobs and power. At the time of the Graltan affair in Leitrim, he too had been denounced from the pulpits as a Bolshevik. Graltan on the run had often hidden in his house, and when he was deported to America the newspapers cried out for Eoin Plunkett to be dispatched as well. He survived, the aura of holiness around his Easter medal protecting him, until one night the locals set fire to his house. The brothers' mother had died giving birth to Patrick and their father had brought them to live with Eoin. After the fire, their father cursed Eoin, took the only suitcase and went to England. The sons never heard from him again. Eoin took them to his sister's house in Kerry near where my own father was born, left them there and was arrested and sent home when trying to board a boat to join the International Brigade in Spain. In 1939, when his grandsons were in their late teens, the police came for him again. He came out of the Curragh Internment Camp, a grey-haired man of sixty-seven, when peace was declared.

The brothers always resented the poverty they grew up in when they knew how easy it would have been for Eoin to secure a well-paid niche. He could barely walk when they got him reluctantly back up to the city but they quickly learnt how much he despised their new activities. Eventually, in desperation, each evening before they took him on their rounds of the estates they would remove his false teeth so that the people mistook his tirades against the smugness of the new state for the standard pieties they expected.

They shipped him home when the bunting came down, and in the next election Patrick Plunkett slipped into the last seat on the twelfth count. Eoin died as the first bombs exploded on Derry's streets. They forgot to remove the tricolour from his coffin when they lowered it down, and shovelled the clay on top of it. The local priest claimed a bedside conversion. I always wondered if he had prised the teeth out first.

In April the party had an emergency Ard-Fheis, giving rise to speculation of a snap election. At the last minute Patrick Plunkett was dropped from the list of speakers. That night, after the leader's speech he arrived at Pascal's house. I could see he had been drinking heavily. The brothers withdrew into the drawing-room, muttering angrily to themselves. After an hour Patrick emerged from the drawing-room and told his driver to go. Through the open door I could hear Pascal on the phone placing a bet with someone. I had been idling in the kitchen for hours, waiting to be told to go home.

When I heard the receiver being replaced I reached for my coat and was zipping it up when Pascal came in.

'You're working late tonight Hanrahan,' he said, his manner abrupt as always in his brother's presence. 'Drive us back into the city.'

I could smell whiskey like a fever in the back of the car as I drove. It was after one o'clock when we got there, the streets almost deserted with the burger huts closed and the nightclubs still churning out music. We drove by Liberty Hall, crossed the river and cruised along Burgh Quay. Near the public toilets they beckoned for me to stop. Three youths leaned on the quayside wall, watching for men, obviously for sale. The eldest might have been sixteen. I could sense the brothers staring at them before they motioned me to move on.

Maybe twenty-five years ago it had been impossible to tell them apart, but the grooming of political power had lent Patrick a veneer of cosmopolitanism at odds with his brother's instinctive raw aggression. That night though, as they sat impassively behind me, it was like the polish had slipped away and they were one again. I drove slowly, with a sickness in my stomach, along the quays and down alleyways where dirty children huddled in groups with bags of glue and plastic cider bottles. Some spat at the slow car, others watched with mute indifference. Neither man spoke beyond instructing me to slow down or drive on. At times we moved at a funeral pace and those badly lit alleyways could have been some ghostly apparition of a dead city which we were driving through. Murky lanes with broken street lights, the ragged edges of tumbledown buildings, a carpet of glass and condoms, of chip papers and plastic cartons and, picked out in the headlights, the hunched figures of children and tramps wrapped in blankets or lying under cardboard, their hands raised to block the glare of headlights.

Twice we paused where a figure lay, down a laneway between the ancient cathedral and the ugly squatting bunkers of the civic offices, before I was ordered to stop. Patrick Plunkett was bundled up in an old overcoat and hat. In the semi-dark of the car he could have been anyone or no one. This is what death looks like when it calls, I thought, watching him in the mirror, a black figure with no face. Pascal got out and approached the youth on the ground who tried to shuffle away when he bent to talk to him. He was perhaps eighteen. I saw him shake his head repeatedly before Plunkett produced two twenties and a ten pound note from his wallet which he held up and then placed carefully back among the wad of notes. Both were still for a moment before the youth picked himself up and folded the blanket under his arm. Plunkett caught his shoulder and, after arguing briefly, the youth turned and carefully hid the filthy covering behind some rubble in the lane.

He sat between the two brothers in the back. I could tell from his face in the mirror how scared he was. He wanted to ask them questions but was intimidated by the brothers' silence. Occasionally Pascal murmured to him, reassuring the youth as you would a frightened animal, or called out directions to me. Otherwise we made the journey in silence.

I thought I knew North County Dublin until that night. I know we passed near Rolestown and much later I glimpsed a signpost for The Naul, but generally the lanes we travelled were too small to be signposted. Two cars could not have passed on them and I had to negotiate by following the ridge of grass which grew down the centre. Just when they seemed to peter out they would switch direction. At one crossroads another set of headlights emerged and began to tail us, and this was repeated again and again until we too caught up with a procession of tail lights streaking out into the darkness ahead of us.

The cars slowed almost to a halt and we turned off the tarmacadam and were bumping our way across gravel and then grass. In the field ahead of us a semi-circle of light was formed by the headlights of parked cars. We took our place and those behind followed until a rough circle of blazing light was completed. Men stood about in the grass. Patrick Plunkett addressed me for the first time since leaving the city.

'Get out!'

He climbed into the driver's seat and donned the chauffeur's hat from the glove compartment which I had never been asked to wear. He slammed the door and fixed his eyes through the windscreen on the trampled floodlit grass. Pascal had got out and was standing beside the open boot with the youth who was now stripped to the waist and shivering. Pascal was rubbing liquid from a bottle on to the youth's chest. He handed it to me with a sponge and plastic container of water, then placed his hand on the youth's shoulder to steer him out into the circle. From the far side of the ring of lights I saw a second youth being led out, as scared looking as the first. I knew the man at his side, a wholesale fish merchant named Collins from Swords who occasionally did business with Plunkett. He called out jeeringly:

'Is that the best you can do Plunkett? You must have fierce weak men up in the city.'

'Are you sure a grand won't bust your business Collins?' Plunkett called back. 'I know it's a lot of money for a small man like yourself to lose.'

The two youths eyed each other, desperate to make a deal between themselves. But even if they had tried to run they would have been pushed back into the ring by the circle of well-fed men who were closing in around them. A referee, stripped to his waistcoat, was rolling up his sleeves.

'Where did you get him?' he asked Plunkett.

'Back of Christchurch.'

'And yours?' He turned to Collins.

'Knackers. Camped out near The Ward.'

'Fifty pounds to the winning boxer. I want twenty-five each off you now.'

He turned to the youths.

'Nothing to the loser. Do you understand? No using your feet, you break when I tell you and the first to surrender is out. Now you've got five minutes.'

We returned to the boot of the car. Plunkett put a jacket over the youth's shoulders and fed him instructions on how to weave and hit. Two men approached us and he walked off to cover their bets. The youth kept glancing at me as though I were his jailer. I wanted to tell him to run but I was too terrified, afraid that if he did escape I would be thrust into the ring in his place. The winning purse was less than the smallest bet being placed around me. The laughter and shouting, as if by an unconscious signal, died down into a hush of anticipation. Plunkett returned and pushed the youth forward.

'Fifty pounds son. Fifty smackers into your hand. Don't let me down now.'

I walked behind, noticing that Patrick had left the car and was standing unobserved a small way off from the crowd. A man staggered over to offer me a slug of Southern Comfort and thump me on the back.

'Good man yourself,' he shouted in my ear. 'I've a hundred riding on your man, but watch it, them knackers fight fierce filthy.'

There was a roar as both youths entered the ring. They circled cagily while the referee encouraged them forward. For over a minute they shadowed each other, fists clenched and raised, tongues nervously exposed. The crowd grew angry at the lack of action. They cursed and called the fighters cowards. Then the Gypsy ducked low to get in close and swung his fist up. He caught the youth above the eye as he moved back and flailed at the Gypsy who danced away. It had begun.

There were no gloves, no rounds, both fighters punching and clinging to each other as the men around them screamed, until after five or six minutes the Gypsy was caught by a succession of blows and fell over on to the ground. I expected the referee to begin a count but Collins just pulled him up and wiped the sponge quickly over his face. Plunkett grabbed the water from me and raised it to his fighter's lips.

'Don't swallow, just spit,' he said. 'It's going to be a long night.'

Then they were thrust back into action, a graceless, headlong collision of blows and head butts. Both bled badly from the face. More frequently now they fell and the fight was stopped for a few seconds. After half an hour, the Gypsy got in under his opponent's defence and rained blows against his rib cage. He stepped back and the youth fell, doubled up on the ground. He kept trying to stay down as Plunkett pulled him up.

'Me ribs mister, they're broken, broken.'

'Get back in there. I've money riding on you. Finish the cunt off or you'll leave this field in a box.'

The youth stumbled forward with one hand clutching his side. Money was flowing on to the Gypsy. He approached, grinning now through the blood, sensing that his ordeal was nearly over, but as he swung his fist the youth caught him with his boot right in the balls and, as he fell to his knees, again in the face. There was a near riot of indignation among the crowd around me, their sense of fair play abused. Both youths knelt on the ground while the referee shouted at Plunkett:

'Once more Plunkett and I'm giving it to Collins. Do you hear me?'

The youth rose reluctantly and looked back to where I stood. I lowered my eyes and walked towards the gate of the field. I could bear to watch no more. To the south the lights of the city were an orange glow in the sky. The wind blew against my face. A tree was growing by itself in the ditch. I pressed my face against its cold bark, remembering suddenly the old woman's story of the oak trees in her wood that she would embrace to find strength in times of crisis. I closed my eyes and I could see her, not as that ancient figure I had abandoned, but a young mother in the early light running between trees. I saw her so clearly, as if her image had always been locked away inside me, part of the other me I never allowed myself to think of. I wanted him back, the person I kept nearly becoming – in her caravan, with Shay in the flat. From the shouts behind me I knew that the Gypsy was finishing it. Every eye would be watching the final grisly moments before clustering round the bookmakers. I wrapped my whole body against the base of the tree. I had nobody left to pray to so I prayed to it and to her and to me: to the living wood itself, to the old woman of the fields, to the memory of someone I had almost once been.

When the noise died down, I turned and walked back. The youth was lying against the side of the car. He was crying. I found his clothes, helped him to dress. I wanted to ask him his name but it seemed too late to do so. I helped him up and opened the back door where the brothers sat.

'Put him in the front,' Pascal shouted.

I eased him gently into the passenger's seat and started the engine.

'Leave us home,' Pascal said, 'then dump that tramp back where you found him. Bring the car into work at lunch-time. One word about this and your family will be living on sawdust.'

I let them out at his house. Both slammed their doors, disgruntled and, now they were alone, bowed their heads together to discuss the fight. I drove into the city. The Mater Hospital was on casualty. It was almost dawn but still the benches were jammed with drunks, with lonely people hoping to fool their way into a bed, with girls in party dresses who cried waiting for word of their friends behind the curtains. He hadn't wanted to go in and, if I hadn't sat there, would have stumbled his way back to his blanket hidden in the laneway.

Even the nurses were shocked at his appearance. They called him in ahead of those waiting. When he rose I pushed whatever money was in my pockets into his hand. I knew that Plunkett had given him nothing. He looked at me but we did not shake hands. I watched the nurses help him on to the bunk and, staring back at me with mistrust, pull the curtain shut.

It was daylight outside. I thought of my brothers and sisters. At twelve o'clock I would be waiting at the garage to drive him, but now I left his car there and walked the two miles home in some futile gesture of penance, even though I knew that nothing would be changed.

DEIRDRE MADDEN

from *Remembering Light and Stone*

I

'I don't belong here.' The thought came to me with such force that I almost said it aloud, at once, but I stopped myself just in time. I know what he would have said, reasonably: 'Do I?'

Later, looking back on that last day in Rome, what I would remember would be the heat and the noise. It was a struggle to be in the city because of that, but there was a curious softness too. The violent heat released the scent of fruit from the stalls as we walked past: melons, peaches, nectarines, plums. The fruit and vegetables were stacked outside the little shops in frail wooden crates. Near Campo Dei Fiori there was a woman who tended a stall, and she was singing as she brushed the city dust from the fruit with a spray of coloured feathers. It was the longest day of the year.

Ted wanted a drink, so we sat down at a table outside a café. We didn't say much to each other as we sat there, but watched the people drift along the hot street in their gaudy summer clothes and heavy jewellery. After a while Ted said to me that, for him, there was always a strong sense of death in the south, because of the very emphasis on life. The sun itself that made the fruit so ripe and big, that seemed to make the people bloom so early and so evidently, mercilessly pushed everything over into decay, so that the fruit quickly rotted, and the people suddenly fell into a graceless old age.

I thought of Franca's daughter, Lucia. She was fifteen, almost a woman and completely at ease with the fact, but I could see what Ted meant. I could see the short duration of that ease, and how there was something frail and uncertain about her whole self, as though she might at any moment topple headlong into being an old woman in a black dress, with nothing to look forward to but death. Time and again I remembered looking into the faces of young women in Italy, and seeing peer back, unbeknownst to them, the faces of the women they would be some fifty years later.

So I understood what Ted meant, and in a way I agreed with him, but I wasn't completely convinced, because I didn't want to be. I associated the north with violence and death, and I had come south to escape that.

Deep down, I knew that what he said was true, and that it was one of the many things people didn't understand about Italy, the people, that is, who came south to Italy, where 'everybody is so happy'. No one wants to shatter the myth of the warm, sensual, happy south, for if we did not believe in that, where would people go to escape the rigour of the north? I had learnt a lot about Italy in the time I had been there, but what I had learnt most of all was how little I understood it, how deceptive a country it was. And more than learning anything about Italy, I had found out more about my own country, simply by not being in it. The contrast with Italy was a help, but in many ways I felt I could have gone anywhere, so long as it was far away and provided me with privacy, so that I could forget all about home for a while, forget all about Ireland, and then remember it, undisturbed.

Once, I visited some limestone caverns up near Trieste, and it reminded me of the Burren, where I grew up. I realized then how much I loved that strange, stark beauty, the bare grey stone and the grey sky, the few stunted trees. I missed that landscape when I lived away from it, and had taken it for granted when I was there.

I looked across the table at Ted, and I thought of how I had no word to define him, or his relationship to me, and I was glad that it was so. I remembered expressions I had heard used when I was growing up, such as 'going steady'. I found phrases like that completely absurd, they sounded to me as quaint and outmoded as 'keeping company'. I hate convenient empty words, they trap you when you use them. Franca used to call him my *fidanzato*, and I didn't like that either. It was a word that smelt of matrimony, and yet it was vague, too. There was no word to describe the degree of distance and intimacy there was between us. I think I realized then that it was coming to an end, and that we wouldn't be together for much longer, but of course I didn't say anything.

The waiter brought me a little black bitter coffee, the sort I hated when I first went to Italy, but which I grew to love. The pleasure and fascination of other countries has never left me, and I hope it never does. One of my most vivid childhood memories, certainly one of the most pleasant, is of the time a Japanese woman came to visit our neighbours. Until then, I had never met a person from such a distant country, and I was completely fascinated by her. One day I went into the house where she was staying, and she was talking to someone on the phone in her own language, and I was amazed to think that for her all those sounds came so easily, she understood so much and knew so much. She gave me a coloured paper fan that smelt of smoke, and on a sheet of strange paper – pale green, with a pearly sheen to it – she wrote with black ink and a little brush the characters that stood for her name – Yuriko – and mine – Aisling. I said that some day I would go to Japan to visit her, but my brother Jimmy teased me about it. He said that I'd hate it there because I'd have to eat raw fish and seaweed. 'You'll have to eat rice with your dinner, too.' That seemed really odd to me, for I had only ever seen rice cooked in milk and served with prunes. He told me that I wouldn't like the tea, because it was green, and that they wouldn't let me put milk in it, I'd have to drink it black. That made me think it was all a lie, for if the tea was green, how could you drink it black? I told Jimmy I didn't believe him, told him I didn't care, and that some day I'd go away, to see other countries. My image of what those countries would be like was strange and limited, as is often the case with children. For years I thought that New York was America, that is, I thought it was all skyscrapers from coast to coast. I was shocked and disappointed when I found out there were trees and fields too. (I had once told Ted this and he had said, 'Forget about kids, Aisling: I've met adults who think everywhere in America looks like Manhattan.') When Yuriko went back to Japan, she sent me a postcard, showing the white cone of Mount Fuji under snow. The sky behind was deep blue, the foreground full of yellow flowers. I kept the card, in a safe place, together with the fan and the sheet of paper with our names on it. For me, they were magical things. When I grew up I did go away, but I never got to Japan. I had almost forgotten Yuriko, it was the first time I had thought of her in years. I wondered where she was now, what she was doing, and if she remembered me.

Ted interrupted my thoughts. He touched my hands, and, nodding, said quietly, 'Look over there.'

He indicated three small girls, shabbily dressed and barefoot, who were each holding large torn pieces of corrugated cardboard. They had approached a smartly dressed woman who was looking in a shop window, and tugged her sleeve to attract her attention. At once she was surrounded. All talking at once, the children held out their hands, demanding alms, while holding the cardboard out flat to create a little shelf between themselves and the woman. She was shocked and disoriented to find herself the centre of attention, when the children suddenly scattered as quickly as they had gathered, the smallest one triumphantly waving a slim leather wallet. The woman screamed as she looked down at her handbag, which hung gaping open from her arm, having been craftily opened and swiftly rifled by little hands. It was, of course, all over in seconds: by the time the woman had started to scream and the people around her noticed what had happened, the children were out of sight.

Ted shook his head. 'You wonder how they keep getting away with it. Reminds me of the first time I came to Italy. I had had all the warnings, and then two days after I arrived, down in the Forum, exactly the same thing. Three hundred dollars in lire gone in ten seconds. Losing the money was bad, going to see the Italian police was almost worse. They just said, "You're the tenth in today." You could see they'd had it with stupid *Americani*, getting mugged and then coming to them, as if there was anything they could do to get the cash back. I almost thought the kids were right, I felt kind of sorry for them, even though the little bastards cleaned me out.'

The city was full of poor children, they were like the pigeons or the wild cats, to be found around all the big monuments, the Colosseum, the Forum, in the big squares and in the streets. Earlier that day, I had seen a tiny girl, without shoes, who walked up and down beside a row of cars which were stopped at traffic lights, begging at the car windows. When the lights changed, she huddled in the middle of the streams of traffic, which made no effort to avoid her, nor, I suppose, did she expect it to. When the lights were red again, she resumed her task, walking patiently from window to window. In the time I watched her, nobody gave her anything.

The preceding evening, just a few hours after we got into Rome, we had been having dinner in a restaurant. We had almost finished the meal, and were talking over coffee and fruit about what we would do the following day. The door opened, and a little girl came in, carrying an armful of red roses, each one sheathed in cellophane. She started to go from table to table, and was rebuffed at each one, the diners often barely looking up from their food to tell her to go away. As she approached our table I said to Ted, 'Buy me one, please.' He asked the little girl how much they cost.

'Two thousand.'

Ted gave her five, and waved away the change. She put the green note in her pocket without a word, handed me a rose, and drifted off to the remaining tables. She had a deep cut above her right eye, her cheek was marked by the last shadow of a bruise, and her whole face showed utter exhaustion. Disappointment and bitterness were stamped upon her features in a way that would have been shocking to see in a woman of forty. She had had enough, and her face expressed the unconscious question: 'If this is life, why was I ever born?' She must have been barely six years old. To show her pity would have been to torment her. The child had reached the door again, and she went out into the night.

I recognized the child. Seeing her made me want to withdraw, and I felt a terrible sense of despair. Some years earlier, I had read an article in a newspaper about child pornography. It was a short article, which described how many children were sold into slavery, how films and photographs were found, showing little children crying, being raped and beaten and cut, showing children being killed. When I read that, it was as if something had fallen over me. Suddenly everything changed, my fingernails on the edge of the newspaper looked different, the sun on the wall, the feel of my feet in my shoes; everything, everything. I wanted all at once not to be a part of a world where such things could happen. I felt guilty, as though simply by being in such a society, I was acquiescing to its evils. I wanted to do something to show that I was turning away irrevocably from such things, that I could not, would not tolerate them.

All this was brought back to me by the sight of the little girls who stole the woman's wallet. My face must have been as dark as my mind while this chain of thoughts absorbed me, for I realized that Ted was looking at me anxiously. He didn't understand, because he said to me, 'Don't worry, Aisling. You'll be all right when we get there.' For a moment, I didn't know what he was talking about, and then I remembered where we were going the following day. 'It's not that at all,' I told him. 'I am looking forward to going back, although I am a bit nervous too.' He didn't ask me what I had been thinking about, and I was grateful for that.

I'll probably never know what brought Ted and me together, nor what then kept us together for that time. I don't think it matters, I think it's best that it remain a mystery, even to me, or perhaps particularly to me. I don't believe in trying to analyse things like that. I knew he was very fond of me, but he was afraid of me too. At first he used to deny it, but then he admitted it. I knew in Rome that it was getting to the point where he was more frightened than fond, and so it probably wouldn't last much longer.

It was too hot to move. I wanted to go on sitting there at the café table. A short distance away, beyond the pavement, the phenomenal traffic of Rome roared past. I was glad I didn't live in Rome, I didn't think I could ever become used to it. It wasn't the idea of living in a big city that put me off, because I had once lived in Paris. In Rome it was a combination of things – the disorganization, the hellish heat, the constant traffic. I remembered how it had shocked me when I had first arrived there, and, even after having lived in Italy for years, I could still evoke from it that feeling of strangeness. It can feel as if I'm looking at everything backwards, down a long tunnel of time.

I remembered standing one day, waiting to cross the road in Rome. I could smell the dust and pollution and could hardly bear the terrible heat which was coming off the vehicles and beating down like a hammer from the sun; the sun was like bronze. Every so often the traffic would stop, snarled up on itself. Suddenly this happened and I found I was looking into the face of a man driving a big white Land Rover. And it was the strangest thing, because I felt that I was looking at a person from an ancient civilization. I saw the whole scene in terms of both time and space, and I saw its absurdity, for there was so much traffic and the jeep in particular was so stupidly big that I knew at once it was all bound to end. It was a completely transient phenomenon, it had only existed for forty years, at most, out of the thousands and millions of years during which there had been life. It was all an aberration, and it was doomed. All the big roads made for it would one day be empty. I looked intently at the man behind the wheel. He looked as innocent as a dead warrior. In his face there was not a trace of doubt, not a hint of the frailty of his own life, his times, his transport. It seemed extraordinary to me that in this city above all, with the evidence all around of broken monuments and vainglorious ruins, people seemed unaware of what would happen. Maybe one of the hardest things is to see beyond your own society, to step out of the collective consciousness of your time, but it teaches you about things as nothing else does. You begin to see your own age not with understanding, perhaps, but with compassion. You see the weakness and smallness of things which are now great or powerful. Sights which might at other times have filled me with contempt now moved me to pity, such as the overdressed women with their jewels and their expensive clothes in the *Caffè Greco*, the pity you might feel for bones found in an ancient tomb, a priceless ring on each fingerbone. I pity them their deaths in a way that they do not pity themselves, and I pity them for their faith in frail mortal things, for not knowing that there will be nothing left but weeds and broken stones.

That afternoon, Ted and I had been to see the frescoes in the Sistine Chapel. They had only been opened to the public again earlier that spring following restoration. Ted had seen them since then, but I hadn't. Looking at them it was easy to believe that they would last for such a long time, but they wouldn't last for ever. No matter how magnificent they are, paintings are made of paint, wood, canvas, clay, and no matter how well they are preserved or restored decay is built into them. Afterwards, because we were so near it, we visited St Peter's. I hadn't been there for years, mainly because I don't like it. As soon as we went in, I could see why. It frightens me. Worse, I feel that I'm supposed to be frightened, that the whole building has been carefully planned to that very end. Usually, I like churches and cathedrals. When I was living in Paris, I used to go to Notre-Dame and the Ste Chapelle quite often, especially in winter. What I was talking about earlier – the facility for stepping out of your own age – is something that these churches lend themselves to well. You can feel a sensibility, a belief in an order which has gone now, but which people long for still, and they visit those churches for exactly that. But sometimes people visit such places because they feel they ought to, because the guidebook tells them to go there. As we walked around St Peter's, I looked at all the other people and I wondered if they liked it, and if so, did they only like it because they felt they should? I suppose all that heavy gilt and marble may appeal to some people. It frightened me. We walked across the wide, empty floors, and looked up at the monstrous, mosaiced cupola. It was too big, and out of proportion. A gothic cathedral, whatever its size, can calm your spirit, and in nature too, a massive tree, a mountain or the ocean itself can have the same effect. I felt, in St Peter's, the terror you sometimes feel in a completely empty landscape.

And perhaps the most foolish thing of all was that I believed I should identify with it. Like the people who felt they ought to admire it, I thought I ought to feel some sort of affinity, because it was 'my' church. I'm still prone to notions like this. I am not a free person. To know it is small consolation.

Nobody was praying. Instead, they were milling about, taking photographs and consulting guidebooks in a variety of languages, and then I noticed a small side chapel, reserved for prayer. I thought of Franca, and I asked Ted to wait for a moment while I went in to pray for her.

On the altar, there was a large gold monstrance, with a host in it, and in front of it, kneeling in an attitude of prayer were two nuns. They were both wearing long blue veils which almost covered them completely, veils which reached the floor with cloth to spare. I couldn't pray: I could hardly contain my anger at seeing those veils, at the crass cynical theatre of it. But then I thought of Franca: she would probably have liked it, been quite impressed by the sight. I think Ted was surprised at how quickly I reappeared.

On that last night in Rome, I couldn't sleep, because of the heat, and because I kept thinking of where we were going the following day, and I was thinking of the churches, all the churches I knew. Some of them still meant a great deal to me, those medieval churches where the raw power of Christianity could speak to me from the anguished face of a painted angel, over the roar of the traffic, in the heat of the night, as I lay there wrapped in a sheet, feeling the pulse of my own heart, and hearing the voice of a tormented angel scream down through the centuries to me.

EOIN MCNAMEE

from *Resurrection Man*

14

Jim Curran left the snooker hall at a quarter past twelve and walked towards the Cliftonville Road. He had been playing snooker. He played every night. It was something a man could lose himself in. The green baize under hooded lights, men standing in the shadows along the wall, a purposeful drawing together, attentive to the passage and reclusive click of the balls. Curran loved the studied movements from place to place around the table, sighting along the cue and selecting their footing with precision as if they were working towards a theoretical end, an abstract perfection. Something a man could seek guidance in.

He appreciated the clarity of thought that he brought away with him when he walked home from the club. He had an exhaustive knowledge of the great sportsmen who had come from the city. People whose names you rarely saw in books. Men of icy control and self-knowledge whose greatest victories grew in his mind as feats of unendurable loneliness. Curran had a deep respect for the sporting figures of the past. Rinty Monaghan. Dixie Dean.

It seemed that he could see the city clearly on nights like this and it was a place of age and memory. He thought about the *Titanic* built in the shipyard, the closed linen mills, the derelict shirt factories, the streets of houses built for workers and other edifices constructed by speculators who seemed to have this modern city in mind, their designs weathered down to create a setting for injured lives; this city like gaunt others they had created on shallow, muddy deltas or desolate coasts guided by infallible principles of abandonment.

At first he didn't see the yellow Escort emerge from a side-street, its motor idling. He had travelled another hundred yards before he became aware of the car following him at walking pace, keeping its distance in a way that seemed obedient, as if it were awaiting a command that he might make. He did not alter his pace. It could be the police. It could be a taxi looking for an address. Nevertheless he looked along the street for shelter, a houselight, some warm billet to offset against the sudden conviction of lasting solitude. There was a row of locked garages to his right and the wall of a motorworks to his left. He could hear the noise of traffic in the distance, a sound he had been unaware of for years coming to him now as if there was something gentle-natured and sorrowing in the distance. It made him think of a country song about mothers that brought a tear to his eye. Thinking about this he stumbled on the pavement and immediately heard the car behind him rev wildly. He began to run. He thought that if he could only reach the end of the street. An image of Roger Bannister breaking the four-minute mile came into his head. A man in flapping white shorts and singlet running with his knees high and elbows tucked, upright and fleet, determined to imbue his passage with dignity, aware that history would demand no less of the moment.

He imagined that he was passing people in the street. A pair of lovers in a doorway fixed in an attitude of solace, a drunk watching him mildly, as though inclined to leniency on the basis that much of life propels men into headlong necessities. He felt that the dead from his past were in the shadows. Parents, brothers, uncles. He had the impression that they wore expressions of strange urging. He felt that the untiring dead were somehow gaining on him now, the soft patter of their ghostly sprints almost audible. When the car drew level with him he knew that he had lost. A man spoke to him from the passenger window.

'What's your hurry, big lad?'

Curran stopped and bent over double, gasping for breath. The car door opened and three men got out. One of them was holding a tyre iron.

'You're coming with us, son.'

'A big trip in the motor car.'

'Fuck's sake mister you're not fit at all. Wee run like that and you can't get a breath.'

'He'll be fit by the time we get done with him, Victor.'

'Fit for fuck-all.'

Curran held up one hand. He wanted permission to catch his breath before speaking, a respite so that he could begin to form words again. Please.

Ryan's father died in December. His mother rang him early in the morning. Your father died during the night, she said. Her voice was weary. It was just another thing her husband had done to alarm her. It was news of an affair. It was sitting at the kitchen table with him while he explained the reasons why they had no money. He had spoken her name just once in the middle of the night using the same tone of long-held grievance which he had used to describe the other disasters in his life. She had left the bed and started a series of calm phone calls. Her response to his death was scripted in the same rich language of irreparable fault which she had used during his lifetime.

As Ryan was packing to travel home the phone rang again. It was Margaret.

'Your mother rang me,' she said, 'I'm sorry.' Ryan wasn't surprised. He knew that Margaret and his mother had become closer since they had separated. He tried to imagine them speaking on the phone to each other, both adept at extracting the marginal satisfactions to be had from disappointment in love.

'How do you feel?'

'I don't know. I wished he was dead so often.'

'That's different.'

It was always one of the subjects they could talk about. Ryan and his father. Margaret defending him. Ryan bitterly identifying with his weaknesses. What had most offended him in the end was the half-hearted way his father had gone about deception, the offhand duplicity. The lies he told were borrowed, makeshift. Ryan and his mother always knew when he wasn't telling the truth. He took on an unconvincing, dispirited expression. A rained-on and hopeless look. His arguments possessed a commanding lack of conviction, delivered in an imperious whine that left them feeling helpless.

'I feel like he's got away with something. I don't believe him. He's my da. He shouldn't have died like that in that well I just did it way of his. I feel like I'm owed some sort of explanation somewhere. I could have forgiven him if he'd died heroically. Called for me at the last moment so he could hold my hand and look up at me so's I could graciously forgive him.'

'Swelling violins, fade to weeping women outside bedroom door. Wise up, Ryan.'

It was what he needed. A voice to cut through the rudimentary panic he felt at his father's death. The feeling of being lost in transit somewhere in a neglected landscape with the likelihood of dark weather ahead.

'It's not anybody's fault,' Margaret said softly. 'I'll see you down there.'

He felt the effort she was making to inject the extra note of gracious summary and took it for heartfelt, whispering her name down the line before she hung up.

It was evening before he left, passing the red-brick semi-detached suburbs on the outskirts of the city that he had once watched from the bus on day-trips as a child, with a feeling that there was something deep-set and mysterious about these houses, a suggestion that part of life at least could be bought. He imagined coming home at night and going under the deep shade of the laburnum at the gate, putting out his fingers to the glass handle of a porch door, being greeted by a mother who approached him with low-keyed and costly cries of love.

The traffic died five miles out of the town. He passed through a succession of small towns. There was sectarian graffiti on the walls, policemen carrying old-fashioned Mausers with wooden stocks and looking like a poorly armed Balkan militia, dull and enduring. Dour churches on the outskirts, shops closed at five, a sense of the future indefinitely postponed.

Then the empty caravan parks on the long stretch outside the town. Sand blowing in from the dunes, pitted aluminium, yellow gas cylinders. It looked like a place for the shiftless, the desperate. He thought of it during the summer. Bare-armed women setting meals on collapsible picnic tables. They looked alert and temperate, putting out paper cups with care and a sense that this was as much as they were permitted, these impaired habitations on the edge of the disconsolate. It was the women who gathered and talked quietly outside the shower-block in the morning as though it was a terminus for the unwary. And it was the women who lay awake at night listening to sand hissing in the caravan chassis and to children making sounds in their sleep to complement that sound, so that they felt a parent's faint dread at their children's access to the windblown and strange.

The esplanade was deserted. The arcades were closed for the winter, cloud gathering out at sea. The front seemed like a location designed for an off-season drama, carefully lit to suggest dereliction and small but ominous happenings.

There were cars lined on either side of the pavement outside the council house. Ryan walked in past strangers, who took his hand or touched his shoulder as he passed. He was aware he was being studied, people giving him their attention as a grave, courteous bounty. The only son. Letting him know that this was no small matter. He hugged his mother without speaking to her and went over to the open coffin. Beneath the waxy glow the plain expectant face. An expression of readiness that seemed to have been laboured over, worked at in the long sinking away from the light. He was shaken by the dead man's air of preparation, the honest facing of death's calm interrogative.

When he raised his head he saw Margaret at the other side of the room. She was looking at him, it seemed, with her breath held as if the face he had lifted to her would disintegrate on exposure to air. He saw that she had lost the weight that she had put on during their six years of marriage – putting it on as a form of protest, he thought at the time. Abandoning that which he was supposed to love in her and withdrawing into a meagre guile, determined to be unworthy.

Later he went outside for air. He leaned against a car smoking a cigarette. It was a still night. The cars gleaming in the dark, reflecting a fragmentary light. The roofs of the houses opposite profiled against the sky. He saw the front door open and Margaret coming down the path. He waited for her to reach him.

'Hello.'

'Hello yourself. What are you doing out here?'

'Nothing sinister. Getting air. Did my mother send you?'

'Shit Ryan, don't talk like that. That sly stuff. Your mother's in there with the aunts. She can't stand their guts. They're wandering around dabbing at the eyes with tissues. Your ma says they're Protestants. Says they've got big margarine faces.'

'How's the job?' She was teaching at a technical college in the city.

'You hear yourself droning. You can't help seeing yourself the way they see you.'

'What way's that?'

'I don't know, frantic, living on some scary edge. They keep pushing. The hell with that though. How's life on the front line? The daring investigative reporter.'

'Strange I suppose. It's like me and Coppinger got all tied up in these knife killings. He'll be lining up suspects in the bar of the Four-in-Hand next. It scares the shit out of me. I want to grow old and report on the Lord Mayor's show.'

'Mouse. How is the greasy old bastard anyhow?'

'Greasy as ever. Seriously though he seems to be getting deeper and deeper in. I hardly ever see him. He's like a character out of a book, knows fate's out to get him.'

'Tell him to be careful from me. You too.' He felt the return of a familiar anger at her reply. The perfunctory tone. He wanted to feel that she was still suffering the loss of him.

'Want to go for a drink?' he asked.

'At your father's funeral?'

'All the more reason.'

'I don't think so. I think I can tell what would happen.'

'Nothing would happen. We'd have a drink is all.'

'Everything would happen. It'd all happen. I think I'm going back to the house. You should too.'

'I'll go in when I'm ready to go in. This is my show.'

'Suit yourself.'

He watched her walk away from him, taking with her the momentary reassurance he had felt, an edifying fury which faded as she left, drawing it after her into the darkness.

He could not remember much about the funeral. A sense that it had been recovered from archives. The documented past painfully reconstructed and enacted to purge a troubling historical remainder. Men with weathered faces, farmers from the mountain hinterland, gathered at points along the route. Scenes of rehearsed grief. The brown coffin's weight and awkward shapes; the resisting bulk designed to stress that death is a difficult terrain to enter.

There was rain as well. Squally cold showers that seemed to occur at crucial moments. Walking from the car to the church, darkening the sky as they stood at the graveside and carrying the priest's voice away into a lost and ruinous place. People coughed and reached for handkerchiefs and exchanged glances which enquired as to how they had found themselves here in the worst of all possible places.

When it was over he walked towards the car park with his mother, holding her by the elbow. Her walk was calm and dignified. She had not cried during the funeral, which surprised him. He wondered what way she had decided to frame her mourning and realized that she had decided to defer to the death as though it was a doctor or a solicitor or other tactful and convincing professional. As he was unlocking the car Margaret approached them. She kissed his mother, gave her a solicitous look. His mother put her hand on Margaret's forearm. These were events which did not include him. He felt their approval of each other. He felt the weight of future exchanges. Phone calls. Shopping trips. He remembered how during their marriage Margaret would swap clothes with his mother and how they would engage in small financial transactions with repayments scrupulously adhered to. It represented a tautness in their relationship. No detail was too small. The world was full of unexpected traps and the smallest event had scope for disaster. This was handed on from mother to daughter: to be adequate to the small tasks at hand, to be serious, to make store against loss.

The two women talked in low voices. Come for the weekend. Ring me if you feel. Tones of urgent arrangement before they turned to the man standing at the driver's door as though he was a task to be shared between them, a shoddy thing to be held and turned against a revealing light.

'Listen,' Margaret said to him, 'give me a ring when you get back.' Her words included his mother so that Ryan didn't know whether he was supposed to ring or whether Margaret was speaking in deference to the older woman. Either way it was an opening, a reward held out for endeavour. As Ryan watched her return to her car he felt the revival of an old lust, strongest when she wore formal dress. The black patent high heels, the long skirt in strict pleats, the tension in her calves under black tights made her look tailored into a sexual geometry, a close-fitting garment of the heart.

Ryan stayed for a few days after the funeral. His mother seemed barely aware of his presence. Occasionally he found her looking at him with an expression of mild regret.

She had made no attempt to remove his father's belongings. His jacket behind the door, the worn shaving brush with dried foam in the bristles, the drawers of clothing. Ryan thought they looked indecent. He thought about personal belongings scattered across open fields after an air crash; an intimate debris, deprived of context, looking hapless and betrayed.

He spent the days walking in the town. The arcades were empty. People walked dogs on the beach when the tide was out. He waited for the feeling that he used to get in winter. The sense of off-season grace; an elaborate nostalgia created by empty cafés and car tyres in the rain and the town's vulnerable infinites of deserted car parks, early darkness.

That Friday night he went down to the Harbour bar, coming in off the street at seven o'clock with rain in his hair. There were only a few men wearing working clothes in the bar. There was a pool table and a poker machine. The television was on with the volume down and he watched it as he waited for the barman. He noticed that one of the men at the end of the bar was staring at him.

He ordered a hot whiskey. He enjoyed being in a bar in the space between the day and the night-time crowd. There was an agreed lull – a grant to the restless and unconvinced.

The man who had been staring at him came over. He was wearing blue overalls and labourer's boots caked in red clay. His face was streaked in building-site dirt and his eyes were so bloodshot it was difficult to detect any white in them. He looked like a model for a lurching, unwieldy rage of earth. He stood in front of Ryan swaying, his fists hanging by his sides.

'Fuck are you looking at?' he said suddenly. Ryan realized that this wasn't political or sectarian. This was not one of the poised and subtle forms of violence he examined for its redemptive qualities. This was an unforeseen primal anger.

'Said what the fuck are you looking at?' the man repeated. Ryan didn't reply. He felt remote as if he had already taken the blow and accepted an obscure guilt.

'I don't know what he's looking at but it's looking back at him anyhow. Leave him be Raymie. Get on away out of the road and give the man peace.'

The man blinked, his eye switching to the speaker behind Ryan's shoulder. He shrugged and walked away. Ryan turned towards the woman's voice. She was vaguely familiar behind the make-up on her round face. The blusher, eye-shadow, lipstick laid on with a heavy hand as though she had earned the right to wear this gaudy face, building it up in the mirror with astute touches until she found herself staring at a knowing and vigilant accessory.

'I thought I was headed for casualty,' Ryan said.

'State he was in he'd of probably fell on his arse lifting his fist. Still and all, it took the woman's touch.' Her laugh had an ashen sound which Ryan hadn't expected.

'Could I get you a drink?'

'I'll get my own. Still and all I'll pull up a stool here. I don't think I'll get much chat out of them others.'

She sat on the stool beside him and ordered a Bacardi and coke. She had a big body which moved easily under a loose blouse, as if it was accustomed to addressing itself to physical certitudes.

'Still,' he said, 'you handled him well.'

'That class of a man's easy. Wee buns. Goes home loaded, wife doesn't talk to him for a week, giving him the old picture but no sound. Inside a day he's eating the face off himself saying sorry and starting to hate her guts. Next thing he's off on the drink again. Doesn't know who he feels worse about.'

'That's pretty harsh.'

'Pretty true.' He noticed that the black eye-liner on her bottom lids gave her the look of a shy nocturnal mammal surprised in headlights, and he remembered where he had seen her before.

'The Ambassador,' he said.

'What?'

'The Ambassador cinema. I used to see you there, Friday, Saturday nights.'

'I don't get you.'

'You're from the town. You used to go to the Ambassador, sit up in the balcony with a crowd. You'd be tossing lit cigarettes into the stalls and all.'

'Maybe. It's a long time ago.'

It seemed that way to Ryan as well but he remembered her as an amateur version of the person beside him, the glow of a cigarette in the back row of the balcony, a girl's laughter out of the darkness. There was little else. A few names, half-seen faces, fragments of voices carried towards him on a dark portage of recollection.

'What's your name?'

'Ryan.'

'I know now. Your da.'

'Aye.'

'I was sorry to hear. He used to teach us swimming down at the baths. We never used to talk all that much. I remember it would of froze the bum off you down there.'

He could see the pool tiling, the rusting iron grilles and dank pipes that filled the pool when the tide was in. He could see the weed-covered handrails, the whole thing like a raised hulk, green and dripping, a sense of horror about it as though ghastly corpses still floated in submerged companionways.

'One of many jobs he couldn't hold on to.'

'You shouldn't speak ill of the dead.'

Margaret had said something similar to him. He resented the incursions upon his father's death. It was a place which now belonged to him; a location in a border country, subject to eerie winds, scant rainfall.

'I'm sorry,' she said. 'My big mouth.'

'That's all right.'

'Were you close?'

'I tried to avoid his mistakes.'

'Did you?'

'I found a whole set of new ones.'

He felt that this was what he needed. Conversation with a strange woman in a bar. Laconic words. Someone to admire him for having survived his father, for having wrestled all that age and weariness and spite from his grasp.

He ordered another drink in the spirit of winter evenings in seaside bars, salt spray blowing against the windows with a frugal, corrosive sound.

*

Afterwards he tried to piece it together. The small dance floor, the music. The bar had gradually filled up without their noticing. Lying back in bed he tried to recall a sequence of events. His head ached. The bedroom stank with the toxic remnant of alcohol. She had said that she was living in the city now. He thought back to the disco, the other dancers with their faces set and exultant. She had mentioned a man. He searched his memory feeling like a dazed survivor wandering in the smouldering wreckage. Holding her above the hips, the material of her dress slipping against the skin, the indentations of her underwear then, the hard and elementary patterns. An old joke he'd made with girls when he was seventeen, leading her into it:

'Do you fuck?'

'Yes, do you?'

'Yes.'

'Then fuck off.'

She had to stop dancing to laugh at this. He moved her towards the exit before she had recovered, forcing her through the crowd in front of them, people stepping out of the way and looking at him strangely as though he had just made a peremptory arrest.

Outside in the car park rain glistening on parked cars, dark, wet tarmac, an unforgiving light between zones of shadow. He pushed her back among the stacked beer kegs and empty crates. It was a setting for small lusts, assignations of guilt and consequence. She was still laughing. He put his hands under her blouse. He had never been with this type of woman before. He touched her breasts, the reposed and forceful weight. He thought of Margaret whose body seemed suddenly scaled down into a model of unnecessary refinement. She had stopped laughing then and begun to respond to his kiss. He felt her begin to take control. When he opened his eyes she was looking at him thoughtfully.

The phone began to ring downstairs and he waited for his mother to answer it. When the ring continued he realized that she must have gone out and pulled on a pair of trousers.

'Ryan?' It was Coppinger. His voice had an echoing quality on the phone as though he was standing in a large, frigid space.

'We've got another knife job. I told you it was going to happen.'

'Congratulations.'

'James Frances Curran, age forty-seven, last seen coming from a snooker hall and headed for the Cliftonville Road. Found after an anonymous phone call. Police have refused to comment but locals say his throat was cut and the body placed in a kneeling position with the head tilted back. I hung around the Royal last night. Seems a very sharp instrument was used. A hunting knife was suggested.'

'It's all there isn't it.'

'Official silence, the body posed. All we can get is cause of death to be established.'

'It's understandable. People would be panicking.'

'Shite. The whole city knows about it anyhow. Do you know what they're calling them? The Resurrection Men.'

'Like the grave robbers?'

'Aye. Wouldn't be surprised if they were putting it about themselves. Droll lads so they are.'

Ryan's mind was crowded with images of horror. His father had told him about the Resurrection Men. Operating out of cheap wharfside boarding houses, smothering the drunk and elderly with pillows and shipping the bodies to medical schools in Edinburgh, their veins pumped full of chemicals from a brass syringe, an abiding stink like a sharp taste in the mouth. These are the lungs, this is the heart. Mothers dead in childbirth, paupers, foundlings, travellers in the uneventful dark, their faces fixed in a loose, formaldehyde gape.

'It suits them. My head's away this morning. Tell me what it means.'

'I'll talk to you when you get back. You any plans?'

'I'm leaving this evening. By the way, Margaret was asking for you.'

'Was she?'

'She said how is the greasy old bastard.' The three of them used to go drinking together. Margaret drunk would argue politics with Coppinger. Fifty years of Protestant rule, housing rights, employment rights. A dominion of the righteous. He would listen to her without comment. Sometimes Ryan thought he encouraged it. It seemed to confirm worries he had about himself. Coppinger had never told Ryan anything about his background except that he had come to the city from the country. Somewhere Ryan had gained an impression of makeshift congregational halls, the just gathering from outlying farms in the darkness, sparse and godfearing. Margaret understood this better than Ryan. The bare, scrubbed places in the soul; work from dawn to dusk, Sabbath observance, the wrath of the righteous.

'Is she gone back to the city?'

'Straight after the funeral.'

'I might give her a ring. She's a good girl, so she is.'

Ryan knew the way that Coppinger regarded her. It was a kind of flattery. It made her see herself baking bread, collecting children from school. A dream of well-regarded and admirable motherhood. Honest, not beautiful, plainspoken. The ancestral pain of love.

'I'll see you tonight in the York,' he told Coppinger, before hanging up.

He replaced the receiver feeling lost. Upstairs he went through his pockets before dressing, searching through the debris of coins, wadded tissues, broken cigarettes. How many times had he stood attempting to reconstruct the events of an evening from these fragments? He thought of dimly lit artifacts, difficult, allusive objects. Among them he came across a damp cigarette packet with her address on it. He had walked her part of the way home. After the car park they were both happy to revert to people who had been brought up in the town. They talked about first kisses, café jukeboxes, small episodes fixed in the resonant dismay of adulthood. They held hands and walked along the esplanade. He asked her if he would see her again. She said no, that her man had just come back from a journey. He asked for her address and she had written it on the cigarette packet. When they reached the end she hailed a taxi and rode away without looking round. As he got into the car to drive back to the city Ryan felt the mood of the night before still with him. His mother did not come to the door to wave him off.

A sea mist hung over the town. People drifting apart, his mother in her armchair, a woman's white blouse in the back of a taxi. The air was soft and moist. People and buildings faded into it, features perceived vaguely, as if the town was temporary, constructed in the vague materials of leave-taking and return.

ANNE ENRIGHT

'(She Owns) Every Thing'

Cathy was often wrong, she found it more interesting. She was wrong about the taste of bananas. She was wrong about the future of the bob. She was wrong about where her life ended up. She loved corners, surprises, changes of light.

Of all the fates that could have been hers (spinster, murderer, savant, saint), she chose to work behind a handbag counter in Dublin and take her holidays in the sun.

For ten years she lived with the gloves and beside the umbrellas, their colours shy and neatly furled. The handbag counter travelled through navy and brown to a classic black. Yellows, reds, and white were to one side and all varieties of plastic were left out on stands, for the customer to steal.

Cathy couldn't tell you what the handbag counter was like. It was hers. It smelt like a leather dream. It was never quite right. Despite the close and intimate spaces of the gloves and the empty generosity of the bags themselves, the discreet mess that was the handbag counter was just beyond her control.

She sold clutch bags for people to hang on to; folded slivers of animal skin that wouldn't hold a box of cigarettes, or money unless it was paper, or a bunch of keys. 'Just a credit card and a condom,' said one young woman to another and Cathy felt the ache of times changing.

She sold the handbag proper, sleek and stiff and surprisingly roomy – the favourite bag, the thoroughbred, with a hard clasp, or a fold-over flap and the smell of her best perfume. She sold sacks to young women, in canvas or in suede, baggy enough to hold a life, a change of underwear, a novel, a deodorant spray.

The women's faces as they made their choice were full of lines going nowhere, tense with the problems of leather, price, vulgarity, colour. Cathy matched blue eyes with a blue trim, a modest mouth with smooth, plum suede. She sold patent to the click of high heels, urged women who had forgotten into neat, swish reticules. Quietly, one customer after another was guided to the inevitable and surprising choice of a bag that was not 'them' but one step beyond who they thought they might be.

Cathy knew what handbags were for. She herself carried everything (which wasn't much) in one pocket, or the other.

She divided her women into two categories: those who could and those who could not.

She had little affection for those who could, they had no need of her, and they were often mistaken. Their secret was not one of class, although that seemed to help, but one of belief, and like all questions of belief, it involved certain mysteries. How, for example, does one *believe* in navy?

There were also the women who could not. A woman, for example, who could NOT wear blue. A woman who could wear a print, but NOT beside her face. A woman who could wear beads but NOT earrings. A woman who had a secret life of shoes too exotic for her, or one who could neither pass a perfume counter nor buy a perfume, unless it was for someone else. A woman who comes home with royal jelly every time she tries to buy a blouse.

A woman who cries in the lingerie department.

A woman who laughs while trying on hats.

A woman who buys two coats of a different colour.

The problem became vicious when they brought their daughters shopping. Cathy could smell these couples from Kitchenware.

Cathy married late and it was hard work. She had to find a man. Once she had found one, she discovered that the city was full of them. She had to talk and laugh and be fond. She had to choose. Did she like big burly men with soft brown eyes? Did she like that blond man with the eyes of pathological blue? What did she think of her own face, its notches and dents?

She went the easy road with a kind teacher from Fairview and a registry office do. She stole him from a coltish young woman with awkward eyes. Cathy would have sold her a tapestry Gladstone bag, one that was 'wrong' but 'worked' all the same.

Sex was a pleasant surprise. It was such a singular activity, it seemed to scatter and gather her at the same time.

Cathy fell in love one day with a loose, rangy woman, who came to her counter and to her smile and seemed to pick her up with the same ease as she did an Argentinian calf-skin shoulder bag in tobacco brown, with woven leather inset panels, pig-skin lining and snap clasp. It was quite a surprise.

The woman, whose eyes were a tired shade of blue, asked Cathy's opinion, and Cathy heard herself say 'DIVE RIGHT IN HONEY, THE WATER'S JUST FINE!' – a phrase she must have picked up from the television set. The woman did not flinch. She said 'Have you got it in black?'

Brown was the colour of the bag. Cathy was disappointed by this betrayal. The weave would just disappear in black, the staining was everything. Cathy said, 'It's worth it in brown, even if it means new shoes. It really is a beautiful bag.' The woman, however, neither bought the brown nor argued for black. She rubbed the leather with the base of her thumb as she laid the bag down. She looked at Cathy. She despaired. She turned her wide, sporting shoulders, her dry, bleached hair, and her nose with the bump in it, gave a small sigh, and walked out of the shop.

Cathy spent the rest of the day thinking, not of her hands, with their large knuckles, but of her breasts, that were widely spaced and looked two ways, one towards the umbrellas, the other at the scarves. She also wondered whether the woman had a necklace of lines hanging from her hips, whether she had ever been touched by a woman, what she might say, what Cathy might say back. Whether her foldings and infoldings were the same as her own or as different as daffodil from narcissus. It was a very lyrical afternoon.

Cathy began to slip. She made mistakes. She sold the wrong bags to the wrong women and her patter died. She waited for another woman to pick up the tobacco-brown bag to see what might happen. She sold indiscriminately. She looked at every woman who came her way and she just didn't know anymore.

She could, of course, change her job. She might, for example, work as a hospital maid, in the cardiac ward, which was full of certainties.

Women did not get heart attacks. They would come at visiting time and talk too much or not at all. She could work out who loved simply or in silence. She could spot those who might as well hate. She would look at their bags without judgement, as they placed them on the coverlets, or opened them for tissues. They might even let a tear drip inside.

Cathy emptied out her building-society account and walked up to the hat department with a plastic bag filled with cash. She said, 'Ramona, I want to buy every hat you have.' She did the same at Shoes, although she stipulated size five-and-a-half. She didn't make a fuss when refused. She stuffed the till of her own counter full of notes, called a taxi and hung herself with bags, around her neck and down her arms. All kinds of people looked at her. Then she went to bed for a week, feeling slightly ashamed.

She kept the one fatal bag, the brown calf-skin with a snap clasp. She abused it. She even used it to carry things. She started to sleep around.

GLENN PATTERSON

from *Burning Your Own*

2

In front of the willow tree, on top of the mound on which it grew, stood a toilet with two red cushions tied to the seat. Through the curtain of branches, Mal could see sheets of tin sloping from the ground into the bushes. He shouted hello, but there was no answer, no sign that anyone was inside. He wavered, his heart pounding. All the way across the dump he had gritted his teeth and tried to blot out thoughts of trained rats. Now, his nerve was failing him. He glanced behind at the expanse of weeds and grass, strewn with ripped garbage bags, spring-burst chairs, sodden mattresses, bottles and cans. He thought of the danger he had already run, the numerous bumps and jolts he had suffered, and somehow it seemed less of a risk to go forward than back again over the junk.

Warily, he mounted the small rise and eased aside the outer branches of the willow tree . . . *Whoosh!* – he was drenched by a shower of water . . . *Whoosh!* – the breath was punched out of him and he was knocked to the ground by a red streak that caught him square in the chest. He thrashed on the grass, soaked and spluttering. By the time he had recovered himself, Francy Hagan was bending over him.

'What the fuck are you doing snooping around here?'

He spat a smokespit and, dragging Mal up by his shirt-front, peered at him with his small black eyes.

'Oh,' he said, somewhat softer, but at the same time releasing his grip so that Mal fell again. 'It's you.'

He walked in the shade of the tree, picking up an empty bucket and a boxing glove on a stick. He saw Mal watching him.

'Booby traps,' he said. 'Fucking nobody's going to take me by surprise.'

Mal lay still for a time, but when he realized that Francy wasn't going to do anything else he stood, mopping his face and hair with his sleeves.

'Well, what *do* you want?' Francy asked him.

'The ones at the bonfire,' he blurted. 'They're coming to get you.'

As soon as the words were out, Mal wondered why he had spoken them. He knew the gang had forgotten about Francy in all their talk. Still, he told himself, maybe another day they would come.

'So they sent you to scare me?'

'Oh, no,' Mal explained, terrified of what might happen if Francy thought he was mixed up with the others. 'No one knows I'm here, I was just warning you.'

Francy almost managed a smile.

'Don't worry about me,' he said. 'I'm not afraid of anyone on this estate. I know things – the first person tries anything on me, I'll . . . Well, just let them try. They haven't seen the half of it yet.'

His manner had become aggressive again. Mal hurriedly changed the subject.

'And I was . . . I was . . . I wanted to ask about the rat.'

That statement surprised him too.

'Bastards,' Francy swore. 'It's dead. I'd to kill it myself.'

He stared past Mal an instant.

'D'you want to see it?' he asked, and nodded to the sloping tin.

Mal shrank inwardly at the thought and his stomach flipped again as he remembered the hatchet and the jumbled stories of miscarriages and sucking cocks. He swallowed, and followed Francy towards the den.

'No, you don't.' Francy held out a big hand to halt him. 'D'you think I'm some sort of headcase letting you in there? Wait outside.'

Passing out through the branches, Mal was engulfed in a torrent of sunlight, pouring from a sudden rent in the low summer cloud. He shivered, inexplicably, and crumpled to his knees, next to the toilet, rubbing his eyes with the backs of his hands. A moment later the rent passed on, leaving the sky once more a shifting waste of white. But long after sunspots had ceased to dance before his eyes, Mal was still gazing straight ahead, bewildered.

Beyond the dump, across the grass, a solid mass of redbrick walled in his vision. Roofs merged in strange teetering formations, half-houses, quarter-houses were grafted on to the sides of others, filling every gap, blinding every alley and driveway. He lived here, but he did not recognize this place, could not reconcile the jumble with the neatly hedged rows he walked through day to day.

'I thought you wanted to see this?'

Francy's voice was suspicious and challenging.

Mal turned guiltily. Francy cradled the rat in his hands; lengths of string and bootlace dangled from his belt where once the hatchet had been. He tugged on the cigarette screwed into the corner of his mouth.

'Might have known you weren't fucking interested.'

Mal had expected anger and was not prepared for the pained, almost sad squint in Francy's eyes.

'I am interested,' he assured him. 'Why'd you have to kill it?'

'Why d'you think?' Francy snapped, sitting down with a thump on the cushioned toilet seat. He laid the rat on the ground beside him and pulled the strings from his belt. 'It was suffering – they cry, you know. There was nothing else I could do, so I broke its neck.'

He began tying together the lengths of string, his thick fingers fashioning knots of his own invention, and Mal's attention returned to the redbricked disorder beyond the fence.

'Do you not think the estate looks funny?'

'No,' Francy said, without raising his head.

'I'd never have believed it could look like that.'

Francy made a clucking noise at the back of his throat.

'There's a lot about this place you wouldn't believe – I could teach you a thing or two.'

He hauled so hard on his cigarette that it smouldered with the dark smell of burning filter.

'Lesson number one: when all that' – he waved a hand in the direction of the houses – 'was still no more than barren fields for cows to shit and sick grass in, the dump was here.'

Mal frowned. It was not so much that he found it difficult to imagine the houses not being there, to rub them out, to pluck the goalposts and the crazy-golf course from the park – though that was hard enough; but to imagine a time before they had ever been . . . The effort made his temples ache dully.

'When the builders came, this was their yard – though even before that it was set apart, distinct. They drove their stakes into the ground, where the fenceposts are now, and behind corrugated iron sheets they erected their workmen's huts and offices.'

In one fluid movement, Francy swivelled the No. 6 butt from the left of his mouth to the centre and spat it some ten yards to indicate the spot.

'There.'

Mal accepted without question that the dogend was well aimed.

'That was the first estate, you know: a compound of diggers, bulldozers, braziers, planks and bricks. Those houses out there all started off in here, every one of them – a million fucking pieces. And there were people of course, the workmen. Each morning they'd clock in at the site and when the weather was too bad for work they'd stay in the huts, drinking tea and playing cards, waiting. Hundreds of them: navvies, asphalters, boys for the drains and the water, others to lay the electric and the gas; and then you're only just up to the house-plots. On top of that lot you've your brickies, chippies, sparks and plumbers, tilers, glaziers, not forgetting every bastard type of foreman, overlooker and white-collar worker you'd care to mention.'

He spat a dry spit.

'Hundreds of them. And they'd be out sometimes in the winter before the fucking sun was right up. Day in, day out, week after week, for months on end, they dug up earth, put down foundations, put down pipes, connected mains and cables, churned cement in hand-turned mixers, laid bricks, battened floors, framed doors, wired up, roofed in and planed off, until the whole fucking lot was finished. Out of nothing from this compound they raised an estate: streets, roads, parks, avenues, drives, cul-de-sacs, houses, detached and semi-detached, on the high ground at the front, terraced row upon terraced row down here at the back. And all in the same time that it takes to make a baby, dipping to dropping.'

His beady eyes probed Mal.

'Except, of course, you can't make a baby with just men, as you well know.'

Mal blushed, looking at the ground. Francy rummaged in his butt box and struck a match.

'For a week it stood like that . . .'

Francy began talking again and Mal, who had expected something else, lifted his head, relieved. Eager too. In Francy's words he had seen the estate grow, brick by brick.

'. . . stood complete and empty, while the workmen dismantled the yard. They loaded the huts and braziers, tarburners, mixers, planks and bricks on to trucks. The stakes surrounding the compound were uprooted and the corrugated iron sheets that had filled the gaps between them were piled high and driven to new sites. And on the last day, with the first cars and vans already nosing along the newly tarmacked streets, a workman steered the sole remaining bulldozer to one end of the now bare yard and there, at the foot of an ancient willow tree, shovelled earth, grass, broken wood and brick-dust and covered in the pisstrench.'

Mal's eyes opened wide in recognition. He jumped to his feet, dusting the seat of his trousers. Francy cackled and hackled a smokespit.

'Man, dear, that was fifteen years ago. The tree hasn't suffered, has it? And the grass grows well enough here.'

He tied a final knot in the strings he had painstakingly been twisting together, attaching a long black football lace to the rope of assorted colours.

'And this rat' – he lifted it by the tail – 'didn't die of fucking pisspoison. Did it?'

'No,' Mal said quietly. 'It didn't.'

'Didn't is fucking right,' Francy snarled. 'It was people killed this rat. Lesson number two: rats never kill for fun.'

He spat, absentmindedly, the cigarette stub he had lit only moments before. It spiralled through the air, trailing smoke, like a strafed bomber, and crashed against the neck of a grass-green bottle.

'That nearly went in,' Mal told him.

'What?' Francy screwed up his face. 'Oh, yeah. I can get them in most times. When I remember.'

Mal didn't doubt it. They watched the butt's glowing tip slide down the glass and fizzle in the long tangled grass, where even at this hour the dew had not yet lifted.

'Anyway' – Francy placed the rat on his lap – 'the story. The builders slipped unnoticed through the back here, while the people, owners of the houses they'd made, entered the estate by the front. And fuck did the people ever come. Can you imagine it?'

Mal tried, couldn't, shook his head.

'They came from everywhere: from Newtownards Road, Beersbridge Road and Ballymacarrett in the east; from Ardoyne, the Oldpark, Legoniel, in the north; from Ormeau, Annadale, Sandy Row, the Village, in the south; and in the west, from Shankill, Springfield, Woodvale – aye, and even a few from the Falls and Whiterock Road.'

Francy winked, leaning forward, licking spittle from the corner of his mouth.

'And we're not yet out of the city limits, haven't begun to consider the ones who came from the towns round about: from Bangor and Lisburn, Carrick, Larne, Ballymena, Downpatrick, Portadown. Beyond that too: from Armagh, Dungannon and Omagh, Enniskillen, Newry, Strabane, Derry – and all the countryside in between; people that had scarcely ever seen a town, never mind a city.'

He paused again.

'You'd think that'd be an end to it, wouldn't you?'

Mal, his mind reeling with the vision of the hordes conjured by Francy bearing down on the empty estate, nodded dumbly.

'Not a bit of it,' he said. 'There were the lost ones as well; the ones who'd emigrated when they were young, had had their fill and now wanted to settle down.'

He shook one end of the rope.

'They felt the tug: felt it in Glasgow, Liverpool, Manchester, Birmingham, London; felt it in Toronto, Chicago, New York, Detroit, Wellington, Sydney, Perth and places whose names you've never in your life dreamed of. They felt the tug, like they all do eventually, and were drawn back to Belfast, to a space less than Belfast: an area of a quarter square mile, a collection of detached, semi-detached and terraced houses, in a network of avenues, parks, cul-de-sacs, roads and streets, raised from nothing out of the fields in the time it takes to make a baby; bounded by main roads on three sides and by a poxy wood, trailing into a dump, at its arse end.'

Francy smiled broadly for the first time. His teeth were yellow, going green at the gums.

'Now, I bet you're wondering why,' he said.

But the question wouldn't have entered Mal's head. He was young and listened to those who were older, even those only a few – or was it more? – years older, like Francy, in the same way that he read books. He followed the words, letting them guide him. The patterns they made were the patterns of his thoughts, he was not aware of any alternatives. Indeed, listening to Francy was like reading a book, or, at least, like hearing teachers talk who had taught so long from the same book that its language had become theirs. Though, of course, teachers didn't swear, and neither did books; not the ones that Mal had read at any rate.

'Well?' asked Francy. 'Aren't you wondering why? Or even how I know all this?'

Mal was young, the words of others were his guides. And now they suggested he wonder why, how.

'Why?' he wondered aloud. 'How?'

Francy rocked back in his seat.

'As to how,' he said, tapping the side of his nose slyly. 'That's for me to know and you to find out. But, as to why . . .'

He closed one eye and tilted his head sideways, scrutinizing Mal.

'Well, look, they grew up in the war, most of the people that bought houses on this estate. In the war or in the thirties. Not much to fucking choose between the two if you're from Northern Ireland. There were riots in the thirties, you know, things that make the stuff today look normal – house-burnings, killings, the lot. Bit like the war, only without the uniforms and on your own doorstep. The war had that going for it: by and large it happened somewhere else. And then, it wasn't as bad as the first one – no trenches, or any of that shit, not the same danger of the men coming home all packed up in their old kitbags. And there was work too in the war, unlike the thirties. So, if you could put up with the blackout, the ration books, and the odd air-raid . . . well, things could've been worse. Still and all, they danced in the streets and sang when it was over. Because we'd won. Good old we.

'But after the celebrations, when the rationing continued and the work didn't, people started to catch themselves on. Whole areas had gone' – he snapped his fingers – 'phut! And there they were having to live in prefabs or with their relatives . . . Suddenly just winning didn't seem to be enough. And it wasn't only the usual sort complained. D'you see what I'm getting at?'

Mal looked as serious as he knew how, but his expression of understanding was hopelessly transparent.

'People,' Francy explained carefully, 'will accept war if you can convince them the hardship's worthwhile. But, they're not going to be too happy when they find out the better world they've been fighting for's just the same old world over again. Right?'

'Right,' Mal agreed.

'So, what do you do?'

Teachertrick. Lull you and lead you with their booklanguage, then spring a question. Mal took his time, recapping all he had heard to avoid any error in his reply.

'You change it?' he offered at length.

Francy's broad purple tongue circled the outer ring of his lips, preening the thick down. He sucked a cavity in the recesses of his mouth, watching Mal.

'Aye,' he said. 'You change it.'

He continued talking, but it seemed to Mal as though he were losing interest in his own story.

'What was needed? Jobs? Jobs it was. Not so many as in the war, but more than before it. And what else? Houses. Can't have people living in the ruined shells from war and riots – pull them down. Pull them down and build modern houses, estates full of them, on the outskirts of the city, away from the old memories. That's what they did. Then, they waited to see what happened. And what happened? The people flocked to them. And they flocked here, to Larkview, to a ready-made community.'

Francy lit a heel-flattened scrap of cigar, puffing on it like it was a cigarette, raising clouds of smoke – green, blue, brown – that obscured his face. Then, with a sudden deep breath, he sucked all the smoke inside him, up his nose, down his throat, exhaling a moment later a single offwhite stream.

'Finished,' he said, rising.

He held the string above his head; it bounced taut, knots tightening with the weight of the rat hanging by its tail.

'What d'you think?'

The rat had already begun to stiffen, but Mal was no longer frightened by it. Its tail, entwined in the lengths of string, was not the whiplash he had always envisaged. After killing the rat, Francy pushed as many of the broken bones as he was able back into place; it bulged awkwardly here and there, but remained intact within its smoothed greybrown fur. Only with the mouth was Francy unable to do anything. The lips were peeled back grotesquely and two small yellow teeth protruded over a strip of pink tongue.

'This,' said Francy, 'is a charm.'

'Really?' Mal asked.

Francy cackled until the phlegm rose in his throat.

'Really and truly. See how useful rats are, even dead ones? If you tie this round you and wear it everywhere you go for a week, it'll not only bring you luck, but tell you, too, what the future holds.'

Mal looked at the ratrope doubtfully. The problem wasn't that he didn't believe what Francy told him (he did, although he wasn't quite sure he understood perfectly) but that, much as his terror of rats had diminished, he couldn't see himself trailing one behind him for a whole week. Francy, however, forestalled his objections.

'Oh, don't worry, I'm not wasting this on you. No chance. Too ashamed to wear a rat, aren't you? I'll bet you'd even be ashamed to be seen with me.'

He took the cigar from the tip of his tongue and flicked the burning end off with a red-haired, orange-stained finger, popping the remainder into his mouth. He chewed noisily, a rivulet of bitsy juice trickling down his chin.

'I wouldn't,' Mal said, his voice little more than a whisper. 'I want to be your friend.'

Francy grinned, teeth now smeared with a film of brown mucus, and spat, heavily this time, straight down. A thick, chewed splodge landed at his feet and he ground it into the grass with his baseball boot.

'The ratcharm will decide,' he said.

He crossed the mound and dragged Mal to his feet. Hitching Mal's shirt, Francy passed the string twice around his waist, knotting one end to a back belt-loop. He let go and the rat thudded on the grass. Mal's jeans were tugged tight against him, with a force that made him first gasp, then colour deeply. Francy swayed from side to side, mumbling incoherently, untied the rat and repeated the ritual on himself.

'Right, then,' he told Mal. 'Fuck off.'

Mal glanced at him, hurt.

'But can't I . . .'

'Come back? A week from now, like I said. And not before, mind. The message of the rat will be clear by then – provided, that is, you don't mention to another living soul that you've been here and seen me. Now, beat it. I've got to find some smokes.'

He birled Mal around so that he faced the houses and placed his open hands at the sides of his head, blinkering his eyes.

'Keep going in a straight line, it's easier. And don't stop till you're at the fence.'

Reluctantly, Mal set off, endeavouring to stick to Francy's path of compacted rubbish, cutting out the worst of the brambles and nettlebanks. This morning, he thought, all of this – the dump, the rats, Francy himself – had been part of another world, a world known to him through others' stories and his own imaginings. One afternoon, the like of which he had never before lived through, had changed all that. Now, he was learning its secrets. And there was the sensation in his privates, when Francy let go the rope, straining his trousers against them. He had glimpsed for an instant the vague outlines of still another world; but the faint image quickly died, and he was left once more with the half-remembered, barely understood mutterings of the older boys.

He had reached the end of the track. It occurred to him that Francy hadn't thought to ask his name. He spun on his heel, intending to go back, but the toilet was gone from before the willow and Francy was nowhere to be seen. He turned again and paused, staring at the estate. It *did* look odd from there. The angle was to blame, of course; he wasn't used to it. He climbed the fence and started up the cul-de-sac to the hill. Tomorrow would be time enough for giving the bonfire another go.

JOSEPH O'CONNOR

from *Cowboys and Indians*

Jimmy and Ruth's flat turned out to be quite something. It was in the vast refurbished attic of a sour-faced Victorian house that looked out over the old Jewish cemetery in Golders Green. The floors were polished and smooth, and stained-glass skylights ran along the roof. All the furniture was black and Jimmy said they'd got it from Shabitat, a joke he had to explain to Eddie, who was new to such things.

Crisps and peanuts and little salty things were laid out in black bowls on the black coffee table. Charlie Parker honked out of the black stereo speakers. Ruth kissed the air on both sides of Eddie's face and hung his leather jacket on the black coat hanger.

'Help yourself to nibbles,' she said, wiggling her ass as she backed through the swing doors and into the kitchen. Her tight black dress looked like it probably had to be put on with the aid of a pulley and winch.

Jimmy breezed into the room wrapped in a black towel, his beer belly flopping over the edge.

'Streuth, Ruth,' he yelped, 'everyone's here already.' He picked up a beer can and said hi to Eddie. 'You know everyone?' he said. 'This is Eddie Virago, folks, late of Dublin town, now one of the great unwashed migrants of the Ryanair generation. He's unemployed by the way, so don't flaunt your fabulous wealth in front of him.' Eddie told him to butt out and put some clothes on.

In addition to Jimmy and Ruth, there were a couple of other old college friends. Well, not exactly friends. People whose faces Eddie knew.

A guy called Creep – nobody knew his real name – whose eyebrows met in the middle, and his girlfriend Fiona who was an assistant subeditor in what she called the trade press – actually, on a magazine called *Meat Trade Monthly*. Eddie remembered them vaguely from Commerce. They'd been one of those couples who hold hands during lectures and snog in the bar. Creep was working as a refuse-sack salesman on what he called 'the northern run'. His girlfriend kept telling him to tell a particular story about a really funny thing that had happened to him up in Carlisle once, but he didn't seem to want to.

'You had to be there,' he explained.

There was another girl, also called Fiona, who wore a yellow cheesecloth blouse and was into the Greens. She was a vegetarian, so the subject of *Meat Trade Monthly* was discreetly avoided. She was working as a fundraiser for the Committee to End Animal Experiments, she said. When Eddie asked what that was like she smiled and said, 'Oh, mustn't grumble.' She had a guy with her who seemed shy and awkward and didn't say much and kept cleaning his fingernails with a toothpick. He was a poet, apparently. Eddie didn't catch his name. He wore black-rimmed glasses like Buddy Holly's, and a black poloneck jumper. He looked like someone who'd come to an Islington fancy dress party, *dressed* as a poet. But in fact, a poet was what he really was.

'In real life,' as he put it.

Things were a little tense while they sat around the room waiting for Jimmy and Ruth to come back. One of the Fionas kept looking at Eddie's face, as though she was trying to remember him from somewhere. Eddie kept hoping she'd stop, but after fifteen minutes he decided to put her out of her misery.

'Yes,' said Eddie, resigned, 'Dean Bean.' Then she snapped her fingers and laughed.

'Oh yeah, that's it.' Eddie sighed. 'He's a real sweetie,' she said, with a demolishing smile, 'so what's he doing now anyway?'

Creep got to talking about wheel clamps for some reason and the poet got down on his knees to leaf through the record collection, occasionally scrutinizing the small print on the back of an album cover. Any time somebody said 'Fiona' the two girls would turn around simultaneously, and everybody would crack up laughing, as though it was really funny. But there were whole minutes of agonizing silence while everyone waited for everybody else to start a conversation, and when Jimmy finally came into the room Eddie was so relieved he could have kissed him.

'Fuck me,' said Jimmy, staring around, 'let's join hands and try to contact the living.' Jammed into a tight pair of stonewash denims, Jimmy looked even fatter than he had the other night.

Jimmy apologized for not having any methylated spirits, a supposedly ironic reference to Eddie's haircut. Then he slapped Eddie hard on the back and laughed.

'Good one, Jim,' said Eddie.

'Only jerking you off, Ed,' he said. 'What'll you have really?'

Eddie said he'd have a gin and tonic.

'Ices and slices?' said Jimmy.

'No,' said Eddie, 'straight up.' Jimmy looked him in the eye. 'Don't even think about it,' said Eddie.

When Ruth came out of the kitchen she asked Eddie not to stand on the rug, if he didn't mind. They'd got it on their holidays in Tunisia, and it was *très* special to them. So Eddie sat on the fat window ledge, listening to the small talk and everybody else stood around the rim of the rug, as though it was a swimming pool full of piranhas. The poet put on Nina Simone.

'Corso didn't get the Beeb job,' said Fiona the vegetarian, and Fiona the carnivore shook her head in dismay, saying if she'd been let down as many times as Corso she'd probably just give up breathing or something. 'Yes,' said the veggy Fiona, 'he's very peed off, waiting for a bit of feedback.' Now he was applying for the Royal Film School at Elmers End. Jimmy said he hadn't a chance, he knew that place well, if you weren't shafting someone on the inside you wouldn't get within spitting distance. Creep laughed, and Eddie asked how Jimmy knew this. He winked boldly, and tapped the side of his nose.

'*Vorsprung durch Technik*,' he said. 'Contacts, Ed.' The poet said that was absolute rubbish. 'No, serio,' said Jimmy, 'we do all their advertising.'

'Shall we?' said Ruth, beckoning towards the door.

'Shall we what?' said Eddie.

'Eat,' she said. 'It's all ready.'

Eddie had never tasted vichyssoise before. He said it was wonderful what Marks and Spencer could get into a can these days, and Ruth told him to fuck off. He told her she was looking very well. She told him to fuck off again. Ruth was in one of her nervous moods.

Jimmy sniffed the wine.

'Rough little vintage,' he said, 'wouldn't like to meet it down a dark alley one night.' Nobody laughed. Jimmy had obviously forgotten, but he'd been making this joke ever since first year, when they used to sometimes chip together for a bottle of Moroccan Hock or Asti Spumante and bring it back to Dean Bean's flat.

Beano's flatmate Johnny Speed had been working for the Simon Community at the time. He'd spend the whole night driving around the streets of Dublin, force-feeding sandwiches and soup to bedraggled winos, only to come home at two in the morning and find everybody in his flat almost as pissed and twice as incoherent as anyone he'd met all evening. Then, when they ran out of cigarettes, he'd break open the ration of Players that each Simon worker got issued for the gasping dossers, and they'd pass them round in frantic gratitude before getting into a fight about who was more middle class than whom. It was, as Dean Bean often said, a beautiful time.

When Ruth brought in the huge dish of steaming nut roast she beamed with anxious pride as everyone said how nice it looked. She looked incredibly nervous now. When she chewed her nails, Eddie noticed her hands trembling. That wasn't like Ruth at all. He wondered if she was alright. She kept smoothing down her hair and looking up and down the table, as though she'd forgotten something. Jimmy put his arms around her and squeezed her shoulders. He told her to chill out.

But it hadn't gone well. Even before the avocado salad was shared out, there was a big argument about the SDP. Ruth said she was going to vote for them because she fancied the ass off David Owen, which was about the most intelligent thing anybody said all night. Both Fionas agreed that the Greens would be getting their vote. They kept saying, 'We've destroyed the planet, we've ruined the world,' in a guilt-tinged voice, as though they, personally, had destroyed the planet and ruined the world. Creep said it didn't make any difference, the whole country was run by the banks anyway. Jimmy said he was staying with Maggie and he didn't give a wank about the Poll Tax. Labour were all very well, but you couldn't trust them on the Unions. He said Scargill had Kinnock by the goolies and he made a squeezing gesture with his right hand, forking a knot of pasta into his mouth.

'I know Maggie's a cunt,' he said, 'but she can do the fucking job, you have to give her that.'

Eddie tucked into his nut roast, and said it was very nice. He just didn't feel like a big political discussion. He kept thinking about Marion, for some reason, hoping she was alright, wondering what she would make of a night like tonight, wondering what these friends would say if they ever met her, not that, of course, they ever would. Ruth asked if he'd had any luck on the job front, and he told her there were a few definite possibilities, nothing confirmed, but fingers crossed. The poet said, 'Isn't "definite possibility" an oxymoron?' Jimmy told him not to be such a pedantic fucker.

After dinner the carnivorous Fiona pulled out a big bag of dope and spliffed up. Jimmy called it 'whacky backy' and that made everybody laugh. It was good stuff. Eddie sucked hard at the damp joint end and felt the blast tingle slowly up from his feet. He felt better.

Jimmy brought a bowl of sliced up kiwi fruit and banana from the kitchen, and Ruth carried in a huge jug of whipped cream. The vegetarian Fiona said she went absolutely crazy for kiwi fruit, just flipped out totally for it, and for some reason the poet laughed, slightly too loud.

Eddie started talking to the poet, who seemed to have been ignoring him all night. He said he'd written some poetry himself. The poet didn't seem to be too interested. Eddie asked who his influences were and he said Oh, people like Ginsberg.

'People *like* Ginsberg,' said Eddie, 'what does that mean?' The poet said it was hard to explain exactly what he meant and in fact he didn't like explaining his work at all. He preferred it to stand or fall by its own abilities.

'A bit like Eddie's hair,' said Jimmy.

Eddie asked if he'd got anything published and the poet said, 'Here and there, little magazines mainly, you probably wouldn't know them.' Eddie said he should enter a poetry competition, but the poet said he didn't agree with competitions for art, as they merely replicated the hierarchical fetishism of bourgeois society at large. That seemed to be the end of that.

Creep started talking about the release of the Guildford Four, and a documentary he'd seen about them during the week. He said it was terrible what had been done to them, and he looked genuinely upset about it. Jimmy held up a glass and said, 'Here's to them,' and everybody nodded devoutly as they chinked their glasses. Ruth said it was an absolute disgrace. The poet said he wouldn't mind spending fifteen years in jail if he was going to get all that money at the end, and both Fionas said that was absolutely crass. He said he'd only been joking, and anyway, all this hypocrisy made him sick. Eddie said he agreed actually.

'What about Nicky Kelly?' he said. 'He was framed, in the land of so-called Saints and Scholars.' There were dodgy things happening in Ireland too, but nobody, Eddie said, nobody seemed to give two tosses about that. There was silence for a moment. Then Creep said that was true, but still. 'Typical,' said Eddie. 'Just typical.'

Northern Ireland came up over the camembert. Some guys had been shot dead in a bar during the week, builders' labourers who'd been working for the British Army. The usual row started then, about whether the old IRA were terrorists or not, compared to the Provos. Creep said they were, that they did all the things the Provos did, kidnapped, killed, tortured. Fiona said this wasn't the case, that she didn't know exactly how to put it, but they'd just been somehow different. The vegetarian Fiona said she was opposed to all violence except in South Africa and the poet said, 'Why, do moral rules stop at the South African border or what?' The whole thing limped back and forth across the table, everyone churning out opinions Eddie had heard a million times before. Eddie couldn't concentrate anyway. He felt embarrassed that he'd gone over the top earlier. He said nothing. And all this talk about Northern Ireland kept bringing him back to Marion. It was weird. He was stoned. But it was true.

He thought about the shape of her face, the way she laughed, the way she held a cigarette, the way she turned the page of a magazine, the way she stirred her coffee, the way he sometimes caught her looking at him, the way she smiled, without showing her teeth and laughed when she was saying something sad. He discovered himself comparing the three girls around the table to her, asking himself, if Marion was here, what would she say about that? He sucked on the joint again and tried to forget her. He couldn't.

Half-way though dessert, the phone rang with a shattering glass sound, interrupting the lethargic discussion that was just breaking out on censorship. And in his irrational state, Eddie was convinced it was going to be her. He was sure. He prepared himself to go out to the phone and take her call.

But then they could hear Jimmy from the hall going 'Serious shit' and 'Heavy duty' and 'Drag city Arizona'. And when he came back in he looked worried. Hugo Rogers was in trouble. He'd gone out to celebrate his new job in Foreign Affairs, pranged the old dear's Volvo on the way home from the Leeson Street strip and run over the foot of a policeman who'd tried to stop him on Baggot Street Bridge. He was in deep shit, and he wanted to get the number of Jimmy's brother, Paul ('Pablo', Jimmy called him), a lawyer.

The room filled with gasps. Somebody asked whether the policeman was hurt.

'Well, he's not over the moon, y'know?' – and Jimmy did his Groucho Marx routine with an invisible cigar.

Eddie said it had only been a matter of time, and that Hugo had always been an irresponsible wanker.

'Eddie,' cautioned Ruth.

'Well,' Eddie said, 'the guy thinks with his dick.'

''Course, you've always been a heartless fucker, Eddie,' said Jimmy, pleasantly, 'you don't care about anything except principle, do you?'

'Principle?' said Eddie. 'The guy ran over a cop, for Jesus' sake.'

'A pig, Eddie, isn't that what you used to call them? A fascist pig?' Ruth started clearing away the dishes. Eddie said that wasn't the point. He said they could all drag up stuff from the past if they wanted to. 'Well, you've changed, haven't you, Ed? The conscience of the middle class, is that what you're passing yourself off as now?'

The vegetarian Fiona followed Ruth into the kitchen, holding the joint in front of her like a crucifix to a vampire.

'You'd know about middle class,' said Eddie.

'Yeah, and you wouldn't. Dragged up in the slums of Ranelagh.'

'My father,' said Eddie, stabbing the air with his finger, 'is working class.'

Jimmy began to clap his hands, slowly, and to speak in the insistent Sean O'Casey accent he reserved for these occasions.

'Oh, it's that time of the evening, is it? Let's drag out Virago Senior, the aulfella made good. Here he is, meladies and gents, not an arse in his proletarian trousers. Take a bow sir, bejayzus, take a bow.' Creep and his girlfriend started playing with the cutlery. The poet took off his glasses, wiped them on a napkin, and put them back on again. 'Ah, yeah,' said Jimmy, 'you've changed, Eddie, old son.'

'You haven't changed,' said Eddie, sourly, 'you never will.' He could feel himself getting drunk now, on top of the stoned feeling that was weighing down his jaw.

'Why don't you write a song about it, Eddie, eh? That'll have them manning the barricades, that'll have the bourgeoisie shaking in their shoes.'

Eddie blushed. Jimmy whinnied with laughter, and everybody else was quiet. Fiona started asking Eddie about his music, but he wasn't in the mood.

'Look,' said Eddie, to Jimmy, 'when I first met you you used to draw penises on newspaper photographs. When did you stop that?' Jimmy hissed a mouthful of smoke across the table.

'I stopped drawing them, Ed, maybe you should stop acting like one.'

Creep sighed loudly, and he said the conversation was becoming a little too heavy.

'Maybe,' said Eddie, 'but he's becoming a fucking caricature of himself.'

'Oooooo,' whined Jimmy, 'you're so sexy when you're butch, Eddie.'

In the kitchen the Fiona with the long hair was slumped over the table, weeping. Eddie stood in the doorway, watching her, but she didn't seem to notice. She was busily telling Ruth how life sometimes made her feel like 'a prawn in aspic', beautiful, delicate, but just slowly rotting away. Ruth kept hugging her and telling her everything would be alright.

Just as Eddie sat down at the kitchen table Fiona's head slipped from Ruth's shoulder. Her body slithered to the floor, and she lay flat out on her side, with one arm pointed out straight, still holding the joint. She looked like the statue of liberty, keeled over in a strong breeze.

Eddie helped Ruth do the dishes. It wasn't that he wanted to. It was just that he wanted to get away from Jimmy, who was busily insisting on showing the poet how the gas central heating worked. They stepped back and forth over Fiona's snoring body as they put the dishes away.

She asked him whether he'd heard from Jennifer. Eddie scoffed.

'What do you think?' he asked. 'You know what she's like.' Ruth said yes, that was true. She asked whether anybody new was flipping his pancake just now and he told her no. Then he said, well, yeah, kind of. She said that was nice, but she didn't ask for any details, which surprised Eddie a little, and even disappointed him too. When he said Jimmy was being a bastard again she looked surprised that he'd even mentioned it.

'You know what he's like,' she shrugged.

The kitchen walls were plastered with photos of Ruth and Jimmy, with the Eiffel Tower sprouting out of their heads, clinking pina coladas on sunset washed balconies, poking their faces through cardboard cut-outs of the Mona Lisa, making eyes across sun-spattered café tables.

When they had put the dishes away, Ruth and Eddie sat in the kitchen for a while, polishing off a bottle of gin. They talked about the old days and Eddie got more and more drunk. At one point he reached across the kitchen table and touched Ruth's hand.

'You know,' he slurred, 'I've always found you very attractive, Ruth, physically.' Ruth peeled his fingers off her sleeve.

'Fuck off, Eddie,' she said.

They went back to the gin, as though nothing had happened. They talked, for some reason, about Ireland's chances in the Eurovision Song Contest, something neither of them knew the first thing about. And after another joint Ruth got a serious case of the munchies. Eddie got some bread and took a pack of butter from the fridge. They sat in silence, eating, for ten minutes, saying nothing, catching each other in the eye and then looking away, as though they had something to feel guilty about.

'Fair play to Ireland,' she said, eventually, 'they invented the first really spread-from-the-fridge butter.'

'Yeah,' said Eddie, 'it's a great country.'

When it was time to go Eddie retrieved his leather jacket from the bedroom. Creep and Fiona were asleep under the coats. Creep woke up and looked at Eddie with a bleary confused gape.

'Oh,' he yawned, 'it's you.' He said he could probably get Eddie a job in National Bags'n'Sacks, if he was stuck. Eddie told him thanks but no thanks, he didn't really think that was his thing. Creep made him take his card anyway, even though Eddie said there was honestly no point. Creep told him if he heard of anything else he'd give him a bell. 'We Paddies have to stick together,' he hiccupped. 'Have to keep the fucking flag flying, Eddie, what?'

Downstairs in the front garden Jimmy was rueful and apologetic. He told Eddie he could crash upstairs if he wanted to. They had a sofabed. Eddie said he'd take a raincheck.

'Come on, Eddie,' he said, 'no hard feelings, man.'

Eddie stuck his hands deep in his pockets and stamped his feet in the cold. Wafer ice had formed over the puddles in the drive and the grass felt crisp underfoot. Jimmy said at least he should let them call a cab, but Eddie said no, he just couldn't afford it.

'We're not all set up like you two,' he pouted. Jimmy said he'd bung him a few quid, but Eddie just shot him one of his best offended looks.

The moon was a hard red eye over Golders Green. Deep blue light seemed to dribble through a hollow sky.

'You know me, Ed,' pleaded Jimmy, 'too much fire water. I'm a fucking Barclays Banker when I'm pissed.'

'Yeah,' said Eddie, 'that's true.'

Jimmy threw his arms around Eddie.

'I love you man, you know that, come on Ed, give me a break.' Eddie told him to relax. He said it was just the dope, he'd been overdoing it lately, too much of it made you aggressive. Jimmy said, yeah, he didn't do it that much any more. 'In fact, I'm really a boring bastard now,' he sighed. 'I mean, it's not as if I don't know that, honestly. I do know that. I'm boring as the fucking Channel Tunnel, Ed, I really am.' They stood in the garden, looking up at the yellow-lit windows of the flat, and at the shadows moving across the curtains. Jimmy looked restless and despondent. He said it was good to see Eddie again, and Eddie said, yeah, yeah, sure it was. Jimmy asked if Eddie was really sure he wanted to go home, and Eddie said, yeah, he was positive, he had things to do next day, people to see. Jimmy looked like he was going to cry. 'Come on back up, man,' he said, 'just for old times' sake. Let's have a nightcap or two and bitch about somebody, eh?'

'No,' said Eddie, 'look, I'm really not in the mood, OK?'

'That sofabed,' Jimmy sighed, 'you know, it cost us three hundred and fifty quid and we've never used it once.'

Eddie said they should trade it in. Then he told him no hard feelings, but he really had to split. Jimmy stood in the gateway, waving sadly, as though Eddie was going off to war. And ten yards down the road, Jimmy called out his name again. Eddie rolled his eyes, and he turned. Jimmy seemed to be suddenly drunk again. He was swaying a little on his feet, one hand on the gate post to steady himself.

'You see all those stars up there, Eddie,' Jimmy hissed, 'you know what they do up there?' Eddie shrugged. 'All those planets out there, man, far away, all silver, you know what we are? We're the shit that all the people on those planets produce. They fire it all out into space, Ed, and it comes down here and that's what we are. Inter-planetary shit, you and me, all of us. That's the truth man, I mean, like, that's what it all comes down to, in the end, as far as I can see. Intergalactic turd, you know what I'm saying?'

Windows began to light up white along the tree-lined street.

'Great, Jimmy,' sighed Eddie, 'that's just great.'

He walked down the road to a phonebox and he called a minicab from there.

FRANK RONAN
'Slade'

We had lived on peaches alone in Monte Carlo, and slept on half the beaches in the northern half of the Mediterranean; had outstayed our welcome in the houses of Italians and watched a naked, muscular Dutchman, with dreadlocks halfway down his glistening black back, play Macbeth in a scaffolding castle on the polder. We played it gay and straight, depending on whom we didn't want to sleep with, for Emma was saving herself for a romantically thin man at Manchester University, and I was just saving myself.

She thought she was in love, and wanted to find out, because her greatest fear was that it would never happen to her, and so I knew, as soon as the novelty of being a Eurobum had worn off, that she would want to go to Manchester. And, Manchester not being a place I had ever dreamed of seeing, we said goodbye on the Lüneburg Heideland, and I looked for an autobahn, to go south again.

I hadn't yet found out that fate is never to be trusted, so when the man in the first car that stopped for me said that he was going to the same town as I was, the very next street indeed, I took it for an omen: a good omen, naturally. He was studying to be a theologian and we passed the long, concrete-hemmed hours with talk of biblical prohibitions, among other things. Had I not been seventeen, and had he not been so polite, a subtext might have floated nearer the surface of our conversation.

In a moment of courage I told him that I was going to Heilbron for love, not simple friendship. I said that I had never been there before and asked him what it was like.

He said that I would soon find out.

The street where he dropped me was badly lit, with railway tracks on one side and small factories down the other. There was only one house. It was a solid, forbidding house, the strength of its presence barely mitigated by the single cherry tree that passed for a front garden. What had been the back garden was now the gherkin pickling factory, and the dormitories for the workers. Frau Jater, the owner, lived in the house still, with her cowed small husband and supercilious children, close to the stench of her own vinegar.

This cherry tree, it transpired, was something of a totem to the Jaters. Old hands, who were spending their second summer in the factory, said that the Jaters venerated the thing as though it were more precious than the house itself, and at cherry time they guarded it, night and day, from phantasmic marauders. They little knew that the real marauders had no designs on the fruit, but were plotting against the tree itself.

It was Jimmy Sullivan who was the leader of the hate campaign against the tree. He would lie on his bunk in the evenings, fantasizing aloud, rambling on ways to kill or maim a cherry tree: axes and petrol and poison pellets drilled deep into the bole. His eyes would narrow and his breathing shallow, as if his secret kink might be dendrocide. He had determined that, on his last day, he would do something, and have his revenge on Frau Jater by harming the thing she loved most. I didn't understand why he hated the woman so much. I had yet to meet her.

I knew of a foolproof, failsafe, undetectable way to commit the crime, but I wasn't saying anything. I had a soft spot for cherry trees, and Jimmy Sullivan's talk made me think, protectively, of the cherry tree at home in Slade; the Morello crouched in the lee of a stone north wall that separated it from the sea and the salt-laden gales. The Morello never did well and my mother often said, as she stretched the fruit to a second pot of jam, that the salt was to blame, and that it wasn't the only thing in her garden that was sickened on account of it.

Since Donald was the only reason I had come to that place, I'd watch him to see if he was more in favour of the tree or against the Jaters, but he had other problems that summer, and was even more disconnected than his usual, ethereal self. Because there wasn't a bed spare, and because I wasn't supposed to be there at all, I slept in the same bed as him, which was how I would have slept for preference in any case. We assumed that it was assumed that we were lovers. And that was fine, because it was part of the elaborate double bluff we played on ourselves. If we didn't mind whether people thought we were poofs that just showed how secure we were in our heterosexuality – at least, how secure Donald was in his heterosexuality, for he was the one person who knew the full extent of my experiments, by which I tried to provoke him into jealousy, or disgust, or passion, or something other than the graciousness of his all-forgiving smile. At Heilbron the smile was less evident, but then, so was he.

Everything stank of vinegar, all the time. There were some who had given up washing themselves and their clothes, as a waste of time, just waiting it out until they were back in the suburban bathrooms of Bray. We had no great need to keep our dignity intact, unlike the Turkish men and the Italian women in the other dormitories, for whom this was life. For us, it was an unpleasant but interesting episode; a way to stretch a grant. We were suffering now to buy beer money for the winter, not to feed a family at home in the hills.

I say we, meaning they. My motives for being in that place were not clear to me. Except that when I had nothing better to do I always chose to be as close to him as possible. I tried to get a job in the factory to begin with, and after that I just hung around, performing little domestic services for Donald to pass the time while he worked, and sat in the town square in the sunshine with an old tramp from Transylvania who, indeed, had overdeveloped canine teeth and the sort of hatchet face you'd associate with a B-movie vampire. He pushed all his possessions before him in a shopping trolley and his feet were mummified in layers of bags and rags. Every day, at the same time, he would spend an hour and a half unwrapping these feet, to wash them in the fountain, before settling to his lunch of sausage. He was a chatty soul, but our conversation was limited because he had worked once on an American airbase, and the only words in English he knew were FuckinGoddam sonofabitch. I wondered sometimes what one had to do to become like him. But, in the end, I decided that I didn't have the bone structure.

I can't remember now what caused the strike. There is a vague recollection that Donald was at the centre of it, but that may be a pathetic, retrospective wish on my part to inflate the importance he had to the world in general. In any case, I'm sure it happened on the day I was sent shoplifting.

'Oh, and nick some cheese, while you're there.'

He threw the instruction at me casually, at the end of a list of things I was to buy in the supermarket. Shoplifting, for the rest of them, was no big deal. The theory was that the Germans were so honest that they suspected nothing. One Northsider had achieved glory by filling a trolley with food and putting a crate of beer on the shelf at the bottom and wheeling the whole thing out of the back door of the shop and all the way home. I had been with Donald when he nicked things. I knew the system: you put the object of your illicit desires on that folding, child-seat thing and, when no one was looking, you knocked it from there into your pocket.

I was an hour in that small supermarket, wheeling that bloody thing up and down the three short aisles, sweating like a racehorse and staring at that obnoxious yellow lump, before I finally had the courage to pocket it and rush to the checkout. The girl in the pale pink overall should have thought I was a madman, but she didn't have the imagination.

All the way back I shook like a greyhound, knowing now what I had long suspected – that I wasn't cut out for crime. At that stage deciding on a career was still a process of elimination. I knew well enough what I wanted to do. I just hadn't worked out a system which combined doing it with eating the odd meal. I tended to be good at the sort of things which were, unfortunately, their own reward. If you could make money by being in love I would have been a tycoon, even at that age.

I waited in the dormitory for the lads to come in for their break. It was that time of day when the sun fell across the bottom of a bed by one of the windows and I lay, with my face in the light, thinking of things to say to Donald. I wanted to tell him never to ask me to steal again, but couldn't work out how to say it without making it obvious that I would have done whatever he asked. In my mind, a balance had to be maintained, lest he should think that I loved him more than he me. Only in my mind for, in retrospect, it was obvious to anyone which of us was tying himself in knots of love.

They came in whooping like revolutionaries. There had been an altercation and someone had called out 'strike', and the whole of the Irish had walked out in a body. Production had been stopped for ten minutes, the Germans had panicked and the lads had won. They were snowed with their success; muscles charged and pupils dilated and the endless, fascinated repetition of the details. It was, in some respects, the first victory in the war against the Jaters.

Hostilities were engaged with whatever weapons came to hand: whoever was on cleaning duty would empty the sweepings into the gherkin vats; whoever was packing the jars into boxes would unscrew each lid a little; whoever had a spanner in their hand would drop it in the works. I suppose, symbolically, hiding me in the dormitory became part of the defiance. Frau Jater took to making surprise visits at odd hours, but we had our lines of defence. The man nearest the door would take his shorts off and stand there naked, which gave me time to jump into a cupboard or under a bed. It got to the stage where I seemed to be staying in the place as a matter of principle.

The night she came round with the police we had plenty of warning from the floor below, and Donald grabbed me by the sleeve and dragged me into the lavatory. While the policemen hammered on the door he pretended to be having faecal difficulties and I jumped out of the window into the arms of Jimmy Sullivan and Con Crowley and sped across the road and the railway tracks, my exit covered, as in all the most thrilling chases, by a hurtling train. What we didn't know was that the police were after an armed robber and if they'd seen me running like that I might have been in real trouble. All good *Boy's Own* stuff, I suppose.

That weekend we went sunbathing in the hills, by the edge of a wood overlooking vineyards, and talked about why vineyards were so ugly, and talked about tumescence, in an academic way, as if that were not the reason I was lying on my stomach to talk about it, and came back down through the steep woods, with that feeling of light-headed satisfaction you get from sunbathing and descent.

He asked me if I had called home yet, and I said that I hadn't. The mention of home, even in the deep, green shadows of that Germanic wood, made me think of the paleness of the light at Slade and the cold, solid colours in the sea and the brittle paleness of the rocks, and details: the plumes of rhubarb flower in the garden and the dead smell of crisp seaweed.

'You'll have to find out,' he said. 'Sooner or later.'

'Will I?'

Finding out was not part of the plan I had in mind. It seemed as good a time as any to let him in on the future I had decided for us.

'We don't have to go back. Neither of us. Why should we? There's nothing left for us there, apart from other people's expectations. For all you know Kay will decide to keep the child and you'll be blackmailed into marrying her. So, you go back – your life is over. If we go on the possibilities are endless.'

I looked at him, trying to gauge his reaction. His face had hardened to a carapace. The steepness of the path was sending small shocks through us with every step. Among the trees, small huts in fenced-off gardens had begun to appear; with coy, tasselled curtains at the windows and winsome garden furniture on the lawns.

'I've decided,' I said. 'I can't go back.'

'Fuck,' he said.

'What?'

He grabbed my elbow and shoulder and pushed me behind a stand of trees.

'The Jaters,' he said. 'I don't think they saw us.'

The Jaters were eating, in the afternoon sunshine, both of them wearing bathing costumes, like Mrs Sprat and Jack undressed. They sat on cushions on plastic chairs and a cloth of purple chenille covered the table. I couldn't help wondering what real harm there could be in people with such a penchant for kitsch.

Donald was hissing like a cat in a corner.

If Donald called home that evening it may well have been that he just wanted to talk to his family; it might not have been the act of betrayal that I took it for at the time. He came back from the phone box down the street, looking grave, looking as though he could have done without having to tell me what he was about to say. For the first time I became aware that I had become a problem to him, on top of everything else: I, who used to be his twin in hedonism. Being made to feel as callow as I did then would be enough to make anyone angry.

I remember he was standing in front of a poster of a dark haired girl, her legs spread in the usual, knickerless pose. Someone, perhaps it was me, had given her one of those speech bubbles we used to nick from public telephones, saying, *Ruf doch mal an*.

'They want to get in touch with you. They know you're here and the message is to phone. It's urgent.'

I was supposed to ask how urgent. I was supposed to hold my head despairingly, say 'Oh my God!' as in the most heart-wrenching dramas. Instead, I was wondering how much further I'd have to go before they wouldn't be able to get a message to me; to tell me news I knew already.

I wouldn't look at him.

'Apparently,' I heard him say, 'if you left now you'd make it for the funeral.'

I was aware, but only just, as though it were happening at a great distance, that he had put his hand on my forearm.

He had been talking softly, out of earshot of the others, who were getting ready to go out drinking for the night. At that, bludgeoned, moment the Frau Jater alarm sounded in the corridor, and Eoin Harvey stripped naked and I, automatically, took a dive beneath the bed we were sitting on.

She came in, backed by two Turks, and announced that they were taking a bed away, ignoring the nudity of Eoin Harvey and the tumult of protests from the lads that there wasn't a bed spare. There was, because someone had left for home that day, and she knew it. Still, with fifteen beds in the room, the chances of her directing her cohorts to remove my hiding place were slim. She looked as surprised as I did when the mattress was removed and we found ourselves staring at each other through the bedsprings. Her astonishment gave me just enough time to leap to my feet and my dignity.

Seldom has screaming felt so good. When I got to the bit about who won the fucking war anyway I was on a roll. Quick as a flash and beyond computation in decibels she reminded me that I was Irish, which opportunity I took to inform her that Irishness had not prevented half my family from joining the British Army for the sole purpose of slaughtering Nazi scum like her. Although, in the first moment of making her acquaintance, I had learned to hate her with all the force that I had failed to comprehend in Jimmy Sullivan, looking back across the years now I would like to think that she enjoyed our exchange as much as I did – but I doubt it. Though I hated her, she despised me, and there is no pleasure in despising.

When Frau Jater had gone and the lads had gone and we had arranged to join them later, I found myself clinging to the small of Donald's back, as he sat on his bed in the near-dark; as my body pumped out of itself a noisy, wet grief that I wanted no part of. Why should I have had to grieve for her when I never wanted her dead in the first place?

Jimmy Sullivan came back for something he had forgotten, and must have mistaken what we were doing for something just as private, and apologized for interrupting. I called him back and he stood in the half-lit door, uncertain.

'Salt,' I said, wiping the back of my salted face on Donald's shirt. 'You can kill the tree with a strong solution of salt, and no one will be the wiser.'

ROBERT MCLIAM WILSON

from *Eureka Street*

In the high-capacity car park outside the shopping mall, Chuckie Lurgan sat behind the wheel of a rented Subaru watching the lugubrious women sitting silently in their cars. It was 9.30 a.m. and, although it was summer, the air was cold. Chuckie was beginning to find American mornings beautiful. On his only morning in New York City the light had been early but already tired, the sun on the buildings smoky and dry, like it didn't have enough gas to get through the day. But the Kansas version of 9 a.m. was enchanting. The ground frost breathed up its wisps like a landful of cigarettes.

Chuckie wound down his window and looked up at the sky. He knew that it was getting thinner. The ozonosphere was degrading at a rate that negated replenishment. The earth was being dug up and scattered with corrosive filth. The seas were being fished out and the people were growing everywhere. Every day a hundred species became extinct. (Chuckie had been watching an environmental TV programme the night before and found himself newly concerned. What had previously seemed the worst kind of style-free tree-hugging now seemed crucial to father-to-be Lurgan.)

Chuckie felt that his skin was crackling and warping under the toxic light of the unfiltered sun. In ten years he felt that he would be bald and shrivelled with radiation. The planet, too, would lose its hair and juice. His own city would warp and buckle. Desert Belfast, dry and dead. He found his eyes begin to water.

He was waiting for Max. She was in the mall deli trying to buy chocolate croissants. At breakfast, that morning, she had mildly desired these croissants. Though he thought it absurdly early in her pregnancy for cravings, Chuckie had strenuously insisted that they drive the twenty miles to the nearest deli. She had grumbled but had complied.

After the old lady had told him about Max's pregnancy, Chuckie had spent a couple of days in his hotel room. For thirty hours he had contemplated fatherhood amongst the cloistered plastics and nylons of the little roadside motel. Then he slept for ten hours, rented a car and drove out to see Max.

When he drove up she was sitting on a rocking chair on her porch. The gentle motion of her chair did not falter as he got out and approached her. His heart failed and surged a hundred times in that thirty-second walk, but Max, Max looked serene. Max looked like she had expected him.

He mounted the porch and stopped a few steps from her chair. She looked blankly at him, rocking gently back and forth. There was no welcome in her eyes but there was no refusal either. The Ulsterman took the initiative.

'Marry me,' said Chuckie Lurgan.

It grew dark and chilly out on the porch while they talked. Max told him about the secret thing that had happened to her when she had run away after her father's death. At the end of those two missing years, she had found herself pregnant and too stoned to know by whom. She promised herself that she would have an abortion but, somehow, she never seemed to get around to it. It was a drag to organize, the telephones, the doctors and the clinics. She didn't have the money. She didn't have the time. There were occasions, late at night, just as she was falling asleep when she knew well that she was leaving it late. But the bed was always warm and it was always nice just to dream the bloody thing away so that she would wake up slim-bellied, unfertilized.

But she left it late past the legal termination date. She was six months gone when she finally decided to give it a go.

But that night she and a retired boxer from Tulsa had a party with some cheap crack. Her arm rested on the bump of her belly as she slotted the needle there. She knew exactly what she was doing but she did it anyway.

The people in the hospital had said bad things to her. She remembered one doctor. A young man, unshaven and weary. His voice had been gentle and he had smiled but she had been startled at the thing that she had seen in his eyes. She saw the shame he felt for her.

She had hit him and scratched his face with her ragged nails. A big nurse had rescued him, thumping her back onto the bed. She called Max a dirty whore, pronouncing it broad in the Southern fashion, making it a much uglier word . . . *hoor*.

And there was much time after that. There was a broken time in big rooms where the walls were cold as floors and no one spoke to her. It was like headaches she had had when she was a girl. She knew that there was a thing to endure and only by thinking of its end would she see it out.

She was only truly frightened when they told her that the child had lived. She wept and chided them. That night she dreamt of monstrous births and repulsive babies. The thing had seemed like a virus in her. She had expelled it. That was enough. They could expect no more of her.

For a week or more, she refused to see the child. The nice doctor, his face still scarred from her nails, made a list of all that she had taken when pregnant. As his hand had written down the second page, she understood what she had done. The child would be a monster, made of chemicals and nightmare. One nurse let it slip that the baby had been born addicted and her fears were confirmed. She saw the loathsome little thing with its lizard eyes glittering with greed and narcotic hunger.

When they brought it to her, she wept as if to die. Her heart was glass and broken. That wizened thing was all that she was. She had made it so.

And it seemed that when her baby died only she was surprised.

This was why she ran back to America when she discovered that she was carrying Chuckie's child. When she finished talking, Chuckie simply asked her gently, caringly, what that had to do with anything. That was then and this was now. He had found it a simple task to persuade her that leaving him was not an option. He found it a simple task to tell her he loved her. He found it a simple task to look at her flawless belly and hope that the child would not, eventually, come to look like him.

The old lady neighbour came round for a while, keen to stay as long as Chuckie. She fought it out for an hour or two but when she looked at the acquiescence in Max's face, she decided it wasn't worth getting tired for. Chuckie spent the next hour and a half gauging the weight of Max's now placid breasts and asking her again to marry him.

He spent a short week there, pitilessly uxorious. He followed Max around the house and yard. He practically helped her to sit and stand. The old lady openly tittered at his excessive attentions. Sometimes Max grew vexed at his solicitude. One night, after the old lady had gone home, she snapped at Chuckie that he should stop clucking. But it was impossible to be long angry with him and within ten minutes she was rolling on top of his comprehensive belly, urgently whispering, *Cluck me, cluck me*, in his ear.

It was a joyous, absurd, consequential week. They spent those days more happily than Chuckie could have thought possible. He was drawn deep into all manner of metaphysical speculation. He found himself considering his own mortality for the first time.

By the time the week had passed Chuckie had grown abashed by such thoughts. He knew himself to be a pragmatic man (actually, he knew himself to be a fat, lazy bastard but he was now too rich to merit that summation). Mystical profundities ill-suited him.

There was something appropriate in his new situation. Something that he felt was more his speed. He was about to have a child – the Ulster Protestant in him guaranteed it would be a son. It was time to provide for his international family. It was time to make some more money.

Chuckie saw Max walking across the parking lot towards him. He felt his customary surge of pleasure to think that this spring-heeled, healthy American woman was his. Her genetic contribution to the child would dilute much of the unwelcome Lurgan inheritance.

Max opened the Subaru's passenger door. 'No chocolate croissants,' she said morosely.

'OK, we'll drive out to Shaneton. You said there was a mall there.'

'Chuck, that's forty miles from here.'

'So what?'

Max glared at him. 'I bought some croissants and I bought some chocolate.'

Chuckie looked question marks.

'We can put them together, Chuck. Or you can have a bite of one and then a bite of the other in quick succession. Mix them in your mouth and it's the same thing.'

'Don't get humpy. This was your craving.'

'It wasn't a craving. I just fancied some.'

'Fair enough.'

'Chuck, stop that. Not in the parking lot.'

Chuckie moved back into his own seat.

'Jesus, Chuck, for a fat guy you're always surprisingly horny.'

He smiled. 'For a horny guy, I'm always surprisingly fat.'

He stared at her. She failed to fall off her seat at his comedy. Max and her mother were the only Americans who did not find him hilarious. 'You love me,' said Chuckie.

'Don't I know it?' replied Max.

That night they talked about the future. They talked about where they would live. Chuckie knew that a return to Belfast was not assured. He would go anywhere that Max took him.

'Here or there. That's the big question, I suppose,' she said, trying to remove his lips from her nipple and bring him back to the point.

He looked up at her vaguely. 'Here, there, makes no difference to me.' He smiled. 'I can turn a buck anywhere. The world's my can of Tennant's.' He moved back to her breast. Max sighed at the thought that she would marry this man. She rubbed her hand on the back of his sparse, almost sandy head. She wondered if this was how it had been for Peggy Lurgan.

'Yeah,' she said, suddenly mindful. 'You should call your mother.'

That night Chuckie called Eureka Street. Caroline Causton answered. She told him that Peggy was out shopping. Chuckie felt a momentary thrill that his mother felt so much better. This brief pleasure was quickly replaced by bewilderment that Caroline should be answering his telephone.

'You think it's better that you still hang around for a while longer?' he hazarded, as vaguely as he could.

'What do you mean?' Her tone was exacting.

Chuckie grew tense. 'Relax, Caroline. I was just asking a question.'

'Am I not welcome or something, Chuckie?'

'Don't be stupid. I'm just trying to work out how my mother is.'

There was a brief silence.

'She's much better but she wants me to be with her. Is that all right with you?'

There was something in her tone that Chuckie didn't like. There was something in her tone that he hated.

'OK, take it easy.'

'I will if you will.'

'Tell her I called, will you? I haven't spoken to her since I left.'

'I'll tell her. She's fine. Don't worry.'

There was another silence. Chuckie had wanted to tell his mother. Now he wished he could wait but he found that the news was too big inside him.

'Caroline, I'm going to be a father.'

'I know.'

'What?'

'Peggy told me.'

'Who told her?'

'That American girl of yours. The night before she left.'

'That's nice.'

'You getting married, then?'

'Aye.'

'Congratulations, son. I've got to go now. You take it easy. 'Bye.'

She hung up. Chuckie felt deflated. His big news had depreciated in value on its first telling. And, although Caroline's tone had been warmer towards the end, there had still been something in it that Chuckie had not liked.

He called the office immediately. He told Luke instead. He hadn't known Luke very long and wasn't yet sure how entirely he liked him but at least the man was graciously animated at Chuckie's momentous news.

'John Evans has been calling again,' Luke told him.

'Who?'

'The billionaire you met on the plane. Jesus, Chuckie, what did you tell him?'

'Why?'

'You must have given him the best snowjob in history. He wants a part of everything we're doing. He calls every day. He's even threatening to fly over. He wants to know what our action is, or something transatlantic like that.'

'What have you told him?'

'Nothing. I was too embarrassed to tell him. This man is a very big cheese. I'd heard of him. He's famous. I wasn't going to tell this Rockefeller about our twig-dipping franchises. I still have a reputation.'

'Don't get poncey.'

'It drove him nuts. Absolutely crazy. I don't think he's used to secrets being kept from him. I think his money usually gets him what he wants.'

'Gimme his number,' said Chuckie grimly.

'Are you sure you're in the right mood for this?'

'Gimme the fucking number.'

Chuckie called Evans but he called Slat first. He called Septic and Deasely, he called his cousin, he even called Stoney Wilson. He called old schoolfriends, old enemies. He called people he had once passed on the street. He told them all that he was going to be a father. Despite the reservations of some about the continuance of the Lurgan genetic strain they were all pleased for him. He felt better. Then he called John Evans. He told him the truth about all the bullshit businesses and the ridiculous ways in which he had raised capital. As he had expected, Evans offered him five million dollars on the spot.

'I'll get back to you,' said Chuckie casually.

Then he went off to make some money.

One week later Chuckie found himself in a swanky high-rise in Denver.

'Mr Lurgan, we get a lot of advice about places we could capitalize,' said a man in a New York suit.

'I don't give advice,' said Chuckie.

'We're worried about the war there,' said another man in a New York suit.

'There's a ceasefire,' retorted Chuckie.

'It could all start again,' suggested yet another besuited man.

'We're worried about what your guys are doing in Israel,' said the last of the three-pieces. Chuckie smiled blankly.

'We do a lot of Jewish business in New York. We don't want to irritate anybody there,' the man explained, only partially.

'Well,' Chuckie began, 'I know what you mean.'

He stopped. He had no idea what the man meant. He stared at that trim, tanned foursome. It struck him that they might actually believe that the IRA were some kind of Arab terrorist group. He changed tack quickly. 'If you think that's a problem, then the best option for you is to invest in this region and thus get some leverage with these ... *Muslim* guys.'

The man with the Arab theory nodded, as though admitting the justice of this point.

'Also, Belfast is a crucial Western port in a vital geographical area.' The men murmured uneasy assent. It took some minutes but Chuckie finally deduced that several had supposed Ireland to be just off the west coast of Africa. He thought hard before he corrected their misapprehension.

An hour later, he had made another eight hundred and seventy thousand dollars. He had persuaded them to give him the money to help buy a factory unit, which Luke had told him they already owned. He would use their money to set up the Stateside utilities companies about which he'd so long dreamt. Irish-American Electricity, the American-Irish Water Company, US Hibernian Gas.

In a week he had bamboozled, bluffed, duped and outwitted a selection of America's finest and hardest-headed businessmen. It had barely troubled him. They knew nothing about his country and sometimes believed wildly inaccurate stories. One man, perhaps thinking of Iceland, thought there were no trees; another firmly believed the island of Ireland to be situated in the Pacific. Chuckie found that their ignorance was not the product of stupidity. These men simply didn't want to know much about the rest of the world. News that was not American was not news. Such had always been the case but now that there had been a couple of ceasefires, Northern Ireland was much televised. It was by no means a lead story but it was on television all the same. Americans found themselves forced to have an opinion. There was a gap, a void between what they actually knew and the opinions they felt they must now hold. Chuckie Lurgan aspired to fill that void.

He was not alone. Jimmy Eve and a coterie of Just Us celebs had flown to Washington immediately after the announcement of the first ceasefire. Despite having less than 12 per cent of the Northern Irish vote, they ambled into the White House and hung out with the President. Chuckie briefly considered telephoning the leader of the low-polling British Liberal Democrats and charging him ten grand for the idea that if he wore a C&A suit and shot a few policemen he'd get an audience with world leaders.

The Americans loved Eve. Several matronly Irish-American women insisted on describing him as hunky, despite his patent lack of physical beauty. The *New York Times* compared him with Clint Eastwood. He had a patchy beard which grew up to his eyes and a mouth like a guppy. There was no way around it, the man looked like a weasel. Chuckie was mystified.

Eve did television shows coast-to-coast. His hairy, carnivorous smile was everywhere. He talked the language of American civil rights to interviewers too ill-educated in their own country's history to notice. He talked about South Africa. He talked about equal rights and democracy. He talked about Eastern Europe. He talked about inclusiveness and parity of esteem. One anchorman asked him when he thought Irish Catholics would be given the vote. Eve fought hard with his temptation to say something like, Never too soon, or, I hope I see it in my lifetime. But he also resisted the temptation to correct the anchorman's profitable error. He just ignored the question and started talking about what a bunch of fuckers the British were.

However, the finest moment came when he was interviewed simultaneously with a stray Ulster Unionist and Michael Makepeace, the leader of the Ulster Fraternity Party, a collection of vegetarian middle-class doctors who did much lamenting and quite a lot of unsatirical body repairing. For twenty minutes, it was the usual back and forward. Chuckie, watching TV in a Minneapolis hotel room, had seen this hundreds of times but America obviously loved the way these guys just bad-mouthed each other so happily. It was like the trailers for a boxing match or like the fake badinage of professional wrestlers. It was fun.

But then something extraordinary happened. The Ulster Unionist had persisted in claiming that the ceasefire was no ceasefire until the IRA gave up their weapons. The man obviously considered it his best, if not only, point. Finally, the anchorman put that very question to Eve. He asked him if there was any chance of IRA arms being handed in. Eve did his usual waffle about democracy and military occupation and Chuckie was about to change the channel when the anchorman turned to the Fraternity leader with his bright but sincere American smile. 'And what about you, Mr Makepeace, will you, too, give up your weapons?'

Chuckie lay back on his bed and howled like a hound. His delight was complete. By the time he regained an upright position, Makepeace's mouth was still moving but sounds still failed to issue. Chuckie heard an off-mike titter, probably from Eve, and he believed – he would always believe – that the leader of the lentil-munching, fête-giving Fraternity Party looked almost pleased that anyone would think he looked butch enough to have a few Kalashnikovs stashed.

As the days passed and Eve received the vital presidential imprimatur, his progress took on some of the glamour and resonance of a rock tour. Chuckie saw him stand outside a Boston public building with the poet Shague Ghinthoss by his side. Both men were shaking hands, their faces turned towards the bank of cameras, their smiles wide. Journalists shouted questions but Eve and Ghinthoss ignored them until one man shouted that he was from Swedish television. At those enchanted words, both men abruptly assumed a tender, sensitive expression, their four eyes pleading and mild. Then they glanced at each other, each man calculating the unlikelihood of the other being the first to a Nobel.

In New York, one dissenting protester, who carried a placard reading *Stop the Punishment Beatings*, was arrested and punitively beaten up by a trio of zealous New York cops. Several of the Just Us entourage could be seen casting admiring glances at the NYPD technique. Just Us were triumphant. America didn't know Protestants even existed. Many thought that Great Britain had actually invaded in 1969. A passing English historian was interviewed and mentioned that the Army had been drafted in to protect Catholics.

'Well, you would say that,' the interviewer replied, an indomitable, investigative smile on his brave and trustworthy American face.

It wasn't so much that real history was rewritten. Real history was deleted. Its place was taken by wild and improbable fictions. Ireland was the land of story and Just Us campaigners had always been the best storytellers. They told the world a simple story. They edited or failed to mention all the complicated, pluralistic, true details. It had always been thus and the world had always loved it.

Theirs was a narrative in which the innocent, godly CATHOLIC Irish were subdued and oppressed by the vicious English and their Protestant plantation spawn. Italian socialists, French Maoists, German Communists and the entire population of Islington swallowed it all whole, but every now and then inconvenient voices were raised. Why do you guys shoot young boys for stealing cars? How socialist is that? And that business of blowing up shops, bars, cafés, it doesn't feel enormously left wing, does it? How come you have to kill so many Irish to liberate the Irish? Although these were infrequent objections, they still nonplussed the boys and girls from Just Us who had no logical riposte.

This simply didn't happen in America. The United States presented a trusting, sentimental face for Jimmy Eve. He puckered up whenever possible. True, in America he diplomatically downplayed Just Us's supposedly socialist credentials. But he hardly had to. The Americans were not going to draw any parallels between Just Us and the spick Commie rebels in South and Central America. Just Us was full of white guys. That was enough.

All this had a superbity that Chuckie could not match but he incorporated Eve's Broadway-hit status into his own spiel. He began to develop two separate *personae* for dealing with these businessmen. If required, he could be the ultimate croppy boy within seconds, lamenting the filthy English invasion of his land. He became the ultimate Catholic, he grew misty-eyed when talking of the Kennedy clan and blessed himself, inaccurately, before signing any documents. He even began to affect a spurious command of spoken Irish until one sharp-eared *Star Trek* fan pointed out that the noises coming from his mouth sounded suspiciously like the Klingon for 'Phasers locked and ready, Captain'.

Alternatively, he sometimes found it useful to assume an entirely English manner. East Coast WASPs responded to this particularly well. They had a vague belief in some vestigial Northern Irish aristocracy. Chuckie knew he sounded more like Perry Mason than James Mason but they seemed to go for it.

There had been one frightening occasion upon which Chuckie had made an initial miscalculation. He had sailed into an important meeting in Boston doing his full Mick routine. 'Top o' the mornin' to yous all, now. What say we get all our aul jawin' done and then we get down to Maloney's for a few o' the fine stuff?'

He was just about to start complaining about the health of his pigs when he noticed the frowns on the faces of the four men around the table. Then he noticed their striped ties and highly polished brown brogues, the pictures of old college rowing eights on the walls. It looked like there were fancy old WASPs in Boston too. His transition was immediate and effortless. He smiled thinly at the only man he'd met previously.

'I do apologize, old boy. I've just been listening to some unspeakable bog-wog called Eve on the motor car wireless. They're always banging on about something or other these days. Drives me barmy, I must confess.'

He sounded dreadful. His phoney David Niven accent was mangled by his customary broad Ulster tones. He thought the men might punch him for taking the piss but, as always, it worked a treat. They gave him some more money.

He saw many parallels between the bullshit that Eve was selling and his own success. Indeed, he began to watch each television appearance that the Irish ideologue made, and as Eve's lies and fantasies became more abhorrent and fantastic – and ever more successful – Chuckie stepped up the wildness of his own approaches. Chuckie Lurgan and Jimmy Eve sold Ireland long and short, begetting their monstrous perjuries in tandem, united in an hallucinatory jubilee of simulated Irishness. Chuckie even began to feel something like a grudging affection for his hirsute counterpart.

This uneasy twinship came to a riotous head near the end of Chuckie's second week away from Max. In Washington to tell some lies about a textile company he wanted to start in Dungiven, Chuckie had become so famous that he gave a newspaper interview. In this piece, he had mentioned that he was a Protestant. Jimmy Eve was in town for a few nights, giving head to any Irish-American congressmen who came his way. Spookily, it was the first time that he and Chuckie had coincided geographically. Eve was scheduled for another multitude of television appearances. The producer of one network show happened to see the little piece about Chuckie and decided, uncharacteristically, that it might be a good idea if, just for once, Eve was confronted by an alternative view. He called Chuckie's hotel and booked him to appear the next night.

Chuckie had been missing Max for near a fortnight. He felt himself growing rather grumpy. He called her every couple of hours but it didn't begin to be anything like enough. He grew mutinous and peevish.

Additionally, on the night before his first television appearance, Chuckie failed to sleep. He was remarkably agitated. All his life, this fame business had been magical to him and now he was about to achieve some small renown on his own part. And, whatever he believed about Jimmy Eve, he could not deny that the man was becoming increasingly famous. Chuckie, veteran Protestant Pope-chum, was familiar with this sensation of reluctant awe.

By the time Chuckie arrived at the television studios the next evening, he was so nervous he had practically stopped breathing. While in Make-up, the producers came to see him and were concerned about his evident anxiety. He could see that they were considering cutting him from the show. He was ashamed. He excused himself and sat unhappily in a cubicle in a nearby restroom.

After a few lonely minutes, he heard footsteps. A cubicle door was opened close by. Chuckie waited, scarcely breathing. The business of defecation had always embarrassed him and he decided to wait until this invisible man had finished his task before he himself could leave.

He grew conscious of strange noises: scrapings and small impacts. Suddenly uneasy, he looked up and saw a man staring down at him, obviously perched on the cistern of the nextdoor cubicle.

'How ya doing?' the man asked, airily.

'Fine. Thanks.'

'You on the show tonight?'

Chuckie nodded.

'Got the jitters?'

Chuckie nodded again.

'Hold up.'

The man disappeared from his position. There were more scuffles and then Chuckie heard a polite knock on his cubicle door. Bewildered, he opened it. The man pushed into the cubicle beside him, locking the door behind him. He took a mirror and some small papers from his pocket. He set them on top of the cistern behind Chuckie's head.

'Outa the way, man. I got just the thing for confidence problems.'

Happily, he proceeded to cut four fat lines of cocaine on the little mirror. He pushed it in Chuckie's direction. 'Go for it, big guy. If you get this in you, you'll be a star. You'll get a fucking Oscar.'

He put a thinly rolled-up dollar in Chuckie's hand. Chuckie stared at the little mirror and its four tracks of powder. Now Chuckie was not altogether a drugs virgin. He'd done a little speed, he'd smoked dope – but rejected it as a thin person's vice. He was, in essence, a conservative man. But he was also an anxious conservative man.

He stuck the tube of money in his nose and inhaled one of the lines of powder. His eyes pricked and his face appeared suddenly delicious. He felt as though he would like to eat his own lips. He put the dollar in his other nostril and hoovered up another track. This time, his very gonads grew elated. He had an ecstatic sense of simplicity. He cursed himself for never having previously investigated the Wonderful World of Cocaine.

The man protested only mildly when he snorted up the last two chunky portions of the substance. Chuckie felt as needy and blameless as a greedy superpig and the man felt a certain evangelical satisfaction at introducing such a keen newcomer (and Chuckie pressed a fistful of money into his hand, which also helped console him).

Chuckie straightened up and strode out of that pisser like another man, like several other men. He felt absolutely fucking tremendous as he was quick to inform the waiting TV people in the make-up room. Surprised at this new super-bullishness, the producers decided that he was ready for broadcast and the make-up artists went to work, dabbing at his sweat patches, smudging his spots, failing to damp the lunatic glitter in his eyes. When they finished their work, Chuckie leapt to his feet and strode unaccompanied into the studio, godlike, austere, filled with glorious chemical rectitude.

Thirty-five minutes later, the interview was coming to an end. On the periphery of his vision, Chuckie could see the floor manager signalling that a countdown was imminent. He was broken-hearted. He tried to look pleadingly at the interviewer but the man paled visibly under his demented gaze. He ignored the crumpled figure of Jimmy Eve and tried to finish what he was saying before they were counted out.

'And the other thing is that it always comes down in the end to cold, hard cash. That phrase is no accident. Those are its attributes. America, fabulous America, understands this. All you wonderful Americans out there don't need to listen to our moronic politicians. You don't listen to your own, why should ours be any different? What America understands is what I understand – making a dollar, cutting a deal. There are no nationalities, only rich and poor. Who gives a shit about nationhood if there's no jobs and no money? Bread before flags, that's what I say. I'm here in America to do a bit of business. It's the real peace. Don't listen to assholes like this.' Chuckie gestured towards the silent Jimmy Eve. 'This man wouldn't know an economic policy if it came up and bit him on the bollocks. Interested Americans should invest in my country. They should give their money to men like me.' Chuckie smiled a ghastly smile.

The tirade continued for another minute or so. Chuckie saw the floor manager counting down the seconds and he helpfully reached some notional full stop. There was a moment's dreadful silence, until the presenter managed to gasp a flabbergasted good night.

The red lights on the cameras went dead and the men and women behind them started to bustle importantly. Chuckie removed his own chest mike, shook hands with the presenter, chucked the Just Us leader under the chin, waved a cheery farewell to all and sundry and went off looking for the man he had met in the toilets.

Jimmy Eve had said nothing during those seventeen and a half minutes of national television. He had made several attempts to speak but Chuckie had charged him down with coked-up exuberance. The politician had sat silently, pale and sweating, while the lunatic Protestant had ranted, only sporadically interrupted by the flailing presenter.

Afterwards, Eve's entourage had been mystified. As they bundled him into a waiting limousine, they quizzed him as to what had gone wrong, why he had not performed. Eve said nothing. He looked close to tears and his forehead was cold and damp. When they reached their hotel, they called a doctor. The doctor could find nothing wrong with Eve although he manifested some of the symptoms of shock.

This was not surprising. Something shocking had occurred. Ever since he had arrived in America, Eve had made a big event out of who would shake his hand and who would not. He had tried to discomfit British government officials and opposing Irish politicians by offering his hand whenever there were cameras around. He knew that these people could not possibly shake his hand and he knew that that looked so unreasonable on American television. There he was, making the ultimate gesture of peace and amity, and those unreasonable reactionaries continued to reject him.

Thus when Chuckie Lurgan had surged into the television studio, Eve had offered his hand in his usual demonstrative and significant manner. He had never heard of this Lurgan guy but he knew he was a Protestant and that he was there to put forward the Unionist position. Thus, he was enormously surprised when this excited fat man took his hand firmly and shook it vigorously. His surprise increased when the man moved close to him and hugged him one-armed in the American fashion, putting his face close to Eve's own.

The two men remained in that position for what seemed like a long time. The smile on Lurgan's face was so joyous and the way he murmured so intimately in Eve's ear led the producers to think that they had been set up and that these men were related. They did not notice Eve's abrupt pallor and immediate sweat. They did not remark the tremble of his hands as he regained his seat.

When Chuckie was seventeen he had suffered a brief fad for rugby football. He began to play for the third fifteen of a club situated in the nearest bourgeois area to Eureka Street. He had not lasted long. Chuckie had not fitted in. His own team-mates disdained him and opposition players treated him with open contempt. Chuckie was neither good enough nor butch enough to reply with any on-the-pitch heroics, but he found a way to unburden himself of some of his resentments.

He began to place himself in the front row of scrums. When both front rows locked shoulders, his face would be inches from that of another player. Chuckie would proceed to hiss nauseating and vile abuse of a nature that sometimes shocked himself. He told these nice middle-class boys that he had had sex with their mothers and sisters, sometimes their fathers and brothers as well. Sometimes he threatened to have sex with the boys themselves, sometimes he threatened them with arcane amputations and extractions: penises lopped off, bottoms burnt, testicles torn apart. Occasionally, to vary the monotony, he did this to one of his own team-mates.

It always worked. It produced in the victim a state of something approaching catatonia. The dazed individual, a rabbit in headlights, would then be haplessly mashed in some hospitalizing tackle. The obscenity or level of threat was not the effective ingredient. What worked so brilliantly was the sheer surprise. These young men were astonished to have their bourgeois pastime invaded so abruptly by this back-street coarseness.

And this was what had produced the uncustomary silence in Jimmy Eve. Fired by a million years' worth of resentment against this duplicitous Nazi (Chuckie had never felt so Protestant before, he had never felt Protestant at all), Chuckie's rage had been massive. He had whispered things so appalling in Eve's ear that he would always prefer to forget exactly what he'd said. It was bound to be his finest performance. The four fat lines of cocaine had helped.

Two days later, Chuckie and Max boarded a 747 bound for London. They had settled the here-or-there question in the way both had known they would. After a difficult parting from the old house in Kansas, during which Max tried to be stoic but blubbed like a baby, they flew to New York and spent a night there. With Max beside him, that city was a different and much more appealing experience.

Once they had boarded the British Airways plane and Chuckie heard the – relatively familiar – accents of the cabin crew, he breathed a sigh of European relief. He had liked America enormously but his last two days had been mayhem. His television appearance had made him briefly famous. Excerpts were shown on other networks; the entire event was even repeated. Other stations called him and asked him to be interviewed in tandem with American politicians, one even offered him a job as their political correspondent. The CLAD (Campaign to Legalize *All* Drugs) called him. Max had to deal with much of this telephone traffic. Her mulishness protected him. He was referred to as the MFG in Irish politics, the Mad Fat Guy. There were even rumours of T-shirts being printed. Jimmy Eve skulked home a week early.

This sudden fame upset Chuckie. It shattered the love for celebrity that had never left him. If someone as unevolved as Chuckie himself could be celebrated, however briefly, then notoriety was not worth the having. It was oddly appropriate to his experience of America. That country ran on the fuel of celebrity. It was the true spiritual currency of the nation. In America, actors and actresses were gods, the populace hung on their every word. Chat-shows were the discourses in which these beings diagnosed for the people.

When first in New York, Chuckie had felt that movie-unease was a feeling restricted to him. Every step he took on those famous pavements was self-conscious. That, he felt, was a visitor's sensation. By the time he got to New York second time around, he had established that this sensation was the common experience of the inhabitants as well. Everyone behaved like the movies they'd seen, like the movies in which they'd want to star. The streets were full of men and women acting out images of what they wanted to be. The cops acted like movie cops. The young bloods acted like movie young bloods. The men in suits were motion-picture men in suits. Chuckie even saw a street-sweeper who wielded his brush with a discernibly cinematic air.

In New York, there was a glitch in reality, a hair in the gate, a speck on the lens.

There were gross parodies of machismo and arcane street competence everywhere he looked.

The fact that Chuckie now knew that everyone on the planet was an infant who watched too many movies meant that he would never be able to stop making money.

But as the aircraft flew away from America and Max rested her head on the plump shelf of his belly, Chuckie knew that making money had, perhaps temporarily, lost its mystique. He needed to look for something else to give substance to his life. As he looked at her slumbering face, he knew he didn't need to search.

COLUM MCCANN

'Breakfast for Enrique'

The only older men I know are the ones who rise early to work. They fish the ocean for sea trout and haddock, flaring out their boats from the wharf before the sun, coming back by mid-morning with huge white plastic barrels full of fish, ready for us to gut. They draw hard on unfiltered cigarettes and have big hands that run through mottled beards. Even the younger ones look old, the hair thinning, the eyes seaward. You can see them move, slow and gull-like, back to their boats when their catch has been weighed, stomping around in a mess of nets and ropes. They don't talk to the fishgutters. They hand us a sort of disdain, a quiet disregard, I believe, for the thinness of our forearms.

I think of them always in the mornings, when the light comes in through my curtains. The light is like an old fisherman in a yellow rain-slicked coat, come to look at Enrique and me, wrapped in our bedsheets.

It's a strange light that comes this morning, older, thicker-wristed, pushing its way through the gap and lying, with its smotes of dust, on the headboard. *Goddamn it, aren't you two just the salt of the earth?* Enrique is curled into himself, the curve of his back full against the spindle of his legs. His hair is all about his face. Stubbled hairs in a riot on his chin. His eyes have collected black bags, and his white T-shirt still has smatterings of spaghetti sauce from yesterday's lunch. I move to brush my lips against his cheek. Enrique stirs a little, and I notice a little necklace of blood spots on the pillow where he has been coughing. *Get up out of bed, you lazy shits.* I smooth Enrique's brow where the sweat has gathered, even in sleep.

I climb naked out of bed, swinging my feet down into my slippers. The floor is cold and I step carefully. Last night I smashed the blackberry jamjar that used to hold our money. The glass splayed in bright splinters all around the room. I move over to the window, and Enrique murmurs into the pillow. The curtains make the sound of crackling ice. The ghosts of old fishermen can tumble in here in droves now if they want, spit their epithets all around the room. *What the hell sort of mess is this? You're late for work, Paddy-boy. No foghorns going off this morning. Gut the fish along the side, asshole.*

Our window looks out to a steep hill of parked cars. This morning they are bumper to bumper. Drivers have turned their steering wheels sideways so their vehicles won't roll down the hill and fling themselves toward the sea. Two weeks ago Enrique and I sold our car for $2,700 to a man with lemon-colored hair, and all the money is gone already. Bags of medicine and a little bit of cocaine. I put our last line on his belly last night, but he was sweating so hard that it was almost impossible to snort it.

I look up the road toward the deli. The white light in the street is slouching on the buildings, spilling over the ironwork railings. What I like most about the street is that people put flower pots in their windows, a colorful daub of Mediterranean greens and reds. Doors are painted in a medley of shades. Curtains get thrown open early in the mornings. There's a cat on the third floor across the street, jet black with a dappled blue bandanna. It is forever cocking its head sideways and yawning in the window. Sometimes I bring home some sea trout and leave it on the doorstep of the house for the owner.

I cover myself with my hand and step out through the French doors. A chill wind is coming up from the waterfront, carrying the smell of salt water and fresh sourdough. Already some of the fishermen will have unloaded their catch and Paulie's fingers will be frantic in his hair. *Where's O'Meara this morning?* they'll say to him. *Has he found himself a gerbil?* The other fishgutters will be cursing over slabs of fillets. Their plastic gloves will be covered in blood. Strings of fishgut will have fallen on their boots. *That bastard's always late anyway.*

I should pull on my old jeans and whistle for a taxi, or hop on the trolley, or ride the bicycle through the hills, down to the warehouse, but the light this morning is curiously heavy, indolent, slow, and I feel like staying.

Enrique is coughing in the bedroom behind me, spitting into the pillow. It sounds like the rasp of the seals along the coastline cliffs farther up the California shore. His skin is sallow and tight around his jaw. The way he thrashes around in the bed reminds me of a baby corncrake I once took home after an oil slick in my hometown near Bantry Bay, continually battering its blackened wings against the cage to get out.

He should wake soon, and perhaps today he'll feel well enough to sit up, read a novel or a magazine. I bend down and pick up the large pieces of shattered glass from the floor. There's a long scar on the wall where I threw the jamjar. *That was smart, O'Meara, wasn't it?* I find two quarters and a few dimes scattered among the glass. There's an Irish five-penny piece on the floor too, an anachronism, a memory.

I flick a tiny shard of glass off my finger, and Enrique tosses again in bed. He is continually thinning, like the eggshell of a falcon, and soon the sheets will hardly ripple. I move to the bathroom and take a quick piss in the sink. Enrique has always said that it's a much better height and there's no risk of splashing the seat. Not too hygienic, but curiously pleasurable. My eyes are bloodshot in the mirror, and I notice the jowly look in my face. When I wash I can still smell yesterday's fish on my hands. We are down to the last bar of soap, and the water that comes through the tap has a red iron color to it. Back in the bedroom I pull on my jeans, a heavy-checked lumber shirt, and my black-peaked hat. I search in the pockets of my jeans and find three more dollars, then check my watch. Another hour late won't really matter. My coat hangs on the bedpost. I lean over him again and tell him that I will be back in a few moments. He doesn't stir. *Ah, isn't that just lovely, O'Meara? Out ya go and get breakfast for Enrique.*

*

The wind at my back hurries me along, down the street, past a row of saplings, over a child's hopscotch chalkmarks, to the deli, where Betty is working the counter. It's an old neighborhood store, the black-and-white floor tiles curled up around the edges. Betty is a large, dark-haired woman – capable, Enrique jokes, of owning her own zip code. She often wears tank tops, and the large flaps of flab that hang down from her underarms would be obscene on anybody else, but they seem to suit her. There's a barker on the other side of town, near City Lights Bookstore, who shouts about 'Sweaty Betty''s shows, but I've never had the guts to go in and see if it's her up there, jiggling onstage in the neon lights. Betty negotiates the aisles of the deli crabways, her rear end sometimes knocking over the display stands of potato chips. When she slices the ham the slabs are as thick as her fingers. There is a bell on the inside of the door, and when I come in she looks up from the cash register, closing the newspaper at the same time.

'The Wild Colonial Boy,' she says. 'What's the rush?'

'Late for work. Just gonna grab a few things.'

'Still working down at the abattoir?'

'The warehouse. Gutting fish.'

'Same difference.' Her laugh resounds around the shop. The tassels on the bosom of her white blouse bounce. Her teeth are tremendously white, but I notice her fingernails chewed down to the quick. The bell clangs and a couple of elderly Asians come in, followed by a man whom I recognize as a bartender down on Geary Street. Betty greets each of them with a fluttering wave.

I move up and down the aisles, looking at prices, fingering the $3.80 in my pocket. Coffee is out of the question, as are the croissants in the bakery case, which are a dollar apiece. An apple tart might do the trick, however. Walking down the rows of food, other breakfasts come back to me – sausages and rashers fried in a suburban Irish kitchen with an exhaust fan sucking up the smoke, plastic glasses full of orange juice, cornflakes floating on milk, pieces of pudding in circles on chipped white plates, fried tomatoes and toast slobbered with butter. In the background Gay Byrne would talk on on the radio, while my late mother draped herself over the stove, watching the steam rise from the kettle. Mornings spinning off on my Raleigh to lectures at University, a bar of Weetabix in my jacket pocket. Once, champagne and strawberries in Sausalito with a lover who clawed his brown moustache between his teeth.

I reach for a small plastic jar of orange juice and a half dozen eggs in the deli fridge, two oranges and a banana from the fruit stand, then tuck a loaf of French bread under my arm. There is butter and jam at home, perhaps some leftover teabags. Betty sells loose cigarettes at twenty-five cents each. Two each for Enrique and me will do nicely. Tomorrow night, when I get my wages from the warehouse – Paulie will be there with his head bent over the checks morosely and some stray old fishermen will be coughing in from their boats – I will buy steak and vegetables. Not too much, though. Enrique has been having a hard time keeping his food down, and the blue bucket sits at the side of our bed, an ugly ornament.

I cart the groceries up to the cash register, and Betty cocks an eye at me.

'How's the patient?' she asks. 'Haven't seen hide nor hair of him in the last three weeks.'

'Still holed up in bed.'

'Any news?'

'None, I'm afraid.'

She shakes her head and purses her lips. I reach into my pocket for the change. 'Can I get four of your smokes please?'

Betty reaches up above her for a box of Marlboro Lights and slides them on the counter, toward me. 'My treat,' she says. 'Don't smoke 'em all at once, hon.' I thank her and tuck them quickly in my shirt pocket. Betty leans over the counter and touches my left hand: 'And tell that man of yours I want to see his cute little Argentinian ass in here.'

'He'll be up and at it in a few days,' I say, putting the groceries in a white plastic bag and hooking it over my wrist. 'Thanks again for the smokes.'

The door clangs behind me, and the street seems to open up in a wide sweep. Twenty cigarettes can make a man's day. I skip through the chalk marks – it's been years since I've hop-scotched – and sit down on the curb, between a green Saab and an orange pickup truck, to light up. Looking down the street I can make out our balcony, above the tops of the cars, but there's no sign of Enrique.

Last night he almost cried when the cocaine coagulated in his sweat, but I scooped some off his belly and onto the mirror. He pushed it away and turned his face to the wall, looked up at a photograph of himself rafting the Parana River. The photo is fading now, yellowing around the edges. The way he leans forward in the boat, going down through a rapid, with his paddle about to strike the water, looks ineffably sad to me these days. He hasn't been near a river in years and hasn't gone outside for almost a month.

In the apartment we have unrolled our sleeping bags and use them as blankets over the bedsheets. Our television set is in the front window of the pawnshop, next to a hunting bow. The trust fund is dry, but Enrique is adamant that I don't call his father. The insurance people are gentle but unyielding. Sometimes I imagine a man at the very tip of Tierra del Fuego reaching his arms out toward the condors that flap their wings against the red air. He wonders where his son has gone.

Enrique sometimes talks of moving to the Pampas. His mind takes him there, and we are building a wooden fence together behind a ranch house. The grasses sweep along with a northward wind. At night we watch the sun swing downward behind a distant windmill.

Late at night he often wakes and babbles about his father's cattle farm. When he was young he would go to the river with his friends. They would have swimming contests, holding against the rapids. Whoever stayed longest in one spot was the winner. In the late afternoons, he'd still be there, swimming stationary in the current, flailing away, without noticing that his friends were already halfway down the river. After the competition, they would stand in the water and catch fish with their hands. Then they'd light a campfire and cook the fish. It was Enrique who taught me how to gut when I first got the job down in the warehouse. With one smooth sweep of the finger you can take out all the innards.

*

When scrambling eggs I always make sure to add a little milk and whisk the fork around the bowl quickly so that none of the small stringy pieces of white will be left when they're cooked. The only disturbing thing about my mother's breakfasts were the long thin raw white pieces. The kitchen is small, with only room for one person to move. I lay the baguette on the counter and slice it, then daub butter on the inside. The oven takes a long time to warm up. In the meantime I boil water and put some teabags in the sunflower-patterned mugs.

I hear Enrique stir out of bed and move slowly toward the window. At first the noise startles me, but I'm glad he's awake. I hope he doesn't cut his feet on the stray glass – the doctor told us that the longer this goes on the harder it will be to stop a cut from bleeding.

Steam has gathered on the glass face of the oven clock. *You're late again, O'Meara, were ya picking petals offa roses?* I peel the oranges and arrange them in segments on the plate. *Or maybe you were spanking the monkey, is that it, O'Meara?* I hear the radio click on and a chair being dragged out onto the balcony. I hope he's put his scarf on under his dressing gown or else the chill will get to him.

I wish I could have seen him when I was down on the street, watched him sitting there, looking out over the white city, his hair dark and strewn like seaweed, the tufts on his chest curling toward his neck, his face chiseled, the scar on his chin worn like the wrongly tied knot of a Persian rug.

The eggs puff up and harden, sticking to the side of the saucepan. I scrape them off with a fork and then arrange the dollops on two plates. I've burnt the bread a little and the water is still not boiled. Amazing thing that, water. The molecules bouncing off each other at a huge rate of speed, passing on energy to one another, giving heat, losing heat. In the warehouse I spend my time thinking about these brutally stupid things, whittling the hours away. *There're lots of people in this town'd be happy to gut fish, bum-boy.* I put the bread on a third plate and wait. When the water finally boils I pour it on the teabags, making sure the little paper tabs stay outside the mugs. I hold the three plates in the shape of a shamrock in my right hand – I was a waiter before I met Enrique – and I grab the handles of both cups with my left forefinger and thumb.

The door to the bedroom is slightly ajar and I push it with my left foot. It opens with a creak but Enrique doesn't turn in his chair on the balcony. Perhaps the traffic is too loud. I see him cough and then spit into one of our flowerpots. He leans back in the chair again. It's a little more gray outside now, the sun blocked by clouds. I see that he has picked up the last pieces of the jamjar and put them on the bedside table. The pillow has been turned over and there are no visible blood spots, but there is a cluster of stray black hairs on the bedsheets. Twenty-seven is too young to be going bald.

I move soundlessly across the room. His head is laid back in the chair now. The curtains on the French windows swish against my leg and the rings tinkle against the rod. I sidle up behind the chair, lean over him, hand him the tea, and he smiles. His face seems weathered, the eyes run into crowfeet, the brow heavy. We kiss and then he blows on the tea, the steam rising up. *Why the hell d'you wear those goddamn bracelets anyway, O'Meara?*

'I thought you were gone already,' he says.

'In a few minutes. I thought it'd be nice to have breakfast.'

'Wonderful.' He reaches out for the plate. 'I'm not sure if I can.'

'It's all right. Eat as much as you like.' I put my own plate down on the balcony floor and close the top button on my shirt to keep out the wind. Cars trundle along the street below. Some kids have taken over the hopscotch court. There is a tremendous freshness to the breeze coming up from the sea and it rifles through the trees. Enrique purses his lips, as if to speak, then lets them fall apart, and he looks along the street again, a small smile crackling the edges of his mouth. The bags under his eyes darken.

'I have some smokes too,' I say. 'Betty gave them to me. And some orange juice if you want it.'

'Great.' Enrique stabs gingerly at the eggs with his fork and moves the pieces of orange around. Then he reaches for a piece of bread and slowly tears the crust off. 'Lovely day, isn't it?' he says, all of a sudden sweeping his arm out to the street.

'Gorgeous.'

'Radio said that the high would be in the sixties.'

'Grand weather for sitting around,' I say.

'Lows tonight in the high forties.'

'We'll sleep well.'

He nods his head and shifts his body gently in the chair. A small piece of crust falls down into the lap of his dressing gown. He reaches for it and lays it on the side of the plate. 'Nice eggs,' he says.

'Wish I didn't have to go to the warehouse.'

'We could just sit here and talk.'

'We could,' I say.

I watch him as he eddies the fork around the plate, but his eyes are drooping already. The cup of tea sits on the floor, by the edge of his chair. He leans his head back against the chair and sighs. His chest thumps like that of a small bird. The beginnings of sweat gather on his brow. I watch as the fork slides across the plate and nestles itself against the clump of food. I look down at the traffic passing beneath us, and all of a sudden I understand that we are in the stream, Enrique and I, that the traffic below us is flowing quite steadily, trying to carry us along, while all the time he is beating his arms against the current, holding still, staying in one place.

He sleeps and the breakfast grows cold.

In a few moments I will go to work and gut everything they bring me, but for now I watch this body of Enrique's, this house of sweat, this weedlot of proteins, slowly being assaulted.

Enrique once told me a story about starfish.

There was an oyster fisherman down the coast from Buenos Aires who farmed his own little area of the bay. He hadn't listened to the generations of fishermen who had gone before him, their advice, their tricks, their superstitions. All he knew was that starfish preyed on oysters. When they were dragged up in his nets he would take them and rip their symmetrical bodies in two neat pieces. He would fling them over the side of the boat and continue fishing. I imagine he was probably a bearded man with a rawboned laugh. But what he didn't know is that the starfish don't die when ripped, they regenerate themselves. For every one he tore, a second one came about. He wondered why there were so many starfish and so few oysters left, until he was told by an older fisherman. From then on, the fisherman left the starfish alone, although he could perhaps have taken them to shore and dumped them behind some big gray rock or in a large silver dustbin on the pier where the children, on the way home from school, would fling them like stones.

There are times these days, strange times spent among these idle thoughts of mine, when I wonder why my fishermen don't come to me in the warehouse, amazed, cigarettes dangling from their lips, two fully grown starfish in their hands, saying, *Look at this O'Meara, look, for Christ's sake, can you imagine this?*

EMMA DONOGHUE

'Going Back'

Cyn kicked the machine systematically. She glanced down at Lou, who was scrabbling under the radiator for a pound coin. 'Come on, wimp, help me kick,' she told him. 'I'm not letting you deflower me without a packet of Thick-Ribbed Ultras.'

Lou's response was to embed his ears between his knees and gasp. Passersby were lingering at the nearby jobs noticeboard, all studious expressions and pencils in hand.

'So much for chivalry,' Cyn announced loudly. 'No rubber no jolly rogering. That's fifty pee I've wasted on you already.'

She slung her scarred jacket over one shoulder and headed for the stairs. Lou hauled his red face up and stumbled after her. Once through the rainbow-muralled doors of the community centre into the noisy Brixton street, they let rip with laughter.

'Pathetic,' Cyn reproached him. 'Didn't they ever teach you how to keep a straight face in that seminary of yours?'

'If they'd taught me how to keep anything straight, sweetie, I wouldn't have been thrown out on my ear.'

'Poor ear,' murmured Cyn, flipping its pointed tip with one finger as they paused at the pelican crossing.

He writhed away. 'That's sexual harassment of a co-worker, that is. And you who always meant to be a separatist.'

'I'm a respectable woman now; I've been seen trying to buy condoms on a public corridor.'

'Yeah, but which of us would have got to wear them?'

Cyn gave him a mistressful scowl. Then the skin around her eyes crinkled. 'Did you spot May from Accounts at the noticeboard, ears flapping? Our reputations are saved.'

They had met at Pride the previous June. Cyn, on a day off from her temping job, leaned her elbows on a steel barrier and watched the crowd whoop by. Lou was one of the boys in gleaming white jockey shorts, funking along behind the Sisters of Perpetual

Indulgence. What made her notice him was the shamrock in relief on the back of his No. 2 shave; when he dropped out for a rest against the barrier, it was two inches from her face. The most testicular of symbols, she commented afterwards. Lou claimed it represented a triad of Celtic goddesses, but, when pressed, could not remember their names.

Then a few weeks later, on her way back from a James Dean double-bill at the Roxy in Brixton, Cyn happened to spot the Rainbow Centre and remembered something that nice boy-germ had said about working there as a set painter. Lou recognized the woman in the navy suit only when she hoisted herself onto the stage and introduced herself as 'Whatshername from the march'. She hadn't been on the boards, she said, since her days of teaching heel-toe in the parish hall under the knobbly crucifix.

August was nearly over when the two of them came face to sweaty face in Oscars. She reached over a line of men and bought them two lime and sodas. In return Lou remembered to tell her that they needed a dance person at the Rainbow to add a chorus of local ten-year-olds to *Fee Foe Fie Fum*.

It was one of Cyn's unspoken superstitions that if you met someone accidentally three times in as many months, the friendship had to happen.

She turned up Monday morning, surprising them both. Over polystyrene cups of tea, her voice relaxed and dipped. Lou's ears recognized it as Irish, and he was suddenly awkward. He wiped his hands on a crusty blue rag. 'You didn't tell me you were one of us.'

'Who's us?' she asked.

'Ah, you know, Gay-lickers. Little green fairies.'

'I've never felt like one of an us.'

Lou let it drop. He led Cyn round the back of the set and pointed out details on a painted dragon to make her laugh.

As the first knot of kids trickled in, she stepped carefully over some chickenwire, introduced herself to them, and began inventing a Digestion Dance for Act II. Smacking her hip for the rhythm, Cyn stopped herself after one '*haon dó trí*', realizing that these kids would have no idea what it meant. Somehow 'one two three' sounded much flatter.

Two months slid by, three and a half, and Cyn was still working at the Rainbow. Or, as they variously called it on idle mornings round the drinks machine, the Rambo, the Brainrow, or the Puddle.

Lou she addressed as her toy-boy, her babe, her gentleman friend, her Martin Luther Queen. He borrowed her big leather jacket; she stole the last mouthful of his tea. The other workers didn't know what to make of them. Cyn and Lou didn't know what to make of themselves, nor did they worry about it.

One Friday in December Lou noticed her mouth sagging at the corners, so he dragged her to Oscars. 'Would you go halves on a packet of crisps?'

She straddled a stool. 'No point, English crisps are horrible. I stay faithful to Tayto Cheese 'n' Onion.'

'So you binge on them when you go back?'

Cyn spun a beermat on a fingertip. 'Haven't been back.'

'In how long?'

'At all.'

Lou curled his feet round the bar of the stool. He tried to take it in. 'What, since whenever?'

'1980. John Paul II was blessing ze young people of Iyerland as my plane took off. I could see the crowd shrinking behind the wing.'

Lou bit the corner off his peanut packet. 'Not even for Christmas?' He heard his voice, like a disappointed child's.

Cyn grinned over her upturned collar. 'I suppose you'll be zooming home to the Mammy on the 23rd of December?'

'And stay till after the New Year's hangover. This year she wants me till Epiphany but I've told her we've a show on.'

'Liar.'

Lou bent his head. 'Let's get the full confession over: I forget all my vegetarian principles when I smell the turkey stuffing.'

'And do you delight the family with your *Queer as Fuck* T-shirt?'

'Ah, get away with you.' Lou's voice sank.

'Let me guess: you're not exactly out to them.'

'Not in so many words, and certainly not in those particular words.' Lou pulled at his ear lobe. 'You've forgotten what it's like back there.'

'I remember too well.' Cyn took a deliberate sip. 'So why fold yourself back into the closet once a year?'

He made a face. 'Because being a bit discreet is better than the ructions it would cause if I said anything. Besides, I couldn't miss the Christmas.'

'Missing it's easy after the first time,' Cyn assured him. 'I get an old friend to send me a box of Tayto each year.'

'But you must feel a bit . . . cut off.'

'Ah get lost laddy.' She looked at him with amusement that had a warning behind it. 'Can you see me ever fitting in?'

Lou frayed the edge of his beermat with one nail. 'You wouldn't have to . . .'

'Listen, I felt more of an exile for twenty years in Ireland than I ever have in the twelve I've been out of it.'

He contemplated the mark his glass had made on the polished wood.

Three hours later their speech was slower, more circuitous. The conversation had meandered through SM, the best temperature to drink Guinness, god, nephews and nieces, and was circling back to Ireland and its many embarrassments.

Lou knew some activists over there working for decriminalization. Cyn tried three times to pronounce the word, and sniggered into her beer. She shut one eye and fixed him with the other. 'What's the Irish age of consent then?' she asked.

His forehead hurt. 'There isn't one. I was telling you, it's a Victorian statute –'

'No,' she interrupted him, 'I mean what's the age of consent for being Irish?'

Lou was massaging his temples, too hard.

'I mean, I don't seem to remember ever being consulted. Correct me if I'm wrong.' She pointed a stubby finger. 'Were you ever asked if you agreed to be Irish?'

He shook his head carefully, once.

'All that cultural baggage foisted' – Cyn paused, checking the word – 'absolutely *foisted* upon us without a by your leave.'

She continued, her finger dipping on every important work like a conductor's baton. 'And what happens if you try and refuse it or leave it behind? Everybody freaks out as if you've dumped a baby in a carrier bag at the airport.'

Lou opened his mouth, but could think of no remark that was not sad or silly.

Suddenly very much the personal secretary, she smoothened out a bus ticket and began a list of Reasons for Not Living in Our Dear Native Isle. It began to expand beyond the limits of the ticket, into rural depopulation and the violent habits of Celtic heroes, so Lou proposed they turn it over and restrict the list to new factors since 1980. On the plus side – Lou insisted there be a plus side, so Cyn drew a narrow margin down the edge of the ticket – all they could think of was crisps.

By the time he came back from the loo, Cyn had sagged over the counter. He could see a tear shining on the wood, and her shoulders were heaving. Putting one arm around her, he tried to shield her from the blank stares of the other drinkers.

After a minute, Cyn sat up and wiped her face on her denim sleeve. 'Sorry.'

'No problem,' he said, too heartily.

'Christ,' she roared, pointing one accusatory finger behind the bar.

'What is it now?'

'Page Three calendar. Typical bloody men. Even bloody faggots like a few bloody tits on the wall.'

Lou got her out the door before the barman could take action. They walked in silence to the Tube.

She cleared her throat with a husky roar. 'Sorry. One pint too many.'

'Sure.'

'It wasn't about anything.'

'Mmm.'

Cyn turned a wet repentant face. 'And what I said about faggots – I didn't mean you. I mean men are shits but you're alright, Lou – Lou.'

'I quite agree.' He pushed her through the turnstile. As she drifted towards the escalator he shouted, 'You will receive my severed balls by the next post in a plain brown wrapper.' He made a few jaws drop, but Cyn glanced over her shoulder and seemed comforted.

By the time they met up after Christmas, Cyn had worked her way through her box of Tayto. The next two shows were planned around gospel choirs rather than dance choruses; Cyn gave herself a week of moody unemployment, loitering in galleries and parks, then rooted out an old pair of navy tights and went back to temping.

One evening her Looptheloop came round to her flat for tuna bake. (Not that he was not a vegetarian, but somehow he always thought of tuna as a vegetable, just like anchovies.) He accepted seconds and thirds, to keep her company. Then they sat in front of the television with the sound turned down, and burped, and laughed in disgust at themselves. Each told the other they looked tired.

'Luther?'

He glanced up, startled by the full name.

She passed him the biscuit barrel. 'Why don't you go out and have a wild passionate affair?'

'No particular reason.'

'You're so post-Aids,' Cyn sighed. 'Have you calmed down after a riotous youth, is that it?'

'Not really. All through adolescence I painted trees. Then the seminary, painting Jesuses.' Lou paused to remember, staring at the television screen, where a man and a woman were silently shouting at each other over a car door.

'And then a few wild oats?'

'No, then I hung around Limerick for a few years, wondering whether I'd go back to the seminary if they asked me. But in the back of my mind I knew well that the priests would never have me back without me volunteering for ECT or something. So finally I rolled up my vocation, left it under the bed, and took the boat over to London.'

'And then some wild oats?' Cyn dipped another gingernut in her tea.

'One or two.'

She rolled her eyes. 'How can I be a faghag if my only fag is so damn respectable? I'm going to enrol you in a nude painting class tomorrow. You're in a rut.'

'Am not.'

'Are so. I can hear it in your voice.'

'You're just projecting your rut onto me.'

'Sounds painful!' she murmured.

Cyn didn't want to talk about herself tonight. She wanted to make fun of models in shampoo ads and maybe play Off the Couch if there was nothing on after *The Golden Girls*. With Lou she could almost touch the sixteen-year-old girl she'd never been.

Lou was sticking out his tongue at her lasciviously. 'Don't you go inventing ruts for me. Those who can't live, counsel.'

Cyn stared into the biscuity dregs of her tea.

It was a cold, clammy evening in March. Lou sat on the Tube, counting the stops, reminding himself not to bend his ticket in case the machine would spit it back at him. He had four layers on to keep out the howling draughts; his face felt damp and hot. Cyn had rung to say he had to come over.

'What, now? Cyn-ful, I'd have to take three Tubes.'

'Please, I'm really sorry but please.'

'OK pet, no worries. Give me an hour.'

Lou watched the grey wall of the tunnel hurtle by. Paper corners of old ads flapped in the breeze as the train came alongside a platform. Things had been strange with Cyn recently. Once they went dancing together in a dyke club which let boys in as friends or slaves on Mondays. He and Cyn had worn matching Pervert T-shirts, and danced like lunatics under a full moon, and in the toilet queue Cyn had told a curious woman that yes, Lou was her son, and she was very proud of him. It was a hilarious night, something to write home about, if his letters to his mother had ever told her anything that mattered.

But ever since, Cyn and he had been getting on each other's nerves. Silences and mishearing and prickliness; it seemed a silly way for a friendship to peter out.

On a lunch break last week, he had consulted Jazz, the counsellor at the Rainbow. Jazz advised sitting down together to share feelings and negotiate new terms. Lou nodded and squirmed. The best thing about friendship was not having to have all those heavy analytical conversations lovers had. Friends could just get on with living it.

His stop; he lunged for the door.

Cyn met him at the top of her stairs but didn't hug him. He had never known her to gabble quite like this. She told him how worried she was about the rumour that her landlord was planning to gentrify the block. Also she was thinking of changing to an agency which didn't mess temps around quite as much. The punnet of imported raspberries was a shocking price, but she had felt an urge to anticipate summer. Which laces did he think would go with her new boots?

Lou stayed patient until the third cup of tea. 'Is anything the matter?'

'No, just wanted to see your ugly mug really.'

'Any time.'

Cyn sat on the arm of the sofa, her arms folded round a big patchwork cushion. Her feet tucked under the leg of his jeans, for anchorage. They watched a gorgeous dancer in a pop video.

'What a sulky face on your woman.'

'It's a man in make-up,' he told her.

'No way.'

They argued the matter idly. She talked as if she had been drinking but her breath smelt of nothing but raspberries. Her fingertips were stained with them.

Lou accepted one, delicate-haired and slightly bruised. He kept his eyes on the television, nodding and keeping the occasional yawn inside his jaw. Only when he realized she was talking about the two of them did he look up and grin at her.

Cyn was telling him stuff he already knew but it was nice to hear it. How interesting it had been this year, something she had never done before, getting to know someone who was gay but of the opposite sex, like having so much in common yet being so far apart. It was the perfect situation for friendship, actually, because she was a completely woman-identified woman and he was, well, she supposed the equivalent phrase was a totally man-identified man, though that sounded a bit fascist, but she meant it in a nice way.

Lou assured her that he took it in a nice way. He stole the third last raspberry from the punnet in her lap.

Cyn was in full flow. How brilliant it was that the two of them could sort of share their thoughts without having them sort of curdled by heteropatriarchal patterns. (And to give her credit, she did grin as she dredged this phrase up from her feminist race memory.) A faggot and a dyke could balance each other, Cyn was explaining to him. They fitted. They knew who they were.

Lou nodded. His eyes slid back to the screen where Wogan was interviewing someone interesting for a change.

And then Cyn forgot what she was saying, forgot herself, and kissed him on the ear.

The rest was a blur to him, afterwards. He could never remember many details of that night. Maybe because he was so curious, so busy watching from outside, that he had not been really involved at all. Or maybe it was as if nature had edited out of his memory an experience irreconcilable with the rest of his life, like some women forget the pain of childbirth. But what Lou would always remember was that slow kiss on the ear that made every hair on his body stand up.

When he woke they were lying back to back. It was oddly comforting, the weight of his hip against the small of her back, her soles against his heels. The bed was damp, the wrinkled sheets still warm; he must have only dropped asleep for a few minutes.

Lou lay awake, not moving a muscle in case the two of them would become aware of each other and have to talk. He wanted to hold still and run it back through his head, but already it was blurring. The strange female shapes, the unexpected timing. And then, after all, the human similarity; the results of hands on bodies turned out to be not so different after all.

He had never been to bed with a woman before. Did it count if she was a lesbian? In some ways, Lou thought, stifling a giggle, it was the most logical choice.

Behind him Cyn shifted, her back pulling awake from his; a draught wound in to separate them. He had to move his leg or it would cramp. He twisted to face her, and rested his head on her shoulder, but lightly.

She found she could hear him thinking, like a pulse in the head on her shoulder.

'Hi,' he said at last, rather squawkily, and Cyn was overwhelmed with fondness for him.

'Hello,' she reassured him.

After a gap of half a minute, Lou got his question over with.

'Was that all right?'

'Yeah.' What a bland word, an insult, a mere grunt. What could she tell him about something so recent and brief that her brain had hardly registered it? 'Rather different from how it used to be,' Cyn added in an undertone.

'When?'

'Fifteen years ago.'

'Fifteen years ago I was taking my first holy communion in velvet knickerbockers.' Cyn cleared her throat. 'I meant with other men.'

'I know.' Lou turned his face up to the cracked ceiling. Silence covered them like a blanket, stifling the words. But if he didn't ask these questions now they would hammer in his head. 'How different, exactly?'

Her face was angled into the pillow. What she said was muffled and he had to ask her to repeat it. 'Not different enough,' Cyn said at last.

'I'm sorry. I mean, that's fine. No sweat.' What was he rabbiting on about? There was sweat everywhere, cooling the sheets against them like a mummy's wrappings.

It wasn't bright enough for Lou to see her eyes, but he could feel their gaze on his skin. 'It's not you, it's me,' she said, as if to a child. 'You're very different from them, you make a totally different . . . shape. But I'm afraid I still can't quite see it.'

He lay still, then scratched his ear. Why was he feeling bleak when it was such a relief? The things he had been dreading, ever since he woke up, were enthusiasm, romance, or a dreadfully earnest renegotiation of the terms.

Lou exhaled a quick prayer to the god he didn't believe in anymore. What he would have liked to say to the woman breathing beside him was a simple thanks that she seemed to have got about as much as he did out of the whole business and no more. But some things couldn't be said, even between friends. 'Tea?' he asked, leaning up on one elbow.

'Please.'

It took two months for them to feel safe enough to curl up on a sofa together. Lou's sofa this time, to avoid memories. It was May, and the sun sifted across the cushions. When he took her hand this time there was a layer of airiness between their bodies; it cushioned them, saved their nerves from jarring. They kept talking. Lou delivered a rant, punctuated with laughter, about the Rainbow's Artistic Director, who was so paranoid about Clause 28 that he had instructed Lou to paint over the giants' moustaches and bandannas in case the Council withdrew funding. By the end of an argument about the Labour Party, Cyn decided that the electricity between them had been earthed and laid to rest. It felt so wonderfully ordinary, her hand lying on his. Laying her head back on one of Lou's granny's cushions, she decided she wouldn't have to unearth that 'Bi Any Other Name' badge after all.

Lou watched her eyelids float in a sea of tiny lines. 'Your accent's coming back these days, you know,' he remarked.

'It is not!'

'Listen to yourself. "'Tis an' all,"' he added in a stage-Oirish quaver.

She grinned and slid farther down the sofa arm, putting her boots up on his jeans. 'Must be your evil influence.'

If he didn't push it now he mightn't get another chance. 'They say it's getting better over there, Cyn-ful.'

'Don't they always.'

'Ah but seriously. The Government are finally going to have to make us legal; they've promised to bring in an equal age of consent by July.'

'Speak for yourself, I was never illegal.'

'They'd have to get you for general indecency.'

'They'd have to catch me first.'

Lou rapped on her soles. 'Stop messing. Why don't you come home with me at the end of June for Pride?'

Cyn opened one eye.

'Dublin has its very own Pride March now, isn't that the cutest thing?'

Her eye shut. 'Dublin's not home. I grew up a hundred and fifty miles away. I've been to Manchester more often than Dublin.'

'Well, think of it as a halfway point, then. Halfway between the Rainbow Centre and your parish hall.'

The cushion dropped to the floor. 'I'd rather think about tandoori chicken. Come on, my treat.'

Lou followed her down the stairwell. The sun was pale yellow, snagged on a city spire; fingers of cloud stroked it as they passed.

'I just can't believe in an Irish Pride March,' Cyn commented, as they crossed the street to avoid a knot of skinheads. 'It'd be a contradiction in terms. Pride is sun on the lions in Trafalgar Square and bobbies in helmets and that transvestite dressed up as Margaret Thatcher.'

'What a traditionalist you are, for a deviant.'

The point struck home. Cyn's walk slowed; her fists went deeper into her pockets. 'Where'd we stay, if we did, which we won't?'

'I'll find a nice queer B&B in Dublin. Separate rooms, I assure you.'

'But of course.' She grabbed his hand, gave it a quick and only partly mocking kiss. 'It'll all be so different from how you remember it.'

'How different exactly?'

'Let me guess what you're going to say: "Not different enough"?'

He caught the edge of a sheepish grin, as she turned her face away.

'Cyn, it's a new decade. Condom machines –'

'– much good that does me –'

'– a female president up in the Park. How about if I pay the price of your ticket if you're not entirely satisfied?'

'You couldn't afford to, unless you've been turning tricks in your lunchbreaks.'

'I know,' sighed Lou, 'but didn't it sound impressive?' The campness left his tone. 'Listen, you have to come back with me. If I went with English mates they wouldn't understand. Ireland's growing up, we have to be there.'

'Oh really? Puberty is not a pretty sight. Tantrums and spots,' Cyn reminded him, folding her arms across her jacket.

'Think of it more like a gorgeous teenager, with very soft eyelashes.'

'Paedophile.'

He pulled a hideous leer.

Cyn yawned as they turned the corner onto the high street. 'I don't know, Lou-Lou, the very idea makes me tired. Wake me up when Ireland starts consenting to us instead of kicking us in the teeth.'

'Any day now,' he promised her, doubtfully.

'I'll believe it when I see it.'

'You'll never see it unless you believe it a bit.'

They wandered down the street past the restaurant, past the pub, coming to no conclusion. Like tails of cloud, their voices winding around and in and out.

BIOGRAPHICAL NOTES

JOHN BANIM was a novelist, playwright and poet. He was born in Kilkenny, and lived both in Dublin and London before returning to his place of birth. He collaborated with his brother Michael on a series of novels.

JOHN BANVILLE was born in Wexford. His books include *Birchwood* (1973), *The Book of Evidence* (1989) and *The Untouchable* (1997). He was for many years literary editor of *The Irish Times*.

LELAND BARDWELL was born in India of Irish parents, and has lived most of her life in Ireland. Her novels include *That London Winter* (1981) and *There We Have Been* (1989). *Dostoevsky's Grave: New and Selected Poems* was published in 1991.

SEBASTIAN BARRY was born in Dublin. He is a poet, playwright and novelist. His plays include *Prayers of Sherkin* (1990) and *The Steward of Christendom* (1995). His novel *The Whereabouts of Eneas McNulty* was published in 1998.

MARY BECKETT was born in Belfast, but has lived in Dublin for many years. She has published two collections of stories, *A Belfast Woman* (1980) and *A Literary Woman* (1990), and one novel, *Give Them Stones* (1987).

SAMUEL BECKETT was born in Co. Dublin, but lived in Paris for most of his life. His plays include *Waiting for Godot* (1953) and *Endgame* (1957); his best-known prose works are the trilogy *Molloy*, *Malone Dies* and *The Unnamable*, published in English in the early 1950s. He won the Nobel Prize for Literature in 1969.

SAM HANNA BELL was born in Glasgow of Irish parents. He worked for the BBC for more than twenty years. His books include *Summer Loanen and Other Stories* (1943) and *The Hollow Ball* (1961). *December Bride* (1951) remains his masterpiece.

DERMOT BOLGER was born in Dublin, where he lives. He is a poet, playwright, novelist and publisher. His novels include *The Woman's Daughter* (1987), *The Journey Home* (1990) and *Father's Music* (1998). *Taking My Letters Back: New and Selected Poems* was published in 1998.

ELIZABETH BOWEN was born in Dublin and divided her time between London and her family house, Bowen's Court, in Co. Cork. Her novels include *The Last September* (1929) and *The Heat of the Day* (1949). Her *Collected Stories* appeared in 1981.

CLARE BOYLAN was born in Dublin, where she still lives. Her novels include *Holy Pictures* (1983) and *Black Baby* (1988). She has also published a number of short-story collections.

MAEVE BRENNAN was born in Dublin but moved to Washington with her family – her father was a diplomat. She was a staff writer with the *New Yorker* for thirty years. Her selected stories, *Springs of Affection*, were published in 1998.

JOHN BRODERICK was born in Athlone. Among twelve novels are *The Pilgrimage* (1961) and *An Apology for Roses* (1973). He travelled widely and spent the last ten years of his life in England.

WILLIAM CARLETON was born near Clogher in Co. Tyrone. He attended a hedge school and later flirted with the priesthood before becoming a full-time writer. *Traits and Stories of the Irish Peasantry*, his best-known book, appeared in 1830.

SHANE CONNAUGHTON was born in Cavan, but has lived in London for many years. He is an actor and screen-writer as well as a fiction-writer. He is the author of a collection of stories, *A Border Station* (1989), and a novel, *The Run of the Country* (1991).

DANIEL CORKERY was born in Cork, where he lived all his life. His fiction includes *A Munster Twilight* (1916) and *The Threshold of Quiet* (1917); his critical work includes *The Hidden Ireland* (1924) and *Synge and Anglo-Irish Literature* (1931).

ANTHONY CRONIN was born in Enniscorthy, Co. Wexford. He has lived in London, Spain and Dublin. He is a poet, critic and novelist. His *New and Selected Poems* was published in 1982. His novels are *The Life of Riley* (1964) and *Identity Papers* (1979).

ITA DALY was born in Co. Leitrim but has lived in Dublin for many years. Her first collection of stories, *The Lady with the Red Shoes*, appeared in 1979. Since then she has published several novels, including *Ellen* (1986) and *Unholy Ghosts* (1996).

SEAMUS DEANE, born in Derry, is best known as a poet and critic. He was the general editor of the *Field Day Anthology of Irish Writing*. He teaches at the University of Notre Dame. His *Selected Poems* appeared in 1988; his novel, *Reading in the Dark*, was published in 1996 and was shortlisted for the Booker Prize.

EMMA DONOGHUE was born in Dublin, but has lived outside Ireland for several years. Her first book, *Stir Fry*, appeared in 1994, when she was twenty-five. Her other books include *Hood* (1995) and *Kissing the Witch* (1997).

MARY DORCEY was born in Dublin. She has published both poetry and fiction. Her first collection, *Kindling*, appeared in 1982. She has written one collection of stories, *A Noise from the Woodshed* (1989), and a novel, *Biography of Desire* (1997).

RODDY DOYLE was born in Dublin, where he still lives. His first three novels – *The Commitments* (1987), *The Snapper* (1989) and *The Van* (1991) – have been collected as *The Barrytown Trilogy*. His novel *Paddy Clarke Ha Ha Ha* won the Booker Prize in 1993.

MARIA EDGEWORTH was born and educated in England but came to Ireland to help run the family estate when she was fifteen. Her first novel, *Castle Rackrent*, was published in 1800. Subsequent novels include *The Absentee* (1812) and *Ormond* (1817).

ANNE ENRIGHT was born in Dublin, where she now lives. She has worked as a television producer and broadcaster. Her books are *A Portable Virgin* (1991) and *The Wig My Father Wore* (1995).

BRIAN FRIEL, born in Omagh, Co. Tyrone, is best known as a playwright. His plays include *Philadelphia, Here I Come!* (1964), *Faith Healer* (1979) and *Dancing at Lughnasa* (1990). *Selected Stories* was published in 1979.

CARLO GÉBLER was born in Dublin and brought up in London. He lives in Co. Fermanagh. His first novel, *The Eleventh Summer*, appeared in 1985. His other novels include *August in July* (1986) and *The Cure* (1994). He has also written travel books about Northern Ireland and Cuba.

OLIVER GOLDSMITH was born in Co. Longford and educated at Trinity College Dublin. He was a poet, playwright and novelist. His best-known poem, *The Deserted Village*, was published in 1770, his best-known novel, *The Vicar of Wakefield*, in 1766.

GERALD GRIFFIN was born and educated in Limerick. He published his first collection of stories, *Holland-Tide*, in 1826 and his best-known novel, *The Collegians*, in 1829. In 1838 he burnt his manuscripts and entered the Christian Brothers.

HUGO HAMILTON was born in Dublin to a German mother and an Irish father, and brought up speaking Irish and German. His novels include *Surrogate City* (1990), *The Last Shot* (1991) and *Sad Bastard* (1998).

DERMOT HEALY was born in Westmeath and brought up in Cavan. His fiction includes a collection of stories, *Banished Misfortune* (1982), and the novel *A Goat's Song* (1995). His memoir *The Bend for Home* appeared in 1996.

AIDAN HIGGINS was born in Co. Kildare. His first novel, *Langrishe, Go Down*, was published in 1966. His other novels include *Balcony of Europe* (1972), *Bornholm Night-Ferry* (1983) and *Lions of the Grunewald* (1993).

DESMOND HOGAN was born in Galway and has lived in London and the west of Ireland. His novels include *The Ikon Maker* (1976), *A Curious Street* (1984) and *A New Shirt* (1986). He has also published two collections of stories and a volume of travel writing.

JENNIFER JOHNSTON was born in Dublin but has lived outside Derry for many years. Her many novels include *The Captains and the Kings* (1972), *How Many Miles to Babylon?* (1974), *The Railway Station Man* (1985) and *The Illusionist* (1995).

NEIL JORDAN was born in Sligo and brought up in Dublin. He is best known as a film director, but he is also the author of a collection of stories, *Night in Tunisia* (1976), and three novels.

JAMES JOYCE was born in Dublin. His long exile was spent in Trieste, Paris and Zurich. *Dubliners*, a collection of stories, was published in 1914, followed by *A Portrait of the Artist as a Young Man* (1916), *Ulysses* (1922) and *Finnegans Wake* (1939).

PATRICK KAVANAGH was born in Monaghan, moved to Dublin in his thirties and lived there for the rest of his life. He is best known as a poet, but his prose works include an autobiography, *The Green Fool* (1938), and a novel, *Tarry Flynn* (1948).

MOLLY KEANE was born in Co. Kildare. She began to write under the pseudonym M. J. Farrell and produced ten novels between 1928 and 1952. She was also a successful playwright. In the 1980s she wrote three more novels, including *Good Behaviour* (1981).

BENEDICT KIELY, born in Co. Tyrone, is a short-story writer, journalist and novelist. He has lived in Dublin for most of his life. His novels include *Land Without Stars* (1946), *Nothing Happens in Carmincross* (1985) and *Proxopera* (1977). *God's Own Country: Selected Stories* appeared in 1993.

MARY LAVIN was born to Irish parents in the United States, coming to Ireland when she was ten. She lived for many years on a farm in Co. Meath. She was the author of two novels and many collections of stories.

EMILY LAWLESS, a poet and novelist, was born in Co. Kildare. Her best-known novel, *Hurrish*, was published in 1886. She also wrote historical romances and a biography of Maria Edgeworth.

JOSEPH SHERIDAN LE FANU was born in Dublin and worked as a journalist and newspaper proprietor. Following the death of his wife, he began to write fiction. His best-known books are *The House by the Churchyard* (1863) and *Uncle Silas* (1864).

MAURICE LEITCH was born in Co. Antrim. He worked for the BBC for many years in both London and Belfast. His novels include *The Liberty Lad* (1965), *Poor Lazarus* (1969), *Stamping Ground* (1975) and *Gilchrist* (1994).

MARY LELAND was born in Cork, where she now lives. She is the author of two novels, *The Killeen* (1986) and *Approaching Priests* (1991), and a collection of stories, *The Little Galloway Girls* (1987).

CHARLES LEVER was born in Dublin and studied medicine at Trinity College Dublin. He lived in North America and Brussels and later in Trieste. His many novels include *Harry Lorrequer* (1840) and *Charles O'Malley* (1841).

EUGENE MCCABE was born in Glasgow, but has lived for most of his life on a farm on the Monaghan–Fermanagh border. He is the author of several plays, including *King of the Castle* (1964). His novels are *Victims* (1976) and *Death and Nightingales* (1992).

PATRICK MCCABE was born in Clones, Co. Monaghan. Among his five novels are *The Butcher Boy* (1992) and *Breakfast on Pluto* (1998), both shortlisted for the Booker Prize.

COLUM MCCANN was born and brought up in Dublin, but lives in New York. He is the author of a collection of stories, *Fishing the Sloe-Black River* (1993), and two novels, *Songdogs* (1995) and *This Side of Brightness* (1998).

JOHN MCGAHERN was brought up in the Irish midlands and has lived for many years in Co. Leitrim. Among his five novels are *The Barracks* (1962) and *Amongst Women* (1990). His *Collected Stories* appeared in 1992.

SEOSAMH MAC GRIANNA was born in Co. Donegal. He fought on the Republican side in the Civil War. His best-known work is a collection of stories, *An Grá agus An Ghruaim* (1929). He worked as a translator from English to Irish. His final years were spent in a mental institution.

TOM MAC INTYRE is a poet, prose-writer and playwright. He has written a number of innovative works for the Irish theatre. His prose works include the collections of stories, *Dance the Dance* (1970) and *The Harper's Turn* (1982).

BERNARD MAC LAVERTY was born in Belfast but has lived for many years in Scotland. His novels are *Lamb* (1980), *Cal* (1982) and *Grace Notes* (1997). He has also published several collections of short stories.

MICHAEL MCLAVERTY was born in Co. Monaghan but lived in Belfast for most of his life, where he worked as a school teacher. He published eight novels and several collections of short stories. His best-known novel is *Call My Brother Back* (1939).

BRYAN MACMAHON was born in Listowel, Co. Kerry, where he lived most of his life working as a school teacher. His first collection of stories, *The Lion-Tamer*, was published in 1948. Other collections include *The Red Petticoat* (1955).

EOIN MCNAMEE was born in Kilkeel in Co. Down and now lives in Co. Sligo. He is a poet, screen-writer and novelist. His best-known work of fiction is *Resurrection Man* (1994).

DEIRDRE MADDEN was born in Antrim. She has lived in France and Italy. Her novels include *Hidden Symptoms* (1987), *Remembering Light and Stone* (1992) and *One by One in the Dark* (1996).

AIDAN MATHEWS was born in Dublin, where he lives, working as a radio producer. He is a poet, playwright and fiction-writer. His collections of stories include *Adventures in a Bathyscope* (1988). His novel *Muesli at Midnight* was published in 1990.

CHARLES ROBERT MATURIN was born in Dublin and studied at Trinity College Dublin, becoming a clergyman. He wrote a number of plays, but his best-known work is the Gothic novel *Melmoth the Wanderer* (1820).

BRIAN MOORE was born in Belfast, but lived most of his life in Canada and then in California. Among his twenty novels are *The Lonely Passion of Judith Hearne* (1956), *The Doctor's Wife* (1976) and *Black Robe* (1985).

GEORGE MOORE was born in Co. Mayo, the son of a landlord. He lived in Paris, Dublin and London. His many novels include *Esther Waters* (1894) and *The Brook Kerith* (1916). His collection of stories, *The Untilled Field*, appeared in 1903. He is the author of a three-volume autobiography, *Hail and Farewell* (1911–14).

LADY MORGAN was born in Dublin. She was a poet, novelist and travel writer. Her best-known novel is *The Wild Irish Girl* (1806). She spent her last years in London.

MARY MORRISSY was born in Dublin and works as a journalist with *The Irish Times*. She has written two books of fiction, a collection of stories, *A Lazy Eye* (1993), and a novel, *Mother of Pearl* (1996).

ROSA MULHOLLAND was born in Belfast. She published her first novel, *Dumara*, in 1864, when she was twenty-three. She was encouraged by Charles Dickens, who printed her early stories in *Household Words*, and by W. B. Yeats, who published her in *Representative Irish Tales*.

VAL MULKERNS was born in Dublin, where she still lives. She worked on the magazine *The Bell* in the 1950s, and has published four novels and a number of collections of stories, including *Antiquities* (1978) and *An Idle Woman* (1980).

IRIS MURDOCH was born in Dublin and educated in England. She lived in Oxford for most of her life. Her many novels include *Under the Net* (1954) and *The Red and the Green* (1965), set in Ireland during the 1916 Rising.

EDNA O'BRIEN was born in Co. Clare and has lived for many years in London. Her novels include *The Country Girls* (1960), *August is a Wicked Month* (1965) and *A House of Splendid Isolation* (1994). She has also published a number of collections of stories and a book on James Joyce.

FLANN O'BRIEN was one of the pseudonyms used by Brian O'Nolan. He was born in Strabane, Co. Tyrone, and lived for most of his life in Dublin, writing a famous column for *The Irish Times*. His best-known novels are *At Swim-Two-Birds* (1939) and *The Third Policeman* (written in 1940 and published after his death in 1967).

KATE O'BRIEN was born in Limerick and lived for many years in Spain, England and the west of Ireland. Her best-known novels are *The Anteroom* (1934), *The Land of Spices* (1941) and *That Lady* (1946).

MÁIRTÍN Ó CADHAIN was born in Co. Galway. In 1939 he was interned for five years for IRA membership. He later worked as a translator and academic. He wrote many short stories and a novel, *Cré na Cille*, published in 1949.

FRANK O'CONNOR was the pseudonym for Michael O'Donovan, who was born in Cork. He took the Republican side and was imprisoned in the Civil War. He was a biographer and playwright, but best known as a short-story writer, his first volume, *Guests of the Nation*, appearing in 1931, when he was twenty-eight.

JOSEPH O'CONNOR was born in Dublin. *Cowboys and Indians*, his first novel, was published in 1991. His other novels are *Desperadoes* (1994), set in Nicaragua, and *The Salesman* (1997). He was also written *The Secret World of the Irish Male* (1994).

PEADAR O'DONNELL was born in Co. Donegal. He fought in the War of Independence and on the Republican side in the Civil War, and later was active on the left. He edited

The Bell for eight years from 1946. He published many novels and three volumes of autobiography.

JULIA O'FAOLAIN was born in London and brought up in Dublin. She has lived outside Ireland for most of her life. Her novels include *Women in the Wall* (1975), *No Country for Young Men* (1980) and *The Judas Cloth* (1992).

SEAN O'FAOLAIN was born in Cork and fought on the Republican side in the Civil War. He published ten volumes of short stories, four novels, five biographies and several prose works. In 1940 he founded the literary magazine *The Bell*.

LIAM O'FLAHERTY was born on Inis Mór in the Aran Islands. He fought in the First World War and was later involved in revolutionary activity in Dublin. He published more than a dozen novels, two volumes of autobiography and more than a hundred and fifty short stories.

DAVID PARK was born in Northern Ireland, where he still lives. His books include a volume of stories, *Oranges from Spain* (1990), and a novel, *The Healing* (1992).

GLENN PATTERSON was born in Belfast, where he still lives. He is the author of four novels, including *Burning Your Own* (1989) and *The International* (1999).

JAMES PLUNKETT was born in Dublin, where he has worked as a trade union official and a television producer. He is the author of three novels, including *Strumpet City* (1969). *Collected Stories* appeared in 1977.

K. ARNOLD PRICE was born in Co. Mayo and spent her childhood in Co. Limerick. She was educated at Trinity College Dublin and later studied in England and France. Her first novel, *The New Perspective*, was published in 1980 when she was eighty-four. Her second novel, *The Captain's Paramours*, was published in 1985.

FRANK RONAN was born in Co. Wexford, but has lived in England for many years. His novels include *The Men Who Loved Evelyn Cotton* (1989), *A Picnic in Eden* (1991) and *Lovely* (1996).

FRANCES SHERIDAN, the novelist and dramatist, was born in Dublin, but moved to London when she was thirty. Her best-known novel, *The Memoirs of Miss Biddulph*, appeared in 1761. *The Discovery* (1763) was her most famous play.

EDITH SOMERVILLE AND MARTIN ROSS. Edith Somerville was born in Corfu, but lived most of her life in Co. Cork; Violet Martin was her cousin, born in Co. Galway, who spent a good deal of time with Somerville. Their first book appeared in 1889 and by the time Violet Martin died in 1915 they had published fourteen titles, including *The Real Charlotte* in 1894.

JAMES STEPHENS, poet and fiction-writer, was born in Dublin. His best-known novels are *A Charwoman's Daughter* and *The Crock of Gold*, both published in 1912. His *The Insurrection in Dublin* is an eyewitness account of the 1916 Rising.

LAURENCE STERNE was born in Clonmel, Co. Tipperary, and spent his early years in Irish garrison towns. He lived thereafter in England. His best-known work is *The Life and Opinions of Tristram Shandy, Gentleman* (1760). *A Sentimental Journey* (1768) describes his travels in France and Italy.

BRAM STOKER was born in Fairview in Dublin. He wrote a dozen novels, of which *Dracula* (1897) is the best known. He worked for many years as a manager for the theatre impresario Sir Henry Irving.

FRANCIS STUART was born in Australia of Irish parents and brought up in Northern Ireland. He fought in the War of Independence and the Civil War on the Republican side. He lived in Berlin during the Second World War. He has written more than twenty novels, including *Black List, Section H* (1972).

JONATHAN SWIFT was born in Dublin and educated at Trinity College Dublin. He became a clergyman, publishing *A Tale of a Tub* and *The Battle of the Books* anonymously in 1704. In 1713 he became dean of St Patrick's in Dublin. He published *Gulliver's Travels* in 1726.

KATHERINE CECIL THURSTON was born in Cork and educated privately by her wealthy parents. Her novels, especially her second, *John Chilcote MP* (1904), were immensely popular during her lifetime.

ROBERT TRESSELL, a pseudonym for Robert Noonan, was born in Dublin. He emigrated to South Africa in his twenties and later lived in England. *The Ragged-Trousered Philanthropist*, his only book, was published in an abridged version in 1914 three years after his death and in full in 1955.

WILLIAM TREVOR was born William Trevor Cox in Co. Cork, and brought up in various towns in provincial Ireland. He has lived in England for many years. His novels include *The Old Boys* (1964), *Mrs Eckdorf at O'Neill's Hotel* (1969) and *Reading Turgenev* (1992). His *Collected Stories* appeared in 1992.

ANTHONY TROLLOPE was born in London. In 1841, at the age of twenty-six, he came to Ireland, where he stayed for the next eighteen years. He wrote forty-seven novels, five volumes of short stories, travel books, biographies and collections of sketches.

OSCAR WILDE was born in Dublin. His only novel, *The Picture of Dorian Gray*, came out in 1891. His plays include *Lady Windermere's Fan* (1892) and *The Importance of Being Earnest* (1895). In 1895 he was charged with homosexual offences and sentenced to two years with hard labour.

ROBERT MCLIAM WILSON was born in Belfast, where he still lives. His novels are *Ripley Bogle* (1989), *Manfred's Pain* (1992) and *Eureka Street* (1996).

ACKNOWLEDGEMENTS

I am grateful to my editor at Penguin, Tony Lacey, who oversaw this project with a mixture of enthusiasm, generosity and patience. I am also grateful to Jon Riley, who commissioned the book, and to Donna Poppy, who copy-edited a difficult manuscript with such skill and, once more, patience. Several other people in Penguin were immensely helpful, and they include Jeremy Ettinghausen, John Hamilton, Keith Taylor, Joanna Seaton, Georgie Widdrington and Nick Wetton. I should also like to thank Ian Rowland and his team at Rowland Phototypesetting Ltd.

In Dublin I wish to thank Fintan O'Toole for some brilliant ideas and constant support; also Brendan Barrington, Catriona Crowe, Aidan Dunne and Tina O'Toole. I am grateful to the staff of the National Library in Dublin, where much of the research for this book was done, especially Noel Kissane; also to the staff of the library of Trinity College Dublin.

COPYRIGHT ACKNOWLEDGEMENTS

JOHN BANVILLE: from *Birchwood* (Minerva, 1992), reprinted by permission of Sheil Land Associates on behalf of the author; from *The Book of Evidence* (Mandarin, 1990), reprinted by permission of Sheil Land Associates on behalf of the author; LELAND BARDWELL: 'The Hairdresser' from *Different Kinds of Love* (Attic Press, 1987), reprinted by permission of Cork University Press; SEBASTIAN BARRY: from *The Whereabouts of Eneas McNulty* (Picador, 1998); MARY BECKETT: 'A Belfast Woman' from *A Belfast Woman* (Poolbeg, 1987), reprinted by permission of the publisher; SAMUEL BECKETT: from *Murphy* (Calder Publications, 1969), © Samuel Beckett Estate, reprinted by permission of the publisher; 'First Love' (Calder, 1973), © Samuel Beckett Estate, reprinted by permission of the publisher; from *Malone Dies* (Calder, 1973), © Samuel Beckett Estate, reprinted by permission of the publisher; 'Company' (Calder, 1982), © Samuel Beckett Estate, reprinted by permission of the publisher; SAM HANNA BELL: from *December Bride* (Blackstaff Press, 1974), reprinted by permission of the publisher; DERMOT BOLGER: from *The Journey Home* (Viking, 1990); ELIZABETH BOWEN: from *The Last September* (Vintage, 1998), © Elizabeth Bowen 1929, 1935, reprinted by permission of Curtis Brown Ltd, London; 'Her Table Spread' from *The Cat Jumps, and Other Stories* (Victor Gollancz, 1934), © Elizabeth Bowen 1934, reprinted by permission of Curtis Brown Ltd, London; CLARE BOYLAN: from *Holy Pictures* (Penguin, 1984); MAEVE BRENNAN: 'The Morning after the Big Fire' from *Springs of Affection* (Flamingo, 1999); JOHN BRODERICK: from *The Trial of Father Dillingham* (Marion Boyars, 1981), reprinted by permission of the publisher; SHANE CONNAUGHTON: 'Topping' from *A Border Station* (Hamish Hamilton, 1989); DANIEL CORKERY: 'Nightfall' from *The Stormy Hills* (Jonathan Cape, 1929; Mercier Press, 1969), reprinted by permission of Mercier Press; ANTHONY CRONIN: from *The Life of Riley* (Secker & Warburg, 1964); ITA DALY: 'Such Good Friends' from *The Lady with the Red Shoes* (Poolbeg, 1980), reprinted by permission of the publisher; SEAMUS DEANE: from *Reading in the Dark* (Cape, 1996); EMMA DONOGHUE: 'Going Back' from *Alternative Loves: Irish Gay and Lesbian Stories*, edited by David Marcus (Martello Books, 1994); MARY DORCEY: 'A Country Dance' from *A Noise from the Woodshed: Short Stories* (Onlywomen Press, 1989); RODDY DOYLE from *The Snapper* (Secker & Warburg, 1990); ANNE ENRIGHT: '(She Owns) Every Thing' from *The Portable Virgin* (Secker & Warburg, 1991); BRIAN FRIEL: 'Foundry House' from *Selected Stories* (Gallery Press, 1979); CARLO GÉBLER: from *The Cure* (Abacus, 1995); HUGO HAMILTON: 'Nazi Christmas' from *Dublin Where the Palm Trees Grow* (Faber, 1996), reprinted by permission of the Peters Fraser & Dunlop Group Ltd on behalf of Hugo Hamilton; DERMOT HEALY: from *A Goat's Song* (Harvill, 1994), reprinted by permission of the publisher; AIDAN HIGGINS: from *Balcony of Europe* (Calder, 1972), © Calder Publications Ltd, reprinted by permission of the publisher; DESMOND HOGAN: 'Memories of Swinging

London' from *The Mourning Thief and Other Stories* (Faber, 1987); JENNIFER JOHNSTON: from *The Captains and the Kings* (Penguin Books, 1990); NEIL JORDAN: 'Night in Tunisia' from *Night in Tunisia and Other Stories* (Vintage, 1993); JAMES JOYCE: 'The Dead' from *Dubliners* (1914; The Corrected Text, Jonathan Cape, 1967), © the Estate of James Joyce, reproduced with the kind permission of the Estate of James Joyce; from chapter 1 of *A Portrait of the Artist as a Young Man* (1916; Penguin Twentieth-Century Classics, 1992), © the Estate of James Joyce, reproduced with the kind permission of the Estate of James Joyce; episode 12, 'Cyclops', from *Ulysses* (1922; Penguin Twentieth-Century Classics, 1992), © the Estate of James Joyce, reproduced with the kind permission of the Estate of James Joyce; 'Anna Livia Plurabelle' from *Finnegans Wake* (Faber, 1939), © the Estate of James Joyce, reproduced with the kind permission of the Estate of James Joyce; PATRICK KAVANAGH: from *Tarry Flynn* (Penguin Books, 1990); MOLLY KEANE: from *Two Days in Aragon* (Virago, 1985), reprinted by permission of the publisher; BENEDICT KIELY: 'Homes on the Mountain' from *God's Own Country* (Minerva, 1993); MARY LAVIN: 'Happiness' from *Happiness and Other Stories* (Constable, 1969); MAURICE LEITCH: from *Stamping Ground* (Secker & Warburg, 1975); MARY LELAND: from *The Killeen* (Hamish Hamilton, 1985); EUGENE MCCABE: 'Music at Annahullion' from *Heritage and Other Stories* (Victor Gollancz, 1978); PATRICK MCCABE: from *The Butcher Boy* (Picador, 1992), reprinted by permission of the Peters Fraser & Dunlop Group Ltd on behalf of Patrick McCabe, and Macmillan Publishers Ltd; COLUM MCCANN: 'Breakfast for Enrique' from *Fishing the Sloe-Black River* (Phoenix, 1994); JOHN MCGAHERN: from *The Barracks* (Faber, 1997); 'The Country Funeral' from *Collected Stories of John McGahern* (Faber, 1992); SEOSAMH MAC GRIANNA: 'On the Empty Shore' from *Irish Writing, 1955*; TOM MAC INTYRE: 'Left of the Door' from *The Harper's Turn* (Gallery Press, 1982); BERNARD MAC LAVERTY: 'Life Drawing' from *A Time to Dance and Other Stories* (Jonathan Cape, 1982); MICHAEL MCLAVERTY: from *Call My Brother Back* (Poolbeg, 1979) © The Estate of Michael McLaverty, reprinted by permission of Maura Cregan, Literary Executor; BRYAN MACMAHON: 'Exile's Return' from *The Red Petticoat and Other Stories* (Macmillan, 1955); EOIN MCNAMEE: from *Resurrection Man* (Picador, 1995); DEIRDRE MADDEN: from *Remembering Light and Stone* (Faber, 1993); AIDAN MATHEWS: 'In the Dark' from *Adventures in a Bathyscope* (Secker & Warburg, 1988); BRIAN MOORE: from *Black Robe* (Grafton Books, 1987); GEORGE MOORE: from *Esther Waters* (1894; Oxford University Press, 1983); 'Home Sickness' from *The Untilled Field* (1903; Gill & Macmillan, 1990), reprinted by kind permission of Colin Smythe Ltd on behalf of the Estate of Christopher Douglas Medley; MARY MORRISSY: 'The Cantilever Principle' from *A Lazy Eye* (Jonathan Cape, 1993); VAL MULKERNS: 'Memory and Desire' from *An Idle Woman and Other Stories* (Poolbeg, 1980), reprinted by permission of the Peters Fraser & Dunlop Group Ltd; IRIS MURDOCH: from *The Red and the Green* (Chatto & Windus, 1984); EDNA O'BRIEN: from *The Country Girls* (Penguin Books, 1998); FLANN O'BRIEN: 'The Martyr's Crown' from *Stories and Plays* (Paladin, 1991), © Evelyn O'Nolan, 1967, reprinted by permission of A. M. Heath & Company; from *At Swim-Two-Birds* (Penguin Books, 1990), © Evelyn O'Nolan, 1967, reprinted by permission of A. M. Heath & Company; from *The Third Policeman* (Grafton Books, 1988), © Evelyn O'Nolan, 1967, reprinted by permission of A. M. Heath & Company; KATE O'BRIEN: from *The Land of Spices* (Virago, 1988), reprinted